The Editor

JACK ZIPES is Professor of German at the University of Minnesota, where he has taught since 1989. He is the recipient of numerous awards, among them Fulbright and Guggenheim fellowships. His many books include *Breaking the Magic Spell: Radical Theories of Folk and Fairy Tales; The Tribals and Tribulations of Little Red Riding Hood: Versions of the Tale in Sociocultural Context; Fairy Tales and the Art of Subversion: The Classical Genre for Children and the Process of Civilization; Don't Bet on the Prince: Contemporary Feminist Fairy Tales in North America and England; The Brothers Grimm: From Enchanted Forests to the Modern World; Happily Ever After: Fairy Tales, Children, and the Culture of Industry;* and *When Dreams Came True: Classical Fairy Tales and Their Tradition.* He is the editor of *The Oxford Companion to Fairy Tales: The Western Fairy Tale Tradition from Medieval to Modern,* among other works.

W. W. NORTON & COMPANY, INC.

Also Publishes

THE NORTON ANTHOLOGY OF AFRICAN AMERICAN LITERATURE
edited by Henry Louis Gates Jr. and Nellie Y. McKay et al.

THE NORTON ANTHOLOGY OF AMERICAN LITERATURE
edited by Nina Baym et al.

THE NORTON ANTHOLOGY OF CONTEMPORARY FICTION
edited by R. V. Cassill and Joyce Carol Oates

THE NORTON ANTHOLOGY OF ENGLISH LITERATURE
edited by M. H. Abrams and Stephen Greenblatt et al.

THE NORTON ANTHOLOGY OF LITERATURE BY WOMEN
edited by Sandra M. Gilbert and Susan Gubar

THE NORTON ANTHOLOGY OF MODERN POETRY
edited by Richard Ellmann and Robert O'Clair

THE NORTON ANTHOLOGY OF POETRY
edited by Margaret Ferguson et al.

THE NORTON ANTHOLOGY OF SHORT FICTION
edited by R. V. Cassill and Richard Bausch

THE NORTON ANTHOLOGY OF WORLD MASTERPIECES
edited by Sarah Lawall et al.

THE NORTON FACSIMILE OF THE FIRST FOLIO OF SHAKESPEARE
prepared by Charlton Hinman

THE NORTON INTRODUCTION TO LITERATURE
edited by Jerome Beaty and J. Paul Hunter

THE NORTON INTRODUCTION TO THE SHORT NOVEL
edited by Jerome Beaty

THE NORTON READER
edited by Linda H. Peterson, John C. Brereton, and Joan E. Hartman

THE NORTON SAMPLER
edited by Thomas Cooley

THE NORTON SHAKESPEARE, BASED ON THE OXFORD EDITION
edited by Stephen Greenblatt et al.

For a complete list of Norton Critical Editions, visit us at
www.wwnorton.com/college/english/nce/welcome.htm

A NORTON CRITICAL EDITION

THE GREAT FAIRY TALE TRADITION: FROM STRAPAROLA AND BASILE TO THE BROTHERS GRIMM

TEXTS

CRITICISM

Selected, Translated, and Edited by

JACK ZIPES

UNIVERSITY OF MINNESOTA

W · W · NORTON & COMPANY · *New York* · *London*

To Alan Dundes and Rudolf Schenda,
two of the most innovative and challenging folklorists of the
twentieth century, in appreciation of their inspiring work

The text of this book is composed in Electra
with the display set in Bernhard Modern.
Composition by PennSet, Inc.
Manufacturing by Courier Companies, Inc.
Book design by Antonina Krass.

Library of Congress Cataloging-in-Publication Data

The great fairy tale tradition : texts, criticism / translated and edited by Jack Zipes.
        p. cm. — (A Norton critical edition)
Includes bibliographical references.

ISBN 0-393-97636-X (pbk.)

1. Fairy tales. 2. Fairy tales — History and criticism. I. Zipes, Jack David. II. Series.

PN6071.F15 G74 2000
398.2 — dc21   00-041897

W. W. Norton & Company, Inc., 500 Fifth Avenue, New York, N.Y. 10110
www.wwnorton.com

W. W. Norton & Company Ltd., 10 Coptic Street, London WC1A 1PU

1 2 3 4 5 6 7 8 9 0

Contents

v

A Note on the Illustrations

There have been hundreds of illustrated books of the classical fairy tales, and they have played a major role in the formation of the great fairy tale tradition. The illustrations included in the present edition have been chosen to provide a small sampling of the diverse and innovative techniques used by artists to project their particular views of the fairy tale discourse. The illustrations for this book have been taken from:

Giambattista Basile, *The Pentamerone; or, The Story of Stories*, trans. John Edward Taylor, illustr. George Cruikshank (New rev. ed. London: T. Fisher Unwin, 1893).

Beauty and the Beast, illustr. Walter Crane (Routledge, 1875).

Fairy Tales of the Brothers Grimm, trans. Mrs. Edgar Lucas, illustr. Arthur Rackham (London: Selfridge, 1911).

Grimms' Fairy Tales, illustr. Charles Folkard (London: Adam and Charles Black, 1911).

Charles Perrault, *Les Contes de Perrault*, preface by J. T. de Saint Germain, illustr. anonymous (Paris: Émile Guérin, ca. 1890).

Giovan Francesco Straparola, *The Facetious Nights of Straparola*, trans. William G. Waters, illustr. Jules Garnier and E. R. Hughes, 4 vols. (London: Lawrence and Bullen, 1894).

The illustration for the cover appeared in Giambattista Basile, *Stories from The Pentamerone*, ed. E. F. Strange, trans. John Edward Taylor, illustr. Warwick Goble (London: Macmillan, 1911).

The early editions of the tales by Straparola and Basile did not contain any illustrations, and the first editions of the tales by the French writers and the Brothers Grimm were sparsely illustrated. It was not until the middle of the nineteenth century that publishers began to include black-and-white ink drawings, woodcuts, lithographs, and paintings in collections of fairy tales. With advances in technology, European and American publishers started to print color illustrations, and they ushered in the golden age of illustration, especially in Victorian England. George Cruikshank, Walter Crane, Jules Garnier, E. R. Hughes, Arthur Rackham, Charles Folkard, and Warwick Goble were among the best British artists at the end of the nineteenth century and beginning of the twentieth. Although Crane created many picture books with several scenes from individual fairy tales, most of the illustrators supplied one drawing for each tale in the book, and the scene they chose tended to highlight and interpret one specific dramatic situation in the tale.

There were also numerous editions with illustrations by unknown artists in England, on the Continent, and in North America. Therefore, I have included several lithographs by an anonymous illustrator from *Les Contes de Perrault*, published by Guérin, who produced various fairy tale books at the end of the nineteenth century.

Introduction

How did literary fairy tales originate? How did they spread? How was their great tradition formed? There are numerous theories about the origins of the fairy tale, but none have provided conclusive proof about the original development of the literary fairy tale. This is because it is next to impossible to pinpoint such proof. It is next to impossible because the fairy tale is similar to a mysterious biological species that appeared at one point in history, began to evolve almost naturally, and has continued to transform itself vigorously to the present day.

It may seem strange to compare the genre of the fairy tale to a natural species. Yet there is a virtue to developing a biological analogy to make sense out of the great tradition of the literary fairy tale. In fact, the literary fairy tale has evolved from the stories of the oral tradition, piece by piece in a process of incremental adaptation, generation by generation in the different cultures of the people who cross-fertilized the oral tales and disseminated them. If we consider that tales are mentally and physically conceived by human beings as material products of culture, then it is possible to analyze how special forms of telling originated as species.

In one of his provocative essays about paleontology, Stephen Jay Gould sought to explain his theory of punctuated equilibrium that has helped him understand speciation, the origin of new and distinct biological populations, and he formulated the following definition: "Species are real units, arising by branching in the first moments of a long and stable existence. A trend arises by the differential success of certain kind of species. . . . Speciation is the real cause of change, not an arbitrary consequence of artificial division of a continuum. Since the causes of branching are so different from those of continuous transformation, trends must receive a new explanatory apparatus under punctuated equilibrium."[1]

Since we know that many different kinds of storytelling existed in antiquity[2] before oral wonder tales came into existence, and since we know that there were many kinds of wondrous oral and literary tales that served to form the hybrid "species" of the literary fairy tale, we can trace a historical evolution of all these tales by examining how bits and pieces of story accumulated in different cultures and then eventually gelled to form a genre. We cannot say with historical precision when the literary fairy tale evolved, but we can trace motifs and elements of the literary fairy tale to numerous types of storytelling and stories of antiquity that contributed

---

1. Stephen Jay Gould, "Opus 200," *Natural History* 8 (August 1991): 18.
2. For a concise history, see Anne Pellowski, *The World of Storytelling*, rev. ed. (Bronx, NY: H. W. Wilson, 1990).

to the formation of a particular branch of telling and writing tales.[3] In the western European tradition, this branching occurred sometime in the fourteenth and fifteenth centuries and led to a special literary genre in the sixteenth century that we today call the literary fairy tale.

Writers and storytellers during the Renaissance began setting a trend by distinguishing a certain type of telling and writing from the main body of storytelling. This type, which can be broadly defined as the oral wonder tale, eventually succeeded to specify and define itself as a separate species and became a literary genre in late-seventeenth-century France. This speciation or evolution of the literary fairy tale can be traced through historical documentation of oral tales and through the comparative analysis of other genres such as myth, legend, anecdote, joke, lais, epic, and so on. As a hybrid genre or species, the fairy tale borrowed from these genres to formulate its own conventions and laws and to stabilize itself throughout Europe by the end of the eighteenth century.

In the course of development, there was a fruitful interaction between oral storytelling and literary reproduction and invention of tales that is often documented in the frames created by the early writers of fairy tales such as Giovan Francesco Straparola in Le piacevoli notti (The Pleasant Nights, 1550/53), Giambattista Basile in Lo cunto de le cunti (known as The Pentamerone, 1634–36), Marie-Jeanne Lhéritier in Oeuvres meslées (Assorted Works, 1696), Marie-Catherine d'Aulnoy in Les contes de fées (The Fairy Tales, 1697), Charles Perrault in Histoires ou contes de temps passé (Stories or Tales of Past Times, 1697), Jean de Mailly's Les illustres fées (The Illustrious Fairies, 1698), Henriette Julie Murat's Histoires sublimes et allégoriques (Sublime and Allegorical Stories, 1699), and others. Of course, the most famous frame of all is that used by Antoine Galland in his translation and adaptation of Les milles et une nuit (The Thousand and One Nights, 1704–17). All the early writers of fairy tales borrowed from other literary and oral tales, and thus their narratives can be regarded as retellings that adapt the motifs, themes, and characters to fit their tastes and the expectations of the audiences for which they were writing. Very little attention has been paid to the depth and extent of their borrowings and the intercultural layers of their tales. In particular, the similarities of the tales and the cycles that developed based on tale types are extremely important to grasp if we want to know more about the origins and stabilization of the literary genre that produced an equilibrium by the nineteenth century. This equilibrium can best be seen in the work of the Brothers Grimm, who created a large and stable body of tales which I designate as the first major equilibrium of the literary genre. It is from this equilibrium that we can look back to see what constituted the literary genre of the fairy tale and look forward to "punctuated" equilibriums, genres that have branched off from the Grimms' model or retellings of the Grimms' tales that have brought about changes in the species.

It is not commonly known that the Grimms' body of tales rests on numerous Oriental, Italian, French, Scandinavian, and Slavic literary and

3. See the important recent study by Graham Anderson, Fairy Tales in the Ancient World (London: Routledge, 2000).

oral stories. However, it is the richness of this intercultural mesh that makes the genre of the fairy tale as species so fascinating and the Grimms' stabilization of the genre so significant. It is this realization that prompted me to collect some of the more significant tales that were published before the Grimms' edition of *Children's and Household Tales* (*Kinder- und Hausmärchen*, 1812–15) and influenced the formation of the Grimms' book as equilibrium of the genre. The period between 1500 and 1815 is key for understanding the genesis of the literary fairy tale, and the significant fairy tales that prefigured the formation of the Grimms' tales have often been neglected. There is, however, a distinct manner in which the Grimms' tales were engendered as equilibrium of the genre, and it involved oral procreation of tales that became very relevant for the survival of people in specific societies, the interaction of oral and literary tales, and the writing down, repetition, and transformation of relevant tales. To a great extent, this process can be traced in the works of Straparola, Basile, d'Aulnoy, Lhéritier, Perrault, and others in this anthology.

The present collection is the first of its kind in any language and brings together unfamiliar fairy tales originally published in Latin, Italian, French, and German before the appearance of the Grimms' tales. And it also includes the familiar Grimms' tales. Not all the stories are strictly speaking fairy tales. Some are humorous folk anecdotes, and others are closely tied to the legend. However, most of them found their way into the French and German classical fairy tale tradition and are highly significant for understanding how the literary genre evolved in Europe and in North America from the sixteenth to the nineteenth century.

The tales are arranged according to types. I have purposely not followed the traditional Aarne-Thompson method of cataloguing the tale types that folklorists use because their system pertains largely to oral folktales and because I have problems with the manner in which they defined their types. Instead, I have arranged the tales according to themes that I thought were most striking and are similar to elective affinities, and I have provided headnotes that explain some of the historical influences that account for the affinities. Unfortunately, I was not able to include every single "pre-Grimm" tale that fit each theme, but I have tried to refer to them in the headnotes.

The headnotes to the tales provide historical background material that addresses the connections between the tales and their authors. The short biographies following the texts of the fairy tales amplify the information presented in the introduction. I have translated all the tales myself, and in each case I have tried to use the first publications or reprints of the first editions. The most difficult tales to translate were those by Giambattista Basile, who wrote them in Neapolitan dialect. Therefore, I used several editions as my sources: Michele Rak's *Lo cunto de li cunti* (1986), which contains the Neapolitan text and a modern Italian translation on opposite pages; Alessandra Burani and Ruggero Guarini's *Il racconto dei racconti* (1994), a modern Italian translation; *The Pentamerone of Giambattista Basile* (1932), translated and edited by N. M. Penzer, and based on a modern translation by the Italian scholar Benedetto Croce. All of these editions have invaluable notes, and wherever I could, I interpreted the notes and incorporated their meaning into the texts of my translation. In addition, I did not seek to annotate the tales in such a thorough manner as did Rak, Burani, Guarini, and Penzer. Scholars interested in pursuing work on Basile can turn to these other editions and translations. Moreover, Nancy Canepa, the leading expert on Basile in the United States, is preparing a complete translation of *Lo cunto de li cunti*, also known as *The Pentamerone*, and I expect her translation to be the definitive one in English with ample notation. All the other Latin, Italian, French, and German texts, while they presented their own difficulties for translation, were not as complex as Basile's extraordinary Neapolitan stories. In some cases, I had already translated the tales, and so I reworked them carefully for this edition.

I have included seven essays for background reading: my own study, "Cross-Cultural Connections and the Contamination of the Classical Fairy Tale"; W. G. Waters's "Terminal Essay" from *The Facetious Nights of Straparola*; Benedetto Croce's "*Lo cunto de li cunti* as a Literary Work"; Lewis Seifert's "The Marvelous in Context: The Place of the *Contes de fées* in Late Seventeenth-Century France"; Patricia Hannon's "*Corps cadavres*: Heroes and Heroines in the Tales of Perrault"; Harry Velten's "The Influence of Charles Perrault's *Contes de ma Mère L'Oie* on German Folklore"; and Siegfried Neumann's "The Brothers Grimm as Collectors and Editors of German Folktales." Waters was one of the first and best scholarly translators of Straparola's tales; Croce, one of the greatest scholars of Italian literature, wrote extensively on Basile and Neapolitan literature; Seifert is one of the foremost American scholars to reinterpret the rise of the French fairy tale as a literary genre in the late seventeenth century; Hannon has made major contributions toward the feminist analysis of the French writers of fairy tales; Velten is one of the first American critics to trace the cross-cultural connections between Perrault and German fairy tales; and the German scholar Neumann provides a comprehensive historical analysis of how the Grimms collected and edited their tales.

In preparing all the material for publication, I was helped by Wolfgang Mieder, one of the world's leading authority on proverbs, who was most generous with his advice, and by Lewis Seifert and Nancy Canepa, whose work in the field of French and Italian fairy tale research respectively is exemplary. Thanks to a research grant from the National Endowment of the Humanities, I was able to devote a great deal of my time to this project in 1998–99. Since I had been dreaming of realizing this project for the past fifteen years and had some difficulty in finding the right publisher for this undertaking, I am deeply grateful to Carol Bemis, my editor at Norton, who was willing to take the plunge and has been most supportive of my work. Finally, for help in seeing the manuscript through production, I should like to express my appreciation to Marian Johnson, Christa Grenawalt, Brian Baker, and Diane O'Connor.

The Texts of
THE GREAT FAIRY
TALE TRADITION

Clever Thieves

Tales about the exploits of thieves were commonly told and published through-out the Medieval and Renaissance periods. Broadly speaking, there were two types of tales: (1) narratives in which the thieves stole for aggrandizement and violated someone else's property—the thieves are depicted in a negative light and are generally punished for their devious and selfish actions; (2) tales in which the heroes do not steal out of social need but to accomplish a particular goal that involves recognition of their skill and cunning—these "admirable" and likeable thieves are often compulsive and seek to celebrate their art. There is also a fascinating version of this kind of master thief in Al-Mas'udi's tenth-century universal history *Muruj al-Dhahab*, first published in English as *El-Mas'udi's Historical Encyclopedia, entitled Meadows of Gold and Mines of Gems* (1841), with a more recent edition, *The Meadows of Gold: The Abbasids*, edited by Paul Lunde and Caroline Stone, published in 1989. In one story, the Caliph Mutawakkil bets the doctor Bakhtishu' that one of the most famous master thieves of his day, who was called by the nickname al-Uqab, "The Eagle," or Abu al-Baz, "Father of the Falcon," can easily steal something from the doctor within three days. If this thief succeeds, the caliph will receive ten thousand dinars. If not, the doctor will be given a country estate. The doctor accepts, and the caliph orders the talented thief, al-Uqab, to steal something precious from the doctor. Although the doctor has his house guarded with great care, the thief manages to steal the doctor himself from his house and carry him to the caliph in a chest. We learn that Al-Uqab succeeded in doing this by mixing a sleeping potion in the food of the doctor's guards. Then he pretended to be an angel who had descended from heaven. He carried a burning torch in one hand and told the doctor that he had been sent by Jesus to take him back to heaven. Consequently, the doctor naively and willingly entered the chest to be taken to heaven. Such histories and legends of thieves circulated throughout the Middle East and Europe. In addition, there were popular books such as François de Calvi's *Histoire générale des Larrons* (1623), often reprinted, which documented the different types of thieves that often served as models in literature. The Grimms' source was primarily a story by Friedrich Stertzing in the journal *Zeitschrift für deutsches Alterthum* 3 (1843). However, it is apparent from the similarities with Straparola's tale that they were familiar with it and may have used it in creating their own tale. Peter Christen Asbjornsen published a version of "The Master Thief" in *Norske Folke-eventyr* (*Norwegian Fairy Tales*, 1841), and it was translated into English and appeared in *Blackwood's Magazine* (November 1851).

GIOVAN FRANCESCO STRAPAROLA

Cassandrino the Thief†

Not very long ago a handsome young rogue named Cassandrino lived in Perugia, an ancient and noble city of Romagna, renowned as a center of learning and lavish living. Cassandrino enjoyed the pleasures of life and was well known in Perugia as a cunning thief. But many of the inhabitants from different social classes made grave and serious charges against him to the chief magistrate of the city because Cassandrino had stolen so many goods from them. The magistrate, however, never punished him, even though he threatened at times to do so, for despite everything, Cassandrino did have a redeeming quality: he never robbed out of mere avarice. Rather he wanted to be in a position every now and then to offer generous and magnificent gifts to those people who showed him favors and treated him with kindness. Indeed, he was so affable, pleasant, and witty that the magistrate loved him very much and would not let a day pass without seeing him.

So Cassandrino continued to lead his partly virtuous and partly degenerate life while the magistrate listened to the just complaints lodged against the young man day after day. No matter what happened, the magistrate could not bring himself to punish Cassandrino because of the great affection he felt for him. One day, however, he summoned Cassandrino to his secret chamber and began to admonish him with friendly words and implored him to put an end to his wayward life and to become more virtuous, warning him of the perilous risks that he was taking. After Cassandrino listened attentively to the magistrate's words, he replied, "Sir, I have clearly understood your friendly and gracious warning, and I know full well that it springs from your affection for me. Therefore, I am most grateful for your advice, but I am distressed that we should be plagued by certain foolish people, jealous of the well-being of others and always ready to do damage to their honor with their spiteful words. These busybodies who spread such tales about me would do better to keep their poisonous tongues between their teeth than to let them run on and harm me."

The magistrate, who did not need much persuasion to believe Cassandrino's story, trusted his words entirely and gave no or little credence to the complaints against him. Due to the affection that he felt for the young man, he closed his eyes so that he would not see anything. Sometime after this last conversation, Cassandrino happened to dine with the provost and began talking about various things that pleased and delighted his friend. Among other things Cassandrino talked about a young man who was so naturally gifted and cunning that there was nothing he could not steal, no matter how well it was hidden or how carefully it was guarded. When the

† Giovan Francesco Straparola, "Cassandrino the Thief'—"Cassandrino, famosissimo ladro e amico del pretore di Perugia, li fura il letto ed un suo cavallo leardo; indi, apprentatoli pre' Severino in un saccone legato, diventa umo da bene e di gran maneggio" (1550), *Favola* II, *Notte prima* in *Le piacevoli notti*, 2 vols. (Venice: Comin da Trino, 1550/53).

magistrate heard this, he said, "This young man can be no one else but yourself, for there is no one as crafty, shrewd, or wily as you are. Well, if you can summon the courage, I promise you one hundred golden florins if, tonight, you manage to steal the bed out of the room in which I sleep."

Cassandrino was somewhat disturbed by the magistrate's proposition and replied, "Signor, you obviously take me for a thief, but I am not a thief, nor am I the son of one. I live by the sweat of my brow and my own industry, and this is how I spend my time. But if it is your desire to cause my death because of this, I shall gladly die because of the affection I have always felt for you and still feel for you."

Cassandrino did not wait for an answer. Instead, he left the magistrate right away, for he wanted very much to respond to his challenge. As a result he ran around the entire day frenetically thinking of a way to steal the bed without being caught. In the midst of his frenzy he managed to concoct a plan. A poor beggar had died that very day in Perugia and had been buried in a grave outside the church of the Franciscans. Therefore, after midnight he went to the beggar's tomb, opened it easily, pulled out the dead body by the feet, and dragged it away. After he stripped the corpse nude, he dressed it again in his own clothes, which fit it so well that anyone would have mistaken the dead beggar for Cassandrino. Then he lifted the corpse on his shoulders as best he could and made his way to the palace. Upon arriving he found a ladder that he had set up before and climbed it with the beggar on his back. Then he began quietly to remove the tiles with an iron crowbar and eventually made a large hole in the ceiling of the room in which the magistrate was sleeping.

The magistrate, who was wide awake in his bed, could clearly hear all that was happening. Even though his roof was being torn to pieces, he did not want to ruin the fun of the game and waited for Cassandrino to enter. "Keep plugging away, Cassandrino," he said to himself. "You're going to be terribly disappointed because you won't get my bed tonight." While the magistrate lay there with his eyes open and his ears alert, expecting that Cassandrino would try to steal the bed, the thief sent the dead beggar through the hole in the ceiling. When the body struck the floor, it made everything shake, causing the provost to jump out of bed and fetch a lamp. Upon seeing the crushed body lying in a heap on the floor, he truly believed that the corpse was Cassandrino's body because he saw the young man's clothes. Immediately he cried out with great regret, "What a miserable sight! Just look at it! How sorry I am! I've caused the boy to die just to satisfy my foolish whim. What will the people say when they know that he died in my house? I had better take some precautions!"

The magistrate continued to lament as he ran to wake his loyal and faithful servant and told him about the unfortunate incident. Then he asked him to dig a hole in the garden and to put the corpse in it so that nobody would ever learn about this ghastly deed. While the magistrate and his servant went to bury the dead body in a grave, Cassandrino, who had silently watched everything from above, let himself down by a rope into the room after he had made sure that nobody was around. Then he made a bundle out of the bed and carried it away with great ease. Soon after the provost had buried the dead body with the help of his servant, he returned to his room and saw that the bed was missing. That night he was not able to sleep much, for he kept thinking about the cunning and skill of the clever thief.

Upon arising the next day, Cassandrino went to the magistrate's palace. When the magistrate saw him, he cried out, "Truly, Cassandrino, you are the most notorious of thieves! Nobody else but you could have stolen my bed with such cunning!"

Cassandrino did not reply and pretended as if nothing had happened, but he was content with himself.

"That was quite the hoax you played on me," the magistrate continued. "But I want you to play another so that I may know how great your mind really is. If you can manage tonight to steal my favorite and dear horse Leardo, I shall give you another hundred florins to add to the hundred that I have already promised you."

Cassandrino listened to the magistrate's request and pretended to be disturbed. He complained loudly that the magistrate had a terrible opinion of him and begged him not to bring about his ruin. Seeing that Cassandrino refused to do what he asked of him, the magistrate grew angry and said, "Well, if you won't do as I ask, don't expect anything else from me but to order you to be hung from a halter on the city wall."

Now Cassandrino realized that he was in a dangerous predicament and that this was not a laughing matter. So, he replied, "I shall do my best to satisfy you, but it's possible that this may exceed my capabilities." Then he asked permission to leave and departed.

As soon as he was gone, the magistrate, who was determined to test Cassandrino's deft ingenuity, called one of his servants and said, "Go to the stable and saddle and bridle my horse Leardo. Then mount him and stay on his back all night. Make sure that you are on your guard and that the horse is not stolen."

Then the magistrate gave orders to another servant to guard the palace itself and to secure all the doors of the palace and the stable with very strong locks.

That night, Cassandrino took all his tools and set out for the main entrance of the palace, where he found the guardian quietly dozing. Since he was very familiar with all the secret places of the palace, Cassandrino let the guardian continue to sleep and went through another passageway. Once he entered the courtyard, he went straight to the stable, which was firmly locked. But with the help of his tools, he easily broke open the door. To his bewilderment, however, he saw the servant sitting on the provost's horse with the reins in his hand. Yet, as he gradually approached the horse, he saw that the fellow was sound asleep, and since he was in such a deep sleep, Cassandrino, the cunning and clever thief, thought of the shrewdest plan imaginable. He carefully measured the height of the horse and then went into the garden where he brought back four thick poles that were normally used to support vines on a trellis. After sharpening them at the ends, he cut the reins which the servant held in his hands and then the harness, the girth, the crupper, and everything else that might hinder him. Afterward he planted one of the poles into the ground with the upper end inserted under one corner of the saddle, he quietly raised the corner of the saddle and placed it on the pole, and he did the same thing on the other three sides. While all this was happening, the servant remained sound asleep and soon rested on the saddle that was set on the four poles firmly planted in the ground. Since there was now no obstacle, Cassandrino haltered the horse and led it away.

Early the next morning the magistrate arose and went straight to the stable, where he expected to find his horse. Instead, he found his servant still in a deep sleep on the saddle propped up by four poles. After the magistrate woke him, he used every possible curse word in the world to heap abuse on him. Right after that he stormed out of the stable.

At the usual hour in the morning, Cassandrino arrived at the palace, and when he saw the magistrate, he gave him a cheerful greeting.

"Truly, Cassandrino," said the magistrate. "You carry away all the laurels among thieves. So, I'm going to call you 'king of the thieves.' However, I want to know once and for all whether you are really as clever and ingenious as I think you are. I believe you know the priest Severino, who lives in the village of Sangallo not far from the city. Well, if you bring him here to me tied up in a sack, I promise to double the two hundred gold florins that I already owe you. But if you fail, you will die."

Now the priest Severino had a good reputation and led an honest life, but he did not have much worldly experience, for he attended only to the affairs of his church and did not care about much else. When Cassandrino saw that the magistrate was not kindly disposed toward him, he said to himself, "This man clearly wants me to die, but perhaps his plan will not work out because I'll find a way to do as he wishes." Once Cassandrino decided to fulfill the magistrate's demand, he began thinking of ways to play a trick on the priest which would serve the purpose he had in mind. Finally, he came up with a plan. First, he went to a friend and borrowed a white stole embroidered with gold and a long priest's robe that came down to the tips of his feet, and he brought these things to his home. Then he built a pair of wings out of a large piece of cardboard and painted them in various colors. He also made a diadem out of tinsel that glistened all around. At nightfall he left the city with his gadgets and went to the village where the priest Severino lived. Once he was there, he hid himself in a thicket with sharp thorns until the day began to dawn. Then Cassandrino put on the robe and placed the stole around his neck. He set the diadem on his head and fixed the wings on his shoulders. Once all this was done, he hid himself once more and did not stir until the time arrived for the priest to go and ring the bell for the Ave Maria. No sooner had Cassandrino finished dressing himself than the priest Severino arrived at the church door with his acolyte. When they entered the church to do the morning service, they left the door open. Cassandrino, who was on the alert, saw that the church door was standing open while the priest was ringing the bell. So, he left his hiding place and went quietly into the church. After he had entered, he went up to the altar and stood upright. Holding open a sack in his hands, he cried out in a soft, low voice, "Whoever seeks the glory of heaven will find it by entering this sack. Whoever seeks the glory of heaven will find it by entering this sack." As he kept repeating these words, the acolyte came out of the sacristy, and when he

saw the white robe and the diadem shining like the sun and the wings as
gorgeous as a peacock's and also heard the words, he was completely
stunned. After he recovered from his shock, he went off to find the priest
and said to him, "Master, I have just seen an angel of heaven in the
church, and he was holding a sack and saying 'Whoever seeks the glory
of heaven will find it by entering this sack.' As for me, master, I've decided
to enter."

The priest, who was not especially well endowed with brains, fully believed his assistant's words, and when he went out of the sacristy, he saw
the angel standing there and listened to his words. Since the priest also
desired to go to heaven, and since he did not want his acolyte to get into
the sack before him, he pretended that he had left his breviary behind
him in his house, and he said to his assistant, "Go home and search my
room for my breviary. I seem to have forgotten it, and I want you to bring
it back."

While the acolyte went to look for the breviary, the priest approached
the angel and crept into the sack with great humility. When Cassandrino,
that cunning, mischievous, and astute rogue, saw that his plan was succeeding nicely, he immediately closed the sack. Then he took off the robe,
the diadem, and the wings, and after making a bundle out of them, he
hoisted it along with the sack on his shoulders and set out for Perugia,
where he arrived when it was still early in the morning.

At the customary hour, Cassandrino presented himself before the magistrate. After he untied the sack, the priest Severino came tumbling out,
more dead than alive, in front of the magistrate and realized right away
that Cassandrino had made a fool out of him. So he began to complain
and cry out that he had been robbed and tricked into the sack and that
Cassandrino had dishonored him. He begged the magistrate to grant him
justice and not let a crime as great as this go without severe punishment
in order to set an example for all other criminals. The magistrate, who
had already grasped what had happened from beginning to end, could not
contain his laughter, and turning to the priest Severino, he said, "My good
father, do not say another word or upset yourself, for you will never lack
for favors from me nor fail to have justice done you. To be sure, I can
plainly see that you've been made the victim of a joke."

The magistrate knew what to say and do to pacify the priest, and after he
took a little purse that contained several gold pieces, he handed it to him
and ordered him to be escorted out of the city. Then, turning to Cassandrino, he said, "Cassandrino, Cassandrino, you've caused quite a stir with
your thieving, and you've become notorious throughout the land. Now, I
want you to take these four hundred golden florins that I promised you because you earned them fair and square. But take care that you live more
modestly than you have been doing. Indeed, if I hear of any kind of complaints against you, I promise you that you will be hanged without mercy."

Thereupon, Cassandrino took the four hundred golden florins, and after
duly thanking the magistrate, he went his way, and he used the money to
set up a trading business and became a wise man who managed his affairs
with great skill.

JACOB AND WILHELM GRIMM

The Master Thief†

One day an old man and his wife sat in front of a wretched-looking hut and sought to relax a while from their work. Suddenly a magnificent coach drawn by four black horses drove up to their home, and out stepped a richly clad gentleman. The peasant stood up and approached the gentleman and asked him what he wanted and how he, the peasant, might be of service to him. The stranger extended his hand to the old man and said, "My only desire is simply once to enjoy a country dish. Prepare some potatoes for me in your customary way. Then I'll sit down at your table and eat them with pleasure."

The peasant smiled and said, "You must be a count or prince or even a duke. Noble people often have such fancies. Your wish shall be fulfilled."

The woman went into the kitchen and began to wash and scrape the potatoes. She intended to make dumplings out of them just the way peasants eat them. While she was working, her husband said to the stranger, "Come into my garden for a while. I must finish something there."

In the garden he had dug some holes and wanted to plant trees in them.

"Don't you have any children who could help you with this work?" asked the stranger.

"No," the peasant answered. "Of course, I had a son, but he has long since departed for the wide world. He was a spoiled boy, clever and crafty, but he never wanted to learn anything and was always playing mischievous pranks on people. Eventually, he ran away, and since then I've heard nothing from him."

The old man took a small tree, placed it in a hole, and stuck a post into the ground next to it. After he had shoveled some dirt into the hole and had stamped it down, he took some twine and tied the stem of the tree to the post at the bottom, in the middle, and on top.

"Tell me," the gentleman asked, "why don't you also tie the crooked and gnarled tree lying over there in the corner. It's bent almost to the ground, and if you tied it to the ground, it would grow straight like these here."

The old man smiled and said, "Sir, you speak according to your experience, and it's apparent that you've not had much to do with gardening. The tree over there is old and knotted. Nobody can make it grow straight anymore. Trees must be raised carefully when they are young."

"It's the same with your son," the stranger remarked. "If you had raised him carefully when he was still young, he would not have run away. By now he must have become old and knotted."

"Certainly," the old man answered, "it's been quite a long time since he left us. He's probably changed."

† Jacob and Wilhelm Grimm, "The Master Thief"—"Der Meisterdieb" (1857), No. 192 in *Kinder- und Hausmärchen. Gesammelt durch die Brüder Grimm* (Göttingen: Dieterich, 1857).

"Would you recognize him if he appeared before you?" the stranger asked.

"Not by his face," the farmer replied, "but he has a mark on him, a birthmark on his shoulder that looks like a bean."

As he said this, the stranger took off his coat, bared his shoulder, and showed the bean to the peasant.

"My God!" exclaimed the old man. "You are indeed my son," and the love for his child roused his heart. "But," he added, "how can you be my son? You're a grand gentleman and live in wealth and luxury. How did you come by all of this?"

"Ah, father," replied the son, "the young tree was not bound to a post and grew up crooked. Now it's too old. It will never become straight again. How did I acquire all this? I became a thief. But don't become alarmed. I am a master thief. There's no such thing as locks or bolts for me. Whatever my heart desires is mine. But I don't want you to think that I steal like a common thief. I only take from the rich, who have more than they need. Poor people are safe. I prefer to give them things rather than to take anything from them. Therefore, I won't touch a thing that doesn't demand effort, cunning, and skill to obtain it."

"Ah, my son," the father said, "I'm not at all pleased by this. Once a thief always a thief. I tell you, nothing good will come of this."

He led him to his mother, and when she heard that he was her son, she wept for joy. However, when he told her that he had become a master thief, two streams of tears flowed down her cheeks. Finally, she said, "Even if he has become a thief, he's still my son, and my eyes are fortunate to behold him one more time."

The gentleman sat down at the table with his parents and once again ate the sparse meal that he had not eaten for such a long time. Then the father said, "If our lord, the count over there in the castle, learns about who you are and what you do, he will not take you in his arms and rock you the way he did when he held you at the baptismal font. Instead he'll let you dangle from the gallows."

"Don't worry, father. He won't harm me, for I know my craft. I'll even go to him myself this very day."

As dusk approached, the master thief climbed into his coach and drove to the castle. The count received him courteously because he thought the thief was a refined gentleman. However, when the stranger revealed himself, the count turned pale and was silent for a while. Finally, he said, "You are my godson. Therefore, I shall allow mercy to prevail over justice, and I shall deal leniently with you. Since you pride yourself on being a master thief, I intend to put your art to a test. However, if you fail, you must marry the ropemaker's daughter, and the cawing of the crows will provide you with music at your wedding."

"My lord," the master thief replied, "think of three very difficult things, and if I don't complete your tasks, you may do with me whatever you wish."

The count reflected for a moment. Then he said, "Well then, for your first task, you are to steal my private horse from the stable. Next you are to take away the sheet from under me and my wife while we are sleeping without our noticing it, and in addition, you are to steal the wedding ring from my wife's finger. For your third and last task, you are to steal the parson and the clerk from the church. Make sure that you have noted all this, for your life depends on it."

The master thief went to the nearest city in the region. There he bought the clothes of an old peasant woman and put them on. Then he stained his face brown and drew wrinkles on it so that nobody would be able to recognize him again. Finally, he filled a small cask with old Hungarian wine and mixed a strong sleeping potion in it. He put the small cask into a basket, which he lifted onto his back. With deliberate steps, he walked with a sway to the castle of the count. By the time he arrived, it had already become dark. He sat down on a rock in the courtyard, began to cough like an old asthmatic woman, and rubbed his hands as if he were freezing. In front of the door to the horse stable there were soldiers lying around a fire. One of them noticed the old woman and called out to her, "Come closer, little mother, and warm yourself at our fire. I'm sure that you don't have a place to sleep for tonight. So you'd better take what you can get."

The old woman tottered over to them and asked them to take the basket from her back. Then she sat down with them at the fire.

"What do you have in your cask, you old bag?" one of the soldiers asked.

"A good drink of wine," she answered. "I earn my living by selling wine. For money and kind words I'll gladly give you a glass."

"Let me have one then," the soldier said, and after he had tasted the wine, he exclaimed, "When wine is good, I always like to have a second!" He let himself be served a second glass, and the others followed his example."

"Hey, there, comrades!" a soldier called out to those who were in the stable. "We have an old lady here who's got wine as old as she is herself. Have a drink too! It'll warm your bellies even better than our fire."

The old woman carried the cask into the stable. One of the soldiers was sitting on the saddled private horse of the count. Another held the reins in his hand, and a third had the horse by the tail. She served them as much as they demanded until the cask ran dry. Shortly after, the reins fell out of the hands of one soldier. He sank to the ground and began to snore. The other one let go of the tail, laid himself down on the ground and snored even louder. The soldier, who sat in the saddle, remained sitting. However, he bent his head forward almost to the horse's neck, and while asleep he blew through his mouth like the bellows of a blacksmith's forge. The soldiers outside had long since fallen asleep on the ground and did not budge. It was if they were made of stone. When the master thief saw that he had succeeded, he gave one soldier a rope in his hand instead of the reins and the other, who held the tail, a straw wisp. But what was he to do with the one who sat on the back of the horse? He did not want to throw him off; otherwise, he would awaken and let out a cry. Soon, however, the thief had an idea. He unbuckled the straps of the saddle, tied the ends of some rope hanging from a ring on the wall to the saddle, and pulled the sleeping rider with the saddle above the horse. Then he fastened the ends of the rope around the posts. He was soon able to release the horse from the chain, but if he had ridden the horse over the stone pavement of the courtyard, the noise would have been heard in the castle. So he wrapped the hoofs of the horse in old rags and led it carefully out of the courtyard. Then he swung himself on top and galloped away from the castle.

At daybreak the master thief jumped on the stolen horse and rode back to the castle. The count had just gotten up and looked out the window.

"Good morning, my lord," the master thief called to him. "Here's the horse that I successfully took from your stable. Just look at how beautifully your soldiers are lying there asleep, and if you go into the stable, you'll see how comfortable your guards have made everything for themselves."

The count had to laugh. Then he said, "Well, you've succeeded this first time, but the second time things will not run as smoothly. And I'm warning you, if I encounter you as a thief, I'll treat you as a thief."

That night, when the countess went to bed, she closed her hand with the marriage ring tightly together, and the count said, "All the doors are locked and barred. I'll stay awake and wait for the thief. If he climbs through the window, I'll shoot him down."

But the master thief went out to the gallows in the darkness and cut down a poor sinner, who had been hanging from the halter, and then he carried him on his back to the castle. There he placed a ladder against the wall that led to the bedroom of the count, put the dead man on his shoulders, and began to climb up the ladder. When he had gotten high enough so that the head of the dead man appeared at the window, the count, who had been on the lookout in his bed, pulled the trigger of his pistol. As he did this, the master thief let the poor sinner fall to the ground. Then he himself jumped down the ladder and hid himself in a corner. The moon was so bright this night that the master thief could clearly see how the count climbed down the ladder and carried the dead man into the garden, where he began to dig a hole in which he intended to bury the dead body.

"Now," thought the thief, "the right moment has arrived." He slipped nimbly out of his corner and climbed the ladder right into the bedroom of the countess.

"My dear wife"—he began talking in the count's voice—"the thief's dead, but he was nevertheless my godson and was more of a rascal than a villain. I don't want to shame him in public, and I also feel sorry for his poor parents. Therefore, I want to bury him myself in the garden before daybreak to keep the affair from becoming known. Now, give me the bedsheet so I can wrap his corpse in it and cart him away like a dog."

The countess responded by giving him the sheet.

"You know what," the thief added. "I feel a touch of generosity. Give me the ring, too. The unfortunate wretch risked his life for it. So let him take it with him into his grave."

She did not want to oppose the count, and though she did it reluctantly, she took off the ring from her finger and handed it to him. The thief made off with both things and arrived safely at home before the count had finished his grave-digging work in the garden.

The next day the count made a long face when the master thief came and brought him the sheet and the ring. "Can you work miracles?" the count asked him. "Who got you out of the grave in which I myself buried you? And who brought you back to life?"

"You didn't bury me," the thief said. "You buried a poor sinner from the gallows," and he told him in detail how everything had happened. The count had to concede that he was a smart and cunning thief. "However, you're not finished yet," he added. "You must still perform the third task, and if you don't succeed, nothing will help you."

The master thief smiled but did not respond. When night fell, he went to the village church with a long sack on his back, a bundle under his arm, and a lantern in his hand. In the sack he had crabs, in the bundle there were very short wax candles. He sat down in the graveyard, took a crab out of the sack, and stuck a wax candle on its back. Then he lit the small candle, set the crab on the ground, and let it crawl around. Next he took a second one out of the sack and did exactly the same thing with this crab and continued working in this manner until he had emptied the sack. After this he put on a long black gown that looked like a monk's cowl, and he pasted a gray beard on his chin. When he was finally unrecognizable, he took the sack in which he had carried the crabs, went into the church, and climbed into the pulpit. The tower clock was just about to strike twelve. When the last stroke of the clock had faded, he cried out with a loud shrill voice, "Hark, you sinful people, the end of everything has come! Judgment Day is near. Hark, hark! Whoever wants to go with me to heaven had better crawl into the sack. I am Peter, who opens and shuts the door to heaven. Behold how the dead ones out there amble and gather their bones together. Come, come and crawl into the sack. The world is going under!"

The cries resounded throughout the entire village. The parson and clerk, who lived closest to the church, had been the first to hear them, and when they caught sight of the lights that were wandering over the graveyard, they realized that something unusual was happening, and they entered the church. They listened to the sermon for a while, and then the clerk nudged the parson and said, "It wouldn't be a bad idea at all if we were to take advantage of this opportunity and together went to heaven in an easy way before Judgment Day actually arrives."

"Indeed," replied the parson, "these were my very own thoughts. If this is your desire, let's be on our way."

"Yes," the clerk answered, "But you, father, take precedence. So I'll follow after you."

The parson went ahead of the clerk and climbed the pulpit, where the thief opened the sack. First the parson crawled inside, then the clerk. Immediately the master thief tied the sack tightly, grabbed it around the middle, and slid it down the stairs of the pulpit. Whenever the heads of the two fools bumped against the steps, the thief called out, "Now we're going over the mountains." Then he dragged them the same way through the village, and when they went through the puddles, he cried out, "Now we're going through wet clouds." And, when he finally dragged them up the castle steps, he cried out, "Now we're on the steps to heaven, and we'll soon be in the outer court." When he arrived at the top, he shoved the sack into a pigeon coop, and when the pigeons fluttered about, he said,

"Just listen to the way the angels are rejoicing and flapping their wings."
Then he bolted the door and went away.

The next morning he went to the count and told him that he had also
completed the third task and had abducted the parson and the clerk from
the church.

"Where have you left them?" the count asked.

"They're lying in a sack up in the pigeon coop imagining that they're
in heaven."

The count himself went up to the coop and convinced himself that the
thief had told the truth. After he had freed the parson and the clerk from
their prison, he went to the thief and told him, "You're an inveterate thief
and have won your wager. You've gotten away with everything this time,
and you've not been harmed. But see to it that you leave my land, for if
you ever set foot on it again, you can count on your advancement to the
gallows."

The inveterate thief took leave of his parents and went forth once more
into the wide world. Since then nobody has ever heard from him again.

Swindled Swindlers

This type of tale is generally referred to as a *Schwank* in German, a farcical tale or comic anecdote, and it was widespread throughout the Medieval period. A Latin poem, "Versus de Unibove," which was published in the Netherlands in the eleventh century, describes how a farmer, mocked by his neighbors, makes fools out of them, and this plot became very common in Italian and French stories of the Renaissance. Elements of the tale can be found in the fourteenth-century Latin collection of tales and anecdotes *Gesta Romanorum*, Giovanni Boccaccio's *Decameron* (1348–53), and Gian Francesco Bracciolini Poggio's *Facetiae* (1438–52). The theme of the clever swindler who does not respect the norms of society is related to many other tales from antiquity that depict a small clever hero who uses his wits to outsmart a giant, ogre, monster, or group of threatening people. These tales tend to be realistic portrayals of peasant life and contain a social critique of the injustices that the poor peasants encountered. For the most part the peasants are portrayed in the farcical tale as carrying out menial tasks such as wood gathering, spinning, weaving, wood chopping, and tending herds of sheep, goats, and geese. The exaggeration serves to highlight their desperate plight, and the ending is often a wish fulfillment in which the clever peasant has plenty of money and plenty to eat. In 1835, Hans Christian Andersen published "Little and Big Klaus," which is closely connected to the Grimms' version "Little Farmer."

GIOVAN FRANCESCO STRAPAROLA

The Priest Scarpacifico†

Not far from Imola, a city plagued by feuds and almost destroyed by them in our time, there was a village called Postema, and the church was administered by a priest named Scarpacifico, a very rich man but also miserly and greedy. His housekeeper was a shrewd and smart woman named Nina, who was so frank that she never hesitated telling any man what she thought was good for him. And because she served the priest Scarpacifico so faithfully and so wisely, he held her in high regard.

Now when the good priest Scarpacifico was younger, he was one of the most vivacious and active men in the region, but as he reached old age, he became more and more exhausted from walking. So the good Nina kept trying to persuade him to buy a horse so that he would live longer. At last, Scarpacifico became convinced by her pleas and arguments and

---

† Giovan Francesco Straparola, "The Priest Scarpacifico"—"Pre' Scarpacifico, da tre malandrini una sol volta gabbato, tre fiate gabba loro; e finalmente vittorioso con la sua Nina lietamente rimane" (1550), *Favola* III, *Notte prima* in *Le piacevoli notti*, 2 vols. (Venice: Comin da Trino, 1550/53).

15

went one day to the market, where he saw a mule, which appeared to suit his needs. So, he bought it for seven golden florins, but there happened to be three boon companions at the market that day, and they were the kind of men who amuse themselves at the cost of others. Therefore, when they saw the priest Scarpacifico buy the mule, one of the crooks said to the others, "Friends, I think that mule over there should be ours."

"How are you going to arrange that?" asked the others.

"Let's station ourselves along the road he must take on his way home," he suggested. "Each of us will be about a quarter of mile apart from the other, and as he passes, each of us will tell him that the mule he's bought is not a mule but an ass. If we are convincing enough and resolute, the mule will be ours."

Accordingly they left the market and stationed themselves along the road as they had planned. When Scarpacifico came along, the first of the swindlers pretended to be on his way to the market and said to the priest, "God be with you, sir!"

"And greetings to you, too, brother," replied the priest.

"Where are you coming from?" asked the thief.

"From the market," answered the priest.

"And what good things have you bought there?" the thief inquired.

"This mule," said Scarpacifico.

"Are you telling the truth, or are you mocking me?" the thief said. "It seems to be that your mule's really an ass."

"How can you say it's an ass?" Scarpacifico replied, and without another word he hurried away. Before he had ridden very far, he met the next crook, who greeted him with "Good morning, sir, and where are you coming from?"

"From the market," answered the priest.

"Is there a good market there?"

"Yes, very good," replied the priest.

"Did you buy something good there?" the thief inquired.

"Yes," responded Scarpacifico, "I bought this mule right here."

"Are you telling the truth?" asked the crook. "They sold that thing to you as a mule?"

"Yes."

"But the fact is that it's an ass."

"What do you mean an ass?" replied Scarpacifico. "If anyone else tells me this, I'll give him the beast as a present right on the spot."

Then he proceeded on his way and encountered the third thief, who said to him, "Good day, master. You must be coming from the market."

"I am," replied Scarpacifico.

"Have you bought something good there?" asked the swindler.

"I bought this mule which I am riding," said Scarpacifico.

"Mule? What do you mean by mule?" said the fellow. "Are you telling me the truth, or are you joking?"

"I'm telling the truth. I'm not joking," maintained Scarpacifico.

"You poor man," said the crook. "Don't you see that it's an ass, not a mule? Oh those greedy thieves, they've swindled you!"

Upon hearing this, Scarpacifico announced, "Two other men I met told me the same thing, and I didn't believe them." Then he got off the mule and said, "Take it. I'm giving you this beast as a present."

The fellow took the mule, thanked the priest for his kindness, and went off to join his companions, leaving the priest to make his way home on foot. As soon as Scarpacifico arrived home, he told Nina how he had bought some kind of horse at the market, thinking it was a mule, but he had actually bought an ass. This was what some people had told him along the way, and so he had given the animal away as a present to the last man he met.

"By Christ!" cried Nina. "Don't you see that they've duped you? I thought you were smarter than this. I swear, they wouldn't have pulled the wool over my eyes the way they've done it to you."

"Well, don't worry yourself about it," said Scarpacifico. "They may have played one trick on me, but I'll play two on them in return. Now that they've fooled me once, you can be sure that these crooks will not be content with that. They'll soon be weaving a new plot to see if they can take advantage of me again."

Now there was a peasant in the village, and he lived near the priest's house and had two goats which were so much alike that it was impossible to tell one from the other. The priest went to the market and bought the two goats from the peasant, and the next day he ordered Nina to prepare a good dinner because he wanted to invite some friends to dine with him. He proposed that she make boiled veal, roast chicken and meat, savory sauces, and a tart that she usually baked for such occasions. Then he took one of the goats, tied it to a hedge in the courtyard, and gave it some fodder. He put a halter on the other and led it off to the market. Once he arrived he was immediately approached by the three swindlers who had stolen his mule.

"Welcome, master," they said, "and what are you going to do here today? Would you like to make another good buy?"

"I've come to buy various provisions," Scarpacifico replied. "Some friends are going to come and dine with me tonight. It would give me great pleasure if you three would come and join my feast."

The three companions willingly accepted Scarpacifico's invitation. Then after the priest had bought everything he needed, he set all the stuff on the back of the goat and said, "Now, go home and tell Nina to boil this veal, roast the chickens and meat, and ask her also to make a tasty sauce with these spices and a delicious tart the way she usually does. Do you understand? Now go in peace."

Then the priest set the goat loose, loaded with all the provisions, and it wandered away, but where it went, no one knows. In the meantime, Scarpacifico and his companions and some other friends strolled about the marketplace until dinnertime. Then they all went to the priest's house, where the first thing they saw on entering the courtyard was the goat which Scarpacifico had tied to the hedge, calmly digesting a meal of grass. The three crooks thought it was the goat which the priest had sent home with the provisions, and they were completely astounded. When they all had

entered the house, Scarpacifico said to Nina, "Have you prepared everything that the goat told you to do?"

The servant understood the gist of his words and replied, "Yes, sir, I
have roasted the lamb and the chickens. I've boiled the veal. I've also
prepared the sauce with spices and baked the tart just as the goat told me."

When the three swindlers saw the roasted chicken, the boiled meat and
the tart, and when they heard Nina's response, they were more astonished
than ever before, and at once they began to ponder how they might steal
the goat. But when the dinner had come to an end and they had not come
up with a way to trick the priest and rob his goat, they said to Scarpacifico,
"Sir, we would very much like to buy your goat."

But the good priest replied that he had no wish to sell it because it was
priceless. But, after a while, he agreed to accept fifty golden florins for the
goat. Believing that the goat was a royal treasure that they had stolen from
under a king's eyes, they immediately handed him the fifty florins. However, the priest said, "I'm warning you. I don't want you to come to me
and complain if the goat doesn't produce exactly what you want at first
because it will take time for the beast to get to know you."

But the three crooks did not bother to reply. They led the goat home
in a cheerful mood, and when they arrived, they said to their wives, "Tomorrow we are going to send you all the food you need to prepare on the
back of this goat."

The next day they went to the town square, where they bought some
chicken and many other things that they needed for dinner, and they
packed all of this on the goat's back and sent it home to tell their wives
what they should do with the food. Once the goat, loaded with all their
provisions, was set free, it departed with great speed and was never seen
again.

When dinnertime arrived, the three swindlers returned home and asked
their wives whether the goat had come back with their provisions and
whether they had cooked everything according to the directions they had
given the goat.

"What fools and numskulls you are!" the women responded. "How
could you ever believe that a beast could do your bidding? You've clearly
been swindled. Since all you do every day is swindle other people, you
were bound to be swindled yourselves!"

When the three companions realized that the priest Scarpacifico had
tricked them and had made away with their fifty golden florins, they exploded in such rage that they wanted to kill him. So they grabbed their
weapons and set out to find him. But the cunning priest, who fully expected that the crooks would come to take his life, kept on the alert for
them and called out to his servant, "Nina, take this bladder which is full
of blood and wear it under your dress. Then when these thieves come, I'll
place all the blame on you and pretend to stab you. But I'll stick the knife
into this bladder, and you must fall down as if you were dead. Then leave
all the rest to me."

No sooner had Scarpacifico finished speaking than the crooks arrived
and went straight for the priest with the intention of killing him. But the
priest said, "My brothers, I don't know why you want to harm me. Perhaps

my servant did something to displease you. I don't know." And, turning toward Nina, he took his knife and stabbed the bladder filled with blood. Then Nina, pretending to have been killed, fell to the ground while the blood gushed in streams all around her. Seeing this strange situation, the priest pretended to repent and started shouting in a loud voice, "What a miserable and unhappy man I am! What have I done? What a fool to have slain the woman who was the prop of my old age? How shall I be able to live without her?"

Suddenly he took a bagpipe made according to his own design, lifted her dress, and placed the pipe between her buttocks. Then he blew with all his might so that Nina quickly revived and jumped to her feet alive and well. When the crooks saw how Nina was restored to life, they put aside their anger, and they bought the bagpipe for two hundred florins and went home much pleased with themselves. Soon after it happened that one of the crooks had an argument with his wife, and in his rage he stabbed her in the breast with his knife and killed her. Immediately the husband took the bagpipe that had been bought from Scarpacifico, placed the pipe between her buttocks, and blew as the priest had done with the hope of reviving her. But he blew his breath in vain, for the miserable woman had departed from this life and had gone to the next. When one of the other companions saw what he had done, he remarked, "What a fool you are! You didn't know how to do it. Let me show you."

So he seized his own wife by the hair and cut her throat with a razor. Then, taking the bagpipe, he blew with all his might but with no better result than the first. Finally, the third crook did exactly the same with his wife so that all three were left without wives. Bursting with anger they headed for the priest's house and were determined not to listen to his tall tales. Instead, they seized him and threw him into a sack with the intention of drowning him in a nearby river. But as they carried him toward a river, something happened that gave them a great scare, and they took flight, leaving the priest Scarpacifico tied up in the sack on the ground.

Soon after a shepherd who was driving his flock to a pasture, happened to pass by, and he heard a sorrowful voice crying out, "They want to give her to me, but I don't want her! I'm a priest, and I can't take her!"

The shepherd was frightened because he did not see where the voice was coming from, and this voice kept repeating the same words over and over again. As he approached it, the priest kept speaking in a loud voice until the shepherd opened the sack and found the priest. When the shepherd asked him why he had been tied up in the sack and why he had been shouting those words so loudly, Scarpacifico said that the lord of the city had insisted on wedding him to one of his daughters, but he did not want to comply because, besides being a priest, he was already too old to marry. The shepherd completely believed every word the priest said and asked, "Do you think, master, that the lord would give his daughter to me?"

"I believe he would," replied Scarpacifico, "provided that you get into this sack and are tied up."

So the shepherd got into the sack, and Scarpacifico tied him tightly and left the place with his sheep. Within that same hour, the three crooks

The Priest Scarpacifico. Jules Garnier, 1894.

returned to the place where they had left the priest in the sack. Without looking into it, they heaved the sack onto their shoulders, carried it to the river, and threw it into the water. Such was the miserable end of the shepherd, who suffered the fate intended for the priest. As the crooks then headed for their home and were talking together along the way, they noticed a flock of sheep grazing nearby. At once they began to plan how they might steal a couple of lambs. But when they approached the flock, they were amazed to see that the priest was tending the sheep, for they had believed he had drowned in the river. So, they asked him how he had managed to get out of the river, and he answered, "You fools! If you had thrown me a little farther into the water, I would have come back with ten times as many sheep as you see here."

When the swindlers heard this, they said, "Oh, master, if you do us a great favor, we'll abandon our crooked ways and become shepherds. We would like you to put us into sacks and throw us into the river."

"Well," answered the priest, "I'm prepared to do anything you wish. In fact, there's nothing in the world that I wouldn't do for you."

After Scarpacifico found three strong and solid sacks made of canvas, he put the three thieves into them and tied them up so firmly that there was no chance of their escaping. Then he threw them into the river. Thus, their unhappy souls went to the place where they were to suffer eternal pain. On the other hand, the priest Scarpacifico returned home a rich man with plenty of money and sheep, and he lived many more years with his Nina in great comfort.

JACOB AND WILHELM GRIMM

Little Farmer†

There once was a village where all the farmers were rich except one who was poor, and he was called Little Farmer. He did not even have a cow, much less the money to buy one. Since he and his wife wanted to own one, he said to her one day, "Listen, I have a good idea. We'll ask our cousin the carpenter to make us a calf out of wood and then paint it brown so that it will look like all the other cows. In time it's bound to get big and become a cow."

His wife liked the idea, and their cousin the carpenter took his plane and saw and built a perfect-looking calf. Then he painted it brown and lowered its head to make it seem that the calf was eating. When the cows were driven out to pasture the next morning, Little Farmer called the cowherd to him and said, "Look, I've got a little calf here, but it's quite small and needs to be carried."

"All right," said the cowherd, and he lifted it in his arms and carried it to the pasture. There he put it down on the grass, and the little calf just stayed at the same spot as if it were eating.

† Jacob and Wilhelm Grimm, "Little Farmer"—"Das Bürle" (1857), No. 61 in *Kinder- und Hausmärchen. Gesammelt durch die Brüder Grimm* (Göttingen: Dieterich, 1857).

"It'll soon be running around by itself," the cowherd said. "Just look at how it won't stop eating."

In the evening, when he wanted to drive the herd back home, he said to the calf, "If you can stand there and eat your fill, then you can also walk on your own four legs. I don't feel like carrying you in my arms again."

Meanwhile, Little Farmer stood in front of his door waiting for his little calf. When the cowherd drove the cows through the village and the little calf was missing, he asked where it was.

"It's still standing and eating in the pasture," said the cowherd. "It didn't want to stop and come with me."

"My God!" said Little Farmer. "I've got to have my calf back."

Then they went back to the meadow together, but someone had stolen the calf, and it was gone.

"It must have gone astray," said the cowherd.

"Don't give me that story!" said Little Farmer, and he took the cowherd to the mayor, who decided that the cowherd was negligent and ordered him to give Little Farmer a cow to replace the missing calf.

Now Little Farmer and his wife had the cow that they had longed for in the past. They were exceedingly happy, but they had no fodder and could not give it anything to eat. So, soon they had to slaughter it, and they salted the meat so it would keep. Then Little Farmer took the cowhide to the city, where he intended to sell it and buy a new calf with the profit. On the way he passed a mill where a raven was sitting with broken wings. Out of pity for the bird, he picked it up and wrapped it in the hide. Just then the weather became bad, and a storm arose with wind and rain. Since he could not continue on his way, he stopped at the mill, where he requested lodging. The miller's wife was alone at the house and said to Little Farmer, "Lie down on the straw over there," and she gave him bread and cheese. Little Farmer ate the food and lay down with the cowhide next to him. Now the miller's wife thought, "I'm sure he's asleep since he was so tired."

Soon the priest arrived, and the miller's wife welcomed him warmly.

"My husband's away," she said. "So let's treat ourselves to a feast!"

Little Farmer's ears perked up when he heard her talking about a feast. He was very disturbed that she had made him put up with bread and cheese. Then the miller's wife brought out four different things: a roast, a salad, a cake, and some wine. As they were about to sit down and eat, there was a knock at the door.

"Oh, God! It's my husband," said the wife. She quickly hid the roast in the tile stove, the wine under the pillow, the salad on the bed, the cake under the bed, and the priest in the hallway cupboard. Then she let her husband in and said, "Thank God you're here again! That's some weather outside. You'd think the world was coming to an end!"

The miller saw Little Farmer lying on the straw and asked, "What's that fellow doing there?"

"Ah," said his wife, "the poor fellow came here in the storm and rain and asked for shelter. So I gave him some bread and cheese and showed him to that place on the straw."

"Well, I've got no objections," said the husband, "but get me something to eat and be quick about it."

"There's nothing but bread and cheese," the wife said.

"I'll eat anything," answered her husband, "even if it's just bread and cheese." Then he glanced over at Little Farmer and called, "Come over here and eat a little more with me!"

Little Farmer did not have to be asked twice but got up and joined the miller in his meal. Afterward, the miller noticed the cowhide wrapped around the raven lying on the floor, and he asked, "What have you got there?"

"I've got a fortune-teller wrapped up inside," answered Little Farmer.

"Can he predict my future?" asked the miller.

"Why not?" responded Little Farmer. "However, he only predicts four things, and the fifth he keeps to himself."

The miller was curious and said, "Let him predict my future."

Thereupon Little Farmer pressed the raven's head so that it cawed "Krr! Krr!"

"What did he say?" asked the miller.

"His first prediction is that there's wine under the pillow," Little Farmer answered.

"Good heavens!" exclaimed the miller, who went over and found the wine. "Go on," he said.

Little Farmer made the raven caw again and said, "His second prediction is that there's a roast in the tile stove."

"Good heavens!" exclaimed the miller, who went over and found the roast.

Little Farmer made the raven caw once more and said, "His third prediction is that there's salad on the bed."

"Good heavens!" exclaimed the miller, who went over and found the salad.

Finally, Little Farmer pressed the raven's head one more time so that it cawed, and he said, "His fourth prediction is that there's cake under the bed."

"Good heavens!" exclaimed the miller, who went over and found the cake.

Now the two of them sat down at the table, but the miller's wife was frightened to death. So she went to bed and took all the keys with her. The miller wanted to know the fifth prediction, but Little Farmer said, "First let's eat these four things in peace, for the fifth is something awful."

So they ate, and afterward they bargained over how much money the miller should pay Little Farmer for the fifth prediction. Finally, they agreed on three hundred talers, and Little Farmer pressed the raven's head one more time so that it cawed loudly.

"What did he say?" asked the miller.

"He said the devil's hiding in the hallway cupboard outside," replied Little Farmer.

"I want the devil out of there at once!" said the miller, and he unlocked the front door. After he forced his wife to turn over the other keys, he gave them to Little Farmer, who opened the cupboard. Then the priest ran out as fast as he could, and the miller exclaimed, "It's true! I saw the black scoundrel with my own eyes!"

At dawn the next morning Little Farmer made off with his three hundred talers. When he returned home, his affairs began to show gradual improvement. He built himself a charming house, and the farmers said, "Little Farmer's surely been to that land where golden snow falls and where people take money home by the shovelful."

So Little Farmer was summoned by the mayor and ordered to reveal where he had gotten his wealth.

"I sold my cowhide in the city for three hundred talers," he said.

When the farmers heard that, they all wanted to take advantage of the opportunity. They ran home, slaughtered all their cows, and then skinned them in order to sell them in the city at a great profit.

"My maid must go first," the mayor declared.

However, when she got to the city, the merchant gave her only three talers for a cowhide, and when the rest of them came, he did not give them even that much.

"What am I supposed to do with all these cowhides?" he asked.

Now, the farmers were furious that Little Farmer had pulled the wool over their eyes, and they wanted revenge. So they went to the mayor and accused the farmer of fraud. The innocent Little Farmer was unanimously sentenced to death by a jury and was to be rolled into the lake in a barrel full of holes. So Little Farmer was led out to the lake, and a priest was brought to read him the last rites. All the others had to leave, and when Little Farmer looked at the priest, he recognized the man who had been with the miller's wife.

"Since I set you free from the cupboard," he said, "you can set me free from the barrel."

Just at that moment the shepherd came by with his flock of sheep, and Little Farmer happened to know that for a long time this man had wanted to become mayor. Therefore, Little Farmer screamed with all his might, "No, I won't do it! Even if the whole world wants it, I won't do it!"

When the shepherd heard the screams, he went over and asked, "What's going on? What won't you do?"

"They want to make me mayor," said Little Farmer, "providing that I get into this barrel, but I won't do it."

"If that's all that it takes to become mayor," said the shepherd, "I'll get in right away."

"If you get in," said Little Farmer, "they'll make you mayor for sure."

The shepherd was happy to comply and got inside. Then Little Farmer slammed the lid down, took the shepherd's flock, and drove it away. Meanwhile, the priest went to the villagers and said he had read the last rites. They then went and rolled the barrel toward the water. When the barrel began to roll, the shepherd cried out, "I'll gladly be the mayor!"

They believed it was no one else but Little Farmer screaming and said, "We believe you, but first we want you to look around down there." And they rolled the barrel into the lake.

Then the farmers went home, and when they returned to the village, Little Farmer came along as cheerful as ever, driving a flock of sheep. The farmers were astonished and said, "Little Farmer, where are you coming from? Are you coming from the lake?"

"Of course," he answered. "I sank down into the water until I reached the bottom. Then I knocked the lid off the barrel and crawled out. There were beautiful meadows with lots of sheep grazing on them. So I brought back a flock of them with me."

"Are there any more left?" the farmers asked.

"Oh, yes," said Little Farmer, "more than you could possibly use."

So the farmers decided to fetch some sheep too, each one a flock, and the mayor declared, "I'm going first!"

They all went down to the lake together, and just then there happened to be in the sky the small flocks of clouds that are called little fleece. They were reflected in the water, and the farmers exclaimed, "We can already see the fleece of the sheep down below!"

The mayor pushed to the front and announced, "I'll dive down first and look around. If everything looks all right, I'll call you."

So he jumped into the water, and there was a big *splash!* It sounded as if he had yelled "Rush!" and the whole group of farmers plunged into the water after him. Thus the entire village was wiped out, and since Little Farmer was the sole survivor and heir, he became a rich man.

Incestuous Fathers

In the western world, the theme of incest took on significance in literature during the eleventh century. Stories dealing with this topic that may have influenced Straparola, Basile, Perrault, and the Grimms appeared in Ser Giovanni Fiorentino's *Il pecorone* (1385) as "Dionigia and the King of England" and in the fifteenth-century verse romance of *Belle Hélène de Constantinople*, of which there are also prose manuscripts. The story of Belle Hélène became very popular and was published in chapbooks and folk collections up to the nineteenth century. There is generally one plot outline that is followed in most of the publications: Emperor Antoine of Constantinople falls in love with his daughter, Hélène, and manages to obtain a papal dispensation so that he may be allowed to marry her. However, Hélène flees to England before the wedding and meets King Henry but does not reveal that she is from a royal family and why she has fled Constantinople. Henry falls in love with her and marries her against his mother's wishes. When the Pope is besieged by the Saracens, Henry goes off to war to help him. While he is absent, Hélène gives birth to twins, but the queen-mother sends a message to her son that Hélène has brought two monsters into the world. Henry writes back that Hélène is to be kept under guard, but his mother changes his message into an execution order. When the duke of Gloucester, who is the acting regent, reads the order, he has Hélène's right hand chopped off as proof that he has slain her. In reality, he sends her off in a boat with her two sons and hangs the hand around the youngest son's neck. In the meantime, he has the hand of his own niece chopped off as replacement, and she is also burned at the stake. After a shipwreck, Hélène's sons are abducted by a wolf and lion who bring them to a hermit who names the boy with the hand around his neck Brac and the other Lion. Meanwhile, Hélène makes her way to Nantes. When Henry learns about Hélène's fate from the duke of Gloucester, he has his mother executed. By chance he meets the emperor Antoine, who is looking for his daughter. Together, Henry and Antoine search for Hélène for a year. At the same time, Brac and Lion commence their quest for their mother. When they come to Tours, they enter the service of the archbishop Martin de Tours, who names them Brice and Martin. Unknown to all, Hélène has also moved to Tours. When Henry and Antoine encounter Brice and Martin in Tours, they notice the hand around one of the boy's necks, and Henry is united with his sons. Soon Hélène comes upon them and she is reunited with her sons, father, and husband, and her hand is restored to her through a miracle.

Many of the motifs in this legend stem from Byzantine and Greek tales and Medieval legends. There is some connection to the marriage customs in the ruling houses in the pre-Hellenistic period. Other important sources are the legend of the famous eighth-century king Offa, John Gower's *Confesso Amantis*, written in the fourteenth century, and Geoffrey Chaucer's *Canterbury Tales* (1387–89). The father's incestuous desire has always been depicted as sinful, and the second half of the story, the transformation of the princess into a mutilated person or squalid, animallike servant, has parallels with the Cinderella tales. However, for the most part the heroine is a princess, and the plot revolves around her fall from and return to royalty. Her purity and integrity are tested, and she proves through a ring or shoe test that she is worthy of her rank. Depending on the attitude of the writer, the incestuous father is punished or forgiven. Sometimes he is just forgotten. The Brothers Grimm based their version on a story that was embedded in Carl Nehrlich's novel *Schilly* (1798). Other literary versions that are related to the topic are Johann Karl August Musäus's "Die Nymphe des Brunnens" ("The Nymph of the Fountain," 1782) and Albert Ludwig Grimm's "Brunnenhold und Brunnenstark" ("Lovely Fountain and Strong Fountain," 1816). There is an old Scottish oral version, "The King Who Wished to Marry His Daughter," published in John Francis Campbell, ed., *Popular Tales of the West Highlands*. Most of the tales dealing with incest are also clearly related to another cycle of tales concerned with "The Maiden without Hands." One of the key literary sources here is Philippe de Rémi's verse romance *La manekine* (ca. 1270), which may have been based on oral tales in Brittany connected to the motif of the persecuted woman.

GIOVAN FRANCESCO STRAPAROLA

Tebaldo†

According to the story that our ancestors told long ago, Tebaldo, prince of Salerno, had a prudent and sagacious lady of good lineage for his wife, and she gave birth to a daughter who, in beauty and manners, was to outshine all the other ladies of the city. However, it would have been better for Tebaldo if his daughter had never seen the light of day, because then he would never have experienced what he did.

At one time, his young wife, wise beyond her years, became ill, and as she was dying, she asked her husband, whom she loved dearly, never to wed another woman unless that lady's finger fit the ring which she herself wore. Well, the prince, who loved his wife just as much as she loved him, swore on his life that he would honor her wish.

After the good princess had died and had been respectfully buried, Tebaldo contemplated marrying again, but he kept in mind the promise he had made to his dead wife and was determined to keep it in some way. Yet, the news that Tebaldo, prince of Salerno, intended to remarry was soon spread abroad and came to the ears of many maidens who were certainly his equal in rank and reputation. But Tebaldo desired very much to fulfill the wish of his dead wife and thus made it a condition that any lady offered to him in marriage had to try on his wife's ring to see whether it fit. However, he did not find a single woman who could meet this condition because the ring was either too big or too small. Consequently, the king rejected all the ladies.

Now it happened one day that Tebaldo's daughter, whose name was Doralice, was with her father, and she noticed her mother's ring lying on

† Giovan Francesco Straparola, "Tebaldo"—"Tebaldo, prencipe di Salerno, vuole Doralice, unica sua figliuola, per moglie; la quale, perseguitata dal padre, capita in Inghilterra, e Genese la piglia pe moglie, e con lei ha doi figliuoli, che da Tebaldo furono uccisi: di che Genese re si vendicò" (1550), *Favola* IV, *Notte prima* in *Le piacevoli notti*, 2 vols. (Venice: Comin da Trino, 1550/53).

the table. So she slipped it on her finger, turned toward her father, and said, "Father, look how well my mother's ring fits my finger!"

Upon seeing this, the prince realized that this was true. But a short time later, Tebaldo was seized by a strange and diabolical idea, namely to take his daughter Doralice for his wife. For a long time, he wavered between saying yes and no. At last, consumed by this sinister scheme and aroused by his daughter's beauty, he summoned her one day and said, "Doralice, my daughter, while your mother was still alive but approaching the end of her days, she asked me with all her heart never to wed again unless I found a woman whose finger fit the ring she herself wore while she was alive. And I swore on my life that I would carry out her wish. This is why I gave a test to all those maidens, but I could not find a single one who could wear your mother's ring except you. Therefore, I've decided to take you for my wife. This way I shall satisfy my own desire without breaking the promise I made to your mother."

Doralice, who was just as pure as she was beautiful, was deeply disturbed when she heard about the evil intentions of her perverse father. But, she was well aware of how vile he could be, and fearing that she might provoke and anger him, she did not answer. Instead, she left his presence with a cheerful face. Since there was no one she trusted as well as her old nurse, who was always there for her, she went to her at once to ask for her advice. When the nurse heard the story of the father's perfidious plans and his evil disposition, she comforted Doralice with kind words, for she knew full well how steadfast and true the maiden was and that she would be ready to endure any torment rather than submit to her lecherous father. Indeed, she promised to help protect her virginity from such a violent and disgraceful threat.

After this conversation, the nurse thought of nothing else but how she might find a solution to help Doralice out of her predicament. She pondered this and that plan, but she did not come up with anything that met her satisfaction. She would have preferred it if Doralice were able to flee and get far away from her father, but she was afraid that Tebaldo was too shrewd and would catch her. If the girl were to fall into his hands after her flight, she felt certain that her father would put her to death.

The faithful nurse mulled over ideas frantically in her mind herself, and finally, she came up with a new plan, and this is what she did: In the chamber of the dead mother there was a beautiful chest, magnificently hand-carved, in which Doralice kept her richest garments and her most precious jewels, and the only person other than Doralice allowed to open this wardrobe was her nurse, who secretly removed all the robes and jewels that were in it. After she moved them somewhere else, she inserted a certain potion into the wardrobe that had a special power: whoever took a spoonful or even less could live for a long time without eating any other food. After doing this, the wise nurse called Doralice, shut her inside, and told her to stay there until such time as God should send her a better fortune and until her father abandoned his bestial plans. The maiden listened to her dear nurse's advice and did exactly as she was told.

In the meantime, Tebaldo, whose ardent desire to marry his daughter had not simmered, made no effort to restrain his unnatural lust. He constantly asked after his daughter, and when he could not find her or discover where she had gone, his rage became so terrible that he threatened to have her killed in some horrible manner.

One morning, a few days later, Tebaldo went into the room where the chest was kept, and when his eyes fell upon it, he could not endure its sight. So, he gave orders with his hand that it was to be immediately removed and sold so that its presence would no longer offend him. The servants were prompt to obey their master's command, and after lifting the chest on their shoulders, they carried it to the great square.

It so happened that a rich and honest merchant from Genoa was at the square, and as soon as he caught sight of the beautiful and splendidly carved chest, he fell in love with it. Indeed, he decided that he would not let it get away from him, no matter how much he might have to pay. So, he approached the servant in charge of selling it, and when the merchant was told the price, he bought it and gave orders to a porter to carry it on board his ship. The nurse, who watched the sale of the chest from a distance, was very pleased with the outcome, even though she was filled with sorrow about losing the maiden. Yet, she consoled herself with the thought that, when it comes to the choice of two great evils, it is always best to choose the lesser of the two.

After the merchant loaded his ship with other valuable goods, he left Salerno and set sail for the island of Britain, known to us today as England. He landed at a port located near a vast plain. He had not been there very long when he saw Genese, who had recently been crowned king of the island and happened to be riding pell-mell along the seashore, chasing a beautiful doe, which ran down to the beach out of fright and threw itself into the waves. The king, exhausted from the long pursuit, decided to rest a while, and upon catching sight of the ship, he asked the merchant for something to drink. Now the merchant pretended not to know he was the king and gave Genese a cordial and appropriate welcome. Eventually he prevailed upon him to come aboard his vessel. When the king saw the beautiful and splendidly carved chest, he was overcome by a great longing to possess it and grew so impatient to call it his own that every hour seemed like a thousand until he could claim it as his own. So he asked the merchant the price and was told that it was extremely expensive. The king, more taken than ever with this precious object, would not leave the ship until they had agreed upon a price. After sending for some money and paying the merchant in full, he took his leave of him and ordered the chest to be carried to the palace and placed in his chamber.

Since Genese was still young at this time, he had not married, and he took great pleasure in hunting every day. Meanwhile, Doralice, who was still hiding inside the chest that had been transported into his bedroom, heard and understood everything that happened in the king's chamber. As she reflected upon the perils of her past, she began to hope that a happier future might be in store for her. Now, when the king left his room for the hunt each morning, Doralice began coming out of the chest and would deftly put the chamber in order by sweeping it and making the bed. Then she would adjust the bed curtains and put on the coverlet, skillfully embroidered with fine pearls, and straighten out the two marvelously ornamented pillows. After this, the beautiful maiden would strew the pretty bed with roses, violets, and other sweet-smelling flowers mingled with Cyprian spices which gave off pleasant odors and had a soothing effect. Day after day Doralice continued to arrange things neatly in the king's chamber without being seen by anyone. As a result Genese was very content, for when he returned from the hunt, it seemed to him as if he were living among all the spices of the Orient.

One day, he asked the queen, his mother, and her ladies-in-waiting which of them had so kindly and graciously adorned his room and freshened it with sweet scents. They all replied that they did not know who had done this, for each morning, when they went to put the chamber in order, they found the bed strewn with roses and violets and pleasant scents. When Genese heard their response, he was very determined to get to the bottom of the mystery, and the next morning he pretended that he was going to visit a castle in a city ten miles away. But, instead of departing, he quietly hid himself in the room, keeping his eyes steadily fixed on everything and waiting to see what might occur. He had not been watching very long when Doralice, looking more beautiful than the bright sun, came out of the chest and began sweeping the room, straightening the rugs, and making sure the bed was tidy. Indeed, she diligently put everything in order as though she had always been accustomed to doing this. Once the beautiful maiden had finished her kind and considerate chores, she sought to return to her hiding place, but the king, who had attentively watched everything, took her by the shoulders and grabbed her hands. Upon seeing how very beautiful she was, fresh as a lily, he asked her who she was. The trembling girl responded that she was the only daughter of a prince, but she had forgotten his name because she had been hiding in the chest so long. Nor would she explain the reason why she had been in the chest. After he had heard her story, the king took her as his bride with the full consent of his mother, and together they had two children.

In the meantime Tebaldo was still possessed by his wicked and perfidious lust, and since he could find no trace of Doralice, search as he would, he began to believe that she must have been hidden in the chest that he had sold. Since she had escaped, she still might be wandering somewhere around the world. Tebaldo was overcome by rage and indignation at the thought, and therefore, he decided to try to discover her whereabouts, and he wanted to find her no matter where she was. He disguised himself as a merchant and took with him a great deal of jewels and precious stones, marvelously wrought in gold. Then, without telling anyone, Tebaldo left Salerno and searched many different countries until he finally met the merchant who had originally purchased the chest. Immediately, Tebaldo asked whether he had successfully sold it and requested to know who had bought the chest. The merchant replied that he had sold the chest to the king of England for double the price that he had paid for it. Upon hearing this, Tebaldo was very happy and now made his way to England. When he landed there, he journeyed to the royal city, where he began displaying his jewels and golden ornaments at the palace wall. Among the items on display were some golden spindles and distaffs, and he cried out, "Spindles and distaffs, ladies!"

Right at that moment one of the ladies-in-waiting was looking out of the window and heard the merchant's cries. When she saw his precious goods, she ran to the queen and told her there was a merchant below selling the most beautiful golden spindles and distaffs that she had ever seen. The queen commanded him to be brought into the palace. So, he climbed the stairs, entered the large hall, and stood before the queen, but she did not recognize her father because she no longer thought about him, while he knew his daughter at once. When the queen saw how marvelous and beautiful the spindles and distaffs were, she asked the merchant how much they cost.

"The price is great," he answered. "But I shall give one of them to your highness for nothing, providing that you will grant me a wish. I should like your permission to spend one night in the same room as your children."

Doralice, pure and trusting, did not suspect that the merchant had anything sinister in mind, and also her attendants persuaded her to grant his wish. But before the servants led the merchant to retire, the queen's attendants decided to give him a cup of wine drugged with opium. When night came and the merchant pretended to be sleepy, one of the ladies conducted him into the chamber of the king's children, where a splendid bed had been prepared for him. Before she left him, the lady asked, "Are you thirsty, my good man?"

"Indeed, I am," he replied.

So she handed him the drugged wine in a silver cup, but the malicious and cunning Tebaldo took the wine and only pretended to drink it. Meanwhile, he really spilled it over his garments and then lay down to rest.

Now there was a side door in the children's room through which it was possible to pass into the queen's chamber. At midnight, when all was still, Tebaldo entered the chamber quietly through this door and, when he reached the queen's bed and found her clothes left on the side, he took a small dagger which he had noticed the day before hanging from her belt. Then he returned to the children's room and killed them both with the dagger, which he immediately put back into its scabbard all bloody as it was. After this he opened a window and let himself down by a rope. Later that morning, as the sun began to rise, he went to a barber and had his long beard shaved off so that he would not be recognized. Then he put on new large and long garments and walked about the city.

As soon as the nurses awakened in the palace at the usual hour to suckle the children, they came to the cradles and found them both lying dead. Immediately they began to scream and to shed a flood of tears. They tore their hair and their garments and laid their breasts bare. The dreadful news was delivered quickly to the king and queen, who ran barefooted and in their nightclothes to the spot. When they saw their dead children, they wept bitter tears.

Soon the news of the two children's murder was spread throughout the city just when a famous astrologer had arrived. By studying the constellations of the various stars, this man could reveal the past and predict the future. When reports about the astrologer's great fame reached the ears of the king, he had the man summoned, and as soon as he arrived at the palace, the king asked whether he could tell him the name of the murderer of the children. The astrologer replied that he could and, whispering secretly in the king's ear, he said, "Your majesty, let all the men and women of your court who wear daggers at their sides appear before you. If among these people you shall find one whose dagger is still stained with blood in its scabbard, that very person is the murderer of your children."

At once the king gave orders that all his courtiers should present themselves, and when they were assembled, he diligently searched with his own hands one by one to see if any one of them might have a bloody dagger, but he could find none. Then he returned to the astrologer and told him all that he had done and that everyone had been searched except his old mother and the queen.

"Your majesty, you must search everywhere," the astrologer replied, "and you must respect nobody. Then you will surely find the murderer."

So the king searched his mother first and found nothing. Then he called the queen, and when he took the dagger, which Doralice was wearing, and drew it from the scabbard, he found it completely covered with blood. Convinced by this proof, the king turned to his wife and exclaimed, "Oh, wicked and despised woman, enemy of your own flesh and blood, traitress to your own children, what drove you to stain your hands in the innocent blood of these babes? I swear to God that you will pay fully for the crime you've committed!"

Although the king was furious and wanted to avenge himself right away by putting her to death in a shameful and disgraceful way, he decided to torment her by making her suffer a long and cruel death. As soon as he came up with an idea, he ordered her to be stripped of her clothes and buried naked up to the chin in the earth. She was also to be fed good and delicious food so that she might live longer and so that the worms might devour her flesh while she was still alive and thus cause her great suffering. The queen, who had endured much misery in the past, knew that she was innocent and faced this torment with patience and dignity.

When the astrologer learned that the queen had been judged guilty and condemned to such a cruel death, he was very happy and satisfied with his work. After he took his leave from the king, he departed from England and returned secretly to Salerno, where he told the old nurse everything that had happened, including how Doralice had been sentenced to a terrible death by her husband. As she listened, the nurse pretended to be joyful, but in her heart she was very sad. Moved by pity and the love which she had always felt for the princess, she left Salerno the next morning by horse. Riding day and night, she soon arrived in England and went directly to the palace where the king was receiving people in a vast hall. The nurse threw herself at his feet and requested a private audience about a matter which concerned the honor of his crown. The king granted her request, took her by the hand, and beckoned her to stand up. Then, after the rest of the company had gone and left them alone, the nurse addressed the king reverently and said, "Your majesty, I want you to know that Doralice, your wife, is my child. She is not, indeed, the fruit of my poor womb, but I suckled and nourished her with my breasts. She is innocent of the crime of which she has been accused, and for which you sentenced her to a cruel and miserable death. And you, when you shall have learned every detail and laid your hands upon the ruthless murderer, you will understand why he slaughtered your children, and you will certainly be moved to pity your wife and free her right away from her long and bitter torment. And if you find that I am lying to you, I shall willingly suffer the same punishment that the wretched Doralice is now enduring."

Then the nurse told the entire story from beginning to end and related point by point what had happened. After the king heard everything, he believed every word she said and gave orders that the queen, who was more dead than alive, was to be taken out of the grave. Then, after careful nursing and treatment by doctors, Doralice recovered her health in a very short time.

While all this was happening, King Genese began great preparations for war throughout his kingdom and gathered together a powerful army which he sent to Salerno. After a short campaign the city was conquered, and Tebaldo, bound hand and foot, was taken back to England and put in prison, where King Genese, who wanted to know the complete truth of his crime, had him tortured. But he confessed to everything without being beaten much. The next day Tebaldo was conducted through the city in a cart drawn by four horses and then tortured with red-hot pincers like Ganelon.[1] After his body had been quartered, his flesh was thrown to ravenous dogs.

And this was how the sad and villainous Tebaldo finished his life, while King Genese and Doralice his queen enjoyed many happy years together. When they died, they left many children behind them.

GIAMBATTISTA BASILE

The Bear†

There was once, it is told, a king of Roccaspra whose wife was the very essence of beauty, but she fell from the horse of health in her best years and collapsed. Before her candle of life was finally extinguished, she called her husband to her and said, "I know that you've always loved me with all your heart. So, now that I've reached my end, show me the depth of your love by promising never to marry again unless you find another woman as beautiful as I have been. Otherwise I shall leave you with a curse wrung from my breasts and shall bear you such hate that I shall carry it with me into the other world."

Now the king loved her more than anything, and when he heard this last wish, he was unable to utter a single cursed word for some time. At last, when he stopped lamenting, he said, "If I ever marry again, may the

---

1. The traitor who deceives Roland in *Chanson de Roland* (*The Song of Roland*, ca. 1100) and brings about the hero's death. Ganelon was later captured by Charlemagne and quartered as punishment for his misdeed.

† Giambattista Basile, "The Bear"—"L'orsa" (1634), *Sesto passatempo della seconda giornata* in *Lo cunto de le cunti overo Lo trattenemiento de peccerille*, De Gian Alessio Abbattutis, 5 vols. (Naples: Ottavio Beltrano, 1634–36).

gout take me! May I be struck dead by a Catalan spear! May I be torn to pieces like Starace![1] For my sake, dismiss the thought from your mind. Don't ever dream that I could love another woman. You were the first woman to carry away my feelings, and you shall take the very last tatters of all my desires with you!"

While he was saying all these words, the poor young woman, whose voice had already rattled with death, rolled her eyes and stretched out her feet.

When the king saw that Patria[2] had been uncorked, a flood of tears was uncorked and flowed from the fountains of his eyes, and he made such a loud hue and cry that his entire court came rushing to the spot. He called out the name of his dearly departed and cursed Fortune, who had carried her away. Then he tore his beard and railed at the stars for causing such a misfortune.

Sometime later, however, seeing the way of the world, he decided to act according to the old sayings. "If your elbow aches, or your wife bellyaches, they are both painful, but they only last a short time." And the other: "It is always good to have two, one in the grave and another at your side."

As soon as night had come out from the drill grounds of the heavens to review the bats, the king began to calculate. "Here my wife is dead and gone from me, and I am now a desolate widower with no other hope for an heir except the poor daughter that she left me. Therefore, I must find some appropriate way of having a son. But how shall I go about this? Where shall I find a woman as beautiful as my wife, when all the others have nothing to show compared with her? What's there to do? Should I go poking all over the place with a stick? Should I search with a bell when nature produced Nardella (may she rest in glory!) and then broke the mold? Alas, I'm trapped in a labyrinth and hemmed in on all sides! But come, I haven't even seen the wolf, and yet I'm running away! I've got to search, look around and listen! Can it be possible that there's no ass in the stable except Nardella? Is this really the end of the world for me? Have famines and plagues killed off all the women? Is their species extinct?"

As soon as he finished saying all this, the king immediately issued a royal proclamation and order announcing that all the beautiful women in the world were to come and take part in a beauty contest because he wanted to marry the most beautiful and bestow a kingdom on her. No sooner had the word spread than women from all parts of the world came to try their luck. Every single hag appeared, no matter how deformed, for once you touch on this subject of beauty, there is not a plague-ridden woman who will give in, nor a sea monster who will yield. Each one stubbornly insists she is the loveliest, and if the mirror tells her the truth,

1. Giovan Vicenzo Starace was the Elected of the People in Naples, who was accused of causing the price of bread to increase during a famine. On May 9, 1585, he was taken from the convent of Santa Maria la Nuova, where he was preparing to call on the viceroy with the other elected officials. He was dragged through the streets and beaten, stabbed, and stripped of his clothing. Eventually his body was torn to pieces.
2. Patria was a lake near Naples and was only open to fishing and hunting at certain times. Generally speaking, the mouth of the lake would be opened to hunters in November.

it is the mirror's fault for not reflecting her as she is, or else the makeup has been badly smeared.

When the city was full of women, the king had them form a line, and he began to walk up and down in front of them like a Grand Turk[3] when he enters his harem to choose the most precious stone on which to whet his damascene blade. He paced back and forth like a monkey who cannot sit still. He brooded and looked at them up and down. The first woman seemed to him to have a crooked forehead; the next had too long a nose; another, too large a mouth; another had big lips; and another was too tall. One was small and malformed; then another was too plump; and yet another much too lean. He did not like the Spanish girl because of her sallow complexion. He disliked the Neapolitan because of the way she walked on her heels. The German seemed to him cold and icy. The Frenchwoman was too capricious. The Venetian was nothing but a shuttle of flax, and her hair was losing its color.

In the end, for either one reason or another, the king sent them away with one hand in front and the other behind. Since none of these pretty faces had pleased him, and he still wanted to hitch himself to a woman, he began turning his thoughts to his own daughter. "Why should I continue this search for Maria all through Ravenna,"[4] he said to himself, "when Preziosa, my daughter, is made from the same mold as her mother? I have this beautiful face at home, and yet I keep going to the ends of the earth to try to find it!"

So, he spoke his mind to his daughter, whose fury and shrieks only heaven alone can describe. In turn, the king flew into a rage and told her, "Lower your voice, and keep your tongue quiet! We shall tie the marriage knot this very night. Otherwise, your ear will be the biggest piece left of you!"

When Preziosa had heard her father's decision, she went back to her room, shed tears about her misfortune, and tore the hair from her head. While she was in the midst of her sad lamenting, an old woman, who had always taken care of her makeup, entered the room and found her in a crazed state. So she listened to Preziosa's tale of woe and then told her, "Keep your spirits up, my daughter, and do not despair. For every evil there is a remedy, except for death. Now, listen to me: tonight when your father tries to play the part of a stallion, although he is more like an ass, put this little stick into your mouth. You will then immediately become a bear and can run away, for he will be so frightened that he will let you escape. Head straight into the woods, where heaven is guarding your future. When you wish to become a woman again, as you are and will always be, take the stick out of your mouth, and you will regain your former shape."

Preziosa embraced the old woman affectionately, had an apron full of flour and some slices of ham and lard brought to her, and then dismissed

---

3. There are many references to the Turks in Basile's tales because of the many wars waged between the Italian principalities and the Turks and also because of the commerce with the Turks.
4. This proverbial saying alludes to a vain and useless search and refers to the unfortunate story of Maria die Brienna, princess of Taranto.

her. When the sun, like an unsuccessful prostitute, began switching quarters in search of new clients, the king summoned some musicians and invited all the courtiers to a great feast. After five or six hours of dancing, the guests sat down at the table and began eating with great appetites. Then the king went to bed, sending word to his bride to bring him the ledger to settle the accounts of love. But Preziosa slipped the stick into her mouth and was immediately transformed into a terrible bear. When she approached in this wondrous form, the king was terrified by this and rolled himself up in the mattress and did not stick his head out, even when morning came.

In the meantime, Preziosa left the palace and set off in the direction of a forest in which the shadows gathered together to disturb the sun at the twenty-fourth hour. It was in those woods that she remained and began holding sweet conversations with the other animals until, one day, the son of the king of Acquacorrente came to hunt in these parts. When he saw the bear, he nearly died of fright, but as soon as he saw that this beast merely walked around him and finally lay down and wagged her tail like a little dog, he took courage and began caressing it, and said, "Cuccia-cuccia, meow-meow, cheep-cheep, ti-ti, grunf-grunf, quack-quack." Finally, he took her home with him, ordered everyone to treat her as they would himself, and had her put in a garden near the royal palace so he could see her as often as he liked from his window.

Now, one day when everybody had left the house and he remained alone, he went to the window to look at the bear. Instead of the bear, however, he saw Preziosa, who had taken the stick from her mouth in order to arrange her hair and was combing her golden tresses. The prince was overcome by the sight of such incredible beauty, and after rushing downstairs, he ran into the garden. But Preziosa, having sensed the danger, put the stick in her mouth and turned back into the bear.

The prince searched the entire garden but was unable to find what he had seen from above and was so crushed by his disappointment that he became extremely melancholy and, after four days, became ill, constantly crying out, "Oh bear, my bear!"

When his mother heard his laments, she thought that the bear had harmed him in some way. So, she ordered her to be killed, but the servants were all so fond of the tame creature, who had succeeded in making even the stones of the street love her, that they disobeyed the queen and refused to harm her. Instead, they took the bear into the woods and told the queen that they had put her to death.

When the prince learned about this, he did incredible things. He jumped out of bed and wanted to make mincemeat of his servants. However, they managed to tell him what really had happened, and in turn, he threw himself onto his horse and searched and searched until he found the bear, whom he brought back to the house again. Leading her into a room, he said, "Oh, mouthful fit for a king, why do you stay cooped in this skin? Oh, candle of love shut in this hairy lantern, why are you driving me cuckoo? Do you want to torment me and watch me burn away slowly? I'm dying from hunger. I have such a great longing for your beauty that I would gladly prostrate myself for it. You can clearly see the proof, for I have shrunk to a third of myself like cooked wine, and I am nothing but skin and bones, for the fever has sewn itself with double thread into my veins! Therefore, lift the curtain of this bristly hide and let me see your beautiful face! Lift, oh lift the leaves off this basket and let me peep at the lovely fruit! Raise this curtain and let my eyes contemplate the display of wonders! Who has shut up such a smooth work of art in a prison woven from bristles? Who has locked up such a treasure in a leather chest? Permit me to gaze at the graceful show and accept all my love as payment, for only a bear's ointment can cure my frayed nerves."

But though he spoke and spoke, he saw that his words were uttered in vain. So, he flung himself back on his bed and had such a terrible fit that the doctors predicted he might not recover. Then his mother, who had no other pleasure in the world, sat down on the side of his bed and said to him, "My son, what has caused this mad fit? Why have you become so melancholy? You are young, loved, noble, and rich. What do you lack, my son? Tell me: your pockets will always remain empty if you are ashamed and behave like a timid person. If you want to marry, then choose, and I shall provide the money to guarantee your pledge. You take, and I'll pay. Don't you see that your sorrows are my sorrows? It is your pulse that beats in my heart. If your blood is filled with fever, I have an apoplectic fit in my brain. Remember, I have no other prop to support me in my old age but you. Therefore, be cheerful for my sake, and make this heart of mine happy. Do not let this kingdom become destroyed, this house ruined, and your mother desolate!"

In response to his mother's words, the prince replied, "There's nothing that can console me but the sight of my bear. Therefore, if you want to see me well again, have her brought into my room. I want no one else to look after me or make my bed and cook my food except her. This pleasure will bring about my cure once and for all."

Although the queen thought it absurd for a bear to act as cook and chambermaid and feared that her son might be out of his mind, his mother had the bear brought into his room in order to please him. The bear walked up to the prince's bed, lifted her paw, and felt his pulse, which terrified the queen, who feared that she would scratch off his nose at any moment. But then the prince said, "My teddy bear,[5] won't you cook something for me and feed me and look after me?"

The bear nodded her head to show that she was going to grant his request. So the mother sent for some chickens and had a little stove lit in the same room. Then a pot of water was set on the stove and brought to a boil. At this point the bear seized a chicken, dipped it into the boiling water, plucked it, cut it into pieces, put one part on the spit and made the rest into such an excellent hash that the prince, who previously had been unable to swallow even a little sugar, finished by licking his fingers. When he stopped swallowing, the bear gave him something to drink with such grace that the queen wanted to kiss her on the face. After this was done and the prince got out of bed to be examined by the doctors, who wanted to see a urine sample, the bear remade his bed and then ran off

5. Basile uses the term "chiappino," which referred to cuddly tame bears.

into the garden, where she gathered a fine bunch of roses and citron-flowers which she spread all over the bed, while the queen said that this bear was worth a treasure and that her son had a bundle of reasons to love her.

The prince took note of all the bear's kind acts, which added fuel to his flames, and if before he had been wasting away by ounces, he was now crumbling away by pounds, so much so that he said to the queen, "Oh mama, my lady, if I cannot kiss this bear, my spirit will leave me!"

The queen, who saw that he was on the point of fainting, turned to the bear and said, "Kiss him. Kiss him, my dear beast. Do not make me see my poor son waste away!"

The bear went up to the prince, who took her by both cheeks and kissed her again and again without stopping. While they stood, cheek to cheek, the stick somehow fell out of Preziosa's mouth, and the prince found the most beautiful thing in the world in his arms. He continued to hold her in his loving arms and cried, "Now you are caught, my squirrel, and you shall not escape again without good reason!"

Preziosa, whose natural beauty was now colored by her blush of modesty, answered, "I am already in your hands. Take care of my honor, for you can slice me, weigh me, and turn me as you like!"

Then the queen spoke and asked the girl who she was and why she had been compelled to lead such a savage life. When Preziosa told her the entire story of how her father had tried to disgrace her, the queen praised her as a good, virtuous girl and told the prince that she would be very content if Preziosa were to become his wife. The prince, who desired nothing else in the world, pledged himself to Preziosa. Consequently, his mother blessed the couple and had their marriage celebrated with a great ceremony and feast. Thus Preziosa was tested on the scales of human justice that showed

Good always comes to those who do good.

CHARLES PERRAULT

Donkey-Skin†

Once upon a time there was a king who was the most powerful in the world.[1] Gentle in peace, terrifying in war, he was incomparable in all ways. His neighbors feared him, while his subjects were content. Throughout his realm the fine arts and civility flourished under his protection. His better half, his constant companion, was very charming and beautiful. She had such a sweet and good nature that he was less happy as king and more

---

† Charles Perrault, "Donkey-Skin"—"Peau d'ane" (1694), in *Griseldis, nouvelle. Avec le conte de Peau d'ane, et celui des souhaits ridicules* (Paris: Veuve de J.-B. Coignard et J.-B. Coignard fils, 1694).
1. Clear reference to King Louis XIV.

happy as her husband. Out of their tender and pure wedlock filled with sweetness and pleasure a daughter was born, and she had so many virtues that she consoled them for their incapacity to have more children.

Everything was magnificent in their huge and rich palace. There was a lovely and sufficient group of courtiers and servants surrounding them. In his stables, the king had large and small horses of every kind that were adorned with beautiful trappings, gold braids, and embroidery. But what surprised everyone on entering the stables was the sight of a master donkey with two large ears in the place of honor. This strange and offensive picture may surprise you, but if you knew the superb virtues of this donkey, you would probably agree that there was no honor too great for him. Nature had formed him in such a way that he never emitted an odor. Instead, he deposited heaps of beautiful gold coins of every kind that were gathered from the stable litter every morning at sunrise.

Now, heaven, which sometimes renders humans content, and which always mixes the good with the bad just like rain may come in good weather, allowed a nasty illness to attack the queen all at once. Help was sought everywhere, but neither the learned physicians nor the charlatans[2] who appeared were able to arrest the spread of the fever that increased day by day. When her last hour arrived, the queen said to her husband, "Before I die, I want you to promise me one thing, and that is, if you should desire to remarry when I am gone . . ."

"Ah!" said the king. "Your concern is superfluous. I'd never think of doing such a thing. You can rest assured about that."

"I believe you," replied the queen, "if your ardent love is any proof. But to make me more certain, I want you to swear that you'll only give your pledge to another woman and marry her if she is more beautiful, more consummate, and wiser than I am."

Her confidence in her qualities and her cleverness were so great that she knew he would regard the promise as an oath and never get married. Indeed, with his eyes bathed in tears, he swore to do everything the queen desired. Then she died in his arms, and never did a king make such a commotion. Day and night he could be heard sobbing, and people believed that he could not keep mourning like this for long and that he wept about his deceased lover like a man who wanted to end this matter in haste.

In truth, this was the case. At the end of several months he wanted to move on with his life and choose a new queen. But this was not an easy thing to do. He had to keep his word, and his new wife had to have more charms and grace than his wife who had been immortalized. Neither the court, with its great quantity of beautiful women, nor the country, the city, or foreign kingdoms, where the rounds were made, could provide the king with such a woman. His daughter was the only one more beautiful, and she even possessed certain attractive endearments that her deceased mother did not have. The king himself noticed this, and he fell so ardently

---

2. Perrault is referring to the numerous con men or merchants who sold medicine and drugs in public places in Paris.

in love with her that he became mad and convinced himself that this love was reason enough for him to marry her. He even found a casuist[3] who argued logically that a case could be made for such a marriage. But the young princess was sad to hear him talk of such love and wept night and day.

Greatly troubled by all of this, the princess sought out her godmother, who lived at some distance from the castle in a grotto of coral and pearls. She was a remarkable fairy, far superior to any of her kind. There is no need to tell you what a fairy was like in those most happy of times, for I am certain that your mother has told you about them when you were very young.

Upon seeing the princess, the fairy said, "I know why you've come here. I know your heart is filled with sadness. But there's no need to worry, for I am with you. If you follow my advice, there's nothing that can harm you. It's true that your father wants to marry you, and if you were to listen to his foolish request, it would be a grave mistake. However, there's a way to refuse him without contradicting him. Tell him that before you'd be willing to abandon your heart to him, he must satisfy some of your desires and give you a dress the color of the sky. In spite of all his power and wealth, and even though the stars may be in his favor, he'll never be able to fulfill your request."

So the princess departed right away and went all trembling to her enamored father. Immediately he summoned his tailors and told them the details on the spot. Then he ordered them to make a dress the color of the sky without delay, or else he would surely hang them all.

The sun was just on the verge of shining the next day when they brought the desired dress, the most beautiful blue of the firmament, and there was not a color more like the sky, and here it was bordered by large clouds of gold. But, the princess was overcome with joy and pain, for she did not know what to say or how to get out of the promise she had made. Then her godmother said to her in a low voice, "Princess, ask for a dress more radiant and exceptional. Ask him for one the color of the moon. He'll never be able to give it to you."

No sooner did the princess make the request than the king said to his embroiderer, "I want a dress that will glisten greater than the star of night, and I want it without fail in four days."

The splendid dress was ready by the deadline set by the king. Up in the sky where the night deployed its stars, the moon was less luxuriant in its dress of silver, and this was highly unusual considering the fact that its vivid illumination made the stars appear pale in the middle of its obedient court.

Admiring this marvelous dress, the princess was almost ready to give her consent to her father, but urged on by her godmother, she said to the enamored king, "I can't be content until I have a dress the color of the sun, even more radiant than this one."

Since the king loved her with an ardor that could not be matched

---

3. A theologian who taught religious morals and was expected to resolve crises of conscience with regard to practical moral questions.

anywhere, he immediately summoned a rich jeweler and ordered him to make a superb garment of gold and diamonds, telling him that if he failed to satisfy the king, he would be tortured to death. Yet, it was not necessary for the king to punish the jeweler, for the industrious man brought him the precious dress by the end of a week. It was so beautiful, bright, and radiant that the blond lover of Clytemnestra,[4] when he drove his chariot of gold on the arch of heaven, would have been dazzled by its brilliant rays.

The princess was so confused by these gifts that she did not know what to say to her father the king. Right then her godmother took her by the hand and whispered in her ear, "There's no need to pursue this path anymore. There's a greater marvel than all the gifts you have received. I mean that donkey who constantly fills your father's purse with gold coins. Ask him for the skin of this rare animal. Since the donkey is the major source of his money, he won't give it to you, unless I'm badly mistaken."

Now this fairy was very clever, and yet, she did not realize that passionate love counts more than money or gold, provided that the prospects for its fulfillment are good. So the skin was gallantly granted the moment the princess requested it.

When the skin was brought to her, she was terribly frightened, and she began to complain bitterly about her fate. Her godmother arrived and explained that, if one does one's best, there is no need to fear. It was necessary to let the king think that she was completely ready to place herself at his disposal and to obey the conjugal law, but at the same time, she was to disguise herself and flee alone to some distant country in order to avoid an impending and certain evil.

"Here's a large chest," the fairy continued. "You can put your clothes, mirror, toilet articles, diamonds, and rubies in it. I'm going to give you my magic wand. Whenever you hold it in your hand, the chest will always follow your path beneath the ground. And whenever you want to open it, you merely have to touch the ground with my wand, and the chest will appear before your eyes. We'll use the donkey's skin to make you unrecognizable. It's an admirable disguise and so horrible that, once you conceal yourself inside, nobody will ever believe that it contains anyone so beautiful as you."

Thus disguised, the princess departed from the abode of the wise fairy early in the morning as the dew began to drop. When the king started preparations for the celebration of the blissful marriage, he learned to his horror that his bride-to-be had fled. All the houses, roads, and avenues were promptly searched, but it was in vain. No one could imagine what had happened to her. Sadness and sorrow spread throughout the realm. There would be no marriage, no feast, no tarts, no sugar almonds. Quite disappointed, the ladies at the court were not to dine anywhere, but the priest was most saddened, for he was to have dined much later and had been expecting a heavy donation at the end of the ceremony.

Meanwhile the princess continued her flight, and her face was made

4. Aegisthus, the Greek hero who helped Clytemnestra kill her husband, Agamemnon, the king of Mycenae.

ugly by dirt. When she extended her hands to people who passed her by and tried to find a place to work, people less refined than she was and more malicious did not want to have anything to do with such a dirty creature when they noticed how much she smelled and how disagreeable she looked. Further and further she traveled and further still until she finally arrived at a farm where they needed a scullion whose job was to wash the dishcloths and clean out the pig troughs. She was put in a corner of the kitchen where the servants, who were insolent and nasty creatures, just ridiculed, contradicted, and mocked her. They kept playing mean tricks on her and harassed her at every chance they had. Indeed, she was the butt of all their jokes and jeers.

On Sundays she had a little more rest, and after finishing her morning chores, she went into her room, closed the door, and washed herself. Then she opened the chest and arranged her toilet articles carefully in their little jars in front of her large mirror. Satisfied and happy, she tried on her moon dress, then the one that shone like the sun, and finally the beautiful blue dress that even the sky could not match in color. Her only regret was that she did not have enough room to spread out the trains of the dresses on the floor. Still, she loved to see herself young, fresh as a rose, and a thousand times more elegant than she had ever been. Such sweet pleasure sustained her and kept her going from one Sunday to the next.

I forgot to mention in passing that there was a large aviary on this farm that belonged to a powerful and magnificent king. All sorts of strange fowls were kept there, such as chickens from Barbary, rails, guinea fowls, cormorants, musical birds, quacking ducks, and a thousand other different kinds that were the match of ten other courts put together. The king's son often stopped at this charming spot on his return from the hunt to rest and enjoy a cool drink. He was more handsome than Cephalus[5] and had a regal and martial appearance that could appropriately make the proudest battalions tremble. From a distance Donkey-Skin watched and admired him with a tender look. Thanks to her courage, she realized that she still had the heart of a princess beneath her dirt and rags.

"What a grand manner he has!" she said, even though he neglected her. "How gracious he is, and how happy the woman who has captured his heart! If he were to honor me with the plainest dress imaginable, I'd feel more decorated than in any of those which I have."

One day the young prince went wandering about adventurously from courtyard to courtyard, and he passed through an obscure hallway, where Donkey-Skin had her humble room. He chanced to peek through the keyhole, and since it was a holiday, she had dressed herself up as richly and superbly as possible and was wearing her dress of gold and large diamonds that shone as purely and brightly as the sun. Succumbing to his desire, the prince kept observing her, and as he watched, he could scarcely breathe because he was filled with such pleasure. Such was her magnificent dress, her beautiful face, her lovely manner, her fine traits, and her young freshness that he was moved a thousand times over. But most of

5. According to Greek mythology, Cephalus, the son of Herse and Hermes, was so handsome that the goddess Eros fell in love with him and carried him up to heaven.

all, he was totally captivated by a certain air of grandeur along with a prudent and modest reserve that bore witness to the beauty of her soul.

Three times he was on the verge of entering her room because of the ardor that overwhelmed him, but three times he refrained out of respect for the divinity he thought he was beholding. So he returned to the palace and became pensive. Day and night he sighed and refused to attend any of the balls even though it was Carnival.[6] He began to hate hunting and attending the theater. He lost his appetite, and everything saddened his heart. At the bottom of his malady was a sad and deadly melancholy. He inquired about the remarkable nymph who lived in one of the lower court-yards at the end of the miserable alley where it remained dark even in broad daylight.

"It is Donkey-Skin," he was told. "But there's nothing nymphlike or beautiful about her. She's called Donkey-Skin because of the skin that she wears on her back. She'd be a real remedy for anyone in love. In short, this beast is almost uglier than a wolf."

All this was said in vain, for he did not believe it. The elements of love had left their mark, and they were constantly on his mind and could not be effaced. However, his mother, the queen, who doted on her only child, begged and pleaded with him to tell her what was wrong. Yet, she pressured him in vain. He moaned, wept, and sighed. He said nothing, except that he wanted Donkey-Skin to make him a cake with her own hands. And so, his mother could only repeat what her son desired.

"Oh, heavens, madam!" they said to her. "This Donkey-Skin is a black drab, more ugly and dirty than the most wretched scullion."

"It doesn't matter," the queen said. "We must fulfill his request, and this is the only thing that should concern us." His mother loved him so much that she would have served him anything on a golden platter.

Meanwhile, Donkey-Skin took some ground flour, salt, butter, and fresh eggs in order to make the dough especially fine. Then she locked herself alone in her room to make the cake. Moreover, she washed her hands, arms, and face and put on a silver smock in honor of the task that she was about to undertake. It is said that, in working a bit too hastily, a precious ring happened to fall from Donkey-Skin's finger into the batter. But some who know the end of this story claim that she dropped the ring on purpose. As for me, quite frankly, I can believe it because, when the prince had stopped at the door and looked through the keyhole, she must have seen him. With regard to this point, women are so alert that nothing can escape their eyes, and they always know what they have perceived. Indeed, I am quite sure and give you my word on it that she was convinced her young lover would gratefully receive her ring.

There was never a cake kneaded so daintily as this one, and the prince found it so good that he began ravishing it immediately and almost swallowed the ring. However, when he saw the remarkable emerald and the narrow band of gold that formed the shape of Donkey-Skin's finger, his heart was ignited by an inexpressible joy. At once he put the ring under

6. The week before the beginning of Lent, devoted in Italy and other Roman Catholic countries and regions to revelry, feasting, and riotous amusement.

his pillow, but his malady continued. Upon seeing him grow worse day by day, the doctors, wise with experience, used their great science to come to the conclusion that he was sick with love.

No matter what one may say about marriage, it is a perfect remedy for lovesickness. So it was decided that the prince should marry. But he deliberated for some time and finally said, "I'll be glad to get married provided that I marry only the person whose finger fits this ring."

This strange demand surprised the king and queen very much, but he was so sick that they did not dare to say anything that might upset him. Now a search began for the person whose finger might fit the ring, no matter what class or lineage. The only requirement was that the woman be ready to come and show her finger to claim her due.

A rumor was spread throughout the realm that, to claim the prince, one had to have a very slender finger. Consequently, every charlatan, desirous of gaining high regard, pretended that he possessed the secret of making a finger slender. Following such capricious advice, one woman scraped her finger like a turnip. Another cut a little piece off. Still another used some liquid to remove the skin from her finger and reduce its size. All sorts of plans imaginable were concocted and put into action by the women to make their fingers fit the ring. The process was begun by the young princesses, marquesses, and duchesses, but no matter how delicate their fingers were, they were too large for the ring. Then came the countesses, the baronesses, and all the rest of the nobility who took their turns and presented their hands in vain. Next came the working girls who have pretty and slender fingers and are well-proportioned. Sometimes it seemed the ring would fit. However, it was always too small or too round and rebuffed everyone with disdain in like manner.

Finally, it was necessary to turn to the servants, the kitchen help, the minor servants, and the poultry keepers, in short, to all the trash whose red and black hands hoped for a happy fate just as much as the delicate hands. Many girls presented themselves with large and thick fingers, but trying the prince's ring on their fingers was like trying to thread the eye of a needle with a rope.

Everyone thought that they had reached the end because Donkey-skin was the only one remaining in the corner of the kitchen. And who could ever believe that the heavens had ordained that she might become queen?

"And why not?" said the prince. "Let her try."

Everyone began laughing and exclaimed aloud, "Do you mean to say that you want that dirty wretch to enter here?"

But when she drew a little hand as white as ivory and of royal blood out from under the dirty skin, and when the destined ring was around her finger and fit perfectly, the members of the court were completely astonished. They were so delirious and astonished that they wanted to take her to the king right away, but she requested that she be given some time to change her clothes before she appeared before her lord and master. In truth, the people could hardly keep from laughing because of the clothes she was wearing.

But when she arrived at the palace and passed through all the halls in her sumptuous dress whose beautiful splendor could not be matched, with

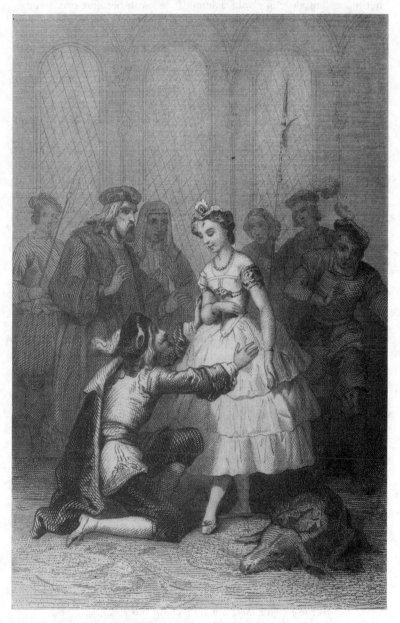

Donkey-Skin. From *Les Contes de Perrault*, ca. 1890.

her blond hair glistening with diamonds, and with her blue eyes so large and sweet filled with a proud majesty and whose gaze always pleased and never hurt, and with her waist so slender and fine that two hands could have embraced it, the ladies of the court showed their feminine politeness and divine courtesy, and all their charms and ornaments dwindled in comparison. Despite the rejoicing and commotion of the gathering, the good king did not neglect to see the many charms of his future daughter-in-law, and the queen was also terribly delighted. The prince, her dear lover, was overcome by a hundred pleasures and could hardly bear the excitement of his rapture.

Preparations for the wedding were begun at once. The monarch invited all the kings of the surrounding countries, who, all radiant in their different attire, left their lands to attend the grand event. Some came from the East and were mounted on huge elephants. The Moors arrived from distant shores, and they were so black and ugly that they frightened the little children. People embarked from all the corners of the world and descended on the court in great numbers. But neither prince nor king appeared in such splendor as the bride's father, who had been in love with her at one time and had purified the fires that had ignited his spirit in the past. He had expurgated all his criminal desires and the odious flame. The little that was left in his soul had been transformed into devoted paternal love. When he saw her, he said, "May heaven be blessed for allowing me to see you again, my dear child."

Weeping with joy, he embraced her tenderly. Everyone wanted to share in his happiness, and the future husband was delighted to learn that he was to become the son-in-law of such a powerful king. At that moment the godmother arrived and told the entire story of how everything had happened and culminated in Donkey-Skin's glory.

It is not hard to see that the moral of this tale is that a child learns it is better to expose oneself to hardships than to neglect one's duty; that virtue may sometimes seem ill-fated, but it is always crowned with success; that strongest reason is a weak dike against mad love and ardent ecstasy; that a lover is not afraid to squander rich treasures; that clear water and brown bread are sufficient nourishment for all young creatures provided that they have good habits; that it is no longer the female under the heavens who imagines herself to be beautiful, and who imagines that, if she had not been mixed up with the three beauties of the famous quarrel between Hera, Aphrodite, and Athena, she would have carried off the honors.[7]

Moral

The tale of Donkey-Skin is difficult to believe,
But so long as there are children on this earth,
And mothers and grandmothers continue to give birth,
This tale will be one to re-conceive.

---

7. Like other Greek goddesses, Hera was jealous of her honor and beauty, and it did not take much to incur her enmity. Shortly before the Trojan War, Paris, the Trojan prince, was asked to judge a beauty contest between Hera, Aphrodite, and Athena. Because he awarded the golden apple to Aphrodite, Hera and Athena were bitter enemies of the Trojans in the ensuing war.

JACOB AND WILHELM GRIMM

All Fur†

Once upon a time there was a king whose wife had golden hair and was so beautiful that her equal could not be found anywhere on earth. Now, it happened that she became sick, and when she felt she was about to die, she called the king to her and said, "If you desire to marry again after my death, I'd like you to take someone who is as beautiful as I am and who has golden hair like mine. Promise me that you will do this."

After the king had promised her that, she closed her eyes and died. For a long time the king could not be consoled and did not think about re-marrying. Finally, his councillors said, "This cannot continue. The king must marry again so that we may have a queen."

Messengers were sent far and wide to search for a bride who might equal the beauty of the dead queen. Yet, they could not find anyone like her in the world, and even had they found such a woman, she certainly would not have had such golden hair. So the messengers returned with their mission unaccomplished.

Now the king had a daughter who was just as beautiful as her dead mother, and she also had the same golden hair. When she was grown-up, the king looked at her one day and realized that her features were exactly the same as those of his dead wife. Suddenly he fell passionately in love with her and said to his councillors, "I'm going to marry my daughter, for she is the living image of my dead wife."

When the councillors heard that, they were horrified and said, "God has forbidden a father to marry his daughter. Nothing good can come from such a sin, and the kingdom will be brought to ruin."

When she heard of her father's decision, the daughter was even more horrified, but she still hoped to dissuade him from carrying out his plan. Therefore, she said to him, "Before I fulfill your wish, I must have three dresses, one as golden as the sun, one as silvery as the moon, and one as bright as the stars. Furthermore, I want a cloak made up of a thousand kinds of pelts and furs, and each animal in your kingdom must contribute a piece of its skin to it." She thought, "He'll never be able to obtain all those furs, and by demanding this, I shall divert my father from his wicked intentions."

The king, however, persisted, and the most skillful women in his realm were assembled to weave the three dresses, one as golden as the sun, one as silvery as the moon, and one as bright as the stars. His huntsmen had to catch all the animals in his entire kingdom and take a piece of their skin. Thus a cloak was made from a thousand kinds of fur. At last, when everything was finished, the king ordered the cloak to be brought and spread out before her. Then he announced, "The wedding will be tomorrow."

† Jacob and Wilhelm Grimm, "All Fur"—"Allerleirauh" (1857), No. 65 in *Kinder- und Hausmärchen. Gesammelt durch die Brüder Grimm* (Göttingen: Dieterich, 1857).

47

When the king's daughter saw that there was no hope whatsoever of changing her father's inclinations, she decided to run away. That night, while everyone was asleep, she got up and took three of her precious possessions: a golden ring, a tiny golden spinning wheel, and a little golden reel. She packed the dresses of the sun, the moon, and the stars into a nutshell, put on the cloak of all kinds of fur, and blackened her face and hands with soot. Then she commended herself to God and departed. She walked the whole night until she reached a great forest, and since she was tired, she climbed into a hollow tree and fell asleep.

When the sun rose, she continued to sleep and sleep until it became broad daylight. Meanwhile, it happened that the king who was the lord of this forest was out hunting in it, and when his dogs came to the tree, they started to sniff and run around it and bark.

"Go see what kind of beast has hidden itself there," the king said to his huntsmen.

The huntsmen obeyed the king's command, and when they returned to him, they said, "There's a strange animal lying in the hollow tree. We've never seen anything like it. Its skin is made up of a thousand different kinds of fur, and it's lying there asleep."

"See if you can catch it alive," said the king. "Then tie it to the wagon, and we'll take it with us."

When the huntsmen seized the maiden, she woke up in a fright and cried to them, "I'm just a poor girl, forsaken by my father and mother! Please have pity on me and take me with you."

"You'll be perfect for the kitchen, *All Fur*," they said. "Come with us, and you can sweep up the ashes there."

So they put her into the wagon and drove back to the royal castle. There they showed her to a little closet beneath the stairs that was never exposed to daylight.

"Well, you furry creature," they said, "you can live and sleep here."

Then she was sent to the kitchen, where she carried wood and water, kept the fires going, plucked the fowls, sorted the vegetables, swept up the ashes, and did all the dirty work. All Fur lived there for a long time in dire poverty. Ah, my beautiful princess, what shall become of you?

At one time a ball was being held in the castle, and All Fur asked the cook, "May I go upstairs and watch for a while? I'll just stand outside the door."

"Yes," said the cook. "Go ahead, but be back in half an hour. You've got to sweep up the ashes."

All Fur took her little oil lamp, went to her closet, took off her cloak, and washed the soot from her face and hands so that her full beauty came to light again. Then she opened the nut and took out the dress that shone like the sun. When that was done, she went upstairs to the ball, and everyone made way for her, for they had no idea who she was and believed that she was nothing less than a royal princess. The king approached her, offered her his hand, and led her forth to dance. In his heart he thought, "Never in my life have my eyes beheld anyone so beautiful!" When the dance was over, she curtsied, and as the king was looking around, she disappeared, and nobody knew where she had gone. The guards who were standing in front of the castle were summoned and questioned, but no one had seen her.

In the meantime, the princess had run back to her closet and had undressed quickly. Then she blackened her face and hands, put on the fur coat, and became All Fur once more. When she went back to the kitchen, she resumed her work and began sweeping up the ashes.

"Let that be until tomorrow," said the cook. "I want you to make a soup for the king. While you're doing that, I'm going upstairs to watch a little. You'd better not let a single hair drop into the soup or else you'll get nothing more to eat in the future!"

The cook went away, and All Fur made the soup for the king by brewing a bread soup as best she could. When she was finished, she fetched the golden ring from the closet and put it into the bowl in which she had prepared the soup. When the ball was over, the king ordered the soup to be brought to him, and as he ate it, he was convinced that he had never eaten a soup that tasted as good. However, he found a ring lying at the bottom of the bowl when he had finished eating, and he could not imagine how it could have got there. He ordered the cook to appear before him, and the cook became terrified on learning that the king wanted to see him.

"You must have let a hair drop into the soup," he said to All Fur. "If that's true, you can expect a good beating!"

When he went before the king, he was asked who had made the soup. "I did," answered the cook.

However, the king said, "That's not true, for it was much different from your usual soup and much better cooked."

"I must confess," responded the cook. "I didn't cook it. The furry creature did."

"Go and fetch her here," said the king.

When All Fur appeared, the king asked, "Who are you?"

"I'm just a poor girl that no longer has a mother or father."

"Why are you in my castle?" the king continued.

"I'm good for nothing but to have boots thrown at my head," she replied.

"Where did you get the ring that was in the soup?" he asked again.

"I don't know anything about the ring," she answered. So the king could not find out anything and had to send her away.

Some months later there was another ball, and like the previous time, All Fur asked the cook's permission to go and watch.

"Yes," he answered. "But come back in half an hour and cook the king the bread soup that he likes so much."

She ran to the little closet, washed herself quickly, took the dress as silvery as the moon out of the nut, and put it on. When she appeared upstairs, she looked like a royal princess. The king approached her again and was delighted to see her. Since the dance had just begun, they danced together, and when the dance was over, she again disappeared so quickly that the king was unable to see where she went. In the meantime, she returned to the little closet, made herself into the furry creature again, and returned to the kitchen to make the bread soup. While the cook was still upstairs, she fetched the tiny golden spinning wheel, put it into the bowl, and covered it with the soup. Then the soup was brought to the king, and he ate it and enjoyed it as much as he had the previous time. Afterward he summoned the cook, who again had to admit that All Fur had made the soup. Now All Fur had to appear before the king once more, and she merely repeated that she was good for nothing but to have boots thrown at her and that she knew nothing about the tiny golden spinning wheel.

When the king held a ball for the third time, everything happened just as it had before. To be sure, the cook now asserted, "Furry creature, I know you're a witch. You always put something in the soup to make it taste good and to make the king like it better than anything I can cook."

However, since she pleaded so passionately, he let her go upstairs at a given time. Thereupon she put on the dress as bright as the stars and entered the ballroom wearing it. Once again the king danced with the beautiful maiden and thought that she had never been more beautiful. While he danced with her, he put a golden ring on her finger without her noticing it. He had also ordered the dance to last a very long time, and when it was over, he tried to hold on to her hands, but she tore herself away and quickly ran into the crowd, vanishing from his sight. However, she had stayed upstairs too long, more than half an hour, and she could not take off her beautiful dress but had to throw her fur cloak over it. Moreover, she was in such a hurry, she could not make herself completely black, and one of her fingers was left white. Then All Fur ran into the kitchen and cooked the soup for the king. While the cook was away, she put the golden reel into the bowl. So, when the king found the reel at the bottom of the bowl, he summoned All Fur and saw the ring that he had put on her finger during the dance. Then he seized her hand and held it tight, and when she tried to free herself and run away, the fur cloak opened a bit, and the dress of bright stars was unveiled. The king grabbed the cloak and tore it off her. Suddenly her golden hair toppled down, and she stood there in all her splendor unable to conceal herself any longer. After she had wiped the soot and ashes from her face, she was more beautiful than anyone who had ever been glimpsed on earth.

"You shall be my dear bride," the king said, "and we shall never part from each other!"

Thereupon the wedding was celebrated, and they lived happily until their death.

Beastly Born Heroes

There are three common motifs in these beast bridegroom fairy tales that had a great circulation in both the oral and the literary traditions in Europe: (1) the parents desperately want to have a child and apparently will accept anything just as long as the wife gives birth; (2) the parents are revolted by their bestial offspring and are put to a test by him; (3) the perspective of the narrative is very much sympathetic to the beast protagonist, who has done nothing to warrant his bestial condition; it is only love and compassion in the form of a tender woman who can preserve the beast's humanity and guarantee his complete transformation into a man. The motif of the young hero who is compelled to wear an animal skin is an ancient one and made its first literary appearance in Sanskrit in the *Pancatantra*, a collection of Indian didactic fables and stories, about 300 C.E. In "The Enchanted Brahmin's Son," a father burns the snakeskin of his son to preserve his humanity. This particular motif can be found in numerous folktales. Generally speaking, however, it is a young woman or her parents who burn the animal skin to set a young man free. The Grimms apparently knew many European literary texts that preceded the final composition of "Hans My Hedgehog," and they based their tale mainly on an oral version told to them by Dorothea Viehmann, wife of a village tailor, who lived near Kassel. In Germany there are two other important versions that bear resemblance to the Grimms' tale and the Italian and French literary tales: Johann Wilhelm Wolf's "Das wilde Schwein" ("The Wild Boar") in *Deutsche Märchen und Sagen* (1845) and Josef Haltrich's "Das Borstenkind" ("The Bristly Child") in *Deutsche Volksmärchen aus dem Sachsenlande in Siebenbürgen* (1885).

GIOVAN FRANCESCO STRAPAROLA

The Pig Prince†

Galeotto, king of Anglia, was a man blessed with great wealth and intelligence. His wife Ersilia, daughter of Matthias, king of Hungary, was a princess whose beauty, virtues, and grace outshone those of all other ladies of the time. Moreover, Galeotto was a wise king who ruled his realm with such justice that no one ever raised a complaint against him. Though he and Ersilia had been married several years, she had not been able to become pregnant, and they were both unhappy about this.

One day, while Ersilia happened to be walking in her garden and pick-

---

† Giovan Francesco Straparola, "The Pig Prince"—"Galeotto, re d'Anglia, ha un figliuolo nato porco, il quale tre volte si marita; e posta giù la pelle procina e diventato un bellisimo giovane, fu chiamato re porco" (1550), *Favola* I, *Notte seconda* in *Le piacevoli notti*, 2 vols. (Venice: Comin da Trino, 1550/53).

ing flowers, she suddenly felt tired. Upon noticing a spot covered with green grass nearby, she went over to it and sat down. Overcome by sleep and soothed by the sweet songs of the birds on the green branches, she fell asleep. Now, by chance, three proud fairies flew by in the air while she was dozing. When they caught sight of the sleeping queen, they stopped, and, gazing at her beauty and charm, they discussed how they might protect her with some spell. Once they reached an agreement, the first fairy said, "I wish that no one will be able to harm her, and that the next time she sleeps with her husband, she will become pregnant and bear a son who will be the most handsome child in the world."

Then the second fairy declared, "I wish that no one will ever have the power to offend her, and that the prince, her son, will become the most virtuous, charming, and courteous man imaginable."

And the third fairy declared, "I wish that she will become the richest and wisest of women, but that the son she conceives will be born in the skin of a pig with a pig's ways and manners, and he will be obliged to live in this shape until he has wed three times."

As soon as the three fairies had flown away, Ersilia awoke, stood up, and returned directly to the palace, taking with her the flowers that she had gathered. A few days later she became pregnant, and when the time of her delivery arrived, she gave birth to a son with limbs like those of a pig. When the news reached the king and queen, they were tormented, and since the king did not wish to disgrace his saintly wife, he felt compelled to have his son killed and cast into the sea. But as he considered the situation, he recognized that this son, whatever he might be, was of his own blood, and he discarded the cruel plans that he had been pondering. Moved by pity mixed with grief, he decided that the son should be brought up and nurtured like a rational human being and not like a beast.

Therefore, the child was nursed with the greatest care, and he would often run to his mother, the queen, and put his little snout and his little paws in her lap. In turn, his compassionate mother would caress him by stroking his bristly back with her hand and embrace and kiss him as though he were a human. Then he would wag his tail and give other clear signs to show how pleased he was by his mother's affection.

When he grew older, the piglet began to talk like a human being and to wander around the city. If he came near any mud or dirt, he would always wallow in it like pigs are accustomed to do and return home covered with filth. When he would approach his father and mother, he would rub his sides against their beautiful garments, defiling them with all kinds of dirt. Nevertheless, they tolerated everything with great patience because he was their only son.

One day he came home covered with mud and filth, as was his custom, and he lay down on his mother's rich robe and said with a grunt, "Mother, I want to get married."

When the queen heard this, she replied, "Don't talk so foolishly. What maiden would ever take you for a husband? You're dirty, and you stink. What baron or knight would ever give his daughter to you?"

But he kept on grunting that he wanted a wife of one sort or another.

Not knowing how to deal with him in this instance, the queen went to the king and said, "What should we do? You see our predicament. Our son wants to marry, but we certainly won't be able to find a maiden who will take him as her husband."

Soon afterward the pig returned to his mother with the same demand and grunted, "I want a wife, and I won't leave you in peace until you bring me the maiden I saw today because she pleases me a great deal."

This maiden was the daughter of a poor woman, who had three daughters, each of whom was very beautiful. When the queen heard this, she summoned the poor woman and her eldest daughter right away and said, "My dear woman, you are poor and burdened with children. If you consent to what I am about to say to you, you will become rich. I have this son who is a pig, and I would like to marry him to your eldest daughter. You don't have to do this out of respect for him because he is a pig, but out of respect for the king and me. Moreover, remember that she will inherit our entire kingdom."

When the young girl heard the queen's words, she was very disturbed and blushed red out of shame. Then she said that she could not possibly agree to the queen's proposition. However, her poor mother pleaded with her so sweetly that she at last consented. So, when the pig came home that day, all covered with dirt, his mother said to him, "My son, we've found a wife for you as you requested."

Then she commanded the bride to be brought into the chamber, and by this time she had been dressed in sumptuous regal attire and was presented to the pig. When he saw how beautiful and charming she was, he was filled with joy, and despite the fact that he was all stinking and dirty, he jumped around her and endeavored to show some sign of his affection by pawing and nuzzling her. But as she felt him soiling her dress, she pushed him aside, whereupon the pig said to her, "Why are you pushing me like that? Didn't I have these garments made for you?"

Then she answered disdainfully, "No, neither you nor any other swine in the whole kingdom of pigs could ever have made this for me."

And when the time for going to bed arrived, the young girl said to herself, "What am I to do with this foul beast? I think tonight, when he falls asleep, I'll kill him."

Now, the pig happened to be nearby and heard these words but said nothing, and when the two retired to their chamber, he got into the sumptuous bed. Stinking and dirty as he was, he lifted and defiled the clean smooth sheets with his filthy paws and snout and lay down next to his wife, pretending to fall asleep, but it was she who fell asleep first. Then he struck her with his sharp hooves and drove them into her breast so forcefully that he instantly killed her.

The next morning he rose early, as was his custom, and he went out into the pasture to feed himself and get dirty. Meanwhile, the queen went to visit her daughter-in-law, and to her great grief, she found that the pig had killed her. When he returned, the queen reproached him bitterly, but he replied that he had only dealt with his wife as she had intended to deal with him. Then he departed with great indignation.

Not many days passed before the pig began once again to beseech the queen to let him marry one of the other sisters. At first the queen would not listen to his request. However, he persisted and threatened to ruin everything in the palace if he could not wed the maiden. When the queen heard this, she went to the king and told him everything, and he answered that perhaps it would be wiser to kill their son before he committed some great crime in the city. Yet the queen, who still loved him like a mother, could not endure the thought of doing away with him, even if he was a pig. So, once again she summoned the poor woman to the palace along with her second daughter, and after she had a long talk with her about giving her daughter in marriage, the second girl consented to take the pig for a husband. Yet things did not go the way that she had desired because the pig killed her the same way he did his first bride, and then he quickly left the palace.

When he returned, he was as dirty as usual and stunk so dreadfully that no one wanted to be near him. The king and queen reprimanded him severely for the crime he had committed, but again he cried out boldly that he had only done to her what she had intended to do to him. Soon thereafter, however, the pig began to plead once again with his mother to let him wed the third sister, who was much more beautiful than the other two. When his request was firmly rejected, he became more insistent than ever, and in the end, he began to threaten the queen with violent and vicious words that he would kill her if she refused to grant him the young girl as his wife. When she heard this shameful and nasty talk, her heart was so torn apart that she feared she might go out of her mind. But she managed to control her feelings and thoughts and summoned the poor woman and her third daughter, whose name was Meldina. Then she said to the girl, "Meldina, my child, I would be greatly pleased if you would consent to marry the pig. You need not pay any respect to him, but to his father and to me. Then, if you're prudent and tolerate him, you may become the happiest and most satisfied woman in the world."

In response, Meldina said with a serene and clear expression that she was quite content to do as the queen requested and thanked her very much for deigning to accept her as a daughter-in-law. Indeed, she realized that she herself had nothing in the world, and it was indeed her good fortune, she said, that she, a poor girl, would become the daughter-in-law of a powerful king. When the queen heard this grateful and amiable reply, she could not keep back the tears for the happiness she felt, but she also feared that the same fate that her sisters had suffered might also be in store for Meldina.

After the new bride was dressed in rich attire and adorned with jewels, she awaited the dear bridegroom, and the pig entered, filthier and muddier than ever. However, she graciously welcomed him by spreading out her precious gown and asking him to lie down by her side. Thereupon, the queen told her to push him away, but she refused and said, "There are three wise sayings, gracious lady, that I recall very well. The first is, it is foolish to waste time by searching for something that cannot be found. The second is, we should never trust anything we hear unless it is reasonable and makes sense. The third is, you should learn to appreciate a rare gift and never let it go once you have it in your hands."

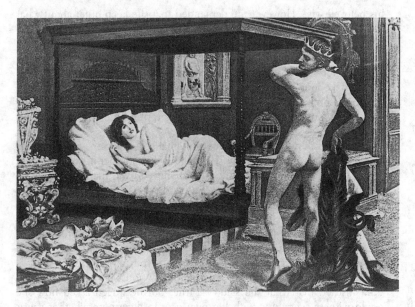

The Pig Prince. Edward Hughes, 1894.

When the pig, who had been wide awake, heard all she had said, he got up and licked her on the face, neck, bosom, and shoulders with his tongue, and she returned his caresses and kisses so that he felt ignited by a warm love for her. As soon as it was time to go to sleep, the bride went to the bed and waited for her dear husband, and it was not long before he arrived, completely muddy and stinking. As soon as he got into bed, she raised the cover and asked him to lie near her and put his head on the pillow, covering him carefully with the nightclothes and drawing the curtains so that he would not feel cold.

When morning came, the pig got up, leaving the mattress covered with excrement, and went out into the pasture to eat. Very soon after, the queen arrived at the bride's chamber, expecting to discover that she had met with the same fate as her sisters. But she found her daughter-in-law cheerful and content, even if the bed was stinking and defiled. So the queen thanked God that her son had at last found a spouse whom he liked.

One day soon after this, when the pig prince was conversing pleasantly with his wife, he said to her, "Meldina, my beloved wife, if I could be completely certain that you could keep a secret, I'd tell you one of mine, something I have kept hidden until now. Since I feel you are very prudent and wise and that you truly love me, I'd like to share this secret with you."

"You may certainly tell me any of your secrets," said Meldina, "for I promise never to reveal them to anyone without your consent."

Since he was sure he could trust his wife, he immediately shook off the dirty and stinking skin of the pig from his body, and he stood there before her as a handsome and attractive young man. That night he lay close to his beloved wife. However, he demanded that she keep quiet about what she had seen, for he had to stay in his miserable shape a while longer. Therefore, when he left the bed, he donned the dirty pig's hide once more.

Of course, as one might imagine, Meldina became immensely happy to have such a handsome and polite young man for her husband. And it did not take long before she became pregnant. In due time she gave birth to a handsome boy, and the king and queen were overjoyed, especially when they found that the child had the form of a human being and not that of a beast.

But the burden of the marvelous and great secret became too much for Meldina to bear, and one day she went to her mother-in-law and said, "Most wise queen, for some time I had believed I was married to a beast, but in fact, you have given me a husband who is the handsomest, the most virtuous, and the most gallant young man that nature has ever created. I want you to know that when he comes to my chamber to lie by my side, he casts off his stinking dirty hide, leaves it on the ground, and is changed into a charming, handsome man. It is impossible for anyone to believe this change if you don't see it with your own eyes."

The queen thought that her daughter-in-law must be joking, but Meldina insisted that what she said was true. So the queen asked how she could witness everything with her own eyes to determine whether it was true, and her daughter-in-law replied, "Come to my chamber tonight when we fall asleep. The door will be open, and you'll find that what I tell you is the truth."

That same night, when the appointed time had arrived and everyone had gone to bed, the queen had some torches kindled and went to her son's chamber accompanied by the king. Upon entering, she saw the pig's skin lying on the floor in a corner of the room, and when she went to the bed, she found a handsome young man who had his arms wrapped around Meldina. To say the least, the queen and king were extremely delighted, and the king ordered the pig's hide to be torn to shreds before anyone was allowed to leave the room. Their joy about the recovery of their son was in fact so great that they almost died from it.

When King Galeotto saw that he had such a fine son and a grandchild as well, he discarded his diadem and his royal robes and had his son crowned king in his place with great pomp. Thereafter, his son was known as King Pig, and to the great satisfaction of all the people in the realm, the young king began his reign, and he lived long and happily with Meldina, his beloved wife.

MARIE-CATHERINE D'AULNOY

The Wild Boar†

Once upon a time there was a king and queen who lived in great sadness because they had no children. Though still beautiful, the queen was no longer young, so she did not dare look forward to having any children. This tormented her a great deal. She slept little and was always sighing and praying to the gods and all the fairies to give her what she wished.

One day while she was strolling in a small woods, she gathered some violets and roses and also some strawberries. As soon as she had eaten some of the strawberries, she was overcome by a profound urge to sleep. So she lay down at the foot of a tree and fell asleep. While she slept, she dreamed that she saw three fairies passing through the air, and they stopped just over her head. The first one looked pityingly at her and said, "Here is a lovely queen, and we would be doing a real service if we were to give her a child."

"I agree," said the second. "Since you are the eldest, why don't you begin?"

"My gift to her," the eldest went on, "is a son, the handsomest, the most amiable, and the best loved in the world."

"As for me," said the other, "I want her to see this son happy in whatever he undertakes, and he will be powerful, intelligent, and just."

When the turn for the third fairy arrived, she burst out laughing and mumbled some words between her teeth that the queen did not hear.

That was her dream. Waking up after a few minutes, she saw nothing in the air nor in the garden. "Alas!" she said. "I don't have enough good fortune to hope that my dream may come true. How grateful I'd be if the gods and good fairies granted me a son!" Gathering some more flowers, she returned to the palace more cheerful than usual. The king noticed this and asked her to tell him the reason. She refused, but he insisted.

"It is not even worthy of your curiosity," she said to him. "It is nothing but a dream, and you will think me very silly if I were to believe in it anyway." Then she told him that while she was asleep, she had seen three fairies in the air, and she recalled what two of them had said, but the third had burst out laughing without her being able to hear what she had muttered.

"This dream pleases me as it must you," said the king, "but that fairy with her wry humor makes me uneasy, for most of them are mischievous, and it is not always a good sign when they laugh."

"As for me," replied the queen, "I believe that signifies neither good nor evil. My mind is filled with my desire to have a son, and thus I imagine a hundred things. Besides, what could happen to him, supposing there were anything true in what I have dreamed? Wouldn't he be endowed with all that can be most advantageous to him? May heaven grant that I

---

† Marie-Catherine d'Aulnoy, "The Wild Boar"—"Le prince Marcassin" (1698), in *Suite des contes nouveaux ou les fées à la mode*, 2 vols. (Paris: Théodore Girard, 1698).

57

receive this consolation!" Thereupon she began to weep. The king assured her that she was so dear to him that she made up for everything.

When some months had passed, the queen knew that she was pregnant. The entire kingdom was given word to say prayers for her. The altars smoked only with the sacrifices offered to the gods for the preservation of such a dear treasure. The assembled states sent deputies to compliment their majesties. All the princes of the blood, the princesses, and the ambassadors were at the court when the queen was brought to bed. The baby garments for the dear child were remarkably beautiful, and the nurse excellent. But the public joy was quickly changed to sadness when, instead of a handsome prince, a little wild boar was born! Everybody shrieked, which frightened the queen very much. She asked what was the matter, but they did not wish to tell her for fear she should die of grief. So, on the contrary, they assured her that she was the mother of a fine boy and that she had cause for rejoicing.

But the king was very distressed. He ordered them to put the wild boar in a sack and throw him to the bottom of the sea so that the memory of an event so revolting might be lost entirely. But afterward he had pity, and thinking it right to consult the queen about this matter, he gave orders for the boar to be fed and did not say a word to his wife until the danger was past that a great disappointment might cause her death. Every day she asked to see her son, and they told her he was too delicate to be brought from his room to her own, and she was satisfied with that explanation.

As for Prince Boar, he felt himself grow like a wild boar with a robust desire to live. They had to provide six nurses for him, three of them dry nurses, in the English fashion. These women kept giving him Spanish wines and cordials to drink, which taught him early to be a connoisseur of the best wines. The queen, impatient to caress her baby, told the king that she was well enough to go as far as the child's room, and that she could no longer live without seeing her son. The king heaved a deep sigh and ordered them to bring the heir to the crown to them. He was swaddled like a child in blankets of gold brocade. The queen took him in her arms and lifted a frill of lace that covered his head, and—alas, she was totally dismayed by the sight! That moment seemed as if it would be the last of her life. She looked with sad eyes at the king, not daring to utter a word.

"Don't torment yourself, my dear queen," he said to her. "I place no blame on you because of our misfortune. It is, no doubt, a trick played by some wicked fairy, and if you give your consent, I shall carry out my first plan, which was to have the little monster drowned."

"Ah, sire!" she said. "Don't make me your accomplice in such a cruel deed. I am the mother of this unfortunate wild boar. I feel the tenderness within me making an appeal for him. Do not harm him, I beg of you. He has already suffered too much by being born a wild boar when he should have been a man."

So deeply did she move the king by her tears and her reasoning that he promised what she requested. Therefore, the ladies who had charge of raising the boar began to take much more care of him because, until then, they had regarded him as a miserable beast soon to serve as food for the fish. It is true that, in spite of his ugliness, his eyes appeared to be full of intelligence. They had taught him to give his little foot to those who came to salute him as others give their hand. They had decked him out with diamond bracelets, and in all his ways there was a certain grace.

The queen could not help but love him. She held him often in her arms, and at the bottom of her heart she thought him pretty, though she dared not utter this for fear they might think her crazy. But she did say to her friends that her son seemed to be of an amiable disposition. She covered him with a thousand knots of rose-colored ribbons, and his ears were pierced. He had a string with which they held him up to teach him to walk on his hind legs. They put shoes on him and silken stockings fastened over the knee to make his legs look longer. He was beaten whenever he wanted to grunt. In short, they weaned him from the habits of wild boars as much as it was possible.

One evening, when the queen was out walking and carrying him in her arms, she passed under the same tree where she had fallen asleep and where she had dreamed all that I have already told. The remembrance of that adventure came back to her mind with great vividness. "Here then," she said, "is the prince so handsome, so perfect, and so happy, that I was supposed to have! Oh deceptive dream! Oh fatal vision! Oh fairies, what did I do for you to mock me so?" She was murmuring these words under her breath when all of a sudden she saw an oak spring up, and a richly dressed lady appeared from it. She looked at the queen in a kindly manner and said, "Great queen, do not grieve at having given birth to the wild little boar. I assure you that there will come a time when he will seem lovely to you."

The queen recognized her as one of the three fairies who had passed through the air while she had been asleep and had stopped and had granted her a son. "It is difficult for me to believe you, madam," she answered. "No matter how much intelligence my son may possess, who could love him with such a face like this?"

Once again the fairy answered, "Do not grieve, great queen, at having given birth to the wild boar. I assure you that there will come a time when he will seem lovely to you." Then she disappeared immediately into the tree and the tree into the earth without it even appearing that there had ever been one in that place.

The queen was very astonished by this new adventure and could not help but hope that the fairies would take some care of the royal beast. She returned quickly to the palace to tell the king what had occurred, but he thought that she had invented this means of making his son less odious to him.

"I see quite well," she said, "from the way you are listening to me that you don't believe me. Yet nothing can be more true than what I have just told you."

"It is very hard," said the king, "to endure the mockery of the fairies. How could they possibly make anything else out of our child than a wild boar? I never think of him without being overwhelmed by grief."

The queen left him, and she was more troubled than ever. She had hoped that the fairy's promises would soften the king's sorrow, yet, he would hardly listen to them. So she withdrew, determined not to speak anymore about her son to him and to leave it to the gods to console her husband.

Meanwhile, the wild boar began to speak like other children: he lisped a little, but that did not diminish the queen's pleasure in hearing him, for she had doubted whether he would ever speak at all. He grew very tall and often walked on his hind feet. He wore long garments covering his legs, and an English cap of black velvet to conceal his head, ears, and a part of his snout. To tell the truth, his tusks were terrible, and his bristles stood up in a fearsome way. His look was proud, and he evoked an awe of absolute command. He ate out of a golden trough in which truffles, acorns, morels, and grass were prepared for him, and no pains were spared to teach him cleanliness and politeness. He was born with a superior mind and he had dauntless courage. Recognizing his qualities, the king began to care more for him than he had until then, and he hired good instructors to teach him all they could. The wild boar was not successful with figure dances, but in round dances and the minuet, where speed and lightness are required, he did wonderfully. As for musical instruments, he knew well enough that the lute and the theorbo[1] were not suitable for him. He loved the guitar and played the flute beautifully. He rode on horseback with astonishing talent and grace. Hardly a day passed that he did not go hunting and would furiously tear apart the fiercest and the most dangerous beasts with his teeth. His masters perceived in him a quick mind and an excellent aptitude for acquiring a perfect knowledge of the sciences. But he still felt the bitter humiliation from the ridicule that his wild boar's face brought upon him so that he avoided appearing in large gatherings.

He was spending his life in happy indifference when, one day, while he was with the queen, he saw a lady enter. She was good-looking and was followed by three very lovely young girls. Throwing herself at the feet of the queen, she told her majesty that she had come to beg her to give them shelter at the court. Her husband's death and great misfortunes had reduced her to extreme poverty, and her birth and her unfortunate condition were well enough known to her majesty to justify the hope that she would take pity on her. The queen was deeply touched at seeing them thus kneeling before her. She embraced them and said she would gladly receive the three girls, the eldest of whom was called Ismene, the second Zelonide, and the youngest Marthesie.[2] She promised to take care of them, assured the mother that she need not be discouraged and that she could remain in the palace, where she would be treated with high regard and could count on the queen's friendship. The mother, charmed by the kindness of the queen, kissed her hand a thousand times and felt a sudden calm for the first time in a long time.

The fame of Ismene's beauty spread through the court and very deeply affected a young knight named Corydon, who was no less famous in his own way than she was in hers. Almost at the same time they felt a secret

1. A large kind of lute with a double neck and two sets of tuning pegs, much in vogue in the seventeenth century.
2. Marthesie was the name of an Amazon from Greek antiquity, and she was the heroine in an opera by André Cardinal Destouces and Antoine Houdar de la Mothe that was performed at Fontainbleu on September 27, 1699.

sympathy linking them to each other. The knight was infinitely charming. He pleased everyone, and everyone loved him. And since this was a match with many advantages for Ismene, the queen looked upon the attentions he paid her with pleasure and approved the way Ismene regarded him. At last their marriage was discussed, and everything seemed pointing that way. They were born for one another, and Corydon neglected nothing in the way of those gallant entertainments and all those necessary gestures that reinforce the ties of two hearts already dedicated to one another.

But Prince Wild Boar had also felt the power of Ismene as soon as he had seen her without daring to declare his passion. "Ah! You boar! You boar!" he cried, looking at himself in a mirror. "With a face as hideous as yours, could you possibly dare to hope that the fair Ismene would think favorably of you? I must cure myself of these feelings, for the greatest of all misfortunes is to love without being loved."

So he avoided her presence with great care, but since he continued to think of her nonetheless, he became terribly melancholy, and he grew so thin that his bones stuck through his skin. But his troubles mounted when he learned that Corydon was openly wooing Ismene, that she held him in high esteem, and that before long the king and queen would be preparing the wedding feast.

Hearing this news, he felt his love increase and his hope diminish, for it seemed easier to please Ismene while she was merely indifferent than now when her heart was committed to Corydon. He understood that silence on his part would be disastrous to him and thus watched for a favorable opportunity to speak with her until he found it. One day, as she was sitting under some pleasant trees singing the words of a song that her lover had made for her, the wild boar approached her, very emotional, and sitting down beside her, he asked if it were true, as he had been told, that she was going to marry Corydon. She answered that the queen had commanded her to receive his attentions, and clearly that would have its consequences.

"Ismene," he said sweetly, "you are so young that I did not think they were planning your marriage. Had I known it, I would have proposed that you marry the only son of a great king who loves you, and who would be overjoyed to make you happy."

Upon hearing these words, Ismene grew pale. She had already noticed that the boar, who was quite naturally shy, had always talked to her with evident pleasure, had given her all the truffles which his wild boar instinct enabled him to find in the forest, and had presented her with flowers with which his cap was generally decked. She was very afraid that he himself might be the prince about whom he was speaking, and she answered, "I am very glad, my lord, not to have known about the sentiments of the son of this great king. It may be that my family, more ambitious than I myself, would have wished to force me to marry him, but I must confess in confidence that my heart belongs entirely to Corydon's so that it can never be changed."

"What!" he replied. "You would refusal a member of the royal crown who would place his fortune at your disposal?"

"There is nothing I would not refuse," she said. "I have more tenderness than ambition, and I beg of you, my lord, seeing that you have dealings with this prince, to make him promise to leave me alone."

"Oh, you wicked creature!" cried the impatient boar. "You know only too well the prince I mean! You can't bear his face, and you don't want to bear the name of Queen Wild Boar. You have sworn eternal faithfulness to your knight, but think of the difference between us. I am not Adonis, I admit, but I am a formidable wild boar. Supreme force is surely worth as much as some mere natural graces. Ismene, think about this. Do not drive me to despair!"

While he was speaking, his eyes seemed to be on fire, and his long tusks clacked against each other with such a noise that it caused the poor girl to tremble. Then the wild boar left. The tormented Ismene, in great trouble, began shedding a flood of tears when Corydon appeared. Until that day they had only known the delights of a mutual tenderness. Nothing had come in their way, and they had reason to hope that their love would soon be crowned. What, then, was this young lover's despair when he saw the grief of his fair mistress? When he asked her to tell him what had happened, she did, and it is impossible to describe the grief he felt when he heard the news.

"I refuse to pursue my happiness at the cost of yours," he said. "If a crown is offered to you, you must accept it."

"Accept it? Great gods!" she cried. "Forget you, and marry a monster! Alas, what have I done that you give me such advice that goes against our friendship and tranquility?"

Corydon was so overcome by grief that he could not answer, but the tears flowing from his eyes were enough to show the condition of his soul. Ismene, deeply aware of their common misfortune, said to him hundreds of times that she would never change, no matter what king in the world was concerned. Touched by her generosity, he told her hundreds and hundreds of times that it would be best to let him die of sorrow and that she should ascend the throne that was offered to her.

While they were engaged in this dispute, the wild boar had gone to the queen and declared that the hope of curing his passion for Ismene had compelled him to keep silent, but that he had struggled in vain, that she was on the eve of her marriage, that he felt he did not have the strength to bear up under such a misfortune, and that, in short, he wished to marry her or to die. The queen was very astonished to hear that the wild boar was in love.

"Have you really thought about what you are saying? Who would want you, my son?" she asked. "And what kind of children could you hope for?"

"Ismene is so beautiful," said he, "that she could not have ugly children, and even if they were to take after me, I am determined to do anything than to see her in another's arms."

"Have you so little sense of delicacy and of your own position," the queen went on, "as to desire a girl whose birth is inferior to your own?"

"And what royal lady is there," he replied, "with so little daintiness as to be willing to marry a miserable pig like me?"

"My son, you are mistaken," answered the queen. "Princesses are less free than anyone else to choose. We shall have you described as fairer than love itself. When the marriage is completed, and we have the lady in our keeping, she will be forced to remain with us."

"I am not capable of such trickery," he asserted. "I would despair at making my wife unhappy."

"Do you believe," cried the queen, "that the young lady whom you desire would be happy with you? The man she loves is worthy of her love, and if there is a difference of rank between a sovereign and a subject, there is no less between a wild boar and the most charming man of the world."

"So much the worse for me, madame," replied the boar, annoyed at the reasons she was using. "Dare I say that you, less than any other, should insist upon my misfortune. Why did you bring me about as a pig? Is it not unjust to reproach me with a thing which I did not cause?"

"I'm not reproaching you," answered the queen, deeply moved. "I only want to show you that if you marry a woman who does not love you, you will be very unhappy, and you will bring her sorrow. If you could but understand how much people suffer from forced marriages, you would not want to risk one. Isn't it better to live by yourself in peace?"

"To do that demands more indifference than I have, madame," he said. "Ismene has touched my heart. She is gentle, and I flatter myself that a careful treatment of her, together with the crown she must hope for, will make her yield. But, however it turns out, if it is my fate not to be loved, I would still have the happiness of possessing a wife whom I love."

The queen found he was so determined to carry out his plan that she gave up trying to dissuade him. She promised to work for the end he desired, and without any delay she sent for Ismene's mother. She knew her disposition: Ismene's mother was an ambitious woman, who would have sacrificed her daughters for an advantage even below that of a crown. As soon as the queen told her that she wanted her son the wild boar to marry Ismene, the woman threw herself at the queen's feet and assured her that the wedding day was for her to choose.

"But her affections are engaged," said the queen. "We have commanded her to regard Corydon as her destined husband."

"Well, madame," answered the old mother, "we shall command her to look on him from now on as the man she will not marry."

"The heart does not always consult the mind," replied the queen. "When once it is really committed, it is difficult to subdue it."

"If her heart had other desires than mine," said Ismene's mother, "I would tear them from her without mercy."

Seeing her so determined, the queen felt that she might safely impose on her the task of making her daughter obey. And, in truth, she hastened to Ismene's chamber, where the poor girl, knowing that the queen had sent for her mother, was anxiously awaiting her return. And one may easily imagine how her anxiety increased when she was told in a callous and decisive manner that the queen had chosen her for her daughter-in-law, that she was forbidden to speak to Corydon anymore, and that, if she disobeyed, she would be strangled. Ismene did not dare answer this terrible threat, but wept bitterly, and the news was spread throughout the kingdom that she was going to wed the royal wild boar, for the queen, who had made the king consent, sent her precious stones with which to deck herself when she came to the palace.

Overcome by despair, Corydon went to Ismene and spoke to her in spite of all that had been done to prevent him from seeing her. When he managed to reach her room, he found her reclining on a couch, her face covered by her handkerchief, which was soaked in tears. Falling on his knees by her side, and taking her hand, he said, "Alas, charming Ismene, you are weeping for my sorrows."

"They are my sorrows, too," she replied. "You are aware, dear Corydon, how I have been condemned. I can only avoid the violence that they are doing to me by death. Yes, I assure you, I would prefer to die rather than give myself to anyone else."

"No," said he. "Live. You will be a queen. Perhaps you will grow used to this hideous prince."

"That I could not do," she said. "I can imagine nothing more terrible in the world than such a husband. His crown does not diminish my sorrows."

"May the gods preserve you from such a disastrous resolution, lovely Ismene," he continued. "Such a drastic step only suits me because I'm going to lose you. I am suffering too much to stop myself."

"If you die," she answered, "I shall not survive you, and I feel a certain consolation in the thought that death at least will bring us together."

While they were talking in this way, the wild boar took them by surprise. The queen had told him what she had done in his favor, and he had hastened to express his joy to Ismene, but the presence of Corydon annoyed him immensely. He was in a jealous and impatient mood, and this brought out the wild boar in him. So he ordered Corydon to be gone and to never appear again at the court.

"What do you mean, cruel prince?" cried Ismene, stopping her lover as he was leaving. "Do you think you can banish him from my heart as you do now from my presence? No, he is planted there too well. Don't you realize that, when you cause me grief, you will be causing your own as well. Here is the man whom I can love. For you I feel only horror."

"And as for me, you cruel creature," said the wild boar, "I am completely in love with you. It is useless to confess all your hate for me. You will still be my wife, and you will only suffer more."

In despair at having brought this fresh unhappiness on his beloved, Corydon went away just at the moment that Ismene's mother came to reprimand her. She assured the prince that her daughter would forget Corydon forever and that there was no reason to delay such a pleasant wedding. The wild boar, no less eager, said he was going to arrange the day with the queen since the king had left the care of this great festive occasion in her hands. The truth was, however, that the king did not want to have anything to do with it, for this marriage seemed distasteful and ridiculous to him. Indeed, he was afraid that the race of wild boars would be perpetuated in the royal house, and he was upset by the blind indulgence which the queen displayed for her son.

The wild boar was afraid that the king might retract the consent that he had given to his marriage with Ismene so all the preparations for the wedding ceremony were hastened. He had knee breeches made for himself with bunches of ribbon at the knee and a perfumed doublet, for there was always a slight odor about him which was difficult to endure. His mantle was embroidered with jewels; his wig was as fair as a child's curls; and his hat was covered with feathers. No one had ever seen such an extraordinary figure, and no one except Ismene, who was unfortunately condemned to marry him, could look at him without laughing. But, alas, young Ismene had little heart to laugh. In vain they promised her splendor. She despised it and was only conscious of the unlucky star under which she had been born.

Corydon saw her passing on her way to the temple looking like a beautiful victim about to be slaughtered. The wild boar was overjoyed and implored her to banish the deep sadness that had overcome her, for he wished to make her so happy that all the queens of the earth would envy her.

"I confess," he said, "that I am not handsome, but it is said that every man is like some animal. Well, I am most like a wild boar. That is my beast. There is no reason to consider me less amiable on that account, for my heart is full of tender feelings and possessed by a strong passion for you."

Without answering, Ismene looked at him with a disdainful air, shrugged her shoulders, and let him guess all the horror she felt for him. Her mother was behind her, threatening her in a thousand different ways.

"Wretched girl," she said, "do you wish to destroy us along with yourself? Don't you fear that the prince's love may turn to fury?"

But Ismene, occupied by her own unhappiness, did not pay the least attention to these words. The wild boar, who had her hand in his, could not stop leaping and dancing, whispering in her ear a thousand tender words.

At last the ceremony was over. After the guests had cried three times, "Long Live Prince Wild Boar! Long Live Prince Wild Boar!" the bridegroom brought his bride to the palace, where all the preparations had been made for a magnificent meal. After the king and queen had taken their places, the bride sat down opposite the wild boar, who devoured her with his eyes, so beautiful did he find her. But she was buried in such deep sadness that she saw nothing of what was going on and heard nothing of the loud sounds of music.

The queen tugged at her dress and whispered in her ear, "My child, cast off that cloud of melancholy if you wish to please us. You look as though this were your funeral, not your wedding day."

"May the gods grant, madame, that this be the last day of my life!" she answered. "You commanded me to give my heart to Corydon. It was your decision, not mine. But, alas! If you have changed your attitude toward him, I have not."

"Do not speak like this," replied the queen. "It makes me blush out of shame and annoyance. Think of the honor my son is doing you, and the gratitude you owe him."

Ismene did not answer but let her head fall gently on her breast as she plunged again into her previous reverie. The wild boar was very distressed at seeing the aversion which his wife felt for him. There were, indeed, moments when he wished his marriage had not taken place, when he even wished to dissolve it on the spot, but his heart refused to consent to any such renunciation. The ball opened. Ismene's sisters shone in splendor. Little did they care for her sorrows in their delight at the brilliant position which the alliance gave them. The bride danced with the wild boar, and it was really frightening to see his face and still more frightening to be his wife. The whole court was so sad that it was impossible to feign joy. The ball did not last long. The princess was conducted to her apartment, and after the ceremony of disrobing, the queen withdrew. The wild boar, who was an impatient lover, retired to bed right away. Ismene said she wished to write a letter, and after entering her private room, she shut the door. The boar cried out to her to write quickly and yelled that this was hardly the right hour to begin a correspondence.

Alas! Upon entering her private room Ismene was shocked to find the unfortunate Corydon before her eyes. He had bribed one of her women to open the door of the secret stair by which he had entered. In his hand was a dagger.

"Don't think, my charming princess," he said, "that I have come to reproach you for abandoning me. When our tender love was in its initial stages, you said your heart would never change. Nevertheless, you have consented to leave me, and I blame the gods more than I do you. But neither you nor the gods can make me bear such a great sorrow. Losing you, princess, there is nothing left for me to do but to die."

No sooner had he uttered these words than he plunged the dagger into his heart. There had been no time whatsoever for Ismene to answer him.

"You die, dear Corydon!" she cried in great anguish. "Then I have nothing left to care about in the world! Its splendors would be hateful to me. The light of day would be intolerable."

She said nothing more but plunged the dagger, still dripping with Corydon's blood, into her bosom, and then she fell dead. In the meantime the wild boar was waiting impatiently for the fair Ismene and was not aware of why she had delayed her return. He called to her as loudly as he could, but there was no answer. He became very angry, and after rising and putting on his dressing gown, he ran to the door of the private room and had the servants force it open. He was the first to enter, and alas! he was astonished to find Ismene and Corydon in such a deplorable condition that he thought he would die of grief and rage. Mixed feelings of love and hate maddened him. He adored Ismene, but he knew that she had only killed herself in order to put a sudden end to the union they had just contracted. The servants ran to the king and queen with the news of what had happened in the prince's apartment. The whole palace rang with laments, for Ismene was beloved and Corydon had been held in high esteem. The king did not rise. He could not bring himself to feel sorry for the wild boar and left it to the queen to console him. So, she made the boar go to bed. She mixed her tears with his, and when he let her have an opportunity to speak and ceased his laments for a while, she tried to make him see that to kill a great passion was well nigh impossible, and that she was persuaded he ought to think himself fortunate in having lost her.

"What does it matter!" he cried. "I wished to have her for my own even if she had been unfaithful to me. I cannot say she sought to deceive me by false caresses. She always showed her horror for me. It is me who has caused her death, and I must reproach myself for all of this!"

When the queen saw how deeply troubled he was, she left him with those persons who pleased him most and withdrew to her own room. In bed she recalled all that had happened since the dream in which she had seen the fairies. "What harm did I do to them to make me suffer so bitterly?" she said. "I was hoping for an amiable and charming son. They made him like a wild boar. He is indeed a monster. The miserable Ismene preferred to kill herself rather than live with him. The king has never had a moment of joy since this unfortunate prince was born. As for me I am overcome by sadness every time I see him."

While she was speaking this way to herself, she saw a great light in her room, and right near her bed she recognized the fairy who had come out of the trunk of a tree in the woods.

"Oh, queen," the fairy said, "why will you not believe me? Didn't I assure you that your wild boar would bring you much satisfaction? Have you no faith in my sincerity?"

"Ah, what am I to believe?" said the queen. "I have yet to see the slightest proof of your words. Why didn't you leave me without an heir for the rest of my life rather than give me one like him?"

"We are three sisters," answered the fairy. "Two of us are good. The other one nearly always spoils the good that we do. It was she whom you saw laughing while you slept. Without us your sufferings would last even longer, but they will have an end."

"Alas! It will be the end of my life or the wild boar's," said the queen.

"I am not allowed to tell you," said the fairy. "I'm only allowed to bring you the comfort of some hope."

Then she vanished. A pleasant fragrance lingered in the room, and the queen convinced herself that a change for the better was about to come.

The wild boar went into deep mourning. He passed many days shut up in his chamber and covered many a page with the record of his deep regrets for the loss he had sustained. He even desired that the following lines should be carved on the tombstone of his wife:

> Oh fate unyielding, cruel decree,
> Ismene is gone for eternity!
> Your eyes are closed in eternal night,
> Your eyes which were so much our light.
> Oh fate unyielding, cruel decree,
> Ismene is gone for eternity!

Everybody was surprised that he kept such a tender memory of a person who had shown so much aversion for him. But gradually he began to frequent the society of ladies and was struck with the charms of Zelonide, Ismene's sister, who was no less charming than she had been and who bore a great resemblance to her. This resemblance pleased him. When he talked to her, he found her full of wit and vivacity. It seemed to him that, if anything could console him for the loss of Ismene, it would be young Zelonide. She was very polite to him, for it never entered her mind that he wished to marry her. Nevertheless, he was determined to do so. And one day, when the queen was alone in her chamber, he went there more cheerful than usual.

"Madame," he said, "I have come to ask a favor of you and at the same time to beg of you not to dissuade me from what is on my mind, for nothing in the world could quench the desire I feel to marry again. Give me your word, I beg you. It is Zelonide I wish to marry. Speak to the king so that the matter can be arranged without delay."

"Ah, my son," said the queen, "what are you planning now? Have you already forgotten Ismene's despair and her tragic death? How can you hope that her sister will love you any better? Are you more lovable than you were, less of a wild boar, less hideous? Be honest with yourself, my son. Do not expose yourself anew every day. When someone is made like you, it's preferable to conceal yourself."

"I agree with you, madame," replied the wild boar. "That's why I would like to have a companion. The owls, the toads, and the serpents find mates. Am I then inferior to vile beasts? But you want to torment me. It seems to me a wild boar is worth more than any of those beasts I have just named."

"Alas, dear child," said the queen, "the gods will testify to the love I bear you, and to the sorrow with which I am overwhelmed when I look at your face. When I set forth all these reasons, it is not because I am bent on tormenting you. When you have a wife, I hope she may love you as much as I do, but there is a difference between the feelings of a wife and those of a mother."

"My mind is made up," said the wild boar. "I beg you, madame, to speak to the king and to Zelonide's mother today so that my marriage may take place as soon as possible."

The queen promised, but when she talked to the king about the matter he told her that she was pitifully weak with regard to her son, and that most certainly even more catastrophes would result from such an unsuitable marriage. Although the queen was as much convinced of the truth of this as he was, she did not, therefore, yield since she desired to keep the promise that she had made to her son. Accordingly, she pressed the king so intensely that he tired of the matter and told her she could do what she wanted, but that if trouble came because of it, she could only blame her own compliance.

On returning to her own room, the queen found the wild boar there awaiting her with the greatest impatience. She told him he might declare his feelings to Zelonide since the king had given his consent, provided that she herself gave hers, for he did not want the authority with which he was clothed to bring misfortune.

"I assure you, madame," said the wild boar with a swaggering air, "you are the only person that thinks so meanly of me. Everyone else praises me and points to a thousand good qualities that I possess."

"Courtiers always do so," said the queen, "and princes are always treated in that fashion. The former do nothing but sing praises, the latter hear nothing but praises sung. How is it ever possible to know one's faults in such a labyrinth? Ah, how happy the great might be if they had friends more dedicated to them because of their person and not their fortune."

"I am not sure, madame," rejoined the boar, "that they would be pleased to hear unpleasant truths. Nobody likes these, no matter what rank they hold in life. Why, for instance, do you always insist that there is no difference between a wild boar and me, that I inspire terror, and that I should go and hide myself? Have I no obligation toward those who bring me solace, who tell me flattering untruths, and who hide the faults you are so anxious to point out?"

"Oh wellspring of vanity!" cried the queen. "We find you wherever we turn our eyes! Yes, my son, you are fair and handsome. I advise you to continue to give gifts to those who tell you so."

"Madame," said the wild boar, "I am very well aware of my misfortunes. I am perhaps more keenly aware of them than anyone else is, but it does not lie in my hands to make myself larger or smaller. Nor can I exchange my boar's head for a man's with flowing locks. I am willing to be reprimanded for ill-temper, impatience, or avarice—in fact, for any defect that can be remedied. But as for my person, you must admit, surely, that I am to be pitied and not blamed."

Seeing that he was growing annoyed, the queen told him that since he was so determined to marry, he could see Zelonide and come to terms with her. Since he did not want to stay with his mother any longer, he ended the conversation quickly and hastened to Zelonide's apartment, where he entered her room unceremoniously. Finding her in the inner room, he kissed her and said, "Little sister, I bring news which I do not think will be displeasing to you. I should like you to marry."

"My lord," she said, "if I marry according to your wishes, I shall be happy."

"The bridegroom in question," he replied, "is one of the greatest princes in the kingdom, but he is not handsome."

"That's not important," she said. "My mother is so hard on me that I shall only be too glad to change my situation."

"He of whom I speak," added the prince, "is very much like me."

Zelonide seemed astonished and looked at him attentively.

"You're not answering me, little sister," he said. "Is it joy or grief that makes you silent?"

"I don't recall, my lord," she replied, "ever having seen anyone at court like you."

"What!" he exclaimed. "You cannot guess that I mean myself? Yes, dear child, I love you, and I have come to offer to share my heart and my crown with you."

"Oh gods! What do I hear?" cried Zelonide in grief.

"What do you hear, ungrateful creature?" said the wild boar. "You hear what should give you more satisfaction than anything else in the world. Could you ever hope to be a queen? I am gracious enough to cast my eyes on you. You should seek to deserve my love, and don't have any foolish ideas about imitating Ismene."

"No," she said, "you need not fear that I shall take my life as she did. But, my lord, there are so many persons more amiable and more ambitious than I am. Why don't you choose someone who would appreciate better the honor you have bestowed on me? I confess to you that my only desire is for a quiet and retired life. Let me determine my own destiny."

"You really don't deserve my violating protocol to raise you to the throne!" he cried. "But a fatal impulse which is beyond my understanding compels me to marry you."

Zelonide's only response was her tears. Thereupon, he left her full of anguish and went to seek his mother-in-law to tell her of his intentions so that she might persuade Zelonide to do what he desired with good grace. He told her about what had just happened between them and about the repugnance that Zelonide had shown for this marriage which was to make her fortune and that of all her family. The ambitious mother knew full well the advantages she might derive from it. When Ismene had killed herself, she had been much more distressed on account of her own interests than because of any tenderness she had felt for her daughter. She was overjoyed that this crass wild boar wished to form a new alliance with her family. So, she threw herself at his feet, embraced him, and thanked him a thousand times for an honor that affected her so deeply. She assured him that Zelonide would be obedient, or if not, she would plunge a dagger in her eyes.

"I must confess," said the wild boar, "that it grieves me to do violence to her, but if I wait until hearts are thrown my way, I may wait for the rest of my life. All the beautiful ladies think me ugly. Nevertheless, I have made up my mind to wed a lovely maiden."

"You are right, my lord," replied the wicked old woman. "You should satisfy yourself. If they are not content, it is only because they do not know how truly advantageous it is for them."

So strongly did she uphold the wild boar that he told her that the matter was therefore fully settled, and that he would turn a deaf ear to the tears and payers of Zelonide. When he arrived home, he selected his most magnificent possessions and sent them to his mistress. Since her mother was with her when they brought her the golden baskets full of jewels, she did not dare to refuse them, but she showed the utmost indifference to all they brought her except to a dagger with a handle set in diamonds. She took it in her hand several times and put it in her belt for the ladies of that country were in the habit of carrying them. Then she said, "I may be mistaken, but isn't this the same dagger that pierced the bosom of my poor sister?"

"We don't know, madame," said the servants to whom she spoke, "but if you think it is, you should never look at it."

"On the contrary," she responded. "I admire her courage. Happy is she who is brave enough to do likewise!"

"Ah, my sister!" cried Marthesie. "What morbid thoughts are passing through your mind? Do you wish to die?"

"No," replied Zelonide firmly. "The altar is not worthy of such a victim, but may the gods be my witness that . . . ." She could say no more, for her tears choked her laments and words.

When he was told how Zelonide had received his gift, the amorous boar was so very angry that he was on the point of breaking off the marriage and never seeing her again. But whether out of tender feelings or pride, he could not bring himself to do so and was determined to carry out his first intention with the greatest possible speed. The king and queen placed him in charge of arranging the great celebration, and he ordered everything on a magnificent scale. Yet, no matter what he did, there was always a certain taste of wild boar in it, which was very extraordinary. The ceremony took place in a vast forest where tables were loaded with venison for all the fierce and savage beasts that might want to come and eat so that they might share in the feast.

Zelonide was conducted there by her mother and sister and found the king, queen, their wild boar son, and the entire court under the thick dark foliage. Then the newly wedded couple swore to each other eternal love. The wild boar would not have found it difficult to keep his word. As for Zelonide, it was easy to see that she obeyed with great repugnancy, though she was able to control herself and partly hide her displeasure. The prince, who liked to look at the bright side, thought she was yielding to necessity, and that she would only think of how she could please him from now on. This idea put him in a good mood again. And when the ball was about to begin, he quickly disguised himself as an astrologer with a long robe. There were only two courtier ladies who participated in the masquerade besides him, and he had them dressed like him so it would be impossible to tell them apart. But it was not all that easy to make such good-looking ladies resemble a vile pig like him.

One of these ladies was the confidante of Zelonide, and the wild boar knew this. It was only out of curiosity that he had planned the disguise. After they had danced a very short *entrée de ballet*—it had to be short because it exhausted the prince—he went up to his new bride and made certain signs, pointing to one of the masked astrologers, which made Zelonide think it was her friend who was by her side and that she was pointing to the wild boar.

"Alas," she said. "I know it only too well. There's that monster whom the gods in their anger have given me for a husband. But if you love me, we shall rid the earth of him tonight."

The wild boar understood from her words that she was referring to some plot which concerned him. So, he whispered in a low voice to Zelonide, "I'll do whatever you want."

"Listen then," she answered. "Here is a dagger he sent me. You must hide it in my room and help me kill him."

The wild boar said little in reply for fear that she might recognize his voice, which was somewhat extraordinary. He took the dagger quietly and left her for a moment.

Afterward he returned without a mask and paid his compliments to her, which she received with a rather embarrassed air, for she was pondering the plan for his death in her mind, and at that moment he was just as anxious as she was.

"Is it possible," he said to himself, "that anyone so young and beautiful could be so wicked? What have I done to her that she would want to kill me? True, I'm not handsome. I eat in a crude fashion. I have some faults. But who doesn't? Though I have the face of a beast, I'm still a man! Indeed, there are many beasts with human faces! Isn't Zelonide, whom I thought was so charming, a tigress, a lioness? Ah, it is difficult to trust in appearances!"

As he was muttering all this between his teeth, she asked him what was the matter. "You are sad, wild boar. Are you regretting the honor you have bestowed on me?"

"No," he said. "I do not change easily. I was thinking of a way to close the ball soon. I am sleepy."

The princess was delighted to see him drowsy, thinking that she would have less trouble in carrying out her plan. When the ball ended, the wild boar and his wife were taken away in a stately chariot. The whole palace was illuminated by lamps in the shape of little pigs, and there was a great ceremony in conducting the wild boar and his bride to their apartment. She was certain that her confidante was behind the curtains, so she went to bed with a silk cord under her pillow. She intended to use it to revenge the death of Ismene and the wrong they had all done to her in forcing her into such a distasteful marriage. In view of the deep silence between them, the wild boar pretended to sleep and snored until all the furniture in the room shook.

"You're asleep at last, you vile pig!" said Zelonide. "The time has come to take revenge on you for your fatal affection. You will die in the dark night."

Quietly she rose and ran to all the corners calling her friend, but of course, she was not there because she had never learned of Zelonide's plan.

"Ungrateful friend!" she cried in a low voice. "You've abandoned me. After giving me such a firm promise, you don't keep it, but my courage will not abandon me."

After uttering these words, she slipped the silk cord around the neck of the wild boar, who had only waited for this moment to jump on her. He gave her two blows of his great tusks on her throat, and she died almost immediately.

Such a catastrophe could not take place without a great deal of noise. Everyone ran and looked at the dying Zelonide with great astonishment. They wanted to help her, but the wild boar placed himself in front of her with a furious air. Meanwhile, the servants ran to fetch the queen, and when she arrived, he told her what had happened and what had forced him to extreme violence against the unfortunate princess.

The queen could not help regretting her fate and said, "I foresaw only too well the trouble that such an alliance would bring with it. Let it, at least, serve to cure you of this marriage frenzy that appears to possess you. We cannot always have every wedding day end with a funeral ceremony."

The wild boar did not answer, for he had fallen into a deep reverie. He went to bed, but he could not sleep, reflecting continually on his misfortunes. Secretly he reproached himself with the death of two of the loveliest beings in the world, and the passion he had for them would awake again ceaselessly to torment him.

"Unhappy wretch that I am!" he said to a young lord with whom he was very close. "I have never tasted happiness in the whole course of my life. Whenever people speak about the throne that I am to occupy, they all say it's a pity that such a fair realm will be in the possession of a monster. If I try to share my crown with a poor girl, she seeks to kill herself or to kill me instead of considering herself happy. If I seek solace from my father and mother, they abhor me and cast nothing but angry looks at me. What am I to do against this despair that's grabbed hold of me? I want to leave the court. I shall go to the deepest paths of the forest and lead the life which befits a wild boar of might and spirit. I shall never play the gallant anymore. The animals will not reproach me for being uglier than they are. It will be easy for me to be king over them, for I have the advantage of reason, which will serve me as a means of mastering them. I shall live more peacefully with them than I do now in a court that I am destined to rule, and I shall not suffer the indignity of marrying a mate who stabs herself or one who wants to strangle me. Ah! I shall flee to the woods and despise the crown they think I am unfit to wear!"

At first his friend sought to dissuade him from such an extraordinary resolution, but he saw that he was so overwhelmed by the continual blows of bad luck that he finally gave up trying to convince him to remain. Consequently, one night when the king and queen had forgotten to keep guard around his palace, the wild boar made his escape without being seen and went into the depths of the forest where he began to lead the life of his wild boar kindred.

The king and queen could not help being touched by a flight which despair alone had driven him to take. They sent out hunters to look for him, but how were they to recognize him? Two or three fierce boars were caught and brought home after much danger, but they caused so much damage at court that it was decided not to run any further risks. A general order was given that no more boars should be killed for fear of encountering the prince.

When the wild boar had left, he had promised his friend to write to him sometimes. Indeed, he had taken writing materials with him, and from time to time people found at the gate of the town a very illegible letter addressed to the young lord. This was a consolation to the queen since it informed her that her son was still alive.

The mother of Ismene and Zelonide felt the loss of her two daughters very deeply. All her magnificent dreams had vanished when they died. She had to bear the reproach of sacrificing them to her ambition. They would have still been alive if she had not used threats to force them to marry the wild boar. The queen no longer regarded her so favorably as she had done before. So the mother decided to live in the country with Marthesie, her only daughter, who was much more beautiful than her sisters had been, and her gentle manners had so much charm that everyone was taken with her.

One day, when this maiden was walking in the forest followed by two waiting women, not far from her mother's house, she suddenly saw an enormous boar about twenty paces from her. Her attendants left her and fled. As for Marthesie, she was so terrified that she remained as motionless as a statue unable to escape.

The wild boar, for it was he, recognized her at once, and he saw that she was nearly dead from fright the way she was trembling. Since he had no wish to terrify her, he stopped and said, "Have no fear, Marthesie, I love you too well to do you any harm. It depends on you only as to whether you will allow me to serve you. You know what injuries I suffered at the hands of your sisters. What a miserable return for my affection, though I must confess that I did deserve their hatred because of my obstinacy in wanting to please and possess them against their wills. Since I have lived in this forest, I have learned that nothing in the world demands more freedom than the heart. I see that all the animals are happy because they live without constraint. I did not know their maxims before. I know them now, and I feel that I would far rather die than enter into an enforced marriage. If the gods, who are angry with me would at last be appeased, if they would make you think favorably of me, I confess, Marthesie, that I would be enchanted to tie my fortunes to yours. But—alas!—what am I proposing? Would you come with a monster like me and enter deep into my cave?"

While the wild boar was speaking, Marthesie summoned up strength enough to answer him. "What's this, my lord?" she cried. "Is it possible that I see you in a condition well beneath your birth? The queen, your mother, never lets a day pass without weeping for your misfortunes."

"My misfortunes!" said the wild boar, interrupting her. "Do not speak that way about my present condition. I've made my choice. It was not easy, but it's done. Don't think, young Marthesie, that a brilliant court will always ensure our lasting happiness. There are joys more delightful, and I repeat, you could help me find them if you were inclined to join me in this wild life."

"And why won't you return to a place where you are still beloved?" she asked.

"Still beloved?" he exclaimed. "No, no, princes covered with disgrace are not loved. Just as people look for thousands of benefits which the great are not in a position to render, so princes are made responsible when their evil fortune happens and are hated infinitely more than other people. But why am I amusing myself in this way? If any of the bears or lions that I know were to pass by and hear me, my reputation as wild boar would be lost. So, make up your mind to come without any other thought than that of passing your best days in the narrow retreat of an unfortunate monster, unfortunate no longer if he has you."

"Wild boar," she responded, "up until now, I have had no reason to love you. If it weren't for you, I would still have two sisters who were dear to me. Let me have time before making up my mind to take such an extraordinary step."

"You may be asking for time only to betray me," he said.

"I am not capable of that," she answered, "and I assure you that from this moment on no one will know I have seen you."

"Will you come back?" he asked.

"Certainly," she replied.

"Ah! But your mother will forbid it. They will tell her you encountered a terrible boar. She will not be willing to let you run any further risks. Come then, Marthesie. Come with me."

"Where will you take me?" she asked.

"Into a deep grotto," he answered. "A stream clearer than crystal runs slowly through it, and there are banks covered with moss and green grass. A hundred echoes respond to the plaints of love-stricken and forsaken shepherds. There we shall live together."

"Perhaps you should say, there I shall be devoured by one of your best friends," she remarked. "They will come to see you and find me, and my last moment will have come. Besides that, my mother, in despair at having lost me, will have her servants search for me everywhere. These woods are too near her house. I would be discovered."

"Let us go wherever you like," he said. "The preparations of a poor wild boar are soon made ready."

"No doubt," she answered. "But mine are more troublesome. I need garments for every season and ribbons and jewels."

"You want loads of trifles and useless things for your toilet. When one has intelligence and reason, isn't it possible to raise oneself above those petty concerns? Believe me, Marthesie, they will add nothing to your beauty, and I feel sure they will tarnish its splendor. Seek nothing for your complexion but the clear fresh water of the streams. Let your hair, with its curls and its exquisite color, its texture finer than the spider's web where the silly fly is caught, be your adornment. Your teeth are as white as pearls and more regular. Be content with their brightness, and leave the trinkets to those who are not so lovely as you."

"I am very pleased by all that you say to me," she answered, "but you will never be able to persuade me to bury myself in the depths of a cave with only lizards and snails to bear me company. Wouldn't it be better for you to come home with me to your father, the king? I promise that they will give their consent to our marriage. I shall be delighted. And if you loved me, shouldn't you want to make me happy and raise me to a lofty position?"

"I love you, beautiful Marthesie," he replied, "but you do not love me. It is ambition that would induce you to take me for a husband, and I have too much delicacy of feeling to reconcile myself to these sorts of sentiments."

"You are naturally inclined to think ill of our sex," replied Marthesie, "but my lord boar, surely it is still something that I promise to cherish a sincere friendship for you. Think about this. You will see me again in a few days at this same place."

The prince took leave of her and withdrew into his dark grotto, very much occupied with what she had said to him. His bizarre star had made him so hateful to those he loved that, until that day, he had never been flattered by a gracious word. This made him much more aware of Marthesie's kindness. Striving for some means to express his love, the idea occurred to him of preparing a repast for her, and several lambs and roebucks felt the force of his carnivorous tooth. Then he arranged them in his cave, waiting for the moment when Marthesie would come to keep her appointment.

With regard to Marthesie, however, she did not know what to decide. If the wild boar had been as handsome as he was hideous, had they loved each other as much as Astreé and Céladon[3] did, it would have been all she could do to spend her best days this way in a terrible solitude, and then the wild boar would have had to have been Céladon. However, she was not engaged. No one up until now had the honor of pleasing her, and she was inclined to live perfectly happy with the prince if he would only leave the forest. At one point she went out to see him at the appointed meeting place. He had never failed to go there several times a day for fear of missing the moment when she would come. As soon as he saw her, he ran to her and crouched at her feet to let her know that wild boars can have most courteous forms of greeting when they so wish.

Then they withdrew to a place apart, and the wild boar looked at her with his little eyes full of fire and passion and said, "What may I hope from your tenderness?"

"You may have great hopes," she replied, "if you decide to return to court, but I confess to you that I do not have the strength to spend the rest of my life cut off from society."

"Ah," said he, "it is because you do not love me. It is true that I'm not lovable, but I am unhappy, and out of pity and generosity, you might do for me what you would do out of inclination for another."

"And how do you know that those feelings have no part in the friendship I have for you?" she answered. "Believe me, wild boar, I am giving good proof of this in consenting to follow you to your father, the king."

"Come to my grotto," said he, "and judge for yourself what I shall have to leave for your sake."

At this proposal she hesitated a little, fearing he might keep her against her will. Guessing what was on her mind, he said, "Don't be afraid, I would never be happy by obtaining my happiness through violence."

Marthesie trusted his word, and so he led her to the far end of the cave, where she found all the animals he had slaughtered to regale her. This kind of butchery made her sick at heart. At first, she turned away her eyes, and after a while she would have left, but the boar put on a masterful air and tone and said, "Lovely Marthesie, I have such powerful feelings for you that I do not want you to leave. May the gods bear witness that you will reign in my heart forever. Insurmountable difficulties prevent me from returning to my father, the king. Please accept my love and trust here. Let this flowing stream, these evergreen vines, this rock, these woods, and all that dwells here bear witness to our mutual oaths!"

Marthesie was not so desirous of pledging herself as he was, but she was shut inside the grotto without means of getting out. Why had she entered?

3. The two ideal lovers, a shepherdess and shepherd, in the novel *Astrée* by Honoré d'Urfé. Written in five parts (1607–28) with contributions by Balthazar Baru, this novel about the trials and tribulations of faithful lovers had a great influence on the notion of *précosité* cultivated in many French fairy tales.

Should she not have foreseen what would happen? She began to weep and to reproach the boar.

"How can I trust your promises," she asked, "when you have already broken your first one?"

"There must be," he said to her with a wild boar smile, "something human mixed with the animal in me. This breaking of my promise for which you blame me, this little trick by which I gained my end—these reveal the man in me. To speak frankly, there is more honor among animals than among men."

"Alas!" she answered. "You have the worst part of both—the heart of a man and the face of a beast. Either be one or the other, and after that I shall make up my mind with regard to what you desire."

"But, beautiful Marthesie," he said, "would you stay with me without being my wife? You may take it for granted that I shall not allow you to leave here."

Her tears and prayers increased, but he was not affected by them. So, after a long struggle, she consented to take him as her bridegroom and assured him that she would love him as fondly as if he were the most charming prince in the world. He was delighted by her pleasant ways. He kissed her hand a thousand times and assured her in his turn that she would not be so unhappy as she had reason to think. Then he asked her if she would eat some of the animals that he had killed.

"No," she said, "that is not my taste. I would prefer your bringing me some fruit."

When he went out, he closed the entrance to the cave so securely that it was impossible for Marthesie to run away. But she had made up her mind as to her lot, and she would not try to escape even if she had been able to do so. In the meantime, the boar loaded three hedgehogs with oranges, sweet limes, citrons, and other fruits. He goaded them by the prickles with which they were covered, and they carried the load to the grotto quite safely. Then he entered and begged Marthesie to help herself.

"Here is your wedding feast, not like the feasts made for your two sisters, but I hope that the less magnificence there is, the sweeter the enjoyment."

"May the gods grant that it be so," she answered. Then, after taking some water in her hand, she drank to the health of the wild boar, and this toast filled him with delight.

The meal was as short as it was frugal, and afterward, Marthesie gathered all the moss and grass and flowers that the boar had brought her and made a bed out of it, hard enough to be sure, on which she and the prince went to sleep. She was most careful to ask him if he liked his pillow high or low, if he had room enough, and on what side he slept best. The good boar thanked her tenderly and exclaimed from time to time, "I would not change my lot with that of the greatest men. At last I have found what I sought. I am loved by the woman I love." He went on to say a hundred pretty things to her, and she was not surprised by this because he always had demonstrated wit. She rejoiced in it because his mind had not been diminished by living in such solitude.

Both fell asleep, but when Marthesie woke up, she had the feeling that her bed was softer than when she lay down. Then touching the boar gently, she found that his head was like a man's, that his hair was long, that he had arms and hands. She could not help wondering, but she fell asleep again, and when it was day, she found that her husband was as much of a wild boar as ever.

They spent the next day like the one before. Marthesie said nothing to her husband about what she had suspected during the night. The hour for retiring came. She touched his head while he was asleep and again found the same change she had found before. Now she was really troubled. She could hardly sleep at all, for she was filled with constant anxiety and always sighing. The boar saw this with real despair.

"You do not love me, Marthesie," he said. "I am an unfortunate wretch whose face disgusts you. I shall die, and it will be your fault."

"It is the opposite, you deceitful barbarian," she responded. "You will be the death of me. The wrong that you are doing me affects me so deeply that I cannot endure it."

"I am doing you a wrong?" he cried. "I'm a deceitful barbarian? What do you mean? You certainly have no reason to complain."

"Do you think that I don't know that you give up your place to a man every night?"

"Wild boars," he said, "especially those like me, are not of such an easy disposition. Don't harbor a thought so offensive to both of us, dear Marthesie. Be assured, I would be jealous of the gods themselves. But perhaps you are dreaming all these things in your sleep?"

Ashamed of having spoken about something so improbable, Marthesie replied that she trusted him, though she had reason to think she was awake when she was touching arms and hands and hair. She did not trust her own judgment, she told him, and she would never talk about this matter with him again. In fact, she cast aside all the suspicious thoughts that came to her. Six months passed with little enjoyment on Marthesie's side, for she never left the cave for fear that she might meet her mother or the servants of her household. Since the poor mother had lost her daughter, she never stopped lamenting. She made the woods resound with her sorrows and with the name of Marthesie. At the sound of her mother's voice, which could be heard almost every day, Marthesie sighed in secret because she was causing so much pain to her mother and was helpless to console her. But the wild boar had given her due warning, and she feared him as much as she loved him. Since she was all sweetness, she continued to show great tenderness to the wild boar, who loved her in a most passionate way. Yet, now that she had also become pregnant and thought that the wild boar race would be perpetuated, her sorrow knew no bounds.

One night, as she lay awake weeping softly, she heard someone talking so near to her that she heard every word even though the voices were very low. It was the good boar, who was praying to someone to be less cruel and to give him the permission for which he had long been asking. The answer was always, "No, no. I will not."

Marthesie was more troubled than ever.

"Who can enter this cave?" she said. "My husband has not revealed this secret to me."

She had no desire to fall asleep again, for she was too curious. The conversation ended, and she heard the person who had been speaking to the prince leave the cave. Shortly after, the wild boar was snoring like a pig. Soon she got up to see if it were easy to move the stone that filled the entrance to the grotto, but she could not move it. Coming back quietly and without a light, she felt something beneath her feet and discovered that it was a wild boar's skin. She picked it up and hid it and waited silently for the outcome of the affair. When dawn had soon appeared, the boar got up, and she heard him fumbling about on all sides. While he was anxiously searching, the day began. She saw him so extraordinarily handsome and well made that she became the most delighted person in the world.

"Ah!" she exclaimed. "Don't continue to make a mystery out of it any longer. I know it. I feel it deep down in my heart. Dear prince, what good fortune has enabled you to become the handsomest of all men?"

At first he was surprised at the discovery she had made, but composing himself, he said, "I shall explain everything to you, my dear Marthesie, and at the same time I confess that I owe this charming transformation to you. It began when the queen my mother was asleep one day in the shade of some trees when three fairies passed over her in the air. They recognized her and stopped. The eldest one gave her a son who was to be intelligent and handsome. The second improved on this gift and added a thousand fine qualities in my favor. The youngest said with a burst of laughter, 'We must vary this affair somewhat. Spring would not be so pleasant if winter did not come before. In order, therefore, that the prince whom you desire should be charming, and may appear more so, my gift to him is that he be a wild boar until he marry three wives, and until the third one find his wild boar's skin.' At these words, the three fairies disappeared. The queen had heard what the first two had said very distinctly, but as for the one who was harming me, she was laughing so much that it was impossible to understand her words. It is only since our wedding day that I myself have been aware of what I have just told you. When I was going in search of you, thinking only of my passion, I stopped to drink at a stream that flows near my grotto. Whether it was clearer than usual, or whether I was looking at my reflection more attentively because of my desire to please you, I felt myself to be so frightful that my eyes filled with tears. Without exaggeration, I shed tears enough to swell the current of the stream, and I said to myself that it was impossible that I would ever please you. Depressed by this thought, I made up my mind to go no further. 'I cannot be happy,' I said, 'if I am not beloved, and I can never be loved by any reasonable creature.' I was muttering these words when I saw a lady approach with a boldness that surprised me, for I have a fearsome look to those who do not know me. 'Wild boar,' she said, 'the hour of your happiness is drawing near, provided that you marry Marthesie, and that she loves you as you are. Be assured that before long you will take off the guise of a wild boar. Beginning with your wedding night, you will discard that skin which is so hateful to you, but you will have to put it on again before daybreak and say nothing to your wife. Be careful to prevent her from knowing anything about it until the time of the great discovery arrives.'

"She told me," he continued, "all that I have already related to you about my mother, the queen. I thanked her very humbly for the good news she brought me and went to seek you with feelings of mixed joy and hope that I had never experienced before. And, when I was so happy as to receive signs of friendship from you, my satisfaction increased in every way, and it was difficult to restrain my impatience to share my secret with you. The fairy, who knew this, used to come at night and threaten me with the greatest misfortunes if I would not keep silent. 'Ah, madame,' I said to her, 'you surely have never loved, or else you would not oblige me to hide anything so delightful from the lady I love most in the whole world.' She laughed at my distress and told me not to grieve, for everything would turn out well. But you must give me back my boar's skin. I must put it on again in case the fairies are angry."

"Whatever happens, dear prince," said Marthesie, "I shall never change toward you. The charming picture of your transformation will always stay with me."

"I feel assured," he said, "that the fairies will not make us suffer long. They are taking care of us. This bed which seems to you to be of moss is made of excellent down and fine wool. It was they who placed all the fine fruit that you have eaten at the entrance of the grotto."

Marthesie did not neglect to thank the fairies for so many favors. While she was expressing her gratitude to them, the wild boar was making the utmost efforts to get into the skin, but it had grown so small that it would not even cover one of his legs. He pulled it this way and that way with his teeth and hands, but in vain. He was very sad and was lamenting his misfortune, for he feared with reason that the fairy who had turned him into a wild boar would come and dress him in the skin again for a long time.

"Alas!" he cried. "Why did you hide this fatal skin, my dear Marthesie? Perhaps it is to punish us that I can't use it as I did before. If the fairies are angry, how can we pacify them?"

Marthesie wept also, and it was very strange for her to weep about his inability to remain a wild boar. At that moment, the grotto shook. Then the roof opened. They saw six distaffs fall, filled with silk, three of them white, and three black, and they all danced together. A voice emanated from them and said, "If the wild boar and Marthesie can guess what these white and black distaffs mean, they will be happy."

The prince pondered for a while, and then he said, "I guess that the three white distaffs mean the three fairies who gave me gifts at my birth."

"And I," said Marthesie, "guess that the three black ones signify my two sisters and Corydon."

All of a sudden the three fairies took the place of the white distaffs. Ismene, Zelonide, and Corydon appeared also. Never was anything so terrifying as this return from the other world.

"We do not come from so far away as you think," they said to Marthesie. "The prudent fairies were kind enough to take care of us. While you were weeping for our deaths, we were being led into a castle where we lacked for nothing but your company."

"What!" said the wild boar. "Didn't I see Ismene and her lover lifeless, and didn't Zelonide perish by my own hand?"

"No," said the fairies. "A charm was on your eyes so that we could deceive you as we wished. These kinds of incidents occur every day. For instance, a husband thinks his wife is at the ball with him, while she is lying asleep in bed. A lover dotes on his fair mistress, while, in truth, she is as hideous as an ape. And another believes he has killed his enemy who is living safely in another country."

"My mind is in a whirl of doubt," said Prince Wild Boar. "It would seem from what you say that one must not even believe what one sees."

"The rule is not always a general one," answered the fairies, "but it cannot be denied that one should suspend one's judgment about many things, and believe that some dose of Faërie may enter into what seems to us most certain."

The prince and his wife thanked the fairies for the lesson they had just received and for preserving the lives of those who were so dear to them.

"But," added Marthesie, throwing herself at their feet, "may I not hope that you will stop making my faithful wild boar wear that vile skin?"

"We have come to assure you of this," they said, "for it is time to return to the court."

Immediately the grotto took the form of a superb tent in which the prince found many valets who dressed him in gorgeous attire. There were attendants for Marthesie, too, and a dress of exquisite work. In addition, she had all she needed to groom her hair and to adorn herself. Then the dinner was served as a meal ordered by the fairies. What need to say more?

Never was there such perfect joy. All the grief the wild boar had suffered did not equal the pleasure of seeing himself not only a man but a wondrously handsome man at that. After they had risen from the table, several magnificent carriages drawn by the finest horses in the world came up full speed. The ladies got into them with the rest of the little company. Guards on horses marched before and behind.

At the court they did not know where this splendid entourage came from. Still less did they know who was in it until a herald announced it in a loud voice to the sound of trumpets and of kettledrums. All the people ran in great delight to meet their prince. Everyone was enchanted with him, and no one wanted to doubt the reality of an event which seemed nevertheless so dubious. The news was carried to the king and the queen, who descended at once to the courtyard. Prince Wild Boar was so much like his father that it would have been difficult to mistake him. And no one did. And never was there more widespread joy. After some months this was further increased by the birth of a son in whose face and character there was not a trace of the wild boar.

HENRIETTE JULIE DE MURAT

The Pig King†

Once upon a time there was a king who ruled a realm whose name I don't know. He married the daughter of a king, who was his neighbor, and she was as beautiful as can be. They lived together for some time without having children, and this saddened the king somewhat because he would have liked to have had a successor. He often went with the queen to a beautiful villa in the country where she enjoyed herself very much because she did not like the court life. She preferred to go into the park and leave her ladies and then stroll by herself in some spot.

One day when she had gone off by herself, she sat down on the edge of a pretty fountain in the shade of a tree surrounded by a lawn covered with flowers. She amused herself for some time by making bouquets of flowers with which she adorned her hair, and she gazed at herself in the liquid glass of the fountain. After a while the murmur of the water and the sweet song of the birds made her drowsy, and she fell asleep. Just at that time three fairies who had attended the birth of a beautiful princess to whom they had given magnificent gifts passed by this spot in their flying chariot. The great beauty of the sleeping queen caused them to stop and take a careful look at her.

"What a charming person," said one of the fairies. "She deserves some sort of gift from us. So I want her to give birth in nine months to the most handsome and most accomplished of all men."

"As for me," said the second, "I shall bestow the perfect gift of tenderness and gallantry on this prince."

"Well, as for me," said the third fairy, who was old and had apparently had very little fun at the banquet from which they were coming, "I wish the prince to be born a pig, and he will remain this way until he has married three women."

"You are quite ridiculous," the first fairy said, "to spoil our work with such malice. You've just done the same to the princess from whom we have come. What was the sense in making her fall in love with a river?"

"It's true," said the second. "You've done this trick more than once. But if my sister agrees, we're not going to let ourselves be bamboozled by you anymore, nor shall we travel in your company."

The malicious fairy laughed mockingly at the other two and departed. Meanwhile the two fairies stayed and sat down next to the queen, who awoke a moment later. She was pleasantly surprised to see such lovely company, for the fairies were incomparably beautiful. The fairy named Bienfaisante said to the queen, "Madame, even though we have not had the honor of your acquaintance before this, we are your best friends."

Thereupon, she told her who they were and what had just happened. In particular, she explained to her the sorrow that would come from the

---

† Henriette Julie de Murat, "The Pig King"—"Le roy porc" (1699), in *Histoires sublimes et allegoriques* (Paris: Floentin Delaulne, 1699).

malicious act of the old fairy Rancune and that they would not be able to
undo what she had done. But they would do their best to help her hide
her child once it was born. The fairy Bienfaisante also told the queen that
she would transform herself into a midwife and would take charge of
raising the child until the bad years had passed.

The queen thanked her as well as her sister Tranquille, and she also
received more instructions regarding this entire affair that she was ordered
to keep secret. Then the fairies withdrew. And the queen showed that it
is not always true that women are incapable of keeping silent, for she did
not tell anyone about what had happened between her and the fairies.

The queen became larger to the great pleasure of the king her husband.
Even though the fairies had promised her their help, she was troubled
when she entered the final stage of her pregnancy because she had become
very large, and she imagined that she was carrying a child in the shape of
a pig in her stomach. While the queen was feeling bothered by these
disturbing thoughts, the king received news that one of the neighboring
princes had attacked one of his frontier outposts and had begun making
hostile acts. He immediately gave orders to engage the enemy forces and
prepared to go to the front himself.

At another time the queen would have regretted her husband's departure, but the circumstances of her pregnancy made her see his leaving
from another viewpoint. Indeed, she could be the mistress of her own
actions during his absence. At last, the king departed at the head of a large
assembly of his troops, and the queen went to the villa in the country in
order to give birth. Before leaving the court, she said to the councillors
that, when the time for giving birth arrived, they were to come to her, and
she would alert them that it was time. Then she summoned the most
expert midwife to come and stay with her, and this was, of course, the
fairy Bienfaisante. The queen had confided her secret in one of her ladies,
and she and the fairy slept in the queen's chamber. That evening the
queen felt sick, and she returned to her room early with her two confidantes without saying anything. Then with their aid she brought a milky
white pig into the world that was the prettiest one that anyone had ever
seen. Of course, she did not do this without weeping tears, but the charitable fairy consoled her by giving her good hope for the future.

As soon as the pig was born, the fairy carried it away without anyone
seeing it, and she brought it to a place that was near the palace and not
far from the queen so that she could come back to her. The next morning
it was announced that the queen's pregnancy had come to an end, and
that there had been a miscarriage. This announcement was taken for gos-
pel truth, and the king was informed about it. Though he was displeased
to hear this news, he had been victorious over his enemies, and when he
returned to his palace, he was greeted with such rejoicing that he forgot
his sorrow. However, Bienfaisante had put the little Pig Prince in a lovely
little stable that was very clean. It had high railings and was outfitted
according to his proportions. There he was nourished with the very best
milk which was given to him in a massive golden trough. Sometimes the
fairy went to the queen's chamber without being seen, and she gave the
queen an account of her son's nourishment. The fairy had given the little

pig the gift of speech, and when he reached an age when he could think
for himself, she taught him all that a prince should know in order to mold
and fuse his mind and manners in accordance with the grandeur of his
birth. She made him acquainted with this grandeur by saying only that he
had to live in the form of a pig for a length of time determined by destiny.
Sometimes the fairy transported the queen to the stable so she could see
her son, whom she caressed a thousand times. This was only done when
she was in the country, and the king was in the city.

Finally, the Pig Prince reached the age of fifteen, and the fairy Bienfaisante allowed him to leave his pigskin in the stable and gave him his
natural form so that he became the most charming prince one had ever
seen. She led him into his palace at night, which she transformed into
daytime when it was night elsewhere. Then sometime before the sun rose
outside, he became a pig again. This was the way in which this good fairy
tricked the malicious Rancune. When the prince was at the palace, he
amused himself marvelously well, and what gave him most pleasure was
the conversation of the beautiful ladies of the court of Bienfaisante, and
he often held some amorous talks with them.

Nearby there was a castle in which a fairy of a low order by the name
of Bourgillonne was living. She had become infatuated with her neighbors,
two very common ladies, and she wanted to procure a fortune for them.
As a result of her efforts, she found a way to get them into Bienfaisante's
palace as chambermaids for the fairy Tranquille, who had given the prince
the gift of gallantry. The young ladies were pretty enough because Bourgillonne had given them proper clothes and jewels which managed to
sparkle, even though they were false. All this along with a good deal of
affectation brought them to the attention of the prince, who was often in
the apartment of their mistress, whom he visited assiduously. Finally, the
prince fell head over heels in love with one of the chambermaids. He
believed that, with his appearance as pig, he would never be loved, and
even though the chambermaid treated him favorably, she always did so
with a great reserve. Indeed, she was not informed about the prince's power
to transform from pig to prince, and moreover, she took him for a minor
lord. Meanwhile, the chambermaid confided in Bourgillonne about his
advances, and the fairy encouraged her to make the prince want to marry
her. Consequently, the chambermaid played her role so well that the poor
prince became taken by her and promised her everything she wanted. Yet,
she was not content with his promises. She wanted results.

The fairy Bienfaisante perceived that her pig was upset by something,
and although she soon guessed the cause, she wanted to learn about it
from him. He had great difficulty confessing it to her, and when he did,
Bienfaisante became angry and told him that the queen his mother would
never consent to a marriage that was so unsuitable.

"But, madame," the prince responded, "I don't know how long I must
live in this horrible form. If I have to spend my entire life as a pig, what
princess would want me?"

The clever fairy, who pursued her point, pretended to give into his bad
reasoning and permitted him to marry the chambermaid without the
queen knowing it. His joy was extreme, and the following night he told

the good news to his beloved. The day after, he married her in the presence of the fairies Bienfaisante and Tranquille, and then the fairies led the newlyweds to a room, where they placed the wife on the bed, and when the prince was undressed, they left. But imagine the surprise of the prince when he got into the bed and found a large paper doll instead of his new wife! His vexation and his shame compelled him to flee to the stable, where he put on his pigskin again. The fairy, who had played this little joke by transporting the chambermaid from that spot, asked the sad pig why he had left his wife so quickly. Then he told her with some anguish mixed with confusion what had happened.

"Well then," said the fairy, "why are you so upset? It must undoubtedly be some superior power that does not want you to consummate a marriage that is regarded to be so ill-matched."

The prince did not pay any respect to these reasons, and he did not want to go to the palace for several days. He remained sad and spent his time in his stable, but the fairy obliged him to leave and took him to the palace, where they doubled the amusements to dissipate his melancholy mood. Meanwhile, he found a very pleasurable means to console himself by falling in love with the second chambermaid more than he had been with the first. She believed that she was happy in his company, even though she secretly accused him of some essential fault and made use of the same means as the other chambermaid to set the same terms with the prince as before.

He did not dare to say anything to Bienfaisante. He wept. He sighed and did not want to eat, so that the fairy was obliged to command him to tell her about everything, which she pretended not to know. When she was informed, she caused him more difficulty than she had caused him before, threatening to alert the queen, who would not be happy about his conduct and his bad taste. But gradually she calmed down and let herself be persuaded by him. The same marriage ceremony was observed, but this time he did not find a doll in his bed but a large cat that fled through a window and broke all the glass.

This second incident led him to despair, and he decided not to return into his pigskin and thus to die. He had been warned by the fairy that, if the sun were to cast its rays on his natural face, he would not be able to avoid death. But Bienfaisante, who was on her guard and who did not see him return, was afraid that her art had betrayed her and that the chambermaid was living with the prince or that the despair of having been tricked a second time might have caused him to do something foolish. She ran across the field to the stable to clarify everything, and she found him in the bed almost drowning in his tears. Despite his condition, she managed to get him out of bed, and when he had put the pigskin back on himself and assumed his piglike figure, she had him drink some water from the River of Oblivion, which completely effaced the memory of all that had happened. The next day he returned to the palace as calm as he had been before the amorous adventures that the fairy had kept concealed from his mother. Instead, the fairy showed him to his mother in his charming figure, and she almost died from pleasure when she saw him.

Some time later, the prince was out walking one night by himself in the gardens of the palace, and he strolled along the bank of a canal where he saw a monstrous carp that stuck its head out of the water and said to him, "Prince, if you are willing to let me conduct you to a certain spot, I shall show you the most surprising and most pleasant thing that a mortal has ever seen."

"But how can you take me anywhere, and where will you take me?" asked the prince.

"You needn't worry," the carp replied. "I give you my word. Nothing will happen to you if you return to this place tomorrow at the same time."

The prince promised him and did not say anything to Bienfaisante about this incident. The next night he appeared at the rendezvous. His friend the carp appeared harnessed to a small boat made out of turtle scales, and the fish told him to enter, which he did. The skillful carp then set off and pulled him in a marvelous fashion, and when the prince had been traveling in this boat for some time, he approached a small island where there was a tiny forest. The carp told him to go there, that he would find a dwarf dressed in an eelskin, who would escort him to a place where he would see what the fish had promised him, that the fish would wait for him at this place, that his escort would take care to warn him when the time came to withdraw, and that he should not worry about anything.

The prince went into the tiny forest where he met the dwarf who was dressed as the carp said he would be. The prince was received with respect and taken to a very dark grotto in which he walked for a long time, preceded by the dwarf, who lit the way with a little glass lamp that did not make great light. The dwarf stopped at a place where he had the prince approach a rock. Then he showed him a small opening through which he could look with two eyes, and he told the prince to keep looking until he came to fetch him.

The prince was as surprised as one could be to see a chamber that was incomparable in its beauty and construction. It was illuminated by many crystal lamps set on chandeliers of amber and coral which had been made in a marvelous way. Sheets of water lost themselves noiselessly in golden sand that formed the floor as well as the lining of the walls. The ceiling was constructed of dangling and moving water. There was a grand mirror with an enamel frame of various colors that depicted flowers on which one saw flies of all kinds, butterflies, caterpillars, glowworms, and spiders made in imitation of nature. The furniture consisted of a Cornelian table, some wooden armchairs decorated with blue rattans, a cabinet made of rubies from the Orient that contained serpentine and chiseled clay vases. A marvelously ornamented bed completed the furnishings of this extraordinary apartment. The curtains were made from a gold fabric covered with a remarkable design of flowers in a melange of pearls and coral. They were hung by golden cords, and at the bottom there were great rings of pearls and coral. The counterside and back were made of the same stuff. The feet of the bed were cut with crystal. There was a young attractive girl wearing a sparkling muslin dress decorated with rose-colored ribbons, and she was putting her hair in order. On her hair was a headdress made of English lace, high and fine, and there was something in lace above the bed, plated in gold and silver. The squares, the powder boxes, the beauty patches, the pads, and all the other small accessories were made of mother-of-pearl garnished with gold.

While the prince was contemplating such rare objects, a door painted with flowers au naturel was opened, and in walked a young lady who appeared to be sixteen or seventeen years old. She was so surprisingly beautiful that the prince almost fainted. Her perfect and well-proportioned figure was the least of her charms. It is impossible to describe the beautiful colors of her skin, the regularity of her features, the sparkle of her eyes and their touching languor, and the mysterious traits of her beautiful lips. Her lovely blond hair was incomparable. Tied with a green and gold ribbon, it fell in a thousand curls around her face and cheeks. Intertwined in her hair were flowers and precious stones. Her dress was made of green crepe streaked with gold that was enriched by pearls. She was leaning lightly on a young and pretty girl dressed like the one who was in the chamber. As soon as she entered, she sat down in an armchair and learned on the Cornelian table. She supported her head with her hand and had a sad and melancholy air about her, while the girls were standing near her and waiting for her orders. Finally, the girl who had entered the room with her said, "Madame, would you like to lie down on the bed? It is late."

"Alas, Miris," the charming young lady sighed and responded, "why should I try to relax when I am certain that I shall not be able to calm myself?"

"Madame," Miris replied, "I would appreciate it if you would permit me to ask you what has caused this sudden change and what has caused you to feel such a way toward your lover? When the river Pactole was taken by your beauty and carried you away with us when we were walking along his banks, I was not surprised by your despair. The agony that you suffered as you were torn out of the arms of your father the king and your mother the queen was understandable. Nor do I blame you for having difficulty adjusting to a place so different in all ways from the place where you were born. The extraordinary face of the river Pactole justifies the torment that you have when you look at him and suffer his signs of passion. But, madame, all of that has become familiar to you. You are apparently pleased by the tender attention of Pactole and the numerous beautiful nymphs and demigods who form your gallant court. You no longer have cause to worry, for all the magnificent preparations that are being made in this vast empire will unite you with a powerful divinity and make you immortal. Who could have changed the inclinations of your heart so suddenly, madame?"

"Here," said the princess as she languidly took a portrait from a diamond box that was in her pocket. "Here is what is causing my trouble and torment. I found this box on a table of a small cabinet in the river's apartment. I had entered alone and was struck by the glistening gems on the box. I picked it up, opened it, and found what you are looking at."

Miris took the portrait, and in order to see it better, she passed it beneath the light of one of the lamps on the table. This enabled the prince to see easily that it was his portrait. He had seen himself often enough in the mirrors of Bienfaisante's palace to recognize himself. If the beauty of the princess had already made him move from admiration to love, he now moved from admiration to joy when he saw that his portrait had produced such overwhelming feelings in the princess's heart that she preferred him over a divinity. While he was indulging himself in this pleasure, Miris and her companion admired the surprising beauty of this portrait.

"Well then, Miris," said the princess, "don't you find a great difference between this charming mortal and the bizarre face of Pactole? And am I to be blamed for giving him the preference in my heart that he deserves?"

"It is true, madame," Miris responded, "that there is a great difference between the god your lover and the mortal who has served as the original for this painting, if it is really true that it can have one, because I believe that this painting is only a figment of the imagination. But suppose, madame, that this portrait was the copy of a real original: you do not know if he has all the qualities that he needs to animate his beauty, and if he is of the right birth and mind, and above all if he has the heart capable of responding to your tender feelings."

"Ah, Miris!" the princess said, as she took back the portrait and looked at it affectionately, "how impossible it would be for the interior of an object so accomplished not to be also as perfect as the charming exterior!"

"Well then, madame," Miris replied, "when everything is as you imagine, what use is all of this since you don't know where this handsome phantom is living? How can you leave something certain for something uncertain?"

"Don't upset me," said the princess, who was now crying. "I have enough to worry about. Pactole has given me only six days in which to make him happy. Let me then hope that the genius of chance that led me to find this fatal painting will also lead me to discover the original."

The prince was on the verge of talking, and he was looking for a way to make himself seen by the princess when the dwarf arrived to warn him that he did not have much time to lose and had to return to the palace. After he closed the opening, he obliged the prince to follow him, and the prince left the spot with great agony, for it was a place where he had abandoned his heart and had seen and heard very surprising things. At last he rejoined the carp, who took him back to the palace. Along the way he asked the carp questions that touched upon the marvels that he had seen, and the carp told him that this beautiful princess was the only daughter of King Authomasis of the Cabalistiques Islands, which were inhabited by philosophers who dealt with secret sciences. The head of the philosophers was a great captain named Gabalis, and he had had some dealings with the fairy Rancune. Together they arranged the marriage of Princess Ondine with their friend the river Pactole. As a reward they received from him the Philosopher's Stone, and with their help, Pactole carried away the princess with her two chambermaids. Since that time King Authomasis had not had any news of her.

The prince asked his escort whether it would be possible to see the incomparable princess again and whether he could be seen.

"This is something that I cannot tell you," said the carp. "But try to come to the bank of the canal every night, and I'll tell you what I can do for you."

The prince thanked the fish and returned to his ugly form in the pigskin, which had never been more intolerable than now. It was in this condition that he became steeped in cruel and pleasant thoughts. He did not tell the fairy about this adventure, but she was well aware of it because the carp and the dwarf did not act without orders from her. Of course, she had her reasons for keeping silent. As soon as the sun set, the prince went to the palace, where he groomed himself with the help of his many servants and made certain adjustments to augment his charms in the hope that he might be seen by the beautiful Ondine. He needed some makeup to restore the natural vivacity of his skin color, which age and troubles of the past night or rather the preceding day had altered. When he had completed all this and had eaten his soup—for he did not eat much when he was in his human shape and was not allowed to eat pork—he went to directly to the bank of the canal, where he walked for some time, or rather where he ran impatiently. Moments are like centuries for lovers. He despaired of seeing his dear and good friend the carp. But at last he watched the water bubble, and the carp appeared. However, the prince did not see the little boat, and this troubled him a great deal, and he was troubled even more when the carp told him that there was nothing that could be done that evening. The princess had been sick the entire day and she was resting. Perhaps she would be better the next day, and the carp promised to keep him informed.

After the carp had said these words, it disappeared and left the poor prince in deep sorrow. However, he consoled himself somewhat with the thought that he had played some role in causing the princess's indisposition. Lovers are the most unjust people in the world, and the proofs of love that they receive from their mistresses make them more happy when their mistresses have to pay more for them. He spent the night and day very sad and very lonesome, and when the moment to go to the palace arrived, he was there and had himself dressed appropriately. Since he believed he had noticed that the princess loved green, he had green added to his garments wherever possible. Then he went to the bank of the canal, and he was overjoyed to find the carp there with the little boat. After the prince stepped gingerly into the boat, his obliging friend, sensing his desires and impatience, took him to the island. When the prince landed, he went straight to the forest, where he found the dwarf, who conducted him like the first time with a small lamp.

"My dear friend," the prince said to him, "can't you provide me with some means to be seen by the princess?"

"That is something that I couldn't tell you," replied the dwarf. "If I receive some new orders, I would gladly carry them out."

The prince quickly looked through the opening into the princess's chamber, which he found illuminated and decorated in the same way that he had previously seen it, but nobody was there. He understood the reason for her absence, attributing it to her health. But while he was steeped in thought, he was soon troubled by a feeling of jealousy. He imagined that she was with his rival, and he sighed about this a few times. Therefore, the arrival of the princess escorted by the river and followed by her two chambermaids increased his sorrow instead of diminishing it. He believed that Pactole had perhaps married her, and that he was going to be the witness of the river's happiness. While his mind is being agitated by these cruel thoughts, let us compose a description of the river Pactole.

He was tall and well-built with handsome traits as far as one could see. His eyes were lively. The color of his skin was just as pale as his lips, which were almost covered with a large blue beard that dropped down to his belt. His long hair and his collars were the same color. He was wearing a sort of jacket that descended to his knees and was made of a light and flexible material, the color of water and gold. His leather boots crafted with grains of gold dust had clusters of lustrous pearls attached to them. At his side he had a saber made of a great fishbone ornamented with gems, and around his waist was a sash of gladiolus and rustic lilies. A crown that was similar in style covered his head. This outfit and this bizarre figure were not without their beauty.

As far as the princess is concerned, she appeared as she did the first time, except that she seemed more sad.

"Madame," Pactole said to her as soon as they had entered the room, "you are subjecting my feelings to a severe test. I have recently been surprised to see that, after you had revealed yourself to be open to my love at the time that I began to show my affections for you, you have become very contrary at the moment that you permitted me to hope that I might be happy."

"My lord," the princess responded, "I have told you already that I am not in a position to dispose of myself without the consent of the king my father, and I believe that after you return me to his arms, you can obtain me from him in the ordinary way, and in this way I shall not be opposed to your legitimate desires."

"Madame," the river said, "gods do not let themselves be used the same way as men. They have the power to satisfy themselves as they will. I have already told you, madame, and I repeat it again. You have only four days to decide."

After he finished speaking, he bade her a sorry farewell and departed. As soon as the princess was alone with her chambermaids, she threw herself down on the bed and burst into a flood of tears and sighs. Her dear Miris knelt down on her knees next to her and tried to console her and told her she would accommodate herself in time.

"No, Miris," the tormented princess said. "No, I shall not consent to give myself to someone other than the charming object of my affection."

"Well, madame," Miris interrupted her, "think about what you are saying and realize that this object to whom you have given your heart is not in your power, and from what I can see, he never will be."

Just as she was talking about him and as the prince was dying to make himself known to the princess, the dwarf came to him and said that he had orders to let him enter the princess's chamber.

"But, my lord," the dwarf added, "when you are there, do not forget where you are, and as soon as you see one of the lamps that are on the table go out, you are to leave immediately."

Upon saying this, he knocked three times on the rock with a cane, and it opened up enough to let the prince slip inside. Indeed, he was so excited that he did not wait for an invitation. He ran and threw himself at the feet of the beautiful Ondine and said to her, "Here I am, madame, this happy mortal whom your heart prefers to that god, and here I am to pay homage to you with my heart and with a throne that I am supposed to occupy one day."

One can imagine the pleasant surprise of the princess, who easily recognized the original of a painting that had made such a strong impression on her heart. She was so ecstatic to see the object of her love next to her that she could not speak. Thus she remained on her bed for a few moments as if she were dumbfounded.

"Charming princess," the prince continued and took her hands with respect, "please get over your astonishment. I am not a ghost. These moments are very precious for me, my princess. Permit me in these moments that I have near you to persuade you that I love you, that I adore you, and that nothing can ever make me change the feelings that I have for you. You are not responding to me, divine Ondine!"

"Oh, my lord!" she said, regarding him with surprise, "excuse me. I am upset. It is true. I found your portrait in a place where no mortal could have brought it, and I am now seeing you yourself at my feet through some supernatural effect. What is even more surprising, you know the most secret feelings of my heart."

Then they began telling each other the most tender things that one can imagine in a similar situation. The prince acquainted her with the powerful protection of the fairy who had taken care of him since his birth and only spoke of her in good terms and without revealing the secret of the pigskin. But he assured her that through the power of this fairy he would get her out of Pactole's power, providing that she consented.

"Alas!" the princess sighed. "I consent and I wish this more than anything in the world."

As they were talking, the prince noticed that a lamp had gone out. He was immediately aware of what he had to do and sighed, "I must leave you, my princess, and I am sorry, but if I do not leave you right away, I might never be able to see you again. I do not know the powerful agent that has enabled me to come to you. But I am aware that it is acting in concert with my heart."

Finally he tore himself from the charming princess, after having given her all his assurances of his eternal love and after having received all that the kindness and the virtue of the princess permitted her to give. She reminded her lover that she only had four days time given to her by Pactole, that she would pretend to show Pactole her affection because she was afraid to irritate him, and that the prince should take Pactole's violent temper into account.

The prince promised her that he would assuredly have news for her the following night. Then he approached Miris, to whom he presented a pocket mirror decorated with diamonds.

"Charming Miris, I beg you not to take the side of the god against a mortal," he said.

She took the mirror and blushed, and she was extremely surprised to see an unknown man, who was acquainted with her name and with her most intimate feelings. The prince also gave to her companion a box of emerald clasps.

As soon as he left, the opening of the rock closed. He embraced the dwarf and was filled with gratitude, and as he was preparing to pay the dwarf his due compliments, the little man warned him to hurry and to return to the palace because he had spent more time with the princess than he had thought. His good friend the carp said the same thing, and the fish rushed him on board the boat, where he saw Bienfaisante, who said to him in a sorrowful air, "Ah, prince, how upset you've made me, and how you've put my art to a severe test! In order to save your life an hour ago, I retained the sun at Thetis."

He wanted to respond to her, but she prevented him by touching him with her magic wand. All of a sudden he found himself back at the stable in his pigskin. The sun came out of the heart of a tide after having frightened a part of the earth by its tardy appearance, which had been perceived by those jealous ones and those lovers as well as those who have the most troubles and who thus get up very early in the morning. The fairy came to her dear pig, who gave her an account of what had happened. When he had finished speaking, she smiled and said, "I should have spared you the trouble of telling me this story because everything that took place in this adventure was due to my orders. The carp and the dwarf are my subjects. It is I who sent your portrait to the beautiful Ondine by a diver to whom I entrusted the box. Ondine is the same princess whose birth I attended, and I and my sister gave her the gifts of soul and spirit, while the wicked Rancune, who made you into a pig, is the one who caused her to be loved and taken away by the river Pactole. Since your birth I have made you and the princess destined for one another, and I hope, with the help of my art, to rescue Ondine from that humid palace, where you have seen her. And in order not to lose time which is precious for us, I hope to lead that princess to my palace tomorrow night, while Rancune is busy helping her friend Gabalis, who has fallen in love with a sylphide.[1] I want you to wait for me in the palace because I don't want to expose you to any danger that your love could cause you."

Soon the night came in which Bienfaisante intended to carry out her promise to the prince, who escorted her to the bank of the canal where the carp was waiting for her with a very large boat. The precaution was useful because the number of persons who were to occupy the boat was more than usual. The prince watched Bienfaisante depart with envy, but the hope that he would soon see the beautiful princess again consoled him. He went to pass the time in his apartment, filled with joy and distress. He remained there for some time, but his impatience led him to return to the bank of the canal, from where he caught sight of the fairy. But oh God! What was to become of him when he saw that the fairy was only accompanied by the princess's chambermaids, who had tears streaming down their cheeks? He thought he would fall into the water, and he had trouble supporting himself at the foot of a marble statue along the bank

1. A spirit who generally inhabits the air and is associated with a slender, graceful woman.

of the canal. After the fairy got off the boat, she said to the prince with anguish, "Ah, prince, I am in despair! Follow me."

As she said these words, she walked toward the palace, where she entered her room and was alone with the prince, who could not utter a single word.

"Ah!" she screamed and stamped her feet. "You have won, cruel Rancune! You have won, and your evil art has triumphed over the justice of my intentions!"

"Ah, madame," the desolate prince said, "do not keep me in such terrible incertitude. What has happened to my princess? Have I lost her? Has the river taken possession of her?"

"No," Bienfaisante answered, "and although the accident that overtook us has hindered me from knowing her fate, I am sure that she is not in Pactole's power. I have not given up trying to find a remedy for the evil that has befallen you. Prince, calm yourself and listen to what has just happened to me. I had entered the princess's chamber by the same opening through which you went yesterday, and I found her fixing her hair with her chambermaids, who had undressed her. Her beautiful hair flowed freely and almost touched the ground. She appeared to be surprised by me, but your visit had begun to accustom her to extraordinary things. She quickly settled down, and since you had already spoken about me, she knew who I was and received me with great civility and even joy. 'Madame,' I said to her, 'the charming prince who adores you must have spoken about me, for I am the fairy who has promised you protection. I have come here myself to assure you of this, and it only depends on you to make the worthy object of your tenderness happy from today on and to discard your oppressor. In order to do this, beautiful princess, you only have to follow me,' 'But, madame,' she answered me in a timid air, 'should I abandon myself to you and let you escort me from this place without any other guarantees but your word, and the king my father . . .' 'The king your father,' I said interrupting her, 'was not consulted by Pactole when he took you from his arms, and I do not see that any more precaution is necessary to return you to his arms, unless you do not want to make him happy.' 'Ah, I would rather die than not make him happy!' she said. 'And since you promise, madame, to return me into the hands of the king my father, there is nothing more that I wish.' 'Then let us go, madame,' I said once more. 'Let us not lose precious moments.' She stood up to follow me, but at that instant, the liquid floor of her chamber opened, and the water put its arms around the hair of the princess and carried her away with such quickness that I was prevented from helping her. The poor chambermaids tore their hair out, and I made them leave that place. I now fear that the malicious fairy Rancune is planning to bring about the marriage of the princess with the river Pactole. Therefore, I transformed all his water into ice up to his bed. The only thing I must do right now is to discover the place where Rancune is keeping the Princess Ondine. I shall do all that I can, and if my art does not manage to help me, I also have recourse to Destiny."

Following this long talk, the fairy obliged the prince to put on his hideous pigskin, and she locked herself in a secret cabinet where the most occult secrets of the art of faerie are kept. We can assume that she was compelled to consult Destiny in his invisible palace. At last she learned that Rancune had put the princess in a tower of love situated in the middle of an obscure forest more than two hundred miles from Bienfaisante's palace. This distance did not dismay Bienfaisante because she had enough carriages and other vehicles with which she could make this journey in one hour. Bienfaisante also learned that there was no entrance to this tower except for a tiny hole through which a bird could pass. After discovering all this, the fairy did not forget to tell the good news to the prince and promised to return to the palace after sunset. She also told him to wait for her in her apartment, and before midnight, he could be assured of seeing his lovely princess again. Excited by such wonderful hope that the fairy had given him, the prince looked forward to the rendezvous.

In the meantime she departed as soon as possible in a light chariot harnessed to two bats, and after she got lost for a little time in the obscure forest, she finally discovered the tower of love that was extremely high and inaccessible. After she got out of her chariot, she rubbed her face with some water that was enclosed in a little bottle that she had attached around her neck with a gold chain, and she became the most beautiful little swallow that one had ever seen. With this form it was easy for her to enter the tower, and she found the sad princess at the very bottom lying on a magnificent bed pouring tears over the portrait of the prince, which she could barely see. This place was lit by only a small lamp, hung high above, and it could cast only a dim light on the princess.

"Alas, fatal painting!" the princess sobbed. "Have I only seen the original so that I will feel the pain of his loss even more cruelly? And also the loss of my liberty? What am I saying about my liberty? Alas, I have only changed my chains. Wasn't I just the prisoner of the river Pactole, and aren't I now the prisoner of that evil Rancune? Miserable Ondine, what is your destiny? That powerful fairy from whom you were to receive such marvelous help has merely added to your woes, hasn't she? Why have you abandoned me in such a pitiful state? I may soon die from all this pain."

"No, beautiful princess. No," said the swallow that hopped on her hand. "You are not going to die, and far from abandoning you, as you have accused me of doing, I have come to help you. I am that fairy whose power you doubt, and it will be through my power that you will be able to get out of this tower built by your enemy and mine. Let us not lose time with superfluous talk."

The fairy showed her the small bottle that she was carrying around her neck and informed her how to use it. The beautiful princess became a swallow like the fairy, and they flew out of the tower. Then they regained their natural forms and returned promptly to the palace. Bienfaisante led the prince into her apartment, where she found the chambermaids, who were overjoyed to see her again after having tormented themselves so much about having lost her. The fairy brought the princess something to eat to refresh her while she sent someone to fetch the prince, who thought he was going to die from joy when he saw his dear princess, who felt just as strongly as he did.

They would have spent a long time together without thinking about anything but recounting their trials and tribulations if the fairy had not warned them that they had to think of more serious things. She said to them that she had sent the fairy Tranquille, her sister, to the king of the Cabalistiques Islands, the father of Ondine, to alert him about what had happened and to bring him with the queen to be present at the marriage of their daughter, and they would be arriving very soon. No sooner did Bienfaisante say this than Tranquille appeared with the king and queen, who were very happy to be reunited with their charming daughter. They were informed about everything, and when Bienfaisante presented the prince to them, they were pleasantly surprised by how handsome he was. Indeed, they received him as a man who was going to be the husband of their daughter.

The fairy did not lose any time and transported herself to the place of the queen mother of the prince, and having entered her chamber without opening the door, she woke her up and quickly told her about what had transpired. Then the queen arose and went to the apartment of the king, who was very surprised to be woken so early in the morning and even more surprised to learn that he had a son and that he had to go right away to attend his wedding with the daughter of King Authomasis. He did not need more than the testimony of two fairies, for Tranquille was also there, to convince him about the truth of this unexpected event. It was also something that gave him great pleasure.

The fairies led them without much ado to their palace, where, without much ceremony, they celebrated the marriage of the prince and princess, who went straight to their bed. While the kings and queens were resting in their magnificent apartments, to which they had been conducted, the fairies ran to the stable where the pigskin was. They tore it into pieces and burned it in a fire composed of vervain, ferns, and herbs before sunrise during the summer solstice. Then, after they gathered the ashes, they had them thrown by the dwarf onto the ice water of Pactole so that the water became as fluid as it was before. When these great things had been accomplished, they went to rest for they needed it.

There was still an hour before sunrise, and thus they had nothing to fear for the prince, who with the help of Bienfaisante had married three times and thus managed to fulfill the ridiculous wish of Rancune. Everyone got up late at the palace because they had gone to bed in early morning. The order of day and night that had been interrupted in order to please the young prince was re-established. The indefatigable fairies were the first to rise. They ordered magnificent feasts to be prepared for the wedding celebrations, and they were also the first to enter the apartment of the newlyweds, to whom they gave some marvelous presents. Then the kings and queens entered, and they were all very happy. The news of these marvelous events soon spread throughout the kingdom. The prince was named Aimantin by Bienfaisante in memory of the tower of love from which she had rescued the beautiful Ondine, his wife.

After they had spent several days enjoying themselves in different ways, the king, who was Prince Aimantin's father, took this beautiful and illustrious company to his capital city, where the young couple were received in triumph and with great acclamation by all the people who were charmed by the prince and the princess. Once again the festivities lasted a long time in the palace of the king, and Rancune had such a violent reaction to the failure of her evil plans that she retired with her good friend Gabalis to the Isle of Oblivion, where they are still living today. Bourgillonne went to beg Bienfaisante to call back the two chambermaids, her flighty friends, which she gladly did because she no longer had any reason to complain about them since they had served to disenchant the prince. And in order to compensate them, the fairy arranged rich marriages for them.

Sometime after the marriage of Aimantin, his father died, and the prince succeeded him to the great pleasure of the subjects of this realm, who could never call him other than King Pig. The beautiful Ondine had children and produced a long line of successors. As for the river Pactole, he suffered so much torment after losing the beautiful Ondine that he almost dried up completely and became a small stream whose location is better known by poets than by a map.

JACOB AND WILHELM GRIMM

Hans My Hedgehog†

Once upon a time there was a farmer who had plenty of money and property, but rich as he was, his happiness was not complete, for he had no children with his wife. When he went into town with the other farmers, they often made fun of him and asked why he had no children. One day he finally got angry, and when he went home, he said, "I want to have a child, even if it's a hedgehog."

Then his wife gave birth to a child whose upper half was hedgehog and bottom half human. When she saw the child, she was horrified and said, "You can see how you cursed us!"

"There's nothing more we can do about it now," said her husband. "The boy must be christened, but we'll never find a godfather for him."

"There's only one name I can think of for him," said the wife, "and that's Hans My Hedgehog."

After he was christened, the pastor said, "He won't be able to sleep in a regular bed because of his quills."

Therefore, they gathered together some straw, spread it on the floor behind the stove, and laid Hans My Hedgehog on it. His mother could not nurse him because he might have stuck her with his quills. So he lay behind the stove for eight years, and eventually his father got tired of him and wished he might die, but he did not die. He just kept lying there.

One day there was a fair in town, and the farmer decided to go to it and asked his wife if she would like anything.

---

† Jacob and Wilhelm Grimm, "Hans My Hedgehog"—"Hans mein Igel" (1857), No. 108 in *Kinder-und Hausmärchen. Gesammelt durch die Brüder Grimm* (Göttingen: Dieterich, 1857).

"Some meat and a few rolls," she said. "That's all we need for the house."

Then he asked the maid, and she wanted a pair of slippers and stockings with clogs. Finally, he went and asked his son, "Hans My Hedgehog, what would you like to have?"

"Father," he said, "just bring me back some bagpipes."

When the farmer returned home, he gave his wife the meat and rolls he had brought. Then he handed the maid the slippers and stockings with clogs. Finally, he went behind the stove and gave Hans My Hedgehog his bagpipes. Upon receiving the bagpipes, he said, "Father, please go to the blacksmith and have him shoe my rooster. Then I'll ride away and never come back."

The father was happy at the idea of getting rid of him and had his rooster shod. When the rooster was ready, Hans My Hedgehog mounted it and rode away, taking some donkeys and pigs with him, which he wanted to tend out in the forest. Once he reached the forest, he had the rooster fly him up into a tall tree, where he sat and tended the donkeys and pigs. He sat there for many years until the herd was very large, and he never sent word to his father about his whereabouts.

As he sat in the tree, he played his bagpipes and made beautiful music. One day a king, who had lost his way in the forest, came riding by. When he heard the music, he was so surprised that he sent his servant to look around to see where the music was coming from. The servant looked around, but all he could see was a small animal, sitting up in a tree, that seemed to be a rooster with a hedgehog sitting on top of it playing music. The king told the servant to ask the creature why he was sitting there and whether he knew the way back to the king's kingdom. Hans My Hedgehog climbed down from the tree and said he would show him the way if the king would promise in writing to give him the first thing he met at the castle courtyard when he returned home.

"No danger in that," thought the king. "Hans My Hedgehog can't understand writing, so I can write whatever I want." The king took pen and ink and wrote something down, and after he had done this, Hans My Hedgehog showed him the way, and the king arrived home safely. When his daughter saw him coming from afar, she was so overcome with joy that she ran out to meet him and kissed him. Then he thought of Hans My Hedgehog and explained to her what had happened: he had been forced to make a promise in writing to a strange creature who had demanded to have the first thing the king met upon returning home. This creature had been sitting on a rooster as though it were a horse and had been playing beautiful music. The king told his daughter that he had, however, written down that Hans My Hedgehog was not to get what he demanded. Anyway, it made no difference, since he could not read. The princess was happy to hear that and said it was a good thing since she would never have gone with him anyway.

Hans My Hedgehog continued tending his donkeys and pigs. He was always cheerful, sitting there perched in his tree, playing his bagpipes. Now it happened that another king came driving by with his servants and courtiers. He too had lost his way, and the forest was so large that he did not know how to get back home. He too heard the beautiful music from afar and told a courtier to go and see what it was. So the courtier went to the tree and saw the rooster sitting there with Hans My Hedgehog on its back, and the courtier asked him what he was doing up there.

"I'm tending my donkeys and pigs, but what can I do for you?"

The courtier asked him whether he could show them the way out of the forest since they were lost and could not make it back to their kingdom. Hans My Hedgehog climbed down from the tree with his rooster and told the old king that he would show him the way if the king would give him the first thing that met him when he returned home to his royal castle. The king agreed and put it in writing that Hans My Hedgehog was to have what he demanded. When that was done, Hans My Hedgehog rode ahead of him on the rooster and showed the way. The king reached his kingdom safely, and as he entered the castle courtyard, there was great rejoicing. His only daughter, who was very beautiful, ran toward him and embraced him. She was very happy to see her old father again and asked him what in the world had kept him so long. He told her that he had lost his way and would not have made it back at all had it not been for a strange creature, half human, half hedgehog, who had helped him find his way out of the forest. The creature had been playing beautiful music. In return for his aid the king had promised to give him the first thing that met him at the castle courtyard. Now he was very sorry that it had happened to be her. However, out of love for her old father, the princess promised him that she would go with Hans My Hedgehog whenever he came.

In the meantime, Hans My Hedgehog kept tending his pigs, and the pigs had more pigs, and eventually there were so many that the entire forest was full of them. Then Hans My Hedgehog decided that he no longer wanted to live in the forest, and he sent word to his father to clear out all the pigsties in the village, for he was coming with such a huge herd of pigs that anyone who wanted to slaughter one could have his pick. On hearing this, his father was distressed, for he had believed that Hans My Hedgehog had long been dead. Nevertheless, Hans My Hedgehog mounted his rooster, drove his pigs ahead of him into the village, and ordered the slaughtering to begin. Whew! There was such chopping and butchering that the noise could be heard for miles around. Afterward Hans My Hedgehog said, "Father, have the blacksmith shoe my rooster one more time. Then I'll ride away and never return as long as I live."

His father, glad that Hans My Hedgehog would never return again, had the rooster shod. When Hans My Hedgehog departed, he set out for the first kingdom, but the king had given his men orders to stop anyone who was riding on a rooster and playing bagpipes from entering the castle. If necessary, they were to use their guns, spears, or swords. So, when Hans My Hedgehog came riding, they attacked him with their bayonets, but he put spurs to his rooster, and the bird rose in the air, flew over the gate, and landed on the ledge of the king's window. He called to the king to keep his promise and give him the princess; otherwise, he would take his life and his daughter's as well. Then the king implored his daughter to go with Hans My Hedgehog to save their lives. So she dressed herself all in white, and her father gave her a coach with six horses, splendid servants, money, and property. She got into the coach and was followed by Hans My Hedgehog, with his bagpipes and his rooster by his side. They then said good-bye and drove away, and the king thought that was the last he would ever see of his daughter, but things happened much differently. When they had gone a little way, Hans My Hedgehog took off her beautiful clothes and stuck her with his quills until she was covered with blood.

"This is what you get for being so deceitful!" he said. "Go back home. I don't want you."

Then he sent her away, and she lived in disgrace for the rest of her life. Meanwhile, Hans My Hedgehog, carrying his bagpipes, continued his journey on his rooster. Eventually, he came to the second kingdom, which belonged to the other king he had led out of the forest. However, this king had ordered his men to present arms and greet him by shouting "Long may he live!" After that they were to escort him into the royal palace. When the king's daughter saw him, she was startled and frightened because he looked so strange. Yet, there was nothing she could do, so she thought, for she had promised her father to go with him. Therefore, she welcomed Hans My Hedgehog, and then they were married. After the wedding ceremony he led her to the royal table, where they sat down together and ate and drank. When evening came and it was time to go to bed, she was quite afraid of the quills, but he said not to be scared because he had no intention of harming her. Then he told the old king to have four men stand watch in front of the bedroom door and to make a big fire, for when he got inside and was prepared to go to bed, he would slip out of his hedgehog's skin. Then the men were to rush in quickly, throw the skin on the fire, and stand there until it was completely consumed.

When the clock struck eleven, he went into the room, stripped off the hedgehog's skin, and left it on the floor. Right after this the men came, picked up the skin, and threw it into the fire. When the fire had consumed it, he was set free and lay in bed just like a human being, but he was pitch black, as if he had been burned. The king sent for his doctor, who rubbed him with special ointments and balms, and gradually, he became white and turned into a handsome young man. When the princess saw that, she was very happy. The next morning they got up in a joyful mood and had a fine meal. Then the marriage was performed again properly with Hans as a human, and the old king bequeathed his kingdom to Hans My Hedgehog.

After some years had passed, Hans took his wife and drove to visit his father. When he told the old man that he was his son, the father said that he had no son. Indeed, he had a son at one time, but he was born with quills, like a hedgehog, and had gone out into the world. Then Hans My Hedgehog revealed himself to his father, and the old man rejoiced and went back with him to his kingdom.

> My tale is done,
> and now, it's on the run.

The Wishes of Fools

Among folklorists, this narrative is categorized as tale-type "The Lazy Boy," and generally speaking, in most renditions, a poor, somewhat dumb and coarse boy is insulted by a young girl or woman of the upper class and eventually marries her due to some miraculous occurrence. Literally hundreds of such tales have been found throughout the world, and they provide evidence that the tale-type existed in oral traditions before Straparola wrote the first literary version. Why the tale-type has been called "The Lazy Boy" is not really clear because the boy is often industrious and kind, even if he is stupid. If anything, he is a luckless hero, whose fortune changes when he helps a fish or an animal. Some scholars have argued that the tale reflects a distinct male perspective in which the luckless hero takes revenge for the castrating remarks of an upper-class woman and then rises to power. Though there is some truth to this interpretation, there is also a strong possibility that the tale stems from class struggle and has another important social aspect: a commoner, who is often degraded by the upper class, takes revenge on the nobility by making off with the king's prize possession. The critique of authoritarian patriarchy is very strong in this tale, and the princess, wrongly accused of having an illicit affair, also learns how oppressive patriarchal rule can be. Here the motif of the miraculous pregnancy, perhaps a mock episode of the immaculate conception, is crucial for understanding the different tales.

The mysterious pregnancy of a daughter was a real concern for many noble families and commoners as well. A woman's body was regarded as a possession of the male, and any violation of a female body was a violation of patriarchal authority. At stake were the legacy and honor of a family. In the cycle of tales that involve a fool, often called Peter or Hans, who seeks his luck by wishing that a princess becomes pregnant, there are other motifs that recall King Lear's harsh treatment of his innocent daughter as well as the cycle of tales that deal with a proud princess or noblewoman who needs to learn humility. Christoph Martin Wieland, one of the most gifted German writers of the eighteenth century, wrote "Pervonte" (1778/79), a remarkable verse rendition of Basile's "Peruonto," which concerns a poor simpleton whose heart is so good that he is blessed by the fairies and thus rises in society. Another interesting German tale written during the romantic period was Heinrich von Kleist's "Die Marquise von O" (1810–11). Though not a fairy tale, it raises all the same questions about a mysterious pregnancy that the tales in this cycle pose.

GIOVAN FRANCESCO STRAPAROLA

Pietro the Fool†

In the Ligurian Sea there is an island called Capraia, which was ruled by King Luciano at one time. Among his subjects was a poor widow named Isotta, who lived with her son Pietro, a fisherman, who unfortunately was crazy, and everyone who knew him called him Pietro the Fool. Though he went fishing every day, he was always unlucky, and never caught any fish. Yet, each time he returned home, he would always run from his boat and shout so that all the people on the island could easily hear him, "Mother, bring out your tubs, big and small, your buckets and pails, I want them all. Your Pietro has brought you quite a haul!"

The poor woman, who trusted her son and believed his words, would get ready to receive the catch. But as soon as he arrived at his mother's house, the fool would stick out his tongue in ridicule and mock her.

Now the widow's house stood just opposite the palace of King Luciano, who had only one child, a beautiful and graceful girl about ten named Luciana. Whenever she heard Pietro the Fool cry out, "Mother, bring out your tubs, big and small, your buckets and pails, I want them all. Your Pietro has brought you quite a haul," she ran to the window and was so amused by his trick that she would nearly die from laughter. But when the fool saw her laugh so hard, he became very irritated and cursed her with vulgar language. But the more Pietro heaped abuse on her, the more she laughed and mocked him the way playful children are apt to do. Pietro, however, went on with his fishing day after day and repeated the same foolish trick on his mother every evening upon his return until one day he caught a large and fat tuna fish. Out of sheer happiness he jumped for joy and shouted, "I'll have a great meal with my mother! I'll have a great meal with my mother!" And he kept repeating these words. Meanwhile, when the tuna saw that he was caught and could not escape in any way, he said to Pietro the Fool, "Ah, my dear brother, I beg of you to be gracious and to spare my life and set me free! Dear brother, what do you want with me? Once you've eaten me, there will be no other benefit. But, if you let me live, perhaps I can help you some way at another time."

Pietro was, however, more in need of food than words, and he hoisted the fish on his shoulders and headed home in order to enjoy the fish with his mother. Nevertheless, the tuna kept imploring Pietro to spare his life, offering him as many fish as he wanted, and he also promised him to do whatever he would like. Though he was a fool, Pietro did not have a heart of stone, and, moved by pity, he was content to set the fish free. So he set it down, pushed it with his arms and legs, and rolled it back into the sea. After having received such a great favor, the fish did not wish to seem

---

† Giovan Francesco Straparola, "Pietro the Fool"—"Pietro pazzo per virtù di un pesce chiamato tonno, da lui preso e da morte campato, diviene savio; e piglia Luciana, figliuola di Luciano re, in noglie, che prima per icantesimo di lui era gravida" (1550), *Favola I, Notte seconda* in *Le piacevoli notti,* 2 vols. (Venice: Comin da Trino, 1550/53).

ungrateful, and so he said to Pietro, "Get into your boat and tilt it so that water can enter."

Pietro climbed into the boat, and leaning on top of one side, he let in so much water and fish that the boat was in great danger of capsizing. When he saw the danger, he easily took care of it and was happy with his haul. After he took as much fish as he could carry, he set out for home. As he approached his dwelling, he cried out, as was his custom, in a loud voice, "Mother, bring out your tubs, big and small, your buckets and pails, I want them all. Your Pietro has brought you quite a haul!"

His mother, however, did not move because she thought that he was only mocking and tricking her as usual. But Pietro continued to shout even louder. So the mother prepared all the pots, fearing that he would do something terribly foolish if he did not find them ready for cooking. When Pietro arrived at home and his mother saw how many splendid fish he brought with him, she was overjoyed and praised him because he had at last come back with a good haul.

Meanwhile, Princess Luciana had heard Pietro cry out, and she had run to the window. Then she began to mock and jeer at him, laughing at his words more boisterously than ever before. Not knowing what else to do, poor Pietro broke into a fit and rage. He left the fish with his mother and rushed back to the seashore and called loudly to the tuna to come and help him. Upon hearing and recognizing Peter's voice, the fish swam toward the shore, thrust his head out of the water, and asked him what he commanded.

"For now," the fool replied, "I only want Luciana, daughter of our King Luciano, to become pregnant."

In less than a wink of an eye, the command was carried out. Within days and then months the virginal womb of the young girl began to grow, and she was not even twelve years old. Soon there were clear signs of a pregnancy. When her mother saw this, she was greatly distressed and would not believe that a child of eleven could be pregnant. Instead, she attributed the swelling to some incurable disease. So, she secretly brought Luciana to be examined by some women who knew how to handle such cases as these. After carefully checking the girl, they came to the conclusion that she was definitely pregnant. The queen, who could not bear such ignominy and suffering, rushed to the king and told him everything. When he heard the news, he felt he would die from grief. He ordered a careful investigation to be made in a secret and fair way to discover who could have violated the child, but nothing was discovered. So, he decided to have his daughter killed to avoid the disgrace and vicious gossip.

However, the queen loved her daughter dearly, and she begged her husband to spare her until the child was born. Then he could do whatever he wanted with her. The king, as her father, was moved by compassion for his only daughter and agreed to let her have the baby. In due time, Luciana gave birth to a beautiful boy, and since he was so handsome the king could no longer bear the thought of getting rid of them. Instead, he ordered the queen to tend and nurse the boy until he was a year old. During that time he grew to become incomparably handsome, and it also occurred to the king that he could try an experiment to find out who the boy's father was.

So, he issued a proclamation that each man in the city who was fourteen or older was to appear at the palace carrying either some fruit or a flower in his hand to attract the child's attention. Whoever did not appear would lose his head.

On the appointed day, in obedience to the proclamation, all the men came to the palace carrying either a fruit or a flower. After they passed before the king, he ordered them to sit down according to their rank. Now, it so happened that one of the young men, as he was going to the palace, had met Pietro the Fool and had said to him, "Where are you going, Pietro? Why aren't you going to the palace like all the others to obey the king's orders?"

"What should I do in such company like that?" he replied. "Can't you see that I'm a poor fellow without a rag to my name? Yet, you ask me to mingle with all those gentlemen and courtiers! No!"

Then the young man jested with him and said, "Come with me, and I'll give you a coat. Who knows, maybe the child will turn out to be yours!"

So Pietro went to the young man's house and was given a coat. After he put it on, he accompanied the young man to the palace. He climbed the stairs and took a place near an exit where he could hardly be seen. By this time all the men had presented themselves to the king and were seated. Then Luciano commanded the child to be brought into the hall, thinking that, if the father were there, his paternal feelings would stir him to indicate who he was. The nurse took the baby in her arms and carried him down the hall where everyone caressed him and dangled fruit and flowers in front of him. But the infant refused them all with a wave of his hand. After the nurse had passed fifty or so men, she turned toward the exit of the palace, and as she moved toward it, the child immediately began to laugh and threw himself forward so vivaciously that he almost fell out of the woman's arms. But since she did not notice anyone near the exit, she walked back down the hall. Then she turned and went down the row of men to the same place, and the child became more excited than ever, laughing and pointing with his finger at the exit.

The king, who had already noticed the child's actions, called to the nurse and asked her who was standing at the exit. The nurse, who could not think of what to say, said that it must be a beggar. When the king commanded the person to be brought to them, he recognized Pietro the Fool at once. The child, who was close to the fool, stretched out his arms and grasped Pietro around the neck and kissed him lovingly. Upon seeing this, the king was tormented. He dismissed the assembly and then commanded Pietro, Luciana, and the child to be put to death. But the queen was very prudent, and she wisely suggested that, if they were all decapitated, this would bring scorn and disgrace down upon the king. Therefore, she persuaded him to have a barrel built as large as possible so all three of them could fit into it. This barrel was then to be cast into the sea and drift at random. Then they would not have to suffer much anguish. This plan pleased the king very much, and he ordered the barrel to be built and all three to be placed inside with a basket of bread, a flask of wine, and a cask of figs for the child. Then they were thrown out into the high sea with the expectation that the barrel would crash against a reef, and they would all drown. But everything turned out much differently than the way the king and queen thought it would.

When Pietro's old mother learned of her son's misfortune, she died of grief a few days later. Meanwhile the unfortunate Luciana, tossed about by fierce waves, shed a flood of tears and could see neither sun nor moon. Since she had no milk to give to her son, who often cried, she soothed him to sleep by giving him a fig. But Pietro did not seem to care about anything and simply ate the bread and drank the wine. Seeing him act this way, Luciana cried, "Alas, Pietro! You see how I am innocently suffering this punishment that you brought on me, and yet you just eat and drink and laugh without worrying about the danger facing us."

"Everything that's happened to you is not my fault," he answered, "but your own. You caused it by continually mocking me and deriding me. But don't lose heart. We'll soon get out of this predicament."

"You're certainly right about that," she said, "because the barrel will soon crash into a reef, and then we'll all drown."

"Be quiet," said Pietro. "I have a secret, and if you knew it, you'd be quite astounded and perhaps delighted as well."

"What secret do you have?" she asked. "Can it possibly help against all this torment?"

"I have a large fish, who will do whatever I command," Pietro stated. "In fact, there's nothing he can't do. He was the one who caused your pregnancy."

"If this is really true," Luciana said, "that would be a good thing. But what is this fish of yours called?"

"I call him simply, 'tuna.'" replied Pietro.

"Well," said Luciana, "let's put your fish to the test. I want you to transfer the power you hold over him to me. Tell him that he is to do my bidding."

"Just as you wish," Pietro responded, and he immediately called the tuna and commanded him to do everything that Luciana asked him to do. Once she had the power over the fish, she ordered him to cast the barrel on one of the safest and most beautiful cliffs on an island near her father's kingdom. As soon as the fish had completed this task, she commanded him to change Pietro from the ugly fool that he was into a wise, handsome young man. But she was not simply content with that. She also wished for a very splendid castle to be built on top of the cliff, and it was to have beautiful lounges, halls, and chambers with a sumptuous garden in the rear full of trees bearing gems and precious pearls. In the middle were two fountains, one that had the freshest water, the other filled with the finest wine. All of this was brought about without delay.

In the meantime the king and queen realized how miserable they were without their daughter and grandson, and they deeply regretted everything, for they were no longer happy or content. They kept thinking how they had abandoned their own flesh and blood to be devoured by the fish. Since they suffered greatly from their anguish and woe, they decided to console themselves by a visit to Jerusalem and the Holy Land. So, they ordered a ship to be prepared for them and had it furnished with all the appropriate things. Then they set sail with a favorable and propitious wind, and before they had gone a hundred miles, they caught sight of a splendid palace on the cliff of a small island. Since this palace was so charming and the island was part of Luciano's kingdom, they decided to visit it.

After they approached an inlet, they weighed anchor and landed on the island. Before they reached the palace, Luciana and Pietro recognized them. So, they went forth to meet them and greeted them with a cordial welcome, but the king and queen did not recognize their hosts, who had been transformed in such a great way. The guests were taken first into the charming palace, which they examined with great care, praising its great beauty, and then they were led by a secret staircase into the garden. The splendor pleased them so much that they swore they had never seen a place as delightful as this one. In the center of the garden was a tree which bore three golden apples on one of its branches. The caretaker of the garden had been ordered by Luciana to guard the apples very carefully. Now, due to some secret means, which I cannot fathom, the most beautiful of these apples was transported secretly into the folds of the king's robe near his bosom. Luciano and the queen were about to take their leave when the caretaker approached and said to Luciana, "Madame, the most beautiful of the three golden apples is missing, and I don't know who took it."

So Luciana gave orders that everyone should be searched carefully, one by one, for such a loss like this was no light matter. After the caretaker had thoroughly searched everyone twice, he came back and told Luciana that the apple could not be found anywhere. Upon hearing these words, Luciana pretended to be very upset, and turning to the king, she said, "Your majesty, do not be angry with me if I ask that even you allow yourself to be searched, for the golden apple that is missing is priceless and the most precious thing that I have in the world."

The king was not suspecting any kind of plot and was certain of his innocence. So, he loosened his robe, and immediately the golden apple fell to the ground. When the king saw this, he was shocked and amazed. He did not know how the golden apple had gotten into his robe. Then Luciana spoke, "Sire, we welcomed and honored you with all the respect fitting your rank. Yet as recompense you robbed our garden of its finest fruit without our knowledge. It seems to me that you have shown yourself very ungrateful."

The innocent king kept trying to prove to her over and over again that he could not have taken the apple. After a while she realized that the right time had come for her to reveal herself to her father and declare him innocent, and she said with tears in her eyes, "My lord, I am Luciana, your unfortunate daughter whom you sentenced to a cruel death along with my child and Pietro the Fool. I am Luciana, your only daughter, who gave birth to a child, though I never slept with a man. This boy here is the innocent child I conceived without sin, and this other is Pietro the Fool. Thanks to a fish called tuna, Pietro has become wise, and the fish also built this superb and stately palace. It was the fish who placed the

golden apple into the folds of your robe, and just as you are innocent of
stealing the golden apple, I am innocent of the pregnancy that he caused
through a magic spell."

After she revealed all this, they wept with joy and embraced each other.
Then they organized a great celebration, and after spending a few days on
the island, they embarked on the ship and returned triumphantly to Capraia, where Pietro was married to Luciana, and the wedding was followed
by a grand feast. He lived with her a long time in great honor and consolation. Then, when Luciano died, he inherited the throne and became
king of the realm.

GIAMBATTISTA BASILE

Peruonto†

A worthy woman of Casoria[1] called Ceccarella had a son called Peruonto, who was the most disgraceful, the most stupid, and the most terrific
blockhead that nature had ever produced. That is why the poor woman's
heart turned darker than a dustcloth, and why she cursed more than a
thousand times that day when her knees had opened the door to that
birdbrain, who was not even worth a dog's bowels. But no matter how
much the unfortunate woman might open her mouth and scream, the
lazybones did not give a shit and would not do a simple damn favor for
her.

At last, after yelling a thousand times at his head, after a thousand outbursts of rage, and a thousand "I tell you" and "I told you" and cries today
and screams tomorrow, she persuaded him to go into the woods and fetch
some logs for the fire. "Now's the time," she said, "to stuff our mouths.
Run and fetch some wood. Don't forget the way, and come back soon. I
want to cook four cabbages dragged out of the ground to drag on our
lives."

The good-for-nothing Peruonto departed, and he left like a condemned
man who walks between two priests of Father Death.[2] He departed and
walked as if he were stepping on eggs with the gait of a sentry counting
his steps and moving very slowly and very softly and a little at a time.
Gradually he made his way into the woods like a crow that is not going
to return.

Soon he reached the middle of a meadow and came to a stream grumbling and murmuring against the lack of discretion shown by the stones
that impeded its way. There he found three boys who had made a quilt
out of grass and a pillow out of flint stone. They were sleeping as if they

---

† Giambattista Basile, "Peruonto"—"Peruonto" (1634), *Terzo passatempo della prima giornata* in
   Lo cunto de le cunti overo Lo trattenemiento de peccerille, De Gian Alessio Abbattutis, 5 vols.
   (Naples: Ottavio Beltrano, 1634–36).
1. A village about four miles northeast of Naples.
2. There was a brotherhood called the Bianchi della Giustizia in Naples, and the members customarily accompanied criminals to execution.

had been slaughtered and were lying under the blazing sun that was frying them.

Seeing that these boys were reduced to a fountain of water in the midst of a red-hot furnace, Peruonto took pity on them and cut some branches of an oak tree with his ax and built a fine bower of leaves over them. Shortly thereafter the boys, who were sons of a fairy, woke up and perceived the courtesy and the kindness of Peruonto. Therefore, they endowed him with a magic power: everything he desired would be granted as soon as he requested it.

After this was done, Peruonto continued on his way into the woods, where he fetched such a gigantic log that it could only be moved by a rope and cable. Seeing that it would be a waste of time to try to carry it on his back, he straddled it and said, "Oh my, if only this log could carry me like a horse!" And, lo and behold, the wood began to pace like a prize Bisignanian[3] horse, and when it reached the king's palace, it twirled and pranced in an incredible way. There were some ladies standing at a window, and when they saw this marvelous steed, they called Vastolla, the king's daughter, who leaned out of the window and watched the whirling and springing of this piece of wood and burst out laughing. This was unusual because she had a melancholy temperament, and nobody remembered her ever laughing this way.

Peruonto raised his head, and when he saw the princess making fun of him, he said, "Oh Vastolla, wait and see! May you one day become pregnant by me!"

And having said this, he gave the log a kick with his boots, and immediately the wood galloped home. But there were so many children who ran after him staring and screaming that, if his mother had not quickly shut the door, they would have killed him with blows of lemons and broccoli.

Meanwhile Vastolla's menstruation stopped, and she began having certain longings and palpitations of the heart. Soon she realized she was pregnant. She concealed her pregnancy as long as possible, but she could not keep this up because her belly had become as large as a keg. When the king became aware of this, he behaved like a mad hatter and called together his councillors.

"You already know that the moon of my honor has grown horns," he said. "You already know that my daughter has provided me with the horns[4] of ink to write the chronicles or rather the debacle of my shame. You already know that she has filled her womb to fill my brow with wrinkles. Therefore, speak to me! Advise me! I'm inclined to deliver her soul from her body before she delivers a bad brood. I'd like her to feel the pains of death before she feels labor pains. I'm disposed toward uprooting her from this world before she plants her germs and seeds in this world."

The councillors, who had consumed more oil than wine and hence were more sober, said, "Truly, she deserves a severe punishment, and the handle of knife that cuts off her life should certainly be made from the horn she has placed on your brow. But now is not the time. If we execute

---

3. The family of Sanseverino di Bisignano was known for breeding superb prize horses.
4. It was customary in those days to make inkstands out of horn, and, of course, Basile is implying that the king has been cuckolded.

Peruonto. George Cruikshank, 1893.

her when she is pregnant, the rash culprit, who has trapped you in the middle of the battle by arming himself on your left and right flanks, will escape by the skin of his teeth. To teach you the politics of Tiberius, he has made you study Cornelius Tacitus.[5] To force you to recognize a dream of infamy that predicts the truth, he has made it come from the gate of horns. Therefore, let us wait for what comes, and we shall see what is at the root of this crime, and then we can think and decide, with a pinch of salt, what we should do."

This advice pleased the king, for he saw that they spoke wisely and appropriately. So, he restrained himself and said, "Let us await the outcome of this affair."

And, when heaven decreed, the hour of birth arrived, and with very easy labor pains, with the first puff of Vastolla's breath into the phial,[6] with the urging of the midwife, with the first squeeze of her womb, two baby boys popped into the lap of the midwife like two golden apples.

The king was also pregnant, but with rage, and he called his councillors so he could, in turn, give vent to his feelings.

"Now my daughter has given birth," he said. "Now's the time to strike!"

"No," said the wise old men, who were all for taking more time. "Let us wait for the boys to grow enough so we can identify the features of their father."

The king, who never wrote a verse without having it corrected by his councillors because he never wanted to scribble across lines, shrugged his shoulders, kept his patience, and waited until the boys were seven years old. Then, once again, he urged his councillors to strike at the base of the trunk and get to the root of everything.

"Since you've not been able to pry the answer from your daughter," one of them said, "and since you've not been able to determine who has falsified your image and altered the crown, we shall now eradicate this blemish. Therefore, we would like you to arrange a grand banquet and order all the nobles and gentlemen of this city to attend. We shall carefully watch with eyes as sharp as a hawk to see what man the children embrace most freely, spurred by nature, because he undoubtedly will be their father, and we shall immediately cart him away like a little pile of crow shit."

This idea pleased the king, who ordered the banquet and invited all the people of rank and importance, and after they had eaten, he had them stand in a line. Then he had the children pace by them, but they paid the men no more attention than Alexander's dog paid to the rabbits.[7] Consequently, the king cursed and bit his lips, and he also stamped his

5. A reference to the contemporary debates concerning the policies of Tiberius in the *Annals* of the Roman historian Tacitus (ca. 55–ca. 117). There is again another playful reference to corns and cuckoldry in the name Cornelius.

6. It was customary for women who were giving birth to blow hard into a phial, vase, or jug to help ease the labor pains.

7. In his *Storia Natural*, Pliny recounts a story about Alexander the Great during his expedition in India. Evidently, Alexander received a dog of immense size as a gift. However, when he wanted to test its courage and strength by exposing it to deer and wild boars, it did not move. As a result, Alexander thought it was a coward and had it killed. Then the former owner sent Alexander another dog, the same breed, and the last of its kind, and he warned the king not to set the dog before small animals like deer and wild boars but only before lions and elephants because the dog would deign to fight only large animals. And, indeed, the dog went on to triumph and prove its valor.

feet out of pain because his shoes were too tight, even though he had other shoes to wear.

However, the councillors said to him, "Gently, your majesty. Don't get upset. Tomorrow we shall hold another banquet, not for the people of rank, but for those from the lower classes. Given women's tendency always to turn to the worst, perhaps we shall find among the merchants of cutlery and the pedlars of paternosters[8] and combs the seed of your anger that we could not find among the gentlemen of the city."

The king liked this idea, and he ordered a second banquet to be prepared, and when the proclamation was announced, all the scavengers, vagabonds, poor strolling players, scoundrels, scamps, ruffians, good-for-nothings, ragamuffins, rascals, thieves, and riffraff of the city appeared. They sat down at a long table as if they were lords and stuffed themselves. Now, Ceccarella had heard about this proclamation, and she began pushing Peruonto to attend the banquet, too. She kept at it until he eventually went to the feast. No sooner did he arrive than the two boys latched on to him and hugged and caressed him many times.

When the king saw this, he plucked out his beard, for he now knew that the apple of his eye, the winning ticket of the lottery, had fallen to an ugly monstrosity who made you nauseous and want to vomit just by looking at him. Moreover, this brute had a shaggy head, owl's eyes, a parrot's beak, and a fish's puss, and he was clothed in rags and tatters so that you could see all his private parts without consulting the doctor Fioravanti.[9] After heaving a deep sigh, the king said, "How could that slut of a daughter of mine have taken a fancy to this sea ogre? How could she have gone off with this hairy fool? Oh you blind, false, disgraceful girl! How could you have changed so much? Why did you become a harlot for this pig in order to transform me into a cuckold? But what are we waiting for? Why are we bothering to think about this? Let her have the punishment that she deserves. You can determine the punishment, but get her out of my sight because I can no longer stand her."

So the councillors got together and sentenced her along with the culprit and the boys: they were to be placed into a barrel and thrown into the sea. This way the councillors could put an end to their lives without dirtying their hands with blood. As soon as the sentence was delivered, the barrel was brought forth, and all four were placed in it. But before it was sealed, some of Vastolla's ladies, who were shedding a flood of tears, put inside a small cask of raisins and dried figs so that the prisoners could nourish themselves for a while. Then after the barrel was closed, it was carried away and thrown into the sea, where it drifted at the mercy of the wind.

After a while, Vastolla, who wept so hard that two streams of tears flowed from her eyes, said to Peruonto, "What a great disgrace to have the cradle of Bacchus as our grave. Oh, if only I knew who meddled with my body

8. Paternosters were beads in a rosary and were special charms. The councillors are implying that a lowborn merchant or a pedlar may have caused the king's daughter's pregnancy.
9. Leonardo Fioravanti (1518–1588), a Bolognese doctor who became very popular especially due to his work *Compendio de' secreti razionali intorno alla medicina, chirurgia ed alchimia* (1564). He was a controversial figure, regarded as a charlatan by some and miraclemaker by others.

and caused me to be cast into this barrel! Alas, I've been spiked without knowing how! Tell me, tell me, you cruel thing, what spell did you use? What magic wand did you wave to cause me to be locked up in this round barrel? Tell me, tell me, what devil spurred you to slip me into this invisible tube where I have no other opening to see through than this disgraceful peephole?"

Peruonto pretended for a while not to hear, but then he eventually answered, "If you want me to tell you, give me some raisins and figs."

Now, in order to get him to speak, Vastolla filled his mouth with one after another. As soon as he had his throat full of raisins and figs, he told her in detail what had happened to him with the three sons of the fairy, then with the log, and finally with her at the window where she had ridiculed him and caused him to wish her pregnant.

After hearing this the poor maiden plucked up her courage and said to Peruonto, "My brother, do we really want to perish in this barrel? Why don't you change this heap into a beautiful ship that could bring us out of danger and to a good port?"

And Peruonto replied, "Give me raisins and figs if you want me to say what you wish."

Vastolla immediately filled his throat, and like a fisherwoman at carnival time,[1] she fished the words fresh out of his mouth using the figs and raisins. And, lo and behold, as soon as Peruonto said what Vastolla desired, the barrel was transformed into a vessel with all the rigging that was necessary for sailing the ship. There you could have seen sailors pulling the sheet, rolling shrouds, steering the helm, preparing the sails, climbing to the crow's nest, crying out "Keep her close to the wind!" or "To the leeside!" There were also sailors sounding the trumpet, firing the canons, and doing this and that.

Now Vastolla was in the ship and swimming in a sea of delight, and since the time had come when the moon wanted to play the game of trading places with the sun,[2] Vastolla said to Peruonto, "My handsome man, change this ship into a beautiful palace so that we shall be more secure. You know the old saying: praise the sea, and stay ashore."

And Peruonto replied, "If you want me to say what you wish, give me some raisins and figs."

And she immediately gave him all he wanted, and Peruonto swallowed them and did what she requested. All at once the ship touched land and became a splendid palace completely furnished and so full of furniture and luxurious things that there was nothing left to be desired. Consequently, Vastolla, who would have sold her life for three pennies before all of this, would not have changed places now with the first lady of the world, especially since she had so many gifts and servants and was treated like a queen. However, she wanted to top off her good fortune and thus asked Peruonto to have the good grace to become handsome and cultivated so that they could enjoy each other with more pleasure. Even if the

---

1. There was a game played during Carnival in which women would dress themselves as fisherwomen and cast lines with rods that had sweets and other objects attached to them.
2. Reference to a game played by children, similar to musical chairs.

proverb says, "Better a dirty husband than an imperious lover," she preferred that he would change his looks to make her the happiest woman in the world.

And Peruonto replied with the same refrain, "Give me some grapes and figs if you want me to say what you wish."

And Vastolla immediately remedied the situation by giving him those purgative figs that helped the constipation of Peruonto's words, and as soon as he said them, he was transformed from a flycatcher into a goldfinch, from an ogre into a Narcissus, from a grotesque character into a dashing young man. When Vastolla saw this, she felt ecstatic and transported to seventh heaven. Squeezing him between her arms, she enjoyed him with great pleasure.

At the very same time that this was taking place, the king, who had never recovered from that disastrous day when he had condemned his daughter, continued to brood and say, "Let me alone." But his courtiers took him on a hunt in order to amuse and distract him. Losing track of time, they were surprised by nightfall. Then the king saw a lantern in a window of a splendid palace and sent a servant to seek lodging. The servant returned with the answer that not only could the king and his retinue stay for dinner but also for the night. Thus, the king went there, and after climbing the stairs and passing through all the rooms, he did not see a living soul except for two boys who danced around him and cried, "Grandpa! Grandpa!"

The king was stunned, amazed, and astonished and felt as if a spell had been cast over him. Then, since he was tired, he sat down at a table and watched invisible hands cover it with a tablecloth and set out all sorts of dishes so that he ate and drank truly like a king, and the two boys kept serving him without interruption. While he remained at the table, he heard the music of lutes and tambourines that penetrated him to his core. When he finished eating, a bed fully adorned with gold appeared. After his boots were taken off, he went to sleep as did all his courtiers, who had eaten very well at one hundred other tables that had been prepared for them in the other rooms.

When morning came and the king was about to leave, he wanted to take the two boys with him. But Vastolla appeared with her husband, and they threw themselves at his feet, begged his pardon, and told him about all their good fortune. The king, seeing that he had gained two grandsons, who were jewels, as well as a son-in-law, who was like a magical fairy, embraced them all one by one. Then he took them to the city, where he arranged a grand feast that lasted many days, and he confessed, in spite of the decisions that he had made:

Man proposes, but God disposes.

MARIE-CATHERINE D'AULNOY

The Dolphin†

Once upon a time there was a king and queen to whom Heaven had given many children, but they loved them only to the degree that they were beautiful and amiable. Among them was a young son called Alidor, who had a decent character but was also unbearably ugly. The king and queen regarded him with a great deal of repugnance and were always telling him to stay out of their sight. And as he began to see that all their caresses were for others and nothing but severity for him, he realized that the only thing left for him to do was to go away in secret. Therefore, he carefully arranged his plans for leaving the kingdom without anyone knowing where he was heading in hope that fortune would treat him better in some other country than his own.

When the king and queen discovered he had gone, they were very upset. They envisioned that he would not be able to make the splendid appearance that befit a prince and that unpleasant things might happen to him, which concerned them more on account of their own reputation than for his sake. They sent some couriers after him with orders to bring him back at once, but he was so careful to choose the most out-of-the-way roads that they followed him in vain, and those who had been ordered to search for him returned to the court only to find that he had been forgotten there. Everyone knew very well how little the king and the queen cared for Alidor and had not loved him as much as they would have loved a happy prince. So, Alidor was no longer mentioned. Besides, who was there to talk about him? Fortune was against him. His kinsfolk hated him, and nobody thought he had the merits that he possessed.

Alidor was just setting out to seek his fortune without knowing very well where he wished to go when he met a handsome young man riding a fine steed, who looked as if he were on a journey. They greeted each other and exchanged some courteous words for a while, speaking only of general matters. After some time the traveler learned from Alidor where he was going.

"But you yourself," Alidor responded, "will you tell me your destination?"

"My lord," he said, "I am a squire in the service of the King of the Woods. I have been sent to fetch some horses from a place not far from here."

"Is he a savage king?" asked the prince. "You call him King of the Woods, and I picture him as spending his life there."

"His forefathers probably lived there, as you say," stated the squire. "As for him, he has a great court. The queen, his wife, is one of the loveliest ladies in the world, and their only daughter, Princess Livorette, is endowed with a thousand charms which enchant everyone who regards her. True,

† Marie-Catherine d'Aulnoy, "The Dolphin"—"Le Dauphin" (1698), in *Suite des contes nouveaux ou les fées à la mode,* 2 vols. (Paris: Théodore Girard, 1698).

she is still so young that she is not aware of all the attention paid her. Nevertheless, one cannot help pay homage to her."

"You've aroused a great desire in me to see her," said the prince, "and to spend some time in such a delightful court. But do they look upon strangers with favor? I do not flatter myself. I know that nature has not blessed me with a handsome face, but in compensation she has given me a good heart."

"Well, you've been provided with a rare virtue," said the traveler, "and I regard it much higher than the other. It is well known that everything is given its true value in our court so that you may go there perfectly certain of being favorably received."

Thereupon he gave him directions as to the road he should take to reach the Kingdom of the Woods, and since he was very obliging and noticed that his companion had an air of nobility which his ugliness could not mar, he gave him the address of some of his friends, who would present him to the king and queen. The prince was very pleased with the courtesy shown him. It promised well for a country if such politeness were characteristic of it, and since he was only seeking a place where he might dwell in anonymity, he preferred to choose the one now suggested to him than any other. He even felt a particular urge on the part of fortune that made him choose it. After taking leave of the traveler, he went on his way, dreaming at times of the Princess Livorette, for he already felt a strong curiosity to see her.

When he arrived at the court of the King of the Woods, the friends of his companion received him hospitably, and the king gave him a fine welcome. He was delighted at having left his own country, for though he was unknown, he could not but be gratified at all the signs of regard shown toward him. It is true that things were much different in the queen's apartment, which he had hardly entered before peals of laughter burst out from all sides. One lady hid her face so as not to look at him; another ran away. But above all, young Livorette was influenced by these examples of bad behavior and let the prince see what she thought of his ugliness. It seemed to him that a princess who laughed in this fashion at a stranger's defects was not very well raised, and secretly he pitied her.

"Alas!" he said. "This is how I was spoiled in my father's house. It must be confessed that princes are unfortunate, seeing how their faults are tolerated. Ahh! Now I understand the poison and realize that we drink big swigs of it every day. Shouldn't this fair princess think it a shame to laugh at me? I come from a distant land to pay respects to her and to attach myself to her court. I could journey farther and spread word about her good qualities or her bad ones. I was not born her subject, and nothing need bind my tongue except her civility. Yet, no sooner does she cast her eyes on me than she insults me with her mocking airs. But, alas! How safe she is from anything that I might say! Never have I seen a maiden as beautiful as she! I admire her. I admire her only too much, and I know only too well that I shall do so all my life."

While he was making these reflections, the queen, who was very obliging, ordered him to come to her and sought to lift his spirits. She spoke pleasantly to him and asked about his country, his name and his adven-

tures. And to all her inquiries, he replied like a man of intelligence and
was quick to answer. She appreciated his character and told him that,
whenever he wished to pay his respects to her, she would see him with
pleasure. She even asked whether he played any kind of game and told
him to come and play basset[1] with her. Since he desired to please her, he
made a point of being present when the queen played. He had plenty of
money and jewels. In all his actions there was an air of nobility which
enabled him to distinguish himself. And though nobody knew who he
was, for he took great pains to conceal his birth, they judged him nonetheless favorably. The princess was the only one who could not endure
him. She burst out laughing in his face. She made faces at him and
was guilty of a thousand tricks typical of her age, which would not have
mattered much from anyone else. But from her it was different. He took
it very seriously, and when he knew her a little better, he uttered his
complaints.

"Don't you think, madame," he said, "that it is somewhat unjust to
mock me? The same gods that made you the most beautiful princess in
the universe made me the ugliest man in the world, and I am their work
as well as you."

"I admit it, Alidor," she said. "But you are the most imperfect work that
ever came out of their hands."

Thereupon she looked straight into his eyes for a long time, and then
she laughed until she made herself sick. The prince, who returned her
look, drank big swigs of the poison that love was preparing for him.

"I must die," he said to himself, "since I cannot hope to please, and I
cannot live without obtaining the good graces of Livorette."

At last he grew so melancholy that everybody pitied him. The queen
noticed it, for he did not play the games in his usual good spirits. She
asked him what the matter was but could draw nothing more out of him
than that he felt an extraordinary languor caused, he thought, by the
change of climate. Therefore, he was determined to go into the country
more often for fresh air. The fact was he could no longer bear to see the
princess every day without hope. He believed he might be cured if he
avoided her, but wherever he went, his passion followed him. He sought
out solitary places, and there he abandoned himself to a profound reverie.
Since the sea was near, he frequently went fishing, but he cast his hook
and net in vain and never caught anything. On his return, Livorette was
nearly always at the window, and when she saw him coming, she used to
call out with a sly little air, "Well, Alidor, and have you brought me some
nice fish for my supper?"

"No, madame," he answered, bowing low, and continued on his way
home in sorrow.

The beautiful princess laughed at him. "Oh, how clumsy he is!" she
said. "He can't even catch a single sole."

Alidor was miserable because of his lack of luck and because the princess constantly laughed at him, and he wanted so much to catch something worth offering to her. He used to go out often in a little sloop, taking

1. A game of cards, resembling Faro.

various kinds of nets with him, and he made every effort to please Livorette. "What bad luck I have!" he said. "Even this pleasurable pastime is ruined! I was only trying to forget the princess by fishing, and now she wants to eat the fish I catch. But fortune is relentless and won't even let me enjoy this little pleasure."

Full of sorrow he sailed out into the sea further than he had ever done before, and throwing out his nets in a determined fashion, he felt that they had suddenly become very heavy and quickly drew them back for fear of tearing them. When he had hauled the net on board, he was curious to see what was struggling inside, and he found a fine dolphin, which he picked up in his arms, delighted at his success. The dolphin tried hard to get away and resisted with surprising strength. Then he pretended to be dead so that Alidor might be put off his guard, but it was no use.

"My poor dolphin," he said, "don't torment yourself any longer. I'm determined to take you home to the princess, and you'll have the honor of being served on her table this evening."

"This will be most disastrous for me," said the dolphin.

"What!" cried the prince in astonishment. "You can speak! Oh merciful gods! What a miracle!"

"If you will be so good and kind as to let me free," the dolphin continued, "I shall do you so many important favors as long as I live that you will never need to repent your kindness."

"And what will the princess have for her supper?" asked Alidor. "Don't you know how exasperating she can be with her irony? She calls me awkward, stupid, and a hundred other things, and for the sake of my reputation I must sacrifice you."

"Well now, a prince who prides himself on the art and pleasure of fishing!" said the dolphin. "If you don't know how to fish well, you think your honor and nobility have been degraded! Let me live, I beg you. Put back your most humble servant, the dolphin, into the water. Do a good deed, and the reward will not be far behind."

"All right, you may go," said the prince, throwing the dolphin into the sea. "I don't expect anything will come from you, neither good nor evil, but I respect your strong desire to live. Let Livorette add even more insults to those she has already heaped on me, if she wants What does it matter? You are an extraordinary fish, and I want to make you happy."

The dolphin disappeared from his sight, and at that moment, the prince felt that all hope of a big haul had vanished, too. Sitting down in the boat and drawing in the oars, which he placed under his feet, he folded his arms and began daydreaming. All of a sudden he was wakened by a pleasant voice which seemed to graze the waves as it rose from the sea.

"Alidor, Prince Alidor," said the voice, "look, and you will see a friend."

As he glanced about him, he saw the dolphin doing somersaults on the surface of the water.

"Everyone must have their turn. It's only fair," said the dolphin. "Only a quarter of an hour ago you were very kind to me. Now ask me to do you a favor, and you will see what I shall do."

"I ask only for a small reward for a great favor," said the prince. "Send me the best fish in the sea."

All at once, without Alidor's casting a net, a huge quantity of salmon, sole, turbot, oysters, and other shellfish came jumping into the boat, and there were so many that Alidor became afraid that they might tip over the boat. "Stop, stop, my dear dolphin," he cried. "I'm overwhelmed by all that you are doing for me, but I fear that your generosity might prove dangerous. Save me, for you see that the situation is serious."

In response, the dolphin pushed the boat to shore, where the prince arrived with all his fish. Four mules could not have carried the amount of fish, so he sat down and began choosing the best when he heard the dolphin's voice:

"Alidor," it said as it thrust up its big head from the water, "are you somewhat satisfied with what I've done for you?"

"How could I not be?" he answered.

"Oh, but you must know," the fish declared, "that I am most grateful for the way you treated me, and for your having saved my life. I have, therefore, come to tell you that every time you want something, I shall be ready to obey you. I have more than one kind of power, and if you believe in me, you will have proof."

"Alas!" said the prince. "What should I wish for? I love a princess, and she hates me."

"Do you want to stop loving her?" asked the dolphin.

"No," replied Alidor. "I don't have the will to stop myself. Make it possible for me to please her, or let me die."

"Will you promise me," continued the dolphin, "never to have any other wife than Livorette?"

"Yes, I promise you," cried the prince. "I have sworn to be faithful to the love I bear for her, and I shall always do all that I can to please her."

"But we must play a trick on her," said the dolphin, "for she does not wish to marry you. She thinks you are ugly and does not really know you."

"I give my consent to this trick," replied the prince, "though I realize that she can never give herself to anyone like me."

"Time might change her mind," said the dolphin, "but let me change you into a canary. It is a disguise that you can discard, whenever you like."

"You are in charge, my dear dolphin," answered Alidor.

"Well, then," continued the fish. "I want you to become a canary!"

And in that very moment the prince saw himself with feathers, claws, and a tiny beak, and he could sing and whistle in an admirable way. Then, wishing himself Alidor again, he found that he was the same as before.

Never was anyone more joyful, and he was burning with impatience to be with the young princess. So, he called to his attendants and ordered them to carry the fish, and together they all set out on the road to the city. Of course, Livorette was on her balcony crying out to him, "Well, Alidor, have you had better luck this time?"

"Yes, madame," he said, showing her the great baskets filled with the finest fish in the world.

"Oh!" she cried, pouting like a child. "I'm very sorry that you've caught so many fish. Now I shall never be able to laugh at you again."

"You'll always find a reason when you desire one, madame," he answered, and he went on his way, giving orders for all the fish to be sent to her. Then after a moment he took the form of a little canary and flew to her windowsill. As soon as she noticed the bird, she went softly toward it and held out her hand to grasp it, but it flew away from her into the air.

"I came from one end of the earth," it said, "where the news of your beauty reached me. But it would not be fair, charming princess, for me to have flown such a great distance just to be treated like an ordinary canary. You must promise never to put me in a cage, to let me come and go, and to have no other prison than your sweet eyes."

"Ah, dear little bird," cried Livorette, "set whatever conditions you like. I promise never to violate any one of them, for I have never seen anything as pretty as you. You speak better than a parrot, and you whistle wonderfully. I love you so much—so much that I am dying to have you as my own."

The canary flew down and landed on Livorette's head and then hopped to her finger, where it not only whistled airs but sang words with accuracy and in the style of the most skillful musician.

"I am enchanted," she said to all the ladies, "by the gift that fortune has just sent me."

Thereupon, she ran to her mother's room to show her the charming canary. The queen was dying to hear it speak, but it wouldn't say a word except to the princess, and it had no mind to please anyone else.

When night arrived, Livorette went to her room with the pretty bird, whom she called Bébé, the canary. She began combing her hair and grooming herself while he perched on her mirror and took the liberty of pecking her eyebrows and sometimes her hands. She was overjoyed by this, and for Alidor, who until then had not tasted any kind of sweetness, he felt as if he were a king and did not want to be anything else but this canary. True, he was sad to see that they wanted to leave him in a room where Livorette's dogs, monkeys, and parrots generally slept.

"What!" he said with a troubled air. "You think so little of me that you have no qualms about abandoning me like this!"

"Do you call this abandonment, dear Bébé," she answered, "when I put you with those creatures I love most?"

Then she went out, but the prince remained perched on the mirror. As soon as it was day, he flew away to the seashore. "Dolphin, dear dolphin," he cried, "let me have a word or two with you. Do not refuse to listen to me."

The obliging fish appeared, gravely riding a wave. When Bébé saw him, he flew toward him and perched gently on his head.

"I know everything you've done, and everything you want me to do," said the dolphin, "but I declare that you are not to enter Livorette's room until she is married to you, and until the king and queen have given their consent. After that I shall look upon you as her husband."

The prince had so much regard for the fish that he did not insist but thanked the dolphin a thousand times for the charming disguise he had procured for him and asked him to remain his friend. Returning to the palace in his feathered shape, he found the princess in her dressing gown.

She had been searching for him everywhere, and not having found him, she was now weeping bitterly.

"Ah, perfidious creature!" she exclaimed. "You've already left me! Didn't I treat you well enough? Haven't I petted you and given you biscuits and sugar and sweets?"

"Yes, yes, my princess," said the canary, who was listening through a hole, "you have shown me some signs of friendship, but you have also been indifferent toward me. Do you think that I am satisfied to sleep near your nasty cat? He would have eaten me fifty times if I had not taken the precaution to keep awake all night to save myself from his claws."

Moved by his words, Livorette looked at him tenderly. Holding out her finger, she said, "Come, Bébé, come, and let's make peace."

"Oh! I don't make up so easily," he answered. "I wish the king and queen to know of this."

"Very well," she said, "I'll take you to their room."

She went at once to find them. They were still in bed and talking about a marriage proposal that would be very advantageous for their daughter.

"Well, dear child," said the queen, "what do you want this morning?"

"It's my little bird," she answered, "who wants to speak to you."

"That is most important," responded the queen, laughing. "But are we in a condition to give a serious audience?"

"Yes, your majesty," replied the canary. "I know that I am not appearing in your court with all the pomp that befits me, but when the fame of the beauty and the charms of the young princess reached me, I set off speedily to request her hand in marriage. Such as you see me, I am king of a little grove, where oranges, myrtles, and honeysuckles grow, the most charming spot in all the Canary Isles. I have a great number of subjects of my own kind, who are obliged to pay me a large tribute of flies and worms. The princess might eat her fill, and she would never want for music, for I am related to some nightingales that would sing their best for her. We would live in your court as long as you liked. I only need, your majesty, a little millet, some rapeseed, and fresh water. When you give the word for us to retire to our own states, distance will not prevent us from receiving news of you and from sending you ours in return. We shall have flying couriers to serve us, and I think I may say without vanity that you will get a great deal of satisfaction from a son-in-law like me."

He ended his speech by whistling two or three tunes and chirping pleasantly. The king and queen laughed until they became sick.

"We have no wish," they said, "to refuse to give Livorette to you. Yes, pretty canary, we give her to you, provided that she consents."

"With all my heart," she said. "I have never been so happy in my life as I am now that I am to marry Prince Bébé."

Thereupon he plucked one of the finest feathers from his wing and offered it to her as a wedding present. Livorette accepted graciously and stuck it in her hair, which was remarkably beautiful. When she returned to her own apartment, she told her ladies-in-waiting that she had some great news for them—that the king and queen had just wed her to a sovereign prince. On hearing this, one of her ladies rushed toward her and embraced her knees. Another kissed her hands. With the utmost eagerness they asked her who the lucky prince was to whom the most beautiful princess in the world was to be given.

"Here he is," she said, drawing out the little canary from the inside of her sleeve and showing them her future husband. At the sight of him, they laughed heartily, and many a jest was made about the perfect innocence of their beautiful mistress. Then Livorette quickly got dressed and returned to her mother's room, for the queen loved her so dearly that she always liked to have her near her. Meanwhile, the canary flew away and assumed his ordinary shape as Alidor so that he might pay his court to the queen.

"Approach," cried the queen, when she saw him, "and congratulate my daughter on her marriage with Bébé. Don't you think that we've found a fine lord for her?"

Alidor entered into the spirit of the jest, and as he was more cheerful than he had been in his life, he said a hundred pretty things, and the queen was very amused by him. But Livorette continued to laugh at him and contradict every word he said to her. It would have made him very melancholy to see her in this mood if he had not remembered that his friend, the fish, was going to help him overcome this aversion.

When the princess went to bed, she would have left the canary in the room with the animals, but he began to grumble and fly around her. He followed her into her own room and perched himself neatly on a piece of porcelain from which the servants dared not chase him for fear of breaking it.

"If you begin to sing too early in the morning, Bébé," Livorette said, "and wake me, I shall not forgive you."

He promised her to be quiet until she ordered him to sing his little song, and with that assurance, they retired for the night. No sooner was the princess in bed than she fell into such a deep sleep that there can be no doubt that the dolphin had a hand in it. She even snored like a little pig, which is not natural for a young lady. But Bébé did not snore. To do so he would first have had to shut his eyes. Leaving the porcelain base, he flew and settled so softly near his charming bride that she did not awake. As soon as day had come again, he took his canary shape and flew away to the edge of the sea, where, as Alidor, he sat down on a smooth little rock covered by sapphire. Then he looked all around to see if his dear friend the dolphin were near. He called him several times, and while he waited, he reflected with pleasure about his happiness.

"Oh fairies," he said, "whose praises we sing, and whose power is indeed so extraordinary, could your art make any other mortal as happy as I am?"

As he was murmuring these words, he felt the rock shaking violently. Suddenly, an old dwarflike woman appeared through an opening. Leaning on a crutch, she waddled toward him. It was Grognette the fairy, who was no better than Grognon.

"Truly, my lord Alidor," she said, "I think you are taking great liberty by seating yourself on my rock. I don't know what should prevent me from throwing you to the bottom of the sea just to teach you that, if the fairies cannot make a happier mortal than you, they can at least make an unhappy one whenever they like."

"Madame," replied the prince, somewhat astonished by her appearance, "I didn't know you lived here. I should certainly have been much more careful with respect to your palace."

"Excuses will get you nowhere," she continued. "You are ugly and presumptuous, and it will give me great pleasure to see you suffer."

"Alas!" said he. "What have I done to you?"

"I don't know myself," she answered. "But I shall treat you as if I did."

"The dislike you bear me is extraordinary," he said, "and if I did not hope that the gods would protect me against you, I would kill myself before you had a chance to fulfill your threats and harm me."

Grognette went on muttering threats and then withdrew into her rock again, which closed up. Deeply distressed, the prince did not want to sit down again and start a fresh quarrel with this ominous dwarf.

"I was too satisfied with my lot," he said, "and now a little fury has arrived to trouble it. What will she do to me? Ah, I don't think she will vent her anger on me. Rather, it will be the beautiful lady whom I love. Oh dolphin, dolphin, I beg you to come and console me!"

At that moment the fish appeared near the shore. "Well, what do you want?" he asked.

"I was coming to thank you for all the favors you have done me. I am now married to Livorette, and in the ardor of my joy, I was rushing to you so you could share my happiness with me when a fairy . . ."

"I know," said the dolphin, "it was Grognette, the most malicious and strangest creature on earth. It does not take much to displease her. All you have to do is to be happy. What makes me even more angry is that she has power, and that she wants to oppose my plans for your good."

"What a strange creature!" replied Alidor. "How have I displeased her?"

"What! You are a man, and you are surprised by human injustice!" the dolphin exclaimed. "In truth, you humans never think of justice. It would be all you could do were you a fish, and even we in our kingdom of the seas are not too just. Every day we see the big ones swallowing up the little. This should not be tolerated, for the smallest herring has its right as a citizen of the water as much as a terrible whale."

"If I interrupt you," said the prince, "it is only to ask if I may ever let Livorette know that I am her husband."

"Enjoy the present without thinking about the future," the dolphin answered.

And, having said these words, he disappeared beneath the water. The prince became a canary again and flew to his dear princess, who was searching for him everywhere.

"What now! Will you always make me upset this way, you little libertine?" she said as soon as she saw him. "I'm afraid that you'll get lost, and then I would die of sorrow."

"No, my Livorette," he replied. "For your sake, I'll never get lost."

"Can you guarantee this?" she continued. "They might lay snares and spread nets for you. Or, if you fell into the trap laid for you by some beautiful lady, how do you know you would return?"

"Oh, what an unjust suspicion!" he said. "You don't know me."

"Forgive me, Bébé," she said smiling. "I've heard tell that little importance is attached to being loyal to a wife, and since I am yours, I'm afraid you might change."

Conversations like these satisfied the canary, for they showed him that he was loved. And yet, he was loved only as a little bird, and at times his delicate heart would be wounded.

"Should I have permitted myself to play this trick on her?" he asked the dolphin. "I know the princess does not love me, that she finds me ugly, and that none of my faults have escaped her. I have every reason to think that she would not wish to have me as a husband. In spite of this, I have become hers. She is bound to heap reproaches on me if, one day, she discovers it. What shall I say to her? I would die of sorrow if I were to displease her."

But the fish said to him, "Your reflections do not jell with your love. If every lover were to do as you do, ladies would never be carried off anymore or be discontended. Enjoy the present, for less happy days are in store for you."

Alidor was very troubled by this warning. He knew quite well that Grognette the fairy still wanted to harm him for having sat down on her rock when she was underneath. He prayed that the dolphin would continue to help him as he had done before.

There was a great deal of talk about the marriage of the princess with a handsome young prince whose realm was not far away, and he sent ambassadors to ask for her hand. Since they received a cordial welcome from the king, this news was most alarming to Alidor, who, without delay, went to the seashore and called his good friend the fish. Once he was there, Alidor revealed his fears to him.

"Just think," he said, "how desperate my situation is! Either I must lose my wife and see her married to another, or I must declare my marriage and be separated from her for the remainder of my life."

"I have no power to prevent Grognette from harming you," said the dolphin. "I am just as desperate as you are, and you cannot be more occupied with your affairs than I am. Yet, pluck up courage. I can tell you nothing more at present, but you may count on my friendship. I shall never fail you."

The prince thanked him with all his heart and went back to the princess. He found her in the midst of her ladies, one holding her head, and another her arm, while she was complaining of an illness. Since he was not in his canary disguise at that moment, he did not dare to go near her, even though her illness made him very anxious. As soon as she saw him, she smiled in spite of all that she was suffering.

"Alidor," she said, "I think I am going to die. It is very unfortunate for me that the ambassadors have come right now because I hear all kinds of good reports about the prince who wants to marry me."

"But, madame," he replied with a forced smile, "have you forgotten that you've chosen a husband?"

"What! My canary?" she said. "Ha, ha! I know he will not be angry. But that will not stop me from loving him tenderly all the same."

"He would perhaps not be content to share your heart with another," said Alidor.

"Well, no matter," Livorette replied. "I shall be pleased to be queen and reign over a great kingdom."

"But, madame," he said, "your canary offered you one."

"Oh, what a charming kingdom!" she answered. "A little jasmine wood! That might do for a bee or a linnet, but not for me. It's not the same thing."

Her waiting women, thinking that she was talking too much for her health, begged Alidor to withdraw. Then they made her lie down, and Bébé came and chided her gently for her infidelity. Since she was not very ill, she went to see the queen. But from that day on, she continued to suffer, and her languor changed her appearance. She grew thin and squeamish. Months passed, and they did not know what to do. In addition, the court was especially troubled because the ambassadors who had come with the demand for her hand were urging her parents to place her in their charge. Then the queen heard of an excellent physician who might be able to cure her. She sent a carriage to fetch him and forbade her servants to tell him the rank of the sick princess so that he might speak more freely about her case. When he arrived, the queen hid herself in order to listen. After he had examined Livorette for a while, he said with a smile, "Is it possible that your court doctors haven't known what has been troubling this lady? The fact is, she will soon give birth to a fine baby boy."

The ladies-in-waiting did not give him time to finish what he was going to say. They heaped reproaches on him, and taking him by the shoulders, they pushed him out of the room and jeered at him. Bébé, who was in Livorette's room, did not think like the others that the country doctor was a fool. Several times it had occurred to him that the princess might be pregnant, and so he went to the seashore to consult his friend, the fish, who seemed to be of the same opinion.

"I advise you," he said, "to go away. I fear that they might find you by her side when she is asleep, and you would both be lost."

"Ah!" said the prince mournfully. "Do you think that I can live apart from her? She is more dear to me than anything else in the world. Why should I be careful about my life? The time is coming when it will be hateful to me. Let me see Livorette or die!"

The dolphin felt pity for him and shed some tears, though dolphins rarely weep. And he did what he could to console his dear friend, for it was all Grognette's fault without a doubt.

In the meantime, the queen related the doctor's prognosis to the king. Livorette was summoned, and she answered all their questions with as much sincerity as innocence. They even spoke to her waiting women, whose testimony was satisfactory in every way. So the worries of the king and queen were put to rest until the day when the princess gave birth to the most beautiful baby in the world. How is it possible to describe the astonishment and the anger of the king, the grief of the queen, the despair of the princess, the anxiety of Alidor, and the surprise of the ambassadors and the entire court? Where did the child come from? No one could tell, and young Livorette knew just as little as the child itself. Certainly it was not a joking matter for the king. His daughter's tears and vows were of no avail. He made up his mind to have her and her son thrown from the top of a mountain onto some rocks with jagged sides where she would die a cruel death. He told the queen what his intention was, but she was so terribly distressed at the thought that she fainted and lay as if she were dead at his feet. The king was touched by her sad condition, and when she came to herself somewhat, he tried to console her, but she told him she would never know a moment of joy or health until he had revoked such a terrible order. Throwing herself on her knees with tears streaming down her cheeks, she begged him to kill her and spare the lives of Livorette and her son. She had the infant fetched on purpose so that the king might be touched by his innocence. Indeed, the lamentations of the queen and the cries of the little child moved him with compassion. Throwing himself into an armchair, he covered his face with his hands, pondered, and sighed a long time before he could utter a word. At last he said to the queen that for her sake he was willing to delay the death of the princess and her son, but she had to understand that it was only being deferred and that nothing but blood could wash away a stain so shameful to their house. The queen thought that much had already been gained in getting the death of her dear daughter and her grandson deferred. So, she made no further demands and gave her consent to have the princess locked up in a tower where the light of the sun could not come and brighten her heart. In that sad place she was left to mourn her cruel fate. If anything could have comforted her in her sorrows, it would have been her perfect innocence. She never saw her child and was given no news of him.

"Just heaven!" she cried. "What have I done to be tormented in such a bitter way?"

Alidor was greatly distressed and was at the end of his strength. Gradually his mind gave way, and he eventually became completely mad. His moans and cries were heard constantly in the woods. He threw away his money and jewels on the road. His clothes were in rags, his hair in tangles, his beard unkempt, and all this, added to his natural ugliness, made him almost horrible to regard. Everyone pitied him a great deal and would have done so even more if the princess's misfortune had not filled the minds of every person in the kingdom. The ambassadors who had come to ask for her hand in marriage sought to take their leave, for they were ashamed in a way for having come to ask for her. In this regard, the king willingly let them depart because their presence was an embarrassment to him. As for the dolphin, he remained hidden in the depths of the sea and did not appear anymore. Thus the field was left free to Grognette, the fairy, to do all the harm she could to the prince and princess.

Although the little prince grew lovelier than the most beautiful day, the king had only saved his life so he could use him to determine who his father was. He said nothing about this to the queen, but one day, he announced that all the courtiers were to bring a gift to amuse his grandson. They all obeyed, and when the king was told that a large number of men had assembled, he led the queen into the large hall where he was accustomed to hold audience. They were followed by the nurse, who carried the lovely child, who was dressed in brocade of gold and silver. Each one of the courtiers stepped forward to kiss his little hand and to give him a gift, among which were a jeweled rose, artificial fruits, a golden lion, an agate wolf, an ivory horse, a spaniel, a parrot, and a butterfly. The child accepted everything with indifference, and although the king seemed not to pay attention, he was nevertheless watching what the boy was doing. In particular, he noticed that he did not show special affection to one man more than another. So, he gave orders for another announcement that, if any man whatsoever failed to come to his court, he would be punished for disobedience. These threats brought a quick response, and the king's squire, who had met Alidor on his travels and who had been his reason for coming to the court, found him deep in the cave in which he generally hid himself ever since he had lost his mind.

"Come, Alidor," the squire called to him. "Do you wish to be the only one not to give anything to the little prince? Haven't you heard the proclamation? Do you wish the king to sentence you to death?"

"Yes, then, I do," replied the poor prince with a wandering look. "Why have you come and disturbed my peace?"

"Don't be angry," said the squire. "I've only come to urge you to make an appearance."

"Yes, I am perfectly dressed for the occasion," Alidor replied with a laugh, "that is, to pay a visit to the royal monkey!"

"If it is only a question of providing you with clothes," said the squire, "I can furnish you with very fine ones."

"Very well," said Alidor, "it is long since I have seen myself dressed in stately apparel."

He came out of the cave and went quietly enough to the squire's house. Since the squire was one of the most magnificent men at court, he gave Alidor a choice of several splendid suits. But no matter what the squire said or did, Alidor went without a tie, hat, or shoes. When he reached the palace door, he realized that he had forgotten that he was supposed to bring a gift for the prince, but he did not trouble himself long about the matter. Seeing a pin lying on the ground, he picked it up to serve as his gift. Then he went hopping into the hall, rolling his eyes, and hanging out his tongue in such a way that one could hardly bear to look at him given his natural ugliness. The nurse, who feared that the baby prince might be terrified, wanted to turn his face the other way and signaled to Alidor to go away. But as soon as the child caught sight of him, he held out his arms and began laughing. He made such an extraordinary scene that Alidor had to be brought to him. Then the child threw his arms around his neck, kissed him a thousand times, and refused to be taken away from him. And Alidor, despite his madness, was no less friendly toward the child.

The king was astonished by this strange event and stood transfixed. He hid his anger from the assembly, but as soon as the audience was ended and without revealing his plans to the queen, he gave commands to two lords, whom he trusted with special confidence, to go and fetch the Princess Livorette from the tower in which she had been languishing for four years. They were to put her into a barrel with Alidor and the little prince, provide them with a pot of milk, a bottle of wine, and a loaf of bread, and fling them into the sea. Horrified at receiving such a cruel order, the lords prostrated themselves at his feet and humbly begged him to spare his daughter and his grandson.

"Alas, sire!" they said. "If your majesty realized how much she has suffered during these past four years, you would think that she had been sufficiently punished without now adding such a cruel death. Remember, she is your only daughter, intended by the gods to wear your crown one day. You are accountable for her life to your subjects. There is great promise in her son. Will you cut him off in his infancy?"

"Yes, I will," said the king, furious at the resistance shown to his command, "and if you do not carry out my orders, you will perish along with her."

The courtiers knew with sorrow that their struggle against the king's decision was in vain, so they withdrew with downcast heads and tears in their eyes. They gave orders that a barrel large enough to contain the princess, her son, and Alidor, and a little supply of provisions was to be procured. Then they went to the tower and found Livorette lying on some straw with irons on her hands and feet. For four years she had not seen the light of day. They greeted her with profound respect and told her the command they had received from her father. Their sobbing was so loud that she could hardly hear what they said. And yet, she understood their message well and mingled her tears with theirs.

"Alas!" she said. "The gods are witnesses of my innocence. I am only sixteen years old. I was destined to wear more crowns than one, and now you are about to cast me to the bottom of the sea like the guiltiest of creatures. But do not think that I am trying to bribe you or that I am begging you to find some pretext to save my life. For many a day the king has accustomed me to long for death. I would willingly die if my poor child could be saved. What crime has he committed? What? Isn't his innocence enough to save him from the fury of the king? Is it possible he is condemned to perish with me? Isn't it enough for my father to take my life? Doesn't one victim satisfy him?"

The lords who were listening to her could not say a word in reply. They could only obey, they said to the princess.

"Well," she answered, "break the chains that bind me. I am ready to follow you."

The guards came and filed off the irons with which her hands and feet were bound, causing her a great deal of pain, but she bore everything with wonderful patience. She left the prison as lovely as the sun rising at dawn, and everyone who saw her admired her courage just as much as her ravishing beauty, which, in spite of all her sorrows, was greater than ever, her languid air becoming her no less than her former vivacity.

Alidor and the little prince were waiting at the seashore, where they had been brought by the guards, the one knowing just as little as the other what was about to be done to them. When the princess saw her son, she took him in her arms and kissed him a thousand times with utmost tenderness. When she was told that it was on account of Alidor that she was to be drowned, she said that she was very glad that they had named the man for whom she cared least in the whole world, and that while preparing her destruction, they were nonetheless justifying her. Alidor began laughing as soon as he saw her.

"Ha, little princess, where are you coming from?" he asked. "Truly, there is a great deal of news. Since your departure, Livorette is no longer at the palace, and I have been raving mad. They say that we are to voyage together to the bottom of the sea. Listen, princess, wake me every morning, otherwise I'll sleep to noon if you don't pay attention."

And he would have said more if Livorette, as with a last effort, had not entered as the first into the barrel, clasping her son in her arms. Alidor threw himself pell-mell inside and rejoiced at setting out for the kingdom of the soles, where the turbot is king. All the while he uttered a stream of nonsense. Then they closed up the barrel, and from the top of a rock that jutted into the sea, they threw it down. All the spectators were sobbing and uttering long cries of despair, and as they withdrew, their hearts were filled with true grief. As for Alidor, he was marvelously calm. The first thing he did was to seize the loaf and eat the entire thing. Then he found the bottle of wine and began to drink it in a cheerful way, singing songs as if he were at some merry feast.

"Alidor," said the princess, "let me at least die in peace, and do not dazzle me with your impertinent joy."

"What have I done to you?" he replied. "Why do you want me to be sorrowful? Do you know that I have a secret to tell you? Somewhere hereabouts, where exactly I do not know, there is a certain fish called a dolphin. He is my best friend and has promised to obey me whenever I command. That is why, my beautiful Livorette, I am not anxious, for I shall call him to help us as soon as we are either hungry or thirsty, or whenever we feel we should like to sleep in some superb palace. He will build one expressly for us."

"Call him then, you naive thing!" the princess said. "Why do you put off something that should not be delayed? If you wait until I am hungry, you will wait a long time. Alas! My heart is too sad for me to think of food. But my son here is dying. He will be suffocated in this vile barrel. So, hurry, please, I beg of you so that I may see if you're telling the truth, for a madman like you may well be deceiving yourself."

Alidor immediately called out, "Ho! Dolphin, my fish, my friend, I command you to come here at once, and obey everything I tell you to do!"

"Here I am," said the dolphin. "Speak."

"Are you there?" asked the prince. "This barrel is so tightly closed that I cannot see."

"Just tell me what you want," said the dolphin.

"I should like to listen to pleasant music," Alidor replied, and at that moment the music began.

"What! Good God!" said the princess with impatience. "You're surely mocking me with your music? Isn't it rather a useless thing to hear fine music when you are drowning?"

"But, princess, you were neither hungry nor thirsty," Alidor responded. "What do you want?"

"Give me your power of commanding the dolphin," she answered.

"Dolphin, dolphin," cried Alidor, "I command you to do all that Princess Livorette desires without failing in any way."

"Very well," said the dolphin. "I shall do so."

And without a moment's delay she told him to carry them to the loveliest island in the world and to build the finest palace that was ever seen on that spot. She asked for enchanting gardens, surrounded by two streams, one full of wine and another of water, with a garden full of flowers and a tree in the middle, whose trunk was to be silver and its branches gold with three oranges growing on it, one diamond, the second ruby, and the third emerald. The palace was to be painted and gilded, and her entire story was to be painted on the walls.

"Is that all?" asked the dolphin.

"It is a good deal," she answered.

"Not very much," he replied, "for it's already done."

"Well, then, I wish you to tell me one thing I don't know and perhaps you do," she replied.

"I understand," the dolphin said. "You want to know who the father of your little prince is. Well, it is Bébé the canary, and Bébé is none other than Prince Alidor, who is with you."

"Ah, my lord dolphin!" cried Livorette. "You're mocking me."

"I swear," he said, "by Neptune's tridents, by Scylla and Charybdis,[2] by all the caverns of the sea, by the shells, by the treasures, by the naiads, and by the happy omens that a desperate pilot gleans when he catches sight of me, and lastly, I swear by yourself, dear Livorette, that I am honest and honorable, and that I do not lie."

"After so many oaths," she said, "I can only believe you, though, to tell the truth, what I have just heard is one of the most surprising things in the world. I order you then to restore Alidor's reason to him, to make him exceedingly intelligent, and to endow his conversations with charm. Let him be a hundred times handsomer than he was ugly, and tell me why you call him prince, for that title sounds pleasant in my ears."

The dolphin obeyed every single command as he had done before. Then he told Livorette about the prince's adventures, who his father and mother were, and all about his ancestors and relatives. Indeed, he had complete knowledge of the past, present, and the future and was as good as any genealogist in the profession. Such fish are not to be found every day. Dame Fortune has her say in the making of them.

While they were talking the barrel landed on an island, and the dolphin had it raised and land onto the shore. As soon as it was there, it opened. The princess, prince, and child were free to come out of their prison. The first thing that Alidor did was to throw himself at his dear Livorette's feet. He had completely recovered his reason, and his wit was a thousand times more charming than it was before. He had grown very handsome, and all his features were changed so much for the better that she hardly recog-

---

2. Scylla is a rock on the Italian side of the Straits of Messina facing Charybdis, on the coast of Sicily. In Greek mythology, Scylla and Charybdis are personified as sea monsters who terrorize mariners. Hence, the phrase indicates the space between two equally dangerous alternatives.

nized him. Tenderly he begged to be forgiven for his transformation into
the canary, excusing himself in a way which was both respectful and affectionate. At last she pardoned a marriage to which she perhaps would
not have consented if he had taken other means of bringing it about. It is
true the dolphin had made him so handsome that she had never seen his
equal at her father's court. He confirmed all the dolphin had told her
about his rank, a matter most essential to the satisfaction of the princess.
In fact, what advantage would there be to be a friend of fairies when one
cannot change one's birth? When heaven does not place us in that position
in which we would have desired to be born, only virtue and merit can
compensate for the loss, but often it is compensated with such generosity
as to bring abundant consolation.

The princess was in the best of moods, for she had been saved from
terrible danger. Deeply aware of this, she gave thanks to the gods. Then
she looked out toward the sea for their good friend, the dolphin, who was
still there. As was her duty, she thanked him for having rescued her, while
the prince was no less grateful. Moreover, their son, who spoke very charmingly and was much more intelligent than children of his age usually are,
complimented him too in a way that delighted the gallant dolphin, who
turned somersaults over and over again to please the little boy.

But suddenly they heard a loud sound of trumpets, fifes, and hautboys,
and the neighing of horses. It was the prince and princess's entourage and
their guards, all in magnificent attire. There were ladies in the carriages
who dismounted to kiss the hem of the princess's robe as soon as they
approached her. She did not want to allow this, seeing that they were
clearly of high rank and deserved her respect. But they told her that the
orders from the dolphin were to acknowledge the prince and princess as
king and queen of the island, where there were many obedient subjects
and much happiness in store for them. Alidor and Livorette were overjoyed
to see the honor paid them by such polite and honest people, and they
responded to their tributes with as much graciousness as dignity. Then
they got into an open carriage drawn by eight-winged horses who carried
them away. First they mounted to the clouds, and then they came down
so gradually that the passengers were hardly aware of the descent. This
way of driving is pleasant, for you are not jolted and need not worry about
fatigue.

They were still near the middle region of the air when they saw a
marvelous palace on the slope of a hill lying along the seacoast. It was so
magnificent that, though the walls were made of silver, they could still see
right into the rooms, which were furnished in the most superb style and
with the most exquisite taste imaginable. The gardens were even more
beautiful. There were countless fountains, and nature had scattered delicious springs all about in profusion. The prince and his wife did not know
which to cherish most, so perfect did each thing seem to them. After they
had entered the palace, they heard from all sides, "Long live Prince Alidor!
Long live Princess Livorette! May their séjour here be filled with pleasures!" The music of instruments and charming voices made for an enchanted symphony as they walked down the halls.

Before long they were served with an excellent meal, which they had needed very badly. The sea air and the way they had been cast adrift had exhausted them terribly. So, once they sat down, they ate their meal with a hearty appetite. When they had finished, the guardian of the royal treasure entered and asked them if they would be pleased to spend a little time after their meal in the neighboring hall. They went and saw along the walls large wells and buckets made of perfumed Spanish leather, ornamented with gold. They asked what they were for, and the guardian told them that streams of metal flowed into these wells, and when money was needed, one just had to let down a bucket and say, "I wish to draw up louis, pistoles, quadruples, crowns, or other coins."

Once the words were spoken, the water took the form that the person wished, and the bucket came up full of gold or silver or coins, and yet, the spring never dried up for those who made good use of it. But there had been several incidents when misers let down the bucket with the intention of amassing gold and keeping it locked up. As a result, they drew up buckets full of frogs and adders to their great horror, and sometimes they were even harmed, depending on the degree of their avarice. The prince and princess admired these wells and considered them as one of the finest and rarest things in the whole world. To test the result they let down the bucket, and it came back filled with little grains of gold. When they asked why the gold was not already coined, the guardian told them they were waiting to know the arms of the prince and princess in order to stamp them.

"Ah!" said Alidor, "we are so indebted to the generous dolphin that we want no other image on them but his."

So, in an instant all the grains were changed into gold pieces with a dolphin stamped on each. Since the hour for retiring had arrived, Alidor, timid and respectful, went to his own room, and the princess and her son to theirs. It was past eleven o'clock the next morning, and the princess was still asleep. The prince had risen early to go on a hunt and wanted to be back again before she would awake. When he learned he might see her without disturbing her, he went to her room, followed by a train of gentlemen carrying great golden vessels filled with the game he had killed. He presented them to his dear princess, who accepted them graciously, thanking him many times for his goodness to her, which gave him the opportunity of telling her that he loved her with more ardor now than ever before, and that he implored her to name the time when their marriage would be celebrated with pomp.

"Ah! My lord," she said, "my mind is made up about this. I shall never consent except with the permission of my royal father and mother."

Never did a lover receive a crueler blow.

"Beautiful princess, do you realize the fate to which you are condemning me?" he asked. "Don't you know that what you desire is impossible? We have just escaped from the fatal barrel into which they had put us to bring about our death, and you are already imagining that they will consent to what I desire. Ah, perhaps you wish to punish me for the passionate feelings I have for you. I am aware that you intend to give your heart and your hand to the prince who sent ambassadors to you at the time when I had become a canary."

"You're quite mistaken about my feelings," she said. "I respect you. I love you, and I have forgiven all the terrible things that you caused me by transforming yourself in a way that you should not have done. Being the son of a king, couldn't you have felt assured that my father would have been pleased to make an alliance with you?"

"Someone with great feelings does not reason with a cold heart," he answered. "I have taken the first step which has led me to happiness, but you are very hard, and if you do not take back the cruel conditions that you have just set, I shall become completely despondent."

"It is impossible for me to take it back," she said. "I must tell you what happened to me this past night. While I was sleeping quietly, I felt someone tugging me roughly. Opening my eyes, I saw a torch which cast a somber light, and then I made out the most hideous little creature in the world looking at me steadily with angry eyes. 'Do you know me?' she said. 'No, madame,' I answered, 'nor do I wish to.' 'Ah! You are joking,' said she. 'No,' I replied, 'I swear I am telling the truth.' 'My name is Grognette, the fairy,' she said. 'I have good reason to be angry with Alidor, who sat down on my rock. In fact, he has a particular gift for displeasing me. I forbid you, therefore, to consider him as your husband until you have your father and mother's consent, and if you disobey me, I shall take my revenge on your son. He will die, and his death will be followed by a thousand other misfortunes which you will not be able to escape.' At these words she blew the flames of fire on me. They covered me, and I thought I was going to be burned, when she said, 'I shall spare you on condition that you obey my orders.'"

The prince knew full well from the name and the description of Grognette that the princess's story was true.

"Alas!" he said. "Why did you ask our friend the fish to cure my madness? Then I was less to be pitied than now. Mind and reason, what purpose do they serve except to make me suffer? Let me go and beg him to take away my reason again. It is more like a burden than anything else."

The princess was deeply moved. She truly loved the prince and found in him all kinds of good qualities and thought that everything he did and said was in perfect grace. She wept, and he could not help feeling joy at the sight of her tears flowing for his sake. It gave him much more pleasure to know her feelings for him than his own for her had given him when he was the canary, and this comforted him so much that he threw himself at her feet and kissed her hands.

"My dear Livorette," he said, "you can be certain that I have no will where you are concerned. In fact, you are completely in charge of my destiny."

Livorette was fully aware of the great value of his submission, and she constantly pondered how she might obtain the permission so necessary for their happiness. In fact, it was the only thing lacking in their lives, for the inhabitants of the island provided them with every pleasure possible. Their rivers were full of fish, their forests, of game, their orchards, of fruit, their fields, of wheat, their meadows, of grass, their wells, of gold and silver. There were no wars and no lawsuits. It was a land where youth, health, beauty, wit, books, pure water, and good wine abounded, and where snuffboxes were inexhaustible! And Livorette was just as much in love with Alidor as Alidor with Livorette.

Every now and then they would go and pay their respects to the dolphin, who was always glad to see them. When they spoke about Grognette, the fairy, and about the orders that she had given to Livorette, and when they begged him to serve them as their friend, he always had some small words of comfort to console them. Yet he made no definitive promises. So two years passed away. Alidor wished to send ambassadors to the King of the Woods and asked the dolphin's advice on the subject, but the dolphin said that Grognette would kill them for sure and that perhaps the gods themselves would intervene in the end in favor of the prince and princess.

Meanwhile, Livorette's mother, the queen, had learned about the deplorable fate of her daughter, her grandson, and Alidor, and her sorrow knew no bounds. Soon she lost all her joy and her health. Every spot where she had once seen the princess recalled her sorrow, and she could not stop heaping endless reproaches on the king.

"Cruel father!" she said. "How could you make up your mind to drown the poor child? She was our only one, and the gods had given her to us. We should have waited until the gods had taken her from us."

For some time the king was philosophical about these reproaches, but at last he himself began to feel the full extent of his terrible act. He missed his daughter no less than his wife did, and secretly he was bitten by remorse for sacrificing his tender feelings for his glorious reputation. Unwilling that the queen should know how he suffered, he endeavored to hide his sorrow under an air of hardness. But as soon as he found himself alone, he would cry out, "My daughter, my dear daughter, where are you? Have I then lost you, the only consolation of my old age? Indeed, I lost you because I wanted to."

At last, overcome one day by the queen's grief and his own, he confessed to her that since that fatal day when he had given orders for Livorette and her son to be cast into the sea he had not had a moment's peace. Her plaintive shadow followed him wherever he went. The innocent cries of her son rang in his ears, and he feared that he might die out of grief. This news made the queen much unhappier than before.

"Now I shall suffer your grief as well as my own. What can we do to find consolation, sire?" she asked.

The king said he had heard tell of a fairy who for some little time back had been living in the forest of bears, and that he would go and consult her.

"I'll gladly make this journey with you," said the queen, "though I'm not sure what I want to ask her since I am certain that our dear little Livorette and the little prince are dead."

"All the same," said the king, "we must see her."

So he ordered his servants to get the royal carriage ready at once and furnish it with everything that might be necessary for a journey of thirty leagues. They set off early next day and soon arrived at the dwelling of the fairy. Since she had read the stars that the king and queen were coming to visit her, she came out right away to greet them.

As soon as the king and queen saw her, they got out of their carriage and embraced her with great signs of friendship. Yet they could not restrain themselves from weeping bitterly.

"Sire," said the fairy, "I know why you have come. You are deeply distressed because you brought about the death of the princess, your daughter. I know of no other remedy for your sorrow than to advise both of you to set out in a good ship for the Island of the Dolphin. It is a long way from here, but you will find there a fruit which will make you forget your grief. I advise you not to lose any time. It is your only means of consolation. As for you, madame," she turned to the queen, "your condition moves me so deeply that your troubles seem as if they were my own."

The king and queen thanked the fairy for her good advice, gave her some valuable gifts, and begged her to have the goodness during their absence to take special care of their kingdom so that none of their neighbors might decide to wage war. She promised all they asked, and they went back to their capital comforted to some degree in that they could look forward to a lessening of their sorrow. Then they ordered a ship to be prepared for the voyage. After they went on board, they set sail for the high sea guided by a pilot who had been on the Island of the Dolphin. For some days the wind was favorable, but afterward, it became so tempestuous and the storm increased to such a pitch that, after being tossed about, the vessel crashed against a rock without there being a chance of saving it. All those who were on board were suddenly separated from each other with no hope of escaping from the terrible danger.

All this time the king was only thinking of his daughter.

"I fully deserve the punishment that the gods are sending me," he said, "since it was I who exposed Livorette and her son to the fury of the waves."

These guilty feelings tortured him so much that he had given up all thought of prolonging his life. Just then he saw the queen on a dolphin's back, for the fish had caught her as she was falling from the ship. She was extending her arms to the king with a burning desire to be reunited with him and hoping that the good dolphin might reach him and save him along with her. And that is just what happened, for at that moment, when the king was on the point of drowning, the good fish approached him, and with the aid of the queen, he managed to pull himself on to the dolphin's back. She was charmed to see him again and told him to pluck up his courage since Heaven was apparently on their side and was bringing them to a safe haven. And, in fact, toward the close of day, the obliging dolphin, who was always at their service, carried them to a pleasant shore on which they landed, no more exhausted than if they had just come from their cabins in the stern of the ship.

It was the very island reigned over by Livorette and Alidor. They happened to be walking along the shore, Livorette holding her son by the hand, and a large retinue following them, when they saw to their great astonishment two people on the dolphin's back. Naturally, they felt obliged to go to them and to offer hospitality to them. But imagine the surprise of the prince and princess when they recognized the king and queen! However, they also realized that they were not recognized in return, which was not extraordinary seeing that the king and queen had not set eyes on their daughter for six years. A girl changes greatly in such a long space of time. And Alidor, far from being ugly and mad, had now become handsome, and his reason had been restored to him. The child, too, had grown. So the king and queen were far from being aware that they had encountered their dear daughter and their grandson.

Livorette had a great deal of difficulty restraining her tears. At every word she said to her father and mother, or that she heard them say, her bosom swelled, and her voice changed its tone every minute, trembling with agitation.

"Madame," the king said to her, "you see at your feet a monarch deeply distressed and a queen in despair. We were shipwrecked nearby, and all those who were with us have perished. We are alone, stripped of all our treasures and with none to help us. We are sad examples of the fickleness of fortune."

"Sire," said the princess, "you could have landed in no better country. We shall be more than glad to help you. Forget your misfortunes, I beg of you. And you, madame," she said to the queen, "permit me to embrace you."

Upon saying this, she threw herself on her neck while the queen pressed her in her arms with such extraordinary tenderness because of her likeness to her dear Livorette that she almost fainted. Alidor invited them to ride in his chariot, and they consented. Then they were driven to the castle, where all the beauty and magnificence filled the king with surprise. There was hardly a moment that went by when some pleasure was not prepared for them. But what gave them most joy was the prince's vessels, which had not been far away from the spot where the shipwreck of the king had taken place, had saved the ship and all on board and brought the crew to the Island of the Dolphin, even while the king was lamenting their death.

At last, one day after they had spent a good amount of time with the prince and the princess, the king begged them to give them the means of returning to their own kingdom.

"Alas!" said the queen. "I shall not conceal from you our misfortune, the saddest that could ever happen to a father and mother."

Thereupon, she told the story of Livorette; the griefs that had overwhelmed them ever since the cruel torture to which the king had condemned her; the advice of the fairy who dwelled in the forest of the bears; and their plan to go to the Island of the Dolphin.

"And here we have reached it by the most extraordinary route possible," the queen continued. "But beyond the pleasure of seeing you, we have found nothing here to comfort us, and the fairy, who induced us to come, did not predict correctly what would happen."

The princess had listened to her dear mother with such pity and natural affection that she could not keep her tears back. The queen was indeed grateful to see how keenly she felt her sorrows. She begged the gods to reward her, and embracing her again and again, she called Livorette her daughter and her child without knowing why.

At last, a ship was ready for them, and the departure of the king and queen was scheduled for the next day. The princess had been keeping one of the most beautiful things about the palace for them to see until the very last. It was the beautiful tree in the flower bed, whose trunk was made of silver and the branches of gold with three oranges of diamonds, rubies, and emeralds hanging from them. There were also three guardians whose duty it was to watch the tree day and night in case someone should attempt to steal it or to carry away the fruit. When Alidor and Livorette had taken the king and queen to this place, they let them admire it leisurely for some time so they could enjoy the beauty of the marvelous tree which was unique in the world. After they had spent more than four hours examining it, they returned to the place where the prince and princess were waiting for them to participate in a superb meal. In the room there was a table with two covers, and when the king asked why, she told him that they wished to have the honor of serving them. So they begged their majesties to be seated. Livorette and Alidor and their child brought wine to the king and queen, serving them on their knees, carving the meat for them, placing it neatly on their plates, choosing the best and the most delicate portions. Meanwhile sweet and pleasant music could be heard. Suddenly, the three guardians of the rare tree entered with a terrified air and with the news that the fine diamond and ruby oranges had been stolen, and it could only have been by those people who had just seen them—which meant the king and queen. They were, of course, offended, and rising from the table, they both said they were willing to be searched before the whole court. The king undid his scarf and opened his vest, while the queen undid her bodice. But to their astonishment, the diamond and the ruby oranges fell down.

"Ah, sire!" cried the princess. "Is this the reward we get for the kind and respectful treatment you have received on our island? It is a bad return for a good welcome from hosts who paid you such great respect."

Confused by this affront, the king and queen tried all sorts of means to justify themselves against the reproaches they received. They protested that they were incapable of committing the theft, that those who accused them did not know them, and that they themselves could not understand how it had all happened.

Upon hearing their words, the princess threw herself at the feet of her father and mother and said, "Sire, I am the unfortunate Livorette, whom you placed in the barrel along with Alidor and my son. You accused me of a crime which I never committed. The misfortune happened to me without my knowing anything more about it than your majesties knew when the oranges were hidden in your bosoms. I beg you to believe all this and to pardon me!"

The hearts of the king and queen were pierced by these words. They lifted their daughter up and all but smothered her so tightly did they clasp her in their arms. Then she presented Prince Alidor and the little prince to them. It is easier to imagine than to describe the joy of these illustrious people.

The wedding of the prince and princess was celebrated in a magnificent manner. The dolphin was present in the shape of a young monarch who was charming and witty. Ambassadors carrying precious gifts were sent to Alidor's father and mother, and they were also assigned the task of telling his parents about all that had happened. The life of the prince and princess was just as long and happy after this as it had been full of sorrow and complications in the beginning. Livorette returned with her husband to her father's kingdom, but her son stayed behind on the Island of the Dolphin.

JACOB AND WILHELM GRIMM

Simple Hans†

Once a king lived happily with his daughter, who was his only child. Then, all of a sudden she gave birth to a baby, and no one knew who the father was. For a long time the king did not know what to do. At last he ordered the princess to take the child and go to the church. There a lemon was to be given to the child, who was to offer it to anyone around him, and that man was to be the child's father and the princess's husband. Everything was arranged accordingly, and the king also gave orders to allow only highborn people into the church.

However, there was a little, crooked hunchback living in the city who was not particularly smart and was therefore called Simple Hans. Well, he managed to push his way into the church among the others without being noticed, and when the child offered the lemon, he handed it to Simple Hans. The princess was mortified, and the king was so upset that he had his daughter, the child, and Simple Hans stuck into a barrel, which was cast into the sea. The barrel soon floated off, and when they were alone at sea, the princess groaned and said, "You nasty, impudent hunchback! You're to blame for my misfortune! Why did you force your way into the church? My child's of no concern to you."

"That's not true," said Simple Hans. "He does concern me because I once made a wish that you would have a child, and whatever I wish comes true."

"Well, if that's the case, wish us something to eat."

"That's easily done," replied Simple Hans, and he wished for a dish full of potatoes. The princess would have liked to have something better. Nevertheless, she was so hungry that she joined him in eating the potatoes. After they had stilled their hunger, Simple Hans said, "Now I'll wish us a beautiful ship!"

No sooner had he said this than they were sitting in a splendid ship that contained more than enough to fulfill their desires. The helmsman guided the ship straight toward land, and when they went ashore, Simple Hans said, "Now I want a castle over there!"

Suddenly there was a magnificent castle standing there, along with servants dressed in gold. They led the princess and her child inside, and

† Jacob and Wilhelm Grimm, "Simple Hans"—"Hans dumm" (1812), was first published as No. 62 in *Kinder- und Hausmärchen. Gesammelt durch die Brüder Grimm* (Berlin: Realschulbuchhandlung, 1812). It was omitted in the following editions due either to its French origins or to its similarity to a poem by Christoph Martin Wieland.

when they were in the middle of the main hall, Simple Hans said, "Now I wish to be a young and clever prince!"

All at once his hunchback disappeared, and he was handsome, upright, and kind. Indeed, the princess took such a great liking to him that she became his wife.

For a long time they lived happily together, and then one day the old king went out riding, lost his way, and arrived at their castle. He was puzzled because he had never seen it before and decided to enter. The princess recognized her father immediately, but he did not recognize her, for he thought she had drowned in the sea a long time ago. She treated him with a great deal of hospitality, and when he was about to return home, she secretly slipped a golden cup into his pocket. After he had ridden off, she sent a pair of knights after him. They were ordered to stop him and search him to see if he had stolen the golden cup. When they found it in his pocket, they brought him back. He swore to the princess that he had not stolen it and did not know how it had gotten into his pocket.

"That's why," she said, "one must beware of rushing to judgment." And she revealed to him that she was his daughter. The king rejoiced, and they all lived happily together, and after his death, Simple Hans became king.

Dangerous Sirens

The stories of sirens, mermaids, nixies, and water nymphs who tempt men as seductresses are widespread throughout the world. One of the most famous incidents related to these powerful creatures can be found in *Homer's Odyssey* when Ulysses is tempted by the sirens. For the most part, the water nymphs are very dangerous as the many German legends about Lorelei in the Rhine River attest. The various versions of these tales about female water spirits depend on the local legends, beliefs, and customs in which the tales originated. In the literary tradition, the water nymph desires to possess men, punish them, or pursue her attraction, and she will only release the man when she is tempted by gold, precious and unique objects, or music. Quite often the man who is captured is saved by his wife. Straparola's tale has, of course, other important motifs such as the bastard who seeks to discover his origins, the animal helpers, and the rescue of a princess from a dragon. Mailly's version remains very close to Straparola's, whereas the Grimms' text was directly based on a fairy tale that Moritz Haupt published in his journal *Zeitschrift für deutsches Altertum* (1842): 358–60. In addition, Ludwig Bechstein's "Der Müller und die Nixe" ("The Miller and the Nixie") in *Deutsches Märchenbuch* (1857) has motifs that are similar to those in the works by Haupt and the Grimms. All of these tales may have been influenced by two earlier versions in Germany: Johann Karl Musäus's "Die Nymphe des Brunnens" ("The Nymph of the Fountain") in *Volksmährchen der Deutschen* (1782–87) and Johann Christoph Matthias Reinecke's "Der Nixen Eingebinde" (The Nixie's Captive") in *Eichenblättern* (1793).

GIOVAN FRANCESCO STRAPAROLA

Fortunio and the Siren†

There was once a man named Bernio, who lived in the outer regions of Lombardy. Though fortune had not been kind to him, he had a good heart and good head on his shoulders. One day he married a valiant and gracious woman named Alchia. Though she was of low origin, she was nevertheless endowed with brains and commendable manners and loved her husband as dearly as any woman could. They desired very much to have children, but God did not grant them this gift perhaps because man does not know what will be best for him when he asks for things. Still,

---

† Giovan Francesco Straparola, "Fortunio and the Siren"—"Fortunio per una ricevuta ingiuria dal padre e dalla madre putativi si parte; e vagabandono capita in un bosco, dove trova tre animali da' quali per sua sentenza è guidardonato; indi, entrato in Polonia, giostra, ed in premio Doralice figliuola del re in moglie ottiene" (1550), *Favola* IV, *Notte terza* in *Le piacevoli notti*, 2 vols. (Venice: Comin da Trino, 1550/53).

they both continued to want a child, and since fortune kept going against them, they decided at last to adopt a child whom they would nurture and raise as their own legitimate son.

So, early one morning they went to a place where young children who had been abandoned by their parents were left, and seeing one that appeared more handsome and charming than the others, they took him home with them, named him Fortunio, and brought him up with utmost diligence and discipline. Now, it so happened—in accordance with the wishes and will of He who rules the universe and tempers and modifies everything—that Alchia became pregnant, and when the time of delivery arrived, she gave birth to a boy who completely resembled his father. As a result, both the mother and the father were incredibly happy and gave their son the name of Valentino.

The boy was well nurtured and educated, and he grew up with good manners and qualities. Moreover, he loved his brother, Fortunio, so much that he despaired whenever he was not with him. But discord, the enemy of everything good, became aware of their warm and fervid friendship, and not being able to tolerate their affection for one another, it intervened and worked its evil so effectively that the brothers soon began to taste its bitter fruits.

One day, as they were fooling around with one another, as boys are apt to do, their play became heated, and Valentino, who could not bear that Fortunio was better in their game, exploded with such anger and fury that he called Fortunio a bastard several times and the son of a vile woman. When Fortunio heard those words, he was very astonished and disturbed, and turning to Valentino, he said, "What do you mean, I'm a bastard?"

In reply, Valentino muttered angrily between his teeth and repeated what he had said. Consequently, Fortunio was so disturbed that he stopped playing and left. He went straight to his so-called mother and politely asked her whether he was the son of Bernio and herself. Alchia responded with a yes, and once she learned that Valentino had insulted Fortunio with vicious words, she scolded the latter soundly and swore that she would punish him severely if he ever did something like that again. But the words that Alchia spoke only aroused suspicion in Fortunio, and he thus became certain that he was not her legitimate son. Indeed, he often sought to test her to see whether he really was her son and to know the truth. Seeing how obstinate Fortunio was and not being able to resist his pleas, Alchia finally told him that he was not her true son, but that he had been adopted and raised in their house for the love of God and to alleviate the faults of her and her husband. Upon hearing these words, Fortunio felt as if he had been stabbed in the heart many times, and he was tormented all the more. He could barely endure the grief, but he could also not bring himself to use violence and to kill himself. So, he decided to leave Bernio's house and to wander around the world to see if fortune would treat him more favorably in time.

When Alchia saw that Fortunio's desire to leave grew stronger each day and that she could not find any way to prevent him from carrying out his plans, she became enraged, cursed him, and prayed to God that if he should ever take a journey by sea, he would be swallowed up by sirens

just as ships are by the stormy and high waves. But Fortunio, driven by
the impetuous wind of indignation and wrath, did not care about the
maternal curse, and without saying farewell to his parents, he departed
and set out in the direction of the west.

As he journeyed, he passed lakes, valleys, mountains, and other wild
places. Finally, early one morning, he came upon a densely covered forest.
As soon as he entered, he found a wolf, an eagle, and an ant quarreling
over the body of a dead stag because they could not agree on how to divide
the meat among themselves. After Fortunio had come unexpectedly upon
the three animals in midst of their hard dispute and none of them willing
to yield to the others, they agreed after a while that the young man should
resolve their argument and give each one of them some part of the meat
that he thought would be most suitable. They also promised to be content
with his final decision and not seek to contradict it, even though it might
seem unjust. Then Fortunio undertook the task, and after he carefully
investigated everything, he divided the prey among them in the following
manner. To the wolf, who was a voracious animal with sharp teeth, he
gave all the bones of the deer and all the lean flesh as reward for his hard
work. To the eagle, a rapacious bird without teeth, he gave the entrails
and all the fat lying around the lean parts and the bones. To the graniv-
orous and diligent ant, which lacked the strength that nature had bestowed
upon the wolf and the eagle, he gave the soft brains as her reward for her
arduous work. Each one of the animals was very content with this just and
reasonable decision, and they thanked Fortunio as best they knew and
could for the favor that he had done for them. And since ingratitude is
the most reprehensible of all the vices, the three animals agreed that the
young man should not depart until they had rewarded him extremely well
for the service he had done them. Thus, after acknowledging the decision,
the wolf said, "My brother, I'm going to give you a certain power so that,
if at any time you want to become a wolf, all you have to say is: 'If only
I were a wolf.' And you will immediately be transformed into a wolf. At
the same time you will be able to return to your former shape whenever
you so desire."

Both the eagle and the ant rewarded him with the same power to assume
their shapes whenever he wanted. Then Fortunio, extremely pleased by
their gifts, thanked the animals as best he knew how and could and took
his leave. He continued his journey until he finally arrived in Polonia, a
noble and populous city, which was at that time under the rule of Odescalco, a powerful and valorous king who had only one child, a daughter
named Doralice. Now, since the king was eager to arrange an honorable
marriage for this princess, he had proclaimed throughout his kingdom that
a great tournament was to take place and the winner in the jousts was to receive Princess Doralice as his bride. Many dukes, counts, and other powerful nobles from all over had already gathered in Polonia to contend for this
precious prize. The first day of the tournament had already passed, and the
jousting was won by a foul Saracen, who was deformed and strange and had
a face as black as pitch. When the king's daughter saw the warped and filthy
figure of the Saracen, she was extremely upset that he had carried away the
honors of the day. Burying her face, crimson with shame, in her tender and

delicate hands, she wept and bemoaned her hard and cruel fate, longing to die rather than to marry the deformed Saracen.

In the meantime, Fortunio entered the city and saw the splendid pomp and the grand competition of the contestants, and when he learned why this glorious tournament was being held, he ardently desired to show his valor in the jousts. But when he realized that he lacked all the equipment necessary for such competition, he lamented his situation. While he was contemplating his predicament, he raised his eyes to the sky and caught sight of Princess Doralice, who was leaning out of one of the large windows of the palace. She was surrounded by a group of lovely and noble dames and damsels and stood out among them like the radiant clear sun does among the lesser lights of heaven.

When it eventually became dark and all the ladies had retired to their apartments, Doralice, sad and alone, went to a small and beautifully decorated chamber. While she was standing by her open window, Fortunio was there below her. As soon as he saw her, he said to himself, "If only I were an eagle!" No sooner did he utter these words than he became an eagle and flew through the window of her chamber, where he became a man again. When he stepped toward Doralice with a light and joyful air to present himself, she was completely bewildered and began to shout in a loud voice as if she were being torn apart by hungry dogs. The king, who was in a nearby apartment, heard her cries and ran to help her. She told him that there was a young man in the room, and he ordered the servants to search every corner. When nothing was found, they all went back to bed. Indeed, Fortunio had changed himself back into an eagle and had flown out of the chamber. However, no sooner had the father returned to his room to rest than the maiden began to shout once more because Fortunio had come back. This time, when the young man heard the girl's cries he feared for his life, changed himself into an ant, and hid himself beneath the blond tresses of the lovely maiden's hair. When King Odescalco heard his daughter's shouts, he ran to her again, but when he found nothing a second time, he was greatly disturbed and threatened her with harsh words that if she were to cry out again, he would play some joke on her that would not be to her liking. Thus he left her in an angry mood and thought that she had imagined seeing one or another of the contestants who, out of love for her, had been killed in the tournament. Fortunio had listened closely to what the king had told his daughter, and when he saw him leave, he discarded the shape of the ant and returned to his own form. As soon as Doralice saw him, she wanted to jump out of bed and scream, but Fortunio prevented her from doing this by placing one of his hands on her lips and whispering, "My lady, I have not come here to dishonor you or steal your virtue. I have come rather to comfort you and to declare myself your most humble servant. But if you cry out, one or two things will happen. Either your reputation and fair name will be tarnished, or you will be the cause of your death and mine. Therefore, oh lady of my heart, do not stain your honor and simultaneously endanger our lives."

While Fortunio was saying these words, Doralice was shedding a flood of tears. She could barely stand this fearful assault. But Fortunio realized

how disturbed the lady was, and he kept talking to her with the sweetest
of words that would have melted a heart of stone. Finally Doralice's stubborn will softened, and she was conquered by his tender way, which pacified her. When she also saw how handsome the young man's face was,
and how strong and well-built his body was in comparison to the ugly,
deformed Saracen, she began to feel tormented again by the thought that
the Saracen as victor might soon possess her. While she was contemplating
her lamentable situation, the young man said to her, "Dear lady, if I had
some way, I would gladly enter the tournament, and I would win the heart
that belongs to the victor."

"If this were to happen, my lord," she replied, "there is indeed none
other to whom I would give myself but you."

Recognizing how ardent and how well disposed he was to her, the princess gave him a great deal of jewels and money, which Fortunio accepted
with all his heart. Then he asked her what garment she wished him to
wear in the tournament, and she said, "Dress in white satin," and he
intended to do as she requested.

On the following day, Fortunio was dressed in polished armor covered
by a coat of white satin that was hand-carved and embroidered with the
finest gold. He mounted a powerful and fiery steed, decked in the same
colors that he wore. Then he rode into the piazza unknown to anyone
there. The people in the crowd had already gathered to watch the grand
spectacle, and when they saw the gallant unknown knight with lance in
hand ready for the joust, everyone stared and marveled at him. Indeed,
they began asking, "Who could this brave and glorious knight be who has
entered the tournament? Does anyone know him?"

In the meantime, Fortunio had joined the lists and called upon his rival
to advance. Then the knights lowered the points of their knotty lances and
charged at each other like two lions let loose upon one another. Fortunio
dealt such a grave blow to the head of the Saracen that the latter was
knocked out of the saddle of his horse and crashed to the ground as if he
had been broken like glass thrown against a wall. No matter what contes-
tant he met that day, Fortunio came away the victor. The princess was
very happy and watched Fortunio intently with the deepest admiration.
She thanked God in her heart for having delivered her from the bonds of
the Saracen and prayed to Him to let Fortunio win all the laurels.

When night arrived, Doralice was summoned to dinner, but she did not
want to go. So she commanded the servants to bring her some delicious
food and precious wine to her chamber, pretending that she did not have
much appetite at present but perhaps she would eat later on. After locking
herself alone in her chamber, she opened the window and watched with
ardent desire for the arrival of her lover. When Fortunio returned like the
previous night, they dined together with great joy. Then he asked her how
she would like him to dress for the tournament the next day, and she
replied, "I would like you to wear green satin embroidered with the finest
threads of silver and gold, and your horse is to be decked in the same
way."

On the following morning Fortunio appeared just as Doralice had requested. He presented himself in the piazza at the appointed time and

demonstrated his valor as he had done on the day before and even more. And everyone shouted that he deserved to win the lovely princess.

When evening came, the princess was very cheerful and happy. She used the same pretext to excuse herself from dinner as she had done the previous day. After locking the door of her chamber and opening the window, she waited for the valorous Fortunio and had a pleasant meal with him. When he asked once more what color he should wear the following day, she answered, "I would like you to wear crimson satin embroidered with gold and pearls, and I would like your horse to be decked in the same fashion because I myself shall be wearing the same colors."

"Lady," replied Fortunio, "if by some chance, I should be somewhat late in making my entry into the lists, do not be astonished, for I shall not be late without good reason."

When the third day came and the tournament began, the spectators awaited the outcome of the glorious contest with great joy, but because of the indomitable power of the gallant unknown knight, none of the contestants wanted to enter the lists against him. Meanwhile, his own whereabouts were not known, and the princess began to suspect something, especially since she did not know where he was. Indeed, she was overcome by so much torment that she fainted and fell to the ground. But as soon as she heard that the unknown knight was approaching the large piazza, her failing spirits began to revive.

Fortunio was clad in rich and sumptuous garments, and his horse was decked with the finest cloth, embroidered with shining rubies, emeralds, sapphires, and large pearls that, according to everyone present, were worth a kingdom. Once the brave Fortunio arrived at the piazza, the people all cried out, "Long live the unknown knight!" and applauded vigorously by clapping their hands. Then Fortunio entered the lists and fought so valiantly that he sent all his opponents to the ground and triumphed in glory. After he had dismounted from his powerful horse, the leading men of the city hoisted him on their shoulders and carried him to the king amid the sound of trumpets and other musical instruments and loud shouts that went up to the heavens. When they had taken off his helmet and shining armor, the king saw a charming young man. Then he summoned his daughter and had them wed. The marriage was celebrated with the greatest pomp, and the party went on for an entire month.

After Fortunio had lived some time with his beloved wife, it appeared to him improper and somewhat deplorable to be so idle, merely counting the hours as they passed like those fools who make nothing out of their lives. Therefore, he decided to depart and go to places where he could demonstrate his valor. So, he prepared a ship and took a large treasure which his father-in-law had given him. Then he took leave of his wife and King Odescalco and embarked on a voyage. Prospering from gentle and favorable winds, he sailed until he reached the Atlantic Ocean. But before he had gone more than ten leagues, the most beautiful siren that had ever been seen appeared at the side of the ship and began singing softly. Fortunio leaned over the side of the ship to listen to her song, and soon he fell asleep. While he was dozing, the siren drew him gently into her arms and plunged with him deep into the ocean. The sailors were not able to save him and broke out into loud cries of sorrow. Grief-stricken and disconsolate, they decked the ship with black cloth and returned to the unfortunate and unhappy Odescalco to tell him about the horrible and lamentable accident they had had at sea.

When King Odescalco, Doralice, and the entire city heard about this, they were overcome with grief and began dressing themselves in black. Soon thereafter, Doralice, who had been pregnant, gave birth to a beautiful boy, who was gently and carefully raised until he was two. At this time, the sad and tormented Doralice, who kept thinking about her beloved and dear husband, began to abandon hope of ever seeing him again. But noble and brave as she was, she decided to test her fortune and to go and search for him on the deep seas, even if her father would not consent to let her depart. She ordered a ship to be prepared for her voyage, and it was well equipped and well armed. She also took with her three apples, marvelously wrought, one made out of brass, another out of silver, and the last out of the finest gold. Then, after she took leave of her father the king, she embarked with her son and sailed into the open sea with a propitious wind.

As the sad lady sailed over a calm sea, she asked the sailors to take her to the very spot where her husband had been snared by the siren, and they carried out her orders. When the ship reached this spot, the child began to shed a flood of tears, and the mother was completely unable to pacify him. So, she took the apple made of brass and gave it to the boy. While he was playing with the apple, the siren noticed him and approached the ship. After she lifted her head out of the foamy waves, she said to Doralice, "Lady, give me that apple, for I'm very much taken by it."

But the princess answered she would not give it to her because it was her child's toy.

"If you will give it to me," the siren said. "I shall show you your husband up to his breast."

When Doralice heard these words, she gave the siren the apple because she desired to see her husband. The siren rewarded her for the precious gift and did as she had promised and showed the husband up to his breast. Then she plunged with him into the depths of the ocean and disappeared from sight.

As Doralice watched everything attentively, she longed to see her husband even more. Not knowing what to do or what to say, she sought comfort with her child, and when the little one began to cry once more, the mother gave him the silver apple. But once again the siren saw the apple and asked Doralice to give it to her. But the princess shrugged her shoulders and said that the apple was her child's toy and could not be given away. Thereupon, the siren said, "If you will give me this apple, which is far more beautiful than the other, I promise to show you your husband down to his knees."

Poor Doralice, who desired to see her husband more than ever, put the love of her husband before that of her son and cheerfully handed the apple to the siren, who kept her promise and then plunged back into the sea with Fortunio. Meanwhile, Doralice watched in silence and uncertainty, and she had no idea how to free her husband. She picked up her child in her arms, tried to comfort herself with him and to still his weeping. Remembering the apple with which he had been playing, the child continued crying so that mother gave him the golden apple to appease him. When the greedy siren caught sight of his apple and saw that it was more beautiful than the other two, she demanded it at once as a gift from Doralice. She insisted so much that the mother conceded against her will and took it away from her son. In return the siren promised that she would show her husband in his entirety, and in order to carry out her promise, the siren came close to the ship carrying Fortunio on her back. Then she rose somewhat above the surface of the water to reveal him from head to foot. However, as soon as Fortunio felt that he was above the water and resting free on the back of the siren, he was filled with joy, and without hesitating a moment, he cried out, "Oh, if only I were an eagle!"

As soon as he said this, he was immediately transformed into an eagle, and he flew to the mast of the ship. All the sailors watched him as he then descended to the main deck and returned to his proper shape. Then he kissed and embraced his wife and his child and all the sailors. Together they all celebrated Fortunio's rescue, and they sailed back to King Odescalco's kingdom. No sooner did they enter the harbor than they began to play their trumpets, drums, castanets, and other instruments that they had with them. When the king heard the music, he was very much astonished and waited with suspense to learn what all this meant. Soon a herald came to announce to the king that his dear daughter had arrived with her husband, Fortunio. When they had disembarked from the ship, they all went to the palace, where they were welcomed with a grand and glorious celebration.

After some days had passed, Fortunio returned to his old home and changed himself into a wolf. Then he devoured Alchia, his wicked mother, and Valentino, his brother, in revenge for the harm that they had done to him. Afterward, he returned to his natural form, mounted his horse, and rode back to his father-in-law's kingdom, where he lived in peace with Doralice, his dear and beloved wife, for many years to the great delight of them both.

JEAN DE MAILLY

Fortunio†

There was once a man whose fortune was not very great, but he was courageous and intelligent and did not consider himself inferior to anyone. He sought a woman who had the same qualities as he did and was not very wealthy, and he married her. Even though they did not have many possessions, they lived together very happily and were satisfied with their lot. They only wanted children to bless their marriage.

After trying for a long time to fulfill their desire in vain, they finally

---

† Jean de Mailly, "Fortunio"—"Fortunio" (1698), in *Les illustres fées, contes galans* (Paris: M-M. Brunet, 1698).

decided to console themselves by adopting a child. Then one day while they were walking along the bank of a river, they noticed a cradle floating on the water. Curious to know what was inside, they got into a boat, and they soon satisfied their curiosity and found what they had been wishing for: it was a baby who appeared to them to be marvelously beautiful and promised to have perfectly regular features which they thought that they could recognize. Since they felt themselves fortunate to have found the baby, they gave him the name of Fortunio and raised him and taught him everything with great diligence.

This child was born with the finest inclinations in the world and did honor to the education that was given him. He satisfied his adoptive parents so much that he became their veritable consolation for not having given birth to their own child. He even became so dear to them that they only thought about augmenting their wealth in order to benefit his future in the world and to be able to leave him a considerable inheritance so he could live with the luster suitable to the noble birth from which he appeared to have come, for he had been wrapped in a magnificent blanket when they found him. But during the time that they were contemplating all this, the amiable wife became pregnant, which did not diminish her or her husband's tenderness for Fortunio. They said to each other that, if Heaven was going to augment their family, they would take care to augment their wealth, and they would consider themselves very content if Heaven gave them a son as charming as the one that was given to them by fortune.

Heaven granted their wishes and gave them a son who could not have been more pretty when he was born. As he grew, he became more and more amiable, and to increase the happiness of his father and mother, he felt a strong friendship for Fortunio, whom he believed to be his older brother, and lived a long time with him in a strong union which would have lasted eternally if a young man, who would at times amuse himself with them, had not told the younger brother that he had reason to complain because his parents treated Fortunio with as much kindness as they treated him, as if Fortunio was their child, which he was not. Indeed, this friend said that Fortunio had been found by his mother and father, who had adopted Fortunio because they had desperately wanted to have their own child. Now that their wishes had been satisfied by his birth, it was only just that they should be more fond of their own son than of Fortunio.

When the young boy learned about this, he took the first opportunity that he had in a little spat with Fortunio to reproach him by saying that he was not his brother and that he was an orphan who had been taken in by his parents out of pity. Fortunio, who had a good heart, was very surprised by this news and went straight to the woman whom he had believed to be his mother until then, and he asked her to tell him if he were truly her son, and if he was, to tell his brother to be quiet because he maintained that he was not her son. She responded that he was truly her son, and that she was going to punish that thoughtless little boy for having harmed him with such insults. But she did not say this strongly enough to convince Fortunio, who had such great suspicions about his sad state that he pressed her so hard that she had to tell him the truth. At the same time, she assured him that he would never be less dear to her than her own son and that she would always have the same affection for him as for his brother.

Since he was of noble birth, he was very aware of how good his parents had been to him and how good they would be in the future, but he was so agitated by what he had just learned that he determined right then and there to go out into the world and perform deeds that would efface the shame of his birth and enable him to procure a better destiny. The woman whom he thought was his mother and who truly loved him did all she could to stop him. But when she saw that all her efforts were in vain, she became vexed and cursed him a thousand times. Indeed, she even wished he would be ensnared by a siren if he ever found himself at sea. In contrast, his father was more kind and approved Fortunio's decision and gave him money to equip himself. After Fortunio assured them of his eternal gratitude, he left and took a path, uncertain of where it would lead him.

He had not traveled very far when he encountered a forest so dense that the sun could not penetrate it. After he entered this forest he found himself in a dilemma, for he did not know which path to take. Just then he noticed a lion, an eagle, and an ant who were arguing among themselves about how to divide the carcass of a deer that they had hunted and killed. These three animals had prudently agreed to take the first man who passed by as a referee in order to avoid a bloody battle among themselves. When they caught sight of Fortunio, they addressed him and asked him to make peace among them and settle the differences that they had in dividing the dead deer. They promised that they would respect his decision without complaining, even if they felt he was unjust.

Fortunio, who was naturally bold, responded without being surprised and told them that he would be pleased to have the opportunity to do these honorable animals a favor. Indeed, so bold was Fortunio that it appeared he himself had been raised among the lions. He asked them if they would grant him their friendship in the event that he decided things fairly, and he received a thousand assurances that they would not only love him but would serve him anytime and anywhere that he had need of them.

Fortunio was charmed by their honest conduct and began to judge this important contest in a manner that would satisfy all their interests. He wanted to part from them in their good graces because, even though he put on a good face, he believed, as a man of good sense, that these animals, polite as they might appear, were not very good company for a man alone. Finally, he began to deliberate how to divide the carcass and was able to satisfy the taste of each one of the animals. In turn, they gave him a thousand thanks and considered themselves very fortunate to have met such a fair judge. Once they had finished making polite compliments, Fortunio began thinking how he might continue his journey, while his new friends were enjoying themselves.

Just at the time that he wanted to take his leave from the animals, a fairy appeared who was so magnificently adorned that he was surprised, for he had never seen anyone as beautiful, and he prostrated himself out of the respect that she had inspired in him. She had a hunting horn

hanging from a scarf which would have made her look like Diana[1] if she
had not told him that she was a fairy who had her palace deep in this
forest. As far as the three animals were concerned, they knew her very well
and had the deepest respect for her.

The fairy was curious to know what had happened between these creatures who were so different and so opposed to each other. So the lion
spoke up and told her about the fair decision that the man whom she saw
before her had made and asked her to be so kind as to use her power to
reward him. The fairy praised Fortunio for the fair decision that he had
made, and as a gift she gave him the power to transform himself into one
of the three animals whenever he had the need to do so and to return to
his own shape whenever he pleased. She was even so touched by his sense
of justice and good appearance that she proposed that he spend some days
with her at her chateau.

Fortunio accepted her offer with respect, for he was on a quest for
adventures. He spent several days at the fairy's palace and enjoyed himself
immensely as one can imagine. Indeed, he was sorry to leave the palace.
But the fairy, who knew that he was destined for great things, gave him
permission to leave after she had given him presents of very precious jewels
as well as good instructions on how he was to conduct himself.

Now that he had the means to make people take notice, Fortunio departed full of hope and stopped at the first city on his way and equipped
himself as a knight. Then he went on many quests, had diverse adventures,
and acquired a great reputation of valor by engaging in famous battles. I
shall recount these adventures another time. For now I want to talk about
the most celebrated and the most fortunate of his deeds since it led to his
conquering the most amiable princess of his century and a realm which
she inherited.

He arrived at the court of this princess just at the time when her father
the king had announced to all the neighboring princess who wanted to
marry his daughter that he had decided to give his daughter as bride to
whoever vanquished all the others in a tournament that was to take place
within a few days. Fortunio arrived at the right time to try his luck, and
he presented himself to the king as a knight who was traveling around the
world to serve in wars and to perform chivalrous deeds. The king told him
that he had arrived at an opportune time to witness a tournament that he
was holding at his court in a few days and he was counting on him to
enter it because nobody was to be excluded. Since his good appearance
reflected that he was highborn, he was received well everywhere. Fortunio
responded to the king that he would do his best not to disappoint the king
and to maintain the good opinion that his majesty had of him. Then he
asked for the liberty to go and pay his respects to the princess. The king
ordered the captain of his guards to go and present him, and he was
received very favorably. The princess was the most charming person in the
world, and on seeing her he was aroused with the desire to conquer her
or to shed his blood to the last drop. He was encouraged by some glances
of the princess which he believed to be favorable, and he pondered how

---

1. A Roman divinity—the moon goddess, patroness of virginity and hunting.

he might make himself agreeable in her eyes by showing his profound respects and assiduity while waiting for the day when he could win her at the tournament.

During the following days he saw the arrival of princes and knights who were seeking to win the princess or die for such a beautiful prize. Never had one seen a grander or more noble assembly. Each man was eager to approach the princess and wanted to express his vows to her for this great day. Some wanted to engage in the tournament out of profound respect for her, and others because of the great love they felt for her and were bold enough to declare it. Fortunio, the most passionate of all, was also the most respectful, and the less he dared to let her see in his eyes what was going on in his heart, the more he feared that he might displease her. But he was the one whom the princess wanted to win the prize, even though he might not be a prince, and there were moments when she judged that he would be the one, whereby his merits would equal those of a prince.

Finally the day of decision arrived or at least the day of destiny arrived for her, and there was an infinite number of princes and knights among the ranks of contestants. The king had decided that they were to draw lots to see who would be the first to enter the lists. He had assigned the judges to regulate everything and settle all the differences that might occur between the contestants. Many princes fought one after the other and destroyed each other. A neighboring prince, strong and valiant, but known as someone without courtesy and scruples, and who was so ugly that he was frightening to look at, entered the lists and defeated all those knights whom he encountered. It was now Fortunio's turn to engage him, but night approached, and the king put off this great battle until the next day. The princess was terribly scared, for she saw that she might fall into the hands of a prince whose reputation horrified her and who was considered to be ferocious. Moreover he had a mean appearance, and she could not see how Fortunio could defeat him.

News had spread that Fortunio was a knight of great valor. Some princes who had seen him in war had said this, but since she knew that he would be faced with a man so formidable, she did not dare hope that he would emerge as the victor. Of course, in the event that Fortunio succeeded in vanquishing the terrible man she hated, she would have preferred to know with certainty whether Fortunio was a true prince. Even though this was a minor concern, she thought it could cause her some difficulty if he were merely a knight. Preoccupied by these diverse thoughts, she went to the window of her apartment and appeared to be very upset. When Fortunio saw her, he went to the door of her apartment to present himself, but her servant told him that she did not want to see anyone.

Moved by her affliction, Fortunio decided to rescue her the next day from the anguish that she was suffering. He went into the street, and after wishing to be changed into an eagle, he was transformed into the bird, and he flew up to the princess's window. Seeing that she was alone, he entered and transformed himself back into his natural form. She was frightened and screamed. Her servants ran to see what was happening, but Fortunio had disappeared, for he had transformed himself into an ant and had slipped into the ruffle of the princess's dress. She had not noticed this and sent her attendants away, saying that she thought that she had seen something but had been mistaken. While Fortunio was hidden in her dress, he heard the princess utter sighs again and mutter some words that made him grasp the horror that she had for the prince who had been the victor in the tournament up until then. She also sighed for the man who seemed to be a simple knight but had touched her heart, and she would have liked to have seen him triumph.

No sooner did the ant understand the princess's sentiments than he said to her, "Do not fear, charming princess. The monster who is frightening you will not possess you, and if you promise not to call your attendants anymore, you will see the man who will rescue you tomorrow and who is the man who respects you more than anyone in the world. Don't be alarmed, princess, when he stands before you."

So Fortunio appeared before her again, and he assured her that he would rescue her from all her fears the next day. "I shall," he said, "be more than happy to have served you and shall be even more happy if, through all my efforts, I can win the reward that the king has promised to the victor."

After this conversation, Fortunio transformed himself into an eagle and flew out of the window. Meanwhile, the princess remained so scared that she had hardly had the strength to get up from her chair. She would never have dreamed that something like this could happen. She had never experienced anything like this and said to herself, "Is it possible that I shall be able to find the help that I need? Was I just dreaming all this?" Fortunio appeared so respectful and so amiable that she could only hope that he would be the victor even though he might only be a simple knight. The manner in which he had entered her room and in which he had left was something that caused her more concern. She had often heard of the power of fairies, and she guessed that a fairy, who might be touched by her misfortune, had probably sent her a defender.

Troubled by all these different worries, she could not think about anything else. So she decided to say that she was sick so she could stay in bed and wait for the following day, which she longed for with hope. She called one of her ladies-in-waiting and sent her to tell her father that she would like to go to bed with his permission because she was suffering from such a great headache that it was impossible for her to see anyone. The king came, and when he found out that the princess's head was on fire, he ordered everyone to let her repose herself, convinced that if she could sleep, her headache would disappear.

It is easy to imagine that, when the princess was left alone, she did not spend a peaceful night of sleep before such a great day on which all the happiness of her life was depending. On the other hand, Fortunio was not worried. He had to fight a formidable prince known for his valor and his force, but Fortunio was inspired by his love and great courage. Moreover, he was under the protection of a powerful fairy!

As soon as the lists commenced the next day, the people saw Fortunio enter. He was riding on the most handsome horse that one had ever seen and was dressed in a splendid suit of armor adorned by gold and jewels.

All the spectators admired him, and the princess recognized him by the great quantity of green ribbons tied in knots to his horse's equipment and by the green feathers on his helmet because he had asked permission to wear this color when he had seen her the previous day.

He assumed a proud position as he waited for his opponent to arrive. This king seemed to be surprised to find someone who would have the audacity to fight him after he had conquered everyone the day before.

"Who are you?" he said. "Who has made you so bold that you dare oppose me? Didn't you see all the men whom I demolished yesterday?"

"Just think about defending yourself," Fortunio responded. "You will not be so fortunate this day as you were yesterday."

They separated from each other to obtain some distance to run at each other, and the first joust ended in triumph for Fortunio, for he pierced his rival's breastplate with his lance and made him bite the dust. Since all the contestants had already been defeated, Fortunio waited in vain for someone else to oppose him, but nobody appeared to dispute the prize that he so well deserved because he had vanquished his rival who had defeated all the other contestants. The people burst into great applause, and the heralds entered into the lists to conduct the happy Fortunio amid trumpets and drums to the foot of the king's throne. Fortunio dismounted and took off his helmet. The princess was charmed to see that it was the knight for whom she felt destined. Indeed, from the very first day that he had arrived at the court, she had felt a strong inclination toward him.

As I have said, the king had been persuaded that Fortunio could only be of high birth and did not hesitate to extend his arm tenderly toward him and to say, "Come, amiable stranger. Here is the princess who is destined for you as the prize for your great victory. You have vanquished a knight whom no other opponent could defeat, and I believe that you have brought great pleasure to the princess, my daughter, to have defeated a man who would not have pleased her, even though he was a king."

Then the king turned to his daughter and said, "Here is the knight who belongs to you, my daughter. It is up to you to reward him for what he did to deserve you. I want you to give him your hand in marriage in two days."

Fortunio threw himself at the feet of the king and begged him to let the princess have the freedom of her choice and to let him have time to win her profound respect by accomplishing some great deeds in her name and in her glory.

"I am not very worthy of this grand princess," he said.

"No," the king replied, "you are more than worthy. Isn't this true, my daughter? Surely, this knight does not displease you."

"I shall have no difficulty," the princess answered, "in obeying your majesty on this occasion or on any other."

So the king was obeyed without repugnance, and the marriage ceremony was soon performed amid feasts and celebrations that lasted one month.

Fortunio spent some years in the arms of love and had everything he desired. But one day, the king decided to go to war against a prince who had usurped the realm of one of the neighboring kings, and he had his navy equipped for battle. Immediately, Fortunio asked the king if he could command the fleet, saying that he wanted to perform some deeds that would make him worthy of the princess, whom he still believed he had not deserved enough. The charming princess burst into tears and wanted to prevent her husband from going off to war. However, the king, who loved glory, approved of Fortunio's plan. So, after saying tender good-byes to his wife, Fortunio embarked, but the captain of his ship unknowingly conducted the fleet to a place on the sea in the empire of sirens. All of a sudden, the queen of the sirens appeared out of the water with a number of her retinue, curious to see who was brazen enough to cross her empire without having asked permission.

This queen was bored of just having tritons[2] for lovers, and she often desired to have a man as a lover, whom she thought would be a hundred times more pleasant. It was therefore not surprising that she was struck by the good looks of Fortunio and that she decided to carry him off with her. To obtain her goal, she made use of her art and sang with such sweetness that Fortunio was drawn to the side of the ship and lost control of his senses. As soon as she saw that he was in the condition that she desired, the queen of the sirens approached the ship and carried him away. The captain and all the sailors were tormented, but since they could find no way to remedy the situation, they turned around and went back to the king to tell him about the terrible misfortune. The captain tried his best to excuse himself by recounting how naive Fortunio was to want to hear the voice of this enchantress even though he had advised him to be on his guard. But Fortunio had been destined to endure this curse because it had been placed on him by the person who had been in charge of his upbringing.

It is impossible to express how upset the king and the princess were by this sad event. But the princess, who was inspired by the fairy, who had taken Fortunio under her protection and everyone connected to him, did not lose hope. She had a secret presentiment that she would see her dear Fortunio again one day, and she decided to search for him throughout the world. Indeed, she wanted to take her son, who was the spitting image of his father, with her, for she could not bear to let him out of her sight. The king yielded to her insistent pleas and consented to let her depart. He had a ship outfitted for her and gave her the same captain who had been in command of Fortunio's ship. After the princess had embarked, she ordered the captain to conduct her to the spot where Fortunio had been abducted.

The fairy, who had inspired the princess to undertake this adventure, appeared to her in a pleasant form and gave her three balls that were of infinite worth. She assured the princess that they had the power to enable her to see the husband whom she loved with such tenderness. But once they had arrived at the designated spot, it was necessary for her to give the balls to her son at three different times to appease him when he cried. Meanwhile, the captain alerted the princess that they had arrived at the

---

2. Imaginary sea monsters of semihuman form, often represented as bearded men with the hind-quarters of fish.

spot that had been fatal for her husband, and she ordered him to weigh anchor. Just then her son began to cry, and she gave him a golden ball plated in diamonds to appease him. The two other balls were made from a great emerald and a great ruby. When the little prince began rolling it on the deck, there was a harmonious music that came from it and astonished everyone on the ship. The sounds attracted the queen of the sirens from her palace, which was built on the sand beneath the sea. She addressed the princess and said to her, "Give me that ball, madame, and I shall be obliged to you."

The princess responded that she would gladly give the ball to her, but it was the ball that she used to amuse her son when he cried.

"Give it to me," the queen said again, "and I shall let you see the head of the man whom you've been seeking."

"For this prize I shall give it to you with all my heart," the princess said. "But what guarantee will you give me so that I know you will keep your promise?"

The queen swore to her that she was incapable of breaking her word, and if she did, she would lose her empire. The princess believed her, and as soon as she gave the queen the ball, she was content to see her dear Fortunio's head down to his shoulders. But it was only for a moment. The queen plunged down into the water and made her lover plunge down with her. The princess was greatly upset that she had been able to see her dear husband for a moment only. She took her son in her arms because he was her consolation. This child, who wanted to run about the deck, began to cry again. This time the queen gave him the emerald ball, and he rolled it like he had rolled the other. Once again a harmonious music could be heard, much sweeter than the music they had all heard before. The queen of the sirens appeared, and she was more touched than ever. She said to the princess that, if she would give her the ball, she would let her see her husband out of the water down to his knees. So, the princess gave her the ball right away, and she saw her husband momentarily, but then he was immediately forced to plunge back into the water. The poor princess did not know what she could do in such an extraordinary situation. She had seen her husband, whom she passionately desired, two times, but he had disappeared so suddenly that she could not say one word to him or hear anything from his lips.

The princess always had recourse to embrace her dear son in her sorrow, and this child cried in her arms like a little desperate soul. Finally, she gave him the last ball, which was made of a ruby, and he rolled it on the deck again. This time they all heard harmonious music that was one thousand times more touching than before, and the queen of the sirens cried out like a person very much in love, "Give me that ball again, and I shall give you whatever you like."

"I want my husband from you," the princess said.

The queen promised to let her see him from head to toe and let her know that she would return him to her one day. As soon as the ball was given, Fortunio gushed forth from the water standing on the back of a triton, and all of a sudden he transformed himself into an eagle and flew to the princess, where he immediately regained his natural form.

When she saw herself tricked, the queen of the sirens dove back down toward her empire and ordered all the sirens and tritons to make the water toss and turn to destroy the ship that was carrying away the man whom she had enchanted, even though he had never taken pleasure in the delights of her palace, of which he had been made master. Since Fortunio knew what the queen was capable of doing when she was enraged, he had the ship sail faster to get beyond the domain of the offended queen. Soon they were beyond it, and when he saw that they were safe, he embraced his charming wife and dear son tenderly and gave hugs to all who contributed to his rescue. The weather was so beautiful and the wind so favorable that the ship returned to port in a few hours.

When the king learned about the good luck of his daughter, he ran to her and his son-in-law, whom he was charmed to see after such a long absence. To celebrate such a happy event, the king could think of nothing else but inviting the people to a grand feast to make his joy more perfect and universal. Fortunio recounted all the marvels of the siren's palace and let his wife know how indifferent he had been toward the caresses of this powerful queen in the middle of her empire. The princess showed him even more tenderness to reward such a rare fidelity, and they delighted immensely in the pleasure of being together after such a cruel separation.

Only one thing was missing to make Fortunio's happiness complete. He wanted to resume his mission and help the neighboring king who had been dispossessed to regain his throne. Thus he asked his father-in-law, the monarch, for some troops to undertake this expedition, and the king gave them to him. He marched against the usurper and defeated him in a series of battles and re-established the king on the throne from which he had been banished. This king, who was very grateful, wanted to share his realm with him, and he asked him to stay at his court and have his wife come and join him. Sensing an extraordinary tenderness for Fortunio, he wanted to know the cause. After examining Fortunio's features and observing a mark that he had above his left eye, it occurred to the king that he could be the son that he had lost while still in his cradle and who had the same mark above his left eye. This child had been kidnapped during a dispute with his spiteful brother, who wanted to be his successor. Therefore, the brother had carried away the child, put him in a cradle, and thrown it into the river. The king, who believed that he recognized his son, knowing that blood never lies, urged Prince Fortunio to tell him what he knew about the beginning of his life. He responded and recounted that he had been raised by some people who lived along the very same river, where the king's son had been abandoned. Therefore, these people were sent for, and when they arrived a few days later and told the king that they had found Fortunio in a rich cradle at the same time that the young prince had been lost, the king recognized Fortunio as his son and proclaimed him as the successor to his throne.

This news was brought to Fortunio's wife and his father-in-law, and it is easy to guess how happy they were to see that fate had found a hero who had deserved the princess by his valor and also by his birth. The people in both realms, between which the prince and princess shared their lives, could think of nothing but celebrating these marvelous events and the merits of a prince who had brought them so much delight. The couple who had saved the prince from perishing in the water when he was a baby were very nicely rewarded for a deed that brought about much happiness for all the people.

JACOB AND WILHELM GRIMM

The Nixie in the Pond†

Once upon a time there was a miller who led a pleasant life with his wife. They had money and property, and their prosperity increased from year to year. Calamity, however, can strike overnight. Just as their wealth had increased rapidly, it also began to decrease each year until the miller could hardly call the mill that he inhabited his own. His problems weighed heavily on him, and when he lay down in bed after working all day, he could not rest. Instead he tossed and turned and worried himself sick. One morning he got up before daybreak, went outside into the open air, and hoped that this would ease his heart. As he walked over the dam of the mill, the first rays of the sun burst forth, and he heard a rushing sound in the pond. When he turned around, he caught sight of a beautiful woman who was rising slowly out of the water. Her long hair, which she clasped by her tender hands over her shoulders, flowed down both sides and covered her white body. He realized that this was the nixie[1] of the millpond and became so frightened that he did not know whether to go or stay. But the nixie raised her soft voice, called him by his name, and asked him why he was so sad. At first the miller was distrustful, but when he heard her speak in such a friendly way, he summoned his courage and told her that he had formerly lived in happiness and wealth but was now so poor he did not know what to do.

"Calm yourself," responded the nixie. "I shall make you richer and happier than you ever were before. But you must promise to give me what has just been born in your house."

Since the miller thought that it could be nothing but a puppy or a kitten, he agreed to give her what she desired. The nixie descended into the water again, and he rushed back to his mill feeling consoled and in good spirits. Just as he was about to enter the mill, the maid stepped out of his house and shouted that he should rejoice, for his wife had just given birth to a little boy. The miller stood still, as if struck by lightning. He realized that the sly nixie had known this and had deceived him. So he bowed his head and went to his wife's bedside, and when she asked him, "Why aren't you happy about our fine little boy?" he told her what had happened to him and what he had promised the nixie. "What good are happiness and wealth," he added, "if I must lose my child? But what can I do?"

† Jacob and Wilhelm Grimm, "The Nixie in the Pond"—"Die Nixie im Teich" (1857), No. 181 in *Kinder- und Hausmärchen. Gesammelt durch die Brüder Grimm* (Göttingen: Dieterich, 1857).
1. A female water elf or nymph.

Even the relatives, who had come to visit them and wish them happiness, did not know what advice to give him. In the meantime, prosperity returned to the house of the miller. Whatever he undertook turned into a success. It was as if the coffers and chests filled themselves of their own accord, and the money kept multiplying overnight in the closet. It did not take long before his wealth was greater than it had ever been before. But he could not rejoice about this with an easy conscience. The consent that he had given to the nixie tortured his heart. Whenever he walked by the millpond, he feared that she might surface and remind him about his debt. He never let his son go near the water. "Be careful," he said to him. "If you just touch the water, she will grab your hand and drag you under." However, as the years passed, and the nixie did not reappear, the miller began to relax.

When his boy became a young man, he was given to a huntsman as an apprentice. Once he learned everything and had become an able huntsman, the lord of the village took him into his service. In the village there was a beautiful and true-hearted maiden who had won the hunter's affection, and when the lord became aware of this, he gave the young man a small house. So the maiden and the huntsman were married, lived peacefully and happily, and loved each other with all their hearts.

Once when the huntsman was pursuing a deer, the animal turned out of the forest and into the open field. The huntsman followed it and finally killed it with one shot. He did not realize that he was close to the dangerous millpond, and after he had skinned and gutted the animal, he went to the water to wash his hands, which were covered with blood. No sooner did he dip his hands into the water than the nixie rose up and embraced him laughingly with her sopping wet arms. Then she dragged him down into the water so quickly that only the clapping of the waves could be heard.

When evening fell, and the huntsman did not return home, his wife became anxious. She went outside to search for him, and since he had often told her that he had to beware of the nixie's snares and that he was never to venture close to the millpond, she already suspected what had happened. She rushed to the water, and when she found his hunting bag lying on the bank of the pond, she was certain she knew what had happened to her husband. She wrung her hands and uttered a loud groan. She called her beloved by his name, but it was all in vain. Then she rushed to the other side of the millpond and called him again. She scolded the nixie with harsh words, but she received no response. The water's surface remained as calm as a mirror. Only the face of the half-moon returned her gaze in silence.

The poor woman did not leave the pond. Time and again she paced around it with quick steps, never resting for a moment. Sometimes she was quiet. Other times she whimpered softly. Finally, she lost her strength, sank to the ground, and fell into a deep sleep. Soon she was seized by a dream.

She was anxiously climbing up a mountain between two huge cliffs. Thorns and briers pricked at her feet. Rain slapped her face, and the wind whipped through her long hair. When she reached the peak, there was an entirely different view. The sky was blue; the air, mild. The ground sloped gently downward, and a neat little hut stood on a green meadow covered by flowers. She went toward the hut and opened the door. There sat an old woman with white hair, who beckoned to her in a friendly way.

At that very moment the poor young woman woke up. The day had already dawned, and she decided to let herself be guided by the dream. So she struggled up the mountain, and everything was exactly as she had seen it in the night. The old woman received her in a friendly way and showed her a chair where she was to sit. "You must have had a terrible experience," the woman said, "for you to have searched out my lonely hut."

The young woman cried as she told her what had happened to her. Then the old woman said, "Console yourself, for I shall help you. Here is a golden comb. Wait until the full moon has risen. Then go to the millpond, sit down on the bank, and comb your long black hair with this comb. When you're finished, set it down on the bank, and you'll see what happens."

The woman returned home, but she felt that the full moon was very slow in coming. Finally, it appeared in the sky. So she went out to the millpond, sat down, and combed her long black hair with the golden comb. And, when she was finished, she set it down on the edge of the water. Soon after, a bubbling from the depths could be heard, and a wave rose up, rolled to the shore, and took the comb away with it. The comb sank to the bottom in no time. Then the surface of the water parted, and the head of the huntsman emerged in the air. He did not speak, but with a sad look, he gazed at his wife. At that very moment, a second wave rushed toward the man and covered his head. Everything disappeared. The millpond was as peaceful as before, and only the face of the full moon shone upon it.

The young woman returned home disheartened. However, the dream came back to her and showed her the old woman's hut. The next morning she set out on her way once again and related her woes to the wise woman, who gave her a golden flute and said, "Wait until the moon comes again. Then take this flute, sit down on the bank, play a beautiful tune, and after you're done, see what happens."

The huntsman's wife did what the old woman told her to do. Just as she set the flute on the sand, there was a sudden bubbling from the depths. A wave rose up, moved toward the bank, and took the flute away with it. Soon after, the water parted, and not only the head of the man became visible but also half his body. He stretched out his arms toward her yearningly, but just as he did this, a second wave rolled by, covered him, and dragged him down into the water again.

"Oh, what's the use!" exclaimed the unfortunate woman. "I'm given glimpses of my dearest only to lose him again! Grief filled her heart anew, but the dream showed her the old woman's hut for a third time. So she set upon her way again, and the wise woman comforted her, gave her a golden spinning wheel, and said, "Not everything has been completed yet.

Wait until the full moon comes, then take the spinning wheel, sit down on the bank, and spin until the spool is full. When you're finished, place the spinning wheel near the water, and you'll see what happens."

The young woman followed the instructions exactly as she had been told. As soon as the full moon appeared, she carried the golden spinning wheel to the bank and spun diligently until there was no more flax left and the spool was completely full of thread. But, no sooner was the spinning wheel standing on the bank than the water bubbled in the depths more violently than ever before. A powerful wave rushed to the shore and carried the spinning wheel away with it. Soon after, the head and entire body of the man rose up high like a water geyser. Quickly he jumped to the shore, took his wife by the hand, and fled. But they had gone barely a short distance when the entire millpond rose up with a horrible bubbling and flowed over the wide fields with such force that it tore everything along with it. The huntsman and his wife could already picture their death. Then, in her fear, the wife called to the old woman to help them, and at that very moment they were transformed—she into a toad, he into a frog. When the flood swept over them, it could not kill them, but it did tear them apart from each other and carry them far away.

After the flood had run its course, and both had touched down on dry land, they regained their human shapes. But neither one knew where the other was. They found themselves among strange people who did not know where their homeland was. High mountains and deep valleys lay between them. In order to earn a living, both had to tend sheep. For many years they drove their flocks through fields and forests and were full of sadness and longing.

One day, when spring had made its appearance on earth again, they both set out with their flocks, and as chance would have it, they began moving toward each other. When the huntsman caught sight of another flock on a distant mountain slope, he drove his sheep in that direction. They came together in a valley, but they did not recognize each other. However, they were glad to have each other's company in such a lonely place. From then on they drove their flocks side by side every day. They did not speak much, but they felt comforted. One evening, when the full moon appeared in the sky and the sheep had already retired for the night, the shepherd took a flute from his pocket and played a beautiful but sad tune. When he was finished, he noticed that the shepherdess was weeping bitterly.

"Why are you crying?" he asked.

"Oh," she answered, "the full moon was shining just like this when I last played that tune on a flute, and the head of my beloved rose out of the water."

He looked at her, and it was as if a veil had fallen from his eyes, for he recognized his dearest wife. And when she looked at him and the light of the moon fell on his face, she recognized him as well. They embraced and kissed each other. And nobody need ask whether they lived in bliss thereafter.

Disguised Heroes

Straparola probably knew the "Story of Grisandole" in the Arthurian romance of *Merlin*, which was translated into Italian as *Historia di Merlino* in 1480 and was reprinted several times up to 1506 in Venice. Straparola's tale plays with the notion of mistaken identities and family honor. Basile's narrative is more ironic and is obviously closer to the oral tradition, while Mme d'Aulnoy and Mme de Murat show that they were clearly influenced by Straparola and sought to address courtly customs in their tales. The disguise of a young woman as man became a common motif in European literature by the nineteenth century and reflected the difficulties that women encountered when they sought to travel alone or wanted to lead independent lives. However, the disguise was always fraught with difficulties because it challenged traditional gender roles and identities. Aside from the two French tales by Mme d'Aulnoy and Mme de Murat, there is also an extended version in Thomas Simon Gueullette's *Les mille et un quarts d'heure, contes tartares* (A Thousand and One Quarters of an Hour, Tartarian Tales, 1715). Shahrukh Husain has collected numerous important European, Asian, and African versions in *Handsome Heroines: Women as Men in Folklore* (1995).

GIOVAN FRANCESCO STRAPAROLA

Constanza/Constanzo†

Thebes is one of the most stately cities of Egypt. It is ornamented with public and private buildings, and there are fields of white fertile crops and plenty of fresh water. Moreover, it abounds in all those things which make for a glorious city. Many years ago it was ruled by a king named Ricardo, a profoundly wise man with great knowledge and valor. Now this monarch desired very much to have some heirs, and thus he married Valeriana, daughter of Marliano, king of Scotland, a beautiful and graceful lady who was, in truth, perfection itself. Together they had three daughters, who were well-mannered, charming, and as beautiful as rosebuds in the morning. One was called Valentia, another Dorothea, and the third Sinella. In the course of time, it became clear to Ricardo that his wife had reached that phase in life when women no longer have children. In addition, his three daughters had reached marital age. Therefore, he decided to arrange for three honorable marriages and to divide his kingdom into three parts.

---

† Giovan Francesco Straparola, "Constanza/Constanzo" — "Ricardo, re di Tebe, ha quattro figliuole: delle quali una va errando per lo mondo, e di Constanza, Constanzo fassi chiamare, e capita nella corte di Cacco, re della Bettinia, il quale per mole sue prodezze in moglie la prende" (1550), *Favola* I, *Notte quarta* in *Le piacevoli notti*, 2 vols. (Venice: Comin da Trino, 1550/53).

So he assigned each daughter a section of the realm and kept enough to sustain himself, his family, and his court. Soon he carried out his plan just as he had conceived it and with the effect that he had desired.

In due time the three daughters were married to three powerful kings, one to the king of Scardona, another to the king of the Goths, and the third to the king of Scythia. As dowry, each daughter was given a third of their father's kingdom. Ricardo himself retained only a small part to satisfy his basic needs. Thus, the good king lived with Valeriana, his beloved wife, in honor and peace. But after a few years had passed, it happened that the queen, from whom the king no longer expected any offspring, became pregnant and gave birth to a beautiful baby girl. Despite the un-expected arrival, the king welcomed her with just as much affection as he had his first three girls. The queen, however, was not so pleased to see another daughter, not because she hated her, but because the kingdom had already been divided into three parts. So, she did not see how they could sufficiently afford to marry her in the same proper way that her sisters had been. After placing a competent nurse in charge of her daughter, the queen ordered this woman to take great care of her, to give her a good education, and to teach her polite and praiseworthy manners appro-priate for a maiden of her rank. As the young girl, who was called Con-stanza, grew up, she became more and more beautiful and well-mannered. She was instructed in so many things by her wise teacher that, by the time she was twelve, she had learned how to embroider, sing, play instruments, dance, and do all those proper things that were expected of a young girl in her position. But she herself was not content with all of this. She also studied literature, which gave her such pleasure and delight that she would spend day and night consuming books, always trying to discover the ex-quisite nature of her reading matter. Besides all of this, she mastered the military arts, learned to ride, wield arms, and joust in tournaments, not like a woman but like a skillful and gifted young man. Indeed, she often came out the victor in many contests just like a valorous knight worthy of such glory.

It was because of all of these virtues, each and every one of them, that Constanza was greatly loved by the king and queen and by all those in their court so that there seemed to be no limit to their affection. When Constanza, however, reached marital age, the king did not have land or money to arrange for an honorable marriage. Since he was greatly sad-dened by this, he conferred with the queen about this matter. But the prudent Valeriana was very content because she regarded the many qual-ities of their daughter as incomparable and comforted the king with sweet and loving words so he calmed down and was firmly convinced that some powerful sovereign, fired with love by the many virtues of their daughter, would eventually consent to wed her, even though they might not be able to provide her with a dowry.

Indeed, before many months had passed, their daughter was sought in marriage by many valiant gentlemen. Among them was Brunello, the son of the marquis of Vivien. Therefore, the king and the queen summoned their daughter, and after she arrived and they were all seated in the royal chamber, the king said, "Constanza, my beloved daughter, the time has now come to arrange your marriage, and we have found a husband for you who should be to your liking. He is the son of the great marquis of Vivien, one of our stewards. His name is Brunello, an attractive young man, admired by everyone for his valor. Moreover, he has not demanded anything from us except our own good grace and your own sweet self, which we consider worth more than any land or treasure in the world. You know, my daughter, that this is the only way I can arrange a marriage for you on account of my poor situation. Therefore, it is our will that you be content with all this."

The daughter, who knew who she was and that she came from a distinguished line of kings and queens, listened attentively to her father's words, and without wasting any time about the matter, she responded, "Your majesty, there is no need to waste many words in replying to your worthy proposal. I only want to address the matter at hand. First, I want to express my gratitude to you for all the affection and good will you have shown me in seeking to provide me with a husband without asking me. Now, with all due respect and obedience, I do not intend to let myself be degraded and fall beneath the progeny of my ancestors, who have always been famous and illustrious, nor do I wish to debase the crown you wear by marrying a husband who is our inferior. You, my beloved father, have produced four daughters, three of whom you have married in the most honorable fashion to three mighty kings, giving them great wealth and land. As for me, I have always been obedient and followed your rules, but I cannot let you arrange an inferior marriage for me. Let me, therefore, tell you in conclusion that I shall never take a husband unless, like my three sisters, I can wed a king of equal rank."

Shortly after this, Constanza shed many tears and took leave of the king and queen. She mounted a mighty steed and set forth from Thebes alone. Fortune was to be her guide as she rode off to an unknown destination. During her journey she decided to change her name from Constanza to Constanzo. She passed over many mountains and by lakes and ponds and saw many lands and heard various languages. She also studied the customs and manners of people who do not live their lives like human beings but more like beasts.

At last, one day at sunset, she arrived at the famous and celebrated city called Constanza, the capital of the region, and at that time under the rule of Cacco, king of Bettinia. After entering the city she began looking at the superb palaces, the straight spacious streets, the streams and large rivers, and the clear, trickling fountains. Then, when she approached the piazza, she saw the spacious and lofty palace of the king, adorned with columns of the finest marble and porphyry. When she raised her eyes somewhat, she saw the king, who was standing on a balcony from which he could see the entire piazza. Taking off her cap from her head, she greeted him with a respectful bow. When the king noticed the graceful and attractive young man down below, he had him summoned and brought into his presence. As soon as Constanzo stood before him, the king asked him where he was from and what his name was. The young man responded with a cheerful expression that he had come from Thebes, which he was forced to leave because of fickle and jealous fortune. He was seeking to join the service of some worthy gentleman and to pledge himself to work for this lord with all the faith and affection that good service required. The king was very pleased by the appearance of the young man and said to him, "Seeing that you already bear the name of my city, I would like you to be a member of my court with no other duty than to be my personal attendant. The young man, who could not have wished for anything better, first expressed his gratitude and then accepted the lord's offer and declared himself ready to undertake whatever the king wished.

So Constanza entered into the service of the king in the guise of a man named Constanzo, and he served him so well and gracefully that everyone who saw him was amazed and astonished. When the queen observed the elegant bearing, the laudable manners, and the discreet behavior of Constanzo, she began to pay more attention to him. Soon she could think only of him day and night, and she would throw such sweet and loving glances at him that, not only a young man but even the hardest rock or the most solid diamond would have been softened. The queen was so much in love with Constanzo that she yearned for nothing else than to be with him alone. Soon a convenient opportunity arose that allowed her to be with him, and she asked him whether it would be agreeable to him to enter into her service, making it known to him likewise that, by serving her, he would gain more than the gold coins she would give him and would be looked upon favorably by the entire court and also be respected and honored.

Constanzo clearly realized that these words the queen uttered did not spring from her good will but from amorous passion. Moreover, being a woman, he could not satisfy the hot unbridled lust which prompted them, and so with a sincere expression, he humbly replied, "Madam, my obligation that binds me to my lord your husband is such that it seems to me I would be doing him a grave injustice if I were to leave his service and disobey him. Therefore, please excuse me, for I am not ready and willing to serve you because I intend to serve my lord until I die, provided that he is satisfied with me."

Then, after taking leave of the queen, he departed. The queen, who was well aware that an oak tree cannot be cut down by a single stroke, tried many times after this with great cunning and art to entice the young man to enter her service. But he was as steadfast and as strong as a lofty tower beaten by tempestuous winds, and nothing could move him. When the queen realized this, her ardent and hot love was converted into mortal bitter hatred so that she could no longer bear the sight of him. She now wanted him dead, and she pondered day and night how she might best get rid of him, but she was very afraid of the king, who loved him and cared for him very much.

Now, in a certain district of the province of Bettinia, there were some savage creatures who were half human. Their upper part resembled that of a man, though they had ears and horns like those of animals. Their lower part was like that of a rough shaggy goat with a little tail twisted and curly like that of a pig. These creatures were called satyrs, and they were so indecent that they often caused great damage to the people in the

country and to their villages and farms. Therefore, the king greatly desired
to have one of these satyrs captured alive and placed under his control.
But there was no one courageous enough to undertake this adventure and
to capture a satyr for the king. Therefore, the queen began to scheme and
sought to bring about Constanzo's death by sending him on a mission to
hunt a satyr. But things did not turn out as she wished because the rug is
sometimes pulled out from under the schemer's feet, and the innocent
person remains standing thanks to divine providence and supreme justice.

The deceitful queen, who was well aware of the king's desire to capture
a satyr, happened to be conversing with him one day about different things,
and while they were talking, she said, "My lord, don't you know that
Constanzo, your faithful servant, is so powerful and strong that he has
enough vigor to go by himself and capture one of those satyrs and to bring
him back to you alive without the assistance of anyone. If this is indeed
the case, you can easily try asking him, and in the course of an hour, you
might have your heart's wish. As a brave and valiant knight, Constanzo
would score a triumph that would guarantee him everlasting fame."

The cunning queen's words pleased the king very much, and he immediately summoned Constanzo to appear before him and said, "Constanzo, if indeed you love me, as you have demonstrated and as everyone
believes you do, you will now fulfill my greatest wish, and you will also
win glory in the bargain. You are certainly aware that, more than anything
else in the world, I desire to have a satyr under my power. Therefore,
seeing how strong and energetic you are, I believe there is no other man
in my entire kingdom who could satisfy my wish as you can. So, if you
love me as you do, you will not refuse my request."

The young man, who knew exactly where this idea had originated, did
not want to disappoint the king. Instead, he sought to please him and said
with a cheerful face, "My lord, your wish is my command. No matter how
weak my powers may be, I shall not stop trying to fulfill your wishes, even
though I might meet with death. But before I begin this perilous undertaking, I request, my lord, that you transport a large vessel into the woods
where the satyrs dwell. It should have a wide mouth, the same size as that
which your servants use when they wash shirts and other kinds of garments.
Besides this, I should like your servants to bring a large cask of good white
wine, the best there is, and also the strongest, and two bags full of the
finest white bread."

The king immediately ordered all that Constanzo required, and then
the young man went into the woods of the satyrs. Once there he took a
copper bucket and began to fill it with wine from the cask, and in turn,
he poured the wine from the bucket into the large vessel which stood
nearby. Next, he took some bread and broke it into pieces which he put
into the vessel full of wine. After this was done, he climbed up a nearby
tree covered with leaves and waited to see what might happen next.

Well, no sooner did Constanzo climb up the tree than the satyrs, who
had smelled the odor of the fragrant wine, began to approach the vessel.
Once they were next to it, they began drinking their bellies full like hungry
wolves when they fall upon young lambs. And after they had filled their
stomachs and had taken enough, they lay down to sleep, and so sound

and deep was their slumber that all the noise in the world would not have roused them. When Constanzo saw this, he descended the tree and quietly went up to one of the satyrs and tied his hands and feet with a rope he had brought with him. Next, without making a sound, he hoisted the creature onto his horse and rode away. While Constanzo was on his return journey with the satyr tightly tied behind him, they came to a village not far from the city at vespers, and the savage, who had recovered from the effects of the wine, woke up and began to yawn as if he were rising from bed. Looking around him, he saw the father of a family and a crowd of people around him. They were about to bury a dead child, and the father was weeping. Meanwhile, the priest, who was conducting the service, was singing. When the satyr gazed at this spectacle, he began to laugh a great deal.

Afterward, when they had entered the city and arrived at the piazza, they saw another crowd of people who were staring attentively at a poor young fellow on the gallows who was about to be hung by the executioner. Again the satyr broke into laughter even louder than before.

Finally, when they reached the palace, everyone began to rejoice and cry out, "Constanzo! Constanzo!" When the satyr saw all this, he laughed louder than ever. After Constanzo was conducted into the chamber where the king, the queen, and her ladies were all waiting, he presented the satyr to the king. Once again the satyr burst into laughter, and he laughed so loud and long that all those who were present were quite astonished. When the king saw how Constanzo had fulfilled his wish, he regarded him with as much affection as any lord has ever extended to a servant. But this only tormented the queen all the more, who had believed that her words might lead to Constanzo's destruction while they only led to greater exaltation. Therefore, not being able to endure the sight of Constanzo's success, the wicked queen decided to set another trap for him. She knew that the king was accustomed to go every morning to the satyr's cell, where he would try to make the creature talk for his amusement. But as yet his efforts had all been in vain. Therefore, she went to the king and said, "Sire, you've gone to the satyr's cell over and over again, and you've exhausted yourself with your attempts to induce him to talk with you so you can amuse yourself. But the beast doesn't want to do this. Why should you then rack your brains about this any longer? Certainly, if Constanzo were only willing, he could easily make the satyr converse and answer your questions."

When the king heard these words, he immediately summoned Constanzo into his presence, and when the young man arrived, the king said, "Constanzo, I am sure you know what great pleasure I get from the satyr you captured for me. Nevertheless, I'm very irritated to find that he is mute and won't answer any of my questions. If you could only do something, I am sure that you'd be able to make him speak."

"Sire," Constanzo replied, "if the satyr is mute, what can I do? It is not within the limits of human power to endow him with speech but divine power. On the other hand, if his speech impediment is not a result of any natural or accidental defect, but comes from stubborn resolve to keep silent, I shall do all I can to make him speak."

Then they went together to the satyr's prison, where they gave him some

Constanza/Constanzo. Jules Garnier, 1894.

good food and even better wine and called out to him, "Eat, Chiappiono!" Indeed, Chiappiono was the name that had been given to the satyr. But the creature only stared at them and did not respond. Then they continued, "Come, Chiappiono, tell us whether you like the capon and the wine." But he still kept silent. Seeing how obstinate the satyr was, Constanzo said, "Well, if you won't answer me, Chiappiono, it will be all the worse for you because I'll let you die of hunger and thirst in this prison."

At this, the satyr shot a side glance at Constanzo.

"Answer me, Chiappiono," Constanzo went on. "If you speak to me, as I hope you will, I promise to set you free from this place."

Then Chiappiono, who had listened with eagerness to all that had been said, answered as soon as he heard mention of freedom.

"What do you want of me?" the satyr asked.

"Tell me," Constanzo replied, "have you enjoyed the wine and food?"

"Yes," said Chiappiono.

"Well, then, please tell me," said Constanzo, "why you laughed in the village street when we saw the dead boy being carried to his grave?"

"I did not laugh at the dead child," Chiappiono answered, "but at the father who was really not his father, and I laughed at the singing priest who was the real father."

Here the satyr indicated that the mother of the child had committed adultery with the priest. Then, Constanzo said, "And now, I would like to know, my Chiappiono, what it was that made you laugh even louder when we arrived at the piazza."

"I laughed," responded Chiappino, "because I saw a thousand or more thieves who had robbed the public of thousands of coins and deserved a thousand gallows. They were standing in the piazza gazing at a poor wretch being led to the gallows, and this poor fellow had perhaps merely stolen ten florins to buy bread for himself and his poor children."

Finally, Constanzo said, "Besides this, I'd like you to tell me what it was that made you laugh longer and louder than ever when we reached the palace?"

"Ah, please don't force me to talk any more at present," said Chiappiono. "Please go away and come back tomorrow, and then I'll tell you certain things that will perhaps be entirely new to you."

Thereupon, the king and Constanzo gave orders that Chiappiono be given good things to eat and drink so that he would be ready to talk all the more the next day. Then they departed.

When the next day arrived, they both returned to see Chiappiono, and they found him breathing and snoring like a fat pig. When they approached him, they cried out to him several times in a loud voice, but Chiappiono, who had filled his belly with a good deal of food, did not respond. Then Constanzo stuck him with a dart which he had in his hand, and the satyr jumped up and asked who was there.

"Now, wake up, Chiappiono!" said Constanzo. "Tell us what you promised you would tell us yesterday. Why did you laugh so loudly when we came to the palace?"

"You know better than I," replied Chiappiono. "It was because they were all shouting 'Constanzo! Constanzo!' while all the time you are Constanza."

The king did not grasp what Chiappiono was inferring, but Constanzo had understood everything and immediately cut him off so that Chiappiono could not continue.

"And when you were conducted to the king and queen," Constanzo quickly said, "what made you laugh so much again?"

"I laughed so much," he said, "because the king, and you as well, believed that the ladies-in-waiting who were serving the queen were really ladies, when most of them were young men."

At this point, the satyr became silent. When the king heard these words, he did not know what to think and said nothing. After leaving the wild satyr, he stood with Constanzo and wanted to know exactly what the satyr had meant by everything he said. After he inquired, he learned that Constanzo was a woman and not a man, and that the beautiful ladies attending the queen were young men, as Chiappiono had said.

Immediately, the king gave orders to have a great fire built in the middle of the piazza, and in front of all the people, he had the queen and her lovers tossed into the fire to burn. In light of the commendable loyalty and true fidelity of Constanza, not to mention her great beauty, the king married her in the presence of all his barons and knights. When he learned who her parents were, he was even more joyful and sent ambassadors to King Ricardo and his wife, Valeriana, and to the three sisters of Constanza to tell them that she was now the wife of a king. When they heard the good news, they were extremely pleased, as might be expected. Thus, the noble and generous Constanza, in reward for the faithful service she rendered, became a queen and lived a long time with Cacco her husband.

GIAMBATTISTA BASILE

The Three Crowns†

Once upon a time there was a king of Vallescossa who could not have children, and thus, wherever he was, he constantly cried out, "Oh Heaven, please send me an heir for my kingdom so that my line will not be desolated!" On one of these occasions, when he was in a garden and loudly lamenting and uttering these words, he heard a voice coming from the bushes that said:

> "King, what do you prefer,
> a daughter, who flees you,
> or a son who destroys you?"

† Giambattista Basile, "The Three Crowns"—"Le tre corone" (1634), *Sesto passatempo della quarta giornata* in *Lo cunto de le cunti overo Lo trattenemiento de peccerille*, De Gian Alessio Abbattutis, 5 vols. (Naples: Ottavio Beltrano, 1634–36).

Bewildered by this proposal, the king did not know exactly what to answer and thought it would be best to consult the wise men of his court. So he immediately went back to his chambers, where he summoned his councillors and ordered them to reflect about his case. One of them answered that it would be advisable to hold honor in higher regard than life. Someone else said that more value should be placed on life as the primary good than on honor, which was a secondary one and therefore should not be regarded in the same way as life. Another maintained that it did not matter if one lost one's life, which flowed away like running water. Nor were riches important, for they were like the columns of life that propped up the brittle wheel of fortune. On the other hand, honor was a durable thing and left its imprint of fame and traces of glory. Therefore, it must be carefully and jealously guarded. Another councillor argued that, since life maintains the lineage of a house, and wealth maintains its greatness, both should be regarded higher than honor, which is an opinion pertaining to virtue, and for a father to lose his daughter through a stroke of bad luck and not through his own fault was not prejudicial to the father's virtue or the honor of the house. Finally, there were other councillors who concluded that honor was not dependent on the blouse of a woman, and moreover, that a just prince must consider the welfare of his people more than his own interests and that a daughter who flees her father causes only a little shame for the father's house, but a malicious son could set the house and the entire realm on fire and bring them down. Therefore, if the king desired children and had these two choices, he should ask for a daughter. In this way he would not endanger his life or the kingdom.

This advice pleased the king, who returned to the garden, and after making his usual lament and hearing the same voice reply, he said, "A girl, a girl." And after he returned to his home in the evening—when the sun invites the hours of the day to take a look at the dwarfs of the Antipodes[1]—he went to bed with his wife, and nine months later he had a beautiful daughter. From that moment on, he had her shut in a solid palace and carefully guarded. These were the precautions he took, as far as he could, to remedy the sad destiny of his daughter, who was raised with all the proper virtues suitable for a royal family. When she was fully grown, he began to arrange a marriage for her with the king of Perditesta. As soon as the marriage agreement was reached, the king's daughter left the palace, which she had never left before, to be sent to her husband. But a whirlwind swept her off her feet, and she was never seen again.

The wind carried her through the air for a long time and finally set her down before the house of an ogress in the middle of a forest that had banished the sun like a person infected with the plague for having killed Python, who was poisonous.[2] There she found an old woman, whom the

---

1. A reference to people of the Antipodes, who, at that time, were thought to be like savages or pygmies, living in America. This was all supposition in Basile's time, but America was considered to be on the opposite side of the globe and to be inhabited by pygmies.
2. Reference to Apollo, who killed the snake Python that guarded the oracle at Delphi. Since the snake was poisonous and Apollo was infected, he had to go to Tempe to be purified. His victory over the Python symbolizes the triumph of the sun or spring over winter.

ogress had left to guard her things, who said, "Oh, how bitter your life is! Do you know where you've arrived? You poor thing! If the ogress of this house returns, your skin will not be worth even three pennies because she eats nothing but human flesh. My life is safe only because she needs my services and because her fangs are loath to bite my poor skin full of cuts from accidents from breaking wind and gravel. But there is something we can do! Here are the keys of the house. Go inside, set the rooms in order, and clean everything. When the ogress returns, hide yourself so that she can't see you. I'll make sure that you get something to eat. In the meantime, who knows? Heaven may help. Time can bring good things with it. Enough: with discretion and patience one can sail into any gulf and survive any storm."

Marchetta—this was the maiden's name—made a virtue out of necessity and took the keys. She entered the ogress's room, picked up the broom, and made the house so clean that one could have eaten macaroni off the floor. Then she took a piece of lard and polished the walnut chests and made them glisten so brightly that you could have seen yourself in the reflection. Next, she made the bed, and when she heard the ogress arrive, she hid herself in a cask in which grain had been stored. Upon finding the place so unusually clean, the ogress was greatly pleased and called the old woman.

"Tell me who has done such a wonderful job of cleaning?" she asked. And, when the old woman answered that she was the one, the ogress commented, "Whoever does what he's not supposed to do has either deceived you or is going to deceive you. You should really cross yourself on this special day. You've done something unusual, and you deserve a great deal of soup."

After saying this, the ogress ate and went forth again. When she returned, she found all the spider's webs cleaned away from the beams, all the copper pots and pans polished and hung neatly on the walls, and all the dirty clothes soaking in water. She felt such incredible joy that she blessed the old woman a thousand times and said, "May heaven always reward you, Madam Pentarosa, so that you prosper and things go well for you, for you have warmed my heart by all your work and by making my place into a doll's house with a bed fit for a bride."

The old woman was ecstatic when she heard such praise and always gave Marchetta chunks of good food such as pieces from a stuffed capon. As soon as the ogress went forth again, the old woman said to Marchetta, "Pay attention because I'm tired of our limping along at this slow pace and want to try your fortune. So I want you to make something with your hands that will change the ogress's mood. But, if she begins to swear by all the seven heavens, don't believe her. However, if she happens to swear by her three crowns, then you can let yourself be seen, for everything will have gone as planned, and you'll see that I've given you advice that only a mother would give."

After hearing these words, Marchetta slaughtered a beautiful goose and made a good stew with its feet. After stuffing it with lard, oregano, and garlic, she stuck the goose on the spit. Then she prepared four gnocchi in a basket and decorated the table with roses and citron leaves. When the ogress returned and saw everything prepared like this, she almost jumped out of her clothes for joy, while calling for the old woman.

"Who did this good work?" she asked.

"Eat," replied the old woman, "and don't ask any questions. It should be enough that you are served and satisfied."

As the ogress ate and enjoyed the good pieces down to the tips of her toes, she began to say, "I swear by the three words of Naples[3] that if I knew who the cook was, I would give him my eyelashes." Then she continued. "I swear by the three bows and arrows that if I got to know him, I would take him to my heart. I swear by the three candles which are lit when a contract is being signed at night; by the three witnesses who are necessary to have a man hung; by the three feet of rope that are used to hang the man; by the three things that drive a man out of his house: stench, smoke, and a nasty woman; by the three things that consume a household: fritters, fresh bread, and macaroni; by the three women and a goose that form a market; by the three primary singers of Naples: Giovanni della Carriola, Compare Biondo, and the King of Music; by the three S's necessary for a lover: solitude, solicitude, and silence; by the three things necessary for a merchant: credit, courage, and luck; by the three types of men that a courtesan cultivates: braggarts, handsome young cavaliers, and blockheads; by the three things important for a thief: vision, slight hands, and fast feet; by the three things that ruin young men: cards, women, and drink; by the three qualities that a constable must have: watchfulness, perseverance, and the ability to arrest someone; by the three things useful for a courtier: pretense, patience, and luck; by the three things a panderer must have: chatter, little shame, and brashness; by the three things a doctor must observe: the pulse, the face, and the chamber pot"—and she could have gone on talking until the next day, but Marchetta, who had been well advised did not appear. Then, finally, the maiden heard, "By my three crowns, if I know who the good housewife who has done so many fine favors for me is, I shall give her more hugs and caresses than she can imagine."

So, Marchetta came out and said, "Here I am!"

When the ogress saw her, she responded, "Well, I'll be darned. You've outsmarted me! You've got a masterly touch, and you've also escaped a good baking in my belly. Now, since you've shown that you know so much and know how to please me, I am more attached to you than to a daughter. So here are the keys of the house and do as if you were the lord and master of this place. I shall make only one condition: this one key fits the door of the last room, and you are never to open it for whatever reason. If you do, you would make my blood rush to my head. Continue to serve me, and you will be rewarded, for I promise you by my three crowns that I shall marry you to a rich man."

Marchetta kissed her hands out of gratitude and promised to work for her like a slave. But when the ogress had departed, she felt strongly pricked

3. Reference to an old proverb that claims three things are necessary for whoever stays at Naples: *vroccole, zuoccole, trapole*—cunning, churlishness, deceit.

by curiosity to see what was inside the forbidden room. Therefore, she opened the door and found three maidens dressed completely in gold, seated on three thrones, who seemed to be asleep. These were the three daughters of the ogress, who had cast a magic spell on them because she knew their lives would be threatened if they were not wakened by the daughter of a king. So, they were locked in the room to protect them from the dangers forecast by the stars.

Now, as soon as Marchetta entered the room, the noise of her footsteps roused them, and when they awoke, they asked for something to eat, and Marchetta went at once and fetched three eggs for each one of them. Then she cooked them and brought them to the maidens. As soon as they felt refreshed, they wanted to go outside, but just at that moment, the ogress arrived and became so enraged that she gave Marchetta a slap in the face. This hurt the maiden so much that she immediately requested permission from the ogress to depart so she could wander about the world and seek her fortune. Now the ogress sought to appease Marchetta with gentle words and said that she had only been joking and would never do anything like this again, but it was impossible to change Marchetta's mind. So the ogress was obliged to let her depart and gave her a ring, telling her to wear it with the stone turned to the inside of her hand and never to look at it unless, when in grave danger, she were to hear her name repeated by an echo. In addition to this, the ogress gave Marchetta some good-looking men's clothes that she had requested. After putting them on, Marchetta set out on her journey and arrived in a forest where night went to fetch wood to warm herself because of the recent frost. Just then she met a king who had been hunting, and when the king saw the handsome young man—this was how Marchetta appeared to him—he asked him where he had come from and where he was going. Marchetta responded by saying he was the son of a merchant, and since his mother had died and his stepmother was so oppressive, he had fled his home. The king was pleased by the frankness and good manners of Marchetta and made her his page and took the "young man" to his palace.

As soon as the queen saw the page, she felt as if a bomb of grace had exploded in the air around her and had ignited all her desires. She tried for a few days, partly out of fear, partly out of pride, which is always riveted to beauty, to conceal the flame of passion and keep the prickly points of love beneath the tail of desire. But she was too short in the saddle to ride herd and to be able to keep down her unbridled desires. This is why she called Marchetta aside one day and began to reveal to him how tormented she felt and to tell him how she had been struck by great pangs of longing as soon as she had seen his handsome figure and that if he would not water the land of her desires, she would soon dry up as would all her hope of living. In addition, she said marvelous things about the beauty of his face and made clear that it would be a mistake by a bad scholar in the school of love if he were to make a blot of cruelty in such a charming book, and he would deserve a spanking of remorse. Aside from praising him to the sky, she added prayers imploring him by all the seven heavens not to leave her in a furnace of sighs and a mire of tears, especially since she kept his beautiful image as a sign in the shop of her thoughts. She followed all this with offers, promising to pay every bit of pleasure with tons of gifts and to keep the bank of gratitude open for whatever such a dear client might need. Finally, she reminded him that she was the queen, and since she was now on the ship, he could not leave her in the middle of the sea without help because she could possibly crash against a reef because of him.

Marchetta listened to these florid words and attacks, these promises and threats, these face-washings and dressing-downs and would have liked to have said that he lacked the key to open the door to her joys. He would have liked to explain that he did not carry the staff of Hermes and thus could not give her the peace that she wanted. But since Marchetta did not want to unmask herself, she replied that it was impossible to believe that the queen wanted to make a cuckold out of a king so worthy as her husband. Moreover, even if the queen did not care about damaging the reputation of her house, he could not and would not commit such a wrong against a master who loved him so much.

When the queen heard this retort to the proclamation of her desires, she said, "All right, but think carefully and plow straight because people of my rank command when they ask, and when they kneel down, they stamp right on your face. Therefore, make sure you know how to keep your accounts and see how much you might profit in this affair! Enough is enough! One more thing I'll tell you, and then I'll leave. When a woman of my stature has been offended, she will try to wash off the stain on her face with the blood of the offender." And with these words and a terrible glare, she turned her back on Marchetta and left the poor maiden confused and frozen in her tracks.

The queen continued her assault on the beautiful fortress a few more days, and when she finally perceived that all her work was in vain, that she had exhausted herself uselessly, that her words had been cast to the wind without bearing any fruit, and that her sighs were made to the empty air, she changed her tune, and her love was transformed into hate, and her desire to enjoy the object of her love was turned into a desire for revenge. So, pretending to cry, she went to her husband and said, "Who would have ever thought, my dear husband, that we were nourishing a snake in our midst? Who would have ever imagined that such a miserable little wretch like that would be so impudent? But you're entirely to blame because of your excessive kindness. If you give a villain an inch, he'll take a foot. In short, everyone wants to piss in the chamberpot. But if you don't give him the punishment he deserves, I'll return to my father's house, and I'll never want to see you or hear your name again!"

"What did he do to you?" asked the king.

"Oh, nothing at all!" the queen replied. "The little rogue just wanted to exact the debt of matrimony that I owe to you, and without any respect, without any fear, without any shame, he had the impudence to come to me and the brashness to ask me for a free way into the field that you have so honorably ploughed."

Upon hearing this news, the king did not see other witnesses because he did not want to question the word and authority of his wife. Instead, he had his guards seize Marchetta at once, and in the heat of the moment, without giving him a chance to defend himself, he condemned him to test the weight of the executioner's sword. When Marchetta was abruptly taken to the place of execution, not knowing what had happened or what crime she had committed, she began to cry out, "Oh, Heaven, what have I done to deserve the funeral of this poor neck before the burial of this wretched body? Who would have ever told me that, without enrolling myself under the banner of thieves and delinquents, I would enter into this palace of Death with three feet of rope around my neck and surrounded by guards? Alas, who will comfort me as I take my last steps? Who will help me in this grave danger? Who will free me from this plight?"

"The ogress!" responded the echo, and when Marchetta heard the reply, she remembered the ring that she wore on her finger and the words the ogress had spoken as she had departed. Now she looked at the stone, which she had never looked at until that moment, and, lo and behold, a voice resounded three times in the air:

"Let her go! She's a woman!"

The voice was so terrifying that neither the guards nor the assistants remained with the executioner, and when the king heard these words that shook the foundations of the palace, he had Marchetta brought to his presence and ordered her to tell the truth, who she was, and how she had happened to come to his country. Spurred by necessity, she told him all the events of her life, how she was born, how she had been locked in a palace, how she had been whisked away by a wind, how she landed at the house of the ogress, how she had left that place, what the ogress had given her and told her, what had happened between her and the queen, and how, not knowing what she had done wrong, she found herself up the creek without any oars.

When the king heard this story and compared it with that which he knew from talking one time with his friend the king of Vallescossa, he recognized Marchetta for what she really was, and at the same time he grasped the maliciousness of his wife, who had put Marchetta in this ugly mess. So, he ordered his wife to be thrown into the sea with a weight tied around her. Then he invited Marchetta's mother and father to a banquet and made Marchetta his wife, and thus he proved:

God will heed
A ship in need.

MARIE-CATHERINE D'AULNOY

Belle-Belle; or, The Chevalier Fortuné†

Once upon a time, there was a very good, mild, and powerful king, but his neighbor, the emperor Matapa, was more powerful. They had waged great wars with one another, and the emperor had won a tremendous battle in the last war. After killing the greater portion of the king's officers and soldiers or taking them prisoner, he besieged and conquered the king's capital city. Consequently, he took possession of all its treasures, and the king had just enough time to save himself with the queen, his sister, who had become a widow at a very early age. She was intelligent and beautiful, and to tell the truth, she was also proud, violent, and difficult to approach.

The emperor sent all the jewels and furniture that had belonged to the king back to his own palace, and he carried away an extraordinary number of soldiers, women, horses, and anything else that he found useful or pleasant. After he had ravaged the greater part of the kingdom, he returned triumphant to his own, where he was received by the empress and the princess, his daughter, with great joy. In the meantime, the defeated king was not inclined to sit down and accept his misfortune lightly. He rallied some troops around him and gradually formed a small army. To increase this army as quickly as possible, he issued a proclamation requiring all the noblemen of his kingdom to come and serve him in person, or to send one of their sons, well-mounted and armed, who would be disposed to support all his ventures.

Now there was an old nobleman, eighty years of age, who lived on the frontier of the kingdom. He was a wise and prudent man, but fortune had not been kind to him so that he found himself reduced almost to poverty after he had been quite wealthy at one time. He would have accepted all this if he had not been compelled to share his fate with three beautiful daughters. They were so understanding that they never complained about their misfortunes, and if by chance they talked about them to their father, it was more to console him than to add to his troubles. They lived with him under a rustic roof without the least desire to seek a better life. When the king's proclamation reached the ears of the old man, he called his daughters to him, looked at them sorrowfully, and said, "What can we do? The king has ordered all the noblemen of his kingdom to join him in order to fight against the emperor, and if they refuse, he intends to levy a heavy tax. I'm not in a position to pay the tax, and therefore I'm in a terrible dilemma. This will either be my ruin or the death of me."

His three daughters were just as much distressed as he himself, but they encouraged him to keep up his spirits, for they were convinced that they would find some way out of this predicament. Indeed, the next morning

---

† Marie-Catherine d'Aulnoy, "Belle-Belle; or, The Chevalier Fortuné"—"Belle-Belle, ou le Chevalier Fortuné," in *Contes nouveaux ou les fées à la mode*, 2 vols. (Paris: Veuve de Théodore Girard, 1698).

the eldest daughter went looking for her father, who was walking sadly in an orchard that he looked after himself.

"Sire," she said, "I've come to ask your permission to join the army. I'm tall and strong enough, and I'll dress myself in male attire and pass for your son. Even if I don't perform any heroic deeds, I'll at least save you the journey or the tax, and that is a great deal in our situation."

The count embraced her affectionately and, at first, objected to such an extraordinary proposition, but she argued so convincingly that there was no other solution that he finally consented. There was nothing to be done now but to provide her with the clothes suitable to the person she was to represent. Her father furnished her with arms and gave her the best of his four plough-horses. Then they said their tender farewells to each other. After traveling some days, she passed through a meadow that had a quickset hedge[1] on its borders. There she saw a shepherdess in great distress. She was trying to drag one of her sheep out of a ditch into which it had fallen.

"What's the matter, good shepherdess?" she asked.

"Alas!" replied the shepherdess, "I'm trying to save my sheep. It's drowning, and I don't have the strength to drag it out."

"Well, I'm sorry about your plight," she said and rode off without offering her any help.

The shepherdess immediately cried out, "Good-bye, disguised beauty!"

Our lovely heroine was totally surprised when she heard that. "How is it possible," she remarked to herself, "that I could be so easily detected? That old shepherdess only saw me for a moment, and yet she knew that I was disguised! Where am I to go now? Everyone will know who I am, and if the king finds out, my shame will be great, and so will his anger. He'll think my father's a coward, who shrinks from danger."

After much reflection, she decided to return home. The count and his daughters were talking about her and counting the days she had been gone when they saw her enter. She told them about the incident with the shepherdess. The good man responded that he had warned her about this and that, if she had listened to him, she would never have set out because it was impossible not to detect a girl in man's clothes. Now this little family was once again in a predicament and did not know what to do. Then the second daughter went to the count in her turn and said, "My sister had never been on horseback, so it's not surprising that she was discovered. If you'll allow me to go in her place, I promise that you'll be satisfied with me."

Nothing the old man could say to oppose her intention had an effect on her. So he was forced to consent, and she put on some other clothes, took other arms, and another horse. After she had equipped herself, she embraced her father and sisters a thousand times and was determined to serve the king bravely. But in passing through the same meadow where her sister had seen the shepherdess and her sheep, she saw her again at the bottom of the ditch trying to drag the sheep out.

"Unfortunate creature that I am!" cried the old woman. "Half my flock

_____

1. A thicket formed of living plants.

has perished this way. If someone would help me, I could save this animal, but everybody flees from me."

"How come you take so little care of your sheep, shepherdess, that they fall into the water?" the fair cavalier asked, and without giving her any other consolation, she spurred her horse and rode on.

The old woman called out after her with all her might, "Good-bye, disguised beauty!"

These words troubled our amazon very much. "What bad luck that she's recognized me too! Now I've experienced what my sister experienced. I'm not any luckier than she was, and it would be ridiculous for me to join the army with such an effeminate appearance that everybody would know who I am!"

She returned at once to her father's house and was quite disturbed at having made such an unsuccessful journey. Her father received her affectionately and praised her for having had the good sense to return. But that did not prevent him from grieving. In addition, he had been put to the expense of purchasing two useless suits of clothes and several other things. The good old man, however, kept his sorrow to himself so that he would not add to that of his daughters.

At length the youngest girl came to him and begged him in the most urgent manner to grant her the same permission he had granted her sisters. "Perhaps," she said, "it's presumptuous of me to hope I'll succeed where they haven't. Nevertheless, I'd like to try. I'm taller than they are, and as you know, I go hunting every day. This exercise qualifies me in some degree for war, and my great desire to relieve you in your distress inspires me with extraordinary courage."

The count loved her more than either of her sisters. She cared for him in such a way that he regarded her as his chief consolation. She read interesting stories to amuse him, nursed him in his illness, and gave him all the game she killed. Consequently, he did all he could to change her mind and argued much more so than he had done with her sisters. "Do you want to leave me, my dear child?" he asked. "Your absence will be the death of me. If fortune should really smile on you, and you should return covered with laurels, I won't have the pleasure of witnessing them. My old age and your absence will bring about my end."

"No, my dear father," said Belle-Belle (for this was her name). "You needn't think I'll be away that long. The war will soon be over, and if I find any other way of fulfilling the king's orders, I won't hesitate to take advantage of them. I want to assure you, if my absence will be upsetting to you, it will be even more distressing to me."

At last he granted her request, and she made a very plain suit of clothes for herself because her sisters' clothes had cost too much, and the poor old count's finances would not allow much more expense. She was also compelled to take a very bad horse since her two sisters had nearly crippled the other two, but all this did not discourage her. She embraced her father, received his blessing with respect, and as her tears flowed with his and those of her sisters, she departed.

In passing through the meadow I have already mentioned, she found the old shepherdess, who still had not yet recovered her sheep, or she was trying to pull another out of the middle of a deep ditch.

"What are you doing there, shepherdess?" Belle-Belle stopped and asked.

"I can't do anything more, my lord," the shepherdess replied. "Ever since daylight I've been trying to save this sheep. It's been all in vain, and I'm so weary, I can scarcely breathe. There's hardly a day that passes when some new misfortune doesn't happen to me, and there's nobody to help me."

"I'm truly sorry for you," Belle-Belle said, "and to prove this, I'm going to help you."

She instantly dismounted from her horse, which was so calm that she did not take the trouble to tie it to anything to prevent its running away. She scratched herself somewhat as she jumped over the hedge. Then she plunged into the ditch and worked so hard that she succeeded in dragging out the sheep. "Don't cry anymore, my good mother," she said to the shepherdess. "Here's your sheep. Despite the fact that it's been in the water a long time, I think it's quite lively."

"You won't find me ungrateful," the shepherdess said. "I know you, charming Belle-Belle. I know where you're going, and what your intentions are. Your sisters passed through this meadow, and I recognized them as well, and I knew what was going on in their minds. But they appeared so heartless and they behaved in such an ungracious way that I managed to interrupt their journey. Things will be different in your case, and I'll prove it to you, Belle-Belle, for I'm a fairy and take pleasure in rewarding those who deserve it. For instance, you have a miserably poor horse, and now I'll give you a real one." She struck the ground as she spoke with her crook, and all at once Belle-Belle heard a neighing behind a bush. She turned quickly and saw the most beautiful horse in the world, which began to run and prance about in the meadow.

Belle-Belle, who was fond of horses, was delighted to see one as perfect as that. The fairy called this fine stallion to her and, touching it with her crook, she said, "Faithful Comrade, I want you to be harnessed better than the emperor Matapa's best horse." Within seconds Comrade had on a saddlecloth of green velvet, embroidered with pearls and rubies, a saddle to match, and a bridle of pearls with a bit and studs of gold. In short, there was not a horse in the world as magnificent as this one. "You've only seen the least remarkable thing about this horse," the fairy said. "He has many other qualities that I'll enumerate. In the first place, he eats only once a week. You don't have to look after him, for he knows the present, the past, and the future. I've had him a long time, and I've trained him as if he were my own horse. Whatever you wish to know, or whenever you need advice, you only have to talk to him. He'll give you such good counsel that most sovereigns would be happy to have ministers like him. Consequently, you must consider him more as your friend than your horse. Lastly, your dress is not to my liking, and I want to give you one more becoming."

She struck the ground with her crook, and a large trunk covered with

Turkey leather appeared. It was studded with gold nails, and Belle-Belle's initials were on it. The fairy looked in the grass for a golden key made in England. She opened the trunk, which was lined with Spanish leather and embroidered in a profuse manner. There were twelve suits of clothes in it, twelve cravats, twelve swords, twelve feathers, and so on; everything in dozens. The coats were covered with so much embroidery and diamonds that Belle-Belle could hardly lift them. "Choose the suit that pleases you the most," the fairy said, "and the others will follow you everywhere. You need only to stamp your foot, saying 'Turkey-leather trunk, come to me full of linen and lace; Turkey-leather trunk, come to me full of jewels and money,' and it will instantly appear before you, whether you are outdoors or in your room. You must also adopt a name, for Belle-Belle will not suit the profession you're about to enter. It occurs to me that you might call yourself the Chevalier Fortuné. But you ought to know who I am. Therefore, I'll appear to you in my usual form." All of a sudden the old woman's skin was discarded, and the fairy appeared so astonishingly beautiful that she dazzled Belle-Belle. Her dress was made of blue velvet, trimmed with ermine; her hair entwined with pearls, and her head, adorned by a superb crown.

Belle-Belle was carried away by her admiration and threw herself at the fairy's feet as a show of her respect and inexpressible gratitude. The fairy raised her and embraced her affectionately. She told her to put on a suit of green-and-gold brocade, and Belle-Belle obeyed her orders. Afterward she mounted her horse and continued her journey so overwhelmed by all the extraordinary things that had just happened that she could not think about anything else.

Eventually she began to wonder about the unexpected good luck that helped her attract the kindness of such a powerful fairy, "Because really," she said, "she didn't need me to save the sheep. A simple stroke of her wand would have brought a whole flock back from the Antipodes, if it had wandered off there. I was very lucky to have been in a position to oblige her. The trifling service I did for her is the cause of all she's done for me. She knew my heart and approved of my sentiments. Ah, if my father could see me now, so magnificent and so rich, how delighted he would be! But at any rate, I'll have the pleasure of sharing the fortune she has given me with my family."

As she finished making these different observations, she arrived in a beautiful city that had a large population. She attracted a great deal of attention, and the people followed her and gathered around her. "Have you ever seen a cavalier more handsome, better built, or more handsomely dressed?" they cried out. "Look how gracefully he manages that superb horse!" They saluted him most respectfully, and he returned their greetings with a kind and courteous air. As soon as he entered the inn, the governor, who had been out walking and had admired him in passing, sent a gentleman to say that he hoped he would come and make his lodgings in his castle. The Chevalier Fortuné (in short we must use this name now when talking about Belle-Belle) replied that since he had not yet had the honor of making his acquaintance, he would not take that liberty. However, he would go and pay him his respects. In addition, Fortuné requested one of

the governor's people, whom he could trust with something of consequence that he wanted to send to his father. The governor responded
immediately and sent him a very trusty messenger, and Fortuné asked him
to come again since his letters were not ready yet.

He shut himself in his room, and stamping with his foot, he said,
"Turkey-leather trunk, come to me filled with diamonds and coins!"
Within seconds it appeared, but there was no key, and where was he to
find it? What a pity to break a lock made of enameled gold of different
colors! Moreover, he could not trust a locksmith. All he would have to do
would be to talk about the chevalier's treasures, and thieves would be there
to rob him, and perhaps they might even kill him.

He looked for the key everywhere, and the more he searched for it, the
less it seemed he would find it. "How disturbing!" he cried. "I won't be
able to make use of the fairy's generosity, nor send my father any of the
things she's given me." While he was musing this way, it occurred to him
that the best thing would be to consult his horse. So he went to the stable
and said in a whisper, "I beg you, Comrade, tell me where I can find the
key of the Turkey-leather trunk."

"In my ear," the horse replied.

Fortuné looked in the horse's ear and saw a green ribbon, which he
drew out and upon which he found the key he needed. He opened the
Turkey-leather trunk, which contained more than a bushel of diamonds
and coins. The chevalier filled three caskets, one for his father, and two
others for his sisters. Then he gave them to the man the governor had sent
to him and told him not to stop, either night or day, until he arrived at
the count's house.

This messenger made great headway, and when he told the old man
that he came from his son, the chevalier, and that he had brought him a
very heavy casket, the count wondered what could be in it because Belle-
Belle had started with so little money that he did not think she was in a
condition to buy anything or even to pay the journey of the man who was
in charge of his present. But after opening her letter and reading all that
his dear daughter had written, he thought he would die from joy. The
sight of the jewels and gold confirmed the truth of the story even more.
The most extraordinary thing was that, when Belle-Belle's two sisters
opened their caskets, they found bits of glass instead of diamonds and false
coins instead of real ones, for the fairy did not want them to benefit from
her kindness. Consequently, they thought their sister was laughing at them
and felt extremely angry at her. However, the count noticed how irritated
they were with her and gave them the greater part of the jewels he had
just received. As soon as they touched them, they changed like the others.
Therefore, they concluded that an unknown power was working against
them and begged their father to keep the rest for himself.

The handsome Fortuné did not wait for the return of his messenger
before he left the city. His business was too urgent and he was bound to
obey the king's orders. He paid his visit to the governor, at whose house
everyone had assembled to see him. His personality and actions revealed
such an air of goodness that they could not help but admire and adore
him. He said nothing except what was pleasant to hear, and there were so

many people around him that he did not know how to account for such
an extraordinary circumstance. Indeed, he was not accustomed to seeing
so many people because he had spent his entire life in the country.

He continued his journey on his excellent horse, which amused him
by telling him a thousand stories or about the most remarkable events in
ancient and modern history. "My dear master," he said, "I'm delighted to
belong to you. I know you possess a good deal of frankness and honor.
I've had my fill of certain people with whom I lived a long time, and who
made me weary of my life because their circle of friends was unbearable.
Among them was a man who pretended to be my friend and who placed
me above Pegasus and Bucephalus[2] when he spoke in my presence. But
as soon as I was out of sight, he treated me as a jaded and sorry horse. He
pretended to admire my faults in order to induce me to commit greater
ones. It's true that one day, when I became tired of his caresses, which
properly speaking were treacherous, I gave him such a severe kick that I
had the pleasure of knocking nearly all the teeth out of his mouth. Whenever I've seen him since then, I've told him with great sincerity that it's
not right for his mouth to be as handsome as others because he opens it
too often to abuse those who do him no harm."

"Ho! ho!" the chevalier cried. "You're full of spirit. Aren't you afraid
that someday in the heat of passion this man will pass his sword through
your body?"

"It wouldn't matter, my lord," Comrade replied. "Anyway, I'd be aware
of his intention before he even knew it himself!"

They were in the midst of this conversation when they approached a
vast forest, and Comrade said to the chevalier, "Master, there's a man who
lives here who may possibly be of great service to us. He's a woodcutter,
and one who has been endowed with gifts."

"What do you mean by that term?" Fortuné interrupted.

"I mean that he's received one or more gifts from fairies," the horse
replied. "You must hire him so he'll accompany us."

Just then they reached the spot where the woodcutter was working, and
the young chevalier approached him with a gentle and winning air. He
asked him several questions about the place they were in, whether there
were any wild beasts in the forest, and whether he was allowed to hunt
there. The woodcutter responded to everything like an intelligent man.
Fortuné then inquired what had happened to the men who had been
helping him chop down so many trees. The woodcutter replied that he
had chopped them down all by himself, that it had taken him only a few
hours, and that he had to cut down many others to make a load for himself.

"What! Do you mean you'll carry off all this wood today?" the chevalier
asked.

"Oh, my lord, this is not difficult, for my strength is extraordinary,"
replied Strongback (which is what people called him).

"So you make a great deal of money, I suppose?" Fortuné said.

2. The name of Alexander the Great's charger, associated with magnificent horses of power. "Pegasus": in Greek mythology, the winged horse that allegedly sprang from the blood of Medusa;
   represented as the favorite steed of the muses, Pegasus is said to bear poets in their flights of
   imagination.

"Very little," the woodcutter replied. "The people are poor in this place. Everyone works for himself without asking for his neighbor's help."

"Since you live in such a poor country," the chevalier remarked, "there is nothing holding you back from leaving and traveling to another. Come with me, and you'll have everything you want. Whenever you think it's time to return, I'll give you money for your journey."

The woodcutter thought he would never get a better offer than this one. So he put down his axe and followed his new master. Then as they were passing through the forest, they saw a man in an open space who appeared to be tying his legs tightly together with some rope so that he could hardly walk. Comrade stopped and said to his master, "My lord, here's another gifted man. You can use him, and I suggest that you take him with you."

Fortuné approached this man and, with his usual grace, asked him, "Why are you tying your legs like that?"

"I'm going hunting," he said.

"What!" the chevalier said, smiling. "Do you mean to say you can run better when your legs are bound like that?"

"No, my lord," he replied. "I'm aware that I won't be very fast, but that's my intention. There's not a stag, roebuck, or hare that I can't outrun when my legs are free. The result is that I always run right by them, and they escape. So I rarely have the pleasure of catching them!"

"You seem to be an extraordinary man," Fortuné said. "What's your name?"

"They call me Swift," the hunter replied, "and I'm well known in this country."

"If you'd like to see another," the chevalier responded, "I'd be very happy if you'd come with me. You won't have difficult things to do, and I'll treat you kindly."

Swift was not particularly well off. So he gladly accepted the offer proposed to him, and Fortuné continued his journey, followed by his new servants.

The next morning he saw a man on the border of a marsh. He was binding his eyes, and the horse said to his master, "My lord, I advise you to hire this man as well."

Fortuné immediately asked him why he was binding his eyes.

"I see too clearly," he said. "I can spot any game more than four miles away, and I always kill more than I wish when I shoot. Therefore, I'm obliged to bind my eyes, for there wouldn't be any game left if I were to catch a glimpse of the animals around me."

"You're very talented," replied Fortuné.

"They call me Sharp Shooter," the man said, "and I'll never abandon this occupation for anything in the world."

"Well, despite what you've just said, I'd like to invite you to travel with me," the chevalier said. "You won't be prevented from exercising your talent."

Sharp Shooter made some objections, and the chevalier had more difficulty in persuading him than the others because sportsmen are generally fond of their freedom. However, Fortuné eventually succeeded and left the marsh with his new servant.

Some days later he passed by a meadow in which he saw a man lying on his side, and Comrade said, "Master, this man is gifted. I can see that you'll need him very much."

So Fortuné entered the meadow and asked the man what he was doing.

"I need some herbs," he replied, "and I'm listening to the grass as it grows to find out which ones I'll need."

"What!" the chevalier remarked. "Are your ears so sharp that you can hear the grass grow and know what's about to sprout?"

"That's why they call me Fine Ear," said the man.

"Very well, Fine Ear," Fortuné continued, "would you like to join me? I'll give you such high wages that you won't have any regrets."

The man was delighted by such an agreeable proposition and joined the others without hesitation. The chevalier continued his journey, and along the way he saw a man whose cheeks were so inflated that they made a very droll effect. He was standing with his face toward a lofty mountain two miles away where fifty or sixty windmills were standing. The horse said to his master, "Here's another of our gifted ones. Do all you can to get him to come with you."

Fortuné, who had a fascinating power over everyone he encountered, approached this man and asked him what he was doing there.

"I'm blowing a little, my lord," he said, "I want to get all those mills working."

"It appears to me you're too far off," the chevalier replied.

"On the contrary," the blower remarked, "I find I'm too near, and if I didn't retain half of my breath, I'd upset the mills, and perhaps the mountains they're standing on. I do a great deal of harm this way without intending to, and I can tell you, my lord, that once, when my mistress had treated me very badly, I went into the woods to indulge my sorrow, and my sighs tore the trees up by their roots and created a great deal of confusion. So, in this region, they now call me Boisterous."

"If they're tired of you," Fortuné said, "and you'd like to come with me, I have some men with me who'd keep you company, and they also possess extraordinary talents."

"I have such a natural curiosity for anything that's unusual," Boisterous replied, "that I accept your offer."

Fortuné was very pleased and proceeded on his way. After passing through a densely wooded country, he came to a large lake that was fed by several springs. On the side of the lake was a man, who was looking at it very attentively. "My lord," Comrade said to his master, "this is the man you need to complete your group. You'd do well if you could induce him to join you."

The chevalier approached him immediately and said, "Will you tell me what you're doing there?"

"My lord," the man replied, "you'll see as soon as this lake is full. I intend to drink it in one gulp, for I'm still thirsty, although I've already emptied it twice."

Accordingly, he stooped down to drink, and in a few minutes there was hardly enough water left for the smallest fish to swim in. Fortuné was just as surprised as his followers. "My, are you always so thirsty?" he asked.

"No," the man said. "I only drink like this when I've eaten something too salty or made a bet. I'm known in this region as Tippler."

"Come with me, Tippler," said the knight. "I'll give you some wine to tipple, which you'll find much better than spring water."

This promise pleased the man very much, and he decided on the spot to join the others. The chevalier had now arrived within sight of the general meeting place set for the king's forces, and he noticed a man eating so greedily that, although he had more than sixty thousand loaves of Gonesse bread in front of him, he seemed determined to eat every last crumb. Then Comrade said to his master, "My lord, all you need is this man. Please make him come with you."

The chevalier approached him, smiled, and said, "Are you determined to eat all this bread for your breakfast?"

"Yes," he replied. "All I regret is that there's so little, but the bakers are lazy fellows and refuse to extend themselves, whether you're hungry or not."

"If you need so much every day," Fortuné remarked, "there is hardly a country you wouldn't bring to the brink of starvation."

"Oh, my lord," replied Eater (as the people called him), "I'd regret it if I always had such a huge appetite. Neither my property nor that of my neighbors would be enough to satisfy it. To tell the truth I only like to feast in this fashion every now and then."

"My friend Eater," Fortuné said, "join me, and I'll give you good cheer, and you won't regret choosing me for a master."

Comrade, who had plenty of good sense and forethought, warned the chevalier to forbid his men to boast about the extraordinary gifts that they possessed. So he lost no time in gathering them around him and said, "Listen to me, Strongback, Swift, Sharp Shooter, Fine Ear, Boisterous, Tippler, and Eater. I would appreciate it very much if you would not tell a soul about your talents. In return, I shall also guarantee to try to make you happy and completely satisfied."

Each one of them took an oath to obey Fortuné, and soon after, the chevalier, who stood out more on account of his natural beauty and his graceful demeanor than on account of his magnificent dress, entered the capital city on his excellent horse and was followed by the finest attendants in the world. He lost no time in procuring uniforms for them, laced all over with gold and silver, and he gave them horses. Then, after taking lodgings in the best inn, he awaited the day set for the review. However, he was now the talk of the city, and the king, who had been made aware of his reputation, was very eager to meet him.

When all the troops assembled on a great plain, the king went there with the queen, his sister, and the entire court. The queen had not given up her pomp despite the misfortunes of the kingdom, and Fortuné was dazzled by so much splendor. But if the king and his sister attracted his attention, they were just as much struck by his incomparable beauty. Everyone asked who that handsome and graceful young gentleman was, and the king, who passed close by him, gave him a signal to approach. In response, Fortuné got down from his horse immediately to make a low bow before the king. He could not help blushing when the king gazed at him so earnestly. This additional color heightened the radiance of his complexion.

"I'd like to know from yourself," he said, "who you are, and what your name is?"

"Sire," he replied, "I'm called Fortuné, without having any reason for bearing this name up to now, for my father, who's a count on the frontier, has been living in great poverty, although he was born of a rich and noble family."

"Fortuné, whoever has served as your godmother," the king replied, "has done well to bring you here. I feel a particular affection for you, and I remember that your father once rendered me a great service. I'll reward him by favoring his son."

"That's quite just of you, brother," said the queen, who had not spoken yet. "And since I'm older than you and know more details than you do about the service that the count of the frontier rendered the state, I request that you let me take care of rewarding this young chevalier."

Fortuné was enchanted by his reception and could not sufficiently thank the king and queen. He did not, however, venture to exaggerate his feeling of gratitude because he believed it would be more respectful to be silent than to talk too much. The little he did say was so correct and so much to the point that everyone applauded him. Afterward he remounted his horse and mixed among the noblemen, who accompanied the king, but the queen called him away every minute to ask him a thousand questions, and, turning toward Floride, who was her favorite confidante, she said softly, "What do you think of this chevalier? Have you ever seen anyone with a more noble demeanor or more regular features? I confess to you, I've never seen anyone more charming."

Floride agreed with the queen wholeheartedly and lavished a good deal of praise on the chevalier, for he was just as charming to her as to her mistress. Fortuné could not help staring at the king from time to time. He was the handsomest prince in the world, and his manners were most engaging. Belle-Belle, who had not renounced her sex with her dress, felt sincerely drawn to him. The king told Fortuné after the review that he feared the war would be a very bloody one, and that he had decided to keep Fortuné near him. The queen, who was present, exclaimed that she had also been thinking the same thing, that he ought not to be exposed to a long campaign, that the place of premier maître d'hôtel was vacant in her household, and that she would give it to him.

"No," the king said. "I intend to make him my squire."

Then they argued with one another as to who would have the pleasure of promoting Fortuné. Since the queen was afraid of revealing the secret emotions that were already exciting her heart, she yielded to the king's wish to acquire the services of the chevalier.

Hardly a day passed that Fortuné did not call for his Turkey-leather trunk and take out a new garment. He was certainly the most magnificent prince at the court. Sometimes the queen asked him how his father could afford to give him such clothes. Other times she would jest with him. "Tell the truth," she said, "you have a mistress, and she's the one who sends you all the beautiful things we see."

Fortuné blushed, and replied respectfully to the various questions the queen put to him. He also performed his duties remarkably well. He had become very appreciative of the king's merits and became more attached to him than he had wanted. "What's my fate?" he said. "I love a great king without any hope of his loving me. Nor will he ever know what I'm suffering."

On his part, the king overwhelmed him with favors, and he found nothing to his liking unless it was done by the handsome chevalier. Meanwhile the queen, deceived by his dress, seriously thought about how she could arrange a secret marriage with him. The inequality of their birth was the only thing that troubled her. However, she was not the only one who entertained such feelings for Fortuné. The most beautiful women at the court were taken with him. He was swamped with tender letters, assignations, presents, and a thousand gallantries, but he replied to all of them with so much indifference that they were certain he had a mistress in his own country. No matter how much he tried to be modest at the great entertainments of the court, he always distinguished himself. He won the prize at all the tournaments. He killed more game than anyone else when he went hunting. He danced at all the balls with more grace and skill than any of the courtiers. In short, it was delightful to see and hear him.

The queen, who was anxious to be spared the shame of declaring her feelings for him by herself, asked Floride to make him understand that the many signs of kindness from a young and beautiful queen ought not to be a matter of indifference to him. Floride was very much taken aback by this task, for she had not been able to avoid the fate of all those who had seen the chevalier, and she thought it would be too nice on her part to give her mistress's interests precedence over her own. So whenever the queen gave her an opportunity of talking to him, she told him only about the queen's bad temperament and what her women took from her instead of speaking about her beauty and great qualities. Floride also told him how unjustly she treated her attendants and how badly she abused the power she had usurped in the kingdom. Finally, she drew a comparison between their feelings and said, "I wasn't born a queen, but really I ought to have been one. I have so much generosity in my nature that I'm eager to do good for everybody. Ah! If I were in that high station," she continued, "how happy I'd make the handsome Fortuné. He'd love me out of gratitude, even if he could not love me from inclination."

The young chevalier was quite dismayed by this conversation, and did not know what to answer. Therefore, he carefully avoided these tête-à-têtes with her, and the impatient queen never failed to ask her what impression she had made for her on Fortuné. "He thinks so little about himself," she said, "and he's so bashful that he won't believe anything I tell him about you, or he pretends not to believe it because he's absorbed by something else."

"I think so too," said the alarmed queen. "But I can't imagine that he'd curb his ambition to advance himself."

"And I can't imagine," Floride replied, "that you'd use your crown to capture his heart. You're so young and beautiful and possess thousands

of charms. Is it necessary for you to take recourse in the splendor of a
diadem?"

"One may have to take recourse in anything possible," the queen replied, "if it becomes necessary to subdue a rebellious heart."

Floride saw clearly that it was impossible to put an end to her mistress's
infatuation in him. Each day the queen expected some positive result from
the confidante's work, but she made so little progress with Fortuné that
the queen was eventually compelled to seek some way of talking with him.
She knew that he usually took a walk very early every morning in a little
wood in front of the windows of her apartment. So, she arose at daybreak,
and as she watched the path he was likely to take, she saw him approaching
with a melancholy and distracted air. Then she called Floride right away.
"You've spoken the truth," she said. "Fortuné is without a doubt in love
with some lady at this court, or in his own country. See how sad he looks."

"I've noticed this sadness in all his conversations," Floride replied, "and
you'd do well if you could forget him."

"It's too late," the queen exclaimed, sighing deeply. "Since he's already
entered that green arbor, let's go there. I want only you to come with me."

The girl did not dare to stop the queen no matter how much she wanted
to do so, for she feared she would induce Fortuné to fall in love with her,
and a rival of such exalted rank is always very dangerous. As soon as the
queen had taken a few steps into the wood, she heard the chevalier singing.
His voice was very sweet, and he had composed these words to a new
melody:

> "How rare a thing it is for love and peace
> To dwell together in the same heart!
> When my joys begin to surge, my fears increase,
> That they, like a morning dream, will soon depart!
> Dread of the future robs my soul of rest,
> Most unhappy I am when most blessed!"

Fortuné had made up these verses out of his feelings for the king, out
of the favor the king had shown him, and out of his fear of being recognized and forced to leave a court that he preferred above all others in the
world. The queen, who stopped to listen, was extremely distressed. "What
shall I do?" she whispered softly to Floride. "This ungrateful young man
doesn't want to honor or please me. He thinks he's happy. He seems
satisfied with his conquest, and he sacrifices me to another."

"He's at that age," Floride replied, "when reason has yet to establish its
rights. If I may venture to give some advice to your majesty, it would be
to forget such a giddy fellow, who's not capable of appreciating his good
fortune."

The queen would have preferred it if her confidante had spoken to her
in a different manner. She cast an angry look at her and hastily moved on
and entered the arbor where the knight was. She pretended to be surprised
to find him there and to be upset at his seeing her in such disarray,
although she had taken great pains to make herself magnificent and attractive. As soon as she appeared, he would have withdrawn out of respect

for her, but she asked him to remain so that he might assist her in walking.

"I was wakened this morning most pleasantly by the singing of the birds. The fine weather and the pure air induced me to go out and listen more closely to their warbling. How happy they are! Alas, all they know is pleasure. Grief does not trouble them!"

"It appears to me, madame," Fortuné replied, "that they're not entirely exempt from pain and sorrow. They're always in danger of the murderous shot or the deceitful snares of hunters. Moreover, there are also the birds of prey which make war against these little innocent ones. When a hard winter comes, freezes the ground, and covers it with snow, they die for want of hemp or millet seed, and every year they have difficulty finding a new mistress."

"So you think, then, chevalier," the queen said, smiling, "that this is a difficulty? There are men who have a fresh one each month in the year, but you appear surprised by this, as if your heart were not of the same stamp, and as if you would not be susceptible to change your heart like this!"

"I'm not able to predict how I'd act," the chevalier said, "for I've never been in love, but I believe that, if I did form an attachment, it would end only when I died."

"You've never loved?" cried the queen, looking so earnestly at him that the poor chevalier changed color several times. "You've never been in love? Fortuné, how can you possibly say this to a queen, who reads in your face and your eyes the passion that occupies your heart? I heard the words you sang to the new melody that's just become so popular."

"It's true, madame," the chevalier replied, "that those lines are my own. My friends ask me every day to write drinking songs for them, although I never drink anything but water. There are others who prefer love songs. So I sing about love and Bacchus, without being a lover or a drinker."

The queen listened to him with so much emotion that she could scarcely keep standing. All that he told her rekindled the hope in her bosom that Floride had sought to extinguish. "I'd think you were sincere," she said, "but I'd indeed be surprised if you hadn't found one lady at this court sufficiently lovely to attract your attention."

"Madame," Fortuné replied, "I try so hard to carry out the duties of my office that I have no time for sighing."

"You love nothing, then?" she responded vehemently.

"No, madame," he said, "my heart is not so gallant. I'm a kind of misanthrope, who loves his liberty and doesn't want to lose it for anything in the world."

The queen sat down and gave him the kindest of looks. "There are some chains so beautiful and glorious," she replied, "that anyone might feel happy to wear them. If fortune has made this your destiny, I'd advise you to renounce your liberty."

As she spoke, her eyes revealed her meaning too clearly for the chevalier to mistake what she meant. He had already very strong suspicions and was now entirely convinced they were right. Fearing the conversation might lead even further, he looked at his watch and moved the hand up a little.

"I must beg your majesty to permit me to go to the palace," he said. "It's time for the king to get up, and he asked me to be there."

"Go, callous youth," she said, sighing profoundly. "You're doing the right thing by paying court to my brother, but remember, it's not wrong to pay some attention to me."

The queen followed him with her eyes, then let them fall. After reflecting on what had just happened, she blushed with shame and rage. Her grief was further augmented by the fact that Floride had witnessed everything, and she noticed an expression of joy on her face, which seemed to tell her she would have done better had she taken her advice instead of speaking to Fortuné. She thought about all this for some time. Then she took her tablets and wrote these lines, which she had set to music by a celebrated court composer:

> Behold! Behold! The torment I endure!
> My victor knows but covers the clue.
> My heart shows, but it can't have a cure,
> Still stung by the shaft he's shot so true.
>
> He's not concealed his coldness or disdain,
> He hates me, and his hate I should return;
> But ah, my foolish heart tries in vain,
> For it only has love for him to burn!

Floride managed to play her part with the queen in a clever way: she consoled her as much as she could and gave her some hope that the queen needed to keep her going. "Fortuné thinks himself so beneath you, madam," she said, "that perhaps he didn't understand what you meant. It seems to me that he's already said a good deal by assuring you that he doesn't love anyone."

It is so natural for us to have certain expectations that the queen was eventually encouraged to think she had a chance with Fortuné. She was unaware that the malicious Floride, who knew all about the chevalier's indifference for her, wished to induce him to speak even more explicitly so that he would offend the queen by his cool answers.

As far as Fortuné was concerned, he was most confused. It seemed to him that he was caught in a cruel predicament. He would not have hesitated to leave the court, if his love for the king had not detained him in spite of himself. He never went near the queen except when she held her court, and then always in the king's entourage. She noticed this change in his conduct instantly, and she gave him the opportunity of paying her some attention several times without his doing so. But one day, as she descended into her gardens, she saw him cross one of the grand avenues and suddenly enter the little wood. She called to him, and he was afraid of displeasing her by pretending not to hear and therefore approached her respectfully.

"Do you remember, chevalier," she said, "the conversation we had together some time ago in the green arbor?"

"I'd never forget that honor," he answered.

"No doubt the questions I put to you then were distressing," she said.

"Ever since that day you've avoided me so that I haven't been able to ask you any more questions."

"Since it was chance alone that gave me that opportunity," he said, "I thought it would be presumptuous of me to seek another one."

"Why don't you say instead that you've been avoiding my presence, you ungrateful man?" Then she added, blushing, "You know quite well how I feel about you."

Fortuné cast down his eyes in an embarrassed and modest manner, and since he hesitated to reply, she continued, "You seem very disconcerted. Go! Don't try to answer me. Your actions speak louder than words."

She would have perhaps said more, but she saw the king coming their way. She advanced toward him, and upon noticing how melancholy he was, she asked him to tell her the reason.

"You know," the king said, "that about a month ago I received news that an enormous dragon was ravaging the country. I thought my soldiers could kill him and issued the necessary orders for that purpose. But they've tried everything in vain. He devours my subjects, their flocks, and anything he encounters. He poisons all the rivers and springs wherever he quenches his thirst and ruins the grass and the herbs that he lies down on."

While the king was talking to her, it occurred to the irritated queen that this would be a good opportunity to take her resentment out on the chevalier. "I'm aware of the bad news you received. As you saw, Fortuné was just with me and told me all about it. But, brother, you'll be surprised at what I have to tell you. He's implored me most insistently to ask you for permission to go and fight this terrible dragon. Indeed, he's so skilled in the use of arms that I'm not surprised he's willing to dare so much. Besides, he's told me he has some secret power that he can use to put the most lively dragon to sleep but that must never be mentioned because it doesn't reveal much courage in the action."

"No matter how he does it," the king replied, "it will bring him great glory and be of great service to us, if he succeeds. But I fear he may be overzealous and it will cost him his life."

"No, brother," the queen added, "there's no need to fear. He's told me some surprising things about all this. You know that he's naturally very sincere, and thus he has no intention of dying so rashly. In short, I've promised to obtain what he wants, and if you refuse him, it will kill him."

"I consent to what you desire," the king said. "But I confess, I'm doing this with a great deal of reluctance. So, now let us call him." He then made a signal for Fortuné to approach and said to him kindly, "I've just learned from the queen that you want to fight the dragon that is devastating our country. It's such a bold decision that I can hardly believe you've considered the danger involved in it."

"I've depicted all this to him," the queen said. "But he's so eager to serve you and to distinguish himself that nothing can dissuade him, and I predict he'll be successful."

Fortuné was very surprised by what the king and queen said to him. He quickly grasped the queen's wicked intentions, but his timidity would not permit him to expose them. So he did not respond and simply let her continue talking. He contented himself by making low bows so that the king thought he was now pleading with him directly to grant him what he desired. "Go, then," the king said, sighing, "go where glory calls you. I know you're very skillful in everything you do, especially in the use of weapons, so perhaps this monster won't be able to avoid your blows."

"Sire," the chevalier replied, "no matter what the outcome of this combat is, I'll be satisfied. Either I'll rescue you from a terrible scourge, or I'll die for you. But grant me one favor that's very dear to me."

"Ask for whatever you wish," said the king.

"May I be bold enough to ask for your portrait," Fortuné said.

The king was very pleased that he would think about his portrait at a time when he should have been occupied with other things, and the queen resented once again that he did not make the same request to her. However, he would have had to possess superabundance of goodness to desire the portrait of such a wicked woman.

The king returned to his palace, and the queen to hers. Fortuné was now in a predicament due to the pledge he had made. So he went to his horse and said, "My dear Comrade, I've got a good deal of news to tell you."

"I know it already, my lord," he replied.

"What shall we do then?" Fortuné asked.

"We must set out right away," the horse said. "Go and get the king's order that will command you to fight the dragon, and then we'll do our duty."

These words consoled our young chevalier, and the next morning he awaited the king in a riding dress that was just as handsome as the others that he had taken from the Turkey-leather trunk. As soon as the king saw him, he exclaimed, "What! You're ready to go?"

"Your commands cannot be executed too quickly, sire," he replied. "I've come to take my leave of your majesty."

The king could not help but feel pity for Fortuné, seeing that he was such a young, handsome, and accomplished gentleman, and that he was about to expose himself to the greatest danger man could ever confront. He embraced him and gave him his portrait surrounded by large diamonds. Fortuné accepted it with great joy, for the king's noble qualities had made such an impression on him that he could not imagine anyone in the world more charming. If Fortuné was upset at leaving him, it was much less from the fear of being devoured by the dragon than from that of being deprived of the presence of one so dear to him.

The king added a general order to Fortune's commission, calling upon all his subjects to aid and assist Fortuné whenever he might be in need. After that, Fortuné took leave of the king and went to the queen so that nothing might be taken amiss. She was sitting at her dressing table and was surrounded by several of her ladies. She changed color when he appeared, and she began reproaching herself for what she had done to him. He saluted her respectfully and asked her if she would honor him with her commands since he was on the point of departure. These last words completely disconcerted her, and Floride, who did not know that the queen had plotted against the chevalier, was thunderstruck. She would have liked to have had a private conversation with him, but he carefully avoided such an embarrassing situation.

"I pray to the gods," the queen said, "that you may conquer the dragon and return triumphant."

"Madame," the chevalier replied, "your majesty does me too much of an honor. You're sufficiently aware of the danger to which I shall be exposed. However, I'm full of confidence. Perhaps, on this occasion, I'm the only one who has hope."

The queen understood very well what he meant. No doubt she would have replied to this reproach if there had been fewer persons present. The chevalier returned to his lodgings and ordered his seven excellent servants to get their horses and follow him since the time had arrived to prove what they could do. There was not one who did not rejoice at being able to serve him. In less than an hour everything was ready, and they set out with him, assuring him they would do their utmost to carry out his commands. In short, as soon as they had reached the open country and had no fear of being seen, each one gave proof of his talent. Tippler drank the water from the lakes and caught the finest fish for his master's dinner. Next, Swift hunted the stags and caught a hare by its ears, despite its vast speed. Sharp Shooter gave no quarter to the partridges and pheasants, and after the game was killed and the fish were taken out of the water, Strongback carried everything cheerfully. Even Fine Ear made himself useful: he found truffles, morels, mushrooms, salads, and fine herbs by listening to where they were growing in the ground. So Fortuné rarely had to pay anything to cover the expenses of his journey. He would have been amused a great deal at the sight of so many extraordinary things, if he had not been so troubled by all that he had just left. The king's qualities continued to impress him, and the queen's malice seemed so great to him that he could not help hating her. As he was riding along lost in thought, he was aroused from his reverie by the shrieks of several poor peasants, whom the dragon was attacking. At the same time, he saw some who had escaped and were running away as fast as they could. He called to them, but they would not stop. So he followed and spoke to them, and he learned that the monster was not far off. He asked them how they had managed to escape, and they told him that water was very scarce in the country. They had only rainwater to drink and had made a pond to conserve it. After making his rounds, the dragon went to drink there and uttered such tremendous roars when he arrived there that he could be heard a mile away. Then everybody became so alarmed that they hid themselves and locked their doors and windows.

The chevalier entered an inn, not so much to rest as to get some good advice from his handsome horse. After everyone had retired, he went into the stable and asked, "Comrade, how are we going to conquer this dragon?"

"My lord," he said, "I'll dream about it tonight, and tell you what I think tomorrow morning."

Accordingly, the next morning, when the chevalier came again, the horse said, "Let Fine Ear listen if the dragon is close by." Fine Ear laid himself down on the ground and heard the roars of the dragon, who was about seven miles away. When the horse was informed of this, he said to Fortuné, "Tell Tippler to go and drink up all the water in the great pond, and make Strongback carry enough wine there to fill it. Then you must put dried raisins, pepper, and several other things around the pond that will make the dragon thirsty. Order all the inhabitants to lock themselves up in their houses. And you, my lord, must stay there and lay in wait with your attendants. The dragon won't fail to come and drink at the pond. He'll like the wine very much, and then you'll see how it will all end."

As soon as Comrade had indicated what was to be done, they all took care of what they had to do. The chevalier went into a house that overlooked the pond. No sooner did he do this than the frightful dragon arrived at the pond and drank a little. Then he ate some of the breakfast they had prepared for him, and he drank more and more until he became quite intoxicated. Finally, he was unable to move and lay on his side. His head hung down, and his eyes were closed. When Fortuné saw him in this state, he knew he did not have a moment to lose. So he emerged from the house, sword in hand, and courageously attacked the dragon. The dragon was wounded on all sides and tried to stand up so he could fall on the chevalier, but he did not have the strength because he had lost too much blood. The chevalier was overjoyed that he had reduced him to this sorry state. He called his attendants to bind the monster with cords and chains so that the king would have the pleasure and glory of putting an end to his life. Once there was nothing more to fear from the beast, they dragged him to the city. Fortuné marched at the head of his little troop, and on approaching the palace, he sent Swift to the king with the good news of his great success. However, it seemed incredible to everyone until they actually saw the monster tied on a machine constructed for the purpose.

The king descended and embraced Fortuné. "The gods have reserved this victory for you," he said. "I feel more joy at your safe return than at the sight of this horrible dragon reduced to this condition, my dear chevalier."

"Sire," he replied, "it would please me if your majesty would give the monster his death blow. I brought him here so you could deliver it."

The king drew his sword and terminated the existence of one of his most cruel enemies. Everybody uttered shouts of joy at such unexpected success. Floride, who had been worrying all the time, soon heard about the return of the handsome chevalier. She ran to tell the queen, who was so astonished and confounded by her love and her hatred that she could not respond to what her confidante told her. She reproached herself hundreds of times for the malicious trick she had played on him, but she preferred to see him dead than so indifferent to her. She did not know whether she should be pleased or sorry that he had returned to the court, where his presence would again disturb her peace.

The king was eager to tell his sister about the extraordinary event, and he entered her chamber, leaning on the chevalier's arm. "Here's the conqueror of the dragon," he said. "He has performed for me the greatest service that I could have ever demanded from a faithful subject. You were the one, madam, to whom he first expressed his desire to fight this monster.

I hope you'll appreciate the courage with which he exposed himself to the greatest danger."

The queen composed herself and honored Fortuné with a gracious reception and a thousand praises. She thought him handsomer than when he went away, and the way she looked at him indicated that her heart was not cured of its wound.

Indeed, she did not want to leave it up to her eyes alone to explain how she felt. So, some days later, as she was hunting with the king, she stopped following the hounds and said she felt suddenly indisposed. Then, turning to the young chevalier, who was near her, she said, "Do me the pleasure of remaining with me. I want to get down and rest a little. Go," she continued speaking to those who accompanied her, "don't leave my brother!" She got off her horse with Floride and sat down by the side of a stream, where she remained for some time in deep silence, trying to think of the best way to start the conversation.

Finally, she raised her eyes and fixed her glance on the chevalier. "Since good intentions are not always obvious," she said, "I fear you did not grasp the motives that induced me to convince the king to send you to fight the dragon. I had a presentiment that never misleads me and felt sure that you'd prove yourself to be brave. Your enemies didn't think highly of your courage because you didn't join the army. That's why it was necessary, I felt, for you to perform some action to stop their tongues from wagging. I should have told you what they had been saying about you, and perhaps I ought to have done so, but I feared the consequences that might have resulted from your resentment. So I thought it might be better for you to silence such evil-minded people by showing your intrepid conduct in danger rather than by exerting influence on them, which would mark you as a favorite not as a soldier. You see now, chevalier, that I wanted to do something that might contribute to your glory, and you'd be very wrong if you were to judge otherwise."

"The distance is so great between us, madame," he replied modestly, "that I'm not worthy of the explanation you've been so kind to give me, nor the care you took to imperil my life for the sake of my honor. The gods protected me with more beneficence than my enemies had hoped, and I'll always regard myself lucky to serve the king or you and to risk my life, the loss of which is a matter of more indifference to me than one might imagine."

This respectful reproach from Fortuné annoyed the queen, for she totally comprehended the meaning of his words, but he was still too pleasant to her for her to feel alienated by such a sharp reply. On the contrary, she pretended to sympathize with his feelings and made him tell her again how skillfully he had conquered the dragon.

Fortuné had taken good care not to tell anyone how his men had helped him defeat the dragon. He boasted that he had faced this redoubtable enemy alone, and that his own skill and his courage, even to the point of rashness, had enabled him to triumph. The queen scarcely paid attention to what he was saying to her and interrupted him to ask whether he was now convinced of her sincere concern in his affairs. She would have pressed the matter further, but he interrupted her and said, "Madame, I hear the sound of the horn. The king's approaching. Does your majesty want your horse to go and meet him?"

"No," she said spitefully. "It's sufficient for you to do so."

"The king would blame me, madame," he added, "if I were to leave you by yourself in such a dangerous place."

"I can dispense with your attention," she replied in an imperative tone. "Be gone! Your presence annoys me!"

At this command, the chevalier made her a dignified bow, mounted his horse, and disappeared from her sight, very concerned about how she would react to this fresh offence. Consequently, he consulted his fine horse. "Let me know, Comrade," he said, "if this queen, who's much too passionate and too angry, is going to find another monster for me."

"No, she won't find another one," the handsome horse replied. "But she herself is more of a dragon than the one you've killed, and she'll certainly put your patience and your virtue to the test."

"Won't she cause me to fall out of favor with the king?" he cried. "That's all I fear."

"I won't reveal the future to you," Comrade said. "You've just got to know that I'm always on the alert."

He stopped speaking, for the king appeared at the end of an avenue. Fortuné joined him and told him the queen had not felt well and had commanded him to stay near her.

"It appears to me," the king said smiling, "you're very much in her good graces, and you speak your mind to her rather than to me, for I've not forgotten that you asked her to procure you the glorious opportunity of fighting the dragon."

"I won't dare to contradict you, sire," the chevalier replied, "but I can assure your majesty I make a great distinction between your favors and those of the queen, and if a subject were permitted to make a confidant of his sovereign, I'd find it a most delightful pleasure to declare my feelings to you."

The king interrupted him by asking him where he had left the queen. Meanwhile, the queen was complaining to Floride of Fortuné's indifference to her. "I'm finding the sight of him more and more hateful!" she cried. "Either he must leave the court, or I must withdraw from it. I can no longer tolerate the presence of an ungrateful youth who has dared to show me so much contempt. Any other mortal would consider himself happy to please a queen who's so powerful in her kingdom! He's the only one in the world who doesn't. Ah! The gods have selected him to disturb the tranquillity of my life!"

Floride was not at all sorry that her mistress was so displeased with Fortuné, and far from endeavoring to oppose her displeasure, she increased it by recalling a thousand other disturbing things that the queen had perhaps not wanted to notice. Thus her rage increased, and she began devising some new way to ruin the poor chevalier.

As soon as the king had rejoined her and expressed his concern about her health, she said, "I confess I was very ill, but it's difficult to remain that way with Fortuné around. He's so cheerful, and his ideas are quite amusing. So I must tell you, he's implored me to obtain another favor from your majesty. He's asked, with the greatest confidence of success, to be allowed to undertake the rashest enterprise in the world."

"What now, sister?" cried the king. "Does he want to fight another dragon?"

"Several all at once," she said, "and he's sure he'll triumph. Do you want me to tell you? Well, then, he boasts he'll compel the emperor to restore all our treasures, and he doesn't even need an army to achieve this."

"What a pity," the king replied, "that this poor boy has to exaggerate so much!"

"His fight with the dragon has made him think of nothing but great adventures," the queen remarked. "But what risk do you run if you permit him again to serve you this way?"

"I risk his life, which is dear to me," the king replied. "I'd be extremely sorry to see him throw it away so recklessly."

"No matter what you decide, he's bound to die," she said. "I guarantee that his desire to go and recover your treasures is so strong he'll pine to death if you refuse him permission."

The king felt deeply distressed. "I can't imagine," he said, "how these pipe dreams got into his head. I'm extremely disturbed to see him in this condition."

"The fact is," the queen replied, "he's fought the dragon and conquered him. Perhaps he'll be equally successful in his adventure. I'm seldom deceived by my presentiments, and my heart tells me he'll also complete this mission successfully. Please, brother, don't oppose his zeal."

"Let him be called," the king said. "At any event, I must inform him about the risk he'll run."

"That's just the way to exasperate him," the queen replied. "He'll think you won't let him go, and I assure you he won't be deterred by any consideration for himself, for I've already said all that can be thought about the subject."

"Well, then," the king cried, "let him go. I consent."

The queen was delighted with this permission and sent for Fortuné. "Chevalier," she said, "thank the king. He's granted you the permission you desired so much—to seek out the emperor Matapa, and by fair words, or by force, recover the treasures that he's taken from us. Prepare to depart with as much speed as you did when you went to fight the dragon."

Fortuné was very surprised and realized to what extreme the queen's malice and fury would drive her. However, he felt pleasure in being able to lay down his life for a king who was so dear to him. So without objecting to this extraordinary task, he knelt and kissed the king's hand; the king, for his part, was moved very much. The queen felt a degree of shame in witnessing the respect with which he received this order to encounter certain death.

"Can it be possible," she said, "that he has some affection for me, and that rather than disavow what I've tried to do on his behalf, he prefers to suffer the harm I've done him without a complaint? Ah! If this were true, I'd wish a good deal of harm to myself for having caused him so much!"

The king said very little to the chevalier. He remounted his horse, and the queen entered her chariot again, feigning a return of her indisposition. Fortuné accompanied the king to the end of the forest and then re-entered it to have some conversation with his horse. "My faithful Comrade," he said, "it's all over. I must die. The queen has planned everything in a way I'd never have expected."

"My charming master," the horse replied, "don't alarm yourself. Although I wasn't present when everything happened, I've known about it for some time. The mission isn't as terrible as you imagine."

"You don't realize that this emperor is the most ruthless man in the world," the chevalier said, "and if I suggest to him that he restore all that he has taken from the king, he'll answer me only by having me strangled and thrown into the river."

"I've heard about his violent ways," Comrade said, "but don't let that prevent you from taking your attendants with you. If you perish there, we'll all perish together. However, I hope we'll have better luck than that."

The chevalier was somewhat consoled by this. He returned home, issued the necessary orders, and then went and received the king's commands along with his credentials. "You'll tell the emperor from me," he said, "that I demand my subjects whom he holds in bondage, my soldiers who are prisoners, my horses which he rides, my goods, and my treasures."

"What shall I offer him in exchange for all these things?" Fortuné asked.

"Nothing," replied the king, "but my friendship."

The young ambassador's memory was not overburdened by his instructions. He departed without seeing the queen, and she was offended by this, but he had no reason to treat her with respect. Anyway, what more could she do to him in her greatest rage than she had already done in her greatest love for him? Feelings of this kind appeared to him to be the most dreadful thing in the world. Her confidante, who knew the entire secret, was exasperated with her mistress for wanting to sacrifice the flower of all chivalry.

Fortuné took all that was necessary for his journey in the Turkey-leather trunk. He was not simply satisfied with dressing himself in magnificent clothes, but he also wanted his seven attendants, who accompanied him, to make as good an appearance. Since they all had excellent horses, and since Comrade seemed to fly through the air rather than to gallop over the ground, they soon arrived in the capital city in which the emperor Matapa resided. It was larger than Paris, Constantinople, and Rome put together and had so many people that all the cellars, garrets, and lofts were inhabited.

Fortuné was surprised to see such a tremendous city. He demanded an audience with the emperor, but when he announced the purpose of his mission, even though he did this with a good deal of grace that made his speech more effective, the emperor could not help smiling. "If you were at the head of five hundred thousand men," he said, "one might listen to you, but they tell me you only have seven."

"I've not undertaken this task, my lord," Fortuné said, "to get you to restore what my master wishes by force but by my very humble remonstrances."

"It doesn't matter which way you choose," the emperor responded.

"You'll never succeed, unless you can accomplish a task that's just come to my mind, and it's this: to find a man who's got such a good appetite that he can eat all the hot bread baked for the inhabitants of this great city for his breakfast."

The chevalier was most pleasantly surprised by this proposal, but since he did not answer right away, the emperor burst into a fit of laughter. "You see," he said, "it's perfectly natural to respond to a ridiculous request with a ridiculous answer."

"Sire," Fortuné said, "I accept your offer. Tomorrow I'll bring a man who'll eat all the fresh bread and likewise all the stale bread in this city. Just order it to be brought into the great square, and you'll have the pleasure of seeing him devour every last crumb."

The emperor agreed, and people talked about nothing but the madness of the new ambassador for the rest of the day. Meanwhile Matapa swore he would put him to death if he did not keep his word.

Fortuné returned to the hotel, where he had taken up his abode, and called Eater to him. "Now's the time for you to prepare yourself to eat bread," he said. "Everything depends on it." Thereupon he told him what he had promised the emperor.

"Don't worry, master," Eater said. "I'll eat until they get tired of feeding me."

Since Fortuné was afraid of any exertion on Eater's part, he forbade him to have supper so he would be better able to eat the breakfast. But this precaution was not really necessary. The emperor, the empress, and the princess took places on a balcony the next morning so that they would have a better view of all that took place. Fortuné arrived with his little retinue, and he saw six large mountains of bread, higher than the Pyrenees, standing in the great square. This sight made him turn pale, but it had the opposite effect on Eater. He was delighted by the prospect of eating so much good bread, and he asked them not to keep the smallest morsel from him and declared nothing would be left, even for a mouse. The emperor and the entire court amused themselves at the expense of Fortuné and his attendants, but Eater became impatient and demanded the signal to begin, which was soon given by a flourish of drums and trumpets. Immediately, he threw himself on one of the mountains of bread, which he devoured in less than a quarter of an hour, and he gulped down all the rest at the same rate. The astonishment was great, and everybody wondered whether their eyes had deceived them, and they had to satisfy themselves by touching the place where they had placed the bread. That day everyone, from the emperor to the cat, was compelled to dine without bread.

Fortuné was delighted with his great success. So he approached the emperor and asked very respectfully if the king was pleased by the way he had kept his word with him. The emperor was rather irritated at being duped this way and said, "Monsieur Ambassador, it won't do to eat so much without drinking. Therefore, you or one of your people must drink all the water out of the fountains, aqueducts, and reservoirs that are in the city, and all the wine that can be found in the cellars."

"Sire," Fortuné said, "you're trying to make it impossible for me to obey your orders. However, I don't mind endeavoring to fulfill this task, if I can expect that you'll restore what I've asked for to the king, my master."

"I'll do it if you succeed in your undertaking," the emperor stated. The chevalier asked the emperor if he would be present. He replied, it would be such an extraordinary event that he would attend the occasion. Thereupon, he got into a magnificent chariot and drove to the fountain of lions, where there were seven marble lions that spouted torrents of water and formed a river. The inhabitants of the city usually crossed this river in gondolas. Now Tippler approached the great basin, and, without taking breath, he drained it as dry as though there had never been any water in it. The fish in the river cried out for vengeance, for they did not know what was happening. Then Tippler turned to all the other fountains, aqueducts, and reservoirs and did the same. In fact, he could have drunk the sea, he was so thirsty. After seeing such an example, the emperor was convinced he could drink the wine as easily as the water, and everybody was too upset and refused to give him any. But Tippler complained of the great injustice they were doing him. He said that he would have a stomachache, and that he not only expected the wine, but also the spirits. Fearing he might appear stingy, Matapa consented to Tippler's request. Fortuné took this opportunity to remind the emperor of his promise. At these words the emperor looked very stern and told him he would think about it.

Now the emperor called his council together and expressed his extreme annoyance at having promised this young ambassador to return all he had won from his master. Indeed, he had thought the conditions he had set for Fortuné would be impossible to fulfill and he would not have to comply with them. After he spoke, the princess, his daughter, who was one of the most lovely creatures in the world, remarked, "You're aware, sire, that up to the present I've beaten all those who have dared to race with me. You must tell the ambassador that if he can reach a certain designated spot before me, you'll stop procrastinating and keep your word with him."

The emperor thought her advice was excellent and embraced his child. The next morning he received Fortuné very graciously and said, "I have one more condition, which is that you, or one of your men, must run a race with the princess, my daughter. I swear by all the elements that, if she's beaten, I'll satisfy your master in every respect."

Fortuné did not refuse this challenge, and after he accepted it, Matapa immediately added that the race would take place in two hours. He informed his daughter that she should get ready. It was something she had done since her childhood, and she appeared in an avenue of orange trees three miles long. It was so beautifully graveled that not a stone the size of a pin's head could be seen on it. She had on a light, rose-colored taffeta dress, embroidered down the seams with gold and silver spangles; her beautiful hair was tied by a ribbon at the back and fell carelessly on her shoulders; she wore extremely pretty little shoes without heels and a belt of jewels, which displayed her figure sufficiently to prove that there never had been one as beautiful as hers. Even the young Atalanta could never have matched hers.

Fortuné arrived and was followed by the faithful Swift and his other attendants. The emperor took his seat with his entire court. The ambassador announced that Swift would have the honor of running against the princess. The Turkey-leather trunk had furnished him with a holland-cloth suit trimmed with English lace, scarlet-colored silk stockings, feathers to match, and some beautiful linen. He looked very handsome in this garb, and the princess accepted him as her competitor. But before they started, she had some sort of liqueur brought to her, which was to strengthen her and give her additional speed. Swift said he ought to have some as well, and that the advantages ought to be equal. "Gladly," she said, "I'm too just to refuse you."

She immediately poured some out for him, but since he was not accustomed to this liquid, which was very strong, it mounted suddenly into his head. Consequently, he turned around two or three times and fell down at the foot of an orange tree and was soon fast asleep. Meanwhile, the signal was given for starting. They had already given it three times, and the princess kindly waited for Swift to wake up. Finally, she thought that it was extremely important to free her father from the predicament he was in, and so she set off with wonderful grace and speed. Since Fortuné was at the other end of the avenue with his people, he was unaware of what was happening until he saw the princess running alone and about half a mile from the finish line. "Ye gods!" he cried, speaking to his horse. "We're lost. I see nothing of Swift."

"My lord," Comrade said, "Fine Ear must listen. Perhaps he'll be able to tell us what's going on."

Fine Ear threw himself down on the ground, and although he was two miles from Swift, he could hear him snoring.

"Truly," he said, "he has no intention of coming. He's sleeping as though he were in bed."

"Ah, what shall we do?" Fortuné cried again.

"Master," Comrade said, "Sharp Shooter must shoot an arrow at the tip of his ear to wake him."

Sharp Shooter took his bow and aimed so well that he pierced Swift's ear. The pain woke him, and as he opened his eyes, he saw the princess nearing the finish line and heard shouts of joy and great applause. At first he was astonished, but he took off and soon regained the ground he had lost by sleeping. It appeared as though the winds were carrying him along, and nobody could follow him with their eyes. In short, he arrived first with the arrow still in his ear, for he did not have the time to take it out.

The emperor was so astonished at the three events which had happened since the arrival of the ambassador that he believed the gods favored Fortuné, and that he had better not defer keeping his promise.

"Approach," he said to Fortuné, "I want you to know from my own lips that I consent to your taking as much of your master's treasures from here as you or one of your men can carry. Indeed, you couldn't have expected that I'd ever do more than that or that I'd let either his soldiers, his subjects, or his horses go."

The ambassador made him a profound bow. He told him that he was very much obliged to him, and that he requested that he give orders to execute his will. Matapa was excessively mortified. He spoke to his treasurer and then went to a palace that he had just outside the walls of the city. Fortuné and his attendants immediately asked for admission into all the places where the king's furniture, rare articles, money, and jewels were deposited. The emperor's servants hid nothing from him, but it was on condition that only one man would carry them. Then Strongback made his appearance, and with his assistance the ambassador carried off all the furniture that was in the emperor's palace, five hundred statues of gold taller than giants, coaches, chariots, and all sorts of things. Everything was taken, and Strongback walked so swiftly, it seemed as though he did not have a pound on his back.

When the emperor's ministers saw that the palace was dismantled to such an extent that there were no longer chairs, chests, saucepans, or a bed to lie on, they rushed to warn him, and you can imagine how surprised he was when he learned that one man carried everything. He exclaimed that he would not put up with this and commanded his guards and musketeers to mount and quickly follow the robbers. Although Fortuné was more than ten miles away, Fine Ear told him that he heard a large body of cavalry galloping toward them, and Sharp Shooter, who had excellent vision, saw them at a distance. Fortuné had just arrived on the banks of a river with his men, and he said to Tippler, "We don't have any boats. If you could drink some of this water, we might be able to ford the river."

Tippler instantly performed his duty. The ambassador was anxious to make the best use of his time and get away, but his horse said to him, "Don't worry. Let our enemies approach."

They appeared on the opposite bank, and since they knew where the fishermen moored their boats, they speedily embarked in them and rowed with all their might. Then Boisterous inflated his cheeks and began blowing. The river became tumultuous; the boats were upset; and the emperor's little army perished without a single soldier escaping to tell the news.

Fortuné's men rejoiced when this happened, and each one of them only thought of demanding the reward he considered he deserved. They wanted to make themselves masters of all the treasures they had carried away, and a great dispute arose among them about how to divide everything.

"If I had not won the race," Swift said, "you'd have had nothing."

"And if I hadn't heard you snoring," Fine Ear said, "where would we have been then?"

"Who would have wakened you if it weren't for me?" Sharp Shooter responded.

"In truth," Strongback added, "I admire your arguments. But it's clear to me that I should have first choice since I've been carrying it all? Without my help, you wouldn't have the opportunity of sharing it."

"You really mean without mine," Tippler responded. "The river that I drank like a glass of lemonade would have baffled you."

"You would have been much more baffled if I hadn't upset the boats," Boisterous said.

"I've been silent up till now," interrupted Eater, "but I must remark that it was I who started the chain of events that have happened. If I had left just a single crumb of bread, everything would have been lost."

"My friends," Fortuné said with a commanding air, "you've all done wonders, but we ought to leave it to the king to acknowledge our services. I'd regret it very much if we were to be rewarded by some other hand than his. Believe me, let's leave all to his will. He sent us to recover his treasures, and not to steal them. Just the thought of it is so shameful that I think it should never be mentioned again. And I assure you, I myself will do everything I can for you so that you'll have nothing to regret, even if the king were to neglect you."

The seven gifted men were deeply moved by their master's remonstrance. They fell at his feet and promised him that his will would be theirs. Soon they moved on and completed their journey. But as they approached the city, the charming Fortuné felt troubled by a thousand different concerns. On the one hand, there was the joy at having performed such a great service for the king, for whom he felt such tender affection, and there was the hope of seeing him and being favorably received. He looked forward to all this with great delight. On the other hand, there was the fear of again irritating the queen and once again suffering torments from her and from Floride. This distressed him very much. When he finally arrived at the court, everyone was overjoyed to see the immense quantity of valuables he had brought back with him, and they followed him with a thousand acclamations. The sounds soon reached the palace, and the king could not believe such an extraordinary event was happening. He ran to the queen to tell her about it. At first she was thunderstruck, but she quickly regained her composure. "You see," she said, "the gods protect him, and he's fortunately succeeded. I'm not surprised that he's always ready to undertake anything that appears impossible to others."

As she uttered these words, she saw Fortuné enter. He informed their majesties about the success of his journey, adding that the treasures were in the park. Since there was so much gold, jewels, and furniture, there was no place large enough to put them in. You can easily imagine that the king demonstrated a good deal of affection for such a faithful, zealous, and charming subject.

The presence of the chevalier and all the successes he had achieved reopened the wound in the queen's heart that had never been quite healed. She thought him more charming than ever, and as soon as she was at liberty to speak to Floride, she began complaining again. "You've seen what I've done to try to destroy him," she said. "I thought it would be the only way of forgetting him. Yet, there's some sort of irrefutable fate that keeps bringing him back to me again. Whatever reasons I had to despise a man so much my inferior, and who's returned my affections with the meanest ingratitude, I can't help but love him still, and I'm determined to marry him privately."

"To marry him!" Floride cried. "I can't believe this! Have I heard you correctly?"

"Yes," the queen replied. "You've heard my intentions, and you must help me. I want you to bring Fortuné to my room this evening. I myself shall declare to him how far I'm willing to go because of my love for him."

In despair at being chosen to assist the queen in her plans to marry Fortuné, she tried everything possible to dissuade the queen from seeing him. She argued that the king would be angry if he came and discovered this intrigue, and that perhaps he would order the chevalier to be executed. At the very least he could condemn him to life imprisonment, and she would never see him again. However, all her eloquence was in vain. She saw that the queen was beginning to get angry, and there was nothing for her to do but obey her.

She found Fortuné in the gallery of the palace, where he was arranging the golden statues that he had brought from Matapa. She told him to come to the queen's room that evening. This order made him tremble, and Floride noticed his distress. "Oh," she said, "how I pity you! What unlucky fate caused the queen to lose her heart to you? Alas! I know one less dangerous than hers, but it's afraid to reveal itself."

The chevalier was not eager for another explanation. He already had too much to endure. Since he was not interested in pleasing the queen, he dressed himself very plainly so that she would not think he was distinguished. Yet, he could not efface his personal qualities, even though he could dispense with his diamonds and his embroideries. He was still charming and remarkable, no matter what he wore. In short, he was incomparable.

The queen went to great pains to heighten the luster of her appearance by an extraordinary display of dress, and she was quite pleased to see how astonished Fortuné was. "Appearances," she said, "are sometimes so deceptive that I'm delighted to have the chance to defend myself against the charges you no doubt brought against me in your heart. When I induced the king to send you to the emperor, it may have seemed as though my object was to destroy you. Nevertheless, believe me, handsome chevalier, I knew how everything would turn out, and I had no other goal than to provide immortal honor for you."

"Madame," he said, "you're too much above me to make it necessary for you to condescend to any explanation. I would never presume to inquire into the motives that induced you to act this way. The king's commands are sufficient justification for me."

"You're making light of the explanation I want to give you," she remarked. "But the time has come to demonstrate how much I care for you. Approach, Fortuné, approach. Receive my hand as a pledge of my faith."

The poor chevalier was totally thunderstruck. Twenty times he was on the point of declaring his sex to the queen, but he did not dare to do so and could only respond to her tokens of love by an excessive coldness. He tried to explain to her the innumerable reasons why the king would be angry if he were to hear that a subject in his own court had ventured to contract such an important marriage without his sanction. After the queen vainly endeavored to remove the obstacles that appeared to alarm him, she suddenly assumed the voice and countenance of a fury; she flew into the most violent rage; she threatened him with a thousand punishments; she heaped abuse on him; she fought and scratched him. Then, she turned her rage on herself. She tore her hair, made her face and throat bleed, and ripped her veil and her lace. Finally she cried out, "Help, guards! Help!" She called them into her room and commanded them to fling that wretch of a chevalier into a dungeon and ran to the king to demand justice for the way that young monster had violated her.

She told her brother that Fortuné had had the audacity some time ago to declare his feelings for her. She had hoped that by being severe toward him and sending him away, she could cure him. As the king might have observed, she used every opportunity she could to have him removed from the court. However, he was such a villain that nothing could change him. The king could see for himself to what extremes he had gone to possess her. She insisted that he be brought to justice and that, if she were denied such satisfaction, she know why.

The manner in which she spoke to the king alarmed him, for he knew that she was one of the most violent women in the world. She had a lot of power and was causing turmoil in the kingdom. Fortuné's rash actions demanded an exemplary punishment. Everybody already knew what had happened, and his own feelings should have prompted him to avenge his sister. But, alas, who was to be the target of his vengeance? It was a gentleman who had exposed himself to numerous perils in his service. Indeed, the king was indebted to him for peace and all his treasures, and he had a particular affection for him. He would have given half his life to have saved his dear favorite. So he explained to the queen how useful Fortuné had been to him, the services he had rendered the kingdom, and his youth, and he used everything else that might induce her to pardon him. Yet, she would not listen and demanded his death. The king realized that he could not possibly avoid having him tried, and thus he appointed the mildest and most tenderhearted judges in hopes that they would view the offence as lightly as possible. But he was mistaken in his assumption. The judges wanted to establish their reputation at the expense of this unfortunate prisoner. Since it was an affair that would attract a great deal of attention in the world, they were prepared to be extremely severe and condemned Fortuné without deigning to hear him: he was sentenced to be stabbed three times in the heart with a dagger because it was his heart that was guilty.

The king trembled at this sentence as though it had been passed on himself. He banished all the judges who had pronounced it, but could not save his beloved Fortuné. The queen triumphed because of the punishment he was to suffer, and her eyes thirsted for the blood of her illustrious victim. The king made various attempts to intercede, but they only served to exasperate her. Finally, the day set for this terrible execution arrived. They went to lead the chevalier from the prison in which he had been placed. He had been living in total isolation and was consequently unaware of the crime that he had allegedly committed against the queen and merely imagined that he was about to be persecuted once again because of his indifference to the queen. What distressed him most was his belief that the king shared the queen's rage against him. Floride was inconsolable at seeing the predicament in which her lover was placed and made a most drastic decision: she was prepared to poison the queen and herself if Fortuné was doomed to die a cruel death. From the moment she knew the sentence, she was overcome with despair, and she thought about nothing but how to carry out her plan. The poison she procured, however, was not as powerful as she desired. Despite the fact that she had given it to the queen, her majesty did not feel the effects and ordered the charming chevalier to be brought into the great square of the palace so that the execution could take place in her presence. The executioners brought him from his dungeon according to custom and led him like a tender lamb to the slaughter. The first object that struck his sight was the queen in her chariot, who wanted to be as close to him as possible in hopes that this blood might spurt out upon her. The king locked himself up in his chamber so that he might freely lament the fate of his beloved favorite.

After they tied Fortuné to the stake, they tore off his robe and his vest to pierce his heart, but you can imagine how astonished everyone was when they uncovered the alabaster bosom of Belle-Belle! Now everybody realized Fortuné was an innocent girl, unjustly accused. The queen was so upset and confused by such a sight that the poison began to have an extraordinary effect. She had a series of long convulsions and only recovered from them to utter agonizing lamentations. The people, who loved Fortuné, had already freed her and ran to announce this wonderful news to the king, who had succumbed to the deepest grief. Now joy took the place of sorrow. He ran into the square and was delighted to see Fortuné's transformation.

The last sighs of the queen subdued his rapture somewhat, but when he thought about her malice he could not feel sorry for her. He decided to marry Belle-Belle in order to repay her for the great debt he owed her, and he declared his intentions to her. You can easily imagine that his wish had been the goal of all that she had ever desired, and that it was not the crown she had wanted but the worthy monarch for whom she cherished the greatest affection for quite some time.

The day was set for celebrating the king's marriage, and Belle-Belle reassumed her female attire. She appeared a thousand times more charming than in the garb of the chevalier. Then she consulted her horse with regard to her future adventures, and he promised her that she would have nothing but pleasant ones. In gratitude for all the good services he had done her, she had a stable built for him made of ebony and ivory, and she installed the very best satin mattress for him to lie down on. As for her seven followers, they were rewarded in proportion to their services. Comrade, however, disappeared, and when they came and told Belle-Belle, the queen was distressed, for she adored him and ordered her attendants to look for her horse everywhere they could. They did this for three whole days, but it was in vain. On the fourth day she was so worried that she got up before sunrise and descended into the garden. Then she crossed the wood and entered a large meadow, calling from time to time, "Comrade! My dear Comrade! Where are you? Have you deserted me? I still need your wise advice. Come back, come back, and give it to me!" While calling out like this, she suddenly noticed a second sun rising in the west. She stopped to gaze at this miracle, and she was immensely astonished as she watched it advance toward her by degrees. Within minutes she recognized her horse, whose trappings were all covered with jewels, and who pranced at the head of a chariot of pearls and topazes, drawn by twenty-four sheep. Their wool was of gold thread and purl[3] and extremely radiant. Their traces were made of crimson satin and covered with emeralds, and their horns and ears were ornamented with carbuncles. Belle-belle recognized her fairy protectress in the chariot, and she was accompanied by the count, her father, and her two sisters, who called out to her. They were clapping their hands and making affectionate signs to her, intimating that they had come to her wedding. She thought she would die from joy, and she did not know what to do or to say to show her delight. She got into the chariot, and this splendid equipage entered the palace, where everything had already been prepared to celebrate the finest wedding ceremony that had ever taken place in the kingdom. Thus the enamored king bound his destiny to that of his mistress, and the story about this charming adventure circulated for centuries and has been passed down to our own.

> The lion roaming Lybia's burning plain,
> Pursued by the hunter, galled by countless darts,
> Is less to be dreaded than that woman vain,
> Whose charms are disdained and foiled in her arts.
>
> Poison and steel are trifles in her eyes,
> As agents of her vengeance and her hate;
> The dire effects that from such passions rise
> You've now seen in Fortuné's strange fate.
>
> Belle-Belle's change saved her innocent soul,
> And struck her royal persecutor down.
> Heaven protects the innocent and plays its role
> By defeating vice and rewarding virtue with a crown.

HENRIETTE JULIE DE MURAT

The Savage[†]

Once upon a time the islands of Terceres were governed by a king named Richardin. He had married a beautiful princess, who was the daughter of the king of Catharactes of the Nile and was called Corianthe. Richardin was passionately in love with her, and since her father the king had not wanted to give her to him because he had promised her to the king of the Fontaines Ameres, whom she did not love, Richardin waged a fierce war until he gained possession of her. Finally, they were able to gain happiness and enjoy one another, for if Corianthe was beautiful, Richardin was the one handsome king in the world who was perfectly suited for her.

3. Thread or cord made of twisted gold or silver wire, used for embroidering and bordering.
† Henriette Julie de Murat, "The Savage"—"Le sauvage" (1699), in *Histoires sublimes et allégoriques* (Paris: Floentin Delaulne, 1699).

Now, one year after their marriage Corianthe gave birth to a baby girl who was as ugly as a beast. This did not please her or the king, because he was convinced that a beautiful daughter would cost less to marry off than an ugly one. She was named Disgrace. One year later, the queen gave birth again to another princess who was just as ugly as the first, causing more sorrow for the king and queen, but they had to be patient and named her Douleur.

Some months later Corianthe became pregnant again, and the king, who feared that she would give birth to another monster, took care to have only beautiful people around the queen and had portraits of beautiful women placed in his apartment wherever he could. He even had original paintings of fictitious beautiful women painted. At last, despite all these precautions, the queen gave birth again to a princess more horrible than the other two, and she was named Desespoir. So there he was, father of three of the most frightening and ugly creatures in his kingdom. He said to the queen that they had better leave it at that, for he did not want to populate the earth with monsters. Thus, they did not bring any more children into the world.

Meanwhile, the princesses grew and reached the age of maturity. They were just as stupid as they were ugly, and the king did not know what to do with this merchandise. Poor Richardin was severely limited. So, he ventured to issue proclamations and had announcements posted throughout his kingdom that if any princes, knights, barons, or noblemen wanted to marry his daughters, he would give them each one of his islands along with the title of king.

For some time nobody responded to the king's offer. Finally, one day, three knights, who were just as much a disgrace to nature as the three princesses, appeared at the court. One had a hunchback and was called Magotin, another was one-eyed and lame and was called Gambille. The third had lost an arm and a leg and was named Trotte-mal. These disfigured men only increased the sorrow of the poor father, but he could not do any better. These knights had a great deal of spirit and had accomplished some fine deeds.

"Alas," the queen said to her husband, "you might be fearful of populating the earth with monsters. But it will be much worse when these six people are united."

"This may not be the result," the king responded. "You can find people every day just like ourselves who are sound and healthy and yet have children that do not turn out well, and on the other hand, there are ugly people who produce very charming children."

"All the better," said the queen.

In the end, Richardin had his daughters marry these men without grand ceremonies, and after he gave them three islands to be their realms, he retired to a house in the country with a decent revenue and a fair-sized entourage. He lived there in a leisurely fashion and had no ambitions, and since he forgot that he did not want to have children, it happened, I don't know how, that Corianthe became pregnant. When she knew for certain, she felt she was being cruelly tormented.

"Alas," she said to the king, "what will happen to this cursed child when

I give birth? If it is a girl once more just as ugly as the others, what shall we do? We have nothing to give her. If it is a prince, what a disaster it will be if he justifiedly wants to possess the estates and realms of his father, for he will have to banish his brothers-in-law."

Richardin saw that she was right, and there was nothing that he could say to her that it seemed would placate her. He only said that the gods would arrange things accordingly, and that it was not necessary to anticipate the worst before it actually happened. Soon thereafter Corianthe brought a princess into the world who was the most beautiful creature in the world. She consoled herself by hoping that her beauty would bring her riches. She was right to think this way because her daughter could not have been more perfect. The more she grew, the more her charms increased, and her intelligence was even greater. Her entire disposition was grand and noble. She could ride horseback perfectly, shoot superbly with the bow and arrow, and was marvelously adept at handling a sword. She loved the sciences, and what was most admirable was that these heroic occupations did not hinder her from excelling in all the arts of her sex: she cooked, drew, and made clothes and did everything perfectly. No one could sing better, play instruments better, or dance better than she did. In sum, Constantine, for that was her name, was a perfect prodigy.

Richardin and Corianthe would have liked to have wed her to some nobleman, but nobody arrived to ask her hand in marriage. She was eighteen years old, and their worries were beginning to mount. The king, who always had fine inspirations, began to think that it might be best to marry the charming Constantine to one of his officers, who was a man without wealth, without good looks, and without much intelligence, and the only advantage to him would be that he might leave her somewhat wealthy after his death. He spoke to the queen about this, and she did her best to make him change his mind, telling him it would be better if they let her alone with the little that she had than to have her share it with a family which would be miserable with her paltry dowry. The queen also said that Constantine was not yet beyond the age when she might meet someone worthy of her merits. But the queen did not make much headway against the king, who was very obstinate. He made his will known to Constantine, who told him with respect that she preferred to remain single than to enter into misalliance of this kind, but the king was inexorable and set the date for her badly matched marriage. The poor princess broke into tears and implored the queen her mother to give her the means to avoid such a calamity, which appeared more hideous than anything in the world. The queen, who saw that she was totally unable to help her, mixed her tears with those of her daughter. Finally, after having wept a great deal, Constantine said to her mother, "Madame, permit me to flee and let God be my guide. Give me some men's clothes, and with this disguise I shall seek an honorable death in a distant country that would be more preferable to me than a shameful life."

Corianthe had a great deal of difficulty agreeing to this expedient, but not seeing any other way free, she consented. The following night they contacted a merchant's ship that was to set sail in two days. The queen gave Constantine some of the king's clothes, and after giving her whatever money she could, which was not very much, she embraced her tenderly and then set her on her way under the protection of the night. Thus the poor princess embarked and sailed with the merchant for Sicily.

When Richardin did not find his daughter, he became enraged against the queen and was sure that she knew what had become of their daughter, but she did not reveal anything. In the meantime Constantine under the name of Constantin arrived in Sicily. When she left the ship, she did not know where she should turn. The little money that she had received from her mother was not sufficient enough to enable her to set up house no matter how mediocre it might be. Finding herself in difficult straits, she went to sleep in a nearby forest. Later she was wakened by something that pushed her, and when she opened her eyes, she saw a beautiful woman dressed as one might paint Diana standing right next to her. She was wearing a loose dress of green and gold, boots of Morocco leather, adorned with gold and with diamond buckles. Her hair was blond and was braided behind with poppy-red and gold ribbons. On her hip she was carrying an ebony quiver that was decorated with gold, filled with arrows, and supported by a magnificent scarf. In her hand she was holding a bow that was just as magnificent. Her headdress consisted of a small morion à la Greek[1] covered with feathers the color of fire.

The princess was pleasantly surprised, but she was even more astounded when this charming person joyfully told her, "Beautiful princess, I have come here to offer the help that you need, and you will have it. Here is a horse," she continued and showed her a most beautiful horse attached to a tree, "and you only have to mount it and let it carry you to a place where you will find asylum."

"Madame," the princess replied with a surprised air, "permit me to ask you who could have told you about me when I am not known in this foreign country?"

"Do not bother yourself about this, my lovely Constantine," the lady said. "I know more about your affairs than you yourself, but I cannot tell you anything more than this."

Upon saying this she embraced the princess tenderly, and after untying the horse, she touched it on the neck and said to it, "Embletin, do your duty."

The princess got on the horse and felt marvelous. After taking her leave from her benefactress with all the proper civility possible, she rode off, and Embletin galloped so softly and at the same time so fast that they were out of the forest in no time. After they crossed a large meadow, she saw the gates of a city where she thought they would enter, but Embletin turned to the right and took her to the bank of a beautiful river, where Constantine found many gentlemen and ladies who were promenading on foot and also riding on horseback. In the middle was a magnificently dressed lord with a handsome face, and he was holding the hand of a young lady dressed in similarly splendid clothes and with a unique beauty.

Constantine, or rather Constantin, since we are now calling her by this name, asked a page who this lord and young lady were. He told her that

---

1. A kind of helmet, without beaver or visor, worn in the sixteenth and seventeenth centuries.

he was the king of Sicily and the princess was his sister. Constantin advanced a little toward the guards on horseback so that he could be seen by the king. As soon as the king caught sight of him, he was attracted by his handsome features, his fine figure, and his strange clothes and he became curious to know who he was. So he commanded one of his officers to ask him to come forward, and the officer carried out his order at once.

Constantin got off his horse with a great deal of grace, and he presented himself before the king in such a noble manner that the monarch was very charmed.

"Who are you, kind stranger?" the king asked the prince. "What has brought you to my country?"

"My lord," Constantin said, "I am a nobleman from the islands of Terceres, and since I have so many brothers and have not received the resources to sustain myself according to my rank, I have been obligated to travel abroad and search for that which fortune has not granted me in my own country."

"This fortune has been quite unjust to have refused you the favors that you deserve," the king responded. "What is your name?"

"My name is Constantin," he said.

"Well then, Constantin," the king answered, "if you would like to live at my court, you will receive the protection that you deserve."

"This is a great honor that you have bestowed on me," Constantin responded. "I accept it with great pleasure, and I shall try with zeal and dedication to deserve at least a part of the grace with which you have honored me."

The king placed him in the hands of his steward and ordered him to equip Constantin with all that was necessary for a gentleman of his stature, and this was done. That evening Constantin appeared before the king in suitable attire. The magnificent clothes he wore revealed once again his beauty and good appearance. The king was charmed by the fine manners of this new gentleman, and also Princess Fleurianne, his sister, could not stop admiring him. In turn Constantin was attentive to her in a courtly fashion and drew everyone's attention. As a result, he made many conquests, but the greatest he made was on the princess so that she felt something that went beyond the ordinary esteem that one would have for someone like him. Since she was wise, however, she hid her feelings.

A short time before this the king of Canary had sent a magnificent ambassador to the king of Sicily to ask for the hand of his sister for Prince Carabut, his only son, who was a hunchback and very unpleasant, and the princess was not very happy about this. But the king of Canary sent magnificent presents, for he was one of the richest kings in the world. Among the things he sent were two hundred canaries of different colors in golden cages, adorned with gems. These birds sang and whistled most divinely, and what was even more marvelous was that they spoke all kinds of languages and told the princess the most pretty things in the world on behalf of their master, who had a great deal of intelligence and gallantry. Yet that did not diminish his ugliness. He arrived at the court, and all his defects along with the charms of the handsome Constantin placed the princess in a cruel predicament. Because of this she became very melancholy. Her brother the king saw this and realized that the unpleasantness of the prince was the cause of this. He could not bear to witness this and was sorry that he had listened to the marriage proposals. He found everything out of proportion. Since the intelligence and spirit of Prince Carabut spoke in his favor, he pressed to have his marriage proposal accepted and for the marriage to take place because he was very much in love with Fleurianne. But the king always eluded him and placed all sorts of difficulties in the prince's way.

Nevertheless, there were a great deal of games and amusements at the court. Races were held, and Constantin always won the prize. If they went hunting, he always took the honors. If there was dancing at a ball, he outdid all the best dancers. Sometimes, if they organized a concert at the princess's apartment, his beautiful voice and the grace with which he touched the instruments caused everyone to admire him. The princess had her ladies sew clothes for him and create some furniture, and Constantin would always give them some new ideas and work with them, something that surprised everyone at the court, but the Princess Fleurianne only felt her passion for him increase. She spoke so well about him to the king at various occasions that one day he said to her, "My sister, I see that you have a high regard for Constantin, and even though I have such a great pleasure in having him near me, I shall gladly deprive myself of him in order to make you a present. You are in need of a squire, and I shall give him to you in that capacity."

The princess could not control herself and blushed out of joy. She quickly recovered and thanked the king in such a way that he realized how much he had pleased her. Now Constantin was introduced into the princess's service in a position that made them inseparable. He was very happy about this, and his sex was less the subject of suspicions in her service than it was in the king's employ. But it did not take long for him to realize that she had feelings for him that would present difficulties of another kind. Thus he had to conceal his identity with great skill.

In the meantime, the king found that he could not postpone his decision anymore, and the Prince Carabut kept pressuring him so much to conclude the marriage arrangements with the princess that the king was obliged to tell him that his natural defects made him repugnant in Fleurianne's eyes, and since he did not want to impose his will on his sister, he advised the prince to keep his distance for some time while he, the king, would redouble his efforts to try to create a more favorable impression on his sister so that she would find the prince more pleasing.

Despite himself, the prince accepted this proposal. At the same time, since he perceived the esteem that the princess had for Constantin, he gave him magnificent presents in order to win Constantin's help. One day, when the princess was promenading in the gardens of the palace away from her ladies, she saw a beautiful diamond on Constantin's finger. "You have a beautiful gem," she said to him. "Where did you get it?"

"The Prince Carabut gave it to me," he replied.

"He is very generous," said the princess, "and if nature had given him a body similar to his soul, one might say that he would be a perfect prince."

"Madame," Constantin said, "the beauty of the soul is always more preferable than that of the body, for the body does not last very long while the soul is eternal."

"This is true," Fleurianne remarked, "but if one is obliged to spend one's life with a monster, no matter what other quality he may have, that person is to be pitied. I can love Carabut as a friend, but I know quite well that I can never love him as my husband. How unjust nature is!" she continued, throwing a languishing glance at Constantin. "How can a prince find himself happy upon receiving from nature a quality that becomes useless because he has been lavished with too much of it?"

After she finished saying this, she lowered her eyes.

Constantin understood her very well, and he responded, "Madame, I wish it were in my power to communicate to Prince Carabut something which would make him more pleasing in your eyes."

"Ah!" the princess exclaimed. "Life would be much easier if we could add those qualities that one lacks to a person's charms! The choice of a princess could transform a prince who lacks certain qualities into a man worthy of her. But she cannot give to a man that which nature has refused to bless with her favors. I have already said more than enough about this subject." She blushed. "I have said too much. It is impossible for me to conceal my feelings that I have expressed despite myself. Yes, my dear Constantin, I must admit that all my tender feelings are for you, and if I were mistress of my destiny, I would not hesitate for a moment to take you for my husband. Since I cannot do this and comply with my obligations as princess at the same time, I am determined never to wed anyone else."

Just as she finished saying these words, and just as Constantin was about to respond, they heard some noise behind a nearby hedge. The princess thought that it was her ladies, but when she turned around, she saw them several steps behind her on the path. When they joined her, they began conversing about things in general which did not really concern her. Carabut also joined them, and he seemed very upset. Then they returned to the palace, and the princess retired to her apartment.

The prince did not stay very long. Constantin was in the antechamber when he left. The prince approached him and said in a low voice, "Constantin, I have a few things that I want to say to you. Follow me."

He obeyed the prince, and they crossed a hall and entered a path that led to one of the far sides of the gardens, where there was a door that led to a remote place. Carabut opened the door, and when they went through this door, Carabut closed it, and they were completely alone.

"You must explain to me," Carabut said, "why the princess has such feelings for you that you do not deserve. I heard the conversation that you just had with her in the garden."

"My lord," replied Constantin, "if you heard the entire conversation, you must know that I am innocent. I am not to blame if . . . ."

"It is useless," the prince said, interrupting him, "to try to justify your actions. I heard enough to be convinced that you are occupying a place in Fleurianne's heart which she refuses to give to me. You must pay for this with your blood."

Upon saying this, the prince drew out his sword, but Constantin's size gave him a great advantage. No matter what he did to avoid this duel, it was impossible, and he became so furious with Carabut that he soon struck him with two blows, and the prince fell down dead. Now Constantin found himself in an embarrassing situation and realized that it would be best for him to flee. He returned to the palace by another way. Then he ran to the stable where Embletin was kept. After mounting the horse, he immediately left the city.

While Constantin was fleeing, Princess Fleurianne had her servants search for him all over, but it was in vain. His absence and the death of the prince made it appear that he was guilty. The king loved Constantin very much and would have liked to ignore everything. He was not angry that he could not find Constantin. However, he sent some men to search for him and gave them secret orders to let him escape if they found him. As far as Fleurianne was concerned, she became despondent, and to conceal her anguish, she pretended to be sick and took to her bed. The king sent ambassadors carrying the body of Carabut to his father, the king of Canary, and they were charged with the task of pacifying him, which was very difficult.

In the meantime, Constantine continued to flee with Embletin, not knowing where she wanted to go. She had already traveled quite some distance day and night without hardly stopping or eating. Finally she entered a dense forest, and the more she advanced, the more dark it became. She kept going for a long time in this darkness and said to herself, "Alas, unfortunate princess, why has destiny reduced you to such a state that you must let yourself be guided by a beast?"

With these and other similar thoughts, she soon found herself in an open area and facing a magnificent chateau. The door of this grand chateau opened by itself, and Embletin entered, crossed a large courtyard, and stopped at the foot of a flight of steps. Constantine dismounted, and Embletin, who was familiar with this place, went straight to the stable, while the princess climbed the stairs. She crossed a vestibule which, as far as she could see, appeared to be beautiful. Next she climbed a large staircase, and after she had gone a few steps, she saw a young man who was holding a torch. He was handsome and gallantly dressed.

"Princess," he greeted her, "the fairy Obligeantine, the lady of this chateau, having been informed of your arrival, has sent me to conduct you to her apartment."

Although somewhat surprised to find that she was known in this place, she expressed her gratitude. She was conducted through a series of rooms that seemed to her astonishingly magnificent. Then her guide opened a door through which she entered alone. It was a chamber beautifully illuminated and magnificent. It was full of large mirrors with jeweled frames. The floor was lined with marigolds, jasmine, and roses. A beautiful lady who was superbly dressed was lying on a bed of silver and green cloth, and the bed was completely covered with flowers. As soon as this lady saw the princess, she extended her arm toward her and said, "Approach, charming princess. Come and enjoy my company. You have earned this rest that destiny has refused you up until now."

The princess approached her and was pleasantly surprised to see the lady, who was the same person who had given her Embletin as a present.

"Ah, madame!" Constantine said as she received the fairy's caresses. "I see that it is to you that I owe the happiness of my life."

Obligeantine revealed to her that she knew everything that had happened at the king of Sicily's court and that she had been expecting her at her chateau after all that she had suffered.

"Go and rest," said the fairy. "We shall talk about everything tomorrow at our leisure."

She showed her a door and told her to push it open. Constantine did this, and she entered into a chamber that was furnished with lovely things. Two young and beautifully dressed damsels welcomed her in a polite manner. They gave her fruit and sweets, and after she ate them, they undressed her and showed her to her bed.

Upon awakening, the same two damsels came to dress her in clothes of her own sex that were lavish and gallant. When Constantine was finished adorning herself, she went into Obligeatine's chamber, where she found the fairy grooming herself. The fairy greeted her with great affection, and after they had their breakfast, many fairies of the first rank came to visit her, and Obligeantine introduced them to the princess. Then she showed Constantine all the beauties of the chateau and the marvelous gardens. The next day she said to her that she wanted her to see all the marvels of the art of faerie. Therefore, she led her into a hall filled with cabinets, mirrors, round tables, girandoles,[2] and splendid chandeliers. At the end of the hall, she opened a door embossed with bronze that led into a large room. The arch and the linings of the walls were composed of swarms of different colors that depicted the sunset on a beautiful day.

"This is the cabinet of Destiny," Obligeantine told the princess, "and you are going to see things that will astonish you and give you a good deal of pleasure. Here you will see," she continued, touching one of the sides of the room with a bronze wand, "what is happening in the realm of a king whom the world knows as Louis the Great. Locked up on the other side is the general destiny of the entire world. This one here is for the particular destiny of a single person."

After saying all this she touched the side of the general destiny three times, and swarms of distinct figures were formed right away, and they represented the most extraordinary events, battles, besieged cities, massacred kings, some natural deaths, some dethroned, happy and sad marriages, the encirclements of cities, the buildings destroyed by earthquakes or wiped out by lightning, the floods of rivers, sea battles, shipwrecks, the change of seasons, the end of the present century where the weakness of the stars and the planets bring about a general disorder of time, and the horoscope of the future century. After all of these particular things were displayed, the destiny of France was revealed, and the figures that were formed represented all the marvels of the king Louis the Great, his numerous conquests, his army, his navy, the portraits of all the great captains who command the troops and their particular actions, the king's immense and inexhaustible riches, his palaces of beautiful enchantment, the mag-

2. Branched supports for candles.

nificence of his court, his beautiful and bountiful family, of which there were already three generations, the polite manners of his subjects, the sublime nature of the sciences and arts which they possess, the grandeur of his cities, the beauty and abundance of his provinces, the flourishing trade that he entertains with all the nations of the earth, and, above all, his generosity par excellence, which renders him protector of the innocent and the oppressed.

But that was nothing in comparison to a pleasant spectacle that appeared: it was a young and beautiful princess who left a great mountain range. She was completely covered with glistening precious stones and was wearing a crown of myrtle on her head and was holding an olive branch in her hand. A lady who had a divine aspect extended her hand to the princess and presented her to the king of France, who received her with open arms, and in turn he presented her to a young prince about the same age, as handsome as Amour, and the grandson of this great monarch, who had designated him as the husband of the princess. Indeed, their union was to conclude a cruel war and bring peace to an infinite number of powerful states aligned by jealousy against the flourishing empire of the king of France.

"Here you have the greatest event of our times," the fairy said to the princess.

After she said these words, she touched the third side and said, "Here is something that concerns you, princess."

Constantine immediately saw the islands of Terceres, the king her father, the queen her mother tormented by the loss of Constantine, her three sisters and their husbands overwhelmed by civil war and domestic strife. Constantine, who was a good person, was touched by these scenes and shed some tears. Next, the fairy showed her the realm of Sicily, and the Princess Fleurianne in the palace of the king. Unfortunately, they wanted to force her to marry a satyr.

"Alas!" Constantine cried. "By killing Carabut, I've delivered the princess into the hands of a monster who is much more terrible than the prince. Isn't there some way to rescue this kind princess?"

"You will be the one," the fairy smiled and said, "to get her out of this predicament again, but the time has not yet arrived."

The last figure that Constantine saw was herself. She was seated on an elevated throne, and the king of Sicily was placing a crown at her feet.

"What does that signify?" asked the princess.

"In time you will know," the fairy responded. After that the cabinet assumed its previous form, and when they left the room, the fairy shut the door. Some days later she said to Constantine that she wanted to see all the courts of the earth and that she was going to commence by visiting the court of France, where they were going to hold the most superb celebration that had ever been organized by mortals. Therefore, Obligeantine had a chariot prepared that was made from the skull of a giant who had been found on her lands and whom she had exterminated through her art. This giant had been ninety-six feet high, and the fairy had the skull crafted in such an admirable way that one could find there all that was necessary with regard to attendants and wheels. Since she only wanted to travel at night, she had it given a black gloss. She harnessed two large mastiffs to it, and they were provided with bat wings from the Indies that were as large as cows. She and the princess were dressed in black crape lined with a golden cloth, and after swallowing an herb which made them invisible and of which they had an ample supply, they departed with their entourage and arrived shortly thereafter at Versailles, right before the marriage of the princess of Savoy. They were present at the ceremony and banquet without being seen, and they ate the fruit and sweets that were served. The fairy pushed the officers who were carrying baskets of dessert, and while they turned around to see who had dared to push them, the fairy and princess took what they wanted from the baskets without anyone noticing. They also watched the princess of Savoy dress, get undressed, and sleep with the prince, and they saw the dressing room of this princess and all her jewels. As they were leaving the chamber, the king also left, and Constantine ran to say something to Obligeantine. Without thinking, she pushed the king, and he was extremely surprised not to see anyone near him. After he looked around with some concern, he continued on his way. Later, the fairy and Constantine were at the ball and at the performance of the opera Issé,[3] which they found very beautiful. Indeed, they thought everything was magnificent in all the apartments, and they thoroughly enjoyed their time at the celebration. The fairy confessed that the magnificence at this court could only be surpassed by faerie art. Every evening they went to the fairy Marline, who lived in an invisible palace near the chateau de Marly.

After having seen the court of France, they moved on to Spain, where they saw nothing worthy of their curiosity, and this was also true in Germany and in the other realms of the North. But they were satisfied enough later by the magnificence of the Great Sultan as well as by the beauties and riches of the seraglios, in which they experienced intrigues and learned about all the secrets. They went to Siam, China, Mongolia, and Persia, and at last they returned to England to see King William, about whom they had heard many different things. They were curious to see the Parliament, but the rigamarole of laws, the trade prices, the taxes for tea, chocolate, coffee, tonnage dues, and their manner of counting in pound sterling made them so dismayed that they quickly went to Paris to relax and amuse themselves at the Tuileries,[4] the opera, and the theater. They realized that they had not been to Venice, and they went there and passed a good part of their time at Corinth. Afterward, they returned to the chateau of the fairy. Even though they had made a great effort to make their trip short, they had been traveling for approximately two months. The beautiful surroundings of the chateau helped them relax from the exhausting voyage. Indeed, they enjoyed one pleasure after the next in this beautiful setting.

While Constantine led such a sweet and peaceful life, conditions were not the same in the realm of the king of Sicily. He had endured a brutal

---

3. This opera by André-Cardural Destouches was a heroic pastoral, produced in 1697 at Fontainebleu, one of Louis XIV's residences.
4. The French royal palace adjacent to the Louvre in Paris, destroyed in 1871 by arson.

war with the king of Canary. Irritated by the death of his son, the king of Canary had added many canaries to his troops so that all the subjects of the king of Sicily thought that they were being smothered by these birds, but fortunately they knew how to make use of the burning cinders of Mount Vesuvius and grilled the birds as if they were pigs. However, the two hundred talking canaries that Carabut had given as a present to Princess Fleurianne gave them a great deal of difficulty. They had escaped their cages and flew to different places in the kingdom. Then they spread such bad rumors that they caused a civil war, which was difficult to put down. After this the king had hardly begun to breathe again when he heard about another ravaging attack from some mountains that were not far from the capital. There was a species of men or rather hideous and cruel monsters, half-men, half-goats, who were causing terrible damage in the neighboring regions. They were carrying away children, eating the animals, and spoiling the crops, and then they would escape to places in the mountains that were inaccessible.

The king decided to go there in person to exterminate this brood. Aside from his guards, who went on horseback and on foot, he took all his noblemen with him, and everyone who wanted to follow him. The mountains where the monsters were dwelling were at the extreme end of a large forest. The king had the paths cleared, and in order to attract the monsters, he dispersed some herds of sheep, cows filled with milk, and wine, which they loved very much. Then he hid behind the trees with his men and waited for the monsters to descend from the mountains. Shortly after this the monsters appeared, and when they began eating the bait, the king and his men attacked them, and because of the surprise, they were able to kill many of the monsters. However, these gruesome creatures began to rally and throw themselves on the king's men with such fury and ease that they killed many of them. They threw them on the buttocks of their horses and pierced their eyes with their powerful hands. They terrified the king's troops with such fierce acts that the troops fled the forest without thinking about the king, who found himself abandoned and surrounded by the monsters. Fortunately, they did not throw the king on the buttocks of his horse as they had done with the others. They menaced him with horrible shouts and tried to trap him with branches that they had cut from trees. But the king was extremely adroit, and he managed to mount a marvelous horse, killing many of the monsters with his sword and javelin until the rest of them fled into the mountains.

When he saw that he was free, he thought about returning to his palace, and since night was approaching, he called out to see if he could be heard by his men, but nobody responded. So he began to ride, when suddenly he saw one of the savage monsters come out from behind a tree and jump very quickly on the rear of his horse. The satyr seized the king from behind and prevented him from using his arms. The king did all he could to free himself, and as he was doing this, he heard the monster say to him, "King, don't be afraid. I won't hurt you if you promise to do what I tell you."

The king, who was surprised to hear the savage speak, responded, "If you do not ask the impossible, I shall promise to do what you wish."

"I only wish," he said, "that you take me with you to your palace, and that you keep me in a place where only you can see me. After I have been with you for some time, I shall tell you some things that will please you very much."

"All right," said the king, "I promise you."

As soon as the king said that, the monster released his grip and sat on the rear of the horse as the king continued riding toward the city. Since it was night, he was able to cross the city without being seen. His men had told everyone that he was dead, and he found the gates of the palace without guards. When he was inside the court, some of his officers caught sight of him and fled out of fear or fright. He took advantage of this situation by going straight to his apartment without being seen, and he entered with the savage, whom he held by the hand. After opening the door to a small room where he kept rare and precious jewels, he left the savage there and said that he would make sure to give him whatever the savage needed. After this he went to the apartment of the princess, his sister, where he found all the noblemen of the court had gathered around her after they had heard the news of his death. He found her in tears, and she uttered a cry when she saw him enter.

"Do not be afraid, madame," he said to her. "The news of my death is due to the cowardice of my officers. Heaven protected me, and I shall pardon their lack of devotion."

The princess embraced him tenderly, and her mood changed quickly from grief to joy. All the officers, who were terribly ashamed of themselves, went and begged his pardon, and he gave it to them. He said nothing about the savage. He had food and drink brought to his chamber under one pretext or another, and when he was alone, he brought everything to the savage, who gave him a thousand hugs and caresses, and he thanked the king and showed him his admiration.

One day, after the monster had been living in the palace for some time, the king brought him some food, and the savage said to him, "My lord, it is now time that I tell you what you must do to become the happiest king on earth. You must say to your subjects that you want to marry, and you are to make all the necessary arrangements for a celebration to fit the occasion. Everyone will be anxious to know whom you are going to marry. The princess, your sister, will want to know, but you are not to reveal anything to anyone. When you are ready and the day has arrived, you are to lock the apartment that you will have prepared for the queen your wife. Then you are to take the key and bring it to me here. I shall then enter it with you and your sister, and you will see what Heaven has decreed for you."

The king was surprised beyond belief, and he did not know what he should do. When the savage noticed his hesitancy, he assured the king by saying, "Don't be afraid, your majesty. Abandon yourself to your destiny, which has been determining things all along."

The king promised the satyr to do everything promptly just as the savage told him, and from that very day on, he began to make plans for his marriage. The princess was astounded by the secret that the king was keeping in regard to his marriage, but he said to her that she would know everything when the time came. Everyone at the court and in the city believed that the king had fallen in love with the daughter of one of his subjects, and that he did not want to say anything for fear that the nobles at his court would not be content. There was hardly a beautiful maiden who did not flatter herself that she was the one who had been chosen by the king to be his fortunate bride.

Finally the day arrived. The day before, the king had taken the key of the apartment for his future queen, and now he was dressed in his ceremonious robes and ordered the princess to appear in her most magnificent dress. All the officers and ladies of honor of the queen had been ordered to be prepared. After the king had been dressed, he entered the small room where the savage had been staying and took him by the arm and led him across his apartment followed by the princess his sister. She was very frightened to see the king holding the arm of this savage. Everyone remained in a profound silence and did not know what to do about such extraordinary behavior. The king opened the apartment of the queen and crossed it to the antechamber. The savage whispered to him to have everyone stop there except for the princess, and this he did. Then the three of them entered the chamber, and the savage closed the door. The king was very surprised to see that the furniture of this apartment had been changed in magnificent ways. Among the things that he saw were twelve large golden baskets ornamented with jewels that were filled with the most beautiful gems and the most beautiful clothes that one can imagine.

They had not been there very long when a door to another small room opened, and in came two ladies whose beauty and appearance were beyond description. But the king was extremely surprised to recognize the traits of the handsome Constantin in one of the beautiful ladies. He was not mistaken because he was seeing the Princess Constantine. The fairy Obligeantine was escorting her, and when Constantine was in front of the king of Sicily, the fairy said, "Your majesty, here is the beautiful Constantine, daughter of the king of the islands of Terceres, who was at your court under the name of Constantin, and whom you took as your friend. It is she whom the gods have predestined as your wife. But this is not the only marvel that is be accomplished here. The savage whom you see is to become the husband of the charming Princess Fleurianne. Now, do not become frightened, madame," the fairy said when she saw the princess's surprise. "This terrible figure is concealing a prince worthy of you. It is the king of the islands of Aimantine, whom an unjust fairy, who wanted to love him against his will, has kept in this form for many years. However, he will be able to discard this form when the marriage of the king of Sicily with Princess Constantine takes place. It will only take your consent, your majesty," she turned to the king, "to rescue this king from the horrible state to which he has been reduced."

The king of Sicily had now had time to recover from his surprise, and his sister, too, and he replied to the fairy, "I consent to everything that you wish, madame, and provided that the beautiful Princess Constantine desires to make me happy, I have nothing more to wish."

The princess gave a sign of her intention with a great deal of modesty and bashfulness, and as soon as the fairy touched the savage with a golden wand, he became the most handsome prince that one had ever seen.

Immediately he threw himself at the feet of the beautiful Fleurianne, and right there and then they showed the most tender affection for one another. The king of Sicily embraced Constantine, and the princess his sister, who had loved her so much as Constantin, did not love her any less as Constantine and showed her tender affection with a bit of confusion. Obligeantine told the king a little about the background of the princess whom he was about to marry, and when she had finished, she said, "It is necessary that you receive King Richardin and Queen Corianthe, who will be arriving at your palace to attend the marriage of their daughter as well as the three queens, her sisters, and the three kings, their husbands, who have been instructed to come under my orders."

Princess Constantine blushed because she thought that the deformity of her family would upset the king. When the fairy observed this, she said, "I anticipated this, and I never do things halfway. Even if your sisters are not as beautiful as you, they are now beautiful enough to adorn this celebration, and thanks to a powerful art that has aided nature, their husbands have also been changed."

Upon saying these words, she began walking and was followed by the king, holding Constantine's hand, and then the king of the islands of Aimantine with Fleurianne. They went into the large hall and crossed the apartment to the great astonishment of the entire court. Finally they arrived at the grand hall of the palace, where all the lords and ladies had gathered, and Constantine was presented to them as their queen.

Everyone was enchanted by her beauty, and everyone was surprised by the resemblance that she had to Constantin. This puzzle as well as the one that concerned the savage was soon explained. Just then the king and queen of the islands of Terceres entered along with their three daughters and husbands, who were now just as beautiful and handsome as they had been ugly and deformed, but their names remained the same. Everyone began embracing one another and admiring one another. The double marriage was then performed to everyone's contentment. The good and obliging fairy did the honors and received great thanks from everyone whom she had obligingly helped. She gave magnificent presents to Queen Corianthe and to her daughters. The celebration was marvelous, and the fairy took care of everything. It was she who brought the husbands and wives to their beds, and since the king of the islands of Aimantine did not have an entourage with him, she arranged to have all this for him when he awoke the next day. The amusements and the tournaments lasted many days, and Magotin, Gambille, and Trotte-mal did miraculously well. The prizes were distributed by the fairy, and there was an infinite abundance of riches.

The celebrations continued for several months, and afterward the king of the Aimantine Islands led his charming wife to his realm with a sumptuous entourage and immense wealth. The three kings of the islands of Terceres returned to their realms, but King Richardin and his queen continued to live in Sicily with the Queen Constantine until the end of their days. Of course, the fairy returned to her magnificent chateau.

Envious Sisters

Though this fairy tale may have originated in the Orient, the source is not clear. Straparola's version was widely known by the French writers at the end of the seventeenth century, and it is clearly the source of Mme d'Aulnoy's and Le Noble's tales. However, it may have even influenced Galland's version. His tale "The Two Sisters Who Envied Their Cadette" was told to him in Paris by a Maronite Christian Arab from Aleppo named Youhenna Diab or Hanna Diab. There was no Arabic manuscript for this tale, and Galland created it from memory after listening to Diab and may have introduced elements from the European tales he knew. His tale "The Two Sisters" in *The Thousand and One Nights* and Mme d'Aulnoy's tale "Princesse Belle-Etoile" had an influence throughout the French and German eighteenth-century chapbooks (*Bibliothèque bleue* and *Blaue Bibliothek*) in Europe and in England. Justus Heinrich Saal published his version entitled "Der wahrredende Vogel" ("The Truth-Speaking Bird") in his book *Abendstunden in lehrreichen und anmuthungen Erzählungen* (1767), and there was also a Scottish adaptation in *Popular Ballads* (1806). The Grimms' source was a tale told in 1813 by a shepherd in a Westfalian dialect, indicating how widespread the fairy tale had also become in the oral tradition. There tend to be four crucial components in the plot of this tale: (1) the wishes of the sisters; (2) the envy of the two older sisters and/or mother-in-law; (3) the abandonment of the children and unjust punishment of the mother; (4) the reunion of the family, often brought about by a singing bird or some magic gift. The bird that reveals the truth is a common motif in many fairy tales throughout the world.

GIOVAN FRANCESCO STRAPAROLA

Ancilotto, King of Provino†

Many years ago there were three charming sisters, courteous and graceful, but low born, who lived in Provino, a very famous and royal city. They were the daughters of Signor Rigo, a baker, who made bread in his oven all the time for other people in the city. His daughters were named Brunora, Lionella, and Chiaretta. One day, when the three sisters were in their garden and looking for something with which to amuse themselves, Ancilotto, the king, passed by with a great company on his way to enjoy some hunting. When Brunora, the eldest sister, saw the honorable entourage, she said to her sisters, Lionella and Chiaretta, "If I could have the

---

† Giovan Francesco Straparola, "Ancilotto, King of Provino"—"Ancilotto, re di Provino, prende per moglie la figliuola d'un fornaio, e con lei genera tre figliuoli; I quali essendo persequitati dalla madre del re, per virtù d'un'acqua d'un pomo e d'un uccello vengono in cognizione del padre" (1550), *Favola* III, *Notte quarta* in *Le piacevoli notti*, 2 vols. (Venice: Comin da Trino, 1550/53).

king's majordomo for my husband, I believe I could quench the thirst of the entire court with one glass of wine."

"And I am certain," said Lionella, "that if the king's private chamberlain were my husband, I could make enough linen from a spindle of my yarn to provide the finest and most beautiful shirts for the entire court."

Then Chiaretta remarked, "And if I had the king himself for my husband, I believe I could give him three children in one birth, two sons and a daughter. Each one of them would have long hair braided below the shoulders and woven together with threads of the finest gold, a golden necklace around their throats, and a star on each of their foreheads."

These words were overheard by one of the courtiers, who rushed to the king and told him what the young girls had said. When the king heard the gist of their conversation, he commanded them to appear before him, and he then interrogated them one by one to determine what they had said in the garden. Thereupon, each of the girls told the king with utmost respect what she had said, and he was very pleased by their responses. Therefore, he wedded Brunora to the majordomo and Lionella to the chamberlain then and there, and at the same time he took Chiaretta as his bride. The hunting was abandoned that day, and everyone returned to the palace, where the marriages were celebrated with the greatest pomp.

However, the mother of King Ancilotto was very displeased by this marriage. No matter how charming Chiaretta was, no matter how beautiful her face was, no matter how graceful and sweet her conversation was, the queen mother did not find her suitable for such a powerful and glorious king because Chiaretta came from such a low and abject family. Nor could she endure the fact that the majordomo and the chamberlain were brothers-in-law of the king, her son. Indeed, her hatred of her daughter-in-law grew so much that she could not stand to see her. Nevertheless, she hid her hatred so as not to offend her son.

After some time had passed, thanks to the will of God, Chiaretta became pregnant, and the king was very pleased, for he expected to see the lovely progeny whom she had promised him. However, just at the time Chiaretta was to give birth, Ancilotto was obliged to journey to a distant country and to dwell there for several days. During his absence, he directed his mother to look after the queen, his wife, and the children, who were soon to be born. Though his mother hated her daughter-in-law, she did not let the king see this and promised him that she would take the greatest care of them.

Soon after the king had departed on his journey, Chiaretta gave birth to three children, two boys and a girl, just as she had promised when she was a maiden. Their hair was braided below their shoulders, and they wore charming golden chains around their necks and had golden stars on their foreheads. The arrogant and malicious queen mother had absolutely no compassion and pity, and she was still burning with pernicious and mortal hatred. So, as soon as the children were born, she made up her mind and was determined to have them secretly killed. This way no one would ever know they had been born, and Chiaretta would be disgraced in the eyes of the king. She was, in addition, not alone in her hatred for Chiaretta, for ever since Chiaretta had become queen and reigning sovereign, Brunora and Lionella had become extremely jealous of their sister and used all their cunning wiles to intensify the great hate of the impetuous queen mother against Chiaretta.

Now, just at the time that Chiaretta gave birth to her children, it happened that three mongrel pups, two males and a female, were born in the courtyard. They had white stars on their foreheads, and there were signs of a frilled collar around their necks. When the two sisters saw this, they succumbed to their diabolical urges. They took the mutts away from the dam and brought them to the queen mother. After they greeted her with due respect, they said, "We know, madame, that your highness has very little love for our sister, and we find this to be just. She is of low origin, and it is not right that your son should have married someone with such low blood as she has. Therefore, knowing how you feel about her, we have brought you these three mongrel pups which were born with stars on their foreheads, and now we await your advice."

These words pleased the queen mother very much, and she immediately decided to bring them to her daughter-in-law, who had not yet seen her children. Then she would tell Chiaretta that the three pups were her own offspring. To make sure that this plot would not be discovered, the wicked woman ordered the midwife to tell Chiaretta that she had indeed given birth to three mongrel pups. Therefore, when the queen mother, the two sisters, and the midwife appeared in her chamber, they said, "Look, oh queen, at the work that you've produced! Make sure that you regard it well so that the king can see the fruit of your womb."

After saying these words, the midwife placed the mongrels by her side. At the same time, she consoled her and told her not to despair because such accidents happened every now and then to persons of high rank. Once these wicked women had accomplished their evil and malicious plan, they had only one thing left to do—bring about the cruel death of the three innocent children. But God was not pleased that they would soil their hands with the blood of their own kin and kept them from murdering them. Instead, they made a chest that was fortified by pitch. Then they put the children into it, closed it, and threw it into the nearby river to let the current take it where it would. Again, God in His justice would not allow these innocents to suffer and hence sent a miller named Marmiato to the bank of the river. When he saw the chest, he hauled it out, opened it, and found three smiling children. Seeing how beautiful they were, he thought they were the children of some noble lady who had committed this crime to hide her shame. So he closed the chest again, hoisted it onto his shoulders, and carried it home, where he said to his wife, Gordiana, "Look what I found in the river. It's a present for you."

When Gordiana saw the children, she graciously accepted them and brought them up as if they had been her own. The couple named one boy Acquirino and the other Fluvio because they had been found in the river. The girl was called Serena.

In the meantime King Ancilotto had been in very high spirits because he believed that he would find three beautiful children on his return home. But things did not work out the way he had thought. When the cunning queen mother saw her son approaching the palace, she went to meet him and told him that his dear wife had given birth to three mongrel pups instead of three children. Then she took him right away into the chamber where his sorrowful wife was resting, and she showed him the pups which were lying beside his wife. In turn, Chiaretta began to shed a flood of tears and denied that the dogs were her offspring, but her wicked sisters confirmed that everything the old mother had said was the truth. When the king heard this, he was greatly disturbed and fell to the ground struck by grief. After he came to himself, he had some doubts, but he eventually trusted what his mother had said. However, since the miserable queen had so patiently suffered from the jealousy of the court with great dignity, he had pity on her and did not sentence her to death. Instead, he ordered her to be brought to a place where she was to wash the pots and pans, and where she was to be fed the rotten garbage that fell to the dirty, stinking ground.

While the unfortunate queen was compelled to spend her life in this filthy place with nothing to eat but rubbish, Gordiana, the wife of the miller Marmiato, gave birth to a son, who was named Borghino and was raised lovingly with the three foundlings. Whenever Gordiana went to cut the hair of the three royal children, she would find many precious stones and great white pearls that would fall out of their long braids. This was why Marmiato was able to give up the humble calling of a miller and why he became rich. Indeed, they could all now enjoy a life of leisure and luxury. But when the three foundlings reached their maturity, they learned that they were not the children of Marmiato and Gordiana but had been found floating in a chest on the river. Thus, they became very discontent and decided to go their way and try their fortune somewhere else. This decision did not please Marmiato and Gordiana because they were deprived of the treasure that fell from the long blond hair and starry foreheads of the children.

Nevertheless, the brothers and their sister left Marmiato and Gordiana and journeyed for a long time until they reached Provino, the city of King Ancilotto, their father. They rented a house right away and began living together and maintained themselves by selling the jewels which fell out of their hair.

One day, the king, who was riding into the country with some of his courtiers, happened to pass the house where the three were living. As soon as they heard that the king was approaching, they ran down the steps and stood bareheaded to give him a respectful greeting. Since they had never seen Ancilotto before, they did not know he was their father. The king, whose eyes were as sharp as a hawk's, looked at them steadily and noticed that they had golden stars on their foreheads. Immediately his heart was moved, and he felt that they might indeed be his own children. So he stopped and said to them, "Who are you, and where do you come from?"

"We are poor strangers who have come to live in this city," they answered humbly.

"I am greatly pleased," answered Ancilotto. "Tell me now, what are your names?"

One of them said, "Acquirino."

The other replied, "Fluvio."

"And I," stated the sister, "am called Serena."

Then the king said, "I would very much like you to dine with me tomorrow."

Though the young people blushed, they could not refuse such a gracious invitation. When Ancilotto returned to the palace, he said to his mother, "Madame, when I was riding today, I encountered by chance two handsome young men and a lovely maiden. They had stars on their foreheads, and if I'm not mistaken, they seemed to be the three children that the Queen Chiaretta had promised me."

Upon hearing the king's words, the wicked old woman smiled somewhat. But she felt as if she had been stabbed in her heart by a knife. Then she summoned the midwife, who had been present at the birth, and said to her in private, "My dear woman, do you know that the king's children are alive and are as beautiful as ever?"

"How can this be?" replied the woman. "Weren't they drowned in the river? How do you know this?"

The queen mother answered, "As far as I can gather from the king's words, they are alive, and I need your help very much. Otherwise, our lives are in danger."

"Don't worry, madame," said the midwife. "I hope to bring about the death of all three of them."

The midwife left and went straight to the house of Acquirino, Fluvio, and Serena. Finding the young maiden alone, she greeted her and talked about many different things. After she had a long conversation with Serena, she said, "My daughter, do you happen to have any water in your house that can dance?"

Serena answered that she did not have any.

"Ah, my daughter," said the midwife, "what beautiful things you would see if you had some! You could wash your face in it, and you would become even more beautiful than you are now."

"And how can I get it?" Serena asked.

"Send your brothers to look for it," replied the midwife. "They will easily find it because it is not far from here."

After saying all this, the old woman departed. When Acquirino and Fluvio returned home, Serena told them about her encounter with the old woman and begged them out of love for her to go and search carefully for some of the precious dancing water. But Fluvio and Acquirino laughed at her request and refused to go because they had no idea where such water was to be found. However, they soon succumbed to the humble pleas of their dear sister, and they took a phial and departed together.

When the two brothers had traveled several miles, they arrived at a clear bubbling fountain where a dove was refreshing itself. When the bird suddenly spoke to them, they were somewhat frightened.

"What are you seeking, young men?" the dove asked.

"We are searching for the precious water that is said to dance," responded Fluvio.

"You miserable souls!" cried the bird. "And who has sent you on this quest?"

"Our sister," said Fluvio.

"Then you will certainly meet your deaths," declared the bird, "for the water you are seeking is guarded by many poisonous beasts that will devour you right away. If you leave the task to me, I'll surely bring some water back to you."

Then the dove took the phial that the brothers were carrying, stuck it under its right wing, and took off in search of the place where the precious water was to be found. Once it arrived there, the dove filled the phial and returned to the brothers, who were waiting for the bird with great anticipation. After receiving the water and thanking the dove for its service, they returned home and gave Serena the water. Then they implored her never to charge them with another task like that because they had almost lost their lives.

A few days later, the king met the two brothers again and said to them, "Why didn't you come to dine with me after accepting my invitation?"

"Gracious majesty," they answered with respect, "we were compelled to undertake an urgent errand."

"Then," said the king, "I shall expect to see you tomorrow without fail."

The young men apologized again, and the king returned to the palace, where he met his mother and told her he had seen the youths with the stars on their heads once more. Upon hearing this the queen mother was very upset, and again she summoned the midwife. She secretly told her all that she had heard and asked her again to find some way out of the danger. The midwife comforted her and told her not to fear because she would make sure this time that they would disappear forever. After leaving the palace, the midwife went directly to Serena's house and found her. Then she asked whether she had obtained any of the dancing water. Thereupon, Serena reported that she had received some from her brothers but not without great danger to their lives.

"That's good," said the woman, "but it would be better if you had the singing apple because you've never seen such a beautiful apple in your life. Nor have you ever heard such sweet and delightful singing."

"But how can I get it?" asked the maiden. "My brothers will never go in search of it because they almost lost their lives and had practically abandoned hope of survival."

"But they still managed to fetch the dancing water for you," said the woman, "and they are not dead. They will get the singing apple for you just as they fetched the water."

Then the old woman took her leave and disappeared. No sooner had the midwife left than Acquirino and Fluvio arrived home, and Serena said to them, "Oh, my brothers, I would really like to see and enjoy the apple that sings so sweetly! If you do not find a way to bring it me, I shall certainly die."

When Acquirino and Fluvio heard these words, they scolded her a great deal and stated that they did not want to risk death again for her sake. But she continued to plead so sweetly and wept so many tears from her heart that her brothers were soon ready to satisfy her wish no matter what might happen. They mounted their horses and rode until they reached an inn. After the brothers dismounted, they asked their host whether he could tell them where the apple that sang so sweetly was to be found. He replied that he knew where it was, but they could not go there because it was in a lovely and pleasant garden guarded by a ferocious beast that used its outspread wings to kill all who approached the garden.

"What, then, should we do?" the brothers asked. "We must fetch this apple no matter what."

"If you do what I tell you to do," said the host, "you will be able to get the apple without fear of the poisonous beast or death. One of you must take this coat that is completely covered with mirrors and put it on. Once you are dressed in the coat, you must enter the garden, which will have its door open. But the other must stay outside and be careful not to be seen. The beast will immediately charge at the one who enters the garden, but once it sees itself in the mirror, it will fall down to the ground. Then the one waiting outside the garden can go to the tree and pluck the singing apple and leave the garden without looking behind."

The young men thanked their host very much, and after they left, they did exactly as he said. Once they obtained the apple, they carried it to their sister and implored her again not to compel them to undertake such dangerous tasks anymore.

After some days had passed, the king saw the young men again and called them to him.

"Why have you disobeyed my orders once more and failed to come and dine with me?" he asked.

Fluvio answered, "We would have come, my lord, but various concerns prevented us from fulfilling your request."

Acquirino said they would be glad to see him, and the king returned to his palace, where he met his mother and told her that he had again seen the two young men, that he felt more certain than ever that they were the children whom Chiaretta had promised him, and that he could not rest until they came and had dinner with him. When the queen mother heard these words, she felt more tormented than before and was completely convinced that she had been discovered. In her pain and grief, she summoned the midwife and said, "I surely thought, my dear woman, that the children would have disappeared by this time, and that I would hear no more of them. But they are alive, and we stand in danger of death. Look into this matter. Otherwise, we are lost."

"Noble lady," said the midwife, "keep up your spirits and don't worry. I shall carry out your orders, and you will no longer hear any news about them."

Full of rage and fury, she left the palace and went straight to Serena. After wishing the maiden a good day, she asked her whether she had obtained the singing apple. Serena responded that she had. Then the cunning midwife said, "Ah, my daughter, you really have nothing if you do not get one more thing that is the most beautiful and the most charming thing in the world."

"Good mother, what can this beautiful and charming thing be?" asked Serena.

The old woman replied, "It is the beautiful green bird that talks night and day and speaks about marvelous things. If you indeed possessed this bird, you could consider yourself happy and lucky."

After saying these words, she departed. Soon after Acquirino and Fluvio arrived, and Serena began to beg them to do her one last favor. When they asked her what this favor might be, she answered, "The beautiful green bird."

Fluvio, who had fetched the apple guarded by the poisonous beast and remembered how dangerous the adventure had been, refused to go in quest of the bird. Though Acquirino also declined for some time, he was finally moved by brotherly love and the flood of hot tears that Serena shed, and he decided to satisfy her wish and was joined by Fluvio. Then they mounted their horses and rode for several days until at last they reached a verdant meadow covered with flowers. In the middle there stood a very tall green tree surrounded by marble statues that appeared to be alive. Nearby there was a little stream that ran through the meadow. On top of the tall tree the beautiful green bird was hopping from branch to branch in lively fashion, uttering words which seemed more divine than human. The young men dismounted from their stallions, which they left to graze at will, and approached the marble statues to examine them, but as soon as they touched them, they themselves were turned into marble.

Now, after Serena had waited several months eagerly anticipating the return of her dear brothers, Acquirino and Fluvio, it appeared that she had lost them, and she gave up hope of ever seeing them again. She deeply regretted what had happened and wept about the unfortunate deaths of her brothers. But now she decided to try her own luck. So she mounted a sturdy horse and started her journey. After riding some distance she reached the place where the green bird made its home on the tall green tree and was talking sweetly on one of the branches. As soon as she had entered the green meadow, she immediately recognized her brothers' horses, which were grazing in the pasture. Casting her eyes on the statues, she saw her brothers, who had been transformed into two statues that resembled them. Serena dismounted, went up to the tree, and grabbed the green bird from behind. Finding himself a prisoner, the bird begged her to let him go and promised that at the right time and place he would show his gratitude to her. But Serena answered that, before she would set him free, he had to restore her brothers to their former state.

"Look, then, under my left wing," replied the bird, "and there you will find a feather much greener than any of the others and marked with yellow. Pluck it out and touch any of the statues with it. Then your brothers will come alive."

Serena raised the wing, found the feather, and did as the bird had told her to do. As soon as she touched the marble statues, one after the other, they immediately became live men. Acquirino and Fluvio saw themselves in their pristine forms and joyfully kissed their sister. Now that this transformation was accomplished, the bird again asked Serena to set him free, promising that, if she granted his wish, he would come to her aid whenever she might call upon him. However, Serena was still not content and declared that before she would set him free, he would have to help them find their father and mother, and that until he did this, he would have to be patient.

In the meantime, Serena and her brothers had already begun quarreling about who should be in charge of the bird, but in the end, they agreed that Serena should take care of the bird, and she tended it with great kindness. Now that they had the beautiful green bird, they mounted their horses and were glad to ride home.

In the meantime King Ancilotto had frequently passed their house and was quite astounded when he did not see them anymore. When he asked the neighbors what had happened to them, all that he could learn was that nobody knew anything, and that the three young people had not been seen for many days. But after they had returned and had been living in their house for a couple of days, the king rode by again and caught sight of them. Then he asked why they had not been seen for so long, and Acquirino responded that they had been involved in some strange incidents, and that was why they had been absent so long. They also asked the king to pardon them for not appearing at the palace as he had desired. Indeed, they were all anxious to make amends for their conduct in the future.

When the king heard about their unfortunate experiences, he had great compassion for them, and he would not leave until all three of them accompanied him back to the palace for dinner. But before they set forth, Acquirino secretly filled a phial with dancing water. Fluvio took the singing apple, and Serena, the talking bird, and they all rode back with the king. Once they arrived, they entered the palace with him in good spirits and sat down to eat at the royal table. The queen mother and the jealous sisters of Chiaretta noticed them. As soon as they saw how beautiful the maiden was and how handsome and charming the young men, whose eyes were shining like bright stars, they were filled with dread because they suspected who they might be.

When they had all finished dining, Acquirino said to the king, "Your majesty, before we take our leave, we should like to show you some things that may delight you very much."

So he poured some of the dancing water into a silver cup and put it on the table while Fluvio put his hand into his bosom and drew out the singing apple, which he placed beside the water. Serena also brought out the green bird and set it on the table. Immediately the apple began to sing most sweetly, and the water danced wonderfully to the music. The king and the courtiers were all so delighted that they burst into laughter. But the wicked queen mother and the jealous sisters grew more troubled and suspicious because they feared for their lives.

At last, when the apple and the water stopped singing and dancing, the bird began to talk and said, "Oh, sacred majesty, what do those people deserve who have plotted the death of two brothers and a sister?"

Then the cunning queen mother cried out before anyone, "Nothing less than death by fire!"

All those present agreed. Then the singing apple and the dancing water raised their voices and said, "Ah, false mother, full of iniquity, your own tongue has condemned yourself, those wicked and envious sisters of the queen, and the vile midwife to this horrible death."

When the king heard these words, he was filled with suspense, and then the bird continued to speak and said, "Oh, sacred majesty, these young people are the three children that you had always longed for. They bear the star on their foreheads, and their innocent mother is the woman who has been forced to live in filth."

Then the king gave orders to have Chiaretta fetched from the squalid place that was her prison and to be clad once more in her royal garments. As soon as this had been done, she was brought into the presence of the king and his court. Though she had been kept in prison for a long time and had been badly treated, she had retained all her former beauty. Then the green bird related the strange story from beginning to end, and when the king knew all that had happened, he tenderly embraced Chiaretta and their three children with tears in his eyes, and the beautiful green bird, having been set free, disappeared altogether.

The next day the king commanded a huge fire to be built in the center of the piazza. Then he had his mother, the two sisters of Chiaretta, and the midwife thrown into it without pity in the presence of all the people who watched them burn to death. And Ancilotto lived happily for many years with his beloved wife and his beautiful children. After choosing an honorable husband for Serena, he bestowed the kingdom on his two sons as his rightful heirs.

MARIE-CATHERINE D'AULNOY

Princess Belle-Etoile and Prince Cheri†

Once upon a time there was a queen who lost everything that constituted her grandeur except her throne and her cases of table settings. One case was made of velvet and embroidered with pearls; the other was made of gold and adorned with diamonds. She kept them as long as she could, but she was reduced to such dire need that she was obliged every now and then to detach a pearl, a diamond, or an emerald and sell it privately to support her servants. She was a widow, left with three daughters, who were very young and very charming. Eventually, she thought that, if she brought them up with the grandeur and magnificence befitting their birth, they would feel the inevitable change in their circumstances more keenly. Therefore, she decided to sell what little property she had left and to go and settle with her three daughters in some country house a long way off, where they might manage to live within their slender means.

However, while passing through a forest infested with thieves, she was robbed and left all but destitute. The poor queen was more disturbed by this last misfortune than by all that she had experienced before, and she realized that she must either work for her bread or perish from hunger. She used to take great pleasure in serving a good meal and knew how to make excellent sauces. She never went anywhere without her little golden spice box, which people would come from great distances to see, and now

---

† Marie-Catherine d'Aulnoy, "Princesse Belle-Etoile and Prince Cheri"—"La Princesse Belle-Étoile et le Prince Chéry," in *Suite des contes nouveaux ou les fées à la mode*, 2 vols. (Paris: Théodore Girard, 1698).

this object, which used to be something amusing for her, provided her with the means of earning a living.

She settled down in a very pretty house near a large city and made wonderful ragouts. The people in those parts were fond of good living, so everybody flocked to her establishment. People talked about nothing but this excellent cook, and they scarcely allowed her time to breathe. In the meantime, her three daughters grew up, and their beauty would also have been the talk of the town, just like the queen's sauces, if she had not kept them in their room, which they were rarely allowed to leave.

On one of the finest days in the year, a little old woman appeared at her house and seemed quite exhausted. She leaned on a stick with her body almost bent in half, and her face was full of wrinkles. "I've come to eat one of your good dinners," she said. "Before I go to another world, I want to be able to boast of something I've really enjoyed in this one." She took a straw chair, seated herself near the fire, and told the queen to make haste. Since she could not do everything herself, she called her three daughters. The first was named Roussette, the second, Brunette, and the third, Blondine. She had named each one after the color of her hair. They were dressed like country girls, in bodices and petticoats of different colors. The youngest was the most beautiful and the most gentle. Their mother ordered one maiden to fetch some young pigeons out of the dovecote, another to kill some chickens, and the third to make the pastry. In short, the old woman was soon given a nice clean tablecloth, a very white napkin, highly polished earthenware, and a fine dinner with several courses. Moreover, the wine was good, there was plenty of ice, and the glasses were constantly rinsed by the fairest hands in the world. All this whetted the appetite of the good little old woman. She became somewhat merry and said a thousand things, and the queen, who appeared to be taking no notice, discovered considerable wit in what she said.

The meal was finished as pleasantly as it began, and as the old woman arose, she said to the queen, "My very good friend, if I had money I'd pay you, but I've been a beggar for a long time. I could have found no such good cheer elsewhere, and all I can promise you is that I'll send you better customers than myself."

The queen smiled and said to her kindly, "Go, my good mother, don't trouble yourself. I always feel paid when I've satisfied someone."

"We're delighted to have waited on you," Blondine said, "and if you'll stay for supper, we'll be even more so."

"How happy are those who are born with such benevolent hearts!" the old woman said. "Believe me, you'll be rewarded. Rest assured that the first wish you make without thinking of me will be fulfilled."

All at once she disappeared, and they were positive she was a fairy. They were astonished by this incident, especially because they had never seen a fairy before. They were frightened and talked about her constantly for five or six months so that whenever they wished for anything, she immediately came into their minds. Therefore, nothing ever happened, and they became very angry at the fairy. But one day, when the king had gone out hunting, he decided to visit the celebrated cook to ascertain whether she was really as gifted as he had heard. As he approached the garden, in which the three sisters were gathering strawberries, they heard the noise, and Roussette exclaimed, "Ah, if I were fortunate enough to marry my lord admiral, I'd venture to say that I'd spin a great deal of thread with my spindle and distaff, and I'd make so much cloth with the thread that he'd never have to purchase any more for the sails of his vessels."

"And I," said Brunette, "if I were fortunate enough to become the wife of the king's brother, I'd venture to say that I'd make him so much lace with my needle that his palace would be filled with it."

"And I," said Blondine, "I'd venture to say that, if the king married me, I'd give him two handsome boys and a beautiful girl. Their hair would fall in ringlets with fine jewels, and they'd all have a radiant star on their foreheads, and a rich chain of gold around their necks."

One of the king's favorites had preceded him to inform the mistress of the house about his majesty's approach. When he heard voices in the garden, he stopped, listened quietly, and was greatly surprised by the conversation of these three beautiful girls. Then he went to the king and amused him by repeating what he had heard. The king laughed and ordered the girls to be brought before him.

They quickly appeared with wonderful grace and good manners, and after they greeted the king with respect and modesty, he inquired whether it were true that they had been holding a conversation with regard to the husbands they desired. They blushed and lowered their eyes, but he pressed them even further to tell the truth. When they did, he immediately exclaimed, "I certainly don't know what power's influencing me, but I won't leave this house until I've married the beautiful Blondine."

"Sire," the king's brother said, "I request your permission to marry this lovely Brunette."

"Grant me the same favor, sire," the admiral said. "I like this redhead very much."

The king was pleased that the chief men of his realm were prepared to follow his example, and he told them he approved of their choices and asked the mother of the young women if she consented. She replied that her greatest hopes were being realized. The king embraced her, and the prince and the admiral followed his example.

When the king was ready for dinner, a table set for seven with gold plates came down the chimney, and it had the most delicious things to arouse one's appetite. The king, however, hesitated before tasting anything, for he feared that the witches had cooked the viands at one of their festivals, and this way of serving it by the chimney appeared to him rather suspicious. The buffet was also set up, and nothing could be seen but basins and vases of gold, so superbly made that the material itself was outdone. At the same time a swarm of bees appeared in crystal hives and began making the most charming music that can possibly be imagined. The whole dining room was filled with hornets, bees, wasps, gnats, and other insects of that description, and they waited on the king with supernatural ability. Three or four thousand flies served him wine without one of them daring to drown itself in it, which demonstrated a moderation and a discipline that was perfectly astonishing. Of course, the queen and her daughters realized that all this came from the little old woman, and they blessed the hour they had met her.

After the banquet, which lasted so long that night surprised the company at table (his majesty was rather ashamed about this, for it appeared as if Bacchus had taken the place of Cupid at this marriage), the king rose and said, "Let's finish this ceremony as we should have begun it." He drew his ring from his finger and placed it on that of Blondine, and the prince and the admiral did the same. The bees sang with increased vigor as the company danced and made very merry, and all those who had come in the king's retinue advanced and saluted the queen and the princess her sister. Yet they treated the admiral's wife with less ceremony, and this disturbed her a great deal, for she was the older sister of Brunette and Blondine and had made the least brilliant match of the three.

The king sent his grand equerry to inform the queen his mother about everything that had taken place and to order his most magnificent coaches to fetch Blondine and her two sisters. The queen-mother was the most cruel and violent woman in the world. When she heard that her son had married without consulting her, and moreover a girl of obscure birth, and that the prince his brother had done the same thing, she flew into such a rage that she frightened the whole court. She asked the grand equerry what motive could possibly have induced the king to make such a degrading match. He answered that it was the hope of becoming the father of two boys and a girl who would be born with long curly hair, stars on their foreheads, and gold chains round their necks. These wonderful things had enchanted him. The queen-mother smiled contemptuously at the naiveté of her son and made several insulting remarks about it that sufficiently demonstrated her outrage.

When the coaches had arrived at the little country house, the king invited his mother-in-law to follow him and promised that she would be treated with the greatest respect. But she thought right away that the court would be like a sea in constant motion and said, "Sire, I've experienced too many things in the world to want to leave the quiet retreat that I had so much difficulty in obtaining."

"What!" the king said. "Do you want to continue running an inn like this?"

"No," she replied. "I'd like an allowance from you to live on."

"At least permit me," the king added, "to give you an establishment and officers to wait on you."

"I thank you, sire," the queen said. "If I live by myself, I'll have no enemies to trouble me, but if I had a house full of domestics, I fear I might find some among them."

The king admired the sense and discretion of a woman who thought and spoke like a philosopher. While he was urging his mother-in-law to accompany him, Roussette, the admiral's lady, managed to hide all the fine basins and gold vases from the buffet in the bottom of her coach and was determined not to lose any of them. But the fairy, who saw everything though nobody saw her, changed them into earthenware. When Roussette arrived at court later and wanted to carry them into her room, she found nothing that was worth the trouble. The king and queen tenderly embraced the prudent mother and assured her that they would do anything in their power for her. Then they left the rural abode and headed toward the city, preceded by attendants playing trumpets, oboes, kettledrums, and other instruments that made noise enough to be heard a long way off. The confidantes of the queen-mother had advised her to conceal her displeasure since it would offend the king, and the consequences might be unpleasant. Therefore, she restrained herself and received her two daughters-in-law with apparent kindness, giving them presents of jewels, and praising whatever they did, whether it was good or bad.

The fair queen and Princess Brunette were united by a close friendship, but Roussette hated them both mortally. "Just look at the good luck of my two sisters," she said. "One is a queen; the other, wife of a prince of royal blood. Their husbands adore them, and I, who am the eldest, and who consider myself a hundred times more beautiful than either one of them, have married a mere admiral, who doesn't care for me half as much as he ought."

The jealousy she felt for her sisters soon made her join the queen-mother's camp, for it was well known that the affection she displayed for her daughters-in-law was but feigned, and that nothing would have given her more pleasure than an opportunity to do them some harm. Now the queen and the princess were both about to give birth when, unfortunately, a serious war broke out, and the king was compelled to depart at the head of his army. The young queen and the princess were obliged to remain behind under the control of the queen-mother, and they asked the king for permission to return to their own mother and to be comforted by her during the cruel absence of their husbands. However, the king could not consent to this. He implored his wife to remain in the palace and assured her that his mother would treat her well. Indeed, he beseeched his mother most earnestly to love and cherish her daughter-in-law, adding that nothing would please him more, that he anticipated being the father of beautiful children, and that he would look forward to obtaining news of their birth.

The wicked old queen was enchanted that her son placed his wife under her care. She promised him she would only think about Blondine's safety and assured him he had nothing at all to worry about on that score. Therefore, he took his departure, but with such a great desire to return quickly that he risked his troops in every encounter, and fortune continually favored his rashness and crowned all his plans with success. However, the queen gave birth to two boys and a girl before the campaign was over, and the princess her sister also gave birth the same day to a beautiful boy, but she died almost immediately after.

Roussette, the admiral's wife, was very busy hatching plans to harm the young queen. When she saw that the queen had become the mother of such lovely children, and she herself had none, her rage increased. She determined to speak at once to the queen-mother, for there was no time to lose.

"Madame," she said to her, "I'm so deeply grateful for the honor your majesty has bestowed on me by showing me some kindness that I'd willingly sacrifice my interests to further yours. I understand how displeased you must be ever since the king and the prince formed such degrading alliances. Now there are four children born to perpetuate the errors of their fathers. Our mother is a poor villager, who was in want of bread, when it occurred to her to turn cook and make fricassees. Take my advice, madame, let us make a fricassee of these little brats, and get them out of this world before they embarrass you."

"Ah, my dear lady admiral," the queen cried embracing her, "how I love you for your sense of justice, and for sharing my well-founded indignation! I had already decided to do what you've suggested. I'm only unclear as to how I should carry out my plans."

"There's no need to trouble yourself, madame," Rousette replied. "My lapdog has just had three puppies, two male and one female. They each have a star on their foreheads, and a mark around their necks, which has the effect of a chain. We must make the queen believe that she's given birth to these little brutes, and take the two boys, the girl, and the prince's son and do away with them."

"Your plan pleases me immensely," the queen-mother exclaimed. "I've already given orders concerning this matter to Feintise, the queen's lady-in-waiting, so that we have only to send for the little dogs."

"Here they are," the admiral's wife said. "I brought them with me."

Upon saying this, she opened a large bag, which she always carried at her side, and pulled out three blind puppies that she and the queen-mother wrapped in fine linen, which was embroidered with gold and ornamented with lace, just as the linen for the royal children should have been. They placed them in a covered basket, and then the wicked old queen, followed by Roussette, proceeded to the young queen's apartment. "I've come to thank you for the beautiful heirs you've given my son," the queen-mother said. "Here are the heads you've formed to wear a crown. I'm not surprised that you promised your husband two sons and a daughter with stars on their foreheads, flowing locks, and chains of gold around their necks. Take them and nurse them yourself, for you won't find any women willing to suckle puppies."

The poor queen, who was completely exhausted from the pangs of childbirth, almost died from grief when she saw the three little beastly dogs and the sort of kennel they made of her bed, in which they lay yelping desperately. She began to weep bitterly. Then she clasped her hands and said, "Alas! madame, don't add to my torment with your reproaches. Nothing could be worse than what's happened to me. I'd have considered myself happy if the gods had permitted me to die before experiencing the disgrace of being mother to these little monsters. Now the king will hate me just as much as he loved me."

Her voice was stifled with sighs and sobs. She did not have the strength to say anything more, and the queen-mother, who continued to heap abuses on her, had the pleasure of spending three hours at the head of her bed as she lay in that wretched condition. At last she left her, and the queen's sister, who pretended to sympathize with her sorrow, told her that she was not the first who had experienced such a catastrophe and that it was clearly a trick of the old fairy who had promised to work such wonders for them. Since it might be dangerous for her to see the king, she advised her to go to her poor mother with her three little brats of puppies. The queen answered only with tears. Indeed, anyone who was not moved by the wretched state to which she was reduced had to have a hard heart! There she was, suckling those filthy whelps under the impression that she was their mother.

The old queen ordered Feintise to strangle the queen's three children and the princess's son and to bury them so secretly that no one would ever be the wiser. But just as she was about to execute this order and was holding the fatal cord in her hands, she cast her eyes on the poor infants and was so struck by their beauty and the extraordinary appearance of the stars that sparkled on their foreheads that she shrank from dipping her hands in such illustrious blood. Consequently, she arranged to have a boat brought around to the seashore and put the four babes into the same cradle with some strings of jewels so that, if fortune should cast them into the hands of someone charitable enough to bring them up, they would be rewarded for their trouble.

The boat was driven by a stiff breeze so far out to sea that Feintise could no longer make it out. At the same time the waves began to rise, the sun was shrouded, the clouds broke into torrents of rain, and a thousand claps of thunder woke the echoes all around. She was certain that the boat would be swamped, and she felt relieved that the poor little innocents would perish. Otherwise, she felt she would always be haunted by the thought that something extraordinary might happen in their favor and betray the role she had played in saving them.

The king, who had been constantly concerned about his dear wife and the state in which he had left her, agreed to a short truce and returned to the city as quickly as he could. He reached the palace twelve hours after the queen had given birth, and when the queen-mother heard of his arrival, she went to meet him, pretending to be grieved. She held him close to her bosom for a long time and bathed his face with her tears. It appeared as if her sorrow had made her speechless. The king trembled from head to foot and dreaded to ask what had happened, for he was sure that some great disaster had occurred. Finally, she made a great effort and told him that his wife had given birth to three puppies, which Feintise immediately produced. The admiral's wife was all in tears, and she flung herself at the king's feet and implored him not to put the queen to death, but to content himself with sending her back to her mother. Indeed, the young queen was already resigned to such a fate and would consider that sentence a great mercy.

The king was so thunderstruck he could scarcely breathe. He gazed at the puppies and was astonished to see the star that each had in the middle of its forehead and the different color of the hair which formed a ring round each of their necks. He sank into a chair, turning over many thoughts in his mind, and was unable to come to any decision. However, the queen-mother put him under so much pressure that he finally decided to banish the innocent queen. Therefore, she was immediately placed in a litter with her three dogs and carried without the least mark of respect to her mother's house, where she arrived all but dead.

Meanwhile, the gods had looked with compassion on the barque in which the three princes and the princess had been sent out to sea. The fairy who protected them had milk instead of rain fall into their little mouths. They suffered nothing from the sudden terrible storm and floated on a sea as smooth as a canal for seven days and seven nights, when a corsair[1] discovered them. Although the captain had been quite some distance from them, he had been struck by the glistening stars on their foreheads, and he boarded the boat, believing it to be full of jewels. Sure enough, he found some, but what moved him even more was the beauty of the four wonderful children. His desire to save them induced him to alter his course and to set sail for home in order to give the children to his wife, who did not have any and had long wished to have some.

His speedy return alarmed her, for he had sailed away on a very long voyage. But when he presented her with such a great treasure, she became ecstatic, and together they admired the wonderful stars, the chains of gold that could not be taken off their necks, and their long ringlets. The woman's astonishment became even greater when she combed their hair, for each time she combed their hair, out rolled pearls, rubies, diamonds, and emeralds that were different sizes and extremely precious. She told her husband about this, and he was just as surprised as she was.

"I'm quite tired of a pirate's life," he said, "and if the locks of these little children continue to supply us with such treasures, I'll give up roaming the seas, for my wealth will be just as great as that of our most celebrated captains. The corsair's wife, whose name was Corsine, was pleased by her husband's decision, and she loved the four infants even more because of it. She named the princess Belle-Etoile, her eldest brother Petit-Soleil, the second Heureux, and the son of the princess, Cheri. The latter was much handsomer than either of the other two boys so that, although he had neither star nor chain, Corsine loved him more than she did his cousins.

Since she could not raise them all without the aid of a nurse, she asked her husband, who was extremely fond of hunting, to catch some very young fawns for her. He had no trouble doing this quickly, for the forest in which they lived was vast and well stocked with deer. After Corsine obtained the fawns, she tied them up to windward, and once the does smelled them, they came to suckle them. Corsine then hid the fawns and put the infants in their place, who thrived remarkably well on the milk of the does. Four of them came to Corsine's dwelling twice a day in search of the princes and princess, whom they took for fawns.

This was how the royal children spent their early childhood. The corsair and his wife adored them so much that they lavished them with attention. The corsair had been well educated, and it had been less from inclination than from the caprice of fortune that he had become a pirate. He had married Corsine when she was in the service of a princess, in whose court she had fortunately cultivated her natural talents. She had excellent manners, and though she lived in a sort of wilderness, where she and her husband lived only off the plunder he brought home from his cruises, she

---

1. A privateer or pirate. The corsairs were generally authorized to cruise along the North African coast and plunder ships.

had not forgotten the customs of polite society. They were most delighted at no longer being obliged to expose themselves to the danger that accompanied the work of a pirate. Indeed, they had become sufficiently rich to abandon this profession, for, as I have already said, there were valuable jewels that dropped from the beautiful hair of the princess and her brothers, and Corsine disposed of them in the nearest town and always brought back a thousand pretty things for her four babies.

As they grew older, the corsair dedicated himself seriously to cultivating the fine natural abilities with which heaven had endowed them, and since he was convinced there were some great mysteries about their birth and the accident that led to his discovering them, he desired to show his gratitude to the gods for the present they had given him by taking great care of their education. So, after making his dwelling more habitable, he drew talented people to his house, and they taught the children various skills which they acquired with a facility that surprised each one of their great masters.

The corsair and his wife never told anyone the story about the four children. They passed them off as their own, although all the actions of the children revealed that they came from more illustrious blood. They were extremely united, unaffected, and courteous; but Prince Cheri showed Princess Belle-Etoile a more ardent and devoted affection than the other two. The moment she expressed a wish for anything, he would attempt even the impossible to please her and very seldom left her side. When she went hunting, he accompanied her. When she stayed home, he always found some excuse for not going out himself. Petit-Soleil and Heureux, who were her brothers, were less tender and respectful. She noticed the difference, and in justice to Cheri, she loved him more than she did the others. As they grew up, their mutual affection increased with their age. At first it resulted in pure pleasure.

"My gentle brother," Belle-Etoile said to him, "if my wishes could make you happy, you'd be one of the greatest kings on earth."

"Alas, sister!" he replied. "Don't begrudge me the happiness I enjoy in your company. I prefer spending one hour with you to all the grandeur you desire for me."

When she made a similar speech to her brothers, they answered frankly that they would be delighted to be kings, and when she tested them by adding, "Yes, I want you to sit on the highest thrones in the world, though I'd never see you anymore," they immediately answered. "You're right, sister, it would be well worth the sacrifice."

"You'd consent, then, in that case not to see me again?" she asked.

"Certainly," they replied, "we'd be content to hear from you every now and then."

When she was alone she thought about these different ways of loving, and she found her own feelings matched theirs exactly, for though Petit-Soleil and Heureux were dear to her, she had no desire to spend the rest of her life with them, while with regard to Cheri, she burst into tears whenever she contemplated the possibility that their father might send him to sea or off to the wars. It was then that love, disguised under the specious form of natural affection, established itself in these young hearts. At fourteen, Belle-Etoile began to reproach herself with the injustice she felt she was doing her brothers by not loving them all in the same way. She imagined that the intentions and caresses of Cheri brought all this about, and she told him to stop seeking ways to please her. "You've already found too many," she said to him graciously, "and you've succeeded in making me feel a great difference between you and our brothers."

What joy he felt at hearing her talk like that! Far from relaxing the attention he paid her, he increased his efforts, and every day he gave her some new and gallant token of his care. They were as yet unaware of the extent and the nature of their affection, when one day some new books were brought to Belle-Etoile. She picked up the first that came to hand, and it was the story of two young lovers, whose love for one another had begun while they thought they were brother and sister.[2] Afterward their love was discovered by their families, and eventually, after experiencing many difficulties, they married each other. As Cheri read remarkably well and not only understood what he read, but had the capacity to convey the full meaning to others, the princess requested him to read to her, while she finished some work in floss-silk which she was eager to complete. Therefore, he read the story, and he was stunned to discover a perfect description of all his feelings. Belle-Etoile was no less surprised. It seemed as though the author had read all that was happening inside her. The more Cheri read, the more agitated he became. The more the princess listened, the more affected she was. Despite all her efforts to control herself, her eyes filled with tears, and they ran down her cheeks. Cheri, too, struggled in vain against his feelings. He turned pale. His voice faltered. Each of them suffered all you can imagine under such circumstances. "Ah, sister," he exclaimed, gazing at her sadly and dropping the book, "how happy Hippolyte was in not being the brother of Julie!"

"We're not so fortunate," she replied. "Alas, don't we deserve to be like them?" As she uttered these words, she felt she had said too much. She stopped in great confusion, and if anything could have crushed the prince it was the state in which he saw her.

From that moment on, they both fell into a profound melancholy without further explanation. To a certain extent, they understood what was happening inside them, and they took pains to conceal their secret from everyone. They themselves would have preferred not knowing about it, and they never talked about it to each other. Still, it is so natural to hope that the princess placed great stock in the fact that Cheri was the only one who did not have a star on his forehead or a chain around his neck, although he had long ringlets, from which jewels fell when they were combed, the same as his cousins.

One day the three princes went out hunting together, and Belle-Etoile shut herself up in a small room which she liked because it was gloomy and she could muse in it more freely than anywhere else. She sat there perfectly still and silent. This room was separated from Corsine's chamber

---

2. Mme d'Aulnoy is referring to her own novel, *L'histoire d'Hypolite, comte de Duglas* (1690), in which Julie de Warwick and Hypolite are in love with one another but wrongly think they are brother and sister and feel guilty about their love for one another.

only by the wainscot, and she thought the princess was out walking. But the princess heard her say to the corsair, "Belle-Etoile is now of an age to be married. If we knew who she was, we could try to arrange a suitable match for her. Or, if we could determine that her brothers were not really her brothers, we would give her to one of them. Indeed, where could she ever find any men so remarkably handsome as they are?"

"When I found them I saw nothing that could give me any idea of their birth," the corsair remarked. "The jewels that were tied to their cradle showed that they belonged to wealthy people. The thing that was most striking was that their ages indicated that they had all been born at the same time, and four at a birth is not at all a common occurrence."

"I also suspect that Cheri is not their brother. He has neither star nor neck chain."

"That's true," replied her husband. "But diamonds fall from his hair like they do from the others. After all the wealth we've amassed thanks to these dear children, the only wish I have left is to discover their origins."

"We must leave it up to the gods," Corsine said. "They've given them to us, and they'll no doubt clear up the mystery in their own good time."

Belle-Etoile listened attentively to this conversation. It is impossible to describe her delight at the hope she had thus been given that she was of high birth. Although she had always respected the couple whom she had considered her parents, she could not help feeling some pain at being the daughter of a corsair. But what excited her imagination even more was the thought that Cheri might not be her brother, and she was burning with desire to talk to him about it and to tell her brothers about the extraordinary news that she had learned.

She mounted a dun-colored horse that had rows of diamonds on its black mane, for she had only to pass a comb once through her hair to obtain jewels enough to decorate an entire hunting equipage. The green velvet harness of her steed was covered with diamonds and embroidered with rubies. As soon as she was in the saddle, she rode off to find her brothers in the forest. The sound of horns and hounds indicated clearly their whereabouts, and she joined them in a few minutes. At the first sight of her, Cheri left the chase and advanced to meet her more quickly than the others.

"What a pleasant surprise, Belle-Etoile!" he cried. "You've finally decided to go out hunting. I thought you couldn't be diverted one instant from the pleasure you derive from the music and the sciences that you've been studying."

"I've so much to tell you that I wanted to see you alone," she replied. "And that's why I've come looking for you."

"Alas, sister!" he said sighing, "what do you want with me today? It seems to me you decided some time ago not to have anything to do with me."

She blushed, lowered her eyes, and continued sitting on her horse, sad and thoughtful, without replying to him. Eventually her two brothers came up, and she roused herself at the sight of them. It was as though she had been in a deep sleep, and now she jumped to the ground and led the way. They all followed her, and when she reached the middle of a little piece of mossy ground, shaded by trees, she said, "Sit down here, and I'll tell you what I've just heard."

She repeated the conversation the corsair had with his wife exactly as she had heard it and told them that it appeared they were not their children. Nothing could exceed the surprise of the three princes! They discussed among themselves what they ought to do. One was for setting off without saying anything; the other was for remaining; and the third wanted to depart, and to tell the couple the reason why. The first maintained that his was the surest way because the money the corsair and his wife made by combing them would induce them to keep them there. The other replied it would be all well and good to leave if they knew where to go and what their situation would be, but he did not want to be a vagabond in the world since that was unpleasant. The last prince added that it would be very ungrateful of them to abandon their rescuers without their consent, but that it would be equally stupid to want to remain with them any longer in the middle of a forest, where they could not learn who they were. Therefore, the best thing would be to speak to them and get them to consent to their departure. They all approved of this suggestion and immediately mounted their horses to seek the corsair and Corsine.

Cheri's heart was encouraged by all that hope could offer in a way that would be pleasant to console an afflicted lover. His love enabled him to gain some insight into the future: he did not believe he was Belle-Etoile's brother, and his feelings that he had been restraining for a long time now found a vent that inspired him with a thousand tender thoughts and charmed him. They approached the corsair and Corsine with looks mixed with joy and anxiety.

"We haven't come," said Petit-Soleil (for he was the spokesman), "to deny the affection, gratitude, and respect we owe you. Although we've learned about the way in which you found us at sea, and that you're not our father or mother, your compassion in saving us, the excellent education you've given us, the care and kindness you have shown us—all this has created such a bond that nothing in the world can free us from our duty to you. We've come, then, to repeat our sincere thanks to you and to implore you to tell us the details about the extraordinary way you found us and to give us your sage advice so that we can act accordingly and will not have to reproach ourselves about what we're about to do."

The corsair and Corsine were very surprised that they had discovered what they had so carefully concealed. "You've been told the truth," the corsair said, "and we must indeed let you know that you're not our children, and that fortune alone threw you into our hands. We have no idea about your birth, but the jewels which were in your cradle indicate that your parents were either great lords or very rich people. As to the rest, what advice can we give you? If you'd consider our affection for you, you'd certainly remain with us and provide consolation in our old age by your pleasant company. If the mansion we've built here doesn't please you, or if living in such seclusion distresses you, we'll go wherever you wish, provided it is not to a court. Our long experience has given us a distaste for courtly society, and you'd also be disgusted. Perhaps, if you knew about the continual troubles, deceits, jealousies, caprices, real evils, and imaginary benefits that you'd encounter there, we could tell you even more about it, but you'd think that our advice was biased. Indeed, we are biased, my children, for we wish you'd remain in this peaceful retreat, although you are your own masters to leave it whenever you like. At the same time, remember you are presently safe in port, and if you venture out on a tempestuous ocean, the troubles nearly always outweigh the pleasures. Life is short, and we often abandon it in the middle of our careers. The glitter of the world is like false diamonds, and we allow it to dazzle us due to some strange fate. We can only obtain the most sterling happiness by knowing how to limit our desires, to love peace, and to seek wisdom."

The corsair would not have ended his remonstrances so soon if he had not been interrupted by Prince Heureux. "My dear father," he said, "we're too eager to discover something about our birth to remain in such a solitary and secluded place. The moral you teach is excellent, and I wish we could profit from it, but some strange fate calls us elsewhere. Allow us to fulfill the course of our destiny, and we'll return to see you and give you an account of our adventures."

At these words the corsair and his wife shed tears. The princes were very moved, and Belle-Etoile in particular, for she had a remarkable disposition and would have never thought of leaving this secluded place if she had been sure that Cheri would have always remained with her. But once they had made up their minds, they thought about nothing else except preparing for their voyage. Since they had been found and rescued on the sea, they hoped it would shed some light on the matter that they were so eager to explore. They each had a horse put on board their little vessel, and after combing their heads until they were sore in order to leave Corsine with as many jewels as they could, they asked her in return to give them the strings of diamonds that were in their cradle. She went to fetch them from her room, where she had kept them very carefully, and she attached them all to Belle-Etoile's dress, whom she embraced incessantly, bathing her face with her tears.

Never has the world seen such a sad separation. The corsair and his wife thought it would kill them. Their grief did not emanate from selfish motives, for they had amassed such a great fortune that they did not wish for anything more. Petit-Soleil, Heureux, Cheri, and Belle-Etoile went on board the vessel. The corsair had had one built for the voyage and equipped in a magnificent manner. The mast was made of ebony and cedar wood; the ropes were made of green silk mixed with gold; the sails of gold and green cloth; and the designs were beautiful. As it sailed out of port, Cleopatra with her Antony, and even all of Venus's galley, would have lowered their flags to it. The princess was seated under a rich canopy near the stern. Her two brothers and her cousin stood close by her, looking more radiant than the planets, and their stars gave off long dazzling rays of light. They decided to sail to the very spot where the corsair had found them and did as they had planned. They made preparations for a grand sacrifice to be made there to the gods and to the fairies in order to obtain their protection and guidance to their birthplace. They were about to immolate a turtledove, but the compassionate princess thought it so beautiful that she saved its life. Moreover, to keep it safe from such a fate in the future she let it fly away. "Depart, little bird of Venus," she said, "and if some day I should need you, please don't forget the kindness I've shown you."

So the turtledove flew away, and once the sacrifice was finished, they began playing such a charming concert that it seemed as though all of nature kept a profound silence in order to listen to them. The waves were still. There was not a breath of wind. Zephyr[3] alone played with the princess's hair and messed her veil slightly. Just then a siren emerged from the water, and she sang so well that the princess and her brothers were charmed by her. After singing several melodies, she turned toward them and said, "Have no fear. Let your vessel go where it wants. Then disembark where it stops, and let all those who are in love continue to love each other."

Belle-Etoile and Cheri felt an extraordinary delight at what the siren had just told them. They were convinced it was intended for them, and while they exchanged understanding looks, their hearts conversed in silence without Petit-Soleil and Heureux noticing anything. The vessel sailed at the pleasure of the wind and the tide. Nothing very extraordinary occurred as it navigated the waters, except that the weather was always beautiful, and the sea always calm. They spent three whole months on their voyage, during which time the enamored Prince Cheri and the princess talked together a great deal.

"I'm feeling very hopeful," he said one day. "Charming Etoile, I'm not your brother! This heart, which knows your power and will never acknowledge another, is not born for crimes. And it would be a crime to love you as I do, if you were my sister, but the generous sire, who came to give us advice, confirmed my opinion about that matter."

"Ah, brother," she replied, "don't rely on signs that are still too obscure for us to understand. What would happen to us if we irritated the gods by encouraging feelings that displeased them? The siren spoke so vaguely that one would have to have a great imagination to interpret what she said as though it applied to us."

"You refuse to do this, cruel one," the disturbed prince said, "not because you respect the gods so much but because you have an aversion for me."

Belle-Etoile did not answer him, and raising her eyes to heaven, she heaved a deep sigh, which he could not help but interpret favorably. It was the time of year when the days were long and sultry. Toward evening the princess and her brothers went on deck to see the sun set in the bosom of the waters, and she sat down. The princes sat down, took their instruments, and began playing a delightful concert. In the meantime, the vessel, driven by a fresh gale, sailed more quickly, and it soon rounded a small point of land that concealed a part of the most beautiful city in the world. Suddenly, as the city came into sight, its appearance astonished our charming young travelers. All the palaces were made of marble and had gilded roofs. The rest of the houses were made of very fine porcelain, and several evergreen trees blended their enamel leaves with the various colors of the

---

3. The west wind or the god of the west wind.

marble, the gold and the porcelain making the travelers eager to enter the port, but they doubted whether their boat could find room because there were so many others that the masts seemed like a floating forest.

However, they managed to do it and landed. All at once, the shore was crowded with people who had seen the magnificent ship. Indeed, the ship that the Argonauts[4] had constructed to capture the golden fleece could not surpass the radiance of this ship. Moreover, the stars and the beauty of those wonderful young travelers enchanted all who beheld them, and they ran and told the king the news. Since he could not believe what he heard, he went to the grand terrace of the palace that looked out on the seashore. From there he could see the princes, Petit-Soleil and Cheri, take the princess in their arms and carry her ashore. Then they got out their horses with their rich harnesses that perfectly matched everything else about the vessel. Petit-Soleil mounted a horse that was blacker than jet. Heureux rode a gray one, Cheri's was as white as snow, and the princess was on her dun-colored steed. The king admired all four of them seated on their horses, which pranced so proudly that they kept everyone at a distance, especially those who would have come too near them. When the princes heard the people say, "There's the king," they looked up and were so struck by his majestic appearance that they made a profound obeisance and passed slowly with their eyes fixed upon him. He also looked earnestly at them and was just as much charmed by the princess's beauty as by the handsome mien of the young princes. He ordered his equerry to offer them his protection and anything else that they might need in a country where they were evidently strangers. They accepted the honor the king conferred on them with respect and gratitude and said they only needed a house, where they could be alone, and that they would be glad if it were one or two miles from the city since they were very fond of walking. The chief equerry immediately gave them one of the most magnificent houses, where they and their entourage were comfortably lodged.

The king was so interested in these four young people he had just seen that he immediately went to the chamber of the queen his mother to tell her about the wonderful stars that shone on their foreheads and everything else that he admired about them. She was thunderstruck and asked him right away how old he thought they might be. He replied fifteen or sixteen, and she showed no signs of uneasiness, but was terribly afraid that Feintise had betrayed her. In the meantime, the king kept walking back and forth and said, "How happy a father must be to have such handsome sons and such a beautiful daughter! What an unfortunate king I am! To be the father of three dogs and to have them as my illustrious heirs! The succession to my crown is certainly well secured."

The queen-mother listened to these words with dreadful anxiety. The radiant stars and the age of these strangers matched the particulars and date of birth of the princess and their sister so perfectly that she strongly suspected she had been deceived by Feintise, and that instead of killing

---

4. The legendary Greek heroes who sailed with Jason in quest of the Golden Fleece. Their ship was called the *Argo*, and the most important single account of the Argonauts' voyage is the *Argonautica* of Apollonius Rhodius, written in the third century B.C.E.

the king's children she had saved them. Since she had great self-control, she gave no sign of what was going on in her mind. She did not even inquire about several things she was anxious to ascertain on that day, but the next morning she asked her secretary to go to the strangers and to examine everything and check whether they really had stars on their foreheads under the pretext of giving orders in the house for their accommodation.

The secretary departed early in the morning and arrived as the princess was at her dressing table. In those days they did not purchase their cosmetics at shops. Those who were fair remained fair, those who were black did not become white. Consequently, he saw her having her hair dressed. As they combed it, her fair tresses, finer than gold thread, fell in ringlets to the ground. There were several baskets around her to prevent the jewels that fell from her hair from being lost. The star on her forehead glistened so strongly they could hardly bear it, and the gold chain around her neck was as marvelous as the precious diamonds that rolled from the crown of her head. The secretary could hardly believe his eyes, but the princess selected the largest pearl she had and asked him to accept it in remembrance of her. It was the one that the kings of Spain esteem so much and is called *peregrina*, that is to say, pilgrim, because it came from a traveler.

The secretary took leave of her and was baffled by such great generosity. Then he paid his respects to the three princes and remained with them for some time in order to obtain as much information as he could about them. When he returned and made his report to the queen-mother, her suspicions were confirmed. He told her that Cheri did not have a star, but that jewels fell from his hair like his brothers, and that in his opinion he was the handsomest. He also told her that they came from a great distance, and that their father and mother had given them only a certain time to see foreign countries. This latter point rather stumped the queen, and she began to think that they might not be the king's children. Thus she vacillated between fear and hope.

Meanwhile, the king, who was very fond of hunting, rode by their house. The grand equerry, who accompanied him, told him in passing that it was there, by his orders, he had lodged Belle-Etoile and her brothers.

"The queen has advised me," the king replied, "not to see them. She's afraid that they've come from some country where a plague is raging, and that they might have brought the infection with them."

"The beautiful young stranger is indeed very dangerous," the grand equerry replied. "But, sire, I would fear her eyes more than the plague."

"To tell the truth," the king said, "I agree with you," and immediately he put spurs to his horse. As he drew near a large salon with open windows, he heard the sounds of instruments and voices, and after listening with great pleasure to a sweet symphony, he advanced again. The sound of horses induced the princes to look out the window, and as soon as they saw the king, they saluted him respectfully and hastened to the door. There they received him with joyful faces and gave him many signs of reverence. They fell at his feet and embraced his knees, while the princess kissed his hands as though she recognized him as their father. He embraced them fervently and could not understand why his heart was so excited.

He told them that they must come to the palace and that he wished them to be his guests and to present them to his mother. They thanked him for the honor he had bestowed on them and assured him that, as soon as their clothes and their equipage were ready, they would come to the court right away.

The king left them to finish his hunting. Then he kindly sent them half the game and took the rest to the queen. "What's this!" she said. "I can't believe you've had such a bad day. You generally kill three times as much game."

"Very true," the king replied. "But I've given some to the handsome strangers. I feel so much affection for them that I'm quite surprised by it. If you hadn't been so alarmed by the idea of a contagious disease, I would have invited them to the palace before this."

The queen-mother was very angry. She accused him of failing to respect her and reproached him for having exposed himself so carelessly. As soon as he left her, she sent for Feintise and then locked herself in her room with her. Once alone with her she seized her by the hair and put a dagger to her throat. "Wretched woman," she said, "I don't know what should prevent my sacrificing you to avenge my just anger. You've betrayed me. You didn't kill the four children I placed in your hands. Confess your crime, and perhaps I'll forgive you."

Feintise was half dead from fright. She threw herself at the queen's feet and told her all that had happened. She thought it impossible that the children were still alive, for the storm that had risen was so terrible that she herself had nearly been killed by the hail. At any event she asked for time, and she would find some means to do away with them, one after the other, without anyone suspecting it.

The queen, who only wanted to see them dead, was slightly appeased. She told Feintise to get to work right away, and indeed, old Feintise, who saw herself in great danger, did everything she had to do. She waited for the time when the princes went hunting. Then she took a guitar under her arm and went and sat down opposite the princess's windows, where she sang the following words:

> "Beauty can surmount things night and day,
> Profit by it while you may:
> Youth soon flies,
> Beauty dies,
> And frosty age blights every flower.
> Ah, what woe
> It is to know,
> We've lost our chains and power!
> In despair we rail at Fate,
> And strive to charm when all too late.

> "Youthful hearts, your time improve,
> Yours the season is for love;
> Youth soon flies,
> Beauty dies,
> And frosty age blights every flower.
> Ah, what woe

It is to know,
We've lost our charms and power!
In despair we rail at Fate,
and strive to charm when all too late."

Belle-Etoile thought the words were very pretty, and she went to the balcony to see who was singing. As soon as she appeared, Feintise, who had dressed herself very neatly, made her a low curtsy. The princess bowed in return, and since she was in a good mood, she asked her if the words she had just heard had been composed about herself.

"Yes, charming young lady," Feintise replied. "I wrote them about me, but if you want to avoid having such lines written about you, I've come to give you some advice that ought to help you."

"And what is it?" Belle-Etoile asked.

"If you'll permit me to enter your chamber," she said, "I shall tell you."

"You can come up," the princess replied.

The old woman immediately went up to her room and entered with a certain courtly air that is never lost when once acquired.

"My fair child," Feintise said, not losing a moment (for she was afraid someone might come and interrupt her), "heaven has made you very lovely—you're endowed with a radiant star on your forehead, and they tell me many other wonderful things about you. But you're still missing one thing that is essential and necessary for you. If you don't have it, I pity you."

"And what is it I need?" she replied.

"The dancing water," our malicious old woman stated. "If I had possessed it, you wouldn't see a white hair on my head, or a wrinkle on my face. I would have had the most beautiful teeth in the world and the most charming childlike manner. Alas! I learned about this secret too late. My charms had already faded. Take advantage of my misfortune, my dear child. It will be a consolation to me, for I feel a most extraordinary affection for you."

"But where shall I find this dancing water?" Belle-Etoile asked.

"It's in the luminous forest," Feintise said. "You have three brothers. Doesn't any one of them love you enough to go and fetch some? Truly they must have very little affection for you. In fact, this matter is of great importance to you since it would allow you to keep your beauty forever."

"My brothers all love me," the princess said. "But there's one of them who would never refuse me anything. Certainly, if this water possesses all the power you describe, I'll reward you according to its value."

The perfidious old woman went away in haste and was delighted at having been so successful. She told Belle-Etoile that she would be sure to come and see her. When the princes returned from the chase, one brought a young wild boar, another a hare, and the third a stag. They laid the spoil at their sister's feet, but she regarded this homage with a sort of disdain, for she was absorbed by Feintise's story. Indeed, her concern was quite apparent, and Cheri, who kept himself busy most of the time by anticipating her moods, noticed how disconcerted she was after being with her less than a quarter of an hour. "What's the matter, my dear Etoile?"

he said. "Don't you like the country we're in? If that's the case, let us depart immediately. Or, perhaps our equipage is not grand enough, the furniture not sufficiently beautiful, or the table not as fine as you like? Speak, I implore you, so that I may have the pleasure of being the first to obey you and to make the others do likewise."

"I'm glad you're encouraging me to tell you what's on my mind," she replied. "Now I can confess that I can no longer live without the dancing water. It's in the luminous forest. If I can obtain it, I'll have nothing to dread from the ravages of years."

"Don't worry, my charming Etoile," he said. "I'll go and get you some of this water, or you'll know by my death that it was impossible to obtain it."

"No," she said. "I'd rather renounce all the advantages of beauty. I'd much rather be frightful than risk such a precious life. I beg you not to think about the dancing water anymore. Indeed, if I have any power over you, I forbid you to go."

The prince pretended to obey her, but as soon as he saw she was occupied by something, he mounted his white horse, which constantly pranced and curveted. He provided himself with money and rich garments. As for diamonds, his hair could furnish him with enough. If he ran his comb through it three times, it would sometimes produce a million. The supply was not always the same, and the princess and her brothers were aware that the state of their mind or that of their health regulated the quantity of the jewels.

Cheri took no one with him so that he would feel more at liberty. If the adventure turned out to be dangerous, he wanted to be able to risk doing it without exposing himself to the remonstrances of a zealous and timid attendant. When suppertime arrived and the princess did not see her brother Cheri, she felt so concerned that she could not eat or drink. She had her attendants search for him everywhere. The two princes, who knew nothing about the dancing water, begged her not to worry herself so much. He could not be far off, for he was fond of indulging himself in daydreams, and he was most likely in the forest. Consequently, the princess was put at ease until midnight, but after that, she lost all patience, and with tears in her eyes, she told her brothers that she was the cause of Cheri's absence, that she had expressed a great desire to have some of the dancing water from the luminous forest, and that he had surely gone there. Upon hearing this news, they decided to send several people after him, and she commanded them to tell him that she wanted him to return.

In the meantime, the wicked Feintise was very eager to know the results of her advice. When she heard that Cheri had already set out, she was delighted, for she was convinced that he would go faster than those who followed him, and that he would encounter some harm. Thus she ran to the palace, full of hope, and told the queen-mother about all that had happened. "I admit, madame," she said, "that I'm now positive they are the three princes and their sister. They have stars on their foreheads and chains of gold around their necks. Their hair is most beautiful, and jewels continually fall from it. I've seen the princess adorned with some that I had put into her cradle, although not so valuable as those that fall from her hair. So I no longer doubt that they've returned despite the fact that I had taken good care to prevent it. But, madame, I'll get rid of them for you, and since it's the only means of making up for my fault, I implore you only to give me time. One of the princes has already gone to search for the dancing water. He'll undoubtedly perish in the attempt, and I'll find similar means to do away with all of them."

"We shall see," the queen said, "whether you're successful. But, you can depend upon it, that's the only way you'll escape my just rage."

Feintise returned more alarmed than ever, racking her brain to think of a way to destroy them. The plan she had adopted with regard to Prince Cheri was one of the most certain, for the dancing water was not easy to obtain. Yet, everyone knew the road that led to the source of the water because it had become so notorious by causing the downfall of all the men who had sought it. Cheri's white horse went astonishingly fast, and he did not spare it because he was so eager to return quickly to Belle-Etoile and please her by the successful result of his journey. He went one week without taking a rest except in the woods under the first tree he came to, and he did not eat anything except the wild fruit he found on his road, scarcely allowing his horse time to graze. At the end of this period, he arrived in a country where he began to suffer a great deal from the heat. Since it was not due to the power of the sun, he had begun trying to determine the cause when he suddenly perceived the luminous forest from the top of a mountain. All the trees were burning without being consumed, and they were spouting flames so far that the country around was a dry desert. In this forest the hissing of serpents and the roaring of lions could be heard, and this astonished the prince a great deal, for it seemed to him impossible that any animal but a salamander could live in this sort of furnace.

After observing this terrible scene for some time, he descended and contemplated his next step, and more than once he gave himself up for lost. As he approached this great fire, he was dying from thirst, and he noticed a spring coming from a mountain and falling into a marble basin. He got off his horse, approached it, and stooped to pour some water into a little golden vase which he had brought with him. He was about to fill it with some of the water that the princess desired when he noticed a turtledove drowning in the fountain. Its feathers were quite wet, and it had lost its strength and was sinking to the bottom of the basin. Cheri took pity on it and saved it. At first he held it by its feet, for it had swallowed so much water it was quite swollen. Then he warmed it with his bosom, dried its wings with a fine handkerchief, and treated it with such skill that the poor dove was soon quite cheerful and quickly got over its fright.

"My Lord Cheri," she said in a sweet and tender voice, "I'm most grateful and obliged to you. This is not the first time I've received crucial help from your family. Now I'm delighted to be in a position to be of service to you. Indeed, I'm very much aware of the purpose of your journey. You've undertaken this quest a bit too rashly, for it would be impossible to guess how many have perished here! The dancing water is the eighth wonder of the world for ladies. It beautifies them, makes them young again, and enriches them. If I were not to be your guide, you'd never reach it, for the spring rises in the middle of the forest, and, gushing out violently, it falls into a deep chasm. The path down the chasm is covered by branches of trees so twined and twisted together that I can't see any way of getting there but by going underground. Rest yourself here, and don't worry. I'll go and order whatever may be needed."

All at once the dove rose up in the air, went away, returned, landed, and flew backward and forward so often that by the end of the day she was able to inform the prince that everything was ready. He took the friendly bird, kissed it, caressed it, thanked it, and followed it on his white horse. No sooner had he gone a hundred yards than he saw two long rows of foxes, badgers, moles, snails, ants, and all sorts of creatures that burrow in the earth. There was such an enormous number that he could not imagine how they had been gathered there.

"It is due to my orders that you see all these subterranean people here," the dove said. "They've been working for you with the greatest diligence, and you'll do me a favor by thanking them." The prince saluted them and told them he would like to see them one day in a less barren place, where he would be happy to entertain them. Each animal appeared pleased by this compliment.

Cheri got off his horse at the entrance to the subterranean passage they had made for him, and after he bent over, he was nearly half his size and groped his way after the kind dove, which conducted him safely to the fountain. There was so much noise that he would have gone deaf if the dove had not given him two of her white feathers, with which he stopped up his ears. He was totally surprised to see this water dance with remarkable precision as though the great dancers Favier and Pécourt[5] had taught it. Of course, they were nothing but old dances such as the Bocane, the Mariée, and the Sarabande.[6] Several birds flew about and sang the tunes that the water wanted to dance to. The prince filled his golden vase and took two swigs, which refreshed him so much that he no longer felt that the luminous forest was the hottest place in the world.

He returned the same way he came. His horse had strayed, but it recognized his voice and returned at full gallop as soon as he called. The prince leapt lightly upon its back, quite proud at obtaining the dancing water. "Gentle dove," he said as he held her, "I don't know what miracle enables you to have so much authority in this place, but I'm very grateful for the way you've allowed me to benefit from it. And since liberty is the greatest of blessings, I restore you to yours in return for the favors you've granted me." Upon saying this, he let her go, and she flew away fiercely as though he had detained her against her will. "How unexpected!" he thought to himself. "You resemble a human being more than a turtledove—one's inconstant, the other's not."

5. Reference to two well-known dancers: Favier Jean, who made his career at the Royal Academy of Music; Guillaume Louis Pécourt (1653–1729), who was also a choreographer and worked at the opera and Royal Academy of Music.
6. These were indeed ancient dances. The Bocane was a slow dance popular up until 1654 and named after a famous dance master. The Mariée and the Sarabande were more lively dances. The latter originated in Spain.

The dove replied to him even though she was high in the air, "Ah! Do you know who I am?"

Cheri was astonished that the dove had answered his thought like that. He was convinced she was very clever and was sorry he had let her go. "She would have been useful to me," he said to himself. "I might have learned many things from her that would have contributed to my happiness." However, he reflected that one should never regret doing a good action, and he felt he was very indebted to her when he thought about the difficulties she had enabled him to surmount in obtaining the dancing water. The top of the golden vase was screwed on so tight that he could not spill the water, nor would it evaporate. As he began amusing himself by thinking how delighted Belle-Etoile would be to get it, and how joyful he would be to see her again, he saw several cavaliers coming at full speed. No sooner did they perceive him than they uttered loud shouts and pointed him out to one another. He was devoid of fear, for he had an intrepid character and could not be shaken easily by any kind of danger. Still, he was annoyed when anyone tried to stop him, and he spurred his horse toward them. Of course, he was pleasantly surprised when he recognized several of his domestics, who gave him some little notes, or, I should rather say, orders. The princess had sent them to him to tell him not to expose himself to the dangers of the luminous forest. He kissed Belle-Etoile's writing and sighed more than once. Then he rushed off to her to relieve her from further worry.

On his arrival, he found her seated under some trees, where she had abandoned herself to her sorrow. When she saw him at her feet, she did not know how to welcome him. She wanted to scold him for acting against her orders, but she also wanted to thank him for the charming present he had brought her. Eventually, her affection prevailed. She embraced her dear brother, and her reproaches were not very severe.

Old Feintise, who was always on the watch, knew through her spies that Cheri had returned, handsomer than he was before he went away, and that the princess, after washing her face with the dancing water, had become so exceedingly beautiful that one could scarcely look at her without dying half a dozen deaths.

Feintise was very astonished and troubled, for she had been convinced that the prince would perish in such a great undertaking. But this was not the time to be discouraged. She watched for the moment when the princess went to a little temple of Diana with a few attendants. Then she approached her and said with an air of great friendship, "How delighted I am, madame, by the happy results of my advice! It's easy to see by looking at you that you're presently using the dancing water, but if I may dare offer you some further advice, you ought to make yourself mistress of the singing apple. It's quite a different thing, for it augments your intelligence so much that you're able to do anything. If you want to persuade anyone, you only have to smell the singing apple. If you want to speak in public, make verses, write prose, be amusing, draw tears, or cause laughter, the apple has all these virtues. And it sings so well and so loud that one can hear it eight miles away without being stunned by it."

"I don't want it!" the princess cried. "You thought of killing my brother with your dancing water. Your advice is too dangerous."

"What, madame!" Feintise replied. "Would you pass up the chance of becoming the wisest and wittiest person in the world? Truly, you can't mean that."

"Ah, what would I have done if they had brought me my dear brother dead or about to die?" Belle-Etoile responded.

"He doesn't have to go," the old woman said. "The others ought to oblige you in their turn, and anyway, the task is not so dangerous."

"Never mind," said the princess, "I don't feel inclined to expose them to the danger."

"Indeed, I feel sorry that you're going to lose such a golden opportunity. But I'm sure you'll think about it. Adieu, madame!" She then withdrew and was very worried about the success of her argument, while Belle-Etoile remained at the feet of the statue of Diana, undecided as to what to do. She loved her brothers, but she also loved herself. She felt that nothing would give her so much pleasure as possessing the singing apple.

She sighed for some time, and then she began to weep. Petit-Soleil was returning from hunting and heard her making noise in the temple. He entered it and saw the princess, who covered her face with her veil, for she was ashamed to be seen with tears in her eyes. After approaching her, he asked her to tell him instantly why she was crying. She refused to do so, saying she was ashamed of herself, but the more she refused, the more he wanted to know.

At last she told him that the same old woman who had advised her to get the dancing water had just told her that the singing apple was even more wonderful because it would give her a great deal of intelligence and she would become a sort of prodigy. Indeed, she would almost give her life for such an apple, but she feared there would be too much danger in getting it.

"There'll be no need to fear for me, I assure you," her brother said smiling. "I'm not at all eager to perform this good service for you! Don't you have enough wit? Come, come, my sister. Forget about it!"

Belle-Etoile followed him and was just as much distressed by the manner in which he had treated her trust as by the realization that it would probably be impossible to obtain the singing apple. Supper was served, and all four sat down at the table. She could not eat, and Cheri, the charming Cheri, who only thought about her, helped her to the nicest morsels and urged her to taste them. Her heart was full. Tears came to her eyes, and she left the table weeping. Belle-Etoile weeping! You gods, what unhappiness for Cheri! He asked what the matter was with her? Petit-Soleil told him about everything in a sarcastic manner that was very insulting to his sister. She was so hurt that she retired to her room and would not speak to anyone all evening.

As soon as Petit-Soleil and Heureux had gone to bed, Cheri mounted his excellent horse without saying a word to anyone. He left only a letter for Belle-Etoile, with orders to give it to her when she awoke. Dark as the night was, he rode at random, not in the least knowing where to find the singing apple.

As soon as the princess arose, they delivered the letter to her. You can easily imagine the anxiety and tenderness she felt on such an occasion. She ran into her brothers' chamber to read the letter to them, and they shared her grief, for they were a very close family. They immediately sent nearly all their attendants after him to induce him to return and to stop the adventure that would undoubtedly be terrible.

In the meantime, the king did not forget the lovely young people of the forest. His walk was always directed toward their abode, and when he passed by and saw them, he reproached them for never coming to his palace. They excused themselves by saying they had not completed their equipage and that their brother's absence prevented them from doing so. They assured him that, upon his return, they would make use of the permission he had given them and pay their respects.

Meanwhile, Prince Cheri was urged on so strongly by his love for the princess that he went at breakneck speed. At dawn he perceived a handsome young man who was reclining under some trees and was reading a book. He addressed him very civilly and said, "Excuse me for interrupting you. I'd like to ask you if you know where I can find the singing apple?"

The young man raised his eyes, smiled graciously, and said, "Do you wish to obtain it?"

"Yes, if it's possible," the prince replied. "Ah, my lord," the stranger remarked, "you're probably not aware of the dangers you'll encounter in such an undertaking. Here's a book that tells all about it, and it makes me tremble when I read it."

"I'm not concerned about that," Cheri said. "The danger doesn't dismay me. Just tell me where I can find the singing apple."

"This book says that it's in a vast desert in Libya and that one can hear it sing eight miles away," the young man stated. "The dragon that guards it has already devoured five hundred thousand people who have had the temerity to go there."

"I'll make the number five hundred thousand and one," the prince replied, smiling. After saluting him, he set out toward the deserts of Libya, and his fine horse, which was of the Zephyrine race, for Zephyr was his grandsire, went like the wind so that the prince made incredible progress. However, he listened in vain and could not hear the singing apple anywhere. He was beginning to get dejected because of the long and pointless journey when he suddenly noticed a poor turtledove fall at his feet. It was not dead yet, but very close to death. Since he saw no one who could have wounded it, he thought, perhaps, it belonged to Venus, and that it had escaped from its dovecote, and that little mischievous Cupid had tried shooting his arrows at it. He took pity on the dove, got down from his horse, and picked it up. After wiping its white wings, which were stained with blood, and taking from his pocket a little gold bottle that contained a remarkable balsam for wounds, he applied just a little to the poor dove. Suddenly it opened its eyes, raised its head, stretched out its wings, and plumed itself. Next, it gazed at the prince and said, "Good day, handsome Cheri, you were destined to save my life, and in return, I am to do you a great favor. You've come looking for the singing apple. This task is difficult and worthy of you, for the apple's guarded by a terrible dragon which has twelve feet, three heads, six wings, and a body made of bronze."

"Ah, my dear dove," the prince said, "how happy I am to see you again, and at a time when I need your help very much. Please don't refuse me, my lovely little creature, because I'd die of grief if I were forced to return without the singing apple. Thanks to your intervention I obtained the dancing water, and now I hope that you'll find some other means that will enable me to succeed in my present undertaking."

"Your words move me," the dove replied tenderly. "Follow me. I'll fly ahead of you and I hope all will go well."

After the prince let her go, they traveled all day long until they arrived close to a mountain of sand. "You must dig here," the dove said. Without a word of resistance, the prince immediately began digging, sometimes with his hands, sometimes with his sword. After working for several hours, he found a helmet, a cuirass, and the rest of a suit of armor with a harness for his horse, all made of glass. "Arm yourself, and fear nothing from the dragon," the dove said. "When he sees himself in all these mirrors, he'll be so frightened that he'll think they're monsters like himself and he'll take flight."

Cheri approved of this plan very much. He put on the glass armor, and taking the dove again, they proceeded together all through the night. At daybreak they heard a most enchanting melody. The prince asked the dove to tell him what it was.

"I'm convinced," she said, "that nothing else but the apple could be so melodious, for it plays all the different parts of music by itself, and without touching any instrument, it appears to play them in a most enchanting manner."

As they drew nearer, the prince thought to himself how he wished the apple would sing something that suited his own situation. Just then he heard these words:

> "Love can subdue the most stubborn heart for you.
> So struggle not to drive him from your breast;
> No matter how cruel she may be whom you pursue,
> Love on, stay brave, and you'll soon be blessed."

"Ah!" he cried, answering these lines. "What a charming prediction! I may hope to be happier one day than I am now. I've just been assured." The dove made no reply to this since it was not born a prattler and never spoke except when absolutely necessary. As he advanced, the beauty of the music increased, and despite the prince's haste, he was sometimes so delighted that he stopped to listen, not thinking of anything else. However, the sight of the terrible dragon, which suddenly appeared, with his twelve feet, and more than a hundred talons, his three heads, and his bronze body, aroused him from this sort of lethargy. The dragon had smelled the prince from far off and expected to devour him as he had everyone who had preceded him, and who had made for some excellent meals. Their bones were piled around the apple tree that carried the beautiful apple, and they were heaped up so high that it was not possible to see the apple.

The frightful beast advanced by leaps and bounds and covered the ground with a froth that was very poisonous. His infernal throat spouted fire and young dragons, which he hurled like darts in the eyes and ears of the knights-errant who had wished to carry away the apple. But when he saw his own alarming figure multiplied hundreds and hundreds of times in the prince's mirrors, it was he that was frightened in his turn. He stopped, and looking fiercely at the prince covered with dragons, he took flight. Cheri saw the good effect of his armor and pursued him to the entrance of a deep chasm, into which the monster threw himself to avoid him. The prince closed the opening tightly and returned with utmost speed to the singing apple. After climbing to the top of all the bones that surrounded it, he looked in wonder at the beautiful tree. It was made of amber, and the apples were topazes. The most beautiful of all, which he had sought so diligently and at so much peril to his life, appeared at the top, and it was composed of a single ruby with a crown of diamonds. The prince was ecstatic and delighted at being in a position to give Belle-Etoile such a perfect and rare treasure. He quickly broke the amber branch, and quite proud of his good fortune, he mounted his white horse, but could not see the dove anywhere. She had flown away as soon as there was no further need of her assistance. Since he did not want to lose any more time due to superfluous regrets, and since he was afraid that the dragon, whose hisses he heard, would find some means of retrieving the apples, he returned to the princess with this prize.

She had not slept a wink during his absence, for she had constantly reproached herself for wanting to have more intelligence than others. Indeed, she was more worried about Cheri's life than her own. "Ah, unfortunate being that I am!" she cried, sighing heavily. "Why was I so conceited? Wasn't it enough that I could think and speak so well that I never did or said anything absurd? I'll be punished soundly for my pride if I lose the man I love. Alas, the gods are perhaps displeased by my love for Cheri, and they intend to take him from me in some tragic way."

Her troubled heart led her to imagine all sorts of terrible things that might happen to him. Then, in the middle of the night, she heard such lovely music that she could not resist rising and going to the window to hear it better. She did not know what to think of it. At first she believed it must be Apollo and the Muses; then, Venus, the Graces, and the Loves. Their symphony approached closer, and Belle-Etoile continued to listen. At last, the prince arrived. It was a beautifully moonlit evening. He stopped beneath the princess's balcony. She had withdrawn upon seeing a cavalier in the distance, but when the apple began singing, "Awake, lovely sleeper," the princess became curious and looked out instantly to see who was singing so well. Once she recognized her beloved brother, she was ready to throw herself from the window to be beside him all the sooner. She spoke so loud that everybody was wakened, and they went to let Cheri in. You can imagine how fast he entered. In his hand was the amber branch that held the wonderful fruit. Since he had smelled it so often, his intelligence had increased so much that nobody in the world could compare with him. Belle-Etoile ran to meet him eagerly. "Do you think that I'm going to thank you, my dear brother?" she said crying with joy. "No, there's nothing worth acquiring if it means exposing you to dangers."

"There's nothing I would not face to give you the slightest gratification," he replied. "Belle-Etoile, I want you to accept this rare fruit. No one in the world deserves it as much as you do. But what can it give you that you don't already possess?"

Petit-Soleil and his brother came and interrupted this conversation. They were delighted to see the prince again, and he gave them an account of his journey, which lasted till morning.

The wicked Feintise had just returned to her little cottage after discussing her schemes with the queen-mother. She was too anxious to sleep quietly, and when she heard the sweet singing of the apple that nothing in nature could equal, she felt sure that the prince had found it. She cried, she groaned, she scratched her face, she tore her hair. Her grief was excessive, for instead of doing harm to those lovely youngsters, as she had intended, her treacherous advice did them nothing but good. As soon as it was day, she learned that the prince had indeed returned, and she went to the queen-mother.

"Well, Feintise," the queen said, "are you bringing me good news? Have the children perished?"

"No, madame," she said, throwing herself at her feet. "But please, your majesty, don't get impatient. I still have innumerable ways to get rid of them."

"Ah, you wretched creature!" the queen said. "You live only to betray me and to spare them."

The old woman protested that this was not the case, and after she had appeased the queen slightly, she returned home to think about her next move.

She allowed some days to pass without showing herself, and at the end of that time she looked for an occasion to encounter the princess while walking in the forest alone and waiting for her brothers. "Heaven crowns you with blessings, charming Etoile," this wicked woman said as she approached her. "I've heard that you've obtained the singing apple. I couldn't be more delighted if such good fortune had happened to myself, for I must confess, I take a great interest in everything that enhances your situation. But I must now give you another piece of advice."

"Ah, keep your advice to yourself!" said the princess, hurrying away from her. "Whatever good it may bring me, it does not make up for the anxiety I suffer as a result."

"Anxiety is not such a great evil," Feintise replied smiling. "There are sweet and tender anxieties."

"Say no more," Belle-Etoile retorted. "I tremble when I think of it."

"Truly," the old woman said, "you're really to be pitied for being the loveliest and most intelligent girl in the world."

"I must beg your pardon once and for all," replied the princess. "I know only too well how terrible I felt during my brother's absence."

"Nevertheless, I must assure you," Feintise continued, "that you still need the little green bird which tells everything: he could inform you about your birth, your good and bad luck. There's nothing, no matter how secret, that he won't find out for you. And when the world says, 'Belle-Etoile possesses the dancing water and the singing apple,' it will say at the same time, 'but she doesn't have the little green bird which tells everything, and without the bird she might as well have nothing.' "

After saying all she intended, Feintise left. The princess became sad and thoughtful and began to sigh bitterly. "This woman is right," she said to herself. "What advantage do I have from the water and the apple, if I don't know who I am, who my parents are, and what fate exposed my brothers and me to the fury of the waves? There must be something very extraordinary in our births that caused us to be abandoned like that. Only the intervention of Providence could have saved us in such danger. What a delight it would be to know my father and mother, to cherish them if they're still living, and to honor their memory if dead!" Tears rolled down her cheeks like drops of morning dew bathing the lilies and roses.

Cheri, who was always more eager to see her than either of his brothers, hurried back as soon as the hunt was over. He was on foot; his bow hung carelessly at his side; he had some arrows in his hand; his long hair was tied by a ribbon. In this guise he had a martial air, which was extremely charming. As soon as the princess saw him, she turned down a dark path so that he would not observe the traces of grief on her face that a lover would be sure to detect. The prince joined her, and no sooner did he look at her than he knew she was in some trouble, and he was very upset by it. He implored her to tell him what was bothering her, but she obstinately refused. Finally, he turned the point of one of the arrows to his heart and said, "You don't love me, Belle-Etoile, and there's nothing left to do but die."

The manner in which he spoke made her so desperate that she could no longer refuse to tell him her secret. However, she revealed it only on condition that he would not risk his life again by trying to satisfy her wants. He promised all she demanded and showed no sign of undertaking this last journey.

As soon as Belle-Etoile had retired to her room and the princes to theirs, Cheri descended, took his horse out of the stable, mounted him, and set out without saying a word to anyone. This news threw the charming family into great consternation. Meanwhile the king, who could not forget them, asked them to come and dine with him. They replied that their brother had just left, and that they would not feel happy or comfortable without him. They promised that when he returned they would not fail to pay their duty at the palace. The princess was inconsolable; the dancing water and the singing apple no longer had any appeal for her. Nothing was amusing to her while Cheri was gone.

The prince went wandering through the world, asking everyone he met if they could tell him where he could find the little green bird that told everything. Most people knew nothing about it, but he met a venerable old man who took him home with him and kindly examined a globe. This was all part of his profession as well as his amusement. He then told him it was in a freezing cold climate, situated on the top of a frightful rock, and he showed him the route he must take. To show his gratitude for his information, the prince gave him a little bag full of large pearls that had fallen from his hair, and taking leave of him, he continued on his journey.

Finally, at dawn the next day, he saw the rock, which was very high and very steep. On its summit was the bird, speaking like an oracle and telling wonderful things. He thought that, if he were nimble, it would be easy to catch the bird, for it seemed very tame. It went and came, hopping sprightly from one point of the rock to another. The prince got off his horse and climbed up very quietly, despite the roughness of the ascent. He looked forward to pleasing his dear Belle-Etoile by capturing the bird.

He was now so close to the green bird that he thought he could lay his hands on it, when suddenly the rock opened, and he fell into a spacious hall as motionless as a statue. He could neither stir nor moan about his deplorable situation. Three hundred knights, who had made the same attempt, were in the same state. The only thing they were permitted to do was to look at each other.

The time seemed so long to Belle-Etoile, and as there were still no signs of her beloved Cheri, she fell dangerously ill. The physicians saw plainly that she was being destroyed by a deep melancholy. Her brothers loved her dearly, and they asked her why she was so sick. She acknowledged that she reproached herself night and day for causing Cheri to depart and that she felt she would die if she did not hear some tidings of him. They were so moved by her tears that Petit-Soleil decided to search for his brother in hope of curing her.

The prince set out and learned where this famous bird was to be found. He flew there; he saw it; he approached it with the same hopes as the others had done, but he was soon swallowed up by the rock and fell into the great hall. The first person he saw was Cheri, but he could not speak to him.

Belle-Etoile recovered her health a little. She hoped to see her two brothers return at any moment, but her hopes were disappointed, and her distress was renewed. She kept lamenting night and day. She accused herself of causing her brothers' misfortunes, and now Prince Heureux took pity on her and was also worried about his brothers. He decided in his turn to go and look for them. He told Belle-Etoile about his intention, and at first she opposed it, but he told her it was but just that he should confront danger in trying to find his brothers, whom he loved so dearly. Thus, after having taken the most affectionate farewell of the princess, he departed, and she remained alone, a prey to the most profound worries.

When Feintise learned that the third prince had gone, she was extremely delighted. She told the queen-mother about it and promised her with more confidence than ever before that she would destroy everyone in this unfortunate family! Meanwhile, Heureux shared the same fate as Cheri and Petit-Soleil—he found the rock, he saw the bird, he fell like a statue into the hall, where he recognized the princes he was seeking without being able to speak to them. They were all arranged in crystal niches and never slept or ate. They were kept in a miserable state of enchantment, for they were only free to think about and bemoan their fate in silence.

Belle-Etoile was inconsolable as she realized that none of her brothers would return. She reproached herself for postponing her own departure.

Without further hesitation she gave orders to her entire household to wait six months, and if neither she nor her brothers returned at the end of that time, they were to go and inform the corsair and his wife about their death. She then dressed herself in male attire, believing she would be less exposed to danger in traveling disguised like this than if she roamed the world as an adventurer of her own sex. Feintise saw her depart on her beautiful horse and was overjoyed. So she ran to the palace to brighten the queen-mother's day with this good news.

The princess had no other armor than a helmet, and she rarely ever raised the visor, for her beauty was so delicate and perfect that no one would have believed (as she wished they would) that she was a cavalier. It was a very severe winter, and the country of the talking bird never felt the happy influence of the sun in any season! Belle-Etoile was dreadfully cold, but nothing could deter her progress. However, all of a sudden she saw a turtledove, scarcely less white or colder than the snow on which it was stretched out. Despite her eagerness to get to the rock, she could not let it die like that. She got off her horse, picked it up, warmed it with her breath, and then placed it on her bosom. The poor little thing did not move, and Belle-Etoile thought it was dead. She felt very sorry for the dove and took it out again. Then she looked at it and talked to it as though it could understand her, "What shall I do, sweet dove, to save your life?"

"Belle-Etoile," the bird replied, "one sweet kiss from your lips will complete the charitable work you've begun."

"I'll give you not only one," said the princess, "but a hundred, if they're needed."

She kissed it, and as the dove revived, it became cheerful and said, "I know you in spite of your disguise, and I want you to know that you've undertaken something that would be impossible for you to accomplish without my assistance. So follow my advice. As soon as you arrive at the rock, don't try to climb it. Remain at the bottom, and begin to sing the best and sweetest song you know. The green bird that tells everything will listen to you and locate where the voice is coming from. You must then pretend to go to sleep. I'll be near you, and when it sees me, it will come down from the top of the rock to peck me. At that moment you'll be able to grab it."

The princess was delighted by this hope. She got to the rock as fast as she could and recognized her brothers' horses grazing. Upon seeing them, her grief set in again. She sat down and cried bitterly for some time, but the little turtledove said so many beautiful things, so consoling to the unfortunate princess that it could relieve any troubled heart imaginable. Therefore, she dried her tears and began to sing so loud and so well that even the princes had the pleasure of hearing her in their enchanted hall.

From that moment on, they felt that there was some hope. The little green talking bird listened and looked around to see where the voice was coming from. It spotted the princess, who had taken off her helmet so that she might sleep more comfortably, and it also saw the dove, who kept flying around her. At this sight the green talking bird flew down gently to peck the dove, but no sooner did it tear out three feathers than it was taken prisoner itself.

"Ah, what do you want to do with me?" it said. "What have I done to you to make you come from such a great distance and to make me miserable? Grant me my liberty, I implore you, and I'll do anything you wish in exchange."

"I want you to restore my three brothers to me," Belle-Etoile said. "I don't know where they are, but since their horses are grazing near this rock, I'm sure you're keeping them prisoner somewhere in this vicinity."

"Under my left wing there's a red feather. Pull it out," the bird said, "and touch the rock with it."

The princess quickly did what she was told. All of a sudden she saw such lightning and heard such a roar of thunder and wind all together that she was dreadfully frightened. Despite her alarm she still held onto the green bird tightly, thinking it might try to escape. She touched the rock with the red feather again, and the third time it split open from top to bottom. Then she entered the hall with a victorious air, and there stood the three princes with many others. She ran toward Cheri, but he did not recognize her in her helmet and male attire, and since the enchantment had not ended yet, he could neither speak nor move. Upon seeing this, the princess questioned the green bird anew, and it replied that she had to use the red feather again and rub the eyes and mouth of all those she wished to disenchant. So she performed this good deed for several kings and royal personages, and especially for our three princes.

They were so grateful for her great beneficence that they all threw themselves at her feet, calling her the liberator of kings. She then realized that her brothers, deceived by her armor, did not at all recognize her. So she immediately took off her helmet, held out her arms to them, and embraced them a hundred times. Then she kindly asked the other princes who they were. Each of them told her his own adventure and offered to accompany her wherever she wished to go. She replied that, though the laws of chivalry might give her a right over the freedom that she had just restored to them, she would not think of taking advantage of it. Thereafter, she withdrew with her brothers so that they could tell each other what had happened to them since their separation.

The little green talking bird interrupted them to beg Belle-Etoile to set him free. She immediately sought the dove to ask her advice, but she could not find her anywhere. She told the bird that she had suffered too much trouble and anxiety on his account, and thus she wanted to continue to enjoy her conquest somewhat longer. All four then mounted their horses, leaving the emperors and kings to walk, for they had been there between two and three hundred years, and their horses had perished.

The queen-mother thought she was relieved from worrying about the return of those lovely young people. Therefore, she renewed her attempts to persuade the king to marry again and pressured him so strongly that at last he decided to marry a princess of his own family. Since it was necessary to dissolve his marriage with the poor Queen Blondine, who lived at her mother's country house with the three dogs, which she had named Chagrin, Mouron, and Douleur because of all the misery they had caused her, the queen-mother sent for her. Consequently, Blondine got into the carriage and took the whelps with her. Dressed in black with a long veil that fell down to her feet, she looked more beautiful than the sun, although she had become pale and thin. Indeed, she rarely slept and never ate but from compliance, and everyone pitied her poor mother. The king was moved so much that he did not dare look at her. Yet, when he recalled that he ran the risk of having no other heirs but the whelps, he consented to everything.

The marriage day was set, and the queen-mother, at the suggestion of the admiral's wife, who always hated her unfortunate sister, commanded Queen Blondine to appear at the ceremony. Everything was done to make it grand and sumptuous, and since the king wanted the strangers to witness this magnificent ceremony, he ordered his principal equerry to go and invite the beautiful youngsters. In the event that they had not returned, he commanded his equerry to leave strict orders that they were to be informed about his wish on their return.

The principal equerry went to look for them, but he did not find them. Since he was aware of the pleasure the king would have in seeing them, he left one of his gentlemen to wait for them in order to conduct them to the palace without delay. When the happy day—the day of the grand banquet—arrived, Belle-Etoile and the princes had returned. The gentleman then told them all about the king's past history: that he had married a poor girl who was completely beautiful and virtuous, but who had had the misfortune of giving birth to three dogs; that he had sent her away, never to see her again, but that he loved her dearly; that he had spent fifteen years without listening to any proposal of marriage, but that the queen-mother and her subjects had urged him strongly to remarry; that he finally decided to marry a princess of the royal blood; and that it was necessary for them to come to the palace right away to attend the ceremony. Belle-Etoile put on a rose-colored velvet dress trimmed with diamonds; her hair fell in large curls on her shoulders and was decorated with knots of ribbons; the star on her forehead shone splendidly; and the chain of gold around her neck, which could not be taken off, seemed to be made of a metal more precious than even gold. No mortal eyes had ever seen anyone more beautiful. Her brothers were attired with equal splendor, but there was something in Prince Cheri's appearance that distinguished him in a special way. All four went in a coach made of ebony and ivory; the inside was lined with cloth of gold; the cushions were made of the same material and embroidered with jewels. The coach was drawn by twelve white horses, and the remainder of their equipage was incomparably beautiful. When Belle-Etoile and her brothers arrived, the delighted king went with his entire court to greet them at the top of the stairs. The apple sang wonderfully, the water danced, and the little talking bird spoke better than an oracle. All four knelt in front of the king, took his hand, and kissed it with as much respect as affection. He embraced them and said, "I'm very much obliged to you, lovely strangers, for coming here today. Your presence gives me great pleasure." With these words he conducted them into a grand salon where several musicians were performing and various tables, splendidly furnished, left nothing to be desired in the way of good cheer.

The queen-mother arrived, accompanied by her future daughter-in-law, the admiral's wife, and a great number of ladies. Among them was the poor queen, who had a long strap of leather round her neck, which was also linked to the three dogs. They conducted her into the middle of the salon, where they had placed a cauldron filled with bones and bad meat that the queen had ordered for their dinner.

When Belle-Etoile and the princes saw this unhappy queen, tears rushed into their eyes even though they did not know her. Either they were thinking about the vicissitudes of such a life, which touched them, or they were moved by an instinct of nature, which often makes itself felt. But what did the wicked queen think about their return that was so unexpected and went against her wishes? She cast such a furious look at Feintise that this woman sincerely wished the earth would open and swallow her up.

The king presented the beautiful young people to his mother, saying a thousand kind things about them. In spite of her uneasiness, she received them graciously and regarded them just as favorably as though she loved them, for deceit was in vogue even at that time. The feast went well, although the king was very distressed to see his wife eating with the whelps like the meanest of all creatures. Yet, he had decided to oblige his mother as much as possible, and since it was she who was forcing him to re-marry, he left her in charge of everything. At the end of the meal, the king addressed Belle-Etoile. "I know," he said, "you've obtained three incomparable treasures. I congratulate you, and I beg you to tell us how you managed to acquire them."

"Sire," she replied, "it's my pleasure to obey you. First of all I was told the dancing water would make me beautiful, and secondly that the singing apple would give me intelligence. Those are the two reasons why I wanted to possess them. With regard to the little green talking bird, there was a different reason. The fact is that we don't know anything about our fatal birth because we were abandoned as children and are not acquainted with our family. Therefore, I hoped that this wonderful bird would enlighten us about this matter which we think of night and day."

"Judging your birth by you yourself," the king said, "it should be most illustrious. But in truth, who are you?"

"Sire," she said, "my brothers and I deferred asking the bird that question until our return. When we arrived, we got your command to come to your wedding. All that I could do was to bring you these three rare things to amuse you."

"I'm very glad you did," the king said. "Let's not put off anything that will be so entertaining."

"You amuse yourself with every foolish thing that's suggested to you," the queen-mother said angrily. "So now we have these nice little brats with their rare items! Truly, nothing could be more ridiculous than to call these items rare. Fie, fie. I don't want these petty strangers, apparently the dregs of society, abusing your credulity. All this is nothing but a juggling trick, and if it weren't for you, they'd never have had the honor of sitting at my table."

Upon hearing these insults, Belle-Etoile and her brothers did not know what to imagine. Their faces flushed with confusion and despair at being offended in front of the entire grand court. But the king told his mother that her remarks were an outrage and begged the beautiful young people not to feel hurt and held out his hand as a token of friendship. Belle-Etoile took a glass basin and poured all the dancing water into it. Immediately they saw the water was stirred up: it skipped about back and forth, heaving like an angry little sea. It varied its color and made the basin move the length of the king's table. Then suddenly it spurted out and sprinkled the chief equerry's face, to whom the young people felt under obligation. He was a man of great merit, but he was very ugly, and he had also lost an eye. As soon as the water touched him he became so handsome that no one recognized him, and his eye was restored. The king, who loved him dearly, was just as much delighted by this incident as the queen-mother was displeased to hear the applause that the princess received. After silence was restored, Belle-Etoile placed the singing apple on the water; it was made out of a single ruby, surrounded by diamonds, with a branch of amber; it began such a harmonious concert that a hundred musicians would have been less effective. This enchanted the king and his entire court, whose admiration increased when Belle-Etoile drew from her muff a little golden cage made from beautiful workmanship, and there was the green talking bird, which fed on diamond dust and drank only the water distilled from pearls. She took it very gently and placed it on the apple, which was silent out of respect, and which wanted to give the bird the opportunity of talking. Its feathers were so beautiful and delicate that they were ruffled when people nearby just opened and shut their eyes. Indeed, they were all shades of green imaginable. Now the bird addressed the king and asked him what he would like to know. "We'd like to learn," the king said, "who this beautiful girl and these three cavaliers are?"

"Oh, king," the green bird answered with a loud and intelligible voice, "she's your daughter, and two of these princes are your sons. The third, called Cheri, is your nephew," and then it told the whole story with wonderful eloquence and without omitting the least circumstance. The king wept, and the tormented queen, who had left the cauldron, the bones, and the dogs, approached gently. She cried for joy and love for her husband and her children, especially because it was impossible for her to doubt the bird's assertions when she saw all the tokens that revealed who they were. The three princes and Belle-Etoile rose up at the end of the account. Then they threw themselves at the king's feet, embraced his knees, and kissed his hands. In turn, he stretched out his arms to them and pressed them to his heart. Nothing could be heard but sighs and exclamations of joy. The king arose, and as he noticed the queen his wife standing timidly against the wall in a most humble posture, he ran to her and gave her a thousand caresses. Finally, he placed a chair for her close to his and made her sit down on it.

Her children kissed her hands and feet a thousand times. Never has anyone seen a more tender and touching sight. Everyone wept and raised their hands and eyes to heaven in thanks for having permitted such important matters to be brought to light. The king thanked the princess who had intended to marry him and gave her a large quantity of jewels. But for the queen-mother, the admiral's wife, and Feintise, there is no telling what he would have done to them if indignation had been his only counsel! The tempest of his rage was beginning to subside when the generous queen, his children, and Cheri implored him to satisfy himself by punishing them more for the sake of an example than for severity. Therefore, he had the queen-mother imprisoned in a tower, but the admiral's wife and Feintise were thrown together into a dark loathsome dungeon, where they had to eat with the three dogs called Chagrin, Mouron, and Douleur. Since they no longer saw their good mistress, the dogs constantly bit those people who were around them. It was in this dungeon that they ended their days, which were sufficiently extended to give them time to repent all their crimes.

As soon as the queen-mother, the admiral's wife, and Feintise were taken to the places designated by the king, the musicians began to sing and play. The rejoicing was unparalleled. Belle-Etoile and Cheri felt more exuberant than anyone else, for they knew the eve of their perfect happiness had arrived. In short, the king, who thought his nephew the handsomest and most accomplished man at court, told him he would not let such a grand day pass without a wedding, and he gave him his daughter. The prince was ecstatic and threw himself at the king's feet, while Belle-Etoile was equally delighted.

It was but just that the old queen, who had lived in solitude for so many years, should now leave it to participate in the public rejoicing. The same little fairy who had come to dine with her and whom she had treated so well entered suddenly to tell her everything that had happened at court. "Let's go there," she continued. "I'll tell you about the care I've taken of your family as we go along."

The grateful old queen got into the fairy's chariot, which was glittering with gold and azure. It was preceded by a military band and followed by a hundred bodyguards, consisting of the first noblemen in the kingdom. The fairy told the queen the history of her grandchildren and how she had never forsaken them. Indeed, she had protected them in the form of a siren and a turtledove, in short, in a thousand various ways. "You see," she said, "a good deed is always rewarded."

The good queen kept kissing her hand to show her gratitude, and she did not know how to express the extent of her joy. At last they arrived at the palace. The king received them with a thousand expressions of friendship. Blondine and the beautiful children were eager (as might be expected) to demonstrate their love for this illustrious lady, and when they realized what the fairy had done for them, and that she was the kind dove who had guided them, they could not find words enough to thank her. To add to the king's satisfaction, the fairy told him that his mother-in-law, whom he had always considered to be a poor peasant, had been born a sovereign princess. It was perhaps the only thing lacking to complete this monarch's happiness. The fête was concluded by the marriage of Belle-Etoile with Prince Cheri. The corsair and his wife were sent for so that they would be even more rewarded for the remarkable education they had given the beautiful children. At last, after having suffered years of trouble and anxiety, everyone was made perfectly happy.

EUSTACHE LE NOBLE

The Bird of Truth†

There was once a nobleman who lived in the country, and he had three perfectly beautiful daughters. A kind fairy had permitted each one of them to have a wish that she would grant. One day as they were taking a walk in a woods and were amusing themselves by gathering strawberries and flowers, they caught sight of the king of Tartelettes, who was amusing himself by killing magpies. This king was so attractive and handsome that they were charmed by him.

"I'd very much like this king to marry me," said the eldest daughter. "Then I would make him richer than ever before because I would wish his entire kingdom to be turned into sugar."

"If I were fortunate enough to become his wife," the second exclaimed, "I would wish all the rivers and all the lakes on his estates to be changed into milk and cream."

"As for me," remarked the youngest, who was more intelligent than her sisters, "if I were his wife, I would wish for nothing but to give birth to three children all at once, two boys and a girl, who would have golden stars on their foreheads."

The king of Tartelettes did not give them any time to discuss their wishes, for he approached them and asked them what the subject of their conversation was. The respect that they had for him as king obliged them to tell the truth. He found the first two wishes so ridiculous that he did not even deign to regard the young ladies who had made them. But the youngest sister's wish pleased him so much that he decided to make her the queen of Tartelettes. As soon as he returned to his palace, he sent some ambassadors to their father to ask his permission to marry the youngest daughter. Since the nobleman had not expected this honor and was a man of good sense, he feared that the king's intentions were not as honorable as the ambassadors would have had him believe. But they managed to put his mind at ease about the king's intentions. Then they took his daughter and drove her in a carriage so that she would arrive at the court as soon as possible.

The king of Tartelettes found such great merit in his future wife that he married her against the wishes of his mother the queen, who did not approve of this marriage. Never before had there been such a magnificent wedding ceremony. The bride wore garments laden with gold; the feast was superb; and all the tables were spread with sugar almonds, little tarts, and custard. Soon thereafter people noticed that the young queen appeared marvelously fertile. Indeed, she became pregnant, and the king of Tartelettes began waiting impatiently for her to give birth when the king of L'Eau Rose declared war against him.

Of course, it is necessary to explain the reason for the differences be-

† Eustache Le Noble, "The Bird of Truth"—"L'oiseau de vérité," in *Le gage touché, histoires galantes* (Amsterdam, 1700).

tween these two princes. The king of Tartelettes had issued a law that prohibited the use of rose water on little tarts and custard throughout his kingdom. This edict had caused the king of L'Eau Rose to become a pauper. Therefore, he raised an army and entered the realm of Tartelettes, where he lived as he wished. As a consequence, the king of Tartelettes summoned his troops to chase this king from his territory and began a campaign to engage his enemy.

In the meantime, the queen gave birth to two princes and a princess who was unusually beautiful. But the queen-mother, who was very wicked and who did not love her daughter-in-law, wrote the king that his wife had brought two male cats and a female cat into the world. When the king heard this news, he was so horrified that, without thinking that the report might have been false, he replied to his mother that she should lock his wife in a tower and drown the three alleged monsters that she had produced. The queen-mother executed his orders right away: she locked the queen in a tower, and after having shut the three babies in a box, she threw it into the river. The water's current carried it through streams to a miller who was fishing. After he opened it, he was astonished to find three babies, and he was even more stunned to hear a voice that said: "I'll take charge of it and relieve you." He looked around on all sides and saw nobody. This made him think that the children were under the protection of some fairy. In consideration of this strange occurrence and the compassion that he had for the sad fate of these infant children, he decided to take them to his mill and raise them as carefully as he could. They seemed so beautiful that he named the boys Beau-Soleil and Bel-Astre and the girl Belle-Etoile. As they grew older, Beau-Soleil and Bel-Astre showed an inclination for wielding weapons. They always held sticks in their hands and did exercises as if they were little musketeers. When the miller noticed this, he did not want to neglect such a natural disposition. He bought them two pistols with powder and bullets. Consequently, they spent their days hunting and killed so many rabbits that this was all that they ate in the mill.

The king of Tartelettes, however, was still at war with the king of L'Eau Rose. One day one would have the advantage; the next day, the other. The war appeared as if it would never end. Another king, named Friand, wanted to act as mediator to arrange a peace. He had an interest in having the two kings cooperate in a reasonable way because he could not eat custard without rose water. Nevertheless, despite all his intelligent efforts, the war continued for another eight years without his being able to stop it. Finally, he thought of an expedient that enabled him to succeed; he convinced the two kings to let the pastry cook Le Coq act as arbiter and to settle their differences. They had him come from Paris, and it did not take a person with such good taste very long to say that one could not eat the tartelettes without rose water, so the peace treaty was signed by the two kings, who stopped their hostilities right away, and ever since that time they lived like two true bosom friends.

After that long and bloody war, the king of Tartelettes returned to his court and desired to see his wife again. But the queen-mother complained and said, "Let that creature stay where she is. Do you want to produce a menagerie of animals?"

The memory of that terrible birth awakened in his mind the horror that he had experienced when he had learned from the messenger what had happened. So the king continued to let the queen suffer her deplorable fate.

Now the king had a passionate love for hunting, and one day while he was hunting with his entire court in a woods, he heard a pistol shot. So, he immediately ordered the captain of his guards to arrest the person who dared to hunt and interrupt his pleasure. The guards set out right away toward the spot where they had heard the shots, and they found Beau-Soleil, who had just killed a rabbit and who had recharged his pistol.

"What's this?" the captain of the guards said to him. "You dare to hunt on the grounds of the king!"

"Do you think that you can stop me?" Beau-Soleil responded.

"I certainly can," declared the captain, and he began to carry out his duty and arrest him. But Beau-Soleil fired his pistol and wounded him, causing the captain to utter a great cry.

Bel-Astre, who was not far from this spot, heard the cry, and thinking that some wolf was devouring his brother, ran to help him. When he saw that the guards were seizing Beau-Soleil, he shot his pistol and wounded the lieutenant. Now the guards ran and disarmed him as they had done with Beau-Soleil, and after they had bound the two together with a cord, they led them to the king of Tartelettes. When the king saw that the captain and lieutenant had been wounded, he became furious and enraged with the two prisoners. But when he noticed that they were very young, very handsome, and very striking, and that they also had a golden star on their foreheads, his fury turned to pity. He had them unbound and pardoned them.

In turn, they saluted his majesty very civilly and talked to him with such intelligence that the king could not stop admiring them and permitted them to hunt with him. Beau-Soleil killed a deer and two partridges with one shot of his pistol. Bel-Astre stopped a wild boar and wounded a hare. Indeed, they appeared so skilled that the king of Tartelettes gave them two horses as a present. Then he asked them who their father was.

"He's a miller, sire," Beau-Soleil responded with respect.

"He can consider himself very happy," the king remarked, "to have such fine children."

"We also have a sister," Bel-Astre said, "who is as beautiful as a duchess, and she also has a golden star on her forehead like us."

After the king had daydreamed a little, he said, "I should very much like to know her. Therefore, I order you to return here tomorrow at the same time and to bring your sister with you."

They returned to the mill loaded with game, and the miller thought that he would die from joy when they told him about everything that had happened. After this, they said to Belle-Etoile: "My sister, this is not all. The king would like to see you."

"Oh, my brothers," Belle-Etoile responded, "if he marries me, you will become the greatest lords of the court. I promise that I'll make you royal pages."

"That's not impossible," Bel Astre said. "You only have to wash up and make a fine impression on him."

"Oh! Don't you worry," she replied. "I shall wash my face and hands with the water from the fountain and with soap."

Early in the morning on the next day, they ran to the meeting spot even though it was after lunch that the king had said he wanted to meet them. While they were waiting for the king, they put Belle-Etoile in a spot of the woods where she began to spin.

With regard to the king of Tartelettes, he had told his mother all about his adventure at dinner after he had returned from the hunt. And his story had caused this wicked queen to feel terribly uneasy. She could not sleep that night. So she summoned the sorceress who had assisted the young queen when she had given birth and told her that the children whom she, the queen, had thrown into the river were not dead and the king, her son, might soon discover the truth.

"You can depend on me," said the sorceress. "I shall prevent the king of Tartelettes from seeing his daughter."

Immediately thereafter she transported herself to the woods where Belle-Etoile was spinning, and after approaching her with a smiling countenance, she asked, "What are you doing here, my beautiful child?"

"I'm waiting for the king," Belle-Etoile responded, "to show him my respects."

"You are not beautiful enough to appear before him," replied the sorceress, "and if you want to become beautiful enough, you must obtain the singing apple."

"And where is this singing apple?" Belle-Etoile asked.

"It is a hundred miles from here," the sorceress responded. "If you want to find it, you must go in that direction and keep following it."

And the sorceress showed her a road that went in the opposite direction to that by which the king had to pass. The sorceress disappeared, and Belle-Etoile called her brothers, who were not far from her, to tell them that a lady had just warned her that she had to obtain the singing apple to please the king of Tartelettes. Beau-Soleil and Bel-Astre, who were naturally curious, declared to their sister that they would be charmed to hear a singing apple. Belle-Etoile saw that they were disposed to accompany her on her way, and so all three took the path that she had been instructed to take. However, no sooner had they traveled half a mile than they encountered a beautiful woman clad in a silver dress. It was the fairy Landrirette, who had presided over their birth and who had taken them under her protection. She stopped them and asked them where they were going.

"We are going to look for the singing apple," they responded.

"Well, then, my children," she said, "I shall save you the trouble of traveling so far."

At the very same time that she spoke those words, she pulled from her pocket an apple that began to sing like an opera singer.

"How pretty it is!" exclaimed Beau-Soleil.

"Ahh, what a charming apple!" Bel-Astre remarked.

Landrirette put the apple in the hands of Belle-Etoile, whose beauty became unsurpassable that very instant.

"Return to the woods," the fairy told them, "and I hope that you will no longer have any difficulties." Just as she finished saying these words, she disappeared.

Belle-Etoile and her brothers turned back on the path and had the apple sing. Once again the sorceress appeared and said to Belle-Etoile, "My pet, you have a beautiful white complexion, but you do not have enough color and seem to be listless."

"What's this? What must I do so that I can be completely beautiful?" Belle-Etoile asked sadly.

"You have the singing apple," the sorceress responded. "Now you must go and search for the dancing water right away."

"Is it far from here?" Belle-Etoile inquired.

"It is a hundred miles from where you found the singing apple," the sorceress replied, and she left them that very moment. Once again they did not deliberate very long before undertaking this journey.

"Now we must travel two hundred miles," Belle-Etoile said.

"So what?" replied Bel-Astre. "We have our pistols. So what do we have to fear?"

"Let's go!" exclaimed Beau-Soleil. "I have a feeling that we shall soon be returning here."

So they departed, and after traveling for a quarter of an hour on the path, Landrirette appeared.

"You're searching for the dancing water," she said. "Well, here it is," and she showed them a small crystal phial of water which was in perpetual motion. "Return to the woods, and I hope that you will no longer have any difficulties."

After saying these words, Landrirette gave them the phial and disappeared. They returned on the path, and now, for the third time, the sorceress approached Belle-Etoile.

"Your beauty is now perfect," she told Belle-Etoile, "and the king will be content with it. But you do not have a mind, and without that, you will not please him."

"Well, I'm going to return to the mill and lock myself up inside," Belle-Etoile exclaimed and burst into tears. "I've heard said that whoever is born without a mind will die because of this."

"No, no, my little one," the perfidious sorceress said. "Console yourself. I love you, and I want to give you the means to have a mind. Go and search for the bird of truth. Follow the path, and you will find it about a hundred miles from the spot where you found the dancing water."

Since Bel-Astre, Beau-Soleil, and Belle-Etoile seemed prepared to undertake this long journey, the sorceress disappeared, firmly convinced that while they were looking for the bird of truth, the king would pass through the woods and would return to his palace without having seen them. But they had not gone more than twenty feet when they perceived the fairy Landrirette once more, and this time she was holding a golden cage.

"Return right away to the woods, my children," she said to them, "for the king is coming. Belle-Etoile, I want you to keep the cage door open, and the bird of truth will enter."

They obeyed the fairy and went to the place, where they were supposed to meet the king of Tartelettes. Just as they arrived, they saw a tiny bird enter into their cage. It was extremely tiny, no bigger than a thumb. Its crop and wings were the color of the sky, and its tail was sprinkled with pearls and diamonds. They locked the cage, and while they were admiring the beauty of this bird, they heard the sound of trumpets. A moment later they saw the king of Tartelettes with his entire court. Beau-Soleil and Bel-Astre presented their sister to the king. If he was surprised by her beauty and her shining star, he was no less surprised by her mind, for ever since the bird of truth had entered the cage, she had the most beautiful and most delicate thoughts in the world, and her expressions were so precise and so noble that the king of Tartelettes no longer doubted that Beau-Soleil, Bel-Astre, and Belle-Etoile were his children. The maliciousness of his mother came to his mind, and he imagined that the queen his wife had been unjustly punished. These thoughts tormented him with such great force that he returned to his palace without hunting and took the three children with him.

When the queen-mother saw them, she turned white, and this confirmed the king's suspicions. However, Beau-Soleil said to the king, "Sire, I beg your majesty to accept a present that I want to give to you."

As he said this, he gave him the apple, which began to sing in a marvelous way. The king of Tartelettes exclaimed, "Mercy, an apple that sings! You can be assured that I shall preserve this rare object."

Then Bel-Astre intervened and said, "Sire, do me the honor and accept my gift as well. It is a phial with water that dances."

"This is indeed surprising," the king of Tartelettes remarked. "I have nothing like this in my cabinet that is so precious!"

"And I," Belle-Etoile exclaimed, "I beg the sovereign king of Tartelettes and Darioles to accept my cage and my bird that I have kept hidden under my apron."

Upon saying this, she revealed the cage made of gold. Everyone found the workmanship of the cage very beautiful, but the little bird seemed even more charming so that they could not take their eyes off it.

"Great king," Belle Etoile continued as she noticed that the king of Tartelettes was regarding the bird with pleasure, "it is not the beauty of this bird that dignifies it as a present for you. Rather, it is the bird's virtue that allows it to speak like an oracle and to reveal the truth."

"This will give me even more pleasure," said the king. "And I should like to know if all three of you were born in a mill."

To satisfy the king's curiosity, Belle Etoile said to her bird:

"Without pretense, without finesse,
Tell the truth, oh beautiful bird."

The bird responded immediately:

"I shall tell all, lovely princess,
If you'll let me free and give me your word."

Belle-Etoile opened the cage, and the little bird hopped out. Then it flew gently into the air and told the story about the three children. The king and his entire court followed the bird with their eyes until it was lost in the clouds. While everyone was watching the bird and listening to it with great attention, the queen-mother poisoned herself and died a miserable death. Nobody wept about it. The king's first concern was to fetch his wife from the tower in which she had been imprisoned. Everyone expected to find her devastated because the queen-mother had only given her pieces of bread and water for food during her long imprisonment. But they were pleasantly surprised when the queen appeared fit and in good health and more beautiful than she had ever been. She told the king that she had put on flesh thanks to the great care of the fairy Landrirette, who brought her quails, partridges, steaks, sugar almonds, and bread every day. The king embraced his wife tenderly and told her that Beau-Soleil, Bel-Astre, and Belle-Etoile were her children and had garments made of gold for her. He also summoned the miller, who was now a widow, and appointed him at first as high constable with better things awaiting him in the future.

ANTOINE GALLAND

The Jealous Sisters and Their Cadette†

There was once a prince of Persia named Khusrau Shah who liked to go on nightly adventures in order to learn about the world. He would often disguise himself and would be accompanied by one of his trusted officers, who would be disguised like him. As they would stroll through the different districts of the city, they would have particular adventures. After some time had passed, his father died from old age, and this prince inherited the throne and became the sultan of Persia.

After the customary ceremonies had been performed that concerned the prince's ascension to the throne, and after the funeral was completed, the new Sultan Khusrau Shah left his palace at two o'clock in the morning. He did this just as much from inclination as he did from a feeling of responsibility to know what was happening in the city. He was accompanied by his grand vizier, and they found themselves in a district where there were only people from the lower classes. As the sultan went through a street, he heard some very loud voices. So he approached the house where the noise was coming from, and as he peered through an open door, he saw a light and three sisters seated on a sofa holding a conversation after dinner. Since their discourse was very lively, he was able to ascertain that they were talking about their wishes.

"If we were sure of having our wishes fulfilled," one of the sisters said, "mine would be to have the sultan's baker as husband. Then I would eat that delicate and excellent bread, which they call the Sultan's Bread, to my heart's content. Now," she turned to a sister, "let us see if your taste is as good as mine."

---

† Antoine Galland, "The Jealous Sisters and Their Cadette"—"Histoire de deux Soeurs jalouses de leur cadette" (1717), in *Les milles et une Nuit*, 12 vols. (Lyon: Briasson, 1717).

"As for me," responded the second sister, "my wish would be to be the wife of the sultan's chef of the kitchen. Then I would eat excellent soup, and since I am quite convinced that the sultan's bread is shared by everyone in the palace, I would also be able to eat it. You see, my sister, my taste is better than yours."

Then the youngest sister, the cadette,[1] who was very beautiful and who was more pleasant and intelligent than her sisters, spoke in her turn.

"For me, my sisters," she said, "I shall not curb my desires in the least. I shall soar as high as I can, and since we are just wishing, I wish to be the wife of the sultan. I would give him a prince whose hair would be gold on one side and silver on the other. When the child cried, his tears would be pearls. Each time he smiled, a rosebud would appear on his ruby lips."

The wishes of the three sisters and especially that of the cadette appeared so unique to the sultan that he decided to fulfill them. Without communicating his intention to the grand vizier, he ordered him to note the house so that he could go to it the next day and fetch the three sisters to his palace. The following day the grand vizier arrived at the house, and after telling the sisters that the sultan wanted to see them without saying anything more than this, he barely gave the three sisters enough time to get dressed. He escorted them to the palace, and when they were presented to the sultan, he asked them, "Tell me, do you remember the wishes that you made last night when you were in such a good mood? Do not try to conceal anything. I want to know."

Upon hearing the sultan's words, the three sisters, who were not expecting this, became greatly confused. They lowered their eyes, and the red that they blushed made the cadette look particularly pleasing, for she was the one who had wished to gain the heart of the sultan. Since their modesty and their fear that they might have offended the sultan by their conversation made them keep silent, the sultan tried to reassure them by saying, "You have nothing to fear. I haven't ordered you to appear here to punish you. Since I see that the question that I have posed has undermined my intention, and since I know each of your wishes, I would like to fulfill them. You who have wished to have me as your husband will be satisfied today. And you others will have the baker of my palace and the chef of my kitchen as your husbands."

As soon as the sultan had declared his will, the cadette set an example for her older sisters and threw herself at his feet to indicate her submission.

"Sire," she said, "since my wish is known to your majesty, I want you to know that it was only done in a manner of speaking and amusement. I am not worthy of the honor that you are bestowing on me, and I beg you to excuse my bold conduct."

The two older sisters wanted to apologize in the same way, but the sultan interrupted them.

"No, no," he said, "there is no other way. Each of your wishes will be fulfilled."

The marriages were celebrated that same day in the manner determined

---

1. In French, the youngest daughter of a family.

by the Sultan Khusrau Shah, but with a great difference. The marriage
celebrations of the cadette were accompanied by pomp and all the signs
of rejoicing that befit the wedding of the sultan and his queen of Persia,
while the other festivities of her sisters were celebrated with the luster that
one could expect as befitting the ranks of the baker and the chef of the
sultan's kitchen. The two older sisters strongly felt the great disproportion-
ate gap between their marriages and that of their cadette. Also, it was this
factor that produced a complex situation: far from being content with the
happiness that they gained, even though each of the older sisters was
granted her wish beyond her hope, they indulged themselves in excessive
jealousy that not only disturbed their joy but was also the cause of many
misfortunes, humiliations, and the most mortifying afflictions for their
younger sister. They had very little time to communicate to one another
what they thought about the preference that the sultan had shown to their
sister to their disadvantage. They were consumed by the preparations of
their marriage. But as soon as they saw each other some days after on a
public path where they had made an appointment to see each other, they
revealed their sentiments.

"Well, then, my sister," the oldest said to the second, "what do you say
about our cadette? It must be nice to be the wife of the sultan!"

"I must confess," said the other, "that I don't understand anything. I
cannot conceive what traits the sultan found in her to become so fascinated
by the eyes that she has. She is only a little monkey, and you know in
what state we have seen her, you and me. Is that a reason for the sultan
not to cast his eyes on you? Just because she has more youth than we
have? You are more worthy of his bed, and he should have been more
just to you than he was to her."

"Sister," responded the older one, "let us not talk about me. I would
have nothing to say if the sultan had chosen you. But the fact that he has
chosen an uncouth girl, this is what distresses me. I shall seek vengeance
when I can, and you have just as much vested interest in this as I do. This
is why I want to ask you to join me so that we can make common cause
in something in which we both have interest. I want you to tell me the
means that you imagine might be suitable to mortify her, and I promise
you to tell you what I desire to do to mortify her as well."

After setting up this pernicious conspiracy, the two sisters saw each other
often, and each time they only discussed the steps that they could take to
cross and even destroy the happiness of their sister the queen. They came
up with many plans, but when it came to executing them, they encountered such great difficulties that they did not want to risk making use of
them. From time to time, however, they visited their sister together, and
with a condemnable hypocrisy, they demonstrated all the signs of friendship that they could imagine to persuade her how enchanted they were to
have a sister in such an exalted position. On her part, the queen always
received them with a show of esteem and consideration that they might
expect from a sister who had not become intoxicated by her dignity, and
who had not stopped loving them with the same cordiality that she had
before.

Some months after her marriage, the queen found herself pregnant, and the sultan showed immense joy. After the news was communicated throughout the palace, this joy spread throughout all the districts of the capital of Persia. The two sisters came to express their compliments, and right then and there, anticipating that she would need a midwife to help her during her confinement, they asked her not to choose anyone but them.

The queen obliged them and said, "My sisters, as you might imagine, I could not ask for anything better if the choice were to depend on me alone. Despite the fact that I am infinitely obliged by your good will, I must submit myself to whatever the sultan orders. Therefore, I suggest that you have your husbands employ their friends to intervene on your behalf with the sultan. And if the sultan speaks with me about it, you can rest assured that I shall not only indicate the pleasure that it would give me, but I would also thank him immensely if he would choose you as midwives."

The two husbands, each in his own way, solicited the support of their protectors at court, and they asked them to use their credit at court to procure the honor to which their wives aspired. These protectors acted so effectively that the sultan promised to think about it. Indeed, the sultan kept his promise, and in a conversation with the queen, he said that it seemed to him that her sisters were more suitable to help her in her confinement than some other strange midwife. But he did not want to nominate them without having her consent. The queen, sensitive to the deference that the sultan was showing her in such an obliging manner, told him, "Sire, I am inclined to do what your majesty commands. But since you have had the kindness to cast your eyes on my sisters, I should like to thank you for the consideration that you have for them out of love for me, and I must confess that I would prefer to have them as my midwives rather than a woman whom I don't know."

Thus the Sultan Khusrau Shah named the two sisters of the queen to become her midwives. From that time on, they walked about the palace with a great joy since they had found the opportunity that they wished to execute their wicked and detestable plan to bring harm to their sister the queen.

When the time of the delivery arrived, the queen gave birth to a prince as beautiful as the day. Neither his beauty nor his delicate nature was able to touch the hearts of the two merciless sisters or cause them to have tender feelings. They wrapped the baby in swaddling clothes somewhat negligently, put him in a small basket, and abandoned the basket in the stream of a canal that passed at the base of the sultan's apartment. Then they produced a dead puppy and reported that the queen had given birth to it. When the sultan heard this unpleasant news, he became indignant and would have taken his anger out on the queen if his grand vizier had not pointed out to him that he could not rightly hold the queen responsible for this bizarre event.

In the meantime, the basket, which was carrying the prince, flowed to the surrounding wall that blocked the view of the queen's apartment, and it continued floating across the palace garden. By chance, the chief caretaker of the sultan's gardens, one of the principal and respected officers of the realm, was walking in the garden along the canal. When he noticed the basket floating in the stream, he called a nearby gardener and said, "Go quickly and fetch me that basket so I can see what is inside."

The gardener departed, and from one of the banks of the canal, he skillfully managed to pull in the basket with a pole, pluck it out of the water, and carry it to the caretaker, who was extremely surprised to see a baby wrapped in swaddling clothes in the basket. Even though the baby had just been born, one could easily see that it had beautiful traits. The caretaker had been married a long time, and though he had a great desire to have children, heaven had not blessed his wishes thus far. Thus, he interrupted his walk and ordered the gardener, who was carrying the child in the basket, to follow him. When he had arrived at his house, which bordered on the palace and the gardens, he went into his wife's apartment.

"Wife," he said, "we do not have children, and look at what God has sent us. I would like you to look after the baby. Send for a nurse right away, and treat him as if he were your own son. I shall recognize him as my own from this moment on."

His wife took the child with joy, and it was a great pleasure for her to be in charge of the baby. The caretaker of the garden did not want to investigate where the baby came from. "I see quite well," he said to himself, "that he has come from the apartment of the queen, but it is none of my business to check what happens there or to cause any trouble in a place where peace is so necessary."

The following year the queen gave birth to another prince. The unnatural sisters had as little compassion for this baby as they did for the older one. They sent this child, too, in a basket down the canal, and they pretended that the queen had given birth to a kitten. Fortunately for the child, the caretaker of the garden was near the canal and had the child carried to his wife and ordered her to take charge of the boy just like she had done with the first. Accordingly, she did this out of her own inclinations, not just because she felt obliged to obey her husband.

The sultan of Persia was just as indignant about this birth as he was about the first. He expressed his resentment and his remonstrances to the grand vizier, who was again able to appease him. Finally, the queen gave birth to a third child, and this time it was a princess. But she had the same fate as her brothers. The two sisters, who had decided not to stop their detestable undertaking until they saw the queen their sister at least rejected, banished, and humiliated, gave the same treatment to this baby and sent her down the canal in a basket. The princess was saved and fetched from a certain death by the compassion and charity of the caretaker of the gardens, just as he had done with the two princes, her brothers, who were nurtured and raised by him and his wife.

Aside from their cruelty, the two sisters were liars and imposters. They made up a story and showed everyone a piece of wood, assuring them falsely that the queen had given birth to a mole. The Sultan Khusrau Shah could not contain himself when he heard about this extraordinary birth.

"What!" he exclaimed. "That woman is unworthy of my bed. She has filled the palace with monsters. Should I even let her live? No, that will not happen. She herself is a monster. I shall purge her from this world!"

Thus he sentenced her to death, and he commanded his grand vizier to carry out his orders. But the grand vizier and the courtiers who were present threw themselves at the sultan's feet and begged him to revoke his sentence. The grand vizier spoke up and said, "Sire, permit me to inform you that the laws that require the death sentence were established to punish crimes. The three births of the queen, which were hardly expected, were not crimes. How can one say that she contributed to them? An infinite number of women have done this and continue to do this. They are to pity but not to punish. Your majesty can abstain from seeing her and can let her live. The anguish in which she will spend the rest of her life after the loss of your good grace will be punishment enough."

The sultan of Persia reflected for a while, and he realized that it would be wrong to condemn the queen to death because of the miscarriages even if they had been true, and indeed, he was under the false impression that they were true.

"Let her live then," he said, "since this is the way it is. I shall give her life, but in a condition that will make her want to desire death more than once a day. I want a lodging built for her next to the door of the main mosque with a window that is always to remain open. She is to be locked in there with a coarse robe, and each and every Muslim who goes to the mosque to say his prayers is to spit in her face. If anyone fails to do this, he will receive the same punishment. To make sure that my command is obeyed, I order you, vizier, to have guards watch over this place."

The tone in which the sultan pronounced this last sentence caused the vizier to withhold any comment. This sentence was executed to the great contentment of the two jealous sisters. The lodging was built and finished. The queen, who was truly worthy of compassion, was locked into it according to the king's orders, as soon as she had recovered from the last birth. She was thus ignominiously exposed to the laughter and scorn of all the people, a treatment that she nevertheless had not deserved, and she suffered with a constancy that drew the admiration and at the same time the compassion of all those who judged things more sanely than the common people.

In the meantime, the two princes and the princess were nurtured and raised by the caretaker of the garden and his wife with the tenderness of a father and mother, and this tenderness increased as the children grew older and bore fruit in the traits of grandeur that appeared in the princess and the princes, especially in the beauty of the princess. Day by day the traits manifested themselves in their docility and their good inclinations that were greater than those of ordinary children and in a certain air that could only be found in princes and princesses. In order to distinguish the two princes according to the order in which they were born, the first was called Bahman, and the second Parviz, names which the ancient kings of Persia had borne. The princess was given the name of Parizad, which many queens and princesses of the realm had also borne.

As soon as the two princes were the right age, the caretaker of the garden gave them a tutor to teach them how to read and write, and their sister, who was also at their lessons, showed such a great desire to learn how to read and write, even though she was younger than they were, that the caretaker, charmed by her disposition, gave her a tutor as well. Aroused by her vivacity and by her sharp intelligence, she became just as skillful in a short time as her brothers. From that time on, the brothers and their sister had the same teachers in the fine arts, geography, poetry, history, and the sciences, and even in the secret sciences. And since they did not find anything difficult, they made such marvelous progress that their tutors were astonished, and soon they had openly to admit that the youngsters had gone further than even they had gone and could not continue with the lessons. In the hours of recreation, the princess also learned how to sing and play many different musical instruments. When the princes learned how to ride horses, the princess did not want to be excluded and participated with them so that she learned to ride a horse, shoot a bow and arrow, and throw a stick or a javelin with the same agility that they could. And she often beat them in some races.

The caretaker of the gardens was overjoyed to see these youngsters so accomplished in all these physical and mental activities. Indeed, they had more than made up for all the costs that he had undertaken for their education, much more than he himself had expected, and he was going to do something more considerable on their behalf. Until then, he had lived happily in the lodging that was at the edge of the palace. Now he bought a country house not far from the city, and this house had a great deal of fertile land, meadows, and woods, and since the house did not appear beautiful and comfortable enough, he began to renovate it, and he did not spare any expense to make it the most magnificent in the area. He went there every day because he hoped his presence would push the many workers whom he had hired to complete their job more quickly. As soon as they had finished one apartment that could be inhabited, he went there and spent as many days as his functions and duties would permit. He added a vast park that was enclosed by little walls and was filled with all sorts of deer so that the princess and the princes could amuse themselves by hunting whenever it pleased them.

When the country house was completely finished and was in a condition to be inhabited, the caretaker of the gardens threw himself at the feet of the sultan, and after having explained to him how long he had been in his service and the infirmities of old age which he was now suffering, he begged him to release him from his service and let him retire. The sultan granted him this favor with a great deal of pleasure because he was satisfied with his service, which had begun under the reign of his father and had continued during his own regime. As he gave his permission, he asked him if there was anything he could do to reward him.

"Sire," the caretaker responded, "I have been overwhelmed by the generous gifts of your majesty and by those of your father, of whom I have a happy memory, so that I have nothing left to desire except to die in the honor of your good graces."

He took leave of the Sultan Khusrau Shah, and then he went to his country house with the two princes, Bahman and Parviz, and the Princess Parizad. As far as his wife is concerned, she had been dead for some years. He himself lived only five or six months more before he died, and it was so sudden that he did not have any time to tell them the truth about their birth, something that he had resolved do as it was necessary to oblige them to continue to live as they had been doing according to their rank and condition and the education that he had given them and to which they were inclined.

The princes, Bahman and Parviz, and the Princess Parizad, who had not known any other father than the caretaker of the gardens, were very despondent, and they arranged the funeral services out of their love for him and out of their filial duties. They were very content that their father had left them so much wealth and property, and they continued to live together. The princes had no desire or ambition to present themselves at the sultan's court in view of the fact that they had no need for a position or commission.

One day while the two princes were away hunting, and the Princess Parizad was resting, a devout Muslim, who was very old, appeared at the door and requested permission to enter to say her prayers because it was the hour to do so. The servants went to ask the princess's permission, and the princess ordered them to let her enter and to show her the oratory which the caretaker had built because there was no mosque in the vicinity. She also commanded that, after the devout woman said her prayers, they should show her the house and the garden.

The devout Muslim entered and said her prayers in the oratory. After she had done this, two of the princess's ladies, who had waited until she had left the oratory, invited her to see the house and the garden. When she indicated to them that she was ready to follow them, they took her from one apartment to the next, and in each one she regarded all the fine furnishings and beautiful designs. They also took her into the garden, which she found so new and well done that she praised the person who had designed everything and remarked that he must have been an excellent master of his art. Finally, she was brought to the princess, who was waiting for her in a grand salon which surpassed in beauty, furnishings, and splendor all the other apartments that she had already admired.

As soon as the princess saw the devout woman enter, she said, "My good mother, please approach and sit down next to me. I am happy and pleased by the opportunity to have a good example and a good conversation with a person like you who has taken such an admirable path by giving yourself to God, and whom everyone should imitate if they were wise."

Instead of sitting down on the sofa, the devout woman wanted to sit on the edge, but the princess would not allow this. She got up from her place and advanced toward her. Then she took her by the hand and obliged her to sit down in the place of honor. The devout woman was pleased by this civility and said, "Madame, I am not accustomed to being treated so honorably, and I am only obeying you because you want it so and because you are the mistress of this house. When she was seated, the conversation did not begin until one of the princess's ladies placed a small low table before them, ornamented with pearls and ebony, which had a porcelain bowl on top filled with cakes and small porcelain cups filled with fresh fruit and dry preserves and drinks.

The princess took one of the cakes and presented it to the devout woman, "My good woman, please take one, eat, and choose the fruit that pleases you. You must need to eat something after the long walk you had to reach here."

"Madame," responded the devout woman, "I am not accustomed to eat such delicate things. And if I eat some, it is only so that I do not refuse that which God has sent me by such a generous hand as yours."

While the devout woman was eating, the princess, who was also eating to follow her example, asked her many questions about her devotion and the prayers that she practiced and about her manner of living. The old woman responded to all these questions with a great deal of modesty, and they moved from one topic to the next until the princess asked her what she thought of the house and whether she found it to her liking.

"Madame," the devout woman replied, "it would be in very bad taste to find fault with what I have found here. The house is beautiful, pleasant, magnificently furnished, uncomplicated, very well arranged, and the decoration could not be any better. With regard to the location, it is set in a pleasant terrain, and one could not imagine a garden that could give more pleasure than this one. Nevertheless, if you permit me to speak openly, I shall take the liberty, madame, to tell you that the house would be incomparable if three things that are missing, in my opinion, were to be found here."

"My good woman," the Princess Parizad responded, "what are those three things? Inform me, I beg you in the name of God. I shall not spare anything to acquire them if it is possible."

"Madame," the devout woman responded, "the first of these three things is the Talking Bird, a unique fowl by the name of Bulbulhezar, which has the power to attract all the birds that sing within his vicinity, and they come and join his song. The second thing is the Singing Tree, whose leaves are like mouths that produce a harmonious concert of different voices and never cease singing. The third thing is the Yellow Water, the color of gold. If one drop is poured into basin prepared expressly for this purpose, and it is placed into any garden whatsoever, it will soon fill this basin to the brim, and then the water will gush upward like geysers and continue to gush and fall back into the basin without a drop falling over the rim."

"Oh, my good mother!" the princess cried. "I owe you a great deal for acquainting me with all these things! They are surprising, and I had never heard anyone ever speak about such rare and also remarkable things. Since I am convinced that you know where they are located, I would appreciate it very much if you would inform me where they are."

The good woman wanted to satisfy the princess, and therefore, she said, "Madame, I would reveal myself unworthy of your hospitality, which you have just shown me with such kindness, if I refused to satisfy your curiosity about that which you want to know. Thus I have the honor of telling you that the three things about which I have just spoken can be found at the same spot within the borders of this realm near India. The path that leads there goes right by your house. It takes twenty days to reach the place. On the twentieth day, it is necessary to ask the first person that you encounter where the Talking Bird, the Singing Tree, and the Yellow Water can be found, and he will instruct you."

After saying these words, the old woman stood up and took her leave. Then she set out on her way. Princess Parizad's mind was so occupied by the information that the devout Muslim woman had just given her that she did not notice that the woman had left. Indeed, the princess was trying hard to retain all that she had learned about the Talking Bird, the Singing Tree, and the Yellow Water and would have liked to have asked her some more questions to gain greater clarification about everything. It seemed to her in effect that what she had just heard from her lips was not sufficient, and if she undertook a quest to find these things, it might be in vain. Despite her frustration, she did not want to send someone to bring back the woman. So she made an effort to remember all that she had heard and not to forget anything. When she believed that nothing had escaped her, she took pleasure in thinking about the satisfaction that she might have if she were to succeed in acquiring these marvelous things. But as she thought about the difficulties and became afraid that she would not succeed, she became terribly upset.

The princess had just reached the end of her thoughts when her brothers returned home from the hunt. They entered the salon, and instead of finding a cheerful face and alert mind, as they usually did, they were astonished to find their sister withdrawn and somewhat tormented, and she did not even raise her head to indicate that she was aware of their presence.

"Sister," Prince Bahman said, "what has happened to the joy and cheerfulness that you've always shown up to now? Are you not feeling well? Has something bad happened to you? Has someone caused you reason to grieve? Tell us so that we can do our duty and remedy the situation or so we can take vengeance on someone who may have had the audacity to offend you, when you deserve the utmost respect."

Princess Parizad remained quiet for some time and did not move. Finally, she raised her eyes, looked at her brothers, and lowered her eyes quickly after saying that nothing was the matter.

"Sister," Prince Bahman insisted, "do not conceal the truth from us. It must be something very grave. It is not possible that, during the little time that we have been away from you, such a great and unexpected change that we see in you could have happened without having some great meaning. Do you expect us not to hold you accountable for an explanation that does not satisfy us? Don't keep us from knowing what has happened, unless you would like us to believe that you are renouncing the friendship and the strong bond and trust that have existed among us until today ever since our tender youth."

The princess, who was far from breaking with her brothers, did not want to leave them with this impression. So she responded, "When I said to you that nothing was bothering me, I was saying that with regard to you, and not with regard to me because it is indeed important to me. Since you are insisting on your rights of friendship and our bonds that are also dear to me, I shall tell you everything. Until now you've believed, just as I have believed, that this house that our father had built was perfect in every way and that there was nothing lacking. However, today I learned that there were three things lacking, and if we had them, it would put this place beyond comparison with all the country houses of the world. The three things are the Talking Bird, the Singing Tree, and the Yellow Water with the color of gold."

After she explained the excellent qualities of these things, she said, "It was a devout Muslim woman who told me about these things and informed me about their location and the path that one must take to find them. You may think that these things are of little consequence to make our house perfect, and that it can still always pass for a very beautiful house, whether we add the three wonderful things or not, and we can thus afford to forget them. You only think about what pleases you. But I cannot prevent myself from revealing to you that, as far as I am concerned, they are necessary, and I shall not be happy until they are in this place. Thus, whether you are interested or not, I beg of you to give me help with your advice so that I may find a way to conquer and acquire these things."

"Sister," Prince Bahman declared, "anything that concerns you concerns us. Your desire to acquire these things is enough to oblige us to take the same interest. But independent of what regards you, we have been intrigued ourselves by what you have said and would also like to satisfy our curiosity. Indeed, I am convinced that our brother feels the same way that I do, and we should all undertake to conquer and acquire these things. Indeed, the word 'conquer' is apropos, as you say, because these things are so important and unique. I shall take charge of this affair. Just tell me the path that I should take and the location, and I shall set out on this journey tomorrow morning."

"My brother," Prince Parviz began speaking, "it is not appropriate that you absent yourself from the house for such a long time since you are the head of the family. I implore my sister to join me and to ask you to abandon your plan and to let me undertake this journey. I shall perform this deed as well as you, and everything will be more in order this way."

"Brother," Prince Bahman responded, "I am convinced of your goodwill and that you could perform this deed as well as I could. But I am determined. I want to do it, and I shall do it. You stay here with our sister, whom I am placing in your care."

The rest of the day was spent in preparing for the journey, and Prince Bahman listened to the information that the princess had received from the devout old woman so that he would not get lost on the way. The next morning Prince Bahman mounted his horse, and Prince Parviz and Princess Parizad, who wanted to see him off, embraced him and wished him luck on his journey. But in the middle of the farewells, the princess remembered one thing that had not occurred to her.

"Brother," she said, "I had not thought about the accidents that might happen during the journey. Who knows if I shall ever see you again? Get off your horse, and don't take this journey. I don't care whether I ever see the Talking Bird, the Singing Tree, and the Yellow Water if it means running the risk of losing you forever."

"My sister," the prince smiled at the sudden fear of Princess Parizad and said, "my mind is made up, and even if it were not, I would decide the same thing again, and you will find that it is good that I've done this. The accidents which you mention only happen to unfortunate people. It may be true that I could be among them. But it could also be that I am among the fortunate who outnumber the unfortunate by a great deal. Since we cannot anticipate the outcome of events and since I may succumb during my travels, the only thing I can leave you with is this knife here."

So Prince Bahman pulled out a knife and presented it in a sheath to the princess.

"Take it," he said, "and from time to time, take it out of the sheath. When you see that it is clean, as you see it now, it is an indication that I am still alive. But if you see a drop of blood on it, you will know that I am no longer alive, and say your prayers to accompany my death."

Princess Parizad was not able to make him change his mind, and the prince said his farewells to her and his brother for the last time, and he rode off on a fine steed, well-armed and well-equipped. He followed the path and did not veer to the left or right. In fact, he crossed all of Persia, and on the twentieth day of his journey he saw a hideous old man on the edge of the trail. He was seated on a tree some distance from a thatched cottage that served him as a retreat against bad weather. His eyebrows were as white as snow as was his hair, moustache, and beard. His moustache covered his mouth, and his long beard dropped almost down to his feet. The nails of his hands and feet were extremely long. His hat was flat and large and covered his head almost like an umbrella. He was dressed only in a simple coarse cloth that was wrapped around him.

This good old man was a dervish who had retired from the world many years ago and had neglected himself in order to devote himself entirely to God so that he finally assumed the appearance that we have just seen. Prince Bahman, who had been on the alert since morning to encounter someone who might inform him of the location of the three things, stopped his horse when he came near the dervish, who was the first man he encountered. Then he dismounted according to the instructions that the devout old woman had given to Princess Parizad. Holding the horse by the bridle, he advanced until he was in front of the dervish and greeted him.

"Good father," he said, "may God grant you long life and grant you all that you desire!"

The dervish responded to the prince, but his words were so unintelligible that he could not understand a word. Since Prince Bahman saw that the dervish's thick moustache caused this difficulty and since he only wanted to obtain the information that he needed from the old man, he took some scissors that he was carrying with him, and after tying his horse to the branch of a tree, he said to the dervish, "My good man, I have something to say to you, but your moustache prevents me from understanding you. You need a haircut, and I request that you let me cut your eyebrows, moustache, and beard, which have disfigured you and make you look more like a bear than a man."

The dervish did not oppose the prince's intentions, and let him cut his hair, and when the prince was finished, he saw that the color of the dervish's skin was fresh and tender, and that he appeared much younger than he seemed to be.

"Good dervish," the prince said, "if I had a mirror, I could show you how much younger you look. Now you are a man, and before it would have been impossible to distinguish what you were."

The compliments that Prince Bahman paid to the dervish made him smile, and now the man repaid the compliment.

"My lord," he said, "whoever you are, I am indebted to you for the kind service that you rendered me. I am now ready to show my gratitude and to do whatever I can for you. You would not have dismounted unless there was something necessary that obliged you to do so. Tell me what it is, and I shall try to satisfy you if I can."

"Good dervish," Prince Bahman said, "I have come from afar, and I am searching for the Talking Bird, the Singing Tree, and the Yellow Water. I know that these three things are somewhere in this vicinity. But I don't know their exact location. If you know, I would appreciate your showing me the path so that I can take one or the other and so that I do not lose the fruit of such a long journey that I have undertaken."

As the prince was speaking, he noticed that the dervish's face changed, that he lowered his eyes, and that he became serious. Instead of responding, the man remained silent, causing the prince to resume talking. "Good father, it seems to me that you haven't heard me. Tell me if you know anything about what I am asking so that I don't lose any time and can seek information somewhere else."

Finally, the dervish broke the silence. "My lord," he said, "I know the path that you are seeking, but because of the friendship that I have developed for you ever since meeting you, and that has become even stronger because of the service that you have rendered me, I am somewhat apprehensive to grant you the satisfaction that you wish."

"What motive could hinder you?" the prince replied. "What difficulty do you find with me so that you can't give me the information?"

"I shall tell you," the dervish said. "It is because the danger that you will face is much greater than you can imagine. A great number of other lords, who were no less brave and courageous than you are, have passed by and asked me the same question that you have asked. After having done everything I could to deter them, they did not want to believe me. I told them the path in spite of myself, submitting to their insistent demands, and I can assure you that they have all failed in their quest, for I have not seen a single one of them return. If you love life and if you want to follow my advice, then do not go any farther, and return home."

But Prince Bahman persisted and said, "I would like to believe that your advice is sincere, and I am obliged to you for the friendship that you are showing me. But no matter what the danger is that you have indicated, nothing is capable of making me change my plan. If someone attacks me, I have good weapons, even if he is more valiant and more brave than I am."

"And what if the attackers," the dervish responded, "cannot be seen, for there are many like that. How are you going to defend yourself against people who are invisible?"

"It doesn't matter," the prince said. "No matter what you say, you cannot convince me to abandon my quest. If you know the way that I have asked,

I implore you once more to tell it to me and not to refuse me this favor."

When the dervish realized that he could not persuade Prince Bahman, who was determined to continue his journey, notwithstanding the good advice that he was giving him, he put his hand into a sack that he had next to him and took out a ball that he gave to the prince.

"Since you won't listen to my advice," he said, "take this ball, and when you have remounted your horse, throw the ball before you and follow it until you come to the foot of a mountain where it will stop. After the ball no longer moves, you are to dismount, and you are to let the reins of the horse drop around its neck. It will remain in the same place and wait for your return. As you climb the mountain on foot, you will see a great number of large rocks to your right and left, and you will hear a great jumble of voices on all sides that will utter a thousand insults to discourage you and to hinder you from climbing all the way to the top. Be on your guard so that you are not frightened, and above all do not turn your head to look behind you. If you do, you will immediately be changed into a black rock similar to the ones that you will see. Those rocks are lords just like you who failed in their undertaking as I have told you. If you manage to avoid the danger that I have only depicted so that you can be aware of it and arrive on top of the mountain, you will find a cage, and in the cage there is the bird that you are seeking. As he talks, you are to ask him where the Singing Tree and the Yellow Water are. I have nothing more to add. Now you know what you have to do, and what you have to avoid. But if you would believe me, you would follow the advice that I have already given you: you would not risk losing your life. Once more, while there is still time to think about it, consider that this loss is irreparable, for you can inadvertently violate the condition that will cause your death."

"I am most grateful for your concern," responded the prince after taking the ball, "but I cannot stop my quest. Naturally, I shall try to benefit from the advice that you have given me and not look behind me as I climb the mountain, and I hope that you will soon be seeing me again, and that I can thank you even more after I have discharged my tasks and acquired what I am seeking."

Upon saying these words, to which the dervish did not respond except to say that it would give him pleasure to see him again and that he wished him good luck, the prince remounted his horse, took his farewell with a nod to the dervish, and threw the ball ahead of him. The ball rolled and continued to roll at the same speed that the prince had thrown it so that he was obliged to ride after the ball at the same speed in order not to lose sight of it. He continued following the ball, and when he was at the foot of the mountain that the dervish had indicated, the ball stopped. So he dismounted, and let the horse stay at this place, even when he threw the reins on its neck. After the prince surveyed the mountain with his eyes and noticed the black rocks, he began to climb, and he had only taken four steps when he began to hear the voices about which the dervish had spoken, and he could not see a soul. Some of the voices cried out: "Where is that fool going? Where is he going? What does he want? Don't let him pass!" Others cried out: "Stop him! Grab him! Kill him!" Then there were even others that shouted like thunder: "Thief! Murderer! Killer!" Then there were some that were just the opposite and had a mocking tone: "No, don't harm the poor boy! Let the beautiful sweet thing pass. Truly, they've been keeping the birdcage just for him!"

Despite these troublesome voices, Prince Bahman climbed for some time at a steady pace and sought to invigorate himself, but the voices increased with such great hubbub and were so close to him, in front and behind, that he was seized by fright. His legs and feet began to tremble. He staggered, and soon, as he saw that he was losing his strength, he forgot the advice of the dervish and turned to save himself from falling. No sooner did he do this than he was changed into a black rock. This transformation had happened to many others before him who had undertaken the same adventure, and his horse was also changed into a rock.

Ever since the departure of Prince Bahman, his sister had attached his knife to her belt so that she could be informed whether he was alive or dead, and she would take it out of the sheath and consult it a few times during the day. At the beginning she was consoled to learn that he was in perfect health; she often conversed about him with Prince Parviz, who would sometimes ask her about news of their brother. Finally, on that fatal day in which Prince Bahman had been transformed into a rock, the princess and prince were talking about him in the evening as was their custom.

"Sister," said Prince Parviz, "please take out the knife, and let us see if there is any news."

The princess took the knife out of the sheath, and as they looked at it, they saw the color of blood on the blade. The princess was overcome by fright and pain, and she threw the knife to the ground.

"Oh, my dear brother!" she screamed. "I've lost you, and it is all my fault! I shall never see you again! How unfortunate I am! Why did I speak to you about the Talking Bird, the Singing Tree, and the Yellow Water? Why did it matter to me to know whether the devout woman found our house beautiful or ugly, perfect or imperfect? Why in heaven's name did she ever come to this place? Hypocrite, trickster, is this the way you pay me for the hospitality that I showed you? Why did you speak to me about the bird, the tree and the water which, completely imaginary as they are, have caused the unfortunate end of my dear brother? Why do I still let myself be entranced by what you told me?"

Prince Parviz was no less tormented by the death of Prince Bahman than Princess Parizad. But he did not want to lose time with useless regrets, for he saw from his sister's laments that she still passionately desired to possess the Talking Bird, the Singing Tree, and the Yellow Water.

"Sister," he said, interrupting her, "we are mourning the loss of our brother in vain. Our lamentations and our pain will not bring him back to life. It is God's will, and we must submit to it and follow his decrees without seeking to comprehend them. Why are you now doubting the words of that devout Muslim woman after you were firmly convinced that everything she said was certain and true? Do you think that she would have spoken to you about these three things if they did not exist and that she invented them expressly to deceive you, who, far from having given her cause, had received her with so much honor and kindness? Let us believe instead that the death of our brother has resulted from his fault, or from some accident that we cannot imagine. Therefore, my sister, his death should not prevent us from pursuing our goal. I had offered to undertake this journey in his place, and I am still inclined to do this. Since his example has not made me change my feelings, I shall be departing tomorrow."

The princess did all she could to dissuade Prince Parviz, imploring him not to expose herself to the danger of losing two brothers instead of one. But he remained unstoppable, despite the remonstrances that she made to him. Before he departed, he did as his brother did and gave her a token so that she would be informed of the success of the journey that he was undertaking. Instead of a knife he left her with a string of a hundred pearls. As he presented her with the pearls, he said, "If you ask the pearls about my condition while I am absent, and if they happen to become fixed so that you cannot move them and they seem to be glued, this will indicate that I shall have suffered the same fate as our brother. But let us hope that this will not occur, and that I shall have the good fortune of seeing you again with the success that you and I expect."

Prince Parviz departed, and on the twenty-first day he encountered the same dervish at the spot where Prince Bahman had found him. He approached him on horseback, and after greeting him, he asked him if he could tell him the location of the Talking Bird, the Singing Tree, and the Yellow Water. The dervish caused him the same difficulties and made the same remonstrances that he had made to Prince Bahman. Then he told him that a young cavalier who had resembled him had passed by and had asked the same questions. This cavalier had convinced him to show him the way because he was so urgent and insistent. So the dervish had explained everything that might guide him and had given him instructions that he had to obey to succeed, but he had not seen him again. According to the dervish, this cavalier had probably suffered the same fate of those men who had been on the same quest before him.

"Good dervish," Prince Parviz said, "I know the cavalier about whom you have spoken. He was my older brother, and I have been informed that he is definitely dead. How he died, I don't know."

"I can tell you," the dervish replied. "He has been changed into a black rock like those others whom I have just mentioned, and you should expect the same transformation unless you observe the good advice that I gave him exactly as I do you—that is, if you still want to persist and are not willing to renounce your resolution, which I implore you to do one more time."

"My good dervish," the prince insisted, "I cannot show you enough how much I appreciate the concern you have about saving my life, even though you do not know me at all, and even though I have not done anything to deserve your kindness. But I must tell you that, before my departure, I gave a great deal of thought to this quest, and I cannot abandon it. So, I beg you to do me the same favor that you did for my brother. Perhaps I shall succeed better in following the same instructions that I expect from you."

"Since I cannot succeed in persuading you to put an end to your quest," the dervish said, "I shall stand up and give you a ball, if my old age permits me and I can support myself. This ball that I have with me will serve you as a guide."

Since he did not want to cause the dervish any more difficulties, Prince Parviz dismounted and advanced toward the dervish, who had just taken a ball out of his sack, in which he had many others. He gave it to the prince and explained how he was to use the ball, just as he did with Prince Bahman. And after having warned him not to be afraid of the voices that he would hear without seeing anyone, no matter how menacing they were, the dervish told him he was to climb until he could see the cage and the bird. Then the dervish took his leave.

The prince thanked the dervish, and when he had remounted his horse, he threw the ball in front of the horse, and he followed its trail. Finally, he arrived at the foot of the mountain, and when he saw that the ball had stopped, he got off his horse. Before he started to climb the mountain, he paused for a moment and recalled all the instructions that the dervish had given him. He summoned his courage and then began to climb, determined to reach the very top of the mountain. No sooner had he taken five or six steps than he heard a voice behind him that appeared to be very near, as if it were a man calling him and insulting him: "Wait, you reckless fool, I'll punish you for being so impertinent!"

As soon as he heard such an outrageous remark, Prince Parviz forgot all about the dervish's instructions. He put his hand on his saber, drew it out of the sheath, and turned around to seek vengeance. But he realized that nobody was there and was immediately transformed into a black rock, and his horse as well.

Ever since the prince had departed, Princess Parizad carried the string of pearls with her every day, and when she did not have anything else to do, she would run the pearls through her fingers one after the other, and even in the night she did this. Each evening she placed the pearls around her neck, and upon awakening in the morning, she would touch them with her hand to make sure that they continued to move one after the other. Finally, the fatal day arrived. It was the moment that Prince Parviz suffered the same destiny as Prince Bahman and was changed into a rock. The princess carried the string of pearls as she usually did, and when she asked what was happening to Prince Parviz, she suddenly felt that the pearls did not move, and she knew that this was the indication that her brother had definitely died just like Prince Bahman. Since she had already decided to depart if this happened, she did not lose any time in bemoaning the situation and expressing her grief and instead made a great effort to repress everything. The next morning, she disguised herself as a man, and after arming and equipping herself, she said to her people that she would return in a few days. She mounted her horse and departed, following the same path that her two brothers had taken.

Since Princess Parizad was accustomed to riding horseback when she went hunting to amuse herself, she was able to put up with the fatigue of the journey more than other women might be able to do. After she had traveled many days like her brothers, she, too, encountered the dervish on the twenty-first day. When she was near him, she dismounted and held the horse by the reins. Then she went to sit next to him, and after greeting him, she said, "Good dervish, would you mind if I rest for a few moments near you and would you also please tell me whether there is a place in the vicinity where I can find the Talking Bird, the Singing Tree, and the Yellow Water?"

The dervish responded, "Madame, since your voice reveals your sex, despite your disguise as a man, and since this is how I should address you, I want to thank you for the greeting and the great honor that you have given me. I know the location of those three things which you have just mentioned, but what is the purpose of your questions?"

"Good dervish," the princess replied, "I encountered a person who told me all about their merits, and thus I am burning with desire to possess them."

"Madame," the dervish said, "you were told the truth. These things are even more surprising and more unique than you probably realize. But this person concealed the difficulties that would have to be overcome to obtain and enjoy them. You would not have undertaken a quest so difficult and so dangerous if you had been well-informed in advance. Believe me. Do not continue. Turn around on your tracks. Don't expect me to contribute to your destruction."

"Good father," the princess said, "I have come from afar, and it would make me very angry to return home without having carried out my plan. You have spoken to me about difficulties and the danger of losing my life. But you have not told me what the difficulties and dangers are. This is what I would like to know so that I can reflect on the situation and see if I can summon the courage, determination, and strength to go ahead with my plan."

So the dervish repeated to Princess Parizad what he had told the princes Bahman and Parviz and even exaggerated the difficulties of climbing to the top of the mountain where the bird was located in his cage. He explained that she had to gain mastery over the bird before it would inform her about the tree and the yellow water. He told her about the noise and the hubbub of the menacing and frightening voices that were heard on all sides without any people appearing and the large number of black rocks that were once brave cavaliers and had been transformed because they had failed to observe the principle condition for succeeding in this quest, which was not to turn and look behind oneself.

When the dervish finished talking, the princess said, "If I understand your talk correctly, the great difficulty in succeeding in this affair is primarily to climb up to the cage without being frightened by the hubbub of voices that are heard without anyone being seen. The second difficulty to overcome involves not looking back. With regard to this last condition, I hope that I can control myself well enough to observe it. With regard to the second, I must confess that the voices, as you describe them, are capable of scaring even the most confident people. But as in all important and dangerous quests, one is not prohibited from using cleverness, and thus I ask you whether I can use it here since this quest is so important to me."

"And what cleverness do you intend to use?" the dervish asked.

"It seems to me," the princess said, "that if I stuff my ears with cotton, the voices will not make much of an impression on me no matter how loud and frightening. They would also have less of an effect on my imagination. My mind would be free and would not be troubled to the point of losing control of my reason."

"Madame," the dervish said, "of all the people up to the present who have asked me about the way to find the Talking Bird, I don't know of any who has made use of cleverness the way that you have proposed. What I do know is that nobody has ever proposed this, and all have perished. If you intend to persist in carrying out your plan, you can test it out and know very soon if it will work. But I still don't advise you to run the risk."

"Good father," the princess said, "nothing will prevent me from persisting in carrying out my plan. My heart tells me that cleverness will succeed, and I am resolved to make use of it. So, the only thing left is for you to inform me what path I should take. I beg you not to refuse me."

The dervish pleaded with her for the last time to reflect about what she was doing. But since he realized that her determination was set, he pulled out a ball, and upon giving it to her, he said, "Take this ball, remount your horse, and after you have thrown it in front of you, follow it in all its twists and turns until it rolls to the mountain that you are seeking and where it will stop. Then you are also to stop and dismount and go on foot to the base of the mountain. You know the rest, so take your leave, and don't forget to benefit from the instructions that I have given you."

After Princess Parizad thanked the dervish and took leave of him, she remounted her horse and threw the ball. Then she followed the path that the rolling ball took. It continued to roll, and finally stopped at the foot of a mountain. The princess got off her horse, stuffed her ears with cotton, and continued on her way by foot. After she studied the path that she would have to take to arrive at the top of the mountain, she began to climb with great intrepidity. She barely heard the voices, and she realized that the cotton was a great help to her. The more she advanced, the more the voices multiplied and became louder, but they never reached the point where they were capable of troubling her. She heard many kinds of insults and sharp bantering with regard to her sex that displeased her and did not make her laugh.

"I shall not take offence, and I'll simply ignore your insults and your mockery," she said to herself. "You can say even worse, and I don't care. You won't prevent me from continuing on my way."

Finally, she reached a place where she saw the cage with the bird in it. In conspiracy with the voices, the bird tried to intimidate her by crying out in a thunderous voice despite the smallness of its body.

"Crazy woman, get back! Don't approach!"

But the princess was actually invigorated when she saw the bird and increased her steps. When she saw that she was very close to her goal, she gave her all to reach the top of the mountain where the ground was flat. She ran to the cage and put her hand on top of it and said, "Bird, I've got you despite yourself, and you won't escape me."

While Parizad took out the cotton that she had used to stuff her ears, the bird said to her, "Brave woman, you need not worry, nor will you suffer the same fate as those who came before you and tried to secure my freedom. Even though I have been locked in this cage, I have not been content with my fate. But if I am destined to be a slave, I would prefer to have you as my mistress more than anyone in the world, for you have acquired me with great courage and dignity. From now on I promise that I shall be completely faithful to you and submit to each and every one of your commands. I know who you are, and I can tell you that you yourself do not know who you are. But a day is coming in which I shall render you a service that I hope will fill you with gratitude. To begin to show you some signs of my sincerity, just tell me what you wish, and I shall be ready to obey you."

The princess was filled with joy, which was somewhat inexplicable because the conquest of the bird had cost her the death of two dear brothers, and she herself had been exhausted and had encountered great dangers. Indeed, she had come out of it all better than when she began the quest despite what the dervish had depicted. Now, when the bird stopped speaking, she said, "Bird, let me indicate to you right away that I shall wish several things that are of major importance to me, and I am charmed that you have demonstrated your willingness to serve me. First, I have been told that there is some Yellow Water near here that has a marvelous quality. I ask you to inform me where this water is located."

The bird told her where she could find the water, which was not very far. She went there, and she filled a small silver flask that she had carried with her. When she returned to the bird, she said, "Bird, there is more. I am also searching for a Singing Tree. Tell me where it is."

"Turn around," replied the bird, "and you will see behind you some woods where you will find this tree."

The woods were not very far, and when the princess went there, she heard a harmonious concert among all the trees that she saw and knew that the singing must be coming from the tree she was seeking. But it was very large and tall. So she returned to the bird and said, "Bird, I have found the Singing Tree, but I cannot uproot it or carry it."

"It is not necessary to uproot it," the bird replied. "It is sufficient if you just take a single branch and carry it and plant it in your garden. It will take root as soon as you plant it in your garden, and in no time whatsoever you will see a tree just as beautiful as the one that you've just seen."

When the princess finally had all three things for which the devout Muslim woman had aroused her ardent desire, she said once again to the bird, "Bird, all that you have done for me thus far is not sufficient. You were the one who caused the death of my brothers, who must be among the black rocks that I saw while climbing the mountain. I want to take them with me."

It seemed that the bird wanted to satisfy her wish but that he had some difficulty in doing this.

"Bird," the princess insisted, "remember that you just told me that you are my slave, and in effect you are, and your life is at my disposal."

"I cannot contest this truth," the bird said. "Although what you have asked of me is so extremely difficult, I shall not let up until I satisfy your wish. Cast your eyes at our surroundings, and see if you can see a jug somewhere."

"I see one," the princess said.

"Pick it up," the bird replied, "and as you descend the mountain, pour a little of the water with which the jug is filled on each black rock. This will be the means for finding your brothers again."

Princess Parizad fetched the jug, and she carried it with her along with the birdcage, the flask, and the branch as she descended the mountain, and she poured a little of the water on each black rock that she encountered. Then each rock changed into a man. Since she did not omit any of the rocks, all the horses as well as her brothers and other cavaliers reappeared. At the end, she recognized Prince Bahman and Prince Parviz, who also recognized her and ran to embrace her. As she was hugging them and expressing her astonishment, she said, "My dear brothers, what are you doing here?"

When they explained to her that they had just fallen asleep, she remarked, "Yes, but without me, your sleep would have continued to last, and it might have lasted until Judgment Day. Don't you remember that you had gone in search of the Talking Bird, the Singing Tree, and the Yellow Water, and that upon arriving here you had seen the black rocks that were strewn all over this place? Look and see if there is one left. All the lords surrounding us and you as well were rocks. Even the horses that are waiting for you had been turned into rocks. And if you would like to know how I performed the miracle to change you back into your original shapes, it was by the water in that jug that I set on the ground over there. That jug was filled with water that I poured on each rock. But first I had to make the Talking Bird, which is in this cage, my slave. In turn, he helped find the Singing Tree from which I took this branch that I am carrying with me. Then the bird told me where the Yellow Water was, and I filled a flask with it. But I did not want to return without bringing you back with me. I compelled the bird by the power that I have over him to give me the means to do this, and he showed me where I could find the jug and how to make use of it the way I did."

As she told her story, the princes realized how much they were indebted to her and showed their gratitude, and the cavaliers who had gathered around them and had heard the same story also showed how grateful they were. Far from being envious of the three things that she had acquired and which they had aspired to conquer, they could only express how grateful they were that she had given back their lives to them, and they declared that they were her slaves and were ready to do whatever she ordered."

"My lords," the princess declared, "if you have paid attention to my story, you will have noticed that I had no other intention but to rescue my brothers. Thus, if you have benefited from this as you have said, you do not owe me anything. For my part I shall take your compliments for the honesty that you want to show me, and I thank you as I should. Moreover, I regard each one of you as free men as you were before your misfortune, and I rejoice with you for the good fortune that you have experienced through me. But do not remain any longer in a place where there is nothing to keep you here for a long time. Get on your horses and return each one of you to your home countries."

Princess Parizad set an example first by fetching her horse where she had left it. Before she mounted the horse, Prince Bahman wanted to relieve her of some of her burden and asked her to give him the birdcage.

"My brother," the princess said, "the bird is my slave. I want to carry him myself. But if you want to take charge of the branch from the Singing Tree, here it is. But hold the cage while I mount, and then give it back to me."

When she was back on the horse and Prince Bahman had given her the cage again, she said to Prince Parviz, "And you, my brother, here is the flask of Yellow Water, which I am placing in your care, if that does not inconvenience you."

The prince took charge of it with pleasure. When the two princes and all the cavaliers were mounted, Princess Parizad waited for someone to take the lead and begin the journey. The two princes wanted to be polite to the lords, and the lords, on their side, wanted to show politeness to the princess. When the princess realized that none of the lords wanted to take the lead, and that the honor was bestowed upon her, she addressed all of the men and said, "My lords, I expect you all to begin riding."

"Madame," one of the cavaliers said in the name of all of them, "we cannot ignore the honor that is due your sex, and after what you have done for us, notwithstanding your modesty, we beg you not to deprive us of the honor of following your lead."

"My lords," the princess said, "I do not deserve the honor that you have bestowed on me, and I only accept it because it is your desire."

As she said this, she began riding, and the two princes and the cavaliers followed her without making distinctions of rank. The troop wanted to see the dervish on their way and to thank him for his kindness and sincere advice. But he was dead, and they did not know whether it was his age or whether it was because he had accomplished his mission after the conquest of the three things which Princess Parizad had just recently acquired. So the contingent of people continued traveling, but it began to diminish each day. In effect, the lords who had come from different countries began to separate when they recognized the road that led to their realms. Each one took leave from the princess and her brothers and reiterated their gratitude, while the princess and her brothers continued the journey until they reached their home.

At first, the princess placed the cage in the garden, and since the salon was to the side, once the bird began to sing, the nightingales, the finches, larks, warblers, goldfinches, and a great number of other birds of this country came to accompany him with their chirping. As far as the branch was concerned, it was planted in the ground at some distance from the house. It took root, and in a short amount of time, it became a large tree, and soon its leaves produced the same harmony and concert as the tree from which it was cut. With regard to the flask of yellow water, the princess had a large basin of beautiful marble built in the middle of the ground floor, and when the basin was finished, she poured all the yellow water from the flask into it. As soon as the water was in the basin it began to

ANTOINE GALLAND

gush and swell, and a geyser began to rise about twenty feet high and then it fell back into the basin without one drop spilling over the rim.

After some days had passed, the princes Bahman and Parviz had recovered from the fatigue of their journey and resumed their old manner of living. Since the hunt was their usual way of amusing themselves, they mounted their horses, and for the first time since their return they did not go riding in their own park but rode two or three miles away from their house. As they were hunting, the sultan of Persia happened to be hunting on the same spot that they had chosen. As soon as they saw the sultan arrive, they stopped hunting because of the great number of cavaliers who appeared in various places, and began to withdraw so that they would avoid encountering him. But they had taken a path which the sultan had taken, and it was so narrow that they could not retreat or turn around without being seen. Thus, in their surprise, they only had time to dismount and prostrate themselves before the sultan. Their faces were against the ground, and they did not lift their heads to look at him. But the sultan, who saw that they were riding fine steeds and were dressed properly as though they belonged to his court, was curious to see what they looked like. He stopped and commanded them to stand up.

The princes got up and stood before the sultan with a free and easy air but with a modest and respectful demeanor. The sultan looked at them for some time from head to toe without speaking. After admiring their fine features and their handsome countenance, he asked them who they were and where they lived.

Prince Bahman began talking first and said, "Sire, we are the sons of the caretaker of your majesty's gardens. Our father is dead, and we are living in a house which he built shortly before he died. He built the house so that we could live in it until we reached the age when we might serve your majesty, and when we might request employment at the proper time."

"From what I see," the sultan said, "you love to hunt."

"Sire," Prince Bahman said, "it has become our favorite custom, and it is one that none of your majesty's subjects should neglect if they want to carry arms in your army in accordance with the ancient customs of this realm."

The sultan was charmed by such a wise response and said to them, "Since this is the case, I would very much like to see you hunt. Come and choose whatever hunt pleases you."

The princes remounted their horses and followed the sultan, and they had not advanced very far when they saw many different beasts appear at one time. Prince Bahman chose a lion, and Prince Parviz chose a bear. They both took off after the beasts at the same time without fear, and this impressed the sultan. They soon found their prey about the same time, and they threw their javelins with such skill that each pierced the beast he was chasing, Prince Bahman, the lion, and Prince Parviz, the bear, and the sultan saw the animals tumble to the ground. Without stopping, Prince Bahman pursued another bear, and Prince Parviz another lion, and a few moments later they pierced these animals and took their lives. They wanted to continue, but the sultan did not permit them. He called them to him, and when they were within range of him, he said to them, "If I let you continue, you would soon destroy all the animals. It is not so much my hunt, however, that I want to save; rather, your lives, which are very precious, for I am convinced by your bravery that you will become very useful to me when the time comes."

The Sultan Khusrau Shah felt such a strong liking for the two princes that he invited them to come and visit him right then and there.

"Sire," Prince Bahman said, "your majesty has bestowed an honor on us that we do not deserve, and therefore, we beg of you to dispense with it."

The sultan did not understand what reasons the princes could have for not accepting the sign of consideration that he had shown them. So he asked them and insisted that they explain why they could not come.

"Sire," Prince Bahman said, "we have a younger sister, with whom we live in great harmony, and therefore, we do not undertake anything or do anything without first consulting her. On her side, she does not do anything without asking for our advice first."

"I praise your strong family spirit," the sultan said. "So consult your sister, and tomorrow, I want you to return and hunt with me and to give me your response."

The two princes returned home, but neither one of them recalled their encounter with the king nor the honor of hunting with him. So neither one bothered to tell the princess that the sultan had invited them to visit him. The next day, when they appeared at the place designated for the hunt, the sultan said, "Well, then, have you spoken with your sister? Has she given her consent to my invitation?"

The princes looked at each other and blushed.

"Sire," Prince Bahman said, "we beg your majesty to excuse us. Neither I nor my brother remembered to ask her."

"Well, then," the sultan responded, "remember about it today, and don't forget to bring me a response tomorrow."

However, the princes did forget about it a second time, and fortunately the sultan was not upset by their negligence. On the contrary, he pulled three small golden balls from a purse. After he put them in the breast pocket of Prince Bahman, he said with a smile, "These balls will prevent you from forgetting a third time what I would like you to do. The noise that they will make this evening when they fall from your belt will make you remember in case you forget as you have done before."

Everything happened as the sultan had anticipated. Without the three balls, the princes would have once again forgotten to speak to Princess Parizad about the invitation. The balls fell from the breast of Prince Bahman when he loosened his belt in preparing to go to bed. As soon as he found Prince Parviz, they went together to the apartment of the princess, who had not yet gone to bed. They asked her pardon for coming so late, and they explained to her all that had happened with the sultan and the reasons why they had to speak to her.

Princess Parizad was alarmed by this news.

"Your encounter with the sultan," she said, "is very fortunate and honorable for you, and in the long run, it could be to your advantage. But it is unfortunate and sad for me. It is certainly out of consideration for me,

I understand, that you have resisted the sultan's wishes. I am infinitely grateful because I know that we feel perfectly the same about our friendship. You have preferred to commit a rude act of impoliteness to the sultan, so to say, than to refuse him honestly because you have believed that it would have a bad effect on our family bonds and unity that we have sworn to maintain. And you imagine that, if you begin seeing him, you will be unconsciously obliged to abandon me for him. But do you think that it is so easy to refuse a sultan what he wishes with such zeal as it appears he does? It is dangerous to refuse whatever sultans desire. Thus, if I were to follow my inclination and were to dissuade you from complying with his wishes, I would only expose you to his resentment and make myself unhappy with you. You see how I feel about this. However, before concluding anything, let us consult the Talking Bird, and let us see what he advises: he is perceptive and prophetic, and he has promised to help us whenever we have difficulties."

Princess Parizad ordered that the cage be brought to her, and after she had explained the difficulty to the bird in the presence of the princes, she asked the bird what the appropriate thing would be to do in this predicament. The bird responded, "It is necessary that the princes comply with the will of the sultan, and in turn, they should even invite him to come to your house."

"But, bird," the princess said, "we love each other, my brothers and I. It is a friendship without parallel. Won't our friendship suffer if we take these steps?"

"Not at all," the bird declared. "It will become even stronger."

"As a result," the princess said, "the sultan will see me."

The bird told her that it was necessary that the sultan should see her, and that everything would turn out for the best.

The next day the princes returned to the hunt, and as soon as the sultan saw them he asked them if they had remembered to speak with their sister. Prince Bahman approached and said, "Your majesty may dispose of us, and we are ready to obey. Not only did we not have any difficult obtaining the consent of our sister, but she herself found it rude that we had deferred to her when it was our duty to respond right away to your majesty. She was very indignant with us, and if we have sinned, we hope that your majesty will pardon us."

"This should not disturb you," the sultan said. "Far from finding what you have done rude, I approve of it very much, and I hope that you will show me the same deference when I shall have some of your friendship."

The princes were somewhat bewildered by the sultan's excessive kindness and could only respond by indicating the great respect that they had for him and the way he had received them. In contrast to his usual routine, the sultan did not hunt very long. Since he had already judged that the princes had plenty of intelligence, bravery, and valor, he was eager to return to the palace so that he would have more freedom to have a discussion with them. He wanted them to ride by his side during the return. This was an honor which created jealousy, especially since the sultan's most notable courtiers were accompanying him. Even the grand vizier was mortified to see the princes placed before him.

After the sultan had entered the capital, the people, who stood alongside the streets, only had eyes for the two princes, Bahman and Parviz, and wondered who they could be, whether they were strangers, or whether they came from the realm.

"Whoever they are," said the majority of the people, "it would have pleased God if the sultan had given us two princes as handsome and fine as these two are. If the births of the queen, who has been suffering for such a long time, had gone well, she would have had two boys about the same age."

The first thing that the sultan did upon arriving in his palace was to lead the princes through the principle apartment, whose beauty, richness, furniture, decorations, and symmetry they praised without affectation. Then they were served a magnificent meal, and the sultan had them eat at his table. They did not want to do this, but they had to obey the sultan's wish. Since the sultan was highly intelligent and had made great progress in the sciences, and particularly in history, he had foreseen that, by modesty and by respect, the princes would not take the liberty to begin the conversation. So, in order to give them the occasion to speak, he began and provided other opportunities during the meal. To his surprise, no matter what subject he touched upon, they displayed such knowledge, intelligence, and discerning judgment that he was in full admiration of them.

"If they were my children," he said to himself, "and given the intelligence they have, if I had given them an education, they would not know any more than they do now, and they would not be more clever or better informed."

In fact, he took such a great pleasure in their conversation that after having stayed longer at the table than he normally did, he went to his room, where he continued to converse with the princes for a long time. Finally the sultan said to them, "Never did I believe that there were young lords in the country that were my subjects and were so well educated, intellectual, and also skillful. Upon my life I have not had a conversation that has brought me so much pleasure as yours. It is time to relax your minds with some entertainment at my court, and since nothing is more capable of clearing away the clouds than music, you are going to hear a concert of voices and instruments that will not be unpleasant to your ears."

Just as the sultan finished speaking, the musicians were ordered to enter and fulfilled the expectations of the sultan with their playing. After the concert came the excellent actors and clowns, who were followed by the dancers, who completed the entertainment.

When the two princes saw that it had become very late, they prostrated themselves at the feet of the sultan and asked permission to withdraw after thanking him for his kindness and the honors that he had bestowed on them. And when the sultan gave them permission to leave, he said, "I shall let you go, and remember that I have only led you to my palace to show you the way so that you can come here yourselves. You are welcome, and the more often you come, the more you will give me pleasure."

Before leaving the sultan, Prince Bahman said, "Sire, may we take the liberty to beg your majesty to do our sister and us the honor of passing by

our house and resting there for a few moments while you are hunting in
the vicinity? It is not worthy of your presence, but sometimes kings do
deign to seek shelter in a cottage."

"A house belonging to young lords like you," the sultan replied, "can
be only beautiful and worthy of you. I shall look forward with great pleasure to seeing you and your sister as hosts, especially your sister, who is
dear to me even though I have not seen her. But I can tell from your
description that she has beautiful qualities, and I shall not delay my visit.
Indeed, I shall come by the day after tomorrow. I shall be spending the
entire morning at the spot where we met the first time. Meet me there,
and you will then serve as my guide to your house."

The princes returned to their home that same day, and after they had
arrived, they told their sister about the honorable reception that the sultan
held for them and that they had not forgotten to invite him to come to
their house and that the day of his visit had been set for the day after
tomorrow.

"If this is the case," the princess said, "we must think of the dinner that
we should prepare that will be worthy of his majesty. Therefore I think we
should consult the Talking Bird. Perhaps he can inform us about certain
dishes that are more pleasing to the taste of his majesty than others."

Since the princes trusted in her opinion, she went to consult the bird
about the meal after they went to bed.

"Bird," she said, "the sultan is doing us the honor of visiting our house,
and we must entertain him. Please inform us how we can fulfill our duty
in a manner that he will be content."

"My good mistress," the bird said, "you have excellent cooks who will
do their best. Above all they should make a plate of cucumbers stuffed
with pearls, which you are to have placed before him, preferably before
any of the other dishes are to be served."

"Cucumbers stuffed with pearls!" Princess Parizad exclaimed with surprise. "Bird, what are you thinking? I have never heard of a dish like that.
Perhaps the sultan could admire this as some magnificent present, but he
will be at the table to eat and not to admire pearls. Moreover, even if I
were to bring out all the pearls that I have, there is not enough to stuff
cucumbers with them."

"My mistress," the bird said, "do what I tell you, and do not worry about
what will happen. Indeed, only good will come of this. As for the pearls,
I want you to go early tomorrow morning to the first tree in your park,
and then you are to dig a hole to the right and you will find as many
pearls as you need."

That very night the princess alerted a gardener to be ready, and early
the next morning, she took him with her and led him to the tree that the
bird had mentioned. Then she ordered him to dig a hole. After the gardener had been digging for a while, he came across something that resisted
his spade and discovered a golden casket that was about the size of two
square feet.

"This is why I brought you here," she said. "Continue digging, and take
care that you do not harm the casket with your blade."

Finally the gardener was able to pull out the casket and place it in the hands of the princess. Since it was shut with strong little latches, the princess opened it, and she saw that it was filled with a large number of medium-sized pearls, but smooth and pure, just the right kind for her purpose. Very happy to have found this treasure, the princess shut the casket, took it under her arm, and went back to the house, while the gardener refilled the hole at the foot of the tree so that the ground was the way it was before.

Each of the princes had seen the princess go into the garden early in the morning from their windows, and they were curious about this since this was not her custom. So as soon as they could get dressed, they went to join her in the middle of the garden. When they saw her carrying something under her arm, they were surprised to see as she drew closer that it was a golden casket.

"My sister," said Prince Bahman, "you were carrying nothing when we saw you go with the gardener, and now we see you return with this golden casket. Is it some treasure that the gardener found, and did he come and tell you about it?"

"My brothers," the princess said. "It is just the opposite. It is I who led the gardener to the casket, and it is I who showed him the spot where he was to dig. You will be even more surprised about what I found when you see what is inside the casket."

The princess opened the casket, and the princes were astonished when they saw that it was filled with pearls, perhaps not so considerable due to their size, but a very great treasure when one considered their perfection and quantity. So, they asked her how she had come to know about this treasure.

"My brothers," she said, "there is a matter that is more urgent that we must take care of. Come with me, and I shall tell you."

"What matter can be more urgent," Prince Parviz asked, "than the matter at hand, which interests us so much? We know nothing other than what we have seen upon encountering you."

So the princess took her place between her brothers, and as they walked back to the house, she told them about her consultation with the bird, as they agreed she would do, about his response, about what she said to him about the stuffed cucumbers, and about how he had told her where they were and how to fetch them. The princess and princes tried to figure out what was behind the bird's plan and why he wanted them to prepare a dish of this kind for the sultan. But after exploring all the possibilities, they finally had to conclude that they did not understand anything. Nevertheless, they had to do everything exactly as he had instructed.

Upon entering the house, the princess called the head chef of the kitchen, and he came to her apartment. After she had given him the menu and orders for the sultan's meal, she said, "Aside from what I just told you, it is necessary that you make me a dish expressly for the sultan's lips. Nobody but you shall prepare this. This dish is a plate of cucumbers that you will stuff with the pearls that you see here."

As she said this, she showed him the pearls. The chef had never heard of a stuffed dish like this and recoiled with a face that indicated what he was thinking.

"I see very well," she said, "that you think I am somewhat mad to order you to make such a dish that you have never heard of before, and one that has certainly never been made before. This is true. I agree. But I am not mad, and I am ordering you to do this with all my good senses about me. Go. Invent something. Do your best, and take the casket with you. Bring it back to me with the pearls that are left over if there are some that you do not need."

The chef did not reply. He took the casket and went away. Finally, on that same day, Princess Parizad gave the orders to make sure that everything was clean, proper, and well arranged in the house as well as in the garden to receive the king in a dignified way.

The following day the princes were at the spot of the hunt when the sultan of Persia arrived. The sultan began the hunt, and continued until the strong rays of the sun, which was reaching its zenith, obliged him to stop. Then, while Prince Brahman rode at the sultan's side to accompany him, Prince Parviz took the lead to show the way. When they were in view of the house, he spurred his horse to ride ahead and alert the princess that the sultan would soon arrive. But the princess's people, whom she had ordered to stand along the path to the house, had already alerted her, and the prince found her ready to receive the sultan.

When the sultan arrived at the court and had dismounted and entered the vestibule, Princess Parizad presented herself and threw herself at the sultan's feet. The princes, who were present, informed the sultan that she was their sister and begged him to accept the respect that she was showing their majesty.

The sultan bent down to help the princess stand up, and for some time regarded and admired her sparkling beauty, which he found dazzling, as well as her fine grace, her air, and everything about her that came from the country in which she was living.

"Your brothers," he said, "are worthy of their sister, and their sister is worthy of her brothers. And judging the interior by the exterior, I am not astonished that your brothers did not want to do anything without consulting their sister. But I hope very much to get to know you better here in this place that has impressed me very much at first sight."

"Sire," the princess responded, "this is only a country house that is only suitable for people like us who have withdrawn from society. It is nothing to compare with the houses of the large cities and even less with the magnificent palaces of the sultans."

"I do not entirely share your sentiments," the sultan said very obligingly. What I have first seen makes me suspect that you may not be right. I shall withhold my judgment until I have seen everything. Therefore, go ahead of me, and show me the way."

The princess led the sultan from the salon to apartment after apartment, and after the sultan had regarded each room with a great deal of attention and had admired the diverse decor, he said, "My beautiful girl, do you call this a country house? The most magnificent cities would soon be deserted if all the country houses resembled yours. I am not at all astounded that you enjoy yourselves here so much and that you are not fond of the city. Now show me the garden. I expect that it will correspond with the house."

The princess opened a door that let out into the garden. What first struck the eyes of the sultan was the geyser of yellow water, the color of gold, that shot into the air. Indeed, he had never seen such a spectacle before and was very surprised by it. Therefore, he admired it for some time and then said, "Where does this marvelous water come from? It is such a pleasure to watch it. Where is the source? And how have you been able to create such an extraordinary geyser? I don't think that there is anything like it in the world. I would like to see this marvel up close."

As he said these words, he kept walking, and the princess continued to show him the garden. Next she led him to the place where the Singing Tree had been planted. As they approached it, the sultan heard a concert that he had never heard before. He stopped and looked about him to see if he could find the musicians, and since he could not see any of them near or far, he nevertheless listened distinctly to the concert and was charmed by it.

"My beautiful girl," he said, "where are the musicians? Are they here on earth? Are they invisible? With such excellent and charming voices, they have nothing to risk in being seen. On the contrary, they would give me a great pleasure."

"Sire," the princess smiled and responded, "there are no musicians who are making this concert that you hear. It is a tree, your majesty, the one right before your eyes. If you take the trouble to advance a few more steps, you will be able to confirm this, and the voices will be even more clear."

The sultan advanced, and he was so charmed by the sweet harmony of the concert that he only wanted to listen to it. Finally, however, he recalled that he had seen the Yellow Water nearby and broke his silence.

"My beautiful girl," he asked the princess, "tell me, please, did you find this admirable tree by chance in your garden? Is it a present that someone made to you, or did you have it come from some distant country? It must have come from afar. Otherwise, I would have heard about it because I am very curious about the rarities of nature. What is its name?"

"Sire," the princess said, "this tree has no other name than the Singing Tree, and it does not grow in this country. It would take too long to tell all about the adventure that brought it here. It is a story that is connected to the Yellow Water and to the Talking Bird that came to us at the same time. After your majesty sees the Yellow Water up close, we can go to the bird, if you wish. If you find it agreeable, I would be honored to tell you the entire story when you have relaxed and recovered from the fatigue of hunting and from the strong rays of the sun, and the bird itself will add something new."

"My beautiful girl," the sultan said, "I am not at all exhausted as you think, and I have been amply rewarded by the marvelous things that you have shown me. I would rather continue and see the Yellow Water, and I am already burning with desire to see and admire the Talking Bird."

When the sultan arrived at the geyser of yellow water, he stood there a long time and stared at the jet, which continued to create a marvelous effect by rising and falling in the basin.

"According to you, my beautiful girl," the sultan said, "this water does not have a source, and it does not come from some place in this region where there is a canal that conducts it underground. I must admit that it is just as unusual as the Singing Tree."

"Sire," the princess said, "it is as your majesty has said. You can see that the water does not come from below the ground because the marble basin is made of one piece, and thus the water cannot come from the side or from above. What makes this water even more remarkable, your majesty, is that I only threw a flask of it into the basin, and due to some extraordinary quality, it came to bubble and then gush as you see."

Finally, the sultan moved away from the basin.

"Well, then, that's enough for the first time," the sultan said. "Now take me to the Talking Bird."

As they approached the salon, the sultan noticed a number of miraculous birds on the trees that were filling the air with their songs and chirping. He asked why they had all gathered here rather than on the other trees of the garden where he had not seen or heard them.

"Sire," the princess responded, "it is because they have come from all parts of the country to accompany the Talking Bird. Your majesty will see that bird in a cage that is placed on one of the windows of the salon when you enter. If you pay attention, you will perceive that his song is much more melodic than that of any of the other birds, even more than that of the nightingale, which cannot even begin to approach him."

The sultan entered the salon, and since the bird was continuing to sing, the princess raised her voice and said, "My slave, here is the sultan. Pay him your respects."

The bird stopped singing right away, and all the other birds stopped as well.

"May the sultan be most welcome," the birds said. "May God give him prosperity and long life!"

Since the meal was being served on the sofa near the window where the bird was placed, the sultan took a seat at the table.

"Bird," he said, "I thank you for your welcome, and I am charmed to find in you the sultan and the king of the birds."

The sultan saw that there was a plate of cucumbers placed before him, and he thought that they were stuffed in the way they usually are. He took the plate with his hand, and he was most astonished to find that they were stuffed with pearls.

"How unique!" he said. "What is the purpose of a stuffing made with pearls. One cannot eat pearls."

He looked at the two princes and the princess to have them explain to him what the significance of the pearls was, but the bird interrupted and said, "Sire, how can your majesty be so surprised by a stuffing made out of pearls that you are viewing with your eyes, when you have so easily believed that your wife the queen gave birth to a puppy, a kitten, and a piece of wood that was made to resemble a mole?"

"I believed all this," the sultan replied, "because the midwives assured me that it was true."

"These midwives, sire," the bird declared, "are the queen's sisters, but they were jealous of how happy you made her and how much honor you bestowed on her by preferring her to them. To satisfy their rage, they abused the gullibility of your majesty. They will confess their crime if you have them interrogated. The two brothers and their sister whom you see before you are your children, whom they abandoned by sending them down the canal in a basket, but they were saved by the caretaker of your gardens, and nurtured and raised in his care."

The bird's story made complete sense to the sultan right away, and he exclaimed, "Bird, I have no difficulty believing that what you have told me is the truth. The inclination that I have felt toward them and the tenderness that I have already felt toward them tell me that they are of my blood. Come to me, my children, come, my daughter, so that I can embrace you and give you the first signs of my love and my paternal tenderness."

He stood up, and after he had embraced the two princes and the princess, one after the other, tears streamed down their cheeks and mixed with one another.

"It is not enough, my children," the sultan said. "You must also embrace one another, not as the children of the caretaker of my gardens, to whom I am eternally grateful for having saved your lives, but also as my children, emanating from the blood of the kings of Persia, and I am convinced that you will maintain this glory in the future."

After the two princes and the princess embraced each other with a new kind of satisfaction, as the sultan wished, the sultan sat down at the table with them again. He ate quickly, and when the meal was finished, he said, "My children, you now know your father in person. Tomorrow I shall take you to the queen, your mother. Prepare yourselves to meet her."

The sultan mounted his horse and returned to his capital as soon as he could. The first thing that he did as soon as he set foot inside the palace was to command his grand vizier to bring charges against the two sisters of the queen as soon as possible. So, the two sisters were taken from their apartments, interrogated separately, put to the test, and then sentenced and condemned to be torn to pieces. All of this was done within less than an hour.

In the meantime, the Sultan Khusrau Shah, followed by all the lords of the court who were present, went to the door of the grand mosque, and after he himself took the queen out of her narrow prison, where she had been languishing and suffering for many years, he embraced her with tears in his eyes because of the pitiful state in which she was and said, "I have come to ask you pardon for the unjust way that I have treated you, and I want to make reparations that I owe you. I have already begun doing this by punishing your sisters for having deceived me with an abominable trick, and I hope that you will regard my gesture complete when I present you to two perfect princes and an amiable and charming princess, who are your children and mine. Come, and assume the position that belongs to you with all the honors that are due to you."

This apology was made before a crowd of innumerable people who had come from everywhere as soon as the first news of the recent events had been spread throughout the city. Early the next morning the sultan and the queen, who had changed the dress of humiliation and affliction that she had been wearing the day before and was now clad in a magnificent dress that suited her, went to the house of the two princes and the princess. And they were followed by their entire court. As soon as they set foot in the house, the sultan presented the princes Bahman and Parviz and the Princess Parizad to the queen and said to her, "Madame, here are the two princes, your sons, and the princess, your daughter. Embrace them with the same tenderness with which I embraced them. They are worthy of me and worthy of you."

Tears were shed in abundance while they embraced and hugged each other. In particular, the queen wept out of consolation and out of joy to embrace her sons and daughter after being tormented for such a long time. The two princes and the princess had prepared a magnificent meal for the sultan, the queen, and the entire court. After they were finished, the sultan led the queen into the garden, where he had her observe the Singing Tree and the beautiful effect of the Yellow Water. With regard to the Talking Bird, she had seen it in its cage, and the sultan had said some words of praise about the bird during the meal.

When there was nothing more that obligated the sultan to remain at this house, he mounted his horse, and Prince Bahman accompanied him on the right, and Prince Parviz on the left. The queen, with the princess on her left, followed the sultan. In this order, preceded and followed by the officers of the court, each person took his place according to rank, and they all headed toward the capitol. As they approached, the people who had come out to see them formed a huge crowd, and they were especially eager to see the queen and shared her joy after such long suffering. In addition, their eyes were riveted by the princes and the princess, whom they cheered with acclamation. Their attention was also drawn by the bird in the cage which Princess Parizad carried with her. They admired the bird's song, which drew many other birds, and all of them followed him by hopping from one tree to the next and perching on the roofs of the houses in the streets of the city.

Finally, the princess Bahman and Parviz and the Princess Parizad were led into the palace with all this pomp. In the evening the splendor was followed by great celebrations in the palace as well as throughout the city, and they lasted for many days.

JACOB AND WILHELM GRIMM

The Three Little Birds†

More than a thousand years ago there were many minor kings in this country, and one of them lived on the mountain called Köterberg. He was very fond of hunting, and one day, when he left his castle and went down the mountain with his huntsmen, he came upon three maidens tending

† Jacob and Wilhelm Grimm, "The Three Little Birds"—"De drei Vügelkens" (1857), No. 96 in *Kinder- und Hausmärchen. Gesammelt durch die Brüder Grimm* (Göttingen: Dieterich, 1857).

their cows. When they saw the king with his men, the oldest pointed at the king and called to the other two, "Hallo, hallo! If I can't have that man over there, I don't want any at all."

Then the second responded from the other side of the mountain and pointed at the fellow walking on the king's right. "Hallo, hallo. If I can't have that man over there, I don't want any at all."

Finally, the youngest pointed at the fellow on the king's left and called out, "Hallo! Hallo! If I can't have that man over there, I don't want any at all."

The two men were the king's ministers, and the king had heard what the maidens had said. After he returned from the hunt, he summoned the three maidens and asked them what they had said the day before on the mountain. They refused to answer, but the king asked the oldest if she would take him for her husband. She said yes, and her two sisters also married the two ministers, for the maidens were all beautiful and had fine features, especially the queen, who had hair like flax.

The two sisters did not bear any children, and once when the king had to take a trip, he asked them to stay with the queen and cheer her up, for she was with child. While he was away, she gave birth to a little boy who had a bright red star as a birthmark. But the two sisters decided to throw the pretty baby boy into the river. After they had thrown him into the water—I think it was the Weser—a little bird flew up in the air and sang:

> "Get ready for your death.
> I'll see what I can do.
> Get ready for the wreath.
> Brave boy, can that be you?"

When the two sisters heard the song, they feared for their lives and ran off. Later the king returned home, and they told him the queen had given birth to a dog, and the king responded, "Whatever God does is always for the best."

However, a fisherman lived by the river, and he fished the little boy out of the river while he was still alive. Since his wife had not given birth to any children, they fed and cared for him.

After a year had passed, the king went on another journey, and the queen gave birth to a second boy during his absence. The two wicked sisters again took the baby away and threw him into the river. Then the little bird flew up into the air once more and sang:

> "Get ready for your death.
> I'll see what I can do.
> Get ready for the wreath.
> Brave boy, can that be you?"

When the king came home, the sisters told him the queen had again given birth to a dog, and he responded as before, "Whatever God does is always for the best."

However, the fisherman fetched this baby out of the water, too, and fed and cared for him.

Once again the king went on a journey, and the queen gave birth to a little girl, whom the wicked sisters also threw into the river. Then the little bird flew up into the air once more and sang:

> "Get ready for your death.
> I'll see what I can do.
> Get ready for the wreath.
> Brave girl, can that be you?"

When the king came back home, the sisters told him the queen had given birth to a cat. This time the king became so angry that he had his wife thrown into prison, where she was forced to stay for many years.

In the meantime, the children grew up, and one day the oldest went out fishing with some other boys, but they did not want him around and said, "You foundling, go your own way!"

The boy was very upset when he heard that and asked the old fisherman whether it was true. Then the fisherman told him how he had been out fishing one day and had found him in the water. The boy then said he wanted to go out and search for his father. The fisherman begged him to remain, but there was no holding him back. At last the fisherman gave in, and the boy went forth. He walked for many days until he came to a large and mighty river, where he found an old woman standing and fishing.

"Good day, grandma," said the boy.

"Why, thank you kindly."

"You'll be fishing here a long time before you catch any fish."

"And you'll be searching a long time before you find your father. How are you going to get across the river?"

"God only knows."

Then the old woman picked him up and carried him across on her back. Once he was on the other side, he continued his search for his father a long time, but he could not find him.

When a year had gone by, the second boy went out looking for his brother. He, too, came to the river, and the same thing happened to him as to his brother. Now only the daughter was left alone at home, and she grieved so much for her brothers that finally the fisherman had to let her go, too. Soon she also came to the large river and said to the old woman, "Good day, grandma."

"Why, thank you kindly."

"May God help you with your fishing."

When the old woman heard that, she treated the girl in a friendly way. She carried her across the river, gave her a stick, and said, "Now, my daughter, just keep going straight ahead, and when you come to a big black dog, you must be quiet. Don't be afraid or laugh or stop to look at it. Then you'll come to a large open castle. You must drop the stick on the threshold and go right through the castle and out the other side, where you'll see an old well. The big tree will be growing from the well, and on the tree a cage with a bird inside will be hanging. Take the cage down and get a glass of water from the well. Then carry both things back the same way you came. When you come to the threshold, pick up the stick, and when you come to the dog again, hit it in the face with the stick, but see to it that you don't miss. Then come back here to me."

The girl found everything as the woman had said, and on her way back from the castle she met her two brothers, who had been searching half the world for each other. They went on together to the spot where the black dog was lying. Then she hit it on the face, and it turned into a handsome prince, who accompanied them to the river. The old woman was still standing there and was happy to see them. She carried all four of them across the river, and then she departed because she had now been released from the magic spell.

The others traveled back to the old fisherman, and they were all glad to have found each other again. Once inside the house, they hung the birdcage on the wall. But the second son was still restless. So he took a bow and went hunting. When he became tired, he took out his flute and began playing a little tune. The king, who was out hunting, too, heard the music and went toward it. When he saw the boy, he said, "Who's given you permission to hunt here?"

"Nobody."

"Who're your parents?"

"I'm the fisherman's son."

"But he doesn't have any children."

"If you think I'm lying, come along with me."

The king did so and asked the fisherman, who told him all that had happened. Suddenly, the little bird in the cage began to sing:

> "Oh, king of noble blood,
> your children are back for good.
> But their mother sits in prison
> with nothing much to live on.
> Her sisters are the wicked ones,
> who took your daughter and your sons
> and left them to the river's fate,
> but the fisherman came 'ere it was too late."

When they heard the song, they were all astounded. The king took the little bird, the fisherman, and the three children with him to his castle, where he had the prison opened and his wife released. However, she had become very sick and was haggard. So her daughter gave her a drink of water from the well, and she regained her health. But the two wicked sisters were burned to death, and the daughter married the prince.

Wild Men

In 1815, the Brothers Grimm published "The Wild Man" in dialect, a tale that they had obtained from a member of the aristocratic family von Haxthausen. The Grimms kept publishing this tale in the following editions of *Children's and Household Tales* until 1843. Then they eliminated it in favor of "Iron Hans," a tale which Wilhelm Grimm virtually wrote by himself using the dialect version of "The Wild Man," another oral story that they had collected from a member of the Hassenpflug family of Kassel, and Friedmund von Arnim's "Iron Hans" in *Hundert neue Mährchen im Gebirge gesammelt* (1844). Wilhelm synthesized literary and oral versions that folklorists have traced to two basic tale-types: 314 (*The Youth Transformed to a Horse*, also known as *Goldener* in German, or *The Golden-Haired Youth at a King's Court*) and 502 (*The Wild Man*), according to *The Types of the Folk-Tale* by Antti Aarne and Stith Thompson. Given the evidence we have from the Brothers Grimm, Wilhelm's "Iron Hans" is mainly based on tales that stem from type 314, *The Golden-Haired Youth*. As usual, there is debate among folklorists about the origins of this type. Some place the tale's creation in India, while others argue that it originated during the latter part of the Roman Empire. However, almost all folklorists agree that, as far as Wilhelm Grimm's version is concerned, the major plot line and motifs of the tale were formed during the Middle Ages in Europe. Furthermore, they were strongly influenced by a literary tradition, in particular a twelfth-century romance entitled *Robert der Teufel* or *Robert le Diable* (*Robert the Devil*), which gave rise to many different literary and oral versions in Medieval Europe.

In *Robert der Teufel*, the Count Hubertus of Normandy and his wife become skeptical about God's powers because they cannot conceive a child. They lose their faith in the Almighty, and the wife says that she would accept a child even if it were provided by the Devil. Indeed, she gives birth to a son named Robert, who is possessed by the Devil and has extraordinary powers. No one can control him, and he cannot master himself. Soon he is known by the name of Robert the Devil. When he turns seventeen and is made a knight, he terrorizes the region and commits many crimes. However, all this changes when his mother tells him to kill her because she is so ashamed of him and herself. She reveals the story of his birth, and he decides to make a pilgrimage to Rome. As repentance for his crimes, a holy hermit tells him that he must live the life of a fool or madman. So Robert travels to the emperor's court, where he acts the fool and lives with dogs. Only the emperor's daughter, who cannot speak, knows that Robert is someone other than he pretends to be. After seven years, a treacherous seneschal attempts to overthrow the emperor with the help of the Saracens. God commands Robert to help the emperor and gives him white armor and a white horse. As a result, Robert saves the Holy Roman Empire, and the emperor's daughter reveals that he is the true savior when his identity is doubted. Eventually, Robert marries the emperor's daughter and returns to Normandy, where he and his wife give birth to a son named Richard.

As can be seen from this summary, this popular romance contains most of the important motifs and features that one can find not only in the Grimms' "Iron Hans," but also in Straparola's "Guerrino and the Wild Man" and Mailly's imitation "Prince Guerini." All these tales are a blend of Christian legendary material and medieval folktales dealing with the golden-haired youth and the mysterious wild man, who may be either a friend, a mentor, or a demonic figure. There are hundreds of oral versions of this tale in France and the Scandinavian countries, and they have spread to North America. One more notable literary version that preceded Wilhelm Grimm's final text is Christian August Vulpius's "Der eiserne Mann, oder: Der Lohn des Gehorsams" ("The Iron Man; or, The Reward of Obedience") in *Ammenmärchen* (1791).

GIOVAN FRANCESCO STRAPAROLA

Guerrino and the Wild Man†

Sicily is a perfect and fertile island and surpasses all the other islands of antiquity. Indeed, it abounds in cities and castles that render it even more beautiful. Many years ago the lord of this island was a king named Filippo Maria, a wise, amiable, and unusual man, who had a courteous, gracious, and beautiful lady as his wife. Together they had one son whose name was Guerrino.

The king took greater delight in hunting than any other man in the country because he was so strong and robust, and the exercise was well suited to him. Now it happened one day that, as he was returning from hunting in company with some of his barons and huntsmen, he saw a large and tall wild man coming out of a dense forest. He was so deformed and ugly that they all gazed at him with amazement. Since his physical strength seemed just as great if not greater than that of any of the men in his company, the king prepared himself for a fight. And together with two of his best barons, he boldly attacked the wild man, and after a long battle they valiantly overcame him. Then they tied his hands and led him back to the palace, where they put him up in a secure chamber locked with very strong keys. Thereupon, the king ordered that he was to be closely watched and guarded. Indeed, the king regarded his captive with so much esteem that he placed the queen in charge of the keys, and he never failed to go to the prison every day to visit the wild man for his own pleasure.

Sometime later the king prepared to go hunting once more, and after having equipped himself with all the necessary things, he departed with a noble company of courtiers. Before he left, he gave the keys of the prison to the queen. During the time that the king was hunting, a great desire overcame Guerrino, who was still a young boy, and he longed to see the wild man. So he took his bow and arrow, which always delighted him,

---

† Giovan Francesco Straparola, "Guerrino and the Wild Man"—"Guerrino, unico figliulo di Filippo Maria re di Cicilia, libera un uomo salvatico dalla prigione del padre; e la madre per temenza del re manda il figliulo in essilio. E lo salvatico uomo, fatto domestico, libera Guerrino da molti ed infinit infortuni" (1550), *Favola* I, *Notte quinta* in *Le piacevoli notti*, 2 vols. (Venice: Comin da Trino, 1550/53).

and he went all alone to the prison bars behind which the monster was compelled to live. When he saw the wild man, he began conversing with him in a civilized way. As they were talking, the wild man began affectionately caressing and flattering the boy. Then, all of a sudden, he adroitly snatched the richly ornamented arrow from the boy's pocket. Immediately, the boy began to weep and could not keep back his tears, pleading with the man to give him back his arrow. But the wild man said, "If you will open the door and free me from this prison, I'll give you back your arrow, but if you refuse, I shall never let you have it."

The boy answered, "How can I open the door for you and set you free when I have no way to do this?"

"If you really would like to release me," said the wild man, "and get me out of this narrow cell, I'd gladly teach you the way to do it."

"But how?" replied Guerrino. "Tell me the way."

"Go to the chamber of the queen your mother," instructed the wild man, "and when you see that she is taking her midday nap, move your hand carefully under the pillow on which her head is resting. Then take the keys of the prison so that she doesn't notice it and bring them here and open my prison door. As soon as you do this, I'll give you back your arrow right away, and perhaps at some future time I'll be able to return your kindness."

Guerrino was eager to regain his gilded arrow, and since he was just a boy, he did not think of anything else. So he promptly ran to his mother and found her asleep. Then he slowly pulled the keys out from under her pillow and returned to the wild man.

"Here are the keys," he said. "If I let you out of this place, you must go as far away as possible so that no one will ever pick up your scent. My father is a great huntsman, and if he should find you and capture you again, he would certainly have you killed right away."

"Trust me, my son," said the wild man. "As soon as you open the prison and make me a free man, I'll give you back your arrow and go so far away from here that neither your father nor any other man shall ever find me."

Guerrino, who was very strong for his age, worked away at the door until it opened. Then the wild man gave him back his arrow, thanked him very much, and went his way. Now, this wild man had been a very handsome young man, and out of despair at not being able to win the lady whom he had ardently loved, he had abandoned his amorous thoughts and urbane pursuits and had taken to living among the beasts of the forest. He had always dwelled in the gloomy woods and dense thickets, eating grass and drinking water like an animal. This is why the wretched man had become covered with a great fell of fair, thick skin, and a long, tangled and heavy beard. Through eating grass, his beard, hard skin, and hair had become so green that they were monstrous to behold.

As soon as the queen awoke, she moved her hand under her pillow to take the keys that she always kept by her side. When she found they were gone, she was quite astonished. After turning the bed upside down without finding any trace of them, she ran like crazy straight to the prison door, which was standing open. Upon realizing that the wild man had escaped, she thought she would die from grief. Returning to the palace, she searched high and low and questioned each and every courtier as to who could have been so audacious and arrogant to have taken the prison keys without her knowledge. But they all responded that they knew nothing whatsoever about the matter. When Guerrino encountered his mother and saw that she was terribly upset, he said to her, "Mother, don't blame any of these people for opening the prison door because, if anyone deserves to be punished, then it is me. I am the one who opened the door."

When the queen heard these words, she was plunged deeper into sorrow than before. Indeed, she feared that the king would kill his son out of anger when he returned from the hunt, for he had attached great importance to the wild man by giving her the keys and charging her to guard them as carefully as she would guard her own person. Therefore, the queen, who created a bigger mistake by trying to avoid the consequences of a smaller one, summoned two of her most trustworthy servants and her son as well. After giving them a great deal of jewels and money and superb horses, she sent them away to seek his fortune elsewhere. At the same time, she implored the servants most sincerely to take great care of Guerrino.

A short time after the son had left his mother, the king returned from the hunt, and as soon as he got off his horse, he went straight to the prison to see the wild man. When he found the door wide open and saw that the wild man had escaped, he exploded into a great rage and made up his mind to slay the person who had committed this atrocious act. Thus he went to the queen, who was sitting in her chamber and asked her who the arrogant and rash person was that had opened the prison door and had enabled the wild man to escape. The queen replied in a meek and trembling voice, "Oh, sire, please don't be upset! Guerrino confessed to me that he was the one who did this." And then she told the king everything that Guerrino had said to her. When the king heard her story, he became very angry. Next she told him that she had been afraid he might slay their son, and thus she had sent him far away accompanied by two of their most faithful servants. In addition she had given them enough jewels and money to serve their needs. After the king had listened to his wife, he felt such constant and painful throbs of anguish that he almost fell to the ground in a mad fit. If it had not been for the courtiers who held him back, he would assuredly have slain his grief-stricken wife on the spot.

Now, when the poor king had regained his composure and calmed his unbridled rage, he said to the queen, "Alas, my wife, what could you have been thinking to send away our son to some foreign land? Did you perhaps believe that I cherished this wild man more than my own flesh and blood?" And without waiting for a reply, he ordered a large troop of soldiers to mount their horses right away, and after he divided them into four companies, they were to carry out a careful search and to try to find the prince. But all their efforts were in vain because Guerrino and the servants were traveling incognito, and they did not let anyone know who they were.

After they had ridden far and crossed valleys, mountains, and rivers, living here and there, Guerrino eventually turned sixteen. Indeed, he became so handsome that he resembled a fresh morning rose. Soon after this, the servants, who accompanied him, conceived a diabolical plot to kill him and take the jewels and money, which they would divide among themselves. This plan, however, came to nothing. Thanks to divine justice, they were unable to reach an agreement among themselves. Then, fortunately, it happened one day that a very handsome and graceful young man came riding their way. He was mounted on a superb steed, decked out in magnificent style, and when he approached, he bowed and saluted Guerrino with great courtesy.

"Most gracious sir," he said, "if you don't mind, I should very much like to join your company."

"Since you have asked with such politeness," Guerrino replied, "I cannot possibly refuse your company. Therefore, it would be an honor for me if you would join us. We are strangers in this country and do not know the roads all that well. Perhaps you may be kind enough to instruct us which way would be the best to take. Moreover, as we ride on together we can discuss the different experiences we have had, and thus our journey will be less boring."

Now this young man was none other than the wild man whom Guerrino had freed from the prison of King Filippo Maria, his father. After wandering through various countries and strange places, he had accidentally encountered a very beautiful fairy, who was somewhat ill. When she gazed at him and saw how deformed and ugly he was, she began to laugh so impetuously at the sight of his ugliness that she burst a boil that had formed near her heart and could have caused her death by suffocation. This was how she was saved and restored to health, and it was as if she had never been afflicted with an illness in the past. Not wishing to appear ungrateful to him, the good fairy desired to repay his great favor and said, "Oh, you deformed and filthy man, since you have been the means of restoring my health, which I so greatly desired, go your way, and you will be changed from what you are into the most polite, the most wise, and the most graceful young man in the world. Moreover, you are to share all the power and authority conferred upon me by nature. Therefore, you will be able to do and to undo whatever pleases you." After giving him a noble and enchanted horse, she bade him farewell and let him go wherever he wanted.

Thus as Guerrino journeyed with the young man, he did not recognize him, but the young man knew who he was. Eventually, they came to a mighty city called Ireland, which at that time was ruled by King Zifroi, who was the father of two lovely daughters with polite manners. In fact their beauty and charms surpassed those of Venus herself. One of the daughters was called Potentiana, and the other Eleuteria. Their father adored them so much that he had eyes only for them.

As soon as Guerrino entered the city of Ireland with the unknown youth and servants, he took lodging at an inn run by a host who was the wittiest fellow in all of Ireland and treated his guests in a most honorable way. The following day the unknown youth pretended that he had to depart and travel to another country. Therefore, he went to take his leave of Guerrino and thanked him cordially for his good company. But Guerrino had formed a strong affection for him and would not let him depart. Indeed, he embraced the young man so tenderly that he agreed to stay.

At this time in the territory around Ireland, there were two very ferocious and frightful animals. One was a wild horse, and the other a mare just as wild. They were so vicious and bold that they not only ravaged and devastated all the cultivated fields, but they also killed all the animals and humans in a miserable way. Due to the ferocity of these animals, the condition of the country was such that no one could be found who wanted to dwell there. As a result, the peasants abandoned their farms and dear homes and went to foreign countries. There was no man strong and powerful enough to face the horses, much less slay them. As the king saw the whole country stripped of food as well as animals and people, he did not know how to remedy the situation. So he became gloomy and cursed his hard and evil fate.

Meanwhile, Guerrino's two servants had not been able to carry out their sinister plan during their journey because they had not reached an agreement among themselves and because of the arrival of the unknown youth. Now, however, they pondered how they might bring about Guerrino's death and gain possession of the money and the jewels.

"Let us see," they said to one another, "if we can find some way to cause our master's death."

But they could not find the means to satisfy themselves because they would be in danger of losing their own lives if they were to kill him in an obvious way. So they decided to speak privately with the innkeeper and tell him that Guerrino was a young man of great prowess and valor. Furthermore, they recounted that he had often boasted in front of them that he could slay the wild horse without danger to himself. They knew that this story would easily reach the ears of the king, who, eager to have the two animals killed and to restore the health of his land, would summon Guerrino to appear before him and would then ask him how he intended to accomplish everything. Since Guerrino would not know what to say or do, he would immediately be put to death by the king. Then the servants planned to take possession of the jewels and money. This was their plan, and they carried it out as they conceived it.

When the innkeeper listened to their story about Guerrino, he became the most cheerful and happy man that nature had ever created. Within seconds he ran to the palace, and after kneeling down before the king and showing due reverence, he said to him secretly, "Sacred king, I'd like you to know that there is a charming wandering knight who is staying in my inn. His name is Guerrino, and while I was talking about various matters with his servants, they told me, among other things, how their master was famous for his great valor and prowess with arms and that there is nobody comparable to him in our day. Indeed, many a time he has boasted about his strength and power and that he could easily overcome the wild horse that is causing so much damage in your kingdom."

When King Zifroi heard these words, he immediately ordered Guerrino to be brought before him. Thereupon, the innkeeper obeyed the king and returned at once to his inn and said to Guerrino that he was to go alone to the king, who had a great desire to speak with him. When Guerrino heard this, he presented himself to the king, and after paying his respects, he asked why the king had asked to speak with him.

"Guerrino," the king replied, "the reason I have sent for you is that I have heard you are a valiant knight, and that there is nobody like you in the world. Indeed, it is said that you could tame the horse that has destroyed and wasted my kingdom without harming yourself or others. If you can summon enough courage to undertake this glorious task and conquer the horse, I promise you on my honor to give you a gift which will make you content for the rest of your life."

When Guerrino heard the king's proposal, he was extremely amazed and denied right away that he had ever said such words. The king was greatly disturbed by Guerrino's answer and declared, "Guerrino, I want you to undertake this task no matter what. If you refuse to comply with my wishes, I shall take away your life."

Guerrino returned to his inn and was very perturbed, but he did not disclose his feelings to anyone. However, the unknown youth noticed that Guerrino was not his customary self and had become melancholy. So he asked him gently why he was so sad and tormented. Then Guerrino, because of the brotherly love he felt for his friend, was unable to refuse this honest and just request, and he told him clearly what had happened to him. As soon as the unknown young man heard this, he said, "Keep your spirits up, and trust me. I'll show you a way to do everything so that you won't perish. Instead, you'll be victorious, and the king's wish will be fulfilled. Therefore, return to the king and ask him to give you the help of a skilled blacksmith. Then order this blacksmith to make four horseshoes for you that must be thicker and broader than the width of two fingers and larger than ordinary horseshoes. Each one is to be fitted behind with two spikes of a finger's length and sharpened to a point. After these shoes are made, you are to have them placed on my steed, which is enchanted. Then you no longer have to worry about anything."

After he listened to these words, Guerrino returned to the king and told him everything that the young man had instructed him to say. The king then summoned a superb blacksmith who was ordered to carry out whatever work Guerrino needed. When they went to the smith's forge, Guerrino ordered him to make the four horseshoes. But when the blacksmith heard Guerrino's instructions, he mocked him and treated him like a madman, for this way of making shoes was quite strange and unknown to him. When Guerrino saw that the blacksmith was inclined to ridicule him and unwilling to obey his instructions, he went to the king and complained that the smith would not carry out his orders. Therefore, the king summoned the blacksmith again and told him that he would be disgraced if he did not carry out Guerrino's orders, and if he did not do this, he would have to carry out the task of killing the horses that had been assigned to Guerrino. Under such pressure by the king, the blacksmith made the horseshoes as instructed by Guerrino.

When the horse was shod and equipped with everything necessary for the mission, the young stranger said to Guerrino, "Now mount my steed, and go in peace. As soon as you hear the neighing of the wild horse, dismount at once, take off the saddle and bridle, and let the horse range at will. You are to climb a high tree and to stay there until the end of the battle."

After receiving these instructions from his dear companion, Guerrino took his leave and departed in good spirits.

Already the glorious news had been spread throughout the city of Ireland that a charming and handsome young knight had set out to capture the wild horse and to present it to the king. All the men and women of the city ran to their windows to watch him ride by. When they saw how handsome, young, and grand he was, their hearts were moved to pity, and they said, "Ah the poor youth! He is riding of his own free will to his death. Certainly it's a terrible sin that he will have to die such a wretched death." And they could not keep back their tears because of the compassion they felt for him.

But the intrepid and manly Guerrino continued cheerfully on his way and arrived at the spot that was inhabited by the wild horse. When he heard its neighing, he got down from his own horse, took off the saddle and bridle, and let it go free while he himself climbed up a great oak tree, where he awaited the outcome of the brutal and bloody contest.

No sooner did Guerrino climb the tree than the wild horse appeared and attacked the enchanted steed. Then the two horses engaged in the fiercest struggle that the world had ever seen. They rushed at one another as if they had been two unchained lions, and they foamed at the mouth as if they had been bristly wild boars pursued by raging hounds. Then, after they had fought valiantly for some time, the enchanted steed gave the wild horse two kicks right on its jaw that was knocked out of its joint so that it could no longer fight or defend itself. When Guerrino saw this, he was extremely pleased and descended the oak. Then he took a halter which he had brought with him, tied the wild horse with it, and led it with its dislocated jaw back to the city, where he was welcomed by all the people with great rejoicing. Just as he had promised, he presented the horse to the king, who, together with all the inhabitants of the city, held a grand victory celebration.

But Guerrino's servants were very upset because their evil plan had miscarried. Therefore, inflamed by rage and hatred, they spread the news once more to King Zifroi that Guerrino had boasted that he could also kill the wild mare with ease. When the king heard this, he assigned the same task to Guerrino as he had done with the wild horse. When the youth, however, refused to undertake the task, which appeared extremely difficult, the king threatened to have him hung by one foot as a rebel against the crown. After Guerrino returned to his inn, he told everything to his companion, who said with a smile, "My good brother, don't worry. Just go and find the blacksmith. Command him to make four more horseshoes, as big as the last, and see that they are duly equipped with good sharp spikes. Then you must do exactly as you did before with the hose, and you will return here with just as great honor as before."

So Guerrino ordered the sharply spiked horseshoes to be made and had them put on the enchanted steed, and then he set forth on his noble mission. As soon as Guerrino arrived at the spot inhabited by the mare and heard her neighing, he did everything exactly as he had done before. When he set the enchanted horse free, the mare charged toward it and attacked it with such fury that it had difficulty defending itself. But it endured the assault and succeeded in giving a sharp kick to the mare that caused her right leg to go lame. So Guerrino descended the high tree into which he had climbed, took the mare and tied her tightly with a halter. Then he mounted his own horse and rode back to the palace, where he presented the wild mare to the king amid the rejoicing and praise of all the people. Everyone was so astonished and attracted by the mare that they ran to see it, but she soon died from the grave injuries that she had suffered in the battle. And this was how the country was freed from the nuisance that had plagued it so long.

Now, when Guerrino had returned to the inn, he was so tired that he lay down to rest, but he could not fall asleep because of some unusual noise that he heard. Therefore, he got up from his couch and noticed that there was something strange beating about inside a jar of honey and not able to get out. So, Guerrino opened the jar and saw a hornet which was beating its wings and unable to free itself from the honey around it. Moved by pity, he picked up the insect and let it go free.

Now King Zifroi had not yet rewarded Guerrino for his two triumphs, but it was apparent to him that it would be disgraceful if he did not reward him. So he summoned Guerrino to appear before him and said, "Guerrino, thanks to you, my kingdom has now been liberated. Therefore, I intend to reward you for the great deed that you have performed for us. But since I cannot conceive of another gift that would be worthy and suitable for your heroic act, I have decided to give you one of my daughters as your wife. I want you to know that I have two, and one is called Potentiana, and she has hair braided in such a beautiful way that it glistens like gold. The other is called Eleuteria, and her long hair glitters like the finest silver. Now, if you can guess which one of my daughters has golden hair after they are veiled, then I shall give her to you as your wife with a great dowry of money. But if you fail, I shall have your head cut off your shoulders."

When Guerrino heard Zifroi's challenging proposal, he was most astonished, and turning to him, he said, "Oh sacred king, is this what you call a prize for all my exhausting work? Is this the reward that you are going to give me after I have liberated your country that had been ravaged and devastated? Alas! I have not deserved such treatment, and it is certainly not worthy of a king such as yourself. But since this is your pleasure and I am in your hands, you can do with me as you wish."

"Go now," said Zifroi. "You're not to bide your time here. You have until tomorrow to make a decision."

Guerrino left the king and became terribly sad. He went to his dear companion and repeated to him everything that the king had said. But his friend did not take all this very seriously and said, "Guerrino, keep up your spirits and trust me because I'll save you from all this. Remember how you saved the hornet a few days ago when it was caught in the honey. Now this same hornet will save you. Tomorrow, after the dinner at the palace, it will fly around the daughter's head with the golden hair three times, and it will buzz. She will drive it away with her white hand. And when you see her do this three times, you will know for sure that this is the one who will be your wife."

"Ah me!" cried Guerrino. "When will the time come when I shall be able to repay you for all the favors you have done me? Certainly, if I were to live a thousand years, I still would only be able to reward you for a very small portion of your favors. But he who is the rewarder of all will compensate for what is lacking in me."

Then his companion answered, "Guerrino, my brother, there is no need for you to repay me for my services. But now is the right time for me to reveal to you who I am. Since you saved me from death, I have felt obliged and have wanted to give you the rewards that you deserve. I want you to know that I am the wild man whom you released from your father's prison out of the kindness of your heart. I am called Rubinetto." And then he went on to tell Guerrino how the fairy had changed him back into a handsome and charming young man.

When Guerrino heard all this, he was astonished. Then, with tears in his eyes, he embraced Rubinetto with tenderness, kissed him, and treated him as if he were his own brother.

Since the time had now come for Guerrino to complete the task set for him by King Zifroi, the two went to the palace. Thereupon, the king gave orders that his two daughters, Potentiana and Eleuteria, were to be brought before Guerrino and were to be covered from head to foot with white veils, and this was done right away. When the two daughters arrived, they looked so much alike that it was impossible to tell them apart. Then the king said, "Now which of these two, Guerrino, do you want me to give you for your wife?"

But Guerrino stood still and wavered. He did not respond to the king. But the king, who was eager to conclude everything, pressured him to speak. He cried out that time was flying and he had to make a decision.

"Most sacred king," said Guerrino, "time may be flying, but you have given me the entire day to make my decision, and the day is not yet done."

And all those present confirmed that Guerrino was only claiming his right. While the king and Guerrino and all the rest stood a long time in anticipation, a hornet suddenly appeared and began to fly and buzz around the heard of Potentiana, who had the golden hair. She appeared to be afraid and raised her hand to drive the hornet away, and when she did this three times, the hornet flew away. But Guerrino remained uncertain a short time, although he had complete trust in his beloved companion Rubinetto's words. Then the king said, "What are you doing, Guerrino? It's now time for you to make up your mind."

Then Guerrino looked carefully first at one maiden and then at the other until he put his hand on the head of Potentiana, who had been pointed out by the hornet.

"Sacred king," said Guerrino, "this one is your daughter with the golden hair."

And when the maiden raised her veil, everyone could clearly see that she was indeed the one, and all who were present and all the people of the city were greatly satisfied. Therefore, King Zifroi gave her to Guerrino as his wife, and they did not depart until Rubinetto was given the other sister. After this Guerrino revealed that he was the son of Filippo Maria, king of Sicily. When Zifroi heard this, he was extremely happy and had the marriages celebrated with great pomp and splendor.

When the news of the marriages reached the father and mother of Guerrino, they were very glad and content because they had believed their son had been lost forever. After Guerrino returned to Sicily with his dear wife and his beloved brother-in-law and sister-in-law, they all received a gracious and affectionate welcome from his father and mother, and they lived a long time in peace and happiness. Eventually Guerrino left behind him beautiful children as the heirs to his kingdom.

JEAN DE MAILLY

Prince Guerini†

The kingdom of Lombardy was once governed by King Philip, and since he was not ambitious and did not keep a gallant court, he spent his life just like one of his most simple subjects and enjoyed the tranquillity that he found with his wife and children. He was mainly concerned about the merits of the queen and the upbringing of his only son, whose name was Guerini, a prince with great promise. If he had some other avocation, then it was hunting, and he often took pleasure in it, even though it was always without passion.

One day when he went hunting with some of his barons, he saw a wild man come out of the forest, and this creature was frightening to behold. The king ordered the savage to be seized, but since it was necessary to fight him in order to overcome the man, the king cried out that they should surround him and try to avoid killing him, for he had already drawn blood from those who had been bold enough to approach him. However, when the wild man saw that he had been surrounded, he surrendered and let himself be put in chains. Then he was taken to a cramped prison which the king had guarded. Since the king was curious to learn about the customs and opinions of savages, he went to visit the man every day with his court. He only wanted to keep him in irons until he saw some signs that the wild man had been tamed and showed that he was disposed to submit to the laws and customs of civilized men. But since the king had not seen any traces yet, and since he was afraid that the wild man would escape if he let people freely enter the prison, he kept the keys with him. Whenever he had to go into the city, he placed his wife in charge of them and emphasized strongly that she was not to give the keys to anyone.

One day when the king went hunting, Guerini, his young son, became curious and went to hold a conversation with the wild man. As he approached the prison window where there was an iron bar, he was holding a very precious arrow in his hand, and the wild man, who wanted to take

---

† Jean de Mailly, "Prince Guerini"—"Le prince Guerini" (1698), in *Les illustres fées, contes galans* (Paris: M-M. Brunet, 1698).

it from him, caressed him and drew him near him so that he could grab the arrow, which he did. The young prince was grief-stricken at having lost his arrow and begged the wild man to return it to him that very instant. The savage responded frankly that, instead of giving it to him, he would break it into pieces if the boy did not open the prison door and find some way to undo his chains.

The young prince, who cherished the arrow above anything else, because his most favorite recreation was to shoot the bow and arrow, wanted to retrieve the arrow no matter what the price was. Moreover, since he was very humane, as one is at that age, he thought it would be a good deed to set a prisoner free, especially this wild man, who had not committed a single crime. But he found it very difficult to obtain the keys to the prison since he knew that his mother, the queen, was taking care of them. However, he thought that if she went to sleep after her dinner, which happened sometimes, he would find it easy to take the keys since he had complete freedom to enter her room at any time. And this is what happened. Then he ran straight to the prison carrying a bunch of keys among which was one also for the chains that the wild man was forced to wear. He did all this without thinking that he would be making his father, the king, angry. So he liberated the savage, who, in turn, placed the arrow in his hands and quickly fled into the forest.

When the queen woke up, she did not find the keys and was greatly upset. She immediately sent an attendant to see if the prison had been opened, and he sent word that it was and that the wild man had disappeared. Now the queen was in great anguish, fearing the rage of her husband, who could be quite violent. She wept. She screamed, and she threatened. She absolutely wanted to know who had been bold enough to enter her room while she was sleeping. Her ladies-in-waiting told her that nobody had entered the room except the prince, her son. They did not dare to mention one of her stewards whom they had also seen enter and who entered very familiarly during the absence of the king. Since this was to be kept a secret, they did not dare to mention his name.

Informed that her son had entered her room, the queen sent someone to look for him. Guerini arrived at once and revealed everything that had happened. The poor tormented queen, fearing that the anger of her husband would be taken out more on her son than on her, decided that he should not be exposed to the rash acts of his father. She called two of the prince's servants whom she believed were very trustworthy, and she told them that Guerini had made a mistake that the king would hardly forgive, and thus she wanted the prince to take a trip to give the king some time to vent his anger and calm down. Since she knew that they were good men, she believed she could place the most precious thing she had in the world in their hands. Then she gave a huge quantity of gold and precious jewels to her son so that he could appear in a good state wherever he went. Finally, she quickly gave him leave to depart, fearing that the king would arrive very soon.

Thus Prince Guerini departed, and when the king arrived soon after and saw that the prison door had been opened, he ran to the queen's apartment full of rage. She went toward him and disarmed his anger by her submission and sweetness. She told him that she alone had been guilty because she had not guarded carefully enough the keys that he had left in her care, that she let them be taken by their son, who could not be blamed, because he was seduced by the urgent pleas of the prisoner, whom he set free. She had judged it better to send their son away for some time because the father would be so irritated that his son had made such a big mistake. So he was now learning about the world to become more wise.

Since the king found that this punishment was too great, he immediately sent his servants all over with orders to assure his son that he gladly pardoned the mistake that he had made in opening the door of the wild man's prison, and that he was very upset by the bad opinion that his son had of him by thinking that he would not show him paternal kindness. Therefore, he implored his son to return home immediately and that his father would certainly die of sorrow if he stayed away for a long time. However, all the care that the king took was in vain because all the men that he sent out into the country returned without being able to learn which route the prince had taken.

In the meantime, Prince Guerini continued traveling with the two servants without knowing really where he was going. He could not have been placed in worse hands than those of these two scoundrels who had decided to kill him and divide his riches. But they had deferred carrying out their detestable plot until they had reached the first forest, where they would have no witnesses to fear. Fortunately, the prince encountered someone who protected him from this great danger. It was a young knight more handsome and stronger than any he had ever seen at his father's court, and who was mounted on such a fine and richly equipped horse that it was clear that this was a man who came from nobility. Thus the prince was inclined to receive this man in a very civil way and accepted his offer to travel together. They entered into a conversation about general things, and since the prince did not know with whom he was speaking, he did not open up to him at first and did not tell him where he was coming from and where he was going.

It was not necessary for Prince Guerini to declare this because the young knight already knew perfectly well what had happened to him and was there to express his gratitude toward him; he was the wild man, whom the prince had set free, and who had experienced a very fortunate adventure in the meantime. He had encountered a fairy, one of those who seek to do good, and perhaps also to show their power. This good fairy had found him asleep deep in a forest and had touched him with a wand that she was carrying in her hand. Then he felt himself pleasantly wakened and one could even say reborn, for he found himself with sentiments that were completely different from the ones he had up till then. Instead of thirsting for blood and carnage, he only thought of leading a gentle life and was ashamed of his natural ferocity. He also noticed that he had a more pleasing figure, and in spite of the proper love that makes us always content with out first condition, he sensed an indescribable joy in the considerable change that he had undergone.

Indeed, the fairy had transformed him and had led him to her palace where she kept him for some days. But since this was a fairy who was concerned about her reputation, she had discharged him for some time and had given him the means to have all that he needed to live well and some secrets of her art. He was given permission to make use of these secrets to acquire the amenities and pleasures of life that he desired. She was very generous and recommended to him that he go and search for Prince Guerini to express his gratitude for having set him free and that it would give her great pleasure if he would do this after she had given him such gifts. Thus it was the fairy who had sent him to encounter his liberator after telling him how to find Prince Guerini.

This is how Prince Guerini began to receive the reward for the good act that he had done out of compassion for those less fortunate than he. The knight, whom he had encountered and whom the fairy had given the name Alcée, told him that he was charmed by his mind and manners. Therefore he was resolved not to leave him and to lead him to a place where he might hope to have some pleasant adventures. Indeed, he took the liberty of saying to him that, from all the qualities he had observed in Guerini, he could not help but be admired wherever he went, and for this reason he advised him to choose the court of a great king, where he could experience adventures worthy of him.

Since the prince did not have any other prospects in view, and since he believed that Alcée was sincere, he asked him to tell him which court he should choose. After some discussion and reflection about the state of affairs of all the neighboring princes, they decided to cross the Alps to go to the court of the king of Arles, whose name was Godefroi, and who had achieved a large reputation in the world because of his knowledge and wisdom. It was also said that he received strangers at his court in a very honorable way. Moreover, it was known that he had two beautiful daughters, and Alcée told Prince Guerini that, since he was so handsome, there was not a lady who could resist him.

The prince, who was young and who was born of nobility, imagined easily that there was hope for him. Therefore, he set in his mind at that very moment that he would please one of the princesses of Arles, and with his heart filled with such a project, they traveled onward and finally arrived at the court of Arles. Some time after their arrival, Prince Guerini presented himself before King Godefroi as a knight who was traveling about the world and was curious to learn what was happening at the king's court. The king wanted to know who he was, and the prince told him that he had reasons for concealing his native country. Thus he only revealed that his name was Guerini and that the knight who was accompanying him was called Alcée, and they were two knights who had taken a vow to search for chivalric adventures and to learn what was important in the world. Since the king saw that they had a good appearance and since they spoke to him with such great assurance about those people reared among princes, he understood that their secret was very advantageous for them and thought that they were of the nobility. Therefore, he bestowed great honors on them and urged his courtiers to treat them in the same way.

The two knights lived peacefully at the court of Arles for some months. Prince Guerini, who had formed his plan, thought about pleasing the older of the two sisters, however, without declaring his intention. For Alcée, though he was not a prince, he had such knowledge of science that the fairy had given him that he did not despair of pleasing the younger sister. But the fairy, who was jealous, did not give up such an amiable knight so easily, one whom she took back with him from time to time to enjoy the delights of her palace.

In the meantime, the courtiers, who had become somewhat disturbed by the qualities of the two strangers, had learned that they prided themselves on being very valorous and that they were looking for an occasion to demonstrate this. So, they proposed to the king that he send them to do battle with the giants who were making his subjects tremble and had ravaged the fields of his domain from time to time. After the giants caused their damage, they would retreat into the mountains where nobody dared to search for them. The king responded to his courtiers that he could not expose the two young men to such great danger unless they desired the glory that they allegedly sought with passion. Nor did he want to order them to undertake such a great expedition unless they were helped by some of his subjects who would volunteer to render their services. At the same time he added that there was nothing he would not give to show his appreciation if they could save his realm from such cruel enemies. He confessed that they were his only hope since his subjects, who had never seen war, were not fit for such daring enterprises.

News was spread throughout the court that the two unknown knights wanted to try to get rid of the giants. Soon this news reached them, and they had not even thought about it. At the same time, the king had declared that he would be eternally grateful to them if they could render him a service so important.

Alcée trusted in the protection of the fairy, who had already done him many favors, and thus he encouraged Guerini to undertake this task. Seeing that Guerini had a great deal of difficulty deciding to run the risk of such a clear danger, Alcée confided in him and told him his secret. After he had told him that he was the wild man who owed him such a great debt and also revealed to him the great debt that the two of them owed to a powerful fairy, who had taken them under her protection, he told him that he had been informed about the plot of his servants, from whom she wanted to protect Prince Guerini by sending Alcée to keep him company. That was why he kept observing the two servants, and since their will may have changed, he did not bother to tell Guerini about this. He added that he was still suspicious of them, and it was necessary to keep them with them and expose them to the fury of the giants when they attacked. That would be a way to punish them for their wicked plot and to make good use of them. The prince was charmed by Alcée's reasoning, which he found very prudent, and, encouraged by the hope of a fairy's protection, he no longer hesitated. So the two of them went to offer their services to the king without losing any time.

Guerini was primarily moved by the passion that he felt for Princess Pintiane and the kindness that she had recently expressed by allowing him to see a little tenderness in her eyes. For his part, Alcée, who found Princess Eleuthrie charming, would have exposed his life to danger a thousand times to win her favor. But he feared that he would be crossed by the fairy, whom he knew was very jealous about this. Yet this did not prevent him from participating voluntarily in this undertaking. He knew that at least the glory would be with him eternally and that he would contribute to the happiness of Prince Guerini, whom he truly loved.

So they went to offer their very humble services to the king, to whom they promised to destroy the race of giants that were devastating his realm, or at the very least to chase them far away. If the king were agreeable, they asked him to give them guides to conduct them and inform them about the mountain retreats of the enemies they were about to combat. They also asked him for the liberty to choose fifteen or twenty men from his guards to serve them for certain occasions during this expedition. There were very few men for such a great undertaking, but the prince, who was leading the excursion, was highly esteemed. Moreover, Alcée had assured him that the fairy, who regarded him as her favorite, would not abandon them on such an important quest.

Thus the two of them confidently set out with a small troop on an expedition that no one would have undertaken without having ten thousand well-armed men. The giants were numerous, and one single one was capable of putting a troop like theirs to flight. They were men of enormous size and miraculous force. Their appearances were so revolting that it was almost impossible to bear their sight. Each one was armed with a club made from a large branch of a tree. Neither animals nor men had ever been able to defeat them. They spent their nights in caves which were closed by great rocks that they maneuvered as they wished. They relished drawing blood, and their clothes were made out of the skins of lions and bears whom they had killed.

These were the enemies that Guerini and Alcée, followed by a small poorly armed troop, were seeking to destroy, and whom they would never have conquered without that helpful fairy who had taken them under her protection. She appeared to them on the first day of their march, and she made herself visible only to Guerini and Alcée, to whom she gave magic lances and helmets to defend themselves and to use when they attacked. On each one of the helmets there was a carbuncle, and she revealed to them how to use the carbuncles to throw forth explosive flames that would bewilder their enemies so that they would not know what was happening, and this would be the downfall of the giants.

The two knights arrived in the mountains with their small army furnished with food for several days. They noticed a cave closed by large rocks and approached the cave with a lot of noise. The giants became curious to see what was happening, and they immediately came out of the cave and vented their first fury on the two servants of Guerini, who had wickedly planned to put an end to their master. What happened was what Guerini and Alcée had hoped would happen: the giants pushed the rocks before them as they exited the cave, and the rocks crushed the two evil servants. But no sooner did the giants advance than the two knights attacked without being seen because of the flashing light produced by the carbuncles. The giants were pierced many times by lances, and they retreated into their caves with dreadful cries. The same thing happened to many other giants the first day of the battle, and those who avoided death gathered that night to take counsel, and the next day they made a signal with a white flag to ask for peace. The knights had two of their men advance to meet two of the giants, who offered to retreat deep into the mountains and to give guarantees never to return to this realm as long as the king let them be masters of the region of the mountain to which they would retire.

Since the king had given Guerini power to speak for him, they reached an agreement provided that the two chief giants let themselves be conducted in chains to the court, where they would remain hostages for some years. Guerini also wanted to take the heads of the dead giants to the court to make their victory known, and the giants agreed. After the prince signed the peace treaty, the giants retreated to the territory that was prescribed, and Guerini and his followers buried the bodies of their own. Then they left the mountains with the hostages and the heads of the giants, which amounted to ten.

The generous fairy, who had contributed so much to the happy success of this expedition, had not demanded any gratitude from Alcée except that he was to go to her palace and spend several days with her after everything had been accomplished. And Alcée kept his promise, not wishing to be ungrateful, which would have been an enormous vice. Indeed, he did this despite the fact that he had a great desire to see the charming princess whom he had wanted to please. He also regretted leaving his dear Guerini, who asked him to take part in the victory celebrations since he had played such a great role in their success. But Alcée, who left him with great sorrow, as one can imagine, assured him that he would soon be seeing him. They separated after embracing each other with great tenderness, and while Alcée went to revisit the generous fairy, Guerini arrived at the court, where he was received with inexpressible rejoicing on the part of the people.

The king and the queen were so grateful for what Guerini had done that they assured him that there was no possible way they could reward him for such a great deed. Princess Pintiane gave him such a favorable welcome that he was charmed. She had been greatly disposed toward him before his departure, and now his glorious return determined everything, and her heart was open to him. Ladies believe that they are obligated to reward glorious acts, and one witnesses many women every day who love very ugly and crude men only because they have acquired a reputation through their arms.

The king, who had developed a high regard for Alcée, asked with some urgency what had become of him. Guerini responded that he would soon be at the court and that some pressing duties had obligated him to take a journey which would take but a few days. In the meantime, he gave an exact account to the king about how brave Alcée was and how much he had contributed to the victory. The king was very relieved to learn that Alcée would return to receive some token of his gratitude. In the meantime he did not forget to hug Guerini or to treat him as best he could. He also gave marvelous presents to all those of his men who had distinguished themselves in the combat according to Guerini's report.

There were many days of feasts and celebrations, and Guerini was pressed by the king to declare what reward he wanted to have, but the prince asked for two days to reflect about it. This was because he wanted to search for an occasion to speak with the princess. He found her, and after telling her about his high birth, he revealed his great love for her and informed her that he had only undertaken the great expedition to show that he deserved her. Now he had success and had satisfied the king, but for him, it was not even enough to be worthy of her. Indeed, the only reward that he desired from the king was the permission to serve her until she felt ready to grant him the one thing that he desired in life, and that depended entirely on her. The princess responded that if it depended on her, the king could give him the reward that he desired whenever he pleased because her father was the master of her will and she would obey him on this occasion without repugnance.

The prince was charmed to hear her speak so favorably about him, and he threw himself at her feet. He swore that he would do the most extraordinary things in order to make himself worthy of the happiness that she was granting him. Since she approved of everything, he would go and tell the king about his birth. Moreover, he intended to be bold enough to ask her hand in marriage as reward even though he had done little to win it. When the king learned that Guerini was the son of a king, he was very satisfied to give his daughter to him, especially since he had become so illustrious after his victory. In fact, he would have given her to him even if he had been a simple knight. The marriage was celebrated a few days later and was followed by great happiness for many years thereafter. The credit of Prince Guerini was so great at this court that, a little time after his marriage, he was able to arrange the union between Princess Eleuteria and Alcée. Finally, to make his happiness perfect, he wanted to acquaint the king and queen with his parents, to whom he owed his life. Therefore, he divided the rest of his life between two courts, and Guerini and the princess took delight in this life. For many centuries thereafter, the glory of their reign was passed on for posterity.

JACOB AND WILHELM GRIMM

The Wild Man†

Once upon a time there was a wild man who was under a spell, and he went into the gardens and wheatfields of the peasants and destroyed everything. The peasants complained to their lord and told him that they could no longer pay their rent. So the lord summoned all the huntsmen and announced that whoever caught the wild beast would receive a great reward. Then an old huntsman arrived and said he would catch the beast. He took a bottle of brandy, a bottle of wine, and a bottle of beer and set the bottles at the river, where the beast went every day. After doing that

† Jacob and Wilhelm Grimm, "The Wild Man"—"De wilde Man" (1815), was first published as No. 50 in *Kinder- und Hausmärchen. Gesammelt durch die Brüder Grimm* (Berlin: Realschulbuchhandlung, 1812). It was omitted in 1843 because of its resemblance to "Iron Hans."

the huntsman hid behind a tree. Soon the beast came and drank up all the bottles. He licked his mouth and looked around to make sure everything was all right. Since he was drunk, he lay down and fell asleep. The huntsman went over to him and tied his hands and feet. Then he woke up the wild man and said, "You, wild man, come with me, and you'll get such things to drink every day."

The huntsman took the wild man to the royal castle, and they put him into a cage. The lord then visited the other noblemen and invited them to see what kind of beast he had caught. Meanwhile, one of his sons was playing with a ball, and he let it fall into the cage.

"Wild man," said the child, "throw the ball back out to me."

"You've got to fetch the ball yourself," said the wild man.

"All right," said the child. "But I don't have the key."

"Then see to it that you fetch it from your mother's pocket."

The boy stole the key, opened the cage, and the wild man ran out.

"Oh, wild man!" the boy began to scream. "You've got to stay here, or else I'll get a beating!"

The wild man picked up the boy and carried him on his back into the wilderness. So the wild man disappeared, and the child was lost.

The wild man dressed the boy in a coarse jacket and sent him to the gardener at the emperor's court, where he was to ask whether they could use a gardener's helper. The gardener said yes, but the boy was so grimy and crusty that the others would not sleep near him. The boy replied that he would sleep in the straw. Then early each morning he went into the garden, and the wild man came to him and said, "Now wash yourself, now comb yourself."

And the wild man made the garden so beautiful that even the gardener himself could not do any better. The princess saw the handsome boy every morning, and she told the gardener to have his little assistant bring her a bunch of flowers. When the boy came, she asked him about his origins, and he replied that he did not know them. Then she gave him a roast chicken full of ducats. When he got back to the gardener, he gave him the money and said, "What should I do with it? You can use it."

Later he was ordered to bring the princess another bunch of flowers, and she gave him a duck full of ducats, which he also gave to the gardener. On a third occasion she gave him a goose full of ducats, which the young man again passed on to the gardener. The princess thought that he had money, and yet he had nothing. They got married in secret, and her parents became angry and made her work in the brewery, and she also had to support herself by spinning. The young man would go into the kitchen and help the cook prepare the roast, and sometimes he stole a piece of meat and brought it to his wife.

Soon there was a mighty war in England, and the emperor and all the great armies had to travel there. The young man said he wanted to go there too and asked whether they had a horse in the stables for him. They told him that they had one that ran on three legs that would be good enough for him. So he mounted the horse, and the horse went off, *clippety-clop*. Then the wild man approached him, and he opened a large mountain in which there was a regiment of a thousand soldiers and officers.

The young man put on some fine clothes and was given a magnificent horse. Then he set out for the war in England with all his men. The emperor welcomed him in a friendly way and asked him to lend his support. The young man defeated everyone and won the battle, whereupon the emperor extended his thanks to him and asked him where his army came from.

"Don't ask me that," he replied. "I can't tell you."

Then he rode off with his army and left England. The wild man approached him again and took all the men back into the mountain. The young man mounted his three-legged horse and went back home.

"Here comes our hobbley-hop again with his three-legged horse!" the people cried out, and they asked, "Were you lying behind the hedge and sleeping?"

"Well," he said, "if I hadn't been in England, things would not have gone well for the emperor!"

"Boy," they said, "be quiet, or else the gardener will really let you have it!"

The second time, everything happened as it had before, and the third time, the young man won the whole battle, but he was wounded in the arm. The emperor took his kerchief, wrapped the wound, and tried to make the boy stay with him.

"No, I'm not going to stay with you. It's of no concern to you who I am."

Once again the wild man approached the young man and took all his men back into the mountain. The young man mounted his three-legged horse once more and went back home. The people began laughing and said, "Here comes our hobbley-hop again. Where were you lying asleep this time?"

"Truthfully, I wasn't sleeping," he said. "England is totally defeated, and there's finally peace."

Now, the emperor talked about the handsome knight who provided support, and the young man said to the emperor, "If I hadn't been with you, it wouldn't have turned out so well."

The emperor wanted to give him a beating, but the young man said, "Stop! If you don't believe me, let me show you my arm."

When he revealed his arm and the emperor saw the wound, he was amazed and said, "Perhaps you are the Lord Himself or an angel whom God has sent to me," and he asked his pardon for treating him so cruelly and gave him a whole kingdom.

Now the wild man was released from the magic spell and stood there as a great king and told his entire story. The mountain turned into a royal castle, and the young man went there with his wife, and they lived in the castle happily until the end of their days.

FRIEDMUND VON ARNIM

Iron Hans†

There was once a king who had a great forest that would not put up with any hunters entering it. Whoever went into it would disappear along with the hounds. Therefore, the king decided not to send any more hunters into the forest and to let the forest alone. But one day a man showed up who wanted to serve the king as hunter.

"It will cost your life," said the king. "I can't really take you in."

"Now, that's my worry," replied the hunter.

So he went hunting with his hound, and when the hound came upon a scent, he sprang over a pool, but a bare arm stretched itself out and dragged the hound down into it. Immediately thereafter some men were sent for from the city, and they had to drain the pool and they found a wild man. Then they brought him into the city to the king, who had a big cage built and locked the wild man inside.

Then he commanded that the wild man was not to be let out of the cage, or if anyone did this, it would cost him his life. Now the king had a prince, who was six years old, and when the prince came to the cage one time, the wild man was playing with a golden ball. Then the prince said, "Give me the ball."

"If you let me out," the wild man said.

"I can't do that. If I do, it will cost me my life."

Meanwhile the king returned from a hunt, and nothing had happened in the forest. The next day they went hunting again, and they found plenty of game. Now the prince went to the cage once more.

"Give me the ball."

"Only when you let me out."

"I'm not allowed to do it," the prince said again, and soon he was irritated that he did not get the golden ball.

On the third day the king and his company went hunting again, and as soon as they were gone, the prince went to the cage once more.

"I really want the ball!" the prince declared.

This time the wild man gave him the ball, and the prince let him out. Then the wild man said, "If you are ever in great trouble, you're to go to the edge of the forest and cry out 'Iron Hans,' and then I'll help you."

When the king returned, he headed straight to the cage, but the wild man was gone. So he went to the queen and immediately asked whether she knew what had happened to the wild man. She was very terrified and stood there petrified because this could cost her her life since the wild man had escaped. Nobody else had been there except the prince, and he must have let him out. Indeed, the golden ball revealed that he had done it.

So the king sent the hunter into the forest with the prince and ordered

† Friedmund von Arnim, "Iron Hans"—"Der eiserne Hans" (1844), in *Hundert neue Mährchen im Gebirge gesammelt* (Charlottenburg: E. Bauer, 1844).

him to kill his son. The hunter went into the woods with him, but he only cut off a finger, shot a young hog, and took out its tongue and heart, which he brought and showed to the king along with the finger. Meanwhile the boy went deeper into the forest and kept crying out, "Iron Hans, do you hear me?"

Finally, Iron Hans came and said,"Come, I'll give you some work to do."

Now he led him to a small spring and said, "You're not to let anything fall into the water. If you do and I come again, you'll regret it."

But his finger hurt him so much that he put it into the water. Immediately it turned to gold. Then Iron Hans returned.

"What have you done to the spring?" asked Iron Hans.

"Nothing, nothing," said the prince.

"You dipped your finger into it," Iron Hans replied. "I'm going away again. If you let anything fall into the water again, it will be too bad for you."

Then the boy took a little piece of hair and dipped it into the water, and it turned gold right away.

"You've dipped some hair into the spring," said Iron Hans when he returned. "Now you'd better believe me. This is the last time that I'm going away. Don't dishonor the spring."

As soon as Iron Hans was gone, the boy dipped his entire head of hair into the spring and now had a splendid golden head as if the sun were really shining upon it. He did not know, however, how he should hide it so that Iron Hans would not see it right away.

"What have you done to the spring?" Iron Hans asked when he came back. "Take off the kerchief!" The boy had put a kerchief on his head. "Go away. You're a disobedient son. But if things go bad for you, you may go to the edge of the forest again and call for me."

Now the boy went away through the forest through thick and thin until he came to the country and finally reached a royal city again. Then he asked where he could find some work, and he found a job in the royal kitchen and became a kitchen helper. But he was supposed to carry the food to the table many times and he always kept a cap on his head.

"When you come to the table," said the king, "you must take off the cap."

"Yes, I know," said the boy, "but I have a horrible-looking head. I have the scabs and can't take off my cap."

This was quite bad for the cook who had hired a helper like this who could not serve at the table. Therefore, he sent the boy to the garden in exchange for the garden helper. There the boy had to dig and work hard. One time the sun shone so strongly that he became hot. So he took off his cap, and when the sun shone upon his head, it glistened so much that it cast a great reflection on the windows. When the princess saw this, she rushed outside to see what was glistening and radiating. It was the gardener's helper with his golden hair.

"My son," she cried, "bring a bouquet of flowers up to my room."

So he made a bundle out of the most ordinary flowers. When the gardener came, he showed them to him and told him that he was supposed to bring the princess a bouquet. The gardener said, "But those are just plain wildflowers."

"Well," responded the boy, "they have a strong scent."

Then he went to the princess, and when he entered her room, she said, "My son, take off your cap."

He did not take it off and said that he had something wrong with his head. But she had seen his head and knew that this was not true. So she tried to tear it off his head. He jumped away from her. She called him back and gave him a handful of ducats as a tip for bringing the flowers. When he returned to the gardener, he said, "I was given some money as a tip, and I'd like to give them to your children so that they can play with them."

The gardener said that was fine with him, for he thought, "Let him first give them to my children!" Then he took the money away from them.

The next day the princess called the gardener's helper again, and he had to make another bouquet. As soon as he entered, she wanted to snatch him and pluck off the cap. However, she didn't get it and gave him another handful of ducats. Then he went away and gave the money to the children once more. On the third day he had to bring her a bouquet again, and again she wanted to take the cap. But he held on to it tightly.

So now the princess decided to have a ball game and invited many people. All sorts of noble and royal people appeared. Meanwhile, the gardener's helper asked the gardener to let him go along. When he was told he could, he went to the forest, called Iron Hans, and asked him to help him get the balls from the princess.

"They're yours already," said Iron Hans as soon as he appeared. Then he gave the gardener's helper a brown horse, a brown coat, and changed him into a knight. Later, when the princess threw out the ball, our dear prince got it. None of the other knights got a ball, for the prince rode back to Iron Hans on his brown steed. On the next day there was another game. So the boy went to the edge of the forest and called Iron Hans. Then he received a white horse and a pure white coat. And again he got the ball, and nobody got one. The king did not know what was happening; nor did the princess. So the third day came, and the king issued an order: if the knight rode off and did not stop, his men were to chop him down, shoot him, or stab him. Meanwhile, the boy went to the edge of the forest again and called out. This time he received a black stallion and a pitch-black coat and had to ride bare-headed. He looked quite charming. Then our dear princess threw the ball again. Fortunately, he got it, and there was a great uproar. Not one nobleman, not one prince, nobody got the ball. But when our prince rode away with it, he was wounded on his leg.

Since everyone was upset again that nobody had gotten the ball again, the gardener said, "My helper was there at the game."

So the king summoned the helper, and he had the three balls.

"Tell me," said the king, "were you the knight who won the ball three times?"

Now he had a wound on his leg, and it was clear that he was indeed the knight.

"Where do you come from?" asked the king.

"I am the prince whose realm has no end," he said, for Iron Hans had told him everything that he was to say. Since he had the balls, however, he got the princess.

Soon he was made vice-king, and he was assured that he would become the ruling king when his father-in-law died. Then the king asked him where he was born.

"The king of Sicily is my father," he said, "and I was banished because I had freed the wild man, who is always ready to help me."

Soon the time arrived for the marriage to be celebrated, and the young man's father was invited. Then the son sat next to his father, and his father-in-law asked what such a father was worth who had a son and had him killed because he had freed a wild man. The young man's father replied that he should have his tongue cut out, for he thought that his son had long since disappeared from the face of the earth.

"You are my father, and I'm the prince," his son revealed himself. "And you will be punished the way that you have chosen."

Now the matter was settled, and the prince became king of both realms.

JACOB AND WILHELM GRIMM

Iron Hans†

Once upon a time there was a king who had a large forest near his castle, and in the forest all sorts of game could be found. One day he sent a huntsman there to shoot a deer, but he did not return. "Perhaps he met with an accident," said the king, and on the following day he sent two other huntsmen into the forest to look for the missing one, but they too did not return. So, on the third day the king assembled all his huntsmen and said to them, "Comb the entire forest and don't stop until you've found all three of them." But these huntsmen were never seen again, nor were the dogs from the pack of hounds that went with them. From that time on nobody dared venture into the forest, and it stood there solemnly and desolately, and only every now and then could an eagle or a hawk be seen flying over it.

This situation lasted for many years, and then a huntsman, a stranger, called on the king seeking employment and offered to go into the dangerous forest. However, the king would not give his consent and said, "The forest is enchanted, and I'm afraid the same thing would happen to you that happened to the others, and you wouldn't return."

"Sire," replied the huntsman, "I'll go at my own risk. I don't know the meaning of fear."

So the huntsman went into the forest with his dog. It was not long before the dog picked up the scent of an animal and wanted to chase it, but after the dog had run just a few steps, it came upon a deep pool and could go no further. Then a long, bare arm reached out of the water,

† Jacob and Wilhelm Grimm, "Iron Hans"—"Der Eisenhans" (1857), No. 136 in *Kinder- und Hausmärchen. Gesammelt durch die Brüder Grimm* (Göttingen: Dieterich, 1857).

grabbed the dog, and dragged it down. When the huntsman saw that, he went back to the castle and got three men to come with buckets and to bale the water out of the pool. When they could see to the bottom, they discovered a wild man lying there. His body was as brown as rusty iron, and his hair hung over his face down to his knees. They bound the wild man with rope and led him away to the castle, where everyone was amazed by him. The king had him put into an iron cage in the castle courtyard and forbade anyone to open the cage under the penalty of death. The queen herself was given the key for safekeeping. From then on the forest was safe, and everyone could go into it again.

One day the king's son, who was eight years old, was playing in the courtyard, and as he was playing, his golden ball fell into the cage. The boy ran over to it and said, "Give me back my ball."

"Only if you open the door," answered the man.

"No," said the boy. "I won't do that. The king has forbidden it." And he ran away.

The next day he came again and demanded his ball. The wild man said, "Open my door," but the boy refused.

On the third day, when the king was out hunting, the boy returned and said, "Even if I wanted to, I couldn't because I don't have the key."

"It's under your mother's pillow," said the wild man. "You can get it."

The boy, who wanted to have the ball again, threw all caution to the winds and brought him the key. It was difficult to open the door, and the boy's finger got stuck. When the door was open, the wild man stepped out, gave him the golden ball, and hurried away. But the boy became afraid, screamed, and called after him, "Oh, wild man, don't go away; otherwise, I'll get a beating!"

The wild man turned back, lifted him onto his shoulders, and sped into the forest with swift strides. When the king came home, he noticed the empty cage and asked the queen what had happened. She knew nothing about it and looked for the key, but it was gone. Then she called the boy, but nobody answered. The king sent people out into the fields to search for him, but they did not find him. By then it was not all that difficult for the king to guess what had happened, and the royal court fell into a period of deep mourning.

When the wild man reached the dark forest again, he set the boy down from his shoulders and said to him, "You won't see your father and mother again, but I'll keep you with me because you set me free, and I feel sorry for you. If you do everything that I tell you, you'll be all right. I have plenty of treasures and gold, more than anyone in the world."

He made a bed out of moss for the boy, and the child fell asleep on it. The next morning, the man led him to a spring and said, "Do you see this golden spring? It's bright and crystal clear. I want you to sit there and make sure that nothing falls in; otherwise, it will become polluted. I'll come every evening to see if you've obeyed my command."

The boy sat down on the edge of the spring, and once in a while he saw a golden fish or a golden snake, but he made sure that nothing fell in. While he was sitting there, his finger began to hurt him so much that he dipped it into the water without meaning to. He pulled it out quickly but saw that it had turned to gold, and no matter how hard he tried, he could not wipe off the gold. It was in vain.

In the evening Iron Hans returned, looked at the boy, and said, "What happened to the spring?"

"Nothing, nothing," the boy answered as he held his finger behind his back so that the man would not see it.

But Iron Hans said, "You dipped your finger in the water. I'll let it go this time, but make sure that you don't let anything else fall in."

At the crack of dawn the next day, the boy was already sitting by the spring and guarding it. His finger began hurting him again, and he brushed his head with it. Unfortunately, a strand of his fair fell into the spring. He quickly pulled it out, but it had already turned completely into gold. When Iron Hans came, he already knew what had happened. "You've let a hair fall into the spring," he said. "I'll overlook it once more, but if this happens a third time, the spring will become polluted, and you'll no longer be able to stay with me."

On the third day the boy sat at the spring and did not move his finger even when it hurt him a great deal. However, he became bored and began looking at his face's reflection in the water. As he leaned farther and farther over to look himself straight in the eye, his long hair fell down from his shoulders into the water. He straightened up instantly, but his entire head of hair had already turned golden and shone like the sun. You can imagine how terrified the boy was. He took his handkerchief and tied it around his head so that Iron Hans would not be able to see it. When the man arrived, however, he already knew everything and said, "Untie the handkerchief."

The golden hair came streaming out, and no matter how much the boy apologized, it did not help. "You've failed the test and can no longer stay here. Go out into the world, and you'll learn what it means to be poor. However, since you're not bad at heart, and since I wish you well, I'll grant you one thing: whenever you're in trouble, go to the forest and call, 'Iron Hans'; then I'll come and help you. My power is great, greater than you think, and I have more than enough gold and silver."

Then the king's son left the forest and traveled over trodden and untrodden paths until he came to a large city. He looked for work there but could not find any. Nor had he been trained in anything that might enable him to earn a living. Finally, he went to the palace and asked for work and a place to stay. The people at the court did not know how they might put him to good use, but they took a liking to him and told him to stay. At length the cook found work for him and had him carry wood and water and sweep away the ashes. Once, when nobody else was available, the cook told him to carry the food to the royal table. Since the boy did not want his golden hair to be seen, he kept his cap on. The king had never seen anything like this and said, "When you come to the royal table, you must take off your cap."

"Oh, sire," the boy answered, "I can't, for I have an ugly scab on my head."

The king summoned the cook, scolded him, and asked him how he could have taken such a boy into his service. He told the cook to dismiss him at once. The cook, however, felt sorry for him and had him exchange places with the gardener's helper.

Now the boy had to plant and water the garden, hoe and dig, and put up with the wind and bad weather. One summer day, while he was working in the garden all alone, it was so hot that he took off his cap to let the breeze cool his head. When the sun shone upon his hair, it glistened and sparkled so much that the rays shot into the room of the king's daughter, and she jumped up to see what it was. Then she spotted the boy and called to him, "Boy, bring me a bunch of flowers."

Hastily he put on his cap, picked a bunch of wildflowers, and tied them together. As he was climbing the stairs, he came across the gardener, who said, "How can you bring the king's daughter a bunch of common flowers? Quick, get some others and choose only the most beautiful and rarest that you can find."

"Oh, no," answered the boy. "Wildflowers have a stronger scent, and she'll like them better."

When he entered her room, the king's daughter said, "Take off your cap. It's not proper for you to keep it on in my presence."

He replied, as he had before, "I've got a scabby head."

However, she grabbed his cap and pulled it off. Then his hair rolled forth and dropped down to his shoulders. It was a splendid sight to behold. He wanted to run away, but the king's daughter grabbed his arm and gave him a handful of ducats. He went off with them, but since he did not care for gold, he gave them to the gardener and said, "Here's a gift for your children. They can have fun playing with the coins."

The next day the king's daughter called to him once again and told him to bring her a bunch of wildflowers, and as he entered her room with them, she immediately lunged for his cap and wanted to take it away from him, but he held it tight with both hands. Again she gave him a handful of ducats, but he did not keep them. Instead, he gave them to the gardener once again as playthings for his children. The third day passed just like the previous two: she could not take his cap from him, and he did not want her gold.

Not long after this the country became engaged in a war. The king assembled his soldiers but was uncertain whether he would be able to withstand the enemy, who was more powerful and had a large army. Then the gardener's helper said, "I'm grown up now and want to go to war. Just give me a horse."

The others laughed and said, "When we've gone, you can have your horse. We'll leave one for you in the stable."

When they had departed, he went into the stable and led the horse out. One foot was lame, and it limped *hippety-hop, hippety-hop.* Nevertheless, he mounted it and rode toward the dark forest. When he reached the edge of the forest, he yelled, "Iron Hans!" three times so loudly that the trees resounded with his call. Immediately the wild man appeared and asked, "What do you want?"

"I want to go to war, and I need a strong steed."

"You shall have what you want and even more."

Then the wild man went back into the forest, and it was not long before a stableboy came out leading a horse that snorted through its nostrils and was so lively that it could barely be controlled. They were followed by a host of knights wearing iron armor and carrying swords that flashed in the sun. The young man gave the stableboy his three-legged horse, mounted the other, and rode at the head of the troop of knights. As he approached the battlefield, he saw that a good part of the king's men had already fallen, and it would not have taken much to have forced the others to yield as well. So the youth charged forward with his troop of iron knights. They broke like a storm over the enemy soldiers, and the young man struck down everything in his way. The enemy took flight, but the young man remained in hot pursuit and did not stop until there was no one left to fight. However, instead of returning to the king, he led the troop back to the forest by roundabout ways and called Iron Hans.

"What do you want?" asked the wild man.

"Take back your horse and your troop, and give me my three-legged horse again."

He got all that he desired and rode home on his three-legged horse. Meanwhile, when the king returned to his castle, his daughter came toward him and congratulated him on his victory.

"I'm not the one who brought about the victory," he said. "It was some unknown knight who came to my aid with his troop."

The daughter wanted to know who the unknown knight was, but the king had no idea and said, "He went in pursuit of the enemy, and I never saw him after that."

She asked the gardener about his helper, and he laughed and said, "He's just returned home on his three-legged horse, and the others all made fun of him crying out, 'Here comes *hippety-hop, hippety-hop* again.' Then they asked, 'What hedge were you sleeping behind?' And he replied, 'I did my best, and without me things would have gone badly.' Then they laughed at him even more."

The king said to his daughter, "I'm going to celebrate our victory with a great festival that will last three days, and I want you to throw out a golden apple. Perhaps the unknown knight will come."

When the festival was announced, the young man went to the forest and called Iron Hans.

"What do you want?" he asked.

"I want to catch the princess's golden apple."

"It's as good as done," said Iron Hans. "You shall also have a suit of red armor and ride on a lively chestnut horse."

When the day of the festival arrived, the young man galloped forward, took his place among the knights, and went unrecognized. The king's daughter stepped up and threw a golden apple to the knights, but only he could catch it. However, as soon as he had it, he galloped away. On the second day Iron Hans provided him with a suit of white armor and gave him a white horse. Once again only he could catch the apple, and again he did not linger long but galloped away with it. The king became angry and said, "I won't allow this. He must appear before me and tell me his name." So the king gave orders that his men were to pursue the knight if he caught the apple again, and if he did not come back voluntarily, they were to use their swords and spears on him.

On the third day the young man received a suit of black armor and a black horse from Iron Hans. Again he caught the apple, but this time the king's men pursued him when he galloped away with it. One of them got near enough to wound him with the point of his sword. Nevertheless, he escaped them, and his horse reared so tremendously high in the air that his helmet fell off his head, and they saw his golden hair. Then they rode back and reported everything to the king.

The next day the king's daughter asked the gardener about his helper.

"He's working in the garden. The strange fellow was at the festival too, and he didn't get back until last night. Incidentally, he showed my children three golden apples that he won there."

The king had the young man summoned, and when he appeared, he had his cap on. But the king's daughter went up to him and took it off. Then his golden hair swooped down to his shoulders, and he was so handsome that everyone was astonished.

"Are you the knight who came to the festival every day in a different-colored armor and caught the three golden apples?" asked the king.

"Yes," he replied. "And here are the apples." He took them out of his pocket and handed them to the king. "If you want more proof than this, you can have a look at the wound that your men gave me as they pursued me. And I'm also the knight who helped you defeat your enemy."

"If you can perform such deeds, you're certainly no gardener's helper. Tell me, who is your father?"

"My father is a mighty king, and I have all the gold I want."

"I can see that," said the king. "I owe you a debt of gratitude now. Is there any favor that I can do for you?"

"Yes," he replied. "You can indeed. You can give me your daughter for my wife."

Then the maiden laughed and said, "He doesn't stand on ceremony, does he? But I already knew from his golden hair that he wasn't a gardener's helper." Then she went over and kissed him.

The young man's mother and father came to the wedding and were filled with joy, for they had given up all hope of ever seeing their dead son again. And while they were sitting at the wedding table, the music suddenly stopped, and the doors swung open as a proud king entered with a great retinue. He went to the young man, embraced him, and said, "I am Iron Hans and was turned into a wild man by a magic spell. But you released me from the spell, and now all the treasures that I possess shall be yours."

Competitive Brothers

Most of the material in these tales can be traced to ancient India, especially the motif of the extraordinary talents acquired by the sons. In the old Hindu collection *Vetalapanchauinsati* (*Twenty-five Tales of a Demon*), there is a story in which a beautiful princess named Somaprabha will marry a man only if he has one of the following qualities: courage, wisdom, or magic power. Three suitors arrive and convince three separate family members that they are suitable for the princess. Each receives a promise that he can marry her. However, when the suitors seek to claim her, there are major problems because the family members had not consulted with one another. But suddenly the princess disappears, and the royal family asks the suitors to help them. The first suitor, the man of wisdom, informs them that a demon has abducted the princess to a forest. The second, the man of magic power, brings them to the forest in a magic chariot. The third, the man of courage, kills the demon. But the question remains: who deserves the princess? The answer is the man of courage because the first two men were created by God to be his instruments and were intended to help him kill the demon. The first European literary version of this tale type was written in Latin by Girolamo Morlini, and Straparola translated it into Italian and adapted it. Given the comic element of the tale and the common problems regarding the education of the sons, it was popular in both the oral and the literary traditions. Basile took delight in the tale and gave it a special twist at the end by having the father win the princess. The social conditions of apprenticeship and the father's concern for the future of his sons served as the social-historical background for the humorous adventures. The individual "trades" that the sons learn formed the basis for other types of folktales. For instance, the son's art of thievery is related to the "art" of other master thieves in the oral and literary traditions of the seventeenth and eighteenth centuries. Other important versions are Eberhard Werner Happel's tale about three peasant sons in his novel *Der ungarische Kriegs-Roman* (*The Hungarian War Novel*, 1685) and Clemens Brentano's important fairy tale "Das Märchen von dem Schulmeister Klopfstock und seinen fünf Söhnen" ("The Fairy Tale about the Schoolmaster Klopfstock and His Five Sons," ca. 1811–15), which was based on Basile's "The Five Brothers." The Grimms had originally begun collecting their fairy tales for Brentano and sent him an important handwritten manuscript with their early tales about 1810. However, Brentano neglected these tales and was planning at that time to translate and to adapt Basile's tales. He sought to give the tales a Germanic tone and setting. Since he liked to play with language, he used many puns and added numerous poems. He managed to complete eleven adaptations, and in "The Fairy Tale about the Schoolmaster Klopfstock and His Five Sons," he depicts a poor schoolmaster whose school burns down. Therefore, he sends his five sons, Gripsgraps (thief), Pitschpatsch (shooter), Piffpaff (pharmacist), Pinkepank (shipbuilder), and Trilltrall (singer, who understands birds), into the world for one year to learn something. When they return, they are accomplished and decide to help rescue the daughter of King Pumpam, who has been kidnapped

335

by the evil King Knarratschki. Once they succeed, there is a debate about who should marry the princess. The sons agree that the father should have her, but Klopfstock does not really want her. The princess is given her choice, and she chooses the "poet" Trilltrall. Then King Pumpam gives Klopfstock half his kingdom, which he, in turn, divides into five parts for his sons.

GIROLAMO MORLINI

Three Brothers Who Become Wealthy Wandering the World†

A poor man, the father of three sons, had nothing to give his sons and could not support them. In order to take the burden from his shoulders, the three hungry sons considered their father's poverty and helpless situation and decided to set out into the world like philosophers with their walking sticks and backpacks to seek their fortune. Therefore, they knelt down before the old man and asked his permission to leave with the promise that they would return within ten years.

The oldest son happened to come upon an encampment of soldiers who were in the middle of a battle and enrolled in the service of a captain. In very little time he became a brave and courageous soldier, and due to his diligence and valor he was soon considered the best among all his comrades. In addition, he learned the art of climbing a vertical wall with two daggers in his hands. The second son reached a harbor where ships were being built. He apprenticed himself to a master who surpassed all the others in shipbuilding, and he soon became so good that his name was known by everyone in the region. Finally, the youngest son became so enraptured by the sweet song of the nightingale that he followed its traces and melodies everywhere, through dark valleys and shadowy meadows, through deep forests and silent, echoing woods into the solitude of the birds. He forgot about returning and made his home in the forest like a primitive man of the woods and spent ten entire years there. Since he constantly mingled with the birds, he learned their language until he mastered it and was honored among the fauns as if he were Feronia[1] or Pan.

On the appointed day for their return home, the two older brothers met at the designated spot and waited for the youngest. When they saw him coming so naked and haggard, they approached him affectionately, embraced him with tears, and shared their clothes with him. When they were eating later in a tavern, a blue jay hopped on a branch and spoke with its squeaking voice: "Let me tell you, my friends, that there is an enormous treasure lying hidden at this corner of the inn, and it has been designated for you for a long time." With these words it flew away. After the youngest translated the bird's speech to his brothers, they dug for it and found the treasure.

---

† Girolamo Morlini, "Three Brothers Who Become Wealthy Wandering the World"—"De fratibus qui per orbem pererrando ditati sunt" (1520), in *Novellae, fabulae, comoedia* (Naples: Joan. Pasquet de Sallo, 1520).

1. Etruscan goddess of the woods who had sacred temples on Mount Soratte and in Lazio.

Blessed in this manner they arrived at their father's house as rich people, and their father received them with open arms and celebrated their return with splendid meals. One day the youngest son heard another bird that said: "In the Aegean Sea there is the island of Chios that is the size of nine hundred stadiums. The daughter of Apollo had a strong castle made out of marble built on this island, and its entrance is guarded by a fire-spitting and poisonspitting serpent, while a basilisk watches over the threshold. Aglaea[2] is imprisoned there with piles of treasures, whose value is so great that there is no way that it can be estimated. Whoever dares to approach this island and climb the tower, he will win the treasure and Aglaea." After saying these words, the bird flew away.

The youngest son explained to his brothers what the bird had said, and they decided to undertake the risk. The oldest brother promised to climb with his daggers. The second promised to build a ship that was as fast as an arrow, and the ship was soon finished. When a favorable wind filled the sails and a promising breeze curled the sea, they climbed into the boat and steered it toward Chios. After landing in the gray dawn, the soldier immediately took his two daggers, climbed the tower, grabbed hold of Aglaea, and sent her down to his brothers by a rope. Then he collected everything together—carbuncles, precious jewels, and gold—and left the empty tower and climbed back down. Then they arrived back in their homeland safe and sound. However, they soon began arguing because of the maiden, and after a long quarrel, the question remained for an arbiter to determine which of the three brothers would have undisputed possession of Aglaea. But I shall let you, dear reader, settle the question.

This novella shows that the mind is more capable than brute strength and that parents should make every effort to endow their children with knowledge.

GIOVAN FRANCESCO STRAPAROLA

The Three Brothers†

There was once a poor man who lived in this glorious city of ours, and he had three sons. However, due to his poverty, he had no way to nourish and support them. Since they became very needy and realized how poverty-stricken their father was and how he was becoming more and more feeble, they decided among themselves to lighten his burden by going out into the world. They planned to wander from place to place with their staffs and a pack of clothes in order to find a way to earn their living and support themselves. So they went and knelt before their father and asked for permission to go and find a way to procure a living, and they promised to return home after ten years. Their father granted their wish, and they

---

2. Greek word for "splendor." Aglaea was the youngest of the Graces and supposedly married Hephaestus, a god of fire.
† Giovan Francesco Straparola, "The Three Brothers"—"Tre fratelli poveri andando pel mondo divennero molto ricchi" (1553), *Favola* V, *Notte settima* in *Le piacevoli notti*, 2 vols. (Venice: Comin da Trino, 1550/53).

set out and traveled until they came to a certain place where it seemed best to separate from one another.

Now the oldest of the brothers went to seek his fortune among some soldiers who were engaged in a war, and he agreed to serve their leader, who was a colonel. In a short space of time, he became skilled in the art of war and was such a brave and valorous fighter that he took a leading role among his companions. So agile and dexterous was he that he could climb the walls of the highest rocks with a dagger in each hand.

The second brother reached a certain seaport where many ships were being constructed. So he went to work for one of the master shipbuilders who was the best in his trade. Within a brief amount of time, he became so skilled and was so diligent that he became famous throughout the country.

The youngest brother heard the sweet songs of a nightingale and decided to follow the traces and songs of the bird through dark valleys and dense woods, lakes and solitary forests, and deserted and uninhabited places. He became so enchanted by the sweet singing of the birds that he forgot the way back to civilization and continued to dwell in the forest. After living there for ten whole years in such solitude, he became like a wild man of the woods. Indeed, he worked so diligently that he became completely accustomed to the place and learned the language of all the birds. He listened to them with great pleasure and understanding and eventually became known as the god Pan among the fauns.

Now, when the designated day for the return home arrived, the older two brothers went to the meeting place and waited for the third brother. When they saw him approaching, his naked body was only covered by his own hair, and they ran to meet him. Out of the tender love they felt for him, they burst into tears, embraced and kissed him, and put some clothes on him. Later, as they were eating, a bird flew onto a branch of a tree and sang the following sweet words: "You men over there who are eating, I want you to know that there is a great treasure hidden beneath the cornerstone of this inn. It has been there a long time and has been predestined for you. Go there and take it."

After saying these words, the bird flew away. Then the brother who was the last to arrive explained to the other two what the bird had said. So they began digging in the place that the bird had indicated and took out the treasure that they found and became fabulously rich. Thus they happily returned to their father, who embraced them and prepared a sumptuous and grand meal.

Sometime later the youngest brother heard the song of another bird which said that, in the Aegean Sea, ten miles or so from land, there was an island known by the name of Chios, upon which the daughter of Apollo had built a very strong castle made of marble. The entrance was guarded by a dragon that spit fire and poison from its mouth. Connected to the castle was a basilisk in which Aglea, one of the most graceful ladies in the world, was imprisoned with a large treasure that she had collected along with a vast amount of money. Whoever made it to this place and climbed the tower would win Aglea and the treasure.

After saying these words, the bird flew away. As soon as the youngest brother interpreted these words, the three brothers decided to go to the island. The first brother promised to climb the tower using his two daggers, and the second agreed to build a very fast ship. All this was accomplished in a short space of time. Then they crossed the sea with good fortune and fair winds and headed to the island of Chios. They arrived one morning just before daybreak, and the first brother used his two daggers to climb the tower. Then he took Aglea, tied her with a cord, and gave her to his brothers. Next, he collected all the rubies and jewels and a heap of gold and descended the tower. Afterward, they all rejoiced, and the three brothers returned home safe and sound with Aglea and the treasure.

But since the lady could not be divided into three parts, a quarrel arose among the brothers as to which one of them should have her. There were many long fights and disputes as to who deserved her. Indeed, to this present day the case is still before the court, and we must await the court's decision. Until that day arrives, it is up to you to decide.

GIAMBATTISTA BASILE

The Five Sons†

Once upon a time there was a good man called Pacione, who had five such inept sons that they were good for nothing. Since their poor father was no longer able to provide for them all, he decided one day to get them off his back and said to them, "My sons, God knows how much I love you. After all, you sprung from my loins, but I am an old man and cannot work much. You're young and eat a great deal, and I can no longer support you as I used to do. Each for himself and heaven for all! It's now time for you to seek a master and learn a trade. But take care that you don't serve a master for more than a year. At the end of this time, I shall expect you back home, and I shall also expect that you will have learned some kind of craft."

When the sons heard this decision, they took some tattered rags to change their clothes, and each went his way in search of his fortune. At the end of the year, at the designated time, they all met at their father's house, where he received them with great embraces. Then he immediately set the table because they were tired and starving, and they sat down to eat.

While they were in the middle of their meal, they heard a bird singing, and the youngest of the five sons got up from the table and went outside to listen. When he returned, the table had been cleared, and Pacione began to question his sons.

"Well then," he said, "warm my heart a little, and let me hear what craft you've learned during the year."

So Luccio, who had become a master thief, said, "I've learned the art

† Giambattista Basile, "The Five Sons"—"I cinque figli" (1634), *Settimo Passatempo della Quinta Giornata* in *Lo cunto de li cunti overo Lo trattenemiento de peccerille*, De Gian Alessio Abbattutis, 5 vols. (Naples: Ottavio Beltrano, 1634–36).

of stealing, and I've now become the top thief in the profession, the commander in chief of all those who rob things from others, the master of rogues, and you cannot find anyone my equal who knows how to stretch and clean out cloaks, pile and take away linen, slip his hand into pockets and empty them, shake and reorder purses, and clean and empty safes. Wherever I arrive, I can show you miracles of things snatched."

"Bravo! My word!" the father responded. "Just like a merchant's swindles, you've learned to exchange counterpoints: receipts burdening your back for a finger's breadth, the stroke of an oar for the turn of a key, a slip knot for a jump from a window. Poor me! It would have been better if I had taught you how to spin because then I wouldn't have this spinning wheel in my belly. Now I'll keep thinking that I might see you from one moment to the next with a paper hat on your head in court or caught in the act with the evidence in your hand, or if you manage to avoid this, I'll see you one day in the end with a rope wringing your neck."

After saying these words, he turned to Titillo, who was his second oldest son, and said, "And you, what fine craft have you learned?"

"Boat building," the son replied.

"All the better," the father remarked. "At least this is an honorable trade, and you can make a living off it. And you, Renzone, what have you learned during this time?"

"I know how to shoot so well with a crossbow that I can hit a bull's-eye," his son answered.

"This, too, is something," the father said. "You can make use of it by hunting and can earn your bread that way."

Next he turned to his fourth son and asked him the same question, and Jacovo responded, "I've learned to recognize an herb that can raise the dead."

"Bravo! Dam Lanfusa!" Pacione responded. "Now we can get out of our misery and make people live longer than the ruins of Capua!"[1]

Finally, Pacione asked his youngest son, who was Menecuccio, what he had learned, and the son replied, "I know how to understand the language of birds."

"So that was why you got up from the table while we were eating," replied the father, "and went out to listen to the chirping of that sparrow. But since you say you understand what the birds say, tell me what you heard from that bird which was sitting on the tree."

"It said," Menecuccio responded, "that an ogre has kidnaped King Altogolfo's daughter and has taken her to a rock, and nobody knows anything more about her. The king has issued a proclamation and announced that he will wed his daughter to whoever finds her and brings her back to him."

"If that's so, we're rich," Luccio cried out, "because I've got more than enough courage to rescue her from the ogre's clutches."

"If you have the courage to do this," the father joined in, "let us go

---

1. The Roman ruins of the amphitheater of Capua were called *lo Verlascio di Capua*. "Lanfusa": the mother of Ferrari, whose name he customarily used to make a curse in Ludovico Ariosto's *Orlando furioso* (*Orlando in a Frenzy*, 1532). Ferrari was one of the many knights who appear in key episodes of *Orlando furioso*.

immediately to the king, and if he will give his word that he intends to keep his promise, we'll offer to rescue his daughter."

And they all agreed to do this. Titillo built a fine boat right away, and they all went on board and set sail for Sardinia, where they were received by the king. After they offered to rescue his daughter, the king confirmed his promise anew. So they sailed onward until they reached the rock, where they fortunately found the ogre stretched out and asleep in the sun with the head of Cianna, the king's daughter, resting on his lap.

As soon as she saw the boat arrive, she began to get up out of joy, but Pacione made a signal to be quiet, and he placed a large stone on the ogre's stomach. Then they helped Cianna get up, and they jumped into the boat and began rowing away in the water. However, they had not gotten very far from the shore when the ogre woke up. Since he did not find Cianna by his side, he looked out toward the sea and saw that a boat was carrying her away. Therefore, he changed himself into a black cloud and soared through the air to catch up with the boat.

Cianna, who knew the ogre's magic arts, perceived that he had hidden himself in the cloud and was about to arrive. She was so frightened that she could barely warn Pacione and his sons before she dropped down dead. Renzone watched the cloud that was advancing, and after seizing his crossbow, he shot straight into the ogre's eye, and the ogre fell in agony like a hailstone *boom!* into the sea. All this time they had been filled with fright and had fixed their eyes on the cloud. Now they turned to look inside the boat to see what had happened to Cianna, and they found her with her feet stretched out and no longer able to play the game of life. When Pacione saw this, he began to pluck his beard and said, "Now we have lost our precious oil and can no longer rest! Now all our efforts have been thrown into the wind and our hope into the sea! She has gone to the heavenly pastures, and her death will cause us to die of hunger. She has said good night to make our days bad. She has cut the thread of her life that will cause the cord of our hopes to be cut! Truly the plans of the poor never succeed! Truly, whoever is born unlucky dies unhappy! Look how we freed the king's daughter! Look how we've returned to Sardinia! Look how we found a wife! Look at how the feasts have been prepared! Look at the scepter, and here we are sitting on our rear ends!"

Jacovo kept listening to this funeral dirge until he saw that this song was lasting too long and that his father was about to provide the counter-point on the lute of sorrow up to the rosary. So he said, "Slowly, Father, because we want to go to Sardinia, where we shall be happier and more satisfied than you think!"

"The Grand Turk can take satisfaction," Pacione responded, "because when we bring this corpse to the father, he will pay us, but not in money, and while others die with a sardonic laugh, we shall die with a sardonic lament."

"Be quiet!" Jacovo replied. "Your brains must have gone wandering! Don't you remember what craft I learned? Let's disembark, and let me look for the herb that I have in mind, and you will see something more than particles of dust."

The father recovered his calm after hearing these words, and he embraced his son. Pulled by desire, he pulled the oars, and in a short time they arrived at the coast of Sardinia, where Jacovo went ashore and found the herb. Then he returned to the boat and squeezed the juice of the herb in Cianna's mouth. All at once she came back to life like a frog who had been in the Grotto of the Dogs and then was thrown into the lake of Agnano.[2]

Then they all rejoiced and went to the king, who could not stop embracing and kissing his daughter and thanking the brave men who had brought her back to him. But when he was asked to keep his promise, the king said, "To whom should I give Cianna? She is not a pie that can be divided into pieces. Out of necessity, someone must take the cherry, and the others will be left with toothpicks."

The oldest son, who was very intelligent, responded, "My lord, the reward should be granted in proportion to each one's labor. Therefore, consider which one of us deserves this dainty morsel, and then decide according to what you think is just."

"You speak like Roland,"[3] responded the king. "Tell me, then, what you have done so that I shall not make a mistake when I judge."

So after each one reported about how he had demonstrated his prowess, the king turned to Pacione and said, "And you, what have you done in this undertaking?"

"It seems to me that I've done a great deal," Pacione replied, "because I've made men out of my sons, and by dint of spurning them, I compelled them to learn those crafts that they now know. Otherwise, they would have wasted their many talents, while now they are bearing fruit."

After hearing one after the other, the king pondered and considered each one's reasons, and when he saw and considered what seemed just, he decided to give Cianna to Pacione because he was the root of his daughter's salvation. After he said and did this, he gave the sons heaps of money to use for their own profit. Then, out of joy, Pacione, the father, became like a young man of fifteen, and he adapted very well to the situation in keeping with the proverb

When two argue, it is the third who benefits.

JACOB AND WILHELM GRIMM

The Four Skillful Brothers†

There was once a poor man who had four sons. When they had grown up, he said to them, "My dear children, you must now go out into the

2. The famous grotto was near Naples; as an experiment, animals were asphyxiated in the carbon anhydrite of the grotto and then submerged in the water of the nearby Lake Agnano to revive them.
3. Noble French hero of the medieval Charlemagne cycle of *chansons de geste.* His heroic deeds were immortalized in the *Chanson de Roland* of the eleventh or twelfth century.
† Jacob and Wilhelm Grimm, "The Four Skillful Brothers"—"Die vier kunstreichen Brüder" (1857), No. 129 in *Kinder- und Hausmärchen. Gesammelt durch die Brüder Grimm* (Göttingen: Dieterich, 1857).

world, for I have nothing to give you. Make your way to foreign countries. Learn a trade and try to succeed as best you can."

So the four brothers got ready for their journey, took leave of their father, and went out of the town gate together. After they had traveled for some time, they came to a crossroads that led in four directions. Then the oldest son said, "We must separate here, but let us meet again at this spot four years from today. In the meantime, we shall try our luck."

So each one went his way, and the oldest met a man who asked him where he was going and what his plans were.

"I want to learn a trade," he answered.

"Then come with me," the man said, "and become a thief."

"No," the oldest son responded. "That's no longer considered an honest trade, and one generally ends up dangling from the gallows."

"Oh," said the man, "you needn't be afraid of the gallows. I'll just teach you how to get what nobody else can otherwise fetch, and I'll show you how to do this without ever being caught."

So the oldest son let himself be persuaded, and the man taught him how to become a skillful thief. The young man became so adroit that nothing was safe from him once he wanted to have it.

The second brother met a man who asked him the same question about what he wanted to learn in the world.

"I don't know yet," he answered.

"Then come with me and become a stargazer. You won't find anything better than this, for nothing will ever remain hidden from you."

The second son liked the idea and became such a skillful stargazer that when he had finished studying and was about to depart, his master gave him a telescope and said, "With this you'll be able to see everything that happens on the earth and in the sky, and nothing can remain hidden from you."

The third brother served an apprenticeship under a huntsman and learned all there was to know about hunting so that he became full-fledged huntsman. His master gave him a gun as a gift upon his departure and said, "You won't miss whatever you aim at with this gun. You'll hit it for sure."

The youngest brother also met a man who spoke to him and asked him about his plans.

"Do you have any desire to become a tailor?"

"Not that I know of," said the young man. "I've never had the least desire to sit bent over from morning till night and to swing the steel needle back and forth."

"Oh, come now!" answered the man. "You really don't know what you're talking about. With me you'll learn a totally different kind of tailoring that's respectable and decent and may even bring you great honor."

The young man let himself be persuaded. He went with him and learned all the basics of the trade from the man, and upon his departure the master gave him a needle and said, "With this you'll be able to sew together anything you find, whether it be as soft as an egg or as hard as steel. And you'll be able to make anything into one complete piece so that not a single seam will show."

When the designated four years were over, the four brothers met together at the crossroads at the same time. They embraced, kissed each other, and returned home to their father.

"Well," said the father delightedly, "look what the wind has blown back to me again!"

They told him what had happened to them and how each had learned a particular trade. As they sat in front of the house under a big tree, the father then said, "Well, I'm going to put you to the test to see what you can do." After this he looked up and said to the second son, "There's a chaffinch's nest up there in the top of this tree between two branches. Tell me how many eggs are in it."

The stargazer took his telescope, looked up, and said, "Five."

Then the father said to the oldest son, "Fetch the eggs without disturbing the bird that's sitting on them."

The skillful thief climbed up the tree and took the five eggs from under the bird, who sat there quietly without noticing a thing. Then he brought the eggs down to his father, who took them and placed one on each corner of the table and the fifth in the middle and said to the huntsman, "I want you to shoot the five eggs in two with one shot."

The huntsman took aim with his gun and shot the eggs just as his father had demanded. Indeed, he hit all five of them with one shot, and he certainly must have had some of that powder that shoots around corners.

"Now it's your turn," said the father to the fourth son. "I want you to sew the eggs together again and also the young birds that are in them, and I want you to repair any damage that the shot has done to them."

The tailor got his needle and sewed just as his father had demanded. When he was finished, the thief had to carry the eggs up to the nest again and put them back under the bird without it noticing anything. The bird sat on them until they hatched, and after a few days the young chicks crawled out of the eggs and had little red stripes around their necks where the tailor had sewn them together.

"Well," said the old man to his sons, "I must praise you to the skies. You've made good use of your time and have learned something beneficial. I can't say which of you deserves the most praise, but if you soon have an opportunity to apply your skills, we'll find out who's the best."

Not long after this there was a great uproar in the country: the king's daughter had been carried off by a dragon. Day and night the king worried about his daughter, and he made a proclamation that whoever brought her back could have her for his wife. The four brothers discussed the situation together. "This could be our chance to show what we can do," they said, and they decided to set out together to free the king's daughter.

"I'll soon find out where she is," said the stargazer, and he looked through his telescope and said, "I already see her. She's sitting on a rock in the sea very far away from here, and next to her is the dragon, who's guarding her."

The stargazer went to the king and requested a ship for himself and his brothers. Together they sailed across the sea until they came to the rock. The king's daughter was sitting there, but the dragon was lying asleep with his head in her lap.

The Four Skillful Brothers. Arthur Rackham, 1911.

"I can't take a risk and shoot," said the huntsman. "I might hit the beautiful maiden at the same time."

"Well, then, I'll try out my skill," said the thief, who crawled to the maiden and stole her from under the dragon so quickly and nimbly that the monster did not notice a thing and kept on snoring. The brothers joyfully hurried off with her, boarded the ship, and sailed away on the open sea.

Upon awakening, however, the dragon discovered that the king's daughter was gone, and snorting furiously, it flew after them through the sky. Just as it was hovering above the ship and about to dive down upon the vessel, the huntsman took aim with his gun and shot it through the heart. The monster fell down dead, but it was so large and powerful that it smashed the entire ship to pieces in its fall. Fortunately, those on board were able to grab hold of some planks and swim about on the open sea. Once again they were in terrible danger, but the tailor, who was always alert, took his marvelous needle and hastily sewed together the planks with a few big stitches. Then he sat down on the planks and collected all the parts of the ship, which he then sewed together in such a skillful way that in a short time the ship was seaworthy once again, and they could sail home safely.

When the king saw his daughter once more, there was great rejoicing, and he said to the four brothers, "One of you shall have the princess for your wife, but you must decide among yourselves which one it's to be."

A violent quarrel soon broke out among the brothers, for each one had a claim. The stargazer said, "If I hadn't seen the king's daughter, all your skills would have been in vain. That's why she should be mine."

The thief said, "Your seeing her would not have helped much if I hadn't fetched her out from under the dragon. That's why she should be mine."

The huntsman said, "The monster would have torn all of you apart along with the king's daughter if my bullet hadn't hit the beast. That's why she should be mine."

"And if I hadn't patched the ship together for you with my skill," the tailor said, "you'd all have drowned miserably. That's why she should be mine."

Then the king made his decision known. "Each one of you has a just claim, and since it would be impossible to give the maiden to each of you, no one shall have her. Nevertheless, I shall reward you with half my kingdom to be divided among the four of you."

The brothers were satisfied with this decision and said, "It's better this way than to be at odds with each other." So each one of them received a portion of the kingdom, and they lived happily with their father as long as it pleased God.

Triumphant Apprentices

The focus in these fairy tales is on the competition between an apprentice and his master. They are somewhat related to the tales about master thieves, except here the master/apprentice situation is the determining factor in the plot. Generally speaking, there is a contest to see who can be most inventive in transforming himself into some kind of an animal, and often it is a battle until death. Similar folktales can be traced back to the Orient and Greek and Roman antiquity. Aristophanes' play *The Clouds* (423 B.C.E.) contains an incident based on the master/apprentice conflict. Such tales were also widespread in the Celtic tradition. An important source is Jean de Boves's fourteenth-century collection of fabliaux *De Barat e de Haimet*. It includes a farcical tale of one thief stealing from a thief who is stealing eggs from a bird's nest. Sometimes the competition is between two sorcerers or magicians, but for the most part, the European literary tales depict a young man who seeks to liberate himself as magician or thief from an older man. The apprentice often receives some help from the magician's daughter, provided that he promises to take her away and marry her because she wants to escape her father's demonic powers. It is not certain whether Straparola was influenced here by the oral tradition, but Le Noble clearly knew Straparola's tale and stylized it according to the French taste of his time. The names that he chooses lend it an allegorical flavor. The romantic literary treatment of this theme, which was transformed into a tale about artistic dedication, is best exemplified in E. T. A. Hoffmann's "Rat Krespel" ("Councillor Krespel," 1819). In 1857 Ludwig Bechstein published a fairy tale, "Der Zauber-Wettkampf" ("The Magic Contest"), which is closer to the plot of the Grimms' tale and concerns a bookbinder's apprentice who outwits his master.

GIOVAN FRANCESCO STRAPAROLA

Maestro Lattantio and His Apprentice Dionigi†

On Sicily, an island which surpasses all others in antiquity, there is a noble city commonly called Messina, renowned for its safe and deep harbor. It was in this city that Maestro Lattantio was born, a man who exercised two kinds of trades and was highly skilled in both. One of these he practiced in public, namely his trade of a tailor, while the other, the art of necromancy, he did in secret.

Now one day Lattantio took the son of a poor man as his apprentice in

---

† Giovan Francesco Straparola, "Maestro Lattantio and His Apprentice Dionigi"—"Maestro Lattantio sarto ammaestra Dionigi suo scolare; ed egli poco impara l'arte che gl'insegna, ma ben quella' sarto teneva ascosa. Nasce odio tra loro, e finalmente Dionigi lo divora, e Violante figliuola del re per moglie prende" (1553), in *Le piacevoli notti*, 2 vols. (Venice: Comin da Trino, 1550/53).

order to make a tailor out of him. This young man was called Dionigi, an industrious and smart fellow, who learned everything as soon as it was taught him. One day, when Maestro Lattantio was alone, he locked himself in his chamber and began conducting experiments in magic. When Dionigi became aware of this, he crept silently up to a crack in the door and saw clearly what Lattantio was doing. As a result, he became so entranced and obsessed by this art that he could only think of necromancy and cast aside all thought of becoming a tailor. Of course, he did not dare tell his master what he had discovered.

When Lattantio noticed the change that had come over Dionigi and how he had become ignorant and lazy and was no longer the skilled and industrious fellow he had been before and no longer paid any attention to tailoring, he dismissed the apprentice and sent him home to his father. Now, since Dionigi's father was a very poor man, he lamented greatly when his son came home again. After he scolded and punished the boy, he sent him back to Lattantio, imploring the tailor to keep him on as an apprentice and saying that he would pay for his board and chastise him if Dionigi did not learn what Lattantio had to teach. Lattantio knew quite well how poor the apprentice's father was and consented to take back the boy. Every day he did his best to teach him how to sew, but Dionigi appeared always to be more asleep than anything else and learned nothing. Therefore, Lattantio kicked and beat him every day, and more than once he smashed his face so that blood streamed all over it. In short, there were more beatings than there were handfuls of food to eat. But Dionigi endured all this with patience and went secretly to the crack in the door every night and watched everything that Lattantio did in his chamber.

When Maestro Lattantio saw what a simpleton the boy was and that he could learn nothing that he taught him, he no longer concealed the magic that he practiced, for he thought that, if Dionigi could not grasp the simple art of tailoring, he would certainly never understand the difficult art of necromancy. This is why Lattantio no longer shunned Dionigi but did everything in front of him. Of course this pleased Dionigi very much. Even though it seemed to his master that he was awkward and simpleminded, Dionigi was easily able to learn the art of necromancy and soon became so skilled and sufficient that he could perform wonders greater than his master.

One day Dionigi's father went to the tailor's shop and noticed that his son was not sewing. Instead, he was performing menial household chores such as carrying the wood and water for the kitchen and sweeping the floors. When he saw this, he was very disturbed and took him out of Lattantio's service and led him straight home. The good father had already spent a fair amount of money so his son would be dressed properly and learn the art of tailoring, but when he saw that he could not prevail upon him to learn this trade, he was very sad and said, "My son, you know how much money I've spent to make a man out of you. But you've never availed yourself of this opportunity to help me. So now I find myself in the greatest of difficulties and don't know how I can provide for you. Therefore, I would appreciate it very much if you could find some honest way to support yourself."

"Father," Dionigi replied, "before anything else I want to thank you for all the money and trouble you've spent on my behalf, and at the same time I beg you not to get upset even though I've not learned the trade of tailoring as you wished. However, I've learned another, which is much more useful and satisfying. Therefore, my dear father, calm yourself and don't be disturbed because I'll soon show you how we can profit from this and how you'll be able to sustain the house and family with the fruits of my art. Right now I shall use magic to transform myself into a beautiful horse. Then you're to get a saddle and bridle and lead me to the fair, where you're to sell me. On the following day, I'll resume my present form and return home. But you must make sure not to give the bridle to the buyer of the horse. Otherwise, I won't be able to return to you, and you'll perhaps never see me again."

Thereupon, Dionigi transformed himself into a beautiful horse, which his father led to the fair and then showed to many people attending the event. All of them were greatly astonished by the beauty of the horse and the feats that it performed. Now, just at that time it happened that Lattantio was also at the fair, and when he saw the horse, he knew that there was something supernatural about it. So, he quickly returned to his house, where he assumed the guise of a merchant, took a great deal of money, and went back to the fair. When he approached the horse, he perceived at once that it was really Dionigi. So he asked the owner whether the horse was for sale, and the old man replied that it was. Then, after much bartering, the merchant offered two hundred gold florins, and the owner was content, but he stipulated that the horse's bridle was not to be included in the sale. However, the merchant used many words and much money to induce the old man to let him have the bridle as well. Then the merchant led the horse to his own house and put him into the stable. After tying him tightly, he began to beat him severely. Indeed, he continued to do this every morning and evening until at last the horse became such a wreck that it was pitiful to behold.

Now Lattantio had two daughters, and when they saw the cruel treatment of the horse by their ruthless father, they were greatly moved and sympathized with the horse. So every day they would go to the stable and fondle and caress it. One day they took the horse by the bridle and led it to the river so that it might drink. As soon as the horse came to the bank of the river, it dashed into the water at once and transformed itself into a small fish and dove deep down. When the daughters saw this strange and unexpected thing, they were stunned. After they returned home, they began to weep tears, beat their breasts, and tear their blond hair. Shortly after this, Lattantio came home and went straight to the stable to beat the horse as he usually did, but he did not find it. Immediately, he burst into a fit of anger and went to his daughters, who were shedding a flood of tears. Without asking why they were crying (because he already had suspected their mistake), he said to them, "My daughters, tell me everything right away, and don't be afraid." As soon as the father heard their story, he took off his clothes and went to the bank of the river, where he threw himself into the water and transformed himself into a tunfish. Immediately, he began pursuing the little fish wherever it went to devour it. When

the little fish saw the vicious tunfish, it was afraid of being swallowed. So
it swam to the edge of the river, changed itself into a precious ruby ring
and leapt out of the water right into a basket carried by one of the handmaidens of the king's daughter, who had been amusing herself by gathering pebbles along the river's bank. It was there that the ring remained
concealed.

When the maiden returned to the palace and took the pebbles out of
the basket, Violante, the only daughter of the king, happened to see the
ruby ring. After picking it up, she put the ring on her finger, and it became
very dear to her. When night came, Violante went to bed wearing the ring
on her finger, but suddenly it transformed itself into a handsome young
man who caressed her white bosom and felt her two firm little round
breasts. The damsel, who had not yet fallen asleep, was very scared and
was about to shriek. But the young man put his hand over her entire
mouth and prevented her from screaming. Kneeling down before her, he
asked her pardon and implored her to help him because he had not come
there to sully her name, but was driven there out of necessity. Then he
told her who he was and the reason why he had come, how he was being
persecuted, and by whom. Violante was somewhat reassured by the words
of the young man, and when she saw how charming and handsome he
was as he stood in the light of the lamp, she was moved to pity and said,
"Young man, in truth you have shown great arrogance by coming here
and even greater impudence by touching restricted areas that are off-limits
to you. However, now that I have heard the full tale of your misfortunes,
and since I'm not made of marble with a heart as hard as a rock, I am
ready and prepared to provide you with any aid that I can honestly give
you, provided that you will promise faithfully to respect my honor."

The young man thanked Violante at once, and since dawn had arrived,
he changed himself once more into a ring, and Violante put it away in a
place where she kept her most precious jewels. But she would often take
it out so that it could assume human form and hold sweet conversations
with her.

One day, the king, Violante's father, was stricken with a serious disease
which could not be cured by any of his doctors, who reported that the
malady was indeed incurable. From day to day, the king's condition grew
worse and worse. By chance, the news of the king's malady reached the
ears of Lattantio, who disguised himself as a doctor, went to the royal
palace, and gained admission to the bedroom of the king. Then, after
asking the king something about his malady and carefully observing his
face, he felt his pulse.

"Sacred king," Lattantio said, "your sickness is indeed grave and serious,
but cheer up. You'll soon recover your health, for I know a remedy which
will curse the deadliest disease in a short time. So, keep up your good
spirits, and don't worry."

Thereupon the king said, "Good doctor, if you cure my disease, I shall
reward you in such a fashion that you may live according to your heart's
content for the rest of your life."

But Lattantio replied that he did not want land or money, but only one
single favor. Then the king promised to grant him anything that might be

within his power, and the doctor replied, "Sacred king, I ask for no other reward than a single ruby stone, set in gold, which is at present in the possession of the princess your daughter."

When he heard this modest request, the king said, "If this is all you desire, be assured that I shall readily grant your wish."

After this, the doctor applied himself diligently to develop a cure for the king, who in the course of ten days found that the malady had disappeared. When the king was completely recovered and in pristine health, he summoned his daughter in the presence of the doctor and ordered her to fetch all the jewels that she had. The daughter did what he commanded; however, she did not bring back the one jewel that she cherished above all others. When the doctor saw the jewels, he said that the ruby, which he desired so much, was not among them and that, if the princess were to search more carefully, she would find it. The daughter, who was already deeply enamored of the ruby, denied having it. When the king heard these words, he said to the doctor, "Go away for now and come back tomorrow. In the meantime, I shall speak to my daughter in such a way that you can count on having the ruby tomorrow."

When the doctor departed, the king called Violante to him, and after the two were alone in a room with the door closed, he asked her in a kindly manner to tell him about the ruby that the doctor wanted to have so much, but Violante firmly denied that she had it. After she left her father, Violante went straight to her own chamber, locked her door, and began to weep. She took the ruby, embraced and kissed it, and pressed it to her heart, cursing the hour in which the doctor had come across her path. As soon as the ruby saw the hot tears which streamed down from the eyes of the princess and heard the sighs which came from her tender heart, it was moved to pity and changed itself into the form of Dionigi, who with loving words said, "My fair lady, to whom I owe my life, do not weep or sigh on my account, for I am beholden to you. Rather, let us find a way to overcome our anguish. Indeed, this doctor who is so keen to get me in his hands is my enemy who wants to do away with me. But since you are so wise and prudent, you will not deliver me into his hands. Instead, when he asks, you are to hurl me violently against the wall, and I shall provide for what may come after."

On the following morning, the doctor came back to the king, and when he heard the unfavorable report, he became somewhat disturbed and affirmed that the ruby was in the damsel's hands. In the presence of the doctor, the king summoned his daughter once more and said to her, "Violante, you know full well that, if it had not been for this doctor's skill, I would not have recovered my health. Moreover, he did not request land or treasure as a reward but only a ruby which is said to be in your hands. I should have thought that, on account of the love you have for me, you would have given me not merely the ruby but your own blood. Therefore, because of the love I have for you, and because of the suffering your mother has undergone for your sake, I implore you not to deny this favor which the doctor requests."

When his daughter had heard and grasped the wish of her father, she withdrew to her room. Then she took the ruby along with many other

Maestro Lattantio. Edward Hughes, 1894.

jewels and went back to her father and showed the stones one by one to the doctor. As soon as he saw the one which he so greatly desired, he cried out, "There it is!" And he extended his hand to pick it up.

But as soon as Violante perceived what he was about to do, she said, "Stand back, doctor, and you'll get the stone!"

Then she angrily took the ruby in her hand and said, "Now that I realize this is the precious and lovely jewel you've been seeking, I want you to know that I would regret losing it for the rest of my life. So I won't give it to you of my own free will but only do so because my father has compelled me to do it."

As she spoke these words, she threw the beautiful ruby against the wall, and when it fell to the ground, it opened immediately and became a fine large pomegranate, which scattered its seeds on all sides when it burst. As soon as the doctor saw the pomegranate seeds spread all over the floor, he immediately transformed himself into a chicken, thinking he could make an end of Dionigi by pecking the seeds with his beak. But he was deceived because one of the seeds hid itself and waited for the right opportunity to change itself into a clever and agile fox which swiftly pounced on the chicken, seized it by the throat, killed it, and devoured it in the presence of the king and princess.

When the king saw all this, he was astonished. But once Dionigi reassumed his proper human form, he told the king everything, and then with full royal consent, he was united with Violante, who became his lawful wedded wife. They lived together many years in tranquility and glorious peace. Dionigi's father rose from poverty to become a rich man, while Lattantio was killed by his own envy and hate.

EUSTACHE LE NOBLE

The Apprentice Magician†

There was once a young man called Alexis who had a promising future. He was perfectly built, handsome as the day is bright. His father and mother had died because of poverty, and he lived with his grandfather named Bonbenêt, who went to some pain to send him to school. It was a shame because Bonbenêt was not rich. Otherwise, he would have given his grandson a wonderful education. However, since he did not have enough money to make Alexis a grand nobleman, he sent him as an apprentice to a tailor whose name was La Rancune.[1] He was a famous tailor, who had a shop like André,[2] and who did not accept less than ten crowns to make a suit. His jerkins[3] were admirable, and he invented new

---

† Eustache Le Noble, "The Apprentice Magician"—"L'apprenti magicien," in *Le gage touché, histoires galantes* (Amsterdam: Jacques Desbordes, 1700).
1. Rancune means "rancor" in French. Le Noble liked to play with names. For instance, Bonbenêt has the meaning of "good simple man," or possibly "good foolish man." Benêt signifies a fool, simpleton, or bumpkin.
2. A well-known and well-established tailor in Paris at that time.
3. Close-fitting garments.

fashions. But there was something unusual about all this because he did not have any boys helping him, and he himself never worked. However, his clothes were always made, and he delivered them on the day that they were promised. People believed that little Robert[4] worked for him.

Alexis worked for him for one year, and Bonbenêt, who visited him on a frequent basis, found him sometimes sweeping the floors, sometimes cleaning the rooms of his master, but never sewing on a table. This state of things grieved the old man so much that he turned yellow like a pumpkin. Indeed, he was not wrong to be unhappy with the tailor, for Alexis knew nothing about sewing and would not have been able to make anything for a simple soldier. So Bonbenêt took him away from La Rancune with the intention of placing him with someone else. Alexis, who had the temperament of an angel, noticed that Bonbenêt was disturbed, and thus he embraced him and said, "Hey, come on, grandpa. Don't get upset. Even if I didn't learn how to make clothes, I did learn something else."

"What could that be?" Bonbenêt asked.

"It's true. It's true," responded Alexis. "I'm not as dumb as I look. I know some droll things. One day, Monsieur La Rancune locked himself in his study, and I was curious. So I peeped through the keyhole, and I saw him do some surprising things. Just think, he only had to say two words that I've been careful to retain, and *zoom!* he assumed the form of a mouse."

"Mother in heaven!" exclaimed Bonbenêt. "What are you telling me? It's not possible."

"Believe me, it's possible," Alexis replied. "And if you want, I'll change myself before your very eyes into a dog this instant."

"Seeing is believing," Bonbenêt said.

Just as he said this, a beautiful lapdog with long silky hair appeared in the room, and it romped about the place. Bonbenêt was most astounded by this transformation, but he loved his grandson with great affection and was afraid that he might remain a lapdog for the rest of his life. Consequently, he said to him two or three times, "My son, turn yourself back into your natural form."

Alexis always obeyed his grandfather and stopped being a dog that very instant.

"What do you think, grandpa?" he said to Bonbenêt. "Isn't it worth more to know this than to know how to make a pair of sleeves? Now you will have nothing to worry about. You looked after me ever since the death of my good father and mother. It's only just that I look after you until your time comes. Tomorrow morning I'll change myself into a handsome horse. You'll take me to the market and try to sell me for a hundred pistoles. But you must remember to bring back the halter to our lodging, and everything will go well."

The next morning Alexis assumed the shape of the most beautiful horse in the world. Bonbenêt led him to the market, where everyone who saw the horse admired it. The horse dealers bargained with Bonbenêt and offered him ninety pistoles, but Bonbenêt would only sell the horse for a

4. In other words, the devil.

hundred. La Rancune, who was not content with the horse that he had at his place, wanted to buy another one and had come to the market. No sooner did he throw a glance at Bonbenêt's horse than he desired to buy it. However, he knew that Bonbenêt was very poor, and he said to himself, "Well now, what's the meaning of this? Either this old man is poor, or he's stolen the horse. But I fear that his grandson has discovered my secret. I had better clear things up."

As he said this, he pulled a cylinder from his pocket that enabled him to recognize his apprentice under the form of the horse. So, he was determined to revenge himself.

"How much do you want for your horse?" he asked the old man.

"One hundred pistoles," Bonbenêt responded. "And you won't have it unless you pay me everything down to the last penny."

La Rancune, who was obsessed with getting revenge on his apprentice, would have given him ten thousand. He counted out one hundred pistoles and gave them to Bonbenêt, who began to take off the halter as he had been told, but La Rancune knew what the consequence would be and said to him, "My good man, let the halter stay where it is. Here's another pistole for a new one."

Bonbenêt took the pistole without realizing that he had done something wrong, and he went back to his lodging to wait for Alexis, who did not have the protection necessary to return. Meanwhile, La Rancune had taken Alexis to his place and attached him by the halter with his nose against the rack of the stable. Instead of caring for him and giving him straw, he gave him some mighty blows with a stick. For the next three days, the tailor treated him this way, and he was on the verge of dying from thirst and hunger when La Rancune's two daughters took pity on him.

"Good God!" said the eldest. "How cruel our father is! Why is he treating this poor beast so badly?"

"I pity the horse," said the younger sister. "Let's bring it something to eat, and let's at least give it a good feeding so that it will have the strength to bear the blows that it's been receiving."

"I agree," the older sister said. "Let's take care of it while our father is absent."

Then they both ran to the stable, gave the horse something good to eat, and afterward they led it to a river to drink. But it escaped their hands as soon as it felt the water, and the thirst that Alexis had been experiencing made him as happy as a fish in water. So Alexis changed himself into a carp to drink at his ease.

"Well, look at that!" The tailor's daughters were astonished. They returned to their house and were deeply troubled for having lost such a beautiful horse and were terrified in advance of the bad consequences they could expect from their father, who would be sure to be angry. Indeed, when he returned home shortly thereafter, his first concern was to run to the stable to beat his horse, but he did not find it there. He wanted to know what had become of it, and his daughters wept in recounting what had happened. He whipped the younger daughter and boxed the ears of the elder. Then he transformed himself into a bird that one calls black-throated diver and went flying over the surface of the river to swallow Alexis, thinking that he had changed himself into a little fish. He ate all the little fish of the river, one after the other, but he did not find his apprentice among them. Then he realized that Alexis must have changed himself into a carp. What was he to do? He took the form of a large net and sank deep down in the water and caught two hundred carp at one fell swoop. He examined them, and when he did not find what he wanted, he dove down into the water a second time. Clearly, with such precise action, the unfortunate Alexis would have been caught in the end if he had not taken the precaution of leaving the water after he had quenched his thirst. In fact, he had anticipated that La Rancune would be told by his daughters where he had escaped and that the tailor would come fishing for him. So he transformed himself right away into a diamond, and through this artifice he managed to elude La Rancune's vigilance and resentment. Meanwhile, La Rancune caught nothing but carp and returned home swearing that he would not die content unless he got rid of his apprentice.

Now, near the river there was a magnificent palace where a king was living with his daughter, who was extraordinarily beautiful. As the princess often took strolls along the bank of the river with her ladies-in-waiting, they perceived one day a stone that was glistening on the shore, and they picked it up. The princess was charmed by it, and she immediately sent it to a jeweler, who made a ring of such great beauty that one had never seen anything like it in the world. Alexis, who was under the form of this ring, was completely comfortable to be in the hands of the king's daughter, but his joy was soon placed in jeopardy.

Due to the power of his art, Rancune knew that Alexis was under the form of the ring and had brought delight to the princess. Therefore, he thought of a way that he could obtain it if the opportunity should present itself. And it soon came, for the king fell sick, and the doctors were unable to cure him with all their medicine. The entire court was greatly worried about this. The king, who had no great desire to die so soon, issued an edict and announced throughout his kingdom that he would give half of his realm and his daughter in marriage to the man who could find the means to cure him.

La Rancune did not miss this opportunity. He went to the king, and after having cured him, he said, "Sire, I know that half of your realm now belongs to me and that the word of a king is inviolable. It is up to me now to marry your daughter. But I don't want to do this. The only reward that I demand, sire, is that the princess give me a ring that she has in her possession."

"What's this?" replied the king. "You are willing to content yourself with such a small reward when you have the right to demand a much greater one?"

"Yes, sire," La Rancune declared. "May God pity me, I have no desire for love, nor am I ambitious."

"Well, then," said the king, "come to my royal session tomorrow, and I shall not only give you the ring but also give you the casket with all my daughter's precious stones."

"Great king," the tailor responded, "you are too generous. I only desire the ring that I have just mentioned, and now that your majesty has promised this to me, I shall count on your word."

In the meantime, the princess, who was unaware of the conversation that Rancune had just had with her father, had locked herself in her room with one of her ladies-in-waiting whom she loved the most to talk about the king's convalescence and about the edict that he had issued.

"How unfortunate princesses are!" she said. "Victims of politics! They are sometimes delivered to men who have not merited the rank or the fortune that they have. For me," she continued weeping, "I have more to complain about than another, for I am about to marry a vile tailor who has a rough beard and is so ugly that I feel that I shall never be able to love him."

Even though the lady-in-waiting was very intelligent, she found this marriage such a poor match that she did not know what to say to the princess to console her. Thus she cried as well, and while they were both downcast, they noticed with astonishment that the stone on the ring of the princess removed itself in front of their eyes. Gradually it took the form of a young man as handsome as Eros, and finally Alexis appeared.

"Don't be frightened, my princess," he said addressing his words to the king's daughter. "And please deign to hear me tell you my misfortunes." After saying this he told them everything in a touching way. "La Rancune," he added, "will ask the king that you give me up as the prize for having healed him. In the name of God, please do not deliver me into the resentful hands of the most barbaric of men. Ah! If you had seen him beat me with his stick in his stable, you would be convinced that it is not without reason that I fear falling into his hands again."

Alexis aroused the compassion of the princess so much that she promised to do her best to avoid delivering him to his enemy.

"But, if my father obliges me to do this," she said sorrowfully, "what do you want me to do?"

"Throw me," Alexis said, "with all your might against the wall, and don't worry about the rest."

Their conversation lasted quite a long time, and the lady-in-waiting, who had a good deal of experience, noticed that the princess found Alexis very charming, and that she wished that it had been him who had cured the king. Since it was late, the princess disrobed, but before she went to bed, she asked Alexis to assume the form of the ring again.

The next morning the king told his daughter what La Rancune's preference was.

"My daughter, you know the debt that I owe to La Rancune. He has let me remain the tranquil possessor of my kingdom, and far from desiring your hand in marriage, he will be content with a certain ring that you have in your casket. Since you have always been very good and obedient, I have no doubt that you will voluntarily give him what he wants."

"My father," the princess responded respectfully, "there's nothing in the world that I would not sacrifice for you with all my heart even if it were just to procure a quarter of an hour of health. But I should not like to give him this ring, with your permission."

"What's this?" the king asked angrily. "You ingrate! Is this the way you respond to the friendship that I've always had for you?"

"My father," the princess replied, "let us talk without getting upset. You are unjust if you accuse me of lacking tenderness for you. All my ladies-in-waiting can tell you that I did not cease weeping during your illness. As for my ring, I must confess that I cannot do without it. La Rancune can take whatever he wants. He can have the part that I have of your crown. It doesn't matter to me. I shall retire to a convent, where I would live more content with my ring than I would be on your throne without it."

"By Jove!" the king said. "How strange this is! How can one love these trifles so much? Well then," he continued with a burst of rage that he could not control, "I'm going to punish you by depriving you of all the precious stones that you love so much and by having you locked up in a tower."

This menace brought the princess to her senses. As soon as she saw that she could not save the ring, she took the casket from her pocket, and after she opened it, La Rancune wanted to carry it away. But the princess repulsed him as the insolent man that he was and said, "Let me do it." Then she showed him a ring and asked him if it was the one that he wanted.

"No," he responded.

"Is it this one?" she asked as she showed him another.

"No," he responded.

Finally, she took out the ring in question. La Rancune reached out his hand brusquely to grab it, but the princess threw it to the ground with all her might. All of a sudden, the ring changed itself into a grenade that exploded, and all its seeds spread on the ground of the room. Then La Rancune showed the entire court what he knew and took the form of a cock and began pecking the seeds one after the other. When he believed that he had swallowed all of them, he promenaded proudly before the princess, who would have liked to have seen him in a stew. Just then a small seed that he had not noticed because it was under a cobweb changed itself all at once into a fox that strangled the cock. The entire court, stunned by this miracle, fell into a profound silence as Alexis abandoned the figure of the fox and returned to his natural form. Then he saluted the king and the princess with such graceful manners that they were charmed by him. The king immediately summoned his council, and after an hour of deliberation, his councillors announced to the king that Alexis was really the cause of his getting well and thus he should marry the princess.

The king, who approved of all that his ministers had advised, said that this appeared just to him. Then he asked his daughter whether she would find it repugnant to marry a man of such low birth.

"Oh, no, my father!" she responded, for she was madly in love with him. "Happiness is more important than richness, and with the exception of birth, Alexis is worth a prince."

So they sent someone to search for Bonbenêt so that he could witness the happiness of his grandson, who married the princess the next day.

The moral that one can take from this tale is that *whoever wants to harm someone else will only harm himself.*

JACOB AND WILHELM GRIMM

The Thief and His Master†

Jan wanted his son to learn a trade. Therefore, he went to church and prayed to the Lord to tell him what would be best for his son. The sexton was standing behind the altar and said, "Thieving, thieving."

So Jan went to his son and told him that he had to learn how to be a thief because the Lord wanted it that way. He then set out with his son to look for a man who knew something about thieving. After they had traveled for a long time, they finally reached a great forest, where they found a little cottage with an old woman sitting inside.

"Do you happen to know a man who's good at thieving?" Jan asked.

"You can learn what you want here," said the woman. "My son's a master thief."

Then Jan talked with her son and asked him whether he was really good at thieving.

"Your son will be taught well," said the master thief. "Come back in a year, and if you can still recognize him, I won't take any money for my services. However, if you don't recognize him, you must give me two hundred talers."

The father went home again, and the son learned all kinds of witchcraft and thieving. When the year was over, the father set out by himself and began fretting because he did not know how he would be able to recognize his son. As he was walking along and fretting, he encountered a little dwarf, who said, "Man, what are you worrying about? You look quite gloomy."

"Oh," Jan said, "I hired my son out as an apprentice to a master thief a year ago. He told me to return about now, and if I can't recognize my son, I must pay him two hundred talers. But if I can recognize my son, I won't have to give him anything. Now I fear I won't be able to recognize him, and I don't know where I'll get the money to pay him."

Then the dwarf told him to take a crust of bread with him and stand beneath the chimney once he was there. "You'll see a basket up on the crossbeam, and a bird will peep out of it. That will be your son."

So Jan went there and threw a crust of black bread in front of the basket, and a bird came out and looked at it.

"Hello there, son, is that you?" said the father.

The son was glad to see his father, but the master thief said, "The devil must have given you the clue! How else could you have recognized your son?"

"Let's go, father," said the boy.

† Jacob and Wilhelm Grimm, "The Thief and His Master"—"De Gaudeif un sien Meester" (1857), No. 68 in *Kinder- und Hausmärchen. Gesammelt durch die Brüder Grimm* (Göttingen: Dieterich, 1857).

Then the father and son set out for home. On the way a coach came driving by, and the son said, "I'm going to turn myself into a big greyhound. Then you can earn a lot of money by selling me."

A nobleman called from the coach, "Hey, my good fellow, do you want to sell your dog?"

"Yes," said the father.

"How much do you want for it?"

"Thirty talers."

"Well, man, that's certainly a lot, but since it's such a fine-looking dog, I'll pay."

The nobleman took the dog into his coach, but after they had driven along for a while, the dog jumped out of the coach window. Now he was no longer a greyhound and went back to his father.

They made their way home together, and on the following day, there was a fair in the neighboring village. So the boy said to his father, "Now I'm going to turn myself into a fine-looking horse, and you'll sell me at the fair. But when you sell me, make sure that you take off the bridle so I can become a human being again."

The father took the horse to the fair, and the master thief came and bought the horse for a hundred talers. However, the father forgot to take off the bridle, and the master thief went home with the horse and put him in the stable. Later, when the thief's maid happened to enter the stable, the horse cried out, "Take my bridle off! Take my bridle off!"

The maid stopped and listened. "My goodness! You can talk!"

She went and took the bridle off, and the horse became a sparrow and flew out the door. Then the master thief also became a sparrow and flew out after him. They met and held a contest in midair, but the master lost and fell into the water, where he turned himself into a fish. The boy also turned himself into a fish, and they held another contest. Once again the master lost, and he turned himself into a rooster, while the boy turned himself into a fox and bit the master's head off. So the master died, and he has remained dead up to this very day.

Brotherly Love

Although there are many romances and tales about dragon slayers in the medieval period, Straparola's tale is the first literary fairy tale to develop this motif along with the theme of brotherly love. There are, of course, many other motifs that occur in the fairy tale and romance tradition: the unintentional injury, the animal helpers, the rescue of the princess, the cutting out of the dragon's tongues, the woman who enchants men with her hair, the sword that protects the honor of the brother's wife, the evil witch, the magic plant or balm that saves one of the brothers, and the reunion of the brothers. All these motifs are used by Straparola, Basile, and the Grimms in slightly different ways, with the animals providing comic relief. Important in each of these tales are the notions of faith and honor. Basile's tale "La cerva fata" ("The Enchanted Doe") is also related to the tales in this group.

GIOVAN FRANCESCO STRAPAROLA

Cesarino, the Dragon Slayer†

Not very long ago in Calabria, there was a poor woman who had a son called Cesarino di Berni, a discreet young man, richly endowed with the gifts of nature more than with those of fortune. One day Cesarino left his home, went into the country, and soon reached a dense forest covered with leaves. Enchanted by the verdant beauty of the place, he entered, and by chance he came upon a rocky cave in which he found a litter of lion cubs, another one of bear cubs, and a third of wolf cubs. Then he took one cub from each of the litters, carried them home and nurtured them with the greatest care and diligence. In time the animals became so closely attached to one another that they could not bear to be apart. Moreover, they had become so docile that they would not hurt a soul. Yet they were by nature wild animals and had only become domesticated by chance.

Once they matured and reached their full strength, Cesarino would often take them hunting with him, and he would always return home carrying a great deal of game. This was how he supported his mother and himself. But when his mother saw her son constantly bringing home so much game, she was quite astounded and asked him how he managed to

---

† Giovan Francesco Straparola, "Cesarino, the Dragon Slayer"—"Cesarino de' Berni con un leone, un orso e un lupo si parte dalla madre e dalle sorelle; e giunto nella Sicilia, trova la figliuola del re che deveva esser divorata da un ferocissimo dracone, e con quelli tre animali l'uccide; e liberata da morte, vien presa da lui in moglie" (1553), in *Le piacevoli notti*, 2 vols. (Venice: Comin da Trino, 1550/53).

catch so many wild beasts. Thereupon, Cesarino answered, "I've caught them with the help of my three animals that you've seen by my side. But I beg you not to tell anyone about this. Otherwise, they might be taken from me."

Shortly thereafter, it happened that the old mother was with a neighbor of hers whom she liked very much, not merely because she was well-off but because she was kind and obliging as well. As they were conversing about this and that, the neighbor said, "How is it that your son manages to catch so many wild beasts?"

And then the old woman revealed everything to her, took her leave, and returned home. No sooner had she departed than the neighbor's husband arrived home. His wife went to meet him with a joyful face and soon told him all that she had just learned. When the husband heard this, he went straight to Cesarino and said to him, "How come you never take companions with you when you go hunting, my son? That's not a good way for a friend to act."

Cesarino did not say anything in reply but simply smiled. The next day, without saying a word of farewell to his old mother or to his beloved sisters, he left home with his three animals and went out into the world to seek his fortune.

After he traveled a very long distance, he arrived at a solitary and un-inhabited spot in Sicily, where he saw a hermitage. After he approached it, he entered the little hut and did not find anyone there. So he set up his lodging with his three animals. He had not been there long when the hermit came back, and when he entered, he saw the animals and was so frightened that he turned to flee. But Cesarino, who had already seen the hermit approaching the hut, cried out, "My father, don't be afraid. You can safely stay in your cell because these animals are tame and won't harm you in any way."

Assured by these words, the hermit decided to stay in his humble cell. Now, Cesarino was very worn out after the long journey, and turning to the hermit, he said, "My father, do you by chance have any bread and wine so that I can regain the strength that I've lost."

"Certainly I have, my son," replied the hermit, "but it's not perhaps the quality that you desire."

Then the hermit skinned and cut up some of the game which he had brought with him and put it on a spit to roast. Afterward, he prepared the table and spread it with the meager food he had at hand and ate his meal heartily with Cesarino. When they had finished eating, the hermit said to Cesarino, "Not far from this place there is a dragon whose poisonous and stinking breath cannot be withstood by anyone or anything, and he has caused such great damage that all the peasants will soon abandon the country. Moreover, every day a human person must be sent to him for his meal. Otherwise, he has announced that he will destroy everyone and everything. By a cruel and evil fate the one chosen by lot for tomorrow is the daughter of the king, who is the most beautiful, virtuous, and courteous maiden alive. Everyone sings her praises, and it is truly a great sin that such an innocent damsel should have to perish in such a cruel way."

After he had listened to the hermit's words, Cesarino replied, "Keep up your good spirits, holy father, and you can depend on me to set the maiden free."

The next morning, almost before the rays of the sun had appeared in the sky, Cesarino took his three animals and went to the spot where the vicious dragon dwelled, and he found the princess, who had already been brought there to be devoured. Without hesitating, he went straight to the maiden, who was shedding a flood of tears, and comforted her.

"Don't cry, my lady," he said. "There is no need to grieve, for I've come to set you free."

But just as he said these words, the rapacious dragon rushed violently from its lair with its jaws wide open and ready to tear the beautiful and delicate maiden to pieces and devour her while she trembled in fear. Then Cesarino, moved by pity, plucked up his courage and urged the three animals to attack the fierce and voracious beast. They fought long and hard until they knocked the dragon to the ground and killed him. Thereupon, Cesarino took a bare knife, cut out the dragon's tongue, and carefully put it into a bag. Then, without saying a word to the damsel, he left and went back to the hermitage, where he told the holy father all that he had done. When the hermit heard the dragon was indeed dead and the young maiden and the country were liberated from the monster, he was extremely happy.

Meanwhile, it so happened that a crude and coarse peasant, who had been wandering about the country, came across the place where the horrible dead beast was lying on the ground, and as soon as he saw the dreadful dragon, he grabbed the knife that he carried on his side and cut the dragon's head from its body. Then he put it in a large sack which he had with him and continued on his way toward the city. As he went along the road at a rapid pace, he caught up with the princess, who was returning to her father, and joined her company. Indeed, he accompanied her into the royal palace and handed her to the king, who almost died from joy when he saw that his daughter had come back safe and sound. Then the peasant, who was very pleased with himself, took off his hat and said to the king, "Sire, I claim your daughter as my wife since I saved her from death."

To show that he was telling the truth, the rogue drew the horrible head of the slain beast from his bag and placed it before the king. When the king saw the monstrous head of the beast that had terrified his kingdom at one time and was now reduced to nothing, and when he realized how his daughter and country had been freed from this dragon, he gave orders for a victory celebration and a superb feast to which all the ladies of the city were invited. Soon, they arrived in splendid garments to offer congratulations on the occasion of the princess's rescue.

Now it so happened that, at the very same time that preparations were being made for the feast and victory celebration, the old hermit was in the city, and news reached him that a certain peasant was to wed the king's daughter as a reward for liberating her from the dragon. When the hermit heard all this, he was greatly distressed and put aside all thought of seeking alms that day and returned to his hermitage, where he told Cesarino what had happened.

When the young man listened to the hermit's story, he became upset and took out the tongue of the slain dragon to show the hermit the clear proof that he himself had killed the wild beast. When the hermit heard his story and was fully convinced that Cesarino was the dragon slayer, he went to the king, took off his ragged cap, and said, "Most sacred majesty, it would be a most detestable thing if a malicious and evil culprit, accustomed to living in caves, were to become the husband of a maiden who is the flower of loveliness, the model of good manners, the mirror of courtesy, and richly endowed in all kinds of virtues. But it is even worse when this rogue seeks to deceive your majesty by pretending that the lies he utters are the truth. Now I, who am very concerned about protecting your majesty's honor and eager to be of service to your daughter, have come here to reveal to you that the man who has boasted about rescuing the princess is not the man who slew the dragon. Therefore, oh sacred majesty, keep your eyes and ears open, and listen to one who has your well-being at heart."

When the king heard the firm convictions of the hermit and also knew that they stemmed from a faithful and devoted subject, he completely trusted the hermit's words. So he had all the celebrations stopped and ordered the hermit to tell him who the true rescuer of his daughter was. The hermit, who wished for nothing better, said, "Sire, there is no need to make a mystery about his name, but if it would please your majesty, I shall bring him here to meet you, and you will see a handsome young man, who is charming, gracious, and praiseworthy. Indeed, he has a noble and honest air about him that no other man his equal can match."

The king, who was already enchanted by the young man, ordered the hermit to bring Cesarino to the palace right away. So the hermit left the palace and returned to his hut, where he told Cesarino everything that had happened. Then the young man took the dragon's tongue, put it into a small pouch, and went to the palace accompanied by the hermit and the three animals. When he presented himself to the king, he knelt down and said, "Sacred majesty, I struggled hard and exhausted myself, but the honor belongs to others. With the help of my three animals, I slew the wild beast and set your daughter free."

Then the king said, "What proof can you give me to show that you really did slay the beast, for another man has brought me the dragon's head, which you see hanging over there."

"I don't ask you to take the word of your daughter," Cesarino answered, "which would certainly be sufficient testimony by itself. I shall simply offer you one token that will clearly prove that I and no other was the slayer of the beast. Look carefully at the head hanging over there, and you'll find that it has no tongue."

Thereupon, the king had the dragon's head examined, and it was discovered to be without a tongue. Then Cesarino took out the enormous dragon's tongue from his pouch, and no one had ever seen one as huge as this one. Indeed, it clearly demonstrated that he had slain the savage beast. After the king had seen the tongue and had heard his daughter's story and had seen some other evidence, he had his guards seize the peasant immediately and ordered them to cut off his head from his body. Then he arranged the marriage of Cesarino with his daughter, and a great feast and celebration were held.

In the meantime, the mother and sisters of Cesarino heard the news that he had slain the wild beast, had rescued the princess, and had been rewarded with the damsel as his wife. Therefore, they decided to travel to Sicily. After boarding a ship and benefitting from a favorable wind, they soon arrived in Sicily, where they were received with full honors. But these women had not been in the country very long before they were consumed by envy of Cesarino's good fortune. Their hatred increased day by day until it reached a point that they became determined to have him secretly murdered. After pondering various plans, they finally decided to take a bone, sharpen its point, and dip it into some poison. Then they planned to place it under the sheets in Cesarino's bed with the point upward so that, when he went to rest and threw himself down on the bed as is the custom of young men, he would stab himself and be poisoned. Once the women made up their minds to do this, they began to carry out their evil plan.

When the time for going to sleep arrived, Cesarino went into the bedroom with his wife, and after taking off all his clothes, he threw himself on the bed and struck his left side against the point of the bone. The wound he received was so deep that his body immediately became swollen because of the poison, and when the venom reached his heart, he died. As soon as his wife saw that her husband was dead, she began to scream and shed a flood of tears. Alarmed by the noise, the courtiers ran to the chamber, where they found Cesarino dead. After they turned his corpse over and over, they found it was swollen and black as a raven. Therefore, they judged that he had been murdered by poison. When the king heard what had occurred, he called for a thorough investigation, but nothing could be found. So he and his daughter and the entire court put on their mourning dress, and he ordered the body of Cesarino to be buried with the most solemn funeral rites.

While all these grand and stately obsequies were being carried out, the mother and sisters of Cesarino began to be very afraid of what the lion, bear, and wolf would do when they found out that their master was dead. So they took counsel with one another, and they decided to seal the ears of the three animals with wax, which they did. But they failed to seal the ears of the wolf entirely, so he was able to hear with one of them. So, while the dead body was being taken to the sepulchre, the wolf said to the lion and the bear, "Comrades, it seems to me that I've got some bad news."

But they did not hear a thing because their ears were sealed. When he repeated his words, they could not understand him any better. Still the wolf kept making signs and gestures to them so that at least they grasped that someone was dead. Then the bear used his hard crooked claws and penetrated the lion's ears deep enough to bring out the seal. Then the lion did the same to the bear and to the wolf. As soon as they could all hear again, the wolf said to his companions, "It seems to me as if I had heard some talking about our master's death."

Thereupon, they left the house together and went straight to the spot where the dead body had been carried to be buried. As soon as the priests and the others who were attending the funeral saw the three animals, they took flight, and the men who were carrying the corpse put it down and did the same. But some others, who were more courageous, stayed to see what would happen.

Immediately, the animals began to work hard with their teeth and claws, and soon they stripped the clothes off their master's body and examined it closely until they found the wound. Then the lion said to the bear, "Now's the time to give us some of that fat that you store in your belly. If we can rub the grease into our master's wound, we can revive him."

"No need to say another word," answered the bear. "I'll open my mouth as wide as I possibly can, and then you can put your paw down my throat and take out as much fat as you want."

So the lion put his paw down the bear's throat while the bear hunched together so that the lion could reach what he wanted. When the lion took out all the grease he needed, he rubbed his master's wound with it on all sides. After the wound had softened somewhat, he sucked it with his mouth and then put a certain herb into it. This herb was so potent that it immediately reached his heart and ignited it. Little by little Cesarino recovered his strength and was brought back to life.

When all the people who were present saw this resurrection, they were amazed and ran straight to the king to tell him that Cesarino was alive. After the king had heard this news, he went to meet him accompanied by his daughter, whose name was Dorothea, and they embraced him and kissed him with great joy. Then they celebrated his return at the royal palace with a great feast.

When the news of Cesarino's resurrection reached his mother and sisters, they were greatly displeased. Nevertheless, they pretended to be very happy and went to the palace. But as soon as they came near Cesarino, his wound immediately opened and gushed forth a good deal of blood. When this happened, the women were bewildered and turned pale. The king saw this and became suspicious of them. So he had them retained, and after they were tortured, they confessed everything, whereupon the king commanded them without indulgence to be burned alive.

Cesarino and Dorothea enjoyed a long and happy life together and left children to rule after them. As for the three animals, they were tended with great care until they died from natural causes.

GIAMBATTISTA BASILE

The Merchant†

Once upon a time there was a very rich merchant who was called Antoniello, and he had two sons, Cienzo and Meo, who looked so much alike that it was impossible to tell them apart. Now it so happened that

† Giambattista Basile, "The Merchant"—"Il mercante" (1634), *Settimo passatempo della prima giornata* in *Lo cunto de li cunti overo Lo trattenemiento de peccerille*, De Gian Alessio Abbattutis, 5 vols. (Naples: Ottavio Beltrano, 1634–36).

Cienzo, who was the older son, had a stone fight with the son of the king of Naples at the Arenaccio[1] and smashed his head. As a result, Antoniello became angry with him and said, "Bravo! You must be proud of yourself! Tell everyone about it! Boast about it, you windbag, and I'll pick you apart. Make sure everyone knows. Look, you've broken something worth six soldini.[2] You've battered the head of the king's son. Didn't you realize that there is some distance between you two, you goat's head? Now, how are you going to get out of this mess? Your life is worth nothing because you've cooked your goose. Even if you returned to where you were born, I wouldn't be able to keep you safe from the long arm of the king. You know full well that his reach is great, and he will do something nasty."

After his father had repeated himself a few times, Cienzo replied, "If you please, my sir, people have always said that it's better to have the police in the house than the doctor. Wouldn't it have been worse if the king's son had broken my head? I was provoked. We are only boys. It all happened in a fight, and it is my first offense. The king is a reasonable man, and after all, what can he do to me? If I don't get the mother, give me the daughter. If I don't get cooked meat, give me raw meat. The whole world is our home, and whoever's afraid should become a policeman."

"What can he do to you?" Antoniello responded. "He can send you out of this world and give you a change of air. He can make you a schoolmaster with a stick twenty-four feet long to make you thrash the fish until they learn how to speak.[3] He can enable you to depart this world with a soaped collar three-feet wide to amuse yourself at the gallows. Instead of touching the lady gallows' hand, you'll feel the hangman's foot.[4] That's why I wouldn't want to be in your shoes, and that's why you should get out of here right away. Don't let anything new or old be known about what you're doing if you don't want to stumble over your own feet. The bird in the field has a better life than the bird in a cage. Here's some money. Take one of the two magic horses that I have in the stable and also one of the magic dogs, and don't delay any longer. It's better to take to your heels than to feel the heels of someone else.[5] It's better to get your legs flying than to have two legs around your neck. In short, it's better to run a thousand feet than to remain here with three feet of rope tying you down. If you don't pack your knapsack and get out of here, neither the lawyer Baldo nor the lawyer Bartolo[6] will be able to help you."

So Cienzo asked for his father's blessing and mounted his horse. With the little dog in his lap, he galloped out of the city. But as soon as he passed through the Capuan Gate,[7] he turned to gaze at the city and began

1. A large area in the eastern part of the city that was the battlefield in the sixteenth and seventeenth centuries for Neapolitan stone fights. These stone fights took place when one district or quarter of the city challenged another to a contest. There were often as many as two thousand people engaged in the battles, and the custom continued up to the twentieth century.
2. An ironic reference to a chamberpot, which was commonly worth six soldini at that time.
3. Basile is using schoolboy slang here and means that the king could send Cienzo to row in a galley.
4. To finish his job more quickly, the hangman often got on the shoulders of the man who was being hung.
5. Meaning the hangman.
6. Reference to two famous lawyers: Baldo degli Ubaldi (1327?–1400) and Bartolo da Sassoferrato (1314–1357).
7. The eastern gate of Naples, which had been moved to that place by Ferrante I of Aragon.

uttering, "Take care of yourself while I am gone, my beautiful Naples! Who knows whether I shall ever see you again with your bricks of sugar and walls of pastry, where the stones are made of manna, the rafters made of sugarcane, and the doors and windows are made of cream puffs. Alas! I shall be separated from you, beautiful Pendino,[8] and it seems as if I shall be like a pendulum swinging in emptiness. My heart is heavy as I leave you, Piazza Larga! I feel as if I'm losing my soul as I bid you farewell, Piazza dell' Olmo. As I part from you, Lancieri, I feel as if a Catalan lance[9] were piercing me. As I tear myself away from you, Forcella, my heart feels as if I had been stabbed to the core. Where shall I find another Porto, sweet harbor of the world's wealth? How shall I find another Gelsi, where the silkworms of love continually weave cocoons of contentment? Where shall I find another Pertuso, the meeting place of all men who amount to something? How shall I find another Loggia, where so much is lodged and pleasure is refined? Alas! I cannot part from you, my Lavinaro, without a stream of tears rushing from my eyes! I cannot leave you, oh Mercato, without marching in terrible pain. I cannot leave you, beautiful Chiaia, without feeling a thousand thrashes being inflicted on my heart! Good-bye carrots and beets. Good-bye fritters and chestnut cakes. Good-bye broccoli and pork. Good-bye tripe and liver, good-bye minced meat and grated cheese, good-bye flower of cities, the glory of Italy, painted egg of Europe, mirror of the world. Good-bye Naples, the *non plus altra*, where virtue has set its stakes and grace her borders! I am leaving you and shall miss your cabbage soups.[1] I am going away from this beautiful village. On my broccoli, I'm leaving you behind."

Upon saying this and making a winter of lament in dog days of sighs, he went his way until evening when he arrived at some woods near Cascano,[2] where he could enjoy silence and shade while the sun kept its mule outside. He found an old house at the foot of a tower and knocked at the door of the tower, but the owner was afraid of robbers and did not open because it was already night. So poor Cienzo was forced to stay in the old house. He tethered his horse in the middle of a meadow and then threw himself down to sleep on a pile of straw which he found inside the house, and his dog lay beside him. But no sooner did he close his eyes than he was wakened by the barking of the dog. Indeed, he heard someone shuffling about in the room, and since Cienzo was courageous and bold, he seized his sword and began to slash about in the darkness. But as soon as he realized that nobody was there and that he was just hitting the wind, he turned to lay down again. However, after a while he felt that his feet were slowly being pulled, and he grabbed his sword once more, got up, and said, "Hold on there! Now I'm really getting annoyed. It's useless to

---

8. Pennino, sometimes Pendino, was a popular district of Naples. Basile was also playing on the word *pennone*, which was a large red standard or pennant with the royal arms. It was carried by a minister of the tribunal on horseback when he accompanied the condemned to the scaffold. All the following references are to places in Naples (Piazza Larga, Piazza dell'Olmo, Lancieri, Porto, Gelsi, Pertuso, Loggia, Lavinaro, Mercato, Chiaia) and together they make up an ironic panegyric to the city.
9. The efficacy of Catalan soliders using lances was notorious in Naples.
1. The cabbage soup was filled with ham, lard, and other ingredients and was regarded as the masterpiece of Neapolitan cooking and praised by numerous local writers.
2. A village near Sessa Aurunca, near Naples.

play these foolish pranks! Let me see you if you have any courage, and stop your antics, for you've met your match!"

After he said these words, he heard an enormous laugh followed by a deep voice that said, "Come down here so I can tell you who I am."

Cienzo was not really alarmed and responded, "Wait, I'll be right there." And he moved forward and groped about until he found a ladder that led into a cellar. As soon as he descended, he found a brightly lit lantern and three deformed creatures who were lamenting bitterly and crying, "My beautiful treasure, now I've lost you!"

Upon seeing this, Cienzo also began to lament and join in the conversation. After he moaned a good while—after the moon had cut the wedge of heaven in half with the hatchet[3] of her rays—the three men who had been groaning said to him, "Go and take the treasure which has been destined for you alone, and make sure you know how to take good care of it."

Once they said this, they vanished on the spot just like that notorious fellow[4] from below who often makes himself invisible. Meanwhile, when Cienzo saw the sun through a hole, he wanted to climb out of the cellar, but he could not find the ladder. Therefore, he began to shout so loudly that the owner of the tower, who had gone to piss between the broken-down walls, heard him. After he asked Cienzo what he was doing down there and then heard what had happened to him, he fetched a ladder, and when he descended, he found a great treasure, half of which he offered to Cienzo. But the young man did not want any of it, climbed out of the cellar, took his dog, and continued his journey.

Soon Cienzo arrived at a lonely and desolate forest that was so gloomy it made you want to writhe. There he found a fairy on the bank of a river which wriggled through the fields and leapt over stones to please the shadows in which it was in love. This fairy was surrounded by a bunch of highwaymen who wanted to deprive her of her honor. When Cienzo saw the evil intention of these rogues, he took his sword and cut them down. The fairy, who watched his deed, overwhelmed him with compliments and invited him to her nearby palace, where she wanted to reward him for his service. But Cienzo said, "Please, it was nothing. Many thanks. I'll take the reward some other time. Right now I'm in a hurry to take care of some important business."

So he took his leave, and after he had journeyed for some time, he came upon the palace of a king so completely draped in black that it saddened one's heart to see it. When Cienzo asked why the palace was covered in black, he was told that a dragon with seven heads had appeared in this country, and it was the most terrible monster that had ever been seen in the world. It had the crest of a cock, the heart of a cat, eyes of fire, mouths of racehorses, wings of a bat, claws of a bear, and a tail of a serpent. "Now, this dragon," he was told, "has swallowed a Christian every day, and he has continued to do this up until today when it is now the

---

3. Allusion to a forbidden weapon used in a game played by two people. The purpose of the game was to slice a bar into two equal parts, and the players took turns at slicing the bars. The player who did not split the bar had the right of first choice of the divided parts.
4. The devil.

turn of Menechella, who is the king's daughter. This is why everyone is tearing out their hair and stamping their feet on the ground in the palace. Indeed, the most beautiful creature in this country is to be swallowed and devoured by this ghastly beast."

After Cienzo heard this, he stepped aside and watched Menechella approaching in a mourning procession. She was accompanied by the ladies of the court and all the women of the country, who were wringing their hands, tearing out their hair by the handful, and weeping about the unfortunate destiny of the poor princess. "Who would have ever thought," they cried out, "that this unfortunate maiden would have to abandon her rich life in the body of this evil beast? Who would have said that this beautiful goldfinch would have to live her life in the cage of the dragon's belly? Who would have thought that this beautiful silkworm would have to leave the seed of the thread of her life in a black cocoon?"

And while they were saying this, the dragon came out of its cave. Oh, mamma mia! How horrible it was! The sun hid itself in the middle of some clouds out of fright. The sky darkened, The hearts of all the people became mummified, and they abandoned the princess. There was such a trembling that a pig's bristle would not have been able to have penetrated them.

When Cienzo saw this, he grabbed his sword, plunged ahead, and sliced off one of the heads of the beast. But the dragon rubbed its neck on a certain herb nearby, and his head was immediately reattached just like a lizard when it reattaches its tail. When Cienzo saw this, he said, "He who fails to grab the initiative will amount to nothing." So he clenched his teeth and gave the dragon such a violent blow with his sword that all seven heads were cut off at once, and they jumped from the dragon's head like chickens from a frying pan. Then he tore out the tongues and put them into his knapsack, while he threw the heads as far away from the body as he could so that they would not join themselves to the necks as they had previously done. Then he took a handful of the herb that the dragon had used to attach his head to his body and put this in his pocket. Finally, he sent Menechella home to her father, and he went to rest in a tavern.

When the king saw his daughter, it is impossible to imagine how happy he was. Upon learning how she had been rescued, he issued a proclamation that whoever had killed the dragon could come and wed his daughter. As soon as a shrewd peasant heard this, he collected the heads of the dragon, took them to the king, and said, "Thanks to my deed, your daughter Menechella was saved! These are the hands that have saved the country from great destruction! Here are the heads that are proof of my valor. Now you must honor your promise."

When the king heard all this, he lifted the crown from his head and placed it on the rogue's noggin, which resembled the head of a robber on top of a pole.[5] Soon the news of this event spread throughout the country until it reached the ears of Cienzo, who said to himself, "I'm quite the

5. The heads of outlaws or criminals were often exhibited in a cage placed on top of a column or hung from a gate. The heads were frequently crowned with gilded pasteboard that the men wore as they were taken to be executed.

blunderer. I grabbed fortune by the hair of her head, and I've let her slip through my hands. One man wanted to give me half a treasure, but I didn't take any account of it, just like a German would pass up a glass of fresh water.[6] The fairy wanted to reward me in her palace, and I paid no more attention to her than an ass would to music. And now I've been summoned by the crown, and I'm standing here like a crazy woman who keeps staring at her spindle, and I let a despicable boor take advantage of me, swindle me, and steal my beautiful winning card."

As he said this, he took a pen from an inkstand, spread some paper, and began to write: "To the most beautiful jewel of all women, Menechella, daughter of King Perditesta. By the grace of Soleone,[7] I saved your life, and now I've heard that another man has taken the credit for my work and boasts that he performed the deed. Since you were present at the event, you can convince your father of the truth and not allow another to obtain the place that I deserve. If you do this, your graciousness as princess will be duly recognized and the strong hand of Skandberg[8] will be rewarded. In closing, I kiss your delicate hands. From the Inn of the Urinate, today Sunday."

After writing this letter and sealing it with some chewed bread, he put it in the mouth of his dog and said, "Run and bring it to the king's daughter, and do not give it to anyone else. It must be delivered only into the hands of the silver-faced maiden."

The dog ran so fast to the royal palace that it seemed to be flying. It climbed the stairs and found the king, who was still holding court with the peasant. When the king saw the dog with the letter in its mouth, he ordered his servants to take the letter. But the dog would not let anyone have it and jumped into Menechella's lap, where it deposited the letter into her hands. Then Menechella rose from her seat, made a curtsy to the king, and gave him the letter to read. Once the king read it, he ordered the dog to be followed to see where it would go and to make its master appear before him in the palace. So two courtiers followed the dog and arrived at the inn, where they found Cienzo. After delivering the king's message, they brought him back to the palace, and when Cienzo stood before his majesty, the king asked him why he boasted of having killed the dragon when the seven heads had been brought by the man who was sitting next to him with the crown on his head.

"This scoundrel deserves to be condemned by royal decree and hung," replied Cienzo. "He should not be wearing the crown, for he has tried brazenly to pull the wool over your eyes. To prove that I'm telling the truth and have saved your daughter and not this billy goat, have the heads to the dragon brought here. Then you will see that none of them can testify in his behalf because they are without tongues. And to convince you of this, I have brought them with me so they can bring about justice."

As he was speaking, he showed the tongues, and the scoundrel was

---

6. The Germans were generally described in Italian sayings as being exceedingly fond of wine.
7. A popular folk expression that appeals to the sun in Leo (lion), the astrological sign.
8. The name given to the national Albanian hero Giorgio Castriota (1403–1468), very popular in the Neapolitan tradition because of the aid that he gave to the king of Naples, Ferrante I of Aragon, in defense of his throne.

petrified and did not know what had happened to him, especially when Menechella pointed to Cienzo and said, "This is the man who saved me! You miserable dog," she said as she turned to the peasant, "what have you done to me?"

When the king heard this, he took the crown from the blockhead and put it on Cienzo's head, and he decided to send the peasant to prison. But Cienzo asked the king to pardon him, repaying his wickedness with kindness. Then the tables were prepared for a royal feast, and when it was finished, Cienzo and Menechella retired to a beautiful bed with fragrant linen, where Cienzo, raising the trophies of his victory over the dragon, entered the citadel of love with a triumphant air.

When morning came—when the sun brandishing the sword of light with two hands in the midst of the stars called out: *Back, you rabble!*— Cienzo got dressed next to a window and saw a beautiful lady at the opposite window. Then he turned to Menechella and said, "Who's the beautiful neighbor who lives in the house across the way?"

"What do you want with that busybody?" his wife replied. "Can't you take your eyes off her? Perhaps your mood has changed? Hasn't your appetite been satisfied enough? Isn't the meat that you have at home good enough for you?"

Cienzo did not say a word and hung his head in shame like the cat caught in the act. He pretended that he had to go out and do something. When he left the palace, however, he went straight to the house of the beautiful lady, who was truly an exquisite morsel just like a tender cheese or a sugar cake. She never moved the pupils of her eyes without producing a tremor of love in the heart of some man, and she never opened the cauldron of her lips without scalding some soul. She never moved her feet without giving a good kick to the back of some poor man who was at the end of the rope of his hope. Besides all these enchanting charms, she also had the power to bewitch whenever she desired, to bind, to fasten, to entangle, to captivate, and to entwine men with her hair, just as she did with Cienzo, who as soon as he set foot in her house was ensnared and tethered like a young colt.

In the meantime, Meo, who was his younger brother, had not received any news from him, and therefore, he wished to go and search for him. After asking permission from his father, he received the other magic horse and dog. So Meo began his journey and arrived one evening at the tower where Cienzo had been, and the owner mistook him for his brother and treated him with great kindness. He also wanted to give him money, but Meo did not want any, for he realized that he was receiving such attention because his brother must have been there. Consequently, he was hopeful of finding him again.

As soon as the moon, the enemy of poets, turned its back on the sun, he set out again and arrived at the fairy's palace. She, too, believed he was Cienzo and overwhelmed him with kindness and kept saying, "You're always welcome here, my young man, for you saved my life."

Meo thanked her for so much kindness and replied, "Excuse me if I do not stay, but I am in a hurry. Farewell until I return."

Happy at having found traces of his brother, he continued on his way

until he arrived at the palace of the king the exact same morning in which
Cienzo had been ensnared by the hair of the deceitful fairy. He entered
the palace and was received with great honor by the servants and was
embraced with great affection by Menechella, who said, "Welcome, my
husband! Morning has gone, and the evening has arrived. When all the
birds go to eat, the owl still sleeps. How come you've been gone so long,
my Cienzo? How can you stay away so long from your Menechella? You
dragged me from the dragon's mouth and threw me into the gullet of
suspicion because your eyes are not always mirroring mine!"

Meo was very astute and realized right away that Menechella was his
brother's wife. So he turned his attention to her and excused himself for
being late. After he embraced her, they went to dine together. And when
the moon appeared like a broody hen calling the stars to peck up the dew,
they went to sleep, and Meo, who respected his brother, divided the sheets
by giving one to her and taking one for himself so that he would not have
to touch his sister-in-law. When Menechella saw this new device, however,
she became gloomy and said to him with the face of a stepmother, "Good
gracious! What's going on here? What game are we playing? What's the
joke? Are we quarreling peasants who have to set boundaries? Are we
enemy armies so we have to dig a trench between us? Are we wild horses
and need a wooden fence to keep us apart?"

Meo, who could count straight up to thirteen, said, "Don't be upset
with me, my darling, but with the doctor who wanted to purge me and
has ordered me to follow a special regime. Moreover, I'm also tired from
hunting and really have returned with my tail between my legs."

Menechella, who was still somewhat wet behind her ears, swallowed
this yarn and went to sleep. But—as night, banished by the sun, was helped
by time to make itself scarce—Meo dressed himself at the same window
where his brother had stood and saw the same lady who had captivated
Cienzo. Since he was also attracted to her, he said to Menechella, "Who
is that coquette leaning out the window?"

And Menechella, very cross, responded, "So, you're continuing again!
If things are like this, then everything's clear! Even yesterday you made
me itch to give that wretch a smack, and I'm afraid that the tongue goes
where the tooth hurts. But you ought to show me some respect. After all,
I am the daughter of the king, and every turd has its own odor! So, there
was a reason last night why you pretended to be such an imperial eagle,[9]
shoulder to shoulder. There was a reason why you retired with your income. Now I understand you: dieting in my bed allows you to feast in
other people's homes. But if I see this, I'll do something crazy and send
chips flying through the air!"

Meo, who had eaten bread from many ovens, calmed her with kind
words. He told her and swore that he would not change his home for the
most beautiful courtesan in the world and that she was the most precious
thing in his heart. Consoled by these words, Menechella went to her
dressing room attended by her ladies to have the wrinkles on her face
smoothed over, to have her hair dressed, to tint her eyelashes, to color her

9. Allusion to the two-headed eagle of the Hapsburg arms.

cheeks, and to deck herself out so that she would appear more beautiful to the man she thought was her husband.

In the meantime, Meo suspected from listening to Menechella's words that Cienzo was in the beautiful lady's home. So he took his dog with him and left the palace and entered the house across the way. No sooner did he arrive than she said, "Hair of my head, bind him!"

But Meo was ready and replied at once, "Dog of mine, eat this woman up!"

And the dog dashed at her and swallowed her down as if she were the yolk of an egg. Then Meo explored the house and found his brother, who was under a spell. So he took two of the dog's hairs and passed them over him. Then Cienzo awoke as if from a deep sleep, whereupon Meo told him all that had happened on his journey up to the very end, including the palace and how he had slept with Menechella because she had mistaken him for Cienzo. He wanted to continue telling him about the divided sheets, but Cienzo, tempted by the devil, grabbed a sword and cut off his head as if it were a cucumber. Since Menechella had heard all the noise, she ran into the house and saw that Cienzo had killed a man who looked just like him. Immediately, she asked why he had done this, and Cienzo said, "Ask yourself, you who have slept with my brother, thinking it was me. This is why I killed him."

"Look at what you've done! Many people are slain by mistake," Menechella said. "You're living proof of that! You really don't deserve your brother because, when he found himself in the same bed with me, he separated the sheets with great modesty, and each one of us slept alone!"

Cienzo sensed that he had done something wrong and had acted too rashly due to a hasty judgment, and he repented. Indeed, he began to scratch his face, but then he remembered the herb used by the dragon, and he rubbed it on his brother's neck. No sooner did he do this than the head was reattached to the neck, and his brother was alive and well. Cienzo embraced him with great joy and asked his pardon for acting so hastily and for having sent him out of this world because he had misunderstood the situation. Then they all went back to the palace together and sent for the brothers' father, Antoniello, and their entire family. Indeed, Antoniello came and became a dear friend to the king, and he saw in his son's life the living proof of the proverb

It is the crooked ship that goes straight to port.

JACOB AND WILHELM GRIMM

The Two Brothers†

Once upon a time there were two brothers, one rich and the other poor. The rich brother was a goldsmith and evil-hearted. The poor brother

† Jacob and Wilhelm Grimm, "The Two Brothers"—"Die zwei Brüder" (1857), No. 60 in *Kinder- und Hausmärchen. Gesammelt durch die Brüder Grimm* (Göttingen: Dieterich, 1857).

earned a living by making brooms and was kind and honest. He had two sons who were twins, and they looked so much alike that they seemed like two peas in a pod. Every now and then the twins went to their rich uncle's house and were given the leftovers to eat.

One day the poor man happened to be in the forest gathering brushwood when he saw a bird pure as gold and more beautiful than any bird he had ever seen. So he picked up a stone, threw it at the bird, and was lucky enough to hit it. However, only a single golden feather dropped to the ground, and the bird flew off. The man took the feather and brought it to his brother, who examined it and said, "It's pure gold," and he gave him a lot of money for it.

The next day the poor man climbed a birch tree to cut a few branches. Just then the same bird flew out, and after the man searched a while, he found a nest with an egg in it. The egg was made of gold, and he took it home with him. Afterward, he showed it to his brother, who once again said, "It's pure gold," and he gave him what it was worth. Finally, the goldsmith said, "I'd like to have the bird itself."

The poor man went into the forest for a third time and saw the golden bird perched on a tree. He took a stone, knocked the bird down, and brought it to his brother, who gave him a huge amount of gold for it.

"Now I'll be able to take care of things," the poor man thought, and went home with a happy feeling.

The goldsmith was clever and cunning and knew exactly what kind of bird it was. He called his wife and said, "Roast this golden bird for me, and make sure that none of it gets lost! I want to eat it all by myself."

Indeed, the bird was not an ordinary creature. It possessed a miraculous power, and whoever ate its heart and liver would find a gold piece under his pillow every morning. The goldsmith's wife prepared the bird, put it on a spit, and let it roast. Now it happened that, while the bird was roasting over the fire, the wife had to leave the kitchen to take care of something else. Just then the two sons of the poor broom maker ran in, stopped in front of the spit, and turned it a few times. When two little pieces dropped from the bird into the pan, one of the boys said, "Let's eat the two little pieces. I'm so hungry, and nobody's bound to notice it."

So they ate two pieces, but the wife returned and saw that they had eaten something.

"What did you eat?" she asked.

"A couple of pieces that fell out of the bird," they answered.

"That must have been the heart and liver," the wife said, and she was horrified. She quickly slaughtered a cock, took out its heart and liver, and put them in the golden bird so her husband would not miss them and get angry. When the golden bird was done, she carried it to the goldsmith, who consumed it all by himself until nothing remained. However, when he reached under his pillow the next morning expecting to find a gold piece, there was nothing there out of the ordinary.

In the meantime, the two boys did not realize how fortunate they had been. When they got up the next morning, something fell on the floor making a tingling sound. Upon looking to see what made the sound, they found two gold pieces, which they brought to their father. He was amazed and said, "How can that have happened?"

When they found another two the following morning and continued to find two every morning thereafter, the father went to his brother and told him the strange story. The goldsmith knew immediately how everything had happened and that the children had eaten the heart and liver of the golden bird. Since he was envious and hard-hearted, he sought revenge and said to the father, "Your children are in league with the devil. Don't take the gold, and don't let them stay in your house any longer. The devil's got them in his power and can also bring about your own ruin."

The father was afraid of the devil, and even though it was painful for him, he led the twins out into the forest and with a sad heart left them there. The two boys wandered about the forest and searched for the way back home, but they repeatedly lost their way and could not find it. Finally, they encountered a huntsman, who asked, "Where do you come from?"

"We're the poor broom maker's sons," they answered and told him that their father no longer wanted them in his house because every morning there was a gold piece under each one of their pillows.

"Well," said the huntsman, "there's nothing really terrible about that as long as you remain good and upright and don't become lazy."

The kind man took a liking to the boys, and since he did not have any sons himself, he took them home with him and said, "I shall be your father and raise you."

So they learned all about hunting from him, and he saved the gold pieces that they found every morning when they got up in case they were to need them in the future. One day, when they were finally grown-up, their foster father took them into the forest and said, "Today you're to be tested in shooting to determine whether I can release you from your apprenticeship and pronounce you full-fledged huntsmen."

They went with him to the raised blind and waited for a long time, but no game appeared. Then the huntsman looked above him, and when he saw some wild geese flying by in a triangle formation, he said to one of the brothers, "Now shoot one from each corner."

He did it and passed the test. Soon after, more geese came flying by in the number two formation. The huntsman told the other brother likewise to shoot one goose from each corner, and he also passed the test. Now the foster father said, "You have completed your apprenticeship, and I pronounce you both full-fledged huntsmen."

At that point the two brothers went into the forest together, discussed their situation, and decided on a plan of action. When they sat down in the evening to eat, they said to their foster father, "We're not going to touch the food or take a single bite until you grant us one request."

"What is your request?"

"Since we're now full-fledged huntsmen," they replied, "we must also prove ourselves. So we want your permission to leave and travel about the world."

"You speak like real huntsmen," said the old man joyfully. "Your desire is my very own wish. Set out on your journey. I'm sure everything will go well for you."

In a merry mood, they now ate and drank together. When the appointed day for their departure arrived, their foster father gave each of them a good gun and a dog, and since he had saved their gold pieces, he had each take as many of them as he desired. Then the old man accompanied them part of the way, and when they were about to take their leave, he gave them a shiny knife and said, "If you should ever separate, stick this knife into a tree at the crossroad. Then if one of you comes back, he can see how his absent brother is doing, for the side of the blade facing the direction he took will rust if he's dying but will stay bright as long as he's alive."

The two brothers set out on their journey and came to a huge forest that was impossible to cross in one day. So they spent the night there and ate what they had in their hunting pouches. On the second day they continued their journey but still did not reach the end of the forest. Now they had nothing more to eat, and one of them said, "We must shoot something, or we'll starve."

He loaded his gun and looked around. When he saw an old hare running nearby, he took aim, but the hare cried out:

> "Dear huntsman, if you let me live,
> two of my young to you I'll give."

Then the hare jumped into the bushes and brought back two young ones. The little creatures were so frisky and charming that the huntsmen did not have the heart to kill them. So they kept them, and the little hares followed at their heals. Soon after, a fox came slinking by, and they were about to shoot it when the fox cried out:

> "Dear huntsmen, if you let me live,
> two of my young to you I'll give."

He also brought two young ones, and the huntsmen had no desire to kill the little foxes. They gave them to the hares for company, and the animals continued to follow the huntsmen. Soon a wolf came out of the thicket, and just as the huntsmen took aim at him, he cried out:

> "Dear huntsman, if you let me live,
> two of my young to you I'll give."

The huntsman added the two young wolf cubs to the other animals, and they all followed the two young men. Then a bear came, and he had no desire to have his days of wandering ended, so he cried out:

> "Dear huntsman, if you let me live,
> two of my young to you I'll give."

Two young bear cubs joined the other animals, and now there were eight of them. Finally, who should come along shaking his mane but the lion! And he also cried out:

> "Dear huntsman, if you let me live,
> two of my young to you I'll give."

He, too, fetched two of his young cubs, and now the huntsmen had two lions, two bears, two wolves, and two hares who followed and served them.

Meanwhile, however, the brothers were still starving, and they said to the foxes, "Listen, you tricky creatures, get us something to eat. After all, we know you're crafty and cunning."

"There's a village not far from here," they answered. "In the past we were able to get many a chicken there. We'll show you the way."

The brothers went to the village, bought themselves something to eat, and had their animals fed. Then they continued on their way. Since the foxes were very familiar with the region and knew exactly where the chicken yards were, they could guide the huntsmen to the right spots. For a while they traveled about, but they could not find jobs that would enable them all to remain together. Eventually, the brothers said, "There's no other way. We'll have to separate."

They divided the animals so that each had a lion, a bear, a wolf, a fox, and a hare. Then they said farewell, took a vow of brotherly love unto death, and stuck the knife that their foster father had given them into a tree. Then one went to the east, the other to the west.

Soon the younger brother arrived with his animals in a city that was completely draped in black crepe. He went into an inn and asked the innkeeper whether he could put up his animals there. The innkeeper gave him a stable that had a hole in the wall. The hare crawled through it and fetched himself a head of cabbage; the fox fetched a hen, and after he had eaten the hen, he went and got a cock as well. However, the wolf, the bear, and the lion were too big to slip through the hole. So the innkeeper took them to a meadow where a cow was grazing, and there they could eat their fill. After the huntsman had taken care of his animals, he asked the innkeeper why the city was draped in black crepe.

"Because our king's only daughter will perish tomorrow," said the innkeeper.

"Is she that sick?" asked the huntsman.

"No," the innkeeper replied. "She's hale and healthy, but she must die nonetheless."

"But why?" asked the huntsman.

"Outside the city there's a dragon living on a high mountain," said the innkeeper. "Every year he has demanded a pure virgin and threatened to lay waste to our entire country if he did not receive one. Now, after many years, all the maidens have been given to him, and there's no one left but the king's daughter. Despite that, the dragon shows no mercy. She must be delivered to him, and that's to be done tomorrow."

"Why doesn't someone slay the dragon?" asked the huntsman.

"Ah," responded the innkeeper, "many, many knights have tried, but they've all lost their lives. The king's promised to give his daughter's hand in marriage to the man who slays the dragon, and this man would also inherit the kingdom after the king's death."

The huntsman said nothing more, but the next morning he took his animals and climbed the dragon's mountain with them. At the top was a small church, and there were three full goblets on the altar with a piece of paper next to them that said, "Whoever drinks these goblets shall become the strongest man on earth and shall be able to wield the sword that lies buried beneath the threshold of the door." The huntsman did not drink the goblets but went outside and searched for the sword in the ground, which he was not able to move. Then he went back inside, drank the goblets, and was now strong enough to pull out the sword and wield it with ease. When the hour came for the maiden to be delivered to the dragon, the king, the marshal, and the entire court accompanied her. From afar she could see the huntsman standing on top of the dragon's mountain. She thought it was the dragon standing there and waiting for her, and she did not want to go. But finally she had to begin the painful journey; the whole kingdom would have been lost otherwise. The king and his court returned home in full mourning, but the king's marshal was assigned to stay there and watch everything from a distance.

When the king's daughter reached the top of the mountain, it was not the dragon standing there but the young huntsman, who comforted her and told her he wanted to save her. He led her into the church and locked her inside. Shortly after, with a great roar, the seven-headed dragon descended on the spot. When he caught sight of the huntsman, he was astounded and said, "What do you think you're doing on this mountain?"

"I've come to fight you," replied the huntsman.

"Many a knight has lost his life here," declared the dragon. "I'll soon finish you off as well!" Then flames shot from his seven jaws.

The flames were intended to set fire to the dry grass, and the dragon hoped to smother the huntsman with the fire and smoke, but the huntsman's animals came running to his aid and stamped the fire out. The dragon then attacked the huntsman, but the man swung his sword so swiftly that it sang in the air and cut off three of the dragon's heads. Now the dragon was really furious. He rose up, began shooting flames directly at the huntsman, and got set to dive down at him. However, the huntsman once again lashed out with his sword and cut off three more heads. The monster sank to the ground and was exhausted. Nevertheless, he tried to charge the huntsman again, but the young man used his last bit of strength to cut off the dragon's tail. Then, since the huntsman could not continue fighting, he called his animals, who tore the dragon to pieces. When the battle was over, the huntsman opened the church and found the princess lying on the ground. She had fainted from fear and fright during the combat. So he carried her outside, where she regained consciousness and opened her eyes. When he showed her the dragon's devastated body and told her she was now free, the princess was overjoyed and said, "Now you will be my very dear husband, for my father promised my hand in marriage to the man who slew the dragon."

The princess then took off her coral necklace and divided it among the animals as little collars to reward them, and the lion received the golden clasp to the necklace. However, her handkerchief with her name embroidered on it went to the huntsman, who proceeded to cut out the tongues of the seven dragon's heads, wrap them in the handkerchief, and put them away carefully.

When that was done, he felt so tired and exhausted from the fire and battle that he said to the maiden, "We're both so drained and overcome with fatigue, perhaps it would be best if we slept a while."

The princess agreed, and they lay down on the ground. Then the huntsman said to the lion, "I want you to keep watch so that no one surprises us in our sleep."

When the huntsman and the princess fell asleep, the lion lay down beside them to keep watch, but he too was tired from the battle. So he called the bear and said, "Lie down beside me. I've got to sleep a little. If anything happens, wake me up."

The bear lay down next to the lion, but he was too tired. So he called the wolf and said, "Lie down beside me. I've got to sleep a little. If anything happens, wake me up."

The wolf lay down next to the bear, but he too was tired. So he called the fox and said, "Lie down beside me. I've got to sleep a little. If anything happens, wake me up."

The fox lay down beside the wolf, but he too was tired. So he called the hare and said, "Lie down beside me. I've got to sleep a little. If anything happens, wake me up."

The hare lay down next to the wolf, but he was tired. However, there was no one left whom he could call on to help him, and soon he fell asleep. Once that happened, they were all asleep and sleeping soundly, the princess, the huntsman, the lion, the bear, the wolf, the fox, and the hare.

Meanwhile, the marshal, who had been assigned the task of watching everything from a distance, did not see the dragon fly off. So, when everything was calm on the mountain, he summoned his courage and climbed the mountain, where he found the dragon lying on the ground and torn to pieces. Not far from there were the king's daughter and the huntsman with his animals. They were all sound asleep, and since the marshal was a wicked and godless man, he took his sword and cut off the huntsman's head. Next he lifted the maiden in his arms and carried her down the mountain. When she awoke, she was petrified, but the marshal said, "I've got you in my power, so you'd better say that it was I who slew the dragon."

"I can't do that," she replied. "It was a huntsman with his animals. They were the ones who did it."

Then the marshal drew out his sword and threatened to kill her if she did not obey him. Thus he forced her to promise that she would do as he commanded. Afterward, he brought her to the king, who was overcome by joy upon seeing his dear daughter alive again when he had thought she had already been torn to pieces by the dragon.

"I've slain the dragon and saved the maiden and the whole kingdom," said the marshal. "Therefore, I claim your daughter for my wife as you promised."

"Is what he says true?" the king asked the maiden.

"Oh, yes," she answered. "It must probably be true, but I insist that the wedding be held in a year and a day and not before." Indeed, she hoped to hear from her dear huntsman by then.

Meanwhile, the animals were still lying asleep beside their dead master on the dragon's mountain. Then a bumblebee came and landed on the hare's nose, but the hare brushed it aside again and continued to sleep. Finally, it came a third time and stung him on the nose so that he woke up. As soon as the hare was awake, he woke the fox, and the fox woke the wolf, who woke the bear, and the bear woke the lion. And when the lion saw that the maiden was gone and his master was dead, he began roaring dreadfully loud and cried out, "Who did that? Bear, why didn't you wake me?"

The bear asked the wolf, "Why didn't you wake me?"

And the wolf asked the fox, "Why didn't you wake me?"

The fox asked the hare, "Why didn't you wake me?"

The poor hare was the only one who did not know what to answer, and the guilt fell on his shoulders. They wanted to pounce on him, but he pleaded with them and said, "Don't kill me! I'll bring our master back to life. I know a mountain where a root grows that cures and heals all kinds of sicknesses and wounds. You only have to stick the root in the sick person's mouth. But it takes two hundred hours to get to the mountain."

"Well, you've got to dash there and back and fetch the root within twenty-four hours," declared the lion.

The hare raced away, and within twenty-four hours he was back with the root. The lion put the huntsman's head back in position, and the hare stuck the root in his mouth. All at once, everything functioned again: his heartbeat and life returned to him. When the huntsman awoke, he was distressed not to find the maiden by his side. "She must have gone away while I was asleep to get rid of me," he thought.

In his great haste, the lion had put his master's head on backward. However, the huntsman was so preoccupied by his sad thoughts about the king's daughter that he did not notice it. Only at noon, when he wanted to eat something, did he realize that his head was on backward. Since he was at a loss to understand how that had happened, he asked the animals. The lion told him that they had all been so tired that they had fallen asleep and that upon awakening they had found him dead with his head cut off. The hare had then fetched the root of life, but the lion in his haste had held his head the wrong way. After saying all that, the lion wanted to correct his mistake. So he tore off the head of the huntsman, turned it around, and the hare healed him again with the root. Nevertheless, the huntsman remained in a gloomy mood. He traveled about the world and made his animals dance before crowds of people. After a year had passed, he happened to return to the same city where he had rescued the king's daughter from the dragon, and this time the city was draped completely in crimson.

"What does all that mean?" he asked the innkeeper. "A year ago the city was draped in black. What's the meaning of the crimson?"

"A year ago the princess was supposed to have been delivered to the dragon," answered the innkeeper. "But the marshal fought and slew the dragon. Tomorrow his wedding with the princess will be celebrated. When the city was in mourning, it was draped in black a year ago, and now, in its joy, the city is draped in crimson."

At noon on the next day, when the wedding was to take place, the huntsman said to the innkeeper, "Do you think, innkeeper, that it might be possible for me to eat bread from the king's table right here at your place?"

"Well," said the innkeeper, "I'd be willing to bet a hundred gold pieces that you can't possibly do that."

The huntsman accepted the wager and put up a pouch with one hundred gold pieces to match the innkeeper's money. Then he called the hare and said, "Go there, my speedster, and fetch me some of the bread fit for a king."

Now, the little hare was the weakest of the animals, and it was impossible for him to pass this task on to any of the others. So, he had to perform it by himself. "My God," he thought, "if I amble down the street by myself, the butchers' dogs will soon be after me!" And it happened just as he thought it would. The dogs chased after him and wanted to tear his good fur to shreds. However, you should have seen the hare run! He sped to the castle and took refuge in the sentry box without the guard noticing him. When the dogs came and tried to get him out, the soldier would take no nonsense from them and hit them with the butt of his rifle so they ran away yelping and howling. When the hare saw the coast was clear, he ran into the palace and straight to the king's daughter. Then he sat down under her chair and scratched her foot.

"Get out of here!" she said, for she thought it was her dog. The hare scratched her foot a second time, and she repeated, "Get out of here!" for she thought it was her dog. But the hare did not let himself be deterred and scratched a third time. Then she looked down and recognized the hare by his coral collar. So she picked him up, carried him into her chamber, and said, "My dear hare, what do you want?"

"My master, the dragonslayer, is here," he answered, "and he's sent me to fetch some bread fit for a king."

The princess was filled with joy. She summoned the baker and ordered him to bring her a loaf of bread fit for a king.

"But the baker must also carry it for me," said the hare. "Otherwise, the butchers' dogs will harm me."

The baker carried the bread up to the door of the inn for the hare. Then the hare stood up on his hind legs, took the loaf of bread in his front paws, and brought it to his master.

"You see, innkeeper," the huntsman said, "the hundred gold pieces are mine."

The innkeeper was astonished, but the huntsman continued to speak. "Well, innkeeper, I've got the bread, but now I want some of the king's roast as well."

"I'd like to see that," said the innkeeper, but he did not want to bet anymore.

The huntsman called the fox and said, "Little fox, go there and fetch me a roast fit for a king."

The red fox knew the shortcuts better than the hare, and he went through holes and around corners without the dogs catching sight of him. Once at the castle he sat under the chair of the princess and scratched her foot. When she looked down, she recognized the fox by his coral collar, carried him into her chamber, and said, "My dear fox, what do you want?"

"My master, the dragonslayer, is here," he answered, "and he's sent me to ask for a roast fit for a king."

She summoned the cook and ordered him to prepare a roast fit for a king and to carry it for the fox up to the door of the inn. There the fox took the dish from him, wagged his tail to brush off the flies that had settled on the roast, and brought it to his master.

"You see, innkeeper," said the huntsman, "bread and meat are here, but now I want to have some vegetables fit for a king." So he called the wolf and said, "Dear wolf, go straight to the castle and fetch me some vegetables fit for a king."

So the wolf went straight to the castle, for he was afraid of no one, and when he reached the princess, he tugged at her dress from behind so that she had to turn around. She recognized him by his coral collar, took him into her chamber, and said, "My dear wolf, what do you want?"

"My master, the dragonslayer, is here," he answered, "and he's sent me to ask for some vegetables fit for a king."

She summoned the cook, who had to prepare some vegetables fit for a king, and she ordered him to carry them for the wolf to the door of the inn. There the wolf took the dish and brought it to his master.

"You see, innkeeper, now I've got some bread, meat, and vegetables, but I also want some sweets fit for a king." So he called the bear and said, "Dear bear, since you're fond of licking sweet things, go and fetch me sweets fit for a king."

So the bear trotted off to the castle, and everyone cleared out of his way. When he reached the sentry box, the guards barred his way with their guns and did not want to let him enter the royal castle. But he stood up on his hind legs and slapped the guards left and right, forcing them to fall apart. Then he went straight to the king's daughter, stood behind her, and growled softly. She looked behind her, recognized the bear, and told him to go with her into her chamber.

"My dear bear," she said, "what do you want?"

"My master, the dragonslayer, is here," he answered, "and I'm to ask for some sweets fit for a king."

She summoned the confectioner and ordered him to make sweets fit for a king and to carry them up to the door for the bear. There the bear licked the sugarplums that had rolled off, stood on his hind legs, and brought them to his master.

"You see, innkeeper," said the huntsman, "now I've got bread, meat, vegetables, and sweets, but I also want to drink wine fit for a king." So he called his lion and said, "Dear lion, since you like to indulge yourself and get tipsy, go and fetch me some wine fit for a king."

When the lion strode down the street, the people fled from him, and when he came to the guards, they wanted to bar his way, but he only had to let out a roar, and they all dashed away. The lion then went to the royal chamber and knocked on the door with his tail. The king's daughter came out and recognized him by the golden clasp of her necklace. She invited him inside and said, "My dear lion, what do you want?"

"My master, the dragonslayer, is here, and I'm to ask for some wine fit for a king."

She summoned the cupbearer and ordered him to give the lion some wine fit for a king.

"I want to go with him to make sure that I get the right kind," said the lion.

He went downstairs with the cupbearer, and when they were below, the cupbearer was about to draw some ordinary wine that the king's servants usually draw when the lion said, "Stop! I want to taste the wine first." He drew half a measure for himself and drank it down. "Now," he said, "that's not the right kind."

The cupbearer glared at him and was cross. Then he went on and was about to offer him wine from another barrel reserved for the king's marshal.

"Stop!" said the lion. "I want to taste the wine first." He drew half a measure for himself and drank it down. "It's better than the first, but it's still not the right kind."

Now the cupbearer was angry and said, "How can a stupid beast understand anything about wine?"

But the lion gave him such a blow behind the ears that he fell hard on the ground. When he got up, he did not utter a word. Instead, he led the lion into a special small cellar where the king's wine was kept solely for his private use. The lion drew half a measure for himself, tasted the wine, and said, "That's the right kind," and he ordered the cupbearer to fill six bottles with the wine. Then they climbed back upstairs, and when the lion left the cellar and stepped outside, he began to stagger back and forth. Since he was a bit drunk, the cupbearer had to carry the wine up to the door for him. There the lion took the basket in his mouth and carried it to his master.

"You see, innkeeper," the huntsman said, "I've got bread, meat, vegetables, sweets, and wine fit for a king, and now I want to dine with my animals."

He sat down at the table, ate and drank, and shared his meal with the hare, the fox, the wolf, the bear, and the lion. The huntsman was in good spirits, for he realized that the king's daughter was fond of him. After the meal was over, he said, "Innkeeper, now that I've eaten and drunk just like a king, I'm going to the king's palace, where I shall marry his daughter."

"How are you going to do that?" asked the innkeeper. "She already has a bridegroom, and the wedding is to be celebrated today."

The huntsman took out the handkerchief that the king's daughter had given him on the dragon's mountain, and it still contained the seven tongues of the monster.

"All I need," he said, "is what I'm holding here in my hand."

The innkeeper looked at the handkerchief and said, "Even if I believe everything else, I can't believe this, and I'm willing to stake my house and everything I own on it."

Then the huntsman took out a pouch with a thousand gold pieces in it, put the pouch on the table, and said, "I'll match your house and property with this."

Meanwhile, the king and his daughter were sitting at the royal table, and the king asked her, "What did all those wild animals want who kept running in and out of the castle?"

"I'm not allowed to say," she answered. "But you'd do well to send for the master of those animals."

So the king sent a servant to the inn and had the stranger invited to the palace. The servant arrived just as the huntsman had concluded the bet with the innkeeper.

"You see, innkeeper," said the huntsman, "the king's sent a servant to invite me to his palace, but I refuse to go the way I am." Then he turned to the servant and said, "Please be so kind to tell the king to send me royal garments, a coach with six horses, and servants to attend me."

When the king heard the answer, he said to his daughter, "What should I do?"

"You'd do well to honor his request and send for him," she said.

So the king sent royal garments, a coach with six horses, and servants to attend him. When the huntsman saw them coming, he said, "You see, innkeeper, my request has been honored," and he dressed himself in the royal garments, took the handkerchief with the seven tongues of the dragon, and drove to the palace. When the king saw him coming, he said to his daughter, "How shall I receive him?"

"You'd do well to go and meet him," she answered.

The king went to meet him and led him up to the palace, while the animals followed behind. The king showed the young huntsman to a place next to him and his daughter. The seat on the other side was taken by the marshal, who did not recognize the huntsman. Just then the seven heads of the dragon were carried out for display, and the king said, "Since the marshal cut off the seven heads of the dragon, I shall give him my daughter to be his wife today."

Then the huntsman stood up, opened the seven jaws, and said, "Where are the seven tongues of the dragon?"

Upon hearing that, the marshal was so frightened that he turned pale and did not know what to reply. Finally, he said, "Dragons have no tongues."

"Liars should have no tongues," said the huntsman. "But the dragon's tongues can prove who the real dragonslayer is."

Then he unwrapped the handkerchief to reveal the seven tongues. When he stuck each tongue back into the mouth where it belonged, each fit perfectly. Next he took the handkerchief, on which the name of the king's daughter had been embroidered, showed it to the maiden and asked her to point out which man she had given it to.

"To the man who slew the dragon," she replied.

Then he called his animals, took off their coral collars and the golden clasp from the lion, and asked the maiden to tell whose articles they were.

"The necklace and the golden clasp were mine," she answered, "but I divided the necklace among the animals who had helped in slaying the dragon."

Then the huntsman said, "After I was weary from the fight, I lay down to rest and sleep, and the marshal came and cut off my head. Then he carried off the king's daughter and pretended it was he who had slain the dragon. To prove that he's been lying, I have brought the tongues, the handkerchief, and the necklace." And then he told how his animals had healed him through a miraculous root and how he had traveled around for a year and had finally come back to the spot where he had learned about the treachery of the marshal, thanks to the innkeeper's story.

"Is it true that this man killed the dragon?" the king asked his daughter.

"Yes," she replied, "it's true. Now I may reveal the marshal's shameful crime, for it has been exposed without my speaking about it. You see, the marshal made me take a vow of silence, and that's why I had insisted upon waiting a year and a day before celebrating the wedding."

The king summoned twelve councillors and ordered them to pronounce judgment on the marshal, and they sentenced him to be torn apart by four oxen. Thus the marshal was executed, and the king gave his daughter to the huntsman and named him viceroy over the entire kingdom. The wedding was celebrated with great rejoicing, and the young king sent for his father and foster father and overwhelmed them with fine gifts. Nor did he forget the innkeeper. He, too, was sent for, and the young king said, "You see, innkeeper, I've married the king's daughter, and your house and property are mine."

"Yes," he said, "by right everything is yours."

But the young king said, "No. I intend to act with mercy, and you shall keep your house and property. Moreover, I want you to retain the one thousand gold pieces as a gift."

Now, the young king and young queen were in good spirits and had a happy life together. He often went out hunting since that gave him pleasure, and his faithful animals always accompanied him. Nearby was a forest, however, that was said to be enchanted. Whoever entered did not return very easily. But the young king had a great desire to go hunting in it, and he kept bothering the old king until he obtained permission to go there. So he rode out with a large retinue, and when he came to the forest, he saw a doe as white as snow and said to his men, "Wait here until I return. I want to hunt that beautiful doe."

He rode into the forest in pursuit of the doe, and only his animals followed him. His men stopped and waited until evening, but he did not come back. So they rode home and said to the young queen, "The young king went hunting after a beautiful white doe in the enchanted forest and did not return."

Upon hearing this she became very worried about him. Meanwhile, he had kept riding after the beautiful doe, never managing to overtake it. Each time he thought he had the doe within his aim, the animal would dart away and run off into the distance, until finally it vanished altogether. When the huntsman realized that he had gone deep into the forest, he took out his horn and blew it. There was no response, however, for his men could not hear it. After night began to fall, he saw that he could not get home that day. So, intending to spend the night there, he dismounted and built a fire near a tree. While he was sitting by the fire and his animals were lying beside him, he thought he heard a human voice. He looked around but did not see anyone. Soon after, he heard a groan that sounded as though it were coming from above. When he looked up, he saw an old woman sitting in the tree moaning and groaning.

"*Oooh! Oooh!* I'm freezing," she cried.

"Climb down," he said, "and warm yourself if you're freezing."

"No, your animals will bite me," she replied.

"They won't harm you, granny," he answered. "Just come down."

However, she was a witch and said, "I'm going to throw down a switch from the tree. If you hit them on their backs with it, they won't hurt me."

Then she threw the switch to him, and when he hit them with it, they immediately lay still and were turned to stone. When the witch was safe from the animals, she jumped down, touched him with a switch, and he was turned to stone. Thereupon she laughed and dragged him and the animals to a pit where there were already many more such stones.

When the young king did not come back at all, the young queen's worries and fears increased. Now, it happened that just at this time the other brother, who had gone to the east when the twins had separated, came to this kingdom. He had been looking for employment and had found none. Therefore, he had been traveling about and having his animals dance in front of crowds of people. Eventually, it occurred to him to take a look at the knife they had stuck into the tree upon their separation to see how his brother was doing. When he got there, his brother's side of the knife was half rusty and half bright. At once he became alarmed and thought, "My brother must have met with a great misfortune. But perhaps I can still save him, for half the knife is bright."

He went off to the west with his animals, and when he arrived at the city gate, the guards approached him and asked whether they should announce his arrival to his wife, for the young queen had been upset for several days about his absence and had been afraid that he had been killed in the enchanted forest. The guards, of course, believed that he was none other than the young king himself because he resembled him so much and also had the wild animals following him. The brother realized that they had mistaken him for his brother and thought, "It's best that I pretend to be him. Then I'll be able to rescue him more easily."

So he let himself be conducted by the guards into the palace and was jubilantly received. The young queen thought for sure he was her husband and asked him why he had stayed away so long.

"I lost my way in the forest and could not find the way back any sooner," he said.

In the evening he was taken to the royal bed, but he placed a double-edged sword between himself and the young queen. She did not know what to make of it, but she did not dare to ask.

He remained there a few days and inquired into everything concerning the enchanted forest. Finally, he said, "I must go hunting there once more."

The king and the young queen tried to talk him out of it, but he insisted and set out with a large retinue. When he reached the forest, he went through everything his brother had experienced. He saw a white doe and said to his men, "Stay here and wait until I return." He rode into the forest, and his animals followed after him. But he could not overtake the doe and went so deep into the forest that he had to spend the night there. After he had built a fire, he heard a groan above him.

"*Oooh! Oooh!* I'm freezing!"

He looked up and saw the same witch sitting in the tree.

"If you're freezing, climb down, granny," he said, "and warm yourself."

"No, your animals will bite me," she replied.

"They won't harm you," he said.

"I'm going to throw you a switch from the tree," she said. "If you hit them with it, they won't hurt me."

When the huntsman heard that, he did not trust the old woman and said, "I won't hit my animals. Either you come down, or I'll come get you!"

"Do you really think you can do something?" she cried. "There's no way you can harm me!"

But he answered, "If you don't come down, I'll shoot you down."

"Go ahead and shoot," she said. "I'm not afraid of your bullets."

So he took aim and fired at her, but the witch was protected against lead bullets, and she let out a shrill laugh. "You'll never hit me!" she exclaimed.

But the huntsman knew just what to do: he took off three silver buttons from his jacket and loaded his gun with them, for her witchcraft was powerless against them. When he now pulled the trigger, she fell from the tree with a scream. Then he put his foot on her and said, "You old witch, if you don't tell me right away where my brother is, I'll pick you up with both my hands and throw you into the fire."

Since she was terribly frightened, she begged for mercy and said, "He's been turned into stone along with his animals, and they're lying in a pit."

He forced her to go with him, and there he threatened her by saying, "You old monkey, now you'd better restore life to my brother and all the other creatures that are lying there, or I'll throw you into the fire!"

She took a switch and touched the stones, and his brother and the animals came back to life again, and many others as well, such as merchants, artisans, and shepherds, who arose, thanked the huntsman for their release, and went home. Meanwhile, when the twin brothers saw each other again, they kissed each other, and their hearts were full of joy. Then they grabbed the witch, tied her up, and put her into the fire. After she had been burned, the forest opened up all by itself and became bright and clear so that one could see the royal castle, which was about a three-hour walk from there.

Now the two brothers headed toward home together and along the way told each other about their adventures. When the younger one said that he was viceroy for the whole kingdom, the other said, "I realized that right away. When I came into the city, I was mistaken for you and shown every royal honor. The young queen thought I was her husband, and I had to sleep in your bed."

When the other heard that, he became so jealous that he drew his sword and cut off his brother's head. However, when he saw his brother lying there and his red blood flowing, he was overcome by remorse.

"My brother rescued me!" he exclaimed. "And in return I've killed him!"

He uttered cries of grief, and then his hare came and offered to fetch the root of life. The hare dashed off and returned at just the right time. The dead brother was brought back to life and did not even notice his wound. When they continued on their journey, the younger brother said, "You look like me, and your animals are like mine. Let's enter from opposite gates and go to the king's chamber at the same time from opposite directions."

So they took separate paths, and simultaneously the guards came from opposite gates to the old king and announced that the young king had returned with his animals from the hunt.

"It's not possible," the king said. "The gates are an hour's walk apart."

Just then, however, the brothers arrived at the palace courtyard from two sides and came upstairs.

"Tell me," the king said to his daughter, "which one is your husband. They look exactly alike, and I can't tell them apart."

The young queen was very upset and could not tell them apart either. Finally, she remembered the necklace that she had given the animals. She searched and found the golden clasp on the lion, and then she exclaimed happily, "The man whom this lion follows is my husband!"

Then the young king laughed and said, "Yes, you've found the right one."

Now they all sat down at the table and ate and drank, and they were in a merry mood. That night, when the young king went to bed, his wife asked him, "Why did you always place a double-edged sword in our bed these last few nights? I thought you might want to slay me."

Then he realized how faithful his brother had been.

Shrewd Cats

This tale is perhaps one of the most popular in the world, and Straparola's version is the first known literary text. It was probably based on an oral tale, but there is no clear evidence of this. However, given the hundreds if not thousands of oral versions of this tale that have circulated in the Mediterranean region, the Orient, Europe, and North America, it is more than likely that Straparola was familiar with a folktale. Cats are not always the magic helpers in the literary and oral versions; there are foxes, jackals, fairies, dead people, and trees that help a commoner rise in society to become rich and a nobleman. The theme of "clothes make the person" is very important, and the helper is sometimes depicted as the protagonist's alter ego. What is most interesting in the versions of Straparola and Basile is that the cats are female, and that Constantino and Caglioso need feminine intelligence and guidance to rise in society. Moreover, the end of Basile's narrative reveals how ungrateful the peasant is, and how the cat rejects his society. Perrault changes the sex of the cat, and he is clearly the protagonist of the tale as master cat, who uses his wits not only to help his master and to survive but to climb the social ladder himself. Perrault's tale was reprinted and spread through chapbooks during the eighteenth century and had a profound influence on most of the literary and oral versions that circulated during that time and later. Ludwig Tieck, the gifted German Romantic writer, used Perrault's version as the basis of his play *Der gestiefelte Kater* (*Puss in Boots*, 1797), and his play had, in turn, an effect on Wilhelm Grimm, who published his version of this tale in the 1812 edition of *Children's and Household Tales*. However, he removed it in the second edition because it was so closely related to Perrault's French text.

GIOVAN FRANCESCO STRAPAROLA

Constantino Fortunato†

There was once a woman named Soriana, who lived in Bohemia. She was extremely poor and had three sons called Dusolino, Tesifone, and Constantino Fortunato. Soriana had nothing of any value in the way of household goods except for three things, and these were a kneading trough that women used in making bread, a board necessary for preparing pastry, and a cat. Feeling the heavy weight of her years burdening her, Soriana saw that death was approaching and consequently made her last will and

† Giovan Francesco Straparola, "Constantino Fortunato"—"Soriana viene a morte, e lascia tre figliuoli: Dusolino, Tesifone e Constantino Fortunato; il quale per virtù d'una gatta acquista un potente regno" (1553), in *Le piacevoli notti*, 2 vols. (Venice: Comin da Trino, 1550/53).

testament, leaving the kneading trough to her eldest son, Dusolino, the pastry board to Tesifone, and the cat to Constantino.

When the mother was dead and buried, the neighbors in the vicinity would at times borrow the kneading trough and at other times the pastry board, depending on their needs. Since they knew that the young men were very poor, they gave them a cake by way of payment, but Dusolino and Tesifone ate it by themselves and gave nothing to Constantino, the youngest brother. And, if Constantino chanced to ask them to give him a little of the cake, they would answer by telling him to go to his cat, who would certainly let him have what he wanted. As a result, poor Constantino and his cat suffered a great deal.

Now it just so happened that this cat was a fairy in disguise, and one day, feeling very sorry for him and a great deal of anger toward his two brothers because of their cruel treatment of him, she said, "Constantino, don't be depressed. I'll take good care of you and find enough provisions for the two of us."

Thereupon, the cat left the house and went into the fields, where she lay down and pretended to be asleep. Indeed, she was so clever that an unsuspecting hare came too close to where she was lying and soon found itself dead in her paws. Then the cat carried the hare to the king's palace, and upon meeting some of the courtiers who were standing around, she told them that she would like to speak to the king.

When the king heard that a cat had requested to have an audience with him, he commanded them to bring the cat into his presence and asked her what she wanted. The cat replied that Constantino, her master, had sent his majesty a hare as a present and begged him to accept the present. With these words, the cat gave the hare to the king, who was pleased to accept it, asking at the same time who this Constantino might be. The cat responded that he was a young man who was the most virtuous and handsome man in the world. Upon hearing this report, the king gave the cat a kind welcome and ordered his servants to bring the cat food and drink of the very best quality. When she had eaten and drunk, the cat deftly filled the bag in which she had brought the hare with all sorts of good provisions, when no one was looking that way. After she took leave of the king, she carried the spoils back to Constantino.

When the two brothers saw Constantino delighting in the food and drink, they asked him to let them have a share, but he paid them back in their own coin and refused to give them a morsel. As a result, the brothers were tormented by envy and wished they had Constantino's good fortune.

Though Constantino was a good-looking young man, he had suffered so much deprivation and distress that his face was rough and covered with blotches that caused him great discomfort. So, one day the cat took him down to the river, washed him and licked him carefully with her tongue from head to foot. She tended him so well that in a few days he was cured of his ailment. The cat still went on carrying presents to the royal palace in the fashion already described, and by those means she managed to provide for Constantino.

But after a while the cat began to find these journeys to and from the palace somewhat tiring. Moreover, she feared that the king's courtiers might become impatient about all of this. So she said to Constantino, "My master, if you will only do what I tell you to do, you will soon find yourself a rich man."

"And how will you manage this?" asked Constantino.

"Come with me," the cat answered, "and don't trouble yourself about anything. I have a plan for making a rich man out of you which cannot fail."

Thereupon the cat and Constantino went to a spot on the bank of the river which was near the king's palace. As soon as they were there, the cat told Constantino to take off his clothes and jump into the river. Then she began to cry and shout in a loud voice, "Help, help, run, run. My lord Constantino is drowning!"

It happened that the king heard the cat's cries, and bearing in mind what great benefits he had received from Constantino, he immediately sent some of his servants to the rescue. When Constantino had been dragged out of the water and dressed by the attendants in attractive garments, he was led into the presence of the king, who gave him a hearty welcome and inquired how he had fallen into the water. But Constantino, due to his agitation, did not know what to reply. So, the cat, who always kept to his side, answered in his stead, "I must tell you, oh king, that some robbers, who had learned through a spy that my master was taking a large amount of jewels and wanted to offer them to you as a present, ambushed him and robbed him of his treasure. Then they threw him into the river to murder him, but thanks to the help of these gentlemen, he has escaped death."

Upon hearing this report, the king gave orders that Constantino was to enjoy the best of treatment, and seeing that he was sturdy and handsome, and convinced that he was very rich, he made up his mind to give him his daughter, Elisetta, as his wife and to endow her with a rich dowry of gold and jewels and sumptuous raiment.

When the wedding ceremony was completed and the festivities were at an end, the king told his servants to load ten mules with gold and five others with the richest garments, and he sent the bride, who was accompanied by a large entourage of people, to her husband's house. When Constantino saw himself so highly honored and loaded with riches, he was greatly troubled because he did not know where to take his bride. Therefore, he asked the cat for her advice.

"Don't be troubled by this matter," said the cat. "I shall provide for everything."

So, as they all set out on their merry journey, the cat left the others and rode on rapidly in advance, and after she had left the company a long way behind her, she came upon some cavaliers whom she addressed as follows:

"Alas! You poor fellows, what are you doing here? Get away from here as quickly as you can. There is a large group of armed men coming along this road, and they'll surely attack and destroy you. See, they are now quite near. Listen to the noise of their horses."

The cavaliers were overcome with fear and said to the cat, "What shall we do?"

"It will be best," she responded, "to do as I tell you. If they should ask you who your master is, you must answer boldly that you serve the Lord Constantino, and no one will harm you."

Then the cat left them, and after riding further, she came upon great flocks of sheep and herds of cattle, and she told the same story and gave the same advice to the shepherds and cowherds who were in charge of the animals. Then, going on still further, she gave the same advice to whomever she happened to meet.

As the cavalcade of the princess passed through the countryside, the gentlemen who were accompanying her asked the cavaliers whom they met what the name of their lord was. Then they asked the herdsmen who the owner of the sheep and oxen was, and the answer given by all was that they served Lord Constantino. As a result, the gentlemen of the escort said to the bridegroom: "So, Lord Constantino, it appears that we are entering your dominions."

Constantino nodded his head to affirm this, and he answered all their queries in the same way so that the company believed him to be enormously rich because of this. In the meantime the cat had ridden on and had come to a fair and stately castle which was guarded by a very weak garrison of guards, whom the cat addressed in the following words: "My good men, my good men, what's it to you? I'm sure you're aware that you're about to be devastated!"

"What are you talking about?" demanded the guards.

"Why, before another hour passes," replied the cat, "your place will be besieged by a great company of soldiers who will cut you in pieces. Don't you already hear the neighing of the horses? Just look at the dust in the air? Unless you desire to perish, take my advice, and you'll be safe from all danger. When the company arrives and you are asked who owns this castle, you must say that it belongs to your Lord Constantino Fortunato."

And when the time came, the guards gave the answer just as the cat had told them to do. The noble escort of the bride had arrived at the stately castle, and certain gentlemen had asked the guards the name of the lord of the castle. They heard the answer that it was Lord Constantino Fortunato. And when the whole company had entered the castle, they were honorably lodged there.

Now the lord of this castle was a certain Signore Valentino, a very brave soldier who only a few days ago had left his castle to bring back the woman whom he had recently married. But as luck would have it, he had an accident on the road somewhat before he came to the place where his beloved wife was residing, and he immediately met with his death. So Constantino Fortunato retained the lordship of Valentino's castle.

Not long after this, Morando, king of Bohemia, died, and by acclamation the people chose Constantino as their king, seeing that he had married Elisetta, the late king's daughter, to whom the kingdom belonged by right of succession. And by these means Constantino rose from poverty or even beggary to become a powerful king, and he lived a long time with Elisetta, his wife, leaving their children to inherit his kingdom.

GIAMBATTISTA BASILE

Cagliuso†

There once lived in my city of Naples an old man who was totally impoverished. He was a wretched beggar without a penny to his name and nothing in his pockets. Indeed, he went about as naked as a louse. When the time came for him to empty the sacks of life, he called his two sons, Oraziello and Cagliuso, to his side and said, "I have been summoned according to the contract that I have with nature to pay my debt. Believe me, if you are Christians, I would be most pleased to leave this Mandracchio¹ of trouble, this pigsty of suffering, if it were not for the thought that I am ruined and leaving you poor like the church of Santa Chiara,² insecure at the five roads of Melito,³ without a penny, cleaned out like a barber's basin, flighty like servants, and dry as a plum stone. You don't even have as much as a fly can carry away on its foot, and even if you were to run a hundred miles, I'm sure you wouldn't manage to obtain a single cent. It is all because fate has brought me to the place where the three dogs shit,⁴ and I have nothing left except my life. And, as you see me, you can write about me because, as you know, I have always yawned for hunger and made crosses⁵ and have gone to bed without candles. Nevertheless, I would like to leave you with some sign of my love at my death. Oraziello, you who are my firstborn, take that sieve which is hanging on the wall. It will be your means to earn a living. And you, Cagliuso, you who are my pup, you are to take the cat. And may both of you remember your father."

Upon saying this, he burst into tears, and after a little while, the father said, "Good-bye. It is night."

Oraziello buried his father with help from charity, and then he took the sieve and went to work here and there. And the more he used his sieve, the more he earned. Meanwhile, Cagliuso took the cat with him and said, "Look at what a poor legacy my father has left me! I have nothing to eat for myself, and now I'll have to feed two mouths. What a misfortune this inheritance is! It would have been better not to have received it."

When the cat, heard this, she said, "You're lamenting too much. You have more luck than you realize because I'm capable of making you rich if I put my mind to it."

As soon as Cagliuso heard this, he thanked her catship, stroked her back three or four times, and placed himself ardently in her charge. Now, the

---

† Giambattista Basile, "Cagliuso"—"Caglioso" (1634), *Quarto passatempo della seconda giornata* in *Lo cunto de li cunti overo Lo trattenemiento de peccerille*, De Gian Alessio Abbattutis, 5 vols. (Naples: Ottavio Beltrano, 1634–36). There is a good likelihood that the name stems from the word *quaglio* (*caglio*), which has different meanings but is related to the term *furbastro*, meaning "clever" or "cunning."
1. A very poor district of Naples.
2. Church and convent in Naples which housed an order of nuns who served the poor.
3. A small place between Naples and Aversa.
4. Common expression used to indicate a destitute condition.
5. According to a popular custom, one placed a finger on one's mouth when one yawned to cross it and thus prevent evil spirits from entering the body.

cat felt sorry for the unfortunate Cagliuso, and every morning, when the sun fishes for the shadows of night with its bait of light on its golden hook, she made her way to the beach at Chiaja or the Fish Rock[6] and, as soon as she spotted some large mullet or fine goldfish, the cat would catch it and carry it to the king, saying, "My Lord Cagliuso, a humble slave of your highness, sends this fish to pay homage to you and says, 'There is no gift large enough for a great lord.'"

The king's face broke into a pleasant smile, one only reserved for those who bring presents, and he answered, "Tell this lord, whom I do not know, that I thank him very much."

Another time the cat ran to a place known for hunting. It was in the marshes near Astroni,[7] and when the hunters shot an oriole, blackbird, or titmouse, she would pick them up and take them to the king with the same message. She repeated this trick many times until, one morning, the king said to her, "I feel myself greatly obliged to your Lord Cagliuso, and I should like to make his acquaintance so that I may repay the affection that he has shown me."

"Lord Cagliuso's desire," the cat responded, "is to place his life and blood at the service of your throne. Tomorrow, without fail, when the sun will have set fire to the stubbles in the fields, he will come to pay homage to you."

When morning came, however, the cat went to the king and said, "Sire, the Lord Cagliuso sends his apologies. He cannot come because last night some of his servants made off with everything and left him without even a shirt to his back."

Upon hearing this, the king immediately ordered some clothes and linen to be taken from his wardrobe and had them sent to Cagliuso. Within two hours, Cagliuso arrived at the palace accompanied by the cat, and once there, the king gave him a thousand compliments and asked him to sit down beside him. Then the king had a splendid banquet prepared for Cagliuso. While they were eating, however, Cagliuso kept turning to the cat and saying, "Oh, pussy, take care that those four rags of mine don't get lost."

"Be silent," replied the cat. "Hold your tongue, and don't talk about those miserable things."

Now the king was prompted to ask whether the cat desired anything, and she responded that she would like to have a small lemon. So the king sent his servants at once to the garden and ordered them to fetch a whole basketful. Shortly after, Cagliuso turned again to pipe the same tune about his rags and tatters, and the cat told him again to shut his mouth. In turn, the king inquired once more whether the cat wanted anything. But this time she had an excuse ready to cover up Cagliuso's poor manners.

At last, after they had finished eating and had chatted at length about this and that, Cagliuso took his leave. Meanwhile, the cat remained with the king, describing the valor, ability, and judgment of Cagliuso and, above all, the great wealth that he had on his estates in Rome and around Lom-

6. Where wholesalers purchased fish from fishermen after they had returned with their catch.
7. Old hunting grounds, marshlands, in the eastern part of Naples not far from Lake Agnano.

bardy. Indeed, the cat maintained, it was because of this that Cagliuso deserved to marry the daughter of a king. In response, the king inquired how much Cagliuso owned, and the cat answered that it was impossible to give an account of the chattel, properties, and household goods of this rich lord because he himself did not know how much he possessed. But if the king wanted to obtain information for himself, he could send some of his people around the region with her. Then they would be able to ascertain that there was no one in the world as rich as her master.

The king immediately called some of his trusty followers and ordered them to follow the cat and gather detailed information about Cagliuso. But the cat used the excuse that she had to find refreshments for them along the road and went out before them. No sooner was she outside the kingdom than she ran ahead. Wherever she encountered flocks of sheep, herds of cows, troops of horses, and droves of pigs, she would say to the shepherds and keepers, "Ho there, pay attention! There is a band of robbers who are ransacking everything they come across in this district. If you want to escape their fury and protect your homes and property, you must say that everything belongs to Lord Cagliuso, and they won't touch a hair on your heads."

And she continued to say the same thing at all the farms that she passed so that wherever the king's people went, they heard the same music like bagpipes. Indeed, everyone kept telling them that all they saw belonged to the Lord Cagliuso. Exhausted from asking the same question over and over again, they returned to the king and told him about the immense riches of Lord Cagliuso. When the king heard all this, he promised a good reward to the cat if she could manage to bring off this marriage. In turn, the cat pretended to shuttle back and forth between the king and Cagliuso until she, at last, arranged the affair.

When Cagliuso came to court, the king gave him a large dowry and his daughter in marriage. After a month of festivities, Cagliuso told the king that he wanted to take his bride to his territories. The king accompanied them to the borders. Then they went onward toward Lombardy, where Cagliuso acted upon the cat's advice and bought land and property and became a baron.

Seeing himself now so tremendously rich, Cagliuso could not thank the cat enough, saying that he owed his life and his greatness to her because of her services and that the tricks of a cat had brought him greater benefits than the cleverness of his father. Therefore, she could do whatever she thought and pleased with his things and life. He promised that, when she died, even in a hundred years, he would have her embalmed and placed in a golden cage and kept in his own room so as to have the memory of her always before his eyes.

Sensing that this was a boast, the cat pretended three days later to be dead, and she lay stretched out at full length on the ground. When Cagliuso's wife saw her, she cried out, "Oh my husband, what a great misfortune! The cat has died."

"May she take all bad luck with her," Cagliuso answered. "Better her than us!"

"What shall we do with her?" asked the wife.

"Take hold of a paw, and we'll throw her out the window," he said.

When the cat heard this gratitude, something that she had never imagined, she started screaming, "So, this is the reward that I get for the lice I have cleaned from your back! These are the thousand thanks for ridding you of the rags from your back that were only fit to hang spindles on! This is what I get in exchange for having worked like a busy spider to clothe you so elegantly and to feed you when you were famished! You miserable creature! You're nothing but a tattered, ragged, threadbare, deceitful wretch! Such is the reward of those who wash the head of an ass! Get out of my sight, and may a curse be on everything that I have done for you because you're not even worth spitting on! What a fine golden cage you've prepared for me! What a beautiful grave you've assigned me! I go and serve you, work and sweat, only to receive this reward! Oh, woe is he who boils his pot for the hope of others! That philosopher put it well when he said, 'Whoever goes to bed an ass, wakes up an ass.' In short, whoever works the most should expect the least. But good words and bad deeds deceive the wise and the foolish."

Upon saying this and shaking her head, the cat departed, and no matter how Cagliuso tried to pacify her, calling out to her with sweet lungs[8] of humility, there was no way the cat would come back. Instead, she kept on running and repeating:

God keep you from all those rich men turned poor
And from those beggars turned rich who have too much more.

CHARLES PERRAULT

The Master Cat;
or,
Puss in Boots[†]

A miller left his three sons all his worldly possessions, which amounted to nothing more than his mill, his ass, and his cat. The division was made quickly. Neither notary nor attorney was summoned or requested, for they would have charged too much and consumed all of the meager patrimony. The eldest received the mill; the second son, the ass; the youngest got just the cat, and naturally, he was upset at inheriting such a poor portion.

"My brothers can now earn an honest living as partners," he said, "but, as for me, I'll surely die of hunger once I have eaten my cat and made a muff of his skin."

The cat, who had heard these words but pretended not to have been

8. Basile uses the expression *polmone*, which was food for cats. In the Naples of his time, the *polmone* was sold by street vendors in the morning, and the cats would come running and collect when they heard the vendor calling out to his customers.

† Charles Perrault, "The Master Cat; or Puss in Boots"—"Le maître chat; ou, Le chat botté" (1697), in *Histoires ou contes du temps passé* (Paris: Claude Barbin, 1697). Perrault uses the French familiar term *maître*, which referred to someone whose social standing was not very high. At the same time, he is playing with the word and using it in the sense of a teacher as master who instructs a young man and determines the events in the story.

listening, said to him with a sober and serious air, "Don't trouble yourself, master. All you have to do is to give me a pouch and have a pair of boots made for me to go into the bushes. Then you'll see that your share of the inheritance is not as bad as you believe."

Although the cat's master did not place much stock in this assertion, he had seen the cat play such cunning tricks as catching rats and mice by hanging himself upside down by the heels or lying in the flour as if he were dead that he was willing to give the cat a chance to help him.

As soon as the cat had what he had asked for, he boldly pulled on his boots, and after hanging the pouch around his neck, he took the strings in his forepaws and went to a warren where there were a great number of rabbits. He put some bran and lettuce into his pouch and, stretching himself out as if he were dead, he waited for some young rabbit, little versed in the wiles of the world, to come and hunt for something to eat in the pouch. He had hardly laid down when his expectations were met. A young scatterbrain of a rabbit entered the pouch, and master cat instantly pulled the strings, caught it, and killed it without mercy. Proud of his prey, he went to the king's palace and demanded an audience. He was ushered up to the royal apartment, and upon entering, he made a low bow to the king and said, "Sire, here's a rabbit from the warren of my lord, the Marquis de Carabas (such was the name[1] he had dreamed up for his master). He has instructed me to present it to you on his behalf."

"Tell your master," replied the king, "that I thank him and that he's given me great pleasure."

Another time the cat went and hid in a wheatfield, keeping the mouth of the pouch open as he always did, and when two partridges entered it, he pulled the strings and caught them both. Then he went directly to the king and presented them to him just as he had done with the rabbit from the warren. The king was equally pleased by the two partridges and gave the cat a small token for his efforts.

During the next two or three months, the cat continued every now and then to carry presents of game from his master to the king. One day, when he knew the king was going to take a drive on the banks of the river with his daughter, the most beautiful princess in the world, he said to his master, "If you follow my advice, your fortune will be made. Just go and bathe in the river that I'll point out to you, and leave the rest to me."

The Marquis de Carabas did as his cat had advised him, without knowing what good would come of it. While he was bathing, the king passed by, and the cat began to shout with all his might, "Help! Help! My lord, the Marquis de Carabas, is drowning!"

At this cry, the king stuck his head out of the coach window and, recognizing the cat who had often brought game to him, he ordered his guards to rush to the help of the Marquis de Carabas. While they were pulling the poor marquis out of the river, the cat approached the royal coach

1. The derivation of this name is not certain. It was known through legend that there was a fool in Alexandria who was referred to as Carabas by the inhabitants of the city, and they mocked him by treating him as if he were a king. The Turkish word *Carabag* designates a beautiful place in the mountains where the sultans and princes would spend the summer months. Perrault might have come upon this term in the *Dictionaire oriental*, edited by Barthélemy d'Herbelot during this time.

and told the king that some robbers had come and carried off his master's clothes while he was bathing, even though he had shouted "Thieves!" as loud as he could. But in truth the rascal had hidden his master's clothes himself under a large rock. The king immediately ordered the officers of his wardrobe to go and fetch one of his finest suits for the Marquis de Carabas. The king embraced him a thousand times, and since the fine clothes given to the marquis brought out his good looks (for he was handsome and well-built), the king's daughter found him much to her liking. And no sooner had the Marquis de Carabas cast two or three respectful and rather tender glances at her than she fell in love with him. Then the king invited him to get into the coach and to accompany them on their drive.

Delighted to see that his scheme was succeeding, the cat ran on ahead and soon came upon some peasants who were mowing a field.

"Listen, my good people," he said. "You who are mowing here, if you don't tell the king that the field you are mowing belongs to my lord, the Marquis de Carabas, you'll all be cut into tiny pieces like minced meat!"

Indeed, the king did not fail to ask the mowers whose field it was they were mowing.

"It belongs to our lord, the Marquis de Carabas," they said altogether, for the cat's threat had frightened them.

"You can see, sire," rejoined the marquis, "it's a field that yields an abundant crop every year."

Master cat, who kept ahead of the party, came upon some reapers and said to them, "Listen, my good people, you who are reaping, if you don't say that all this wheat belongs to my lord, the Marquis de Carabas, you'll all be cut into tiny pieces like minced meat!"

A moment later the king passed by and wished to know who owned all the wheatfields that he saw there.

"Our lord, the Marquis de Carabas," responded the reapers, and the king again rejoiced about this with the marquis.

Running ahead of the coach, the cat uttered the same threat to all whom he encountered, and the king was astonished at the great wealth of the Marquis de Carabas. At last master cat arrived at a beautiful castle owned by an ogre, the richest ever known, for all the lands through which the king had driven belonged to the lord of this castle. The cat took care to inquire who the ogre was and what his powers were. Then he requested to speak with him, saying that he could not pass so near his castle without doing himself the honor of paying his respects to him. The ogre received him as civilly as an ogre can and asked him to sit down.

"I've been told," said the cat, "that you possess the power of changing yourself into all sorts of animals. For instance, it has been said that you can transform yourself into a lion or an elephant."

"It's true," said the ogre brusquely, "and to prove it, watch me become a lion."

The cat was so frightened at seeing a lion standing before him that he immediately scampered up into the gutters of the roof, and not without difficulty and danger, for his boots were not made to walk on tiles. Upon noticing that the ogre shortly resumed his previous form, the cat descended and admitted that he had been terribly frightened.

Puss in Boots. From *Les Contes de Perrault*, ca. 1890.

"I've also been told," said the cat, "but I can't believe it, that you've got the power to assume the form of the smallest of animals. For instance, they say that you can change yourself into a rat or mouse. I confess that it seems utterly impossible to me."

"Impossible!" replied the ogre. "Just watch!"

And immediately he changed himself into a mouse which began to run about the floor. No sooner did the cat catch sight of it than he pounced on it and devoured it.

In the meantime, the king saw the ogre's beautiful castle from the road and desired to enter it. The cat heard the noise of the coach rolling over the drawbridge and ran to meet it.

"Your majesty," he said to the king, "welcome to the castle of my lord, the Marquis de Carabas."

"What!" exclaimed the king. "Does this castle also belong to you, Marquis? Nothing could be finer than this courtyard and all these buildings surrounding it. If you please, let us look at the inside of it."

The marquis gave his hand to the young princess, and they followed the king, who led the way upstairs. When they entered a grand hall, they found a magnificent banquet, which the ogre had ordered to be prepared for some friends who were to have visited him that very day. But they did not presume to enter when they found the king was there. The king was now just as much delighted by the accomplishments of the Marquis de Carabas as his daughter, who doted on him, and realizing how wealthy he was, he said to him, after having drunk five or six cups of wine, "The choice is entirely yours, Marquis, whether or not you want to become my son-in-law."

After making several low bows, the marquis accepted the honor the king had offered him, and on that very same day, he married the princess. In turn, the cat became a great lord and never again ran after mice, except for his amusement.

Moral

Although the advantage may be great
When one inherits a grand estate
Passed on from father to son,
Young men often find their industry,
Combined with ingenuity,
Leads to greater prosperity.

Another Moral

Though the miller's son did quickly gain
The heart of a princess whose eyes he tamed,
As he charmed her in a natural way,
It's due to good manners, looks, and dress
That inspired her deepest tenderness
And always help to win the day.

JACOB AND WILHELM GRIMM

Puss in Boots†

A miller had three sons, a mill, a donkey, and a cat. The sons had to grind grain, the donkey had to haul the grain and carry away the flour, and the cat had to catch the mice. When the miller died, the three sons divided the inheritance: the oldest received the mill, the second the donkey, and nothing was left for the third but the cat. This made the youngest sad, and he said to himself, "I certainly got the worst part of the bargain. My oldest brother can grind wheat, and my second brother can ride on his donkey. But what can I do with the cat? Once I make a pair of gloves out of his fur, it's all over."

The cat, who had understood all he had said, began to speak: "Listen, there's no need to kill me when all you'll get will be a pair of poor gloves from my fur. Have some boots made for me instead. Then I'll be able to go out, mix with people, and help you before you know it."

The miller's son was surprised the cat could speak like that, but since the shoemaker happened to be walking by, he called him inside and had him fit the cat for a pair of boots. When the boots were finished, the cat put them on. After that he took a sack, filled the bottom with grains of wheat, and attached a piece of cord to the top, which he could pull to close it. Then he slung the sack over his back and walked out the door on two legs like a human being.

At that time there was a king ruling the country, and he liked to eat partridges. However, there was a grave situation because no one had been able to catch a single partridge. The whole forest was full of them, but they frightened so easily that none of the huntsmen had been able to get near them. The cat knew this and thought he could do much better than the huntsmen. When he entered the forest, he opened the sack, spread the grains of wheat on the ground, placed the cord in the grass, and strung it out behind a hedge. Then he crawled in back of the hedge, hid himself, and lay in wait. Soon the partridges came running, found the wheat, and hopped into the sack, one after the other. When a good number were inside, the cat pulled the cord. Once the sack was closed tight, he ran over to it and wrung their necks. Then he slung the sack over his back and went straight to the king's castle. The sentry called out, "Halt! Where are you going?"

"To the king," the cat answered curtly.

"Are you crazy? A cat to the king?"

"Oh, let him go," another sentry said. "The king's often very bored. Perhaps the cat will give him some pleasure with his meowing and purring."

When the cat appeared before the king, he bowed and said, "My lord,

† Jacob and Wilhelm Grimm, "Puss in Boots"—"Der gestiefelte Kater" (1812), was published as No. 33 in *Kinder- und Hausmärchen. Gesammelt durch die Brüder Grimm* (Berlin: Realschulbuchhandlung, 1812).

the Count"—and he uttered a long, distinguished name—"sends you his regards and would like to offer you these partridges, which he recently caught in his traps."

The king was amazed by the beautiful, fat partridges. Indeed, he was so overcome with joy that he commanded the cat to take as much gold from his treasury as he could carry and put it into the sack. "Bring it to your lord and give him my very best thanks for his gift."

Meanwhile, the poor miller's son sat at home by the window, propped his head up with his hand, and wondered why he had given away all he had for the cat's boots when the cat would probably not be able to bring him anything great in return. Suddenly, the cat entered, threw down the sack from his back, opened it, and dumped the gold at the miller's feet.

"Now you've got something for the boots. The king also sends his regards and best of thanks."

The miller was happy to have such wealth, even though he did not understand how everything had happened. However, as the cat was taking off his boots, he told him everything and said, "Surely you have enough money now, but we won't be content with that. Tomorrow I'm going to put on my boots again, and you shall become even richer. Incidentally, I told the king you're a count."

The following day the cat put on his boots, as he said he would, went hunting again, and brought the king a huge catch. So it went every day, and every day the cat brought back gold to the miller. At the king's court he became a favorite, so that he was permitted to go and come and wander about the castle wherever he pleased. One day, as the cat was lying by the hearth in the king's kitchen and warming himself, the coachman came and started cursing. "May the devil take the king and princess! I wanted to go to the tavern, have a drink, and play some cards. But now they want me to drive them to the lake so they can go for a walk."

When the cat heard that, he ran home and said to his master, "If you want to be a rich count, come with me to the lake and go for a swim."

The miller did not know what to say. Nevertheless, he listened to the cat and went with him to the lake, where he undressed and jumped into the water completely naked. Meanwhile, the cat took his clothes, carried them away, and hid them. No sooner had he done it than the king came driving by. Now the cat began to wail in a miserable voice, "Ahh, most gracious king! My lord went for a swim in the lake, and a thief came and stole his clothes that were lying on the bank. Now the count is in the water and can't get out. If he stays in much longer, he'll freeze and die."

When the king heard that, he ordered the coach to stop, and one of his servants had to race back to the castle and fetch some of the king's garments. The count put on the splendid clothes, and since the king had already taken a liking to him because of the partridges that, he believed, had been sent by the count, he asked the young man to sit down next to him in the coach. The princess was not in the least angry about this, for the count was young and handsome and pleased her a great deal.

In the meantime, the cat went on ahead of them and came to a large meadow, where there were over a hundred people making hay.

"Who owns this meadow, my good people?" asked the cat.

"The great sorcerer."

"Listen to me. The king will be driving by, and when he asks who the owner of this meadow is, I want you to answer, 'The count.' If you don't, you'll all be killed."

Then the cat continued on his way and came to a wheatfield so enormous that nobody could see over it. There were more than two hundred people standing there and cutting wheat.

"Who owns this wheat, my good people?"

"The sorcerer."

"Listen to me. The king will be driving by, and when he asks who the owner of this wheat is, I want you to answer, 'The count.' If you don't do this, you'll all be killed."

Finally, the cat came to a splendid forest where more than three hundred people were chopping down large oak trees and cutting them into wood.

"Who owns this forest, my good people?"

"The sorcerer."

"Listen to me. The king will be driving by, and when he asks who the owner of this forest is, I want you to answer, 'The count.' If you don't do this, you'll all be killed."

The cat continued on his way, and the people watched him go. Since he looked so unusual and walked in boots like a human being, they were afraid of him. Soon the cat came to the sorcerer's castle, walked boldly inside, and appeared before the sorcerer, who looked at him scornfully and asked him what he wanted. The cat bowed and said, "I've heard that you can turn yourself into a dog, fox, or even a wolf, but I don't believe that you can turn yourself into an elephant. That seems impossible to me, and this is why I've come: I want to be convinced with my own eyes."

"That's just a trifle for me," the sorcerer said arrogantly, and within seconds he turned himself into an elephant.

"That's great, but can you also turn yourself into a lion?"

"Nothing to it," said the sorcerer, and he suddenly stood before the cat as a lion. The cat pretended to be terrified and cried out, "That's incredible and unheard of! Never in my dreams would I have thought this possible! But you'd top all of this if you could turn yourself into a tiny animal, such as a mouse. I'm convinced that you can do more than any other sorcerer in the word, but that would be too much for you."

The flattery had made the sorcerer quite friendly, and he said, "Oh, no, dear cat, that's not too much at all," and soon he was running around the room as a mouse.

Then the cat ran after him, caught the mouse in one leap, and ate him up.

While all this was happening, the king had continued driving with the count and princess and had come to the large meadow.

"Who owns the hay?" the king asked.

"The count," the people all cried out, just as the cat had ordered them to do.

"You've got a nice piece of land, count," the king said.

Afterward they came to the large wheatfield.

"Who owns that wheat, my good people?"

"The count."

"My! You've got quite a large and beautiful estate!"

Next they came to the forest.

"Who owns these woods, my good people?"

"The count."

The king was even more astounded and said, "You must be a rich man, count. I don't think I have such a splendid forest as yours."

At last they came to the castle. The cat stood on top of the stairs, and when the coach stopped below, he ran down, opened the door, and said, "Your majesty, you've arrived at the castle of my lord, the count. This honor will make him happy for the rest of his life."

The king climbed out of the coach and was amazed by the magnificent building, which was almost larger and more beautiful than his own castle. The count led the princess up the stairs and into the hall, which was flickering with lots of gold and jewels.

The princess became the count's bride, and when the king died, the count become king, and the puss in boots was his prime minster.

Virtuous Queens

There are strong indications from a tale entitled "The Maiden Who Laughs Roses and Weeps Pearls" in the Greek oral tradition that Straparola may have been familiar with a similar folktale in Italy. His tale combines numerous motifs common in other folk- and fairy tales such as the wish for a child, the special gifts of Biancabella, the jealous stepmother, the rescue of the innocent maiden in the woods, and the exposure of the evil stepmother. Mailly's tale is based closely on Straparola's narrative, but he made important changes in keeping with the courtly tradition of France. Although Pompeo Sarnelli wrote a similar tale about a snake maiden and her loyal servant in *Posilecheata* (1684), there are not many literary fairy tales that follow the design of Straparola's text.

GIOVAN FRANCESCO STRAPAROLA

Biancabella and the Snake†

A long time ago in Monteferrat there was a powerful marquis by the name of Lamberico, who was very wealthy, but who had no children. Though he wanted very much to have some, God had not granted his wish. Now one day as his wife went walking to amuse herself in one of the gardens, she became very tired and sat down at the foot of a tree, where she fell asleep. While she dozed sweetly, a little grass snake crawled to her side and slipped in beneath her clothes without her ever feeling a thing. Then it entered her vagina and carefully made its way into her womb, where it rested quietly. Shortly thereafter, the marquis's wife became pregnant, to the great delight and pleasure of everyone in the city. When the time for the delivery arrived, she gave birth to a baby girl who had a grass snake wrapped around her neck three times. As soon as the midwives, who had assisted in the birth, saw this, they were very frightened, but the snake, without doing any harm to the infant's neck, untwined itself, slid to the ground, and made its way into the garden.

When the infant was given a bath and was cleaned and made beautiful, she was wrapped in a pure white blanket, and gradually the midwives began to see that there was a beautifully crafted gold necklace around her neck. It was so fine and lovely that it seemed to radiate from between the

† Giovan Francesco Straparola, "Biancabella and the Snake"—"Biancabella, figliuola di Lamberico marchese di Monferrato, viene mandata dalla matriga di Ferrandino, re di Napoli, ad uccidere. Ma gli servi le troncano le mani e le cavano gli occhi; e per una biscia viene reintegrata, e a Ferrandino lieta ritorna" (1550), *Favola* III, *Notte terza* in *Le piacevoli notti*, 2 vols. (Venice: Comin da Trino, 1550/53).

skin and flesh just like the most precious jewels are accustomed to shine from sparkling crystal. Moreover, it went around the child's neck just as many times as the little snake had done.

Due to her beauty, the little girl was given the name of Biancabella,[1] and she grew up with such good and gracious qualities that it seemed she was more divine than human. Now, when she turned ten years old, she happened to go out on a balcony with her nurse and saw a garden full of roses and all kinds of lovely flowers. Since she had never seen it before, she asked the nurse whose garden it was. Then the nurse replied that it was a place her mother called her own and often went there to amuse herself. Thereupon, the girl said, "I've never seen anything as beautiful as this garden. I'd like to go for a walk there."

Then the nurse took Biancabella by the hand and led her into the garden. At one point she separated from the girl, sat down under the shade of a leafy beech tree, and fell asleep, allowing the girl to enjoy herself in the garden. Delighted by the lovely place, Biancabella ran here and there and gathered flowers. Finally, she felt tired and sat down under the shade of a tree. No sooner did the child settle down on the ground than a grass snake appeared and crawled close to her side. As soon as Biancabella saw it, she was very frightened and was about to cry out when the snake said, "Be quiet and don't move. You needn't be afraid because I am your sister and was born on the same day you were born, and Samaritana is my name. If you will obey my commands, I'll make you happy, but if, on the other hand, you disobey me, you'll be the most unhappy and dissatisfied maiden the world has ever seen. So go your way now without any fear, and tomorrow I want you to bring two buckets into the garden, one filled with pure milk, and the other with fine rose water. Make sure that you come alone and do not bring any company with you."

When the snake was gone, the girl stood up and went back to her nurse, who was still sleeping. After having wakened her, she returned with her to the palace without telling her anything about what had happened. The following day Biancabella was alone with her mother in a room, and the mother noticed that her daughter looked unhappy. Thereupon, she said, "Biancabella, what is bothering you? You've got such a sad face! You were happy and lively before, but now you seem gloomy and distressed."

"There's nothing wrong with me," Biancabella replied. "I just want to take two buckets into the garden, one filled with pure milk and the other with rose water."

"Why have you been troubling yourself about such a small matter?" the mother asked. "Don't you know that everything here is at your disposal?" Then her mother ordered two beautiful buckets to be brought to her, one filled with milk and the other with rose water, and then she had them carried into the garden.

When the designated time arrived, Biancabella went all alone to the garden. After she opened the door, she went in and closed the gate behind her. Then she sat down on the ground at the spot where the two buckets had been placed. As soon as she had taken her place, the snake appeared

1. In Italian, the name means "beautiful, blond girl."

Biancabella and the Snake. Edward Hughes, 1894.

and approached her. Immediately she ordered Biancabella to strip off all her clothes, and once this was done, she was to step naked into the bucket filled with milk. Once this was done, the snake washed her from head to toe with the white milk and licked her all over with her tongue, curing all her defects. After Biancabella stepped out of the milk, she went into the one filled with rose water, and she was given a scent that made her feel very fresh. After she put on her clothes, the snake ordered her expressly not to tell anyone what had happened, not even her father or mother. It was the snake's intention that no other woman in the world was to match Biancabella in beauty or in graciousness. And therefore, she endowed her with an infinite number of qualities, and then she departed.

After Biancabella left the garden, she returned home. When her mother saw that her daughter had become more lovely and beautiful than any other young lady in the world, she was astonished and did not know what to say. Therefore, she asked her what she had done to make herself so beautiful, but Biancabella did not know what to respond. Then her mother took a comb and began to comb and shape her daughter's blond hair. Suddenly, pearls and precious stones fell from her head, and when Biancabella went to wash her hands, roses, violets, and all kinds of bright flowers tumbled from them with such sweet odors that the place was like the earthly paradise. After seeing all this, her mother ran to Lamberico, her husband, and, full of maternal pride, she said, "My lord, we have a daughter who is the nicest, the most beautiful, and the loveliest that nature has ever produced. Aside from her divine beauty and loveliness, which everyone can clearly see, there are pearls, gems, and other precious jewels that fall from her hair. And what is even more marvelous, roses, violets, and all kinds of flowers tumble from her white hands and emit sweet odors to all who happen to be nearby. I would never have believed any of this if I had not seen it with my own eyes."

Her husband, who was, by nature, incredulous, was not inclined to trust his wife's words at all and made fun of her story and derided her. But she urged him so vigorously to believe her that he wanted to get to the bottom of her story. So he summoned his daughter into his presence and found even more things than his wife had described, and as a result he became exceedingly happy and proudly declared that there was not a man in the world worthy of marrying her.

Very soon the fame and glory of Biancabella's lovely and immortal beauty spread throughout the world, and many kings, princes, and dukes came from all over to win her love and to wed her. But none of them were considered worthy enough to have her because each one proved to be lacking in some respect. Finally, however, Ferrandino, king of Naples, arrived and his prowess and illustrious name radiated like the sun among the smaller stars. As soon as he presented himself to the marquis, he requested his daughter's hand in marriage. Seeing that Ferrandino was handsome and charming besides being a powerful prince with great land and wealth, he gave his consent to the nuptials. Therefore, he summoned his daughter, and the two were married without delay by the joining of hands sealed by a kiss.

No sooner were the marriage rites completed than Biancabella recalled the loving words which her sister Samaritana had said to her. So she withdrew from her husband under the pretext that she had certain things to do, and she went to her chamber and locked the door. Then she walked through a secret passage into the garden, where she began to call Samaritana in a low voice. But her sister did not appear as she had done before, and Biancabella was quite astonished by this. After she searched every place in the garden without finding her, she was very distressed. Indeed, she knew that Samaritana's disappearance had come about because she had not followed her sister's orders in some way. Therefore, she was greatly saddened and returned to her chamber. After opening the door, she went to rejoin her husband, who had been waiting a long time for her, and sat down beside him. Since all the ceremonies were now done, Ferrandino took his bride with him to Naples, where they were given an honorable reception by the city with great pomp and glorious celebrations.

Now it so happened that Ferrandino had a stepmother, who had two ugly and nasty daughters, and she had desired to marry one of them to the king. But, when all hope was taken from her fulfilling her wish, her rage and anger against Biancabella became so fierce that she could hardly bear to look at her or listen to her. Nevertheless, she managed to pretend to love her and show her affection.

About this time, as fate would have it, the king of Tunis had assembled a mighty army and navy and declared war against Ferrandino. (Whether he did this because Ferrandino had won Biancabella as his wife or for some other reason, I don't know.) In fact, he had already crossed the borders of the kingdom of Naples with his powerful army. Therefore, it was necessary for Ferrandino to take up arms to defend his realm and confront his foe. So after placing Biancabella, who was now pregnant, in the care of his stepmother and looking after his affairs, he set out with his army.

Soon thereafter the malicious and impetuous stepmother made plans to kill Biancabella. She called two of her most loyal servants and commanded them to take Biancabella with them to some place for her amusement and they were not to leave until they had killed her. Moreover, to make sure that her servants would carry out her orders, the stepmother demanded some sign of her death. These servants, who were ready to do anything evil, did indeed follow their mistress's instructions. Pretending that they wanted to take Biancabella to some place where she could amuse herself, they conducted her to some woods, where they prepared to kill her. But when they saw how lovely and gracious she was, they were moved to pity and decided not to murder her. But they cut off both her hands from her body and tore her eyes out of her head to prove to the stepmother that Biancabella had been killed by them. When the odious and cruel woman examined the proof, she was very pleased and paid them for their work. Now the wicked stepmother sought to put another evil plan into effect, and she spread the rumor throughout the kingdom that her two daughters were dead, one from consumption, and the other from a boil near her heart that had caused her to suffocate to death. In addition, she announced that Biancabella had become so distraught because of the king's departure that she had had a miscarriage. Then she was allegedly overcome by tertian fever,[2] which had destroyed her health so much that there was more cause to fear her death than to hope for recovery. In truth, however, the wicked and cunning woman's plan was to keep one of her own daughters in the king's bed, pretending that she was Biancabella and suffering gravely from the fever.

Meanwhile, Ferrandino had already engaged the enemy and had dispersed the army of his foe, and he soon returned in glorious triumph. He had thought he would find his beloved Biancabella full of joy and cheer, but instead he found her lying in bed, feeble, pale, and deformed. When he approached the bed and gazed at her face, he was stupefied to see how devastated she had become. He could scarcely imagine that the woman he saw there could be Biancabella. Then he had some servants comb her hair, and instead of the gems and precious jewels that usually fell from her blond hair, large lice appeared and kept eating away at her. No longer did violets and sweet-smelling roses tumble from her hands, but there was filth and a stench that turned the stomach of all who saw her. But the wicked stepmother comforted him and said that all these things were due to the long sickness that had produced such effects.

In the meantime, the miserable Biancabella, without hands and blind in both eyes, was alone in that desolate place and suffered greatly from her affliction. She constantly called her sister Samaritana to help her, but there was no answer except for a resounding echo that reverberated through the air. One day, however, as the unhappy maiden continued to live in great agony, deprived of all human aid, a very old man entered the woods. He was benevolent and compassionate, and when he heard a sad and lamentable voice, he made his way toward the place from where it came and found a blind maiden with her hands cut off, bemoaning her sad fate. When the good old man saw her, he could not bear to leave her alone like that among the branches, thorns, and brambles. Overcome by fatherly love, he led her to his home and placed his wife in charge of her and asked her to take good care of the maiden. Then he turned toward his three daughters, who shone like three bright stars, and instructed them earnestly to keep her company and to show her all the affection that she might need. But the wife, who was not as kind and merciful as her husband, burst into anger against her husband and cried out impetuously, "Husband, what do you want us to do with this blind and maimed woman? Most likely she's deserved the treatment that she received."

But the old man answered indignantly, "Do what I tell you to do. If you refuse, don't expect to call this place my home."

Some time later, while the tormented Biancabella happened to be conversing about various things with the wife and three daughters and she was reflecting about her misfortunes, she asked one of the maidens to do her a favor and comb her hair. But, when the mother heard this, she became very angry because she did not want her daughter to become her servant in any way whatsoever. However, the daughter was more compassionate than her mother, and she also recalled her father's instructions. In addition, she sensed that there was something noble about Biancabella. So,

2. A fever characterized by the occurrence of a paroxysm every third day.

she took off her apron from around her waist, and after spreading it on the floor beside Biancabella, she gently began to comb her hair. No sooner did she begin combing her than pearls, rubies, diamonds, and precious jewels began to fall from her blond strands of hair. When the mother saw this, she was amazed and filled with awe. All the hatred she had felt for her was turned into love. When the old man returned home, they all ran to embrace him and rejoiced with him over the unexpected good luck that would help out of poverty. Then Biancabella asked them to fetch a bucket of clear water and wash her face and her maimed arms. Immediately thereafter, roses, violets, and other flowers tumbled from her arms in great abundance. Therefore they all thought she must be some divine person and certainly not human.

Some time after this Biancabella decided to return to the place where the old man had first found her. But he and his wife and daughters had seen how much they benefitted from her presence, and so they caressed her and showed her a great deal of affection and begged her sincerely not to leave them. Indeed, they gave her many reasons why she should stay. But she had firmly made up her mind and was determined to leave no matter what, but she did promise them to return. When the old man heard this, he took her without further delay to the place where he had found her. Then she asked the old man to depart and come back there at dusk so she could return with him to his house.

As soon as the old man had left her, the unfortunate Biancabella began to wander about the woods and call for Samaritana. Her cries and lamentations reached the high heavens. But, even though Samaritana was very near her sister and had never abandoned her, she refused to answer her. Seeing her words scattered in the wind, the miserable Biancabella cried out, "What am I to do in this world without eyes and hands and without the hope of human help?"

In a state of frenzy, she abandoned all hope of salvation, and as she became more and more desperate, she sought to commit suicide. But since she did not have any means to put an end to her life, she walked toward a nearby pool of water with the intention of drowning herself. When she reached the bank of the pool and was about to throw herself into the water, she heard a thunderous voice cry out, "What are you doing? By no means are you to take your life. You must keep it for some better end."

Alarmed by this voice, Biancabella felt her hair stand on end. But it appeared to her that she knew the voice, and so she plucked up courage and said, "Who are you and why are you talking to me this way?"

"I am Samaritana," the voice replied, "your sister, for whom you've been calling all this time."

When Biancabella heard these words, she answered in a fervid voice broken by sobs, "Ah, my sister! I beg you. Help me! If I disregarded your advice in the past, please pardon me. Indeed, I have made a mistake out of ignorance and not out of malice. If I had done it out of malice, divine providence would not have tolerated it very long."

When Samaritana heard her sister's sorrowful lamentations and saw how maltreated she had been, she comforted her. Then she gathered some marvelous herbs and spread them on her eyes so she could see again. After that she joined hands to her arms, and they were sound again. Finally, Samaritana discarded the squalid snakeskin and revealed herself as a beautiful young lady.

The sun had already begun to conceal its glittering rays, and the evening shadows had begun to appear when the old man had made his way back to the woods at a quick pace. When he arrived, he found Biancabella with a forest nymph. As he gazed into Biancabella's bright face, he was stunned and could not believe it was her. But when he was sure it really was her, he said, "My daughter, weren't you blind and without hands this morning? How have you been able to heal yourself so quickly?"

"It wasn't me who did it," Biancabella answered, "but my sister, who's sitting next to me. Thanks to her powers and graciousness, I've been healed."

Thereupon, the two sisters stood up and went happily with the old man to his house, where his wife and three daughters gave them a most cordial welcome.

Many, many days later, Samaritana and Biancabella and the old man, his wife and three daughters decided to move to the city of Naples to live there. When they came across a vacant place near the king's palace, they thought it would make a perfect spot for their lodging. That night, Samaritana picked up a laurel twig and hit the ground with it three times and said certain words. No sooner had the sounds of the words faded than the most beautiful and superb palace arose from the ground. Nothing like it had ever been seen before.

The next morning Ferrandino, the king, got up early and looked out of his window. When he caught sight of the rich and marvelous palace, he was amazed and stunned. He called his wife and his stepmother to come and see it, but they were displeased because they suspected that something bad was going to happen to them. While Ferrandino was standing and carefully examining all the parts of the palace, he raised his eyes to a window and noticed two ladies inside whose beauty was such that the sun would have been jealous of them. No sooner did he catch sight of them than his heart began to throb because it seemed to him that one of them resembled Biancabella. And when he asked who they were, he was told that they were two ladies who had been exiled from their home, and that they had come from Persia with all their possessions to live in the glorious city of Naples. So Ferrandino sent a messenger to inquire if they would not mind if he and the ladies of his court paid them a visit, and they replied that they would be delighted, but that they were also aware that it would be more proper and respectful if they, as subjects, should go to him, rather than he, as lord and king, should visit them.

Such a polite answer made the king even more eager to pay them a visit. Thereupon, Ferrandino summoned the queen and the other ladies of the court to accompany him on a visit to the two ladies. Although the stepmother and her daughters refused to go at first, because they felt an impending doom, they all went to the palace of the two ladies, who welcomed them in a cordial and respectful way. Then they showed the visitors their sumptuous lodgings, the spacious halls, and the richly decorated chambers whose walls were lined with alabaster and fine porphyry and adorned with figures that seemed very lifelike. After they had visited the entire palace, the beautiful Biancabella approached Ferrandino and asked him sweetly whether he would deign to come one day with his queen to dine with them. The king, whose heart was not made of stone and was magnanimous and liberal by nature, graciously accepted the invitation. After thanking the ladies for the cordial reception they had given him, the king and queen departed together and returned to their own palace.

Now, when the day of the dinner arrived, the queen and the stepmother got dressed in their royal garments and were accompanied by various ladies of the court. Then they went to do honor to the magnificent dinner that was prepared for them. After the seneschal gave them water to wash their hands, he led the king and queen to a separate table more eminent than the others but at the same time near to them. Then he seated all the rest of the guests according to their rank, and soon they all dined merrily and joyfully together.

When the splendid dinner was finished and all the tables had been cleared, Samaritana stood up and said, "Your majesty, to avoid falling into boredom, I suggest that someone propose something that will give us pleasure and make us happy."

The guests all agreed, but no one dared to propose anything. When Samaritana saw they were all silent, she said, "Since no one has any suggestions, I should like to ask, with your majesty's permission, one of our maidens to provide you with a little entertainment." Then she called a damsel named Silveria and ordered her to take a lyre in hand and to sing something in honor of the king and worthy of his praise. The damsel followed her lady's orders and picked up the lyre. Standing before the king, she began to play with inspiration while singing the story of Biancabella from beginning to end while never mentioning her name. After the song was completed, Samaritana stood up again and asked the king what would be a fitting punishment for those culprits who had committed such a grave atrocity. Then the stepmother, who thought she might cover up her misdeed by a prompt and ready reply, did not wait for the king to give his answer, but boldly called out, "They deserve to be cast into a burning furnace, and nothing less!"

Then Samaritana's face grew red as embers and she answered furiously, "You are the very wicked and cruel women who caused all these terrible things! You've condemned yourself by your own words, you malevolent and malicious creature!" Then Samaritana turned to the king with a look of joy on her face and said, "This lady here is your Biancabella. This lady is your wife whom you loved so dearly. This is the lady without whom you could not live."

Then, to prove that her words were true, Samaritana ordered the three daughters of the old man to comb Biancabella's wavy blond hair in the presence of the king. No sooner did they begin than precious and valuable gems sprang from her hair, and sweet-smelling flowers and morning roses tumbled from her hands. And to convince the king even more, Samaritana showed him Biancabella's white neck lined by a chain of the most delicate gold that grew naturally between the skin and flesh and sparkled like crystal.

Thanks to these clear signs and evidence, the king recognized Bianca-bella as his true wife and began to weep and embrace her with tenderness. But before he left the palace, the king had a red-hot furnace kindled and had the stepmother and her daughters thrown into it. This was how they were punished for their sins and how their lives came to a miserable end. Soon thereafter the old man's three daughters were honorably wed. Then King Ferrandino lived a long life with Biancabella and Samaritana and left legitimate heirs behind him to inherit the kingdom.

JEAN DE MAILLY

Blanche Belle†

Lamberie, marquis of Montserrat, governed his realm in such a way that he became very prosperous. Indeed, everything succeeded as he wished. With the exception of one thing that he passionately desired, he possessed everything that could make a man happy. But he could never have children, and this caused the marquise, his wife, and him great sorrow. The marquise once heard people talking about the birth of Romulus, which antiquity attributed to a simple conversation that Rea Silvia,[1] his mother, had with a sylph. The marquise wished a thousand times to have the same adventure, and it did not matter how, but she wanted to efface the shame of not being a mother.

One day when she was alone in her garden and her imagination was full of sylphs, she fell asleep and had a dream that gave her great pleasure. She thought that she had spent a pleasant night with a sylph, who was as handsome as love, and she woke up convinced very much that she was pregnant. Indeed, she was not mistaken. Nine months later she gave birth to a beautiful and marvelous baby girl. Since husbands have a bizarre habit of not approving when their wives have mysterious conversations, even with sylphs, the marquise kept her secret to herself and let the marquis flatter himself that he was the father of this charming little princess, whom they called Blanche Belle because she was both beautiful and very white.

After some time passed, she became so beautiful that she was the marvel of marvels. She was also raised with such care that she was soon admired by everyone in Monsterrat. News of her beauty spread throughout Italy, that there was no woman as perfect as she, and there was not a single monarch who did not seek her hand in marriage. Aside from all these pleasant features that made her so desirable, Blanche Belle was very much attached to the sylph to whom she owed a gift of infinite worth, for each morning that she awoke and opened her eyes, a pearl dropped from each

† Jean de Mailly, "Blanche Belle"—"Blanche Belle" (1698), in *Les illustres fées, contes galans* (Paris: M.-M. Brunet, 1698).
1. Mailly's version of Romulus's birth is somewhat misleading. Rea Silvia was the daughter of Numitor, king of Alba Longa. Her uncle Amulius deposed her father and appointed her a vestal virgin so she would be prevented from bearing rightful heirs to the throne. However, she was seduced by Mars and gave birth to the twins, Romulus and Remus, who eventually overthrew Amulius.

one, and the first word that she uttered each day would be accompanied by a ruby that would tumble from her lips, and these jewels were a source of immense wealth.

Since the marquis knew he had such a beautiful means to accumulate a good deal of money, he became very difficult when it came to deciding which prince might make her happy. Before separating from her, he thought he would use the present state of things to renovate his house so that it would flourish, and he amassed such a great treasure that he would never lack for anything for the rest of his life. After taking this precaution, he decided to contemplate who, among all the princes who wanted Blanche Belle as his wife, was the most worthy of possessing such a beauty and such grandeur. He even consulted his charming daughter, whom he loved tenderly, and after having learned that she had no inclination to marry, and that none of the men who had sighed for her touched her heart, he was no longer in a hurry to decide on a husband, hoping that, with the virtues and wonderful secret that she had, she could always choose a man that would please him when she developed the desire to marry.

She was in this nonchalant phase for some time when the most charming prince that the sun ever illuminated appeared at the court of Casal. His name was Ferdinand, king of Naples, and he was visiting all the courts of Italy. He had started in Milan and had come from Milan to Casal full of curiosity. As soon as he saw Blanche Belle, all his plans were altered to please her. On her side, the princess found him so amiable that, when the marquis asked her what she thought of him, she confessed frankly that she would not be angry if a prince of his kind were to think about her for his wife, and she declared to the marquis her father that she would be ready to obey him if he commanded her to listen favorably to the king when he offered her his heart.

At the same time, the king of Naples thought of some means to make himself agreeable to the marquis and the princess his daughter and did not have any difficulty in succeeding. The inclinations on both sides to form an alliance were so great that his proposal was accepted as soon as it was made. The marriage was celebrated in great splendor. The marquis was satisfied to have found a great king as son-in-law, and the princess his daughter was charmed by the valor of the king her husband and thought she was the most happy person in the world. Since the king wanted to show his people the charming princess who was his pride and joy, they departed for Naples. As she was splendidly beautiful, and her clothes were bedecked with pearls and rubies, the people were dazzled by such a magnificent appearance and adored their incomparable queen. Consequently, the king was so happy that he could not even express his joy. Now, in addition to the acclamation of everyone in the large city, he also had the most charming princess in the world. But since we have yet to see eternal happiness, it is not surprising that theirs became troubled.

The king of Tunis, upon hearing that Ferdinand was the master of such a rare treasure, decided to kidnap her. He was so fascinated by all that he heard about Queen Blanche Belle's beauty and the gift that produced pearls and rubies every day that he brought together a great army to make war against Ferdinand. Concerned about protecting Blanche Belle's life as well as his crown, he sent her to a chateau that was deep in the woods, and he asked his mother, the widow of the king his father, and a daughter that his mother had from another marriage to accompany Blanche Belle. They gladly agreed to do this since they were very happy to have this occasion to carry out a wicked plan that they had been contemplating against Blanche Belle from the very first day that she had appeared in Naples.

This old queen hated Blanche Belle to death because she occupied a place that she had wanted to fill with her daughter, for whom Ferdinand had shown some good will while his father had been alive, even to the point of making her hope that he would marry her when his father was dead. Neither the old queen nor her daughter had ever accused the king of infidelity, but they were to be feared. The king should have realized that a concealed hate is all the more dangerous and that a woman abandoned for another rarely pardons the insult that she claims that a man has given her. Blanche Belle's adventure is a good example of this.

As soon as the old woman had this charming person in her power and in a chateau where she was the mistress, she only thought about getting rid of her and putting her daughter in her place. But how would it be possible to deceive the eyes of the king and send the queen to a place where he would never be able to find her? No matter how wicked the old queen was, she was not wicked enough to kill a person who gave her a thousand caresses every day, or perhaps she did not want to make the king irreconcilable if he were to discover one day how she had deceived him. Given all the complications of such a great plan, the old queen thought it would be better to seek out the help and advice of an illustrious fairy, who had contributed a great deal toward making her queen by her magic. This fairy had always taken a particular interest in her since her birth, and thus she went to see her. The fairy had her palace in the most dense part of the woods, and when the queen went there, she took her daughter with her. After she had consulted her and had received some good advice, she said one day to Blanche Belle that she wanted to take her to the most beautiful place that she had ever seen. It was, she said to her, a beautiful meadow surrounded by canals where the water was so beautiful that it was a pleasure to see it. These canals were also filled with all kinds of fish. At the end of the meadow, she continued to speak, there was a chateau in which one of her old friends was living, and she wanted her to make her acquaintance, but they could only see this friend at her chateau because she was so old that she hardly went out. Then to make Blanche Belle more curious, she said that her friend was as wise as the fairies, and she would tell her upon looking at her hand what would happen to the king of Tunis's undertaking and the most considerable things that were bound to happen in the course of her life. What young person would not be curious to know what was going to happen to her husband, whom she loved tenderly and who was exposed to the vicissitudes of war? Is there anybody who does not want to know about the future? Therefore, it is not surprising that the young queen let herself be seduced and taken to a place where she would have spent the rest of her life in a sad state if the sylph had not presided over her birth and had not had the power to rescue her.

This sylph was the son of a fairy more powerful than the friend of the old queen and had never refused the sylph anything, and this sylph was also the most accomplished of all her children.

Since the old queen believed that Blanche Belle would never find the means to escape from the hands of her friend the fairy, she brazenly took her there, and as soon as the young woman arrived, she found herself locked in an apartment of the palace. The fairy let her know that this was a just punishment for the infidelity that she had caused the king to commit in regard to the daughter of the old queen, whom he had promised to marry. But nothing else would happen to her other than the loss of her lover, who did not belong to her anyway, and she would be served in her apartment in such a way that she would have everything she desired.

Blanche Belle realized that she was in an isolated place and at the mercy of an old woman whom she did not know and who appeared to be very powerful from what she could gather from the great quantity of black men and dwarfs who wore collars like slaves. It is not surprising that a young person would be scared in a situation like this and that she took recourse in submission and prayer in order to try to preserve her life. The fairy assured her that she had nothing to fear and even promised her to do all that she could to make her captivity tolerable. It is true that, aside from having Blanche Belle served with great respect in her apartment, she ordered her life to be made comfortable and allowed her to listen to music and read books. Thus she sweetened her solitude, but she placed merciless guards at the door of her apartment so that she would never be able to exit.

The old queen returned to her chateau with her daughter, whom her friend the fairy had transformed with her art into a person that perfectly resembled Blanche Belle so that everyone would be deceived. The old queen said that she had left her daughter with her friend who had wanted her to provide company for her. Indeed, she said that she had gladly left her daughter there because her friend had promised to make her heiress of her chateau and all her wealth. There was nothing now to desire but to make this new princess familiar with all Blanche Belle's manners because the resemblance was already perfect. So the old queen took care to instruct her, and she hoped that the king would be satisfied with her. There was, however, only one defect that she did not know how to remedy. The fairy did not have the power to grant her the gift of pearls and rubies that Blanche Belle had. But the queen mother had taken the precaution of gathering together a large amount that Blanche Belle had produced, and she believed that would be a way to deceive the king for a long time. Moreover, she knew that he did not make much of this kind of wealth, and there was some hope that he would regard her with more nonchalance when he returned victorious after defeating the king of Tunis, as it seemed that he would, and he would augment his fortune considerably by this victory.

Indeed, the king returned very soon to Naples after a total victory, and he sent a message right away that he wanted to see his charming Blanche Belle. The old woman set out at once with great confidence in the measures that she had taken to make her daughter queen, and she was sure that her daughter would fill the position of queen for the rest of her life. The fraud was so skillfully done that the king, from the very first day, believed that he possessed his charming Blanche Belle again. However, he did notice that there was something missing, and he believed that she had lost some of her charms. Unconsciously, this thought caused him to develop a great aversion toward her, and soon he found himself overcome by melancholy and sadness without being able to decipher the reason. Finally, this melancholy went so far that he could no longer find any pleasure at court and decided to go on a hunt with just a few people. He chose the chateau and the forest where he had sent the queen during the war. Each day that he went hunting, he went past an unfamiliar chateau, but he was not in a mood to think much about it. He was so distracted that he was not curious about anything. He was not even particularly interested in the hunt. Such was the morbid condition of the king until one day he was suddenly attracted by a voice that he heard coming from the unknown chateau, a voice that he thought he recognized. He did not know the precise location of the voice, and thus he approached the chateau and saw a person who extended her arms and asked for help. The sounds of her voice penetrated his heart, and as he approached even closer, he felt a surge of excitement that he had felt when he first met Blanche Belle. Finally, he realized that he was seeing the true love of his life. But he was somewhat shocked to see someone in this chateau whom he believed was in Naples, and after reflecting about this sudden change of his heart, he did not know whether he was seeing some kind of dream.

His surprise became even greater when he saw this person in the air and saw that she was descending very softly and landing right by his side. His heart told him that she was the true Blanche Belle, and he threw himself at her feet. After embracing her tenderly, the two of them stood there for some time without being able to say a word and without being able to let go of each other. When the first rushes of joy passed, Blanche Belle told the king what had happened to her and how she felt herself being lifted into the air and carried to him by some unknown force. Indeed, she owed this rescue and flight to the sylph, who had presided over her birth. He had come to rescue her from this captivity to which she thought she was condemned for life, and he brought about her perfect happiness, which she would have missed a thousand times more than the loss of her freedom.

The king, who was more in love with her than he had ever been, deferred taking vengeance in order to take his charming Blanche Belle to the chateau where he was keeping a small court. Indeed, he wanted to take her away from a place where he did not know whether there was still something to fear. The next day he assembled his council and revealed the wickedness of the old queen and the fraud that she and her daughter had committed. He also complained about the fairy who had employed her powers to help them, and after hearing the advice of all the members of his council, who recommended a severe punishment, he ordered that the old queen and her daughter were to be banished forever from his realm and that the fairy's chateau was to be demolished. But the queen and her daughter had already fled before the sentence could be carried out against them. In addition, the men who were given orders to demolish the fairy's chateau searched for it in vain. It appeared as if it had been transported somewhere else, and wherever it was, it was serving as the refuge for the old queen and her daughter, who were spending the rest of their lives regretting that they had committed a useless crime and had left King Ferdinand the happiest of monarchs with his charming Blanche Belle, for whom his love increased every day during the course of a long life. Never had such a marvelous love as theirs been seen before.

Magic Helpers

The tales by Basile and the Grimms in this section contain three important fairy tale motifs: the son's banishment from the home, his apprenticeship, and the demonstration of his skills. In this respect, the two tales bear a similarity to those tales in which sons go out into the world to learn a craft, especially in the humorous way in which the protagonists manage to bumble their way through life. It is as if the heavens were protecting them. In some of the oral versions, it is the devil who helps the awkward and naive youngest brother. In his adaptations of Basile's tales, Clemens Brentano, the German Romantic poet, wrote a hilarious, political version of "The Ogre" entitled "Das Märchen vom dem Dilldapp" ("The Fairy Tale about Dilldapp," wr. 1805–11, rev. 1815). Composed during the French occupation of the Rhineland, this fairy tale exhibits strong anti-French sentiments and contains comical poems and poetry. Dilldapp is a bumbling fool who lives with his mother, a poor seamstress named Frau Schlender (sloppy), and his three sisters, Andrienne, Saloppe, and Kontusche (all names that indicate clumsiness and neglect). Dilldapp is chased out of the house and enters the service of a Popanz (a monster). Though the good-natured Dilldapp is still clumsy and foolish, he delights the Popanz, and after four years, the monster gives him a donkey that discharges gold and jewels to take home to his mother. Similar to Basile's story, an innkeeper steals the donkey, and three years later, the same innkeeper steals a magic napkin that produces gold and jewels. Finally, after another three years pass, Dilldapp is given a magic club that beats people on command, including its owner, and he learns his lesson by testing it on himself. Then he travels to the inn and allows the innkeeper to rob him, but soon after he orders the club to beat the thief until he returns the donkey and the napkin. Now that Dilldapp has these magic gifts, he returns home and chases away the French. His sisters are given good German names (Else, Thusnelda, and Siegelinde), and he provides for his mother and becomes a wealthy man.

GIAMBATTISTA BASILE

The Ogre†

They say that there was once a respectable woman named Masella, who lived in the town of Marigliano.[1] Aside from having six revolting unmarried daughters like six beanpoles, she had a son who was such a useless blockhead that he was not even capable of playing the simplest games. As a

---

† Giambattista Basile, "The Ogre"—"Il racconto dell'orco" (1634), *Primo passatempo della prima giornata* in *Lo cunto de li cunti overo Lo trattenemiento de peccerille*, De Gian Alessio Abbattutis, 5 vols. (Naples: Ottavio Beltrano, 1634–36).
1. A town about fifteen miles from Naples in Terra di Lavoro.

result, she was like a sow with a bar stuck in her mouth, and not a day passed without her squealing, "What are you doing in this house, you cursed creature? You're not worth the bread you eat! Get out of here, you piece of nothing! You bothersome Maccabeus![2] You bring nothing but trouble. Disappear, you peanut brain. Somebody switched my cradle, and instead of a beautiful chubby little boy, I got a fat pig."

But despite all of Masella's rants, Antonio, for that was his name,[3] just whistled. When his mother finally realized that there was no hope of Antonio changing his life, she washed his head without soap, picked up a rolling pin, and started to take the measure of his jacket. Antonio, who really did not expect this, felt as though he were being measured for a coffin and escaped from her hands. He took to his heels and kept running until midnight when the lights begin to illuminate the shops of the moon, and he arrived at the foot of a mountain so high that it played leapfrog with the clouds. As he looked around, he saw, lo and behold, an ogre sitting at the large roots of a poplar tree next to a grotto decorated by pumice stones, and mamma mia, how ugly this ogre was! He resembled a dwarf with the body of a broomstick, and his head was larger than an Indian pumpkin. His forehead was covered with warts; his eyebrows were knitted; his eyes squinted. His nose was dented with two nostrils that looked like sewers, and his mouth was as large as a millstone, and two tusks dropped from it and went all the way down to his ankles. His chest was hairy, and his arms were like skein winders; his legs like a rooster's; and his large feet like a duck's. Altogether he resembled an evil spirit, a devil, an ugly ragamuffin, a real ghost who would have sent shivers up the spine of Orlando, scared a Skandeberg,[4] and made a brave fighter turn pale.

But Antonio, who had not moved a sling's throw, simply nodded his head and said, "Good day, sir. How are things going? How are you doing? Would you like anything? How far is it from here to where I have to go?"

When the ogre heard these rambling remarks, he began to laugh, and since he liked Antonio's ridiculous humor, he asked, "Do you want to enter my service?"

"How much do you want a month?" Antonio responded.

"If you serve me decently," the ogre declared, "we'll reach an agreement, and you won't have cause to complain."

After they came to terms this way, Antonio started serving the ogre, and he found that the food was thrown on the ground, and as far as work was concerned, Antonio acted like a lazy dunce so that he became as fat as a Turk at the end of four days, as round as an ox, as alert as a cock, red as a lobster, green as a garlic, huge as a whale and so massive and sturdy that he could no longer see. But after two years he became tired of this fat life, and he had a great desire and longing to visit Marigliano once more. Whenever he thought about his little house, he felt himself almost re-

---

2. A stupid and coarse person.
3. Reference to St. Antonio, but in the common usage of Basile's time, the name Antonio had the meaning of "fool," "bumpkin," or "dolt."
4. The name of the Albanian national hero Giorgio Castriota (1403–1468), who was famous in the Neapolitan tradition because he had supported the king of Naples, Ferrante I of Aragon, in defense of his throne.

gressing to the way he was before. The ogre, who could see into his vitals and sensed that he had an itch to travel and a frustrated appetite, called him aside and said, "Antonio, my boy, I know that you have a burning desire to see your own flesh and blood again. So, since I love you, and since you are the apple of my eye, I'd like you to take this trip and enjoy yourself. Now, I want you to have this ass which will grant you relief during your exhausting journey, but be careful never to say, 'Gee up! Drop your load!' If you do, you'll regret it. I swear by the soul of my grandmother."

Antonio took the ass, and without even saying good-bye, he jumped on it and trotted away. But he had not gone more than a hundred paces when he dismounted from the ass and said, "Gee up! Drop your load!" And he had hardly opened his mouth when the little ass began to drop from his rear end pearls, rubies, emeralds, sapphires, and diamonds each as large as a nut. Antonio's jaw remained wide open, and he stared at this beautiful heap, this superb diarrhea, this rich dysentery of the little ass. Indeed, he was extremely happy and filled a little sack with these jewels. Then he remounted the beast and continued riding until he arrived at an inn, where he dismounted. The first thing that he said to the innkeeper was, "Tie up this ass in the manger and give it something good to eat, but make sure that you don't say, 'Gee up! Drop your load!' or you'll regret it. And take these small things in my sack and keep them in a safe place."

The innkeeper was one of the heads of the Arts and Crafts Guild,[5] a sly fox, a man of integrity and perception, to be sure, and when he heard these extravagant orders and saw the jewels worth millions, he became curious to learn the meaning of the words. Therefore, he gave Antonio a good meal and as much to drink as possible, and then he had him lie down in a corner between a sack and a cloth blanket. As soon as the innkeeper saw Antonio close his eyes and begin snoring, he ran to the stable and said to the little ass, "Gee up! Drop your load!" and with the medicine of these words, the ass performed his usual operation, spilling pieces of gold from its body and squirting jewels. When the innkeeper saw this precious excrement, he decided to switch asses and swindle the ignoramus Antonio, deeming that it would be easy to dazzle, deceive, dupe, cheat, swindle, hoodwink, confuse, pull the wool over the eyes of such a dumb ox, boor, blockhead, dolt, and simpleton who had fallen into his hands.

When Antonio awoke the next morning—when Aurora went to empty the chamberpot of her old man, completely full with red sand, at the window of the Orient—he rubbed his eyes with his hands and stretched his arms for half an hour with sixty yawns and farts in the form of a dialogue. Then he called the innkeeper and said, "Come here, my friend, short bills make for a long friendship, and we'll remain friends and let the purses quarrel. Make out the bill, and the account will be settled."

So the innkeeper reckoned so much for the bread, so much for the wine, this for the soup, that for the meat, five for the ass's stable and ten for the bed and fifteen for the tip. Then Antonio laid out the money, took the false ass with a sack of pumice stones in place of the jewels, and headed

5. The corporations of arts and trades were headed by consuls and the "four of the craft," who were regarded as experts in their respective fields. They were powerful and shrewd.

toward his home. Before he set foot inside the house, he began to scream as if he had been stung by nettles. "Run, mother, run, for we're rich! Prepare the linen, spread the sheets, lay down the covers, and you'll see treasures!"

His mother was very happy and opened the closet where she kept her daughters' trousseaux and took out sheets so fluffy that a breath of air could have carried them away, linen that smelled very sweetly, and covers that dazzled the eye. All were spread on the ground, and then Antonio got on top of the ass and sung out, "Gee up! Drop your load!" But despite all the "Gee ups!" and "Drop your loads!" the ass paid as little attention to these words as it would to the sounds of a lyre. Antonio repeated these words three or four times, but they were like words thrown to the wind, and thus he picked up a good stick and sought to urge the poor beast to do its thing. He beat and whipped the miserable animal so much that it let everything go and dropped a beautiful disgusting yellow load on the white sheets.

Poor Masella, who watched the ass liberate its body and had hoped to have been relieved of her poverty, was now left with a payment so abundant that it stunk up the entire house. Right then and there she grabbed a stick and did not give Antonio any time to show her the pumice stones. Instead she gave him a good thrashing. As a result he immediately ran away and went straight to the ogre.

When the ogre saw him coming more in a trot than in a walk, he knew right away what had happened because he had magic powers. So he gave him a juicy scolding for letting himself be swindled by an innkeeper. Indeed, he called Antonio a good for nothing, fit only for his mother's aprons strings, a dupe, a drudge, a dunce, a worthless creature, a laughingstock, a peanut head, a simpleton, an idiot, and a blunderer, who had accepted a beast that stunk of rancid mozzarella for an ass lubricated with treasures. In turn, Antonio swallowed the pill and swore never again to let himself be cheated or mocked by any living creature.

After a year had passed, Antonio had the same dolorous yearning and desperate desire to see his family again. The ogre, who had an ugly face but a generous heart, gave him permission to depart and made him a present of a fine table napkin and said, "Bring this napkin to your mother, and make sure that you don't behave like an ass as you did with the ass. Until you reach home, don't say either 'Open, napkin' or 'Close, napkin.' Otherwise, if something unfortunate happens to you, it will be your own fault. Now go with many greetings and come back soon."

So Antonio departed, but not very far from the grotto he set the napkin on the ground and said, "Open, napkin." Once it was open, there appeared a great deal of very lovely, very magnificent, and very elegant things that were a wonder to behold. As soon as he saw them, Antonio said right away, "Close, napkin." Once it was closed with everything in it, he headed straight to the same inn. As soon as he entered, he said to the innkeeper, "Take this napkin, and keep it safe for me. But make sure that you don't say, 'Open, napkin' or 'Close, napkin.'"

The innkeeper, who was a cunning rascal, said, "Leave it to me." After he gave Antonio a good meal and enough to guzzle so he would drink himself into a stupor, he sent him off to sleep. Then he took the napkin and said, "Open, napkin," and after the napkin opened, it spilled out so many valuable things that he was dazed. Consequently, he found another napkin similar to the magic one and switched them. When Antonio awoke the next morning, he continued his journey and went at a fast pace. As soon as he arrived at his mother's house, he said, "Now we can laugh in the face of poverty. Now I've found the remedy for all our misery, rags, and tatters."

After saying all this, he spread the napkin on the ground and began to cry out, *"Open, napkin."* But he could have repeated himself from here until eternity. It was a waste of time, for it did not spill out either crumbs or specks of straw. Seeing that the entire affair was going against him, he said to his mother, "What a stroke of bad luck! The innkeeper cheated me again. But just wait, because he and I are two. It would be better for him if he had never been born! It would be better for him if he had been run over by a cart! May I lose all my best possessions if, when I pass his inn the next time, I don't smash his place to smithereens to repay him for stealing my jewels and my ass."

When his mother heard these new foolish remarks, she became enraged and said, "Stop it, and get out of my sight! Go break your neck somewhere! Take off. You've ripped apart my guts, and I can't stand you anymore. My hernia swells up, and my goiter grows each time you appear. Stop coming here. From now on this house is like fire for you. I wash my hands of you and consider that I never spewed you forth into this world."

Poor Antonio, who saw the lightning, did not want to wait for the thunder, and as if he had been nabbed stealing laundry, he lowered his head, raised his heels, and galloped straight to the ogre. When the ogre saw him arrive very slowly and making muffled sounds, he played some other music for him and said, "I don't know what keeps me from tearing out one of your eyes. You spitface, blowhard, rotten piece of meat, hen's ass, tattler, trumpet of Vicaria![6] You have to proclaim every little thing to the world! You have to vomit everything in your body and can't even contain chickpeas. If you had kept your mouth shut at the inn, nothing would have happened to you, but you use your tongue like the pulley of a windmill, and you've crushed the happiness that I bestowed upon you with my own hands!"

Poor Antonio put his tail between his legs and swallowed the music, and he remained peacefully in the ogre's service another three ears thinking no more of his home than of becoming a count. However, in time he was bitten by the bug again, caught a fever, and longed to return home. Therefore, he asked the ogre for permission to depart. Since the ogre did not want to be bothered, he was happy to let him depart and gave him a finely crafted club and said, "Carry this club with you and keep it as a souvenir of me. But take care that you do not say *'Rise up, club!'* or *'Settle down, club!'* because I don't want to get mixed up in your affairs."

Antonio took the club and said, "Don't worry. I've grown my wisdom teeth and know how many pairs make three oxen. I'm no longer a boy, and whoever seeks to cheat Antonio will have to kiss his own elbow."

6. Reference to the public crier at the court of Vicaria at Naples. He issued the proclamations of the court to the sound of the trumpet.

Thereupon the ogre responded, "The finished work is all the praise a master needs. Words are spoken by women, and deeds are accomplished by men. You'll be more convincing when I've seen your deed. You've listened to me more than a deaf man: a man who is warned is already half saved."

As the ogre continued to talk, Antonio began heading toward his home. But he had not gone half a mile when he said, "*Rise up, club!*" But these words were not just words but a magic spell because the club began to work like a lathe on poor Antonio's back as if it were possessed by a mischievous imp, and the blows poured from the open sky, one after the other. The wretched Antonio, who felt pounded and thrashed like a Cordovan hide,[7] said quickly, "*Settle down, club!*" and the club stopped playing the counterpoint on the music sheet of his spine. Now that he had learned at his own expense, he said, "Anyone who tries to flee will be made lame because I won't let the opportunity escape me! The person who deserves to get a beating hasn't gone to bed yet!"

After he had muttered this, he arrived at the same inn where he was received with the best welcome in the world because the innkeeper knew what sauce could be made with this pigskin. Upon entering, Antonio said to the innkeeper, "Take this club, and keep it safe for me, but make sure that you don't say, '*Rise up, club!*' because you'll endanger yourself. Listen carefully and don't complain about Antonio because I'm keeping out of this, and nothing will be my fault."

The innkeeper was very pleased about this third piece of good luck and filled Antonio full of soup and made sure he emptied a pitcher of wine. As soon as he threw Antonio on a bed, he ran and picked up the club. Then he called his wife to watch the beautiful show and said, "*Rise up, club!*" And the club began to demolish the spines of the innkeeper and his wife with a whack here and whack there that sounded like thunder, and the beating continued so hard and the couple found themselves in such a terrible predicament that they ran, followed by the club, to wake Antonio and ask for mercy.

When Antonio saw that his plan had been a success and that the macaroni had fallen into the cheese,[8] and the broccoli into the lard, he said, "There's no remedy. You'll be beaten to death by the club unless you restore my things to me."

The innkeeper, who had been soundly beaten, cried out, "Take all that I have and take away this burdensome beating from my back!"

Once Antonio made sure that he had all that had been stolen from him and that everything was in his hands, he said, "*Settle down, club!*" And the club stopped and settled nearby. Then Antonio took the donkey and other things and went to his mother's house, where he had the ass perform a regal show with his rear end and tested the napkin. Then he amassed a great deal of money, married off his sisters, made his mother rich, and proved the truth of the saying:

God helps madmen and boys.

---

7. Goat leather from the Spanish city of Cordova, considered as fine as Moroccan leather when tanned.
8. Old Neapolitan proverb. Now it is more customary to say "the cheese on top of the macaroni."

JACOB AND WILHELM GRIMM

The Magic Table, the Golden Donkey, and the Club in the Sack†

In days of old there was a tailor who had three sons and only one goat. Since they all lived on goat's milk, she had to be fed well and be taken out each day to graze somewhere. The sons took turns doing this, and one day the oldest son led her to the churchyard, where the finest grass was growing. He let her graze there and run about. In the evening, when it was time to go home, he asked her, "Goat, have you had enough?"

The goat answered:

> "Oh, my, I'm stuffed!
> Enough's enough.
> *Meh! Meh!*"

"Then let's head for home," said the boy. He took her by the rope, led her back to the barn, and tied her up.

"Well," said the old tailor, "did the goat have a proper feeding?"

"Oh," answered the son, "she's really stuffed. I can tell she's had more than enough."

But the father wanted to make sure of everything himself. So he went down to the barn, patted the precious creature, and asked, "Goat, have you had enough?"

The goat replied:

> "How can I have eaten enough
> when the ground was dry and horribly rough
> and the leaves and grass were much too tough?
> *Meh! Meh!*"

"What's this I hear!" the tailor exclaimed, and he ran upstairs to his son. "You liar!" he yelled. "You said the goat had enough to eat, and yet you let her starve!" And in his rage he grabbed his yardstick from the wall, gave his son a good beating, and drove him out of the house.

The next day it was the second son's turn, and he chose a place near the garden hedge where only the very best grass was growing, and the goat combed it clean. In the evening, when the son wanted to go home, he asked, "Goat, have you had enough?"

The goat answered:

> "Oh, my, I'm stuffed!
> Enough's enough.
> *Meh! Meh!*"

† Jacob and William Grimm, "The Magic Table, the Golden Donkey, and the Club in the Sack"—
"Tischendeckdich, Goldesel und Knüppel aus dem Sack" (1857), No. 36 in *Kinder- und Hausmärchen. Gesammelt durch die Brüder Grimm* (Göttingen: Dieterich, 1857).

"Then let's head for home," said the boy, and he pulled her home and tied her up in the barn.

"Well," said the old tailor, "did the goat have a proper feeding?"

"Oh," answered the son, "she's really stuffed. I can tell she's had more than enough."

Since the tailor did not trust his son, he went down to the barn and asked, "Goat, have you had enough?"

The goat replied:

> "How can I have eaten enough
> when the ground was dry and horribly rough
> and the leaves and grass were much too tough?
> *Meh! Meh!*"

"The godless scoundrel!" the tailor screamed. "How could he let such a good creature starve?" And he ran out, grabbed his yardstick, and beat his second son out of the house.

Now it was the third son's turn, and he wanted to do a good job. He looked for bushes with the finest leaves and let the goat eat them. In the evening, when he wanted to go home, he asked, "Goat, have you had enough?"

The goat answered:

> "Oh, my, I'm stuffed!
> Enough's enough.
> *Meh! Meh!*"

"Then let's head for home," said the boy. He led her into the barn and tied her up.

"Well," said the old tailor, "did the goat have a proper feeding?"

"Oh," answered the son, "she's stuffed. I can tell she's had more than enough."

Since the tailor did not trust him, he went downstairs and asked, "Goat, have you had enough?"

The wicked animal replied:

> "How can I have eaten enough
> when the ground was dry and horribly rough
> and the leaves and grass were much too tough?
> *Meh! Meh!*"

"Oh, you pack of liars!" the tailor exclaimed. "One as devious and unreliable as the next! You're not going to make a fool out of me anymore!" And in his rage he lost control of himself, ran upstairs, and gave his son such a terrible beating with his yardstick that the boy ran out of the house.

Now the old tailor was alone with his goat. The next morning he went down into the barn, petted the goat, and said, "Come, my dear little goat, I myself shall take you out to graze."

He took her by the rope and led her to green hedges, clusters of yarrow, and other things that goats like to eat.

"This time you can eat to your heart's content," he said to her, and let

her graze until evening. Then he said, "Goat, have you had enough?"
The goat answered:

> "Oh, my, I'm stuffed!
> Enough's enough.
> *Meh! Meh!*"

"Then let's head for home," said the tailor, and he led her into the barn
and tied her up. Just as he was about to leave, he turned around once
more and said, "Now you've really had enough for once!"
But the goat was just as ornery to him as usual and cried out:

> "How can I have eaten enough
> when the ground was dry and horribly rough
> and the leaves and grass were much too tough?
> *Meh! Meh!*"

When the tailor heard that, he was stunned, and he realized he had
driven his sons away without cause.
"Just you wait!" he exclaimed. "You ungrateful creature! Sending you
away would be much too mild a punishment for you. I'm going to brand
you so you'll never be able to show your face among the honest tailors
anymore."
He ran upstairs in great haste, fetched his razor, lathered the goat's head,
and shaved it smooth as the palm of his hand. And, since he thought the
yardstick would be too good for her, he got out his whip and gave her
such a thrashing that she leapt high in the air and dashed away.
When the tailor was all alone in his house, he fell into a great depression
and wished his sons were there again. But no one knew where they had
gone. Meanwhile, his oldest son had been taken on as an apprentice with
a carpenter. He worked hard and learned diligently, and when the time
came for him to depart and begin his travels as a journeyman, the master
gave him a little table that did not appear to be anything special and was
made out of ordinary wood. However, it had one good quality. Whenever
one put it down and said, "Table, be covered," it would immediately be
covered by a clean tablecloth, and on it would be a plate with a fork and
a knife, and dishes with roasted and stewed meat, as much as there was
room for on the table, and a large glass of sparkling red wine to tickle
one's throat. The young journeyman thought, "That's enough to keep you
going for the rest of your life!" Naturally, his spirits were high as he set
out on his travels in the world. He did not care whether an inn was good
or bad or whether he would find something to eat or not. If he had no
desire to stop at an inn, he just went into a field, a forest, or a meadow,
wherever he liked. Then he took the little table off his back, set it down
before him, and said, "Table, be covered!" In seconds everything his heart
desired was there.
After some time had passed, he decided to return to his father in the
hope that his father's anger might have subsided and that he might be
glad to see him with his magic table. Now, it happened that on his way
home he stopped at an inn which was filled with guests. They greeted

him warmly and invited him to sit down and eat with them; otherwise he might have trouble getting something to eat so late.

"No," the carpenter said, "I don't want to take away your last few morsels. Instead, I'd prefer you to be my guests."

They all laughed and thought he was joking with them, but he set up his little table in the middle of the room and said, "Table, be covered!"

Within seconds the table was covered with much better food than the innkeeper could have produced, and the guests inhaled the lovely aroma with their nostrils.

"Help yourselves, dear friends," said the carpenter, and when the guests realized he meant it, they did not have to be asked twice. They drew up their seats, pulled out their knives, and plunged in bravely. What astonished them was that a new dish appeared by itself as soon as one dish became empty. The innkeeper stood in a corner and watched everything without knowing what to say, but he thought, "I could certainly use a cook like that in my business."

The carpenter and his companions enjoyed themselves until late into the night. Finally, they went to sleep, and the young journeyman put his magic table against the wall and went to bed too. The innkeeper's thoughts, however, left him no peace, and he recalled that there was an old table in the storage room that looked just like the magic one. He went and got it and then switched it quietly with the magic table. The next morning the carpenter paid for the lodging and packed the table on his back without realizing that he had the wrong one. He set out on his way and at noon came to his father, who welcomed him with great joy.

"Well, my dear son, what have you learned?" he asked him

"Father, I've become a carpenter."

"That's a good trade," replied the old man, "but what have you brought back with you from your travels?"

"Father, the best thing I've brought back is this table."

The tailor examined it from all sides and said, "I can't say that you've made a masterpiece. It's just a shabby old table."

"But it's a magic table," answered his son. "When I put it down and tell it to be covered, the most delicious dishes appear at once, and wine as well. It will warm your heart with joy. Just invite all our friends and relatives. I'll provide them with good refreshments and a fine meal. My table will give them more than enough to eat."

When the company was assembled, he set the table in the middle of the parlor and said, "Table, be covered!" But the table did not move an inch. It remained there as any ordinary table that cannot understand speech. The poor journeyman now realized that his table had been switched, and he was ashamed at having to appear like a liar. His relatives laughed at him, but they were forced to return home without having anything to eat or drink. His father got out his sewing material again and resumed working, while the son found a job with a master.

The second son had gone to a miller to serve an apprenticeship. When his years were up, the master said, "Since you've done such a good job, I'm going to give you a special kind of donkey. He doesn't draw carts, nor does he carry sacks."

"Well, what's he good for?" asked the young journeyman.

"He spits gold," the miller replied. "If you set him on a piece of cloth and say, 'Bricklebrit,' the good animal will spit out gold pieces from the front and behind."

"That's a wonderful thing," said the journeyman, who thanked his master and went out into the world. Whenever he needed money, he only had to say, "Bricklebrit" to his donkey, and it would rain gold pieces, which he picked off the ground. Wherever he went, only the best was good enough for him, and the more expensive the better, for his purse was always full. After he had traveled about in the world for some time, he thought, "You really ought to seek out your father. If you return to him with the gold donkey, he's bound to forget his anger and give you a nice welcome."

It so happened that he stopped at the same inn at which his brother's magic table had been switched. He led his donkey by the bridle, and the innkeeper wanted to take the animal from him and tie it up, but the young journeyman said, "Don't bother yourself. I'll lead my gray steed into the stable myself and tie him up because I must know where he is."

The innkeeper found this strange and thought that whoever had to take care of his donkey himself did not have much money to spend. But when the stranger reached into his pocket, took out two gold coins, and told him to buy something very good for him, the innkeeper's eyes opened wide. He promptly ran and brought out the best food he could find. After the meal the guest asked the innkeeper what he owed him, and the innkeeper, who had no scruples about chalking up double the amount, charged him another couple of gold pieces. The journeyman reached into his pocket, but his gold had just run out.

"Wait a minute, innkeeper," he said. "I just want to go and fetch some gold."

As he left, he took the tablecloth with him, and the innkeeper did not know what to make of that. Since he was curious, he sneaked after him, and when the guest bolted the stable door, the innkeeper peeped through a knothole. The stranger spread the tablecloth out under the donkey and said, "Bricklebrit," and instantly the animal began to spit so much gold from the front and the rear that it was like a good rainfall.

"The devil take me!" said the innkeeper. "What a way to mint ducats! I wouldn't mind having a money purse like that!"

The guest paid his bill and went to sleep, but the innkeeper crept into the stable, led the money-maker away, and tied up another donkey in its place. Early the next morning, the journeyman departed with a donkey that he thought was his gold donkey. At noon he arrived at his father's house, and the father was delighted to see his son again and gave him a nice welcome.

"What have you made of yourself, my son?" asked the old man.

"A miller, dear father," he replied.

"What have you brought back with you from your travels?"

"Nothing but a donkey."

"There are plenty of donkeys here," the father said. "I really would have preferred a good goat."

"Yes," responded the son, "but this is not an ordinary donkey. It's a gold donkey. If I say 'Bricklebrit,' the good animal spits out enough gold to cover a piece of cloth. Just call our relatives together, and I'll make them all rich people."

"I like the idea," said the tailor. "Then I won't have to torture myself anymore with this sewing."

He himself ran off to gather the relatives together. As soon as they were all assembled, the miller told them to make room. Then he spread his piece of cloth on the floor and brought the donkey into the parlor.

"Now, pay attention," he said, and cried out, "Bricklebrit!" But what fell were not gold pieces, and it was quite clear that the animal knew nothing about the art of making gold, for there are very few donkeys who become so accomplished. The poor miller made a long face. He realized that he had been cheated and apologized to his relatives, who went home as poor as they had come. As for the old man, there was nothing left to do but resume tailoring, and the son hired himself out to a miller.

The third brother had become an apprentice to a turner,[1] and since this is a craft that demands great skill, his apprenticeship had lasted the longest. During this time he had received a letter from his brothers in which they told him about their terrible experiences with the innkeeper who had stolen their magical gifts on the last night before they were to arrive home. When he finished his apprenticeship as turner and was about to set out on his travels, his master gave him a sack because he had done such a good job.

"There's a club in the sack," said the master.

"I can carry the sack on my back, and it may come in handy, but what can I do with the club? It will only make the sack heavy."

"I'll tell you," responded the master. "If someone threatens to harm you, you just have to say, 'Club, come out of the sack,' and the club will jump out at the people and dance on their backs with so much spirit that they won't be able to move a bone in their body for a week. And the club won't let up until you say, 'Club, get back in the sack.' "

The journeyman thanked him, swung the sack over his shoulder, and if anyone came too close to him and threatened him, he would say, "Club, come out of the sack," and the club would immediately jump out and dust off the fellow's coat or jacket without waiting for him to take it off, and then it would finish off all the others, one by one. And that would all happen so quickly that it would be over before one had any time to think.

It was evening when the young turner arrived at the inn where his two brothers had been cheated. He put his knapsack down on the table in front of him and began to tell stories about the remarkable things he had seen in the world.

"Yes," he said, "some people come across such things as a magic table, a gold donkey, and the like. These are wonderful things and not to be laughed at, but they're nothing compared to the treasure I've acquired. And I've got it right here in my sack."

The innkeeper pricked up his ears. "What in the world could that be?"

1. A craftsman who makes different kinds of articles and instruments with a lathe.

he thought to himself. "Perhaps the sack is filled with jewels. There's no reason why they shouldn't be mine as well, for all good things come in threes."

When it was bedtime, the guest stretched himself out on the bench and put his sack underneath his head as a pillow. When the innkeeper thought the guest was sound asleep, he went over to him and cautiously tugged and pulled at the sack to see if he could quietly replace it with another. But the turner had been waiting for this moment, and just as the innkeeper was about to make a final hearty tug, he cried out, "Club, come out of the sack!"

Immediately, the club jumped out of the sack and beat the innkeeper all over his body until the seams of his clothes burst. The innkeeper screamed for mercy, but the louder he screamed the harder the club beat in rhythm on his back until the innkeeper eventually fell to the ground exhausted. Then the turner said, "If you don't give me the magic table and the gold donkey, the dance will soon begin again."

"Oh, no!" the innkeeper exclaimed. "I'll gladly return everything to you. Just have that cursed hobgoblin crawl back into the sack!"

"Mercy shall prevail over justice this time," said the journeyman, "but you'd better watch your step in the future." Then he cried out, "Club, get back in the sack!"

The next morning the turner took the magic table and the gold donkey and continued his journey home to his father. The tailor was delighted to see him again and asked him what he had learned in foreign countries.

"Dear father," he replied, "I've become a turner."

"That's a craft that demands a lot of skill," said the father. "What have you brought back with you from your travels?"

"A precious thing, dear father," he replied. "A club in a sack."

"What!" exclaimed the father. "A club! That's not worth the trouble! You can chop off a club from any old tree."

"But not this kind, father. If I say, 'Club, come out of the sack,' the club will come out and start dancing vigorously on anyone who threatens me, and the club won't stop until the person is lying on the ground and begging for mercy. You see, this club helped me get back the magic table and the gold donkey that the thieving innkeeper stole from my brothers. Now, I want you to invite both of them and all our relatives, for I'm going to provide them with food and drink and fill their pockets with gold as well."

Although the old tailor did not entirely believe him, he gathered all the relatives together. The turner spread out a piece of cloth in the parlor, led the gold donkey inside, and said to his brother, "Now, dear brother, speak to him."

The miller said, "Bricklebrit," and within seconds there were gold pieces pouring onto the cloth as though there had been a sudden thunderstorm. Moreover, the donkey did not stop until they all had more than they could carry. (I can tell from the look on your face that you would have liked to have been there, too.) Then the turner fetched the table and said, "Now, dear brother, speak to it."

No sooner did the carpenter say "Table, be covered," than it was covered and offered an abundance of the finest dishes. Never in his life had the old tailor enjoyed such a meal as the one held in his house that day. All the relatives stayed late into the night, and they were merry and happy. The tailor locked up his needle and thread and his yardstick and flat iron in a cupboard and lived with his sons in joy and splendor.

But whatever happened to the goat that was to blame for the tailor's driving out his three sons? Let me tell you.

She was so ashamed of her bald head that she ran to a foxhole and crawled inside. When the fox came home, a pair of eyes glared at him out of the darkness. He became so frightened that he ran away. When he encountered the bear, he looked so upset that the bear said, "What's the matter, brother fox? Why are you making such a face?"

"Oh," answered Red Fox, "a gruesome beast is sitting in my cave, and he glared at me with his fiery eyes!"

"Well, we'll soon get rid of him," said the bear, and he went to the cave and looked inside. But when he saw the fiery eyes, he too was struck by fear. He wanted nothing to do with the gruesome beast and took off. Soon he met the bee, and when the bee noticed that the bear was looking very pale, she said, "Bear, you look so miserable. What's happened to your good spirits?"

"It's easy for you to talk," the bear responded, "but there's a gruesome beast with glaring eyes in Red Fox's house, and we can't drive him out."

"I feel sorry for you, bear," the bee responded. "You and the fox barely acknowledge me when you see me because I'm such a poor weak creature. Still, I think I can help you."

She flew into the foxhole, landed on the goat's smooth-shaven head, and stung her so hard that the goat jumped up screaming "*Meh! Meh!*" and ran like mad out into the world. And to this day nobody knows what has become of her.

Foolish Peasants

In the folk tradition, there are thousands of tales that depict the foolish peasants known as Hans, Jack, Peter, Else, Gretel, Lizzy, or Katy, who generally survive all kinds of adventures despite their stupidity and naiveté. In particular, they cannot understand or use language very well, and there is a humorous cycle of oral and literary tales in which the foolish peasant understands everything he hears in a literal sense and acts accordingly. When these fools try to think, they actually cause more damage. Their actions have disastrous results, and often it is the peasant's mother, husband, or wife who has to beat some sense into the dumb person to order his or her life. In some cases, the foolish people are sent to a madhouse or wander off and get lost forever.

GIAMBATTISTA BASILE

Vardiello†

Grannonia of Aprano[1] was a woman of very sound judgment, but she had a son called Vardiello who was the most unfortunate and simple-minded fellow in the village. However, since a mother's eyes are blind and dazzled, and since she had such a profound love for him, she constantly tended him and stroked him as if he were the most handsome creature in the world.

Now Grannonia had a hen which was about to hatch chickens, and she had placed all her hope in this bird because she expected it to hatch a good brood and to bring her handsome earnings. Since she had to go on an errand, she called her son and said to him, "My handsome boy, apple of my eye, listen to me. Keep your eye on this hen, and if she gets up to peck around for food, be alert and make sure that she returns to her nest. Otherwise the eggs will get cold, and then you'll have neither eggs nor chicks."

"Leave it to me," said Vardiello. "You don't think I'm deaf, do you?"

"Another thing, blessed son," his mother remarked, "there's a jar with some poison on the cupboard. Make sure that you keep away from it, because, if you touch it, you'll wind up stretched out on your feet."

"May heaven help me," replied Vardiello. "I won't go near the poison,

† Giambattista Basile, "Vardiello"—"Vardiello" (1634), *Quarto passatempo nella prima giornata* in *Lo cunto de li cunti overo Lo trattenemiento de peccerille*, De Gian Alessio Abbattutis, 5 vols. (Naples: Ottavio Beltrano, 1634–36).
1. A village between Naples and Aversa.

but you've been wise to think about it and warn me because I could have eaten it, and there would have been nothing left of me."

Then the mother left, and Vardiello was alone, and so as not to lose any time, he went into the garden to make holes which he covered with sticks and dirt so that children would fall into them. In the middle of his work he saw that the hen had begun walking about outside the henhouse. So he began to cry out, "Shoo, shoo! Come here. Get away from there."

But the hen did not move a claw, and Vardiello, who saw that the hen was as stubborn as a mule, began to stamp his feet at her and continued to yell, "Shoo, shoo!" After he stamped his feet, he threw his cap at her. After the cap, he flung a rolling pin, which hit her full force, and she died with her feet stretched out. When Vardiello saw this terrible catastrophe, he tried to think how he could repair the damage, and making a virtue out of necessity, he took down his pants and sat right down on the nest to keep the eggs warm, but he squashed the eggs all at the same time and made an omelette out of them. Realizing that he had now caused double trouble, he wanted to hit his head against a wall. Yet, in the end, since every pain finishes in the mouth, his stomach rumbled, and he decided to stuff it with the hen. So, after plucking the feathers and sticking the hen on a good spit, he lit a fire and began to roast it. When it was almost done, he sought to prepare everything in time. So he spread a beautiful linen cloth over an old chest, took a jug, and went down into the cellar in order to tap some wine from a barrel. As he was in the taproom, he heard a noise, a crash, a crumbling of the house as though an armed cavalry were storming through the house. Frightened, he looked about and saw that a tomcat had seized the chicken with the entire spit, and another cat was running after it and screeching for its share.

In order to stop another disaster, Vardiello threw himself like an unchained lion onto the cat, but in his haste, he left the wine barrel open, and after playing hide and seek with the cat throughout the house, he recovered the hen, but the barrel was now empty. When Vardiello returned to the cellar, he saw his beautiful mess, and tears streamed from his eyes just as the wine had streamed from the barrel. Now he really had to use his head to repair the damage so that his mother would not notice how much had been destroyed. So he took a sack filled to the brim with flour and spread and scattered it all over the floor. Despite all this, he counted the number of disasters on his fingers and thought that his mother would certainly stop loving him after she saw all these asinine and incredible things that had happened. Therefore, he courageously decided that his mother should not find him alive, and he took down from the cupboard the jar of candied nuts that his mother had told him was filled with poison. Then he emptied the jar, and with his stomach full, he got into the oven.

Meanwhile his mother returned, and after knocking at the door for some time, she realized that nobody heard her. So she gave the door a kick, entered, and called her son with a loud voice. Again no one responded, and she sensed that something bad had happened. Therefore, she yelled even more loudly, "Vardiello, Vardiello, are you deaf? Don't you hear me? Are you paralyzed? Why don't you come? Has the cat caught your tongue? Why don't you answer? Where are you, gallows face? Where have you vanished to, bad seed? If only I had strangled you in my belly before giving birth to you!"

When Vardiello heard this uproar, he finally cried out in a pitiful little voice, "Here I am, inside the oven. And you'll never see me again, mama."

"Why not?" asked the poor mother.

"Because I've poisoned myself," the son replied.

"Alas," Grannonia responded, "how did you do it? What could have caused you to do such a thing? Who gave you the poison?"

So Vardiello told her one by one all the wonderful things that he had done and had caused him to want to die and to abandon this world. When his mother heard this, she felt miserable and unfortunate, and it was all she could do to get Vardiello out of his melancholy mood. Since she loved him with all her heart, she gave him other sweet things to eat to make him forget the incident with the candied nuts, which were not poison but were actually medicine for the stomach. Thus, after calming him with some kind words and a thousand caresses, she pulled him out of the oven and gave him a good piece of cloth that he was to go and sell. At the same time, she told him not to do business with anyone who talked too much.

"Fine!" said Vardiello. "You can count on me. I'll do well by you."

Thereupon, he took the cloth and headed toward the city of Naples, where he strolled through the streets crying, "Cloth for sale! Cloth for sale!"

But whenever anyone asked him, "What kind of cloth is this?" he responded, "You're not the right one. You talk too much." And if someone else asked, "How much is the price of the cloth?" he told him that he was a talker, and all his chatter gave him a headache and made him deaf.

Finally, Vardiello saw a plaster statue in the courtyard of a house that had been abandoned because it was haunted by a goblin. The poor fellow was exhausted and worn out from walking so much. So he sat down on a little bench. Since he did not see anyone entering or leaving the house that seemed like a ransacked village, he was somewhat astounded and said to the statue, "My friend, does anyone live in this house?"

Seeing that the statue did not respond and seemed to be a man of few words, Vardiello added, "Would you like to buy this cloth? I'll give you a good deal."

When the statue continued to be silent, he said, "My word, I've found the man I was looking for! Well, take this cloth and have it inspected. Then you can tell me your price. I'll return tomorrow for the money."

After saying this, Vardiello left the cloth where he had been sitting, and the very first boy who entered the courtyard to do nature's work found this treasure and ran off with it. Meanwhile, Vardiello returned to his mother without the cloth and told her what had happened. She thought she was going to have a heart attack and cried out, "When are you going to get your head on straight? Look at what you've done to me! Are you aware of what you've done? But I'm to blame because I was too tender-hearted and should have punished you with a good spanking the very first time you did something wrong. Now I realize that the merciful doctor does not heal the wound. But if you keep on doing all this, you'll end up by destroying us, and we'll all have to pay for it."

In response Vardiello said, "Be quiet, mama. It's not how you think. You'll soon have newly minted coins in your pocket. Do you think that I'm from the hick village Joio[2] and don't know what I'm doing? Wait until tomorrow. It's not very far from here to Belvedere,[3] and you'll see whether I can put a handle to this shovel."

The next day—when the shadows of the night left the country, pursued by the sun's constables—Vardiello went to the statue in the courtyard and said, "Good day, sir. Are you now ready to give me the money for the cloth? It's time to pay me."

But when he saw the statue remained silent, he grabbed a stone and fired it with all his might and hit the statue right in the middle of its chest so that a vein broke, and this was his salvation because, when the plaster crumbled, Vardiello discovered a pot full of gold coins which he seized with his two hands, and he ran at breakneck speed to his home crying out, "Mama, mama, look at all the gold coins I have. Look! Just look!"

When his mother saw the money and knew that her son would probably spill the beans to everyone in the world, she told him to stand at the door and watch for the man who sold ricotta because she wanted to buy some milk. Vardiello, who was a glutton, sat down at once while his mother went upstairs, and from the window above she showered him with bunches of grapes and dry figs for more than half an hour. Vardiello gathered them up and screamed, "Mama, mama, get out the basins, bring out the wash-tubs, prepare the baskets. If this rain continues, we'll become rich." And after he had stuffed his belly full with the raisins and figs, he went upstairs to sleep.

Now it happened one day that two scoundrels who were always in trouble were at court and quarreling about a gold coin that they had found on the ground when Vardiello arrived and said, "What asses you are to quarrel about a single gold coin like this! It's nothing compared to the pot full of gold coins that I found!"

When the judge heard this, his ears perked up, and he questioned Vardiello about how, when, and with whom he had found the money. And Vardiello responded, "I found the pot in the courtyard of a house next to the man who didn't speak. It was the very same day that it rained raisins and dry figs."

Surprised by this ridiculous reply, the judge ordered Vardiello to be seized and taken to the hospital,[4] where he could be better judged. This was how the son's ignorance made his mother rich, and his mother's sound judgment could remedy her son's stupidity. Indeed, we can clearly see that

it's difficult to smash a ship on the rocks
when navigated by a good pilot.

2. A village in the province of Salerno called Ioio, now called Gioi. It was known as a very savage and primitive place and became a symbol of obtuseness and simplemindedness.
3. The name of a castle erected on one of the volcanic hills near Pozzuoli by Frederick II; Basile uses the name as a pun: *un bel vedere* = a beautiful sight.
4. The reference is to the Ospedale degli Incurabili (the Hospital of the Incurables) in Naples, which also treated the insane.

JACOB AND WILHELM GRIMM

Freddy and Katy†

Once there was a man named Freddy and a woman named Katy who got married and began living together in wedlock. One day Freddy said, "I'm going to the field, Katy. When I return, I want some roast meat on the table to take care of my hunger and a cool drink for my thirst."

"Just run along, Freddy," Katy answered. "Just go. I'll have everything ready the way you want it."

When noontime drew near, she got a sausage from the chimney, put it in a frying pan, added butter, and set it on the fire. The sausage began to fry and sizzle, and while Katy was standing there and holding the handle of the pan, she began thinking, and it occurred to her, "You could go down into the cellar and draw the beer before the sausage is done." Therefore, she fixed the pan so it would not tip, took a tankard, and went down into the cellar, where she began to draw the beer. As the beer was flowing into the tankard and Katy was gazing at it, she suddenly recalled, "Hey, the dog's upstairs, and since he's not tied up, he could get the sausage from the pan. Oh, it's a lucky thing I thought of that!"

She ran up the cellar stairs in a jiffy, but her spitz had already grabbed the sausage with his jaws and was dragging it along the ground. Still, Katy was quick to act: she ran after him and chased him a long way over the fields, but the dog was faster and gripped the sausage tightly as he dashed off with it beyond her reach.

"What's gone is gone," said Katy, who turned back home. Since she was tired from running, she walked very slowly and cooled herself off. In the meantime, the beer continued to flow from the keg, for Katy had forgotten to shut the tap. When the tankard became full and there was no more room in it, the beer flowed over onto the cellar floor until the whole keg was empty. As soon as Katy reached the top of the stairs, she saw the accident and cried out, "Heavens! How are you going to keep Freddy from noticing it?"

She thought for a while until she finally remembered a sack with fine wheat flour that was still up in the loft. It had been bought at the last fair, and she thought it would be a good idea to fetch it and sprinkle it over the beer. "Yes," she said, "a stitch in time saves nine." She climbed up to the loft, brought down the sack and threw it right on the tankardful of beer, causing it to topple. Now even Freddy's drink swam about in the cellar. "That's quite all right," said Katy. "They all belong in the same boat together." Then she scattered the flour all over the cellar. When she was finished, she was tremendously pleased with her work and said, "How clean and neat everything looks here!"

† Jacob and Wilhelm Grimm, "Freddy and Katy"—"Der Frieder und das Katherlieschen" (1857), No. 59 in *Kinder- und Hausmärchen. Gesammelt durch die Brüder Grimm* (Göttingen: Dieterich, 1857).

At noon Freddy came home and said, "Well, wife, what have you made for me?"

"Oh, Freddy," she answered, "I wanted to fry a sausage for you, but while I was drawing the beer in the cellar, the dog came and made off with the pan. Then, while I was chasing the dog, the beer ran over, and as I went to dry up the beer with the wheat flour, I knocked over the tankard. But don't get upset, the cellar is all dry again."

"Katy, Katy!" he said. "You shouldn't have done that! Just think! You let the sausage be carried off, you let the beer run out of the keg, and on top of it, you squandered our fine flour!"

"Well, Freddy, I didn't know that. You should have told me."

"If that's the way your wife is," Freddy thought, "then you'd better take precautions." Now, Freddy had saved up a nice sum in talers that he had finally changed into gold, and he went to Katy and said, "Look, these here are yellow chips, and I'm going to put them into a pot and bury them in the stable under the cow's manger. Make sure you keep away from them, or I'll teach you a lesson!"

"Don't worry, Freddy," she said. "I promise not to touch them."

Soon after, while Freddy was away, some peddlers came to the village selling clay pots and bowls, and they asked the young woman whether she wanted to trade with them.

"Oh, you're so kind," she said. "I don't have any money and can't buy anything. But if you can use yellow chips, I'll make a trade with you."

"Yellow chips? Why not? But we'd have to have a look first."

"Well, just go into the barn and dig under the cow's manger, and you'll find the yellow chips. I'm not allowed to go there."

The scoundrels went there, dug up the ground, and found pure gold. Then they put it into their pack and ran off, leaving the pots and bowls behind in the house. Katy thought she should make use of her new kitchenware, but since there was already so much of it in the kitchen, she knocked the bottoms out of the new pots and hung them as ornaments on the poles of the fence all around the house. When Freddy came and saw the new ornaments, he asked, "Katy, what have you done?"

"Well, Freddy, I bought them with the yellow chips that were buried under the cow's manger. I didn't go near them myself. I made the peddlers dig them up."

"Oh, wife!" said Freddy. "What have you done? They weren't yellow chips. They were pure gold, our entire fortune! You shouldn't have done that."

"Well, Freddy," she said. "I didn't know that. You should have told me before."

Katy stood there a while and tried to think of something. Finally, she said, "Listen, Freddy, we can get the gold back. Let's run after the thieves."

"All right," said Freddy. "Let's try it, but take some butter and cheese so that we have something to eat along the way."

"Yes, Freddy, I'll take some along."

They set out on foot, and since Freddy was faster, Katy trailed after him. "It's to my advantage," she thought. "If we turn back, then I'll have a head start." Now she came to a hill where there were deep wagon ruts on both sides. "Just look!" said Katy. "They've trampled and torn apart the poor earth so that it's all beaten up! It will never get well again as long as it lives." Out of the kindness of her heart, she took out the butter and smeared the ruts on the right and left so they would not be hurt as much by the wheels. While she was performing this charitable work and was bending over, a cheese rolled out of her pocket and down the hill.

"I've already climbed up the hill once," said Katy, "and I'm not going down again. Let some other cheese run down and bring it back."

So she took another cheese and rolled it down the hill. However, this cheese did not come back either. So she sent a third one after it and thought, "Perhaps they don't like to walk alone and are waiting for company." When all three of them failed to return, she said, "I'm not sure what all this means, but it's possible that the third one didn't find the way and has gone astray. I'll just send a fourth to call them all back."

The fourth did not do the job any better than the third. Then Katy became so annoyed that she threw the fifth and sixth down the hill too, and they were the last she had. For a while she stood and waited for them to come back, but when they did not return, she said, "Oh, you're just the right ones to send in search of death because you really drag your feet. Do you think I'm going to wait for you any longer? I'm moving on, and you can catch up with me. You've got younger legs than mine."

Katy went on and found Freddy, who had stopped to wait for her because he wanted something to eat.

"Now let's have some of the food you brought along."

She handed him the dry bread.

"Where's the butter and cheese?" her husband asked.

"Oh, Freddy," said Katy, "I smeared the ruts with the butter, and the cheese will soon be here. One got away from me, and so I sent the others after it."

"You shouldn't have done that, Katy," said Freddy. "Just think! You smeared the butter on the road, and you let the cheese roll down the hill!"

"Well, Freddy, you should have told me."

They ate the dry bread together, and Freddy said, "Katy, did you lock up the house before you left?"

"No, Freddy, you should have told me before."

"Well, then, go home and lock it up before we continue on our way. Also, bring something else to eat with you. I'll wait for you here."

As Katy began walking back, she began thinking, "Freddy obviously wants something else to eat. Since he doesn't like butter and cheese, I'll bring him some dried pears in a handkerchief and a jug full of vinegar to drink."

When she was about to leave the house again, she bolted the upper half of the door and took the lower half off the hinges. Then she carried it on her back because she thought the house would be safer if she kept the door with her. Then she took her time walking back since she thought to herself, "Freddy will have all the more time to rest himself."

Once she reached her husband again, Katy said, "There, Freddy, now you have the house door, and you'll be able to keep the house safe yourself."

"Oh, God!" he said. "What a clever wife I've got! She takes off the lower half of the door so that anyone can walk in, and she bolts the upper half. Now it's too late to go home again, but since you brought the door here, you'll carry it the rest of the way yourself."

"I don't mind carrying the door, Freddy, but dried pears and the jug of vinegar are too heavy for me. I'll hang them on the door and let the door carry them."

Now they went into the forest to look for the thieves, but they did not find them. When it finally became dark, they climbed up into a tree to spend the night. No sooner were they sitting up high than some men came along who tend to carry off things that do not want to be carried away and who tend to find things before they are lost. They camped out right beneath the tree in which Freddy and Katy were sitting. They made a fire and began to divide their loot. Freddy climbed down the other side of the tree and gathered some stones, after which he climbed back. He wanted to throw the stones at the thieves to kill them. However, he missed, and the thieves cried out, "Soon it will be morning, and the wind's knocking down the pinecones."

Katy was still carrying the door on her back, and since it was so heavy and weighing her down, she thought the dried pears were to blame and said, "Freddy, I've got to throw the dried pears down."

"No, Katy, not now," he answered. "They could give us away."

"Oh, Freddy, I've got to! They're too heavy for me!"

"Well, then, do it, for all I care!"

She rolled the pears down between the branches, and the thieves said, "Here come some bird droppings."

Shortly afterward, since the door was still very heavy on her back, Katy said, "Oh, Freddy, I've got to pour out the vinegar."

"No, Katy, you mustn't do that. It could give us away."

"Oh, Freddy, I've got to! It's too heavy for me."

"Well, then, do it, for all I care!"

So she poured out the vinegar, and it splattered all over the thieves. "The dew's already falling," the men said to one another.

Finally, Katy thought, "Could it be the door that's been weighing me down?" And she said, "Freddy, I've got to throw the door down."

"No, Katy, that could give us away."

"Oh, Freddy, I've got to. It's too heavy for me."

"No, Katy, hold on to it tight."

"Oh, Freddy, I'm going to let it drop."

"All right!" Freddy answered irritably. "Let it drop for all I care!"

The door fell down with a great crash, and the thieves below cried out, "The devil's coming down the tree!"

They cleared out and left everything behind. Early the next morning, when Freddy and Katy came down the tree, they found all their gold again and carried it home.

When they were home once more, Freddy said, "Katy, you've got to be industrious and work hard now."

"Yes, Freddy, of course I will. I'll go into the field and cut down the fruit."

When Katy went into the field, she said to herself, "Should I eat before I cut. I think I'll eat!" So Katy ate and became tired from eating. When she started to cut some fruit, she began daydreaming and cut all her clothes to pieces—her apron, her dress, and her blouse. Upon snapping out of her dream, she stood there half naked and said to herself, "Is that me, or is it someone else? Oh, that's not me!"

Meanwhile, it was already night, and Katy ran into the village and knocked on her husband's window.

"Freddy!" she called out.

"What is it?"

"I'd like to know if Katy's inside."

"Yes, yes," answered Freddy. "She's probably lying down asleep."

"Good," she said. "Then I'm clearly at home already," and she ran off.

Outside the village Katy came across some thieves who were planning a theft. She went up to them and said, "I want to help you steal."

The thieves thought she knew her way around the region and agreed to let her join them. Then Katy went in front of the houses and called out, "Folks, do you have anything you want stolen?"

"This won't do!" thought the thieves, and they wished they could get rid of Katy.

"There's a turnip patch owned by the parson outside the village," they said to her. "We want you to go there and pull some of the turnips for us."

Katy went to the patch and began to pull up some turnips, but she was so lazy that she remained in a crouched position. Soon a man came by, stopped, watched her, and thought the devil was tearing up all the turnips in the patch. So he ran to the parson in the village and said, "Parson, the devil's in your turnip patch, and he's tearing up all your turnips."

"Oh, God!" exclaimed the parson. "I've got a lame foot and can't run out to expel him."

"I'll carry you on my back," said the man, and he carried him out to the field. When they got to the turnip patch, Katy straightened herself up.

"Oh, it's really the devil!" the parson cried out, and they both rushed off. Indeed, since his fright was so great, the parson was able to run faster with his lame foot than the man who had carried him with his two sound legs.

The Revenge and Reward
of Neglected Daughters

There are thousands of oral and literary versions of "Cinderella," one of the most popular fairy tales in the world. Motifs of the Cinderella tale-type can be found in Greek and Roman mythology. There is also a Sanskrit version of the fifth century C.E. underlying Kalidasa's drama *Sakuntala*. There are indications that the tale may have originated in ancient China or Egypt. The shoe or slipper test may have been connected to a marriage custom in which the bridegroom takes off the bride's old shoes and replaces them with new ones. But this thesis has never been completely verified, and depending on the society and customs, shoes are used in many different ways in marriage celebrations. In the various literary versions, the shoes are leather, gold, silver, and glass. Perrault invented the glass slippers most likely as an ironic joke since a glass slipper was likely to break if it were to fall off a foot. What most of the tales, oral and literary, have in common is the conflict between a young girl and her stepmother and siblings about her legacy. Cinderella must prove that she is the rightful successor in a house in which she has been deprived of her rights. She receives help from her dead mother in the guise of doves, fairies, and godmothers. Belief in the regeneration of the dead who can help the living in the form of plants or animals underlies one of the key motifs of the fairy tale. In the European literary tradition, which first began with Bonaventure des Périers's *Les nouvelles recréations et joyeux devis* (*New Recreations and Joyous Games*, 1558), it is clear that Basile played a role in influencing Perrault and d'Aulnoy, who, in turn, had some effect on the Grimms' tale. Significant in Basile's tale is the active role that Cinderella plays in determining her future: she kills her stepmother and stops her father's ship from returning from Sardinia. Some of this activism, in contrast to Perrault's narrative, can be seen in the Grimms' version. Since there were so many different versions by the time the Grimms composed their "Cinderella"—for instance, they may have also been influenced by the Bohemian version "Laskopal und Miliwaka" in *Sagen der Böhmischen Vorzeit aus einigen Gegenden alter Schlösser und Dörfer* (*Legends of the Bohemian Early Period from some Regions of old Castles and Villages*, 1808)—it is difficult to establish one source for their work in particular. Clearly, many different literary and oral tales fostered a huge Cinderella cycle in the East and the West. Alan Dundes's *Cinderella: A Folklore Casebook* (1982) provides valuable background information and discussions about the cycle and different interpretations. The early literary work of Basile, Mme d'Aulnoy, and the Grimms certainly played a role in the creation of nineteenth-century plays and musical adaptations such as Nicolas Isouard's popular fairy opera *Cendrillon* (1810), as well as in the equally successful opera *La cenerentola* (1817) by Gioacchino Antonio Rossini.

GIAMBATTISTA BASILE

The Cat Cinderella†

Once upon a time there was a prince who was a widower, and he had a daughter who was so dear to him that he saw the world through only her eyes. At one point he hired a sewing teacher who taught her small chain work, open sewing, hem stitching, and fringes and showed her more affection than words can describe. But the father soon remarried, and he took a rambunctious, evil, and diabolical woman as his wife, and this wicked lady was so repulsed by her stepdaughter that she began throwing her sour glances, making wry faces, and scowling at her. As a result, Zezolla, for that was the daughter's name, became frightened and kept complaining to her teacher about how badly her stepmother was treating her and said, "Oh God, if only you could be my dear little mama since you are so affectionate and fond of me!"

Since Zezolla continued to sing this little song, she succeeded in putting a bug in her teacher's ear until the woman was spurred by the devil and said, "If you want to pursue this crazy idea, I shall become your mother, and you'll become so dear to me that you'll be the apple of my eye."

She wanted to continue talking, but Zezolla said, "Excuse me if I interrupt you. I know you love me very much. There's no need to say anymore. Just teach me what I have to do because I'm new at this. You write the orders, and I'll carry them out."

"Well, then," her teacher said, "listen carefully. Pay attention, and you'll succeed in baking bread as white as flowers. As soon as your father leaves the house, tell your stepmother that you want one of those old dresses from the large chest in the closet so you won't spoil the one that you are wearing now. Since she prefers to see you in rags and tatters, she will open the chest and say, 'Hold the lid.' And you're to hold it while she searches inside. Then you must let it fall right away, and it will break her neck. Once she's gone, you know that your father would even forge money to please you. So when he is being affectionate with you, ask him to take me as his wife. Then your fortune will be made, for you'll be the mistress of my life."

After Zezolla had heard this, every hour seemed a thousand years, and then she carried out her teacher's plans exactly as she had advised. When the mourning period for her stepmother's death had ended, she began to sound out her father about marrying the teacher. At first, the prince thought she was joking, but his daughter kept pricking him with the flat end of the pin until she stuck him with the point and he yielded to Zezolla's words. So he wed Carmosina, the teacher, and arranged for a great celebration.

Now, while the newlyweds were involved with one another, Zezolla

† Giambattista Basile, "The Cat Cinderella"—"La gatta Cenerentola" (1634), *Sesto passatempo della prima giornata* in *Lo cunto de li cunti overo Lo trattenemiento de peccerille*, De Gian Alessio Abbattutis, 5 vols. (Naples: Ottavio Beltrano, 1634–36).

went out on the terrace of her house, and a dove flew onto a wall and said to her, "Whenever you desire anything, send a message to the dove of the fairies on the island of Sardinia, and you will have it at once."

For five or six days, the new stepmother smothered Zezolla with caresses and had her sit at the place of honor at the table. She gave her the best tidbits and dressed her in the most beautiful clothes. But after a short period of time, she forgot the favor that Zezolla had done for her and banished it from her mind. (Oh, how sorry the soul that has such an evil mistress!) Then she began to bring her own six daughters upstairs. Until then she had kept them in hiding, but now she worked on her husband until they won his affection, and he let his own daughter fall out of his heart. Things always go from bad to worse. Soon she was reduced to taking a room next to the kitchen and went from the canopy to the hearth, from the luxury of silk and gold to rags, from the scepter to the spit. Indeed, she changed not only her condition but even her name and was no longer called Zezolla but Cat Cinderella.

Now it so happened that the prince had to go to Sardinia on urgent business for the state, and he asked his six stepdaughters, Imperia, Calamita, Fiorella, Diamante, Colombina, and Pasquarella, one by one, what they would like him to bring back to them from his trip. One after another they asked for a dressing gown, a headdress, cosmetics, amusing games, and for this thing and that. Finally, almost as if he were mocking her, he asked his daughter, "And what would you like?"

"Nothing," Zezolla replied. "But give my regards to the dove of the fairies and ask her to send me something. And, if you forget, I wish that you will not be able to move either forward or backward. Remember what I've said. Woe to you if you don't keep your promise!"

The prince departed, took care of his business in Sardinia, bought what his stepdaughters had requested, and forgot all about Zezolla. But when he had embarked on his ship and it was ready to sail, the ship was not able to leave the port, and it seemed that there was some obstacle preventing it from moving. The captain of the ship, who was almost desperate, became exhausted from trying to get the ship to move and fell asleep. In his dreams he saw a fairy who said to him, "Do you know why you can't move the ship out of the port? Well, it's because the prince who is on board your ship has not kept the promise that he made to his daughter. He has remembered all the other promises except the one that he made to his own flesh and blood."

When the captain awoke, he told his dream to the prince, who was upset by his negligence. So he went to the grotto of the fairies, and after giving the greetings from his daughter, he asked that they send something to her. Then, lo and behold, a beautiful young woman who resembled a standard-bearer came out of the grotto and told him to thank his daughter for her warm regards and that she wanted his daughter to enjoy herself because she cared so much for Zezolla. As she said this, she gave him a date tree, a spade, a golden can, and a silk napkin and told him that the tree was to be planted, and the other things were to be used to cultivate the plant. The prince was astounded by these gifts, took his leave from the fairy and turned to journey toward his country. When he arrived, he gave his stepdaughters what they had requested, and lastly he gave Zezolla the gifts that the fairy had sent. Well, she almost jumped out of her skin for joy. She immediately planted the date tree in a beautiful pot with the help of the spade, and then she watered it and dried it with the silken napkin day and night. Within four days it grew to the size of a woman, and a fairy came out of the tree and said, "What would you like?"

Zezolla replied that she wished to leave the house every now and then without her sisters knowing it. The fairy replied, "Just go to the pot whenever you like and say,

> Oh my golden date tree,
> With the golden spade I've dug you,
> With the golden can I've watered you,
> With the silken napkin I've dried you.
> Now strip yourself and dress me!

And when you want to undress, change the last line and say, 'Strip me and dress yourself!' "

Soon after there was a festival day, and the teacher's daughters left the house in full blossom, decked out, made up, all ribbons, bells, trinkets, all flowers, perfume, and roses. Zezolla ran at once to the pot and uttered the words that the fairy had taught her. Within seconds she was dressed like a queen and was placed on a horse and accompanied by twelve neatly dressed pages. Then she traveled to where her sisters had gone, and their mouths drooled with envy when they saw the beauty of this splendid dove.

Now it so happened that the king appeared at this same place, caught sight of the incredible beauty of Zezolla, and was immediately enchanted by her. He told his loyal servant to find out all he could about this remarkable beauty, who she was, and where she lived. The servant immediately began to follow her, but when she realized this, she threw down a handful of gold coins from the date tree that she had obtained for this purpose. When the servant saw the coins on the ground, he forgot to follow the horse because he wanted to fill his pockets with the money. Meanwhile, she rushed home and slipped out of the clothes in the way that the fairy had taught her. Later, when the ugly sisters arrived, they told her all about the beautiful things they had seen to vex her.

At the same time the servant returned to the king and told him about the incident with the money, and the king became enraged and told him that he had thrown away his pleasure for some shitty coins and at the next festival he was at all costs to find out who the beautiful maiden was and where this lovely bird made her nest.

When the next festive occasion arrived, the sisters got dressed up in elegant fashion. Then they departed, and the despised Zezolla was left at the hearth. But she quickly ran to the date tree and uttered the usual words. Lo and behold, a group of damsels appeared carrying different objects such as a mirror, a small bottle of squash water,[1] curling tongs, rouge, hairpins, dresses, a diadem, and a necklace. After they made Zezolla as beautiful as the sun, they put her in a coach drawn by six horses and

1. A cosmetic oil made from certain kinds of squash.

accompanied by footmen and pages in livery. When she arrived at the same place as the other celebration, she astonished her sisters and kindled a fire in the breast of the king.

Later, as she was leaving the party, she threw a bunch of pearls and jewels on the ground when she noticed that the servant had started to follow her. Since they were things that one could not ignore, he stopped to pick them up, and this gave her time to reach home and undress as usual. The servant returned to the king very downcast, and the king said, "By the soul of my ancestors, if you don't find this maiden, I'll give you a sound beating, and I'll give you as many kicks in your ass as you have hairs in your beard!"

When the next festive occasion arrived, the sisters left the house, and Zezolla went to the date tree and repeated the magic phrase. This time she was dressed in splendid fashion and placed in a golden coach with so many servants around her that she seemed to be a whore surprised during a promenade and arrested by constables who surrounded her.[2] Then she went and made her sisters' mouths water. When she left this time, the king's servant tied himself to the coach with a cord. When Zezolla saw that he was alongside the coach, she said to the coachman, "Use the whip!" And the coach began to race ahead, and the pace was so rapid that she lost a slipper[3] that was the most beautiful and valuable shoe that had ever been seen. The servant was not able to keep up with the coach that went flying away, but he managed to pick up the slipper from the ground, brought it to the king, and told him what had happened.

The king took the slipper in his hand and said, "If the foundation is so lovely, what must the house be like? Oh beautiful candlestick, where can the candle be that consumes me? Oh tripod of the beautiful cauldron in which my life is boiling! Oh beautiful corks[4] attached to the fishing line of Cupid with which he has caught this soul! Behold, I embrace you and hold you tightly, and if I cannot reach the plant, I shall adore the roots, and if I cannot possess the capitals,[5] I shall kiss the base. You have already captured a white foot; now you have taken hold of a melancholy heart! Through you she who rules my life is taller by half a foot,[6] and through you my life grows in sweetness as long as I regard and possess you."

After he poured out these words, the king summoned the scribe and ordered the trumpeters to sound the *taratara* and spread the royal proclamation that all the women in the land were to come to a public celebration and a banquet which he intended to give. When the appointed day arrived, my but there was an abundance of food and great feasting! Where did all the tarts and cakes come from? Where did all the stews and

2. The whores frequently broke a law in Naples that forbade them to ride in carriages along the public walks or in gondolas along the beach at Posillipo. If they were caught by the police, they were arrested and taken to prison.
3. Basile uses the Neapolitan term *chianiello* or *pianella*, which was a patten and slipped over the shoes and had high heels. Pattens had gone out of fashion by the end of the seventeenth century. Instead of using the unfamiliar word "patten," I am using "slipper."
4. The corks of the slippers.
5. Probably a reference to the architectural supports of arches that were placed high in buildings or hallways.
6. The pattens or slippers had high heels.

meatballs come from? Where did all the macaroni and ravioli come from? There was more than enough stuff to fill an entire army.

Soon all the women arrived—the nobles and the commoners, the rich and poor, young and old, beautiful and ugly—and after they had finished their due, the king said the *prosit*[7] and began trying the slipper on all his guests one by one to see whether it would fit any of the ladies so that he might recognize the maiden he was looking for from the form of the slipper. But he could not find the foot that fit and became desperate. However, after he ordered everyone to be silent, he said, "Return tomorrow to do penance with me one more time. But if you truly love me, do not leave a single woman home, no matter who she may be."

Then the prince said, "I have a daughter, but she always looks after the hearth because she is worthless and a disgrace and doesn't deserve to sit at the table where you eat."

"Well, it will be my pleasure," said the king, "to have her first on my list."

So they took their leave, and the next day they all returned, and Zezolla came with Carmosina's daughters. As soon as the king saw her, he had the impression that she was the one he desired, but he did not let on how he felt.

When they finished digesting their meal, it was time for the slipper test. As soon as it came near Zezolla, it threw itself at the foot of the little painted egg of Cupid just as iron is attracted to the magnet. When the king saw this, he ran and took Zezolla in his arms and led her to sit on the throne beneath the canopy, where he put the crown on her head and ordered everyone to bow and curtsy to her as their queen. When the sisters saw this, they burst with rage and did not have the stomach to bear the agony of their breaking hearts. So they slipped off home to their mother, confessing, in spite of themselves, that

you must be mad to oppose the stars.

CHARLES PERRAULT

Cinderella;
or,
The Glass Slipper†

Once upon a time there was a gentleman who took the haughtiest and proudest woman in the world for his second wife. She had two daughters with the same temperament and the exact same appearance. On the other hand, the husband had a daughter whose gentleness and goodness were

---

7. The *profizio* or the "proficiat" was like a toast that inaugurated the ceremony.
† Charles Perrault, "Cinderella; or, The Glass Slipper"—"Cendrillon ou la petite pantoufle de verre," in *Histoires ou contes du temps passé* (Paris: Claude Barbin, 1697).

without parallel. She got this from her mother, who had been the best person in the world.

No sooner was the wedding over than the stepmother's ill-humor revealed itself. She could not abide the young girl, whose good qualities made her own daughters appear all the more detestable. So she ordered her to do all the most demeaning tasks in the house. It was she who cleaned the plates and the stairs, who scrubbed the rooms of the mistress and her daughters. She slept on a wretched straw mattress at the top of the house in a garret, while her sisters occupied rooms with parquet floors and the most fashionable beds and mirrors in which they could regard themselves from head to toe. The poor girl endured everything with patience and did not dare complain to her father, who would have only scolded her since he was totally under the control of his wife. Whenever she finished her work, she used to sit down near the chimney corner among the cinders.[1] Consequently, she was commonly called Cindertail. The second daughter, however, was not as malicious as her elder sister, and she dubbed her Cinderella. Nevertheless, Cinderella looked a thousand times more beautiful in her shabby clothes than her sisters, no matter how magnificent their clothes were.

Now the king's son decided to hold a ball and to invite all the people of quality. Our two young ladies were included in the invitation, for they cut a grand figure in this country. Of course, they were very pleased and began planning and choosing what would be the best gowns and the best headdresses to wear. This meant more misery for Cinderella because she was the one who ironed her sisters' linen and set their ruffles. Nothing was talked about but the style in which they were to be dressed.

"I'll wear my red velvet dress," said the elder sister, "and my English point-lace trimmings."

"I only have my usual petticoat to wear," said the younger, "but to make up for that I'll put on my gold-flowered mantua[2] and my necklace of diamonds which are quite impressive."

They sent for a good hairdresser to make up their double-frilled caps and brought their patches[3] from the best artisan. They summoned Cinderella and asked her opinion, for she had excellent taste. Cinderella gave them the best advice in the world and even offered to dress their hair for them, which they were glad to accept. While she went about it, they said to her, "Cinderella, wouldn't you like to go to the ball?"

"Alas! Ladies, you're playing with me. That would not befit me at all."

"You're right. People would have a great laugh to see a Cindertail at a ball!"

Any other person but Cinderella would have messed up their hairdos, but she was good-natured and dressed them to perfection. They could eat nothing for nearly two days because they were so excited with joy. More than a dozen laces were broken in making their waists as small as possible, and they were constantly standing in front of their mirror. At last the happy

1. Symbol of humiliation and penitence.
2. A silk dress coat.
3. Small pieces of black silk or court-plaster worn on the face in the seventeenth and eighteenth centuries either to cover a blemish or to show off the complexion by contrast.

day arrived. They set off, and Cinderella followed them with her eyes as long as she could. When they were out of sight, she began to cry. Her godmother, who came upon her all in tears, asked what was troubling her.

"I should so like—I should so like—" she sobbed so much that she could not finish the sentence.

"You'd like to go to the ball. Is that it?"

"Ah, yes!" said Cinderella sighing.

"Well, if you'll be a good girl, I shall enable you to go." She led her into her chamber and said, "Go into the garden and bring me a pumpkin."

Cinderella left immediately, gathered the finest pumpkin she could find, and brought it to her godmother, unable to guess how the pumpkin would enable her to go to the ball. Her godmother scooped it out and left nothing but the rind. Then she struck it with her wand, and the pumpkin was immediately changed into a beautiful coach gilded all over. Next she went and looked into the mousetrap, where she found six mice, all alive. She told Cinderella to lift the door of the trap a little, and as each mouse ran out, she gave a tap with her wand, and the mouse was immediately changed into a fine horse, producing a fine-looking team of six handsome, dappled mouse-gray horses. Since she had some difficulty in choosing something for a coachman, Cinderella said, "I'll go and see if there's a rat in the rattrap. We could make a coachman out of him."

"You're right," said her godmother. "Go and see."

Cinderella brought her the rattrap, which contained three large rats. The fairy selected one among the three because of its ample beard, and after she touched it, the rat was changed into a fat coachman who had the finest moustache that had ever been seen. Then she said, "Go into the garden, where you'll find six lizards behind the watering pot. I want you to bring them to me."

Cinderella had no sooner brought them than her godmother transformed them into six footmen, who immediately climbed up behind the coach in their braided liveries and hung on there as if they had done nothing else all their lives. Then the fairy said to Cinderella, "Well, now you have something to take you to the ball. Are you satisfied?"

"Yes, but am I to go in these dirty clothes?"

Her godmother merely touched her with her wand, and her garments were instantly changed into garments of gold and silver covered with jewels. She then gave her a pair of glass slippers, the prettiest in the world. When she was thus attired, she got into the coach, but her godmother advised her above all not to stay past midnight, warning her that, if she remained at the ball one moment too long, her coach would again become a pumpkin; her horses, mice; her footmen, lizards; and her clothes would resume their old appearance. She promised her godmother she would not fail to leave the ball before midnight, and so she departed overcome with joy.

Upon being informed that a grand princess had arrived whom nobody knew, the king's son went forth to greet her. He gave her his hand to help her out of the coach and led her into the hall, where the company was assembled. All at once there was dead silence; the guests stopped dancing, and the fiddlers ceased to play, so engrossed was everybody in regarding the beauty of the unknown lady. Nothing was heard but a low murmur, "Oh, how lovely she is!" The king himself, old as he was, could not take his eyes off her and whispered to the queen that it was a long time since he had seen anyone so beautiful and so pleasant. All the ladies were busy examining her headdress and her clothes because they wanted to obtain some similar garments the very next day, provided they could find materials as beautiful and artisans sufficiently clever to make them.

The king's son conducted her to the place of honor and then led her out to dance. She danced with so much grace that everyone's admiration was increased. A very fine supper was served, but the prince could not eat anything because he was so engrossed in watching her. She went and sat beside her sisters and showed them a thousand civilities. She shared oranges and citrons with them that the prince had given her, and her sisters were quite surprised because they did not recognize her at all. While they were conversing, Cinderella heard the clock strike a quarter to twelve. She immediately made a low curtsy to the company and departed as quickly as she could.

As soon as she arrived home, she went to look for her godmother, and after having thanked her, she said she wished very much to go to the ball again the next day because the king's son had invited her. While she was busy in telling her godmother all that had happened at the ball, the two sisters knocked at the door, and Cinderella went and opened it.

"How late you are!" she said to them, yawning, rubbing her eyes, and stretching as if she had only just awoken. However, she had not had the slightest inclination to sleep since she had left them.

"If you had been at the ball," said one of her sisters, "you would not have been bored. The most beautiful princess attended it—the most beautiful in the world. She paid us attention over a thousand times, and she also gave us oranges and citrons."

Cinderella was beside herself with delight. She asked them the name of the princess, but they replied that nobody knew her and that the king's son was stumped and would give anything in the world to know who she was. Cinderella smiled and said, "She was very beautiful, then? Heavens! How fortunate you are! Couldn't I have a chance to see her? Alas! Jayotte, would you lend me the yellow gown you wear every day?"

"Indeed," said Jayotte, "I like that! Lend my gown to a dirty Cindertail like you! I'd have to be quite mad to do something like that!"

Cinderella fully expected this refusal and was delighted by it, for she would have been greatly embarrassed if her sister had lent her the gown. The next day the two sisters went to the ball, and so did Cinderella, even more splendidly dressed than before. The king's son never left her side and kept saying sweet things to her. The young lady enjoyed herself so much that she forgot her godmother's advice and was oblivious when the clock began to strike twelve, for she did not even think it was eleven. She rose and fled as lightly as a fawn. The prince followed her but could not catch her. However, she dropped one of the glass slippers, which the prince carefully picked up. Cinderella reached home out of breath without coach or footmen, and in shabby clothes. Nothing remained of her finery, except one of her little slippers, the companion to the one that she had dropped. The guards at the palace gate were asked if they had seen a princess depart. They answered that they had only seen a poorly dressed girl pass by, and she had more the appearance of a peasant than a lady.

When the two sisters returned from the ball, Cinderella asked them if they had enjoyed themselves as much as the first time and if the beautiful lady had been present. They said yes, but that she had fled as soon as the clock had struck twelve, and she had been in such haste that she had dropped one of her glass slippers, the prettiest in the world. The king's son had picked it up and had done nothing but gaze upon it during the remainder of the evening. Undoubtedly, he was very much in love with the beautiful person who had worn the slipper.

They spoke the truth, for a few days later the king's son issued a proclamation accompanied by the sound of trumpets that he would marry the lady whose foot exactly fit the slipper. They began by trying it on the princesses, then on the duchesses, and so on throughout the entire court. However, it was all in vain. Soon it was taken to the two sisters, who did their utmost to force one of their feet into the slipper, but they could not manage to do so.

Cinderella, who witnessed their efforts and recognized the slipper, said with a smile, "Let me see if it will fit me."

Her sisters began to laugh and ridicule her. The gentleman who had been entrusted to try the slipper looked attentively at Cinderella and found her to be very beautiful. So he said that it was a proper request and that he had been ordered to try the slipper on everyone without exception. He asked Cinderella to sit down, and upon placing the slipper on her little foot, he saw it go on easily and fit like wax.

The astonishment of the two sisters was great, but it was even greater when Cinderella took the other little slipper out of her pocket and put it on the other foot. At that very moment the godmother arrived, and she gave a tap with her wand to Cinderella's clothes, which became even more magnificent than all the previous garments she had worn. The two sisters then recognized her as the beautiful person they had seen at the ball. They threw themselves at her feet begging her pardon for the harsh treatment they had made her endure.

Cinderella raised and embraced them, saying that she forgave them with all her heart and begged them to love her well in the future. Dressed just as she was, she was now conducted to the young prince. He found her more beautiful than ever, and a few days later he married her. Cinderella, who was as kind as she was beautiful, gave her sisters apartments in the palace and had them married the very same day to two great noblemen of the court.

Moral

Woman's beauty is a treasure
That we never cease to admire,
But a sweet disposition exceeds all measure
And is more dear than a precious gem's fire.
Now the fairy's gift to Cinderella, according to the story,

Was what she taught the girl about love and glory,
And she did it so well that Cinderella became queen.
(Indeed, this story has a moral to be esteemed.)

Beautiful ladies, it's kindness more than dress
That can win a man's heart with greater success.
In short, if you want to be blessed,
The real fairy gift is graciousness.

Another Moral

It's undoubtedly a great advantage
To have wit and a good deal of courage,
Or if you're born with common sense
And other worthwhile talents
That heaven may discharge.
But all of these may prove useless
And you may indeed need others
If you think you can have success
Without godfathers or godmothers.

MARIE-CATHERINE D'AULNOY

Finette Cendron†

Once upon a time there was a king and a queen who had managed their affairs very badly. Consequently, they were driven out of their kingdom and had to sell their crowns to support themselves. Soon after, they also had to part with their wardrobes, their linen, their lace, and all their furniture, piece by piece. The brokers became tired of purchasing their goods, for every day something else was sent to them for sale. When the royal couple had disposed of nearly everything, the king said to the queen, "We've lost our own country and no longer have any property. So now we must do something to earn a living for ourselves and our poor children. Think a little about what we can do. Up to now the only profession I've known is that of a king, which is a very pleasant one."

The queen had a lot of good sense, and she asked for a week to think the matter over. At the end of that time, she said to the king, "Sire, there's no need for us to be unhappy. You only need to make nets, with which you can catch both fowl and fish. When the lines wear out, I'll spin new ones. With regard to our three daughters, they're downright idle girls who still think of themselves as fine ladies and would like to continue living in that style without working. We must get them away from here, so far away that they'll never be able to find their way back again because we cannot possibly support them as well as they would like to be."

The king began to weep when he found he had to separate himself from

† Marie-Catherine d'Aulnoy, "Finette Cendron"—"Finette Cendron" (1697), in *Les contes de fées,* 4 vols. (Paris: Claude Barbin, 1697).

his children. He was a kind father, but the queen was mistress. Therefore, he agreed to whatever she proposed. "Get up early tomorrow morning," he said to her, "and take your three daughters wherever you think fit."

While they were thus plotting together, the Princess Finette, who was the youngest daughter, listened at the keyhole, and when she discovered her father and mother's plans, she set off as fast as she could in the direction of a big grotto that was a considerable distance from where they lived and was the abode of the fairy Merluche, who was her godmother.

Finette had taken two pounds of fresh butter, some eggs, some milk, and some flour to make a nice cake for her godmother to make sure she would be given a warm reception. She began her journey in good spirits, but the further she went, the more exhausted she grew. The soles of her shoes were worn completely through, and her pretty little feet became so sore that it was sad to see them. Indeed, she became so tired that she sat down on the grass and cried. Just then, a beautiful Spanish horse came by, already saddled and bridled. He had more than enough diamonds on his saddlecloth to purchase three cities. When he saw the princess, he stopped and began to graze quietly beside her. Bending his knees he appeared to pay homage to her. Thereupon, she took him by the bridle and said, "Gentle Hobby, would you kindly carry me to my fairy godmother's? You'd do me great service, for I'm so weary that I feel ready to die. If you help me on this occasion, I'll give you good oats and good hay and a litter of fresh straw to lie upon."

The horse bent himself almost to the ground, and when young Finette jumped upon him, he galloped off with her as lightly as a bird until he stopped at the entrance of the grotto, as if he had known where to go to. In fact, he knew well enough, for Merluche herself had foreseen her goddaughter's visit and had sent the fine horse for her.

As soon as Finette entered the grotto, she made three respectful curtsies to her godmother. Then she took the hem of her gown, kissed it, and said to her, "Good day, godmother, how are you doing? I've brought you some butter, milk, flour, and eggs to make you a cake according to our country custom."

"You're welcome, Finette," the fairy said. "Come here so I may embrace you." She kissed her twice, and this delighted Finette a great deal, for Madame Merluche was not one of those fairies you can find by the dozen. "Come, goddaughter," she said, "you'll be my little lady's maid. Take down my hair and comb it." The princess took her hair down and combed it as adroitly as possible. "I know full well why you've come," Merluche said. "You overheard the king and queen talking together about how they might abandon you, and you want to avoid this disaster. Here, you have only to take this skein of thread, which will never break. Fasten one end of it to the door of your house, and keep the other end in your hand. When the queen leaves you, you'll easily find your way back by following the thread."

The princess thanked her godmother, who gave her a bag full of fine dresses all made of gold and silver. She embraced her, placed her again on the pretty horse, and in two or three minutes he carried Finette to the door of her parents' cottage.

"My little friend," Finette said to the horse, "you're very handsome and clever. Your speed is as great as the sun's. I thank you for your service, and you may now return to the place you came from."

She entered the house quietly and hid her bag under her pillow. Then she went to bed without appearing to know anything that had taken place. At break of day the king woke his wife. "Come, come, madam," he said. "Get ready for your journey."

She got up right away, took her thick shoes, a short petticoat, a white jacket, and a stick. Then she summoned her eldest daughter, who was named Fleur d'Amour; her second, who was named Belle-de-Nuit; and her third, named Fine-Oreille, whom they familiarly called Finette.[1] "I've been thinking all last night that we ought to go and see my sister," the queen said. "She'll entertain us in splendid fashion. We can feast and laugh as much as we like there."

Fleur d'Amour, who was in despair at living in a desert, said to her mother, "Let us go, madam, wherever you please. Just as long as I can walk somewhere, I don't care." The two others agreed and took leave of the king. They set off all four together and walked so far—so very far that Fine-Oreille was very afraid her thread would not be long enough, for they walked nearly a thousand miles. She always kept behind the others, drawing the thread skillfully through the thickets.

When the queen thought her daughters would not be able to find the way back, she entered a dense forest and said to them, "Sleep, my little lambs, I'll be like the shepherdess, who watches over her flock for fear the wolf might devour them." They laid themselves down on the grass and went to sleep. Then the queen left them there, believing she would never see them again. Finette had shut her eyes but had not gone to sleep. "If I were an evil-natured girl," she said to herself, "I'd go straight home and leave my sisters to die here, for they beat me and scratch me until they draw blood. Yet, despite all their malice, I won't abandon them." She aroused them and told them the whole story. They began to cry and begged her to take them with her, promising that they would give her beautiful dolls, a child's set of silver plates, and all their other toys and candy. "I'm quite sure you'll do nothing of the kind," Finette said. "Nevertheless, I'll behave as a good sister should." After saying this, she rose and followed the thread with the two princesses so that they reached home almost as soon as the queen.

While they were at the door, they heard the king say, "It troubles my heart to see you come back alone."

"Pshaw!" said the queen. "Our daughters were much too great a burden for us."

"If you had brought back my Finette," the king said, "I might have felt consoled about the loss of the others, for they love nothing and nobody."

At that moment they knocked at the door—*rap, rap*. "Who's there?" asked the king.

---

1. "Fleur d'Amour": Flower of Love. "Belle-de-Nuit": Beauty of the Night. "Fine-Oreille": Shrewd Listener; "Finette" generally means "little clever girl."

"Your three daughters," they replied. "Fleur d'Amour, Belle-de-Nuit, and Fine-Oreille."

The queen began to tremble. "Don't open the door!" she exclaimed. "It must be their ghosts, for it would have been impossible for them to find their way back alive."

The king, who was as great a coward as his wife, called out, "You're lying! You're not my daughters!"

But Fine-Oreille, who was a shrewd girl, said to him, "Papa, I'll stoop down, and if you look at me though the hole made for the cat to come through, and if I'm not Finette, I agree to be whipped."

The king did as he was told, and as soon as he recognized her, he opened the door. The queen pretended to be delighted to see them again and said that she had forgotten something and had come home to fetch it, but that she would surely have returned to them. They pretended to believe her and went up to a snug little hayloft in which they always slept.

"Now, sisters," Finette said, "you promised me the doll. Give it to me."

"Don't hold your breath, you little rogue," they said. "You're the reason why they king cares so little for us."

Thereupon, they grabbed their distaffs and beat her to a pulp. After they had beaten her as much as they wanted, they let her go to bed. However, since she was covered with wounds and bruises, she could not sleep and heard the queen say to the king, "I'll take them in another direction, much further, and I'm positive they'll never return."

When Finette heard this plan, she rose very quietly to go and see her godmother again. She went into the chicken yard, where she took two hens and a cock and wrung their necks along with two little rabbits that the queen was fattening on cabbages for a feast on the next suitable occasion. She put them all into a basket and set off, but she had not gone a mile, groping her way and quaking with fear, when the Spanish horse approached at a gallop, snorting and neighing. She thought it was all over for her and that some soldiers were about to seize her. However, when she saw the beautiful horse all alone, she jumped on top of him and was delighted to travel so comfortably, especially since she arrived almost immediately at her godmother's.

After the usual ceremonies, she presented her with the hens, the cock, and the rabbits, and asked for her good advice, since the queen had sworn she would lead them to the end of the world. Merluche told her goddaughter not to trouble herself and gave her a sack full of ashes. "Carry this sack in front of you," she said, "and shake it as you go along. You'll walk on the ashes, and when you wish to return, you'll only have to follow your footsteps, but don't bring your sisters back with you. They're too malicious, and if you do bring them back, I'll never see you again."

Finette said farewell to her and was given millions of diamonds in a little box, which she put in her pocket to take with her. The horse was ready and waiting and carried her home as before.

At daybreak the queen called the princesses. They came to her, and she said to them, "The king isn't very well, and I dreamed last night that I ought to go and gather some flowers and herbs for him in a special country where they grow to great perfection. They'll help him recuperate. So let's go there right away."

Fleur d'Amour and Belle-de-Nuit, who never thought their mother intended to lose them again, were quite grieved at hearing these tidings. Yet, they had to go, and they went further than any journey had ever been made. Finette, who never said a word, kept behind and shook her sack of ashes with such wonderful skill that neither the wind nor the rain spoiled them.

The queen was perfectly convinced that they would not find their way back again, and one evening when she observed that her three daughters were fast asleep, she used the opportunity to leave them and returned home. As soon as it was light and Finette found her mother was gone, she woke her sisters. "We're alone," she said. "The queen has left us."

Fleur d'Amour and Belle-de-Nuit began to cry. They tore their hair and beat their own faces with their fists. "Alas! What will become of us?" they exclaimed.

Finette was the best-hearted girl in the world, and therefore, she took pity on her sisters once again. "Look how I'm leaving myself vulnerable," she said to them. "When my godmother furnished me with means to return, she forbade me to show you the way and told me that, if I disobeyed her, she'd never see me anymore."

Belle-de-Nuit threw herself on Finette's neck; Fleur d'Amour did the same, kissing her so affectionately that it required nothing more to bring all three back together to the king and the queen. Their majesties were greatly surprised at the return of the princesses, and they discussed their situation all night long, while their youngest daughter, who was not called Fine-Oreille for nothing, heard them concoct a new plan that involved the queen taking them on another journey the next morning. Again Fine-Oreille ran to wake her sisters.

"Alas!" she said to them. "We're lost! The queen is determined to lead us into some wilderness and leave us there. I offended my godmother for your sakes, so I don't dare to go to her for advice as I used to do."

They were in a terrible situation and asked each other, "What shall we do, sister? What shall we do?"

At last, Belle-de-Nuit said to the two others, "Why should we worry ourselves? Old Merluche doesn't possess all the brains in the world. Some other folks may have a little. We only have to take plenty of peas with us and drop them all along the road as we go, and we'll be sure to trace our way back."

Fleur d'Amour thought it was a remarkable idea, and they loaded themselves with peas by filling all their pockets. But instead of peas, Fine-Oreille packed her bag full of fine clothes and the little box of diamonds, and as soon as the queen called them, they were ready to go. Then she said to them, "I dreamed last night that in a country which is unnecessary to name, there are three handsome princes, who are waiting to marry you. I'm going to take you there to see if my dream was true."

The queen went first and her daughters followed her, dropping their peas without fear, for they made sure of being able to find their way home. This time the queen went further than she had ever gone before, and during one dark night she left the princesses and reached home very weary, but very happy for having gotten rid of such a great burden as her three daughters. After sleeping until eleven o'clock in the morning, the three princesses awoke, and Finette was the first to discover the queen's absence. Although she was perfectly prepared for it, she could not help crying, especially because she trusted much more in the power of her fairy godmother than in the cleverness of her sisters for her return. In her fright she went to them and said, "The queen's gone. We must follow her as soon as possible."

"Hold your tongue, you little hussy!" replied Fleur d'Amour. "We can find our way well enough when we choose. There's no need to make such a fuss, sister."

Finette did not dare to answer. However, when they did try to retrace their steps, there were no signs or paths to be found. Since there were immense flocks of pigeons in that country, they had eaten up all the peas. The princesses began to cry and scream with grief and terror. After spending two days without food, Fleur d'Amour said to Belle-de-Nuit, "Sister, don't you have anything to eat?"

"Nothing," she replied.

She put the same question to Finette.

"Nor do I," she answered, "but I've just found an acorn."

"Ah! Give it to me," one sister said.

"Give it to me," said the other.

Each insisted on having it.

"An acorn will not go far among the three of us," Finette said. "Let us plant it, and maybe a tree will spring from that which may be useful to us."

Although there was little chance of a tree growing in a country where none were to be seen, they agreed. The only things they could find to eat were cabbages and lettuces, and this was what the princesses lived on. If they had been very delicate, they would have died a hundred times. They slept almost always in the open air, and every morning and evening they took turns watering the acorn and saying, "Grow, grow, beautiful acorn!"

Indeed, it began to grow so fast that you could see it grow. When it had reached a certain size, Fleur d'Amour tried to climb it, but it was not strong enough to bear her. She felt it bend under her weight, and so she came back down again. Belle-de-Nuit was no more successful. Since Finette was lighter, she managed to get up and remained there a long time.

Her sisters called to her, "Can you see anything, sister?"

She answered, "No, I can't see a thing."

"Ah, then, the oak is not tall enough," said Fleur d'Amour.

So they continued to water it and say, "Grow, grow, beautiful acorn!" Finette kept climbing it twice a day, and one morning, when she was up in the tree, Belle-de-Nuit said to Fleur d'Amour, "I've found a bag which our sister has hidden from us. What can be in it?"

Fleur d'Amour replied, "She told me it contained some old lace she had brought along to mend."

"I believe it's full of candy," Belle-de-Nuit said. Since she had a sweet tooth, she decided to look. When she opened the bag, she actually found a good deal of old lace belonging to the king and queen, but hidden beneath it were the fine clothes the fairy had given to Finette and the box of diamonds.

"Well, now! Was there ever such a sly little rogue?" exclaimed Belle-de-Nuit. "We'll take out all the things, and put some stones in their place."

They did this right away. When Finette rejoined them, she did not notice what they had done, for she never dreamed of decking herself out in a desert. She only thought about the oak, which quickly became the finest oak that the world has ever seen. One day, when she had climbed it and her sisters as usual had asked her if she could see anything, she exclaimed, "I can see a large mansion, so beautiful, so very beautiful that I can't find the words to describe it. The walls are made of emeralds and rubies, the roof of diamonds. It's all covered with golden bells and weathercocks that whirl about as the wind blows."

"You're lying," they said. "It can't be as beautiful as you say."

"Believe me," Finette replied. "I'm not a liar. Come and see for yourselves. My eyes are quite dazzled by it."

Fleur d'Amour climbed up the tree. When she saw the château, she could talk about nothing else. Belle-de-Nuit, who had a great deal of curiosity, climbed in her turn and was just as enchanted as her sisters at the sight of the château.

"We must certainly go to this palace," they said. "Perhaps we'll find some handsome princes who'd be happy to marry us."

They spent the whole evening long talking about this subject and lay down to sleep on the grass. But when Finette seemed to be fast asleep, Fleur d'Amour said to Belle-de-Nuit, "I'll tell you what we should do, sister. Let's get up and dress ourselves in the fine clothes Finette has brought here."

"That's a good idea," Belle-de-Nuit said.

So they got up, curled their hair, powdered it, put patches on their cheeks, and dressed themselves in the beautiful gold and silver gowns all covered with diamonds. What a magnificent sight they made!

Finette was unaware of her wicked sisters' theft. So when she took her bag with the intention of dressing herself, she was greatly distressed to find nothing in it but flint stones. At the same time, she saw her sisters shining like suns. She wept and complained about their treachery, but they only laughed and joked about it.

"I can't believe," she said to them, "that you'd have the gumption to take me to the château without dressing and making me as beautiful as you are?"

"We have barely enough for ourselves," Fleur d'Amour replied. "You'll get nothing but blows if you annoy us."

"But," Finette continued, "the clothes you have on are mine. My godmother gave them to me. They don't belong to you."

"If you say one more word about it," they responded, "we'll hit you on the head and bury you without anyone being the wiser!"

Poor Finette did not dare provoke them. She followed them slowly, walking a short distance behind them, as if she were only their servant.

The nearer they approached the mansion, the more wonderful it appeared to them.

"Oh," Fleur d'Amour and Belle-de-Nuit said, "what fun we'll have! What splendid dinners we'll get! We'll dine at the king's table, but Finette will have to wash the dishes in the kitchen, for she looks like a scullion. If anybody asks who she is, we must take care not to call her sister. We must say she's the little cowherd in the village."

Of course the lovely and sensible Finette was distressed at being treated so badly.

Once they reached the castle gate, they knocked at it. It was opened immediately by a terrifying old woman. She had just one eye, which was in the middle of her forehead, but it was bigger than five or six ordinary ones. Her nose was flat, her complexion swarthy, and her mouth so horrible that it was frightening to see. She was fifteen feet high and had a waist thirty feet wide. "Unfortunate wretches!" she said to them. "What's brought you here? Don't you know that this is the ogre's castle, and that all three of you would scarcely make do for his breakfast? But I'm more good-natured than my husband. Come in. I won't eat you all at once. You'll have the consolation of living two or three days longer."

Upon hearing the words of the ogress, they began to run hoping to escape, but one of her strides was equal to fifty of theirs. So she ran after and caught them, one by the hair, and the others by the nape of the neck. Then she tucked them under her arm, took them into the castle, and threw all three into the cellar, which was full of toads and adders and strewn with the bones of those the ogres had eaten. Since the ogress desired to eat Finette right away, she went to fetch some vinegar, oil, and salt to make her into a salad, but when she heard the ogre approaching, she felt that the princesses were so white and delicate that she wanted to eat them all herself. So she popped them quickly under a large tub, from which they could only look through a hole.

The ogre was six times as tall as his wife. When he spoke, the building shook, and when he coughed, it was like peals of thunder. He had just one great filthy eye, and his hair stood all on end. He used a huge log of wood for a cane and had a covered basket in his hand, from which he pulled fifteen little children he had stolen on the road and swallowed them like fifteen freshly laid eggs. When the princesses saw him, they trembled under the tub. They were afraid to cry, lest they be heard, but they whispered to each other, "He'll eat us alive. How can we possibly save ourselves?"

The ogre said to his wife, "You know, I smell fresh meat. Give it to me."

"That's a good one!" the ogress said. "You always think you smell fresh meat. It's your sheep that have just passed by."

"Oh, you can't fool me," the ogre said. "I smell fresh meat for certain, and I'll search everywhere for it."

"Search," she said. "You won't find anything."

"If I do find something, and you've hidden it from me," the ogre replied, "I'll cut your head off and make a ball out of it."

She was frightened by this threat and said, "Don't be angry, my dear little ogre. I'll tell you the truth. Three young girls came here today, and I've put them in a safe spot, but it would be a pity to eat them, for they know how to do everything. I'm old and need some rest. You can see that our fine house is very dirty, that our bread is badly made, and your soup rarely pleases you. Moreover, I myself no longer appear so beautiful in your eyes ever since I began working so hard. These girls will be my servants. I beg you not to eat them just now. If you should desire one of them some other day, they'll always be within your reach."

The ogre was very reluctant to promise that he would not eat them immediately. "Let me do what I want," he said, "I'll only eat two of them."

"No, you won't eat them."

"Well, then, I'll only eat the smallest."

"No, you won't touch a single one of them," she replied.

At last, after a lot of bickering, he promised he would not eat them, but she thought to herself, "When he goes hunting, I'll eat them and tell him they managed to escape."

The ogre came out of the cellar and told his wife to bring the girls to him. The poor princesses were practically dying with fright, and the ogress tried to comfort them. When they were brought before the ogre, he asked them what they could do. They answered, they could sweep, sew, and spin exceedingly well; that they could make ragouts so delicious that people would even be tempted to eat the plates; and as for bread, cakes, and patties, people had been known to order them from a thousand miles round. Since the ogre was fond of good cooking, he said, "Aha! Set these good housewives to work immediately. After you light the fire, how do you know when the oven is hot enough?"

"I throw some butter into it, my lord," Finette replied, "and then I taste it with my tongue."

"Very well," he said, "light the oven fire then."

The oven was as big as a stable because the ogre and ogress ate more bread than two armies could eat. The princess made a terrific fire, and the oven was as hot as a furnace. In the meantime, the ogre, who was present and waiting for his new bread, ate a hundred lambs and a hundred little suckling pigs. Fleur d'Amour and Belle-de-Nuit were making the dough. "Well," the great ogre asked, "is the oven hot?"

"You shall see, my lord," said Finette. She threw in a thousand pounds of butter and then said to him, "It should be tasted with the tongue, but I'm too short to reach it."

"I'm tall enough," the ogre said as he stooped and thrust his body so far into the oven that he could not keep his balance. So all the flesh was burned off his bones. When the ogress came to the oven, she was astounded to find her husband a mountain of cinders!

Fleur d'Amour and Belle-de-Nuit, who saw that she was very distressed, consoled her to the best of their ability, but they feared her grief would subside too soon, and once her appetite returned, she would make a salad out of them as she had been about to do before. "Don't be discouraged, madam," they said to her, "you'll find some king or some marquis who'll be delighted to marry you."

She smiled a little, showing her teeth, which were longer than most people's fingers. When they saw her in such a good mood, Finette said to her, "If you would take off these horrible bearskins that you wrap yourself in, and follow the fashion, we'll dress your hair to perfection, and you'll look like a star."

"Come," the ogress said, "let's see what you can do. But rest assured that, if I find any ladies more lovely than me, I'll make mincemeat out of you!"

Thereupon, the three princesses took off her cap and began combing and curling her hair while they entertained her with their chatter. But Finette took a hatchet and struck her from behind with such a blow that her head was sliced clean off her shoulders. Never was there such delight! The three princesses climbed to the roof of the mansion to amuse themselves by ringing the golden bells. Then they ran into all the apartments, which were made of pearls and diamonds with costly furniture, and could have died from pleasure. They laughed, they sang, they had all they wanted: corn, marmalade, fruit, and dolls in abundance. Fleur d'Amour and Belle-de-Nuit went to sleep in beds of brocade and velvet and said to each other, "Look at us! We're richer than our father was when he possessed his kingdom. But we want to be married, and nobody will dare to come here. People probably think this mansion is still a cutthroat place because they don't know that the ogre and the ogress are dead. We must go to the nearest city and show ourselves in our fine dresses, and soon we'll find some honest bankers who'd be quite glad to marry princesses."

As soon as they were dressed, they told Finette that they were going to take a walk and that she must stay home and cook and wash and clean the house, so that they would find everything as it should be on their return. If not, she would be beaten within an inch of her life!

Poor Finette, whose heart was full of grief, remained alone in the house, sweeping, cleaning, washing and crying all the time without resting. "How unfortunate," she said, "that I disobeyed my godmother! All sorts of bad things have happened to me. My sisters have stolen my precious dresses and have adorned themselves with my ornaments. If it weren't for me, the ogre and his wife would be alive and well at this moment. What have I gained from killing them?"

After saying all this she sobbed until she almost choked. Shortly afterward her sisters returned loaded down with Portugal oranges, preserves, and sugar. "Ah!" they said to her. "What a splendid ball we've been to! How crowded it was! The king's son was among the dancers, and we received a thousand compliments. Come, take our shoes off and clean them. It's one of your tasks."

Finette obeyed them, and if by accident she let a word drop in the way of complaint, they jumped at her and beat her almost to death. The next day they went out again and returned with an account of new wonders.

One evening, when Finette was sitting in the chimney corner on a heap of cinders, not knowing what to do, she examined the cracks in the chimney and found a little key in one of them. It was so old and so dirty that she had the greatest trouble cleaning it. After she had done so, she found it was made of gold and assuming that a golden key ought to open some beautiful little box, she ran all over the mansion trying it in all the locks. Eventually she found it fit the lock of a casket which was a masterpiece of art. When she opened it, she found it full of clothes, diamonds, lace, linen, and ribbons worth immense sums of money. She did not say a word to her sisters about her good luck but waited impatiently for their departure the next day. As soon as they were out of sight, she dressed and adorned herself until she looked more beautiful than the sun and the moon together.

It was thus in this altered condition that she went to the ball where her sisters were dancing, and though she was not wearing a mask, she had changed so much for the better that they did not recognize her. As soon as she appeared, a murmur arose throughout the gathering. Some were full of admiration, others of jealousy. She was asked to dance and surpassed all the other ladies in grace as much as she did in beauty. The mistress of the mansion came to her, and after making a respectful curtsy, she asked her name so that she would always have the pleasure of remembering such a marvelous person. Finette replied civilly that her name was Cendron. Now there was not a lover who did not leave his mistress for Cendron, not a poet who did not write verses about Cendron. Never did such a little name cause so much commotion in such a short time. The echoes repeated nothing but the praises of Cendron. People did not have eyes enough to gaze at her, nor tongues enough to extol her.

Fleur d'Amour and Belle-de-Nuit, who had previously created a great sensation wherever they had appeared, observed the reception accorded to this newcomer and were ready to burst with spite. But Finette extricated herself from all such rivalry with the best grace in the world. Her manners seemed to be those of one born to command. Fleur d'Amour and Belle-de-Nuit, who never saw their sister except with her face covered with soot from the chimney and looking as dirty as a dog, had completely forgotten how beautiful she was. Consequently, they did not have the least idea who she was. Like all the rest, they paid their respects to Cendron, and as soon as she saw the ball was nearly over, she hurried away, returned home, undressed herself quickly, and put on her old rags.

When her sisters arrived, they said to her, "Ah, Finette, we've just seen a young princess who is perfectly charming! She's not a baboon like you. She's as white as snow with a richer complexion than the roses. Her teeth are pearls, and her lips coral. She was wearing a gown that must have weighed more than a thousand pounds. It was all gold and diamonds. How beautiful, how charming she was!"

Finette said in a low voice, "So was I, so was I."

"What are you muttering there?" her sisters asked.

She repeated in an even lower tone, "So was I, so was I."

This little game was played for some time. Hardly a day passed that Finette did not appear in a new dress, for the casket was a fairy one, and the more you took out, the more it was filled and everything was so highly fashionable that all the ladies dressed themselves in imitation of Finette.

One evening, when Finette had danced more than usual and had delayed her departure to a later hour, she was so anxious to make up for lost time and get home a little before her sisters that she walked too fast and lost one of her slippers, which was made of red velvet and embroidered with pearls. She tried to find it on the road, but the night was so dark, her search was in vain, and she entered the house wearing a slipper on only one of her feet. The next day, Prince Chéri, the king's eldest son, went out hunting and found Finette's slipper. He had it picked up, examined it, admired its diminutive size and elegance, turned it over and over, kissed it, took care of it, and carried it home with him. From that day on, he refused to eat and became thin. His looks underwent a great change: he was as yellow as a quince, melancholy, and depressed. The king and queen, who were totally devoted to him, had the choicest game and the best confiture brought in from everywhere. But they meant nothing to him. He looked at everything and would not utter a word when his mother spoke to him. They summoned the best physicians from everywhere, even as far as Paris and Montpellier. When they arrived, they examined the prince, and after observing him constantly for three days and three nights, they came to the conclusion that he was in love and that he would die if they did not find the only remedy for him.

The queen, who completely doted on her son, burst into tears because she did not know the object of his love and could not help him marry her. She had the most beautiful ladies she could find brought into his room, but he would not deign to look at them. At last she said to him, "My dear son, you're going to be the cause of our death, for you're in love, and you're hiding your feelings from us. Tell us whom you love, and we'll give her to you, even if she's just a simple shepherdess."

The prince took courage from the queen's promise and drew the slipper from under his pillow. Upon showing it to her, he said, "Look, madam, this is the cause of my malady. I found this little, soft, delicate, and pretty slipper as I went out hunting, and I refuse to marry anyone but the woman who can wear it."

"Well, my son," said the queen, "there's no need to trouble yourself. We'll organize a search for her."

She rushed to the king with this news. He was very surprised and immediately ordered a proclamation to be made with the sound of drum and trumpet: all single women were to come and try on the slipper, and she whose foot fit the slipper would marry the prince. Upon hearing this, the women washed their feet with all sorts of waters, pastes, and pomades, some ladies actually had them peeled, while others starved themselves in order to make their feet smaller and prettier. They went in crowds to try on the slipper, but no one could get it on, and the more they came and failed, the more the prince's suffering increased.

One day, Fleur d'Amour and Belle-de-Nuit dressed themselves in such a superb fashion that they looked astonishingly beautiful.

"Where are you going?" asked Finette.

"We're going to the big city where the king and queen reside," they replied. "We're going to try on the slipper the king's son has found. If it fits one of us, the prince will marry her, and then one of us will become queen."

"And why can't I go?" Finette responded.

"Really! You're pretty stupid!" they said. "Go! Go and water our cabbages. That's all you're fit for."

Right then and there Finette decided it would be a good idea to put on her finest clothes to go and take her chance with the rest, for she had a slight suspicion that she would be successful. What troubled her was that she did not know her way, for the ball she had attended had not been held in the big city. Nevertheless, she dressed herself in magnificent fashion. Her gown was made of blue satin and covered with stars in diamonds. She had a sun made of them in her hair, and a full moon on her back, and all these jewels glistened so brightly that it was impossible to look at her without blinking. When she opened the door to go out, she was quite surprised to see the pretty Spanish horse which had carried her to her godmother's. She patted him and said, "You're most welcome, my little hobby. I'm much obliged to my godmother, Merluche." He knelt down, and she mounted him like a nymph. He was covered all over with golden bells and ribbons. His saddlecloth and bridle were priceless, and Finette was thirty times more beautiful than fair Helen of Troy.

The Spanish horse galloped off in a sprightly manner, his bells went *ting, ting, ting*. When Fleur d'Amour and Belle-de-Nuit heard their sounds, they turned around and saw her coming. They were completely taken by surprise, for they now recognized her both as Finette and as Cendron. As they turned around, they were splashed, and their fine dresses dripped with mud. "Sister!" Fleur d'Amour cried to Belle-de-Nuit, "I say, that's Finette Cendron!"

The other echoed the cry, and Finette passed so close to them that her horse splashed them all over and turned them into a mass of mud. Finette laughed at them and said, "Your highnesses, Cendrillon despises you just as you deserve it."

Then she passed them like a shot and disappeared. Belle-de-Nuit and Fleur d'Amour looked at each other. "Are we dreaming?" they said. "Who could have supplied Finette with clothes and a horse? What a miracle! She's got luck on her side. She'll put on the slipper, and we'll have made a long journey in vain."

While they were bemoaning their situation, Finette arrived at the palace. The moment she appeared, everybody thought she was a queen. The guards presented arms, the drums beat, and the trumpets sounded a flourish. All the gates were flung open, and those people who had seen her at the ball preceded her and cried out, "Make room! Make room for the beautiful Cendron, the wonder of the world!"

It was in this state that she entered the room of the dying prince. He cast his eyes on her, and enraptured by her sight, he wished fervently that her foot would be small enough to fit into the slipper. She put it on instantly and produced its fellow, which she had brought with her for this purpose. Shouts immediately arose of "Long live the Princess Chéri! Long live the princess who will be our queen!"

The prince got up from his couch and advanced to kiss her hand. She thought he was handsome and very intelligent. He paid her a thousand courteous attentions, and the king and queen were informed of the event. They came in all haste, and the queen took Finette in her arms, called her her daughter, her darling, her little queen! They gave her some magnificent presents, and the generous king added many more. They fired the guns, and violins, bagpipes, and every sort of musical instrument began playing. Nobody talked about anything else except dancing and rejoicing. The king, the queen, and the prince begged Cendron to consent to let the marriage take place immediately.

"No," she said, "I must first tell you my story," which she did in a few words. When they found that she was born a princess, there was another burst of joy that was almost the death of them. Then, when she told them the names of the king and queen, her father and mother, they recognized them as the sovereigns whose dominions they had conquered. They informed Finette about this fact, and she immediately vowed that she would not consent to marry the prince until they had restored the estates of her father. They promised to do so, for they had upward of a hundred kingdoms, and one more or less was not worth talking about.

In the meantime, Belle-de-Nuit and Fleur d'Amour arrived at the palace. The first news that greeted them was that Cendron had put on the slipper. They did not know what to do or say. Then they decided to go back again without seeing her, but when Finette heard they were there, she insisted they should come in, and instead of berating them and punishing them as they deserved, she got up and advanced to meet them, embraced them tenderly, and then presented them to the queen. "Madam," she said to her, "these are my sisters. They are very charming, and I ask you to love them."

They were so confused by Finette's kindness that they were left speechless. She promised them they could return to their own kingdom, which the king would restore to their family. At these words, they threw themselves on their knees before her and wept for joy.

The wedding was the most splendid that had ever been seen. Finette wrote to her godmother and put the letter along with valuable presents on the back of the pretty Spanish horse. The letter requested that she go and visit the king and queen, tell them about their good fortune, and inform them that they could now return to their kingdom. The fairy, Merluche, performed this errand most graciously so that Finette's father and mother regained their estates and her sisters later became queens just like her.

> If it's revenge on the ungrateful you want to see,
> Then follow Finette's wise policy.
> Do favors for the undeserving until they weep.
> Each benefit inflicts a wound most deep,
> Cutting the haughty bosom to the core.
> Finette's proud, selfish sisters suffered more,
> When by her generous kindness overpower'd,
> Than if the ogres had made them into a mess,
> For she overcame them with her kindness.
> From her example then this lesson learn,
> And give good for evil in your turn
> No matter what wrong may awake your wrath,
> There is no greater vengeance than this kind path.

JACOB AND WILHELM GRIMM

Cinderella†

The wife of a rich man fell ill, and when she felt her end approaching, she called her only daughter to her bedside and said, "Dear child, be good and pious. Then the dear Lord will always assist you, and I shall look down from heaven and take care of you." She then closed her eyes and departed.

After her mother's death, the maiden went every day to visit her grave and weep, and she remained good and pious. When winter came, snow covered the grave like a little white blanket, and by the time the sun had taken it off again in the spring, the rich man had a second wife who brought two daughters with her. They had beautiful and fair features but nasty and wicked hearts. As a result, a difficult time was ahead for the poor stepsister.

"Why should the stupid goose be allowed to sit in the parlor with us?' they said. "Whoever wants to eat bread must earn it. Out with this kitchen maid!"

They took away her beautiful clothes, dressed her in an old gray smock, and gave her wooden shoes.

"Just look at the proud princess and how decked out she is!" they exclaimed with laughter, and led her into the kitchen.

They expected her to work hard there from morning till night. As a result, she had to get up before dawn, carry the water into the house, make the fire, cook, and wash. Besides this, her sisters did everything imaginable to cause her grief and make her look ridiculous. For instance, they poured peas and lentils into the hearth ashes so she had to sit there and pick them out. In the evening, when she was exhausted from working, they took away her bed, and she had to lie next to the hearth in ashes. This is why she always looked so dusty and dirty and why they all called her Cinderella.

One day it happened that her father was going to the fair and asked his two stepdaughters what he could bring them.

"Beautiful dresses," said one.

"Pearls and jewels," said the other.

"And you, Cinderella?" he asked. "What do you want?"

"Father," she said, "just break off the first twig that brushes against your hat on your way home and bring it to me."

So he bought beautiful dresses, pearls, and jewels for the two stepsisters, and as he was riding through some green bushes on his return journey, a hazel twig brushed against him and knocked off his hat. So he broke off that twig and took it with him. When he arrived home, he gave his stepdaughters what they had requested, and Cinderella received the twig from the hazel bush. She thanked him, went to her mother's grave, planted the twig on it, and wept so hard that the tears fell on the twig and watered it.

† Jacob and Wilhelm Grimm, "Cinderella"—"Aschenputtel" (1857), No. 21 in *Kinder- und Hausmärchen. Gesammelt durch die Brüder Grimm* (Göttingen: Dieterich, 1857).

Soon the twig grew and quickly became a beautiful tree. Three times every day Cinderella would go and sit beneath it and weep and pray, and each time a little white bird would also come to the tree. Whenever Cinderella expressed a wish, the bird would throw her whatever she had requested.

In the meantime, the king had decided to sponsor a three-day festival, and all the beautiful young girls in the country were invited so that his son could choose a bride. When the two stepsisters learned that they too had been summoned to make an appearance, they were in good spirits and called Cinderella.

"Comb out our hair, brush our shoes, and fasten our buckles!" they said. "We're going to the wedding at the king's castle."

Cinderella obeyed but wept because she, too, would have liked to go to the ball with them, and so she asked her stepmother for permission to go.

"You, Cinderella!" she said. "You're all dusty and dirty, and yet you want to go to the wedding? How can you go dancing when you've got no clothes or shoes?"

When Cinderella kept pleading, her stepmother finally said, "I've emptied a bowlful of lentils into the ashes. If you can pick out all the lentils in two hours, you may have my permission to go."

The maiden went through the back door into the garden and cried out, "Oh, you tame pigeons, you turtledoves, and all you birds under heaven, come and help me pick

> the good ones for the little pot
> the bad ones for your little crop."

Two white pigeons came flying to the kitchen window, followed by the turtledoves. Eventually, all the birds under heaven swooped down, swarmed into the kitchen, and settled around the ashes. The pigeons bobbed their heads and began to peck, peck, peck, peck, and all the other birds also began to peck, peck, peck, peck, and they put all the good lentils into the bowl. It did not take longer than an hour for the birds to finish the work, whereupon they flew away. Happy because she thought she would now be allowed to go to the wedding, the maiden brought the bowl to her stepmother. But her stepmother said, "No, Cinderella. You don't have any clothes, nor do you know how to dance. Everyone would only laugh at you."

When Cinderella started crying, the stepmother said, "If you can pick two bowlfuls of lentils out of the ashes in one hour, I'll let you come along." But she thought, "She'll never be able to do it."

Then the stepmother dumped two bowlfuls of lentils into the ashes, and the maiden went through the back door into the garden and cried out, "Oh, you tame pigeons, you turtledoves, and all you birds under heaven come and help me pick

> the good ones for the little pot,
> the bad ones for your little crop."

Two white pigeons came flying into the kitchen window, followed by the turtledoves. Eventually, all the birds under heaven swooped down, swarmed into the kitchen, and settled around the ashes. The pigeons bobbed their heads and began to peck, peck, peck, peck, and all the other birds also began to peck, peck, peck, peck, and they put all the good lentils into the bowl. Before half an hour had passed, they finished their work and flew away. Happy because she thought she would now be allowed to go to the wedding, the maiden carried the bowls to her stepmother. But the stepmother said, "Nothing can help you. I can't let you come with us because you don't have any clothes to wear and you don't know how to dance. We'd only be ashamed of you!"

Then she turned her back on Cinderella and hurried off with her two haughty daughters. When they had all departed, Cinderella went to her mother's grave beneath the hazel tree and cried out:

"Shake and wobble, little tree!
Let gold and silver fall all over me."

The bird responded by throwing her a gold and silver dress and silk slippers embroidered with silver. She hastily slipped into the dress and went to the wedding. She looked so beautiful in her golden dress that her sisters and stepmother did not recognize her and thought she must be a foreign princess. They never imagined it could be Cinderella; they thought she was sitting at home in the dirt picking lentils out of the ashes.

Now, the prince approached Cinderella, took her by the hand, and danced with her. Indeed, he would not dance with anyone else and would not let go of her hand. Whenever someone came and asked her to dance, he said, "She's my partner."

She danced well into the night, and when she wanted to go home, the prince said, "I'll go along and escort you," for he wanted to see whose daughter the beautiful maiden was. But she managed to slip away from him and got into her father's dovecote. Now the prince waited until her father came, and he told him that the unknown maiden had escaped into his dovecote. The old man thought, "Could that be Cinderella?" And he ordered a servant to bring him an ax and pick so he could chop it down. However, no one was inside, and when they went into the house, Cinderella was lying in the ashes in her dirty clothes, and a dim little oil lamp was burning on the mantel of the chimney. Cinderella had swiftly jumped out of the back of the dovecote and had run to the hazel tree. There she had taken off the beautiful clothes and laid them on the grave. After the bird had taken them away, she had made her way into the kitchen, where she had seated herself in the gray ashes wearing her gray smock.

The next day, when the festival had begun again and her parents and sisters had departed, Cinderella went to the hazel tree and cried out:

"Shake and wobble, little tree!
Let gold and silver fall all over me."

The bird responded by throwing her a dress that was even more splendid than the one before. And when she appeared at the wedding in this dress, everyone was amazed by her beauty. The prince had been waiting for her, and when she came, he took her hand right away and danced with no one but her. When others went up to her and asked her to dance, he said, "She's my partner."

When evening came and she wished to leave, the prince followed her, wanting to see which house she went into, but she ran away from him and disappeared into the garden behind the house. There she went to a beautiful tall tree covered with the most wonderful pears, and she climbed up into the branches as nimbly as a squirrel. The prince did not know where she had gone, so he waited until the father came and said, "The unknown maiden has slipped away from me, and I think she climbed the pear tree."

The father thought, "Can that be Cinderella?" And he ordered a servant to bring him an ax and chopped the tree down, but there was no one in it. When they went into the kitchen, Cinderella was lying in the ashes as usual, for she had jumped down on the other side of the tree, brought the beautiful clothes back to the bird, and put on her gray smock.

On the third day, when her parents and sisters had departed, Cinderella went to her mother's grave again and cried out to the tree:

> "Shake and wobble, little tree!
> Let gold and silver fall all over me."

The bird responded by throwing her a dress that was more magnificent and radiant than all the others she had received, and the slippers were pure gold. When she appeared at the wedding in this dress, the people were so astounded they did not know what to say. The prince danced with no one but her, and whenever someone asked her to dance, he said, "She's my partner."

When it was evening and Cinderella wished to leave, the prince wanted to escort her, but she slipped away from him so swiftly that he could not follow her. However, the prince had prepared for this with a trick: he had all the stairs coated with pitch, and when Cinderella went running down the stairs, her left slipper got stuck there. After the prince picked it up, he saw it was small and dainty and made of pure gold.

Next morning he carried it to Cinderella's father and said, "No one else shall be my wife but the maiden whose foot fits this golden shoe."

The two sisters were glad to hear this because they had beautiful feet. The oldest took the shoe into a room to try it on, and her mother stood by her side. However, the shoe was too small for her, and she could not get her big toe into it. So her mother handed her a knife and said, "Cut your toe off. Once you become queen, you won't have to walk anymore."

The maiden cut her toe off, forced her foot into the shoe, swallowed the pain, and went out to the prince. He took her on his horse as his bride and rode off. But they had to pass the grave where the two pigeons were sitting on the hazel tree, and they cried out:

> "Looky, look, look
> at the shoe that she took.
> There's blood all over, and the shoe's too small.
> She's not the bride you met at the ball."

He looked down at her foot and saw the blood oozing out. So he turned his horse around, brought the false bride back again, and said that she was definitely not the right one and the other sister should try on the shoe. Then the second sister went into a room and was fortunate enough to get all her toes in, but the heel was too large. So her mother handed her a knife and said, "Cut off a piece of your heel. Once you become queen, you won't have to walk anymore."

The maiden cut off a piece of her heel, forced her foot into the shoe, swallowed the pain, and went out to the prince. He took her on his horse as his bride, and rode off with her. As they passed the hazel tree, the two pigeons were sitting there, and they cried out:

> "Looky, look, look
> at the shoe that she took.
> There's blood all over, and the shoe's too small.
> She's not the bride you met at the ball."

He looked down at her foot and saw the blood oozing out of the shoe and staining her white stockings all red. Then he turned his horse around and brought the false bride home again.

"She isn't the right one either," he said. "Don't you have any other daughters?"

"No," said the man. "There's only Cinderella, my dead wife's daughter, who's deformed, but she can't possibly be the bride."

The prince told him to send the girl to him, but the mother responded, "Oh, she's much too dirty and really shouldn't be seen."

However, the prince demanded to see her, and Cinderella had to be called. First she washed her hands and face until they were clean, and then she went and curtsied before the prince, who handed her the golden shoe. She sat down on a stool, took her foot out of the heavy wooden shoe, and put it into the slipper, which fit her perfectly. After she stood up and the prince looked her straight in the face, he recognized the beautiful maiden who had danced with him.

"This is my true bride!" he exclaimed.

The stepmother and the two sisters were horrified and turned pale with rage. However, the prince took Cinderella on his horse and rode away with her. As they passed the hazel tree, the two white pigeons cried out:

> "Looky, look, look
> at the shoe that she took.
> The shoe's just right, and there's no blood at all.
> She's truly the bride you met at the ball."

After the pigeons had made this known, they both came flying down and landed on Cinderella's shoulders, one on the right, the other on the left, and there they stayed.

On the day that the wedding with the prince was to take place, the two false sisters came to ingratiate themselves and to share in Cinderella's good fortune. When the bridal couple set out for the church, the oldest sister was on the right, the younger on the left. Suddenly the pigeons appeared

Cinderella. Arthur Rackham, 1911.

and pecked out one eye from each of them. And as they came back from
the church later on, the oldest was on the left and the youngest on the
right, and the pigeons appeared and pecked out the other eye from each
sister. Thus they were punished with blindness for the rest of their lives
due to their wickedness and malice.

The Power of Love

The incarceration of a young woman in a tower (often to protect her chastity during puberty) was a common motif in various European myths and became part of the standard repertoire of medieval tales, lais, and romances throughout Europe, Africa, and the Orient. In addition, the motif of a pregnant woman who has a strong craving for an extravagant dish or extraordinary food is very important. In many peasant societies, people believed that it was necessary to fulfill the longings of a pregnant woman; otherwise, something evil like a miscarriage or bad luck might occur. Therefore, it was incumbent on the husband and other friends and relatives to use spells or charms or other means to fulfill the cravings. Basile's tale about a pregnant woman who is desperate for a certain vegetable delicacy (parsley, cabbage, rapunzel) was one of the most popular tales in the oral and literary tradition, and there have been many different versions of this narrative up to the present. It is apparent that Mlle de la Force was acquainted with his tale, and there is a very important retelling of this story embedded in Mme d'Aulnoy's "The White Cat" (1697). At one point, a young prince meets an enchanted cat, who was once a princess, and she explains to him why and how she was transformed into a cat. She recounts that, when her mother had been pregnant with her, she had taken a journey and had become so desirous to eat some fruit from the fairy garden that she promised the fairies her baby. Her father protested, and the queen herself regretted her actions. However, the fairies took the princess and built a tower for her without an entrance. The fairies entered the tower on the back of a dragon. The princess was never told about her parents, and her only companions were a talking parrot and a talking dog. One day a prince discovered the tower, and the princess and the prince fell in love. The fairies discovered their love and decided that the princess had to marry someone of their own kind, a monstrous fairy king. So the princess and prince decided to flee with the help of the parrot and the dog, and they got married. However, the fairies found them. The prince was devoured by a dragon, and the princess wanted to take her own life, but the fairies transformed her into a white cat. In conclusion, the white cat explains that only when she finds a prince who resembles her dead lover will she be able to regain her human form. As in many of d'Aulnoy's tales, she was concerned here in critiquing forced marriages and courtly customs that did not allow for tender love. "The White Cat" enjoyed a limited popularity in an abbreviated form as a chapbook. The dominant plot was carried in the literary tradition by Mlle de La Force's version, which may have influenced a similar German tale published by Friedrich Immanuel Bierling in 1765. On the other hand, Schulz's version of "Rapunzel" was definitely based on Mlle de la Force's tale, and he, in turn, had a strong influence on the Grimms, who refined their version but also eliminated any indication that Rapunzel had intercourse with the prince in the tower. Ludwig Bechstein included a "Rapunzel" tale, influenced by the Grimms, in his *Deutsches Märchenbuch* (1845) and Vittorio Imbriani published an important Italian version, "Prezzemolina," influenced by Basile, in *Novellaja fiorentina (Florentine Ta-*

les, 1871). The most complete coverage of the Rapunzel cycle is in *Rapunzel: Traditionen eines europäischen Märchenstoffes in Dichtung und Kunst* (1993). Aside from invaluable historical background information and bibliographies, the book contains two excellent essays on the illustrations to "Rapunzel" and many color reproductions of the illustrations.

GIAMBATTISTA BASILE

Petrosinella†

Once upon a time there was a pregnant woman named Pascadozia, who leaned out a window overlooking the garden of an ogress, and she saw a beautiful bed of parsley. All at once she had such a craving to have some of the parsley that she felt she would faint. Try as she might, she could not resist her desire and kept watch until the ogress left her house. Then she went down into the garden and picked a handful of parsley. When the ogress returned home and wanted to make a sauce, she noticed that someone had cut some parsley and said, "May I break my neck if I don't catch this intruder and make him repent! I'll teach him to eat off his own plate and not to mess with other people's pots."

Nevertheless, poor Pascadozia continued to go into the garden until, one morning, she was surprised by the ogress, who was bitter and furious and said, "I've caught you in the act, you slippery thief! Perhaps you think you pay the rent for this garden, and that's why you brazenly come and pick my herbs? But, if I must, I swear that I'll send you all the way to Rome to do penance!"

The unfortunate Pascadozia tried to excuse herself by saying that it was not because of gluttony or greed that she had been prompted by the devil to commit this sin but because she was pregnant, and she had been afraid that her baby would have parsley on its face when it was born. Moreover, she told the ogress that she should actually be grateful that she had not given her a sty in the eye for not gratifying the wish of a pregnant woman.[1]

"The bride wants more than just words!" replied the ogress. "You won't get anywhere with this chatter. Your life may be over and done with unless you promise to give me your baby after it is born, boy or girl, whichever it is."

Poor Pascadozia was desperate, and to avoid the danger threatening her, she swore with one hand on the other that she would do as the ogress demanded. Then the ogress let her go free.

When the time came, Pascadozia gave birth to a beautiful baby girl, who was a jewel and was called Petrosinella[2] because she had a pretty birthmark on her breast, the shape of a tuft of parsley. She grew up nicely day after day, and when she turned seven, she began to go to school. Each

---

† Giambattista Basile, "Petrosinella"—"Petrosinella" (1634), *Primo passatempo della seconda giornata* in *Lo cunto de li cunti overo Lo trattenemiento de peccerille*, De Gian Alessio Abbattutis, 5 vols. (Naples: Ottavio Beltrano, 1634–36).
1. Reference to a popular superstition: whoever did not grant the wish of a pregnant woman would be punished with the *orzaiuolo*, a reddening and swelling of the eyelids.
2. In Neapolitan dialect, *prezzemolina*, meaning "parsley."

time that she crossed the street, however, she met the ogress, who said to her, "Tell your mother to remember her promise!"

And each time that Petrosinella repeated this message, it haunted her mother so much that she could not stand the music any longer and said to her daughter, "If you meet the same old woman, and she asks you about this cursed promise, tell her the answer is, 'Take her.' "

Petrosinella, who knew nothing whatsoever about nothing, met the ogress, and as soon as she innocently passed on her mother's message, the ogress seized her by the hair and took her into a forest where not even the horses of the sun entered because they did not pay to have the right to graze in the shade. The ogress locked Petrosinella in a tower that she had built through her magic powers, and this tower had neither doors nor stairs but only a little window. It was through this window that the ogress climbed in and out of the tower, using Petrosinella's long hair—and it was very long hair indeed—just as the ship boy climbs on the rigging of the mast.

Now one day it so happened that, when the ogress was away from the tower and Petrosinella stuck her head out of the window and let her hair down to be bleached by the sun, a prince passed by the tower. When he saw golden banners that called his soul to enlist in Amour's service and saw the face of a captivating siren that surfaced in the middle of the precious waves, he fell head over heels in love with so much beauty. Consequently, he sent a memorial of sighs in which he declared that he had totally surrendered his castle to her charms. And the negotiations between the two went so well that the prince received many nods in exchange for the kisses from his hand, smiles for his bows, thankful glances for his kind offers, hope for his promises, and gracious words for his courteous behavior. All this continued for several days, and after they became more familiar with one another, they decided to meet at night when the moon plays hide and seek with the stars. Petrosinella was to give the ogress a narcotic to make her sleep and then pull the prince up by her hair.

After they agreed about their plan, the appointed time arrived, and the prince reached the tower, where he gave a whistle, and Petrosinella let her hair down. Then he grabbed the tresses with both his hands and said, "Lift me up!" And she pulled him up, whereupon he jumped through the little window into the room, and there he made a little meal out of the saucy parsley of love. Later, before the sun instructed his horses to jump through the hoop of the zodiac, he descended by the same ladder of gold and went his way.

Petrosinella and the prince continued to have many more meetings until one of the ogress's cronies noticed them, and taking on the troubles of Rosso[3] and poking her snout into other people's shit, she told the ogress to be on her guard because Petrosinella was making love with a certain young man. Indeed, she suspected that things had already gone too far,

---

3. The reference is to the notorious sixteenth-century Florentine thief named Rosso; legend has it that when he was being taken to the gallows in a cart, he was so shaken up due to the bad pavement of the street that he asked the guard to tell the magistrate to have the road repaved because it was a shame for the condemned to arrive at the gallows with their insides turned upside down by the ride.

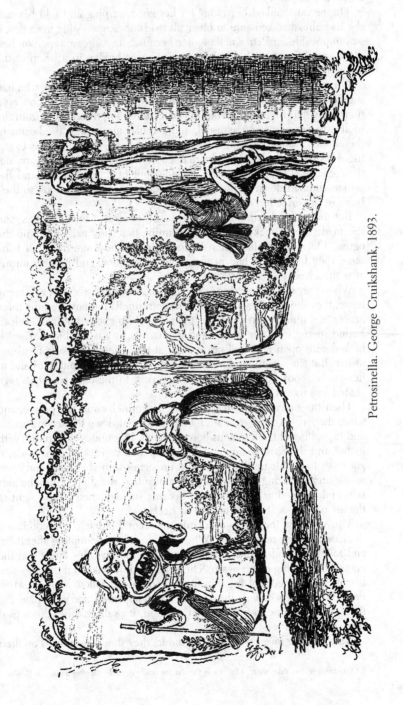

Petrosinella. George Cruikshank, 1893.

for she had seen continual hustling and bustling back and forth, and she feared that if the ogress did not rein them in, they would abandon the house before May.[4]

The ogress thanked her crony for her good warning and told her that she had already taken care to block all roads of escape. Aside from this, it was impossible for Petrosinella to flee because she had cast a spell on her: if the girl did not get hold of the three acorns hidden in a beam of the kitchen, it would be a waste of her effort to try to escape.

But while the ogress was chatting with her crony, Petrosinella, who had suspected the neighbor and was on the alert, heard their entire conversation. So, when night spread out her black robes to protect them from the moths, the prince came as usual, and she had him search the beams in the kitchen, where he found the acorns. Of course, she knew how to use them because they had been enchanted by the ogress. Now, to carry out their escape, Petrosinella made a ladder out of rope, and she and the prince climbed down to the bottom of the tower, and they took to their heels in the direction of the city.

But the crony saw them leave and began to scream for the ogress, and she made such a racket with her screaming that she finally woke up the ogress. Once she realized that Petrosinella had fled, she descended the same rope ladder that had been tied to the window and began running after the lovers.

When they saw her chasing after them and moving faster than a runaway horse, they thought they were lost. But Petrosinella remembered the three acorns and quickly threw one on the ground. Lo and behold, a Corsican hound sprang from the acorn, and mama mia, it was terrible looking! It barked with open jaws and ran straight at the ogress to make a meal out of her. But she was more devious than the devil, and she put her hand in her pocket, took out some bread, and gave it to the dog so that its rage abated and its tail dropped.

Then the ogress continued pursuing Petrosinella and the prince, and when the girl saw the ogress advancing, she threw down the second acorn, and lo and behold, a ferocious lion appeared. It pounded the ground with its tail and shook its mane, and after it opened its jaws two feet wide, it got ready to gobble up the ogress. But the ogress turned around, and upon seeing an ass grazing in the middle of a meadow, she slipped into the ass's skin and charged at the lion, who became so frightened by the sight of the ass rushing at it that it took to its heels.

This was how the ogress overcame the second obstacle and continued to chase after the poor couple. When they heard her trampling after them and saw the cloud of dust that she raised to the sky, they knew that the ogress was coming closer again. The ogress had not taken off the ass's skin because she feared that the lion might continue to follow her, and when Petrosinella threw down a third acorn, a wolf appeared, and without giving the ogress any time to find another solution, it swallowed her down as if she were an ass.

Now that the lovers were out of trouble, they slowly continued on their

---

4. According to the old custom, May 4 was the day for removals and changing houses in Naples.

way until they reached the prince's kingdom, where, with the kind permission of his father, the prince made Petrosinella his wife and proved that, after many trials and tribulations,

one hour in a safe harbor
can make you forget one hundred years of storms.

CHARLOTTE-ROSE DE LA FORCE

Persinette†

After a long period of courtship, two young lovers were married, and nothing could equal their ardor. They lived content and happy, and to complete their felicity, the young wife became pregnant, and this brought great joy to their little household. They had strongly desired to have a child, and their wish was now fulfilled.

Within the vicinity of their house there lived a fairy who was fond of cultivating a beautiful garden filled with different kinds of fruits, plants, and flowers. At the time of this story, parsley was very rare in this country, and the fairy had it brought from the Indies. Indeed, one could not find any parsley in that country except in her garden.

Now the expectant wife had a great desire to eat some parsley, and since she knew that it would be difficult to satisfy her wants because nobody was allowed in the fairy's garden, she became so sad and wretched that her husband could barely recognize her with his own eyes. He kept insisting and urging her to tell him what had brought about such a huge change not only in her spirits but in her body, and after resisting for some time, his wife finally confessed that she had a great desire to eat some parsley. Her husband sighed and was troubled by this desire, which would indeed be difficult to satisfy. Nevertheless, since nothing appears difficult if one is in love, he walked along the walls of the garden day and night to try to find a way to climb over. But it was impossible because they were so high.

Finally, one evening, he saw that one of the doors to the garden was open. He crept through quietly, and he was so happy that he grabbed a fistful of parsley as fast as he could. Then he left as he had entered and carried the loot to his wife, who ate the parsley with avidity. Two days later she felt an even greater desire to eat some more.

To be sure, the parsley must have been extremely delicious at that time.

The poor husband returned to the garden many times afterward but in vain. Eventually, however, his perseverance was rewarded, for he found the door to the garden open again. He entered and was extremely surprised to find the fairy herself, who snarled at him because he had been so audacious as to set foot in a place where admission was not simply granted to anyone who thought he could enter. The bewildered young man fell

† Charlotte-Rose de la Force, "Persinette"—"Persinette" (1698), in *Les contes des contes* (Paris: S. Bernard, 1698).

to his knees, begged her pardon, and told her that his wife would die if she could not eat a little parsley, for she was pregnant, and her desire was thus understandable and indeed forgivable.

"Well, then," said the fairy, "I'll give you as much parsley as you like if you will give me your child when your wife gives birth."

After a short deliberation, the husband gave his promise, and he took as much parsley as he liked.

When the time of the birth arrived, the fairy went to be near the mother, who gave birth to a daughter, whom the fairy called Persinette. She wrapped her in sheets of gold and sprinkled her face with some precious water which she had in a crystal vase that immediately made her the most beautiful creature in the world. After performing these ceremonies to make the child beautiful, the fairy took little Persinette to her home and raised her with the utmost care imaginable. Before Persinette reached the age of twelve, she was a marvel to behold, and since the fairy was fully aware of what fate had in store for her, she decided to shield her from her destiny.

In order to accomplish her goal, she used her magic to build a silver tower in the middle of a forest. This mysterious tower did not have a door by which one could enter it. There were large and beautiful apartments that were so bright it seemed as if the sunlight penetrated them, but they actually received the day through the fire of the carbuncles that glistened in all the chambers. The fairy had splendidly provided everything necessary for life, and all the rarest things were gathered together in this place. Persinette had only to open the drawers of her dressers, and she would find the most beautiful jewels. Her wardrobe was just as magnificent as that of the queens of Asia, and she was always the first to start the most recent fashion. Alone in this beautiful residence, she had nothing to desire other than some company. Except for that, all her desires were anticipated and fulfilled.

Needless to say, the food at all the meals was the most delicious one could imagine, and I assure you that, even though she did not know anyone except the fairy, she was not bored in her solitude. She read, painted, played musical instruments, and entertained herself with all the things that a girl knows how to do when she has been perfectly educated.

The fairy ordered her to sleep at the top of the tower, where there was one single window, and after helping Persinette get settled in this charming solitude, she descended via this window and returned to her own home. Meanwhile, Persinette amused herself with a hundred different things, and even when she was merely searching around in her caskets, she felt fully occupied. Indeed, how many people would like to feel as contented as she was!

The view from the window of the tower was the most beautiful in the world because one could see the sea from one side, and from the other, the vast forest, two sights that were unusual and charming. Since Persinette had a divine voice, she liked to sing aloud. This was one of the ways she entertained herself, especially during the hours she awaited the arrival of the fairy, who came to see her very often, and when the fairy was at the bottom of the tower, she used to say, "Persinette, let your hair down so I can climb up."

One of the great beauties of Persinette was her hair, which was thirty yards long and did not cause her any discomfort. It was as blond as gold and braided with ribbons of all colors. And when she heard the fairy's voice, she would undo her hair and let it fall down, and the fairy would climb up.

One day, Persinette was alone at her window, and she began to sing in the most extraordinary way. Just at this very moment, a young prince happened to be hunting in the forest. He had lost the rest of his company in pursuit of a stag. Upon hearing such a pleasant voice in this wilderness, he approached the tower and saw the young Persinette. Her beauty moved him. Her voice captivated him. He went around that fatal tower twenty times, and when he could not find an entrance, he thought he would die of agony, for he had fallen in love. But since he was daring, he kept looking for a way to scale the tower.

As far as Persinette was concerned, she became speechless upon gazing at such a charming man. She looked at him a long time, but all at once she withdrew from the window, believing that he was a kind of a monster, for she remembered that she had heard of some men who could kill with their eyes, and she had found his looks to be very dangerous.

When the prince saw that she had disappeared, he became despondent and began making inquiries in the nearby village, where he was told that a fairy had built that tower and had locked up a young girl in it. So he prowled around it every day, until he finally saw the fairy arrive and say: "Persinette, let your hair down so I can climb up." At that very instant, he watched the beautiful girl undo her long plaits of hair, and soon after he saw how the fairy mounted by taking hold of the hair. To be sure, he was very surprised by this unusual manner of making a visit.

The next day, when he knew that the usual hour for the fairy to enter the tower had passed, he waited impatiently until nightfall. Then he went under Persinette's window and disguised his voice admirably to make it sound like the fairy's, and he said, "Persinette, let your hair down so I can climb up."

Poor Persinette, deceived by the sound of this voice, ran to the window and undid her beautiful hair. The prince climbed up, and when he was at the top and looked at her through the window and saw how marvelously beautiful she was up close, he thought he would fall back down to the bottom. Nevertheless, he recovered his natural boldness and jumped into the chamber. Then he bowed down before Persinette and embraced her knees with an ardor that was to persuade her of his love. But she was frightened. She cried, and the next moment she trembled, and there was nothing that could calm her, for her heart was full of all the love she could possibly feel for this prince. Meanwhile, he was saying all the most beautiful things in the world to her, and she responded by showing her confusion, which in turn gave hope to the prince. Finally, he became bolder and proposed to marry her right then and there, and she consented without hardly knowing what she was doing. Even so, she was able to complete the ceremony.

Now the prince was happy, and Persinette grew accustomed to loving him. They saw each other every day, and in a short time she became pregnant. Since she had no idea what this condition meant, she was upset. Although the prince knew, he did not want to explain it to her for fear of tormenting her. But the fairy had come to see her, and no sooner did she look at her than she recognized the malady.

"Ah, how unfortunate for you!" she said. "You've made a great mistake, and you're going to be punished for it. Fate has had its way, and all the precautions I took were in vain."

After saying all this, she asked Persinette in an imperious tone to confess all that had happened. And Persinette complied with her eyes filled with tears. Upon hearing her story, the fairy did not appear to be moved by Persinette's touching story about how she fell in love, and taking her by her hair, she cut off the precious braids. After doing this, she made Persinette climb down the tower by using her braids, and she followed her through the window. When they were at the bottom, she covered Persinette in a cloud that carried both of them to the seaside and deposited them at a spot that was very isolated but pleasant enough. There were meadows, woods, a brook with fresh water, and a small bit made of foliage that always remained green. Inside there was a bed made of shrubs, and on the side was a basket filled with unusual biscuits that were continually replenished. Such was the place to which the fairy had conducted Persinette, and she left her there after severely reproaching her. These reproaches seemed to Persinette a hundred times more cruel than her own woes.

It was in this place that she gave birth to a little prince and a little princess, and it was in this place that she nursed them and had all the time in the world to cry about her misfortune.

But the fairy did not find this vengeance sufficient enough. She also wanted to punish the prince as well. As soon as she left the wretched Persinette, she returned to the top of the tower and began singing the way Persinette usually did. The prince was fooled by this voice, and when he returned to see Persinette, he asked her to lower her hair so that he could climb up the way he was accustomed to doing. The perfidious fairy had expressly cut Persinette's hair for this purpose and let it down for him. When the poor prince appeared at the window, he was more distressed than surprised by not finding his mistress, and he searched for her eyes.

"You reckless fool!" the fairy said to him. "Your crime is immense. Your punishment will be terrible!"

But the prince shrugged off these menacing threats and responded, "Where is Persinette?"

"She's no longer here for you!" the fairy replied.

And invoking her power, she caused the prince to throw himself from the top of the tower. Although his body should have broken into a thousand pieces when it reached the ground, the only agony he suffered was the loss of his sight.

The prince was horrified when he realized that he could no longer see. He remained for a time at the foot of the tower, groaning and repeating Persinette's name a hundred times. Then he began groping about and tried to proceed as best he could. Slowly he gained confidence and could make his way in the dark world he now inhabited. For a long time he did not encounter anyone who could help and guide him. He nourished himself by eating herbs and roots that he found when he became hungry.

At the end of some years, he was walking about one day, when he found himself more troubled by his love and suffering than usual. He went to sleep under a tree and was consumed by sad reflection, a cruel preoccupation for someone who deserved a better fate. But suddenly he was wakened from his reverie by a charming voice. The first sounds pierced his heart, producing sweet feelings that he had not experienced for a long time.

"Oh gods!" he cried out. "It's Persinette's voice!"

He was not mistaken. Without realizing it, he had reached her solitary spot. She was seated at the door of her cabin and was singing a song about her unfortunate love. Her two children, more beautiful than the day was bright, were playing a little distance from her. They moved about until they came upon the tree under which the prince had been sleeping. No sooner did they see him than one and then the other ran and hugged him a thousand times.

"It's my father!" they said at one and the same time and called their mother. In fact, they made such a cry that she came running, for she could not imagine what the matter could be. Until that very moment nothing had ever happened in that solitary place.

Imagine her surprise and joy when she recognized her dear husband! It is impossible to describe it. She uttered a piercing cry above him and quite naturally burst forth into tears. But what a miracle! No sooner had her precious tears fallen on the prince's eyes than he regained his full vision. Now he could see just as clearly as he had seen before, and all this was due to the tenderness of the impassioned Persinette, who took him into her arms. He responded with endless hugs, more than he had ever given her before.

It was touching indeed to see the handsome prince, the charming princess, and the lovely children express such ecstatic joy and tenderness. The rest of the day continued just as pleasant, and when night came, this little family finally realized it was time to eat. However, when the prince took a biscuit, it turned into stone. He was terror-stricken by this miracle and sighed with pain. The poor children cried, and the distraught mother wanted at least to give them some water, but it changed into crystals. What a night! They believed this terrible time would last forever.

When the sun appeared, they got up and decided to gather herbs. But to their astonishment, the herbs turned to toads and venomous snakes. The most innocent birds became dragons, and vixens flew around them, glaring at them in a terrifying way.

"I can't go on like this!" the prince cried. "My dear Persinette, I did not want to find you only to lose you in such a terrible way."

"Let us die together, my dear prince," she responded, embracing him tenderly, "and let us make our enemies envious by the sweetness of our death."

The poor little children were in their arms, all of them so faint that they were on the brink of death. Who would not have been touched by the sight of this dying poor family? They needed a miracle.

Fortunately, the fairy was finally moved, and recalling at this moment all the tenderness that she had once felt for the amiable Persinette, she flew to the spot where they were and appeared in a glittering golden chariot covered with gems. She summoned the now fortunate lovers, each of them at one side of her, and after placing their charming children on magnificent pillows at their feet, she transported them to the palace of the prince's father, the king. There was no end of rejoicing. The handsome prince, whom his parents had long believed lost, was received like a god, and he found himself quite content to be settled after the torments of his stormy life. Nothing in the world could be compared to the happiness in which he lived with his perfect wife.

> Oh, tender couples learn to view
> How advantageous it is always to be true.
> The pains, the work, the most burdensome worry,
> All this will eventually turn out quite sweet,
> When the ardor is shared in a love complete.
> Together there's nothing a couple can't do,
> And fortune and fate will be overcome too.

FRIEDRICH SCHULZ

Rapunzel†

Two young people who were in love with one another were finally able to become man and wife after they had overcome some objections to their relationship by their relatives. They were extremely delighted by this and lived together like two happy doves. They became even more delighted when they gradually learned that the young woman was carrying something in her belly. She had always desired to bring an heir into this world, and now, she thought, her wish would be fulfilled.

Not far from this couple there lived a fairy who was totally devoted to her beautiful garden and her lovely flowers, bushes, and shrubs. Whenever she planted seeds, wonderful things would appear, and among them were rapunzel lettuces, which were very rare at that time. The fairy had ordered them from overseas, and her garden was the only one in the entire country that had rapunzel.

Now the young woman developed a huge craving to eat some rapunzel, and she knew full well that it was difficult to obtain some because nobody was allowed to enter the fairy's garden. But the young woman grieved so much about this and became so haggard that her own husband could barely recognize her. One day he asked her why she was grieving so much, and after she tried very long to conceal everything from him, she confessed that she had a strong desire to eat rapunzel salad.

Her husband heaved a deep sigh, for he regretted that she had a craving that would be so difficult to fill. But since he loved her very much and

---

† Friedrich Schulz, "Rapunzel"—"Rapunzel" (1790), in *Kleine Romane*, vol. 5 (Leipzig: Georg Joachim Göschen, 1790).

since love overcomes everything, he walked around the fairy's garden day and night and searched for a place to climb over the walls. But they were so high that he was unable to do it. Finally, one evening, he saw the garden door open. He quietly slipped inside and was fortunate to be able to pull out a handful of rapunzel without being caught. He ran away quickly and brought it to his wife, who made a salad out of it and hungrily gobbled it down. The rapunzel tasted so delicious that the next day her craving for it was three times as great as it was before. Indeed, in those days rapunzel still tasted wonderful.

Her poor husband went back to the garden, but he was unable to gain entrance two days in a row. His wife began to waste away again until he finally found the garden door open again and went inside. But before he knew what was happening, the fairy stood before him and asked him what he thought he was doing in her garden, for he knew that nobody was allowed to enter.

He was very frightened and fell to her feet begging her not to harm him, and he explained to her that he had no choice, for his wife would die if she did not get a handful of rapunzel to eat. She was pregnant, and the fairy was probably very well aware of that.

"Good," said the fairy, smiling and merciful, "you can have as much rapunzel as you want if you let me have your child when your wife gives birth."

The man thought about this for a while, and then he consented. Now he could take as much rapunzel as he wanted, and his wife loved him even more than before. When she finally gave birth, the fairy appeared before her bed. The baby was a girl, and she was called Rapunzel. The fairy wrapped her in a blanket embroidered with gold and silver. Then she sprinkled her with some precious water that she was carrying in a little can, and the baby became the most beautiful child under the sun. Then the fairy took her home and raised her with great care, and the girl became quite a wonder to behold before she was twelve years old.

However, since the fairy knew that there had been a bad constellation of the stars when Rapunzel was born, she decided to do all she could to protect the girl. Therefore, she used her magic powers to create a high silver tower in the middle of the forest, and this tower did not have a door through which one could enter and exit, but it did have a small window toward the top. Moreover, the rooms inside were so bright that it seemed as if the sun were shining for there were great carbuncles which illuminated everything.

The young Rapunzel found everything there that one needed to lead a splendid and joyous life. Nothing but magnificent things! She only had to open her caskets or drawers, and there were rings, diamonds, and pearls. Her closets were filled with such precious clothes that the empress of Russia would not have been ashamed to wear anything from them. Everything was totally in fashion. Nevertheless, Rapunzel was totally alone there, and she lacked company. If she had only had some, everything would have been perfect. For her meals she had boiled and roasted meat, marzipan and almonds and sugar cookies. It all tasted delicious, and she also enjoyed eating it all.

Since she knew nobody except the fairy, she did not wish to make the acquaintance of anyone else. Indeed, she spent her time in good ways. She read, painted, played, sewed, and knitted. In short, she did everything that a properly raised daughter usually does. The view from her window was magnificent. On the one side she could see the open sea, and on the other side, the dense black forest, and both appeared beautiful.

Rapunzel had a glorious voice, and she liked to sing, especially when she knew that the fairy would be coming, and the fairy came quite often. When she stood at the bottom of the tower, she would always say, "Rapunzel, let your hair down so I can climb up!"

Rapunzel's hair was the most beautiful part of her. It was thirty yards long, and she did not mind having such heavy hair. It was blond just like the finest gold and woven into braids and tied with beautiful ribbons. As soon as she heard the fairy, she would wind the braids first around a hook in the window and then let the hair down so the fairy could climb up.

One time when Rapunzel was alone and stood at her window, she began to sing in a wonderful voice. Just at that time a young prince out on a hunting expedition was passing by, and when he heard her, he tiptoed near the tower and saw the beautiful Rapunzel. She was so lovely that she appeared to be an angel, and he fell in love with her. He walked around the tower ten times, and when he could not find a door, he lamented so much that he almost died of grief. But Rapunzel was also taken by him when she saw how handsome this young man was. She looked at him for a long time and was very astounded. But then she suddenly stepped back from the window and closed it because she thought he might be a monster, for she had heard that there were such things which could kill you with their eyes, and she had felt that there was something wrong with the way he looked at her.

The prince wanted to die when he saw her disappear all at once. He went to a nearby hut of a charcoal burner and asked all about the tower. Then he was told that a fairy had built it, and that she had locked a young beautiful maiden inside it. This story made him even more curious, and he came each day to the tower and crawled around it. One time he saw the fairy in front of it and heard her say, "Rapunzel, let your hair down so that I can climb up!"

He immediately observed how the beautiful maiden let her long braids down, and how the fairy climbed up. He was astonished by the strange way the fairy visited her, and he took special note of it. The next day, when he thought that the hour had passed for the fairy to make her usual appearance, he waited impatiently until dusk. Then he went beneath Rapunzel's window, imitated the voice of the fairy, and said through a pipe, "Rapunzel, let your hair down so I can climb up!"

Poor Rapunzel did not suspect anything bad. So she went to the window and let her braids down. Then the prince climbed up, and when he was on top and stood in the window, he thought he would fall back down again because Rapunzel was so beautiful. But he summoned his courage, which was not difficult for him as a prince, jumped into the room, fell to Rapunzel's feet, embraced her knees, and said things to her to make her trust him.

However, she was afraid and screamed pitifully and did not stop until she was just as much in love with the prince as he was with her, and then everything became quiet. He told her many beautiful things, and she was stunned and did not answer. This gave him hope, and finally he was so bold as to propose marriage to her, and he wanted to have her right away. She said yes, without knowing why it was happening and without knowing how, and she did not really want to know where. What good behavior!

The prince was overjoyed. Rapunzel grew accustomed to loving him, and they saw each other every day. But it was not long before her dresses no longer fit her. The prince realized that nothing good would come of this, but he did not want to say anything for fear that she would become upset. But when the fairy appeared and Rapunzel complained to her that all her clothes had become too tight for her, the fairy grasped what was happening and said, "You unfortunate child, you've made a great mistake, and you'll be punished for it! You cannot escape your fate, and my precautions were to no avail."

With a wrinkled brow, she ordered Rapunzel to confess everything. And poor Rapunzel did this and sobbed pitifully as she did. The fairy remained unmovable, and Rapunzel told her very touching things about how she loved the prince, and how he loved her. But the fairy cried out, "Even worse!" Finally, she took Rapunzel's braids in her hand and cut them in one slash. Then she tied them to the window and had Rapunzel climb down first, and she followed. Once they were at the bottom, she wrapped herself and Rapunzel in a cloud and flew with her to the seashore, where the fairy had the cloud set them down in a beautiful region. There were meadows, woods, clear springs, brooks, and a small hut made out of evergreen trees. Inside was a litter of dry foliage, and next to it was a basket with very special bread that never became empty. The fairy gave her Rapunzel a good scolding and left her alone, and this hurt Rapunzel more than anything else that had happened to her. Later it was here that she gave birth to a small prince and princess, and it was here she nursed the two little worms and wept that their father was not with them.

In the meantime, the fairy was not satisfied simply to punish the mother. The father was also to get his share, and she wanted to get the prince in her hands. So, when she left Rapunzel, she returned to the tower and began to sing the way Rapunzel had sung. The prince came and believed that it was her. He called out, "Rapunzel, let your hair down so I can climb up!"

Now the fairy had cut off her hair for this purpose and let the braids down. When the prince appeared, he was disturbed not to find Rapunzel and searched for her with yearning looks. But the fairy glared at him angrily and said, "You impertinent thing! You've made a horrible mistake, and now you're going to be cruelly punished for it!"

But he did not pay attention to her threats and ran around wringing his hands and kept crying out, "Where is she? Where is she?"

"She's lost for you!" said the fairy.

Out of grief the prince jumped out of the tower, and he would have broken his neck, but he was lucky in his fall and only lost both his eyes. He was quite puzzled that he could not see anymore and remained lying at the bottom of the tower for some time. He kept weeping and saying nothing but "Rapunzel! Rapunzel!" Finally he stood up and felt his way along the paths with great effort until he learned how to move about much better. So he continued walking, oh, I don't know how long, and he was unable to find anyone to guide him. When he was hungry, he ate grass and roots, even though he was not at all used to doing this. After a year passed, he was once again strongly overcome by thoughts of Rapunzel and his misfortune. He lay himself down beneath a tree and abandoned himself to his sad memories. But all of a sudden he was aroused by a beautiful voice which could not have been far away from him. The voice penetrated deep into his heart and caused feelings to stir that he had not had for a long time.

"Oh, dear God," he said as he stretched out his hands. "That's the voice of my Rapunzel!"

And he was right, for he had gradually wandered and reached the isolated spot where she was living. She sat in front of her hut and sang something about her unfortunate love story. A pair of children as beautiful as little angels were playing nearby in the grass. Since they had gone somewhat further away, they saw the prince lying under the tree and ran to him. No sooner did they look into his face than they hugged him and kept crying, "You're our father!"

They called their mother and yelled so loudly that she came running and could not understand what was happening because until then she had not been disturbed by anything in her solitude. But how astonished she was and how joyful she was to see her husband suddenly appear before her! It is impossible to describe the scene. She uttered a great cry and embraced him, and she burst into tears out of joy. And it was indeed a miracle: no sooner had some of her tears fallen on the eyes of the prince than they were healed and he could see again as clearly as he had seen before. He owed this great luck to the love of his Rapunzel, whom he also loved again more passionately than he had ever loved her before.

This was a very touching scene as the handsome prince, the beautiful princess, and their two children made such a display of their happiness that they all cried out of joy, and the day continued in this cheerful spirit. When evening came, however, everyone in this small family was somewhat hungry. The prince reached into the basket and thought that he would pull out some bread, but unfortunately it was a stone. He was terrified by this strange occurrence and sighed. The two children wept because their bread had been changed into stone. The poor mother wanted at least to give them a few drops of water, but the water had changed into crystal. What a horrible night it was! They believed that it would last forever. As soon as it was daylight, they stood up and wanted to look for roots. But, alas! The roots turned into snakes and worms. They wanted to catch birds, and even the smallest of the birds became common ravens, hoopoe, and vultures.

"Now we are done for, dear Rapunzel," said the prince. "We've found each other again only to see ourselves starve."

"Then let us die!" she exclaimed and pressed herself to him. "And our friends will envy us because we shall have fallen asleep so gently."

The two poor children sat on their laps and were so exhausted that they could not even weep. A stone would have been moved to tears if it had witnessed this scene. But help soon arrived. The fairy could not help but be touched, and her love for Rapunzel led her to seek a reconciliation. She came riding through the air on a magnificent carriage, had them all get in, sat them down on splendid pillows, and carried them to the castle in which the prince's father was holding court.

When they arrived, everyone became ecstatic because the prince had returned, for he had long since been regarded as lost, and his father wanted to marry another woman in order to have a second son. Now he dropped that plan because it was no longer necessary. His son was now extremely happy because he had been so unhappy, and he loved Rapunzel more than ever before and she him because they had lost one another. Here is where their story ends.

JACOB AND WILHELM GRIMM

Rapunzel†

Once upon a time there was a husband and wife who for quite some time had been wishing in vain for a child. Finally, the dear Lord gave the wife a sign of hope that their wish would be fulfilled. Now, in the back of their house, the couple had a small window that overlooked a splendid garden filled with the most beautiful flowers and herbs. The garden, however, was surrounded by a high wall, and nobody dared enter it because it belonged to a sorceress who was very powerful and feared by all. One day when the wife was standing at the window and looking down into the garden, she noticed a bed of the finest rapunzel lettuce. The lettuce looked so fresh and green that her mouth watered, and she had a great craving to eat some. Day by day this craving increased, and since she knew she could not get any, she began to waste away and look pale and miserable.

Her husband became alarmed and asked, "What's wrong with you, dear wife?"

"Ah," she responded, "I shall certainly die if I don't get any of that rapunzel from the garden behind our house."

Her husband, who loved her, thought, "Before I let my wife die, I'll do anything I must to make sure she gets some rapunzel."

That day at dusk he climbed over the wall into the garden of the sorceress, hastily grabbed a handful of rapunzel, and brought it to his wife. Immediately, she made it into a salad and ate it with great zest. But the rapunzel tasted so good to her, so very good, that her desire for it was three times greater by the next day. If she was to have any peace, her husband knew he had to climb into the garden once more. So at dusk he scaled the wall again, and just as he landed on the other side, he was given a tremendous scare, for he stood face-to-face with the sorceress.

† Jacob and Wilhelm Grimm, "Rapunzel"—"Rapunzel" (1857), No. 12 in Kinder- und Hausmärchen. Gesammelt durch die Brüder Grimm (Göttingen: Dieterich, 1857).

"How dare you climb into my garden and steal my rapunzel like a thief?" she said with an angry look. "You'll pay for this!"

"Oh!" he cried. "Please, let mercy prevail over justice. I did this only because I was in a predicament: my wife noticed your rapunzel from our window, and she developed such a great craving for it that she would have died if I hadn't brought her some to eat."

Upon hearing that, the sorceress's anger subsided, and she said to him, "If it's truly as you say, then I shall permit you to take as many rapunzel as you like, but only under one condition: when your wife gives birth, I must have the child. You needn't fear about the child's well-being, for I shall take care of it like a mother."

In his fear, the man agreed to everything, and when his wife had the baby, the sorceress appeared at once. She gave the child the name of Rapunzel and took her away.

Rapunzel grew to be the most beautiful child under the sun. But when she was twelve years old, the sorceress locked her in a tower located in a forest. It had neither door nor stairs, only a little window high above. Whenever the sorceress wanted to get in, she would stand below and call out:

> "Rapunzel, Rapunzel,
> let down your hair for me."

Rapunzel's hair was long and radiant, fine as spun gold. Every time she heard the voice of the sorceress, she unpinned her braids and wound them around a hook on the window. Then she let her hair drop twenty yards, and the sorceress would climb up on it.

A few years later a king's son happened to be riding through the forest and passed by the tower. Suddenly, he heard a song so lovely that he stopped to listen. It was Rapunzel, who passed the time in her solitude by letting her sweet voice resound in the forest. The prince wanted to climb up to her, and he looked for a door but could not find one. So he rode home. However, the song had touched his heart so deeply that he rode out into the forest every day and listened. One time, as he was standing behind a tree, he saw the sorceress approach and heard her call out:

> "Rapunzel, Rapunzel,
> let down your hair."

Then Rapunzel let down her braids, and the sorceress climbed up to her.

"If that's the ladder one needs to get up there, I'm also going to try my luck," the prince declared.

The next day, as it began to get dark, he went to the tower and called out:

> "Rapunzel, Rapunzel,
> let down your hair."

All at once the hair dropped down, and the prince climbed up. When he entered the tower, Rapunzel was at first terribly afraid, for she had never laid eyes on a man before. However, the prince began to talk to her in a friendly way and told her that her song had touched his heart so deeply that he had not been able to rest until he had seen her. Gradually, Rapunzel overcame her fears, and when he asked her whether she would have him for her husband, she saw that he was young and handsome and thought, "He'll certainly love me better than old Mother Gothel." So she said yes and placed her hand in his.

"I want to go with you very much," she said, "but I don't know how I can get down. Every time you come, you must bring a skein of silk with you, and I'll weave it into a ladder. When it's finished, then I'll climb down, and you can take me away on your horse."

They agreed that until then he would come to her every evening, for the old woman came during the day. Meanwhile, the sorceress did not notice anything, until one day Rapunzel blurted out, "Mother Gothel, how is it that you are much heavier than the prince? When I pull him up, he's here in a second."

"Ah, you godless child!" exclaimed the sorceress. "What's this I hear? I though that I had made sure you had no contact with the outside world, but you've deceived me!"

In her fury, she seized Rapunzel's beautiful hair, wrapped it around her left hand several times, grabbed a pair of scissors with her right hand, and *snip, snap* the hair was cut off, and the beautiful braids lay on the ground. Then the cruel sorceress took Rapunzel to a desolate land where she had to live in great misery and grief.

On the same day that she had banished Rapunzel, the sorceress fastened the braids that she had cut off to the hook on the window, and that evening, when the prince came and called out,

> "Rapunzel, Rapunzel,
> let down your hair,"

she let the hair down.

The prince climbed up, but instead of finding his dearest Rapunzel on top, he found the sorceress, who gave him vicious and angry looks.

"Aha!" she exclaimed with contempt. "You want to fetch your darling wife, but the beautiful bird is no longer sitting in the nest, and she won't be singing anymore. The cat has got her, and it will also scratch out your eyes. Rapunzel is lost to you, and you will never see her again!"

The prince was beside himself with grief, and in his despair he jumped off the tower. He escaped with his life, but he fell into some thorns that pierced his eyes. Consequently, he became blind and strayed about in the forest, where he ate only roots and berries and did nothing but mourn and weep about the loss of his dearest wife. Thus he wandered for many years in misery. Eventually, he made his way to the desolte land where Rapunzel was leading a wretched existence with the twins, a boy and a girl, to whom she had given birth. When he heard a voice that he thought sounded familiar, he went straight toward it, and when he reached her, Rapunzel recognized him. She embraced him and wept, and when two of her tears dropped on his eyes, they became clear, and he could see again. Then he escorted her back to his kingdom, where he was received with joy, and they lived happily and contentedly for a long time thereafter.

Terrible Curses and
Lucky Princes

Basile's tale combines several important motifs that can be found in both the oral and the literary traditions: the breaking of the pot or jug, the curse of the old woman, the three impossible tasks that the hero must perform, the miraculous help generally from the daughter of the oppressor, the magic flight of the lovers, the forgotten bride, and the final recognition of the true bride. The Grimms' version was written in dialect and does not indicate a direct influence by Basile. Other German versions are Ludwig Bechstein's "Der goldene Rehbock" ("The Golden Doe," 1845) and Johann Wilhelm Wolf's "Das goldene Königsreich" ("The Golden Royal Realm," 1851). There is a strong indication that the king, ogre, or oppressor must seek a young man to set a daughter free from a curse. It is only through the man that the daughter can escape a baleful existence.

GIAMBATTISTA BASILE

The Dove†

Once upon a time there was a forest of figs and poplars eight miles from Naples in the direction of Astroni,[1] and it was so dense that the rays of the sun could not penetrate it. Within this forest there was a little dilapidated house inhabited by an old woman who lacked as many teeth as she was burdened by years and who had a lump as high on her back as her fortunes were low. She had a hundred wrinkles on her face, but her pockets were smooth, and although her head was completely silver, she not possess a single silver coin to cheer her spirits. Indeed, in order to support herself she went around to the cottages of the region in search of alms.

However, even nowadays people give a purse of money more readily to loafers and spongers than three pennies to a poor needy person, and it was then very difficult for her during threshing time just to get a plate of beans even though there was so much abundance in those parts and few homes were without tons of food. Well, people say, "an old kettle has a crack or a hole in it" and "God sends flies to an old horse" and "the fallen tree, a hatchet, a hatchet." Eventually, the old woman managed to take home a few beans, wash them, and stick them in a clay pot. Then she placed the

† Giambattista Basile, "The Dove"—"La colomba" (1634), *Settimo passatempo della seconda giornata* in *Lo cunto de li cunti overo Lo trattenemiento de peccerille*, De Gian Alessio Abbattutis, 5 vols. (Naples: Ottavio Beltrano, 1634–36).
1. A village to the east of Naples near Lake Agnano.

pot outside on the windowsill while she went to look for four small logs in the forest to cook them.

While she was gone, it so happened that the king's son, Nardaniello, who had been out hunting, passed by the cottage. When he saw the pot on the windowsill, he was overcome by the desire to take a shot at it and made a wager with his attendants to see who had the best aim and could break the pot with a stone. Thus they began flinging stones at the innocent pot, and after three or four throws, the prince hit it in the middle, smashed it to pieces, and celebrated with joy.

Just as the prince and his retinue were about to leave, the old woman returned, and when she saw the bitter disaster, she began to scream and curse him, "What are you boasting about? Why are you so proud, you goat of Foggia?[2] Just because you knocked down the pot? You son of a witch, you've dug the grave of your own flesh! You wretched blockhead, how could you sow my beans out of season? Even if you don't have a drop of compassion for my misery, you should at least have some respect for your own interests and not have thrown your family's coat of arms on the ground. Nor should you have crushed beneath your feet that which should be on your head! But go, get out of here! I pray to heaven on my bare knees and with all my heart that you fall in love with the daughter of some ogress who will make you cook and boil until you burn. May your mother-in-law always be on your back so that you'd prefer to be dead than alive. May you be so captivated by the beauty of the daughter and bewitched by the spell of the mother that you will not be able to flee but will be compelled to remain and suffer the deadly torments of that ugly harpy who will command your services with blows from a stick and will give you such stale bread that you will sigh more than four times for my beans that you've thrown to the ground."

The curses of this wretched old woman sprouted wings and flew at once to heaven so that in spite of the usual proverbs—"curses of an old woman are to be sown behind you" and "the coat of a cursed horse shines"—the curses hit the prince right on his nose, and he was lucky to keep the skin on his back. Indeed, after two hours had passed, he became separated from his retinue, and he came across a remarkably beautiful girl who was gathering snails and amusing herself by singing the ditty,

> "Come out, come out little horn,
> Your mama wants you dishorned, dishorned.
> Now, be a good little boy."[3]

When the prince saw this imprint of nature's most precious sources appear before him, this bank of the richest deposits of heaven, this arsenal of the most mighty forces of Love, he did not know what had hit him, and when the rays of her eyes emanating from her sparkling crystal face landed on the fuse of his heart, they ignited him so that he became a

2. Foggia was the center of the plateau of Puglia, and flocks came down from the Abruzzi mountains to this place during the winter. This was also the place where the shepherds had to pay their feudal tributes. So, proverbially speaking, to be in Foggia was similar to being horned or cuckolded.

3. A little rhyme that children used to sing as part of a game to stimulate snails to put out their horns. It was common not only in Italy but also in Spain and France.

furnace in which the stones of his plans to build a house of hope were about to be baked.

Filadoro, for this was how the girl was called, reacted just as quickly. The prince was a handsome young man, and he pierced her heart to the core so deeply that they both sought mercy from the other with their eyes, and while they remained tongue-tied, their glances were like the trumpets of the court messenger who blared the secret of their souls. They both stayed like this for a while, and since their throats were parched, they were unable to utter one cursed word. Finally, the prince uncorked his vocal chords and said, "From what meadow has this flower of beauty sprouted? From what sky did this dew of grace come showering down? From what mine has this treasure of beauty been taken? Oh happy forests! Oh fortunate woods! You inhabitants of this luxury, illuminated by this luminary of the feasts of love! Oh woods, oh forests, I see that you don't make handles for brooms here, crosspieces for pitchforks, or lids for chamberpots, but rather doors for the temple of beauty, beams for the house of the graces, and lances to make the arrows of love!"

"Lower your voice, my cavalier," Filadoro answered. "You are too gracious because your virtues, not my merits, have produced the epitaph of praises that you have lavished upon me. I am a woman who knows my own measure, and I don't want any other person to measure me. But such as I am, beautiful or ugly, dark or fair, thin or fat, chatty or mute, a harpy or a fairy, a little doll or a toad, I am completely at your service because you have captured my heart with your handsome figure. Your beautiful face has totally enraptured me, and I am now your slave and will serve you in chains from here to eternity."[4]

These phrases were not words but the sounds of a trumpet calling the prince to sit down and eat at the table of amorous delights, and they also roused him to take to his horse[5] for the battle of love. Once he realized that he was offered a finger of affection, he took the hand and kissed the ivory prong that had pierced his heart. In response to the prince's gesture, Filadoro's face appeared like that of a countess or rather like the face in a portrait in which one sees a mixture of the scarlet of shame, the cherry rose of fear, the blue sea of hope, and the vermillion of desire.

Nardaniello wanted to continue this exchange, but he was interrupted, for in this gloomy life there is no wine that provides satisfaction without causing disgust, no delicious broth of contentment without the scum of misfortune. Indeed, while Nardaniello was feeling so wonderful, lo and behold, Filadoro's mother suddenly appeared, and she was an ogress so ugly that nature had made her a model of monsters. She had hair like a broom of dried branches not for cleaning houses of dirt and cobwebs but for blackening and smoking men's hearts. Her brow was like the whetstone of Genova[6] used to sharpen the knife of fear that slashes one's breast. Her eyes were like comets that predict trembling of the limbs, spasms of the heart, shivering of the spirit, colic of the soul, and collapse of the body

---

4. This was often a formulaic and highly complimentary way of ending letters during that period.
5. Allusion to a military call.
6. Rich glittering black stone found on the coast of Genova and used for sharpening the blades of weapons.

because she carried terror in her face, fright in her looks, thunderous roars in her steps, and diarrhea in her words. Her mouth had tusks like those of a wild boar and as large as a shark's. Moreover, she was convoluted like someone suffering from convulsions, and she slobbered like a mule. In short, from head to toe, she looked like the very image of ugliness—a hospital of maimed limbs. Certainly, the prince must have been carrying some story of the lovers Marco and Fiorella[7] sewn in his doublet; otherwise he would have died at the sight of her.

All at once, the ogress grabbed Nardaniello by his cloak and said, "Stand still, you bird! You've been caught!"

"Who are your witnesses that will testify against me, you scum of the earth!" Nardaniello responded and wanted to draw his sword made of fine steel, but he stood frozen just like a lamb that has seen a wolf: he could neither move nor say peep, and the ogress dragged him to her house like an ass led by the halter.

As soon as they arrived there, the ogress said, "You had better work like a dog, if you don't want to die like a pig, and as for your first chores, I want you to dig up and sow this piece of land outside the house by the end of the day so that it reaches the level of this room. Beware that if I return this evening and don't find the work done, I'll swallow you up." Then she told her daughter to take care of the house and left to gossip with the other ogresses in the woods.

When Nardaniello found himself reduced to such a miserable state, he let loose a flood of tears that poured down onto his chest, and he cursed his fate which had caused this bad turn of events. On the other hand, Filadoro consoled him and told him to cheer up because she would give her blood to help him. Moreover, she declared, he should not curse his destiny which had brought him to that house where he was so deeply loved by her. Indeed, she accused him of not reciprocating the love that she felt for him because he was so despondent.

"I'm not sorry for having been reduced to riding an ass instead of a horse," the prince responded. "I'm not sorry for being forced to exchange my royal palace for this cottage, banquet tables for a piece of bread, my cortege of servants for my service by contract, the scepter for a hoe, my frightening armies to being frightened by an ugly stinking woman. I can bear my fate and disgrace as long as I can be with you and behold you with these eyes. But what grieves my heart is that I must spit on my hands a hundred times and dig dirt when before I never had to lift my finger to do anything, and *quod peius*,[8] I must do more work than a pair of oxen could achieve in one day. And if I don't finish the work by this evening, I'll be eaten by your mother. But if I then suffer by losing my unfortunate body, it will be mainly because I shall be separated from your beautiful appearance."

Filadoro dried his eyes and said to him, "My life, believe me, you won't have to work any other field than the garden of love, and you need not

7. Allusion to a popular tale about two faithful lovers that Neapolitan dialect writers often cited in their works. However, the text and plot of the tale have never been discovered.
8. What is worse (Latin).

fear that my mother will ever touch a hair of your head. You have Filadoro, and you need not worry because, if you don't realize it, I am a fairy and can curdle water and darken the sun. Enough is enough! Cheer up because the ground will be dug up and cultivated by this evening without you lifting a finger."

Upon hearing this, Nardaniello said, "If you are a fairy, as you've said, oh beauty of the world, why don't we just go away from here since you know that I would love to make you the queen of my father's house?"

"A certain constellation of stars is preventing this solution right now," Filadoro replied. "But this influence will soon pass, and then we shall be happy."

Between this sweet conversation and a thousand others the day passed. Then the ogress returned and called to her daughter from the road, "Filadoro, let down your hair!" She did this because the house did not have stairs, and she always climbed up by her daughter's hair. When Filadoro heard her mother's voice, she undid her hair and let it down, making a staircase of gold for a heart of iron. As soon as the ogress jumped into the room, she ran to the garden, and when she found that it had been completely cultivated, she was astounded, for it had seemed impossible to her that such a delicate young man could have done the work of a dog.

The next morning, after the sun was just about to appear to take a little air to freshen itself from the humidity caused by the river of India, the old woman got ready to leave the house, and before she did, she told Nardaniello that he had to chop seven stacks of wood that were in a little room by evening, and each piece was to be cut in four. Otherwise, she would make mincemeat out of him and eat him in a stew for her supper.

When the poor prince heard this intimidating command, he almost died from spasms. When Filadoro saw that he was turning pale and about to faint, she said, "What a coward you are! Congratulations! You'd be afraid of your own shadow!"

"Does this seem like nothing to you," answered Nardaniello, "to chop up seven stacks of wood, each piece into four parts, by this evening? Alas, before I ever manage this, I'll be chopped in half to fill the stomach of that miserable old woman!"

"Believe me," Filadoro responded, "you won't have to exert yourself. The wood will be chopped and piled neatly. In the meantime, be in a good mood, and don't chop your jaws and bother with your complaints!"

Now, when the sun closed its shop of rays and stopped selling light to the shadows, the old woman returned home and had the stairs fall down as usual. Then she climbed up and found the wood all chopped and began to suspect that her daughter had caused this checkmate.

On the third day, the ogress gave Nardaniello a third test: she told him that he had to empty a cistern containing one thousand barrels of water because she wanted to refill them with fresh water, and he had to do this by evening; otherwise she would make hash out of him and eat him with a tasty sauce. When the old woman left, Nardaniello began his lamenting again, and when Filadoro saw that the chores were being increased and that the old woman was loading more work on the poor man as if he were an ass and causing him more troubles and woes, she said to him, "Be quiet! The constellation of the stars that was creating an obstacle for my magic art has changed. Before the sun says its farewell, we shall say to this house, be well. Enough, because tonight my mother will find the cottage empty. I want to depart with you, dead or alive."

When the prince, who had been on the verge of dying, heard this news, he regained his calm, embraced her, and said, "You are the north wind that keeps this boat from danger, my soul. You are the mainstay of my hopes!"

So, when it was almost night, Filadoro dug a hole beneath the garden that led to a large tunnel, and they escaped through it and headed in the direction of Naples. As soon as they reached the grotto of Pozzoli,[9] Nardaniello said to Filadoro, "My darling, it would not be proper for you to go to my palace on foot and dressed as you are. Therefore, wait for me in this inn, and I'll return soon with horses, a coach, attendants, clothes, and other things."

So Filadoro remained at the inn, while he went off to the city. In the meantime, the ogress returned to the house, and when Filadoro did not respond to her usual call, she ran quickly into the woods, cut down a large pole, leaned it against the window, and climbed like a cat up into the house. She searched high and low, inside and outside, and when she did not find anyone, she went into the garden and found the hole that led through the tunnel and opened out onto a piazza. So angry was she that she tore out all her hair, cursed her daughter and the prince, and prayed to heaven that Nardaniello would forget her daughter at the first kiss that he received from anyone.

But let us leave the old woman to utter her pastoral paternosters, and let us return to the prince, who had in the meantime arrived at the palace. Since he had been regarded as dead, he set the entire house astir by his arrival, and everyone ran to meet him and cried out, "Finally! Welcome back! You've been saved! How good to see you back!" as well as a thousand other fond words.

When he began climbing the stairs, he met his mother midway, and she embraced him and gave him a kiss.

"My son! My jewel! Apple of my eye!" she exclaimed. "Where have you been? Why have you stayed away so long? You scared us all to death!"

The prince did not know what to answer because, as he was about to tell her all about his misfortunes, he forgot everything that had happened to him after his mother had kissed him with her butterfly lips. Indeed, all this was due to the ogress's curse.

Once the prince was home again, the queen now wanted to put a stop to his habit of hunting and spending so much time in the woods. Therefore, she proposed that he get married, and he answered, "That's all fine with me. I'm ready and prepared to do anything you want, mother."

"That's what all good sons are expected to do," the queen replied, and

9. The tunnel of the hill at Posillipo that connects Pozzoli to Naples and was built during the time of Augustus and restored many times since then.

so they agreed that in four days the bride would be brought to the house. She was a lady of nobility from Flanders, and she happened to be in the city at that time.

Soon great feasts and banquets were arranged, but in the meantime, Filadoro saw that her husband had failed to return to the inn, and though I don't know how, news of the celebrations reached her ears, probably because everyone was talking about the news everywhere. So that night, when the innkeeper's son went to bed, she took his clothes hanging at the head of his bed, left her clothes behind, and dressed herself like a man. Then she went off to the court of the king, and since the cooks had so much work to do and needed help, they hired her as a scullery boy.

The next morning, when the sun, seated on the bench of the sky, showed the privileges accorded it by nature, stamped by the seal of light, and when the sun began to sell its medicine to clear people's sight[1] the bride arrived to the sound of bagpipes and flutes. The tables were set up, and everyone sat down to enjoy themselves. The drinks began to flow, and the steward prepared to cut a large English cake that Filadoro had prepared with her own hands. All of a sudden, out flew a dove from the cake, and it was so beautiful that the guests forgot about eating and stared in astonishment at its marvelous beauty. Then, with a most piteous voice, the bird began talking to the prince: "Have you eaten cat's brains[2] and have you forgotten all about Filadoro's love for you? Have you lost your memory about all the deeds she performed for you, and you can't remember them? Is this the way you repay all the favors she did for you, you ungrateful fool! Is this the way you repay her after she rescued you from the clutches of the ogress and gave you your life and her own? Is this the great reward that you are giving this unfortunate girl for the devoted love she has shown you? Tell her to get up and go away! Tell her to gnaw on some bones until the roast arrives! Oh how miserable is the woman who trusts the promises of men too much, for they always bring ingratitude to their words, forgetfulness to kind deeds, and disregard of their debts! Behold, the poor girl thought that she would bake a cake with you, and now she's being played with as though she were a pancake. She believed that she would play 'Ring around the Rosy' with you, and instead you're playing 'Take a Giant Step to Nowhere' with her. She thought she would break a glass with you, and instead you've broken the chamberpot. Get out of here. Don't you worry, miserable welcher! Once the curses that this unfortunate girl heaps on you with all her heart fall on you with full force, you'll realize what it means to swindle a girl, to make fun of her, to deceive an innocent thing. You'll learn what it means to carry out mean jokes, to pull her leg by attaching a sheet on her back while she was actually carrying you on her back, to crush her under your feet while she was carrying you on her head. You left her where they do all the dirty work while she was serving you. But if heaven has not put a blindfold over its eyes, if the gods have not put plugs in their ears, they will see the wrong you have done

1. Allusion to the charlatans and quacks who, like medicine men, would use their privileges to try to dupe people.
2. Popular belief at that time maintained that people who ate cat brains lost their memory.

to her, and when you least expect it, the vigil and the feast will arrive, lightning and thunder, fever and diarrhea. Beware! Make sure that you eat well, amuse yourself as you like, have fun and celebrate with your little bride because poor Filadoro, who is spinning the thin thread of her life, will break it and leave the field open to you to enjoy your new wife."

After the dove said these words, she flew out of the window, and the wind carried her far away. When the prince heard the piercing cries of the dove, he remained motionless for a long time. Finally, he asked where the cake had come from, and when the steward told him that a scullery boy, who had been hired for the occasion, had prepared it, the prince summoned the boy to appear before him. When Filadoro arrived, she threw herself at the feet of Nardaniello and let loose a torrent of tears and could only say, "What have I done to you, you miserable cur?! What have I done to you?"

Aroused by Filadoro's beauty and stirred by her magic powers, he began to remember the pledges that he had made to her in the court of love, and he immediately had her rise and sit next to him. Then he told his mother about the great debt that he owed to this beautiful maiden, how much she had done for him, and the promise he had given her that was necessary to keep.

Since the mother had only this son, whom she cherished, she said, "Do whatever you please, provided that you save the honor of this young lady whom you've taken as a bride, and provided that you do as she pleases."

"Please don't worry on my account," the bride responded. "To tell you the truth, I was feeling ill at ease in this country. Now that heaven has fortunately intervened, I would like to return to my country of Flanders, with your consent, and to find the ancestors of those glass flasks[3] that are used in Naples, where, thinking I was about to kindle the right flame of my life,[4] I almost extinguished the light of my life."

The prince was very happy about her response and offered her a ship and escort. Soon thereafter Filadoro was dressed as a princess. The tables were cleared. The musicians came, and the ball began and lasted well into the evening. But, when the earth had draped itself in mourning for the obsequies of the sun, and the torches were brought out to light the stairs, they suddenly heard a great ringing of bells, and the prince said to his mother, "This must be some fine masquerade to honor our celebration. By my faith, the Neopolitan cavaliers are very ceremonious, and whenever it's necessary, they do things in a big way."

But while they were talking about this, a horrible-looking masked figure appeared in the middle of the hall. It was a woman about three feet tall and wider than a barrel, and when she arrived in front of the prince, she said, "I want you to know, Nardaniello, that your mischief and bad behavior brought about all the misfortune that you have experienced. I am the ghost of that old woman whose pot you broke and who died of hunger. It was I who heaped the curse on you so that you would be forced to serve

3. Reference to great terracotta flasks of wine used in Flanders and in Germany; also an ironic allusion to the heavy drinking that allegedly took place in northern countries.
4. Literally, to drink a bottle.

an ogress, and my prayers were answered. But thanks to this beautiful fairy, you succeeded in getting out of that predicament and were cursed once more by the ogress who caused you to forget Filadoro once you were kissed after your escape. Your mother's kiss made Filadoro vanish from your mind, but she is now at your side again thanks to her art. However, I've returned to curse you again and to make you remember the harm you've done to me: May you always find before you my beans that you knocked to the ground and may you prove the proverb true that 'he who sows beans will grow horns.'"

Upon saying this, she disappeared like quicksilver, leaving no smoke behind her.

When the fairy saw the prince turn pale, she bolstered his spirits by saying, "Don't be afraid, my husband. Listen and forget. If it is a magic spell, I can annul it. Don't worry, I'll drag you out of the fire!"

Soon after she said this, the celebration was finished, and they went to bed. Later, the prince confirmed his new pledge by having two witnesses[5] sign it, and the past trials and tribulations made the present delights more pleasurable in view of the fact that in the crucible of experiences of the world.

> He who stumbles but does not fall
> takes a step forward in life.

JACOB AND WILHELM GRIMM

The Two Kings' Children†

Once upon a time, there was a king who had a little boy, and according to the constellation of the stars, it was predicted that he would be killed by a stag when he turned sixteen. One day, when he had reached that age, the huntsmen went out hunting with him in the forest, but the prince got separated from them. Suddenly he saw a big stag and kept trying to shoot it without much success. Finally, the stag ran away and led him on a chase until they were out of the forest. All at once a big, lanky man was standing there instead of the stag and said, "Well, it's a good thing I've got you now. I wore out six pair of glass skates chasing after you and could never catch you."

He took the prince with him and dragged him across a large lake toward a big royal castle. Once there the prince had to sit down at a table and eat something with the man. After they had eaten together, the king said, "I've got three daughters, and I want you to watch over the oldest one for me from nine in the evening until six in the morning. Each time the clock strikes the hour, I shall come and call you. If you don't answer me, you'll

---

5. In Neapolitan dialect, Basile is playing with *dui testemmonie: i testicoli* = testicles.
† Jacob and Wilhelm Grimm, "The Two Kings' Children"—"De beiden Künigeskinner" (1857), No. 113 in *Kinder- und Hausmärchen. Gesammelt durch die Brüder Grimm* (Göttingen: Dieterich, 1857).

be put to death in the morning. However, if you answer me, you shall have my daughter for your wife."

When the young people went up to the bedchamber, there was a stone statue of Saint Christopher standing there, and the king's daughter said to it, "My father will come at nine o'clock and every hour until the clock strikes six. If he asks anything, I want you to answer him in place of the prince."

The stone Saint Christopher nodded his head very fast, then more and more slowly until it came to a stop.

The next morning the king said to the young prince, "You've done well, but I can't give you my daughter. Now, I want you to watch over my second daughter. Then I'll consider giving you my oldest daughter for your wife. I shall come every hour on the hour, and when I call, you must answer me. If you don't answer, your blood will flow."

The prince went with the second daughter up to the bedchamber where there was a stone statue of Saint Christopher, much larger than the first, and the king's daughter said to it, "If my father asks a question, I want you to answer."

The big stone Saint Christopher nodded his head very fast, then more and more slowly until he came to a stop. The prince lay down on the threshold, put his hand under his head, and went to sleep.

The next morning the king said to him, "You've done well, but I can't give you my daughter. Now I want you to watch over my youngest daughter. Then I'll consider giving you the second for your wife. I shall come every hour, and when I call, answer me. If you don't answer me when I call, your blood will flow."

Again the prince went with the youngest daughter up to the bedchamber, and there stood a Saint Christopher, much bigger and taller than the other two. The king's daughter said to the statue, "If my father calls, I want you to answer."

The big, tall Saint Christopher nodded his head for a good half hour before he came to a stop, and the prince lay down on the threshold and fell asleep.

The next morning the king said, "Indeed, you kept watch very well, but I can't give you my daughter yet. Now, I've got a very large forest, and if you cut it down for me between six this morning and six this evening, I'll consider giving her to you."

The king gave him a glass ax, a glass wedge, and a glass mattock. When the prince reached the forest, he began chopping right away, and the ax broke in two. Then he took the wedge and began hitting it with the mattock, but it splintered into tiny pieces the size of grains of sand. This made the prince very downcast, for he thought he would now have to die. So he sat down and wept.

At noon the king said, "One of you girls must bring him something to eat."

"No," said the oldest, "we won't bring him anything. Let the one he watched over last take him something."

So the youngest daughter had to go and bring him something to eat. When she reached the forest, she asked him how everything was going.

"Oh," he said, "things are going very badly."

She told him to come over to her and have a little something to eat.

"No," he responded. "I can't, for I have to die, and I don't want to eat anymore."

She spoke kindly to him and implored him to try. So he went over to her and ate something. After he had eaten, she said, "Now I'll louse you a little, and then you'll feel much better."

When she loused him, he became so tired that he fell asleep. Then she took her kerchief, made a knot out of it, and struck the ground three times with it.

"Workers, come out!" she cried.

Suddenly numerous gnomes appeared from beneath the earth and asked the princess what her command was.

"In three hours' time," she said, "this forest must be cut down, and the wood stacked in piles."

The gnomes went and called all their relatives to come out and help them with the work. Then they started, and within three hours everything was finished, and they went and reported to the king's daughter. Once again she took out her white kerchief and said, "Workers, go home!" And they all vanished on the spot.

When the prince woke up, he was very happy, and she said, "When the clock strikes six, you're to go home."

He did as she had said, and the king asked him, "Have you cut down the whole forest?"

When they were sitting at the table, the king said, "I can't give you my daughter for your wife yet. You must do something else."

The prince asked what he had to do.

"I have a very large pond," said the king. "You must go there tomorrow morning and clean it out so that it glistens like a mirror, and there must be all kinds of fish in it."

The next morning the king gave him a glass scoop and said, "You must be finished with the pond by six o'clock."

The prince departed, and when he reached the pond, he struck the scoop into the muck, and the end broke off. Then he tried a pickax, but it broke as well, and he became discouraged. At noon the youngest daughter brought him something to eat and asked him how everything was going. The prince said that things were going very badly, and he was bound to lose his head. "All the tools broke apart on me again."

"Oh," she said, "you should come and eat something first; then you'll feel much better.

"No," he said, "I can't eat. I feel too sad."

But she spoke so kindly to him that he finally had to come and eat something. Once again she loused him, and he fell asleep. She took her kerchief once more, tied a knot in it, and struck the ground three times with it. "Workers, come out!" she cried.

Suddenly numerous gnomes appeared and asked her what she desired.

"In three hours' time, the pond must be all cleaned up and must shine so brightly that you can see your own reflection in it. Then you must fill it with all kinds of fish."

The gnomes went off and called all their relatives to come and help them.

Once again she took her kerchief and struck the ground three times. "Workers, go home!" And they all vanished on the spot.

When the prince woke up, the pond was finished, and just as the king's daughter was about to leave him, she told him to go home at six o'clock. When he got there, the king asked, "Have you finished the pond?"

"Yes," said the prince. "Everything's fine."

When they were sitting at the table again, the king said, "Indeed, you finished the pond, but I can't give you my daughter yet. You must first do one more thing."

"What's that?" asked the prince.

"I've got a big mountain with nothing on it but thornbushes. I want them all cut down, and then you must build the most magnificent castle imaginable, and all the proper furnishings must be in it."

When the prince got up the next morning, the king gave him a glass ax and glass drill to take with him and told him that he had to be finished by six o'clock. As the prince began to chop the first thornbush with the ax, it broke into little pieces that flew all around him. And the drill also turned out to be useless. Then he became very dejected and waited to see if his beloved would come again and help him out of this desperate situation.

At noon she came and brought him something to eat. He went to meet her and told her everything that had happened. Then he ate something, let her louse him, and fell asleep. Once again she took her kerchief and struck the ground with it three times. "Workers, come out!" she cried.

Numerous gnomes again appeared and asked her what she desired.

"In three hours' time," she said, "you must cut down all the thornbushes and build the most magnificent castle imaginable on the mountain, and all the proper furnishings must be in it."

They went off and called all their relatives to come and help, and they finished everything in due time. Then they went and reported to the king's daughter, whereupon she took the kerchief and struck the ground three times with it. "Workers, go home!" she said, and they all vanished on the spot.

When the prince woke up and saw everything, he was as happy as a lark. Since the clock had just struck six, they went home together, and the king asked, "Is the castle finished now?"

"Yes," said the prince.

When they were sitting at the table, the king said, "I can't give you my youngest daughter until the two oldest are married."

The prince and the king's daughter were very sad, and the prince did not know what to do. Then one night he went to the king's daughter, and they ran away together. After they had gone a short distance, the daughter looked around and saw her father pursuing them. "Oh," she said, "what shall we do? My father's after us, and he'll soon catch up. Wait, I'll turn you into a rosebush and myself into a rose, and I'll protect myself by hiding in the middle of the bush."

When the father reached the spot, there was a rosebush with a rose standing there. When he tried to pluck the rose, the thorns pricked his fingers, so he had to return home. His wife asked him why he had not brought back the couple. He told her that he had almost caught them, but then had lost sight of them and had found only a rosebush and a rose where he had thought they were.

"If you had only plucked the rose," the queen said, "the bush would have come along."

So he went away to fetch the rose. In the meantime, the two had made their way far over some fields, and the king had to run after them. Once again the daughter looked around and saw the father coming after them. "Oh," she said, "what shall we do now? Wait, I'll turn you into a church and myself into a pastor. Then I'll stand in the pulpit and preach."

When the king reached the spot, a church was standing there, and a pastor was preaching in the pulpit. So he listened to the sermon and returned home. The queen asked him why he had failed to bring back the couple with him, and he replied, "I ran after them a long time, and just as I thought that I had caught up with them, I came upon a church with a pastor preaching in the pulpit."

"You should have taken the pastor with you," said his wife. "The church would have come along. It's no use sending you anymore. I'll have to go myself."

After she had gone a long way and saw the two from afar, the king's daughter looked around and saw her mother coming. "We've run out of luck now, " she said. "My mother herself is coming. Wait, I'll turn you into a pond and myself into a fish."

When the mother reached the spot, there was a large pond, and a fish was leaping about in the middle of it. The fish stuck its head out of the water, looked around, and was as merry as could be. The mother tried very hard to catch the fish, but she was unable to land it. Then she got so angry that she drank the entire pond dry just to catch the fish. However, she became so sick that she had to spit out the water, and she vomited the entire pond out again. "It's plain to me that I'm helpless against you." So she made her peace and asked them to return with her, which they did. Now the queen gave her daughter three walnuts and said, "These will help you in your greatest need."

Then the young couple set off again. After they had walked for ten hours, they had approached the castle where the prince came from, and nearby was a village. When they arrived in the village, the prince said, "Stay here, my dearest. I'll go to the castle first and then come back to fetch you with a carriage and servants."

When he got to the castle, everyone was happy to see him again. He told them he had a bride, who was now in the village, and he wanted to go fetch her in a carriage. They harnessed the carriage right away, and several servants climbed on back. Just as the prince was about to get in, his mother gave him a kiss, and he forgot everything that had happened and everything he wanted to do. The mother then ordered them to un-harness the carriage, and they all went back into the castle. Meanwhile, the king's daughter sat in the village and waited and waited. She thought the prince would come and fetch her, but no one came. Finally, she hired herself out at the mill that belonged to the castle. She had to sit by the river every afternoon and wash the pots and jars. Once the queen came out of the castle and took a walk along the river. When she saw the beautiful maiden, she said, "What a lovely girl! She's quite appealing!" Then everyone around her took a look, but nobody recognized her.

The king's daughter served the miller as maid honestly and faithfully for a long time. Meanwhile, the queen had found a wife for her son, and she came from a country far away. When the bride arrived, they were to be married right away, and crowds of people gathered to see the event, and the maid asked the miller if she might go and watch too.

"Go right along," said the miller.

Before she left, she cracked open one of the three walnuts and found a beautiful dress inside. She put it on, wore it to the church, and stood near the altar. When the pastor was about to bless them, the bride looked to one side and saw the maid dressed as a lady standing there. Then she stood up and said that she would not marry until she had a dress as beautiful as the lady's. So they returned home and sent servants to ask the lady if she would sell the dress. No, she told them, she would not sell it, but they might be able to earn it. They asked her what they would have to do, and she said that they could have the dress if she could sleep outside the prince's door that night. They said yes, she could do that, but the servants were ordered to give the prince a sleeping potion.

The king's daughter lay down on the threshold and whimpered all night: she had had the forest cut down for him, she had turned him into a rosebush, then a church, and finally a pond, and yet he had forgotten her so quickly. The prince did not hear a thing, but her cries woke the servants, who listened but did not know what to make of it all.

When they got up the next morning, the bride put on the dress and went to the church with the bridegroom. Meanwhile, the beautiful maid opened the second walnut, and she found a dress more splendid than the first, put it on, and wore it to church, where she stood near the altar. Then everything happened as on the previous day. Once again the maid lay down in front of the prince's door, but this time the servants did not give the prince a sleeping potion but something to keep him awake, and he went to bed. The miller's maid whimpered once more, as she had before, and told him about all the things that she had done for him. The prince heard it all and became very sad, for he remembered everything that had happened. He wanted to go to her right then and there, but his mother had locked the door. However, the next morning he went straight to his beloved and told her what had happened and begged her not to be angry with him for having forgotten her for so long. Then the king's daughter opened the third walnut and found a dress that was even more beautiful than the other two. She put it on and went to the church with her bridegroom. Groups of children gathered around them and gave them flowers and placed colored ribbons at their feet. After they were blessed at the wedding, they had a merry celebration, but the false mother and false bride were sent away.

And the lips are still warm on the last person who told this tale.

The Father's Betrayal

Self-mutilation to preserve virginity or to keep a religious vow has been a common theme in the East and West and can be traced back to antiquity. The fairy tales that involve a maiden who has her hands cut off or cripples herself in some way because of a father who betrays her or wants to sleep with her are related to the fairy tales about incest. Here the plot generally concerns a father who threatens his daughter sexually or makes a bargain with a mysterious power that seeks to attain control over her. She has her hands cut off and runs away. After meeting a prince in a chance encounter, often in his garden as she is seeking something to eat, she weds him, but her jealous mother-in-law or the demonic power from whom she has escaped interferes with her life when she gives birth to a son and her husband is far away fighting a war or taking care of some urgent business. She is forced to flee with her son into a forest, where she miraculously recovers her hands in a solitary spot. Her husband returns from his journey and learns how he has been deceived. He pursues his wife and is reunited with her and his son. There were numerous medieval tales in Europe based on the fifteenth-century legends and chapbooks generally printed under the title *La belle Hélene de Constantinople*, the legends about the powerful King Offa of the eighth century, and those may have influenced Giovanni Fiorentino's "Dionigia and the King of England" and Basile's "The Maiden Without Hands." In France, Philippe de Rémi wrote an important verse romance, *La manekine* (ca. 1270), which may have been influenced by French folktales with the motif of the persecuted woman in Brittany. The plot of de Rémi's verse romance is highly significant because it combines motifs that can be found in all the literary tales about incestuous and traitorous fathers: after ten years of marriage, the king and queen of Hungary have a daughter whom they name Joie. Soon thereafter, however, the queen becomes sick, and before she dies, she makes her husband promise her that he will not marry unless he finds a woman who looks just like her. Once she is dead, the nobles of Hungary search for a beautiful woman to match the dead queen. Years pass, but they cannot find one until a nobleman realizes that Joie has flowered into the spitting image of her mother. The nobles of Hungary want the king to marry his daughter, but he at first refuses until he eventually falls in love with Joie and explains to her that he must marry her to follow his dead wife's wish. However, Joie cuts off her left hand and throws it into the river. According to the law of the land, the king was not allowed to marry a woman who was missing a part of her body. Furious, the king commands that she be burned at the stake, but when he departs for a distant castle, his steward takes pity on Joie and puts her on a small boat and sets her out to sea. She arrives in Scotland, where she is taken to the young king's court. Though she is missing a hand and keeps quiet about her past, the king is taken by her beauty and desires to wed her. In contrast, his mother is jealous of her and threatens her. When the king becomes aware of this, he takes Joie under his protection and marries her. His mother retreats to her own castle in the country. When Joie becomes pregnant, the king wants to win some glory in a tournament in France, and he departs. Joie gives birth to a handsome son named John, and his steward sends a messenger to France to inform the king about the happy news. However, the queen mother intercepts the message and changes it to read that the queen had given birth to a monstrous creature. When the king reads this message, he writes back that his steward should preserve their lives. Once again, however, the queen mother intercepts the message and exchanges it for one that instructs the steward to have Joie and her son burned at the stake. But the steward burns two wooden statues instead and sets Joie out to sea with her son in a ship without masthead and sail. Somehow the ship manages to make its way to the Tiber River and land in Rome, where a kindly senator takes care of Joie and her son. When the king of Scotland returns home from France, he learns about his mother's treachery and has her buried in a wall alive. Then he sets off in search of his wife and son, and after seven years of wandering, he is reunited with them in Rome. In the meantime, Joie's father, the king of Hungary, has arrived in Rome to beg pardon from the Pope for his sin, which has been weighing on his conscience. While he is there, Joie miraculously finds her left hand in a fountain and is happily reunited with her father. Finally, the Pope prays that Joie's left hand be re-attached, and lo and behold, this is what occurs.

GIOVANNI FIORENTINO

Dionigia and the King of England†

One of the kings of France had a daughter by the name of Dionigia, who was the most beautiful and lovely woman of her time, and her father, who wanted to arrange a marriage with a wealthy man, intended to give her to a very distinguished German nobleman, who was seventy years old. But the maiden did not want him, and since her father decided to marry her against her will, she kept thinking of some way to flee. So one night she dressed herself as a pilgrim, rubbed her face with some herbs that changed the color of her skin, took some precious jewels that her mother had left her when she had died, and went to the seacoast. There she boarded a ship that carried her to the island of England.

The next morning, when her father the king discovered she was missing, he sent his men out to search the entire city and the entire realm. Since they could not find her, he thought that she had drowned herself out of grief. However, as soon as the maiden had landed, she made her way to a city and came to a convent. It was the richest on the island, and the prioress was related to the king of England. Once she was there, the maiden told the prioress that she would like to become a nun, and the prioress asked her who she was, whose daughter, and where she came from. Dionigia answered that she was the daughter of a good French bourgeois family, that her father and mother were dead, and that she now wanted to dedicate herself to serving God after having journeyed about the world for some time. Since she seemed to be so gentle and lovely, the

---

† Ser Giovanni Fiorentino, "Dionigia and the King of England"—"Dionigia e il re d'Inghilterra" (1385), in *Il pecorone* (Milan: Giovanni Antonio, 1554; rep. and ed. by Enzo Esposito, Ravenna: Longo, 1974).

prioress decided to take her as a novice and partly as her servant and said, "My daughter, I would very much like to accept you, but it is best that you first try out our rules and life, and if our house pleases you, you may wear the habit."

Dionigia was very satisfied with this proposal, and she entered the convent and served the prioress and the other sisters with so much humility that all those who were living there loved her very much and admired her beauty and good manners. Indeed, they all said that she must certainly be a lady of high birth.

A short time thereafter it so happened that the king of England, whose father had recently died, was traveling through his dominions and came to this convent in order to visit his relative, the prioress, and she welcomed him with great honors. While he was staying there, he caught sight of Dionigia, who made an indescribable impression on his heart, and he asked the prioress who she was. In response, the prioress reported how and when Dionigia had come to her and how virtuous and accommodating her behavior was. Upon hearing this, the king decided to make her his wife, but when he informed the prioress of his intention, she replied that she was reluctant to permit this in view of the fact that she did not know who Dionigia was. Moreover, it was more suitable for him to marry the daughter of some king or emperor. However, he responded by arguing that she must truly be the daughter of a great lord, given her gentle manners, her virtuousness, and her beauty.

"This is indeed how she is," the prioress answered.

"I want her just as she is, no matter what she is," said the king.

Thereupon, the prioress had the maiden summoned to her and said, "Dionigia, God has bestowed great fortune on you. Listen to what it is: the king of England wants to wed you."

When the maiden heard this, she blushed and said that there was absolutely no way she could agree to this and that she wanted to become a nun. Therefore, she begged the prioress never to speak about such things again. The prioress reported this to the king, but he remained completely determined to make Dionigia his wife and to clear away all the obstacles.

When the prioress saw that he was so determined, she spoke to Dionigia for a long time and used such great persuasion that the young lady became satisfied and yielded. So the king married her in the presence of the prioress. After he took his leave from the prioress and returned with his wife to London, he celebrated with a great feast in his castle and invited all his barons. There was not a single one of them who did not fall in love with her at the first sight of her great beauty, her purity, and her noble demeanor.

But the mother of the king, who did not approve of his choice, refused to take part in the marriage festivities and departed in anger for one of her country estates. In the meantime, the king became so entirely enraptured of Dionigia that he loved her more than he loved his own life. Soon thereafter she became pregnant, but the king had to depart with an army for another island to put down an uprising. Before he took leave of his wife, however, he urged his viceroy to take good care of her and to honor her as queen and to send him a report about the birth. Then he departed from England.

In due time, Dionigia gave birth to twin boys, and the viceroy reported this in a letter to his lord. The messenger, who was carrying the letter, came to the castle where the queen mother was living, and he interrupted his journey there and informed the queen about the birth of the two children. Furious about this news, the queen switched the letter and wrote to her son that Dionigia had given birth to two little monkeys, who were the most nasty and deformed creatures one had ever seen.

The next day, after she rewarded the messenger, she ordered him to stop by and speak to her on his return. He promised to do this and then set out on his journey. He rode on his horse until he came to the front lines of the battle and gave the letter to his lord. When the king read it and learned about what had happened, he was stunned. Nevertheless, he wrote to his viceroy that he should find a nurse for the boys and that he should not stop treating his wife with love and care until his return, which would be soon. After he handed the letter to the messenger, he remained upset and in pain. When the messenger received the letter, he made his way, as he had promised, to the queen mother's castle, where he spent the night. While he was asleep, the queen took the letter from him. After she had read it and learned from the contents that the king had not ordered the death of her daughter-in-law, she was deeply disturbed. In place of the correct message, she wrote a false letter which said: "When you receive this letter, you are to kill my wife and the two children because I know that the children are not mine."

She stuck the letter in the pocket of the messenger, who was still asleep, and the next morning, after she showed him some favors, she sent him on his way. The messenger, who was unaware of what she had done, set out, and when he arrived at the viceroy's place in London, he gave him the letter. The viceroy was totally astounded as soon as he read the letter and asked him who had given him the letter.

"The king himself," the messenger replied, "and let me tell you that he was completely speechless when he read your message."

When the viceroy heard this news, he began to weep bitter tears and went to the young queen with tears in his eyes. Then he showed her the letter and said, "Read this message, your majesty."

As soon as the queen read the letter, she began to weep loudly and said, "Oh, how wretched my life is! I've never had one hour of happiness!"

Then she took her boys in her arms and said, "My dear children, how miserable your fate is! What sin have you committed that you must die?"

And she broke out into the saddest laments and kissed her poor little ones, who were as beautiful as stars. The viceroy wept with her and moaned and did not know what to do. Turning to the queen, he said, "My lady, what do you intend to do and what do you want me to do? You've seen what my lord has written. But I would never dare lay a hand on you. Therefore, take your children with you in secret, and I'll escort you to the harbor. There you can board a ship and depart with God's grace. Fate will lead you to some other coast where you will be happier than you are here."

Dionigia agreed, and the following night she secretly took her children, went to the harbor, approached the captain of a ship, and said, "Take me away from here and sail your ship to Genova. I shall pay you well."

The viceroy made sure that the captain would take care of the queen, gave him money, and took leave from her with tears in his eyes.

Thanks to favorable winds the ship brought the unfortunate woman to Genova in a short time, and after she had sold some of the jewels that she possessed, she hired two nurses and two maids and set out for Rome, where she carefully looked after her two boys. She named one of them Carlo and the other Lionetto and led a virtuous life. Moreover, she raised her children so diligently that all the people who came into contact with them were astonished by their good looks and qualities as they grew up. Indeed, she had them taught by skilled teachers in all the sciences and arts that were appropriate for a nobleman, and when they became older, she let them frequent the papal court without saying whose children they were.

When the Pope heard about the virtuous and holy life of this woman and saw how gracious and handsome her sons were, he showed them great favors and made certain that they were provided for in a sumptuous manner so that they had servants and horses and could lead a good life. Now it so happened that the Pope wanted to undertake an overseas campaign against the Saracens[1] and summoned all the kings and lords of Christianity, among them the kings of France and England, to appear personally in Rome because he wanted to hear their advice about this undertaking. Thus the two kings found themselves in Rome due to the Pope's bidding.

But first it must be told that the king of England, after he had conquered the island that had revolted against him and returned home to London, asked his viceroy about his wife and children. The viceroy responded that he had carried out his written orders, but not all of them because the king had written that they should be killed, and the viceroy had only banished them from the kingdom. Then he showed the king the letters as proof. The king became furious and wanted to know who had been the cause of these events. When he learned that it had really been his own mother, he was enraged and had her executed. Soon after he sent messengers all over his dominions to look for his wife, and when he learned that she had given birth to two handsome boys, he almost died from grief. Nobody could speak to him for a long time, and nobody could cheer him up, so great was the love for his wife, whom he had lost in such an unfortunate way.

After he had received the summons from the Pope to go to Rome with the king of France, he went to France and then went with the king of France to Rome, where they were received with great honors by the Pope. While they took a walk in the city, it so happened that they were recognized by Dionigia—the king of France as her brother (for her father had died in the meantime), and the other as her husband. Thereupon, she went straight to the Pope and said to him, "Most blessed Father, your Holiness knows that I have never wanted to reveal the origins of my children or my own identity. However, now the time has come to do this, and

---

1. Name used by Christians to designate non-Christians as heathens or pagans—generally applied to Arabs during the Crusades.

I shall do it and let your Holiness decide what the consequences will be. Therefore, I want your Holiness to know that I was born as the daughter of the king of France and am the sister of the present king, who is here in Rome. Since my father wanted to force me to marry an old man, I fled boldly to England, where I found refuge in a convent. It was there that the king of England saw me. He fell in love with me and married me without knowing who I was, and within a year I gave birth to twins. Since he was absent during this time, he sent an order to the viceroy that he was to kill me and my two poor children, denying that they were his. But his minister helped me to escape, and I fled to Rome, where, as your Holiness knows, I have dedicated my time to raising these two unfortunate children."

After she had said all this, she was silent. In response, the Pope offered her consolation and dismissed her. Then he sent for the two kings and the twins and addressed the king of France: "Do you know these boys, my illustrious king?"

"No," he replied. "I give you my word."

After the Pope received the same answer from the king of England, he turned to both kings and informed them about what had happened and urged the king of England to accept them as his sons, and the king of France, as his nephews, and indeed, they were accepted by them with great joy and jubilation. And when they asked the Pope about the mother, the Pope summoned her, and she embraced her brother many times without saying one word to her husband. When he demanded to know why she did not embrace him, she replied, "I am acting this way because of the cruelty with which you treated me."

Then the king wept and told her what had happened and who had been the cause of everything and how he had taken revenge on her. Since Dionigia accepted this explanation, they celebrated the most beautiful and happiest feast in the world, and during this jubilant celebration they remained several days in Rome and enjoyed themselves. Soon, however, the Pope saw that it was time to separate, and Dionigia said to her husband, "I am placing your two sons in your care, and may you go with God. I want to remain here to save my soul, and I don't want to return to the world."

Her husband replied that he would never leave Rome without her, and they had a big argument. But the Pope and her brother, the king of France, intervened and implored her so earnestly and so long that she decided to return home with her husband, and he was the happiest of men. After they finally took their leave from the Pope, they traveled with the king of France to France, where there were great festivities. Some time later, they went to England.

GIAMBATTISTA BASILE

The Maiden Without Hands†

When the king of Pietrasecca was left a widower and did not have a woman at his side, the devil put it into his head to wed his own sister, who was named Penta. Therefore, he called her to him one day, and when they were alone, he said, "My sister, a man of sound judgment never allows anything of value to leave his house. Moreover, you can never know how things will be when strangers enter your house. Indeed, I've thought a great deal about this matter, and this is why I've decided to take you as my wife. You fit my desires, and I know your character. So, I expect you to be content to do this inlaid work,[1] to become my partner, to make this pact, and to accept the doctor's prescription because we shall be happy together."

When Penta heard these disturbing words, she was outraged and changed color because she never thought her brother would ever jump to such an extreme and try to give her a couple of rotten eggs when he himself needed a hundred fresh eggs[2] to cure himself of this madness. She remained silent for a while and pondered how she could answer such an improper and impertinent request. Finally, she could no longer control her patience and said, "You may have lost your senses, but I don't want to lose my modesty! I'm astonished to hear these words escape from your lips! If you've said them as a joke, they're asinine. If they are sincere, they stink and are obscene. I find it revolting that you have the tongue to utter these shameful things, and that my ears must hear them. I, your wife? What's happened to you? What are you doing? Since when do people make such salads? Such messes. Such a hotchpotch of a mixture? Where do you think you are? In the cuckoo land of Joio?[3] Aren't we related, or am I to imagine that we are like cheese cooked in oil?[4] Pay attention! Woe to you if you ever let such words slip out of your mouth again because I'll do something incredible! If you do not consider me like a sister, I shall no longer consider you as a brother!"

After saying this, she fled to her room, locked the door behind her, and did not see her brother for more than a month. The wretched king was left to walk around as though his face had been hit by a sledgehammer. He was worn out and shameful like a boy who has broken a jug, and as confused as a servant when a cat has run off with some meat. However, after many days had passed, he called Penta once more to pay taxes to his

---

† Giambattista Basile, "The Maiden Without Hands"—"La penta mano-mozza" (1634), *Secondo passatempo della terza giornata* in *Lo cunto de li cunti overo Lo trattenemiento de peccerille*, De Gian Alessio Abbattutis, 5 vols. (Naples: Ottavio Beltrano, 1634–36).
1. A partnership between two traders.
2. One of the cures for the insane at the Hospital of the Incurables (*Oespedale degli incurabili*) at Naples was to have them eat a hundred eggs as nutrients while drawing water from a well. To complete the therapy, they were periodically beaten.
3. Reference to the village of Ioio or Ioi, now called Gioi, in the province of Salerno; Ioio had a notorious reputation and was regarded as wild and primitive. Thus, the village became associated with simpletons and dunces.
4. Cheese and oil are two ingredients that do not mix and hence cannot be related.

uncontrollable desires. Since she wanted to know what it was in particular about her that attracted her brother, she went to him and said, "Brother, I have looked and looked at myself in the mirror, and I have not found anything about my face that could possibly deserve your love. Indeed, I'm not one of those tasty dishes that excite the appetite of people."

"My Penta," the king answered, "you are very beautiful from head to toe, but more than anything else, your hands are what have made me crazy about you. Like forks they draw out the core of my heart from my breast. Like hooks they lift the bucket of my soul from the well of this life. Like pincers they grip my spirit tightly while Love smoothes it like a file. Oh hands, oh beautiful hands, ladles that pour out sweetness, pliers that extract desires, shovels that dig up this heart!"

He wanted to say more, but Penta responded, "All right. I've heard enough. Now wait a moment. Don't go away. I'll be back shortly."

Then Penta returned to her room, called a slave who was not very bright in the head, gave him a knife and a handful of coins, and said to him, "Ali, cut my hands off. I've got a secret remedy and want to make my hands more white!"

The slave believed he was doing her a favor and sliced off her hands cleanly with two blows. Afterward, she had them put into a porcelain bowl and sent with a silk cloth to her brother with a message telling him to enjoy the hands that he desired so much and wishing him good health and many sons. When the king saw how he had been treated, he became so furious that he immediately had a chest built and smeared with tar. Then he ordered his sister to be thrust inside and the chest to be thrown into the sea.

Tossed about by the waves, the chest eventually landed on a beach where some fishermen, who were pulling in their nets, found it and opened it up. To their surprise they discovered Penta, who was more beautiful than the moon when it has finished Lent at Taranto.[5] Therefore, Masiello, who was the chief and most important man in the group, took her to his house and told his wife, Nuccia, to look after her and treat her well. However, Nuccia was the mother of suspicion and jealousy, and as soon as her husband left, she stuck Penta back into the chest and threw it once more into the sea.

Battered about by the waves, the chest was rocked back and forth until it came within sight of a ship on which the king of Terraverde was sailing. When he saw something floating on the waves, he turned the ship in that direction and had a small boat lowered into the water to fetch the chest and bring it on board. When they opened it, they found that unfortunate maiden, and after the king saw such a living beauty in that coffin of death, he believed he had found a great treasure even though his heart wept that a casket full of such jewels of Love should be without handles. Then he took her to his kingdom and gave her a position as lady-in-waiting to the queen, whom Penta served as best she could with her feet, even cooking for her, threading needles, starching her collars, and combing her hair so

5. The full moon is implied. Taranto is a port town where the fishing is excellent. One can therefore spend Lent there, abstain from eating meat by indulging in fish meals, and grow round and fat.

that the queen grew fond of her and treated her as if she were her own daughter.

But after some months had passed, the queen was summoned to appear before the bench of Fates to pay the debt of nature, and she called the king to her side and said, "In just a short time, my soul will dissolve the marriage tie that is fastened to my body. Therefore, take care of yourself, my husband, and let us stay in touch. But if you love me and want to make me happy when I go to that other world, I want you to do me a favor."

"Just command me, my darling," the king said. "If I can't give you witnesses[6] of my love for you in life, I shall give you a sign of how much I love you in death."

"Now, since you've promised me this," the queen responded, "I beg you with all my heart to marry Penta after I close my eyes and turn to dust. Even if we do not know where she comes from, one can tell that she is from fine stock by her good manners."

"I hope you live another hundred years," the king said. "However, if you must say 'good night' to make my days gloomy, I swear to you that I shall take Penta for my wife. And it doesn't matter to me that she doesn't have hands and is a bit thin. It's always better to take less from unfortunate creatures."

He whispered these last words in a low voice so that his wife had difficulty hearing him. But after the queen had extinguished the candle of her days, the king took Penta as his wife, and they planted the seeds for a baby boy that very night.

However, it soon became necessary for the king to take another voyage by sea to the kingdom of Altoscoglio, and after the king took his leave of Penta, he set sail. Nine months later Penta brought a shining baby into the world, and the entire city was illuminated. Then the king's councillors sent a fast vessel to notify the king, but this boat became trapped in such a terrible storm that it was tossed by the waves up to the stars and deep down to the bottom of the sea. Finally, thanks to the grace of heaven, it landed on the beach where Penta had once been given shelter by the compassion of a man and then driven away by the cruelty of a woman. As luck would have it, that same woman, Nuccia, was on the beach washing the clothes of her son. Since she was curious to know about the affairs of other people, as is the nature of women, she asked the captain of the vessel where he came from, where he was going, and who sent him. And the captain said, "I'm coming from Terraverde and going to Altoscoglio to find the king of Terraverde and to give him a letter that was entrusted to me. I believe that his wife has written to him, but I don't have the faintest idea what it is about."

"And who is the wife of the king?" asked Nuccia.

"As far as I know," the captain responded, "they say that she is a remarkably beautiful maiden called Penta the Handless because she was found in a chest at sea, and thanks to her lucky stars, she has become the

6. Basile was fond of the pun *li testemmonie* (witnesses): *i testicoli* (testicles).

king's wife. But I don't know why she has written to him so urgently. All I know is that I must set off at full sail to get there quickly."

After the treacherous Nuccia heard this, she invited the captain to have a drink, and once she got him drunk, she took the letter out of his pocket and brought it to a student, one of her clients,[7] who read it to her. As she listened, she almost died with envy and could not hear one syllable without heaving a sigh. Afterward, she had this same student forge the handwriting and report that the queen had given birth to a little dog, and the councillors were awaiting orders to do what was necessary. When the letter was written and sealed, Nuccia put it back into the captain's pocket. As soon as he awoke and saw that the weather had improved, he set sail with the stern to the southwest wind. When he arrived, he gave the letter to the king, who replied right away and instructed the councillors to cheer up the queen and tell her that she was not to have even an ounce of regret because these events were decided by heaven, and no man had better argue with the stars. When he was done, the captain was sent on his way, and two days later he arrived at Nuccia's place again. She gave him many compliments and a great deal to eat, and once more she filled him with drink so that he became intoxicated and lay down to sleep. Then Nuccia put her hand into his side pocket, found the king's letter, and had the student read it to her. Then she had him write a new letter for the councillors of Terraverde, who were ordered to burn the mother and her son as soon as they read it.

After the captain had slept off the effects of the wine, he departed, and when he arrived at Terraverde, he presented the letter to the councillors, but when they opened it, there was a great deal of murmuring among the wise old men. They discussed the matter a very long time and concluded that either the king had become crazy or he had been bewitched, because he had a pearl of a wife and a jewel of an heir, and he could not possibly want to make ashes out of them for the teeth of Death. Therefore, it seemed better to them to choose a middle way, and thus they decided to send the queen and her son away and told her to vanish so that nobody would ever hear the slightest thing about them. So the queen was given a handful of coins to support herself and her child. As a result, the councillors sent a treasure away from the royal chest. They sent away a light from the city and two props from the king her husband's hopes.

Poor Penta found herself expelled even though she was not a prostitute, the relative of a bandit, or a troublesome student.[8] She took her baby son in her arms, bathed him in milk and tears, and set off in the direction of Lagotorbido, which was ruled by a magician. When he saw this beautiful maimed maiden who maimed everyone's heart, who waged more war with the two stumps of her arms than Briareus[9] with a hundred hands, he wanted to hear the entire story of the misfortunes that she had experienced, from the very beginning when her brother had made her food for the

7. A suggestion that Nuccia is indeed a loose woman.
8. The three categories of people that were most often banished from the kingdom of Naples.
9. The giant who had a hundred hands and fifty heads and who helped Zeus in his battle against the Titans; cited in Homer's *Iliad*.

fishes because she had refused to be his food of flesh until the day that she set foot in his kingdom.

After the magician heard this sad and bitter tale, he could not stop crying, and the compassion that entered his eardrums was exhaled in sighs through the air holes of his mouth. At the end of her story, he comforted her with gentle words and said, "Keep up your good spirits, my daughter, for no matter how damaged the house of the spirit becomes, it will always stand on its two feet with the support of hope. Therefore, don't let your spirits get down because heaven sometimes pushes human misfortunes to the brink of ruin in order to make the happy end seem more marvelous. Therefore, don't worry because you have found a mother and father in me, and I'll help you even if it costs my own blood."

Poor Penta thanked him and said, "It doesn't matter if heaven pours down misfortune and torrents of woe on me now that I am under the roof of your generosity, for you are a powerful and worthy man. Just your kind appearance has warmed my heart."

And after a thousand polite words on one side and a thousand thanks on the other, the magician gave her a splendid apartment in his palace and ordered that she be treated like a daughter. The next morning he issued a proclamation in which he stated that whoever came to his court and told the most impressive tale of a great misfortune would be given a crown and a golden scepter that were worth more than a kingdom.

When this proclamation spread throughout Europe more people than there were caterpillars arrived at the magician's court to try to win the rich prizes. One man told how he had served at a court his entire life, and after having lost lye and soap, his youth and health, he was dismissed with a payment of mere cheese. Another said that he had been treated unjustly by a superior, and it had not been possible to complain about the bad treatment. So he had been compelled to swallow the pill without venting his anger. Another man wept because he had invested all his wealth in a ship, and it took just a small bad wind to wipe out his entire investment. Then there was a man who lamented that he had spent all his life pushing a pen without gaining anything useful from it, and above all he had given up all hope because his efforts with the pen had brought him very little fortune while the materials necessary for making inkstands[1] had become worth a small fortune in the world.

In the meantime, the king of Terraverde had returned home and found that everything had gone sour. He reacted to the bad news like an unchained lion and would have skinned all his councillors if they had not shown him his letter. When he saw the forged handwriting, he had the messenger summoned, and after the captain told him what he had done during the voyage, the king realized that Masiello's wife had done all the damage, and so he quickly armed a galley and sailed in person to that beach.

When he found Nuccia, he used his courtly manners to draw the entire story from her, and when he learned that the cause of everything was her jealousy, he ordered her to be made into a candle. So she was waxed and greased and stuck on top of a great pile of dry wood that was set afire.

---

1. Allusion to horns and cuckoldry. Inkstands were made out of horns.

When he saw that the fire had licked its red tongue around the wretched woman and had swallowed her, he got up and set sail.

While he was on the high seas, he came across a ship that was carrying the king of Pietrasecca, who, after they had exchanged a thousand courtesies, told the king of Terraverde that he was sailing to Lagotorbido because he had heard of the proclamation made by the king of that place, and he wanted to try his fortune. Indeed, he believed that nobody in the world had experienced the agony and bad fortune that he had.

"If that's the case," responded the king of Terraverde, "I can beat you with my feet tied, and I can beat all the unfortunate contestants, no matter how many there are. If most people measure torment by the yards, I can measure mine by miles. Therefore, I want to come with you, and let us compete like gentlemen: whichever one of us wins the prizes, he will divide them with the other as a good comrade should."

"Gladly," said the king of Pietrasecca, and after they shook on it, they journeyed to Lagotorbido, where they landed and presented themselves to the magician. In turn, he received them with the honor due their crowned heads. Indeed, he had them seated beneath the canopy and told them a thousand times how welcome they were to his kingdom. When he heard that they had come to try their fortune in the contest of the unfortunate men, he wanted to know how heavy their agony was and how they had been subjected to suffer the storm of sighs.

So the king of Pietrasecca began by telling about the love he had developed for his own flesh and blood, what his honorable sister had done to herself, and how he had acted like a dog when he had her locked in a tarred chest and had it thrown into the sea. Since then his conscience had been torturing him because of all the wrong that he had done on the one hand, and on the other, he was tormented by the loss of his sister and shame and grief. Consequently, if all the sorrows of the souls in hell were to be put into one still, they would still not produce a quintessence of all the suffering that his heart had experienced.

When the king had finished speaking, the other began and said, "Alas! Your sufferings are mere sugared tarts, cake, and candy compared to the pain I feel because that same Penta the Handless, whom I found in a chest like a Venetian candle to burn at my funeral, became my wife, and after she bore me a handsome baby boy, I had them almost burned alive due to the maliciousness of an evil woman! Oh thorn in my heart! Oh torment that will never leave me in peace! Even though saved, they were both sent away and banished from my kingdom, and now I find myself empty and unable to enjoy anything. I don't know why the donkey of my life, burdened by so much suffering, doesn't collapse under the weight."

After the magician heard one king speak after the other, he sensed that one of them was the brother and the other the husband of Penta, and thus he called Nufriello, the little boy, and said, "Go kiss the feet of your lord and father!"

The boy obeyed the magician, and when the king saw how gentle and graceful the boy was, he threw a beautiful golden chain around his neck. Then the magician turned to the boy again and said, "Go kiss the hand of your uncle, my dear boy."

And the handsome boy obeyed right away, and the uncle, astounded by the easy manners of the youngster, gave him a beautiful jewel and asked the magician if he were his son, and the magician replied that he should ask the mother.

Penta, who had been hiding behind a curtain, had witnessed all that had happened and came out like a lost little dog who, finding its master after being away many days, barks, licks him, wags its tail, and makes a thousand other signs to show its joy. Now she ran back and forth between her brother and her husband, drawn to one because he was her flesh and blood and the other because of love. She embraced one and the other with such great joy that it is difficult to describe their feelings. In any case, they made a concert of three with their disjointed words and interrupted sighs. At the first interval in this music, they began caressing the boy, and the father and the uncle took turns hugging and kissing him and flew into raptures. When everything had been said and done all around, the magician concluded with these words.

"Only heaven knows how much my heart rejoices to see Lady Penta consoled since she deserves to be cherished for her good qualities. This is why I made every effort to draw both her husband and brother here and to serve them as their devoted slave.[2] Since man is bound by his word just as the ox is by his horns, and since the promise of a good man is a contract, I declare that the king of Terraverde has suffered to the brink of death, and therefore, I intend to keep my word and give him not only the crown and scepter that were announced in the proclamation but also my kingdom. I do not have any children or complications in my life. With your permission, I should like to have as adopted children this beautiful couple, husband and wife, and you will be dear to me as the pupils of my eyes. And now, since there should be nothing left to be desired, and since I want to please Penta, I would like her to put her stumps beneath her apron, and then, when I ask her to bring them forth, she will have two hands more beautiful than ever before."

Penta followed his instructions, and everything happened just as the magician had said it would, and they were all unbelievably happy and beside themselves with joy, especially her husband, who considered this good fortune better than the other kingdom that the magician had given him. After a few days of great celebrating had passed, the king of Pietrasecca returned to his kingdom, and the king of Terraverde transferred the rights to rule his kingdom to his younger brother, while he remained with the magician, and in comparison to the finger of suffering that he had experienced, he now received arms of joy, and thus he provided testimony to the world that

> *unless you've tasted bitterness first,*
> *you can never know what sweetness is.*

---

2. A formulaic expression of fidelity or indebtedness often used at the end of letters and in conversation.

JACOB AND WILHELM GRIMM

The Maiden Without Hands†

Little by little a miller fell into poverty, and soon he had nothing left but his mill and a large apple tree behind it. One day, as he was on his way to chop wood in the forest, he met an old man whom he had never seen before.

"There's no reason you have to torture yourself by cutting wood," the old man said. "I'll make you rich if you promise to give me what's behind your mill."

"What else can that be but my apple tree?" thought the miller, and he gave the stranger his promise in writing.

"In three years I'll come and fetch what's mine," the stranger said with a snide laugh, and he went away.

When the miller returned home, his wife went out to meet him and said, "Tell me, miller, how did all this wealth suddenly get into our house? All at once I've discovered our chests and boxes are full. Nobody's brought anything, and I don't know how it's all happened."

"It's from a stranger I met in the forest," he said. "He promised me great wealth if I agreed in writing to give him what's behind our mill. We can certainly spare the large apple tree."

"Oh, husband!" his wife exclaimed in dread. "That was the devil! He didn't mean the apple tree but our daughter, who was behind the mill sweeping out the yard."

The miller's daughter was a beautiful and pious maiden who went through the next three years in fear of God and without sin. When time passed and the day came for the devil to fetch her, she washed herself clean and drew a circle around herself with chalk. The devil appeared quite early, but he could not get near her, and he said angrily to the miller, "I want you to take all the water away from her so she can't wash herself anymore. Otherwise, I have no power over her."

Since the miller was afraid of the devil, he did as he was told. The next morning the devil came again, but she wept on her hands and made them completely clean. Once more he could not get near her and said furiously to the miller, "Chop off her hands. Otherwise, I can't touch her."

The miller was horrified and replied, "How can I chop off the hands of my own child!"

But the devil threatened him and said, "If you don't do it, you're mine, and I'll come and get you myself!"

The father was so scared of him that he promised to obey. He went to his daughter and said, "My child, if I don't chop off both your hands, the devil will take me away, and in my fear I promised I'd do it. Please help

† Jacob and Wilhelm Grimm, "The Maiden Without Hands"—"Das Mädchen ohne Hände" (1857), No. 31 in *Kinder- und Hausmärchen. Gesammelt durch die Brüder Grimm* (Göttingen: Dieterich, 1857).

me out of my dilemma and forgive me for the injury I'm causing you."

"Dear father," she answered, "do what you want with me. I'm your child."

Then she extended both her hands and let him chop them off. The devil came a third time, but she had wept so long and so much on the stumps that they too were all clean. Then he had to abandon his game and lost all claim to her.

Now the miller said to his daughter, "I've become so wealthy because of you that I shall see to it you'll live in splendor for the rest of your life."

But she answered, "No, I cannot stay here. I'm going away and shall depend on the kindness of people to provide me with whatever I need."

Then she had her maimed arms bound to her back, and at dawn she set out on her way and walked the entire day until it become dark. She was right outside a royal garden, and by the glimmer of the moon she could see trees full of beautiful fruit. She could not enter the garden because it was surrounded by water. Since she had traveled the entire day without eating, she was very hungry. "Oh, if only I could get in!" she thought. "I must eat some of the fruit or else I'll perish!" Then she fell to her knees, called out to the Lord, and prayed. Suddenly an angel appeared and closed one of the locks in the stream so that the moat became dry and she could walk through it. Now she went into the garden accompanied by the angel. She caught sight of a beautiful tree full of pears, but the pears had all been counted. Nonetheless, she approached the tree and ate one of the pears with her mouth to satisfy her hunger, but only this one. The gardener was watching her, but since the angel was standing there, he was afraid, especially since he thought the maiden was a spirit. So he kept still and did not dare to cry out to speak to her. After she had eaten the pear, and her hunger was stilled, she went and hid in the bushes.

The next morning the king who owned the garden came and counted the pears. When he saw one was missing, he asked the gardener what had happened to it, for the pear was not lying under the tree and had somehow vanished.

"Last night a spirit appeared," answered the gardener. "It had no hands and ate one of the pears with its mouth."

"How did the spirit get over the water?" asked the king. "And where did it go after it ate the pear?"

"Someone wearing a garment as white as snow came down from heaven, closed the lock, and dammed up the water so the spirit could walk through the moat. And, since it must have been an angel, I was afraid to ask any questions or to cry out. After the spirit had eaten the pear, it just went away."

"If it's as you say," said the king, "I shall spend the night with you and keep watch."

When it became dark, the king went into the garden and brought a priest with him to talk to the spirit. All three sat down beneath the tree and kept watch. At midnight the maiden came out of the bushes and walked over to the tree and once again ate one of the pears with her mouth, while the angel in white stood next to her. The priest stepped forward and said to the maiden, "Have you come from heaven or from earth? Are you a spirit or a human being?"

"I'm not a spirit, but a poor creature forsaken by everyone except God."

"You may be forsaken by the whole world, but I shall not forsake you," said the king.

He took her with him to his royal palace, and since she was so beautiful and good, he loved her with all his heart, had silver hands made for her, and took her for his wife.

After a year had passed, the king had to go to war, and he placed the young queen under the care of his mother and said, "If she has a child, I want you to protect her and take good care of her, and write me right away."

Soon after, the young queen gave birth to a fine-looking boy. The king's mother wrote to him immediately to announce the joyful news. However, on the way the messenger stopped to rest near a brook, and since he was exhausted from the long journey, he fell asleep. Then the devil appeared. He was still trying to harm the pious queen, and so he exchanged the letter for another one that said the queen had given birth to a changeling. When the king read the letter, he was horrified and quite distressed, but he wrote his mother that she should protect the queen and take care of her until his return. The messenger started back with the letter, but he stopped to rest at the same spot and fell asleep. Once again the devil came and put a different letter in his pocket that said they should kill the queen and her child. The old mother was tremendously disturbed when she received the letter and could not believe it. She wrote the king again but received the same answer because the devil kept replacing the messenger's letters with false letters each time. The last letter ordered the king's mother to keep the tongue and eyes of the queen as proof that she had done his bidding.

But the old woman wept at the thought of shedding such innocent blood. During the night she had a doe fetched and cut out its tongue and eyes and put them away. Then she said to the queen, "I can't let you be killed as the king commands. However, you can't stay here any longer. Go out into the wide world with your child and never come back."

She tied the child to the queen's back, and the poor woman went off with tears in her eyes. When she came to a great wild forest, she fell down on her knees and prayed to God. The Lord's angel appeared before her and led her to a small cottage with a little sign saying "Free Lodging for Everyone." A maiden wearing a snow white garment came out of the cottage and said, "Welcome, your highness," and took her inside. She untied the little boy from her back and offered him her breast so he could have something to drink. Then she laid him down in a beautifully made bed.

"How did you know that I'm a queen?" asked the poor woman.

"I'm an angel sent by God to take care of you and your child," replied the maiden in white.

So the queen stayed seven years in the cottage and was well cared for.

By the grace of God and through her own piety, her hands, which had been chopped off, grew back again.

When the king finally returned from the wars, the first thing he wanted to do was to see his wife and child. However, his old mother began to weep and said, "You wicked man, why did you write and order me to kill two innocent souls?" She showed him the two letters that the devil had forged and resumed talking. "I did as you ordered," she said, and she displayed the tongue and the eyes.

At the sight of them, the king burst into tears and wept bitterly over his poor wife and son. His old mother was aroused and took pity on him.

"Console yourself," she said. "She's still alive. I secretly had a doe killed and kept its tongue and eyes as proof. Then I took the child and tied him to your wife's back and ordered her to go out into the wide world, and she had to promise me never to return here because you were so angry with her."

"I shall go as far as the sky is blue, without eating or drinking, until I find my dear wife and child," the king said. "That is, unless they have been killed or have died of hunger in the meantime."

The king wandered for about seven years and searched every rocky cliff and cave he came across. When he did not find her, he thought she had perished. During this time he neither ate nor drank, but God kept him alive. Eventually, he came to a great forest, where he discovered the little cottage with the sign "Free Lodging for Everyone." Then the maiden in white came out, took him by the hand, and led him inside.

"Welcome, your majesty," she said, and asked him where he came from.

"I've been wandering about for almost seven years looking for my wife and child, but I can't find them."

The angel offered him food and drink, but he refused and said he only wanted to rest a while. So he lay down to sleep and covered his face with a handkerchief. Then the angel went into the room where the queen was sitting with her son, whom she was accustomed to calling Sorrowful, and said, "Go into the next room with your child. Your husband has come."

So the queen went to the room where he was lying, and the handkerchief fell from his face.

"Sorrowful," she said, "pick up your father's handkerchief and put it over his face."

The child picked the handkerchief up and put it over his face. The king heard all this in his sleep and took pleasure in making the handkerchief drop on the floor again. The boy became impatient and said, "Dear mother, how can I cover my father's face when I have no father on earth. I've learned to pray to 'our Father, who art in heaven,' and you told me that my father was in heaven and that he was our good Lord. How am I supposed to know this wild man? He's not my father."

When the king heard this, he sat up and asked her who she was.

"I'm your wife," she replied, "and this is your son, Sorrowful."

When the king saw that she had real hands, he said, "My wife had silver hands."

"Our merciful Lord let my natural hands grow again," she answered.

The angel went back into the sitting room, fetched the silver hands, and showed them to him. Now he knew for certain that it was his dear wife and dear son, and he kissed them and was happy.

"A heavy load has been taken off my mind," he said.

After the Lord's angel ate one more meal with them, they went home to be with the king's old mother. There was rejoicing everywhere, and the king and queen had a second wedding and lived happily ever after.

The Art of Good Conduct

Many folktales and fairy tales in the Middle Ages and Reformation concerned the protection of chastity, and by the eighteenth century it was a common theme in bourgeois tragedies and early novels. Generally speaking, the particular conflict involves an upper-class man who wants to seduce a virtuous woman from the bourgeoisie or peasantry, although "noble" men also pursued "noble" women as well. It is not clear whether there was a specific oral or literary source for Basile's amusing story about a smart merchant's daughter who not only protects her own chastity but rescues the family's honor. But it is clear that Mlle Lhéritier knew his story and adapted it to suit her moral perspective and to address the "battle of the sexes" in French society at the end of the seventeenth century. Unlike Basile, she has a sparse sense of humor, is very didactic, and has very little pity for the prince.

GIAMBATTISTA BASILE

Sapia Liccarda†

Once upon a time there was a very rich merchant named Marcone, who had three beautiful daughters, Bella, Cenzolla, and Sapia Liccarda. One day he had to go away on a business trip, and knowing that the two elder sisters were gossips and loved to gaze[1] out the window all day, he nailed up all the windows in the house. Then, before he departed, he gave each daughter a ring with a certain stone that became stained if the wearer were to do something shameful.

But no sooner did the merchant leave Villaperta, for that was the name of the town, than the two elder sisters began to climb the windows and lean out from the top despite the fact that Sapia Liccarda, who was the youngest, became terribly upset with them and yelled at them that their house was not like those in the disreputable quarters of Gelsi, Duchessa, Fondaco del Cedro, or Pisciaturo[2] and that they should stop acting like fools and flirts.

Now, just opposite their house was the palace of the king, who had three sons, Cecciariello, Grazullo, and Tore.[3] When they caught sight of

---

† Giambattista Basile, "Sapia Liccarda"—"Sapia Liccarda" (1634), *Quarto Passatempo della Terza Giornata* in *Lo cunto de le cunti overo Lo trattenemiento de peccerille*, De Gian Alessio Abbattutis, 5 vols. (Naples: Ottavio Beltrano, 1634–36).
1. The Neapolitan text uses the expression *cavallesse fenestrere*, meaning unbridled mares who are always flirting at the window.
2. All places of amusement or slums in Naples.
3. Diminutives of Francesco, Orazio, and Salvatore.

these maidens, who were very lovely, they began to make signs with their
eyes, and the signs changed into hand kisses, and the kisses into words,
and the words into promises, and the promises into action so that they all
agreed to a meeting one evening. So, when the sun retired with his retinue
because it did not want to compete with the night, the three brothers
scaled the house of the sisters, and the two older brothers quickly hit it off
with the two older sisters. However, when Tore sought to take Sapia Liccarda, she fled and slipped like an eel into a room. Then she barricaded
herself inside so that it was impossible to open the door. Consequently,
the poor boy was left to watch his brothers enjoy their dainty morsels,
and while they were filling their sacks at the mill, he had to hold the
mule.

The next morning, when the birds, the trumpeters of dawn, sounded
the signal "To horse!" so that the hours of the day could begin to mount
their saddles, the brothers departed. Two of them were very content and
satisfied, while the third was most despondent because of the bad night
that he had spent in the house.

Well, soon thereafter, the two sisters became pregnant, and Sapia Liccarda told them how dreadful their pregnancy was, and as they grew bigger
each day, she kept repeating her reprimands every hour, always concluding
with a warning that the lizard's belly[4] would bring them conflict and ruin,
and when their father returned from his trip, they would see the sheep
dance away.

Meanwhile, Tore's desire for Sapia grew, partly because of her beauty,
partly because she had offended and tricked him. So he got her elder
sisters to agree to help him trap her when she least expected it. As a
result, they sought to find a way to induce her to go to his home, and
one day they called to her and said, "Sister, what's done is done. If
advice would pay off, it should either cost more or be regarded more
highly. If we had listened to your wise words, we would not have lowered
the honor of our house, nor would our bellies be as enlarged as you see.
But how can we remedy all this? The knife has been plunged up to the
hilt. Things have gone too far. Our goose is cooked. But we can't believe
that you will let your anger get the better of you, and that you would like
to see us abandon this world. Please have compassion for our situation, if
not for us, then at least for the poor creatures that we are carrying in our
bellies."

"Heaven knows," replied Sapia Liccarda, "how much my heart weeps
for the sin that you have committed when I think of the present shame
and the punishment that awaits you when our father returns and finds
what misfortune has struck this house. I would give my right hand if I
could make all this go away. But since the devil has blinded you, tell me
what I can do as long as it does not compromise my honor. Blood cannot
become water, and after all is said and done, I cannot deny my own flesh
and blood, and the compassion I feel for your situation moves me so much
that I would offer my very own life to remedy what has happened."

4. Basile is drawing an analogy with another expression, the lizard's eye (*occhio di ramarro*), which
was used by other writers of his time to denote a flirting and seductive eye.

After Sapia Liccarda had spoken, the sisters answered, "We don't desire any other token of your affection other than your obtaining some of the bread that the king eats. Indeed, we have developed such a craving for it that, if we do not satisfy this longing, there is a danger that our children will be born with a loaf of bread on their noses. Therefore, if you are a Christian, you'll do us this favor, and tomorrow morning, when it is still dark, we shall let you down from the window through which the king's sons entered, and we shall dress you like a beggar so that nobody will recognize you."

Moved by her compassion for the poor creatures in their bellies, Sapia Liccarda dressed herself in tattered clothes, and when the sun lifted the trophies of light to celebrate his victory over night, she went to the palace with a flax comb on her shoulders and begged for a little piece of bread. When she obtained her alms, she wanted to return to her house. However, she encountered Tore because he had known all about her arrival and recognized her right away. But, while he endeavored to seize her, she unexpectedly turned her back, and his hands grabbed the teeth of the comb and were scratched so badly that they remained sorely scraped for several days.

So the sisters received the bread, but poor Tore's hunger increased. Thus the sisters conspired once more with Tore, and after a couple of days, they began once more to prompt Sapia to help them because they had a craving for two pears from the royal garden. So their poor sister put on another disguise and went into the garden, where she found Tore, who immediately knew who she was, and when he heard that she wanted the pears, he personally climbed the tree, and after he had thrown a few pears into Sapia's apron, he wanted to climb down and seize her, but she took away the ladder and left him dangling on a branch shouting at the crows. If a gardener had not by chance arrived to gather two heads of lettuce, he might have remained there all night.

Well, thanks to the grace of heaven, the two sisters gave birth to two boys and said to Sapia, "We are completely ruined, lovely sister, unless you decide to help us because our father will soon return, and when he finds what a disservice we have done this house, he will tear us to shreds. Therefore, we ask you to go out once more, and we shall lower these two babies in a basket. Then you can carry them to their fathers, who will look after them."

Although it seemed to Sapia Liccarda that she should not have to put up with so much trouble because of the foolish behavior of her sisters, she was full of tender loving care and let herself be persuaded to go down into the street. Then the babies were lowered, and she carried them to the rooms of their fathers. Since they were not there, she placed each one into a bed, as she had been instructed. Then she entered Tore's room and put a large stone in his bed and returned home.

When the princes returned to their rooms found the babies with the names of the fathers written on tags sewn to their clothes, they were over-joyed, while Tore was all in knots because he had been the only one of the brothers not to procreate and have a son. So he went into his room to sleep, and when he threw himself down on his bed, he hit his head on the stone with such force that a huge lump soon appeared.

In the meantime, the merchant returned home from his long trip, and when he looked at the rings of his daughters, he found those of the two elder sisters completely stained, and he made a terrible scene. He wanted to take his sword to them, torture them, and beat them to find out what had happened. But just then all three of the king's sons came and asked his permission to marry his daughters. At first he did not understand what was happening, and he believed they were playing a joke on him. Finally, he learned what had been going on between them and about the sons of his daughters. Consequently, he considered himself very lucky and arranged to celebrate the weddings that very night.

However, even though Tore was eager to marry Sapia, she was revolted by the idea and remembered all the tricks she had played on him. Indeed, she thought that every herb is not mint, and the coat was not without hairs. Therefore, she quickly made a fine statue of sugar paste, put it into a huge basket, and covered it with some clothes. In the evening, when everyone was dancing and feasting, she pretended to feel faint and went to her room before the others. Then she had the basket fetched into the room with the excuse that she wanted to change clothes, but she put the statue in the bed beneath the sheets and hid herself behind the curtain and waited to see what would happen.

When the hour arrived for the married couples to go to sleep, Tore entered the room and went to the bed in which, he thought, Sapia was lying. "Now you'll pay for all the disgusting things that you've done to me, you bitch!" he exclaimed. "Now you'll see what it's like for a cricket to compete with an elephant! Now you'll pay for everything! I want you to remember the flax comb, the ladder that you took away from the tree, and all the other insulting things that you did!"

As he said this, he grabbed a dagger and stabbed her from one side to the other. Then, still not content, he said, "I'm going to suck your blood as well!" So he pulled the dagger from the skin of the statue, licked it, and smelled the sweetness and aroma of the musk with which it was covered. As a result, he repented having stabbed a maiden so sweet and fragrant and began to lament his anger and uttered words that would have moved even a stone to tears. He declared that his heart was gall, and his dagger, poison to have tarnished a maiden so sweet and gentle. After moaning for a long time and reaching the point of desperation, he raised his hand with the same dagger to do away with himself. But Sapia quickly jumped from her hiding place, grabbed his hand, and said, "Stop, Tore, put down your hand! Here is the piece of flesh that you were bemoaning! Here I am, alive and well, in order to see you safe and sound! Please don't think that I am hard or that I have a thick skin if I've treated you badly and displeased you. I only did this to test you and to try your constancy and fidelity." And she told him that she had played this last trick on him to squash the fumes of an angry heart, and thus she begged his pardon for all that had happened.

The bridegroom embraced her with great affection and had her lie down beside him. Then they made peace together. Indeed, after experiencing so many trials and tribulations, Tore appreciated Sapia's unavailability even more than the great readiness of her two sisters, for as the poet says,

neither naked Cythera,[5]
nor wrapped-up Cynthia,[6]
the middle way is always regarded the best way.

MARIE-JEANNE LHÉRITIER

The Discreet Princess; or, The Adventures of Finette[†]

During the time of the First Crusade, a king of some country in Europe decided to go to war against the infidels of Palestine. Before undertaking such a long journey, he put the affairs of his kingdom into such good order and placed the regency in the hands of such an able minister that he was entirely at ease. What worried this king most, though, was the care of his family. He had recently lost his wife, who had failed to give birth to a son before her death. On the other hand, he was the father of three princesses, all of marriageable age. My chronicle has not indicated what their true names were. I only know that people were quite simple during these happy times and customarily gave eminent people surnames according to their good or bad characteristics without much ado. Thus they called the eldest princess *Nonchalante*, the second *Babbler*, and the third *Finette*.[1] All of these names suited the characters of the three sisters.

There was never anyone more indolent than Nonchalante. The earliest she ever woke up was one in the afternoon, and she was dragged to church in the same condition as when she got out of bed. Her clothes were all in disarray, her dress, loose, no belt, and very often she wore one slipper of one kind and one of another. They used to correct this mistake during the day, but they could never prevail upon this princess to wear anything but slippers, for she found it extremely exhausting to put on shoes. Whenever Nonchalante finished eating, she would sit down at her dressing table, where she would remain until evening, and then she employed the rest of her time until midnight playing and eating. After that, it took almost as long in undressing her as it did in getting her dressed. She never succeeded in going to bed until it was daylight.

Babbler led a different kind of life. This princess was quite vivacious and spent very little time caring about her looks, but she had such a strong propensity for talking that, from the very moment she woke up to the time she fell asleep again, her mouth was never shut. She knew everything

---

5. One of Aphrodite's surnames, which is derived either from Cythera in Crete or from the island of Cythera, where the goddess is said to have first landed.
6. Surname of Artemis, derived from Mount Cynthus on the island of Delos.
† Marie-Jeanne Lhéritier, "The Discreet Princess; or, The Adventures of Finette"—"L'Adroite Princesse, ou les aventures de Finette" (1696), in *Oeuvres meslées* (Paris: J. Guignard, 1696).
1. In French, the name *Finette* indicates a clever or cunning young woman.

about the bad households, the love liaisons, and the intrigues not only at the court, but also among the most petty of the bourgeoisie. She kept a record of all those wives who stole from their families at home in order to make a more dazzling impression when they went out into society. She was informed precisely about what a particular countess's woman and a particular marquis's steward earned. In order to be on top of all these insignificant affairs, she listened to her nurse and seamstress with greater pleasure than she would listen to an ambassador. Finally, she shocked everyone, from the king, her father, down to his footmen, with her pretty stories. She did not care whom she had for a listener provided she could only talk. Such a longing to talk had another bad effect on this princess. Despite her high rank, her familiarity emboldened the young men around the court to talk sweetly to her. She listened to their flowery speeches without much fuss and merely so that she could have the pleasure of responding to them. No matter what the cost was, she had to hear others talk or gossip herself from morning till night.

Neither Babbler nor Nonchalante ever bothered to occupy herself by thinking, reflecting, or reading. They never troubled themselves about household chores or entertained themselves by sewing or weaving. In short, these two sisters lived in eternal idleness and never bothered to stimulate their minds or use their hands.

The youngest of the three sisters had a very different character. Her thoughts and hands were continually active, and she had a surprising vivacity that was put to good use. She knew how to sing and dance and play musical instruments to perfection. She was remarkably nimble and successful in all those little manual chores with which people of her sex generally amuse themselves. Moreover, she put the king's household into perfect order and prevented the pilfering of the petty officers through her care and vigilance, for even in those days princes were cheated by those who surrounded them.

Finette's talents did not stop there. She had a great sense of judgment and such a wonderful presence of mind that she could immediately find ways to get out of any kind of predicament. By using her insight, this young princess had discovered a dangerous trap that a perfidious ambassador had set for the king, her father, in a treaty that he had almost signed. To punish the treachery of this ambassador and his master, the king changed the articles of the treaty, and by wording it in the terms that his daughter dictated to him, he, in turn, deceived the deceiver himself. Another time the princess discovered some cheating by a minister against the king, and through the advice she gave her father, he managed to foil this disloyal man. On several other occasions, this princess gave indications of how perceptive she was and what a fine mind she had. In fact, the people called her *Finette* exactly because she gave so many signs of her intelligence.

The king loved her far more than his other daughters and depended so much on her good sense that, if he had not had any other child but her, he would have departed without feeling uneasy. However, his faith in Finette's good behavior was offset by his distrust of his other daughters.

Therefore, to make sure that his family would be safeguarded in the way he believed he had safeguarded his subjects, he adopted the following measures that I am now going to relate.

The king was on very intimate terms with a fairy, and he went to see her in order to express the uneasiness he felt concerning his daughters.

"It's not that the two eldest, whom I worry about, have ever done the least thing contrary to their duty," he said. "But they have so little sense, are so imprudent, and live so indolently that I fear that they will get caught up in some foolish intrigue during my absence or do something foolish merely to amuse themselves. As for Finette, I'm sure of her virtue. However, I'll treat her as I do her sisters to make everything equal. This is why, wise fairy, I'd like you to make three distaffs out of glass for my daughters. And I'd like you to make each one so artfully that it will break as soon as the daughter to whom it belongs does anything against her honor."

Since this fairy was extremely skillful, she presented the king with three enchanted distaffs within seconds, and she took great care to make them according to his specifications. But he was not content with this precaution. He put the princesses into a high tower, which had been built in a very secluded place. The king told his daughters that he was ordering them to live in that tower during his absence and prohibited them from admitting any people whatsoever. He took all their officers and servants of both sexes from them, and after giving them the enchanted distaffs, whose qualities he explained to them, he kissed the princesses, locked the doors of the tower, took away the keys, and departed.

You are perhaps going to believe that these princesses were now in danger of dying from hunger. Not at all. Care had been taken to attach a pulley to one of the windows of the tower, and a rope ran through it, to which the princesses tied a basket that they let down to the ground every day. Provisions were placed into this basket on a daily basis, and after they pulled up the basket, they carefully carried the rope into their room.

Nonchalante and Babbler led a life of despair in this desolate place. They became bored beyond expression, but they were forced to have patience because they had been given such a terrible picture of their distaffs, and they feared that their least slip might cause them to break.

As for Finette, she was not bored in the least. Her needlework, spinning, and music furnished her with sufficient amusement. Besides this, the minister who was governing the state gave orders to place into the basket letters that kept the princesses informed about what was happening in the kingdom or outside it. The king had given his permission, and the minister paid his respects to the princesses by doing exactly what the king had ordered. Finette read all the news with great attention and enjoyed this. But her two sisters did not deign to participate in the least. They said they were too sorrowful to have the strength to amuse themselves with such trivial things. They needed cards to entertain themselves during their father's absence.

Thus they spent their time sadly by grumbling continually about their destiny, and I believe they even said that it was much better to be born happy than to be born the daughter of a king. They often went to the windows of the tower to see at least what was happening in the country, and one day, when Finette was very absorbed in some pretty work in her room, her sisters were at the window and saw a poor woman clothed in rags and tatters at the foot of the tower. She cried out to them about her misery in very pathetic tones and begged them with her hands joined together to let her come into the castle. Moreover, she told them she was an unfortunate stranger who knew how to do a thousand things and would serve them with utmost fidelity. At first the princesses recalled their father's orders not to permit anyone to enter the tower, but Nonchalante was so weary of tending to herself, and Babbler was so bored at having nobody to talk to but her sisters, that the desire of one sister to be groomed carefully by someone and the eagerness of the other sister to have somebody to chat with made them decide to admit this poor stranger.

"Do you think," Babbler said to her sister, "that the king's order was meant to include this unfortunate wretch? I believe we can admit her without anything happening."

"Sister, you may do whatever you please," Nonchalante responded.

Babbler had only waited for her sister to consent, and she immediately let down the basket. The poor woman got into it, and the princesses pulled her up with the help of the pulley.

When this woman was before their eyes, her horrible and dirty clothes almost turned their stomachs. They would have given her others, but she told them she would change her clothes the next day. At present, she could think of nothing but her work. As she was saying these words, Finette entered the room and was stunned to see this unknown person with her sisters. They told her the reasons that had induced them to pull her up, and Finette, who saw that she could do nothing about it, concealed her disappointment at this imprudent action.

In the meantime the princesses' new servant explored the castle a hundred times under the pretext of doing her work, but in reality it was to see how things were arranged in it because this creature, covered by rags, was none other than the oldest son of a powerful king, a neighbor of the princesses' father. Moreover, this young prince was one of the most artful and cunning people of his time and completely controlled his father, the king. Actually, this did not require much dexterity because the king had such a sweet and easy disposition that he had been given the surname Gentle. And as for this young prince, who always acted with artifice and cunning, the people called him Rich-in-Craft, a name that they shortened to Rich-Craft. Fortunately, he had a younger brother who had as many good qualities as Rich-Craft had bad ones. Despite their different characters, however, there was such a tight bond between these two princes that everyone was surprised by it. Aside from the younger prince's good qualities, his handsome face and graceful figure were so remarkable that he was generally called Bel-a-Voir.

It was Rich-Craft who had instigated the deceitful act of his father's ambassador who had tried to change the treaty, an act that had been foiled by Finette's quick mind. Ever since she had turned the tables on them, Rich-Craft, who had not shown a particularly great love for the princess's father before this, had developed an even stronger aversion for him. Thus, after he had learned about the precautions that the king had taken in

regard to his daughters, he decided to have some pernicious fun by undermining the prudence of such a distrustful father. Accordingly, Rich-
Craft invented some pretext to obtain permission from his father to take a
journey, and he found the means that would enable him to enter the
tower where these princesses were confined, as you have already seen.

In examining the castle, Rich-Craft observed that it was very easy for
the princesses to make themselves heard by people passing by, and he
concluded that it was best for him to stay in his disguise all day because,
if they realized who he was, they could easily call out to the people outside
and have him punished for his rash undertaking. Therefore, he remained
dressed in his rags all day long and pretended to be a beggar woman. That
night, however, after the princesses had dined, he discarded his rags and
revealed himself dressed as a cavalier in rich attire all covered with gold
and jewels. The poor princesses were so frightened by this sight that they
all began to run from him as fast as they could. Finette and Babbler, who
were very nimble, quickly reached their rooms, but Nonchalante, who was
not accustomed to moving fast, was soon overtaken.

As soon as Rich-Craft threw himself at her feet, he declared who he was
and told her that the reputation of her beauty and the sight of her portraits
had induced him to leave a pleasant court in order to pledge his devotion
and propose to her. Nonchalante was at such a loss for words that she
could not answer the prince, who was still kneeling. Meanwhile, he kept
saying a thousand sweet things and made a thousand protestations, and he
ardently implored her to take him that very moment for her husband. Due
to her weak backbone, she did not have the strength to argue with him,
and she told Rich-Craft nonchalantly that she believed him to be sincere
and accepted his proposal. She observed no greater formalities than these,
which concluded the marriage, but at the same time, she lost her distaff,
for it broke into a thousand pieces.

Babbler and Finette were extraordinarily anxious. They had made it
back to their rooms separately and had locked themselves in. These rooms
were at some distance from each other, and since each of the princesses
knew nothing about the other's fate, they did not sleep a wink all night
long.

Next morning, the wicked prince led Nonchalante into a ground apartment which was at the end of the garden. This princess told him that she
was very concerned about her sisters, though she dared not show herself
to them for fear they would criticize her for her marriage. The prince told
her he would make sure that they would approve and, after talking some
more, he locked Nonchalante in her room. Then he searched carefully
all over the castle to locate the other princesses. It took some time before
he could discover in what rooms they had locked themselves, but eventually Babbler's longing to talk all the time caused the princess to speak
and grumble to herself. Therefore, Rich-Craft went up to the door, looked
through the keyhole, and spoke to her. He told her everything that he had
previously told her sister and swore that he had only entered the tower in
order to offer his hand and heart to her. He praised her wit and beauty in
exaggerated terms, and Babbler, who was convinced that she had great
qualities, was foolish enough to believe everything the prince told her. She

answered him with a flood of words that showed how receptive she was. Certainly this princess must have had an extraordinary capacity for speaking to have acquitted herself as she did, for she was extremely faint after not having eaten a morsel all day. In fact, she had nothing fit to eat in her room because she was extremely lazy and had not thought of anything but endless talking. She never took any precautions, and whenever she needed anything, she usually depended on Finette, who was as hardworking and careful as her sisters were indolent and imprudent. That charming princess always kept an abundance of fine biscuits, pies, macaroons, and confiture of all sorts and her own making in her room. Since Babbler did not have this advantage, she felt hunger pangs and was moved by the protestations that the prince made through the door. At last, she opened it, and when it was open, that seducer was the consummate actor and played his role perfectly, for he had had a lot of practice.

Given her hunger, they decided to leave this room and went to the pantry, where he found all sorts of refreshments because the basket had furnished the princesses every day with more than enough. Babbler was still at a loss to know what had happened to her sisters, but she convinced herself—and I am not sure what her reasons were—that they were both locked up in Finette's room and had all they needed. Rich-Craft used all the arguments he could to substantiate this belief and told her that they would go and find the princesses toward evening. She was not entirely in agreement with him on this matter and said they would go and find them as soon as they had finished eating.

In short, the prince and princess began eating with big appetites, and when they were finished, Rich-Craft asked to see the most beautiful apartment in the castle. He gave his hand to the princess, who led him there, and when they entered, he began to exaggerate the love he had for her, and the advantages she would have in marrying him. He told her, just as he had done with her sister Nonchalante, that she should accept his proposal immediately because, if she were to see her sisters before she had accepted him for her husband, they would certainly oppose it. Since he was one of the most powerful of the neighboring princes, he would most probably seem to them better suited for her elder sister than for her, and her elder sister would never consent to a match she herself might desire with all imaginable ardor. After many words that signified nothing, Babbler acted just as extravagantly as her sister had done: she agreed to become Rich-Craft's wife and never thought about what would happen to her glass distaff until after it shattered into a hundred pieces.

Toward evening Babbler returned to her room with the prince, and the first thing she saw was her glass distaff all broken into pieces. She was very troubled by this sight, and the prince asked why she was so concerned. Since her passion for talking made her incapable of holding her tongue about any subject, she foolishly told Rich-Craft the secret about the distaff, and the prince had a pernicious joy because the princesses' father would thus become totally convinced about the bad conduct of his daughters.

Meanwhile, Babbler was no longer in the mood to search for her sisters. She had reason to fear that they would not approve of her conduct, but the prince himself proposed that he would undertake this task and told her he knew how to win their approval. After this assurance, the princess, who had not slept at all that night, grew very drowsy, and when she fell asleep, Rich-Craft turned the key and locked her in her room as he had previously done with Nonchalante.

Once this devious prince had locked up Babbler, he went into all the rooms of the castle, one after another, and when he found them all open except one that was locked from the inside, he concluded that that was where Finette had gone. Since he had created a string of compliments, he went and used the same things at Finette's door that he had used with her sisters. But this princess was not so easy to dupe as her elder sisters, and she listened to him for a good while without responding. At last, realizing that he knew she was in that room, she told him that, if it were true that he had such a strong and sincere affection for her as he would like her to believe, he should go down into the garden and shut the door after him. Then she would talk to him as much as he wanted from the window of her room that overlooked the garden.

Rich-Craft would not agree to this, and since the princess continued to persist in refusing to open the door, this wicked prince lost his patience. So, he fetched a large wooden log and broke the door open. However, he found Finette armed with a large hammer, which had been accidentally left in a wardrobe in her room. Finette's face was red with emotion, and her eyes sparkled with rage, making her appear even more enchanting and beautiful to Rich-Craft. He would have cast himself at her feet, but as she retreated, she boldly said to him, "Prince, if you approach me, I'll split your skull with this hammer."

"What's this I hear, beautiful princess!" Rich-Craft exclaimed in his hypocritical tone. "Does the love I have for you inspire you with such hatred?"

He then began to speak to her from one end of the room to the other and to describe the passionate ardor that the reputation of her beauty and wonderful wit had aroused in him, and he added that the only reason he had put on such a disguise was to offer his hand and heart. He told her she ought to pardon the violent love that caused him to break open her door. Finally, he tried to persuade her, as he had her sisters, that it was in her interest to take him for a husband as soon as possible, and he assured her he did not know where her sisters had gone. This was because his thoughts had been wholly fixed on her, and he had not gone to the trouble of looking for them.

The discreet princess pretended to be appeased and told him that she must find her sisters, and after that, they would do what had to be done together. But Rich-Craft answered that he could not agree to search for her sisters until she had consented to marry him, for her sisters would definitely oppose their match due to their seniority. Finette, who had good reason to distrust this treacherous prince, was made even more suspicious by this answer. She trembled to think of what had happened to her sisters and was determined to revenge them with the same stroke that might enable her to avoid a disaster which she imagined they had suffered. So, this young princess told Rich-Craft that she would gladly consent to marry him, but since she was of the opinion that marriages made at night always turned out to be unhappy, she requested that he postpone the ceremony until the next morning. She added that she would certainly not mention a word of this to her sisters and asked him to give her only a little time to say her prayers. Afterward she would take him to a room where there was a very good bed, and then she would return to her own room until the morning.

Rich-Craft was not very courageous, and as he watched Finette, still armed with the large hammer, with which she played like a fan, he consented to what she proposed and went away to give her some time to meditate. No sooner was he gone than Finette rushed to make a bed over the hole of a drain in one of the rooms of the castle. This room was as clean as any other, but all the garbage and dirty water of the castle were thrown down the hole of that drain, which was very large. Finette put two weak sticks across the hole and then made a nice clean bed on top of them. After that she quickly returned to her room. A few minutes later Rich-Craft made his appearance, and the princess led him into the room where she had made his bed and then retired.

Without undressing, the prince hastily threw himself onto the bed, and his weight immediately broke the small sticks all at once. He began falling down to the bottom of the drain and could not stop himself. Along the way he received twenty blows on his head and was bruised all over. The prince's fall made a great noise in the pipe, and since it was not far from Finette's room, she knew that her trick had worked, and she felt a secret joy that gave her a great deal of pleasure. Indeed, it is impossible to describe the pleasant feeling she had as she heard him muttering in the drain. He certainly deserved that punishment, and the princess had every reason to feel satisfied.

But her joy was not so overwhelming as to make her forget her sisters, and her first concern was to go and look for them. It was quite easy to find Babbler. Rich-Craft had double-locked that princess in her room and had left the key in the door. So Finette entered eagerly, and the noise she made startled her sister and threw her into a great state of confusion. Finette told how she had defeated the wicked prince, who had come to insult them, and on hearing that news, Babbler was thunderstruck. Despite the fact that she engaged in idle talk, she had been foolish enough to have ridiculously believed every word Rich-Craft had told her. The world is still full of such dopes like her. However, she managed to cover up the extent of her sorrow and left the room with Finette to look for Nonchalante.

They went into all the rooms of the castle, but could not find her. At last Finette thought to herself that she might be in the garden apartment, where, indeed, they found her half dead with despair and fatigue, for she had had nothing to eat the entire day. The princesses gave her all the assistance she needed. Then they recounted their adventures to each other, and Nonchalante and Babbler were overcome with mortal sorrow. Afterward, all three went to take a rest.

In the meantime, Rich-Craft spent the night very uncomfortably, and when day came, he was not much better. The prince found himself in the underground sewers, and he could not see how horrible they were because the light could not penetrate this underground terrain. Nevertheless, after he had struggled painfully for some time, he found the end of the drain which ran into a river at a considerable distance from the castle. Once there he was able to make himself heard by some men who were fishing in the river, and they dragged him out in such a state that he aroused the compassion of these good people.

Rich-Craft ordered the men to carry him to his father's court to recover from his wounds in peace and quiet, and the disgrace that he had experienced caused him to develop such an inveterate hatred for Finette that he thought less about getting well than he did about revenge.

Meanwhile, Finette spent her time very sadly. Honor was a thousand times dearer to her than life, and the shameful weakness of her sisters had thrown her into such despair that it was difficult for her to regain her equanimity. At the same time, the princesses' bad state of health, which was a result of their worthless marriages, put Finette's courage to test.

Rich-Craft, who had long since been a cunning villain, continued to hatch ideas since this incident so that he could become even more villainous. Neither the drain nor the bruises disturbed him as much as the fact that he had encountered someone more clever than he was. He knew about the effects of his two marriages, and to tempt the princesses, he had great boxes full of the finest fruit placed beneath the windows of the castle. Nonchalante and Babbler, who often sat at the windows, could not help but see the fruit, and they immediately felt a passionate desire to eat some. So, they insisted that Finette go down in the basket to get some of the fruit for them. The kindness of that obliging princess was so great that she did as they requested and brought back some fruit, which they devoured with great avidity.

The next day, there were fruits of another kind, and again the princesses wanted to have some. And again Finette complied with kindness. But Rich-Craft's officers, who were hiding, and who had missed their target the first time, did not fail the second time. They seized Finette and carried her off in plain view of her sisters, who tore out their hair in despair. Rich-Craft's guards carried out his orders so well that they were able to take Finette to a country house right away, where the prince was residing in order to regain his health. Since he was so infuriated with this princess, he said a hundred brutal things to her, which she answered with a courage and greatness of spirit indicative of the heroine that she was. At last, after having kept her prisoner for some days, Rich-Craft had her brought to the top of an extremely high mountain, where he immediately followed her. It was there that he announced to her that they were going to put her to death in a manner that would sufficiently avenge all the injuries she had caused him. Then the wicked prince demonstrated his barbaric nature by showing her a barrel lined with penknives, razors, and hooked nails stuck all around the inside. He told her that, in order to punish her the way she deserved, they were going to put her into that barrel and roll her from the top of the mountain down into the valley. Though Finette was no Roman, she was no more afraid of this punishment than Regulus[2] was at the sight of a similar destiny. This young princess retained her courage and presence of mind. However, instead of admiring her heroic character, Rich-Craft became more enraged than ever and was determined to put a quick end to her life. With that intention in mind, he stooped to look into the barrel, which was to be the instrument of his vengeance, to see whether it was properly furnished with all its murderous weapons.

Finette, who saw that her persecutor was absorbed in his examination of the barrel, lost no time, but very swiftly pushed him into it and rolled him down the mountain without giving him any time to know where he was. After this she ran away, and the prince's officers, who had seen with extreme grief how cruelly their master would have treated this charming princess, did not make the slightest attempt to stop her. Besides, they were so frightened by what had happened to Rich-Craft that they could think of nothing but how to stop the barrel that was rolling pell-mell down the mountain. However, their efforts were all in vain. He rolled down to the bottom, where they drew him out with wounds in a thousand places.

Rich-Craft's accident made his father, the gentle king, and his brother, Prince Bel-a-Voir extremely sad. As for the people of their country, they were not at all moved by this since Rich-Craft was universally hated. They were even astonished to think that the young prince, who had such noble and generous sentiments, could love his unworthy elder brother. But that was due to the good nature of this prince, who was strongly attached to all the members of his family. And Rich-Craft was always wise enough to show him such signs of affection that this prince would never have forgiven himself if he had not responded with good feelings. Therefore, Bel-a-Voir was extremely grieved by the wounds his brother had received, and he did not leave a thing undone to cure him as soon as possible. Yet, despite all the care everyone took, nothing did Rich-Craft any good. On the contrary, his wounds seemed to grow worse every day, and it appeared that he would be suffering from them for a long time.

After escaping from this terrible danger, Finette returned safely to the castle, where she had left her sisters, but it was not long before she was faced with new troubles. Each of her sisters gave birth to a son, and Finette was very embarrassed by such a predicament. However, her courage did not abate, and her desire to conceal the shame of her sisters made her determined to expose herself to danger once more, no matter how bad it might be. To accomplish her plan, she took every precaution that prudence could suggest. She disguised herself as a man and put the children of her sisters into boxes in which she made little holes so they could breathe. Then she took these boxes and others and went on horseback to the capital of the gentle king, where Rich-Craft was then dwelling.

When Finette entered the city, she learned how generously Bel-a-Voir was paying for the medicine given to his brother. Such generosity had attracted all the charlatans in Europe to this court. At that time, there were

2. Roman general and statesman regarded as a model of heroic endurance. Marcus Atilius Regulus flourished during the third century B.C.E. Captured by the Carthaginians during the Punic Wars, he was tortured to death.

a great many adventures without jobs or talent who pretended to be remarkable men endowed by heaven to cure all sorts of maladies. These men, whose whole science consisted of bold deceit, found great credence among the people because they knew how to create an impression by their outward appearance and by the bizarre names they assumed. Such doctors never stay in the place where they were born, and the benefit of coming from a distant place is often considered to be something positive by the common people.

The ingenious princess, who knew all this, gave herself a very strange name and let it be known that the Chevalier Sanatio had arrived with marvelous secrets to cure all sorts of wounds, no matter how dangerous and infected. Bel-a-Voir immediately sent for this supposed chevalier, and Finette came with all the airs of one of the best doctors in the world and said five or six words in a cavalier way. She was perfect. At the same time, the princess was surprised by the good looks and pleasant manners of Bel-a-Voir, and after conversing with him some time with regard to Rich-Craft's wounds, she told him she would go and fetch a bottle with some extraordinary liquid, and in the meantime, she would leave two boxes she had brought there that contained some excellent ointments and were very appropriate for the wounded prince. After the supposed physician left and did not return, everyone began to feel very anxious. At last, as they were going to send for him, they heard the crying of young infants in Rich-Craft's room. This surprised everybody, for it had not seemed that children were there. However, they listened attentively, and they found that the cries came from the doctor's boxes. The noise was, in fact, caused by Finette's little nephews. The princess had given them a great deal to eat before she came to the palace, but since they had now been there a long time, they wanted more and expressed their needs by singing a doleful tune. Someone opened the boxes, and the people were greatly surprised to find two pretty babes in them. Rich-Craft realized immediately that Finette had played a new trick on him and threw himself into a rage. His maladies got worse because of this, and the people saw that they would not be able to prevent his death.

Bel-a-Voir was overcome with sorrow, but Rich-Craft, treacherous to his last breath, thought he could exploit his brother's affection.

"You've always loved me, prince," he said, "and you're now lamenting my loss. I can have no greater proof of your love for me. It's true I'm dying, but if you've ever really cared for me, I hope you'll grant me one thing that I'm going to ask of you."

Bel-a-Voir, who found himself incapable of refusing anything to a brother in such a condition, gave him his most solemn oath that he would grant him whatever he desired.

As soon as he heard this, Rich-Craft embraced his brother and said to him, "Now I shall die contented since I'll be revenged. After I die, I want you to marry Finette. You'll undoubtedly obtain this wicked princess for your wife, and the moment she's in your power, I want you to plunge your dagger into her heart."

Bel-a-Voir trembled with horror at these words and repented the imprudence of his oath. But now was not the time to retract it. He did not want his despair to be noticed by his brother, who died soon after. The gentle king was tremendously affected by his death. His subjects, however, were far from regretting Rich-Craft's death, and they were extremely glad that his death guaranteed the succession of the crown for Bel-a-Voir, whom everyone considered worthy of that position.

Once again, Finette had returned safely to her sisters, and soon thereafter, she heard of Rich-Craft's death. Then, some time later, news reached the three princesses that the king their father had returned home. He rushed to the tower, and his first wish was to see the distaffs. Nonchalante went and brought the distaff that belonged to Finette and showed it to the king. Then after making a very low curtsy, she returned it to the place from where she had taken it. Babbler did the same, and Finette, in her turn, brought out her distaff, but the king was suspicious and wanted to see them all together. No one could show hers except Finette, and the king fell into such a rage against his two eldest daughters that he immediately sent them away to the fairy who had given him the distaffs, asking her to keep his daughters with her as long as they lived and to punish them the way they deserved to be.

To begin the punishment of these princesses, the fairy led them into a gallery of her enchanted castle, where she had ordered the history of a vast number of illustrious women to be painted who had made themselves famous by leading busy and virtuous lives. Due to the wonderful effects of fairy art, all these figures could move and were in motion from morning until night. Trophies and emblems in honor of these virtuous ladies could be seen everywhere, and it was tremendously mortifying for the two sisters to compare the triumph of these heroines with the despicable situation to which their unfortunate imprudence had reduced them. To complete their grief, the fairy told them very gravely that, if they had occupied themselves like those they saw in the pictures, they would not have gone astray in such an unworthy way that had brought about their fall. She told them that idleness was the mother of all vice and the source of all their misery. Finally, the fairy added that to prevent them from ever falling into the same bad habits again and to make up for the time they had lost, she was going to occupy them in a good way. In effect, she obliged the princesses to employ themselves in work that was most coarse and mean. Without any regard for their complexion, she sent them to gather peas in the garden and to pull out the weeds. Nonchalante could not help but fall into despair at leading a life that did not at all correspond to her inclinations, and she soon died from sorrow and exhaustion. Babbler, some time after, found a way to escape from the fairy's castle by night, broke her skull against a tree and died in the arms of some peasants.

Finette's good nature caused her to grieve a great deal over the fate of her sisters, and in the midst of her sorrow, she was informed that Prince Bel-a-Voir had requested her hand in marriage from the king her father, who consented without notifying her, for in those days the inclination of the partners was the last thing one considered in arranging marriages. Finette trembled at the news. She had good reason to fear that the hatred that Rich-Craft had felt toward her might have infected the heart of a brother, who was quite dear to him, and she was worried that this young prince only sought to victimize her for her brother's sake. Since she was so concerned about this, the princess went to consult the wise fairy, who appreciated her fine qualities in the same way she had despised Nonchalante's and Babbler's bad habits.

The fairy would reveal nothing to Finette and only remarked, "Princess, you're wise and prudent. Up to now you've taken the proper precautions with regard to your conduct, and that has enabled you to bear in mind that distrust is the mother of security. Remember to keep thinking seriously about the importance of this maxim, and you'll eventually be happy without needing the help of my art."

Since she was not able to get anything more out of the fairy, Finette returned to the palace extremely upset. Some days later she was married by an ambassador in the name of Prince Bel-a-Voir, and she was conducted to her spouse in a magnificent equipage. After she crossed the border, she was greeted by the people in the first two cities of King Gentle's realm in the same manner, and in the third city she met Bel-a-Voir, who had been ordered by his father to go and welcome her. Everybody was surprised to see the prince's sadness at the approach of a marriage for which he had shown such a great zeal. Indeed, the king had to reprimand him and send him to meet the princess against his inclinations.

When Bel-a-Voir saw her; he was struck by her charms, but he complimented her in such a confused manner that the courtiers, who knew how witty and gallant this prince was, believed that he had been so strongly moved by being in love that he had lost his presence of mind. The entire city shouted for joy, and there were concerts and fireworks everywhere. After a magnificent supper, preparations were made for conducting the royal couple to their apartment.

Finette, who kept thinking about the maxim which the fairy had revived in her mind, had a plan in her head. She won over one of the women, who had the key of the closet belonging to the apartment that was designated for her, and she privately gave orders to that woman to carry some straw, a bladder, some sheep's blood, and the entrails of some animals that had been prepared for supper into that closet. Then the princess used some pretext to go into that closet and made a figure out of the straw into which she put the entrails and the bladder full of blood. Then she dressed it up in a woman's nightclothes. After she had finished making this pretty dummy, she rejoined her company, and some time later, she and her husband were conducted to their apartment. When they had allowed as much time at the dressing table as was necessary, the ladies of honor took away the torches and retired. Finette immediately placed the straw dummy in the bed and went and hid herself in a corner of the room.

After heaving two or three deep sighs, the prince now approached the bed, drew his sword, and ran it through the body of the supposed Finette. All at once he saw the blood trickle out, and the straw body did not move.

"What have I done?" Bel-a-Voir exclaimed. "What! After so many cruel struggles—after having weighed everything carefully in my mind whether I should keep my word at the expense of a dreadful crime, I've taken the life of a charming princess whom I was born to love! Her charms captivated me the moment I saw her, and yet I didn't have the strength to free

The Discreet Princess. From *Les Contes de Perrault*, ca. 1890.

myself from an oath, which a brother, possessed by fury, had exacted from me by surprising me in an insidious way. Ah, heavens! How could anyone think of punishing a woman for having too much virtue? Well, Rich-Craft, I've satisfied your unjust vengeance, but now I'll revenge Finette by my own death. Yes, beautiful princess, this same sword shall—"

As he was saying these words, Finette heard the prince looking for his sword. He had dropped it in the excitement and now searched for it to thrust through his body. But since she did not want him to commit such a foolish act, she cried out, "My prince, I'm not dead! Your good heart made me anticipate your repentance, and I saved you from committing a crime by playing a trick that was not meant to harm you."

She then told Bel-a-Voir about the foresight she had had in regard to the straw figure. The prince was ecstatic to find Finette alive and admired the prudence she had shown on all occasions and expressed his gratitude to her for preventing him from committing a crime which he could not think about without horror. He could not understand how he could have been so weak and why he had not sooner discovered the futility of those wicked oaths which had been exacted from him by a trick.

However, if Finette had not always been convinced that distrust is the mother of security, she would have been killed, and her death would have caused that of Bel-a-Voir. Then afterward, people would have discussed the prince's strange emotions at their leisure.

Long live prudence and presence of mind! They saved this couple from the most dreadful of misfortunes in order to provide them with the most lovely destiny in the world. The prince and princess always retained the greatest tenderness for each other and spent a long succession of beautiful days in honor and happiness that would be difficult to describe.

Rewards and Punishments for Good and Bad Girls

This cycle of tales is often referred to as "The Kind and the Unkind Girls," and it was widespread in both the oral and the literary tradition throughout the world from the fifteenth century on, largely because of its simple moral statement. The dissemination of the tale and its various folklore versions have been studied meticulously in Warren E. Roberts's *The Tale of the Kind and Unkind Girls* (1994). One of the earliest literary versions can be found in George Peele's play *The Old Wives' Tale* (ca. 1591–94). Almost all the tales follow the same plot: a good-natured, beautiful stepsister is compelled, like Cinderella, to do all the work around the house, and at one point she loses a spindle or some article necessary for her household chores. In order to retrieve this object, she descends into a well or a hole and finds herself in a strange land. During her journey in this realm, she meets three animals, things, or trees, or a mix of three, and kindly helps them. Because she behaves so well in this realm, she is rewarded by an old woman, a witch, fairies, or a powerful spirit. Sometimes she is offered a small or large box, or asked to leave through a dingy or magnificent door. She always chooses the more humble "gift." The good girl returns home, and when she speaks, jewels and precious stones fall from her lips, or she finds that the box is filled with gold. The stepmother sends her ugly, nasty daughter to this same realm, but because she is unkind, she returns and spits out vipers and toads, or she finds a box filled with snakes. Sometimes the good girl finds a husband, who comes upon her by chance and is attracted by her beauty and, of course, by the jewels that she produces. The bad girl is generally punished by death or madness. In some variants, the good girl does not descend into another world. Rather, she treats an old haggard woman kindly at a well, and her stepsister does just the opposite. Basile's tale was undoubtedly based on an oral version, and it is clear that Mlle Lhéritier was familiar with his tale, which she made into a much more didactic narrative, as she was wont to do. Since she knew Perrault, there is a good chance that her tale influenced his "The Fairies" to a certain degree. Mme Leprince de Beaumont was certainly aware of their works by the time she wrote "Aurore and Aimée," and while extolling the virtues of a young woman, she demonstrated how the virtues were to be used to serve men. Most important, her didactic story was one of the first literary fairy tales created specifically for children. Another important version that predated the Grimms' "Mother Holle" was Benedikte Naubert's "Der kurze Mantel" ("The Cloak") in *Volksmährchen der Deutschen* (1789). There were numerous folk- and fairy tales about friendly and unfriendly fairies after the Grimms published their *Kinder- und Hausmärchen* in Germany, and the most popular and didactic was Ludwig Bechstein's "Die Goldmaria und die Pechmaria" ("The Gold Maria and the Coal Maria") in *Deutsches Märchenbuch* (1845).

GIAMBATTISTA BASILE

The Three Fairies†

In the village of Marcianise[1] there was a widow called Caradonia, who was envy's own mother, and whenever she saw something good happen to a neighbor, she would feel a lump in her throat. Indeed, she could not hear about someone else's good luck without becoming disturbed. If she saw anyone happy, woman or man, she would burst out sobbing.

This woman had a daughter called Grannizia, who was the quintessence of ugliness, the better part of a sea monster, the very flower of rotten casks. She had a headful of lice, ruffled hair, plucked temples, a smashed forehead, swollen eyes, a warty nose, decayed teeth, a mouth like a fish, a beard like a goat, the throat of a magpie, breasts like bags, a crooked back, arms like fishing reels, bowed legs, and ankles like cauliflowers. In short, from head to toe she was a beautiful specimen of deformity, a pest, and an ugly brute. To top it all off, she was the size of a dwarf, a tiny creature, a pigmy. But despite all this, the cockroach appeared beautiful to her mother.

Now it so happened that the good widow married a certain Micco Antuono, a very rich landowner of Panecuocolo,[2] who had twice been the magistrate and mayor of this town. He was greatly admired by the townspeople, who depended on him a great deal. Micco Antuono also had a daughter, whose name was Cicella, and she was the most marvelous and beautiful creature that you could possibly find in this world. She had smiling and captivating eyes, tempting lips that sent everyone into ecstasy, and a throat of milky white that caused convulsions. In short, she was charming, witty, lively, and appetizing. She exhibited so many lovely wiles, manners, gestures, politenesses, and ways of talking that one's heart would burst its rib cage just at the sight of her. But what's the use of all this babble? It's enough to say that she seemed drawn by a painter's brush. She was perfect.

But when Caradonia realized that, compared to Cicella, her daughter seemed like a kitchen rag next to the very best velvet cushion, the bottom of a greasy pot next to a Venetian mirror, or a harpy next to Fata Morgana,[3] she began to look askance at Cicella and was surly with her. Nor did things end here, for she spit out the abscess born in her heart and was no longer able to hold on to the umbilical cord of envy. As she began to let loose, she let loose openly and tormented the poor girl. She dressed her daughter

† Giambattista Basile, "The Three Fairies"—"Le tre fate" (1634), *Decimo passatempo della terza giornata* in *Lo cunto de li cunti overo Lo trattenemiento de peccerille*, De Gian Alessio Abbattutis, 5 vols. (Naples: Ottavio Beltrano, 1634–36).

1. A village belonging to the hamlet of Capua, now in the district of Caserta.
2. A village near Casoria that has had various names: Cuculum, Panicocoli, and, more recently, Villarica. The names were changed by the inhabitants of the village because of the association of *cuocolo* with the meaning "arrogance."
3. The most famous of the Italian fairies or *fata*; known in English as Morgan Le Fay. She is a sorceress in Ludovico Ariosto's *Orlando furioso* (1532), and in Italian folklore she also appears as an underwater enchantress.

in a skirt of embroidered serge and in a silk bodice and her stepdaughter in the worst rags and tatters in the house. She gave her daughter white bread from a bakery, and her stepdaughter, stale and hard crusts. She kept her daughter like the Savior's vase[4] and made her stepdaughter run all over the house, up and down, sweeping the floors clean, wiping the dishes, making the beds, washing the clothes, feeding the pigs, looking after the donkey, and emptying the night chamber. And the good girl did all these things diligently and efficiently, and to please her stepmother, she worked as fast she could and did not spare herself.

But as luck would have it, one day when the girl went to throw out the garbage outside the house, she went to a steep precipice, where she accidentally dropped the entire basket down the side and looked all around to see how she might recover it. All of a sudden—what was it? what was it?—she saw a monstrous figure and could not tell whether it was Aesop in person[5] or the devil himself. Actually, it was an ogre with coal-black hair like the bristles of a wild boar that dropped all the way down to his feet. He had a rugged temple in which every wrinkle seemed to have been dug by a plough. He had thick hairy eyebrows, and his eyes were sunken in their sockets and full of some kind of stuff so that they looked like dirty shops beneath the two large awnings of the eyelids. Two large tusks stuck out of his mouth, which was distorted and full of drivel. His chest was covered with warts in a forest of hair that could have filled a mattress. To top it all off, he had a hunchback, a great belly, thin legs, and crooked feet, and anyone who saw him would cringe with fright.

Despite the fact that this evil spirit took Cicella's breath away, she summoned her courage and said, "My good man, if you could help me get that basket which I've dropped, may you become rich."

And the ogre replied, "Climb down, my girl, and you will get it."

So the brave girl began descending the precipice by holding on to the roots tightly and grabbing the stones until she reached the bottom, where she found something incredible—three fairies, one more beautiful than the next. Their hair was spun with gold. Their faces glistened like the full moon. Their eyes spoke oceans of words. Their lips bespoke topics to be filled with sweet kisses. What more? Their throats were soft; their breasts, tender; their hands, smooth; their feet, delicate. And grace provided the gilded frame for such beauty.

It is difficult to describe the affection and politeness with which Cicella was welcomed. The fairies took her hand and led her to a subterranean house fit for a king. There they seated her on Turkish carpets and smooth velvet cushions stuffed with chunks of yarn. One after the other, the fairies placed their heads in her lap and asked her to comb their hair, and while she delicately did this work with a glistening comb of buffalo horn, each one of the fairies asked, "Lovely girl, what do you find in my little head?"

And she politely responded, "I'm finding nits and lice and pearls and rubies."

4. Reference to the cup of the Last Supper, which was first kept at Jerusalem and then at Valenza in Spain.
5. Greek slave who allegedly created the fables first recorded by Demetrius Phalareus in the fourth century B.C.E. Aesop was said to be a hunchback and extremely ugly.

The good manners of Cicella pleased the fairies very much, and after these illustrious women rearranged their loose hair, they took her with them hand in hand and showed her all the magnificent and beautiful things in their enchanted palace. There were chests with marvelous inlays of chestnut wood and hornbeam and with jeweled lids of horse leather and pewter corners. There were walnut tables that glistened so much you could see your face in them, shelves with sparkling dishes, curtains with green flowers painted on them, leather chairs with backs, and many other things so splendid that anyone else would have been bedazzled on seeing them. But Cicella regarded them as if they simply belonged there and admired the splendor of the house without gasping and exclaiming that it was a miracle.

Finally, they took her into a wardrobe entirely filled with rich clothes, and they showed her petticoats made from Spanish cloth, dresses with puffed velvet sleeves lined with gold, covers from Catalonia garnished with enameled jewels, vests with stripes of taffeta, crowns of natural flowers and ribbons, oak leaves, shells, half moons, tongues of serpents, necklaces with stones of turquoise and white glass, ears of corn, lilies and feathers to wear on one's head, enamel rubies inlaid with silver, and a thousand other things to wear around the neck, and they told the girl to choose something to her liking and to take as much as she wanted from those things.

But Cicella was as humble as oil and did not take anything valuable. Instead, she selected a gown that was not worth more than three pennies, and when the fairies saw this, they asked, "Which door do you want to use as your exit, sweet girl?"

Cicella curtsied so low that she almost soiled herself on the ground, and then she said, "It's enough for me if I can leave through the stable door."

So the fairies embraced her and gave her a thousand kisses. Then they clothed her in a splendid dress completely embroidered with gold. They fixed her hair in the Scotch fashion, decorated the tresses of her hair with ribbons and trinkets, and her hair looked like a meadow of flowers with a chignon in the form of a colorful parrot's crown and dangling curls. Then they accompanied her to the door, which had a massive gold frame encrusted with diamonds, and they said, "Go, dear Cicella, we hope to see you marry well! Go, and when you pass through this door, raise your eyes, and see what's above."

After the girl paid her respects, she left, and when she was under the arch of the door, she looked up, and a marvelous thing happened: a golden star fell on her head, and thus, like a horse with a neat and sparkling star on its forehead, she returned to her stepmother and told her everything that had happened from the beginning to the end. But this tale was like a beating to such an envious woman, and the stepmother became so perturbed that she immediately made Cicella show her the place where she had met the fairies. Then she sent her fish-faced daughter off to them. When the ugly girl arrived at the enchanted place and found those three gems of fairies, they asked her right away to inspect their hair and tell them what she found.

"Lice as big as chickpeas," she replied, "and nits by the spoonful."

The fairies were angered and revolted by the vulgar manners of the ugly peasant girl, and they realized that they were in for a bad day, but they pretended not to be disturbed. So they took her to the room with all the luxurious items and told her to take the best thing she saw. When Grannizia saw that she was offered a finger, she took the whole hand and grabbed the most beautiful dress in the wardrobe.

When the fairies saw that things were going from bad to worse, they remained upset. Nevertheless, they wanted to see how far the girl would go and said to her, "Which exit would you like to use, beautiful girl?"

And, with a brazen face, she said, "Only the best will do."

Seeing the presumption of this vile thing, they did not give her even a pinch of salt and sent her on her way.

"When you pass beneath the stable door," they said, "look up at the sky and watch what happens to you."

So Grannizia left and waded through the middle of manure, and when she raised her head, an ass's testicle fell on her forehead and stuck to her skin so that it looked like a craving that her mother had experienced when she had been pregnant.

Slowly but surely Grannizia made it back home. As soon as her mother saw her, her mouth foamed like a mad dog, and she had Cicella undress, gave her rags to wear, and sent her to take care of the pigs, while she dressed her own daughter in Cicella's fine clothes. In the meantime, Cicella, with great calm and the patience of an Orlando,[6] put up with this miserable life. Oh cruelty, which might move the stones of the street! How could those lips worthy to pronounce words of love be forced to sound the trumpet and cry, "Here, piggy, piggy! Here ducky wucky!" How could that beauty worthy to be placed among elegant suitors be placed among swine? How could that hand worthy of bridling a hundred souls be forced to drive a hundred sows with a stick? May that person have a thousand accidents for sending that poor girl into the accidental woods where, under the roof of the shadow of the woods, fear and silence took refuge from the sun.

Now it so happened that heaven, which knocks down the presumptuous and raises the humble, sent a nobleman of great stature to this region. His name was Cuosemo, and when he saw a jewel in the mud, a Phoenix among the swine, and a beautiful sun among the broken clouds of those rags, he became infatuated with her. So he immediately inquired where she came from and where she lived, and without losing any time, he spoke with the stepmother and asked to marry Cicella, promising to give her thousands of gold coins as a dowry.

Caradonia did not blink an eye and accepted the offer, thinking of her own daughter. Then she told him to return in the evening because she wanted to invite her relatives to the wedding. Cuosemo went away very happy, and every hour seemed to him to be a thousand years while he waited for the sun to go to sleep in the bed of silver prepared for him by the river of India so that he, in turn, could go to sleep with that other sun who was scorching his heart. In the meantime, Caradonia had tossed Ci-

6. Reference to the hero of Ludovico Ariosto's *Orlando furioso* (1532).

cella into a barrel and had sealed her inside with the intention of scalding her to death. Since she had already left the pigs, she now wanted to cook her like a pig in hot water.

Now as night began to fall and it became as dark as the snout of a wolf, Cuosemo, whose heart had been palpitating and who had been dying to squeeze his dearly beloved in his arms with great passion, set off happily toward her home. Along the way he said to himself, "This is the right moment to go and slice the tree that love has planted in the middle of my breast so I can take out and enjoy the sweet manna. This is the right moment to dig up the treasure that Fortune has promised me. There's no time to lose, Cuosemo. When you've been promised a good sow, run quickly with a rope. Oh night, oh happy night, oh friend of lovers, oh body and soul, oh ladle and spoon, oh love, run, run at breakneck speed so that, under the cover of your shadows, I can seek refuge from the flames that are consuming me!"

Soon after uttering these words, he arrived at Caradonia's house and found Grannizia in the place of Cicella, an owl in the place of a goldfinch, a weed in the place of a budding rose. Although she had been dressed in Cicella's clothes and one might have said, "Dressed up like Ceppon, he will seem like a baron," she still looked like a cockroach in a cloth of gold. None of the rouge, the makeup, the daubing, and the grooming of the mother had succeeded in removing the scurvy from her head, the sties from her eyes, the freckles from her face, the cavities from her teeth, the warts from her throat, the pimples from her breasts, the crud from her heels, and the stench that one could smell a mile away.

When the bridegroom saw this monstrosity, he was at a loss to grasp what had happened, and he reeled backward as if he had seen the devil himself. "Am I awake, or am I seeing things upside down?" he said to himself. "Am I myself or somebody else? What are you seeing, poor Cuosemo? Have you shit in your pants? This is not the face that I saw this morning and that took my breath away. This is not the picture that was stamped on my heart! What can this be, oh Fortune? Where oh where is that beauty who caught me by her hook? Where is the beauty that drew me like a windlass?[7] Where is the beauty that pierced my heart like an arrow? I know that neither women nor cloth should be chosen by candlelight, but I chose this one in broad daylight! Alas! The gold of this morning has revealed itself to be copper, and the diamonds are glass. The beard has been reduced to a whisker!"

Cuosemo muttered and mumbled these and other words between his teeth. Nevertheless, under the circumstances, he was compelled to give a kiss to Grannizia, but it was if he were kissing a decrepit vase. He approached her and retreated three times before he put his lips to the mouth of his wife. As he stood by her side, it seemed to him that he was at the seaside of Chiaia[8] in the evening, when those worthy women bring their

---

7. A mechanical device working on the principle of the wheel and axle; used for various purposes, as for raising a bucket from a well or weighing the anchor on board ship.
8. A district of Naples where women carried excrement to the sea in the evening because the drains and sewers did not function properly. The stench was terrible, and the evening hours were called the "dumping hours."

tributes to the sea, and these tributes are the very opposite of the perfumes of Arabia. However, since the sky dyed his white beard black to make himself seem younger, and since he was far from his land, Cuosemo was obliged to take his wife to a house not far from the borders of Panecuocolo to spend the night. Once there he spread a sack over two barrels and went to sleep with his wife.

But who can describe the terrible night that the two passed together? Although it was a summer night and did not last longer than eight hours, it seemed to them the longest night of winter. On one side, the bride was restless. She spat, coughed, tossed, and gave a few kicks. At one point, she sighed and made signs that she wanted to collect the rent of her house. But Cuosemo pretended to snore and retreated to the far side of the bed so that he would not have to touch Grannizia. However, he fell out of his sack and into the chamberpot, and everything ended in stench and shame. Oh, how many times did the bridegroom curse the sun's dead[9] for not speeding up the time to pull him out of this mess! How desperately did he implore night to break her neck, and the stars to vanish so that dawn would arrive and he could get up from the side of his wretched bride!

As soon as dawn did indeed arrive to chase out the chickens and awake the rooster, he jumped out of bed and quickly jumped into his pants so he could run back to Caradonia's house to return his daughter and pay her for the taste of the pudding with a broom handle. When he entered the house, he did not find her because she had gone to fetch wood for the fire that she wanted to make to boil her stepdaughter, who was still sealed in the tomb of Bacchus instead of reclining in the cradle of Cupid as she deserved.

Cuosemo searched all over for Caradonia, and when he did not find her, he yelled, "Hey, where are you?"

To his surprise, a tabby cat, sleeping by the hearth, began to meow and reply: "Meow! Meow! Your wife is sealed in that barrel. Meow!"

Cuosemo approached the barrel and heard a low, muffled groan. Therefore, he seized an ax near the fireplace and chopped open the barrel. The opening of the barrel was like the opening of the curtain of a stage when a goddess enters to deliver the prologue. I don't know how Cuosemo managed not to drop dead on the spot when he saw such splendor. Indeed, as soon as he gazed at her, he remained paralyzed for a long time as if he had just seen the devil. Then he came to himself and ran to embrace her. "Who put you in this horrible place, oh jewel of my heart?" he asked. "Who hid you from me, oh hope of my life? What is this? How is this possible, a splendid dove in a cage of hoops? How is it that I had a griffin at my side? What happened? Tell me, my sweet one. Cheer up! Pour out your heart to me!"

Cicella responded by telling him all that had happened without leaving out a single thing: she recalled everything that she had suffered in the

---

9. According to Neapolitan custom and perhaps other Italian customs, people did not direct a curse against the person they wished to offend but against that person's next of kin (mother, sister, brother, etc.) and against those dead people whose memory the person cherished.

house since the day her stepmother had set foot in it until the moment that Bacchus had entombed her in that barrel to take her life. After Cuosemo heard all this, he had her crouch down and hide behind the door, and when he had put the barrel together again, he went and fetched Grannizia. Then he stuck her into the barrel and said to her, "Stay inside a while. I want to weave a magic spell to keep the evil spirits from touching you."

After saying this, he sealed the barrel tightly, embraced his wife, put her on a horse, and carried her off to Pascarola, which was his country. In the meantime, Caradonia returned with a huge bundle of wood, made a great fire, and placed a large cauldron of water on it. As soon as the water began to boil, she poured it through a hole in the barrel and completely scalded her daughter, who gnashed her teeth as if she had eaten Sardinian herbs,[1] and her skin peeled off her just like a snake shedding its skin. When it seemed to Caradonia that Cicella had been bathed from head to toe, she broke open the barrel and saw—Oh, what a sight!—her own daughter cooked by a cruel mother. Immediately, Caradonia began tearing her hair, scratching her face, beating her breast, wringing her hands, hitting her head against a wall, and stamping on the ground. She made such a racket and so much noise that the entire village ran to see her. But she ranted and raved like a madwoman, and nobody could find words to console her and calm her down. All of a sudden she ran to a well and—*splash!*—she plunged headfirst into it and broke her neck, showing how true the proverb is:

Whoever spits at heaven will get splattered back in his face.

MARIE-JEANNE LHÉRITIER

The Enchantments of Eloquence; or, The Effects of Sweetness†

During the time when there were fairies, ogres, spirits, goblins, and other phantoms of this kind in France—it is difficult to mark the specific time, but that does not matter—there was a nobleman of great esteem who passionately loved his wife. (And this is the reason again why I cannot guess the time period.) His wife did not love him any less. He was a good man who deserved her love. They lived together happy enough for fifteen or sixteen years, but death separated them. The lady died, and she left only one daughter behind her. She had been very beautiful, and her daughter was no less beautiful and had a thousand pleasant traits ever since her birth. Indeed, her skin was so lily white and so dazzling that she was called Blanche.

---

1. Considered bitter.
† Marie-Jeanne Lhéritier, "The Enchantments of Eloquence; or, The Effects of Sweetness"—"Les enchantements de l'éloquence; ou, Les effets de la douceur," in *Oeuvres meslées* (Paris: J. Guignard, 1696).

Her mother had not been very wealthy, but her father had inherited and acquired a good deal of money. But he did not have much when his wife died because his business affairs had taken a turn for the worse during his marriage. So his daughter saw herself reduced to nothing, for her dowry consisted only of her whiteness and her beauty. But ordinary things are not a great help when one is looking to make an important match.

Blanche's father had been very tormented by his wife's death and felt he could not be consoled until he wed again. Since his daughter was still too young to have a husband, he decided that he should think about himself first, and he gave serious thought about his choice. The bad state of his business made him lean toward a rich marriage. Therefore, he soon became attached to a widow who was neither beautiful nor young, but very wealthy. This woman had only one daughter, and her husband had been a financier who had known all the tricks of the trade and had used them to become extremely rich. To be sure they came from honorable bourgeois families, and they had never been divided by questions of social rank. Indeed, the mother had taken great care to conserve the customs and the manners of the family into which she had been born and had given her daughter a similar education to the one that she had received. Hence, her daughter had a rough and strong character, and her manners were unpolished. In short, mother and daughter were the most common and most rustic creatures in that society. Moreover, it was easy to discern that they were extremely ambitious, but badly brought up, and they had ideas so ridiculous that they would do a hundred extravagant things where one could perceive mistakes inspired by their pompous behavior and vanity.

Given their dispositions, it is easy to judge that Blanche's father, who had the title of marquis, was received by the widow with joy, for she desired to have a grand name and agreed to marry him within a few days. Her new husband, who had only wanted the best in marrying this woman, realized with great dismay, from the very first day of his marriage, that the marquise had many exhausting faults. But since he was a man who preferred to keep the peace with everyone and also had a character that allowed himself to be governed by a woman just like her, he lived very well with her provided that he remained under her foot, never contradicted her, and allowed her to have absolute power in all their affairs. He consoled himself for her unpleasant moods with the sweet things that her wealth had procured for him. He tolerated her outbursts of anger philosophically, and when he saw that she was about to pout and cry, he would withdraw into his study, where he loved to read.

Only Blanche was to be pitied in all ways. Her stepmother had an incredible aversion toward her and felt great despair when she saw that Blanche's beauty made the deformity of her daughter appear even worse and caused her to be scorned by everyone. Indeed, Alix (this was the name of the daughter of the financier) was just as terribly ugly as she was boorish. Despite this, her mother loved her to the point of idolatry and sacrificed everything just to make her content. To make matters worse, Alix hated Blanche a hundred times more than her mother did. Therefore, she employed all the means imaginable to cause her grief. Her mother wanted to place Blanche in a convent, but Alix, who always wanted to see Blanche the victim of her tricks, prevented her mother from pursuing this plan. Indeed, she feared that when Blanche was no longer in their view, some obliging friend might reveal Blanche's merits and bring about a splendid marriage for her, something which Alix feared more than death.

Thus it was decided that Blanche was to remain in their home and that she was never to visit anyone or receive visits. They took precautions to conceal her from all the honorable people who came to the house, and in order to cover her beauty she was obliged to occupy herself by cleaning rooms and working in the kitchen. It is useless to recount all the astonishing details that concern Blanche's tenderness except to say that she displayed an admirable docile character, very rare in such a beautiful person. She had a good nature and was willing to do all kinds of disagreeable chores that her stepmother gave to her. Blanche added a luster to everything that she touched, and nobody could starch collars and arrange high collars the way she could. She performed all these things with such agility that I am sure if she lived in our times, she would know perfectly well how to smooth all the folds in dresses and would attract a large group of ladies who are always in mortal fear that their dresses are not in their proper forms no matter how much care they have given to making certain that their folds are correct. Blanche would have given complete symmetry to this ornament so useful to the beautiful women in the country of pygmies, and she would have outdone Mme D., with whom no coquette would dare to compete, because she had the fortunate talent of knowing how to groom herself the very best way and to make the finest headdresses in the universe. This superb ability and her good nature would attract a great number of ladies because she would do part of their grooming, and she would do their hair the way she did her own. But let us drop these remarks and continue our story.

Not only did the stepmother and Alix give her a thousand exhausting jobs, but they also treated her with such negligence that she would have become entirely revolting if she had not been naturally disposed to being clean and dressing properly. Thus, despite all their efforts to make her appear deformed by giving her clothes that did not fit and straightening her hair, she still appeared as beautiful as Eros. Even though Alix was completely covered with gold and jewels and had a carefully groomed hairstyle, she scared all the people who saw her because the excess of her cosmetics made her more ugly and gave her a bad appearance.

Still, she could not stay at home. She was incessantly seen taking promenades, at the theater, and at balls. She could not stop showing off her pomp at all these places. But if she found pleasure by attracting the looks of some of the bourgeois people, she was more mortified to hear the pages or the musketeers who continually made some piquant remarks that revealed the truth behind her back. During that time there were many musketeers, young officers, and other madcap fellows who had the ridiculous habit of coming and watching the women who appeared near them and making a thousand impertinent remarks in a loud voice if they did not find the ladies as beautiful as their taste demanded. Therefore, one can judge how these flippant men exercised their fine talents by making piercing jests when they saw the repulsive figure of Alix. But what one cannot easily imagine is that she took revenge on Blanche for the insults that she received. Thinking that, if there were no beautiful women in the world, her ugliness would not be exposed to the same scorn, she increased her aversion toward lovely Blanche and pushed her mother to cause her step-daughter more grief.

Despite the natural sweetness of Blanche, all this bad treatment made her so bitter that she intended to leave the house no matter what price she had to pay. But since she detested making scenes, and since she loved her father so much and hoped to be able to find some way to escape her slavery with decorum, she lost the determination to leave and did not want to cause trouble. So once again she summoned her patience, and her father, who loved her very much, but who did not have the resolve to oppose the boorish manner in which he saw his daughter treated, softened her sorrows by sharing them, praising her virtue, and consoling her by promising her that heaven would see to it that she would be happy one day. His consolation supported the constancy of Blanche during her trou-bled time. Since she was prohibited from participating in society and all sorts of amusements, she found a means to enjoy herself in her room by reading. She accumulated a good many novels. I do not know what kind they were, but she could not completely enjoy them as one might believe because she could only read at night. Her stepmother kept her busy the entire day. Even though she had to curtail her sleep in order to have time to read, it did not prevent her from relaxing with a good book, and when-ever she could find some time during the day, she would rush back to her room to continue reading.

Her stepmother, who observed her every move, became suspicious when she saw her go off by herself into her room, and she wanted to know what held such a powerful attraction for her there. So she surprised her one day as she was reading one of the most beautiful passages of a novel that was very well written and highly imaginative. The marquise should have been touched to view this innocent pleasure to which Blanche had been reduced. But since the marquise hardly knew how to read, she pounced on the book and tore it out of Blanche's hands. After she had read the title with a great deal of difficulty because it was a forbidding Greek name and she pronounced it poorly, she finally realized that it was a novel, and she began to kick up a strange fuss, when, fortunately for the poor girl, her father entered her room. Without giving her husband any time to speak, the stepmother cried out with all her might, "Well then, Monsieur Rasineux, with all your sweet talk about pedigree, see how you've raised this mutt of yours. I have just surprised her reading a book of love on the sly."

The marquis, who had a bit more courage on this day than he ordinarily had, responded to his wife after he had looked at the book: "Blanche knows very well how to enjoy herself with this reading. You have taken away all her pleasures. She cannot do better than to take advantage of whatever opening she has to expand her mind and to develop her manners. I am enchanted when I see girls of quality who occupy themselves by reading. If they apply themselves by doing this, they are not so much at a loss when it comes to making use of their leisure time. They do not run from one theater to another and from one gambling casino to another."

The marquise, who knew that her daughter was more fond of gambling than all other pleasures, thought that her husband meant to attack Alix by what he said. Therefore, she raised her voice and replied, "Truly, I am of the opinion that one should prevent ladies of quality, who have plenty of property, to amuse themselves by letting them get carried away by their imagination. That is perhaps good for common ladies who come from the ruined nobility and have to resort to these pleasures to find happiness. But as for those women who have much more money than those poor fools, they should be permitted to do as they see fit. Those damsels who do not have a penny only know how to keep house and always occupy themselves by doing this. If they want to read, then they should only read good books, not those that teach them bad things."

"One does not learn bad things," Blanche's father replied brusquely, "in the beautiful novels that I see my daughter reading." Indeed, he had a better taste than his daughter did, and he loved novels even more than she did. "On the contrary," he said, "one only finds great sentiments and beautiful examples in them. Vice is always punished, and virtue is always rewarded. One could even say that the reading of novels is better for very young people than that of history itself because history is always completely subjected to truth and sometimes presents images that are shocking for one's morals. History depicts men as they are, and the novels present men as they should be, and they engage readers to aspire toward perfection. At the very least one cannot deny that novels, when well-made, teach readers about the world and polite language. Blanche has already cultivated enough disposition to speak appropriately, and I hope that the reading of pleasant works will succeed in giving her the custom of always speaking like this."

The stepmother, who did not understand anything about her husband's philosophy and who was a sullen creature, could not abandon the severe attitude she had toward Blanche. Nor could she let the marquis complete his defense of novels because it was all Greek to her.

"Why are we looking for difficulties when there are none?" she replied. "My goodness gracious! So what if your daughter reads all by herself and it gives her pleasure and you, too? But if the chores of my household are not done punctually as they are supposed to be done, I'll know very well where to place the blame."

She left them, and this beautiful conversation was finished just like that. But Blanche's father was not mistaken. In a short time his beautiful daughter was able to add perfectly polite manners to her natural sweetness. One could not express oneself more pleasantly and more justly than she did, whether it was in dealing with intellectual matters or other affairs. Neither Alix nor her mother was envious of these advantages because they were too crude to understand the delicate nature of what she said. Therefore they only continued to be hurt by her agreeable qualities, and more than ever before they thought of ways that they could make her lose them.

During the beautiful summertime, the marquis and his entire family went to the country. It was there that Blanche's stepmother did all she could to torment her. She compelled her to do all the rustic chores, but despite the fact that she continually exposed Blanche to the sun, the color of her skin did not change, and she did not get sunburnt. Her stepmother became consumed by spite when she saw that nothing was capable of making her ugly, and her plans were always being spoiled. Finally, after all the means that she had tried had failed, she ordered her one day to go and search for some water that was to be used for cleaning the entire house.

The fountain was quite a distance from the house, but Blanche was accustomed to being patient, and she undertook this repugnant task as she usually did, with great equanimity: to go and fetch water was a task that was not any more humiliating for her than hundreds of others that she had been given. Besides, she saw other damsels doing this, for the customs of that time were very different for certain things than they are now, and their example gave her consolation, whether she wanted it or not, to be like these damsels of the country and to serve the needs of her father's house. But even though she was very patient, she had difficulty in keeping back the tears when she considered that the overwhelming work that was being imposed on her was being done to drive her to desperation and to destroy her. That was her sorrow. Nevertheless, she had the example of her neighbors, and she had also read somewhere that the daughters of kings during the time of Homer had done the washing, and that Achilles had also enjoyed cooking. So, Blanche went to fetch water without saying a word whenever water was needed in the house.

The fountain where she went to fetch the water was surrounded by the most beautiful landscape in the world, but it was dangerous to stay there too long because it was near a forest where the wolves came very often and ran about. Rumor had it that this was the reason that the stepmother loved so much to send her there. People had warned this amiable girl many times about the danger to which she was exposing herself. But even though the wolves did not do what she feared most, the warnings would have been useless for her because she could not make her stepmother listen to reason.

After having been there many times without finding beasts or people, she went to the fountain one day and saw a furious wild boar rushing toward her, even though it was not being pursued by anyone, and she was seized by fright. However, she was not so frightened that she did not think about saving herself. So she took flight, and she had just managed to reach some bushes when she felt a blow on her shoulder that knocked her to the ground. At the same time the wild boar passed right by her without hurting her and hid in the forest.

As she was making an effort to stand up despite the pain that she felt, she heard someone cry, "What! Beautiful child, it was you whom I injured and not the wild boar! How unhappy I am!"

Just then Blanche saw a young man who was clad in rich garments, and he approached her to help her get up. Even though the blood that she was losing made her pale, the hunter quickly realized that she possessed an extraordinary beauty, and he was touched by her sweet and engaging air despite the rustic nature of her clothes. He did not amuse himself by paying her a compliment. Rather, he was more judicious and thought about saving her right away. He tore his handkerchief, and even his tie, in order to try to stop the blood from flowing. The story has it that Blanche's eyes caused a wound in the hunter, but I have difficulty believing that this happened at the very first moment. If the chronicle tells the truth, then it is more likely that the hunter was just as easy to ignite as his weapon.

Some critics might say that the hunter could not have had a gun because there was no such thing as gunpowder or artillery during the time of fairies. I know some scrupulous scholars who never let a story finish without making a fuss about this anachronistic contradiction. But if I wanted to engage in an argument with a critic who is not very intelligent, I could tell him that the madames fairies could very well have performed one of their miracles. We shall soon see other marvels. They could have done one there, especially in favor of the hunter concerned here, who was the godson of Melusine, Logistille, and I don't know of how many other of the most celebrated of those obliging ladies.

However, it is true that the wound in Blanche's arm was not caused by a firearm, for a historian must always tell the truth. As far as I know, it was a dart or a javelin that the prince wanted to throw at the wild boar. . . . But I believe that I have not told you yet that the hunter was a prince. Well, then, it does not matter. I shall tell you as much as I know about his genealogy. However, at present we had better return to poor Blanche, whom we have left much too long in a state of semiconsciousness on the grass.

When she saw herself in the hands of such a doctor, she was frightened and confused, and this caused the hunter as much pain and suffering as she had. He gave her as much help as he could, and he was so overcome by admiration and agony that he could not speak a word. Finally, after he had put the best possible bandage on the beautiful girl's wound that he could and after having glanced at her face ten or twelve times to make sure that she was out of danger of fainting, the stranger said to her, "How extreme is my happiness and misfortune today! What happiness to have met such a charming person as you! What bad luck to be the cause of all your sufferings!"

"You are the innocent cause of my sufferings," Blanche responded. "Such a minor wound does not deserve to disturb your peace of mind."

"If you were only an ordinary girl," the stranger replied, "I would have also been upset for having wounded you. So, you must judge now that I am even more disturbed upon having found such an extraordinarily amiable person like you."

Without responding to such sweet talk, Blanche said, "I must say, my lord, that you are being much too generous. If I had been killed, it would not have been your fault. It would have been an act of destiny. Moreover, when a girl like me dies, it is not a great loss, and it should not cause you to get upset, for your life seems to me one of the fine lives that are useful to the state. If I may also say, people of my character will gladly sacrifice our useless days to maintain your precious days that are necessary for the public welfare in your capacity as nobleman, which I gather you are.

Please grant me the favor that I ask of you, my lord, and do not upset yourself about this incident. Indeed, I reproach myself for having caused you the sorrow that I have caused."

The stranger, who had taken Blanche for a peasant because of her clothes, or a maiden from the village at the most, was greatly surprised when he heard the manner in which she spoke. But he was even more touched by her sweetness than by her politeness. This young prince was naturally very forceful, and he felt that if someone, no matter how innocent, had injured him in the way that he had just hurt this beautiful girl, he would have had no regard for that person and would have revenged himself terribly against the person who had harmed him. The less he was capable of moderate behavior, the more he admired such moderation in other people. Thus, Blanche became the mistress of his soul, and this example shows the very truth of one of Quintilian's[1] maxims:

> If beauty is what sets off the alarm,
> it is sweetness that completes the charm.

The prince was so enchanted by this point that the flood of thoughts that overcame his imagination caused him to become silent for some time, and he only broke the silence to say some more gallant things to Blanche. Nevertheless, he did not reveal to her the great impression that she had made on his heart for fear of alarming such a beautiful person whom he realized was very modest in her responses as well as sweet and polite. In the meantime, the prince was very concerned that his people had not yet rejoined him. He had become lost during the hunt, and he was about to lose his patience because none of his attendants was nearby and he wanted to send someone quickly to find a coach to carry Blanche to wherever she wanted to go. He showed her how upset he was and told her what he wanted to do, but beautiful Blanche said, "My lord, I implore you with all my heart not to do this. If you have any consideration for me, which you have already shown, I assure you that you could not do me any greater pleasure than to leave me without thinking about me and not to speak to anyone about our encounter and my wound. I have the very best reasons in the world to ask you to do this, and I expect that I shall be able to return to my father's home with ease once I have rested somewhat."

After the prince made some kind protests, he said to her, "Well, then, if this is what you wish, I shall submit to your orders. But I cannot obey your command that will restrict me from thinking about you, my charming lady."

Upon uttering these words, the prince remounted his horse and left Blanche, who was astounded, weak, and confused by thoughts that sent her into a state of reverie. Finally, she stood up and set out on her way, and after some difficulty, she arrived at her father's house just at the moment when they were about to send someone to see what was keeping her at the fountain so long. Her stepmother began by making a fuss, but when Blanche told her that she had had an accident and was wounded by a

---

1. Marcus Fabius Quintilianus (35 C.E.–96 C.E.), Latin writer and teacher whose major work, *Institutio Oratoria* (ca. 95 C.E.), made a major contribution to educational theory.

wild boar, and that if a passerby had not helped her, she would have died on the spot, her stepmother was obliged to be silent. The marquis was very troubled to hear this news. He ran to his daughter, had her brought to her bed, and was resolved not to join his wife until Blanche had the proper care. Thus, this beautiful young lady was in good hands.

So now, let us return to the prince and his genealogy. He was related to Urgande, cousin of Magus, grand-nephew of Merlin, and was the godson of the wise Lirgandée and the most wise fairies, as I have already told you. With regard to the rest, it was not known which country would be his future realm because certain sources say that he was the son of the duke of Normandy. Others maintain that he was the duke of Brittany. Other memoirs record that it was the count of Poitiers who was his father. All of this incertitude is due to the fact that we have no idea where the fountain was located from which Blanche fetched the water. Actually, it does not matter much. All we have to know is that all the sources agree that the hunter who wounded Blanche was the son and heir of the king of this country.

Since the young prince was very much occupied by the adventure that he had just had, he no sooner rejoined his attendants than he sent one of his most clever stewards to the village to inquire about Blanche's background. The steward was quick to carry out his task, and when he returned to the prince, he gave his lord an exact account of Blanche's birth, her inclinations, and the troubles of this young beauty. The prince was charmed to learn that she came from a family of illustrious nobles, and he began to think of taking steps to make her happy since it seemed to him that she was worthy of such happiness.

Blanche was as beloved in the village where her father was the lord as Alix was hated. Thus the peasants had told the steward a hundred amusing stories regarding the beautiful qualities of Blanche and the shocking faults of Alix. The steward was a very alert and lively man and did not forget one word of all the things that the peasants had told him, and he repeated the stories to the prince with the exact same expressions and naiveté of the peasants so that the prince as lover was entertained and felt the same tender feelings that the hero of a novel normally has.

The first concern of the prince was to cure Blanche of the wound that he had caused her. But even though he came from a family very knowledgeable in faerie art, he was not very adept in this art himself, and he sought help from one of his godmothers, to whom he went and told about his adventure. He did not reveal his love for Blanche, and he only requested a cure for this beautiful young lady. But he requested this with such ardor, and he spoke about Blanche's merits with such exaggeration that a woman of the world, without being a fairy and without knowing anything about magic, would have easily guessed that he was in love. Indeed, it was not very difficult for this good fairy to discover this, and since she truly loved her godson, it was very easy for her to set everything aright, for it was a pleasure for her to see Blanche and to check to see whether she was worthy of the feelings that she had inspired in a heart which had been insensitive to tender feelings up until that time.

Dulcicula, for that was the name of the fairy, went and prepared a magical balm which cured mortal wounds within twenty-four hours. Then she assumed the form of an old peasant woman, and in this disguise she went and presented herself at the door of the house in which Blanche was residing. The first person whom she encountered was Alix, to whom she said quite civilly in a country style that she had a wonderful secret and wanted to offer her services to the marquis for his daughter.

"What have you said to me, you old fool?" Alix responded brutally. "I believe that all the vermin of the village have become mad and are seeking to help this monkey-face Blanche. I don't know why they are making such a fuss and running around so bewildered. That good beast is not even worth a box at the cemetery. A good sheepdog deserves a better spot for dying than she does."

Dulcicula was extremely surprised to see a damsel completely covered with gold and jewels speaking in such a strange jargon. But this fairy, who was sweetness itself, was more upset by Alix's natural wickedness than by her boorish manners. She did not respond to this brutal damsel, and when she learned that the marquis was not at home, she addressed herself to a woman who was in charge of caring for Blanche. This woman led the fairy to the bed of the sick girl. Dulcicula kept up her disguise and told her that her accident had touched her, and that she had come right away from her village to offer her a balm that would cure all kinds of wounds very quickly.

Blanche, who was very intelligent and who was well aware of the superstitions and mistakes made by the common people, believed that the balm about which the old woman spoke was one of the remedies of which the peasants were fond. These remedies were called the little innocent remedies because one has to be in effect innocent to make use of them. However, this amiable girl, in keeping with her character, responded to the fairy, "You are very obliging, my good mother, to leave all your chores to come and attend me. I don't know how I can reward your zeal since I am not in a position right now to do what I would like to do. But I shall tell my father about you, and I hope that he will take your good will into account. I should like to thank you for the balm, but I am in the hands of doctors, and I cannot change remedies from one day to the next."

Dulcicula, charmed by Blanche's sweetness and honest manners, did not feel insulted by the bad opinion that she had of her balm, but she pressed her to take it with such ardor and confidence that the beautiful girl agreed because of the peasant woman's good nature and because she saw how affectionate the woman was. So the fairy put some of the enchanted balm on Blanche's wound, and because of its marvelous powers, it was not very long before the beautiful young lady began to feel completely relieved. Afterward, they engaged in a conversation, and Dulcicula continued to admire Blanche's sweetness and other lovely qualities that complemented her beauty, and this admiration produced a good result. The fairy held a cane which she seemingly used to support herself, but it was a magic wand which she used to bring about all the miracles of her art. She touched Blanche with this wand as if by chance, and she gave her the gift of always being more intelligent than she was before, and more sweet, amiable, and beneficent, and she also gave her the most beautiful voice in the world. Soon after she left the room of the beautiful sick girl accompanied by the woman who had been in charge of her care.

Now she turned to Alix and her case, and she learned that this grumbler was also a flirt as well as being ugly and malicious. Since she always appeared in a shocking manner and made a hundred grimaces and a hundred distortions to make herself appear pleasant, people ironically called her *beautiful Alix*. The woman who looked after Blanche also told her that, whenever people saw a girl putting on an affected air and acting impertinently, they said everywhere that she *is acting just like beautiful Alix*.

After being informed all about Alix in such fine terms, she happened to encounter her alone in the courtyard. So she approached her and said to her in a civil way, "Mademoiselle, I would appreciate it if you would tell me where I might find the door to this house."

Alix responded angrily and said, "Nothing could be worse than to have an old driveling woman ask me questions like this!"

Without answering, the fairy followed Alix and let her wand fall on her as if it were unintentional, and she gave her the gift of always being hot-tempered, disagreeable, and spiteful. This was only to guarantee that she would keep the qualities that she already had. Indeed, right then and there, Alix became so enraged when the wand touched her that she thought of hitting the good peasant woman. She managed at least to pour out a torrent of insults, and the fairy, who had worked her magic, simply retired.

In the meantime, Blanche no longer felt any sharp pains since the peasant woman had applied the magic balm, and she thought about the adventure in the woods. She still had a vivid impression of the pleasant manners and the good looks of the hunter. It seemed to her that she had never read in all her novels about a marvelous adventure like the one she had. She would have liked to have known who the hunter was, but all her thoughts only amounted to a simple curiosity and wonder on her part. Do not believe that she had anything else on her mind; otherwise you would be doing her an injustice.

As far as the prince was concerned, he was entirely in love with her. When Dulcicula told him more about Blanche's merits, the fire of his passion intensified, and he was so carried away that if it had not been for the fear of his father the duke, he would have immediately gone to fetch the unfortunate beauty and led her triumphantly back to the palace. But he had to moderate his feelings and find some way to satisfy them in his mind.

In about twenty hours, Blanche found that she was perfectly cured, and some days later the merciless stepmother sent Blanche to the fountain again. As she was about to fill a bucket with some water, she saw a lady who was radiant, and she stood out more because of her grand air and grace than by her appearance, even though she was dressed in a magnificent and gallant manner. This lady approached Blanche and said to her, "My dear child, I would appreciate it if you would give me something to drink."

"I am sorry to be caught unaware, madam," Blanche responded in a pleasant way. "I can only offer you water in this jug, which is not appropriate for you."

At the same time, Blanche leaned over the side of the fountain, rinsed the jug with care, and then filled it with water, which she offered to the lady with good grace. After the lady drank the water, she thanked Blanche in a very civil way. She found Blanche's manners so admirable that she engaged her in a conversation and covered a thousand pleasant and fine topics that Blanche was not at a loss to discuss. She responded with such spirit, sweetness, and politeness that she succeeded in charming this lady. As you probably have already guessed, this lady was also a fairy, but you do not know that she was called Eloquentia Nativa.[2] This name may appear to some people to be somewhat strange like a Greek name. But, as you can very well see, it is a Latin name. However, whether it is Greek or Latin, it does not matter. This fairy had this unfermented bouru name, and it should not astonish anyone: all the fairies have unusual names. So then, Eloquentia Nativa was deeply impressed by Blanche's eloquence and obliging manners, and she decided to reward her magnificently for the little favor that this beautiful girl had done for her with such a good heart and such graciousness. The wise fairy put her hand on Blanche's head and gave her a present: from now on, each time that Blanche finished speaking, pearls, diamonds, rubies, and emeralds were to come out of her mouth. Then the fairy said good-bye to this amiable damsel, who returned calmly to her house carrying the jug full of water.

No sooner was Blanche in the presence of her stepmother than this lady asked her in a bitter tone what had kept her so long again at the fountain. Blanche responded, "The kindest lady that I've ever seen came there, and I gave her some water."

Upon her saying these words, a bunch of sparkling pearls and jewels came pouring out of her mouth.

"What is going on here?" cried the marquise.

Blanche told her eloquently and innocently all about the encounter with the lady and about the conversation that she had had with the admirable stranger. But as Blanche told her story and paused every now and then, even though the pauses were very short, a pile of jewels more precious than the next would fall from her mouth, and everyone rushed to gather all that Blanche spread on the floor with her mouth. No one was startled by these bonbons that she dispersed, and she took her turn as well to gather some, and even though she was not interested in doing this, she subconsciously assumed the habit of speaking in terse sentences. It is impossible to describe the marquis's joy, and that is why I shall not talk about it.

In the meantime, the marquise, who was just as surprised as she was disturbed, became determined to send her daughter to the fountain the next time, for she imagined that she would also meet the unknown lady there and that this lady would grant her daughter the same favor that she had granted Blanche. People at that time were just like people are today and did not do justice to things. People wanted grace without making the

2. Born eloquent (Latin).

effort to earn it. So, this woman told her plan to Alix, who was more brutal than ever, and she responded in impertinent terms and told her mother that she must be joking if she wanted to give her this chore, and that she would do nothing of the kind. Her mother told her that she absolutely wanted her to do it and that it was for her own good that she was sending her to fetch water. Finally, after Alix said a thousand other foolish things, she prepared to go there.

She dressed herself as if she were going to a ball, took a jug of gold, the most beautiful in the entire house, and set out for the fountain, where she soon arrived in pompous fashion. Eloquentia Nativa was also near the water. Ever since she had discovered the beautiful solitude of this place, she took great pleasure in frequenting it. But on this particular day she had assumed the figure of a pleasant peasant woman, had a naive air about her, and was wearing a county dress. Indeed, Eloquentia was not any less beautiful in a simple appearance than when she was wearing a splendid dress. On the contrary, when she made the right adjustments, she revealed her full beauty.

Alix sat down at the edge of the fountain, and the pretty peasant woman, who was thirsty because she had been walking for a long time, approached the girl. Alix had a common mind and was only impressed by people in magnificent dress, to whom she rendered as much honor as she could. Therefore, she regarded the peasant woman with disdain and did not deign to honor her, even though Eloquentia was very reverent toward her. The fairy did not become discouraged by that.

"Look at this trash!" Alix responded with anger. "I see that one comes here expressly to water animals. Truly, do you think that these golden jugs were made for your mug. Get out of here, you strawhead. Turn around, and if you are thirsty, go and drink in the trough for our cattle."

"You are rather brusque, mademoiselle," the fairy replied. "Have I done anything to offend you that you should treat me like this?"

Alix stood up, placed her hands on her hips, and cried out with all her might, "I believe that you want to argue with me, you pestilent beast! But I have no desire to have my ears warmed by you, and if you ever pass by our house, I shall make sure that you get a nice beating."

The good fairy was most indignant because of the brutal treatment of this creature and wanted to punish her on the spot in a manner so that she would remember with horror how she had poured out a flood of insults from her verminous tongue. She touched Alix with her magic wand, and the girl fell to the ground. While she was in this condition, the fairy gave her a present, or rather her punishment. With each word that she said, toads, snakes, spiders, and other vile beasts were to come out of her mouth and would frighten anyone who saw this. Right after this, Eloquentia left this spot and left Alix on the ground raging against her.

This wicked young lady waited a long time for the splendid woman from whom she expected favors. However, when she realized that she was waiting in vain, she got up and returned home. Her mother was burning with impatience to see her again, and as soon as Alix appeared at the door, the marquise ran to her. "Well, then," she said, "did you have a good meeting?"

"Yes," Alix said, "it was quite necessary to send me there to dance attendance."

As she said these words, a bunch of snakes, toads, and mice flowed from Alix's mouth.

"Where did you get this, you unfortunate girl?" her mother cried.

Alix wanted to respond, but there came another flood of vile beasts. The mother and her daughter went inside the house, where they saw that the beautiful present that Alix had received was a curse without remedy, and everyone was able to see this indignant person with utmost aversion. Even her mother could not prevent this

In the meantime, the prince, who had been very attentive with regard to everything that concerned Blanche, learned about the fortunate gift that she had received from a fairy. Since he knew the power and the generosity of Eloquentia Nativa, who was also one of his godmothers, he knew that it was she who that had produced this miracle. So he used this miracle as a pretext to see Blanche at the court. Thus, he asked Eloquentia if she would go and fetch this beautiful damsel about whom he had heard such marvelous things.

"Do you know," the fairy smiled and said, "that it was me who did this?"

"No," he replied. "But I should like to offer you a thousand thanks, for I am passionately in love with this young beauty."

"You know the zeal with which I have obliged you," the fairy remarked. "But you do not have to thank me on this occasion. I did not know that you had taken an interest in Blanche. You did not play a role in what I did for her. The sweetness and the politeness of this amiable girl charmed me. Her conversation is completely admirable. Nothing can equal the fine style of her expressions, and I wanted pearls and jewels to flow from her mouth to mark the sweetness and brilliance that I found in her words."

The prince was enchanted to hear Blanche's eloquence praised by a fairy whom he esteemed a thousand times more for her taste and talents than her rhetoric. So now Eloquentia Nativa left her godson and went to the house of Blanche's father. He was besieged by an incredibly large crowd of people. The magnificent things that flowed from Blanche's mouth had attracted more people than the things that came from the mouth of any great speaker in parliament, as beautiful as they might be. The people were right. It is more pleasant to see precious gems come from the beautiful small mouth of Blanche than to watch the creamy words that come from the big mouths of thunderous orators who at one time had been so popular in Athens.

To the great dismay of the crowd who stood around Blanche, Eloquentia had her get into a carriage and took her to court. It was there that the prince demonstrated his tender feelings for her, and Blanche was not insensitive. Since her marvelous gift had made this beautiful person more rich than all the best princesses of the universe, the prince married her with the applause of the duke his father and all the people of his realm.

Blanche's father, who was overcome by joy, was now looked upon most favorably by the court and no longer had to suffer from the whims of his wife. She did not dare to cause him grief after the elevation of his daughter.

The envious Alix, who had always been driven to despair by anything that made Blanche happy, had even more to suffer than her mother or anyone. She left her mother's house in rage and wandered from province to province, where she was the object of aversion and rejected by everyone. She experienced hunger and want wherever she went, and finally, after having suffered a great deal, she died of misery in some bushes while Blanche triumphed. Indeed, the beautiful Blanche's happiness lasted her entire life, which was very long. Her fate and the fate of Alix only prove what I had first proposed in this tale:

> *Sweet and polite language*
> *Is worth more than a rich dowry.*

CHARLES PERRAULT

The Fairies†

Once upon a time, there was a widow who had two daughters. The older one was often mistaken for her mother because she was so much like her in looks and character. Indeed, both the mother and this daughter were so disagreeable and haughty that it was impossible to live with them. The younger daughter, who looked exactly like her father and took after him in her kindness and politeness, was one of the most beautiful girls that has ever been seen.

Since we naturally tend to be fond of those who resemble us, the mother doted on her elder daughter while she had a dreadful aversion toward the younger one. She made her eat in the kitchen and work from morning till night. Among the many things that this poor child was forced to do, she had to go to a place about a mile from their house twice a day to fetch water from a spring and bring it back in a large jug. One day, when she was at the spring, a poor woman came up to her and asked her for a drink.

"Why, of course, my good woman," she said, and the pretty maiden at once stooped and rinsed out the jug. Then she filled it with water from the clearest part of the spring and offered it to the woman, keeping the jug raised so that she might drink more easily.

After she had finished drinking, the good woman said, "You are so beautiful, so good and kind, that I can't resist bestowing a gift on you"— for she was a fairy who had assumed the form of a poor village woman in order to discover just how kind this young girl could be—"I shall give you a gift," continued the fairy, "that will cause every word uttered from your mouth to become either a flower or a precious stone."

When this beautiful girl arrived home, her mother scolded her for returning so late.

"I'm sorry for having taken so long," the poor girl said, and on her

---

† Charles Perrault, "The Fairies"—"Les fées," in *Histoires ou contes du temps passé* (Paris: Claude Barbin, 1697).

The Fairies. From *Les Contes de Perrault*, ca. 1890.

saying these words, two roses, two pearls, and two large diamonds fell from her mouth.

"What do I see there!" said her mother completely astonished. "I believe I saw pearls and diamonds dropping from your mouth. Where do they come from, my daughter?" (This was the first time she had ever called her *my daughter*.)

The poor child naively told her all that had happened while countless diamonds fell from her mouth during the course of her story.

"Upon my word," said the mother, "I must send my daughter. Come here, Fanchon! Do you see what's falling from your sister's mouth when she speaks. Wouldn't you like to have the same gift? You only have to go and fetch some water from the spring, and if a poor woman asks you for a drink, you're to give it to her nicely and politely."

"You'll never get me walking to the spring!" the rude girl responded.

"I'm insisting," her mother replied, "and you'd better go this instant!"

She left and sulked as she went. With her she took the most beautiful silver bottle in the house. No sooner did she arrive at the spring than she saw a magnificently dressed lady, who emerged from the forest and asked her for a drink. This was the same fairy, who had appeared to her sister, but she now put on the airs and the garments of a princess to see just how rude this girl could be.

"Do you think I came here just to fetch you a drink?" the rude and arrogant girl said. "Do you think that I carried this silver bottle just to offer a drink to a fine lady! If you ask my advice, you'd better get your own drink if you want one!"

"You're not at all polite," the fairy replied without anger. "Well, then, since you're not very obliging, I'll bestow a gift on you so that every word uttered from your mouth will become either a snake or a toad."

As soon as her mother caught sight of her, she cried out, "Well, then, daughter!"

"Well, then, mother," her rude daughter responded, spitting two vipers and two toads from her mouth.

"Oh heavens!" her mother exclaimed. "What do I see? Your sister's to blame, and she'll pay for it!"

She dashed off to beat her, but the poor child fled and took refuge in a nearby forest. The king's son, who was returning from a hunt, encountered her, and observing how beautiful she was, he asked her what she was doing there all alone and what had caused her to weep.

"Alas, sir! My mother has driven me away from home."

Seeing five or six pearls and just as many diamonds fall from her mouth, the king's son asked her to tell him where they came from. She told him the entire story, and the king's son fell in love with her. When he considered that such a gift was worth more than a dowry anyone else could bring, he took her to the palace of the king his father, where he married her.

As for her sister, she made herself so hated that her own mother drove her out of the house. This wretched girl searched about in vain for someone who would offer her shelter, and finally she went off to a corner of the forest where she died.

Moral

Diamonds and gold
Can do wonders for one's soul.
Yet, kind words, I am told,
Are worth more on the whole.

Another Moral

Since virtue demands great effort,
One must be patient and good-natured.
Sooner or later there'll be a reward
That comes when it's least expected.

JEANNE-MARIE LEPRINCE DE BEAUMONT

Aurore and Aimée†

There was once a lady who had two daughters. The oldest was called Aurore, and she was as beautiful as the day, and she had a good character. The second, who was given the name Aimée, was just as beautiful as her sister, but she was malevolent and only did bad things. The mother had also been very beautiful, but she began to lose her looks as she got older, and this caused her a great deal of grief. Aurore was sixteen years old, and Aimée was twelve at this time. Since the mother did not want to look old, she left the city where everyone knew her and sent her oldest daughter to the country because she did not want anyone to know that she had such an old daughter. She kept the younger daughter with her and went to another city, where she told everyone that Aimée was only ten years old and that she had given birth to her when she was fifteen.

Since the mother kept fearing that someone might still discover her deception, she decided to send Aurore even further away to a distant country. The person who accompanied her daughter left her in a large forest, where she fell asleep when she sat down to rest. When Aurore awoke and realized that she was all alone in this forest, she began to weep. It was almost night, and after getting up, she searched for a way out of the forest. But instead of finding a path, she became even more lost than she was before. Finally, she saw a light in the distance, and after running toward it, she found a small cottage. Aurore knocked on the door, and a shepherdess opened it and asked her what she wanted.

"My good woman," Aurore said, "for mercy's sake, I beg your permission to let me spend the night in your cottage, for if I stay in the forest, the wolves will eat me."

"With all my heart, my beautiful girl," the shepherdess responded. "But tell me, why are you in this forest so late at night?"

Aurore told the woman her story and said, "Aren't I unfortunate to have

† Jeanne-Marie Leprince de Beaumont, "Aurore and Aimée"—"Aurore et Aimée" (1756), in *Magasin des enfants* (Lyon: Reguillat, 1756).

a mother so cruel! Wouldn't it have been better if I had been born dead than to live and to be so badly treated! What did I do to the good Lord to be so miserable?"

"My dear child," the shepherdess replied, "you should never say anything against God. He is omnipotent and wise, and he loves you. And you must believe that he would not permit your misfortune without having your welfare in mind. Trust in him, and remember that God protects the good, and when terrible things happen to them, they are not calamities. Stay with me, and I shall serve you like a mother, and I shall love you like my daughter."

Aurore was happy to accept this proposal, and the following day, the shepherdess said to her, "I am going to give you a flock of sheep to lead to the meadow, but I am afraid that you will be bored. Therefore, take this spindle, and you can spin to amuse yourself."

"Mother," Aurore responded, "I am a young woman of quality. So I do not work."

"Well, then, take a book," the shepherdess said to her.

"I don't like reading," Aurore replied and blushed. That was because she was ashamed to admit to the fairy that she did not know how to read as one should. However, she had to tell the truth, and she said to the shepherdess that she had never wanted to learn how to read when she had been little, and she had never had the time to learn when she became big.

"You must have had very important things to do," said the shepherdess.

"Yes, mother," Aurore replied, "I went promenading every morning with my good friends. After dinner I dressed my hair. In the evening I would attend our gatherings, and afterward I would go to the opera or theater. Finally, I went dancing at a ball."

"You certainly kept yourself occupied with important matters," the shepherdess said. "And I am sure that you were never bored."

"I beg your pardon, mother," Aurore responded. "It did happen when I was left alone for a quarter of an hour. I would be bored to death. But when we went to the country, it was much worse. I spent the entire day dressing and undressing myself and combing my hair just to amuse myself."

"You're not happy in the country," the shepherdess said.

"Neither was I happy in the city," Aurore responded. "If I gambled, I lost my money. If I was at a gathering, I saw that my friends were better dressed than I was, and that made me even more sorry. If went to a ball, I was mainly occupied by watching for the faults of the other dancers who might be better than I was. In short, I've never spent a day without having some kind of grief."

"Do not complain any more about Providence," the shepherdess said. "By leading you into this desolate place, it has caused you more sorrows than pleasure. But that is not all. You would have been even more troubled in the long run because one does not remain young forever. The times of balls and the theater pass by. When you become old, and you still want to attend parties and gatherings, the young people make fun of you. Besides, you can no longer dance and do not dare to dress yourself up. So you are bored to death and very despondent."

"But, my good mother," Aurore said. "One cannot really remain alone. The day appears longer than a year if you do not have company."

"I beg your pardon, my dear," the shepherdess said. "I'm all alone here, and the years seem as short as the days. If you want, I shall teach you the secret of never boring yourself ever again."

"I would like this very much," Aurore said. "You may command me as you judge best. I shall obey."

The shepherdess made use of Aurore's goodwill and wrote on a piece of paper all that she was to do. The entire day was divided among prayers, reading, work, and walks. There was no clock in the forest, and Aurore did not know what time it was. But the shepherdess told time by the sun and called Aurore for lunch.

"Mother," the beautiful girl said, "you're eating early. We only got up a short time ago."

"However, it is two o'clock," responded the shepherdess with a smile. "We have been up for five hours. But, my daughter, if you make good use of your time, it passes quickly, and you never get bored."

Charmed by not feeling bored, Aurore applied herself with all her heart to reading and working. She found herself a thousand times more happy by doing her country chores than she had been in the city.

"I see well," she said to the shepherdess, "that God does everything for our best. If my mother had not been unjust and cruel to me, I would have remained ignorant. And vanity, idleness, and the desire to please would have made me wicked and unhappy."

Aurore had been at the shepherdess's home for one year when a brother of the king came hunting in the woods where she was tending sheep. He was called Ingénu, and he was the best prince in the world. But the king, his brother, who was called Fourbin, was not like him, for this king only took pleasure in deceiving his neighbors and maltreating his subjects. Ingénu was charmed by Aurore's beauty and told her that she would make him happy if she agreed to marry him. Aurore found him very kind, but she knew that good girls do not listen to men who speak to them in that way.

"Monsieur," she said to Ingénu, "if what you say is true, then you will seek out my mother, who is a shepherdess. She lives in the little cottage that you will find down there. If she would like you to become my husband, I should like this as well, for she is so wise and so reasonable that I shall never disobey her."

"My beautiful girl," Ingénu replied, "I shall gladly go and ask your mother permission to marry you. But I do not want to marry you if you are against this. If your mother agrees that you can be my wife, this may cause you grief, and I would rather die than to cause you any suffering."

"A man who thinks this way has virtue," Aurore said, "and a daughter cannot be unhappy with a virtuous man."

Ingénu left Aurore and went to look for the shepherdess, who knew his virtues and gladly gave her consent to this marriage. So he promised her to return in three days to see Aurore with her, and after giving the shepherdess a ring as guarantee, he departed the most happy man in the world. However, Aurore was very impatient to return to the cottage. Ingénu had appeared to her so amiable that she feared that the woman whom she called her mother had rebuffed him. But the shepherdess told her, "It is not because Ingénu is a prince that I have consented to your marriage with him, but because he is the most honest man in the world."

Aurore waited with great impatience for the prince's return, but the second day after his departure, as she was collecting the sheep, she unfortunately fell into a thicket and scratched her face all over. She quickly looked at her face in a stream and was afraid because blood ran down both her cheeks.

"How unfortunate I am," she said to the shepherdess, upon returning home. "Ingénu will be coming tomorrow, and he will no longer love me because I look so horrible."

The shepherdess smiled and said to her, "If the good Lord has allowed you to fall, then it is undoubtedly for your own good because you know that he loves you, and he does his best for you."

Aurore realized her fault, for she knew she should not complain about Providence and said to herself, "If Prince Ingénu does not want to marry me because I am no longer beautiful, I would have evidently not been happy with him."

However, the shepherdess washed her face, and she pulled out the thorns that had been stuck into it. The next morning Aurore was frightful because her face was horribly swollen, and it was impossible to see her eyes. At ten o'clock in the morning a carriage stopped in front of the cottage, but instead of Ingénu, it was the King Fourbin who descended. One of the courtiers who had been hunting with the prince had told the king that his brother had encountered the most beautiful maiden in the world, and he wanted to marry her.

"You are quite presumptuous to want to marry without my permission," Fourbin had said to his brother. "To punish you, I shall marry this girl if she is as beautiful as one says."

When Fourbin entered the shepherdess's cottage, he asked her where her daughter was.

"Here she is," the shepherdess replied, showing him Aurore.

"What! That monster over there," the king cried. "Don't you have another girl to whom my brother gave a ring?"

"Here it is on my finger," Aurore said.

Upon hearing those words, the king burst out laughing and said, "I didn't know that my brother had such poor taste. But I am charmed to be able to punish him."

As he said this, he commanded the shepherdess to place a veil on Aurore's head, and then he had his brother, Prince Ingénu, summoned to the cottage, where he said, "My brother, since you love this beautiful Aurore, I want you to marry her right away."

"As for me," Aurore said, ripping off the veil, "I don't want to deceive anyone. Look at my face, Ingénu. I have become quite horrible in three days. Do you still want to marry me?"

"You seem even more amiable in my eyes than ever before," the prince said. "I recognize that you are even more virtuous than I believed."

As he said this, he gave her his hand, and Fourbin laughed hysterically. He ordered them to be married in the field. Then he said to Ingénu, "Since I don't love monsters, you can live with your wife in this cabin. I forbid you to bring her to court."

Then the king got back into his carriage and left Ingénu, who was beside himself with joy.

"Well, then," said the shepherdess to Aurore, "do you still think that you were unfortunate to have fallen? Without this accident, the king would have fallen in love with you, and if you would not have married him, he would have had Ingénu killed."

"You are right, mother," Aurore responded. "Nevertheless, I have become so ugly that I am frightful, and I fear that the prince will regret having married me."

"No, I assure you," Ingénu declared. "One can accustom oneself to an ugly face, but one can never accustom oneself to a bad character."

"I am charmed by your sentiments," the shepherdess said. "But Aurore will become beautiful again. I have a special water that will heal the wounds on her face."

Indeed, at the end of three days, Aurore's face became as it was before, but the prince requested that she always wear her veil, because he was afraid that his wicked brother would carry her off if he saw her again. However, Fourbin, who wanted to marry, had many portraits of beautiful women brought to him, and he became enchanted by one of Aimée, the sister of Aurore. Therefore, he commanded her to appear at his court, and he married her.

Aurore was very disturbed when she heard that her sister had become queen. She did not dare to go out any longer because she knew how wicked her sister was and how much she hated her. At the end of one year, Aurore had a son whom she called Beaujour, and she loved him with all her heart. When this little prince began to speak, he demonstrated so much spirit that his parents were most pleased. One day when he was in front of the door with his mother, she fell asleep, and when she awoke, she could no longer find her son. She uttered great cries and ran all over the forest searching for him. The shepherdess had great difficulty reminding her that nothing ever happened that was not for her own good, and she did her best to console her. But the next day Aurore was obliged to admit that the shepherdess was right. Fourbin and his wife, enraged that they could not have children, sent some soldiers to kill their nephew. Upon seeing that they could not find him, they put Ingénu, his wife, and the shepherdess into a boat and sent them out into the sea so that they would never be heard of again.

This time Aurore believed that she should consider herself very unfortunate, but the shepherdess continued to repeat that God always did everything for the best. Since the weather was very beautiful, the boat sailed calmly for three days and approached a city which was on the seacoast. The king of this city was engaged in an enormous war, and his enemies were going to attack the next day. Ingénu, who was very courageous, asked

the king for some troops, and he made many sorties. Finally, he was fortunate enough to kill the leader of the enemy who was besieging the king's
city. Once the soldiers saw that they had lost their commander, they fled,
and the king who had been besieged took Ingénu as his son because he
did not have any children. This was in due recognition for Ingénu's brave
deeds. Four years later, they learned that Fourbin had died out of grief
because he had married such a wicked wife, and the people, who hated
her, banished her with shame from the country. Then they sent ambassadors to Ingénu to offer him the crown. So he embarked with his wife
and the shepherdess, but they became caught in a huge storm and were
shipwrecked on a deserted island. Since Aurore had become wise after
everything that had happened to her, she did not complain and thought
that it was for their good that God had caused this shipwreck. They placed
a large pole on the shore, and the white apron of the shepherdess was
attached on top of the pole so that passing ships might catch sight of this
and provide them with help. During that evening they saw a woman come
toward them, and she was carrying a small child. When Aurore looked at
the child, she recognized her son, Beaujour, and asked the woman how
she had come upon this child. The woman responded that her husband
was a pirate and had kidnapped the child, but they were shipwrecked near
this island, and she had managed to save the child with her arms. Two
days later, there were ships that came in search of the bodies of Ingénu
and Aurore because people had thought they had perished, and the sailors
saw the white apron. So they came to the island and took the king and
his family to their kingdom. And now, no matter what accident happens
to Aurore, she never complains because she knows from experience that
things that appear to us as misfortunes are often the cause of our happiness.

JACOB AND WILHELM GRIMM

Mother Holle†

A widow had two daughters, one who was beautiful and industrious, the
other ugly and lazy. But she was fonder of the ugly and lazy one because
she was her own daughter. The other had to do all the housework and
carry out the ashes like a cinderella. Everyday the poor maiden had to sit
near a well by the road and spin and spin until her fingers bled.

Now, one day it happened that the reel became quite bloody, and when
the maiden leaned over the well to rinse it, it slipped out of her hand and
fell to the bottom. She burst into tears, ran to her stepmother, and told
her about the accident. But the stepmother gave her a terrible scolding
and was very cruel. "If you've let the reel fall in," she said, "then you'd
better get it out again."

The maiden went back to the well but did not know where to begin.
She was so distraught that she jumped into the well to fetch the reel, but

---

† Jacob and Wilhelm Grimm, "Mother Holle"—"Frau Holle" (1857), No. 24 in *Kinder- und Hausmärchen. Gesammelt durch die Brüder Grimm* (Göttingen: Dieterich, 1857).

she lost consciousness. When she awoke and regained her senses, she was in a beautiful meadow where the sun was shining and thousands of flowers were growing. She walked across the meadow, and soon she came to a baker's oven full of bread, but the bread was yelling. "Take me out! Take me out, or else I'll burn. I've been baking long enough!"

She went up to the oven and took out all the loaves, one by one with the baker's peel.[1] After that she moved on and came to a tree full of apples. "Shake me! Shake me!" the tree exclaimed. "My apples are all ripe."

She shook the tree until the apples fell like raindrops, and she kept shaking until they had all come down. After she had gathered them and stacked them in a pile, she moved on. At last she came to a small cottage where an old woman was looking out of a window. She had such big teeth that the maiden was scared and wanted to run away. But the old woman cried after her, "Why are you afraid, my dear child? Stay with me, and if you do all the housework properly, everything will turn out well for you. Only you must make my bed nicely and carefully and give it a good shaking so the feathers fly. Then it will snow on earth, for I am Mother Holle."[2]

Since the old woman had spoken so kindly to her, the maiden plucked up her courage and agreed to enter her service. She took care of everything to the old woman's satisfaction and always shook the bed so hard that the feathers flew about like snowflakes. In return, the woman treated her well: she never said an unkind word to the maiden, and she gave her roasted or boiled meat every day. After the maiden had spent a long time with Mother Holle, she became sad. At first she did not know what was bothering her, but finally she realized she was homesick. Even though everything was a thousand times better there than at home, she still had a desire to return. At last she said to Mother Holle, "I've got a tremendous longing to return home, and even though everything is wonderful down here, I've got to return to my people."

"I'm so pleased that you want to return home," Mother Holle responded, "and since you've served me so faithfully, I myself shall bring you up there again."

She took the maiden by the hand and led her to a large door. When it was opened and the maiden was standing right beneath the doorway, an enormous shower of gold came pouring down, and all the gold stuck to her so that she became completely covered with it.

"I want you to have this because you've been so industrious," said Mother Holle, and she also gave her back the reel that had fallen into the well. Suddenly the door closed, and the maiden found herself up on earth, not far from her mother's house. When she entered the yard, the cock was sitting on the well and crowed:

> *Cock-a-doodle-doo!*
> My golden maiden, what's new with you?

---

1. A baker's shovel used for sliding loaves of bread and pastry into and out of the oven.
2. Whenever it snowed in olden days, people in Hessia used to say that Mother Holle was making her bed [*Grimms' note*].

She went inside to her mother, and since she was covered with so much gold, her mother and sister gave her a warm welcome. Then she told them all about what had happened to her, and when her mother heard how she had obtained so much wealth, she wanted to arrange it so her ugly and lazy daughter could have the same good fortune. Therefore, her daughter had to sit near the well and spin, and she made the reel bloody by sticking her fingers into a thornbush and pricking them. After that she threw the reel down into the well and jumped in after it. Just like her sister, she reached the beautiful meadow and walked along the same path. When she came to the oven, the bread cried out again, "Take me out! Take me out, or else I'll burn! I've been baking long enough!"

But the lazy maiden answered, "I've no desire to get myself dirty!"

She moved on, and soon she came to the apple tree that cried out, "Shake me! Shake me! My apples are all ripe."

However, the lazy maiden replied, "Are you serious? One of the apples could fall and hit me on my head."

Thus she went on, and when she came to Mother Holle's cottage, she was not afraid because she had already heard of the old woman's big teeth, and she hired herself out to her right away. On the first day she made an effort to work hard and obey Mother Holle when the old woman told her what to do, for the thought of gold was on her mind. On the second day she started loafing, and on the third day she loafed even more. Indeed, she did not want to get out of bed in the morning, nor did she make Mother Holle's bed as she should have, and she certainly did not shake it hard so the feathers flew. Soon Mother Holle became tired of this and dismissed the maiden from her service. The lazy maiden was quite happy to go and expected that now the shower of gold would come. Mother Holle led her to the door, but as the maiden was standing beneath the doorway, a big kettle of pitch came pouring down over her instead of gold.

"That's a reward for your services," Mother Holle said and shut the door. The lazy maiden went home covered with pitch, and when the cock on the well saw her, it crowed:

> *Cock-a-doodle-do!*
> My dirty maiden, what's new with you?

The pitch did not come off the maiden and remained on her as long as she lived.

Magical Transformations

The transformation of young men into beasts, for whatever reason, was a popular motif in oral and literary fairy tales in the East and West. In this cycle, two or three brothers are changed into beasts generally representing air, sea, and land. The youngest brother (or brother-in-law) will either need them to assist him while he is on a mission to rescue a princess or try to free them from their enchantment. So, it is a combination of his courage and compassion and their willingness to help him that brings about a happy resolution. It is doubtful whether the Grimms knew the Basile version, but in 1850, they took Friedmund von Arnim's "The Castle of the Golden Sun," which had a choppy style closer to the oral tradition, refined it, and added it to their collection. Another important German literary version was Johann Karl August Musäus's "Die Bücher der Chronika der drei Schwestern" ("The Books of the Chronicles of the Three Sisters") in *Volksmährchen der Deutschen* (1782–87).

GIAMBATTISTA BASILE

The Three Animal Kings†

Once there was a king of Verdecolle who had three daughters as beautiful as jewels, and they were passionately loved by the three sons of the king of Belprato. However, the sons had been changed into three animals by a fairy's curse, and King Verdecolle refused to allow them to marry his daughters.

As a result of his decision, the first son, who was a fine falcon, used his magic powers to summon all the birds to meet in parliament. Soon they began to arrive—chaffinches, wrens, yellowhammers, goldfinches, tomtits, screech owls, lapwings, skylarks, cuckoos, jackdaws, and other kinds of feathered creatures. Then the falcon sent them out to destroy the best part of King Verdecolle's trees until not a single leaf or flower was left on their branches.

The second son, who was a stag, called goats, rabbits, hares, hedgehogs, and all the other animals of the country to run and trample on all the plowed and cultivated fields of the king until there was not a blade of grass left growing.

The third son, who was a dolphin, made a pact with one hundred sea monsters, and they created such a storm that it swamped the coast until not a single boat remained intact.

† Giambattista Basile, "The Three Animal Kings"—"I tre re bestie" (1634), *Terzo passatempo della quarta giornata* in *Lo cunto de li cunti overo Lo trattenemiento de peccerille*, De Gian Alessio Abbattutis, 5 vols. (Naples: Ottavio Beltrano, 1634–36).

When the king saw that things were getting worse and worse, and that he was unable to remedy the damage caused by the three wild lovers, he decided to quell his doubts and let the sons marry his daughters. But the sons did not want any celebration or music and intended to carry the girls away from this kingdom. Before they departed, however, Queen Grazolla gave each one of her daughters the exact same ring as a present and said that, if they ever should become separated for a long period of time and then chanced to meet anyone of their kin, they would be able to recognize whether they were truly related by means of the rings. After this, they said their farewells and departed.

The falcon carried Fabiella, the eldest sister, to a mountain so high that it stretched beyond the clouds and was always dry because it never rained. Then he brought her into a magnificent palace, where she lived the life of a queen. The stag carried Vasta, the second daughter, to a forest that was so dense that the shadows, when summoned by night to form part of her retinue, could not find their way out. This was the place where Vasta lived according to her rank in an incomparably beautiful house with a garden. The dolphin swam with Rita, the third sister, on his back to the middle of the sea, where they found a mansion on top of a rock that could have housed three crowned kings.

In the meantime, Grazolla gave birth to a baby boy whom she named Tittone. As he grew up, he kept hearing his mother lament the loss of her three daughters, who had married animals, and he kept hearing her long for news of them. So, when he reached the age of fifteen, he became eager to go out into the world to see if he could find some trace of them. After a long discussion with his father and mother, he convinced them to let him go, and the queen gave him another ring similar to the one she had given to her daughters. In addition, Tittone had an escort and all the equipment that was necessary and befitting a prince of his rank.

There was not a hole in Italy, a dark closet in France, or a part of Spain that he did not search. Moreover, he traveled through England, crossed Flanders, and visited Poland. In short, he traveled east and west, leaving behind all his servants either in inns or in hospitals and went through all his money. Finally, he found himself on the mountain inhabited by the falcon and Fabiella. As he gazed at the palace and was enraptured by its beauty, which was constituted by cornerstones of porphyry, walls of alabaster, windows of gold, and tiles of silver, he was noticed by his sister, who had him brought to her. Then she asked him who he was, where he came from, and how he had happened to come to this country. When Tittone told her the name of the country and the name of his father and mother, Fabiella recognized him as her brother and was even more sure of this when she compared the ring that he was wearing on his finger with the one that her mother had given her. Therefore, she embraced him with great joy, but since she was afraid that her husband would be disturbed by his arrival, she hid him away. When the falcon returned home, Fabiella said that she had recently been stirred by a longing to see her family, and the falcon responded, "Let it pass, my dear wife. It's not possible until conditions permit."

"At least," said Fabiella, "let us send for someone from my family to console me."

And the falcon replied, "And who would want to make such a long journey to see you?"

"And if someone were to come," she asked, "would it displease you?"

"And why should it displease me?" the falcon responded. "Just as long as he were of your own flesh and blood, that would be enough for me. He certainly would find favor in my eyes."

When Fabiella heard these words, she summoned her courage and brought her brother out of his hiding place and presented him to the falcon.

"Five and five are ten," said the falcon. "Love can pierce a glove just as water seeps through boots! Welcome! You are the master of this house, and your word is our command!" And the falcon gave orders that Tittone should be treated and served just like himself.

But after Tittone spent two weeks on the mountain, he had a great desire to continue his search for the other sisters. Therefore, he asked permission from his sister and brother-in-law to leave, and the falcon gave him one of his feathers and said, "Carry this feather with you, and take good care of it because, if you should find yourself in a predicament, it will be worth a treasure to you. Keep it safe, and if you need something important, throw it on the ground and say, 'Come, come,' and you'll find a reason to be grateful to me."

Tittone wrapped the feather in some paper and put it in his purse. After a thousand compliments, he departed, and he walked a great distance until he came to the forest where the stag was living with Vasta. By this time he had become very hungry, and so he entered the garden to pick some fruit and was seen by his sister, who recognized him as he had been recognized by Fabiella. Then she introduced him to her husband, who gave him a grand welcome and treated him like a prince. After two weeks passed, Tittone was eager to depart and search for the last sister, and the stag gave him one of his hairs and repeated the same words that the falcon had used when he gave him the feather.

Tittone set out again with a handful of money that he had received from the falcon and also with more coins that the stag had given him. He kept walking until he could go no further because of the sea. So he now embarked on a boat with the intention of looking for traces of his sister on every island. After he took off, he kept sailing until he reached the island where the dolphin was living with Rita. As soon as he landed, he was seen and recognized by his sister just as he had been by the two other sisters, and his brother-in-law welcomed him with great courtesy. Later, when he wanted to depart to see his father and mother, the dolphin gave him one of his scales and told him the same thing that the other animals had said.

When Tittone reached land, he mounted a horse and began his journey once more. But he had not traveled more than a mile when he entered a forest that was a highway of fear and shadows and kept up a perpetual market of terror and darkness. Soon he saw a large tower in the middle of a lake whose water kissed the feet of the trees hiding their hideous roots

from the sun. At one of the windows of the tower, he caught sight of a
beautiful maiden at the feet of a horrible dragon that was asleep. When
the maiden noticed Tittone, she called to him in a low and pitiful voice
and said, "My handsome young man, perhaps you have been sent from
heaven to comfort me in my misery in this place where I never see a
Christian face. Rescue me from the clutches of this tyrannical serpent who
abducted me from my father, the king of Chiaravalle, and who has confined me in this wretched tower where I am withering away and turning
sour!"

"Alas!" said Tittone. "What can I do to help you, my beautiful lady?
How can I get across this lake? How can I scale this tower? How can I
attack this ugly dragon whose very sight is so fearful and terrifying that he
gives one the runs. But wait a moment, and we shall see if I can chase
away this serpent with the help of some friends. 'Step by step,' said Gra-
dasso.[1] Now we shall see whether our cup brims over or whether it is
empty!"

Right after having said these words, he threw the feather, the hair, and
the scale that his brothers-in-law had given him on to the ground and said,
"Come, come." All of a sudden, as if there were a summer shower that
brings out the frogs, the falcon, the stag, and the dolphin appeared all at
once and cried out, "Here we are! What's your command?"

Upon seeing them, Tittone responded with great joy, "The only thing
that I desire is to rescue that poor maiden from the clutches of the dragon,
to get away from that tower, to destroy everything, and to take that beautiful
maiden home with me as my wife."

"No need to talk anymore," responded the falcon. "The bean grows
where you least expect it. Now we shall make him spin on a coin in the
coral, and you'll see that he won't have much space to move about."

"Let's not lose any time," added the stag. "It's best to eat trouble and
macaroni while they're hot."

So the falcon summoned a flock of winged griffins that flew into the
window of the tower, seized the maiden, and carried her across the lake
to Tittone, who was waiting for her with his brothers-in-law. If she had
seemed to him to be a moon from afar, she was now as beautiful as the
sun up close. While he embraced her and said many lovely words to her,
the dragon awoke, hurled himself through the window, and began swimming toward Tittone to devour him. Then the stag had a band of lions,
tigers, panthers, bears, and wildcats appear, and they made mincemeat out
of the dragon with their claws. After this was done, Tittone wanted to
depart, but the dolphin said, "I also want to do something to serve you."
So, to make sure that nothing of that accursed and miserable place would
be remembered, he had the sea rise like a tidal wave, and it swept over
the shore and battered the tower with such force that the tower crumbled
and was completely leveled.

When Tittone saw this, he thanked his brothers-in-law as best he could
and asked his bride-to-be to do the same, because, thanks to them, she
had been rescued from such great danger. But the animals interrupted and

1. Words used in an old Italian game.

said, "Actually, we must thank this beautiful maiden because she is the cause of our regaining our natural form. When we were born, a curse was placed on us because our mother had insulted a fairy. We were condemned to remain in the form of animals until we managed to free a king's daughter and help her overcome some difficulties. Now the time that we've longed for has arrived! The apple is now ripe enough to bite! We already feel a surge of fresh air in our breasts and new blood in our veins!"

As they were saying this, they were transformed into three handsome young men, one after another, and they ardently embraced their brother-in-law and shook the hand of the maiden, who was filled with joy to the point of ecstasy. Meanwhile, Tittone remarked, "Oh my Lord, why couldn't my mother and father participate in this glorious moment? They would be so delighted if they could see three such handsome and charming sons-in-law in front of them!"

"Night is still not here," the brothers-in-law responded. "Since we were so ashamed by our looks, we felt obliged to shun the sight of people, but now, thank heaven, we can mix among the people, and we want everyone to come together under one roof and live there happily with our wives. Therefore, let us quickly be on our way, and before tomorrow's sun has unpacked the merchandise of its rays at the customhouse of the East, we shall be with our wives."

Since there was nothing but Tittone's flayed horse to carry them, and since they did not want to go by foot, the brothers made a magnificent carriage drawn by six lions appear. All five of them climbed into the carriage, and after they had traveled the entire day, they arrived that evening at an inn, and while they were waiting for their dinner, they passed the time reading the many ignorant signs that people had written on the walls.[2] Finally, after they had all eaten, they went to bed, but the three brothers only pretended to sleep. Instead, they got up and traveled the entire night, and in the morning, when the stars, like bashful maidens who have just married, retire so as not to see the sun, they returned to the same inn with their wives, where they all kept embracing and rejoicing to celebrate their reunion. Then all eight of them got into the same carriage, and after a long journey, they arrived at Verdecolle, where they were received with incredible affection by the king and queen, who had not only recuperated their son, whom they thought they had lost, but also acquired interest with three sons-in-law and regained their three daughters and a daughter-in-law as well, four columns in the temple of beauty.

Then they sent word to the king of Belprato and to the king of Chiaravalle to inform them of what had happened to their children. They both came to the celebrations that were prepared, thus putting the fat of their joy into the broth of their happiness and putting an end to all the past troubles because

an hour of content
can make you forget a thousand years of torment.

---

2. Similar to graffiti, marks would be made in charcoal on the walls of the inns by people who came by or frequented the inns.

FRIEDMUND VON ARNIM

The Castle of the Golden Sun†

There was once a mother who had three sons. She wished the first to be enchanted into the king of the eagles, and he had to be an eagle twenty-two hours a day and a human for two hours. She wished the second to be enchanted into the king of the fish, and he had to be a fish twenty-two hours a day and a human for two hours. The third son ran away to avoid his mother's enchantments.

In the meantime, he had heard about the castle of the golden sun where there was a princess waiting to be saved. Twenty-three men had already found their death there, and the field was open for a twenty-fourth. So he set out for the castle and came to a large forest where he lost his way. When he looked around, he saw two giants who waved to him. After he went over to them, he saw that they were fighting over a hat. The giants explained to him that they were both equally strong and could not agree who should have the hat. So they wanted him to decide.

The young man had them give him the hat, and he said to them that he would walk some distance away from them and then they were to come running to him. Whoever arrived first was to receive the hat. However, they had told him that the hat was enchanted. Whoever put it on his head could wish to be taken to wherever he wanted. So the young man kept walking without calling the giants. All of a sudden he put the hat on his head and wished to be at the castle of the golden sun.

When he arrived there, he gazed at the princess, but she looked terrible. Then he said to her, "If I had known that you looked so horrible, I would have never come here."

However, she fetched a mirror and told him to look at it so that he could see how beautiful she would be if he were to rescue her. After he looked into the mirror, he said, "That's good! What do I have to do?"

"Down from the castle there's an ox standing at a spring," the princess said and explained that his first task was to kill the ox. When the ox was dead, he had to watch out. A fiery bird would fly from it, and this bird would carry a glowing egg with it. When the bird felt itself under attack, it would let the egg drop, and wherever it fell, it would burn everything until the egg had melted and could no longer be found. But there was a ball in the egg, and if he could obtain it, then the spirit that had power over her would be pacified. She would be saved, and he would become king of the castle of the golden sun.

He did what the princess had told him to do and killed the ox. When the fiery bird wanted to fly away, however, his brother, the eagle, came and pecked at the bird with his beak so that the bird had to let the egg drop. It fell right into a fisherman's hut near some water, for the eagle had

† Friedmund von Arnim, "The Castle of the Golden Sun"—"Vom Schloß der goldenen Sonne," in *Hundert neue Mährchen im Gebirge gesammelt* (Charlottenburg: Egbert Bauer, 1844).

forced the bird to fly near the water. The hut began to burn and was beginning to smell from all the smoke. Now the brother who was a whale came to help and spat one wave of water after the next so that the egg was cooled off and no longer burned. Since the egg had been cooled off so quickly, its shell had cracked open so that the youngest brother could easily take the ball from it. He brought the ball to the spirit. The princess was rescued, and he was now king of the castle of the golden sun.

JACOB AND WILHELM GRIMM

The Crystal Ball†

Once upon a time, there was a sorceress who had three sons, and they loved each other dearly. But the old woman did not trust them and thought they wanted to steal her power. So she changed the oldest son into an eagle. He had to make his home in the mountain cliffs, and sometimes he could be seen gliding up and down in the sky and making circles. The second son was changed into a whale that lived deep in the ocean, and one could see him only when he sometimes sent mighty jets of water high into the air. Both sons reverted to their human shape for just two hours every day. Since the third son feared that his mother might change him too, and he might become a wild animal, perhaps a bear or a wolf, he sneaked away in secret. Indeed, he had heard that at the castle of the golden sun there was an enchanted princess who was waiting to be rescued. However, he would have to risk his life. Twenty-three young men had already suffered a miserable death, and only one more would be allowed to try to rescue her. After that, nobody would be permitted to come. Since he had a courageous heart, he decided to search for the castle of the golden sun.

He had already traveled a long time and had not been able to find it, when he got lost in a large forest and could not find his way out. Suddenly he noticed two giants in the distance, who waved to him with their hands, and as he approached them, they said, "We're quarreling over this hat and who should get it. Since we're each just as strong as the other, neither one can defeat the other. Now, small people are smarter than we are, so we want you to make the decision."

"How can you quarrel over an old hat?" the young man asked.

"You don't know the powers it has. It's a wishing hat. Whoever puts it on can wish himself to be anywhere he wants, and within seconds he'll be there."

"Give me the hat," the young man said. "I'll go off some distance from here, and when I call you, run to me, and whoever wins the race will get the hat." He put the hat on his head and went off. However, he thought

† Jacob and Wilhelm Grimm, "The Crystal Ball"—"Die Kristallkugel" (1857), No. 197 in *Kinder- und Hausmärchen. Gesammelt durch die Brüder Grimm* (Göttingen: Dieterich, 1857).

about the king's daughter, forgot the giants, and kept going. Once he sighed with all his heart and cried out, "Oh, if only I were at the castle of the golden sun!" And no sooner had he uttered these words than he was standing on top of a high mountain in front of the castle gate.

He entered the castle and strode through all the rooms until he reached the last one, where he found the king's daughter. However, he was horrified when he saw her: her face was ash gray and full of wrinkles, and she had dreary eyes and red hair. "Are you the king's daughter whose beauty is praised by the entire world?" he exclaimed.

"Ah," she replied, "this is not my real condition. Human eyes can see me only in this ugly form. But look into this mirror so you'll know what I look like. The mirror can't be fooled, and it will show you my image as it truly is."

She handed him the mirror, and he saw the reflection of the most beautiful maiden in the world, and he saw tears rolling down her cheeks out of sadness. Then he said, "How can you be saved? I'm afraid of nothing."

She replied, "Whoever gets the crystal ball and holds it in front of the magician will break his power, and I'll return to my true form. But," she added, "many a man has gone to his death because of this, and you, my young thing, I'd feel sorry if you placed yourself in such great danger."

"Nothing can stop me," he said, "but tell me what I must do."

"I want you to know everything," the king's daughter answered. "When you descend the mountain on which the castle stands, there'll be a wild bison at the bottom next to the spring. You will have to fight it. And, if you should be so fortunate as to slay this beast, a firebird will rise from it. This bird carries a glimmering egg in its body, and the egg has a crystal ball as a yolk. However, the bird will not let go of the egg unless it is forced to. And, if the egg falls onto the earth, it will set everything on fire and destroy everything near it. The egg itself will melt along with the crystal ball, and all your efforts will have been in vain."

The young man descended the mountain and reached the spring, where the bison snorted and roared at him. After a long battle the young man pierced the bison's body with his sword, and the beast sank to the ground. The firebird immediately rose from the bison and tried to fly away, but the eagle, the brother of the young man, who flew through the clouds, dived after the bird and chased it toward the ocean. There the eagle hit the bird so hard with his beak that the bird was forced to let the egg fall. However, it did not fall into the ocean but on top of a fisherman's hut standing on the shore, and the hut began to smoke right away and was about to burst into flames. Then waves as large as houses rose up in the ocean, swept over the hut, and vanquished the flames. The other brother, the whale, had swum toward the shore and driven the water onto the land. When the fire was out, the young man searched for the egg and was fortunate enough to find it. Indeed, it had not melted yet, but the shell had cracked open due to the sudden cooling from the water, and he could take out the crystal ball, which was undamaged.

When the young man went to the magician and held the ball in front of him, the latter said, "My power is destroyed. From now on you are king of the castle of the golden sun. You can also restore your brothers to their human forms."

So the young man hurried back to the king's daughter, and as he entered her room she stood there in all her magnificent beauty, and they exchanged rings with each other in a joyful celebration.

The Fate of Spinning

The importance of spinning in the economy of Europe from the medieval period to the end of the nineteenth century can be documented in the thousands of folk- and fairy tales that were disseminated by word of mouth and through print. The most popular "spinning" tale is, of course, "Rumpelstiltskin," and like many tales about spinning, it reveals how important spinning could be for women: a good spinner could rise in social status and find a husband that would reward her efforts. This is the case even in Basile's comical version, "The Seven Pieces of Bacon Rind," in which the peasant girl hates spinning and cannot spin well. Indeed, there are different perspectives about the value of spinning for women in these tales, and many of them which were probably originally told by women in spinning rooms reveal how the spinners would actually like not to spin anymore, but use their spinning to entangle a man and to weave the threads and narrative strands of their own lives. The origins of the figure and the name "Ricdin-Ricdon" or "Rumpelstiltskin" have never been conclusively determined. Sometimes the character is a demonic figure; sometimes it is a magical gnome, dwarf, or spirit. Basile's female protagonist relied on the magical intervention of fairies. Mlle Lhéritier was undoubtedly familiar with Basile's tale, but she changed it immensely to address important social issues concerning the diligence and value of a young woman who unwittingly makes a bargain with the devil. The Grimms were well aware of her tale, but they also knew many others that had an influence on their various spinning tales. Johannes Praetorius (a pseudonym for Hans Schultze) published a humorous version in his book *Abentheurlichen Glücks-Topf* (*The Adventurous Lucky Pot*, 1669); Sophie Albrecht's "Graumännchen oder die Burg Rabenbühl" ("The Little Gray Man or the Castle Rabenbühl," 1799) was strongly influenced by Mlle Lhéritier's "Ricdin-Ricdon"; August Ey combined some motifs of "Beauty and the Beast" in his version "Die goldene Rose" ("The Golden Rose") in his *Harzmärchenbuch* (1862). Sometimes motifs from tales that deal with persecuted heroines were combined with motifs of demonic figures and the guessing of names to form a tale similar to "Rumpelstiltskin." For instance, Ignaz and Joseph Zingerle published "Cistl im Korbl" ("Cistl in the Little Basket") in *Tirols Volksdichtungen und Volksbräuche* (*The Folk Poetry and Customs of Tyrol*, 1852); it uses motifs from the Grimms' "All Fur" and tales about a demonic helper. In the English tradition, Rumpelstiltskin generally goes by the name of Tom-Tit-Tot, and there are hundreds of different versions of this tale in Great Britain, as the English folklorist Edward Clodd has shown in his book *Tom Tit Tot: An Essay of Savage Philosophy* (1898). Joseph Jacobs published one of the best texts of "Tom Tit Tot" in *English Fairy Tales* (1890).

GIAMBATTISTA BASILE

The Seven Pieces of Bacon Rind[†]

There was once an old beggar woman who went from door to door with a distaff in her hand seeking alms and spitting at people along the way. Since it is only by craft and deceit that one lives half the time (and by deceit and craft the other half), she said to some dimwitted and gullible women that she wanted to make a nice fat soup for her skinny daughter, and she managed to get seven small pieces of bacon rind from them. Then she carried the bacon rinds home as well as a nice bundle of twigs that she picked up from the ground. She gave all of this to her daughter to cook while she went back to beg a few heads of cabbage from some gardeners so they could make some soup.

Her daughter, Saporita, took the pieces of bacon rind, and after she scraped off the skin, she put them in a pot to cook. But as soon as they began to stir in the pot, they also stirred her appetite because the smell that arose from the pot was a mortal challenge on the battlefield of the appetite and a request for information by the bank of her throat. Though she kept trying to resist, she was finally provoked by the odors from the pot, aroused by her own gluttony, and strangled by the hunger gnawing at her. In the end, she let herself try a little piece, which tasted so good that she said to herself, "Whoever wants to lead a life dictated by fear should become a policeman! I'm going to throw care to the winds! Let's eat, come what may. After all, it's only bacon rind. What could happen to me? The skin on my back is tough enough to pay for the rind."

Upon saying this, she swallowed the first piece, and feeling her stomach grumble for more, she grabbed a second piece. Then she pecked at the third, and gradually, she tried one after the other until she had nibbled away all seven pieces. After she had made a mess of things, she realized what a mistake she had made and imagined that the bacon might stick in her throat. So she began thinking of ways to trick her mother. At last she decided to take an old shoe and cut the sole into seven pieces and put them into the pot. When her mother returned home, she brought a bunch of cabbage and other vegetables. After chopping them into bits, stalks and all so as not to waste anything, she waited for the water to boil and then threw all the vegetables into the pot. Then she added a little leftover grease that the coachman had given her out of charity after he had greased a carriage. Next she had her daughter spread a cloth over a chest of old poplar wood, and after taking out two stale pieces of bread from a little sack, she pulled down a wooden bowl from a shelf and crumbled the bread over the vegetables with the pieces of leather. As she began to eat, she immediately felt that her teeth were not made for shoe leather and that the bacon rinds had undergone some new Ovidian metamorphosis

[†] Giambattista Basile, "The Seven Pieces of Bacon Rind"—"Le sette cotennine" (1634), *Quarto passatempo della quarta giornata* in *Lo cunto de li cunti overo Lo trattenemiento de peccerille*, De Gian Alessio Abbattutis, 5 vols. (Naples: Ottavio Beltrano, 1634–36).

586	GIAMBATTISTA BASILE

and had been transformed into the gizzards of a buffalo. Therefore, she turned to her daughter and said, "What kind of trick have you played on me, you cursed sow? What disgusting stuff have you put into this soup? Do you think that my stomach's become an old shoe and you want to provide me with new soles? Quick! Confess right now and tell me what's happened; otherwise, you'll wish that you'd never been born because I'll break every bone in your body."

Saporita began to deny everything, but this only increased the wrathful cries of the old woman. So she placed the blame on the vapors of the pot that had blinded her eyes and had induced her to make this mistake. Seeing that her meal had been poisoned, the old woman grabbed a broom-stick and began to lather her daughter, whacking her more than seven times, and began chasing her all around the house.

Just then a merchant happened to be passing by and heard the daughter's screams. So he entered the house, and seeing how badly the old woman was treating her daughter, he took the broom out of her hand and said, "What has this poor girl done that you want to kill her? Is this your way of punishing her, or your way of taking her life? Have you found her breaking a lance,[1] or breaking open your money box? Aren't you ashamed of treating this poor girl in this way?"

"You don't know what she's done," replied the old woman. "This shameless girl knows that I'm a poor beggar, and she has no consideration for me. She's going to ruin me with her doctors and druggists. I told her that, when it turns warm, she's not to work so hard; otherwise she'll fall sick, and I won't be able to help her. But the impertinent thing wanted to fill seven spindles this morning, despite my words of warning, and I'm afraid that this would harm her heart, and she'd have to spend a few months in bed."

When the merchant heard this, he began imagining how this industrious girl could work wonders as the fairy of his house. So he said to the old woman, "Forget your anger because I'd be glad to remove this danger from your house. I'll take your daughter as my wife and bring her to my home where she will live like a princess. Thank heaven, I raise my own chickens and breed pigs. I also have pigeons, and the house is so full that you can hardly move about without bumping into something. Heaven has blessed me, and the evil eye has been kept far from my house. I have bushels of grain, sacks of flour, jugs of oil, pots and bladders of grease, strings of bacon lard, shelves filled with jars, stacks of wood, piles of coal, a chest filled with linen, a bridal bed, and to top it all off, I can live the life of a lord because of the rent I charge for land and the interest I receive. Besides that, I've invested some money at the fair, and if things go well, I'll become a rich man."

When the old woman saw this good fortune rain down on her when she least expected it, she took Saporita by the hand and gave her to him according to the customs of Naples.[2] "Here she is," she said. "From this

1. A sexual metaphor.
2. In the Neapolitan wedding ceremony, the bride's mother held up her daughter's hand to have the wedding ring placed on her finger.

moment on and for thousands of years, may she be yours. May you enjoy good health and have many handsome sons."

The merchant put his arm around Saporita and took her home with him. He could not wait for the next market day to arrive so he could go and do some shopping. When Monday finally came, he got up early in the morning and went to the farmers' market, where he bought twenty huge rolls of flax, brought them to Saporita, and said, "Now, spin to your heart's content. You needn't fear another crazy old woman interfering with your work like your mother, who broke your bones because you filled the spindles. For every twenty spindles, I'll give you twenty kisses. For every roll of linen that you make for me, I'll give you my heart. So, enjoy your work, and as soon as I return from the fair in twenty days, I hope to find twenty rolls of spun flax, and I'll give you a beautiful pair of red sleeves trimmed with green velvet!"

"Go! Get out of here already," Saporita responded in a low voice. "Now I'm in a jam! Run and grab the ring! If you expect a shirt made by my hands, you might as well provide yourself now with scrap paper! Understand? Do you think that I'm a devil or witch and can spin twenty rolls of flax in twenty days? May the ship be cursed that carried me to this port! Forget it! Take your time because the flax will be spun only when liver grows bristles and when the ape grows a tail."

Now, while the husband was away, Saporita, who was just as gluttonous as she was lazy, did not do any work at all. Instead, she took some sacks of flower and flasks of oil and made cakes and fritters. From morning until night she nibbled like a mouse and guzzled like a pig. When the day of her husband's return finally came, she became constipated by fear at the thought of the noise and squabbling there would be when the merchant found that the flax had not been spun but that the chests and pitchers were empty. So she took a very long pole and wrapped a roll of flax around it with all its tow and hemp. Then she stuck a large pitchfork into an Indian gourd and tied the pole to the balustrade of the terrace. Finally, she began to lower this portly spindle to the ground, while she kept by her side a large pot of macaroni swimming in water into which she dipped her fingers. As she spun the strands of flax as smooth as a ship's ropes, she dipped her fingers into the pot, and with each dip, she squirted the water at passersby just as mischief makers do at Carnival time.[3] By chance, some fairies arrived on the spot and were so amused by this atrocious scene that they nearly died from laughing. As a result, they cast a magic spell so that the flax in the house was immediately spun and turned into bleached white cloth. All this happened in the blink of an eye so that Saporita swam in the grease of happiness when she saw this good fortune rain down upon her.

Nevertheless, she wanted to make sure that her husband would not cause her any more grief. So she fetched a bunch of nuts, spread them in her bed, and jumped in. When the merchant arrived, she began to groan and turn from side to side, cracking the nuts so loudly that it seemed she

---

3. The week before Lent, devoted in Italy and other Roman Catholic countries to revelry and riotous amusement.

was breaking her bones. Immediately, her husband asked her how she felt, and she responded in a low voice of distress, "I couldn't be worse, my husband. There's not a whole bone left in my body! Do you think it's easy as pie to spin twenty rolls of flax in twenty days and to weave it into cloth as well? Now you won't have to pay for a midwife, my husband, and as for discretion, the ass has eaten it! When I'm dead, don't do anything more like this, mama mia! This is why I'll never work like a dog anymore. I don't want to empty the spindle of my life just to fill all your spindles!"

The husband began caressing her and said, "Just get well, my dear wife, because I cherish your beautiful texture of love more than all the cloth of the world! Now I realize that your mother was right to punish you for exhausting yourself so much, for you've lost your health. But keep up your spirits. I'll spend a bundle of money to get you back on your feet. I'm going to fetch the doctor."

As soon as he said that, he went to look for Dr. Catruopolo. In the meantime, Saporita gulped down the nuts and threw the shells out of the window. When the doctor came, he took her pulse, looked at her face, examined her urine, and smelled the chamberpot. Then he concluded, with the oath of Hippocrates and Galen,[4] that her sickness was due to an abundance of blood and lack of work. The merchant thought that this was ridiculous, and he placed a coin in his hand and sent him away stinking mad. When the merchant told Saporita that he wanted to fetch another doctor, she said to him that it was not necessary because just seeing him again had been enough to make her feel better. Therefore, her husband embraced her and told her that, from then on, she was not to do anything to exhaust herself since it was not possible to grow grapes for good Greek wine and cabbage[5] at the same time.

The barrel full and the slave girl drunk

MARIE-JEANNE LHÉRITIER

Ricdin-Ricdon[†]

Once there was a king who reigned over one of the most beautiful kingdoms of Europe, whose name, however, historians can no longer trace. The king was known for his sense of justice, rectitude, and paternal love for his subjects, and thus he had acquired the glorious name of King Prud'homme, which during those times signified a king full of integrity and honor. This king was married to a lady who also had many virtues. Since she was especially lively and active and constantly occupied herself with some pleasant work, the people called her Queen Laborieuse. The

4. Ironic reference to the doctor's oath. Hippocrates was a famous Greek physician born about 460 B.C.E. Galen was a celebrated doctor born at Pergamus in Asia Minor at the end of the second century C.E.
5. Wherever cabbage grew, it was impossible for the fine Greek vines to take root.
† Marie-Jeanne Lhéritier, "Ricdin-Ricdon"—"Ricdin-Ricdon" (1705), in *La tour ténébreuse et les jours lumineux* (Paris: Veuve de Claude Barbin, 1705).

king and queen had an only son whose inclinations were basically just as virtuous as those he had received at birth, but since this young prince had inherited the vivacity of the queen his mother and was not obliged to work during his youth, he expended his energies in pleasure. He took a great liking to the theater, the balls, the tournaments, and hunting parties. In short, he was extremely eager to do anything that would furnish him pleasure of a diverse kind, and thus he came to be known by the name of Amourjoie.

The king and queen regarded their son's manner of amusing himself as innocent and did not oppose his penchant for pleasure. Indeed, they felt that the eagerness he displayed for amusements would be but a passing phase of his youth. Aside from this, the prince was very likeable, and it was clear from all his actions that he had a fiery spirit.

What surprised most people, however, was that such a vivacious prince had not yet fallen in love and did not respond to affairs of the heart as something significant. The only desire of his heart was to participate at the gallant festivals and in the hunts, and he found only these things stimulating because they tended to be unique and different. Sometimes, while pursuing a stag, he would become separated from the rest of his hunting party, and sometimes he would become so famished before he could find any of his people again that he would enter the home of the first country gentleman or the first peasant that he encountered on his way. Since he ordinarily did not reveal who he was, he often had some bizarre adventures that he enjoyed a great deal. Later he would relate them to his father at the court with extreme delight.

One day, when he had again been separated from his people, he came across a village that appeared to be deserted. Suddenly he saw a dazzlingly beautiful young maiden emerge from a garden. An old woman with an unpleasant face was dragging her violently toward a rustic cottage across from the garden on the other side of the road. The young woman had a distaff packed with linseed at her side and was holding in the folds of her dress a bunch of flowers that she had gathered in the garden. The old woman tore the flowers away from her, threw them down on the ground in the middle of the road, and gave the beautiful girl some harsh blows. Then she took her by the arm again and said to her in a furious tone, "Let's go! Let's go, you miserable little creature! Back to the house! I'm going to teach you there what it means to be so insolent and disobedient to me!"

The prince, who had stopped briefly to watch this spectacle, approached the old woman just as she was about to enter the cottage, and he asked her in a gentle voice, "Why are you abusing this young girl, my good woman? What has she done to make you so angry?"

The peasant woman, who was in a fit of fury and did not like anyone to mix into her affairs, was about to respond to the prince in an insolent way. But when she glanced at his garments and judged by their splendor that the person wearing them had to be a person of distinction, she controlled her fury and contented herself by answering in a bitter voice, "My lord, I'm quarreling with my daughter because she always does the opposite of what I tell her to do. I don't want her to spin anymore, and yet

she spins from morning until night and is so diligent that nobody can
match her work. And I was only scolding her the way you saw me doing
because she spins too much."

"What!" said the prince. "Is that a reason to complain about this poor
child? Ah, truly, my good woman, if you dislike girls because they enjoy
spinning too much, you just have to give your daughter to my mother the
queen, who finds this occupation most pleasant and loves girls who know
how to spin. The queen will make your daughter rich."

"Alas, my lord," responded the old woman, "if this conceited snip here,
with her pretty skills, seems suitable for your good queen, you can have
her right away, for she has been a burden to me for a long time, and I'd
like to get rid of her."

Just as she was finishing her words, part of the prince's hunting party
rejoined him, and he said to one of his valets to place the beautiful girl
on the rump of the horse behind him. The young maiden's face was still
covered with tears because of the old woman's threats and treatment, but
her crying did not distract at all from her charms. The prince tried to
console her by assuring her that with the skills she possessed she could
not fail to find a great deal of favor in the eyes of the queen. However,
the poor girl was so bewildered by the numerous men surrounding her
that she did not even hear half of what the prince said to her. Her mother
watched her departure without evincing the slightest sign of care about
the destiny of her daughter, while the villagers could not open their eyes
wide enough as they watched her in the middle of all those great lords
garnished with gold. They were the prince's petty officers who were leading
her to the queen, and hence she was the envy of all the young peasant
girls of the region.

Along the way the prince learned that the beautiful girl's name was
Rosanie, and as soon as they arrived at the palace, he presented her to the
queen as the most skillful and diligent spinner in the entire kingdom. The
queen gave her a kind welcome, regarded her attentively, and praised even
her modest and touching charms, which greatly mortified certain ladies of
the court who prided themselves on their perfect beauty. The queen provided lodgings for Rosanie in the palace, where there was a suite of rooms
completely filled with large masses of the best filace[1] in the world. There
was hemp from Syria and Brittany and flax from the isle of Ithaca, Picardy,
and Flanders. In fact, there was even that famous incombustible flax out
of which one can make a marvelous cloth that the most scorching fire
cannot damage. Rosanie was told, as if it were good news, that she only
had to choose among the flax and hemp, and she could set to work whenever she wished. Then someone added that it should make no difference
to her since she was stronger and more skillful than anyone else, and the
queen wanted to keep her a long time and do a great deal of good for her
and had destined her to spin everything in the apartment.

When the poor girl was alone, she fell into utmost despair, for she had
such an insurmountable aversion to the metier of spinning that she regarded just a few hours of this work as an atrocious punishment and ob-

1. Medieval term for thread; also spelled *filaze*.

ligation. It is true that, when she was courageous enough to make a great effort to occupy herself with spinning, she performed the work with infinite skill. Her yarn was perfectly even and fine, but she spun so slowly that, even if she could have ultimately gathered together her strength and retained her assiduity from morning until night, she hardly would have been able to spin more than half a spindle of yarn each day.

Given her disposition, one can judge the pain that she felt in respect to the queen's attitude. Rosanie did not know how she would be able to get herself out of this predicament, which was actually created by her malicious mother. However, she was glad to be out of the hands of her mother, who only had harsh feelings toward her. The gracious and kind welcome by the queen had captivated her imagination. The court, where she had just arrived, and which she only viewed in a flash of lightning, seemed to her already a most pleasant place to stay. She was charmed by all the objects her eyes encountered; she also realized that she could only sustain herself at the court by showing what a nimble spinner she was; and she felt only too well that she did not have the talent for this. Preoccupied by these cruel thoughts, she did not sleep a wink that night. Nor did the prince sleep. The stimulating charms and naive grace of Rosanie had attracted him so strongly and had made such a striking impression on his heart that he spent the entire night envisaging nothing but that charming girl.

However, as soon as it became day, the queen sent a message to Rosanie ordering her to come and talk with her. Everyone was in full dress in the queen's chambers that morning, and therefore, when Rosanie arrived, a group of ladies avidly cast their glances at her face. The king, who had not seen her until then and who happened to be there at that moment, regarded the young beauty assiduously and bestowed various praises on her. The prince, who was also in his mother's chambers and who thought her even more beautiful than his father did, did not, however, say anything. Despite the simplicity of her violet corset and the rustic manner of her coiffure, Rosanie truly captivated the eyes of all those who regarded her, for she had a fine and well-shaped figure and free and easy manner about her. Indeed, despite her lack of education, she did not have the awkward air of a village maiden. Her hair was the most beautiful ash blond, and her white face was ornamented by glistening blue eyes which were just as soft as they were alert. Her nose was perfectly proportioned, and she had a small mouth, pleasantly shaped. Moreover, she had splendid teeth, as is necessary to be perfectly beautiful, and her complexion was dazzling white and enriched by a tinge of red that made her glitter. Even with her remarkably regular features and glowing complexion one still could see the lively charms of her face and her personality and whatever else contributed to the soul of beauty.

Even though she had not slept that night, she did not seem to be at all downcast. The confusion that she experienced on being exposed this way to the view of numerous people at the court made her blush so that each of her attractive features was only heightened and brought out to its best. Therefore, it was clear to see, even though she was just a spinner and had been obligated to stay within four walls, her complexion had been pro-

tected from the ravages of sunburn. Those ladies who considered themselves beautiful felt extremely spiteful toward Rosanie, and they tried to
find some faults with her face and figure, while the astonished young men
conceived a thousand ridiculous plans to win her. In sum, no matter how
one viewed her, she drew the attention of the entire court.

Before the king departed, he advised the queen to give another dress to
the beautiful spinner since hers was too bizarre and different from those
of all the other young women at the palace. The queen responded that
she had already given some thought to this, and in effect, a few hours
later, a servant brought Rosanie a dress and the proper headdresses that
perfectly conformed to the prevailing mode at the court of King
Prud'homme. The queen's chambermaids dressed her and combed her
hair with a great deal of care. Afterward, they showed her exactly how she
was to go about grooming herself and fixing her clothes from now on. The
garments fitted her splendidly, and she appeared in perfect dress at the
temple, where the prince saw her. He found her more beautiful than ever
and heaped praise on her for all to hear. All those people at the court who
had not seen her in the queen's chambers regarded her with eager curiosity, and since all remembered her name and since the king had called
her the beautiful spinner, this flattering name stuck with her, and in less
than twenty-four hours she set the fashion at the court and in the city so
that there was not a single conversation in which the beautiful spinner did
not enter for some reason.

Nevertheless, even though there were a hundred young beautiful
women at the court jealous of her good fortune and tired of hearing everyone talk about her so much, the young maiden in question, who had
caused so much jealousy, was experiencing some sad moments. During
the course of the first day that she spent at the palace, she had found a
way to excuse herself from spinning, which she found intolerable, by saying she had cramps in her fingers. The anxiety that she felt about the
constraining work for which she was destined was canceled out by the
delight she had in being so richly dressed and in hearing her beauty
praised a thousand times.

The queen's ladies-in-waiting, most of whom were no longer young and
no longer boasted about being beautiful, took a great liking to Rosanie.
And she responded to their affection with docility and great compliance.
They promenaded with her all over the palace and even in different places
of the city, and these walks were a great distraction for this new member
of the court, whose eyes were not accustomed to seeing so many magnificent things. Yet when she returned in the evening to that fatal apartment
filled with flax, she was repelled by that odious sight and sank once again
into a state of despair. Still, she was able to regain some of her tranquillity
and to sleep much better than she had slept the other night. The next
day, after she had arisen, she thought about putting on the beautiful
clothes that the queen had given her. But she did not remember how to
get dressed properly in the way that the queen's chambermaids had taught
her. Therefore, she tried twenty different times to make herself appear
tolerably well-dressed but could not succeed. Finally, after so many fruit-
less attempts, she decided to let her headdress and garments stay on her

in an odd and awkward manner. Greatly depressed by her lack of success, she sought to compensate for it in some other way. So she loaded her distaff and began to spin, but her hand was just as slow as it ordinarily was. Despite all the efforts she made, she only succeeded in spinning a quarter of a spindle of yarn from ten o'clock, the time that she finished getting dressed, until twelve-thirty, when a messenger arrived from the queen saying that her majesty wanted to see her work.

Right after Rosanie received the message, she burst out into tears. Then she tried to think up a new excuse that might help her out of this predicament. Therefore, when she appeared before the queen, she was downcast and told her that she was depressed because she had been overwhelmed by a violent attack of rheumatism that affected her arm and prevented her from doing her work in her usual assiduous manner. She added that she had tried with all her might to overcome this malady and had tried twenty different times to use the distaff and the spindle. But it had been all in vain. Despite her perseverance, she had been able to spin only a small amount of yarn, which she showed the queen. Now, Queen Laborieuse found her work remarkably beautiful, and it confirmed her opinion of Rosanie's dexterity. Since the queen was a good woman, she told Rosanie not to force herself to work and added that she wanted her to see her chief doctor. However, Rosanie feared that the doctor might discover that nothing was wrong with her and told the queen that she did not need any kind of remedy for this malady. It would not take long for her to recover, because, whenever she had been incapacitated by such an attack before, she had only needed to rest for it to pass. The queen was satisfied with this reason, but right after Rosanie withdrew, the queen's workers, who were very jealous of the great favors that the queen had suddenly shown the newcomer at the court, remarked very loudly that the cramps and rheumatism most assuredly resulted from the queen's orders. Most likely, this beauty, who everyone believed was so skillful and diligent, was nothing but a clumsy and dawdling worker.

Poor Rosanie, who had heard these remarks, was greatly afflicted by them. Moreover, to complete her disgrace, the queen's daughters and other ladies-in-waiting, who noticed how poorly she had dressed herself and placed her headdress, burst out into great peels of laughter and made a thousand jokes about her violet bodice and short skirt, which she had worn the other day. Indeed, they maintained that it had been a great mistake to take those things away from her since they suited her better than the garments of a young lady of the court.

Rosanie could not withstand such vexatious provocations. So she left the palace and went in the direction of the gardens, where she kept on walking until she found herself in a very dense wood at the end of the park. Once there she felt herself so exhausted that she promptly sat down at the edge of a rippling stream that wound its way through the wood. She began to mope and ponder her bad fortune and what role it had played in bringing about the sad state that she was in. For a moment, she almost decided to return to her mother, no matter how hard and savage she was. But when she thought about the harsh way in which her mother had constantly treated her ever since she had lost her father, she reproached herself for having the slightest idea of returning. Considering that she was very young and curious about the world, she felt an aversion to staying in the village and to the life-style there, and the court had not diminished this aversion, even though she had been there only a short time. On the other hand, she saw clearly that the queen would become indignant and expel her from the palace with shame and perhaps punishment if she realized that Rosanie had deceived her about her skill in spinning. However, she saw that the truth was about to manifest itself. She was defeated and worn out. She could no longer feign cramps or rheumatism with success. She did not want to wait for those people who envied her to make her into their laughingstock.

Given these cruel reflections, she abandoned herself completely to her despair, and she said to herself that there was nothing left for her to do but to die. With this idea in mind, forgetting her weariness, she stood up to walk to a high pavilion at the other end of the wood, which the ladies had shown her the other day during their promenade. She intended to climb to the top of this open pavilion and then throw herself to the ground from a window. Nevertheless, the natural love that she had for life, her thoughts about her tender youth, and above all, the secret complaisance that she felt for her beauty, all this made her weep as she thought about her death and as she sought to walk very slowly toward the fatal spot where she had condemned herself to die.

As she was about to cross a path that led to the pavilion, she suddenly saw a very large, dark, and well-dressed man emerge before her. He was somber in appearance but had a jovial and gracious air about him as he spoke.

"Where are you going, my pretty child?" he said. "It seems to me that I see tears streaming from your eyes. Tell me what's bothering you. It would have to be something extraordinary for me not to be able to help you."

"Alas!" responded Rosanie. "There's nothing anyone can do against the troubles that have overwhelmed me. Therefore, it's useless for me to reveal anything to you."

"Perhaps," replied the stranger, "help is not so impossible as you think in your despair. At the very least you can relieve yourself by talking about your troubles. Tell me all about them. There's nobody better you can confide in than me."

"Since you insist," answered Rosanie, "I'll tell you about my entire destiny."

"I had the misfortune of being born under obscure circumstances. My father was a peasant, a good man, full of integrity and intelligence, and he developed a fine reputation among the inhabitants of the village and among the people of the surrounding villages so that they asked him to arbitrate all their differences. Since he was very reserved and never liked to talk much, he was called Disantpeu. My father, who had a tender love for me, had once been in the army and had even won the confidence of his captain. That is why he did not have those repulsive rustic manners and speech that people have who never leave their village. Ever since my childhood he took a great deal of care to teach me all that he knew, and if I have a great love for virtue and am somewhat intelligent, I owe it all to him, for my mother is a frightfully coarse woman, Moreover, she never took any pains to teach me what she knew. In fact, she was always hard with me and disliked me. All her tenderness was reserved for my brother.

"Despite my village background and the apparent weakness of my education, I have the feelings and inclinations of someone much above my state of birth. Of course, the fact that I am of low birth causes me great despair. The only consolation that I have for my low birth resides in my fair features. They allow me to hope that I might have a happy future. When I was only twelve years old, I would often go to a spring or brook where I would keep telling myself that I would never ever stay put beneath a thatched roof. Given such ideas, I very much scorned the compliments that the young boys of the village gave me. However, I had barely turned fourteen when my father received some of the best proposals for my hand that a person of my rank could hope for. When he told me about them, I broke out into tears and told him forcefully that I would prefer to die than to enter into any marriages of that kind. Fortunately, thanks to his love for me, he was kind enough not to force me to accept any of the proposals. My mother complained about this a great deal and kept saying that he was spoiling me by blindly complying with my will. Yet, despite her words, he did not change and become terrible. On the contrary, he often reproached my mother for not loving me and asserted that only her son was dear to her. Alas! It did not take long for her to prove the truth of my father's words. He went on a journey and did not inform us why or where he was going. But he assured us that he would return soon. However, he must have died during this unfortunate journey, for a great deal of time has passed, and he should have returned to us by now.

"Ever since then, my mother began regarding herself as my absolute mistress, and she has treated me as harshly as possible. Finally, two days ago, after scolding me cruelly for not having spun enough, she was dragging me toward our cottage and threatening me furiously when the king's son happened to pass by our door and ask why she was abusing me in such a terrible way. She answered him mockingly and told him that it was because I spun too much. The prince thought she was serious and believed her, and since our queen is favorably disposed toward all kinds of work, and among all things takes a great delight in diverting herself by spinning, the prince immediately asked my mother whether she would give me to the queen. My mother was overjoyed to get rid of me and placed me in the hands of the prince's men right on the spot. Then they presented me to the queen as the best and most diligent spinner in the entire kingdom, but I am truly the last person in the world to possess such qualities as those. Nevertheless, the queen believed that I had them and gave me such a terrible amount of work to do that just the sight of it sends shivers up my spine. I believe that she has gathered together all the best flax in the world in order to overwhelm me. Given how much I hate spinning and my slowness in this metier, I don't know where to begin or how I should finish such boring and consuming work. On the other hand, I have no other choice if I want to stay at the court, where I am pleased to be one of the queen's workers. Alas! How happy I was at first when I found myself at the palace and heard my beauty praised. I recalled the dreams of vanity from my youth and flattered myself that some nobleman at the court or, at least, one of the royal officers would be sufficiently taken by me to want to marry me and share his fortune. I even believed for a few moments— oh, what a presumptuous idea!—that the prince would regard me with eyes full of passion. Oh! And now, what is left of all that? How depressing it is to feel that I don't have the skill to dress myself properly and thus distort the gifts that nature has bestowed upon me. Moreover, I don't have the skill to spin quickly, and because of all this I'll be expelled in shame by the queen and will become the laughingstock of all the envious young women who had previously trembled because of my beauty and the favors that I had received.

"So, monsieur," Rosanie continued, "although you don't know me, you can clearly see that there is no remedy for my troubles. However, I hope to end my torments through some fatal means which I shan't reveal."

"But," responded the stranger, "what if, instead of these fatal means, someone were to give you some sweet and pleasant means to settle these troubles, wouldn't you feel a good deal of obligation to this person and wouldn't you do this person a favor in return?"

"I'd do anything I could reasonably do," Rosanie answered right away. "With the exception of my honor and duty, there is nothing that I wouldn't sacrifice to show my gratitude."

"Since you feel the way you do," the stranger responded, "I should like to oblige myself to serve you and with pleasure. But before I do this, let us agree upon the exact conditions. Now, look at the wand that I'm holding in my hand, and take it in your hand."

Rosanie took this wand and regarded it. It was very small and made of some unfamiliar, gray-brown wood that was very bright. It was adorned by a changing stone that was neither a ruby nor a cornelian, nor any other stone known to her. In short, it was impossible to tell what the stone or wood was. After Rosanie inspected the wand for some time, she returned it to the stranger, who said to her, "Look at this wand very carefully. It has remarkable powers. As soon as you touch flax and hemp very hard, it will spin as much of it as you want each day and provide as fine a quality as you wish. It also has another feature—as soon as you touch wool, silk, or canvas, it produces the most beautiful tapestry in the world and works of petit-point[1] that excel those made by the best of manufacturers. I'll lend you this marvelous wand for three months," he continued, "provided that you agree with the terms that I am about to say to you. If, in three months from today, three months to this very day, I return to retrieve my wand and you say to me, 'Take it, Ricdin-Ricdon. Here is your wand,' I'll take back my wand without your being obligated to me in any way whatsoever. But, if on the appointed day, you cannot recall my name, and you simply say to me, 'Here, take back your wand,' I shall be master of your destiny and lead you wherever I please, and you will be obligated to follow me."

Rosanie thought for a few moments about how she should respond. It seemed to her that it would be easy to retain the name Ricdin-Ricdon and

1. Embroidery made with a bent stitch.

that it would not be risky to accept the propitious help of this marvelous wand. She was already imagining the secret delight that she would have in watching the astonished faces of her vain opponents when she produced the beautiful yarn spun by the wand. However, she was troubled by one thing: she imagined that the artlessness with which she dressed herself and groomed her hair had detracted greatly from the advantages provided by her beauty. It would be a torment to stay in the palace dressed and groomed so unbecomingly. All these thoughts prevented her from responding to the stranger immediately, but finally she said to him, "Monsieur Ricdin-Ricdon, I shall accept your proposal if you will include one more condition. That is, along with the virtue of producing beautiful yarn and tapestries, I would like your wand to be able to transform my coiffure and dress so that they have a fine appearance that will please everyone. If you can enrich the properties of your wand, already so useful, with a virtue as necessary to beautiful women as food, you can consider our agreement settled."

"Ah!" exclaimed Ricdin-Ricdon, "nothing is easier than to grant you what you demand. My comrades and I never refuse the fair sex the virtue of looking just as they would like. That goes without saying among us. This is why you see girls of twelve already capable of grooming themselves in a remarkable way and adjusting a beauty patch on themselves just as judiciously as a woman of fifty. Therefore, I declare that as soon as my wand touches your coiffure and garments, they will have a first-rate appearance and flutter so gracefully that they will entrance all the handsome young men."

"Then I accept your proposition," Rosanie said.

"But you must swear an oath," Ricdin-Ricdon responded.

"Well, then, I swear," she answered. "You have my solemn word."

"That will do," said Ricdin-Ricdon, "and now that I have your promise in such good form, I am your servant until we see each other again."

Upon saying these words, he returned the wand to her and departed. As soon as Rosanie had the wand at her disposal, the first thing she did was to touch her coiffure and clothes. Then she looked at herself in the nearest stream and found herself so beautiful and so well-dressed that she was immensely grateful for the agreement that she had just concluded and remembered every detail. Her eyes caressed the obliging wand, and she said to herself with great delight that she had just acquired a very useful article at very little cost.

Immersed in diverse thoughts, she walked through the wood and park and returned to the palace. No sooner did she reach the ground floor than she encountered the prince. He had not seen her during the day, but certain malicious jesters, who inundated the court, had not failed to tell him about the clumsy manner in which the beautiful spinner dressed and groomed herself. The prince had listened to everything without a smile. Indeed, he did not dare show them how much he was convinced that Rosanie was always charming no matter what garments she wore, for he feared too much that they would discover the feelings that he had for this beautiful young maiden.

As soon as he saw her, he was just as enchanted by her attractions as always, and upon examining her appearance and seeing how perfect she looked, he turned toward one of those cold jesters, who had exhausted him some hours ago with an insipid story about Rosanie that he had believed to be very funny, and the prince made a hundred subtle and pointed remarks about the slander and insipidity of his story. Then he greeted Rosanie with such great chivalry that it seemed as if she were one of the most distinguished people at the court. As he passed by, he asked her obligingly as if she had seen the waterworks, and when she responded no, he told her that he would have them played for her the next day. Then Rosanie made a low curtsy and withdrew to her apartment, overjoyed to have such a marvelous wand in her possession, but her ecstasy caused her to forget the name of the man who had given it to her. That night her joy prevented her from sleeping, just as her sorrow had done the first night she had spent in the palace. And during all those hours that she should have been sleeping, her mind was only occupied by pleasant ideas that made her more content than the most gratifying dreams could ever have done.

When morning arrived, she got up, and her wand was at her service instantly just like Coquette, the most skillful of the chambermaids and her favorite. Then she hastened to test the wand's powers on a small batch of the queen's flax, which, through the virtue of this enchanted stick of wood, immediately became a pound of yarn like the most beautiful yarn of Flanders. Charmed by the great success of the wand, Rosanie took a part of the yarn that she had spun and kept it to show the queen that evening so that she would see from it that she was the most assiduous and diligent worker in the world. Later, she watched the waterworks that had been ordered by the prince, and they had not been as good as they were that day for a long time. When the day was over, she waited for the queen at the passage where she normally began her walk. When the queen appeared, Rosanie told her that the cramps and rheumatism were gone and that she had spent the day working. Therefore, she had taken the liberty of coming to her in order to show her the work that she had accomplished. The queen took the yarn and regarded it with eagerness. However, since the sun had set and the halls had not been illuminated, the queen gave orders for the torches to be lit right away. Consequently, once she could see, she was enchanted by the beauty of Rosanie's yarn and enjoyed herself for such a long time by examining it and talking all about the yarn that she forgot all about the promenade that she normally took for an hour. Finally, she remarked that she did not want any of her ladies at the court to murmur or say anything against the beautiful spinner anymore. At the same time, she said many gracious things to Rosanie and ordered her to come to her the next day at her morning audience. That night Rosanie slept very well, and the next morning she did not fail to be in the queen's chambers on time, and she brought with her the other part of the pound of yarn that she had spun.

"Madame," she said to the queen, as she presented her the yarn, "since I saw that my little work had the good fortune of pleasing you and it could perhaps contribute sometimes to diverting you, I spent the night making something new for you so you can see how zealous I am."

"Ah, poor child!" exclaimed the queen as she turned toward her lady of honor, "she is just as affectionate as she is skillful and diligent. But, my child," she turned back to address Rosanie, "I don't want you to make a habit of spending the night like this. It will ruin your health that seems so solid and excellent."

"Yes, madame," Rosanie answered, "it will be an honor for me to work a great deal for you, and I shan't harm myself. I have the good health and strength of a girl of seventeen, and at that age there is nothing that can trouble me. I only beg you to be so kind as to permit me to entertain you for a few hours each day. If you grant this permission, it will not cost me anything to spend the night working."

The queen assured Rosanie that, if she did not stay awake the entire night, she would grant Rosanie some time to entertain her each day. After receiving the queen's guarantee, Rosanie answered, "Until I had shown you what I can do with the distaff and the spindle, I didn't dare tell you that I can weave tapestry just as well as I can spin yarn. Now that you have seen a sample of my spinning, I'll be so free to tell you that, if you would like to give me some wool, silk, and canvas, I'll weave all kinds of tapestries and do some petit-point for you, as you wish."

"Truly," the queen exclaimed, "this little girl has prodigious talents! Go, my child," she continued, "go and gather strawberries in the garden with my ladies. Later I'll give you all that you will need to make some tapestries, and you can work on it tomorrow."

"Before I go, madame, I have another favor to ask of you. Would you be so kind to give orders that I am to be left alone and undisturbed while I am at work in the apartment that you have given me? I cannot tolerate anyone watching me while I work because it upsets my concentration."

"Consider your request granted," the queen responded. "I'll give orders so that you'll be completely free and have your peace and quiet."

When the conversation had concluded, Rosanie withdrew and spent the rest of the day amusing herself, and that night she slept quite well. Even though she had forgotten the name of the man who had given her the wand, she did not think about this a great deal. And when she did ponder it, she was not very much troubled, for she was sure she would remember the name once she took the trouble to recall it. Besides, she had been given three months, and she wanted to profit from this time and use the wand in peace. Indeed, these three moths appeared to her to be just as long as half a century might appear to someone else.

Meanwhile, the prince only thought about his love for her. The pleasure that he had previously taken from his amusements was no longer so sweet. To go hunting or to the theater seemed insipid to him, and he was bored by everything at the court unless Rosanie happened to be present. The object of all his wishes was to see her, talk to her about his tender feelings, and prove his love for her by some great feat that would move her heart. Nevertheless, he did not dare to express these wishes as much as he was inclined to do for fear that the people at the court would notice the zealousness of his emotions. But, despite the precautions that he took, the majority of the old courtiers had already discerned his true feelings, and this discovery contributed toward their showing Rosanie a great deal of attention and consideration. As far as the young men were concerned, they did not have the slightest idea that the prince was attracted to this young beauty, and they mainly thought about her as the object of a pleasant conquest.

Meanwhile, the queen ordered one of her ladies, named Vigilentine, to accompany Rosanie everywhere she went and to serve as her mother. Vigilentine was delighted by this assignment. She found Rosanie totally charming, and it gave her great pleasure to teach Rosanie all she knew about polite manners and to exhort her to conduct herself well in all the proceedings at the court. Since this woman had a good deal of intelligence and practical experience, she was able to show Rosanie how to become cultivated in a very short time.

Now, in the capital city of King Prud'homme's realm, there was a public garden in which the beautiful ladies from the court and the city exhibited their attractions in great pomp. All the gallant young men displayed themselves to their best there, and the coy young women judged themselves in different ways in this garden. The air was so hot and inflamed that not even the four winds would cool it. One ran the risk of becoming more intoxicated by all the flowery talk than by the flowers themselves. Vigilentine did not take Rosanie to this tempestuous place until she had instructed her on how to avoid all the dangers. Aside from Rosanie's good taste and gallant clothes, all brought about through the help of the wand, Vigilentine's lessons made her assume a modest appearance, mixing her charms and radiant air so that she appeared to be a remarkable person, suited to inspire just as much respect as love. She was regarded with jealous eyes by four or five beautiful women, who were à la mode and had come from the provinces to the capital with plans to find their fortune through tying the nuptial knots with some fine young man. Relying on their attractive features, they imagined that they just had to appear in this large city, where the most cultivated, wealthy, and distinguished men of high rank lived, and these men would come running and offer them their hearts and hands in marriage. However, they had been poorly informed that the men were moved more by two beautiful eyes than by the luster of gold. In vain they made a thousand efforts to advertise their charms all over with great fanfare. Hardly anyone thought of them in terms of a solid matrimonial bond, and in spite of all the care they took, the only thing left for them was the frivolous glory of being courted by foreigners obsessed by these giddy creatures, who were secretly bid on by the financiers. The only thing in their favor was that the public rendered justice to their virtue and was persuaded that they truly knew how to guard themselves against the many different traps that had been set for them.

Ordinarily, these beautiful women would have been divided against themselves, but they united their forces against Rosanie. The flattery that she received from all sides, the acclamations that she produced when she appeared in public, made those other young ladies extremely bitter. They could not tolerate without becoming upset that some rustic villager had come and taken over the empire of beauty that each one of them claimed to deserve. At least they now desired to share it among themselves. Since each one of them had a following, their different supporters went to great lengths to decry Rosanie's charms in all their conversations. One found her nose too long; the other thought her mouth too large. Someone else said her eyes were patched-up and considered her complexion too dark. They spread their stories with such cleverness that all those people who had never seen Rosanie, or who had only caught a glimpse of her, were deceived by the false pictures. As a result, they began saying to each other that the queen's beautiful spinner, who was the talk of the entire city, was not such a marvelous beauty after all. On the contrary, she had many faults, and one should be cautious about expressing admiration for her. However, despite all the trouble her opponents took to spread these notions, they disappeared as soon as Rosanie appeared. Those people who had already seen her once regarded her now with more attention and found her more beautiful than ever. Those people who had only heard rumors about her recognized, once they saw her, that there had been a great deal of malice or bad taste in the pictures that had been painted of her. Vigilentine took her to the theater, and the crowd that filled this vast edifice overwhelmed her with such loud applause that she was embarrassed about it and even upset. To be sure, she was not angry that the people admired her, for she was no different than most beautiful women, who always desire praise. However, Vigilentine had told her that nothing was more fatal for a young woman than to be noticed too much, and since people regarded her too much, Vigilentine decided that it would be best not to go on public walks or to the theater all that often. Such a resolution made Rosanie very sad because she enjoyed those places where there were so many stimulating things to see.

However, she soon had something to console her for this minor disappointment, and this was due to the fortunate success of her wand. Even though she spent most of the day by amusing herself and taking walks, she always found enough time to have this obliging wand do the tasks of the most skilled worker. Thus, she continued to show the most beautiful yarn in the world to the queen, and when eight or ten days passed after she had been given wool, silk, and canvas, she also produced some tapestry that was more beautiful and better made than the work of Arachne.[2] The queen, whose passion for such work was sometimes a bit extreme, was ecstatic when she saw Rosanie's tapestry. She bestowed great praise on her and gave her a good many caresses, and after that day, the beautiful girl was overwhelmed by gestures and signs of favor. It seemed that one even forgot that she came from an extremely low-born family, for she was placed with the maidens of honor at all the celebrations held at the court. And even here she was considered to be among the most distinguished of these young ladies, who were very much irritated by this except one whose name was Sirene. This young woman had a very pleasant face and a generous soul. She paid justice to Rosanie's beauty and dexterity, and instead of scorning her because of her low birth, she said that one should give her more credit for her virtue and sweetness than a person born into an illus-

---

2. In Greek mythology, Arachne is the woman of Lydia who challenged the goddess Athena to a weaving contest. Enraged by her presumption, Athena destroyed Arachne's fine work, whereupon Arachne hanged herself. Then Athena turned her into a spider.

trious family, who is not obliged to cultivate noble sentiments and conduct. This just young lady had such a charming and beautiful voice and sang in such a pleasant way that she acquired the name Sirene. Moreover, the people at the court considered her temperament just as sweet as her voice. Rosanie, who sensed how favorably disposed Sirene was toward her, developed true feelings of friendship for her. In response, Sirene was always gracious and obliging and acted this way out of inclination and joy, something that her companions only did out of politics and with vexation. Not only were they ashamed that they were obliged to behave courteously to Rosanie, but also, as I have already said, they were annoyed by the distinguished honors and lavish praise that were given to her.

The prince was delighted by the consideration that the people at the court had given to his love. Though he was satisfied, however, he was also bothered by the difficulty he encountered in revealing to her the tender feelings he felt for her. He had happily succeeded in managing to see her often and could not complain about this. However, he was not able to get her alone and converse with her for a single moment. Nor was he among those who were permitted to enter her apartment, and whenever she left it, Vigilentine was always at her side. Furthermore, he had organized some balls in vain. Ordinarily, one can find a way to speak to the woman one loves at a ball, but Rosanie did not know how to dance. Although she had been given a dancing master soon after she had arrived at the palace, she had barely had enough lessons to learn how to make a good curtsy. So, since she did not know how to dance, she was obliged to be a spectator and stay in the middle of a group where it was hardly possible to find a suitable occasion to reveal his feelings toward her. To be sure, the prince had sought to make her understand his sentiments through a thousand gallant acts and diverse hints whenever he spoke, and to be sure, he had noticed a hundred small things that she had said and other things that she would have killed herself about if he had heard them. But it was not enough for a love as passionate as his to be known by that which he had aroused in her. He wanted to know for sure whether he had made some favorable impressions on her heart. He saw with great resentment that many of the men of the court and city had already dared to declare their feelings in front of Rosanie and right under the eyes of Vigilentine. He even knew that an ambassador, forgetting the dignity of his position, had been so bold as to want to tempt her virtue by offering her a prodigious sum of money to be his mistress. Of course, this was extremely disturbing for this beautiful maiden, who had always cultivated nothing but noble and elevated feelings.

Aside from this, she was very much a child in her inclinations and in the pleasures she took out of life. She had a boundless love for ribbons, dogs, and birds. Whenever the ladies had a serious conversation, she would become impatient in a very short time, and she amused herself best with girls of her own age. If she loved a play at the theater, it was not so much for the play itself but because she enjoyed seeing such a large group of bustling people gathered together in one spot. The poor girl understood very little of the satirical lines in a comedy, and even less of the political allusions and the tender poetry of a tragedy. And if it were not for the pleasure of seeing and being seen, she would have preferred to have amused herself in a more interesting way by playing blindman's buff or climusette[3] than attending the theater and seeing such plays as *Cinna*, *Iphigenia*, or *The Misanthrope*. Nevertheless, although she still had certain childish inclinations, just as she was naturally tender and affectionate, she did not allow herself to respond to the ardent zeal of the prince. Her penchant for virtue set her in opposition to the feelings that she had for such an amiable lover. She continually told herself that his elevated rank compelled her to close her eyes toward his love and accomplishments, since his high rank was an invincible obstacle that would prevent them from ever being united in a sacred bond. Amidst all these reflections, the beautiful Rosanie continued to make the wand spin and weave with marvelous success and to use the wand so that people would admire her graceful and fine appearance. She also succeeded in learning how to dance very well, even though she did not have the benefit of magic in the lessons that she received. Indeed, she had no other advantage here but a good dance master. On the other hand, although she was given the same benefits when they taught her how to read and write, her progress here was weak. She found forming letters and tracing their characters very boring, and she did not have the strength to apply herself to something that did not amuse her at all.

Meanwhile, the prince was burning with impatience to reveal his ardent feelings to Rosanie, at least for a few moments without constraints. He was so annoyed by the way he was forced to restrain himself that he fell into a bad mood. Now, among the more assiduous young men at court, there was a very bright chevalier by the name of Bonavis, who had been endowed with many fine qualities. The prince confided his wishes in him, and Bonavis, who was ingenious, quickly found a means to help him. He accompanied his lord wherever he went, and thus, when the prince encountered Rosanie, Bonavis cleverly managed to occupy Vigilentine in a conversation about a matter that seemed to be of great importance to her. Then the prince was at his leisure to talk to Rosanie about his love. He drew such moving and tender pictures that she was very touched. But such was the sensitivity of this beautiful young woman that she told him he must extinguish this ardor since, despite all his accomplishments, she would never stoop so low to become his mistress. Moreover, it was clear to her that she had not been born high enough to become his wife. The prince responded that it was no longer something new to see kings marry a villager and that nobody would see anything strange in a bond tied together by love and merit. Rosanie, who did not understand the figurative manner of speaking customary in the theater, grasped these words perfectly well because they emanated from the mouth of a lover whom she cherished. The prince assured her with conviction that his love was more ardent than that of all those who had ever loved before. He solemnly declared that he would rather renounce his claim to the throne than to give her up. He swore so many oaths that no matter what might happen, he would never marry anyone but her, and in waiting for her he would

---

3. An old French game.

make only the same solemn vows with the same respect that he would make to the highest princess on earth. In short, he spoke in such a passionate and natural manner that Rosanie let herself be convinced that his love was sincere and pure, and she gave him permission to talk to her about it from time to time provided that it was with the respect that he had promised and that he was resolved to remain as loyal to her as he had promised.

The amorous prince swore to her again that he would never think about pleasing anyone except her, that he had feelings only for her, and he swore all this to her with the most terrible of oaths.

Ever since that day, after the hearts of those two lovers had reached an understanding, their eyes were in perfect agreement, too, and often gave tender signs of their secret feelings. Bonavis knew how to arrange for diverse conversations to take place, but he was not always able to succeed with such skill in covering up the prince's attachment to Rosanie. Therefore, the king and queen were warned about this. However, the king was not worried about his son's inclination, which he regarded as passing fancy. As for the queen, she had so much confidence in Rosanie's virtuousness that she did not have the slightest fear that their attachment would be fatal. The prince made every effort to conceal his love from the eyes of the court, but he did not succeed very well. Love is one of those turbulent passions that one can only conceal under the veil of discretion, and even then, only rarely.

As soon as Rosanie's opponents had been informed about her illustrious conquest, their jealousy and hate toward her doubled. Among those young women who let herself be swayed by such unjust feelings, none was more tyrannized by them than one of the queen's handmaidens, who had been secretly in love with the prince for a long time. This young woman, whose name was Penséemorne, was somewhat beautiful and had a great deal of ambition, a violent penchant for love, and a dark soul. Furthermore, she was just as vindictive as she was crafty. As long as she saw that the prince was indifferent toward all the beautiful women at the court, she consoled herself about not being able to touch a heart that no one at the court could move, and she flattered herself that, if he were ever to leave himself open to love, he would lean toward her. She counted a great deal on the strength of her charms. Moreover, she had made so many advances to the prince that she could not believe that they had been lost on him, especially since she had done so much for him. However, when she saw that the prince, who had been the sole object of her desires, not only responded to her tender advances with ingratitude but also had given himself to an odious rival, whom she already hated more than death, all her love turned into fury, and she only concerned herself with plans for a savage revenge. In order to succeed, she sought out a pernicious sorceress who had already acted in her interests but who, however, had not been able to use the secrets of art to make the prince fall in love with her.

"In spite of your good intentions," Penséemorne told her as she approached her, "you have not been able to further the cause of my love. But I know that you will be able to use your great art now to help me with my vengeance. So, I want you to make that ingrate of a prince perish because he has scorned me, and at the same time, I want you to make my unworthy rival perish in a terrible way because he has preferred her over me."

The sorceress assured her that she would assume these vengeful feelings as though they were her own and promised to serve her as best she could.

In the meantime, the prince, whose tender feelings had been more satisfied than they had ever been, began pursuing his customary pleasures once again. He went hunting deep in a forest, and as was often the case, he became separated from his party while pursuing an animal with too much zeal. After he had killed it, he found himself unexpectedly in front of the door to a magnificent palace. He was very surprised to see such a splendid edifice in such a desolate spot. But his astonishment increased even more when he saw a dazzling beautiful lady in magnificent dress come out of the palace. She was followed by many other ladies, who seemed to attend her with great respect. This beautiful lady approached him in a gracious manner and said, "Prince, if you love glory, and if you have sympathy for the troubles of the unfortunate, for their interests and yours, enter into this palace with me, and do not refuse to listen to me."

Without saying a word, the prince made a low bow and offered his hand to her. They entered the palace and went to an apartment where gold and precious stones were glistening in emulation of one another. The prince showed the lady how impatient he was to hear her story and to learn whether there was some service he could render this unfortunate woman. After she asked him to sit down, she said the following:

"You see before you, my lord, an unhappy princess, the closest relative and heir of a king who during his lifetime was master of a fertile kingdom, which was, however, taken over by a cruel tyrant fifteen years ago. If you think carefully about the picture I am painting, you will undoubtedly recognize the Realm of Fiction, which the barbarian Songecreux seized after having defeated and killed King Planjoli in the last battle fought by that amiable king. The queen Riante-image, wife of King Planjoli, was taken prisoner. She was pregnant at that time, and the tyrant had her child killed after she gave birth, and he has kept that poor queen in captivity ever since. I was still in my cradle when King Planjoli was dethroned, and due to his death and that of his child, I found myself heir to the Realm of Fiction. Fortunately, my mother, who was a most highborn princess, found a way to remove me from that tyrant's power, and a wise sorcerer, master of this palace, provided us as a retreat with a solitary chateau that often served as an asylum for illustrious people in distress. My mother raised me in that chateau with all possible care, but a year ago, I had the misfortune of losing my mother, and the wise sorcerer became my only support. He led me to this superb palace, where I am served with the splendor worthy of my rank. But a short time ago he discovered through the secrets of his art that the time had arrived for me to regain possession of my kingdom and to punish the usurper, provided that I find a protector of royal blood, who would use his valor and arms for me and would protect my interests under certain conditions that the sage magician would propose. I saw your portrait, my lord," the unknown princess added and lowered her eyes, "and I could tell at once that you had something great to offer us. So I asked my wise adviser to make you a proposal regarding this matter. Now, I am going to withdraw for a few moments, and he will come and discuss everything with you. I shall be most happy if the eloquent speech of this generous old man will be able to make you kindly disposed toward my view so that you will take an interest in my affair."

Upon saying these words, the princess retired, and soon thereafter an old man appeared. He had nice looks but was gaunt and emaciated, undoubtedly due to his old age.

"Prince," he said, after greeting him in a respectful manner, "the great qualities with which you have been endowed have made me take an interest in you, and I would gladly employ the power of my art for your happiness and glory. Therefore, please deign to let yourself be guided by me. The beautiful princess, whom you have just seen, has the most tender feelings for you. She is heiress to a great kingdom, and it is entirely up to you to unite her crown to that which heaven has destined you, if you want the advice and help of Labouréelamboy, which is how I am called. Here you have," he continued as he pulled a ring from his finger, "a ring that has the power of bringing constant victory to the person who wears it. If you have any enemies, they will succumb to your force as soon as you have this ring. There is nothing of merit that can withstand its power. And if you will swear eternal love to our princess, I shall give this rare ring to you as a present. As soon as you place yourself at the head of a powerful following of the princess that has formed itself in the Realm of Fiction against the tyrant Songecreux, you will conquer him and then have a hundred new triumphs after his defeat. You will become master of the dominions of various kings and one of the greatest conquerors who has ever lived on this earth."

The prince had listened to this speech in extreme astonishment, and as soon as he saw that the sorcerer had finished talking and was waiting for a response, he said to him without hesitating a moment, "I cannot offer my love to any woman. My heart and my loyalty are already committed to a charming lady whom I shall love until I breathe my very last gasp of breath. However, despite this, I am prepared to offer my compassion and best wishes to the beautiful princess whom I have just seen, and I am willing to fight against her enemies. However, I do not want to accept your ring. I love glory, and a victory in a battle of arms appears to me as the most exciting thing in the world. Therefore, I shall seek victory with all possible zeal, but I want to triumph only through my own courage and the strength of my arm. Therefore, I shall refrain from accepting the help of a supernatural power."

"You are very fastidious, my lord," replied Labouréelamboy. "I know a great deal of princes and generals who would go to a great deal of trouble to obtain that which you are rejecting. But even if you disdain the help of my art, do not scorn my advice, which comes from experience. I have lived a long time so that it seems to me that I have acquired a certain right to give advice to people of your age. So then, please bear with me when I tell you that the vain scruples you have because of the oath that you have given to another beautiful woman should not prevent you from offering your heart to the heiress of the Realm of Fiction. The princess has a powerful following in her dominions. You only have to put yourself at the head of this party, and it is certain that you will triumph over the tyrant without the help of the ring that you have rejected. After his fall, you will marry the princess, and by this marriage you will acquire a crown that you will one day join to the one for which you are destined. Moreover, you will be performing a generous act in favor of an amiable princess who has the most passionate and tender feelings for you."

The prince continued to respond that his heart and fidelity were no longer his. He could no longer dispose of them. Meanwhile, he was greatly surprised when the princess suddenly returned. Her face was totally covered with tears, and she precipitously threw herself on her knees and said to him, "Oh, my lord, if my weak attractions are not able to move you, then at least have compassion for my misfortunes and my tender feelings. I shall die if you continue to disdain the ardent proof of my feelings for you."

The prince was utterly confused and in an extremely embarrassing situation. He had fallen to his knees just as soon as the princess had. But when he lifted her up and stood up himself, he remained silent and anxious as he regarded her. He saw a face that radiated great charm, but which, nevertheless, bore an expression of pain. He secretly accused himself of being a barbarian for being so cold in his response to the wishes of such a charming person. On the other hand, the tender love and the sacred oaths that committed him to Rosanie appeared vividly to his mind and did not permit him to have the least spark of fire for the princess. Therefore, he followed his inclinations and fidelity, and he believed at the same time that he could satisfy the princess with his generosity and polite manners.

"A beauty such as yours, madame," he said, "deserves undivided love and a completely tender heart. I no longer have power over my heart. The strongest ties and my oaths of fidelity have committed me to a lady worthy of all my tender feelings. Nevertheless, if I cannot give you my heart, madame, I shall consecrate all my profound respect for you and dedicate all the efforts of my arm for you. So, let us go, madame. Let us depart. I shall be delighted to go and support the zeal of your loyal subjects, and I shall spill my blood with joy to vanquish the usurper of your crown."

"You ingrate!" the princess exclaimed in rage. "I am going to leave you. I don't want your help if you refuse to give me your heart. It is only your heart alone that I desire. Alas! My love, my wrath . . ."

As she was uttering these words, a dazzling, beautiful young child appeared all at once in the room. He was carrying a sort of golden scepter in his hand, and once he touched the princess and the sorcerer with it, they immediately began to flee with terrible shrieks. He also touched the walls of the room, and just as he did this, the palace disappeared and the prince found himself in the middle of the forest surrounded by trees with only this charming child in front of him.

"Prince," he said, "I have just dissipated the fatal illusion that clouded your mind in order to reward your gracious fidelity, which you demonstrated by keeping your oath. If heaven severely punishes liars, then it is only just that people of good faith are equally rewarded. Indeed, you deserve divine grace for the way you proved yourself toward Rosanie. I want you to know that the creature that was just before you in the guise of a beautiful princess was a demon occupying a ghostly body through the magic spell of a perfidious sorceress. This dark spirit disguised as a princess sought to deceive you by saying she was the heiress to the Kingdom of Fiction. In fact, all the relatives of King Planjoli are old, and he left behind only a single child, whose identity will become known one day. The old man who appeared to you was also a demon like the one who pretended to be a princess. If your heart had been seduced by the beauty of the princess, or by the flattering promises of the old man, and if you had violated the oath that you had sworn to the lady of your tender feelings, these cruel demons would have immediately taken possession of you, and you would have remained in their power for centuries. But since you have graciously triumphed over all their attacks, heaven wants to liberate you once and for all from their traps to reward your victory and to crown your fidelity. So, take this, sincere lover," the charming child continued, "here is a ring that is completely different from the one that the seductive spirit wanted to give you. His was the ring of falsehood, while this is the ring of truth. Wear it always, and it will prevent the dangerous illusions of hell from ever obtaining power over you, and you will see the sorcerers and demons performing their dark operations without them ever realizing that you see them."

After saying these words, the charming child made a gracious gesture, put the ring on the prince's finger, and then disappeared. Throughout all this, the prince had been so thunderstruck and so speechless that he was only able to demonstrate his feelings to this child, who had seemed to be divine, by signs of respect and gratitude. After the child's departure, the prince managed to gather himself together, and he gave thanks to heaven with a great deal of ardor for having helped him avoid the terrible dangers that had threatened him that day. After he began walking, he sounded his horn in order to find his retinue, which he eventually found. Once he had returned to the palace, the charms of Rosanie's presence and the tender innocence that he discerned in her beautiful eyes made him forget all about the troubling incidents that had upset him during the hunt.

Meanwhile, Penséemorne and the sorceress, her confidante, were distressed because their vengeful act had failed. They had counted a great deal on the palace in the solitary forest, for it was, in effect, a result of their malice. Indeed, since they had counted such a great deal on this enchanted palace, they watched the prince slip through their net in mortal agony. Penséemorne was so disturbed by the feeble power of the sorceress's magic that she resolved to revenge herself in the most pernicious human way possible that cunning and wickedness could inspire. Since she had spies all around Rosanie and all those who took an interest in this beautiful maiden, she knew that the ambassador who had made her that terribly insulting offer was just as in love with Rosanie as before. She even knew that he could not control his feelings and that he would be willing to sacrifice the greatest portions of his fortune for her.

In effect, once this minister became convinced that it was impossible to possess Rosanie except through marriage, he decided to wed her. After

asking her pardon for the offensive way that he had behaved toward her
at first, he offered her his hand and assured her that the minor annoyance
she might have in spending her life in a foreign country would be completely eased by the luster of her rank and by the boundless complaisance
that her husband would eternally have for her. Rosanie told the ambassador that she was very obliged and honored that he wanted to marry her.
However, she declined the honor because she could never think of separating herself from the queen, her mistress, to whom she was passionately
attached, and from whom she had received such kind treatment. The
ambassador, who was a violent man, was enraged by this response. Nevertheless, he pretended he was not angry and contented himself by coming
to the decision that he would fulfill his love, no matter what it might cost.

When Penséemorne learned that Rosanie had rejected a marriage that
was very advantageous for a person of her rank, she burst into an indescribable fury: "How could this audacious peasant think," she exclaimed,
"that a lord so young, handsome, and wealthy like the ambassador was not
sufficient for her! From what I can see, she wants to sit on the throne,
and she will settle for nothing less than lovers who wear crowns on their
heads. Ah, believe me, I shall knock this insolent and proud creature from
her high horse!"

With this in mind, she called for the ambassador's confidant, who was
on her side. This confidant gave his master the idea of abducting Rosanie,
and the ambassador, madly in love and extremely spiteful, gave his approval to this daring plan right away. He finished by saying, "Once I leave
King Prud'homme's realm, I shall be delighted to take this beautiful booty
with me."

Totally preoccupied by all the arrangements necessary to carry out his
plan, he chose a time for the abduction when the king and prince had
taken a trip to a country villa, while the queen could not accompany them
because of some indisposition. The palace was thus much less full than it
normally was.

One evening, when Rosanie had caught a breath of fresh air in the
public park and was returning with Vigilentine to the castle through the
kitchen courtyards, four masked men seized Rosanie brusquely and
dragged her through a hidden door. All of a sudden she found herself on
a deserted street, and in spite of her cries and resistance, they forced her
into a carriage which then departed with such great speed that it seemed
to be flying. After the carriage had traveled for some time, escorted by a
number of cavaliers, it stopped at a relay station for some fresh horses.
Then the sad and despondent Rosanie saw the audacious ambassador who
had planned the abduction climb into the carriage, whereupon she increased her cries and tears.

"Don't torture yourself," he said to her. "I have no intention whatsoever
of harming you. I only want to conduct you to my country, where I shall
give you a worthy rank by marrying you and turning your destiny into a
fortunate one."

"Ah, my lord!" Rosanie cried out with a voice interrupted by tears. "No
matter what your intentions are, they are no longer valid once you begin
to employ force to achieve them. In the name of all that you cherish in

the world, please bring me back to the queen, my mistress. If you do this, I shall be so obligated that I shall have much more sympathy for your desires than I've had up to now, and this will sway me to leave my queen to spend my time with you. But if I don't return, what will this great queen think of me? Alas! She will believe that I consented without asking her advice on how to dispose of my destiny. In the name of God, my lord, permit me to go and eliminate her suspicions."

"No, no, you ingrate," responded the ambassador. "I'm not going to let go of you. I see your trick. Once you are away from me, you will mock my love again. After having gone to so much trouble to determine my fortune, I shall be on my guard and won't let you get away from me."

"You wicked creature!" Rosanie replied. "Since you have little regard for my prayers, I shall not demean myself anymore by begging you. But I hope that heaven will help me get away from your unworthy hands and will not let your crime go unpunished."

While they were holding this discussion, the carriage kept going with inconceivable speed. However, since the driver was so concerned with driving as fast as he could, he lost the way and did not follow the route that his master had ordered him to take. Once he realized this, he sought to regain the right road, but when he began to turn the carriage with a great deal of force, it broke, and Rosanie was thrown into the middle of the road near a wood of full-grown trees. Since she was not injured or at all terrified by this accident, she regarded it as a fortuitous sign. Meanwhile, the ambassador swore furiously at the squire, the driver, and all the rest of his men, who got off their horses and tried to pull the carriage upright and set it back on the road. This predicament gave Rosanie more courage, and she uttered cries with all her might to attract the attention of some peasants. She would have liked to have fled, but it was impossible for her to do so. The ambassador had ordered his servants to hold on to her arms. Now she was afraid that her cries had been in vain, and wavering between hope and fear, she constantly looked up at the clear moon, which was very radiant that night, and watched for someone to appear. It was not long before she saw three men emerge from the wood.

"My lords!" she cried out in a loud voice as soon as she saw them appear. "Please help an unfortunate girl who is being abducted against her will!"

Immediately, the three strangers drew their swords and went to do combat with the ambassador and his men, who did not have time to get back on their horses. All the blows delivered by the three strangers were mortal. One of the strangers distinguished himself through his incomparable skills and valor. It was he who killed the confidant and two other men. The ambassador was enraged and began in turn to fight like a furious lion. The brave stranger took him on with the same vigor with which he had begun the combat, and even though he was wounded on his left shoulder, he gave the ambassador such a terrible blow that he fell down at his feet. As soon as the rest of the ambassador's men saw that the minister was dead, they all took flight. Then the valiant stranger approached Rosanie, who was chilled with fright and trembling with horror at seeing so much blood shed on her behalf.

"You are free, my beautiful maiden," he cried. "Your kidnappers have vanished."

At the sound of this voice, Rosanie suddenly became ecstatic and felt more joy than she had ever felt before. Indeed, she recognized her dear prince as the person who had liberated her. You cannot imagine all the tender things that the two lovers had to say to each other. The prince was enchanted that he had been given the opportunity to save the woman he loved. And Rosanie could not stop praising her illustrious defender. The two men who were with the prince were the loyal Bonavis and a gentleman of the royal house who was also a great confidant of the prince so that Rosanie did not have to feel constrained by their presence.

They bandaged the prince's wound, which fortunately was only a minor cut. When the brave and sensitive prince recognized the ambassador, he at first agonized over the fact that he had killed a man whose position gave him sacred rights because of the title that distinguished him. But when he thought about how this unworthy minister had forfeited his privileges by his odious behavior, he congratulated himself on the fact that he had been chosen by heaven to punish him for so flagrantly violating the rights of the people in his dominions, indeed, in the palace of a king who had treated him with great generosity and consideration.

Meanwhile, the prince, though inconvenienced by his wound, helped the charming Rosanie to walk, and he escorted her to the king's country seat, which was at the other end of the forest from which he had come. While they walked she told him the entire story of her kidnapping, and in his turn, he related to this beautiful maiden how he had been overcome by sorrow caused by their separation, and realizing that he would not be able to sleep, he had resolved to spend a good part of the night catching a breath of fresh air in the forest with the two men whom she saw when she encountered him. No sooner had the prince placed Rosanie in the hands of two ladies at the chateau than he was told that one of the queen's chevaliers had just arrived and wanted to speak to him as soon as possible. This nobleman informed him that someone had kidnapped Rosanie from the palace, practically under the queen's very own eyes, and the queen was distressed and upset by such insolence. Therefore, she wanted to alert the prince and the king so that they could take the proper measures to stop the kidnapper and punish him, even though she had already given the best possible orders about that. However, the prince sent the nobleman right back to his mother with the story about the fortunate coincidence that led to his saving Rosanie and punishing her kidnapper.

The next day the king returned to his capital city and brought back the beautiful spinner to the queen. The pleasant maiden was received with such signs of kindness and benevolence that the envious Penséemorne was practically dying with rage. To crown her despair, she discovered that not only had Rosanie been saved through the prince's valor, but she had also had the good fortune to have escaped the abduction. Even though Penséemorne had been led to see through different obvious signs that heaven was opposed to her vengeance, she did not stop seeking to satisfy it, and once again she took some new steps in her effort to succeed.

Meanwhile, in spite of the joy that Rosanie felt in being rescued from her kidnapper by a dear lover who was showered with glory, she was disturbed by a secret anxiety that she could barely conceal. Sirene, who increasingly demonstrated a tender friendship for her, perceived how agitated Rosanie was and wanted to know what the cause was. However, Rosanie did not want to confide in her about her problems, nor was the wrong to be reserved in this instance. Her trouble stemmed from the fact that her memory was failing her, and she sensed that the date set by the man with the wand was approaching day by day so that he would soon come to seek his precious stick of wood. Her mind had still not recalled the man's bizarre name even though she had made a thousand endeavors for sometime now to recall it. Yet it was always in vain, and she knew that, if she did not remember his name, she was bound by her inviolable oath to follow him wherever he wanted to lead her, and her recent abduction made her feel more than ever the mortal anguish of being eternally separated from the prince.

Even though Rosanie still had difficulty in forming the letters of the alphabet, she wanted to see whether these letters could help her recall the name she passionately sought. She went through great pain and applied herself as best she could until she wrote down *Racdon*, then *Ricordon*, and finally *Ringaudon*. In some instances, she was on the verge of joy because she thought she was about to find the name. But then she would fall into despair, convinced that the names her memory recalled were nowhere near the right and proper name. Tired of making her memory work with such little success, she abandoned all the writing and was plunged once more into sadness.

Meanwhile, Penséemorne intended to give her a reason to become even more anguished. Incensed that not only had the prince escaped her vengeance but he had also enabled Rosanie to escape it, the cruel Penséemorne wanted to gratify her fury by having this young hero killed. Since this wicked young lady was beautiful, highborn, and extremely wealthy, she had many suitors. But most of them were men without titles, money, or manners, and their characters were just as poor as their fortunes. Among these decadent lovers Penséemorne chose three, and she spoke to each one of them in private, saying, "If you perform this task that I ask of you, I shall marry you, and you will become my lord and command my fortune as well. Since the prince has insulted me, my anger can only be appeased by his death. You must follow him closely and take his life during one of those times that he gets separated during a hunt. Two of my friends will accompany you to provide you with support. I shall give each one of you magic swords made by a wise sorceress who is a friend of mine. Thanks to the power of her art, she has made a sword that will always enable you to wound your opponent and not be wounded yourself. And she will also use her magic powers to prevent it from ever being discovered that you have killed the prince."

After Penséemorne had finished talking to each one of these lovers separately, not one of these villains refused her horrible propositions. Therefore, she gave them the swords over which the sorceress had mumbled a magic spell, and then all three prepared to carry out the abominable assassination that Penséemorne had demanded. However, ever since the prince had escaped the traps that she had set for him in the enchanted palace, Penséemorne no longer counted with certainty on the power of magic and only trusted it to a minor extent. She was convinced that she needed the combination of supernatural powers with three heavily armed men to take the life of a single man whom they would attack at their advantage. The sorceress's help was thus an extra precaution because she thought it would be easier for her three loves to kill the prince with special swords.

In the meantime, the king took a trip to his country residence without the queen and the prince, and the young lover, whose wound had completely healed, was now so disturbed by Rosanie's gloomy mood that he decided to go hunting to distract himself from the troubles that this beautiful maiden gave him. More preoccupied by his cares concerning Rosanie than by the hunt, the prince became separated from his party and was so steeped in his thoughts that nightfall surprised him before he could rejoin his retinue. As he passed through a desolate spot near an old ruined castle, which seemed inhabitable, he noticed that there were nevertheless many lights in this palace. He approached the windows of the halls, which were broken and hence completely open, and when he peered through the trees that surrounded them, he saw in the glimmer of a totally violet bright light many men with repulsive faces and bizarre garments. In the middle of them there was a gaunt, dark man with a ferocious and terrifying face. However, he appeared to be in a very cheerful mood, for he sauntered and jumped around with inconceivable agility. The prince shuddered with dread on viewing these atrocious creatures and was convinced that they were from hell. Nevertheless, he remembered that he was wearing the ring of truth and was not afraid of their odious power. Among the group gathered around the hideous man in the middle was a woman who was pleading with him.

"No," he said. "My power does not extend to him. A celestial spirit, my sworn enemy, is protecting him against me and clearly demonstrated to me a short while ago that I cannot have much luck under the name of Labouréelamboy. My other name is much more advantageous. I've already acquired a great number of beautiful young women under this name, and I hope that, tomorrow at this very hour, I'll again have acquired one who is worth more than all the others."

After saying these words, this dreadfully horrible man began to leap about and sing a ditty with a terrible voice:

> If a young and tender female,
> Loving only childish pleasures,
> Had fixed it in her mind
> That my name is Ricdin-Ricdon,
> She would not fall into my trap.
> But the beautiful lass will soon be mine,
> For my name has slipped her mind.

Once the demon, for that was what it in effect was, had finished his pretty song, he turned once more to the woman with whom he had been speaking.

"Since men are educated and more cultivated than women, we ordinarily have more trouble in seducing them than we have in duping the gullible sex unless we make use of this sex to get men to fall into our traps. On the other hand, men often cause women to fall into our snares. I myself have acquired more young girls by exploiting their desire to appear beautiful and to groom themselves than twenty of my comrades who have tried one hundred other means to capture them. And this powerful passion that makes them want to acquire beauty and elegance with such fury stems from their boundless desire to captivate men. This is why I've said that it is very often men who cause women to become our spoils. For example, I am certain that your good friend is not going to escape us. Aren't I right? Isn't it her outrageous passion to please a man that will make her our booty? But who would have believed that this young prince who has charmed her has rendered all the devices ineffectual that we have used against him? Nothing has been able to induce him to break the oath of fidelity that he swore to his mistress, and he has never been tempted by anything of value and glory derived from magic. On the contrary, his two virtuous deeds have led to his acquisition of a defender who makes all the powers of hell useless against him. Thus you're imploring my help in vain. I cannot make him perish. Neither you nor I can harm him. Everything regarding him will take its natural course."

As the prince listened to these words, he recognized that the person he heard was the demon who had spoken to him in the guise of an old man, and he was just as certain that the woman was the sorceress, who was planning something wicked against him, just like the celestial child had warned him she would. He was tempted for a few seconds to act right away and punish this wicked women and all the other villains gathered there. But he abandoned this idea immediately because he felt these miserable creatures were not worth his vengeance. He thought more about getting far away from this odious group and trying to rejoin his men or, at least, finding his way out of the forest.

He had not walked for a very long time when he was abruptly attacked by three men who suddenly jumped out of a thicket. The prince defended himself with valor and heroic intrepidity. He quickly reached a tree against which he leaned so that he could not be attacked from the rear. There he fought with so much courage, skill, and success that, after he had killed one of his adversaries and knocked another to the ground, he saw the third one take flight. He had no intention of pursuing this man but only thought of continuing on his way. He was very tired, and moreover, he had received a wound on his arm, causing him to lose a great deal of blood and feel quite weak. In short, after he had gone some distance, he fortunately encountered some of his men, who were quite surprised to find him so weak, tired, and wounded. In spite of his condition, he mounted a horse and flew instantly to the palace, where he found his mother terribly concerned about him. The queen was visibly upset when she saw that he was wounded, even though the doctors, who had come to attend him, assured her that it was not very serious. In spite of all their assurances, Rosanie was also very distressed by his condition.

Meanwhile, nobody could guess who was behind this abominable assassination attempt against such a gentle and obliging prince. He himself could not unravel the mystery. Even though he had been aware of the feelings that Penséemorne had for him and knew she was unhappy that he had not responded to her, he could not imagine in the least that she would be capable of such a wicked deed.

Now, while the prince had been the uneasy spectator at the witches' Sabbath and had been the object of a wicked lover's fury, his father had been having a very pleasant time. In fact, he had learned about some secrets and events that gave him immense joy. The same day that the prince was exposed to those sinister dangers, the king received a messenger who demanded an audience for a charming and beautiful lady who had a dazzling air about her. When the king granted her permission to enter, he was extremely struck by her radiant features. She was accompanied by an old man with a goodly countenance, who appeared to be a man of quality, and another man who seemed to be a villager with a prudent and honest air that predisposed people to him.

"My lord," the lady said to the king, "you see before you a queen who has come to pay you the homage that she owes you and your wife for your services."

"I don't believe, madame," the king responded, "that either the queen or I have had the pleasure of rendering you a single service."

"It is true," replied the lady, "that I have not personally received the favors for which I have come to thank you. But they have been bestowed upon someone who is more dear to me than myself, for I am speaking about my daughter, the princess Rosanie."

"What, madame?" cried the king. "The beautiful Rosanie is your daughter! That is very difficult to believe. Even though this charming creature is still almost a child, you are too beautiful and youthful for me to believe that you are her mother."

"My lord," replied the lady, "I know how to deal with the obliging sweet things that you have said. They are gallant and gracious lies which men of an elevated rank have made into a pleasant custom of politeness. But, my lord, if you deign to listen to me, I shall tell you some serious truths, which I believe will surprise you a great deal."

"It will be my pleasure to listen to you," replied the king.

So she began by saying, "You see in me, my lord, Queen Riant-image, widow of King Plantjoli, whose sad fate is well known to everyone. When the cruel Songeoreux defeated and killed my husband, he seized his throne, locked me up in an obscure prison, and only thought about strengthening his hold on our realm. Since he knew that I was pregnant, he decided to have my child killed if I gave birth to a boy. But if it was a girl, he wanted to look after her life with great care so that his son, who was still young at that time, could marry her one day. When I learned about the tyrant's sinister plans, I shuddered at the thought of either one of the fates he had in mind for my unborn child. I shed a flood of tears when I reflected on what the barbarian would do to a son, and I was no less distressed when I thought about giving birth to a daughter, for she would one day have to endure the sad fate of forming an odious union with the son of a detestable tyrant. I resolved that, no matter what the child's sex was that heaven was sending me, I would try to remove the child from the tyrant's power, even if it were to cost me my life.

"The loyal chevalier whom you see before you," the queen continued, pointing to the old man, who appeared to be a man of quality, "had always been devoted to me with just as much zeal as intelligence. In fact, he was always so profoundly wise and prudent in all his actions that people gave him the name Longuevue, which stuck to him. Well, this chevalier, who had escaped the cruelty of the tyrant through a disguise, won over some of my guards and found a way to come and speak to me in my prison. Delighted to see him, I took the appropriate steps to give him my child as soon as it was born. The tyrant had ordered that I was to be treated with a great deal of care because of my pregnancy. Therefore, the governor of the fortress in which I was imprisoned made sure that I had all the necessary comforts and was treated with kindness so that I would remain in good health. When I realized that I was close to giving birth, I expressed an extreme desire to eat a pie made of wild boar. The governor wanted to have my wish satisfied right away, and one of my clever ladies arranged it so that the loyal Longuevue, disguised as a peasant, was charged with the responsibility of making this pie. Longuevue gave it to my guards, who carried it to me. After we opened it, my chambermaid and I, we found a dead baby who had recently been born. All this was according to the plan that I had conceived with Longuevue. The prudent chevalier had also given me the means to conserve the body of this innocent child until the time that I would need to show it. Soon thereafter I happily gave birth to a daughter who had a birthmark on her arm above her elbow in the shape of a rose. Consequently, I gave her the name Rosanie right after her birth. My chambermaid hid the princess in a secret spot and placed the dead baby next to me. Then she immediately began to shed tears, cry for help, and tell everyone that I had just given birth to a dead baby.

"When they brought the news to the tyrant, he did not feel sorry, for the dead baby had been a boy. And since there was still a large mass of people who hated Songecreux and his tyranny, they spread the news that I had given birth to a boy whom he had killed. Meanwhile, the guards put the dead child into a coffin. But my chambermaid took him out, placed my live daughter in his place, and got rid of the dead body by throwing it away without anyone ever having the slightest suspicion. Finally, they carried away the coffin, and even though we had given my daughter a great deal of nourishment, I trembled with fear that her cries might betray our secret. But thanks to our immense good luck, she did not cry. Longuevue, who had gained the trust of the governor through his cleverness, was placed in charge of the burial, which took place without a ceremony. As soon as he could, Longuevue took Rosanie from the coffin, and thanks to heaven's protection, he found her in the best of health. From then on he took very good care of the child and did not rest until he had left the country that suffered under the barbarian Songecreux's tyrannical rule. What happened after this, my lord, I shall let the noble Longuevue tell you himself."

When the queen had finished speaking, Longuevue resumed her narrative and addressed the king as follows:

"I left the Realm of Fiction without encountering any trouble, my lord, and along with the little princess, I took with me a wet nurse, whom I passed off as her mother. But even though I had taken great care in choosing this woman, I concealed the baby's true birth from her and the destiny of the child whom she was nursing. I arrived in your dominions, my lord, and I crossed a good part of your country without meeting a person who seemed to me suitable for entrusting the precious creature who was under my charge. Meanwhile, I would have been delighted to have been able to place her in good hands, for it was imperative for me to return to the Realm of Fiction to protect the interests of the queen and princess.

"Finally, one day, in order to give the nurse and the princess some rest, I stopped under some trees on the edge of a large road that served two or three villages. While the nurse was sitting, I walked along the trees, and I was already quite some distance from the nurse, when I heard two peasants walking behind me, and one said to the other, 'Well, then, obstinate Disantpeu, are you going to stay in that mood that has caused such an uproar?'

" 'What do you want me to say?' said the other peasant. 'I'm just satisfied with pitying the bad luck of my neighbor without blaming him for it, nor am I all too curious to find out what has caused it. So, you see, I don't know a thing about it and can't answer your questions.'

" 'Come on!' the other peasant replied. 'None of the other people from your village have such a closed mouth like yours. I know very well what I want to know without your telling me. But since you don't want to tell me anything, I'm going to move faster and arrive in your village before you. That will give me some time to talk with the other villagers. Anyway, I can't stay there too long. Since you are burdened by your child and cannot go as fast as I can, I'm going to leave you.'

"With these words, the peasant left the other and began to walk as fast as he could. When I saw the peasant with the child was all alone, I approached him and began asking many questions. I learned that this child was his daughter, and that his wife had given birth to her about a month ago. Since his wife had something wrong with her breasts, he had been obliged to bring their child to a wet nurse in a village some distance away from theirs. Now that his wife's breasts had completely healed, he was bringing back his daughter because she could now nurse perfectly well. I listened to his story with a great deal of attention, and the man's appearance pleased me very much. I believe, my lord, that you will find that I was right when you get to know this good peasant, who is the same old man whom you see behind the queen, my mistress. I learned again that he had been given the name Disantpeu because of his penchant for silence and reserve. All of this predisposed me in his favor, and I resolved to hire him to be Princess Rosanie's guardian without revealing to him the secret of her birth. Of course, I made considerable promises to him and gave him a lot of gold and precious stones and, among other things, an immensely valuable bracelet from the queen as a means to recognize the princess one day. After having engaged Disantpeu and assuring him that the child who was to be in his charge would one day make him and his family wealthy, I demanded that he never tell anyone about this incident, not even his wife, and he took an oath, swearing that he would act exactly according to my orders, and here is what we did so that our secret would remain between us.

"Since the child of Disantpeu was the exact same age as Rosanie, we decided that he would take the princess to his wife as though she were their very own child, whom he had just brought back from the village where she had been nursed during his wife's sickness. We were certain that he would be able to fool the mother because she had only seen her child the moment she had given birth. I myself went and carried Disantpeu's daughter to Rosanie's nurse, and I took the princess from her arms and placed her in the hands of the good peasant. We agreed, Disantpeu and I, that I would take the nurse to a comfortable home in a village that he named about six miles from where we were, and I assured him that I would take care of his daughter as if she were my very own. After these guarantees, he gave me his daughter, and I, in turn, presented her to Rosanie's nurse and told this good woman that I had just exchanged babies. She was extremely surprised by this, and I told her that I had my reasons for doing it. Then I led her to the very next village, where I found lodgings for her. Right after this I went straight to the peasant's village in order to inquire about his character, and I learned that it was the best that I could have hoped for. After this I returned to the nurse and escorted her and the baby to the village named by Disantpeu, and after arranging for comfortable quarters there, I returned to the Realm of Fiction. I found that Queen Riante-image was still imprisoned and that the barbarian Songecreux continued to exercise his tyranny as usual. Meanwhile, various people who hated Songecreux came together and formed a party, but this party was not powerful enough to declare itself openly against the tyrant. It was imperative to strengthen this movement. Although some loyal followers of the late king and I spent all our energy in doing this, we were not able to succeed, and many years rolled by before we were in a position to act. Since Songecreux was so totally tyrannical and bizarre, he had seized hold of the minds of the people. Moreover, since there were only distant heirs of the late king, people found it discouraging not to have a leader, and I did not dare reveal anything about Rosanie's birth for fear that someone might betray the secret and the tyrant would find a way to take her life. Meanwhile, I received news about her often enough, and I managed to convey everything to the queen with a great deal of difficulty. But this news was the only consolation that the queen had in her sad captivity.

"Some time after I had returned to the Realm of Fiction, the nurse of Disantpeu's daughter informed me that the baby had died. Disantpeu also wrote me about this death, and as I was making arrangements to return the nurse to her country, namely the Realm of Fiction, she, too, died in the village where I had left her without ever knowing about the true origins of Rosanie's birth. Her death was an even greater guarantee that the secret would remain safe, and thus it remained enshrouded in profound silence for a long time. But finally the day came when the family of Songecreux, which had become extremely numerous, had committed too many atrocious acts that reawakened the hate which many people felt toward the tyrant. The party, which had always detested him, still existed and was still united, and without a lot of fanfare, it had become much larger and stronger so that its members finally saw themselves in a position to take action against Songecreux.

"Their first act was to attack and destroy the principle fortresses of Songecreux, and they began a campaign under the command of General Belles-idées, who had led many victorious armies during the regime of the late king. At first, this general made considerable progress and defeated Songecreux's troops in two battles. But the tyrant did not surrender. Instead, he requested help from different kingdoms of Europe and auxiliary troops from the Arab countries. The Arab troops distinguished themselves with such great exploit that, after they had defeated and wounded General Belles-idées, it was believed that they would destroy all the loyal subjects of King Planjoli and Queen Riante-image down to the last person. It is also true that they promised, if they were allowed to plunder the Realm of Fiction up to *A Thousand and One Nights*, that they would guarantee Songecreux an eternal victory. However, a general named Bongout from the country of Politesse had arrived to join his troops with those of General Belles-idées, and our party was reinforced once again. Despite the numerous squadrons of the Arabs and their fantastic forms, their troops were forced to yield to Belles-idées and Bongout.

"When I saw that the party of the deceased king had rebounded so well, I announced to the commanders that their former king had left an heir and informed them about the birth of Rosanie. However, since we thought that there still might be traitors among our troops, we did not think it appropriate to divulge this secret for fear that the princess might somehow be sacrificed. Instead, we resolved to send a messenger in search of Disantpeu so that he would verify what I said to the leaders of the former king's party. As for the queen, it would be a joy to hear the testimony from such an illustrious person as she was. Since the tyrant had changed the governor and guards of the fortress where she was held prisoner, it had been impossible for me to obtain any news about her.

"So, then, we sent for Disantpeu, but as soon as he had crossed the border into the Realm of Fiction, he had been taken prisoner by Songecreux's soldiers. Meanwhile, we continued our progress, and despite the prudence and intrepidity of our commanders and the bravery of our soldiers, we could not overcome the strong resistance that faced us as quickly as we had thought. Therefore, it took us ten days before we could crush the tyrant's forces. Fortunately, we found Disantpeu, and then, once we had taken the fortress where the queen was prisoner, we had the immense joy of rescuing her. Of course, she was in ecstasy when she learned from Disantpeu that Princess Rosanie's soul was just as beautiful as her face. Since the tyrant Songecreux had fled the Realm of Fiction after his last defeat with all his possessions, we declared to the people of this kingdom that they were going to regain their true queen in the person of a girl that the former king had left behind. They received this news with infinite joy, for the memory of King Planjoli was extremely dear to the citizens of the Realm of Fiction. They had given a thousand enormous signs that they would be delighted to live under a princess who descended from his bloodline.

"Queen Riant-image felt that the moment when she would see her daughter could not come soon enough, and consequently she wanted to accompany us so that she could enjoy the pleasure of the reunion as soon as possible. Therefore, we left the government in the hands of Belles-idées and Bongout. The queen-mother made the long journey with a huge retinue, and when she arrived in your dominions, Disantpeu first led us to his village, where the queen believed that she would find Rosanie and surprise her. But we learned in that village, my lord, that your wife, Queen Laborieuse, had invited her to your court and, under the name of the beautiful spinner, Rosanie had received a thousand signs of kindness from this great queen and yourself. At the same time, we learned that you were at your country seat, so the queen, my mistress, hastened here with great zeal in order to thank you for all you have done for Rosanie."

"Yes, my lord." Queen Riante-image resumed talking. "This is why I have come. I would like to repeat again that I cannot thank you enough, and I had thought that I would be able to thank your wife at the same time, for I believed that she was in this chateau with you. And I counted on finding my daughter with the queen as well."

"No, madame," the king responded. "Princess Rosanie is not here, but it will not take long for you to see this charming princess. She is staying with the queen in my capital city, and I shall accompany you there tomorrow. But, madame," he added, "I don't know how we shall be able to apologize to you and your daughter for all the mistakes we made, not knowing how highborn your daughter was."

At the close of this discussion, the king gave orders to prepare the carriages and equipment, and after treating the queen and her retinue in regal fashion, they set out the next day for the capital city.

Meanwhile, Rosanie was going through mortal agony. Although she was greatly distressed about the prince's wound and cared greatly for such a dear lover, his wound was not her major concern. Rather, she saw the dreadful instant approaching minute by minute when the master of the magic wand would come and demand his fatal stick. She had still not recalled the name of this stranger, and she knew that the inviolable commitment of her word and oath would oblige her to follow him wherever he wished to lead her. Streams of tears flowed down her cheeks when she thought she might be forever parted from the queen who had showered her with so much kindness and benevolence and for whom she felt such a sincere attachment. She would also miss the presence of the pleasant Sirene. She would also be angry to be pulled away from Vigilentine's care, but she was torn with pain most of all when she thought that she would be eternally condemned to never see the prince again and to be separated from him. It is impossible to express all that she suffered when she thought about such a cruel separation, and she could not stop weeping the entire night.

The next morning, while still preoccupied by such gloomy thoughts, the queen sent her a messenger, who told her that the queen wanted to see her in the prince's chamber. As soon as the queen saw her enter, she cried out, "I have some strange news for you, my dear Rosanie! Alas, there's a monster among my ladies of honor!"

After saying this, the queen informed her about what she had recently learned and revealed that one of the prince's attackers had dragged himself in a wounded condition to the very next village. The doctors told him that he was going to die from his wounds, and upon hearing such bad news, this miserable man began swearing against Penséemorne, who had convinced him to commit such an odious and criminal act. Thereupon, he recounted all the circumstances that led up to the attack. Then, after he saw the dead bodies of his companions carried out of the forest, he died, heaping hateful curses on his guilty mistress. Apparently, someone alerted this unworthy girl of the villain's confession, and immediately thereafter, Penséemorne left the palace in a fury, flew to the wicked sorceress, and began insulting her. Then after strangling her, she strangled herself.

Rosanie trembled a thousand times as she listened to this story. When the queen had finished, she told Rosanie that she was going to the temple and consequently wanted her to entertain and distract her son so that he would feel less pain from his wound. So she ordered Rosanie and Sirene to stay and amuse him and requested that Sirene also sing. Of course, this pleasant girl sang with great charm, but neither the prince nor Rosanie heard her at all. They were so preoccupied by something else that they were insensitive to the sweetness of music. Realizing that they were both very much distracted, Sirene stopped singing, got up, and went to the window to look at the swans that were gliding on the river and swimming over to eat bread crumbs from the hands of some of the palace officers. As soon as the prince believed that only Rosanie could hear his words, he quickly said to her, "Beautiful Rosanie, why have you become so terribly sad? You seemed to have plunged yourself into gloom. Can't my ardent feelings with all their tenderness provide you with some joy? That is, unless you've become totally insensitive to my love?"

"My lord," Rosanie replied, "do you believe that I can see you in such pain and that I can think about all the dangers you've been exposed to without feeling extreme sorrow?"

"But the dangers have passed," responded the prince, "and even I don't have the slightest fear that there will be any more trouble. And since I don't want to hide anything from you, charming Rosanie, I want you to learn how I was so fortunate to have escaped these dangers."

After saying these words, he told her about his adventure in the enchanted palace of the forest, the traps that had been set for him by that princess who had pretended to be so unfortunate, and the ring of truth that had been given to him by the unknown marvelous child. Following this, he told her the story about his other adventure at the old, ruined palace and all the diabolic ranting that he had heard. Finally, he came to the point of his story where he recalled the ditty sung by the demon, and he repeated it to Rosanie word for word:

> If a young and tender female,
> Loving only childish pleasures,
> Had fixed it in her mind
> That my name is Ricdin-Ricdon,
> She would not fall into my trap.
> But the beautiful lass will be mine,
> For my name has slipped her mind.

After he repeated this verse, Rosanie uttered such a loud cry that he was at first frightened, and she also startled the ladies who were regarding the swans so that they turned their heads. However, the prince was reassured when he heard Rosanie exclaim once again with joy, "Heaven be praised for its infinite kindness to me!"

The prince asked her to explain the meaning of her words, but he realized that she did not want to disclose anything in front of the two ladies who had approached them when they heard her cry. However, when they returned to the window, Rosanie told the prince all about her adventure with the wand, while trying to recover from her fright on learning that this man, whom she had promised to follow, was a demon, for she had not suspected anything of the kind. The prince could not restrain himself from criticizing her a little for having come to an agreement so easily with a man whom she had not known in any way. But since one is always ready to excuse anything that is done by someone one loves, he blamed the imprudent act on her extreme youth and on her lack of experience. Meanwhile, she was delighted beyond belief because his memory had helped her escape the greatest danger of her life. The prince even wrote down the name of Ricdin-Ricdon on a slate right then and there and gave it to Rosanie, who could not find words enough to express her gratitude.

"My lord!" she said to him. "Your abundant valor had already saved me from the hands of a cruel kidnapper. But today your excellent memory has pulled me out of the grasp of an enemy much more formidable."

After she finished expressing how grateful she was to her illustrious lover, she went to join the ladies who were at the window and then brought them back to the prince. One of them did not stay too long, but Sirene remained with Rosanie, and the three of them had a pleasant conversation. Toward noon, in the middle of a lively discussion, a venerable old man, dressed simply but properly, entered the prince's room. As soon as Rosanie saw him, she ran to him with open arms, crying out, "Oh, my dear father! What joy to be able to embrace you after thinking you were dead! My lord," she continued, addressing the prince, "please pardon the ecstasy of a girl who has just seen the best father in the world once more and the one most worthy to be cherished. In spite of the obscurity of his rank, I am not ashamed to admit that I was born from him. He is such an honest man and has such noble integrity that the honesty and elevated feelings with which nature endowed him make up for the lowliness of his birth. I should also like to ask him, my lord, as I am sure you would, too, about my mother, whom I have not forgotten, despite the rough treatment that she gave me."

"Madame," responded the old man, "you are not my daughter. You have too many beautiful qualities to have come from a man like me. You are the daughter of a great king, who is dead. However, the queen, your mother, who has just arrived in this palace, and who is presently with Queen Laborieuse, will come here to embrace you and verify all that I have just told you."

Rosanie was so surprised by his words that she was at first speechless.

But finally, when she regained control of herself, she cried out, "Oh, pity me! What is going on, father? Do you want to deny this integrity which has been a part of you all your life and deceive the prince to whom I have just boasted about your honest character with such great pleasure?"

"I am not deceiving anyone, madame," replied the old man. "The queen, your mother, who, I see, has just entered this room, will testify to this."

Indeed, just then, Queen Riante-image, King Prud'homme, Queen Laborieuse, and Lord Longuevue entered the prince's chamber along with many other illustrious people who were transported by delight. Queen Riante-image was speechless to find Rosanie so beautiful, and she hugged her tenderly in her arms. The charming girl kissed her mother's hands, soaking them with tears of joy. Meanwhile, the king and Longuevue told her about her renowned birth and all about her destiny. She was much less impressed by the throne and the glory of reigning than by the great pleasure and opportunity she would have to offer a scepter to a lover who had planned to offer her a crown, even though she had been a mere villager. As for the prince, he felt such a range of different sweet and glorious emotions that he could hardly stand it: he complimented himself for having been able to distinguish the merit and charms of Rosanie despite the thick veils in which her servile condition enveloped her. He was delighted to have made himself loved by this beautiful maiden, ecstatic to have performed two considerable services for her, and in the flattering hope that he would be united with her soon, he only envisaged the joy of being with her as she had been, without the luster of the throne that fortune had just given her.

After Riante-image had poured out all her tender feelings for some time, Longuevue and Disantpeu approached Rosanie and said, "Please grant us permission, madame, to show your mother, the queen, the mark that you have on your arm and that inspired the name that you bear."

"Oh!" cried out Riante-image. "I don't need any proof to recognize my own blood! If I had not had the testimony of such honest men as you both are, I still would have recognized her because she resembles my former husband so much, and this resemblance is sufficient enough to convince me that she is my daughter."

However, in spite of what the queen said, the chambermaid who had saved Rosanie's life when she was born approached that charming princess and, after rolling up the sleeve of Rosanie's dress, she showed the company an arm that was whiter than alabaster. Everyone stood up and surrounded the new princess, and they saw the figure of a little rose perfectly represented on her arm above her elbow. The two queens began once more to hug her. Then Disantpeu presented Queen Riante-image with the bracelet of diamonds and other precious stones that Longuevue had given him when he placed Rosanie in Disantpeu's trust. The queen-mother handed them to her daughter, who received them with respect.

"Now you see, madame," Disantpeu said with a laugh to Rosanie, "that I was completely right to refuse all those good matches that were proposed to you at the village. I knew that, even if you had never been recognized, the least valuable of these precious stones that I was keeping for you would have made you richer than all the possessions of those suitors put together."

Rosanie said a thousand grateful things to her good protector, assured him that she would show her appreciation in many different ways, and added that, since his wife had been her nurse, she, too, would receive a great deal of wealth as well as their son. The young princess did not forget to say many gracious things to Longuevue and the loyal chambermaid as well. She gave one hundred caresses to Sirene, who from that moment on was regarded as the new queen's favorite. As soon as calm had been a little restored in this beautiful company, King Prud'homme did not wait long before he requested Rosanie's hand in marriage for his son from Queen Riante-image. Of course, she consented right away, and the day of the marriage was set at a time that satisfied the two lovers and the two mothers.

Following this, they dined in splendor, and after the meal, they all withdrew to their rooms to rest. Rosanie had not been in her room a long time when a messenger came to tell her that a man dressed in black with a very somber face wanted to speak with her. She gave the order to let him enter, and as soon as she saw him, she recognized him as the man who had given her the wand. Even though she knew his name, the sight of him made her shudder, for she knew how dangerous he was. Without saying a single word, she stood and fetched the wand and handed it to him. "Here it is, Ricdin-Ricdon," she said. "Here is your wand."

The evil spirit, who had not expected to hear this, disappeared while uttering terrible howls. And thus he was duped, something that happens to him often when those whom he tries to ensnare have not had criminal intentions when entering agreements with him and have not realized that he actually wants to acquire their souls.

Rosanie spent many long years with the prince in a perfect union and in extreme happiness. They arranged a marriage between Bonavis and Sirene, who remained their favorites. They heaped gifts upon all those who rendered them service. Longuevue, Disantpeu, the queen's chambermaid, and Vigilentine were very content with the tokens of gratitude that they received. This admirable couple was loved by most of their subjects and by the most noble, all of whom were delighted to see the descendants of King Planjoli and Queen Riante-image reign over them.

However, since it is difficult to please all people's minds equally, and since it is almost impossible to keep all people's votes together, the party of Songecreux rises up from time to time and becomes powerful enough to cause disruptions that affect the capital city itself. It is even said that, in spite of the gracious manners of the legitimate sovereigns of the country and the care taken by the generals Belles-idées and Bongout, the followers of Songecreux will never be able to be entirely destroyed.

JACOB AND WILHELM GRIMM

Rumpelstiltskin†

Once upon a time there was a miller who was poor, but he had a beautiful daughter. Now it happened that he was talking with the king one time, and in order to make himself seem important, he said to the king, "I have a daughter who can spin straw into gold."

"That is an art that pleases me!" the king replied. "If your daughter is as talented as you say, then bring her to my castle tomorrow, and I'll put her to a test."

When the maiden was brought to him, he led her into a room that was filled with straw. There he gave her a spinning wheel and spindle and said, "Now get to work! If you don't spin this straw into gold by morning, then you must die." Then he locked the door himself, and she remained inside all alone.

The miller's poor daughter sat there feeling close to her wits' end, for she knew nothing about spinning straw into gold, and her fear grew greater and greater. When she began to weep, the door suddenly opened, and a little man entered.

"Good evening, mistress miller, why are you weeping so?"

"Oh," answered the maiden, "I'm supposed to spin straw into gold, and I don't know how."

The little man then asked, "What will you give me if I spin it for you?"

"My necklace," the maiden said.

The little man took the necklace and sat down at the wheel, and *whizz, whizz, whizz*, three times round, the spool was full. Then he inserted another one, and *whizz, whizz, whizz*, the second was full. And so it went until morning, when all the straw was spun, and all the spools were filled with gold. The king appeared right at sunrise, and when he saw the gold, he was surprised and pleased, but his heart grew even greedier. He locked the miller's daughter in another room that was even larger than the first and ordered her to spin all the straw into gold if she valued her life. The maiden did not know what to do and began to weep. Once again the door opened, and the little man appeared and asked, "What will you give me if I spin the straw into gold for you?"

"The ring from my finger," answered the maiden.

The little man took the ring, began to work away at the wheel again, and by morning he had spun all the straw into shining gold. The king was extremely pleased by the sight, but his lust for gold was still not satisfied. So he had the miller's daughter brought into an even larger room filled with straw and said to her, "You must spin all this into gold tonight. If you succeed, you shall become my wife." To himself he thought, "Even though she's just a miller's daughter, I'll never find a richer woman anywhere in the world."

† Jacob and Wilhelm Grimm, "Rumpelstiltskin"—"Rumpelstilzchen" (1857), No. 55 in *Kinder- und Hausmärchen. Gesammelt durch die Brüder Grimm* (Göttingen: Dieterich, 1857).

Rumpelstiltskin. Charles Folkard, 1911.

When the maiden was alone, the little man came again for a third time and asked, "What will you give me if I spin the straw into gold once more?"

"I have nothing left to give," answered the maiden.

"Then promise me your first child when you become queen."

"Who knows whether it will ever come to that?" thought the miller's daughter. And since she knew of no other way out of her predicament, she promised the little man what he had demanded. In return, the little man spun the straw into gold once again. When the king came in the morning and found everything as he had wished, he married her, and the beautiful miller's daughter became a queen.

After a year she gave birth to a beautiful child. The little man had disappeared from her mind, but now he suddenly appeared in her room and said, "Now give me what you promised."

The queen was horrified and offered the little man all the treasures of the kingdom if he would let her keep her child, but the little man replied, "No, something living is more important to me than all the treasures in the world."

Then the queen began to grieve and weep so much that the little man felt sorry for her. "I'll give you three days' time," he said. "If you can guess my name by the third day, you shall keep your child."

The queen spent the entire night trying to recall all the names she had ever heard. She also sent a messenger out into the country to inquire high and low what other names there were. On the following day, when the little man appeared, she began with Kaspar, Melchior, Balzer, and then repeated all the names she knew, one after the other. But to all of them, the little man said, "That's not my name."

The second day she had her servants ask around in the neighboring area what names people used, and she came up with the most unusual and strangest names when the little man appeared.

"Is your name Ribsofbeef or Muttonchops or Lacedleg?"

But he always replied, "That's not my name."

On the third day the messenger returned and reported, "I couldn't find a single new name, but as I was climbing a high mountain at the edge of the forest, where the fox and the hare say good night to each other, I saw a small cottage, and in front of the cottage was a fire, and around the fire danced a ridiculous little man who was hopping on one leg and screeching:

"Today I'll brew, tomorrow I'll bake.
Soon I'll have the queen's namesake.
Oh, how hard it is to play my game,
for Rumpelstiltskin is my name!"

You can imagine how happy the queen was when she heard the name. And as soon as the little man entered and asked, "What's my name, your highness?" she responded first by guessing, "Is your name Kunz?"

"No."

"Is your name Heinz?"

"No."

"Can your name be Rumpelstiltskin?"

"The devil told you! The devil told you!" the little man screamed, and he stamped so ferociously with his right foot that his leg went deep into the ground up to his waist. Then he grabbed the other foot angrily with both hands and ripped himself in two.

JACOB AND WILHELM GRIMM

The Three Spinners†

There was once a lazy maiden who did not want to spin, and no matter what her mother said, she refused to spin. Finally, her mother became so angry and impatient that she beat her, and her daughter began to cry loudly. Just then the queen happened to be driving by, and when she heard the crying, she ordered the carriage to stop, went into the house, and asked the mother why she was beating her daughter, for her screams could be heard out on the street. The woman was too ashamed to tell the queen that her daughter was lazy and said, "I can't get her to stop spinning. She does nothing but spin and spin, and I'm so poor that I can't provide the flax."

"Well," the queen replied, "there's nothing I like to hear better than the sound of spinning, and I'm even happier when I hear the constant humming of the wheels. Let me take your daughter with me to my castle. I've got plenty of flax, and she can spin as much as she likes."

The mother was delighted to give her consent, and the queen took the maiden with her. After they reached the castle, she led the maiden upstairs to three rooms that were filled with the finest flax from floor to ceiling.

"Now, spin this flax for me," she said. "And if you finish all this, you shall have my oldest son for your husband. It doesn't matter to me that you're poor. You work industriously and you never stop. That in itself is dowry enough."

The maiden was deeply frightened, for she could not have spun the flax even if she were to live three hundred years and sit there every day from morning till night. Therefore, when she was left alone, she began to weep and sat there for three days without lifting a finger. On the third day the queen came back to the room, and when she saw that nothing had been spun, she was puzzled. But the maiden made up an excuse and said she had been so tremendously upset about leaving her mother's house that she had been unable to begin working. The queen accepted this excuse, but upon leaving she said, "Tomorrow you must begin your work for me."

When the maiden was alone again, she did not know what to do or where to turn. In her distress she went over to the window and saw three women coming in her direction: the first had a broad flat foot, the second had such a large lower lip that it hung down over her chin, and the third had an immense thumb. They stopped in front of her window, looked up,

---

† Jacob and Wilhelm Grimm, "The Three Spinners"—"Die drei Spinnerinnen" (1857), No. 14 in *Kinder- und Hausmärchen. Gesammelt durch die Brüder Grimm* (Göttingen: Dieterich, 1857).

and asked the maiden what the matter was. She told them about her predicament, and they offered to help her.

"We'll spin your flax for you in no time at all," they said. "But only if you invite us to your wedding and are not ashamed of us. Moreover, you must call us your cousins, and let us eat at your table."

"With all my heart," she responded. "Just come in and get to work right away."

She let the three odd women in and cleared a place for them in the first room where they could sit down and begin their spinning. One drew out the thread and began treading the treadle, the other wet the thread, and the third twisted it and struck the table with her finger. Whenever she struck it, a reel of yarn dropped to the ground, and it was always most delicately spun. The maiden concealed the three spinners from the queen, and every time the queen came, the maiden showed her such a large amount of spun yarn that there was no end to the queen's praise for her. When the first room was empty of flax, they moved on to the second and then the third until it too was cleared of flax. Now the three women took their leave and said to the maiden, "Don't forget what you've promised us. Your good fortune will depend on it."

When the maiden showed the queen the empty rooms and the large piles of yarn, the queen arranged for the wedding, and the bridegroom was happy to get such a skilled and industrious wife and gave her tremendous praise.

"I have three cousins," said the maiden, "and since they've done many good things for me, I'd like to invite them to the wedding. Please allow me to do this and let them sit at our table."

The queen and the bridegroom said, "Why, of course, we'll allow this."

When the feast was just about to begin, the three women entered in bizarre costumes, and the bride said, "Welcome, dear cousins."

"Ahh!" said the bridegroom. "How did you ever come by such ghastly looking friends?"

Then he went to the one with a broad flat foot and asked, "How did you get such a flat foot?"

"From treading," she answered. "From treading."

Next the bridegroom went to the second and asked, "How did you get such a drooping lip?"

"From licking," she answered. "From licking."

Then he asked the third one, "How did you get such an immense thumb?"

"From twisting thread," she answered. "From twisting thread."

Upon hearing this the prince was alarmed and said, "Never ever shall my beautiful wife touch a spinning wheel again."

Thus she was able to rid herself of the terrible task of spinning flax.

JACOB AND WILHELM GRIMM

The Lazy Spinner†

A man and his wife lived in a village, and the wife was so lazy that she never wanted to do any work. Whenever her husband gave her something to spin, she never finished it, and whatever she did spin, she did not wind but left it tangled on the bobbin. If her husband scolded her, she used her quick tongue and said, "How can I wind yarn if I don't have a reel? You go into the forest first and fetch me one."

"If that's what's the matter, then I'll go into the forest and get some wood for a reel."

Upon hearing this, his wife became anxious because she would have to wind the yarn and start spinning again if he found the wood to make a reel. So she gave the matter some thought and came up with a good idea. She secretly followed her husband into the forest, and just as he climbed up a tree to select and cut the wood, she crawled into some bushes below him, where he could not see her, and called up:

"He who chops wood for reels shall die in strife.
She who winds yarn shall be ruined all her life."

The husband listened, laid down his ax for a moment, and wondered what all this could possibly mean. "Oh well," he said, "you must have been hearing things. No need to frighten yourself about nothing." So he took his ax again and was about to begin chopping when he heard the voice from below once more:

"He who chops wood for reels shall die in strife.
She who winds yarn shall be ruined all her life."

He stopped again, and in his fear and terror, he tried to grasp what was happening. After some time had passed, his courage returned. He reached for his ax a third time and was about to chop when he heard the voice cry out loudly for a third time:

"He who chops wood for reels shall die in strife.
She who winds yarn shall be ruined all her life."

This was too much for him, and he lost all desire to chop the wood. He quickly climbed down the tree and made his way home. His wife ran as fast she could via the byways to get home before he did. When he entered the living room, she acted innocent, as if nothing had happened, and said, "Well, did you bring me a nice piece of wood for a reel?"

"No," he said, "I've realized that it makes no sense to wind," and he told her what he had encountered in the forest, and from then on he left her in peace.

Yet some time later the husband began complaining again about the

---

† Jacob and Wilhelm Grimm, "The Lazy Spinner"—"Die faule Spinnerin" (1857), No. 128 in *Kinder- und Hausmärchen. Gesammelt durch die Brüder Grimm* (Göttingen: Dieterich, 1857).

messy condition of the house. "Wife," he said, "it's a disgrace the way you just leave your spun wool on the bobbin."

"You know what," she said. "Since we haven't managed to get a reel, you go up to the loft, and I'll stand here below. Then I'll throw the yarn up to you, and you throw it back down to me. That way we'll have a skein."

"Yes, that'll work," said her husband. So they did this, and when they were finished, he said, "We've got the yarn skeined, and now it needs to be boiled as well."

His wife became uneasy again and said, "Yes, indeed, we'll boil it first thing tomorrow morning," but she was really thinking up a new trick. Early the next morning she got up, made the fire, and set the kettle on it, but instead of putting the yarn in the kettle, she put in a clump of tow[1] and let it boil. After this she went to her husband, who was still lying in bed, and said to him, "I've got to go out a while. So I want you to get up and look after the yarn that's in the kettle on the fire. Make sure you do this right away, and watch things closely for if the cock crows and you're not paying attention, the yard will become tow."

The husband agreed since he certainly did not want anything to go wrong. He got up as fast as he could and went into the kitchen. But when he reached the kettle and looked inside, he was horrified to discover nothing but a clump of tow. Then the husband was as quiet as a mouse, for he thought that he had done something wrong and was to blame. In the future, he no longer mentioned yarn and spinning. But you yourself must admit that his wife was a nasty woman.

---

1. Uncleansed wool or flax.

Good at Heart and Ugly as Sin

Similar to the cycle of tales that depict kind and unkind girls, these tales about compassionate beautiful and nasty ugly maidens depict the rewards that await a certain type of behavior. Here the theme of the "true bride" is crucial, and in this regard the frame tale of Basile's *Pentamerone* is related to the tales of good and ugly girls. The traditional plot concerns a young girl who is beset by difficulties and must overcome them if she is to be wed. Once the good girl accomplishes a valorous deed or does some kind act, it appears that she will be able to marry her "prince charming." However, she is generally tricked and replaced by the nasty girl, her stepsister, or sister, and compelled to do menial tasks until her brother or friend reveals her true identity. Sometimes she manages to bring about the revelation herself. Indeed, once the true bride is discovered, she attains her rightful position, and the ugly girl is punished. Mme d'Aulnoy's "Rosette" (1797) shows some similar motifs while the Grimms' "Die Gänsemagd" ("The Goose Girl") has much the same structure as "The White Bride and the Black Bride," except in "Die Gänsemagd" a princess is replaced by a servant, and there is not as much emphasis on appropriate behavior and the rise in social class.

GIAMBATTISTA BASILE

The Two Cakes†

Once upon a time there were two sisters, Luceta and Troccola, who each had a daughter, one called Marziella and the other Puccia. Marziella was as beautiful in appearance as she was good at heart. In contrast, using the same comparison with a slight change, Puccia was as ugly as sin and just as evil at heart. In this respect she resembled her mother because Troccola was a harpy through and through.

Now one day it happened that Luceta wanted to cook a few carrots in order to fry them with some green sauce, and she said to her daughter, "Marziella, my dear, please go to the fountain and fetch a pitcher of water for me."

"Certainly, mother," replied her daughter. "But if you love me, give me a cake because I'd like to eat one while I drink some fresh water."

"Gladly," her mother said, and she took out a nice piece of cake that was in a basket hanging on a hook, for they had been baking the day before, and she gave it to Marziella. Then the girl placed a pitcher on a

---

† Giambattista Basile, "The Two Cakes"—"Le due pizzette" (1634), *Settimo passatempo delle quarta giornata* in *Lo cunto de li cunti overo Lo trattenemiento de peccerille*, De Gian Alessio Abbattutis, 5 vols. (Naples: Ottavio Beltrano, 1634–36).

632

pad that was on top of her head and went to the fountain, which, like a charlatan on top of a marble bench and with the sound of running water, was selling the secrets which drive away thirst. As Marziella began filling the pitcher with water, an old woman arrived, and she was indeed so old it seemed that she was acting out the tragedy of time on the stage of a great hunchback, and when she saw the nice piece of cake which Marziella was about to bite, she said, "My pretty girl, may heaven send you good fortune if you give me a bit of that cake."

Marziella, whose behavior was like that of a queen, said, "You may have all of it, my worthy woman, I'm only sorry that it's not made of sugar and almonds. Even then I'd give it to you with all my heart."

When the old woman saw how caring Marziella was, she said, "Go, and may heaven repay you for the kindness that you've shown me. I pray that the stars will make you eternally happy and content, and that when you breathe, roses and jessamine will come out of your mouth, when you comb your hair, pearls and rubies will fall from your head, and when you put your feet on the ground, violets and lilies will spring up."

Marziella thanked the old woman and returned home. After her mother finished cooking, they paid their natural debt to their bodies. The next morning, when the sun displayed her luminous merchandise that she brought from the Orient to the marketplace of the celestial fields, Marziella began combing her hair and saw pearls and rubies rain down into her lap. To be sure, her joy was immense, and she called her mother. After they put the jewels in a casket, Luceta went and sold a good deal of them to a jeweler, who was a friend of hers.

In the meantime, Troccola came to visit her sister, and when she found Marziella so excited about pearls and bustling about, she asked her when and where she had discovered them. Since she was the type of girl who could not possibly muddy clear water and perhaps had never heard of that proverb which says never exert yourself beyond your own strength, never eat as much food as you want, never spend all that you have, and never say as much as you know, she told her aunt all that had happened to her. Upon hearing this, Troccola did not bother waiting for her sister because every hour seemed to her to be a thousand years. Instead, she rushed home, where she gave her daughter a cake and sent her to fetch some water.

Puccia found the same woman at the fountain, and when the lady asked her for a piece of the cake, Puccia revealed her true beautiful character and responded, "Do you think I have nothing else to do but give you a piece of my cake? Do you take me for an ass? Why should I share my stuff with you? Get away! Teeth are closer to us than relatives."

Upon saying this, she gulped down the cake in four bites and made the old woman drool. When the lady saw the last piece vanish and her hope also buried with the cake in the girl's stomach, she became enraged and said, "Be gone! And when you breathe, may you snort like a doctor's mule.[1] When you comb your hair, may bunches of lice fall from your head. When

---

1. It was customary during this period for doctors to travel on mules and to be accompanied by their assistants on foot.

you set your feet on the ground, may thistles and coarse fern sprout up!"

So Puccia took the water and returned home, where her mother was eagerly waiting for the moment to comb her hair. She put a fine towel on her daughter's lap and bent her head over it. Then she began combing her hair, and lo and behold, she saw a torrent of those alchemical beasts that can even stop quicksilver.[2] Down they came, and when her mother witnessed this, flames and smoke exploded from her mouth and nostrils, adding the fire of wrath to the snow of her envy.

Sometime after this Marziella's brother, Ciommo, was at the court of the king of Chiunzo,[3] and when he heard some people talking about the beauty of various ladies, he joined the conversation without being asked and asserted that, if his sister were to appear, all the other beautiful women might as well go and jump off a bridge. Aside from her physical beauty, which formed the counterpoint to the *canto fermo*[4] of her beautiful soul, she also had something special about her hair, mouth, and feet bestowed upon her by a fairy. When the king heard Ciommo's boasting, he told him to bring his sister to the court, and if he found her as beautiful as Ciommo had reported, he would take her for his wife.

Since this appeared to Ciommo as an opportunity he could not possibly pass up, he quickly sent a messenger with a letter to his mother, telling her what had happened and asking her to come at once with her daughter so that they would not let this good fortune escape them. However, Luceta was very sick, and therefore, she asked her sister to do her a favor and accompany Marziella to the court of Chiunzo, not realizing that she was entrusting the sheep to the wolf.

When Troccola saw that things were falling into her hands so nicely, she promised her sister that she would take the young girl to her brother and make sure that she arrived safe and sound. Therefore, she embarked with Marziella and Puccia on a ship, and when they were in the middle of the sea and the sailors were sleeping, she threw Marziella into the water. When the girl was about to sink to the bottom, a beautiful siren arrived, took her in her arms, and carried her away.

When Troccola arrived at Chiunzo's court, Ciommo greeted Puccia as if she were Marziella because he had not seen his sister for a long time and could not recognize her. Then he took her right away to the king, who ordered her hair to be combed. As this was done, the king saw those beasts, who were the enemies of truth and always offend witnesses,[5] fall out of her hair. He looked at her face and saw that she was breathing very hard from the exhausting voyage and that foam was coming from her mouth that resembled the slime from a washtub. When he glanced down at her feet, he saw a meadow of stinking grass that made him want to vomit at the sight.

As a result of this disaster, the king sent Puccia and her mother packing,

---

2. Mercury was used at this time to cure cases of lice and to disinfect people's heads.
3. Chiunzo was a mountain near Tramonti; it had become proverbially associated with people such as kings or mayors who thought they were important.
4. A plainchant or simple melody of the ancient hymns and chants of the church.
5. As usual, Basile's use of the term *i testimoni* (witnesses) is a play on *i testicoli* (testicles), and hence the lice are true enemies.

and out of spite, he punished Ciommo by making him tend the geese at the court. Of course, Ciommo was despondent and could not understand what had happened. So he took the geese to the seashore and let them wander freely along the beach while he sought refuge in a hut where he wept about his fate until it was time to go to sleep. Meanwhile, as the geese were running about on the beach, Marziella came out of the water and fed them with almond pastry and gave them rose water to drink so that they all became as fat as sheep and could hardly open their eyes.

This continued for some time, and in the evening the geese began gathering in a garden under one of the king's windows and singing,

> "Honk, honk, honk,
> How beautiful the sun, how beautiful the moon,
> But she who feeds us is most beautiful of all!"

Since the king began hearing this goose serenade every evening, he summoned Ciommo and wanted to know where, how, and what he fed the geese. And Ciommo replied, "I give them nothing to eat except the fresh grass off the fields."

But this answer did not ring true to the king, and he had a trusty servant follow him to see where he took the geese. After following Ciommo's footsteps, the servant saw him enter the hut and let the geese wander off by themselves to the beach. No sooner did they arrive than Marziella came out of the sea, and I don't think that there was any lady as beautiful as she was as she arose from the heavens, not even Venus, the mother of that blind boy, who, as the poet says, seeks no other alms than tears. When the servant witnessed all this, he was struck by astonishment and became ecstatic. Then he ran back to his lord and told him all about the beautiful spectacles that he had seen on the stage of the beach.

The king's curiosity was aroused by the words of the servant, and he was induced to go to the beach and to see this beautiful sight for himself. So, the next morning, when the cock, that leader[6] of the birds, had aroused his feathered friends to arm all living creatures against the night, Ciommo arose and went with his geese to his usual place, and the king was right behind him. After Ciommo stopped at the hut, the king continued on his way without him and followed the geese to the seashore. Then the king saw Marziella rise out of the water and give the geese some almond cakes to eat and some rosewater in a bowl to drink. Afterward she sat down on a rock and began combing her hair. All of a sudden, pearls and rubies fell by the handful, while a cloud of flowers drifted from her mouth, and a Syrian carpet of lilies and violets formed beneath her feet.

After the king had witnessed all of this, he summoned Ciommo and asked him whether he knew this beautiful girl, and Ciommo recognized her and ran to embrace her. Then, in the presence of the king, Ciommo listened to the entire story of Troccola's treachery and how that ugly pest's jealousy had driven this beautiful flame of love to live in the waters of the sea.

It would be impossible to describe the pleasure of the king in finding

---

6. Basile uses the term *capopopolo*, a reference to the organizers of popular uprisings.

such a beautiful jewel, and turning toward her brother, he said that Ciommo had truly had good reason to praise her so much and that he, the king, found her two thirds more beautiful than Ciommo had described her. Therefore, he considered her to be more than worthy to become his wife if she would be content to accept the scepter of his kingdom.

"Oh, if only Sol in Leo[7] would allow this and let me come and serve as the vassal of your crown!" Marziella answered. "But don't you see the golden chain attached to my feet with which the siren keeps me prisoner? If I take too much air and spend too much time on the beach, she drags me back to my rich slavery enchained by gold."

"How can we get you out of this and free you from the clutches of this siren?" asked the king.

"If you could saw the chains silently with a file, then I would be able to slip out of them," Marziella responded.

"Expect me tomorrow morning," the king declared. "We'll settle this affair, and I'll bring you to my palace, where you will be the apple of my eye, the treasure of my heart, and the light of my soul."

After they exchanged pledges with a touch of their hands, she went back into the water, and he into the fire so that he could not sleep a wink until it was day. So when that black demon of night came out to dance the tubba catubba[8] with the stars, the king could not close his eyes but ruminated about Marziella's beauty with the jaws of his memory and pondered all the marvels of her hair with his mind, the miracles of her mouth, and the marvels of her feet. Testing the gold of her charms on the touchstone of his judgment, he found that it was twenty-four carat. Then he cursed the night that was taking so long in finishing its embroidery of the stars, and he cursed the sun for not having arrived sooner with its carrier of light so that he could enrich his house with the goods that he desired, so that he could bring the gold mine that produced pearls into his room, and the pearl shell that brought forth flowers.

Now, while he was lost in the sea of his thoughts contemplating the beautiful maiden in the sea, the sappers[9] of the sun finally began to level the road so that the sun could pass with his army of rays. Then the king got dressed and went with Ciommo to the beach, where they found Marziella. Using the file he had brought with him, the king personally severed the chain from the feet of his beloved while creating an even stronger chain that bound his own heart. Then he helped her into the saddle of a horse he had brought with him—that lady who already rode in his heart —and he set out with her for the royal palace, where he had arranged for all the beautiful women of the country to welcome her and honor her as their mistress.

After the marriage of the king to Marziella, and the grand festivities, the king ordered Troccola to be thrown into the flames along with the many

---

7. Reference to the zodiacal sign of Leo. Solleone was the hottest day of the year, and the expression reflected a popular belief in the sun.
8. Reference to an ancient dance.
9. Sappers generally formed part of the army in those days and went ahead of the main force to eliminate natural obstacles that might stand in the way of their advance.

barrels that were burned for the celebration, and thus she paid for the treacherous way that she had treated Marziella. Then Luceta was brought to the kingdom, where she and Ciommo were given the privilege of living in the palace in royal fashion. But Puccia was banished and forced to wander about as a beggar. Indeed, since she had selfishly refused to share her abundant cake, she was now always in need of bread, for this is the will of heaven:

He who feels no pity finds no pity.

JACOB AND WILHELM GRIMM

The White Bride and the Black Bride†

A woman was walking with her daughter and stepdaughter over the fields to cut fodder when the dear Lord came toward them in the guise of a poor man and asked, "Which is the way to the village?"

"If you want to know," said the mother, "then look for it yourself." And her daughter added, "If you're worried about not finding it, then take a signpost with you."

However, the stepdaughter said, "Poor man, I'll show you the way. Come with me."

Since the mother and daughter had infuriated the dear Lord, he turned his back on them and cursed them so that they became black as night and ugly as sin. But God showed mercy to the poor stepdaughter and went with her to the village. When they drew close to the village, he gave her his blessing and said, "Choose three things for yourself, and I'll grant them to you."

The maiden said, "I'd like to be as beautiful and pure as the sun," and in no time she was as white and beautiful as the day.

"Then I'd like to have a money purse that is never empty," and the dear Lord gave her that as well but said, "Don't forget the best thing of all."

And she replied, "For my third wish, I want to live in the eternal kingdom of heaven after my death."

This wish was also granted, and then the Lord parted from her.

When the stepmother arrived home with her daughter and saw that they were both as black as coal and ugly, while the stepdaughter was white and beautiful, her heart turned even more evil, and she could think of nothing but how she might harm her stepdaughter. However, the stepdaughter had a brother named Reginer, whom she loved very much, and she told him everything that had happened.

One day Reginer said to her, "Dear sister, I want to paint your picture

† Jacob and Wilhelm Grimm, "The White Bride and the Black Bride"—"Die weisse und die schwarze Braut" (1857), No. 135 in *Kinder- und Hausmärchen. Gesammelt durch die Brüder Grimm* (Göttingen: Dieterich, 1857).

so that I may always see you before my eyes. My love for you is so great that I want to see you constantly."

"All right," she said, "but I beg of you not to let anyone else see the picture."

So he painted a portrait of his sister and hung it in his room, which was in the royal castle, because he served the king as coachman. Every day he stood in front of the portrait and thanked God for his dear sister's good fortune.

It happened that the king's wife had just died, and she had been so beautiful that the king was greatly distressed because her equal could not be found anywhere. The court servants had noticed, however, that the coachman stood in front of a beautiful portrait every day, and since they envied him, they reported it to the king, who ordered the portrait to be brought to him. When he saw how the portrait resembled his wife in each and every way and was even more beautiful, he fell desperately in love with it. Consequently, he summoned the coachman and asked him whose picture it was. The coachman said that it was his sister, and the king decided to marry no other woman but her. He gave the coachman a carriage and horses and magnificent golden clothes and sent him to fetch his chosen bride.

When Reginer arrived with the news, his sister rejoiced, but the black maiden was jealous of her good fortune and became terribly annoyed. "What's the good of all your craftiness," she said to her mother, "if you can't bring about such good luck for me?"

"Be quiet," said the old woman. "I'll soon make things turn your way."

And through her witchcraft she clouded the eyes of the coachman so that he became half blind, and she stopped up the ears of the white maiden so that she became half deaf. After this had been done, they climbed into the carriage, first the bride in her splendid royal garments, then the stepmother with her daughter, while Reginer sat on the box to drive. When they had gone some distance, the coachman cried out:

> "Cover yourself, my sister dear,
> don't let the rain get you too wet.
> Don't let the wind blow dust on you.
> Take care, for you must look your very best
> when you appear at your good king's request."

The bride asked, "What's my brother saying?"

"Ah," replied the old woman. "He said you should take off your golden dress and give it to your sister."

Then she took it off and put it on her sister, who gave her a shabby gray gown in return. They continued on their way, and after a while, the brother called out again:

> "Cover yourself, my sister dear,
> don't let the rain get you too wet.
> Don't let the wind blow dust on you.
> Take care, for you must look your very best
> when you appear at your good king's request."

The bride asked, "What's my brother saying?"

"Ah," replied the old woman. "He said you should take off your golden bonnet and give it to your sister."

Then she took off the bonnet, put it on the black maiden, and sat with her hair uncovered. They continued on their way, and after a while her brother called out once more.

> "Cover yourself, my sister dear,
> don't let the rain get you too wet.
> Don't let the wind blow dust on you.
> Take care, for you must look your very best
> when you appear at your good king's request."

The bride asked, "What's my brother saying?"

"Ah," replied the old woman. "He said you should take a look out of the carriage."

Just then they happened to be crossing a bridge over a deep river. When the bride stood up and leaned out the window of the carriage, the other two pushed her out, and she fell into the middle of the water. At the very instant that she sank out of sight, a snow white duck arose out of the smooth glittering water and swam down the river. Since the brother had not noticed a thing, he kept driving until they reached the court. Then he brought the black maiden to the king as his sister and really thought it was her because his eyes were so clouded and he could only go by the glimmer of the golden clothes. When the king saw how abysmally ugly his intended bride was, he became furious and ordered the coachman to be thrown into a pit full of adders and snakes. However, the old witch managed to charm the king and deceive him through witchcraft so that he allowed her and her daughter to stay. Indeed, the daughter gradually appeared quite nice to him, and thus he actually married her.

One evening, while the black bride was sitting on the king's lap, a white duck swam up the drain to the kitchen and said to the kitchen boy:

> "Light a fire, little boy, light it quick,
> for I must warm my feathers and not get sick."

The kitchen boy did as he was asked and lit a fire on the hearth. Then the duck came and sat down next to it, shook herself, and cleaned her feathers with her beak. While she sat there and made herself comfortable, she asked, "What's my brother, Reginer, doing?"

The kitchen boy answered:

> "With snakes and adders in a pit,
> that's where he's been forced to sit."

Then she asked, "What's the black witch doing in the house?"

The kitchen boy answered:

> "She's nice and warm.
> Indeed, the king has got her in his arms."

The duck said, "God have mercy!" and swam back down the drain. The next evening she came again and asked the same questions, and on the third evening as well. The kitchen boy could not bear this any longer, went to the king, and revealed everything to him. The king, however, wanted to see for himself and went to the kitchen on the following evening. When the duck stuck her head out through the drain, he took his sword and cut her head off by the neck. All at once she turned into a most beautiful maiden and looked like the portrait that her brother had made of her. The king rejoiced, and since she was standing there soaking wet, he had fine clothes brought to her, which she put on. Then she told him how she had been betrayed through guile and deceit and how ultimately she had been thrown into the water.

Her first request was to have her brother taken out of the snakepit. When the king had fulfilled this request, he went into the room where the old witch sat and asked, "What kind of a punishment does a woman deserve if she does something like the following?" Then he told her all about the past events. Yet she was so distracted that she did not realize what was going on and said, "She deserves to be stripped naked and put into a barrel studded with nails. Then a horse should be hitched to the barrel and sent running out into the world."

This is what happened to her and her black daughter. But the king married the beautiful white bride and rewarded the faithful brother by making him a rich and respected man.

Faithful Sisters

One of the most popular motifs in the oral and literary tradition of Europe is the innocent sister who seeks to rescue and/or become acquainted with her brothers, who were banished from her family upon her birth. The Grimms were familiar with the Basile version, and they also published two other tales in their collection that dealt with this theme—"Die sechs Schwäne" ("The Six Swans") and "Die sieben Raben" ("The Seven Ravens"). In the Grimms' Ölenberg manuscript, "The Twelve Brothers" has the title "Twelve Brothers and the Little Sister." The original handwritten version was recorded by Jacob while Wilhelm prepared the text for the 1812 publication. The pattern of the oral tale is basically retained, but Wilhelm's reworking of the narrative emphasizes two personal factors: the dedication of the sister and brothers to one another, and the establishment of a common, orderly household in the forest, where they live peacefully together. Aside from reinforcing notions of industry, cleanliness, and order, Jacob and Wilhelm were obviously drawn to the tale because of its theme: *several brothers* and *one sister* overcome adversity after separation from their parents (not unlike the situation in which the Grimms, their brothers, and single sister found themselves). The parents are never mentioned again—the loss is permanent—and it is clear that the brothers and sister, whose reputation is restored at the end, will have a new home and live together in contentment. The underlying social issue in these tales involves the legacy of a family and the right of succession and inheritance. Depending on whether a society was based on primogeniture or ultimogeniture, the older children might be sent away from the family so that the youngest could inherit the family property. There is also a possibility that the tale stemmed from societies that were based on matrilineal rites. Ludwig Bechstein includes versions of "The Seven Ravens" and "The Seven Swans" in *Deutsches Märchenbuch* (1845).

GIAMBATTISTA BASILE

The Seven Doves†

Once upon a time in the village of Arzano[1] there was a good woman who gave birth to a son every year so that, when the number reached seven, the boys resembled the flute of Pan with seven holes each a little bigger than the next. As soon as the sons had grown and lost their first set

---

† Giambattista Basile, "The Seven Doves"—"I sette colombelli" (1634), *Ottavo passatempo della quarta giornata* in *Lo cunto de li cunti overo Lo trattenemiento de peccerille*, De Gian Alessio Abbattutis, 5 vols. (Naples: Ottavio Beltrano, 1634–36).
1. A hamlet near Casoria; now part of the commune of Naples.

of ears,[2] they said to their mother, Jannetella, who was pregnant once again, "Listen, dear mother, if you don't give birth to a girl after so many sons, we've decided to leave this house and wander about the world like the sons of a blackbird."

When their mother heard this bad news, she prayed to heaven to drive this whim out of their minds and to help her avoid losing her seven precious gems. When the time came for her to give birth, however, her sons said to her, "We are going to withdraw to the top of that hill over there and wait on a cliff. If you give birth to a boy, put a pen and inkstand on the windowsill. If you give birth to a girl, put a spoon and distaff there. If we see the signal that it's a girl, we'll return home and spend the rest of our lives under your wing, but if we see that it's a boy, forget us, for we shall spread our wings!"

The sons departed, and heaven granted Jannetella's wish: she gave birth to a girl. Then she told the midwife to make the agreed-upon signal to her sons, but the midwife was in such a daze and so distracted that she set the pen and inkstand on the windowsill. When the seven brothers saw this, they set out on their way and continued traveling for three years until they arrived at a forest, where the trees danced the *Imperticata*[3] with sticks and leaves to the sound of a river which played the counterpoint on the stones. In the middle of this forest there was a house that was inhabited by a blind ogre. Some time ago, while he was asleep, he had his eyes torn out by a woman, and consequently he was now an enemy of that fair sex so that he devoured all the women he managed to catch.

When the young men arrived at the ogre's house, they were exhausted from their journey and dying of hunger. So they indicated to the ogre that they would appreciate for pity's sake if he could give them some morsels of bread. The ogre responded that he would gladly give them food if they would enter his service. Indeed, he told them that they would have nothing more to do than to lead him around like a little dog, each taking a turn once a week. When the ogre spoke these words, it seemed to the seven brothers that they had found both a mother and a father in him, and they agreed to enter his service. So, as soon as the ogre had memorized their names, he would call out Giangrazio, Cecchitiello, Pascale, Nuccio, Pone, Pezillo, or Carcavecchia, depending on whom he needed. In return for their service, he assigned them a room on the ground floor of the house, and he provided them with all the food they needed.

In the meantime, their sister grew up, and when she learned that her brothers had gone out into the world because of the midwife's mistake, and that there had been no news of them since then, she convinced herself that she should go and search for them. She kept on insisting on this so much that her mother finally yielded to her request. So she dressed her daughter like a pilgrim and bade her farewell.

Cianna, for that was her name, traveled about for a long time and kept

---

2. Ironic reference by Basile, implying that children lose ears the way they lose teeth.
3. This was a dance performed during Carnival time. Holding sticks or poles garlanded with flowers, the dancers wore costumes and masks and danced under the windows of the nobles, who threw them money.

asking place after place whether anyone had seen seven brothers. After taking many different roads, she finally heard something about them at an inn, and she had someone show her the road that led to the forest. Finally, one morning, when the sun was using his penknife to scratch out the mistakes that night had made on heaven's papers, she arrived at the ogre's house. With great joy the brothers recognized her at once, and they cursed the pen and ink that had led them astray and caused so much misfortune. After they embraced her a thousand times, they warned her that she had to stay locked in their room so that the ogre would not see her. In addition, she was to give part of her food by hand to a cat that was in their room; otherwise, the cat could cause trouble for her.

Cianna wrote these words of advice in the notebook of her head and shared everything she had in good camaraderie with the cat, splitting everything in half and saying "This is for me. This is for you. This is for the king's daughter." She always divided everything, even down to the last crumb.

Now it so happened that the brothers went out hunting to help the ogre, and they left her with a basket of chickpeas to cook. When she was cleaning the peas, she unfortunately discovered a nut which became the stone of scandal that smashed her peace because she put it into her mouth without giving half to the cat. So, out of spite, the cat ran over to the fire and pissed on it until the fire went out. When Cianna noticed this, she did not know what to do and ran out the room, despite the warning of her brothers, and went straight to the ogre's apartment, asking him for fire.

When the ogre heard a woman's voice, he cried out, "You may take a giant step! Wait a while, and you'll find what you seek!"

After saying this, he took a whetstone, greased it with oil, and began sharpening his tusks. When Cianna saw that she was heading in the wrong direction, she took a torch, ran back into her room, and barricaded the door with bars, chairs, stools, chests, rocks, and anything else she could find in the room. As soon as the ogre had finished sharpening his teeth, he ran down to the room, and finding it closed, he began giving it some vicious kicks to knock it down. As he was making all this noise, the seven brothers arrived and were confronted with this disaster while the ogre began calling them traitors because their room had become the gathering place of his enemies. Giangrazio, the oldest and the most sensible of the brothers, saw that there was now a bad turn of events and said to the ogre, "We don't know anything about this incident. Perhaps this wretched woman entered our room by chance while we were out hunting. But since she has barricaded herself behind this door, come with me, and I'll take you to a passageway from where we can attack her in the rear without her being able to defend herself."

So he took the ogre by the hand and brought him to an extremely deep pit. Then he gave him a shove, and the ogre fell down to the bottom of the pit. Immediately thereafter the brothers covered him with dirt. When they were finished, they made their sister open the door and gave her a sound scolding for the mistake she had made and for exposing herself to such danger. They warned her that in the future she had better be more careful, and they specifically told her not to gather grass near the spot where the ogre was buried; otherwise they would all be turned into seven doves.

"May heaven keep me from bringing you into such danger!" Cianna replied.

Thus they took over the ogre's possessions and became the lords of the entire house, where they lived happily and waited for the winter to pass. They agreed that once the sun had bestowed a green robe embroidered with flowers as a gift to the earth to celebrate his conquest of the house of Taurus,[4] they would start on their journey home.

It so happened, however, that while the brothers were off collecting wood in the mountains to protect themselves from the cold that was growing more severe every day, a poor pilgrim wandered into the forest. At one point he began mocking a mandrill on a pine tree, and the mandrill responded by throwing a pinecone at him that hit him on his head and caused such a large bump that the poor man began shrieking like a lost soul. When Cianna heard the noise, she rushed out of the house. Filled with pity for the man, she quickly picked some rosemary from a bush growing on the ogre's grave. Then she chopped up the rosemary, boiled it with bread and salt, and prepared a plaster for his wound. Afterward she gave him a light meal and sent him on his way. But as she was setting the table in preparation for her brothers' return, she suddenly saw seven doves who said to her, "It would have been better if you had kept your hands to yourself instead of picking that cursed rosemary which is making us fly away to the seashore! Sister, you are the cause of all our bad luck! How could you have forgotten our warning? What's happened to your brains? Thanks to you we've become birds and are now prey to the claws of kites, falcons, and hawks. Thanks to you we are the companions of bee-eaters, blackcaps, goldfinches, screech owls, long-eared owls, jays, magpies, white throats, linnets, bitterns, shrikes, larks, moor hens, woodcocks, siskins, golani, chaffinches, gold-crested wrens, tits, red-crested ducks, wrynecks, rock doves, wagtails, paposce, white-collared flycatchers, dabchicks, wrens, purple herons, white wagtails, garganey seals, morette, paperchi, and hoopoes! What a fine thing you've done! Now, if we return to our home country, we'll find nets and traps prepared to catch us. Just so you could heal the head of a pilgrim you've broken the heads of your seven brothers! Unless you find the Mother of Time, who can show you the way to solve our predicament, there is no hope for us!"

Cianna felt like a plucked quail for the mistake she had made, and she asked her brothers for pardon. Indeed, she offered to travel around the world until she found the home of the old Mother of Time. So, she implored her brothers to stay inside the house the entire time she was gone, and then she set out.

Despite the fact that she went by foot, Cianna never felt tired as she traveled because her desire to help her brothers prompted her to move along like a pack mule, and she covered three miles an hour. Finally, she

---

4. Zodiacal constellation represented pictorially as the forepart of the bull. The sun enters the constellation on May 14.

reached a beach where the sea was beating the rocks with the stick of the waves because they did not want to do the Latin homework that had been assigned them. All of a sudden she saw a huge whale who asked her, "What are you looking for, my beautiful maiden?"

"I'm looking for the home of the Mother of Time."

"Well, let me tell you what to do," responded the whale. "Go straight ahead along the shore, and at the first river that you come across, you'll find someone who will show you the way. But please do me a favor: when you have found the good old woman, ask her how I can swim about safely without crashing into the rocks and landing on the sand so many times."

"Leave it to me," Cianna said and thanked the whale for his directions. Then she began to trot along the beach, and after a long journey, she arrived at the river, which like a treasury officer was pouring money into the bank of the sea. Then she took the path that followed the course of the river until she arrived in a beautiful countryside where the meadows imitated the sky and spread out a green mantle studded with flowers like the stars. Soon Cianna encountered a mouse, who asked, "Where are you going all by yourself, beautiful maiden?"

"I'm searching for the Mother of Time," she replied.

"You've got a long way to go," the mouse said. "But don't feel discouraged. There is an end to everything. Just keep walking toward those mountains which, like the free lords of these fields, have assumed the title of your 'Highness,' and then you'll be able to obtain more information about what you're searching for. But please do me a favor: when you arrive at the old woman's house, ask her to tell you how we can find a way to free ourselves from the tyranny of the cats. Then I shall always be at your command, for I shall be indebted to you as your slave."

After Cianna promised the mouse to do this favor, she advanced toward the mountains. Although they seemed to be close, she thought she would never reach them. However, she managed to arrive, and since she was very tried, she sat down on a rock where she watched an army of ants transport a large supply of grain, and one of them turned to Cianna and said, "Who are you, and where are you going?"

And Cianna, who treated everyone in a gentle fashion, said, "I'm an unfortunate girl who is looking for the Mother of Time because of a matter very close to my heart."

"Keep going straight ahead," the ant replied, "until you reach a point where the mountains open up into a wide plain, and there you'll learn more. But please do me a great favor: ask the old woman what we ants should do to live a little longer because it seems to me one of the great follies of this life on earth is that we have to work so hard to collect and store so much food for such a short life that, like a swindler's candle, is extinguished in the very middle of its best years."

"Don't worry," said Cianna. "I'll certainly repay the kindness you've shown me."

After Cianna walked beyond the mountains, she found herself on a beautiful plain, and she continued traveling for a long time until she reached a large oak tree, a testimony to antiquity, the sweet dessert of that bride, who was happy at one time, and the morsel that time gives to this bitter age to make up for the lost sweetness. Then the oak, making lips out of its bark and a tongue out of its sap, asked Cianna, "Where are you going in such a hurry, my little girl? Come and rest in the shade of my branches."

Cianna thanked him very much, but excused herself, saying that she was in a rush to find the Mother of Time. When the oak heard this, he said, "You are not very far now. You just have to walk one more day, and you'll see a house on a mountain, where you'll find the woman you've been seeking. But, if you are as kind as you are beautiful, please try to discover what I must do to regain my lost honor because I used to provide nourishment for great men while now I am merely food for pigs."

"Leave it to me," Cianna responded. "I'll see what I can do to help you."

After she said this, she continued on her way without stopping until she arrived at the foot of a killjoy mountain that poked its head through the clouds just to annoy them. There she found an old man who had become so tired from walking that he had stretched himself out in the middle of some hay. When he saw Cianna, he recognized her right away as the girl who had tended to the bump on his head. When he heard what she was searching for, he told her that he was also on his way to Time to bring him the rent of the land that he had cultivated. He also said that Time was a tyrant who usurped everything in the world and wanted to receive tribute from everyone, and in particular from those men of his age. Now, since he had been treated so well by Cianna, he told her that he would repay her kindness a hundred times over by giving her good advice about what to do when she arrived at the top of the mountain. Unfortunately, he was unable to accompany her there because his age had compelled him to descend rather than ascend the mountain and obliged him to remain at the foot of the mountain to settle his accounts with the clerks of Time, who are exhaustion, misfortune, and illness, in order to pay his debt to nature. Thus he continued to say, "Now, listen carefully, my beautiful innocent daughter. Right on top of the mountain you will find a house that is so old it is impossible to recall when it was built. The walls are cracking. The foundations are crumbling. The doors have been eaten away by worms. The furniture is moldy. In short, everything is falling to pieces and is wasting away. You can see broken columns and damaged statues. Nothing's been left intact except for a coat of arms quartered over the door where you can see a serpent chewing its tail, a stag, a crow, and a phoenix.[5] As soon as you enter, you will perceive on the ground quiet files, saws, scythes, and pruning hooks and hundreds and hundreds of pails of ashes like special pots with names written on them like Corinth, Saguntum, Carthage, Troy, and a thousand other ruined cities whose ashes are kept in memory of their famous epochs. Now, when you come close to this house, hide yourself somewhere until you see Time come out, and when Time leaves, you are to go inside, and you will find an extremely old woman whose chin touches the ground and whose lump touches the sky. Her hair, like the hair of a musty gray horse, hangs down to her heels.

5. Symbols of time, speed, return, and rebirth.

Her face resembles a head of lettuce and is filled with creases that have become stiff by the starch of time. She will be sitting on a clock attached to a wall, and she will not be able to see you because her eyelids are so heavy that they bury her eyes. As soon as you enter, you are to take the weights off the clock and then to call the old woman and ask her to tell you what you desire. In turn, she will quickly call for her son to devour you. But since the clock that she sits on will have lost its weights, he will not be able to move, and therefore, she will be compelled to tell you what you want. But do not trust any of the promises that she makes unless she swears by the wings of her son. Then you can believe her and do as she says, and you will be satisfied."

While the poor old man said these words, his body decayed like the body that has been lying in a vault and then is brought into the light of day. Cianna took the ashes and mixed them with a small amount of her tears. Then she dug a hole and buried them, praying to heaven to grant them peace and quiet. Afterward, she began climbing the mountain and ran out of breath. Once she arrived, however, she waited for Time to leave the house. He was an old man with a very long beard and wore a mantle of rags and tatters that had many labels sewn on it with the names of various people. In addition, he had enormous wings and ran so fast that Cianna immediately lost sight of him. But she could now enter the house, and though she was frightened by what she saw in that dingy hole, she grabbed the weights right away and told the old woman what she wanted. In turn, the old woman screamed and called for her son, but Cianna said, "You can knock your head against the wall all you want, but you will certainly not see your son because I have the weights of the clock in my possession."

When the old woman realized there was nothing she could do, she tried to deceive her by saying, "Let go of them, my dear. Don't stop my son's movements. Nobody in the world has ever done that. Let the weights go. May God protect you. I promise you by the nitric acid that my son uses to corrode everything, I won't harm you."

"You're wasting your time," Cianna responded. "You had better say something else if you want me to let go of them."

"I swear to you by the teeth which gnaw everything that moves. I'll tell you all that you want to know," she said.

"I don't believe the slightest thing you said," Cianna asserted, "because I know you're trying to deceive me."

Finally, the old woman said, "All right, I swear by those wings which fly everywhere that I shall provide you with more pleasure than you can imagine!"

So Cianna let go of the weights and kissed the old woman's musty and moldy hands. Seeing how polite the girl was, the old woman said, "Hide yourself behind that door, and when Time returns, I'll get him to tell you what you want to know, and when he goes out again—he can never stay still in one place for long—you can slip away. But don't make a sound, for he is such a glutton that he does not even spare his own children, and if there is nothing else to eat, he eats himself and then regenerates himself."

After Cianna had done what the old woman had told her to do, Time came dashing in, light and fast, and he gulped down everything and anything he could get his hands on, even the plaster on the walls. Then, as he was about to leave, his mother asked him the questions that Cianna had given to her and implored him, by the milk she had given him, to respond point by point to all her questions. After a thousand pleas, her son responded, "All right, tell the tree that it will never be cherished as long as it keeps treasures buried beneath its roots. Tell the mice that they will never be safe from cats until they tie bells around their legs so they can hear them coming. Tell the ant that wants to live a hundred years that she is not to fly because, when an ant is about to die, it begins to sprout wings. Tell the whale to make the best of things and become friends with the sea rat who never loses his way and will always guide him. Tell the doves that, when they make their nest on the column of wealth, they will turn back into their original shapes."

After saying all this, Time began to run his usual course, and Cianna took her leave of the old woman. As soon as she descended the mountain and reached the plain, the seven doves arrived at the same time, for they had been following the trail of their sister. Since they were tired from such a long flight, they all went to rest themselves on the horn of a dead ox, and no sooner did they touch the ox with their claws than they turned back into the handsome young men that they had been before. Astonished as they were by this transformation, they soon learned from the answer that Time had given their sister that the horn, as a symbol of plenty, was the column of wealth to which Time had referred. Then after the brothers celebrated their reunion with their sister, they began their return home on the same path by which Cianna had traveled to this region.

When they came back to the oak tree, they told it what Time had said, and the tree asked them to take away the treasure beneath its roots because it had caused the acorn to lose its reputation. So the seven brothers found a spade in a garden and dug beneath the tree until they found a large jar of gold coins. Then they divided the treasure equally among themselves and their sister so that they could carry it with them more easily. Since they were very tired from travelling and transporting all the heavy gold, they became sleepy and lay down to rest next to a hedge. Soon, however, a band of thieves came upon them, and when they saw those unfortunate travelers with their heads on sacks of money, they tied them hand and foot to some trees, took the money, and left them to weep not only about the wealth that they had just found and then let slip through their fingers, but also about their lives. Without the possibility of finding help, they ran the risk of dying from hunger or satisfying the hunger of some beast.

While they were lamenting their bad luck, the mouse arrived, and they told her Time's answer. Then, to repay the favor she had received, the mouse nibbled through the cords with which they were bound and set them free.

Then the brothers and their sister proceeded on their way, and after a while they came across the ant, who listened to the advice of Time. The mouse also asked Cianna why she was so sad and pale, and Cianna told the ant all about their misfortune and how the thieves had tricked them.

"Listen," the ant responded, "now I have the opportunity to repay you for the favor you did for me. I want you to know that, when I was carrying a load of grain beneath the ground, I saw the hole where the murderous dogs hide the things they steal. They've dug a hole beneath an old building, and they store all their loot there. Right now they have gone off to rob someone, and I can take you and show you the place so that you can regain your treasure."

Thereupon, they all went in the direction of some houses that were in ruins, and the ant showed the seven brothers the opening to a hole into which Giangrazio, the bravest of the brothers, was lowered. After he found all the money that had been taken from them, he passed it on to the others, and they quickly headed toward the seashore, where they encountered the whale. Then they gave him the advice which Time, the father of good advice, had given them, and while they were standing there and chatting about their journey and all that had happened to them, they suddenly saw the robbers appear on the horizon armed to the teeth, for they had followed their trail.

"Alas!" they cried. "This time they'll leave no trace of us because they're armed and will skin us alive!"

"Don't be afraid," the whale replied. "I'll get you out of this jam to repay you for the affection and kindness that you've shown me. Get on my back quickly, and I'll carry you off to a safe place."

When the poor brothers and their sister saw their enemies breathing down their backs and saw that they were up to their necks in water, they mounted the whale, and after he passed through some reefs, he carried them until they were within sight of Naples. But he could not land because the water was too shallow. So he said, "Where do you want me to leave you along the Amalfi Coast?"

And Giangrazio replied, "Listen, we would prefer not to land along here, my good fish. We are not too happy about disembarking along this coast because at Massa they just greet you and move on. At Sorrentino they just grit their teeth. At Vico they just bring you bread. At Castellmare there are no friends or companions."[6]

So, to please them, the whale turned toward the Salt Rock,[7] where he left them, and from there, they managed to signal a fishing boat that picked them up and carried them ashore. Then they returned to their own country safe, sound, and rich, and they consoled their mother and father. Thanks to Cianna's goodness, they enjoyed a happy life proving the truth of the old proverb:

Good things happen to those who forget the good they've done.

6. Old sayings that are still in common usage on the peninsula of Sorrento.
7. Basile was very familiar with this region and may have been born on Posilipo. The rock is just off the cape of Posilipo.

JACOB AND WILHELM GRIMM

The Twelve Brothers†

Once upon a time a king and a queen lived together peacefully and had twelve children, all boys. One day the king said to his wife, "When you give birth to our thirteenth child and it's a girl, the twelve boys are to die so she may have all the wealth and the kingdom for herself."

He even had twelve coffins made and filled with wood shavings. Each was fitted with a death pillow, and all the coffins were locked in a room. The king gave the key to the queen and ordered her never to say one word about this to anyone. She then sat and lamented the entire day. Her youngest son, Benjamin, whose name she had taken from the Bible, was always with her, and he asked, "Dear mother, why are you so sad?"

"My lovely child," she replied, "I'm not allowed to tell you."

But he gave her no peace until she opened the room and showed him the twelve coffins already filled with wood shavings. She then said, "My dearest Benjamin, your father had these coffins made for you and your eleven brothers. If I give birth to a girl, all of you will be killed and buried in them."

As she was telling him this, she wept, and her son consoled her by saying, "Don't weep, dear mother. We'll find a way to help ourselves and get away from here."

Then she said, "Go into the forest with your eleven brothers. I want you to find the tallest tree and take turns sitting on top. You're to keep watch and look toward the castle tower. If I give birth to a little boy, I'll raise a white flag, and then you'll be able to return. If I give birth to a little girl, I'll raise a red flag, and then you're to flee as fast as you can. And may the good Lord protect you. I'll get up every night and pray that you're able to warm yourselves by a fire in the winter and that you don't suffer from the heat during the summer."

After she gave her blessings to her sons, they went out into the forest, where they took turns keeping watch. Each one sat on top of the tallest oak tree and looked toward the tower. When eleven days had passed and it was Benjamin's turn, he saw a flag being raised. However, it was not a white one but a bloodred flag announcing that they were to die. When the brothers heard that, they became angry and said, "Why should we suffer death because of a girl? We swear we'll get our revenge. Whenever we find a girl, her blood will flow."

Then they went deeper into the forest, where it was darkest. There they found an abandoned little cottage, which was bewitched.

"We shall dwell here," they said, "and you, Benjamin, since you're the youngest and weakest, shall stay at home and keep house. We others shall go out and search for food."

So they went off into the forest and shot hares, wild deer, birds, little

† Jacob and Wilhelm Grimm, "The Twelve Brothers"—"Die zwölf Brüder" (1857), No. 9 in *Kinder-und Hausmärchen. Gesammelt durch die Brüder Grimm* (Göttingen: Dieterich, 1857).

pigeons, and whatever was fit to eat. They brought this to Benjamin, who had to prepare it nicely for them so they could satisfy their hunger. They lived together for ten years in this little cottage, and the time passed quickly for them.

Meanwhile, the daughter that their mother, the queen, had brought into the world had grown to be a little girl. She had a kind heart and beautiful features and a gold star on her forehead. One time, when there was a great deal of washing to do, she saw twelve boy's shirts among the things to be washed and asked her mother, "Whose shirts are these? They're much too small for father."

Her mother answered her with a heavy heart and said, "Dear child, they belong to your twelve brothers."

"Where are my twelve brothers?" the girl asked. "I've never heard of them until now."

"Only God knows where they are," she answered. "They're wandering somewhere in the world." She took the girl, opened the room, and showed her the twelve coffins with the wood shavings and the death pillows. "These coffins were destined for your brothers," she said, "but the boys departed secretly before you were born." And then she told her everything that had happened.

"Dear mother," the girl said, "don't weep. I'm going to look for my brothers."

So she took the twelve shirts and went straight into the great forest. She walked the whole day, and by evening she came to the bewitched cottage. When she entered, she found a young boy who asked, "Where have you come from and where are you going?" He was astonished by her beauty, her royal garments, and the star on her forehead.

"I'm a princess," she responded, "and I'm looking for my twelve brothers. I'm prepared to continue walking as far as the sky is blue until I find them."

She showed him the twelve shirts, and Benjamin realized she was his sister.

"I'm Benjamin," he said, "your youngest brother."

She began to cry for joy, and they kissed each other and lovingly hugged each other. But then he said, "Dear sister, there's still a problem. We agreed that any maiden who came our way would have to die, for we had to leave our kingdom on account of a girl."

"I'll gladly die," she said, "if I can save my twelve brothers by doing this."

"No," he responded. "You will not die. Sit down under this tub and wait until our eleven brothers come back. Then I'll settle everything with them."

She did as he said, and when it was night, the others came back from the hunt and found their meal ready. After they sat down at the table and began eating, they asked, "What's new?"

"You don't know?" Benjamin said.

"No," they replied.

"You're in the forest the whole day," he continued, "while I stay at home. Yet I still know more than you."

"Then tell us!" they cried out.

"Only if you promise me that the first girl we meet will not be killed," he said.

"Yes!" they all exclaimed. "Now tell us."

"Our sister is here!" he said, and he lifted up the tub, and the princess came crawling out in her royal garments. She had the gold star on her forehead and was very beautiful, gentle, and delicate. In their joy they embraced and kissed her, for they loved her with all their hearts.

Now she stayed at home with Benjamin and helped him with the work. The eleven brothers went into the forest, caught wild game, deer, birds, pigeons so they would have something to eat, and their sister and Benjamin made sure that their meals were prepared. They fetched the wood for cooking, gathered herbs to go along with the vegetables, and put the pots on the fire so dinner was always ready when the eleven brothers came home. Moreover, they kept the little cottage in order and put nice clean white sheets on the little beds. All this kept the brothers satisfied, and they lived with their sister in great harmony.

One day the two at home had prepared a wonderful meal, and when they were all together, they sat down, ate, drank, and were full of joy. Now, there was a small garden next to the bewitched cottage, and in it were twelve lilies, also called students. Since she wanted to please her brothers, the sister plucked the twelve flowers with the intention of giving one to each brother at the end of the meal. But right after she had plucked the flowers, the twelve brothers were instantly changed into twelve ravens and flew away over the forest, while the cottage and the garden vanished as well. Now the maiden was all alone in the wild forest, and when she looked around, an old woman was standing near her and said, "My child, what have you done? Why didn't you leave those twelve flowers alone? They were your brothers, and you've changed them into ravens forever."

"Is there no way to save them?" the maiden asked as she wept.

"No," the woman said. "That is—there's only one way in the entire world, but it's so hard, you won't be able to free them. You see, you would have to remain silent for seven years and neither speak nor laugh. If you utter but a single word and there is just an hour to go in the seven years, everything will be in vain, and your brothers will be killed by that one word."

"I know for sure," the maiden spoke with her whole heart, "that I shall save my brothers."

She went and searched for a tall tree. After climbing it, she sat down and began spinning and did not say a word or laugh. Now, it so happened that a king was hunting in the forest. He had a big greyhound that ran up to the tree where the maiden was sitting. The dog began jumping around, yelping and barking at her. The king then went over to the tree and saw the beautiful princess with the gold star on her forehead. He was so enraptured by her beauty that he called up to her and asked her if she would be his wife. She did not respond but nodded a little with her head. Then he climbed up the tree himself, carried her down, put her on his horse, and took her home. The wedding was celebrated with great splendor and joy, but the bride did not speak or laugh.

After they lived together for a few years, the king's mother, who was an evil woman, began to slander the young queen and said to the king, "The maiden you brought home with you is nothing but a common beggar girl! Who knows what godless mischief she's been secretly plotting? If she's mute and can't talk, she could at least laugh every now and then. Anyone who doesn't laugh must have a bad conscience."

At first the king did not want to believe this, but the old woman kept at it so long and accused the maiden of so many wicked things that the king finally let himself be convinced and sentenced his wife to death. A huge fire was made in the courtyard, and the young queen was to be burned in it. The king stood upstairs at a window and watched everything with tears in his eyes since he still loved her. When she was already bound to the stake and the fire was licking her clothes with its red tongues, the final second of the seven years expired. Suddenly a whirring noise could be heard in the air, and twelve ravens came flying toward the yard and swooped down. Then, just as they touched the ground, they turned into her twelve brothers whom she had saved. They tore apart the fire, put out the flames, freed their dear sister, and hugged and kissed her. Now that she was allowed to open her mouth and talk, she told the king why she had been silent and had never laughed. The king was glad to hear she was innocent, and they all lived together in harmony until their death. The evil mother was brought before the court and put into a barrel that was filled with boiling oil and poisonous snakes. Indeed, she died a horrible death.

Faithful Servants

The key motifs of this tale (the deep friendship of one man for another, the kidnapping of a bride for a prince, the defense of a prince by a loyal servant, and the sacrifice of children) can be found in the Bible, ancient Indian and Greek literature, and the European oral tradition. Basile's "The Raven" had a direct influence on Carlo Gozzi's play *Il corvo* (*The Raven*, 1761), and the Grimms were probably familiar with both Gozzi's and Basile's versions. The tale focuses on a double sacrifice: the brother/servant's loyal dedication to his master, which brings about his self-sacrifice; the king's sacrifice of his two sons. The loyalty of the brother/servant is thus presented as an example of heroic behavior, while the blood sacrifice of the sons stemmed from a folk belief that the blood of innocent children could work wonders in healing people. There is also another important Italian literary version by the Florentine writer Lorenzo Lippi, who wrote the poem "Il malmantile racquistato" ("The Bad Cloth Recovered") in 1650. It was a parody of Torquato Tasso's *Gerusalemme liberata* (*Jerusalem Liberated*, 1581) and was published posthumously in 1676. In the seventh *cantare*, there is a tale that concerns a nobleman who cuts his finger, and when he sees his blood on a white napkin, he craves a wife with similar coloring. When his brother Brunetto learns about this, he departs to find such a woman for his brother, and he eventually makes his way to a garden where he is told by two old men that he will find her. However, these men warn him that he must later prevent the maiden from drinking. If Brunetto reveals his knowledge when he stops her from drinking, he will be turned to stone. Of course, he is turned to stone and then disenchanted in the end.

GIAMBATTISTA BASILE

The Raven†

Once upon a time, there was a king of Frattombrosa called Milluccio, who was so fond of hunting that he neglected the most important affairs of the state and his house to follow the trail of a hare or the flight of a thrush. He continued to pursue these ways until one day fate led him into a forest with such a squadron of dense trees and thick soil that the cavalry of the sun could not penetrate it. While he was in this forest, he came upon a magnificent marble rock where he found a raven that had just been killed. When the king saw the bright red blood splashed on the bleached white stone, he heaved a sigh and said, "Oh heaven! If only I

---

† Giambattista Basile, "The Raven"—"Il corvo" (1634), *Nono passatempo della quarta giornata* in *Lo cunto de li cunti overo Lo trattenemiento de peccerille*, De Gian Alessio Abbattutis, 5 vols. (Naples: Ottavio Beltrano, 1634–36).

could have a wife as white and red as this stone and with hair and eyebrows as black as the feathers of this bird!"

He became so enraptured by this idea that he formed a counterpart to this stone that appeared to be a marble stone making love to another marble stone. Unfortunately, this whim took root in his head, and he nourished it with the pap of desire. In a short time, it transformed itself from a toothpick into a pole, from a jujube[1] into a pumpkin, from a barber's stove into a glass worker's furnace, and from a dwarf into a giant so that Milluccio could think of nothing else but that image which captured his heart and became set like a stone within stone. No matter where he turned his eyes he found the same image before him locked within his heart, and he forgot all other matters since there was nothing else on his mind except the marble. Indeed, he thought about it so much that he began to waste away and grew very thin because this stone was a millstone that crushed his life. It was the porphyry[2] in which the colors of his days were mixed. It was the flint stone which kindled the flame of his soul. It was the loadstone which magnetized him. Finally, it was the gallstone in his bladder that caused him great anguish.

At one point, his brother Jennariello became concerned when he saw him so pale and wan, and he said to him, "Brother, what's come over you? Your eyes seem tormented, and desperation is written all over your pale white face. What's happened to you? Speak, you can vent your feelings with your brother! You know you can die from the fumes of coal in a closed room. Powder contained in a mountain can blow into pieces if it's compressed. Scabs can cause an infection of the blood when they are stuck there. Gases trapped in the body produce farts and colic. Why don't you open your mouth and tell me what you are feeling? You can rest assured that I would stake a thousand lives to help you if I could."

Munching words and sighs, Milluccio thanked him for his great concern and told him that he had no doubts about his love, but there was no remedy for his sickness. This was because it stemmed from a stone on which he had sown the seeds of desire without the hope of fruit. It was a stone from which he could not even hope for a fungus of joy, a stone of Sisyphus[3] which he pushed to the top of his mountain of prospects only to see it roll right down *plop!* to the bottom.

However, his brother kept pleading with him until Milluccio told him all about his love, and when Jennariello heard his story, he consoled him as best he could. He told him to cheer up and not let himself become steeped in melancholy thoughts because he was going to see if he could satisfy his brother's longing, for he had decided to travel around the world until he found a woman who was the exact image of the stone. Immediately thereafter, Jennariello had a large ship outfitted with merchandise, dressed himself as a merchant, and journeyed to Venice, the mirror of Italy, home of virtuous men, and the great book of wonders of art and

1. An edible berry.
2. The stone that painters used to grind their colors.
3. In Greek mythology, the king of Corinth, noted for his cunning. Because of an impious act against the gods, he had to spend eternity in a futile attempt to push an enormous rock to the top of a hill. Once he neared the top, the rock was fated to roll down again.

nature. After he procured a safe-conduct permit for travel in the Levant,[4] he set sail for Cairo. When he arrived at that city, he saw a man carrying a beautiful falcon and immediately bought it to take back to his brother, who was very fond of hunting. After a little while, he saw another man with a splendid horse, and he bought it as well. Since he was now exhausted from his voyage, he went to spend the night in a tavern to refresh himself.

The next morning, when the general of light gave the command to the army of stars to strike their tents in the camp of the sky and to abandon their posts, Jennariello began walking around the city and glancing sharply at everything like a lynx. He looked carefully at this woman and that woman to see if he could, by chance, find a face of flesh that might resemble the face of stone. While he was wandering about haphazardly, always turning around like a thief afraid of the police, he encountered a beggar who was carrying an entire infirmary of bandages and a shop of rags on his back and who said to him, "My good sir, you have such a frightened look. Is anything wrong?"

"Do you think you're the one I should speak to about my business?" responded Jennariello. "When I bake my bread, I'll tell my story to the police first."

"Slowly, my boy," the beggar said. "Man's flesh is not sold by the pound. If Darius had not told his troubles to a stable boy, he would never have become king of Persia.[5] Therefore, it wouldn't be such a big deal if you were to tell a poor beggar about your affairs. No twig is too meager to help you clean your teeth."

Jennariello felt that the man's words made good sense, and he told him his reasons for coming to this county and what he was so diligently seeking.

When the beggar heard all this, he responded, "Now you'll see, my son, just how necessary it is to take everyone into account! Even though I may be no more than rubbish, I am still as useful as manure to fertilize the garden of your hopes. Now listen: I shall go and use the excuse of begging some alms to knock at the door of a beautiful maiden, the daughter of a magician. Open your eyes wide, look at her, contemplate her, glance at her, consider her, measure her, and you may find the image of what your brother desires."

Right after he said this, the beggar knocked at the door of a house not far from there, and the maiden, whose name was Liviella, opened it and tossed him a piece of bread. As soon as Jennariello saw her, he was convinced that she was the exact image of the model that Milluccio had described. Therefore, he gave the beggar a goodly amount of alms and went back to the tavern, where he disguised himself as a peddler of laces and trinkets. Then he filled two baskets with all kinds of treasures of the world, went to Liviella's house, and paced back and forth in front of it, shouting out "wares for sale" until the maiden called him to the door. Then Liviella looked at all the beautiful small nets, pieces of linen, rib-

---

4. The eastern part of the Mediterranean, with its islands and adjoining countries.
5. Reference to a story that Herodotus tells about Oebares, the stable groom, in his *Storie* (ca. 443 B.C.E.–ca. 425 B.C.E.).

bons, veils, lace, trinkets, blankets, buckles, pins, jars of rouge, and caps
fit for a queen that Jennariello was carrying in the baskets. She examined
and re-examined all his merchandise, and when she asked him to show
her some other pretty things, he responded, "Signora, I only carry common
stuff of little value in these baskets. But if you would deign to come to my
ship, I could show you things that are out of this world because I have
beautiful treasures worthy of a great lord."

Liviella, who had enough of that curiosity that was typical of her sex,
told him, "Alas! If my father were not away, I would come and look at
them."

"It's all the better that he's away," responded Jennariello. "Perhaps your
father would not grant you this pleasure, and I promise to show you splendid items that will astound you. What wonderful necklaces and earrings!
What belts and bodices! What combs! What bracelets! What embroidery!
In short, you'll be amazed by all these things."

After Liviella had listened to his description of such luxurious items,
she called a companion to come with her to the ship. When they arrived,
Jennariello kept her enchanted by showing her many beautiful things that
he had brought with him while he deftly had the anchor lifted and the
sails set. When Liviella finally took her eyes off the merchandise, she saw
that they were far from land and had already traveled several miles. Realizing much too late that she had been tricked, she began to do what
Olympia had done but in reverse.[6] Olympia lamented because she had
been abandoned on a rock whereas Liviella lamented because she was
abandoning the rocks.

However, Jennariello told her who he was and where he was taking her
and where good fortune was waiting for her. Aside from that, he described
how handsome Milluccio was, his valor, and his virtues. Finally he told
her all about the love with which she would be received. He said and did
so much that she calmed down and even became eager for the wind to
speed up and carry them quickly to see the colors of the design that Jennariello had painted.

While they were happily sailing along, they suddenly heard the waves
murmuring beneath the ship, and even though these waves spoke in low
voices, the captain of the ship heard them and cried out, "Everyone, be
on the alert! A storm is brewing! My God help us!"

His words were borne out by the whistling of the wind. Suddenly the
sky became covered with clouds, and the sea was turned into rippling
water. Since the waves were curious to learn all about other people's business, they came on board the ship, uninvited to the wedding. The sailors
began bailing out the water with ladles into tubs, and some used the
pumps. Since the sailors realized that all their lives were at stake, they
helped take care of the rudder, the sails, and the ropes. Meanwhile, Jennariello climbed up to the mast with his telescope to see if there might
be some safe place where they could weigh anchor. While he was looking
through his two-feet tube across a distance of one hundred miles, he saw

6. Reference to Ludovico Ariosto's *Orlando Furioso* (1532), Canto X, in which Olympia is abandoned
   by Bireno.

a pair of doves fly by and then land on their masthead. The male cried out, "Rooky, rooky!"

"What's the matter, husband," her mate answered. "Why are you croaking so much?"

And the dove said, "That poor prince has bought a falcon, and as soon as it is in the hands of his brother, it will scratch out his brother's eyes. But if he does not give it to his brother, or if he warns him, the prince will be turned into a piece of marble."

Soon after this, the dove began crying out once again, "Rooky, rooky!" and his mate asked him, "Why are you still croaking? Is there something else?"

And the dove said, "Yes, there's something else. He also bought a horse, and as soon as his brother mounts it, he will break his neck. But if the prince does not give it to him or warns him, he will be turned into a piece of marble. Rooky, rooky!"

"Alas! How many *rooky rookies* are you going to utter?" asked his mate. "What else is in store for them?"

And the dove replied, "The prince is bringing a beautiful bride to his brother, and when they go to bed with one another the first night, they will be attacked and devoured by a horrible dragon. But if the prince does not bring the bride to his brother or warns him, he will be turned into marble."

By the time the dove had finished speaking, the tempest had stopped, and the fury of the sea and the rage of the wind had passed. But a much greater storm began to stir in Jennariello's heart because of what he had heard. He was tempted many times to throw all the things that he was bringing to his brother into the sea so that they would not cause his destruction. On the other hand, he thought of himself because he, too, was affected by all this, and he feared that if he did not bring these things back to his brother or if he warned him he would be turned into marble. So he decided to take care of himself first and then his brother because the shirt is a closer fit than the vest.

When they reached the port of Frattombrosa, Jennariello found his brother on shore already because the king had seen the ship arrive and was waiting for it with happy anticipation. When he saw that his brother had brought the desire of his heart and when he compared the two faces in his mind and saw that there was not the slightest difference, he was so overjoyed that he was almost crushed to death by the enormous weight of the happiness he felt. After embracing his brother with great affection, he asked him, "What is that falcon that you are carrying on your wrist?"

"I bought it as a present for you," Jennariello replied.

And Milluccio said, "I can see that you love me very much since you're always trying to do things that please me. Certainly, even if you had brought me a treasure, it would not have pleased me more than this falcon!"

And just as Milluccio was about to take it in his hand, Jennariello rapidly took out a knife that he was carrying by his side and cut off its head. The king was astonished by his actions and thought his brother must be mad to have done this absurd thing. But because he did not want to spoil the happy mood of his return, he did not say a word.

Now, when Milluccio saw the horse and asked Jennariello whose animal it was and heard that it was his, he wanted to mount it right away. So he ordered someone to hold the stirrup for him, but Jennariello suddenly cut the horse's legs with a knife. This act, too, angered the king, for it appeared that his brother had done it out of spite, and Milluccio began to boil with rage, but he also thought that it was not the right moment to let himself get upset. Indeed, he did not want to displease his wife upon their first meeting. For his part he could not get enough of her and kept gazing at her and squeezing her hand.

Once they arrived at the royal palace, the king invited all the lords and ladies of the city to a grand celebration, and soon the hall seemed like a beautiful riding school full of horses prancing and turning in circles with a group of foals that appeared to be ladies. When the ball and the huge banquet were finished, they all went to bed.

Jennariello, who had no other thought in his head than to save his brother, hid behind the bed of the newlyweds, and he remained on guard and waited for the arrival of the dragon. Finally, at midnight a dreadful dragon entered the room. His eyes were spitting flames, and his mouth was puffing smoke, and he was so frightening that he would have made good publicity for a peddler selling a druggist's remedies against fear. Jennariello had a Damascene sword by his side, and he began using it to slash about at random, back and forth, and one of his blows was so violent that he cut one of the pillars of the king's bed in half. At the sound of the noise, the king was awakened, and the dragon vanished.

When Milluccio saw his brother with the blade in his hand and the pillar cut in half, he began to scream, "Guards! Come look! Someone, come look! Help! Help! My treacherous brother has come to kill me!"

There was a group of guards who slept in the antechamber, and when they heard these cries, they came running and seized Jennariello. After they tied him up, the king ordered them to take him to the prison right away. Then, as soon as the sun opened the bank to pay the creditors of the day with the deposits of the light, the king called together his council. He recounted all the events that had taken place that coincided with the evil actions demonstrated by Jennariello, who allegedly had killed the falcon and horse out of spite, and the council sentenced him to death. Even the pleas of Liviella were not able to soften the heart of the king, who said, "You can't love me very much, my wife, if you care more for your brother-in-law than for my life. You saw with your own eyes how this murderous dog came to slice me into pieces with a sword so sharp that it could have cut a hair in two. If it had not been for the pillar of the bed that protected me—Oh pillar of my life!—you would already be a widow now!"

After saying this, he gave orders for the sentence to be carried out. When Jennariello heard about these orders and saw that he was going to suffer such a bad thing for having done such good, he did not know what to do. If he did not talk, things would indeed go bad for him, and if he talked, things would be worse. It is bad to have a case of scabs, but ringworm is worse. Whatever he did, it would be like falling from a tree into the mouth of a wolf. If he remained silent, he would lose his neck under the ax. If he talked, he would finish his days as a slab of stone. Finally, after many exhausting reflections, he decided to recount the entire story to his brother, and since he had to die in any case, he thought the best solution would be to reveal the truth to his brother and end his days as an innocent man rather than keep the truth to himself and be banished from this world as a traitor.

So, Jennariello sent a message to the king that he wanted to talk to him about an important matter that concerned the state. Soon after, he was conducted into the king's presence, and he began with a long preamble about the love that had always shown his brother. Next he told him about the trick that he had played on Liviella in order to please the king. Then he explained to him what he had heard from the doves and why he had killed the falcon to prevent his brother's eyes from being scratched out and had kept silent so that he himself would not be changed into marble. But while he was saying these words, he felt his legs stiffen and turn into marble. When he continued to talk about the horse in the same way, he could clearly be seen to stiffen miserably and became marble up to his waist, a thing for which he would have paid for in cash at another time, but now his heart wept about it. Finally, when he talked about the incident with the dragon, he turned completely into stone and stood like a statue in the middle of the hall. When the king saw this, he realized his mistake and how hasty he had been to judge his brother who was so good and caring. As a result, he went into mourning for more than a year, and each time he thought about his brother, he burst into a flood of tears.

In the meantime, Liviella gave birth to two sons who were the most beautiful children in the world. After several months passed, the queen took a trip into the countryside to amuse herself, and the king found himself with the boys in the middle of the hall looking at that statue. Milluccio had tears in his eyes as he recalled the blunder he had made that had caused him to lose the flower of men. All of a sudden, a large old man entered the hall. He had hair down to his shoulders and a beard that covered his chest, and after bowing before the king, he said, "What would your highness pay if your handsome brother could return to the way he was?"

"I would give my entire kingdom!" the king replied.

"This is not a thing that can be paid for with wealth," the old man declared. "It concerns life, and life must be paid for with life."

The king, partly moved by the love he felt for Jennariello, and partly because of the guilt that he felt for all the damage he had caused, answered, "Believe me, good sir, I would exchange my life for his, and if he could come out of this stone, I would be glad to be cast into it."

Upon hearing these words, the old man said, "It is not necessary to change your life into cement. It is a long and weary process to bring up a man, and thus, it is good enough to take the blood of your sons and pour it over this statue, and that would bring your brother back to life."

In response the king said, "Indeed, children can be made again. Since we have the mold of these little ones, we can make some others. I would prefer to have my brother because I can never hope to have another like him!"

As soon as he said this, he sacrificed the two innocent lambs on a miserable idol of stone that he had brought before him. After he bathed the statue with their blood, it immediately became alive, and the two brothers embraced each other and were beside themselves with joy. Soon thereafter the king had the two unfortunate boys placed in a coffin to be buried in due honor, and just as this was happening, the queen returned. Quickly the king had his brother hide, and when his wife entered, he said to her, "What would you give, dear heart, to have my brother come back to life?"

"I would give the entire kingdom," she responded.

Then the king retorted, "Would you give the blood of your sons?"

"Certainly not," the queen declared, "because I would not be so cruel as to destroy the treasures of my heart with my own hands!"

"Alas!" the king continued. "I've cut the throats of our sons so that my brother could return to life! This was the price I had to pay for Jennariello's life!"

Upon saying this, he showed her their sons in a coffin, and when the queen saw this grim spectacle, she began to shriek like a madwoman: "Oh my children! Oh my props of my life! Oh joys of my heart! Oh fountains of my blood! Who has stained the windows of the sun with your blood?[7] Who, without a doctor's license, has slashed the major vein of my life? Alas, my children, my hope has been torn asunder, my light darkened, my sweetness made bitter, my crutch lost! You have been pierced by a knife, while I have been stabbed by grief. You are drowned in blood, and I in tears! Alas, to give life to an uncle, you have murdered a mother because I cannot weave the web of my days without my boys, the beautiful counterweights of the loom of this unfortunate life! The organ of my words will have the breath taken out of it now that the bellows have been taken from it. Oh, my children, my children, why don't you answer your mother, who had already given you the blood from her body some time ago and now gives you the blood from her eyes? Since fate has dried up the fountain of my joy, I no longer have any reason in the world to love. I shall now come to you and follow in your footsteps!"

Upon saying these words, Liviella ran to a window to throw herself out, but at that very moment her father entered through it on a cloud and cried out, "Stop, Liviella! Everything is now finished after this journey, for I have revenged myself on Jennariello for having stolen my daughter from my house and accomplished the three things I wanted to do. Indeed, I have made Jennariello stand in a statue of stone for many months like a shelled fish. I have punished you for not showing me respect and letting yourself be carried away on a ship, and hence I caused your sons, two jewels, to be slaughtered by their own father. Finally I punished the king

---

7. Reference to the offense of painting red marks on the outside of houses. This staining or marking was considered a grave insult and led to many acts of violence. Therefore, it became a criminal violation.

for being carried away by his whim—just like the whim of a pregnant woman—by making him the cruel judge of his brother and then the executioner of his sons. But since I only wanted to shear you all and not to flay you, I now want to transform all the poison into a sweet cake. Therefore, go and fetch your children, who are my children and are as beautiful as ever, and you, Milluccio, embrace me. I accept you as son and son-in-law, and I pardon Jennariello for his offence because he did all those things he did to serve a worthy brother."

When the magician finished speaking, the children arrived, and their grandfather could not embrace and kiss them enough. During this happy scene, Jennariello, the last character, also entered. After having survived a tempest, he was now swimming in the broth of macaroni. But despite the fact that he went on to experience all the pleasures one can have in life, he never forgot the dangers of the past and often reflected on the mistakes of his brother. In this regard, he realized how careful a man must be to avoid pitfalls because

all human judgment is false and twisted.

JACOB AND WILHELM GRIMM

Faithful Johannes†

Once upon a time there was an old king who was sick, and he thought, "This will surely be my deathbed." Then he said aloud, "Tell Faithful Johannes to come to me."

Faithful Johannes, his most cherished servant, had been given his name because of his lifelong loyalty to the king. When he reached the old man's bedside, the king said to him, "Most Faithful Johannes, I feel that my end is drawing near, but I am not worried about anything except my son. He is still young in years and doesn't always know what's best for himself. You must promise to teach him everything he should know and be his foster father, or I shall not be able to close my eyes in peace."

"I shall not forsake him," Faithful Johannes reassured him, "and I shall serve him faithfully even if it costs me my life."

"Now I can die in comfort and peace," the old king said, and then added, "After my death you're to show to him the entire castle—all the rooms, halls, and vaults, along with the treasures that are in them. But I do not want you to show him the room at the end of the long hallway, where the portrait of the Princess of the Golden Roof is hidden. If he sees that portrait, he'll fall passionately in love with her and lose consciousness for a while, and then he'll be obliged to undertake great risks because of her. You must protect him against this."

Once again Faithful Johannes assured the old king he would keep his promise. The king then became silent, laid his head on his pillow, and

† Jacob and Wilhelm Grimm, "Faithful Johannes"—"Der getreue Johannes" (1857), No. 6 in *Kinder- und Hausmärchen. Gesammelt durch die Brüder Grimm* (Göttingen: Dieterich, 1857).

died. After the old king was buried, Faithful Johannes told the young king what he had promised the old king on his deathbed and said, "I intend to keep my promise and remain just as faithful to you as I was to your father, even if it costs me my life."

When the mourning period ended, Faithful Johannes said to him, "It's now time for you to see what you've inherited. So I shall show you the castle of your forefathers."

He led the young king all around the castle, upstairs and down, and let him see all the treasures and splendid rooms. But there was one room he did not open, for it contained the dangerous portrait, which was placed in such a way that one would see it the moment the door was opened. Furthermore, it was such a wonderful painting that it appeared to be real and alive, and there was nothing more beautiful or more lovely in the whole world. Now, the young king quickly noticed and Faithful Johannes kept passing by one door, and therefore he said, "Why don't you ever open this door for me?"

"There's something in there that would horrify you," Faithful Johannes replied.

"I've seen the entire castle," the king said, "and I also want to know what's in there."

He went and tried to open the door by force, but Faithful Johannes restrained him and said, "I promised your father before his death that you would not see what is inside this room. It could cause great misfortune for you and me."

"No, that can't be!" the young king responded. "If I *don't* get in, it will certainly be the end of me because I won't be able to rest day or night until I've seen what is inside this room with my own eyes. You won't get me to move from this spot unless you unlock the door."

When Faithful Johannes saw there was nothing he could do, he picked out the key from the large bunch he was carrying. His heart was heavy, and he heaved many sighs as he opened the door. He made sure that he entered first because he intended to cover the portrait with his body so the king would not see it. But what good did that do? The king stood on his tiptoes and looked over his shoulder. When he glimpsed the maiden's magnificent portrait, which glistened with gold and jewels, he fell to the ground unconscious. Faithful Johannes lifted him up, carried him to his bed, and was very concerned.

"Disaster has struck," he thought. "Good Lord, what will come of it all?" Then he gave the king some wine to refresh him, whereupon he regained consciousness. The first words he spoke were, "Oh, who is that beautiful maiden in the picture?"

"That's the Princess of the Golden Roof," answered Faithful Johannes.

"My love for her is so great," continued the king, "that even if all the leaves on all the trees were tongues, they wouldn't be able to express how I feel. I intend to risk my life to win her, and since you're my most Faithful Johannes, you must help me."

It took the servant a long time to determine how they might proceed, for it was difficult to gain access to the princess. Finally, he thought of a way and said to the king, "Everything she has around her is made of gold—

the tables, chairs, dishes, cups, bowls, and all the household utensils. There are five tons of gold in your treasury. Have the goldsmiths of your kingdom make one ton of it into different kinds of vessels and utensils and into all sorts of birds, wild game, and marvelous animals that will please her. Then we'll take all this and travel there to try our luck."

The king had all the goldsmiths summoned to him, and they had to work day and night until the most magnificent things were ready. When the golden objects were all loaded on board a ship, Faithful Johannes put on the clothes of a merchant, as did the king so that he would not be recognized. Then they sailed across the sea, and they kept sailing until they came to the city where the Princess of the Golden Roof made her home.

Faithful Johannes told the king to stay on board the ship and to wait for him. "I may come back with the princess," he said. "So make sure that everything's in order. Have the golden vessels set out on display and have your men decorate the entire ship."

He then gathered together all kinds of golden trinkets in his apron, went ashore, and began walking toward the royal castle. When he reached the courtyard, a beautiful maiden was standing at the well. She had two golden buckets in her hands and was drawing water. Just as she turned around and got ready to carry the sparkling water away, she noticed the stranger and asked him who he was.

"I'm a merchant," he answered, while opening his apron so she could see what was in it.

"Goodness, what beautiful golden trinkets!" she exclaimed. Then she put the buckets down and examined the treasures, one after the other. "The princess must see these things," she remarked. "She takes so much pleasure in golden objects that I'm certain she'll buy all you have."

She took him by the hand and led him up to the palace, for she was the chambermaid. When the princess saw the wares, she was delighted and said, "They're so beautifully wrought that I'll buy everything you have."

But Faithful Johannes said, "I'm only a rich merchant's servant. What I have is nothing compared to what my master has on his ship. Indeed, he has the most artful and precious things that have ever been made in gold."

The princess wanted everything brought up to the castle, but he said, "There is such a huge number of objects that it would take many days to do this. Besides, your palace is not large enough, for you would need many more rooms to display all the articles."

Now her curiosity and desire were roused even more so that she finally said, "Take me to the ship. I'll go there myself to look over your master's treasures."

So, feeling very happy, Faithful Johannes conducted her to the ship. When the king caught sight of the princess and saw that she was even more beautiful than her portrait, he felt as though his heart would burst. After she climbed aboard the ship and the king led her inside the cabin, Faithful Johannes remained behind with the helmsman and ordered the ship to cast off: "Set all sails so that our ship will fly like a bird!"

Inside the cabin the king showed the princess the golden vessels, and each and every piece: the cups, the bowls, the birds, the wild game, and the marvelous animals. She looked at everything for many hours, and in her joy she did not notice that the ship had sailed. After she had examined the last piece, she thanked the merchant and wanted to go home. But when she stepped out on deck, she saw that the ship was on the high seas, far from land, and racing forward at full sail.

"Oh!" she cried out in horror. "You've deceived me! I'm being kidnapped, and I'm in the hands of a merchant no less! I'd rather die!"

But the king seized her hand and said, "I'm not a merchant. I'm a king, and I'm not inferior to you in birth. I tricked you and carried you off by stealth because I was overwhelmed by my love for you. The first time I saw your portrait, I fainted and fell to the ground."

When the Princess of the Golden Roof heard this, she felt more at ease, and her heart went out to him in such a way that she consented to be his wife.

While they were sailing on the high seas, however, Faithful Johannes saw three ravens flying through the air as he was sitting and playing music in the bow of the ship. When they approached, he stopped playing and listened, for he understood their language quite well. One of them cried out, "My, he's bringing the Princess of the Golden Roof home with him!"

"Yes," responded the second, "but he doesn't have her yet."

"You're wrong, he does," the third said. "She's sitting right beside him in the ship."

Then the first raven began to speak again. "What good will that do him? When they reach land, a horse as red as a fox will come trotting up to him, and the king will want to mount it. But, if he does, the horse will ride off with him and soar into the air so he'll never be able to see his maiden again."

"Is there no way he can be saved?" asked the second.

"Oh, yes, if someone else jumps on the horse quickly, takes out the gun that's bound to be in the saddle holster, and shoots the horse dead. This way the young king will be saved. But who knows that? And, even if someone knows it and tells it to the king, that person will be turned into stone from the tips of his toes to his knees."

"I know still more," the second raven said. "Even if the horse is killed, the young king will not keep his bride. When they go to the castle together, he will find a ready-made bridal outfit in a basin. It will look as if it were woven out of gold and silver, yet it's nothing but sulfur and pitch. If he puts it on, it will burn him down to the very bone and marrow."

"Is there no way that he can be saved?" asked the third raven.

"Oh, yes," said the second. "Someone must grab the shirt with gloves, throw it into the fire, and let it burn. Then the young king will be saved. But what good will that do? Whoever knows this and tells the king will be turned to stone from his knees to his heart."

"I know still more," said the third raven. "Even if the bridal outfit is burned, the king will not be able to keep his bride. After the wedding, there will be a ball, and when the young queen begins to dance, she will suddenly turn pale and fall down as if she were dead. If no one lifts her up, draws three drops of blood from her breast, and spits them out, she will die. But whoever reveals what he knows will have his entire body turned to stone from top to bottom."

After having talked about all this, the ravens flew away. Faithful Johannes had understood everything they had said, and from then on he became silent and sad. For if he did not tell his master what he had heard, the young king would be doomed, but if he did reveal everything to his master, he himself would have to pay with his life. Eventually he said to himself, "I must and shall save my master even if it means my own destruction."

When they went ashore, everything started to happen the way the ravens had predicted. A splendid horse, red as a fox, came galloping toward them.

"Well, now, what's this?" said the king. "This horse will carry me to my castle."

As the king was about to mount it, Faithful Johannes jumped in front of him and swung himself quickly into the saddle. Then he pulled the gun out of the saddle holster and shot the horse dead. The king's other servants disliked Faithful Johannes and cried out, "What a crime! Why did he have to kill that beautiful creature that was to carry the king to his castle?"

But the king declared, "Be quiet and let him go! He's Johannes, my most faithful servant, and who knows what good may come of this?"

Now they went into the castle, and there was a basin in the hall. The ready-made bridal outfit was lying in it and looked as though it were made of gold and silver. The young king went over and was about to pick it up when Faithful Johannes shoved him aside, grabbed it with gloves, tossed it into the fire, and let it burn. Once again the other servants began to murmur and say, "Just look! Now he's even burned the king's bridal outfit."

But the young king declared, "Who knows what good may come of this? Let him go. He's Johannes, my most faithful servant."

After the wedding was celebrated, the dance began, and the bride took part in it. Faithful Johannes paid close attention and kept looking at her face. All of a sudden she turned pale and fell to the ground as if she were dead. Then he rushed over to her, lifted her up, and carried her into a room, where he laid her on a bed, then knelt down and sucked three drops of blood from her right breast and spat them out. No sooner had he done this than she began breathing again and regained consciousness. The young king had seen all this, but he was puzzled by Faithful Johannes's actions and became angry.

"Throw him into prison!" he declared.

The next morning Faithful Johannes was condemned to death and led to the gallows. As he stood there about to be executed, he said, "Every condemned man is usually allowed to say one last word before he dies. May I also have this right?"

"Yes," answered the king. "I shall grant you this right."

Then Faithful Johannes said, "I've been unjustly sentenced to death, for I've always served you faithfully," and he told him how he had heard the ravens' conversation on the sea and how he had been compelled to do all those things to save his master.

The king then cried out, "Oh, my most Faithful Johannes, pardon! Pardon! Bring him down from there!"

But the moment after Faithful Johannes had uttered his last words, he had fallen down and had been turned into stone. The king and queen were greatly grieved by this, and the king said, "Oh, how poorly I've rewarded such great fidelity!"

He ordered the stone figure to be carried up to his bedroom and placed beside his bed. Whenever he looked at it, he would weep and say, "Oh, if only I could bring you back to life, my most Faithful Johannes!"

After some time had passed, the queen gave birth to twins, two little boys, who grew up and became the queen's delight. One day, when the queen was at church and the two children were sitting and playing near their father, the king looked at the stone figure and sighed, "Oh, if only I could bring you back to life, my most faithful Johannes!"

Then the stone began to speak and said, "Yes, you can bring me back to life if you're willing to sacrifice what you love most."

"I'd give everything I have in this world for you!" the king responded.

The stone continued, "If you cut off the heads of your two children with your own two hands and rub their blood on me, I shall be brought back to life."

The king was horrified when he heard that he himself would have to kill his precious children. He recalled, nevertheless, the great fidelity of Faithful Johannes and how he had died for him. So the king drew his sword and cut off his children's heads with his own hand. And, after he had rubbed the stone with their blood, it came to life, and Faithful Johannes stood before him once again, alive and well.

"Your loyalty will not go unrewarded," he said to the king, and he took the children's heads, put them back in place, and rubbed the wounds with their blood. Within seconds they were whole again and were running around and playing as if nothing had happened to them. The king was overjoyed, and when he saw the queen coming, he hid Faithful Johannes and the two children in a large closet. After she entered, he said to her, "Did you pray while you were in church?"

"Yes," she answered, "but I could only think of Faithful Johannes and how unfortunate he was because of us."

"Dear wife," he said, "we can bring him back to life, but it will cost our two little sons, whom we shall have to sacrifice."

The queen became pale, and her heart trembled greatly. However, she said, "We owe this to him because of his great fidelity."

The king rejoiced when he saw that she felt as he did. He went over to the closet, opened it, and brought out the children and Faithful Johannes.

"God be praised!" he said. "Faithful Johannes has been saved, and our sons have been restored to us as well."

Then he told her what had happened, and they all lived happily together until the end of their days.

The Taming of Shrews

The taming of a proud princess or aristocratic woman who thinks that she is too good to marry any man, especially one who is beneath her in social rank, became an important didactic motif in the medieval oral and literary tradition. In fact, the shaming of a princess by a gardener, fool, lower-class man, or prince disguised as a beggar or peasant became a motif in many oral and literary tales beginning in the medieval period. For the most part, the tales about so-called shrews represented a patriarchal viewpoint of how women, particularly courtly women, were to order their lives according to the dictates and demands of their fathers/husbands. In addition, the women fulfill the wish-dreams of men's imaginations, and the sadism of the tale is often concealed by the humorous manner in which a haughty woman must learn "humility." In the thirteenth-century erotic tale written in middle high German verse "Diu halbe bir" or "Die halbe Birne" ("Half a Pear"), there is a mighty king who decides to offer his daughter in marriage to the knight who shows his valor and wins a tournament. When a knight named Arnold wins the tournament, he is invited to a feast where pears are served, one for two people. He cuts a pear in half without peeling it. After he eats his half, he offers the princess the other half, and she is so insulted that she berates him before all the guests. Arnold is enraged and departs, swearing revenge. He returns later as a court fool and is allowed to enter the princess's salon to entertain her and her ladies. She becomes so sexually aroused by his antics that she yields to his amorous advances. Then Arnold leaves, discards his disguise, and returns to the court as knight. When the princess sees him again, she begins to mock him as the knight with half a pear. However, he responds with a retort that makes her aware of his amorous conquest of the night before. Consequently, he compels her to become his wife. A similar version can be found in the fourteenth-century Icelandic legend "Clárus" written by Jón Halldórsson. Shakespeare used the motif in *The Taming of the Shrew* (1605), and Luigi Allemanni's novella *Bianca, figliuola del conte di Tolosa* (*Bianca, Daughter of the Count of Toulouse*, 1531) had a direct influence on Basile. The popularity of the literary tales had a strong influence on the oral tradition, and the mutual development of different versions led to Hans Christian Andersen's "The Swineherd" (1842) and Ludwig Bechstein's "Vom Zornbraten" ("About the Angry Roast") in *Deutsches Märchenbuch* (1857). Ernst Philippson's *Der Märchentypus von König Drosselbart* is an excellent study of the folklore and literary background of this tale-type.

GIAMBATTISTA BASILE

Pride Punished†

There was once a king of Solcolungo whose daughter, Cinziella, was as beautiful as the moon, but every ounce of her beauty was offset by a pound of pride. The result was that she was always inconsiderate of other people, and her poor father, who desired to have her wed, could not find a husband to satisfy her, no matter how good or great the man was.

Among the many princes who came to ask for her hand in marriage was the king of Belpaese, who left nothing undone to win the affection of Cinziella. But the more he gave of himself to serve her, the less he received as a reward for his efforts. The more tokens of his love he deposited, the less she showed her desires for him. The more he bared his soul to her, the less she opened her heart to him. The poor man went to her practically every day and asked her, "When, oh cruel woman, after so many melons of hope have turned into pumpkins, shall I find one that is red? When, oh ferocious bitch, will the storms of your cruelty abate so that I can have a favorable wind to steer the ship of my plans to your port? When, after so many assaults of pleas and entreaties, shall I be able to plant the banner of my amorous desires on the wall of your beautiful fortress?"

But all these words were thrown to the wind. Cinziella had piercing eyes that could look through stones, but she did not have the ears to listen to the complaints that this wounded man uttered. Therefore, she treated him poorly, as if he was some miscreant who had cut down her vines. At last, the miserable gentleman realized that Cinziella's cruelty had reduced him to the level of a common scoundrel, and he decided to leave with his retinue. Before his departure, however, he said indignantly, "I've been burned enough by the flames of love!" And he solemnly swore to take revenge on this cold-blooded Saracen[1] in such a way that she would repent for ever having tortured him so much.

So when the king of Belpaese returned to his country, he grew a beard and dyed his hair. After a few months had passed, he went back to Solcolungo disguised as a peasant. Then he bribed some people at the palace and became one of the king's gardeners. Soon thereafter he was working one day in the garden as best he could, and he went to a spot beneath Cinziella's windows and spread out an imperial robe completely studded with gold and diamonds. When her attendants saw it, they immediately ran and told their mistress about it. In turn, she sent one of them to ask the gardener whether he wanted to sell the robe. He answered that he was neither a merchant nor a clothes dealer, but he would gladly give it to her as a gift provided she would let him sleep one night in the princess's hall. After hearing this request, Cinziella's ladies-in-waiting said to her,

---

† Giambattista Basile, "Pride Punished"—"La superbia punita" (1634), *Decimo passatempo nella quarta giornata* in *Lo cunto de li cunti overo Lo trattenemiento de peccerille*, De Gian Alessio Abbattutis, 5 vols. (Naples: Ottavio Beltrano, 1634–36).
1. Name used by Christians to designate non-Christians as heathens or pagans; generally applied to Arabs during the Crusade.

"What's there to lose in satisfying the gardener's request, signora? If you do it, you'll be able to obtain that robe which is fit for a queen!"

Cinziella let herself be caught on the hook that has caught better fish than herself. Upon agreeing, she received the robe and then granted his favor. The next morning the gardener put a gown of the same kind on the same spot, and when Cinziella saw it, she sent word that she wanted to buy it and would give him whatever he wanted. The gardener replied that he would not sell it, but he would gladly give it to her as a gift if she would let him sleep in her antechamber. And in order to complete her outfit, she let herself be induced to grant his request.

Finally, the third day came, and before the sun arrived to strike a light on the tinder of the fields, the gardener spread a beautiful vest that matched the gown on the same spot. Cinziella saw it just as she had seen the others, and she said, "I can only be happy if I obtain this vest!"

So she summoned the gardener to come to her and said, "My good man, it is imperative that you sell me that vest which I saw in the garden. I would give my heart for it."

The gardener responded, "I won't sell it, my lady, but if you would like, I'll give you the vest and also a diamond necklace, if you let me sleep one night in your room."

"Now you are really acting like a boor!" said Cinziella. "Wasn't it enough for you to have slept in the hall and then the antechamber? Now you want my room. Soon you'll even want to sleep in my bed!"

The gardener answered, "My lady, I'm just as attached to my vest as you are to your room. If you want to call me, you know how to reach me. I'd be content to sleep on the ground, something that one would not deny even to a Turk. If you were to see the necklace that I would give you, perhaps you would pay me a better price."

Partly prompted by her own interests and partly urged by her attendants, who were helping the dog climb the obstacle, Cinziella let herself be persuaded and consented to his request. So, when evening came—when night like a leather maker threw the tanning water over the skin of heaven so that it became dark—the gardener took the vest and necklace and went to the princess's apartment. After giving her these things, he was given a seat in a corner of the room, and Cinziella told him, "Now you stay put there, and don't move if you want to stay in my good graces." Then she drew a line with some charcoal and added, "If you pass this line, you'll leave your head behind!"

After she said these words, she had the curtains of her bed drawn for her and went to sleep. As soon as the king-gardener saw that she had fallen asleep and it seemed as if the right moment to work the fields of love had arrived, he got into bed beside her. Then, before the mistress of the place could wake up, he gathered the fruits of love. And when Cinziella was finally aroused and saw what had happened, she did not want to add to the wrong that had been done by committing another. Nor did she want to ruin her entire garden just for the sake of ruining the gardener. So she made a vice out of necessity and resigned herself to the mess and found pleasure in the fault. Now she who had rejected crowned heads showed no concern about being under the hairy feet of a boor because that was what the king appeared to be, and this is what Cinziella thought he was.

During the course of this activity, Cinziella became pregnant, and seeing her belly grow larger day by day, she told the gardener that she thought she would be ruined if her father got wind of this affair. Therefore, they had to think of some way to avoid this danger. The king responded that the only remedy he could think of for this problem would be to go away together. He told her that he could take her to the house of a lady for whom he used to work, and she would be able to provide accommodations for her until she gave birth.

Realizing what a bad state she was in due to the sin of her pride, which had left her smashed against the rocks, Cinziella let herself be persuaded by the king's words. She left her house and placed herself in the hands of fate. So, after a long journey, the king brought her to his own home and told his mother about all that had happened. He then asked her to keep up the pretense because he wanted Cinziella to pay for her pride. Thus, he had her installed down in one of the stables of the palace and made her lead a miserable existence with little to eat but bread.

One day, when the king's servants were preparing to bake bread, the king ordered them to call Cinziella to help them. At the same time he told her to try to steal some buns so they could still their hunger. Thus, while the poor Cinziella was removing some bread from the oven, she secretly moved her hand to steal a bun and put it into her pocket. But at that very moment, the king arrived, dressed in his own clothes, and he said to the servants, "Who said you could let that dirty little girl into this house? Don't you see from her face that she's a thief? Put your hands in her pockets, and you'll find the proof of the crime!"

After they searched her pockets and found the proof, they gave her quite a scolding and barked and yelled at her the entire day. In the meantime, the king put on his gardener disguise again and found her sad and sorry in the stable because of the insults that she had received. But he told her not to bother about it because necessity is the tyrant of men, and as the Tuscan poet Petrarch put it,

> the starving beggar
> is often brought to do things that in a better state
> he would condemn in others.[2]

He told her that, since hunger drives the wolf from the forest, she was certainly excused for doing what would not be proper for others. Therefore, he instructed her to go back up to the palace because the lady of the place was cutting some cloth, and Cinziella should offer to help to see if she could get hold of some pieces because she was close to giving birth and would need a thousand things.

Cinziella did not know how to say no to her husband, for such is how she regarded him, and therefore, went up to the palace and took a place among the maids to cut cloth, napkins, shirts, and caps. While doing this she stole a scrap of the cloth and put it under her dress. But the king

---

2. Reference to *Rime*, Canzone XVI: "Che 'l poverel digiuno: da Ben mi credea passar tempo omai," by Francesco Petrarch (1304–1374).

arrived and once again yelled at her as he had done with the bun. He ordered her to be searched, and they found the stolen scraps on her. So she had to swallow another heap of insults. It was as though she had stolen a bundle of clean linen, the way they screamed at her, and then she returned to the stable.

Once again the king reappeared in his disguise, and when he saw her so desperate, he told her not to let herself be overcome by melancholy because everything in the world is a matter of opinion, and she should try a third time to find some little things for herself since she would soon be giving birth. He told her that this time would be a good occasion to acquire something, and he went on to say, "Your mistress is going to wed her son to a lady from a foreign country, and she wants to send her a ready-made dress of brocade and gold cloth. They say that the bride is just your size, and they have to cut the dress to fit your measurements. So it will be easy for you to slip some of the scraps into a bag. Then we can sell them and live off the earnings."

Cinziella did what her husband ordered her to do, and she stuck some of the rich brocade into her bosom just when the king arrived and made a big scene. He had Cinziella searched, and after they found the stuff, they kicked her out with great shame. But once again the king quickly disguised himself as the gardener, and he ran down to the stable to console her. With one hand he tormented her, and with the other, he caressed her out of love so she would not be driven to despair.

Now, the poor Cinziella had suffered so much agony, she thought she was receiving the punishment of heaven for her arrogance and pride. Indeed, she had stepped all over so many princes and kings, she was now being treated like a tramp. Since she had been deaf to her father's words of advice, she was now obliged to blush with shame at the jeers of the servants. Then the anger that emanated from that shame began to produce the first labor pains.

When the queen was advised that Cinziella was about to go into labor, she had her brought up to the palace and showed compassion for Cinziella's condition. She had her put into a bed embroidered with gold and pearls and in a room with gold tapestry. Cinziella was stunned when she saw herself transported from a stable to a royal chamber, from a dung heap to a luxurious bed, and she did not know what was happening to her, and why she was suddenly given broth and cakes to make her stronger for the time when she was to give birth.

Thanks to the benevolence of heaven, Cinziella soon gave birth to two lovely boys without much pain, and the babies were the most splendid you could ever see. No sooner had she delivered the boys, however, than the king entered and said, "What's going on in your heads? Do you want to put a horse's saddle on an ass? Why are you giving a bed to such a dirty slut? Here, give her a few smacks with this stick and get her out of the bed quickly! Then fumigate the room with rosemary to take away the stench!"

When the queen heard this outcry, she said, "No more, my son, no more! You've tormented this poor girl long enough. You should be satisfied now that you've made a wreck out of her with so much punishment. If, by now, you don't feel repaid for all the scorn that she showed you at her father's court, then these two jewels which she has given you should at the very least pay her debt."

While saying this, she had the babies brought into the room. They were the dearest things in the world, and when the king saw how lovely the boys were, his heart was touched by tenderness, and he embraced Cinziella. Then he revealed to her who he was and what he had done out of indignation because she had treated him so poorly. But from now on he intended to raise her on a pedestal. The queen, too, embraced her as her daughter-in-law and daughter, and they both gave her such great compensation for her two boys that this one sweet moment of joy seemed to make up for all the past anguish she had suffered. But she always remembered to keep her sails low and always recalled

pride comes before the fall.

JACOB AND WILHELM GRIMM

King Thrushbeard†

A king had daughter whose beauty was beyond comparison, but she was so proud and haughty that no suitor was good enough for her. Indeed, she rejected one after the other and ridiculed them as well. Once her father held a great feast and invited all the marriageable young men from far and wide to attend. They were all lined up according to their rank and class: first came the kings, then the dukes, princes, counts, and barons, and finally the gentry. The king's daughter was led down the line, and she found fault with each one of the suitors there. One was too fat for her. "That wine barrel!" she said. Another was too tall. "Tall and thin, he looks like a pin!" The third was too short. "Short and fat, he's built like a vat!" The fourth was too pale. "He resembles death!" The fifth was too red. "What a rooster!" The sixth did not stand straight enough. "Green wood, not good enough to burn!"

There was not a single man whom she did not criticize, but she made the most fun of a good king who stood at the head of the line and had a chin that was a bit crooked.

"My goodness!" she exclaimed and laughed. "He's got a chin like a thrush's beak!" From then on, everyone called him Thrushbeard.

When her father saw that she did nothing but ridicule people, and that she scorned all the suitors who were gathered there, he was furious and swore that she would have to marry the very first beggar who came to his door. A few days later a minstrel came and began singing beneath the windows to earn some money. When the king heard him, he said, "Have him come up here."

The minstrel, who was dressed in dirty, tattered clothes, entered the hall

† Jacob and Wilhelm Grimm, "King Thrushbeard"—"König Drosselbart" (1857), No. 52 in *Kinderund Hausmärchen. Gesammelt durch die Brüder Grimm* (Göttingen: Dieterich, 1857).

and sang in front of the king and his daughter. When he was finished, he asked for a modest reward.

"Your singing has pleased me so much," the king said, "that I shall give you my daughter for your wife."

The king's daughter was horrified, but the king said, "I swore I'd give you to the very first beggar who came along, and I intend to keep my word."

All her objections were to no avail. The minister was fetched, and she was compelled to wed the minstrel. When that was done, the king said, "It's not fitting for you to stay in my palace any longer since you're now a beggar woman. I want you to depart with your husband."

The beggar took her by the hand, and she had to go with him on foot. When they came to a huge forest, she asked:

> "Tell me, who might the owner of this forest be?"
> "King Thrushbeard owns the forest and all you can see.
> If you had taken him, it would belong to you."
> "Alas, poor me! What can I do?
> I should have wed King Thrushbeard. If only I knew!"

Soon they crossed a meadow, and she asked again:

> "Tell me, who might the owner of this forest be?"
> "King Thrushbeard owns the forest and all you can see.
> If you had taken him, it would belong to you."
> "Alas, poor me! What can I do?
> I should have wed King Thrushbeard. If only I knew!"

Then they came to a large city, and she asked once more:

> "Tell me, who might the owner of this forest be?"
> "King Thrushbeard owns the forest and all you can see.
> If you had taken him, it would belong to you."
> "Alas, poor me! What can I do?
> I should have wed King Thrushbeard. If only I knew!"

"I'm not at all pleased by this," said the minstrel. "Why are you always wishing for another husband? Do you think I'm not good enough for you?"

Finally, they came to a tiny cottage, and she said:

> "Oh, Lord! What a wretched tiny house!
> It's not even fit for a mouse."

The minstrel answered, "This house is mine and yours, and we shall live here together."

She had to stoop to get through the low doorway.

"Where are the servants?" the king's daughter asked.

"What servants?" asked the beggar. "You must do everything yourself if you want something done. Now, make a fire at once and put the water on so you can cook me my meal. I'm very tired."

However, the king's daughter knew nothing about making a fire or cooking, and the beggar had to lend a hand himself if he wanted anything done in a tolerable fashion. After they had eaten their meager meal, they

King Thrushbeard. Arthur Rackham, 1911.

went to bed. But the next morning he got her up very early because she had to take care of the house. For a few days they lived like this and managed as best they could. When they had consumed all their provisions, the man said, "Wife, we can't go on this way any longer. We've used everything up, and we're not earning a thing. You've got to weave baskets."

He went out to cut some willows and brought them home, but the rough willows brushed her tender hands.

"I see that won't work," said the man. "Let's try spinning. Perhaps you'll be better at that."

She sat down at the spinning wheel and tried to spin, but the hard thread soon cut her soft fingers, and blood began to flow.

"See now," said the man. "You're not fit for any kind of work. I made a bad bargain when I got you. But let's see how things go if I start a business with pots and earthenware. You're to sit in the marketplace and sell the wares."

"Oh," she thought, "if some people from my father's kingdom come to the marketplace and see me selling wares, they'll surely make fun of me!"

But there was no way to avoid it. She had to obey her husband if she did not want to die of hunger. The first time everything went well. People gladly bought her wares because she was beautiful, and they paid what she asked. Indeed, many gave her money and did not even bother to take the pots with them. So the couple lived off their earnings as long as they lasted. Then her husband bought a lot of new earthenware. His wife sat down with it at a corner in the marketplace, set her wares around her, and offered them for sale. Suddenly, a drunken hussar[1] came galloping along and rode right over the pots so that they were all smashed to pieces. She began to weep and was paralyzed with fear.

"Oh, what's going to happen to me?" she exclaimed. "What will my husband say?"

She ran home and told him about the accident, and he responded by saying, "In heaven's name, who would ever sit down at a corner in the marketplace with earthenware? Now stop your weeping. I see full well that you're not fit for proper work. I've already been to the king's castle and have asked whether they could use a kitchen maid, and they've promised me to take you on. In return you'll get free meals."

Now the king's daughter became a kitchen maid and had to assist the cook and do the most menial kind of work. She sewed two little jars inside her pockets and carried home the leftovers so they could have some food to live on. One day it happened the king's oldest son was celebrating his wedding, and the poor woman went upstairs, stood outside the door of the large hall, and wanted to look inside. When the candles were lit, each guest entered, one more exquisitely dressed than the next, and everything was full of splendor. With a sad heart she thought about her fate and cursed her pride and arrogance for bringing about her humiliation and great poverty. Sometimes the servants threw her pieces of the delicious dishes they were carrying in and out of the hall, and she could also smell

---

1. One of a body of light cavalry regiments organized first in Hungary in the fifteenth century.

the aroma of the food. She put the pieces into her pockets and intended to carry them home.

Suddenly the king's son entered. He was dressed in velvet and silk and had a golden chain around his neck. And, when he saw the beautiful woman standing in the doorway, he grabbed her by the hand and wanted to dance with her, but she refused. Indeed, she was horrified because she saw it was King Thrushbeard, who had courted her and whom she had rejected with scorn. Although she struggled, it was to no avail, for he pulled her into the hall. Then the string that held her pockets together broke, and the jars fell out, causing the soup to spill and the scraps of food to scatter on the floor. When the people saw that, they laughed a good deal and poked fun at her. She was so ashamed that she wished she were a thousand fathoms under the earth. She ran out the door and tried to escape, but a man caught up with her on the stairs and brought her back. When she looked at him, she saw it was King Thrushbeard again, and he said to her in a friendly way, "Don't be afraid. I and the minstrel who lived with you in the wretched cottage are one and the same person. I disguised myself out of love for you, and I was also the hussar who rode over your pots and smashed them to pieces. I did all that to humble your proud spirit and to punish you for the insolent way you behaved toward me."

Then she shed bitter tears and said, "I've done a great wrong and don't deserve to be your wife."

However, he said, "Console yourself. The bad days are over. Now we shall celebrate our wedding."

The chambermaids came and dressed her in splendid clothes, and her father came along with his entire court, and they wished her happiness in her marriage with King Thrushbeard. Then the real rejoicing began, and I wish that you and I had been there, too.

Lucky Bumpkins

Ever since antiquity, the goose has been regarded as a symbol of fertility and domestic bliss. The goose is generally passive, an object that is sought, but in the farcical tale, it assumes a more active role, and there are many erotic and obscene folktales in which the goose is a phallic symbol associated with magic power. Numerous fairy tales from the oral and the literary tradition depict how the youngest son, the youngest daughter, or the good-natured naive protagonist is given a goose as a reward for a kind act. The gift of a miraculous goose is a strange one, but fits the humorous tone of all the tales in this cycle. The key plot motifs involve the reward of simpletons/bumpkins for their goodness, the magic goose that binds people to it, and the rise in social class of the simpletons. There is no indication that the Grimms knew the Basile tale. Their version was based on various oral tales that they collected in 1810 and 1819. Later, Ludwig Bechstein published a similar tale, "Schwan, kleb an" ("Swan, Stick to It") in *Deutsches Märchenbuch* (1857).

GIAMBATTISTA BASILE

The Goose†

Once upon a time there were two sisters reduced to such squalor and poverty that they only managed to subsist by spitting on their fingers to work the spindle from morning until night and by selling what they could from their spinning. But, in spite of this wretched existence, they did not let the billiard ball of necessity knock down the billiard ball of their honor. Consequently, heaven, which is just as generous in rewarding the good as it is niggardly in punishing the bad, induced these two poor girls to go to the market to sell some skeins of thread and then to buy a goose with the little money they received. So they did this and brought the goose home. Indeed, they took such a liking to it right away that they treated it as if it were their own sister and had it sleep in their bed with them.

The next morning, which was a fine day, the good goose began to relieve itself by dropping golden ducats in piles, and it made pile after pile until the girls managed to fill a large chest with the money. This excrement was so abundant that they soon began to raise their heads high and assumed beaming appearances. Soon thereafter some of their neighbors came together one day and started chatting about this change, and they said, "Have you seen, neighbor Vasla, how Lilla and Lolla, who just the

† Giambattista Basile, "The Goose"—"La papera" (1634), *Primo passatempo della quinta giornata* in *Lo cunto de li cunti overo Lo trattenemiento de peccerille*, De Gian Alessio Abbattutis, 5 vols. (Naples: Ottavio Beltrano, 1634–36).

678

other day did not even have a place to die in, have become so neat and polished that they dress and act like fine ladies? Have you seen all those chickens and slabs of meat that are always hanging in their window and that glitter in front of our noses? What can this mean? Either they've opened up the cask of their honor, or they've found a treasure!"

"I'm struck dumb as a mummy by this," answered Perna. "They were almost dying of hunger, and now I see them so rejuvenated and sturdy that it seems as if I'm dreaming."

After talking about this and other things, their envy got the best of them, and they decided to dig a tunnel which led from their house to the room of these two girls so that they could keep an eye on them and satisfy their curiosity. Well, they kept spying so much that one evening, when the sun beats the ships in the Indian Ocean with the stick of its rays to allow the hours of the days to relax, they saw Lilla and Lolla place a sheet on the ground. Then the sisters had the goose hop on to it, and suddenly the good bird began to squirt out heaps of money so that the eyes of the neighbors popped out of their heads, and their tongues hung out of their mouths.

The next morning, when Apollo with his stick of gold implores the shadows to go away, Pasca went to visit the girls, and after running around in circles a thousand times and going back and forth, she came to the point and asked them to lend the goose because she had recently bought some goslings and believed that the goose would help them adjust to her house. She kept speaking and pleading so urgently that the two simple-minded sisters, either because they were so naive that they did not know how to say no or because they did not want to arouse the suspicion of their neighbors, lent her the goose on the condition that she bring it back right away.

When Pasca joined her friends, they quickly spread a sheet on the ground and had the goose hop onto it. But instead of revealing a mint that coined tons of money, the goose opened the pipes of a latrine and decorated the white sheet with yellow lumps in such a filthy way that the stench could be detected throughout the neighborhood just like the odor of kettles of boiling soup on Sunday.

After watching this sight, the neighbors thought that, if they treated the goose well, it might still produce the substance of the philosopher's stone that they so greatly desired, and thus they stuffed many things down its throat. Then they put the goose on another clean sheet, but if the bird had demonstrated how lubricated it was before, she now revealed that she had dysentery because of what she had been forced to digest. As a result, the neighbors burst into a rage and wrung the goose's neck. Then they threw it out the window into an alley where the garbage was usually thrown.

But fortune makes beans grow when you least expect it, and thus by chance a king's son, who had gone out hunting, happened to pass by and was overcome by an upset stomach. So he dismounted and gave his sword and horse to a servant and entered the alley to relieve himself. After having done this, he could not find any paper in his pocket and noticed the freshly killed goose. So he decided to use a part of the bird instead, but the goose was not dead and suddenly stuck its beak into the prince's buttocks so that he began to yell for his servants to come and help him. When they arrived and tried to detach the goose from his flesh, they found it was impossible because the goose was attached like a feathered Salmacis to a Hermaphroditus[1] of skin. Since the prince could not bear the pain and saw that all the efforts of his servants were being swept away by the wind, he had himself carried back to the royal palace, where all the doctors were called for a consultation in front of the two subjects. The doctors did their best to remedy this accident, rubbing ointments, applying pincers, and spreading powder. But the goose was like a closed mint that would not let any more cash flow, or a leech that would not loosen its grip even when acid was used on it. As a result, the prince issued a proclamation stating that whoever succeeded in prying him loose from the irritating creature would receive half his kingdom if a man, or he would marry her, if a woman.

Well, you should have seen all the people who came to poke their noses into the matter! But the more remedies they tried, the more the goose kept its beak stuck in the poor prince's buttocks. It seemed as if all the prescriptions of Galen, the aphorisms of Hippocrates, and the remedies of Mesua[2] had allied themselves against the posteriora of Aristotle[3] to torment the unfortunate prince. But, as fate would have it, Lolla, the younger of the sisters, happened to be among those people who had come to try their luck. As soon as she saw the goose, she cried out, "My little beaky! My little beaky!"

As soon as the goose heard this voice that she loved, it loosened its grip and flew into Lolla's lap and began to kiss and embrace her, not worrying about having exchanged the buttocks of a prince for the lips of a peasant girl.

When the prince saw this wondrous sight, he wanted to know how everything had happened the way it had. So, after he was told the entire story and what kind of trick the neighbors had played, he had them flogged in public and banished from the country. Then he took Lolla for his wife with her dowry of the goose which continued to supply them with treasures. In addition, he found a very rich husband for Lilla. Thus they remained the happiest people in the world, and all this happened despite the neighbors, who had wanted to block the sisters from taking the road of wealth that heaven had sent them, and who had inadvertently opened another road which led Lolla to become queen. As we can see,

an obstacle in life is often a big help.

1. Salmacis fell in love with Hermaphroditus, and when he would not return her love, she prayed to the gods to be allowed to remain united to him forever.
2. A famous Arab doctor who died in the middle of the ninth century and was the physician of the Caliph Harun-al-Rashid. His works were translated into Latin and Italian and published continually in the fifteenth century.
3. Reference to Aristotle's *Analytica posteriora* (*Posterior Analytics*), in which he discusses the proper structure of scientific knowledge. Aristotle lived from 384 to 322 B.C.E. His writings are based on notes taken from his lectures by students. Basile is playing with the title of Aristotle's work and associating it with a rear end.

JACOB AND WILHELM GRIMM

The Golden Goose†

There was once a man who had three sons, and the youngest, who was called Simpleton, was constantly mocked, disdained, and slighted. Now, one day it happened that the oldest brother decided to go into the forest to chop wood, and before he went, his mother gave him a nice, fine pancake and a bottle of wine so that he would not have to suffer from hunger or thirst. When he reached the forest, he met a gray old dwarf, who wished him good day and said, "Give me a piece of the pancake from your pocket, and let me have a drink of wine. I'm very hungry and thirsty."

However, the clever son answered, "If I give you my pancake and my wine, then I won't have anything for myself. So get out of my way," and he left the dwarf standing there and went farther into the forest. When he began chopping down a tree, it did not take long for him to slip and cut himself in the arm. So he had to return home and have his arm bandaged. All this happened because of the gray dwarf.

Shortly thereafter the second son went into the forest, and the mother gave him a pancake and a bottle of wine just as she had given the oldest. The second son, too, met the gray old dwarf, who asked him for a piece of the pancake and a drink of wine. But the second son also spoke quite sensibly. "Whatever I give you, I'll be taking from myself. So get out of my way." Then he left the dwarf standing there and went farther into the forest. Soon his punishment came as well. After he had whacked a tree a few times, he struck himself in the leg. Consequently, he had to be carried home.

Then Simpleton said, "Father, let me go now and chop some wood."

"Your brothers hurt themselves doing that," said the father. "So I want you to steer clear of the woods, especially since you know nothing about chopping down trees."

However, Simpleton kept insisting until his father finally said, "Go ahead. Perhaps you'll learn something from experience."

The mother gave him a pancake made out of water and ashes along with a bottle of sour beer. When he went into the forest, he, too, met the gray old dwarf, who greeted him and said, "Give me a piece of your pancake and a drink out of your bottle. I'm very hungry and thirsty."

"I have only a pancake made of ashes and some sour beer," answered Simpleton. "If that's all right with you, let's sit down and eat."

So they sat down, and when Simpleton took out his cake made of ashes, it turned out to be a fine pancake, and the sour beer was good wine. After they had eaten and drunk, the dwarf said, "Since you have such a good heart and gladly share what you have, I'm going to bestow some good luck on you. There's an old tree over there. Just go and chop it down, and

---

† Jacob and Wilhelm Grimm, "The Golden Goose"—"Die goldene Gans" (1857), No. 64 in *Kinder- und Hausmärchen. Gesammelt durch die Brüder Grimm* (Göttingen: Dieterich, 1857).

you'll find something among the roots." Then the dwarf took leave of him.

Simpleton went over and chopped down the tree. When it fell, he saw a goose with feathers of pure gold lying among the roots. He lifted the goose up and carried it with him to an inn, where he intended to spend the night. Now the innkeeper had three daughters, and when they saw the goose, they were curious to know what kind of strange bird it was. Moreover, they each wanted to have one of its golden feathers. The oldest thought, "I'll surely find an opportunity to pluck one of its feathers."

At one point Simpleton went out, and the oldest daughter seized the goose by its wing, but her hand and fingers remained stuck to it. Soon afterward the second sister came and also intended to pluck a golden feather. However, no sooner did she touch her sister than she became stuck to her. Finally, the third sister came with the same intention, but the other two screamed, "Keep away! For heaven's sake, keep away!"

But she did not grasp why she should keep away and thought, "If they're there, I see no reason why I can't be." So she ran over, and when she touched her sister, she became stuck to her, and all three had to spend the night with the goose.

The next morning Simpleton took the goose in his arm, set out, and did not bother himself about the three sisters who were stuck to the goose. They were compelled to run after him constantly, left and right, wherever his legs took him. In the middle of a field they came across the parson, and when he saw the procession, he said, "Shame on you, you naughty girls! Is that the right way to behave?"

Upon saying that, he grabbed the youngest sister by the hand and attempted to pull her away, but when he touched her, he also got stuck and had to run along behind them. Shortly afterward the sexton came by and saw the parson trailing the three girls on their heels. In his amazement, he called out, "Hey, parson, where are you off to in such a hurry? Don't forget that we have a christening today!"

The sexton ran up to the parson, and as soon as he touched his sleeve, he became stuck like the others. Now the five of them had to trot after Simpleton, one stuck to the other, and they approached two farmers who were coming from the fields with their hoes. The parson called out to them to help them and to set them free. However, as soon as they touched the sexton, they got stuck, and now there were seven of them trailing Simpleton and his goose.

After some time Simpleton came to a city ruled by a king who had a daughter who was so serious, she never laughed. Consequently, the king issued a decree that whoever could make her laugh would have her for his wife. When Simpleton heard that, he went before the king's daughter with his goose and its followers, and when she saw the seven people all attached to one another and running along, she burst out laughing, and it appeared as if she would never stop. So Simpleton demanded the princess as his bride, but the king had no desire to have him for a son-in-law and raised all kinds of objections. Eventually, he said that Simpleton would first have to produce a man capable of drinking the contents of a cellar full of wine before he could wed his daughter.

Now, Simpleton quickly remembered the gray dwarf, for he thought that he might be able to help him. Therefore, he went out into the forest, right to the spot where he had chopped down the tree. There he saw a man with a sad face sitting and moping. Simpleton asked what was bothering him so much, and he answered, "I'm terribly thirsty and don't seem to be able to quench my thirst. I can't stand cold water, and just now I emptied a barrel of wine, but that was like a drop on a hot stone."

"Well, I can help you," said Simpleton. "Just come with me, and you'll be able to drink your fill."

He led him to the king's cellar, and the man rushed over to the large barrels and set to work: he drank so much that his sides began to hurt, but before the day was over, he had emptied the entire cellar. So once again Simpleton demanded his bride, but the king was perturbed that such a common fellow, whom everyone called Simpleton, was to have his daughter. Therefore, he set a new condition: now Simpleton had to produce a man who could eat a mountain of bread.

Simpleton immediately reacted by going directly into the forest. There, on the same spot as before, he saw a man sitting who was pulling in a belt around his waist. The man made an awful face and said, "I've eaten an oven full of coarse bread, but what good is that when I'm as hungry as a lion. My stomach's still empty, and I have to pull in my belt if I don't want to die of hunger."

Simpleton was glad to hear that and said, "Get up and come with me. You will eat your fill."

He led him to the king's courtyard, where the king had gathered all the flour of the entire kingdom and had ordered it to be baked into a tremendous mountain. However, the man from the forest stepped up to it, began eating, and consumed the whole mountain in one day. Now for the third time, Simpleton claimed his bride, but the king found another way out and demanded a ship that could sail on land and water.

"As soon as you come sailing back in it," he said, "you shall have my daughter for your wife."

Simpleton went straight into the forest and encountered the gray old dwarf to whom he had given his cake.

"I've drunk and eaten for you," said the dwarf. "Now I'll also give you the ship. I'm doing all this because you treated me so kindly."

Then he gave him the ship, and when the king saw it, he could no longer prevent him from marrying his daughter. The wedding was celebrated, and after the king's death, Simpleton inherited the kingdom and lived happily ever after with his wife.

The Fruitful Sleep

Since there is little indication that there was an oral tradition of "sleeping beauties" in the medieval period, the first formation of this tale was probably in the fourteenth-century French prose romance *Perceforest*, which contains an episode entitled "L'histoire de Troylus et de la belle Zellandine." The romance was composed by an anonymous author, and it is in the grail tradition. In chapter 46 of book 3, there is an episode that deals with the birth of Princess Zellandine. She is given various gifts by three goddesses but is sentenced to eternal sleep when one of them is offended. Zellandine is destined to prick her finger while spinning and then to fall into a deep sleep. As long as a chip of flax remains in her finger, she will continue to sleep. Troylus meets her before she pricks her finger and falls in love with her. The love is mutual, but Troylus must perform some adventures before seeing her again. In the meantime, Zellandine pricks her finger, and to protect her, her father, King Zelland, places her completely nude in a tower that is inaccessible except for one window. When Troylus returns to King Zelland's court, he discovers what has happened to Zellandine, and with the help of a kind spirit, Zephir, who carries him up through the window, he manages to gain entrance to Zellandine's room. There, urged on by Venus, he gives way to his desire and has sexual intercourse with Zellandine. Then he exchanges rings with Zellandine and departs. Nine months later she gives birth to a child, and when the child mistakes her finger for her nipple, he sucks the flax chip out of it, and she awakes. After grieving about her lost virginity, Zellandine is comforted by her aunt. Soon after a birdlike creature comes and steals her child. Again Zellandine grieves, but since it is spring, she recovers quickly and thinks about Troylus. When she looks at the ring on her finger, she realizes that it was he who had slept with her. Some time later Troylus returns from his adventures to take her away with him to his kingdom. The episode between Zellandine and Troylus served as the basis for two Catalan versions, *Blandin de Cornoualha* and *Frayre de Joy e Sor de Plaser* during the fourteenth century. It is more than likely that Basile was familiar with *Perceforest*, and there is clear evidence that Perrault was acquainted with Basile's *Pentamerone*. Once Perrault's version circulated through the chapbooks of the Bibliothèque Bleue, it began enjoying widespread oral circulation. The Grimms were aware of both oral and literary versions, and they refined the tale by omitting the rape and the incident with the evil mother-in-law. They also gave the sleeping beauty a name which they adopted from "L'histoire d'épine" (1731), a tale written by the Count Antoine Hamilton, but Hamilton's story had nothing to do with the classic plot of the sleeping beauty. On the other hand, Mme d'Aulnoy's "La biche au bois" ("The Doe in the Wood," 1798) shows some similarities, especially the opening incident, when a fairy is offended. The "offended fairy" plays a role in numerous fairy tales, but she is particularly crucial for all the versions of "Sleeping Beauty," which became one of the most popular tales of the nineteenth century and was adapted for the stage and made into an opera by Engelbert Humperdinck in 1864 and Carl Reinecke in 1876. The most famous nineteenth-century musical adaptation was Peter Ilyich Tchaikovsky's ballet *The Sleeping Beauty* (1890).

GIAMBATTISTA BASILE

Sun, Moon, and Talia†

Once upon a time there was a great lord, and after the birth of his daughter, whom he named Talia, he called together all the wise men and prophets of his kingdom to foretell her destiny. After they consulted with one another, these men concluded that her life would be endangered by a tiny piece of flax. As a result, the king prohibited flax, hemp, or anything similar from being brought into his house in order to prevent anything disastrous from happening.

One day, however, when Talia was grown up and leaning out a window, she saw an old woman pass by and was surprised to see her spinning. Up to that moment Talia had never seen a distaff or a spindle, and the woman's spinning delighted her immensely. She became so curious that she had the old woman come up to her room, and when Talia took the distaff in her hand, she began pulling the thread herself. Unfortunately, a tiny piece of flax got stuck in her fingernail, and she fell down dead on the ground.

When the old woman saw what had happened, she ran down the stairs and out of the house. After the father heard about this unfortunate incident, he paid for the bucketful of sour wine with a barrel of tears. Then he had Talia deposited on a velvet chair under a brocaded canopy in a palace that was situated in the middle of the country. Finally, he locked the door to the palace and left it forever since it was a place of such agony that he wanted to obliterate any sign of it from his memory.

Some time later a king was out hunting in this region, and his falcon escaped and flew into a window of the palace, and since the bird did not return when it was called, the king ordered one of his attendants to knock at the door, thinking that someone was living there. But after he had knocked for a long time, the king sent a servant to find a ladder that was used in the vineyards so that he could climb up himself and see whether there was someone inside. And after he climbed up and entered the palace and walked all over, he was perplexed that he had encountered not a single living soul in the place. Finally, he reached the room in which Talia was sitting, as if under a magic spell, and as soon as the king saw her, he thought she was asleep. So he called to her, but she did not awake, no matter how much he touched her or cried out to her. Her beauty, however, set him afire, and he carried her in his arms to a bed, where he gathered

---

† Giambattista Basile, "Sun, Moon, and Talia"—"Sole, Luna e Talia" (1634), *Quinto passatempo della quinta giornata* in *Lo cunto de li cunti overo Lo trattenemiento de peccerille*, De Gian Alessio Abbattutis, 5 vols. (Naples: Ottavio Beltrano, 1634–36).

the fruits of love and then left her asleep in the bed. Afterward he returned to his kingdom, where, for a long time, he forgot about all that had happened.

In the meantime, nine months later to be exact, Talia gave birth to twins, one a boy, the other a girl, two dazzling gems. They were looked after by two fairies, who appeared in the palace and put the babies to their mother's breast. One time, when one of the babies wanted to suck her breast and could not find it, she began to suck a finger and sucked so hard that she made the tiny piece of flax come out of the finger. Thus, Talia awoke as if from a deep sleep, and when she saw the two jewels by her side, she clasped them to her breast and held on to them as dear as life. In the meantime, she did not know what had happened, or how she had come to be alone in the palace with two babies at her side. Nor did she have any idea about who was bringing them things to eat.

About this same time, the king, who had now remembered Talia, took the opportunity of going on a hunt in order to see her, and when he arrived at the palace, he found her awake with the two masterworks of beauty, and he went out of his mind for joy. Then he told Talia who he was and what had happened, and thus they developed a friendship and strong bond between them, and he remained several days. Then he took leave of her with the promise to return and take her with him to his kingdom.

Once he was back in his palace, he kept talking about Talia and her children. Whenever he sat down at a meal, the name of Talia and then the names of her two children, Sun and Moon, were on his lips. Even when he went to bed, he continued to call one or the other name. The king's wife had already suspected that something was wrong due to her husband's long hunting trips, which caused his frequent absence, and now, when she heard him continually mention the names of Talia, Moon, and Sun, she began to burn with fever, but this fever was not caused by sunstroke. So she summoned the king's secretary and said, "Listen to me, my son, you are caught between Scylla and Charybdis,[1] between the door post and the door, between the stick and the prison. If you tell me the woman with whom my husband is in love, I'll make you a rich man. If you hide anything from me, you'll never be found again, dead or alive."

Since the secretary was partly terrified with fear and partly prompted by his own interest, which is always a bandage over the eyes of honor, a twisting of justice, and a horse kick in the face of loyalty, he told her everything and called a spade a spade. So the queen sent this same man in the king's name to Talia to inform her that the king wanted to see his children. Since this gave Talia great pleasure, she sent them off. But the queen, who had the heart of Medea, ordered the cook to cut their throats and make them into various tasty dishes to serve to her unfortunate husband to eat. However, the cook, who had a tender heart, saw these two lovely golden apples and took pity on them. So he entrusted them to his wife, who hid them. Meanwhile, the cook slaughtered two goats and made a hundred different dishes out of them. When the king arrived home, the

1. See above, p. 128, n. 2.

queen took great delight in serving him the dishes, and while the king was eating and enjoying them, he exclaimed, "Oh, how delicious this is, by the life of Lanfusa![2] How tasty the other dish is, by the soul of my grandfather!"

Meanwhile, the queen kept saying to him, "Eat away! You're only eating what's your own."

The first two or three times that the king heard this refrain, he ignored it, but since the music continued, he finally responded, "I know I'm eating what's mine! You never brought anything into this house!"

Then he got up in a rage and went into the country to calm his anger. But the queen was not satisfied with what she had done, and she called the secretary again and sent him to fetch Talia, pretending that the king wanted to see her. So, Talia came immediately because she had been longing to see the light of her eyes, not knowing that fire was awaiting her. As soon as the queen saw Talia, her face became like the embittered visage of Nero, and she said, "Welcome, Signora Troccola![3] So you are that fine piece of goods, that noxious weed that my husband is enjoying! You are the bitch that has driven my head bonkers! Well, you've landed in purgatory, and I'm going to make you pay for all the harm you've done to me!"

When Talia heard this, she tried to excuse herself and say that it was not her fault that her husband had taken possession of her territory while she had been asleep. But the queen did not want to hear excuses and had a huge fire built in the courtyard of the palace and ordered that Talia be thrown into it. Realizing that things had taken a turn for the worse, Talia knelt down before the queen and begged her to give her time at least to take off the clothes she was wearing. The queen consented, not out of pity for Talia but because she wanted to salvage the clothes, which were embroidered with gold and pearls. So she said, "You may undress."

While Talia began to undress, she uttered a cry with each article of clothing she took off. After she had discarded her robe, her dress, and her bodice and was about to take off her petticoat, she shrieked for the last time. As they were dragging her off to make ashes out of her to be used for washing the pants of Charon,[4] the king arrived, and when he saw this spectacle, he wanted to know what was happening and where his children were. But his wife, who blamed him for everything, told him that she had made him eat them. As soon as the poor king heard this news, he was in despair and began to moan: "Alas! I myself am the wolf who's eaten my own sheep! Why didn't my veins recognize the fountains of my own blood? You renegade Turk! You're no better than a dog! Get out of here! You'll pay for your crime! I don't even have to send your tyrant face to the coliseum[5] to do penance!"

2. Mother of the knight Ferrau and wardress of his prisoners in Ludivoco Ariosto's *Orlando Furioso* (1632). Basile uses this oath a few times as a common expression for swearing on one's mother's life.
3. From the Neapolitan *trocula*, meaning a busybody or chatterer. "Nero": Roman emperor (37 C.E.–67 C.E.), known for his cruelty.
4. In Greek and Roman mythology, the ferryman who conveyed the shades across the river Styx.
5. The amphitheatre of Vespasian at Rome, built ca. 75 C.E. Gladiatorial combats were held in the coliseum until 404. Persecuted Christians were allegedly thrown here to beasts.

After saying this, he ordered her to be thrown into the very same fire she had built for Talia, and the secretary was also burned to death with her, for he had assisted her in this bitter game and had helped her weave this wicked web. The king also wanted to do the same to the cook because he thought he had cut up his children, but the cook threw himself at the king's feet and said, "To tell the truth, sire, there should indeed be no other reward for such a deed but a burning furnace, no other voucher but a spike up my behind, no other treatment but annihilation and devastation in the middle of a fire. Indeed, it would also be a great honor for me as a cook to have my ashes mixed with the ashes of a queen! But this is not the great gift that I expect for having saved your children from that spiteful dog who wanted to kill them and wanted to return them to the very same body which brought them into this world."

When the king heard these words, he thought he was losing his grip on himself. He thought he was dreaming and could not believe his ears. Finally, he turned to the cook and said, "If it's true that you've saved my children, you can be sure that I shall put an end to your turning spits in the kitchen. I'll give you a place in the kitchen of my heart, where you can fiddle with my desires as you wish, and I'll give you such a great reward that you will call yourself the luckiest man in the world."

While the king was saying these words, the cook's wife, who had witnessed her husband's predicament, brought Moon and Sun to their father, who played the game of three with his wife and children, giving them a round of kisses, one after the other. Then, after giving a great reward to the cook and appointing him as his steward, he married Talia, and she enjoyed a long life with her husband and children, and after all her trials she realized.

even when asleep
a person can be struck by luck.

CHARLES PERRAULT

Sleeping Beauty†

Once upon a time there was a king and a queen who were quite vexed at not having any children. Indeed, they were so vexed that it is impossible to find words to express their feelings. They visited all the baths in the world. Vows, pilgrimages, everything was tried, and nothing succeeded. At length, however, the queen became pregnant and gave birth to a daughter. There was a splendid christening, and all the fairies that could be found in the realm (seven altogether) were asked to be godmothers so that each would give the child a gift. According to the custom of the fairies in those days, the gifts would endow the princess with all the perfections you can imagine.

† Charles Perrault, "Sleeping Beauty"—"La belle au bois dormant" (1697), in *Histoires ou contes du temps passé* (Paris: Claude Barbin, 1697).

After the baptismal ceremonies, the entire company returned to the king's palace, where a great banquet was held for the fairies. Places were laid for each, consisting of a magnificent plate with a massive gold case containing a spoon, a fork, and a knife of fine gold, studded with diamonds and rubies. But as they were all about to sit down at the table, an old fairy could be seen entering the palace. She had not been invited because she had not left the tower in which she resided for more than fifty years, and the royal couple had supposed that she was either dead or enchanted. The king ordered a place to be set for her, but there was no possibility of giving her a massive gold case such as the others had because there had been only seven made expressly for the seven fairies. The old lady thought that she was being slighted and muttered some threats between her teeth. One of the young fairies, who chanced to be near her, overheard her and, thinking that she might wish the little princess some bad luck, went and hid herself behind the tapestry as soon as they rose from the table in order to have the last word and repair any evil the old woman might do as soon as possible. Meanwhile, the fairies began to bestow their gifts upon the princess. The youngest fairy decreed that she should be the most beautiful person in the world; the next fairy, that she should have the temperament of an angel; the third, that she should evince the most admirable grace in all she did; the fourth, that she should dance to perfection; the fifth, that she should sing like a nightingale; the sixth, that she should play every instrument in the most exquisite manner possible. Finally, the turn of the old fairy arrived, and her head was shaking more with malice than with age as she declared that the princess was to pierce her hand with a spindle and die of the wound. This terrible gift made the entire company tremble, and there was not one person present who could refrain from tears. At this moment, the young fairy stepped out from behind the tapestry and uttered these words in a loud voice, "Comfort yourselves, king and queen, your daughter shall not die. It's true that I don't have sufficient power to undo entirely what my elder has done. The princess will pierce her hand with a spindle. But instead of dying, she'll only fall into a deep slumber that will last one hundred years. At the end of that time, a king's son will come to wake her."

In hope of avoiding the misfortune predicted by the old fairy, the king immediately issued a public edict forbidding all the people to spin with a spindle or to have spindles in their houses under pain of death.

After fifteen or sixteen years had passed, the king and queen went away to one of their country residences, and one day the princess happened to be running about the castle. She went from one chamber up to another, and after arriving at the top of a tower, she entered a little garret where an honest old woman was sitting by herself, spinning with her distaff and spindle. This good woman had never heard of the king's prohibition with respect to spinning with a spindle.

"What are you doing there, my good woman?" asked the princess.

"I'm spinning, my lovely child," answered the old woman, who did not know her.

"Oh, how pretty it is!" the princess responded.

"How do you do it? Let me try and see if I can do it as well."

No sooner had she grasped the spindle than she pricked her hand with the point and fainted, for she had been hasty, a little thoughtless, and moreover, the sentence of the fairies had ordained it to be that way. Greatly embarrassed, the good old woman called for help. People came from all quarters; they threw water on the princess's face; they unlaced her stays; they slapped her hands; they rubbed her temples with Queen of Hungary's water,[1] but nothing could revive her. Then the king, who had run upstairs at the noise, remembered the prediction of the fairies and wisely concluded that this must have happened as the fairies said it would. Therefore, he had the princess carried to the finest apartment in the palace and placed on a bed of gold and silver embroidery. One would have said she was an angel, so lovely did she appear, for her swoon had not deprived her of her rich complexion: her cheeks preserved their crimson color, and her lips were like coral. Her eyes were closed, but her gentle breathing could be heard, and that indicated she was not dead. The king commanded that she be left to repose in peace until the hour arrived for her waking.

The good fairy, who had saved her life by decreeing that she should sleep for one hundred years, was in the kingdom of Mataquin, twelve thousand leagues away. When the princess met with her accident, she was informed of it instantly by a little dwarf who had a pair of seven-league boots (that is, boots which enable the wearer to cover seven leagues at a single stride). The fairy set out immediately, and an hour afterward, she was seen arriving in a chariot of fire drawn by dragons. The king advanced and offered his hand to help her out of the chariot. She approved of all that he had done. Yet, since she had great foresight, she thought to herself that, when the princess awoke, she would feel considerably embarrassed at finding herself all alone in that old castle. So this is what the fairy did.

With the exception of the king and queen, she touched everyone in the castle with her wand—governesses, maids of honor, ladies-in-waiting, gentlemen, officers, stewards, cooks, scullions, boys, guards, porters, pages, footmen; she also touched all the horses in the stables, their grooms, the great mastiffs in the courtyard, and little Pootsie, the princess's tiny dog lying on the bed beside her. As soon as she had touched them, they all fell asleep, and they were not to wake again until the time arrived for their mistress to do so. Thus they would all be ready to attend upon her if she should want them. Even the spits that had been put down to the fire, laden with partridges and pheasants, went to sleep, and the fire as well.

All this was done in a moment, for the fairies never lose much time when they work. Then the king and queen kissed their dear daughter without waking her and left the castle. They issued a proclamation forbidding anyone to approach it. These orders were unnecessary, for within a quarter of an hour the park was surrounded by such a great quantity of trees, large and small, interlaced by brambles and thorns, that neither man nor beast could penetrate them. Nothing more could be seen than the tops of the castle turrets, and these only at a considerable distance. Nobody doubted but that this was also some of the fairy's handiwork so that the

---

1. An alcoholic mixture named after Isabelle, the queen of Hungary, because it had such a wondrous effect on her and was used to treat all kinds of ailments.

princess might have nothing to fear from the curiosity of strangers during her slumber.

At the end of the hundred years, a different family from that of the sleeping princess had succeeded to the throne. One day the son of the king went hunting in that neighborhood and inquired about the towers that he saw above the trees of a very large and dense wood. Each person responded to the prince according to the story each had heard. Some said that it was an old castle haunted by ghosts; others, that all the witches of the region held their Sabbath there. The most prevalent opinion was that it was the abode of an ogre, who carried away all the children he could catch and ate them there at his leisure, since he alone had the power of making a passage through the wood. While the prince tried to make up his mind what to believe, an old peasant spoke in his turn and said to him, "Prince, it is more than fifty years since I heard my father say that the most beautiful princess that has ever been seen is in that castle. He told me that she was to sleep for a hundred years and was destined to be awakened by a chosen king's son."

Upon hearing these words, the young prince felt himself all on fire. There was no doubt in his mind that he was destined to accomplish this wonderful adventure, and impelled by love and glory, he decided on the spot to see what would come of it. No sooner had he approached the wood than all those great trees and all those brambles and thorns opened on their own accord and allowed him to pass through. Then he began walking toward the castle, which he saw at the end of the long avenue that he had entered. To his surprise, the trees closed up as soon as he passed by them, and none of his attendants could follow him. Nevertheless, he continued to advance, for a young and amorous prince is always courageous. When he entered a large courtyard, everything he saw was enough to freeze his blood with terror. A frightful silence reigned. Death seemed to be everywhere. Nothing could be seen but the bodies of men and animals stretched out and apparently lifeless. He soon discovered, however, by the shining noses and red faces of the porters that they were only asleep; and their goblets, which still contained a few drops of wine, sufficiently proved that they had dozed off while drinking. Now he passed through a large courtyard paved with marble, and he ascended the staircase. As he entered the guard room, he saw the guards drawn up and standing in line, their carbines shouldered, snoring their loudest. He traversed several apartments with ladies and gentlemen all asleep; some standing, others seated. Finally, he entered a chamber completely covered with gold and saw the most lovely sight he had ever looked upon—there on a bed with curtains open on each side was a princess who seemed to be about fifteen or sixteen and whose radiant charms gave her an appearance that was luminous and supernatural. He approached, trembling and admiring, and knelt down beside her. At that moment, the enchantment having ended, the princess awoke and bestowed upon him a look more tender than a first glance might seem to warrant.

"Is it you, my prince?" she said. "You have been long awaited."

Charmed by these words, and still more by the tone in which they were uttered, the prince hardly knew how to express his joy and gratitude to

Sleeping Beauty. From *Les Contes de Perrault*, ca. 1890.

her. He assured her that he loved her better than he loved himself. His words were not very coherent, but they pleased her all the more because of that. The less there is of eloquence, the more there is of love. He was much more embarrassed than she was, and one ought not to be astonished at that, for the princess had had time enough to consider what she should say to him. There is reason to believe (though history makes no mention of it) that the good fairy had procured her the pleasure of very agreeable dreams during her long slumber. In short, they talked for four hours without having said half what they had to say to each other.

In the meantime, the entire palace had been roused at the very same time as the princess had been. They all remembered what their tasks were, and since they were not all in love, they were dying with hunger. The lady-in-waiting, as hungry as any of them, became impatient and announced loudly to the princess that dinner was ready. The prince assisted the princess in rising; she was fully dressed and most magnificently, but he took care not to tell her that she was attired like his grandmother, who also wore stand-up collars. Still, she looked no less lovely.

They passed into a salon of mirrors in which stewards of the princess served them supper. The violins and oboes played old but excellent pieces of music, notwithstanding that it was a hundred years since they had been performed by anybody. And, after supper, to lose no time, the chaplain married them in the castle chapel, and the maid of honor pulled the curtains of their bed closed.

However, they did not sleep a great deal. The princess did not have much need of sleep, and the prince left her at sunrise to return to the city, where his father had been greatly worried about him. The prince told him that he had lost his way in the forest while hunting, and that he had slept in the hut of a charcoal burner who had given him some black bread and cheese for his supper. The king, his father, who was a trusting soul, believed him, but his mother was not so easily persuaded. Observing that he went hunting nearly every day and always had some story ready as an excuse when he had slept two or three nights away from home, she was convinced that he had some mistress. Indeed, he lived with the princess for more than two years and had two children by her. The first was a girl named Aurora, and the second, a son, called Day because he seemed even more beautiful than his sister.

In order to draw some sort of confession from him, the queen often said to her son that he ought to settle down. However, he never dared to trust her with his secret. Although he loved her, he also feared her, for she was of the race of ogres, and the king had married her only on account of her great wealth. It was even whispered about the court that she had the inclinations of an ogress, and when she saw little children passing, she had the greatest difficulty in the world to restrain herself from pouncing on them. Hence, the prince refused to say anything about his adventure.

Two years later, however, when the king died, and the prince became his successor, he made a public declaration about his marriage and went in great state to fetch the queen, his wife, to the palace. With her two children on each side of her, she made a magnificent entry into the capital. Some time afterward the king went to war with his neighbor, the Emperor

Cantalabutte. He left the regency of the kingdom to his mother, the queen, and placed his wife and children in her care. He was likely to spend the entire summer in battle, and as soon as he was gone, the queen-mother sent her daughter-in-law and the children to a country house in the forest so that she might gratify her horrible longing more easily. A few days later, she followed them there, and one evening she said to her steward, "I want to eat little Aurora for dinner tomorrow."

"Ah, madame!" exclaimed the steward.

"That is my will," said the queen (and she said it in the tone of an ogress longing to eat fresh meat), "and I want her served up with *sauce Robert*."[2]

The poor man plainly saw that it was useless to trifle with an ogress. So he took his knife and went up to little Aurora's room. She was then about four years old, and when she skipped over to him, threw her arms around his neck with a laugh, and asked him for some sweets, he burst into tears, and the knife fell from his hands. Soon he went down again into the kitchen court, killed a little lamb, and served it with such a delicious sauce that his mistress assured him she had never eaten anything so good. In the meantime, he carried off little Aurora and gave her to his wife to conceal in the lodging she occupied at the far end of the kitchen court.

A week later, the wicked queen said to her steward, "I want to eat little Day for supper."

Determined to deceive her as before, he did not reply. He just went in search of little Day and found him with a tiny foil in his hand, fencing with a large monkey, though he was only three years old. He carried him to his wife, who hid him where she had concealed his sister. Then he cooked a very tender little goat in place of little Day, and the ogress thought it most delicious.

Thus far all was going well, but one evening this wicked queen said to the steward, "I want to eat the queen with the same sauce that I had with her children."

This time the poor steward despaired of being able to deceive her again. The young queen was now twenty years old, not counting the hundred years she had slept. Her skin was a little tough, though it was white and beautiful. Thus, where in the menagerie was he to find an animal that was just as tough as she was?

To save his own life he resolved he would cut the queen's throat and went up to her apartment intending to carry out this plan. He worked himself up into a fit and entered the young queen's chamber dagger in hand. However, he did not want to take her by surprise and thus repeated very respectfully the order he had received from the queen-mother.

"Do your duty!" said she, stretching out her neck to him. "Carry out the order given to you. Then I shall behold my children, my poor children, whom I loved so much."

She had thought they were dead ever since they were carried off without explanation.

2. A well-known sauce that Rabelais described in the sixteenth century. It consisted of onions, mustard, vinegar, pepper, and salt, mixed with butter, and it was generally used with pork, duck, and rabbit.

"No, no, madame!" replied the poor steward, touched to the quick. "You shall not die, and you shall see your children again, but it will be in my own house, where I have hidden them. And I shall again deceive the queen-mother by serving her a young hind in your stead."

He led her straight to his own quarters, and after leaving her to embrace her children and weep with them, he went and cooked a hind which the queen ate at supper with as much appetite as if it had been the young queen. She felt content with her cruelty and intended to tell the king on his return that some ferocious wolves had devoured the queen, his wife, and two children.

One evening when she was prowling as usual around the courts and poultry yards of the castle to inhale the smell of fresh meat, she overheard little Day crying in a lower room because the queen, his mother, wanted to slap him for having been naughty, and she also heard little Aurora begging forgiveness for her brother. The ogress recognized the voices of the queen and her children, and furious at having been duped, she gave orders in a tone that made everyone tremble and commanded that a large copper vat be brought into the middle of the court early the next morning. When it was done, she had the vat filled with toads, vipers, adders, and serpents, intending to fling the queen, her children, the steward, his wife, and his maidservant into it, and she commanded that they be brought forth with their hands tied behind them.

There they stood, and the executioners were preparing to fling them into the copper vat when the king, who was not expected so early, entered the courtyard on horseback. He had ridden posthaste, and in great astonishment, he demanded to know the meaning of the horrible spectacle. Nobody dared to tell him, and then the ogress, enraged at the sight of the king's return, flung herself headfirst into the vat and was devoured by the horrible reptiles that she had commanded to be placed there. The king could not help but feel sorry, for she was his mother, but he quickly consoled himself in the company of his beautiful wife and children.

Moral

To wait so long
And want a man refined and strong
Is not at all uncommon.
And yet to wait one hundred years
Without a tear, without a care,
Makes for a very rare woman.

So here our tale appears to show,
How marriage deferred,
Brings joy unheard,
Nothing lost after a century or so.
But others love with more ardor,
And wed quickly out of passion.
Whatever they do, I won't deplore
Nor shall I preach a lesson.

JACOB AND WILHELM GRIMM

Brier Rose†

In times of old there lived a king and queen, and every day they said, "Oh, if only we had a child!" Yet, they never had one.

Then one day, as the queen went out bathing, a frog happened to crawl ashore and say to her, "Your wish will be fulfilled. Before the year is out, you will give birth to a daughter."

The frog's prediction came true, and the queen gave birth to a girl who was so beautiful that the king was overjoyed and decided to hold a great feast. Not only did he invite his relatives, friends, and acquaintances, but also the wise women in the hope that they would be generous and kind to his daughter. There were thirteen wise women in his kingdom, but he had only twelve golden plates from which they could eat. Therefore, one of them had to remain home.

The feast was celebrated with tremendous splendor, and when it drew to a close, the wise women bestowed their miraculous gifts upon the child. One gave her virtue, another beauty, the third wealth, and so on, until they had given her nearly everything one could possibly wish for in the world. When eleven of them had offered their gifts, the thirteenth suddenly entered the hall. She wanted to get revenge for not having been invited, and without greeting anyone or looking around, she cried out with a loud voice, "In her fifteenth year the princess will prick herself with a spindle and fall down dead!"

That was all she said. Then she turned around and left the hall. Everyone was horrified, but the twelfth wise woman stepped forward. She still had her wish to make, and although she could not undo the evil spell, she could nevertheless soften it.

"The princess will not die," she said. "Instead, she shall fall into a deep sleep for one hundred years."

Since the king wanted to guard his dear child against such a catastrophe, he issued an order that all spindles in his kingdom were to be burned. Meanwhile, the gifts of the wise women fulfilled their promise in every way: the girl was so beautiful, polite, kind, and sensible that whoever encountered her could not help but adore her.

Now, on the day she turned fifteen, it happened that the king and queen were not at home, and she was left completely alone in the palace. So she wandered all over the place and explored as many rooms and chambers as she pleased. She eventually came to an old tower, climbed its narrow winding staircase, and came to a small door. A rusty key was stuck in the lock, and when she turned it, the door sprang open, and she saw an old woman in a little room sitting with a spindle and busily spinning flax.

"Good day, old granny," said the princess. "What are you doing there?"

---

† Jacob and Wilhelm Grimm, "Brier Rose"—"Dornröschen" (1857), No. 50 in *Kinder- und Hausmärchen. Gesammelt durch die Brüder Grimm* (Göttingen: Dieterich, 1857).

"I'm spinning," said the old woman, and she nodded her head.

"What's the thing that's bobbing about in such a funny way?" asked the maiden, who took the spindle and wanted to spin too, but just as she touched the spindle, the magic spell began working, and she pricked her finger with it.

The very moment she felt the prick, she fell down on the bed that was standing there, and she was overcome by a deep sleep. This sleep soon spread throughout the entire palace. The king and queen had just returned home, and when they entered the hall, they fell asleep, as did all the people of their court. They were followed by the horses in the stable, the dogs in the courtyard, the pigeons on the roof, and the flies on the wall. Even the fire flickering in the hearth became quiet and fell asleep. The roast stopped sizzling, and the cook, who was just about to pull the kitchen boy's hair because he had done something wrong, let him go and fell asleep. Finally, the wind died down so that not a single leaf stirred on the trees outside the castle.

Soon a brier hedge began to grow all around the castle, and it grew higher each year. Eventually, it surrounded and covered the entire castle, causing it to become invisible. Not even the flag on the roof could be seen. The princess became known by the name Beautiful Sleeping Brier Rose, and a tale about her began circulating throughout the country. From time to time princes came and tried to break through the hedge and get back to the castle. However, this was impossible because the thorns clung together tightly as though they had hands, and the young men got stuck there. Indeed, they could not pry themselves loose and died miserable deaths.

After many, many years had gone by, a prince came to this country once more and heard an old man talking about the brier hedge. Supposedly, there was a castle standing behind the hedge, and in the castle was a remarkably beautiful princess named Brier Rose, who had been sleeping for a hundred years, along with the king and queen and their entire court. The old man also knew from his grandfather that many princes had come and had tried to break through the brier hedge, but they had got stuck and had died wretched deaths.

"I'm not afraid," said the young prince. "I intend to go and see the beautiful Brier Rose."

The good old man tried as best he could to dissuade him, but the prince would not heed his words.

Now the hundred years had just ended, and the day on which Brier Rose was to wake up again had arrived. When the prince approached the brier hedge, he found nothing but beautiful flowers that opened of their own accord, let him through, and then closed again like a hedge. In the castle courtyard he saw the horses and the spotted hunting dogs lying asleep. The pigeons were perched on the roof and had tucked their heads beneath their wings. When he entered the palace, the flies were sleeping on the wall, the cook in the kitchen was still holding his hand as if he wanted to grab the kitchen boy, and the maid was sitting in front of the black chicken that she was about to pluck. As the prince continued walking, he saw the entire country lying asleep in the hall with the king and queen by the throne. Then he moved on, and everything was so quiet that he could hear himself breathe.

Finally, he came to the tower and opened the door to the small room in which Brier Rose was asleep. There she lay, and her beauty was so marvelous that he could not take his eyes off her. Then he leaned over and gave her a kiss, and when his lips touched hers, Brier Rose opened her eyes, woke up, and looked at him fondly. After that they went downstairs together, and the king and queen woke up along with the entire court, and they all looked at each other in amazement. Soon the horses in the courtyard stood up and shook themselves. The hunting dogs jumped around and wagged their tails. The pigeons on the roof lifted their heads from under their wings, looked around, and flew off into the fields. The flies on the wall continued crawling. The fire in the kitchen flared up, flickered, and cooked the meat. The roast began to sizzle again, and the cook gave the kitchen boy such a box on the ear that he let out a cry, while the maid finished plucking the chicken.

The wedding of the prince with Brier Rose was celebrated in great splendor, and they lived happily to the end of their days.

Abandoned Children

The history of the Grimms' text reveals how assiduously the Grimms, particularly Wilhelm, sought to influence our notions of socialization and the rearing of children through the constant revision of a fairy tale. In essence, his story seeks to apologize for the abandonment of the children (as do many others) and depicts women as threatening figures while it apologizes for the father's behavior. There has always been a close connection between the rationalization process of writing and the reception of fairy tales. In the case of "Hansel and Gretel," Wilhelm heard the story from Dortchen Wild, daughter of a pharmacist in Kassel about 1809. The Grimms indicated in their notes that they knew Charles Perrault's "Le petit poucet" ("Little Tom Thumb," 1697), which has a similar plot, as well as other folk versions. By the time Wilhelm wrote the next version, for the second edition of 1819, he was also familiar with Giambattista Basile's "Ninnillo and Nennella" (1634). Wilhelm constantly revised the tale in each edition, making it more Christian in tone and placing greater blame on a stepmother for the abandonment. However, the most dramatic changes occur in the fifth edition of 1843, after Wilhelm had read August Stöber's Alsatian tale "Das Eierkuchenhäuslein" ("The Little Pancake House," 1842). What is fascinating here is that Stöber collected his tale from an informant who probably had read or heard the Grimms' literary tale of "Hansel and Gretel" and had changed it for his or her purposes. Stöber himself cites the Grimms' edition as his literary source. (Interestingly, one of Stöber's changes is the transformation of the stepmother back into the biological mother, who does not die, but greets the children with her husband at the end. Both parents regret what they did to the children.) Wilhelm, who read Stöber's collection of tales, *Elsäsisches Volksbüchlein* (*The Little Alsatian Folk Book*, 1842), reappropriated from the Alsatian dialect certain phrases, sayings, and verses that he believed would lend his tale more of a quaint and folksy tone. By the time the last edition of *Kinder- und Hausmärchen* was printed in 1857, Wilhelm had made so many changes in style and theme that the tale was twice as long as the original manuscript of 1810.

The popularity and importance of the tales in this cycle, which can be found throughout Europe in the oral and literary tradition, are due to the theme of child abandonment and abuse. Although it is difficult to estimate how widespread child abandonment was, it is clear that famines, poor living conditions, and lack of birth control led to the birth of many unwanted children. In the Middle Ages, it was common for children who could not be nourished to be abandoned in front of churches, in special parts of village squares, or in the forest. Sometimes the abandonment and/or abuse was due to the re-marriage of a man or woman who could not tolerate the children from a previous marriage. When the children are abandoned in the fairy tales, they do not always have an encounter with a witch, but they do encounter a dangerous character who threatens their lives, and they must use their wits to find a way to return home. Given the manner in which the tale celebrated the patriarchal home as haven, "Hansel and Gretel" became one of the most favorite of the Grimms' tales in the nineteenth century. Ludwig Bechstein wrote a similar version in his *Deutsches Märchenbuch* (1857), probably based on the Grimms' tale, while Engelbert Humperdinck produced his famous opera *Hänsel und Gretel* in 1893. The most thorough treatment of this tale-type is Regina Böhm-Korff's *Deutung und Bedeutung von "Hänsel und Gretel"* (1991). This study traces the historical development of different versions and pays careful attention to the motif of food and famine in the tale as well as to the motif of abandonment.

GIAMBATTISTA BASILE

Ninnillo and Nennella†

There was once a father called Jannuccio who had two children, Ninnillo and Nennella, and they were his heart's delight. But, when death with the silent file of Time sawed away the prison bars of his wife's soul, things changed, and he took an ugly woman as his wife who was a malicious bitch. No sooner did she set foot in the house of her husband than she began to act as a temperamental thoroughbred and said, "Have I come to pick the lice off the children's heads of another woman? That's the limit! I don't need this mess! Why should I listen to these whiny brats around me? Ah, I would rather have broken my neck than to come to this hellhole where I eat badly and sleep worse because of these annoying brats. It's unbearable! I came here to be your wife not your servant! You had better search for a way to get rid of these pests; otherwise you'll be rid of me! Better to blush once than to turn white a hundred times. Now let's settle this affair because I'm really determined to get something out of this or to end it once and for all!"

The poor husband, who was somewhat fond of this woman, said to her, "Don't be angry, my wife. Sugar is expensive. Tomorrow morning, before the cock crows, I'll put an end to your woes and make you happy."

And so the next morning, before dawn had hung the red Spanish cover out of the window of the East to shake out the fleas, he took the children by the hand and carried a fine basket of things to eat on his arm. Then he led them into a forest where an army of poplar and beech trees were besieging the shade. When they arrived at this spot, Jannuccio said, "My dear children, I want you to stay here. Eat and drink and make yourselves happy. If you need something, follow the trail of ashes which I've been strewing. This is the thread that will lead you out of the labyrinth and carry you to your home."

After giving each a kiss, he went back home crying. Then, when all the animals, admonished by the guards of night, paid the rent to nature for space to take a needy repose, the children—perhaps because they were frightened of staying alone in that desolate place where the waters of the river thrashed the impertinent stones that appeared at their feet, causing

† Giambattista Basile, "Ninnillo and Nennella"—"Ninnillo e Nenella" (1634), *Ottavo passatempo della quinta giornata* in *Lo cunto de li cunti overo Lo trattenemiento de peccerille*, De Gian Alessio Abbattutis, 5 vols. (Naples: Ottavio Beltrano, 1634–36).

a racket that would have given the shivers even to some manly braggart—advanced slowly along the path of ashes, and it was already midnight as they quietly entered their home.

When Pasciozza, their stepmother, saw them, she did not behave like a woman, but like an infernal fury so that her shrieks reached heaven. She wrung her hands and stamped her feet like a restless horse and said, "What a wonderful thing this is! Where did these stinking brats spring from? Can't we use some mercury to remove them from this house? Is it possible you want to keep them just to drive me to my death? Get out of here, and get them out of my sight this instant! I don't want to wait for the music of the hens or the crowing of the cocks! If you don't do this, you can go brush your teeth alone while I sleep somewhere else, and tomorrow morning I'll head back to the house of my parents because you don't deserve me! I didn't bring all this beautiful furniture into this house to see some stinking behinds crap on it, and I didn't deposit such a rich dowry to become a slave to children who are not my own!"

When the unfortunate Jannuccio saw that the ship was in troubled waters and that things were getting too hot, he took the children back into the forest at once. Then he gave them another basket with little things to eat and said, "Now you see, my little ones, how much this bitch of a wife hates you. Ever since she entered my house, she has been your ruin, and she's stuck a nail into my heart. Therefore, stay in this forest, where the trees are more gentle and will provide a roof to protect you from the sun, where the river is more merciful and will give you water to drink without poisoning you, where the earth is more kind and will give you a mattress of grass on which you can lie down without worrying about danger. And when you need something to eat, you only have to follow this path of bran that I've scattered straight ahead to search for help."

After he said this, he turned his face so that his children would not see him crying and so that he would not scare the little creatures. Later, after the children had finished eating all the stuff that was in the basket, they wanted to return home. But since an ass—the son of bad luck—had gobbled up the bran that had been spread on the ground, they lost their way and wandered around in the middle of the forest for several days, eating acorns and chestnuts that had fallen to the ground from the trees.

Now, since heaven always stretches out a hand to protect the innocent, a king happened to arrive in the forest on a hunting expedition. When Ninnillo heard the barking of the dogs, he became so frightened that he hid inside a hollow tree, while Nennella began to run so fast that she left the forest and soon found herself at the seashore, where some pirates had landed to gather some food. They carried her off to their captain, who, in turn, brought her to his wife, whose baby girl had just died, and she began raising Nennella as her own daughter.

But let us return to Ninnillo, who was hidden in the hollow tree and surrounded by dogs that were barking so loudly that the prince sent one of his men to see what was happening. When he reached the tree, he found a handsome young boy who was so young that he could not even tell who his father or mother was. So the king had him put on the horse of one of his hunters and brought him to his palace, where he raised him with great care and had him educated in all disciplines, and among other things he had him instructed in the art of carving so that in three or four years he became so talented that he could split a hair in two.

In the meantime, people had discovered that the captain with whom Nennella was living was actually a pirate, and they wanted to send him to prison. But he had made friends with some law clerks, and they informed him about this threat at the right moment. So he was able to flee with his entire family. But it was perhaps heaven's way of doling out justice that he who had committed crimes on the high sea should have to pay the penalty for them on the sea. Thus, after the pirate had embarked with his entourage on a tiny ship, a strong gust of wind and furious waves swept over the vessel in the middle of the sea so that the ship capsized and all were drowned. The only survivor was Nennella because she, unlike the pirate's wife and children, had not been guilty of any crimes on the sea. She managed to escape because an enchanted fish appeared right next to the ship just at the moment it capsized, and the fish opened its mouth and swallowed her down.

Now, just when the girl thought that her days were done, she found some astonishing things in the belly of this fish—beautiful fields, delightful gardens, and a stately mansion with all the comforts that enabled her to live like a princess. Meanwhile, this same fish carried her toward a rocky island where the king had gone to get away from the scorching and sultry heat of summer and enjoy some cool air. A grand banquet was being prepared, and Ninnillo went to the terrace of the palace that overlooked the reefs below to sharpen some carving knives, for he took pleasure in displaying his skills and being recognized for his achievements.

When Nennella saw him from the throat of the fish, she cried out these pitiful words: "My brother, my brother, your knives are sharpened. The tables have been set. But regretfully I am living without you and wallowing in a fish's jaw."

At first, Ninnillo did not pay any attention to these words, but the king, who was on another terrace, turned to listen to this lament. When he saw the fish and heard the same words a second time, he was so astonished that he became breathless. Then he sent several servants to see whether they could find a way to trap the fish and drag it ashore. But it was to no avail. So, after hearing the words "my brother, my brother" constantly repeated, he asked all the people in his company if any of them had ever lost a sister. Ninnillo began to respond as if in a dream, recalling that, when the king had found him, he had had a sister with him, but since then he had never received any news about her. The king told him to approach the fish and to see what the matter was. Perhaps fortune was beckoning him.

So Ninnillo went to the fish, which propped its head on a reef and opened its mouth six feet wide to let Nennella come out of it. She was so beautiful that she seemed to be a nymph who, in a scene from some interlude, suddenly springs out of an animal due to a magician's powers of enchantment. When the king asked what the meaning of all this was, Nennella began to tell him about some of their past troubles and about their stepmother's hatred of them. Yet, neither she nor her brother could

Ninnillo and Nennella. George Cruikshank, 1893.

remember their father's name or the place of their home. Consequently, the king issued a proclamation announcing that whoever had lost two children by the names of Ninnillo and Nennella in a forest would receive good news if they came to the royal palace.

Jannuccio, who had been sad for a long time and inconsolable because he believed that the children had been eaten by wolves, ran with great joy to the king's palace to tell him that he was the one who had lost these children. After he explained how he had been compelled to take his children into the forest, the king gave him a good scolding, calling him a sheep and a spineless man to have allowed a woman to run all over him, causing him to lose two jewels such as his children were. But after having broken his head with these words, the king applied a bandage to his wounds by letting him see his two children, whom the father could not stop kissing and embracing for half an hour. Then after the king had him take off his coarse clothes and dressed him as a gentleman, he summoned Jannuccio's wife to the palace. When he showed her the two golden ears of corn and asked her what a person would deserve if that person harmed these two innocents or put their lives in danger, she responded, "I would shut that person in a barrel and have it rolled down a mountain."

"Well, you will have it your way," the king said. "The goat has turned and butted herself. Indeed, you've pronounced your own sentence, and now you'll pay the penalty for having borne such hatred toward your beautiful stepchildren!"

So the king gave orders for the sentence to be carried out. Afterward, he found a gentleman who was very rich and one of his vassals, and he gave him Nennella to be his wife, and he gave the daughter of another rich man to Ninnillo. In addition, he provided them with a sufficient allowance so that they and their father could live without wanting anything in the world. Enclosed in a barrel, the stepmother closed her own life crying through a peephole as long as she had some breath left in her:

> Though justice may be delayed,
> it is heavy-handed when it comes,
> and makes the punishment fit the crime.

CHARLES PERRAULT

Little Thumbling†

Once upon a time there was a woodcutter and his wife who had seven children, all boys. The eldest was but ten years old, and the youngest only seven. People were astonished that the woodcutter had had so many children in such a short time, but the fact is that his wife did not mince matters and seldom gave birth to less than two at a time. They were very

---

† Charles Perrault, "Little Thumbling"—"Le petit poucet" (1697), in *Histoires ou contes du temps passé* (Paris: Claude Barbin, 1697).

poor, and their seven children were a great burden to them since not one was able to earn his own living.

What distressed them even more was that the youngest son was very delicate and rarely spoke, which they considered a mark of stupidity instead of good sense. Moreover, he was very little. Indeed, at birth he was scarcely bigger than one's thumb, and this led everyone to call him Little Thumbling. This poor child was the scapegoat of the family and was blamed for everything that happened. Nevertheless, he was the shrewdest and most sensible of all the brothers, and if he spoke but little, he listened a great deal.

One year there was a very bad harvest, and the famine[1] was so severe that these poor people decided to get rid of their children. So one evening, when they were all in bed and the woodcutter was sitting by the fire with his wife, he said to her with a heavy heart, "It's plain to see that we can no longer feed our children. I can't let them die of hunger before my eyes, and I've made up my mind to lose them tomorrow in the forest. We can do this without any trouble when they are amusing themselves by making bundles of sticks. We only have to disappear without their seeing us."

"Ah!" the woodcutter's wife exclaimed. "Do you really have the heart to abandon your own children?"

Her husband tried in vain to convince her how their terrible poverty necessitated such action, but she would not consent to the deed. She was poor, but she was their mother. However, after reflecting on how miserable she would be to see them die of hunger, she finally agreed and went to bed weeping.

Little Thumbling had heard everything they said, for he had been lying in his bed and had realized that they were discussing their affairs. So he had gotten up quietly, slipped under his father's stool, and listened without being seen. He went back to bed and did not sleep a wink the rest of the night because he was thinking over what he should do. He rose early the next morning and went to the banks of a brook, where he filled his pockets with small white pebbles, and then returned home.

Later they set out all together, and Little Thumbling revealed nothing of what he had heard to his brothers. They entered a very dense forest, where they were unable to see each other once they were ten paces apart. The woodcutter began to chop wood, and his children picked up sticks and made bundles. Seeing them occupied with their work, the father and mother gradually stole away and then fled all at once by a small winding path. When the children found themselves all alone, they began to scream and cry with all their might. Little Thumbling let them scream since he was fully confident that he could get home again after having dropped the little white pebbles he had in his pockets all along the path.

"Don't be afraid, brothers," he said. "Our father and mother have left us here, but I'll lead you safely home. Just follow me."

---

1. There was a series of major famines during the seventeenth century in France: 1660, 1661, 1662, and 1675. In the years 1693–94, when Perrault wrote his first fairy tale, there were famines that were accompanied by epidemics.

They followed him, and he led them back to the house by the same road that they had taken into the forest. At first they were afraid to enter the house. Instead, they placed themselves next to the door to listen to the conversation of their parents.

Now, after the woodcutter and his wife had arrived home, they had found ten crowns that the lord of the manor had sent them. He had owed them this money for a long time, and they had given up all hope of ever receiving it. This money had put new life into them because these poor people had actually been starving. So the woodcutter had sent his wife to the butcher's[2] right away, for it had been many a day since they had eaten anything. She had bought three times as much as was necessary for the supper of two persons, and when they had sat down at the table again, the woodcutter's wife had said, "Alas! Where are our poor children now? They would make a good meal out of our leftovers. But it was you, Guillaume, who wanted to lose them. I told you we'd repent it. What are they doing now in the forest! Alas! Heaven help me! The wolves have probably eaten them already! What a monster you must be to get rid of your children this way!"

The woodcutter lost his temper, for she repeated more than forty times that they would repent it and that she had told him so. He threatened to beat her if she did not hold her tongue. It was not that the woodcutter was not perhaps even more sorry than his wife, but that she browbeat him. He was like many other people who are disposed to women who can talk well but become very irritated by those women who are always right.

"Alas!" His wife was all in tears. "Where are my children now, my poor children!"

She uttered these words so loudly that the children, who were at the door, heard her and began to cry, "Here we are! Here we are!"

She rushed to open the door for them, and embracing them, she exclaimed, "How happy I am to see you again, my dear children! You're very tired and hungry. And how dirty you are Pierrot! Come here and let me wash you."

Pierrot was her eldest son, and she loved him most of all because he was somewhat red-headed, and that was the color of her hair too. They sat down to supper and ate with an appetite that pleased their father and mother. They all talked at once and related how frightened they had been in the forest. The good souls were delighted to see their children around them once more, and their joy lasted just as long as the ten crowns. But when the money was spent, they relapsed into their former misery and decided to lose the children again. And to do so effectually they were determined to lead them much further from home than they had done the first time.

They tried to discuss this in secret, but they were overheard by Little Thumbling, who counted on getting out of the predicament the way he

---

2. The eating of meat was considered a luxury for peasants, and going to the butcher's was a sign of celebration. The normal diet of poor woodcutters and peasants consisted of bread, soup, vegetables, pork, and sometimes poultry, if times were good.

had done before. Yet, when he got up very early to collect the little pebbles, he found the house door double locked. He could not think of a thing to do until the woodcutter's wife gave them each a piece of bread for their breakfast. Then it occurred to him that he might use the bread in place of the pebbles by throwing crumbs along the path as they went. So he stuck his piece in his pocket. The father and mother led them into the thickest and darkest part of the forest, and as soon as they had done so, they took a side path and left them there. Little Thumbling was not at all worried, for he thought he would easily find his way back by means of the bread which he had scattered along the path. But he was greatly surprised when he could not find a single crumb, for the birds had eaten them all up. Now the poor children were in great trouble. The further they wandered, the deeper they plunged into the forest. Night arrived, and a great wind arose which filled them with fear. They imagined that they heard wolves howling on every side of them, and that they were coming to devour them. They scarcely dared to turn their heads. Then it began raining so heavily that they were soon drenched to the skin. With each step they took, they slipped and tumbled into the mud. They got up all covered with mud and did not know what to do with their hands. Little Thumbling climbed up a tree to try and see something from the top of it. After looking all around him, he saw a little light like that of a candle, but it was far away on the other side of the forest. He got down from the tree, and when he had reached the ground, he could no longer see the light. This was a great disappointment to him, but after having walked on with his brothers for some time in the direction of the light, he saw it again as they emerged from the forest. At last they reached the house where the light was burning but not without having been frightened, for they had often lost sight of it, especially when they had descended into some valleys. They knocked at the door, and a good woman came to open it and asked them what they wanted. Little Thumbling told her that they were poor children who had lost their way in the forest and begged her for a night's lodging out of charity. Seeing how lovely the children were, she began to weep and said, "Alas! My poor children, don't you know where you've landed? This is the dwelling of an ogre who eats little children!"

"Alas, madam!" replied Little Thumbling, who trembled from head to toe just as all his brothers did. "What shall we do? It's for sure that the wolves of the forest will devour us tonight if you refuse to take us under your roof. That being the case, we'd rather be eaten by your husband. Perhaps he'll take pity on us if you're kind enough to plead for us."

The ogre's wife, who believed she could manage to hide them from her husband till the next morning, allowed them to come in and led them to a spot where they could warm themselves by a good fire, for there was a whole sheep on the spit roasting for the ogre's supper. Just as they were beginning to get warm, they heard two or three loud knocks at the door. It was the ogre, who had come home. His wife immediately made the children hide under the bed and went to open the door. The ogre first asked if his supper were ready and if she had drawn the wine. With that he sat down to his meal. The mutton was all but raw, but he liked it all the better for that. He sniffed right and left saying that he smelt fresh meat.

"It must be the calf that you smell. I've just skinned it," said his wife.

"I smell fresh meat, I tell you," replied the ogre, looking suspiciously at his wife. "There's something here I don't understand." Upon saying these words, he rose from the table and went straight to the bed. "Ah!" he exclaimed. "This is the way you deceive me, cursed woman! I don't know what's holding me back from eating you also! It's a lucky thing that you're an old beast! Here's some game that comes just in time for me to entertain three ogre friends of mine who are coming to see me in a day or two."

He dragged the boys from under the bed one after the other. The poor children fell on their knees, begging for mercy, but they had to deal with the most cruel of all the ogres. Far from feeling pity for them, he was already devouring them with his eyes and said to his wife that they would be perfect as dainty bits once she had made a good sauce for them. He went to fetch a large knife, and as he approached the poor children, he whetted it on a long stone that he held in his left hand. He had already grabbed one of the boys when his wife said to him, "Why do you want to do it at this hour of the night? Won't you have time enough tomorrow?"

"Hold your tongue," the ogre replied. "They'll be all the more tender."

"But you already have so much meat," his wife responded. "Here's a calf, two sheep, and half a pig."

"You're right," the ogre said. "Give them a good supper to fatten them up, and then put them to bed."

The good woman was overjoyed and brought them plenty for supper, but they could not eat because they were so paralyzed with fright. As for the ogre, he seated himself to drink again, delighted to think he had such a treat in store for his friends. So he emptied a dozen goblets, more than usual, which affected his head somewhat, and he was obliged to go to bed.

The ogre had seven daughters who were still quite young. These little ogresses had the most beautiful complexions due to eating raw flesh like their father. But they had very small, round gray eyes, hooked noses, and large mouths with long teeth, extremely sharp and wide apart. They were not very vicious as yet, but they showed great promise, for they had already begun to bite little children to suck their blood. They had been sent to bed early, and all seven were in a large bed, each having a golden crown on her head. In the same room, there was another bed of the same size. It was in this bed that the ogre's wife had put the seven little boys to sleep, after which she went to sleep with her husband.

Little Thumbling, who had noticed that the ogre's daughters had golden crowns on their heads, and who feared that the ogre might regret not having killed him and his brothers that evening, got up in the middle of the night. He took off his nightcap and those of his brothers, went very softly, and placed them on the heads of the ogre's seven daughters, after having taken off their golden crowns, which he put on his brothers and himself so that the ogre might mistake them for his daughters, and his daughters for the boys whose throats he longed to cut.

Everything turned out exactly as he had anticipated, for the ogre awoke at midnight and regretted that he had postponed until the next morning what he might have done that evening. Therefore, he jumped right out of bed and seized his large knife. "Now let's go," he said, "and see how our little rascals are doing. We won't make the same mistake twice." So he stole up to his daughters' bedroom on tiptoe and approached the bed in which the little boys were lying. They were all asleep except Thumbling, who was dreadfully frightened when the ogre placed his hand on his head to feel it as he had in turn felt those of his brothers.

After feeling the golden crowns, the ogre said, "Upon my word, I almost made a mess of a job! It's clear I must have drunk too much last night." He then went to the bed where his daughters slept, and after feeling the little nightcaps that belonged to the boys, he cried, "Aha! Here are our sly little dogs. Let's get to work!" With these words he cut the throats of his seven daughters without hesitating. Well satisfied with his work, he returned and stretched himself out in bed beside his wife. As soon as Little Thumbling heard the ogre snoring, he woke his brothers and told them to dress themselves quickly and follow him. They went down quietly into the garden and jumped over the wall. As they ran throughout the night, they could not stop trembling and did not know where they were going.

When the ogre awoke the next morning, he said to his wife, "Go upstairs and dress the little rascals you took in last night."

The ogress was astonished by her husband's kindness, never suspecting the sort of dressing he meant her to give them. Thus she merely imagined that he was ordering her to go and put on their clothes. When she went upstairs, she was greatly surprised to find her daughters murdered and swimming in their blood. All at once she fainted (for this is the first thing that most women do in similar circumstances). Fearing that his wife was taking too long in carrying out the task he had given her to do, the ogre went upstairs to help her. He was no less surprised than his wife when he came upon the frightful spectacle.

"Ah! What have I done?" he exclaimed. "The wretches shall pay for it, and right now!" He then threw a jugful of water in his wife's face, and after reviving her, he said, "Quick! Fetch me my seven-league boots[3] so I can go and catch them."

After setting out, he ran far and wide and at last came upon the tracks of the poor children, who were not more than a hundred yards from their father's house. They saw the ogre striding from hill to hill and stepping over rivers as easily as if they were the smallest brooks. Little Thumbling noticed a hollow cave nearby and hid his brothers in it, and while watching the movements of the ogre, he crept in after them. Now the ogre, feeling very tired because his long journey had been to no avail, needed to rest, especially since seven-league boots make the wearer very exhausted. By chance he sat down on the very rock in which the little boys had concealed themselves. Since the ogre was quite worn out, he soon fell asleep and

---

3. Magic boots common in European folklore. The boots adjust to the size of the wearer and allow the wearer to cover seven leagues, or twenty-one miles, in one step. The boots are mainly worn by giants and are often stolen by small and cunning heroes.

began to snore so terribly that the poor children were just as frightened as they had been when he had grabbed the large knife to cut their throats.

Little Thumbling was not as much alarmed and told his brothers to run straight into the house while the ogre was sound asleep and not to worry about him. They took his advice and quickly ran home. Little Thumbling now approached the ogre and carefully pulled off his boots, which he immediately put on himself. The boots were very large and very long, but since they were fairy boots, they possessed the quality of increasing or diminishing in size according to the leg of the person who wore them. Thus they fit him just as if they had been made for him. He went straight to the ogre's house, where he found the wife weeping over her murdered daughters.

"Your husband is in great danger," Thumbling said to her. "He's been captured by a band of robbers who have sworn to kill him if he doesn't give them all his gold and silver. He saw me just at the moment they had their daggers at his throat, and he begged me to come and tell you about his predicament and to ask you to give me all his ready cash without holding anything back. Otherwise, they'll kill him without mercy. Since time was of the essence, he insisted I take his seven-league boots, which you see me wearing, so that I might go faster and also so that you'd be sure I wasn't an imposter."

The good woman was very much alarmed by this news and immediately gave Thumbling all the money she could find, for the ogre was not a bad husband to her, even though he ate little children. So, loaded down with the ogre's entire wealth, Little Thumbling rushed back to his father's house, where he was received with great joy.

There are many people who differ in their account of this part of the story, and who assert that Little Thumbling never committed the theft, and that he only considered himself justified in taking the ogre's seven-league boots because the ogre had used them expressly to run after little children. These people argue that they got their story from good authority and had even eaten and drunk in the woodcutter's house. They maintain that, after Little Thumbling had put on the ogre's boots, he went to the court, where he knew they were anxious to learn about the army and the outcome of a battle that was being fought within two hundred miles of them. They say he went to the king and told him that if he, the king, so desired, he would bring back news of the army before dusk. The king promised him a large sum of money if he did so. Little Thumbling brought news that very evening, and since this first journey gave him a certain reputation, he earned whatever he chose to ask. Not only did the king pay most liberally for taking his orders to the army, but numerous ladies gave him anything he wanted for news of their lovers, and this was the best source of his income. Occasionally he met some wives who entrusted him with letters for their husbands, but they paid him so poorly and this amounted to such a trifling that he did not even bother to put down what he got for that service among his receipts.

After he had been a courier for some time and saved a great deal of money, he returned to his father, and you cannot imagine how joyful his family was at seeing him again. He made them all comfortable by buying newly created positions[4] for his father and brothers. In this way, he made sure they were all established, and at the same time, he made certain that he did perfectly well at the court himself.

Moral

No longer are children said to be a hardship,
If they possess great charm, good looks, and wit.
If one is weak, however, and knows not what to say,
Mocked he'll be and chased until he runs far away.
Yet, sometimes it's this child, very least expected,
Who makes his fortune and has his honor resurrected.

JACOB AND WILHELM GRIMM

Hansel and Gretel†

A poor woodcutter lived with his wife and his two children on the edge of a large forest. The boy was called Hansel and the girl Gretel. The woodcutter did not have much food around the house, and when a great famine devastated the entire country, he could no longer provide enough for his family's daily meals. One night, as he was lying in bed and thinking about his worries, he began tossing and turning. Then he sighed and said to his wife, "What's to become of us? How can we feed our poor children when we don't even have enough for ourselves?"

"I'll tell you what," answered his wife. "Early tomorrow morning we'll take the children out into the forest where it's most dense. We'll build a fire and give them each a piece of bread. Then we'll go about our work and leave them alone. They won't find their way back home, and we'll be rid of them."

"No, wife," the man said. "I won't do this. I don't have the heart to leave my children in the forest. The wild beasts would soon come and tear them apart."

"Oh, you fool!" she said. "Then all four of us will have to starve to death. You'd better start planing the boards for our coffins!" She continued to harp on this until he finally agreed to do what she suggested.

"But still, I feel sorry for the poor children," he said.

The two children had not been able to fall asleep that night either. Their hunger kept them awake, and when they heard what their step-mother said to their father, Gretel wept bitter tears and said to Hansel, "Now it's all over for us."

"Be quiet, Gretel," Hansel said. "Don't get upset. I'll soon find a way to help us."

---

4. During Louis XIV's reign, his director of finances, Louys Phélypeaux, set up a system in which titles and official positions could be bought by the bourgeoisie. In this way, the royal treasury could benefit. Here Little Thumbling buys positions to secure the future of his family.

† Jacob and Wilhelm Grimm, "Hansel and Gretel"—"Hänsel und Grethel" (1857), No. 15 in Kinder- und Hausmärchen. Gesammelt durch die Brüder Grimm (Göttingen: Dieterich, 1857).

When their parents had fallen asleep, Hansel put on his little jacket, opened the bottom half of the door, and crept outside. The moon was shining very brightly, and the white pebbles glittered in front of the house like pure silver coins. Hansel stooped down to the ground and stuffed his pocket with as many pebbles as he could fit in. Then he went back and said to Gretel, "Don't worry, my dear little sister. Just sleep in peace. God will not forsake us." And he lay down again in his bed.

At dawn, even before the sun began to rise, the woman came and woke the two children.

"Get up, you lazybones!" she said. "We're going into the forest to fetch some wood." Then she gave each one of them a piece of bread and said, "Now you have something for your noonday meal, but don't eat it before then because you're not getting anything else."

Gretel put the bread under her apron because Hansel had the pebbles in his pocket. Then they all set out together toward the forest. After they had walked a while, Hansel stopped and looked back at the house. He did this time and again until his father said, "Hansel, what are you looking at there? Why are you dawdling? Pay attention, and don't forget how to use your legs!"

"Oh, father," said Hansel, "I'm looking at my little white cat that's sitting up on the roof and wants to say good-bye to me."

"You fool," the mother said. "That's not a cat. It's the morning sun shining on the chimney."

But Hansel had not been looking at the cat. Instead, he had been taking the shiny pebbles from his pocket and constantly dropping them on the ground. When they reached the middle of the forest, the father said, "Children, I want you to gather some wood. I'm going to make a fire so you won't get cold."

Hansel and Gretel gathered together some brushwood and built quite a nice little pile. The brushwood was soon kindled, and when the fire was ablaze, the woman said, "Now, children, lie down by the fire, and rest yourselves. We're going into the forest to chop wood. When we're finished, we'll come back and get you."

Hansel and Gretel sat by the fire, and when noon came, they ate their pieces of bread. Since they heard the sounds of the ax, they thought their father was nearby. But it was not the ax. Rather, it was a branch that he had tied to a dead tree, and the wind was banging it back and forth. After they had been sitting there for a long time, they became so weary that their eyes closed, and they fell sound asleep. By the time they finally awoke, it was already pitch-black, and Gretel began to cry and said, "How are we going to get out of the forest?"

But Hansel comforted her by saying, "Just wait a while until the moon has risen. Then we'll find the way."

And when the full moon had risen, Hansel took his little sister by the hand and followed the pebbles that glittered like newly minted silver coins and showed them the way. They walked the whole nightlong and arrived back at their father's house at break of day. They knocked at the door, and when the woman opened it and saw that it was Hansel and Gretel, she said, "You wicked children, why did you sleep so long in the forest? We thought you'd never come back again."

But the father was delighted because he had been deeply troubled by the way he had abandoned them in the forest.

Not long after that the entire country was once again ravaged by famine, and one night the children heard their mother talking to their father in bed: "Everything's been eaten up again. We only have half a loaf of bread, but after it's gone, that will be the end of our food. The children must leave. This time we'll take them even farther into the forest so they won't find their way back home again. Otherwise, there's no hope for us."

All this saddened the father, and he thought, "It'd be much better to share your last bite to eat with your children." But the woman would not listen to anything he said. She just scolded and reproached him. Indeed, whoever starts something must go on with it, and since he had given in the first time, he also had to yield a second time.

However, the children were still awake and had overheard their conversation. When their parents had fallen asleep, Hansel got up, intending to go out and gather pebbles as he had done before, but the woman had locked the door, and Hansel could not get out. Nevertheless, he comforted his little sister and said, "Don't cry, Gretel. Just sleep in peace. The dear Lord is bound to help us."

Early the next morning the woman came and got the children out of bed. They each received little pieces of bread, but they were smaller than the last time. On the way into the forest Hansel crumbled the bread in his pocket and stopped as often as he could to throw the crumbs on the ground.

"Hansel, why are you always stopping and looking around?" asked the father. "Keep going!"

"I'm looking at my little pigeon that's sitting on the roof and wants to say good-bye to me," Hansel answered.

"Fool!" the woman said. "That's not your little pigeon. It's the morning sun shining on the chimney."

But little by little Hansel managed to scatter all the bread crumbs on the path. The woman led the children even deeper into the forest until they came to a spot they had never in their lives seen before. Once again a large fire was made, and the mother said, "Just keep sitting here, children. If you get tired, you can sleep a little. We're going into the forest to chop wood, and in the evening, when we're done, we'll come and get you."

When noon came, Gretel shared her bread with Hansel, who had scattered his along the way. Then they fell asleep, and evening passed, but no one came for the poor children. Only when it was pitch-black did they finally wake up, and Hansel comforted his little sister by saying, "Just wait until the moon has risen, Gretel. Then we'll see the little breadcrumbs that I scattered. They'll show us the way back home."

When the moon rose, they set out but could not find the crumbs because the many thousands of birds that fly about the forest and fields had devoured them.

"Don't worry, we'll find the way," Hansel said to Gretel, but they could not find it. They walked the entire night and all the next day as well, from morning till night, but they did not get out of the forest. They were now also very hungry, for they had had nothing to eat except some berries that they had found growing on the ground. Eventually they became so tired that their legs would no longer carry them, and they lay down beneath a tree and fell asleep.

It was now the third morning since they had left their father's house. They began walking again, and they kept going deeper and deeper into the forest. If help did not arrive soon, they were bound to perish of hunger and exhaustion. At noon they saw a beautiful bird as white as snow sitting on a branch. It sang with such a lovely voice that the children stood still and listened to it. When the bird finished its song, it flapped its wings and flew ahead of them. They followed it until they came to a little house that was made of bread. Moreover, it had cake for a roof and pure sugar for windows.

"What a blessed meal!" said Hansel. "Let's have a taste. I want to eat a piece of the roof. Gretel, you can have some of the window since it's sweet."

Hansel reached up high and broke off a piece of the roof to see how it tasted, and Gretel leaned against the windowpanes and nibbled on them. Then they heard a shrill voice cry from inside:

> "Nibble, nibble, I hear a mouse.
> Who's that nibbling at my house?"

The children answered:

> "The wind, the wind; it's very mild,
> blowing like the Heavenly Child."

And they did not bother to stop eating or let themselves be distracted. Since the roof tasted so good, Hansel ripped off a large piece and pulled it down, while Gretel pushed out a round piece of the windowpane, sat down, and ate it with great relish. Suddenly the door opened, and a very old woman leaning on a crutch came slinking out of the house. Hansel and Gretel were so tremendously frightened that they dropped what they had in their hands. But the old woman wagged her head and said, "Well now, dear children, who brought you here? Just come inside and stay with me. Nobody's going to harm you."

She took them both by the hand and led them into her house. Then she served them a good meal of milk and pancakes with sugar and apples and nuts. Afterward, she made up two little beds with white sheets, where-upon Hansel and Gretel lay down in them and thought they were in heaven.

The old woman, however, had only pretended to be friendly. She was really a wicked witch on the lookout for children and had built the house made of bread only to lure them to her. As soon as she had any children in her power, she would kill, cook, and eat them. It would be like a feast day for her. Now witches have red eyes and cannot see very far, but they have a keen sense of smell, like animals, and can detect when human beings are near them. Therefore, when Hansel and Gretel had come into her vicinity, she had laughed wickedly and scoffed, "They're mine! They'll never get away from me!"

Early the next morning, before the children were awake, she got up and looked at the two of them sleeping so sweetly with full rosy cheeks. Then she muttered to herself, "They'll certainly make for a tasty meal!"

She seized Hansel with her scrawny hands and carried him into a small pen, where she locked him up behind a grilled door. No matter how much he screamed, it did not help. Then she went back to Gretel, shook her until she woke up, and yelled, "Get up, you lazybones! I want you to fetch some water and cook your brother something nice. He's sitting outside in a pen, and we've got to fatten him up. Then, when he's fat enough, I'm going to eat him."

Gretel began to weep bitter tears, but they were all in vain. She had to do what the wicked witch demanded. So the very best food was cooked for poor Hansel, while Gretel got nothing but crab shells. Every morning the old woman went slinking to the little pen and called out, "Hansel, stick out your finger so I can feel how fat you are."

However, Hansel stuck out a little bone, and since the old woman had poor eyesight, she thought the bone was Hansel's finger. She was puzzled that Hansel did not get any fatter, and when a month had gone by and Hansel still seemed to be thin, she was overcome by her impatience and decided not to wait any longer.

"Hey there, Gretel!" she called to the little girl. "Get a move on and fetch some water! I don't care whether Hansel's fat or thin. He's going to be slaughtered tomorrow, and then I'll cook him."

Oh, how the poor little sister wailed as she was carrying the water, and how the tears streamed down her cheeks!

"Dear God, help us!" she exclaimed. "If only the wild beasts had eaten us in the forest, then we could have at least died together!"

Early the next morning Gretel had to go out, hang up a kettle full of water, and light the fire.

"First we'll bake," the old woman said. "I've already heated the oven and kneaded the dough." She pushed poor Gretel out to the oven, where the flames were leaping from the fire. "Crawl inside," said the witch, "and see if it's properly heated so we can slide the bread in."

The witch intended to close the oven door once Gretel had climbed inside, for the witch wanted to bake her and eat her, too. But Gretel sensed what she had in mind and said, "I don't know how to do it. How do I get in?"

"You stupid goose," the old woman said. "The opening's large enough. Watch, even I can get in!"

She waddled up to the oven and stuck her head through the oven door. Then Gretel gave her a push that sent her flying inside and shut the iron door and bolted it. *Whew!* The witch began to howl dreadfully, but Gretel ran away, and the godless witch was miserably burned to death.

Meanwhile, Gretel ran straight to Hansel, opened the pen, and cried out, "Hansel, we're saved! The old witch is dead!"

Then Hansel jumped out of the pen like a bird that hops out of a cage when the door is opened. My how happy they were! They hugged each other, danced around, and kissed. Since they no longer had anything to fear, they went into the witch's house, and there they found chests filled with pearls and jewels all over the place.

"They're certainly much better than pebbles," said Hansel, and he put whatever he could fit into his pockets, and Gretel said, "I'm going to carry some home, too." And she filled her apron full of jewels and pearls.

"We'd better be on our way now," said Hansel, "so we can get out of the witch's forest."

When they had walked for a few hours, they reached a large river.

"We can't get across," said Hansel. "I don't see a bridge or any way over it."

"There are no boats either," Gretel responded, "but there's a white duck swimming over there. It's bound to help us across if I ask it." Then she cried out:

> "Help us, help us, little duck!
> We're Hansel and Gretel, out of luck.
> We can't get over, try as we may.
> Please take us across right away!"

The little duck came swimming up to them, and Hansel got on top of its back and told his sister to sit down beside him.

"No," Gretel answered. "We'll be too heavy for the little duck. Let it carry us across one at a time."

The kind little duck did just that, and when they were safely across and had walked on for some time, the forest became more and more familiar to them, and finally they caught sight of their father's house from afar. They began to run at once, and soon rushed into the house and threw themselves around their father's neck. The man had not had a single happy hour since he had abandoned his children in the forest, and in the meantime his wife had died. Gretel opened and shook out the apron so that the pearls and jewels bounced about the room, and Hansel added to this by throwing one handful after another from his pocket. Now all their troubles were over, and they lived together in utmost joy.

My tale is done. See the mouse run. Catch it, whoever can, and then you can make a great big cap out of its fur.

Inconvenient Marriages

Scholars have endeavored for years to determine who the originator of this tale was, Mlle Bernard or Perrault, but they have never produced conclusive proof. One thing is certain: though the tale used certain motifs from the oral tradition, it is apparently a literary product which was conceived by Bernard and Perrault to comment on marriages of convenience in French upper-class society at the end of the seventeenth century. The major folk influence came from the beast bridegroom tales in which a young woman is generally compelled to live with and/or marry a monstrous creature. Both Mlle Bernard and Perrault treat this theme in ironic manner, and in contrast to the traditional happy end of fairy tales, they leave the reader wondering whether marriage to an intelligent hideous creature is worth the sacrifice of true love, no matter how intelligent one becomes. In this case, Perrault's tale is more an apology for the marriage of convenience while Mlle Bernard's narrative is a scintillating critique. Mme Le Prince de Beaumont's treatment of this theme reflects a more conservative position since she was concerned with domesticating young women so that they could advance in upper-class society.

CATHERINE BERNARD

Riquet with the Tuft†

A grand nobleman of Grenada, whose wealth was worthy of his birth, experienced a domestic calamity that poisoned all the treasures that made up his fortune. His only daughter, who was born with beautiful features, was so stupid that her beauty itself only served to make her appear distasteful. Her actions were anything but graceful. Her figure, though slender, made an awkward impression since it lacked spirit.

Mama—that was the name of this girl—did not have enough intelligence to know that she was not intelligent, but there was enough to let her feel that she was disdained, even though she could not figure out why. One day, when she was out walking by herself—an ordinary habit for her— she saw a man hideous enough to be a monster emerge from the ground. As soon as she caught sight of him, she wanted to flee, but his words called Mama back.

"Stop," he said to her. "I've got some unpleasant things to tell you, but I've also got something nice to promise you. Even with your beauty you

---

† Catherine Bernard, "Riquet with the Tuft"—"Riquet à la houppe" (1697), in *Inès de Cadoue* (Paris: Jouvenol, 1696). The etymology of the name Riquet is not certain. Mlle Bernard came from Normandy, and in that region *riquet* referred to someone who was a hunchback or disfigured. It is also possible that *riquet* is the diminutive of *Henriquet*, or "little Henry."

717

have something—and I don't know what's caused it—that makes people disregard you. It has to do with your incapacity to think, and without my making a value judgment, this fault makes you as inferior as I am, for my body is like your mind. That's the cruel thing I had to say to you. But from the stunned manner in which you're looking at me, I think I've given your mind too little credit, since I fear I've insulted you. This is what makes me despair when I approach the subject of my proposition. However, I'm going to risk making it to you. Do you want intelligence?"

"Yes," Mama responded in a manner that might have indicated no.

"Very good," he said. "Here's the way. You must love Riquet with the Tuft. That's my name, and you must marry me by the end of a year. That's the condition that I'll impose on you. Think it over. If you can't, repeat the words that I'm going to say to you as often as possible. They'll eventually teach you how to think. Farewell for a year. Here are the words that will dissipate your indolence and at the same time cure your imbecility:

> "Love can surely inspire me
> To help me shed stupidity,
> And teach me to care with sincerity,
> If I have the right quality."

As Mama began to utter these words in the proper way, her figure stood out to her advantage; she became more vivacious, her movements more free, and she kept repeating the verse. She went to her father's house and told him something coherent, then a little later, something intelligent, and finally, something witty. Such a great and rapid transformation could not be ignored anymore by those people who were interested in her. Lovers came in droves, and Mama was no longer alone at the balls or during promenades. Soon she made men unfaithful and jealous. People talked only about her and for her.

It was easy for her to find someone more handsome than Riquet with the Tuft among those men who found her charming. The mind that he had given started to turn against her benefactor. The words that she conscientiously repeated filled her with love, but the effect was contrary to Riquet's intentions: the love was not for him.

She favored the most handsome of those men who sighed for her, and he was not the best match with regard to his wealth. Thus, her father and mother, who saw that they had wished this misfortune on their daughter by desiring she should have a mind, and who realized that they could not deprive her of it, thought at least they should give her lessons against love. But to prohibit a young and pretty person from loving would be like prohibiting a tree from bearing leaves in the month of May. She only loved Arada a little more—that was the name of her lover.

She made sure not to tell anyone about how she happened to obtain her mind. Her vanity caused her to keep this a secret. Thus, she had enough intelligence to understand the importance of hiding the mystery of how she managed to become so intelligent.

However, the year that Riquet with the Tuft had given her to learn how to think and decide whether she wanted to marry him was about to end. With great anguish, she awaited this deadline. Her mind, now a baneful gift, did not let one single torturous circumstance escape her. To lose her lover forever, to be under the power of someone about whom the only thing she knew was his deformity, and which was perhaps his least fault, and finally to become engaged to marry someone and to accept his gifts that she did not want to return—these thoughts kept passing through her mind.

One day, when she was contemplating her cruel destiny and had wandered off alone, she heard a huge noise and subterranean voices singing the words that Riquet with the Tuft had taught her. She shuddered when she heard them, for it was the signal of disaster. Soon the ground opened. She descended gradually and saw Riquet with the Tuft surrounded by people who were just as deformed as he was. What a spectacle for a person who had been pursued by the most charming men in her country! Her torment was even greater than her surprise. She let loose a flood of tears without speaking. It was the only human thing she did that was beyond the control of the mind that Riquet with the Tuft had given her. In his turn, he looked at her with sadness.

"Madame," he said to her, "it's not difficult to see that I'm more distasteful to you than when I first appeared before your eyes. I myself am bewildered by what has happened in giving you a mind. But, in the last analysis, you're free, and you have the choice of marrying me or returning to your former condition. I'll send you back to your father's house the way I found you, or I'll make you mistress of this kingdom. I am king of the gnomes, and you would be queen, and if you can excuse my shape and overlook certain things that are distasteful, you could have an enormous number of other pleasures here. I am master of all the treasures locked up in the earth, and you would be mistress of these treasures. With gold and intelligence, who could want more from life? I'm afraid that you've developed some kind of false squeamishness. I'm afraid that I'll appear meager in the midst of all my riches. But if I and my treasures don't please you, just speak up. I'll take you away from here and bring you home because I don't want anything to trouble my happiness here. You have two days to become acquainted with this spot and to decide my fate and yours."

After leading her into a magnificent apartment, Riquet with the Tuft left her alone. She was attended by gnomes of her sex, whose ugliness did not repel her as much as that of the men. They entertained her with a meal and good company. After dinner she saw a play in which the deformed actors prevented her from developing an interest in the subject of the drama. That evening a ball was held in her honor, but she attended it without desiring to please anyone. Indeed, she felt a natural disgust that would not pay back Riquet with the gratitude he deserved, nor could she show her appreciation for all the pleasures he provided even under threat.

In order to save herself from this odious husband, she would have returned to her stupidity without feeling grief if she had not had a lover, but it would have meant losing a lover in a most cruel manner. It was also true that she would lose her lover by marrying the gnome—she would never be able to see Arada, speak with him, or send him news about herself, for Riquet would suspect her of infidelity. In sum, by getting rid of the man she loved, she was going to marry a husband who would always be odious even when he was pleasant. Moreover, he was a monster. Thus, the decision was a difficult one to make. When the two days were over, her mind was not any more made up than it was before. She told the gnome that it had been impossible for her to reach a decision.

"That's a decision against me," he told her. "So now, I'll return you to your former condition that you didn't dare to choose."

She trembled. The idea of losing her lover through the disdain he would show her had such a powerful influence over her that she felt compelled to renounce him.

"Well, then!" the gnome said to her. "You've decided. It must be up to you."

Riquet with the Tuft did not make it difficult. He married her, and Mama's intelligence increased even more through this marriage, but her unhappiness increased in proportion to the growth of her mind. She was horrified to have given herself to a monster, and it was never possible for her to comprehend how she could spend one moment with him.

The gnome realized very well how much his wife hated him, and he was hurt by it, even though he prided himself on the force of his mind. This aversion was a constant reproach about his deformity and made him detest women, marriage, and curiosity so much so that he had become totally distraught. He often left Mama alone, and since she was reduced to just thinking, she thought it was necessary to convince Arada with his own eyes that she was not unfaithful. She knew he could get to this place because she easily had managed to get there. At the very least it was necessary to send him news about herself and explain her absence because of the gnome who had abducted her. Once Arada saw him, he would know she was loyal. There is nothing impossible that a woman who has a mind and is in love cannot do. So she won over a gnome who carried news about her to Arada. Fortunately, this was still during the time that lovers were faithful to one another. He had become despondent over Mama's absence without becoming bitter about it. His mind was not even plagued by harmful suspicions. He maintained that, if he died, he would not have the least negative thought about his mistress and did not want to seek a cure for his love. It is not difficult to believe that, with such feelings, he was willing to risk his life to find Mama as soon as he knew the place where she was. Nor did she forbid him to go there.

Mama's cheerfulness returned gradually, and her beauty made her even more perfect, but the gnome's love caused her consternation. He had too much intelligence, and he knew Mama's repugnance for him too well to believe that she had become accustomed to being there and had become sweeter so suddenly. Mama was imprudent enough to get dressed up, and he did himself more than enough justice to realize that he was not worthy of this. So he searched as long as he could until he discovered that there was a handsome man hiding in his palace. As a result, he thought up an extremely fine way to revenge himself and take care of him. First, Riquet ordered Mama to appear before him.

"It doesn't amuse me to make complaints and reproaches," he said. "I let human beings have their share of them. When I gave you a mind,

I presumed I would enjoy it. However, you've used it against me. Still, I won't deprive you of it completely. You've submitted to the law that was imposed on you. But even if you did not break our agreement, you didn't observe it to the letter. Let us split the difference. You shall have a mind during the night. I don't want a stupid wife, but you shall be stupid during the day for whomever you please."

All at once Mama felt a dullness of mind that she did not understand anymore. During the night, her ideas were aroused again, and she thought about her misfortune. She cried and was not able to console herself or find the ways through her wisdom to help herself.

The following night she noticed that her husband slept very soundly. She placed an herb on his nose that increased his sleep and made it last as long as she wished. She got up and moved away from the object of her wrath. Led by her dreams, she went to the place where Arada was dwelling. She thought that he might perhaps be looking for her, and she found him in a lane where they had often met and where he asked her all kinds of things. Mama told him about her misfortunes, and they were alleviated by the pleasure she had in relating them to him.

The next night they met at the same place without being followed, and their meetings continued for such a long time that their misfortune now enabled them to taste a new kind of happiness. Mama's mind and love provided her with a thousand ways to be charming and to make Arada forget that she lacked intelligence half the time.

Whenever the lovers felt the dawn of day approaching, Mama went to wake the gnome. She took care to remove the herbs that made him drowsy as soon as she was near him. When daylight arrived, she became an imbecile again, but she used the time to sleep.

Such a relatively happy condition could not last forever. The leaf that made Riquet sleep also made him snore, and a servant, who was half asleep and half awake, thought his master was grumbling. He ran to him, saw the herbs that had been placed on his nose, and removed them since he thought they were disturbing him—a cure that was to make three people unhappy all at the same time. Riquet saw that he was alone, and he searched for his wife in a rage. Either chance or his bad luck led him to the place where the two lovers had abandoned themselves to each other and had sworn eternal love to one another. He did not say anything except to touch the lover with a wand that transformed his shape into something similar to his own. And after having numerous go-rounds with him, Mama could no longer distinguish who her husband was. She lived with two husbands instead of one and never knew to whom she should address her lamentations for fear of mistaking the object of her hatred for the object of her love.

But perhaps she hardly lost anything there. In the long run lovers become husbands anyway.

CHARLES PERRAULT

Riquet with the Tuft[†]

Once upon a time there was a queen who gave birth to a son so ugly and so misshapen that for a long time it was doubtful whether he possessed a human form. A fairy, who was present at his birth, however, assured everyone that he could not fail to be pleasant because he would have a great deal of intelligence. She even added that he would be able to impart the same amount of intelligence to that person he came to love best by virtue of the gift she had just bestowed upon him. All this somewhat consoled the poor queen, who was very much distressed at having brought such a hideous little monkey into the world. It is true that, as soon as the child was able to speak, he said a thousand pretty things, and that there was an indescribable air of intelligence in all his actions that charmed everyone. I had forgotten to say that he was born with a little tuft of hair on his head, and this was the reason why he was called Riquet with the Tuft, Riquet being the family name.

At the end of seven or eight years, the queen of a neighboring kingdom gave birth to two daughters. The first that came into the world was more beautiful than daylight. The queen was so delighted that people feared her great joy might cause her some harm. The same fairy who had attended the birth of little Riquet with the Tuft was also present on this occasion, and to moderate the queen's joy, she declared that this little princess would have no intelligence whatsoever, and that she would be as stupid as she was beautiful. The queen was deeply mortified by this, but a few minutes later her chagrin became even greater still, for she gave birth to a second child who turned out to be extremely ugly.

"Don't be too upset, madame," the fairy said to her. "Your daughter will be compensated in another way. She'll have so much intelligence that her lack of beauty will hardly be noticed."

"May heaven grant it," replied the queen. "But isn't there some way to give a little intelligence to my older daughter, who is so beautiful?"

"I can't do anything for her, madame, in the way of wit," said the fairy, "but I can do a great deal in matters of beauty, and since there's nothing I would not do to please you, I shall endow her with the ability to render any person who pleases her with a beautiful or handsome appearance."

As these two princesses grew up, their qualities increased in the same proportion, and throughout the realm everyone talked about the beauty of the older daughter and the intelligence of the younger. It is also true that their defects greatly increased as they grew older. The younger daughter became uglier, and the older more stupid every day. Either she gave no

---

[†] Charles Perrault, "Riquet with the Tuft"—"Riquet à la houppe" (1697), in *Histoires ou contes du temps passé* (Paris: Claude Barbin, 1697). It is possible that Perrault used the name Riquet in the same way that Mlle Bernard did, to refer to a disfigured person. However, some scholars have argued that it was a malicious reference to Pierre-Paul de Riquet (1604–1680), a protégé of Jean-Baptiste Colbert (1619–1683), powerful controller general of finances under Louis XIV, who promoted the construction of the canal at Languedoc. Perrault had taken a dislike to him.

answer when addressed, or she said something foolish. At the same time, she was so awkward that she could not place four pieces of china on a mantel shelf without breaking one of them or drink a glass of water without spilling half of it on her clothes. Despite the great advantage beauty has for a young person, the younger sister almost always outshone the elder whenever there were social functions. At first, everyone gathered around the more beautiful girl to watch and admire her, but they soon left her for the more intelligent sister to listen to a thousand pleasant things. People were astonished to find that, in less than a quarter of an hour, not a soul would be standing near the elder sister while everyone would be surrounding the younger. Though very stupid, the elder sister noticed this and would have willingly given up all her beauty for half the intelligence of her sister.

The queen, discreet as she was, could not help reproaching her elder daughter whenever she did stupid things, and that made the poor little princess ready to die of grief. One day, when she had withdrawn into the woods to bemoan her misfortune, she saw a little man coming toward her. He was extremely ugly and unpleasant but dressed in magnificent attire. It was the young Riquet with the Tuft. He had fallen in love with her from seeing her portraits, which had been sent all around the world, and he had left his father's kingdom to have the pleasure of seeing and speaking to her. Delighted to meet her thus alone, he approached her with all the respect and politeness imaginable. After paying the usual compliments, he remarked that she was very melancholy.

"I cannot comprehend, madame," he said, "how a person so beautiful as you are can be so sad as you appear. Though I may boast of having seen an infinite number of lovely women, I can assure you that I've never beheld one whose beauty could begin to compare with yours."

"It's very kind of you to say so, sir," replied the princess, and there she stopped.

"Beauty is such a great advantage," continued Riquet, "that it ought to surpass all other things. If one possesses it, I don't see anything that could cause one much distress."

"I'd rather be as ugly as you," said the princess, "and have intelligence than be as beautiful and stupid as I am."

"There's no greater proof of intelligence, madame, than the belief that we do not have any. It's the nature of that gift that the more we have, the more we believe we are deficient in it."

"I don't know whether that's the case," the princess said, "but I know full well that I am very stupid, and that's the cause of the grief which is killing me."

"If that's all that's troubling you, madame, I can easily put an end to your distress."

"And how do you intend to manage that?" the princess asked.

"I have the power, madame, to give as much intelligence as anyone can possess to the person I love the most," Riquet with the Tuft replied. "And as you, madame, are that person, it will depend entirely on you whether or not you want to have so much intelligence, for you may have it only if you consent to marry me."

Riquet with the Tuft. From *Les Contes de Perrault*, ca. 1890.

The princess was thunderstruck and did not say a word.

"I see," said Riquet with the Tuft, "that this proposal torments you, and I'm not surprised. But I'll give you one full year to make up your mind."

The princess had so little intelligence and at the same time she had such a strong desire to possess a great deal that she imagined that the year might never come to an end. So she immediately accepted the offer made to her. No sooner did she promise Riquet with the Tuft that she would marry him twelve months from that day than she felt a complete change come over her. She found she possessed an incredible facility to say anything she wished and to say it in a polished yet easy and natural manner. She commenced right away and maintained an elegant conversation with Riquet with the Tuft. Indeed, she was so brilliant that Riquet with the Tuft believed that he had given her more wit than he had kept for himself.

When she returned to the palace, the whole court was at a loss to account for such a sudden and extraordinary change. Whereas she had formerly said a number of foolish things, she now made sensible and exceedingly clever observations. The entire court rejoiced beyond belief. Only the younger sister was not very much pleased, for she no longer held the advantage of intelligence over her elder sister. Now she merely appeared as a very ugly woman by her side, and the king let himself be guided by the elder daughter's advice. Sometimes he even held the meetings of his council in her apartment.

The news of this change spread abroad, and all the young princes of the neighboring kingdoms exerted themselves to gain her affection. Nearly all of them asked for her hand in marriage, but she found none of them sufficiently intelligent, and she listened to all of them without promising herself to anyone in particular. At last a prince arrived who was so witty and handsome that she could not help feeling attracted to him. Her father noticed this and told her that she was at perfect liberty to choose a husband for herself and that she only had to make her decision known. Now the more intelligence one possesses, the greater the difficulty one has in making up one's mind firmly about such a matter. So she thanked her father and requested some time to think it over.

By chance she took a walk in the same woods where she had met Riquet with the Tuft to ponder what she had to do with greater freedom. While she was walking, deep in thought, she heard a dull sound beneath her feet, as if there were many people running busily back and forth. After listening more attentively, she heard someone say, "Bring me that cooking pot." Another, "Give me that kettle." Another, "Put some wood on the fire." At that very same moment, the ground opened, and she saw below what appeared to be a large kitchen full of cooks, scullions, and all sorts of servants necessary for the preparation of a magnificent banquet. A group of approximately twenty to thirty cooks came forth, and they took places at a very long table set in a path of the woods. Each had a larding pin in hand and a cap on his head, and they set to work, keeping time to a melodious song. Astonished at this sight, the princess inquired who had hired them.

"Riquet with the Tuft, madame," the leader of the group replied. "His marriage is to take place tomorrow."

The princess was even more surprised than she was before, and suddenly she recalled that it was exactly a year ago that she had promised to marry Prince Riquet with the Tuft. She was indeed taken aback. The reason that she had not remembered her promise was that, when she had made it, she had still been a fool, and after receiving her new mind, she had forgotten all her follies. Now she hardly advanced another thirty steps on her walk when she encountered Riquet with the Tuft, who appeared gallant and magnificent, like a prince about to be married.

"As you can see, madame," he said, "I've kept my word to the minute, and I have no doubt but that you've come here to keep yours. By giving me your hand, you'll make me the happiest of men."

"I'll be frank with you," the princess replied. "I've yet to make up my mind on that matter, and I don't believe I'll ever be able to do so to your satisfaction."

"You astonish me, madame," Riquet with the Tuft said.

"I can believe it," the princess responded, "and assuredly, if I had to deal with a stupid person—a man without intelligence—I'd feel greatly embarrassed. 'A princess is bound by her word,' he'd say to me, 'and you must marry me as you promised to do so.' But since the man with whom I'm speaking is the most intelligent man in the world, I'm certain he'll listen to reason. As you know, when I was no better than a fool, I could not decide whether I should marry you. Now that I have the intelligence which you've given me and which renders me much more difficult to please than before, how can you expect me to make a decision today which I couldn't make then? If you seriously thought of marrying me, you made a big mistake in taking away my stupidity and enabling me to see clearer than I saw then."

"If a man without intelligence," Riquet with the Tuft replied, "would be justified, as you have just intimated, in reproaching you for your breach of promise, why do you expect, madame, that I should not be equally allowed to do the same in a matter that affects the entire happiness of my life? Is it reasonable that intelligent people should be placed at a greater disadvantage than those who have none? Can you presume this, you who have so much intelligence and have so earnestly desired to possess it? But let us come to the point, if you please. With the exception of my ugliness, is there anything about me that displeases you? Are you dissatisfied with my birth, my intelligence, my temperament, or my manners?"

"Not in the least," replied the princess. "I admire you for everything you've just mentioned."

"If so," Riquet with the Tuft responded, "I'll gain my happiness, for you have the power to make me the most pleasing of men."

"How can that be done?" the princess asked.

"It can be done," said Riquet with the Tuft, "if you love me sufficiently to wish that it should be. And, to remove your doubts, you should know that the same fairy who, on the day I was born, endowed me with the power to give intelligence to the person I chose also gave you the power to render handsome the man you loved and on whom you desired to bestow that favor."

"If that's so," the princess said, "I wish with all my heart that you may become the most charming and most handsome prince in the world, and I bestow this gift on you to the fullest extent of my power."

No sooner had the princess pronounced these words than Riquet with the Tuft appeared to her eyes as the most handsome, most strapping, and most charming man she had ever seen in the world. There are some who assert that it was not the fairy's spell but love alone that caused this transformation. They say that the princess, having reflected on the perseverance of her lover, on his prudence and all the good qualities of his heart and mind, no longer saw the deformity of his body or the ugliness of his features, that his hunch appeared to her nothing more than the effect of a man shrugging his shoulders, and that his horrible limp that she had perceived appeared to be nothing more than a slight sway that charmed her. They also say that his eyes, which squinted, seemed to her only more brilliant from that defect, which passed in her mind for a proof of the intensity of his love, and, finally, that his great red nose had something martial and heroic about it. However this may be, the princess promised to marry him on the spot, provided he obtain the consent of the king, her father.

On learning of his daughter's high regard for Riquet with the Tuft, whom he also knew to be a very intelligent and wise prince, the king accepted him with pleasure as a son-in-law. The wedding took place the next morning just as Riquet with the Tuft had foreseen and in accordance with the instructions that he had given a long time before.

Moral

That which you see written down here
Is not so fantastic because it's quite true:
We find what we love is wondrously fair,
And we find what we love intelligent, too.

Another Moral

Nature very often tends to place
Beauty in objects likely to amaze
With colors that art can never achieve.
Yet all this cannot have such an effect on the heart
As that invisible charm, hard to chart,
A charm only love can perceive.

JEANNE-MARIE LEPRINCE DE BEAUMONT

Spirituel and Astre†

Once upon a time there was a fairy who wanted to marry a king, but since she had a very bad reputation, the king preferred to risk exposing

---

† Jeanne-Marie Leprince de Beaumont, "Spirituel and Astre"—"Spirituel et Astre" (1756), in *Magasin des enfants* (Lyon: Reguilliat, 1756).

himself to all her anger than to become the husband of a woman whom nobody held in high regard. Indeed, nothing could be so troublesome for an honest man than to have a despicable wife.

Now a fairy by the name of Diamantine arranged to have this king marry a young princess whom she had raised, and she promised to defend him against the fairy called Furie. But, shortly after this, Furie was named the queen of the fairies, and her power greatly surpassed that of Diamantine so that she now had the means to avenge herself. Therefore, when the young queen was about to give birth, Furie appeared on that very day and wished the queen's son to be the ugliest boy imaginable when he came into the world. Diamantine, who was hiding in a space behind the young queen's bed and the wall, tried to console her after Furie had departed.

"Have courage," she said to her. "In spite of your enemy's malicious act, your son will be very happy one day. I want you to call him Spirituel, and not only will he have as much intelligence as possible, but he will be able to give as much as he wants to the person he loves most."

Nevertheless, the little prince was so ugly that nobody could look at him without being frightened. When he was able to express himself at a reasonable age, everyone desired to hear him talk, but they closed their eyes, and the people, who don't know what they want most of the time, developed such a strong hate for Spirituel that the king was obliged to name their second as his heir after the queen had given birth to him. Spirituel ceded the throne to his brother without a murmur, and he retreated into solitude, where he studied to improve his knowledge and was extremely happy. But the fairy Furie had not settled her account with him yet. She wanted him to be miserable, and this is what she did to make him lose his happiness.

Furie had a son called Charmant. She adored him even though he was the most stupid young man in the world. Since she would stop at nothing to make him happy, she abducted a princess who was perfectly beautiful. However, so that she would not be rebuffed by the stupidity of Charmant, she made her become as dumb as he was. This princess, who was called Astre, lived with Charmant, and even though they were sixteen years old, they could never learn to read.

Now Furie had a portrait made of Astre and carried it herself to a little house where Spirituel was living with just one servant. And her malicious plan turned out to be successful, for even though Spirituel knew that the Princess Astre was in the palace of his enemy, he fell so much in love with her that he decided to go there. At the same time, he recalled his ugliness, and he realized that he was the most unhappy creature in the world because he was certain he would seem horrible in the eyes of this beautiful maiden. So, he resisted his desire to see her for a long time until his passion finally got the better of his reason and he departed with his valet. Astre was promenading in the garden with her governess, Diamantine, when she saw the prince approach. All at once she uttered a great cry and wanted to run away. But Diamantine prevented her from doing this, and she hid her head in her hands and said to the fairy, "My dear woman, please have that nasty man go away. He frightens me to death."

The prince wanted to take advantage of the moment in which she had her eyes closed to make her a well-chosen compliment, but it was as if he were speaking Latin. She was too stupid to understand it.

"You've done enough for the first time," Furie said to the prince. "You may now retire to an apartment that I've had prepared for you, and you will have the pleasure of seeing the princess at your ease."

Perhaps you believe that Spirituel would have said something insulting to that wicked woman, but he had too much intelligence for that. Moreover, he was too agitated. Then later, matters became even worse when he overheard a conversation between Astre and Charmant. She said so many foolish things that she no longer appeared as beautiful as she had before, and thus he decided to forget her and return to his solitude. When he sought to take his leave from Diamantine, he was greatly surprised when the fairy said he would not be allowed to leave the palace, and she knew of some means to bring the princess to love him.

"I am greatly obliged to you," Spirituel responded. "But I am in no great hurry to get married. I admit that Astre is charming, yet it is only when she does not talk. The fairy Furie has cured me of my love for her by making me hear one of her conversations. I shall take her portrait with me since it is so admirable and always keeps silent."

"You are disdaining her in vain," Diamantine replied. "Your happiness depends on your marrying the princess. Let me tell you a secret that only your mother and I know: when you were born, I endowed you with the power of giving intelligence to the person you love the most. Therefore, you only have to wish for Astre to become a highly intelligent person, and she will then be perfect, for she is the best child in the world and has a great heart."

"Ah, madame," Spirituel said, "you are going to make me very miserable. Astre will become too amiable for my peace of mind, and I shall have too little to please her. However, I shall sacrifice my happiness for hers, and I shall wish her all the intelligence that depends on me."

"That is very generous," Diamantine said, "and I hope that this good deed will not remain unrewarded. Go to the palace garden at midnight. It is the time when Furie is obliged to sleep, and she loses all her powers for three hours."

The prince retired, and Diamantine went to Astre's room, where she found the young lady seated, her head in her hands, as if she were having a profound dream. When Diamantine called her, Astre said to her, "Ah, madame! If you could see what has just happened within me, you would be very surprised. It's as if I were suddenly in a new world. I can think, I can reflect!"

"Very good!" Diamantine remarked. "You will have time to think, for you will be marrying Prince Charmant in two days, and then you will be able to study everything at your convenience."

"Oh, my dear woman," Astre responded with a sigh. "Is it possible that I shall be condemned to marry Charmant? He is so stupid, so stupid, that he makes me tremble. But please tell me, why didn't I know about his stupidity before this?"

"It's because you yourself were a fool," the fairy said. "But look, there is Prince Charmant right now."

Indeed, the prince entered her room with a nest of sparrows in his hat.

"Imagine that!" he said. "I've just left my teacher in a great fit of anger because I had been emptying out this nest instead of doing my lesson with him."

"But your teacher is right to be angry with you," Astre told him. "Isn't it shameful for a young man of your age not to be able to read?"

"Oh, you bore me just as much as he does," Charmant responded. "I've got other things to do than to occupy myself with all that learning. I prefer a paddle or a ball than all the books in the world. Good-bye. I'm going to play some shuttlecock and battledore."[1]

"And am I supposed to become the wife of this man when he is so dumb?" Astre asked. "I assure you, my good woman, that I would rather die than to marry him. What a difference there is between him and the prince whom I recently met. It's true that he is very ugly, but when I recall his conversation, it seems to me that he is no longer so horrible. Why isn't he as good-looking as Charmant? But when all is said and done, what's the use of good looks? A sickness can ruin them. Old age causes good looks to fade for sure. What happens then to those who do not have minds? In truth, my dear woman, if I had to choose, I would prefer that prince despite his ugliness over the stupid man they are making me marry."

"I am very pleased to see you think in such a reasonable manner," Diamantine said.

As soon as midnight sounded, the good fairy proposed to the princess to descend into the garden, where they went and sat down on a bench. Soon Spirituel joined them, and he was overjoyed when he heard Astre speak. Indeed, he was convinced that he had given her as much intelligence as he himself had. On her side, Astre was enchanted by the prince's conversation. But when Diamantine informed her about how much she was obliged to Spirituel for her ability to think, her gratitude made her forget his ugliness even though she saw it perfectly well, for it was as clear as the moon.

"I am greatly obliged to you!" she told him. "How may I repay you?"

"It's easy to do," the fairy responded. "You can become Spirituel's wife. It only depends on you to give him just as much beauty as he has given you intelligence."

"I would be very angry to do this," Astre responded. "Spirituel pleases me exactly as he is. I don't care whether he is handsome. He is amiable, and that's enough for me."

"I am going to transport you to Spirituel's realm," the fairy said. "His brother is dead, and the hate that Furie had inspired in the people against him no longer exists."

In fact, the people were happy to see Spirituel return, and he only had to spend three months in his kingdom for the people to accustom themselves to his looks. But they never ceased to admire his intelligence.

---

1. A game similar to badminton. A shuttlecock was a cork stuck with feathers and batted with a paddle called a battledore.

Bloodthirsty Husbands

Many historians and literary critics have endeavored to identify Bluebeard as a real person and have associated him with a man named Gilles de Rais, a bloodthirsty murderer of the seventeenth century. However, the facts of Gilles de Rais's life and the stories told about him do not really correspond to the character and events in Perrault's tale. If anything, Perrault borrowed numerous motifs from the oral folktale tradition to form his original tale: the marriage with a repulsive figure, the curiosity of the woman (Pandora's box), the bloody key as a sign of disobedience, and the delay of the execution. Similar to his version of "Little Red Riding Hood," Perrault's tale of "Bluebeard" places the blame of near violence on the wife's curiosity. It is symbolically implied through the stained key that, if she had not been curious, Bluebeard might not have tried to murder her. In contrast, the French and German folktale variants in the oral tradition that led to the production of the Grimms' "Fitcher's Bird" and "The Robber Bridegroom" depict a more active heroine, who is capable of saving her own life as well as her sisters. These oral tales predated Perrault's literary "Bluebeard" and were known in France and Germany. Quite often they involve a young woman who is obliged to marry a horrible-looking man, or she becomes engaged to him, and she becomes suspicious of his strange behavior. When she finds herself in difficulty, she often uses talking birds or dogs to carry messages that will save her. Sometimes she uses disguises or other ruses to outwit a murderous bridegroom, and the key symbol is not a key but an egg. Not only did the Grimms know Perrault's "Bluebeard" and various oral versions, but they were familiar with Ludwig Tieck's play *Ritter Blaubart* (*The Knight Bluebeard*, 1797). By the time the Grimms published their first edition of *Children's and Household Tales*, the two strands of the tales, the curious maiden in "Bluebeard" and the active, courageous heroine in "The Robber Bridegroom" and "Fitcher's Bird," had been woven into many different oral and literary versions in the nineteenth century. Ludwig Bechstein published two in his *Deutsches Märchenbuch* (1857), and the literary adaptations in France led to Anatole France's witty adaptation, "Les sept femmes de la Barbe-Bleue d'après des documents authentiques" ("The Seven Wives of Bluebeard according to Authentic Documents," 1909), in which Bluebeard is depicted as the unwitting victim of avaricious and adulterous wives, and to Béla Bartók's famous opera, *Duke Bluebeard's Castle* (1911).

CHARLES PERRAULT

Bluebeard†

Once upon a time there was a man who had fine town and country houses, gold and silver plates, embroidered furniture, and gilded coaches. Unfortunately, however, this man had a blue beard, which made him look so ugly and terrible that there was not a woman or girl who did not run away from him.

Now, one of his neighbors, a lady of quality,[1] had two daughters, who were perfectly beautiful, and he proposed to marry one of them, leaving the choice up to the mother which of the two she would give him. Yet, neither one would have him, and they kept sending him back and forth between them, not being able to make up their minds to marry a man who had a blue beard. What increased their distaste for him was that he had already had several wives, and nobody knew what had become of them.

In order to cultivate their acquaintance, Bluebeard took the sisters, their mother, three or four of their most intimate friends, and some young people who resided in the neighborhood to one of his country estates[2] where they spent an entire week. Their heads were filled with nothing but excursions, hunting and fishing, parties, balls, entertainments, and feasts. Nobody went to bed; the whole night was spent in merry games and gambols. In short, all went off so well that the youngest daughter began to find that the beard of the master of the house was not as blue as it used to be, and that he was a very worthy man.

Immediately upon their return to town the marriage took place. At the end of a month Bluebeard told his wife that he was obliged to take a journey concerning a matter of great consequence, and it would occupy him at least six weeks. He asked her to amuse herself as best as she could during his absence and to invite her closest friends, to take them into the country with her if she pleased, and to offer them fine meals.

"Here are the keys to my two great storerooms," he said to her. "These are the keys to the chests in which are kept the gold and silver plates that are only used on special occasions. These are the keys to the strong boxes in which I keep my money. These open the caskets that contain my jewels. And this is the passkey to all the apartments. As for this small key, it is for the little room at the end of the long corridor on the ground floor. Open everything, and go everywhere except into that little room, which I forbid you to enter. My orders are to be strictly obeyed, and if you should dare to open the door, my anger will exceed anything you have ever experienced."

---

† Charles Perrault, "Bluebeard"—"La barbe bleue" (1697), in *Histoires ou contes du temps passé* (Paris: Claude Barbin, 1697).

1. This lady was undoubtedly of the nobility, but she was probably either widowed or poor, and thus she was eager to have one of her daughters marry a rich man.

2. If one was from the wealthy nobility or bourgeoisie, it was customary at that time from Italy to France to maintain a country estate which became the family seat. Since Bluebeard is immensely wealthy, he has several country estates.

She promised to carry out all his instructions exactly as he had ordered, and after he embraced her, he got into his coach and set out on his journey. The neighbors and friends of the young bride did not wait for her invitation, so eager were they to see all the treasures contained in the mansion. They had not ventured to enter it while the husband was at home because they had been frightened of his blue beard. Now they began running through all the rooms, closets, and wardrobes, each apartment exceeding the other in beauty and richness. Then they ascended to the storerooms, where they could not admire enough the number and elegance of the tapestries, the beds, the sofas, the cabinets, the stands, the tables, and the mirrors in which they could see themselves from head to foot. Some mirrors had frames of glass, and some of gilt metal, more beautiful and magnificent than had ever been seen. They could not desist from extolling and envying the good fortune of their friend, who in the meanwhile was not in the least entertained by the sight of all these treasures because of her impatience to open the little room on the ground floor. Her curiosity increased to such a degree that, without reflecting how rude it was to leave her company, she ran down a back staircase in such haste that she nearly broke her neck two or three times. Once at the door of the room she paused for a moment, recalling her husband's prohibition, and thinking that some misfortune might strike her for her disobedience. But the temptation was so strong that she could not withstand it. Therefore, she took the small key, and with a trembling hand, she opened the door of the little room.

At first she could discern nothing, the windows being closed, but after a short time she began to perceive that the floor was all covered with clotted blood that reflected the dead bodies of several women suspended from the walls. These were all the wives of Bluebeard, who had cut their throats one after the other. She thought she would die from the fright, and the key to the room, which she had taken from the lock, fell from her hand. After recovering her senses a little, she picked up the key, locked the door again, and went up to her chamber to compose herself. Yet she was unsuccessful because she was too upset. Then she noticed that the key to the room was stained with blood. She wiped it two or three times, but the blood would not come off. In vain she washed it, and even scrubbed it with sand and grit. But the blood remained, for the key was enchanted, and there was no way of cleaning it completely. When the blood was washed off one side, it came back on the other.

That very evening Bluebeard returned from his journey and said that he had received letters on the road informing him that the business on which he had set forth had been settled to his advantage. His wife did all she could to persuade him that she was delighted by his speedy return. The next morning he asked her to return his keys. She gave them to him, but her hand trembled so much that he did not have any difficulty in guessing what had occurred.

"Why is it," he asked, "that the key to the little room is not with the others?"

"I must have left it upstairs on my table," she replied.

"Bring it to me without fail and right now," said Bluebeard.

After several excuses she was compelled to produce the key. Once Blue-beard examined it, he said to his wife, "Why is there some blood on this key?"

"I don't know," answered the poor woman, paler than death.

"You don't know?" Bluebeard responded. "I know well enough. You wanted to enter the room! Well, madame, you shall enter it, and you shall take your place among the ladies you saw there."

She flung herself at her husband's feet, weeping and begging his pardon, with all the signs of true repentance for having disobeyed him. Her beauty and affliction might have melted a rock.

"You must die, madame," he said, "and immediately."

"If I must die," she replied, looking at him with eyes bathed in tears, "give me a little time to say my prayers."

"I shall give you a quarter of an hour," Bluebeard answered, "but not a minute more."

As soon as he had left her, she called her sister and said to her, "Sister Anne"—for that was her name—"go up, I beg you, to the top of the tower and see if my brothers are coming. They promised me that they would come to see me today. If you see them, give them a signal to make haste."

Sister Anne mounted to the top of the tower, and the poor distressed creature called to her every now and then, "Anne! Sister Anne! Do you see anything coming?"

And sister Anne answered her, "I see nothing but the sun making dust, and the grass growing green."

In the meantime, Bluebeard held a cutlass in his hand and called out to his wife with all his might, "Come down quickly, or I'll come up there."

"Please, one minute more," replied his wife, who immediately repeated in a low voice, "Anne! Sister Anne! Do you see anything coming?"

And sister Anne replied, "I see nothing but the sun making dust, and the grass growing green."

"Come down quickly," roared Bluebeard, "or I shall come up there!"

"I'm coming," answered his wife, and then she called, "Anne! Sister Anne! Do you see anything coming?"

"I see," said sister Anne, "a great cloud of dust moving this way."

"Is it my brothers?"

"Alas! No, sister, I see a flock of sheep."

"Do you refuse to come down?" shouted Bluebeard.

"One minute more," his wife replied, and then she cried, "Anne! Sister Anne! Do you see anything coming?"

"I see two horsemen coming this way," she responded, "but they're still at a great distance." And a moment afterward she exclaimed, "Heaven be praised! They're my brothers! I'm signaling to them as best I can to hurry up."

Bluebeard began to roar so loudly that the whole house shook. So his poor wife descended to him and threw herself at his feet, all disheveled and in tears.

"It's no use," said Bluebeard. "You must die!"

Then he seized her by the hair with one hand and raised his cutlass with the other. He was about to cut off her head when the poor woman turned toward him, and fixing her dying gaze upon him, she implored him to allow her one short moment to collect herself.

"No, no," he said, "commend yourself as best you can to heaven." And lifting his arm . . .

At this moment there was such a loud knocking at the gate that Bluebeard stopped short. The gate was opened, and two horsemen were seen entering right away. With drawn swords they ran straight at Bluebeard, who recognized them as the brothers of his wife—one a dragoon, the other a musketeer.[3] Consequently, he fled immediately and hoped to escape, but they pursued him so quickly that they overtook him before he could reach the step of his door, where they passed their swords through his body and left him dead on the spot. The poor woman was nearly as dead as her husband and did not have the strength to rise and embrace her brothers.

It was found that Bluebeard had no heirs, and so his widow inherited all his wealth. She employed part of it to arrange a marriage between her sister Anne and a young gentleman, who had loved her a long time. Another part became the captains' commissions for her two brothers. The rest she used for her marriage to a very worthy man, who made her forget the miserable time she had spent with Bluebeard.

Moral

Curiosity, in spite of its appeal,
May often cost a horrendous deal.
A thousand new cases arise each day,
With due respect, oh ladies, the thrill is slight:
As soon as you quench it, it goes away.
In truth, the price one pays is never right.

Another Moral

Provided one has common sense
And learned to grasp complex texts,
This story bears evidence
Of taking place in the past tense.

No longer are husbands terrible to see,
No longer do they demand the untarnished key.
Though he may be jealous and dissatisfied,
A husband tries to do as he's obliged.
And whatever color his beard may be,
It's difficult to know who the master may be.

3. A *dragon* (dragoon) was a cavalryman or cavalier, and the *dragons*, who carried bayonettes, pistols, and swords, were organized in 1668 as the mobile part of the army to lead advances. The *mousquetaires* (musketeers) of the king were re-organized in 1668 into two companies. They also rode horses, carried muskets, and wore uniforms of either gray or black with large white crosses on them.

JACOB AND WILHELM GRIMM

Bluebeard†

There was once a man who lived in a forest with his three sons and beautiful daughter. One day a golden coach drawn by six horses and attended by several servants came driving up to his house. After the coach stopped, a king stepped out and asked him if he could have his daughter for his wife. The man was happy that his daughter could benefit from such a stroke of good fortune and immediately said yes. There was nothing objectionable about the suitor except for his beard, which was all blue and made one shudder somewhat whenever one looked at it. At first the maiden also felt frightened by it and resisted marrying him. But her father kept urging her, and finally she consented. However, her fear was so great that she first went to her brothers, took them aside, and said, "Dear brothers, if you hear me scream, leave everything standing or lying wherever you are, and come to my aid."

The brothers kissed her and promised to do this. "Farewell, dear sister, if we hear your voice, we'll jump on our horses and soon be at your side."

Then she got into the coach, sat down next to Bluebeard, and drove away with him. When she reached his castle, she found everything splendid, and whatever the queen desired was fulfilled. They would have been very happy together if she could only have accustomed herself to the king's blue beard. However, whenever she saw it, she felt frightened.

After some time had passed, he said to her, "I must go on a great journey. Here are the keys to the entire castle. You can open all the rooms and look at everything. But I forbid you to open one particular room, which this little golden key can unlock. If you open it, you will pay for it with your life."

She took the key and promised to obey him. Once he had departed, she opened one door after another and saw so many treasures and magnificent things that she thought they must have been gathered from all over the world. Soon nothing was left but the forbidden room. Since the key was made of gold, she believed that the most precious things were probably kept there. Her curiosity began to gnaw at her, and she certainly would have passed over all the other rooms if she could have only seen what was in this one. At last her desire became so strong that she took the key and went to the room. "Who can possibly see when I open it?" she said to herself. "I'll just glance inside." Then she unlocked the room, and when the door opened, a stream of blood flowed toward her, and she saw dead women hanging along all the walls, some only skeletons. Her horror was so tremendous that she immediately slammed the door, but the key popped out of the lock and fell into the blood. Swiftly she picked it up

---

† Jacob and Wilhelm Grimm, "Bluebeard"—"Blaubart" (1812), was published in *Kinder- und Hausmärchen. Gesammelt durch die Brüder Grimm* (Berlin: Realschulbuchhandlung, 1815). It was omitted in 1819 because of its French origins.

and tried to wipe away the blood, but to no avail. When she wiped the blood away on one side, it appeared on the other. She sat down, rubbed the key throughout the day, and tried everything possible, but nothing helped: the bloodstains could not be eliminated. Finally, in the evening she stuck it into some hay, which was supposed to be able to absorb blood.

The following day Bluebeard came back, and the first thing he requested was the bunch of keys. Her heart pounded as she brought the keys, and she hoped that he would not notice that the golden one was missing. However, he counted all of them, and when he was finished, he said, "Where's the key to the secret room?"

As he said this, he looked straight into her eyes, causing her to blush red as blood.

"It's upstairs," she answered. "I misplaced it. Tomorrow I'll go and look for it."

"You'd better go now, dear wife. I need it today."

"Oh, I might as well tell you. I lost it in the hay. I'll have to go and search for it first."

"You haven't lost it," Bluebeard said angrily. "You stuck it there so the hay would absorb the bloodstains. It's clear that you've disobeyed my command and entered the room. Now, you will enter the room whether you want to or not."

Then he ordered her to fetch the key, which was still stained with blood.

"Now, prepare yourself for your death. You shall die today," Bluebeard declared. He fetched his big knife and took her to the threshold of the house.

"Just let me say my prayers before I die," she said.

"All right. Go ahead, but you'd better hurry. I don't have much time to waste."

She ran upstairs and cried out of the window as loudly as she could, "Brothers, my dear brothers! Come help me!"

The brothers were sitting in the forest and drinking some cool wine. The youngest said, "I think I heard our sister's voice. Let's go! We must hurry and help her!"

They jumped on their horses and rode like thunder and lightning. Meanwhile, their sister was on her knees, praying in fear.

"Well, are you almost done?" Bluebeard called from below, and she heard him sharpening his knife on the bottom step. She looked out the window but could only see a cloud of dust as if a herd were coming. So she screamed once again, "Brothers, my dear brothers! Come help me!"

And her fear became greater and greater when Bluebeard called, "If you don't come down soon, I'll be up to get you. My knife's been sharpened!"

She looked out the window again and saw her three brothers riding across the field as though they were birds flying through the air. For the third time she screamed desperately and with all her might, "Brothers, my dear brothers! Come help me!"

The youngest brother was already so near that she could hear his voice. "Calm yourself. Another moment, dear sister, and we'll be at your side!"

But Bluebeard cried out, "That's enough praying! I'm not going to wait any longer. If you don't come, I'm going to fetch you."

"Oh, just let me pray for my three dear brothers!"

However, he would not listen to her. Instead, he went upstairs and dragged her down. Then he grabbed her by the hair and was about to plunge the knife into her heart when the three brothers knocked at the door, charged inside, and tore their sister out of his hands. They then drew out their sabers and cut him down. Afterward he was hung up in the bloody chamber next to the women he had killed. Later, the brothers took their dear sister home with them, and all Bluebeard's treasures belonged to her.

JACOB AND WILHELM GRIMM

The Robber Bridegroom†

Once upon a time there was a miller who had a beautiful daughter, and when she was grown-up, he wanted to arrange a good marriage for her with a man who would provide for her in an appropriate way. "If the right suitor comes along and asks to marry her," he thought, "I shall give her to him."

It was not long before a suitor appeared who seemed to be very rich, and since the miller found nothing wrong with him, he promised him that he could wed his daughter. The maiden, however, did not love him the way a bride-to-be should love her bridegroom, nor did she trust him. Whenever she looked at him or thought about him, her heart shuddered with dread.

One day he said to her, "You're my bride-to-be, and yet you've never visited me."

"I don't know where your house is," the maiden replied.

"My house is out in the dark forest," said the bridegroom.

She tried to make excuses and told him she would not be able to find the way. But the bridegroom said, "Next Sunday I want you to come out and visit me. I've invited the guests, and I shall spread ashes on the ground so you can find the way."

When Sunday arrived and the maiden was supposed to set out on her way, she became very anxious but could not explain to herself why she felt so. She filled both her pockets with peas and lentils to mark the path. At the entrance to the forest, she found that the ashes had been spread, and she followed them, while throwing peas right and left on the ground with each step that she took. She walked nearly the whole day until she came to the middle of the forest. There she saw a solitary house, but she did not like the look of it because it was so dark and dreary. She went inside and found nobody at home. The place was deadly silent. Then suddenly a voice cried out:

---

† Jacob and Wilhelm Grimm, "The Robber Bridegroom"–"Der Räuberbräutigam" (1857), No. 40 in *Kinder- und Hausmärchen. Gesammelt durch die Brüder Grimm* (Göttingen: Dieterich, 1857).

"Turn back, turn back, young bride.
The den belongs to murderers,
Who'll soon be at your side!"

The maiden looked up and saw that the voice came from a bird in a cage hanging on the wall. Once again it cried out:

"Turn back, turn back, young bride.
The den belongs to murderers,
Who'll soon be at your side!"

The beautiful bride moved from one room to the next and explored the entire house, but it was completely empty. Not a soul could be found. Finally, she went down into the cellar, where she encountered a very, very old woman, whose head was constantly bobbing.

"Could you tell me whether my bridegroom lives here?" asked the bride.

"Oh, you poor child," the old woman answered. "Do you realize where you are? This is a murderers' den! You may think you're about to celebrate your wedding, but the only marriage you'll celebrate will be with death. Just look! They ordered me to put this big kettle of water on the fire to boil. When they have you in their power, they'll chop you to pieces without mercy. Then they'll cook you and eat you because they're cannibals. If I don't take pity on you and save you, you'll be lost forever."

The old woman then led her behind a large barrel, where nobody could see her.

"Be still as a mouse," she said. "Don't budge or move! Otherwise, it will be all over for you. Tonight when the robbers are asleep, we'll escape. I've been waiting a long time for this chance."

No sooner was the maiden hidden than the godless crew came home, dragging another maiden with them. They were drunk and paid no attention to her screams and pleas. They gave her wine to drink, three full glasses, one white, one red, and one yellow, and soon her heart burst in two. Then they tore off her fine clothes, put her on a table, chopped her beautiful body to pieces, and sprinkled the pieces with salt. Behind the barrel, the poor bride shook and trembled, for she now realized what kind of fate the robbers had been planning for her. One of them noticed a ring on the murdered maiden's little finger, and since he could not slip it off easily, he took a hatchet and chopped the finger off. But the finger sprang into the air and over the barrel and fell right into the bride's lap. The robber took a candle and went looking for it, but he could not find it. Then another robber said, "Have you looked behind the barrel as well?"

Immediately the old woman called out, "Come and eat! You can look for it tomorrow. The finger's not going to run away from you."

"The old woman's right," the robbers said, and they stopped looking and sat down to eat. The old woman put a sleeping potion into their wine, and soon they lay down in the cellar, fell asleep, and began snoring. When the bride heard that, she came out from behind the barrel and had to step over the sleeping bodies lying in rows on the ground. She feared she might wake them up, but she got safely through with the help of God. The old woman went upstairs with her and opened the door, and the two of them scampered out of the murderers' den as fast as they could. The wind had blown away the ashes, but the peas and lentils had sprouted and unfurled, pointing the way in the moonlight. They walked the whole night, and by morning they had reached the mill. Then the maiden told her father everything that had happened.

When the day of the wedding celebration came, the bridegroom appeared, as did all the relatives and friends that the miller had invited. As they were all sitting at the table, each person was asked to tell a story. The bride, though, remained still and did not utter a word. Finally, the bridegroom said, "Well, my dear, can't you think of anything? Tell us a good story."

"All right," she said. "I'll tell you a dream. I was walking alone through the forest and finally came to a house. There wasn't a soul to be found in the place except for a bird in a cage on the wall that cried out:

> " 'Turn back, turn back, young bride.
> The den belongs to murderers,
> Who'll soon be at your side!'

"Then the bird repeated the warning.

(My dear, it was only a dream.)

"After that I went through all the rooms, and they were empty, but there was something about them that gave me an eerie feeling. Finally, I went downstairs into the cellar, where I found a very, very old woman, who was bobbing her heard. I asked her, 'Does my bridegroom live in this house?' 'Oh, you poor child,' she responded, 'you've stumbled on a murderers' den. Your bridegroom lives here, but he wants to chop you up and kill you, and then he wants to cook you and eat you.'

(My dear, it was only a dream.)

"The old woman hid me behind a large barrel, and no sooner was I hidden than the robbers returned home, dragging a maiden with them. They gave her all sorts of wine to drink, white, red, and yellow, and her heart burst in two.

(My dear, it was only a dream.)

"One of the robbers saw that a gold ring was still on her finger, and since he had trouble pulling it off, he took a hatchet and chopped it off. The finger sprang into the air, over the barrel, and right into my lap. And here's the finger with the ring!"

With these words she produced the finger and showed it to all those present.

The robber, who had turned white as a ghost while hearing her story, jumped up and attempted to flee. However, the guests seized him and turned him over to the magistrate. Then he and his whole band were executed for their shameful crimes.

JACOB AND WILHELM GRIMM

Fitcher's Bird†

Once upon a time there was a sorcerer who used to assume the guise of a poor man and go begging from house to house to catch beautiful girls. No one knew where he took them since none of the girls ever returned.

One day he appeared at the door of a man who had three beautiful daughters. He looked like a poor, weak beggar and carried a basket on his back as though to collect handouts in it. He begged for some food, and when the oldest daughter came out to hand him a piece of bread, he had only to touch her, and that compelled her to jump into his basket. Then he rushed away with great strides and carried her to his house in the middle of a dark forest. Everything was splendid inside the house, and he gave her whatever she desired.

"My darling," he said, "I'm sure you'll like it here, for there's everything your heart desires."

After a few days had gone by, he said, "I must go on a journey and leave you alone for a short time. Here are the keys to the house. You may go wherever you want and look at everything except one room, which this small key here opens. If you disobey me, you will be punished by death." He also gave her an egg and said, "I'm giving you this egg for safekeeping. You're to carry it wherever you go. If you lose it, then something awful will happen."

She took the keys and the egg and promised to take care of everything. When he was gone, she went all around the house and explored it from top to bottom. The rooms glistened with silver and gold, and she was convinced that she had never seen such great splendor. Finally, she came to the forbidden door. She wanted to walk past it, but curiosity got the better of her. She examined the key, which looked like all the others, stuck it into the lock, turned it a little, and the door sprang open. But what did she see when she entered? There was a large bloody basin in the middle of the room, and it was filled with dead people who had been chopped to pieces. Next to the basin was a block of wood with a glistening ax on top of it. She was so horrified by this that she dropped the egg she had been holding in her hand, and it plopped into the basin. She took it out and wiped the blood off, but to no avail: the blood reappeared instantly. She wiped and scraped, but she could not get rid of the spot.

Not long after this, the sorcerer came back from his journey, and the first things he demanded from her were the keys and the egg. When she handed them to him, she was trembling, and he perceived right away by the red spots on the egg that she had been in the bloody chamber.

"Since you went into that chamber against my will," he said, "you will go back in, against your will. This is the end of your life."

---

† Jacob and Wilhelm Grimm, "Fitcher's Bird"—"Fitchers Vogel" (1857), No. 46 in *Kinder- und Hausmärchen. Gesammelt durch die Brüder Grimm* (Göttingen: Dieterich, 1857).

He threw her down, dragged her along by her hair, cut off her head on the block, and chopped her into pieces so that her blood flowed on the floor. Then he tossed her into the basin with the others.

"Now I shall fetch the second daughter," said the sorcerer.

Once again he went to the house in the guise of a poor man and begged. When the second daughter brought him a piece of bread, he caught her as he had the first, just by touching her. Then he carried her away, and she fared no better than her sister, for she succumbed to her own curiosity. She opened the door to the bloody chamber, looked inside, and had to pay for this with her life when the sorcerer returned from his journey.

Now he went and fetched the third daughter, but she was smart and cunning. After he had given her the keys and the egg and had departed, she put the egg away in a safe place. Then she explored the house and eventually came to the forbidden chamber. But, oh, what did she see? Her two dear sisters lay there in the basin cruelly murdered and chopped to pieces. However, she set to work right away, gathered the pieces together, and arranged them in their proper order: head, body, arms, and legs. When nothing more was missing, the pieces began to move and join together. Both the maidens opened their eyes and were alive again. Then they all rejoiced, kissed, and hugged each other.

When the sorcerer returned, he demanded his keys and egg right away, and when he could not discover the least trace of blood, he said, "You've passed the test, and you shall be my bride."

But he no longer had any power over her and had to do what she requested.

"All right," she answered. "But first I want you to carry a basket full of gold to my father and mother, and you're to carry it on your back by yourself. In the meantime I shall prepare for the wedding."

Then she ran to her sisters, whom she had hidden in a little chamber.

"The time has come when I can save you," she said. "The villain himself will carry you back home. But as soon as you get there, you must send me help."

She put her two sisters into a basket and covered them completely with gold until nothing could be seen of them at all. Then she called the sorcerer to her and said, "Now take the basket away. But don't you dare stop and rest along the way! I'll be keeping an eye on you from my window."

The sorcerer lifted the basket onto his back and went on his way. The basket, however, was so heavy that sweat ran down his face. At one point he sat down and wanted to rest a while, but one of the sisters called from the basket, "I can see through my window that you're resting. Get a move on at once!"

Whenever he stopped along the way, he heard a voice and had to keep moving. Although he had run out of breath and was groaning, he finally managed to bring the basket with the gold and the two maidens to their parents' house.

Back at his place, the bride was preparing the wedding feast and sent invitations to all the sorcerer's friends. Then she took a skull with grinning teeth, decorated it with jewels and a wreath of flowers, carried it up to the attic window, and set it down so it faced outward. When everything was ready, she dipped herself into a barrel of honey, cut open a bed, and rolled around in the feathers so she looked like a strange bird, and it was impossible to recognize her. Afterward she went out of the house, and on the way she met some of the wedding guests, who asked:

"Where are you coming from, oh, Fitcher's bird?"
"From Fitze Fitcher's house, haven't you heard?"
"And what may the young bride be doing there?"
"She's swept the whole house from top to bottom.
Just now she's looking out the attic window."

Finally, she met the bridegroom, who was walking back slowly. He also asked:

"Where are you coming from, oh, Fitcher's bird?"
"From Fitze Fitcher's house, haven't you heard?"
"And what may the young bride be doing there?"
"She's swept the whole house from top to bottom.
Just now she's looking out the attic window."

The bridegroom looked up and saw the decorated skull. He thought it was his bride and nodded and greeted her in a friendly way. However, once he and his guests were all gathered inside the house, the bride's brother and relatives arrived. They had been sent to rescue her, and they locked all the doors of the house to prevent anyone from escaping. Then they set fire to the house, and the sorcerer and all his cronies were burned to death.

Dangerous Wolves and
Naive Girls

Although Perrault's source has never been clearly identified, there were oral folktales that predated his literary tale, and they stem from southern France and northern Italy. Paul Delarue and Charles Joisten have published numerous articles indicating that there was a cycle of tales based probably on some kind of initiation ritual in sewing communities. In a composite tale called "The Grandmother," a young peasant woman takes some bread and milk to her grandmother. At a crossroads in the woods, she meets a werewolf, who asks her whether she is going to take the path of the pins or the path of the needles. She generally chooses the path of the needles. He rushes off to the grandmother's house and eats her, but he also puts some of her flesh in a bowl and some of her blood in a bottle before getting into the grandmother's bed. When the girl arrives, the werewolf tells her to refresh herself and eat some meat from the bowl and drink some wine. A cat or something from the fireplace condemns her for eating the flesh of her grandmother and drinking her blood. Sometimes there is a warning. All at once the werewolf asks her to take off her clothes and get into bed with him. She complies, and each time she takes off a piece of her clothing, she asks what she should do with it. The werewolf replies that she should throw it into the fireplace because she won't be needing it anymore. When the girl finally gets into bed, she makes several astonishing observations such as "My, how hairy you are, granny," until the customary "My, what a big mouth you have, granny." When the wolf announces, "All the better to eat you, my dear," she declares that she has to relieve herself. He tells her to do it in bed. But she indicates that she has to have a bowel movement, and so he ties a rope around her leg and sends her into the courtyard through a window. Once there the smart girl unties the rope and ties it around a plum tree and then runs off toward home. The werewolf becomes impatient and yells, "What are you doing out there, making a load?" Then he runs to the window and realizes that the girl has escaped. He runs after her, but it is too late, and she makes it safely to her home.

It is unclear whether Perrault knew this oral tale about a courageous and cunning girl who was proving that she was ready to become a seamstress and could handle needles and wolves. But it is clear that he must have known some version like this and transformed it into a tale in which a naive bourgeois girl pays for her stupidity and is violated in the end. Both Perrault's tale and the oral folk version became popular in the eighteenth century, and Perrault's tale was translated into English, German, and Russian. In 1800, Ludwig Tieck published *Leben und Tod des kleinen Rothkäppchens* (*Life and Death of Little Red Cap*), and he was the first to introduce a hunter who saves Red Cap's life. The Grimms also felt sympathy for Little Red Cap and followed Tieck's example in their version. In addition, they added a second didactic part to show that the grandmother and Little Red Cap learned their lesson. Following the publication of the Grimms' more optimistic "Little Red Cap," writers have chosen either their version or Perrault's tale to adapt in hundreds of different ways, and these two tales have also entered the oral tradition. Some of the more important literary versions in the nineteenth century are F. W. N. Bayley, "Little Red Riding Hood" (1846); Ludwig Bechstein, "Rotkäppchen" ("Little Red Cap," 1853); Alphonse Daudet, *Le roman du chaperon rouge* (*The Romance of Little Red Riding Hood*, 1862); Richard Henry Stoddard, *The Story of Little Red Riding Hood*, 1864; Alfred Mills, "Ye True Hystorie of Little Red Riding Hood," 1872; Harriet Childe-Pemberton "All My Doing; or, Little Red Riding Hood over again," 1882; and Charles Marelle, "La veritable histoire du Petit Chaperon d'or" ("The True History of Little Golden-Hood," 1888). These versions and others can be found in Jack Zipes, *The Trials and Tribulations of Little Red Riding Hood* (1983); Alan Dundes's *Little Red Riding Hood: A Casebook* is an excellent collection of essays pertaining to the tale.

CHARLES PERRAULT

Little Red Riding Hood†

Once upon a time, there was a little village girl, the prettiest that had ever been seen. Her mother doted on her, and her grandmother even more. This good woman made her a little red hood which suited her so well that she was called Little Red Riding Hood wherever she went.

One day, after her mother had baked some biscuits, she said to Little Red Riding Hood, "Go see how your grandmother's feeling. I've heard that she's sick. You can take her some biscuits and this small pot of butter."

Little Red Riding Hood departed at once to visit her grandmother, who lived in another village. In passing through the forest she met old neighbor wolf, who had a great desire to eat her. But he did not dare because of some woodcutters who were in the forest. He asked her where she was going, and the poor child, who did not know that it is dangerous to stop and listen to a wolf, said to him, "I'm going to see my grandmother, and I'm bringing her some biscuits with a small pot of butter that my mother's sending her."

"Does she live far from here?" the wolf asked.

"Oh, yes!" Little Red Riding Hood said. "You've got to go by the mill, which you can see right over there, and hers is the first house in the village."

† Charles Perrault, "Little Red Riding Hood"—"Le petit chaperon rouge" (1607), in *Histoires ou contes du temps passé* (Paris: Claude Barbin, 1697). The title in French was *Le petit chaperon rouge*, which literally means "little red cap." The term "riding hood" was used in the first English translation of 1729 and has stuck ever since. The *chaperon* was a little cap worn by women and girls of the bourgeoisie of this period, and Perrault used it to signify how the girl (and the grandmother) wanted to be like the "bourgeois," and it thus identifies her with the bourgeoisie. There are many other interpretations of the *chaperon*. For instance, the term *grand chaperon* indicated an older lady who was supposed to escort young women. The fact that Little Red Riding Hood only has a small *chaperon* indicates that she does not have enough protection. The color red is, of course, most important. Not only does it signify menstruation or the coming of age of a young girl, but it was also associated with the devil. In the Middle Ages and Reformation, the red sign or hat was used to stigmatize social nonconformists or outcasts.

"Well, then," said the wolf, "I'll go and see her, too. You take that path there, and I'll take this path here, and we'll see who'll get there first."

The wolf began to run as fast as he could on the path that was shorter, and the little girl took the longer path, and she enjoyed herself by gathering nuts, running after butterflies, and making bouquets of small flowers that she found along the way. It did not take the wolf long to arrive at the grandmother's house, and he knocked:

"Tic, toc."

"Who's there?"

"It's your granddaughter, Little Red Riding Hood," the wolf said, disguising his voice. "I've brought you some biscuits and a little pot of butter that my mother's sent for you."

The good grandmother, who was in her bed because she was not feeling well, cried out to him, "Pull the bobbin, and the latch will fall."

The wolf pulled the bobbin, and the door opened. He pounced on the good woman and devoured her quicker than a wink, for it had been more than three days since he had eaten last. After that he closed the door and lay down in the grandmother's bed to wait for Little Red Riding Hood, who after a while came knocking at the door:

"Toc, toc."

"Who's there?"

When she heard the gruff voice of the wolf, Little Red Riding Hood was scared at first, but she thought her grandmother had a cold and responded, "It's your granddaughter, Little Red Riding Hood. I've brought you some biscuits and a little pot of butter that my mother's sent for you."

The wolf softened his voice and cried out to her, "Pull the bobbin, and the latch will fall."

Little Red Riding Hood pulled the bobbin, and the door opened.

Upon seeing her enter, the wolf hid himself under the bedcovers and said to her, "Put the biscuits and the pot of butter on the bin and come lie down beside me."

Little Red Riding Hood undressed and went to get into bed, where she was quite astonished to see the way her grandmother was dressed in her nightgown, and she said to her, "What big arms you have, grandmother!"

"The better to hug you with, my child."

"What big legs you have, grandmother!"

"The better to run with, my child."

"What big ears you have, grandmother!"

"The better to hear you with, my child."

"What big eyes you have, grandmother!"

"The better to see you with, my child."

"What big teeth you have, grandmother!"

"The better to eat you with."

And upon saying these words, the wicked wolf pounced on Little Red Riding Hood and ate her up.

Moral

One sees here that young children,
Especially pretty girls,
Polite, well-taught, and pure as pearls,
Should stay on guard against all sorts of men.
For if one fails to stay alert, it won't be strange
To see one eaten by a wolf enraged.
I say a wolf since not all types are wild,
Or can be said to be the same in kind.
Some are winning and have sharp minds.
Some are loud or smooth or mild.
Others appear just kind and unriled.
They follow young ladies wherever they go,
Right into the halls of their very own homes.
Alas for those who've refused the truth:
Sweetest tongue has the sharpest tooth.

JACOB AND WILHELM GRIMM

Little Red Cap†

Once upon a time there was a sweet little maiden. Whoever laid eyes upon her could not help but love her. But it was her grandmother who loved her most. She could never give the child enough. One time she made her a present, a small, red velvet cap, and since it was so becoming and the maiden insisted on always wearing it, she was called Little Red Cap.

One day her mother said to her, "Come, Little Red Cap, take this piece of cake and bottle of wine and bring them to your grandmother. She's sick and weak, and this will strengthen her. Get an early start, before it becomes hot, and when you're out in the woods, be nice and good and don't stray from the path; otherwise, you'll fall and break the glass, and your grandmother will get nothing. And when you enter her room, don't forget to say good morning, and don't go peeping into all the corners."

"I'll do just as you say," Little Red Cap promised her mother. Well, the grandmother lived out in the forest, half an hour from the village, and as soon as Little Red Cap entered the forest, she encountered the wolf. However, Little Red Cap did not know what a wicked sort of an animal he was and was not afraid of him.

"Good day, Little Red Cap," he said.

"Thank you kindly, wolf."

"Where are you going so early, Little Red Cap?"

"To grandmother's."

"What are you carrying under your apron?"

† Jacob and Wilhelm Grimm, "Little Red Cap"—"Rotkäppchen" (1857), No. 26 in *Kinder- und Hausmärchen. Gesammelt durch die Brüder Grimm* (Göttingen: Dieterich, 1857).

Little Red Cap. Arthur Rackham, 1911.

"Cake and wine. My grandmother's sick and weak, and yesterday we baked this so it will help her get well."

"Where does your grandmother live, Little Red Cap?"

"About a quarter of an hour from here in the forest. Her house is under the three big oak trees. You can tell it by the hazel bushes," said Little Red Cap.

The wolf thought to himself, "This tender young thing is a juicy morsel. She'll taste even better than the old woman. You've got to be real crafty if you want to catch them both." Then he walked next to Little Red Cap, and after a while he said, "Little Red Cap, just look at the beautiful flowers that are growing all around you! Why don't you look around? I believe you haven't even noticed how lovely the birds are singing. You march along as if you were going straight to school, and yet it's so delightful out here in the woods!"

Little Red Cap looked around and saw how the rays of the sun were dancing through the trees back and forth and how the woods were full of beautiful flowers. So she thought to herself, "If I bring grandmother a bunch of fresh flowers, she'd certainly like that. It's still early, and I'll arrive on time."

So she ran off the path and plunged into the woods to look for flowers. And each time she plucked one, she thought she saw another even prettier flower and ran after it, going deeper and deeper into the forest. But the wolf went straight to the grandmother's house and knocked at the door.

"Who's out there?"

"Little Red Cap. I've brought you some cake and wine. Open up."

"Just lift the latch," the grandmother called. "I'm too weak and can't get up."

The wolf lifted the latch, and the door sprang open. Then he went straight to the grandmother's bed without saying a word and gobbled her up. Next he put on her clothes and her nightcap, lay down in her bed, and drew the curtains.

Meanwhile, Little Red Cap had been running around and looking for flowers, and only when she had as many as she could carry did she remember her grandmother and continue on the way to her house again. She was puzzled when she found the door open, and as she entered the room, it seemed so strange inside that she thought, "Oh, my God, how frightened I feel today, and usually I like to be at grandmother's." She called out, "Good morning!" But she received no answer. Next she went to the bed and drew back the curtains. There lay her grandmother with her cap pulled down over her face giving her a strange appearance.

"Oh, grandmother, what big ears you have!"

"The better to hear you with."

"Oh, grandmother, what big hands you have!"

"The better to grab you with."

"Oh, grandmother, what a terribly big mouth you have!"

"The better to eat you with!"

No sooner did the wolf say that than he jumped out of bed and gobbled up poor Little Red Cap. After the wolf had satisfied his desires, he lay down in bed again, fell asleep, and began to snore very loudly. The huntsman[1] happened to be passing by the house and thought to himself, "The way the old woman's snoring, you'd better see if something's wrong." He went into the room, and when he came to the bed, he saw the wolf lying in it.

"So, I've found you at last, you old sinner," said the huntsman. "I've been looking for you a long time."

He took aim with his gun, and then it occurred to him that the wolf

---

1. In German the term for huntsman used by the Grimms was *Jäger*. A *Jäger* was not simply a huntsman but a gameskeeper hired by the lord of a grand estate to patrol the grounds and forest and make sure that there was no poaching or illegal activity. In other words, he was, among other things, a kind of policeman.

could have eaten the grandmother and that she could still be saved. So he did not shoot but took some scissors and started cutting open the sleeping wolf's belly. After he made a couple of cuts, he saw the little red cap shining forth, and after he made a few more cuts, the girl jumped out and exclaimed, "Oh, how frightened I was! It was so dark in the wolf's body."

Soon the grandmother came out. She was alive but could hardly breathe. Little Red Cap quickly fetched some large stones, and they filled the wolf's body with them. When he awoke and tried to run away, the stones were too heavy so he fell down at once and died.

All three were delighted. The huntsman skinned the fur from the wolf and went home with it. The grandmother ate the cake and drank the wine that Little Red Cap had brought, and soon she regained her health. Meanwhile Little Red Cap thought to herself, "Never again will you stray from the path by yourself and go into the forest when your mother has forbidden it."

There is also another tale about how Little Red Cap returned to her grandmother one day to bring some baked goods. Another wolf spoke to her and tried to entice her to leave the path, but this time Little Red Cap was on her guard. She went straight ahead and told her grandmother that she had seen the wolf, that he had wished her good day, but that he had had such a mean look in his eyes that "he would have eaten me if we hadn't been on the open road."

"Come," said the grandmother. "We'll lock the door so he can't get in."

Soon after, the wolf knocked and cried out, "Open up, grandmother. It's Little Red Cap, and I've brought you some baked goods."

But they kept quiet and did not open the door. So Grayhead circled the house several times and finally jumped on the roof. He wanted to wait till evening when Little Red Cap would go home. He intended to sneak after her and eat her up in the darkness. But the grandmother realized what he had in mind. In front of the house was a big stone trough, and she said to the child, "Fetch the bucket, Little Red Cap. I cooked sausages yesterday. Get the water they were boiled in and pour it into the trough."

Little Red Cap kept carrying the water until she had filled the big, big trough. Then the smell of sausages reached the nose of the wolf. He sniffed and looked down. Finally he stretched his neck so far that he could no longer keep his balance on the roof. He began to slip and fell right into the big trough and drowned. Then Little Red Cap went merrily on her way home, and no one harmed her.

Love Conquers All

This tale, "The Orange Tree and the Bee," was typical of Mme d'Aulnoy's work in which she combined numerous fairy tale motifs to compose a narrative about true and natural love between born aristocrats. Her use of the two names Princess Aimée and Prince Aimé makes her intentions quite clear. The most important literary and folk motifs are two sea disasters that cause the lovers to meet on the same island; the cannibals who want their son to marry; the swapping of the cannibals' children, which Perrault used in "Little Tom Thumb"; the stealing of the cannibal's magic wand; and the magic transformation. In *Fabulous Identities* (1998), Patricia Hannon makes a keen observation that applies to most of Mme d'Aulnoy's tales involving metamorphosis: "Aulnoy's enchanted bodies become a theater for self-discovery as well as a conduit for knowledge. Because the world is explored and thus known through the ever-changing body, the latter plays an active role in the quest for knowledge and truth. The fluid boundaries of the metamorphosed self enable the journeys away from the court into forests and countrysides of counter-identities" (79). As in most of her tales, Mme d'Aulnoy had the fairies bring about the final happy resolution in court, where identities are temporarily stabilized. Mme d'Aulnoy's tale was circulated in abbreviated form by the *Bibliothèque Bleue* beginning in 1717 and translated into German in Friedrich Immanuel Bierling's *Das Cabinet der Feen*, 9 vols. (1761–66). Since the Grimms sought to reproduce mainly German folktales and saw clearly how close "Okerlo" was to Mme d'Aulnoy's literary tale, they omitted it after publishing it in their first edition of 1812.

MARIE-CATHERINE D'AULNOY

The Orange Tree and the Bee†

Once upon a time there was a king and a queen who lacked nothing but children to make them happy. Since the queen was already old, she had given up all hope of having any. However, it was just then that she became pregnant, and in due time she gave birth to the most beautiful girl the world has ever seen. There was great joy in the palace, and each person tried to find a name for the princess that would express their feeling toward her. At last, they called her Aimée.

The queen had the name of Aimée, daughter of the king of the Happy Island, engraved upon a turquoise heart. Then she tied it around the princess's neck, believing that the turquoise would bring her good fortune. Yet,

† Marie-Catherine d'Aulnoy, "The Orange Tree and the Bee"—"L'oranger et l'abeille" (1697), in *Les contes de fées*, 4 vols. (Paris: Claude Barbin, 1697).

751

the turquoise failed to work in this case. One day, when the nurse sought to amuse herself, she asked the king's sailors to take her and the princess out to sea in the finest summer weather. However, all at once there was such a tremendous tempest that it was impossible to land. Since she was in a little boat, only used for pleasure trips close to shore, it was soon ripped to pieces. The nurse and all the sailors perished. The little princess, who was sleeping in her cradle, remained floating on the water and was ultimately thrown by the waves onto the coast of a very pretty country. There were very few people inhabiting this country since the ogre Ravagio and his wife, Tourmentine, had come to live there, and they ate up everybody they could find. The ogres are terrible people: once they have tasted fresh meat (this is how they refer to human flesh), they will hardly ever eat anything else, and Tourmentine always discovered some secret way of attracting a victim, for she was half fairy.

When she caught the scent of the poor little princess a mile away, she ran to the shore to search for her before Ravagio could find her. They were equally greedy, and you have certainly never seen such hideous figures, each with one squinting eye in the middle of the forehead, a mouth as large as that of an oven, a huge flat nose, long donkey ears, hair standing on end, and humps in front and behind. However, once Tourmentine saw Aimée in her rich cradle, wrapped in swaddling clothes of gold brocade, playing with her little hands, her cheeks resembling a white rose mixed with a carnation, and her little vermilion smiling mouth half open, which seemed to smile at the horrid monster who had come to devour her, the ogress was overcome by a feeling of pity that she had never experienced before. So, she decided to nurse the baby, and if she was going to eat it, she would not do it right away. She took the child in her arms, tied the cradle on her back, and returned to her cave. "Look, Ravagio," she said to her husband, "here's some fresh meat, very plump, very tender. But if you know what's good for you, you'd better not touch it with your teeth— it's a beautiful little girl. I'll raise her, and we'll marry her to our son. Then they'll have some extraordinary little ogres to keep us amused in our old age."

"Well said," replied Ravagio. "You're as wise as you are great. Let me look at the child. She seems beautiful to look at."

"Don't eat her!" said Tourmentine, putting the child in his great clutches.

"No, no," he said. "I'd sooner die of hunger."

Here, then, were Ravagio, Tourmentine, and the young ogre, caressing Aimée in such a humane manner that it was a kind of miracle to behold. But the poor child, who only saw these deformed creatures around her and missed her nurse, began to curl her lip and cry with all her might. Ravagio's cave echoed with these cries, and Tourmentine, fearing the noise would frighten the baby even more, took her and carried her into the wood with her children following her. She had six—each one uglier than the next. As I mentioned before, she was half fairy, and she used her power by taking a little ivory wand and wishing for whatever she wanted. So she took the wand and said, "I wish, in the name of the royal fairy Trufio, that the most beautiful doe in our forests, gentle and tame, would leave its fawn, and come here immediately to nurse this little creature that fortune has sent me."

Immediately a doe appeared, and since the little ogres gave her a warm welcome, she approached the princess and began suckling her. Then Tourmentine carried her back to her grotto with the doe skipping and gamboling after them. The child kept looking at it and petting it. When she was in her cradle and cried, the doe was always there ready to feed her, and the little ogre rocked her.

This was how the king's daughter was raised while being mourned by her parents night and day for many years. Finally, the king became firmly convinced that she had drowned and thought of choosing an heir. He spoke to the queen about this matter, and she told him to do what he judged proper. Since her dear Aimée was dead, she had no hope of having any more children, and she told him he had waited long enough. Fifteen years had elapsed since she had the misfortune of losing her daughter, and it would now be folly to expect her return. The king decided to ask his brother to choose among his sons the one he thought most worthy to reign and to send him to his kingdom without delay. He gave his ambassadors this message and all the necessary instructions, and they departed. They had to sail a great distance and embarked on some fine vessels. The wind was favorable so that they soon arrived at the palace of the king's brother, who ruled over a large kingdom. He welcomed them very graciously, and when they asked his permission to take back one of his sons to succeed their master, the king, he wept for joy. Since his brother left the choice to him, he told them he would send him the one he would have taken for himself, which was his second son, whose inclinations were so well suited to the greatness of his birth that the king found him perfect in every manner possible. They sent for Prince Aimé (for this was his name), and no matter how prejudiced in his favor the ambassadors had been, they were completely astonished when they saw him. He was eighteen years old, and Cupid, the young god of love himself, could not match his beauty, but it was a beauty which detracted nothing from that noble and martial air that inspires respect and affection. He was told how eager the king, his uncle, was to have him near him and how the king, his father, wanted him to depart soon. So they prepared his equipage, and he took his leave and put to sea.

Let him sail on. Let fortune guide him! We shall now return to Ravagio and see what has been happening with our young princess.

Her beauty increased as she grew older, and one could certainly say that love, the graces, and all the goddesses combined never possessed so many charms. Whenever she was in the dark cave with Ravagio, Tourmentine, and the young ogres, it seemed that the sun, stars, and skies had descended into it. The cruelty of these monsters had the effect of making her even gentler. From the moment she was aware of their terrible inclination for human flesh, she always tried to save the unfortunate people who fell into their hands, so much so that she often exposed herself to the ogres' fury. She would have been destroyed by them had not the young ogre guarded her like the apple of his eye. Ah, what love will not do! This little monster's nature had become softened by seeing and loving this beautiful princess.

But, alas, how she suffered when she thought she would have to marry this detestable lover! Although she knew nothing about her origin, she had guessed rightly from her rich clothes, the gold chain, and the turquoise that she was highborn, and from the feelings of her heart, she believed this to be more than true. She could not read, write, or speak any language but the jargon of the ogres. She lived in perfect ignorance of all worldly matters, yet she possessed such fine principles of virtue and such sweet and unaffected manners; it was as though she had been brought up in the most refined court in the universe.

She normally wore a tigerskin dress that she had made for herself. Her arms were half naked, and she carried a quiver and arrows over her shoulder, and a bow at her side. Her blond hair was fastened only by a plaited band of sea-rushes and floated in the breeze over her neck and shoulders. She also wore buckskins made of the same rush. In this attire, she walked about the woods like a second Diana, and she would never have known she was beautiful if the crystal fountains had not offered themselves to her as innocent mirrors. Still, whenever she gazed into the fountains, she did not become vain or think more highly of herself. The sun had a similar effect on her complexion as on wax—it made it whiter—and the sea air could not tan it. She never ate anything but what she caught in hunting or fishing, and under this pretext she often stayed away from the cave to avoid looking at the most deformed objects in nature. "Heavens!" she cried, shedding tears. "What have I done to make you sentence me to become the bride of this cruel little ogre? Why didn't you let me perish in the sea? Why did you save a life that must be spent in this most deplorable manner? Don't you have any compassion for my grief?"

This was the way she addressed the gods and asked for their aid. When the weather was rough, and she thought the sea had cast some unfortunate people on shore, she would carefully go and assist them and prevent them from approaching the ogres' cave. Well, one night there was a fearful storm, and the next day she arose as soon as it was light and ran toward the sea. There she saw a man who had his arms locked around a plank and was trying to reach the shore, despite the violence of the waves that continually turned him back. The princess was most anxious to help him, and she made signs to him pointing to the easiest landing places, but he did not see or hear her. Sometimes he came so close that it appeared he had but one step to make, when a wave would cover him and he would disappear. At last he was thrown onto the sand and lay stretched out without any motion. Aimée approached him, and in spite of his deathlike appearance, she gave him all the assistance she could. She always carried certain herbs with her, and their odor was so powerful that they could revive anyone from the longest fainting fit. She pressed them in her hands and rubbed some of them on his lips and temples. He opened his eyes and was so astonished at the beauty and dress of the princess that he could hardly tell whether it was a dream or reality. He spoke first, and she responded. They could not understand each other and stared at one another with a good deal of attention mingled with astonishment and pleasure. The princess had seen only some poor fishermen whom the ogres had snared and whom she had saved, as I have already said. What could she have possibly thought when she saw the most handsome man in the world in the most magnificent attire? Indeed, it was none other than the prince Aimé, her first cousin, whose fleet had been driven by a tempest and had crashed to pieces against these shoals. Their crews had been left to the mercy of the winds and waves, and they had either perished or been cast on unknown shores. The young prince, for his part, was most astonished at seeing such a beautiful creature in such savage attire and in such a deserted country. When he thought about the princess and ladies he had so recently seen on his departure, he was only more convinced that the being he now beheld surpassed them all by far. In this mutual astonishment, they continued to talk without being able to understand each other; their looks and their actions were the sole interpreters of their thoughts. Yet, after a few moments, the princess suddenly remembered the danger confronting this stranger, and her face revealed great distress and melancholy. The prince feared that she was falling sick and showed great concern. He wanted to take her hand, but she pushed him away and endeavored, as best she could, to impress upon him that he must go away. She began to run away from him, then returned and made signs for him to do the same. Accordingly he ran away from her and returned. When he returned, she was angry with him. So she took her arrows and pointed them at her heart to indicate that he would be killed. He thought she wished to kill him and thus knelt on one knee awaiting the blow. When she saw that, she did not know what to do, or how to express herself. Looking at him tenderly, she said, "Are you to become a victim of my frightful hosts? Must these very eyes, which now gaze on you with so much pleasure, see you torn to pieces and devoured without mercy?"

She wept, and the prince was at quite a loss to comprehend the meaning of her actions. She succeeded, however, in making him understand that she did not wish him to follow her. She took him by the hand and led him to a cave in a rock that opened toward the sea. It was very deep: she often went there to bemoan her misfortunes, and sometimes she slept there when the sun was too strong to allow her to return to the ogres' cave. Since she was clever and skillful, she had furnished it by hanging butterfly wings of various colors on the walls. In addition, she had spread a carpet of sea-rushes on canes that were intertwined with one another to form a sort of couch. Clusters of flowers were placed in large and deep shells, answering the purpose of vases, which she filled with water to preserve her bouquets. There were a thousand pretty little things she had manufactured, some with fish bones and shells, and others with the sea-rush and cane. Despite their simplicity, these articles were so exquisitely made that it was easy to judge that the princess had good taste and ingenuity. The prince was completely surprised by it all and thought that she lived in this place. Just being there with her delighted him, and although he was not at ease enough to express the admiration he felt for her, it already seemed he preferred this simple girl's company to all the crowns ordained by his birth and the will of his relations.

Making him sit down, she indicated that she wished him to remain there until she could procure something for him to eat. Then she unfastened the band from her hair, put it around the prince's arm, tied him to the couch, and left. He was dying to follow but was afraid of displeasing her. So he abandoned himself to thoughts that he could not entertain in the presence of the princess. "Where am I?" he asked. "What country has fortune led me to? My vessels are lost, my people are drowned, and I've nothing left. Instead of the crown that was offered me, I find a gloomy rock, where I'm taking refuge. What will become of me here? What sort of people shall I find? If I'm to judge from the person who's helped me, they're all divinities. But going by the fear she had when she thought I might follow her—the rude and barbarous language which sounded so terrible from her beautiful mouth—I believe something even more unfortunate will happen to me than has already occurred." He then focused his mind entirely on reviewing all the incomparable charms of the young savage. His heart was on fire, and he became impatient waiting for her return, for her absence appeared the greatest of all evils to him.

In fact, she returned as quickly as she possibly could. She had thought of nothing but the prince; and such tender feelings were so new to her that she was not on her guard against that with which he was inspiring her. She thanked heaven for having saved him from the dangers of the sea, and she prayed that he would be preserved from the danger he ran by being so near to the ogres. She was so excited and she had walked so rapidly that when she arrived, she felt rather oppressed by the heavy tigerskin which served as her mantle. When she sat down, the prince placed himself at her feet and was concerned that she was suffering, even though he was certainly worse off than she was. As soon as she recovered from her faintness, she displayed all the delicacies she had brought him: among them were four parrots and six squirrels, cooked by the sun; and strawberries, cherries, raspberries, and other fruits. The plates were made of cedar and eagle wood, the knife of stone, the table napkins of large leaves of trees, very soft and pliable. There was a shell to be used as a cup, and another filled with beautiful water. The prince expressed his gratitude to her by all the signs he could make with his head and hands, and she made him understand with a sweet smile that all his actions pleased her. But once the hour of separation arrived, she made it perfectly clear to him that they had to part, and they both began to sign and hide their tears from each other. She arose and would have gone, but the prince uttered a loud cry and threw himself at her feet begging her to remain. She saw clearly what he meant, but she rebuffed him with a little air of severity, and he knew he had better learn to obey her soon.

To tell the truth, he spent a miserable night, and the princess did not fare any better. When she returned to the cave and found herself surrounded by the ogres and their children, and when she looked at the frightful little ogre that was to become her husband and thought of the charms of the stranger she had just left, she felt inclined to throw herself into the sea. Moreover, she was afraid that Ravagio or Tourmentine would smell fresh meat, and that they would go straight to the rock and devour Prince Aimé.

These various fears kept her awake all night. At daybreak she arose and nearly flew to the seashore, loaded with the best of everything: parrots, monkeys, and bustards,[1] fruits, and milk. The prince had not undressed. He had suffered so much from fatigue at sea and had slept so little that he had fallen into a doze toward the morning. "What!" she said, as she woke him. "I've been thinking of you ever since I left you. I didn't even close my eyes, and you're able to sleep!"

The prince looked at her and listened without understanding her. In his turn he declared, "What joy, my darling," he said, kissing her hands, "what joy it is to see you again! It seems ages ago since you left this rock."

He talked some time to her before he remembered that she could not understand him. When he remembered, he sighed heavily and was silent. She then picked up the conversation and told him she was dreadfully alarmed that Ravagio and Tourmentine would discover him; that she could not believe he would be safe in the rock for any length of time; that if he went away she would die, but that she would sooner consent to that than expose him to be devoured; that she implored him to flee. At this point, tears filled her eyes; she clasped her hands in front of him in the most supplicating manner. Since he could not understand in the least what she meant, he became desperate and threw himself at her feet. At last she kept pointing to the way out so that he understood part of her signs, and he in his turn explained to her that he would rather die than leave her. She was so touched by this proof of the prince's affection that she took the chain of gold with the turquoise heart from her arm, the one that the queen, her mother, had hung round her neck, and tied it around his arm in the most gracious manner. Despite the exhilaration he felt from this gesture, he did not fail to notice the letters engraved on the turquoise. He examined them carefully and read, "Aimée, daughter of the king of the Happy Island."

Never was anyone more astonished than he was, for he knew that the little princess who had perished was called Aimée. He was convinced that this heart belonged to her, but he was not sure whether this beautiful savage was the princess, or whether the sea had thrown this trinket onto the sands. He looked at Aimée with the most extraordinary attention, and the more he looked at her, the more he discovered a certain family expression and features. And the particular tender feelings of his heart led him to believe that the savage maiden must be his cousin.

She was completely astonished by his actions as he lifted his eyes to heaven in a token of thanks, looking at her and weeping, taking her hands and kissing them vehemently. He thanked her for her generosity, and as he refastened the trinket on her arm, he indicated to her that he would prefer to have a lock of her hair, which he requested but had great trouble in obtaining.

Four days passed in this way. Every morning the princess brought him the food he needed. She remained with him as long as she possibly could, and the hours passed by quickly, even though they could not converse together. One evening, when she returned rather late and expected to be scolded by the terrible Tourmentine, she was very much surprised at the

1. Large birds, mainly found in Europe. In America, they are referred to as Canadian geese.

warm welcome she received. Upon finding a table covered with fruit, she asked if she could have some. Ravagio told her that they were intended for her, that the young ogre had been gathering them, and that it was now time to make him happy, for he wished to marry her in three days. What tidings! Could there be any in the world more dreadful for this charming princess! She thought she would die of fright and grief, but she concealed her affliction and replied that she would obey them without reluctance, provided they would give her a little longer time.

Ravagio became angry and said, "What's to prevent me from devouring you?"

The poor princess fainted with fear in the claws of Tourmentine, and the young ogre, who loved her dearly, entreated Ravagio on her behalf so much that he eventually appeased him. Aimée did not sleep an instant; she waited impatiently for daylight. As soon as it appeared, she flew to the rock, and when she saw the prince, she uttered sad cries and wept profusely. He remained almost motionless. In four days, his love for the beautiful Aimée had grown as much as it would have taken a usual feeling four years to grow, and he was dying to ask her what had happened. She knew he could not understand her and could think of no mode of explanation. At last she untied her long hair, put a wreath of flowers on her head, and taking Aimé's hand, she made signs to show what they intended to do. Indeed, he understood the impending catastrophe and realized that they were going to wed her to someone else.

He felt that he had reached the end of his rope and would die especially because he did not know the roads or have the means to save her. Nor did she, and so they shed tears together, looked at each other, and mutually indicated that it would be better to die together than to be separated. She stayed with him until evening, but when night came sooner than expected and she became lost in thought on her way back to the ogres, she did not pay attention to the paths she was taking and entered a part of the wood very seldom frequented. It was there that a long thorn pierced her foot deeply, and lucky for her she was not far from the cave. However, she had a great deal of trouble in reaching it, since her foot was covered with blood. Ravagio, Tourmentine, and the young ogres came to her assistance. She suffered a lot of pain when they pulled out the thorn. They gathered herbs and applied them to her foot, and she retired, very anxious about her dear prince, as may be imagined. "Alas!" she said. "I won't be able to walk tomorrow. What will he think if he doesn't see me? Thanks to my efforts, he now knows they intend to have me wed, and he'll think I haven't been able to prevent it. Who'll feed him? No matter what he does, it will be his death. If he comes looking for me, he's lost. If I send one of the young ogres to him, Ravagio will learn about it." She burst into tears and sighed. When she arose early in the morning, it was impossible for her to walk. Her wound was too painful, and Tourmentine, who saw her crawling out, stopped her and said if she took another step she would eat her.

In the meantime, the prince realized that the usual hour for their meeting had passed, and he became distressed and frightened. The faster the time flew, the more his fears increased. All the torments in the world seemed less terrible to him than the anxieties that his love caused him.

He forced himself to be patient, but the longer he waited, the less hope he had. At length he decided to die and rushed out determined to seek his charming princess, no matter what the risk was. He did not know where he was going as he walked, and he followed a beaten path that he saw at the entrance of the wood. After walking for about an hour, he heard a noise and saw the cave with thick smoke coming from the entrance. He thought he might obtain some information there. So he entered and had scarcely taken a step when he saw Ravagio, who instantly seized him with immense strength and would have devoured him, if the cries he uttered in self-defense had not reached the ears of his dear love. At the sound of that voice she felt nothing could stop her. She rushed out of the hole she slept in and entered that part of the cave where Ravagio was holding the poor prince. She was pale and trembling as though she herself was about to be eaten. She threw herself on her knees before Ravagio and begged him to keep this fresh meat for the day of her marriage with the young ogre, and she herself would eat him. At these words Ravagio was so content to think the princess would follow their customs that he let go of the prince and locked him up in the hole where the young ogres slept. Aimée requested that she be allowed to feed him so that he would not get thin and would honor the nuptial repast. The ogre consented, and she took the best of everything to the prince. When he saw her enter, his joy made him forget his wretched condition, but his grief returned when she showed him her wounded foot. They wept together for some time. The prince could not eat, but his dear mistress cut such delicate pieces with her own hands and gave them to him with so much kindness that it was impossible to refuse them. She made the young ogres bring fresh moss, which she covered with birds' feathers, and led the prince to understand it was for his bed. When Tourmentine called her she could only bid adieu to him by stretching out her hand. He kissed it with tender feelings that cannot be described, and in her eyes he read the expression of her feelings.

Ravagio, Tourmentine, and the princess slept in one of the recesses of the cave. The young ogre and five little ogres slept in the other, where the prince was. It is the custom in Ogreland that the ogre, ogress, and the young ogres always sleep in their fine gold crowns. This is the only luxury in which they indulge themselves, and they would rather be hanged or strangled than forego it. When they were all asleep, the princess, who was thinking of her lover, remembered that, although Ravagio and Tourmentine had given her their word of honor that they would not eat the prince, it would all be over for him if they felt hungry in the night (which was almost always the case when there was fresh meat near them). The anxiety fostered by this horrid thought troubled her to such a degree that she felt she might die from fright. After contemplating the situation for some time, she got up, quickly threw on her tigerskin, and groped her way out into the open without making any noise. Then she entered the cave where the little ogres were asleep. She took the crown from the head of the first one she came to and put it on the prince, who was wide awake, but did not dare to show it, for he was not sure who was performing this ceremony. Afterward, the princess returned to her own little bed. No sooner had she crept into it than Ravagio, dreaming of the good meal he might have made of the prince, and his appetite increasing while he thought of it, arose in his turn and went into the hole where the little ogres were sleeping. Since he could not see clearly and was afraid of making a mistake, he felt about with his hand and threw himself on the one who was not wearing a crown. Then he crunched him as he would a chicken. The poor princess, who heard the cracking of the bones of the unfortunate creature he was eating, swooned and became extremely afraid that it might be her lover. For his part, the prince, who was much nearer, was a prey to all the terrors that arise from such a predicament.

Morning relieved the princess of her terrible anxiety. She quickly sought the prince and through sign language made him clearly understand her fears and how eager she was to keep him safe from the murderous teeth of these monsters. She spoke kindly to him, and he would have uttered a thousand kinder words to her, but for the arrival of the ogress, who came to look at her children. When she saw the cave filled with blood and her youngest ogre missing, she uttered horrible shrieks. Ravagio soon found out what he had done, but the evil could not be remedied. He whispered to her that he had been hungry and had chosen the wrong one, for he thought he had eaten the fresh meat.

Tourmentine pretended to be pacified, for Ravagio was cruel, and if she had not taken his apology in good stride, he very likely would have devoured her. But alas, the beautiful princess continued to be tormented by her anxiety. She was constantly thinking about how to save the prince, and he could only think about the frightful place this charming girl was living in. He knew he would never leave the place so long as she was there. Death would have been preferable to separation. He indicated this to her by repeated signs while she implored him to flee and save his own life. They shed tears, pressed each other's hands, and vowed in their respective languages that they would be faithful to each other and love each other eternally. She could not resist showing him the clothes she had on when Tourmentine found her and also the cradle she was in. The prince recognized the arms and emblem of the king of the Happy Island. He was ecstatic when he saw this, and the princess noticed how joyful he became, which led her to believe that he had learned something important from the sight of this cradle. She was dying to know what it meant, but how could he make her aware of whose daughter she was and how closely they were related? All she could make out was that she had great reason to rejoice.

The hour for retiring arrived, and they went to their beds as they had on the previous night. The princess was prey to the same misgivings. So, she got up quietly, went into the cave where the prince was, gently took the crown from one of the little ogres, and put it on her lover's head, who did not dare detain her, no matter how much he wanted to. Indeed, he was prevented by the respect he had for her as well as the fear he had of displeasing her. The princess was smart to put the crown on Aimé's head. Without this precaution he would have been lost. The barbarous Tourmentine was startled out of her sleep and began thinking about the prince, whom she considered more beautiful than the day and very tempting food. She was so afraid that Ravagio would eat him alone that she thought she would beat him to it. Without uttering a word, she glided into the young ogre's cave, where she gently touched those that had crowns on their heads (the prince was among them), and one of the little ogres was gone in three mouthfuls. Aimé and his lady-love heard everything and trembled with fear, but Tourmentine, after having accomplished her purpose, now wanted only to go to sleep. So they were safe for the rest of the night.

"Heaven help us!" the princess cried. "Give me some idea about how we can get out of our terrible predicament!"

The prince prayed as fervently. Sometimes he felt inclined to attack the two monsters and fight them. But what hope did he have of winning against them? They were as tall as giants, and their skin protected them from pistol shots, so he came to the more prudent conclusion that cunning alone could extricate them from this frightful predicament.

As soon as it was day, and Tourmentine found the bones of her little ogre, she filled the air with dreadful howls. Ravagio appeared to be in as much despair. A hundred times they were on the verge of throwing themselves on the prince and princess and devouring them without mercy. Though the prince and princess had hidden themselves in a dark little corner, the cannibals knew full well where they were. Of all the perils they had encountered, this seemed to be the most imminent. Aimée racked her brains and all at once remembered that the ivory wand which Tourmentine possessed performed wonders. Why this was so, she herself could never tell.

"If these surprising things could occur despite her ignorance," the princess said, "why shouldn't my words have just as much effect?"

Inspired by this idea, she ran to the cave in which Tourmentine slept and looked for the wand, which was hidden in a hole. As soon as she had it in her hand, she said, "I wish, in the name of the royal fairy Trufio, to speak the language of the man I love!" She would have made many other wishes, but Ravagio entered, and the princess stopped talking. Instead, she put the wand back and returned very quietly to the prince. "Dear stranger," she said, "your troubles affect me much more than my own do!"

When the prince heard these words, he was struck with astonishment. "I understand you, adorable princess!" he said. "You're speaking my language, and I hope that you, in your turn, understand that I'm more worried about you than about myself, and that you're dearer to me than my life, than the light of day, than all that is most beautiful in nature!"

"My expressions are more simple," the princess replied, "but they aren't any less sincere. I feel I'd give everything in the rocky cave on the seashore, all my sheep and lambs—in short, all I possess—for the pleasure of beholding you."

The prince thanked her a thousand times for her kindness and begged her to tell him who had taught her in such a short time to speak a language that she had not known in such a perfect manner. She told him about the power of the enchanted wand, and he informed her about her birth and their relation to each other. The princess was ecstatic, and since nature had endowed her with such marvelous intelligence, she expressed it in such choice and well-turned phrases that the prince was more in love with her than ever.

They did not have much time to arrange their affairs. It was a question of flight from these disturbed monsters and of seeing an asylum for themselves as fast as they could. They promised to love each other forever and bring about harmony in their lives the moment they were able to be married. The princess told her lover that, as soon as she saw Ravagio and Tourmentine were asleep, she would fetch their great camel. Then they would get on it and let heaven conduct them wherever it desired. The prince was so delighted he had difficulty containing his joy. Many things that still alarmed him were offset by the charming prospect of the future.

Finally the night they had desired so long arrived. The princess took some meal and kneaded it with her white hands into a cake in which she put a bean. Then she picked up the ivory wand and said, "Oh, bean, little bean! I wish, in the name of the royal fairy Trufio, that you may speak, if it be necessary, until you're baked." She put this cake in the hot cinders and then went to the prince, who was waiting most impatiently in the miserable lodging belonging to the young ogres. "Let's go," she said. "The camel is tethered in the wood."

"May love and fortune guide us," the prince replied in a low voice. "Come, come, my Aimée, let's seek a happy and peaceful abode." It was moonlight, and she had put the ivory wand in a safe place. When they found the camel, they set out on the road not knowing where they were going. In the meantime, Tourmentine, who was full of grief, kept turning about without being able to sleep. She put out her arm to feel if the princess was in her bed yet, and not finding her, she cried out in a voice of thunder, "Where are you, girl?"

"I'm near the fire," answered the bean.

"When are you coming to bed?" Tourmentine asked.

"Soon," the bean replied. "Go to sleep, go to sleep." Tourmentine was afraid of waking Ravagio and stopped speaking. But two hours later she again felt Aimée's little bed and cried out, "What, you little rascal, you won't come to bed?"

"I'm warming myself as much as I can," the bean answered.

"I wish you were in the middle of the fire for all the trouble you're causing," the ogress added. "I'm there," the bean said, "and nobody has ever warmed himself nearer."

They continued talking for a while, and the bean kept up the conversation, like a very clever bean. Toward morning, Tourmentine again called the princess, but the bean was baked and did not answer. This silence made her uneasy. So she got up very angry, looked about her, called, alarmed everybody, and began searching everywhere. No princess! No prince! No little wand! She shrieked so loudly that the rocks and valleys echoed again and again. "Wake up, my poppet! Awake, dear Ravagio! Your Tourmentine has been betrayed. Our fresh meat has run away."

Ravagio opened his eye and sprang into the middle of the cavern like a lion. He roared, he bellowed, he howled, he foamed. "Quick, quick! Give me my seven-league boots so I can pursue our fugitives. I'll catch them and swallow them before they can get very far."

So he put on his boots, which carried him seven leagues with one stride.

Alas! How was it possible to run fast enough and escape such a runner? You may be surprised that with the ivory wand they could not go faster than he did, but the beautiful princess was a novice in fairy art. She did not know all she could do with such a wand, and it was only in extreme cases that she was afforded sudden insights.

They were now delighted to be together and to be able to understand each other. They were also extremely hopeful that they would not be pursued. However, as they advanced, the princess caught sight of the terrible Ravagio and cried out, "Prince, we're lost! Look, there's that frightful monster coming toward us like a thunderbolt!"

"What shall we do?" the prince exclaimed. "What will become of us? Ah, if I were alone, I wouldn't care about my life, but yours, my dear mistress, is threatened."

"Unless the wand helps us, there's no hope," Aimée remarked in tears. "I wish," she continued, "in the name of the royal fairy Trufio, that our camel would become a pond, that the prince would become a boat, and myself an old woman who rows the boat."

Immediately, the pond, the boat, and the old woman were there, and Ravagio arrived at the water's edge. "Hola, ho! Old mother," he cried, "have you seen a camel and a young man and woman pass by here?"

The old woman, who kept her boat in the middle of the pond, put her spectacles on her nose, and as she gazed at Ravagio, she made signs to him that she had seen them, and that they had passed through the meadow. The ogre believed her, and he went off to the left. Then the princess wished for her natural form again, and she touched herself with the wand three times and struck the boat and the pond. She and the prince became young and beautiful again. They quickly mounted the camel and turned to the right so that they would not encounter their foe.

While proceeding rapidly and hoping to find someone who could tell them the road to the Happy Island, they lived off the wild fruit of the country, drank water from the fountains, and slept beneath the trees, even though they feared that wild beasts could come and devour them. But the princess had her bow and arrows, with which she would have tried to defend herself. The danger was not so terrible as to prevent them from enjoying the exhilaration of being released from the cave and finding themselves together. Ever since they could speak the same language, they said the prettiest things in the world to each other. Love generally quickens the wit, but in their case, they needed no such assistance because they each had a thousand natural charms and unique ideas constantly at hand.

The prince told the princess that he was extremely eager to reach either his or her royal father's court as soon as possible, especially since she had promised to become his wife, provided that their parents consented. What you will have some difficulty perhaps in believing is that, while waiting for this happy day, and being with her in forests and solitude, where he was at complete liberty to make her any proposals he desired, he conducted himself in such a respectful and prudent manner that the world has never witnessed so much love and virtue together in one person.

After Ravagio had scoured the mountains, forests, and plains, he returned to his cave, where Tourmentine and the young ogres impatiently awaited him. He was carrying five or six people who had unfortunately fallen into his clutches.

"Well," said Tourmentine, "have you found and eaten those runaways, those thieves, that fresh meat? Didn't you at least save me one of their hands or feet?"

"I believe they must have flown off into the sky," replied Ravagio. "I ran like a wolf everywhere without encountering them. I only saw an old woman in a boat on a pond, who gave me some tidings about them."

"What did she tell you then?" Tourmentine asked impatiently.

"That they had gone to the left," Ravagio replied.

"My word, you've been deceived!" she said. "I suspect you actually spoke to them. Go back, and if you find them, don't give them a moment's grace!"

Ravagio greased his seven-league boots and set out again like a madman. Our young lovers were just emerging from a wood in which they had passed the night. When they saw the ogre, they were both greatly alarmed. "My Aimée," said the prince, "our enemy is here. I feel I have enough courage to fight him. Do you think you have enough courage to flee by yourself?"

"No," she cried, "I'll never forsake you. How can you be so unkind? How can you doubt my love for you? But let's not lose any time. Perhaps the wand may help us. I wish," she cried, "in the name of the royal fairy Trufio, that the prince be changed into a picture, the camel into a pillar, and myself into a dwarf."

The change was made, and the dwarf began to blow a horn. Ravagio approached with rapid strides and said, "Tell me, you little abortion of nature, have you seen a fine young man, a young girl, and a camel pass by here?"

"Ah, I'll tell you," replied the dwarf. "I know that you're searching for a fine chevalier, a marvelously fair dame, and the beast they rode on. I saw them here yesterday at this spot enjoying themselves happily and joyously. The fine chevalier received the praise and guerdon[2] of the jousts and tournaments, which were held in honor of Melusine,[3] whose features are depicted here. Many high-born gentlemen and good knights broke their lances here on hauberks,[4] helmets, and shields. The contest was rough, and the guerdon was a most beautiful clasp of gold, richly beset with pearls and diamonds. On their departure, the unknown dame said to me, 'Dwarf, my friend, without much ado, I'd like you to do me a favor in the name of your fairest lady-love.' 'It won't be denied,' I said to her, 'and I grant it to you, on the sole condition that it's within my power.' 'In case, then,' she said, 'that you should meet the great and extraordinary giant whose eye is in the middle of his forehead, ask him most courteously

---

2. A reward or a recompense.
3. A fairy from French folklore, also known as Mélisande. After she punished her father, who had offended her mother, by imprisoning him in a large mountain, she herself was punished and sentenced to assume the shape of a serpent from the waist down every Saturday.
4. A piece of protective armor, generally for the neck and shoulders.

to go his way in peace and leave us alone.' With that, she whipped her palfrey,[5] and they departed."

"Which way?" Ravagio asked.

"By that verdant meadow on the edge of the wood," said the dwarf.

"If you're lying, you filthy little reptile," the ogre replied, "you can be sure that I'll eat you, your pillar, and your portrait of Melusine."

"There's no villainy or falsehood in me," said the dwarf. "My mouth doesn't lie. No one alive can convict me of fraud. But go quickly, if you want to kill them before the sun sets."

The ogre strode away. The dwarf resumed her own figure and touched the portrait and the pillar, which also became themselves again. What joy for the lover and his mistress!

"Never have I felt such terrible anxiety, my dear Aimée!" the prince said. "As my love for you increases every moment, so do my fears when you are in danger."

"As for me," she said, "it seems to me that I wasn't afraid, for Ravagio never eats pictures, and I alone was exposed to his fury, and my figure was not appetizing. No matter what, I would have given my life to protect yours."

Ravagio hunted in vain and could not find the lover or his mistress. Tired as a dog, he retraced his steps to the cave.

"What! You've returned without our prisoners?" Tourmentine exclaimed, tearing her bristling hair. "Don't come near me, or I'll strangle you!"

"I saw nothing," he said, "but a dwarf, a pillar, and a picture."

"My word," she continued, "it was them! I was very foolish to leave my vengeance in your hands, as though I were too little to undertake it myself. Now I'll go! I'll put on the boots this time, and I'll go just as fast as you."

She put on the seven-league boots and started off. What chance did the prince and princess have of traveling quickly enough to escape these monsters with their cursed seven-league boots? They saw Tourmentine coming, dressed in a serpent's skin with startling motley colors. On her shoulder she carried a terribly heavy mace of iron, and as she looked around her carefully, she would have seen the prince and princess, had they not been in the thickest part of a wood at that moment.

"The matter's hopeless," said Aimée, weeping. "Here comes the cruel Tourmentine, whose sight chills my blood. She's more cunning than Ravagio. If either of us were to speak to her, she'd know us and eat us up without much ado. Our trial will soon be over as you can imagine."

"Love, love, do not abandon us!" the prince exclaimed. "Can you find more tender or more pure hearts than ours in your realm? Ah, my dear Aimée," he continued, taking her hands and kissing them fervently, "can it be that you're destined to perish in such a barbarous manner?"

"No," she said, "no. I have a certain feeling of courage and firmness that reassures me. Come, little wand, do your duty. I wish, in the name of the royal fairy Trufio, that the camel become a tub, that my dear prince

5. A small saddle horse for ladies.

become a beautiful orange tree, and that I become a bee that hovers around him."

As usual, she struck three blows for each, and the change took place so suddenly that Tourmentine, who had arrived on the spot, did not notice it. The horrible fury was out of breath and sat down under the orange tree. The princess bee took delight in stinging her in a thousand places, and although her skin was very hard, the sting pierced it and made her cry out. To see her roll and flail about on the grass one would have thought her a bull, or a young lion, tormented by a swarm of insects, for this one was worth a hundred. The prince orange tree was dying with fear the princess would be caught and killed. At last, Tourmentine, covered with blood, went away, and the princess was about to resume her own form when, unfortunately, some travelers passed through the wood and saw the ivory wand. It was such a very pretty-looking thing that they picked it up and carried it away. Nothing could be any more unfortunate than this. The prince and princess had not lost their speech, but it was of little use to them in their present condition! The prince was overwhelmed with grief and uttered lamentations that greatly added to his dear Aimée's distress.

"How wretched I am," he exclaimed, "to be locked up within the bark of a tree. Here I am, an orange tree, without any power to move. What will become of me, if you abandon me, my dear little bee? On the other hand, why must you fly so far from me? You'll find a most pleasant dew on my flowers, and drops sweeter than honey. You'll be able to live on this. My leaves will invite you to couch in them, and you'll have nothing to fear from the malice of spiders!"

As soon as the orange tree stopped uttering complaints, the bee replied to him like this:

"Fear not, prince, that I should range.
There's nothing my faithful heart can change.
Let your thoughts now form a sign
To show how you have conquered mine."

She added to that, "Have no fear that I'll ever leave you. Neither the lilies, nor the jasmines, nor the roses, nor all the flowers of the most beautiful gardens would induce me to be unfaithful to you. You'll see me continually flying around you, and you'll know that the orange tree is just as dear to the bee as Prince Aimé was to Princess Aimée."

In short, she shut herself up in one of the largest flowers, as though in a palace, and true love, which is never without its consolation, found some even in this union. The wood in which the orange tree was situated was the favorite promenade of a princess who lived nearby in a magnificent palace. She was young, beautiful, and witty: they called her Linda. She refused to marry because she was afraid she would not always be loved by the man she might choose for a husband. And, since she was very wealthy, she built a sumptuous castle where she admitted only ladies and old men (more philosophers than gallants) and prevented young cavaliers from coming near.

One day, when the heat kept her in her apartments somewhat longer than she had wished, she went out in the evening with all her ladies and took a walk in the wood. The pleasant odors from the orange tree surprised her. She had never seen one, and she was delighted to have found it. She could not understand how she had happened to come upon it in such a place. Soon the entire company surrounded it, and Linda forbade anyone to pick a single flower. They carried the tree into her garden, and the faithful bee followed it. Linda was enchanted by its delicious scent and seated herself beneath it. Before returning to the palace, she was about to gather a few of the blossoms, when the vigilant bee sallied out humming from under the leaves, where she remained as sentinel, and stung the princess so severely that she very nearly fainted. That put an end to depriving the orange tree of its blossoms, and Linda returned to her palace, quite ill.

When the prince was at liberty to speak to Aimée, he said, "What made you so mad at young Linda, my dear bee? You've stung her cruelly."

"How can you ask such a question?" she replied. "Don't you have enough sensitivity to understand that you shouldn't offer any sweets except to me, that all that's yours belongs to me, and that I defend my property when I defend your blossoms?"

"But," he said, "you see them fall without being distressed. Wouldn't it be just the same to you if the princess adorned herself with them, if she placed them in her hair, or put them in her bosom?"

"No," the bee said in a sharp tone, "it's not at all the same thing to me. I know, ungrateful one, that you feel more for her than you do for me. There's also a great difference between a refined person, richly dressed, and of considerable rank in these parts, and an unfortunate princess whom you found covered with a tigerskin, surrounded by monsters who could only give her crude and barbarous ideas, and whose beauty is not great enough to enslave you."

And then she cried, as much as any bee is capable of crying. Some of the flowers of the enamored orange tree were made wet by her tears, and his distress at having disturbed his princess was so great that all his leaves turned yellow, several branches withered, and he thought he would die.

"What have I done, then," he exclaimed, "my beautiful bee? What have I done to make you so angry? Ah! Doubtless, you'll abandon me. You're already weary of being linked to one so unfortunate as I am."

They spent the night exchanging reproaches, but at the break of day a kind zephyr[6] who had been listening to them brought about a reconciliation and could not have done them a greater service. In the meantime, Linda, who was dying to have a bouquet of orange flowers, arose early in the morning, descended to her flower garden, and went to gather one. But when she extended her hand, she felt herself so violently stung by the jealous bee that she lost heart. She returned to her room in a very bad temper.

"I can't make out," she said, "what kind of a tree this is that we've found. Whenever I try to take the smallest bud, some insects that guard it pierce me with their stings."

6. The west wind.

One of her maids, who had some wit and was very lively, said laughingly, "I would advise you, madam, to arm yourself as an Amazon, and follow Jason's[7] example, when he went to win the golden fleece, and courageously take the most beautiful flowers from this pretty tree."

Linda thought there was something amusing in this idea, and she immediately ordered them to make her a helmet covered with feathers, a light cuirass, and gauntlets,[8] and to the sound of trumpets, kettledrums, fifes, and oboes, she entered the garden, followed by all her ladies, who were armed like she was, and who called this fête "the Battle of the Bees and Amazons." Linda drew her sword very gracefully. Then, striking the most beautiful branch of the orange tree, she said, "Appear, terrible bees, appear! I come to defy you! Are you valiant enough to defend that which you love?"

But Linda, and all who accompanied her, were taken aback when they heard a pitiful "Alas!" issue from the stem of the orange tree and saw blood flowing from the severed branch!

"Heavens!" she cried, "what have I done? What marvel is this?" She took the bleeding branch and vainly attempted to join the pieces together. However, she felt herself seized by a terrible fright and anxiety.

The poor little bee was desperate when this sad accident happened to her dear orange tree. She was about to rush out and would have met with death at the point of the fatal sword in her attempt to avenge her dear prince. But she preferred to stay alive for him and remembered a remedy that he would need. So she begged him to let her fly to Arabia so she could bring back some balm for him. After he consented to her going there, and they said their tender and affectionate farewells, she started for that part of the world with instinct alone for her guide. But to speak more correctly, love carried her there, and as he flies faster than the swiftest of winged creatures, he enabled her to complete this long journey very quickly. She brought back the wonderful balm on her wings and with her little feet, and soon she cured her prince. It is true that he was cured not so much by the excellence of the balm as by the pleasure it afforded him in seeing the princess bee take so much care of his wound. She applied the balm every day, and he needed a great deal, for the severed branch was one of his fingers. Indeed, if Linda had continued her assault, he would soon have had neither legs nor arms. Oh, how acutely did the bee feel for the sufferings of the orange tree! She reproached herself with being responsible because of the impetuous manner in which she had defended its flowers. On the other hand, Linda was alarmed at what she had done and could neither sleep nor eat. At last, she decided to send for some fairies in hope that they would enlighten her about a matter that seemed so extraordinary. She despatched ambassadors, loaded with splendid presents, to invite them to her court.

Queen Trufio was one of the first who arrived at Linda's palace. No one was as skilled as she in fairy art. She examined the branch and the

---

7. Greek hero, leader of the Argonauts, who went on a quest for the Golden Fleece of Colchis, a valuable trophy that brought distinction to Jason.
8. Gloves worn as part of medieval armor. "Cuirass": a piece of armor for the body, originally made of leather.

orange tree; she smelt its flowers and detected a human scent, which surprised her. She did not leave a spell untried and employed some so powerful that all at once the orange tree disappeared, and they saw the prince, handsomer and more strapping than any other man in the world. At this sight Linda was petrified. She felt herself struck with admiration and with such a special feeling for him that she soon lost her former indifference.

But the young prince could think of nothing but his charming bee and threw himself at Trufio's feet. "Great queen," he said, "I'm infinitely indebted to you, for you have given me new life by restoring me to my original form. But if you want me to be indebted to you for my peace and happiness—a blessing even greater than the life you've returned to me—restore my princess to me!" Upon uttering these words, he took hold of the little bee, whom he had never stopped gazing at.

"You shall be satisfied," the generous Trufio answered. She began performing her spells again, and the Princess Aimée appeared with so many charms that there was not a single lady there who did not feel envious. Linda herself was uncertain as to whether she ought to be pleased or angered by such an extraordinary incident, particularly by the transformation of the bee.

Finally, her reason got the better of her feelings, which were nipped in the bud. She embraced Aimée a thousand times, and Trufio asked her to tell about her adventures. She was under too much obligation to her to refuse this request. The graceful and easy manner with which she spoke interested the whole assembly, and when she told Trufio she had performed so many wonders by virtue of her name and her wand, there was an exclamation of joy throughout the hall, and everyone begged the fairy to complete this great work. Trufio, on her side, felt extremely glad at hearing all she heard and embraced the princess with her arms.

"Since I was so useful to you, without knowing you," she said to her, "you may judge, charming Aimée, now that I know you, how much I'm inclined to serve you. I'm a friend of the king, your father, and of the queen, your mother: let's go right now in my flying chariot to the Happy Island, where both of you will be welcomed as you deserve."

Linda begged them to remain one day with her, during which time she gave them very costly presents, and the Princess Aimée took off her tigerskin to wear dresses of incomparable beauty. Let all now imagine the joy of our happy lovers. Yes, let them imagine it, if they can, but to do that, they must have experienced the same misfortunes, have been among ogres, and have undergone as many transformations.

At last, they departed. Trufio conducted them through the air to the Happy Island, where they were received by the king and queen as the last persons in the world they had ever expected to see again, but whom they beheld with the greatest pleasure. Aimée's beauty and prudence, added to her intelligence, made her the wonder of the age. Her dear mother loved her passionately. The fine qualities of Prince Aimé's mind were no less appreciated than his handsome person. The wedding was celebrated, and never in the world was anything so magnificent. The graces attended in their festive attire. The loves were there, without even being invited, and by their express order, the eldest son of the prince and princess was named *Faithful Love*. Since then they have given him many other titles, and under all these various names it is very difficult to find a Faithful Love such as that which sprang from this charming marriage. Happy are those who encounter him without any misunderstandings.

> *Aimée with her lover alone in a wood*
> *Conducted herself with great discretion.*
> *To reason she listened—temptation withstood,*
> *And lost not a jot of her prince's affection.*
> *Believe not, fair ones, who would captivate hearts,*
> *That Cupid needs pleasure alone to retain him.*
> *Love oft from the lap of indulgence departs,*
> *But prudence and virtue will always enchain him.*

JACOB AND WILHELM GRIMM

Okerlo†

A queen put her child out to sea in a golden cradle and let it float away. However, the cradle did not sink but floated to an island inhabited only by cannibals. When the cradle drifted toward the shore, a cannibal's wife happened to be standing there. Upon seeing the child, who was a beautiful baby girl, she decided to raise her for her son, who would wed her one day. But she had a great deal of trouble hiding the maiden carefully from her husband, Old Okerlo, for if he had laid his eyes on her, he would have eaten her up, skin and bones.

When the maiden had grown up, she was to be married to the young Okerlo, but she could not stand him and cried all day long. Once when she was sitting on the shore, a young handsome prince came swimming up to her. Since they each took a liking to the other, they exchanged vows. Just then the old cannibal's wife came, and she got tremendously angry at finding the prince with her son's bride. So she grabbed hold of him and said, "Just wait! We'll roast you at my son's wedding."

The young prince, the maiden, and Okerlo's three children had to sleep together in one room. When night came, Old Okerlo began craving human flesh and said, "Wife, I don't feel like waiting until the wedding. I want the prince right now."

However, the maiden had heard everything through the wall, and she got up quickly, took off the golden crown from one of Okerlo's children, and put it on the prince's head. When the old cannibal's wife came in, it was dark. So she had to feel their heads and took the boy that was not wearing a crown and brought him to her husband, who immediately ate him up. Meanwhile, the maiden became terribly frightened, for she thought, "As soon as day breaks, everything will be revealed, and we'll be in trouble." She got up quietly and fetched seven-mile boots, a magic

---

† Jacob and Wilhelm Grimm, "Okerlo"—"Okerlo" (1812), was first published as No. 70 in *Kinder-und Hausmärchen. Gesammelt durch die Brüder Grimm* (Berlin: Realschulbuchhandlung, 1812).

wand, and a cake with a bean that provided answers for everything. After that she departed with the prince. They were wearing the seven-mile boots, and with each step they took, they went a mile. Sometimes they asked the bean, "Bean, are you there?"

"Yes," the bean said. "I'm here, but you'd better hurry. The old cannibal's wife is coming after you in some other seven-mile boots that were left behind!"

The maiden took the magic wand and turned herself into a swan and the prince into a pond for the swan to swim on. The cannibal's wife came and tried to lure the swan to the bank, but she did not succeed and went home in a bad mood. The maiden and the prince continued on their way.

"Bean, are you there?"

"Yes," the bean said. "I'm here, but the old woman's coming again. The cannibal explained to her how you duped her."

The princess took the wand and changed herself and the prince into a cloud of dust. Okerlo's wife could not penetrate it and again had to return empty-handed, while the maiden and the prince continued on their way.

"Bean, are you there?"

"Yes, I'm here, but I see Okerlo's wife coming once more, and she's taking tremendous steps!"

The maiden took the magic wand for the third time and turned herself into a rosebush and the prince into a bee. The old cannibal came and did not recognize them because of their changed forms. So she went home.

But now the maiden and the prince could not regain their human forms because the maiden, in her fear, had thrown the magic wand too far away. Yet their journey had taken them such a long distance that the rosebush now stood in a garden that belonged to the maiden's mother. The bee sat on the rose, and he would sting anyone who tried to pluck it. One day the queen happened to be walking in the garden and saw the beautiful flower. She was so amazed by it that she wanted to pluck it. But the little bee came and stung her on her hand so hard that she had to let go of the rose. Yet she had managed to rip the flower a little, and suddenly she saw blood gushing from the stem. Then she summoned a fairy to break the enchantment of the flower and the bee, and the queen then recognized her daughter again and was very happy and delighted. Now a great wedding was held, and a large number of guests were invited. They came in a magnificent array, while thousands of candles flickered in the hall. Music was played, and everyone danced until dawn.

"Were you also at the wedding?"

"Of course I was there. My hairdo was made of butter, and when I was exposed to the sun, it melted and was muddled. My dress was made from a spider's web, and when I went through some thornbushes, they ripped it off my body. My slippers were made of glass, and when I stepped on a stone, they broke in two."

Compassionate Sisters and
Ungrateful Demons

Wilhelm Grimm read Caroline Stahl's fairy tale "The Ungrateful Dwarf" some time during the early 1820s and adapted it for publication in Wilhelm Hauff's *Mährchenalmanach für Söhne und Töchter gebildeter Stände auf das Jahr 1827*, which was actually published in 1826. He made many changes by creating more of a harmonious bourgeois home life for Snow White and Rose Red, giving the dwarf greater characterization, and adding the love story. In 1837, Wilhelm added it to the *Children's and Household Tales*, and it has become one of the more popular tales, especially for children. It is a good example of how both Stahl and Wilhelm Grimm sought to "domesticate" and adapt the fairy tale for children. There are no known previous oral versions, but Grimm's text has fostered numerous versions since its publication.

CAROLINE STAHL

The Ungrateful Dwarf†

A very poor couple had many, many children, and they had great difficulty feeding them all. One time the children went into the forest to look for wood. One of the girls, by the name of Snow White, happened to lose her way and became separated from the others. Then to her astonishment she met an ugly dwarf who could not have been more than a yard high. He had chopped down a tree and wanted to split it in two. Indeed, he had already made a deep crack in the wood and had slipped a peg inside to keep it open. However, this peg, and I don't know how, had fallen out, and the crack had quickly closed, catching and clamping a large part of the dwarf's enormously long beard so that he stood there trapped. When he saw the girl, he called to her for help, and Snow White was also ready to help him, but try as she might, she was not able to pull the beard out of the crack in the tree.

Then Snow White offered to run quickly to her home and fetch her father, but the dwarf forbade this. Instead, he ordered her to get some scissors in order to cut off the beard. She obeyed and ran off. Soon she returned and freed him by cutting off the part of the beard that had been caught. Immediately thereafter, the dwarf pulled out a sack with money from beneath the tree, and although it would have been proper for him

† Caroline Stahl, "The Ungrateful Dwarf"—"Der undankbare Zwerg" (1818), in *Fabeln, Mährchen und Erzählungen für Kinder* (Nuremberg, 1818).

to have politely thanked his rescuer and to have given her a rich reward from his bundle of money, he did neither one nor the other but crept away grumbling about his accident without a greeting or word of thanks. Snow White just looked at him depart and then she herself scooted away.

Not long after this Snow White went to the river with her sister Rose Red to fish and to catch crabs. All of a sudden she saw the dwarf again, and this time the line of a fishing rod was completely entangled in his beard. At the same time a fish had bitten the hook and pulled the squeaking dwarf into the water. The girls grabbed hold of the little man in order to keep him on shore, but it was impossible to unwind the beard from the line, and the big fish, which was much larger than the fisherman, continued to pull. Then Snow White told her sister to stand there and hold on tight to the dwarf while she ran home and fetched some scissors.

She ran like lightning back and forth and cut the line of the fishing rod, and part of the beard was also lost. Consequently, the dwarf grumbled a great deal, grabbed a sack with the most beautiful pearls and, just like the first time, revealed himself to be ungrateful and impolite and left. But the girls kept fishing and hunting for crabs and did not think any more about the crass little man.

Some time later it happened that the girls were sent to the city in order to fetch something. When the girls were crossing the field, they noticed an eagle which had attacked the dwarf they knew so well and wanted to carry him off. Rose Red and Snow White threw stones at the bird, and since that did not help, they grabbed hold of the little man and tried to tear him away from the eagle, and neither side wanted to let go of the prey. But then the evil dwarf shrieked in such a dreadful way that the eagle became frightened and abandoned him. This time the dwarf had a sack full of jewels with him, and he departed unceremoniously like the first time.

It was not long before the girls found the dwarf again, and this time he was in the paws of a bear, who was about to mash him. They cried out in fright, and the bear hesitated and looked. Then the dwarf begged, "Oh, dear merciful bear, don't eat me! I'll even give you my sacks of gold, pearls, and jewels. Do you see the girls over there? They are young and juicy and tender. They are much more of a tasty morsel than I am. Take them instead and eat them!"

The girls were paralyzed with fright when they heard the ungrateful dwarf's words. However, the bear did not pay any attention to their words. Rather, he roared and ate him skin and hair and then went on his way.

Now the girls found the sacks with pearls, gold, and jewels, which they dragged with great effort to the parents, for the sacks were very heavy. All of a sudden they were as rich as the richest princes and bought beautiful castles and estates, and Snow White and Rose Red as well as their siblings could now study and learn a lot and acquire beautiful clothes and things. However, nobody felt sorry for the nasty dwarf, for he had certainly deserved what fate had in store for him.

JACOB AND WILHELM GRIMM

Snow White and Rose Red†

A widow lived all alone in a small cottage, and in front of this cottage was a garden with two rosebushes. One bore white roses and the other red. The widow had two children, who looked like the rosebushes: one was called Snow White and the other Rose Red. They were pious and kind, more hardworking and diligent than any other two children in the world. To be sure, Snow White was more quiet and gentle than Rose Red, who preferred to run around in the meadows and fields, look for flowers, and catch butterflies. Snow White stayed at home with her mother, helped her with the housework, or read to her when there was nothing to do. The two children loved each other so much that they always held hands whenever they went out, and when Snow White said, "Let us never leave each other," Rose Red answered, "Never, as long as we live." And their mother added, "Whatever one of you has, remember to share it with the other."

They often wandered in the forest all alone and gathered red berries. The animals never harmed them and, indeed, trusted them completely and would come up to them. The little hare would eat a cabbage leaf out of their hands. The roe grazed by their side. The stag leapt merrily around them. And the birds sat still on their branches and sang whatever tune they knew. Nothing bad ever happened to the girls. If they stayed too long in the forest and night overtook them, they would lie down next to each other on the moss and sleep until morning came. Their mother knew this and did not worry about them.

Once, when they had spent the night in the forest, and the morning sun had wakened them, they saw a beautiful child in a white, glistening garment sitting near them. The child stood up, looked at them in a friendly way, but went into the forest without saying anything. When they looked around, they realized that they had been sleeping at the edge of a cliff and would have certainly fallen over if they had gone a few more steps in the darkness. Their mother told them that the child must have been the angel who watches over good children.

Snow White and Rose Red kept their mother's cottage so clean that it was a joy to look inside. In the summer Rose Red took care of the house, and every morning she placed two flowers in front of her mother's bed before she awoke, a rose from each one of the bushes. In the winter Snow White lit the fire and hung the kettle over the hearth. The kettle was made out of brass but glistened like gold because it was polished so clean. In the evening, when the snowflakes fell, the mother said, "Go, Snow White, and bolt the door." Then they sat down at the hearth, and their mother put on her glasses and read aloud from a large book, while the two girls sat and spun as they listened. On the ground next to them lay a little lamb

---

† Jacob and Wilhelm Grimm, "Snow White and Rose Red"—"Schneeweisschen und Rosenrot" (1857), No. 161 in *Kinder- und Hausmärchen. Gesammelt durch die Brüder Grimm* (Göttingen: Dieterich, 1857).

and behind them sat a white dove with its head tucked under its wing.

One evening, as they were sitting together, there was a knock on the door, as if someone wanted to be let in. The mother said, "Quick, Rose Red open the door. It must be a traveler looking for shelter."

Rose Red pushed back the bolt, thinking that it would be some poor man, but instead it was a bear. He stuck his thick black head through the door, and Rose Red jumped back and screamed loudly. The little lamb bleated, the dove fluttered its wings, and Snow White hid herself behind her mother's bed. However, the bear began to speak and said, "Don't be afraid. I won't harm you. I'm half frozen and only want to warm myself here a little."

"You poor bear," the mother said. "Lie down by the fire and take care that it does not burn your fur." Then she called out, "Snow White, Rose Red, come out. The bear won't harm you. He means well."

They both came out, and gradually the lamb and dove also drew near and lost their fear of him. Then the bear said, "Come, children, dust the snow off my coat a little."

So they fetched a broom and swept the fur clean. Afterward, he stretched himself out beside the fire and uttered growls to show how content and comfortable he was. It did not take them long to all become accustomed to one another, and the clumsy guest had to put up with the mischievous pranks of the girls. They tugged his fur with their hands, planted their feet upon his back and rolled him over, or they took a hazel switch and hit him. When he growled, they just laughed. The bear took everything in good spirit. Only when they became too rough did he cry out, "Let me live, children!

> "Snow White, Rose Red,
> would you beat your suitor dead?"

When it was time to sleep and the others went to bed, the mother said to the bear, "You're welcome, in God's name, to lie down by the hearth. Then you'll be protected from the cold and bad weather."

As soon as dawn arrived, the two girls let him go outside, and he trotted over the snow into the forest. From then on, the bear came every evening at a certain time, lay down by the hearth, and allowed the girls to play with him as much as they wanted. And they became so accustomed to him that they never bolted the door until their black playmate had arrived.

One morning, when spring had made its appearance and everything outside was green, the bear said to Snow White, "Now I must go away, and I shall not return the entire summer."

"But where are you going, dear bear?" asked Snow White.

"I must go into the forest and guard my treasures from the wicked dwarfs. In the winter, when the ground is frozen hard, they must remain underground and can't work their way through to the top. But now that the sun has thawed and warmed the earth, they will break through, climb out, and search around, and steal. Once they get something in their hands and carry it to their caves, it will not easily see the light of day again."

Snow White was very sad about his departure. She unlocked the door, and when the bear hurried out, he became caught on the bolt and a piece of his fur ripped off, and it seemed to Snow White that she saw gold glimmering through the fur, but she was not sure. The bear hurried away and soon disappeared beyond the trees.

Some time after, the mother sent the girls into the forest to gather firewood. There they found a large tree lying on the ground that had been chopped down. Something was jumping up and down on the grass near the trunk, but they could not tell what it was. As they came closer, they saw a dwarf with an old withered face and a beard that was snow white and a yard long. The tip of the beard was caught in a crack of the tree, and the little fellow was jumping back and forth like a dog on a rope and did not know what to do. He glared at the girls with his fiery red eyes and screamed, "What are you standing there for? Can't you come over here and help me?"

"How did you get into this jam, little man?" asked Rose Red.

"You stupid, nosy goose," answered the dwarf, "I wanted to split the tree to get some wood for my kitchen. We dwarfs need but little food. However, it gets burned fast when we use those thick logs. We don't devour such large portions as you coarse and greedy people. I had just driven in the wedge safely, and everything would have gone all right, but the cursed wedge was too smooth, and it sprang out unexpectedly. The tree snapped shut so rapidly that I couldn't save my beautiful white beard. Now it's stuck there, and I can't get away. And all you silly, creamy-faced things can do is laugh! Uggh, you're just nasty!"

The girls tried as hard as they could, but they could not pull the beard out. It was stuck too tight.

"I'll run and get somebody," Rose Red said.

"Crazy fool!" the dwarf snarled. "Why run and get someone? The two of you are already enough. Can't you think of something better?"

"Don't be impatient," said Snow White. "I'll think of something." She took a pair of scissors from her pocket and cut off the tip of his beard. As soon as the dwarf felt that he was free, he grabbed a sack filled with gold that was lying between the roots of the tree. After he lifted it out, he grumbled to himself, "Uncouth slobs! How could you cut off a piece of my fine beard? Good riddance to you!" Upon saying this, he swung the sack over his shoulder and went away without once looking at the girls.

Some time after this Snow White and Rose Red wanted to catch some fish for dinner. As they approached the brook, they saw something like a large grasshopper bouncing toward the water as if it wanted to jump in. They ran to the spot and recognized the dwarf.

"Where are you going?" asked Rose Red. "You don't want to jump into the water, do you?"

"I'm not such a fool as that!" the dwarf screamed. "Don't you see that the cursed fish wants to pull me in?"

The little man had been sitting there and fishing, and unfortunately the wind had caught his beard so that it had become entangled with his line. Just then a large fish had bitten the bait, and the feeble little dwarf did not have the strength to land the fish, which kept the upper hand and pulled him toward the water. To be sure, the dwarf tried to grab hold of the reeds and rushes, but that did not help much. He was compelled to follow the movements of the fish and was in constant danger of being dragged into the water, but the girls had come just in the nick of time. They held on to him tightly and tried to untangle his beard from the line. However, it was to no avail. The beard and line were meshed together, and there was nothing left to do but to take out the scissors and cut off a small part of his beard. When the dwarf saw this, he screamed at them, "You birdbrains! You've disfigured my face like barbarians. It was not enough that you clipped the tip of my beard. Now you've cut off the best part. I won't be able to show myself among my friends. May you both walk for miles on end until the soles of your shoes are burned off!" Then he grabbed a sack of pearls that was lying in the rushes, and without saying another word, he dragged it away and disappeared behind a rock.

It happened that, soon after this, the girls were sent by their mother to the city to buy thread, needles, lace, and ribbons. Their way led over a heath which had huge pieces of rock scattered here and there. A large bird circled slowly in the air above them, flying lower and lower until it finally landed on the ground not far from a rock. Right after that they heard a piercing, terrible cry. They ran to the spot and saw with horror that the eagle had seized their old acquaintance the dwarf and intended to carry him away. The girls took pity on him and grabbed hold of the little man as tightly as they could. They tugged against the eagle until finally the bird had to abandon his booty. When the dwarf recovered from his initial fright, he screeched at them, "Couldn't you have handled me more carefully? You've torn my coat to shreds. It was thin enough to begin with, but now it's got holes and rips all over, you clumsy louts!" Then he took a sack with jewels and once more slipped under a rock into his cave.

The girls were accustomed to his ingratitude and continued on their way. They took care of their chores in the city, and when they crossed the heath again on their way home, they surprised the dwarf, who had dumped his sack of jewels on a clean spot, not thinking that anyone would come by at such a late hour. The evening sun's rays were cast upon the glistening stones, which glimmered and sparkled in such radiant colors that the girls had to stop and look at them.

"Why are you standing there and gaping like monkeys?" the dwarf screamed, and his ash gray face turned scarlet with rage. He was about to continue his cursing when a loud growl was heard and a black bear came trotting out of the forest. The dwarf jumped up in terror, but he could not reach his hiding place in time. The bear was already too near. Filled with fear, the dwarf cried out, "Dear mister bear, spare my life, and I'll give you all my treasures! Look at the beautiful jewels lying there. Grant me my life! What good is a small, measly fellow like me? You wouldn't be able to feel me between your teeth. Those wicked girls over there would be better for you. They're such tender morsels, fat as young quails. For heaven's sake, eat them instead!"

The bear did not pay any attention to the dwarf's words, but gave the evil creature a single blow with his paw, and the dwarf did not move again.

The girls had run away, but the bear called after them, "Snow White, Rose Red, don't be afraid! Wait. I'll go with you!"

Then they recognized his voice and stopped. When the bear came up to them, his bearskin suddenly fell off, and there stood a handsome man clad completely in gold. "I am the son of a king," he said, "and I had been cast under a spell by the wicked dwarf, who stole my treasures. He forced me to run around the forest as a wild bear, and only his death could release me from the spell. Now he has received his justly earned punishment."

Snow White was married to the prince, and Rose Red to his brother, and they shared the great treasures that the dwarf had collected in his cave. The old mother lived many more peaceful and happy years with her children. Indeed, she took the two rosebushes with her, and they stood in front of her window, and every year they bore the most beautiful roses, white and red.

The Redeemer

Though Albert Ludwig Grimm created the first literary version of this tale, he depended on folk motifs that can be traced back to antiquity and the Orient, particularly Persia and Turkey: the youngest son who sets out to redeem his decadent brothers; the animal helpers who repay his kindness; the marriage of the three brothers, recalling the cycle of tales "seven brides for seven brothers." Grimm was familiar with Georg Messerschmid's verse romance *Vom edlen Ritter Brissoneto* (*The Noble Knight Brissoneto*, 1559), and it probably served as the model for his tale. The Brothers Grimm were aware of "The Three Princes" as early as 1809, and they incorporated it with many changes into the first edition of *Children's and Household Tales* in 1812 without giving Albert Ludwig Grimm credit. Ludwig Bechstein published a version similar to the Grimms' tale entitled "Die verzauberte Prinzessin" ("The Enchanted Princess") in *Deutsches Märchenbuch* (1857).

ALBERT LUDWIG GRIMM

The Three Princes†

In ancient times, there lived in the Orient a king who had three sons. From childhood on, the two older brothers were wild and mischievous, but clever. On the other hand, the youngest was obedient and good, and not so clever as his brothers.

When the oldest of the princes turned eighteen, his father gave him a horse, armor, and sword and let him depart to see the world and to prove his worth as a knight in foreign countries. So he rode away, far and wide, and lived extravagantly and dissolutely and never came home. He forgot his father and did not send any news about how he was doing. Soon the second of the princes became eighteen, and his father also gave him a horse, armor, and sword and let him ride out into the world to see foreign countries and to prove his worth as a knight and to search for his older brother. He, too, rode away and did just like his brother: He did not return home, nor did he send any news about how he was doing. Therefore, the old king became sad, and thinking his sons were both dead, he pined away and grieved about his loss.

Now when the third son also turned eighteen, he went to his father one day and requested that the king also give him a horse and a sword and let him ride out in the world the way his brothers had done. But the old king

† Albert Ludwig Grimm, "The Three Princes"—"Die drei Königsöhne" (1808), in *Kindermährchen* (Heidelberg: Mohr und Zimmer, 1808).

wept, embraced his son, and said, "Do you want to leave me and get lost as well just like your brothers have abandoned me? No, you are my only child, and I need you as a prop in my old age."

So the youngest son withdrew his request, although he did not want to. A few days later, however, the old king had a marvelous dream: He stood in his garden, so it seemed to him, and two olive trees were growing. At the beginning they were beautiful and appeared to be healthy. Then they began to decay, and the fruit fell from their branches. The leaves became yellow, and the branches seemed to be withered. All of a sudden, a palm tree shot up high quickly between the two and provided shade for the sick olive trees and poured its dew on them. Then they became healthy and fresh again.

One morning, as a result of this dream, the king summoned his fortune-tellers and wise men to interpret the dream for him. The fortune-tellers said, "The two olive trees are your two oldest sons, and the palm tree is your youngest son. The two olive trees quickly became withered just as your two sons have become ruined. So you must let your palm tree, your youngest son, depart so that he can assist his brothers. Otherwise, you will lose them."

When the king heard this, he gave his youngest son a horse and a sword and, with tears in his eyes, he let him go. However, as the youngest prince went out into the world and rode far and wide, he felt good in the open country, and he saw many lands and people. Indeed, wherever he went, he proved himself to be a brave knight. Thus he continued traveling and visiting distant lands, until one night, he entered a dense forest and could not find his way out. As he was riding, he suddenly encountered two men. When he asked them the way out of the forest, he recognized his two older brothers and was happy to see them. However, they began to chide him and said, "If we, who are much more clever than you, can hardly make our way through the world, how do you expect to do so, when you are so simpleminded? Indeed, the two older princes were more worldly, and the youngest lacked such worldly experience.

It was now evening. Very seldom did a ray of the setting sun penetrate the fir trees that stood at the edge of the forest. The three princes deliberated together which way they should take to reach an inn. Finally, they decided to head for the top of the mountain to see if they could catch a glimpse of a house or an open field from there. As they were riding, they came upon an anthill, and the older brothers wanted to turn it over to see how the little insects carried their eggs. But the youngest brother got off his horse and prevented them from doing this. And as they continued on their way, the king of the ants said to him, "Whoever you may be, stranger, I want to thank you for preventing your traveling companions from causing us tiny insects a great misfortune. If I can ever be of service to you, just come here, and you will see how glad I shall be to help you."

Then they went further and came to a lake which was covered with a flock of ducks. The older brothers wanted to run here and there and kill a few so that they could have a good evening meal. But the youngest brother protected them and said, "Leave the poor ducks alone! We'll find something to eat this evening."

So they left the ducks in peace. But when they went by them, the king of the ducks swam toward them and thanked the youngest prince.

"If I can ever be of service to you," he said, "I shall be glad to help you."

Thereupon they went further and came to an oak tree in which some bees had built their hive. There was so much honey in the hive that the honey dripped down onto the trunk of the tree. As the two oldest brothers saw this, they wanted to make a fire in the hollow of the tree so that the bees would die and they could get the honey. But the youngest brother prevented them and said, "Let the poor bees alone! Don't kill them just for the sake of a little honey!"

As the brothers then continued on their way, the queen of the bees flew out of the hive and thanked him.

"If I can ever be of service to you," she said, "you just have to command! I shall be glad to help you."

Then they went further and arrived at an old castle where they wanted to spend the night. However, the castle was built in a very strange way, and there was nothing living in it. They went through the gate, and the youngest brother brought his horse to the stable where nothing but stone horses were standing. Next they climbed some stairs to an inner courtyard which was laminated with marbles, and the three entrances were lined with pillars. The first was lined with silver, the second with gold, and the third with diamonds. After they went through the first entrance, they came to a row of rooms in which everything, walls and utensils, was made out of chased silver. They went through all the rooms and found a door at the end that was sealed with three locks. But they could see into the chamber through a little shutter, and there, sitting at a table, was an old hoary little man whose beard dropped to his feet. They called to him, but he did not hear. They called to him a second time, but he still did not hear. And when they called to him a third time, he stood up, opened the door, came out, and greeted them in a friendly fashion. In the evening, he showed them the best hospitality and gave them beds with silk curtains for their place to sleep. But he did not say one word and did not answer their questions. Nevertheless, the princes felt content that they had found such good accommodations.

When they awoke the next morning, each one lay, to be sure, in a beautiful room, but each room was locked, and they could not get out of their rooms. The hoary little man with the long beard stood by the oldest brother and signaled him to follow him. He did so but he was very anxious, and they went through the golden entrance and came into a large spacious hall, in which everything was made of chased gold. Then the old man pointed with his black cane to some words which were written over the door:

> Each stranger who crosses the threshold of this castle must try to complete three chores. If he succeeds in carrying them out, his fortune will forever be made. If he does not succeed, then he will be transformed into stone and must stand on that spot where the last ray of the sunset will shine upon him until the hour of salvation.

After the oldest prince had read these words, he desired to know what the first chore was and stood between fear and hope, not knowing whether he could accomplish it. Then the old man touched the wall with his cane, and a door sprang open. The prince saw a painting that portrayed the region where the king of the ants had spoken to the youngest brother. Beneath the painting stood the words:

> Three thousand pearls, the chief jewels of the Princess Pyrola and her two sisters, are lying scattered here in the moss. You must gather them all together, and not a single one can be missing!

The prince recognized the region and rushed to the spot, where he began zealously collecting the pearls. But by noon he had only gathered a hundred. As the sun began to set, he had only three hundred, and when the last ray of the sun hit him, he sunk to the ground and was turned to stone.

The next morning the gray old man stood by the second prince and signaled him with his black cane to follow him, and he did this. Then the little old man also showed him the inscription over the door in the golden hall and the painting. The brother also rushed to the spot and zealously collected the pearls until evening. But he had barely gathered three hundred of the tiny pearls together when the sun set, and he sank to the ground and was turned to stone like his brother.

Now the third morning came, and the hoary little man stood by the youngest prince and led him into the hall. He had him read the inscription over the door and showed him the painting. Then he signaled him to leave because he was standing there so sadly. So the third prince departed and saw the tiny, tiny pearls scattered and hidden in the moss. When he saw this and realized that it was impossible to gather all of them, he sat down, wept bitterly, and grieved about his poor father, who had now lost all his children. And as he was weeping and lamenting, he heard a voice call out to him, "Why are you crying, dear stranger?"

Then he looked up and saw the king of the ants and told him about his troubles. But the king of the ants said, "Is that all that's bothering you? Oh, then just calm yourself. You'll soon be helped!"

As soon as he said this, he went into the anthill and returned with more than five thousand ants who collected the pearls and loaded them into the youngest prince's hat. And when he had all of them up to the very last one, the king of the ants said to him, "Go back! You have them all. And don't bother to thank me, for you have deserved more than this little favor."

Then the youngest prince ran into the castle and brought the little man the pearls. The hoary little man was amazed by this and led him into the golden hall again and touched another wall, which opened up. Once again there was a painting, which depicted the lake on which the flock of ducks had been swimming, and beneath the painting were the words:

> At the bottom of this lake lies the key to the bedchamber of the Princess Pyrola and her two older sisters. You must find this before sunset.

The prince recognized the lake and rushed to the spot, where he undressed and waded into the water in order to search for the key. However, as he was about to plunge into the water, the king of the ducks swam over to him and asked, "What is your desire, dear stranger?"

Then the prince told him what he was looking for in the lake, and the king of the ducks answered, "The lake is too deep for you. Let me take care of the lost key for you!"

And he commanded all the ducks to dive down into the water and search for the key. And they dove down and soon brought the lost golden key in their beaks back to the surface. Then the king of the ducks presented it to the prince and said, "Take it and don't thank me. You have deserved more than this little favor."

The prince rushed back to the castle and brought the key to the hoary little man. No sooner had he taken the key from the youngest son than he found his speech again and thanked the prince with tears of joy.

"For over two thousand years," he said, "I have been compelled to sit here alive but silent in this castle and wait for salvation. Now you have only one more chore, fortunate stranger, but it is the most difficult. If you complete it, your fortune is made!"

Then the youngest prince asked him what it was.

"I have three daughters," the gray old man said. "I am the king of this enchanted castle and land. A magic spell has been cast over my three daughters by their own mother, who was an evil fairy, and for two thousand years they have been lying in a deep deathlike sleep. The oldest, Rubina, was enchanted by a piece of sugar; the second, Briza, by some syrup; and the youngest, Pyrola, by a spoonful of honey. All my daughters look identically alike, and they all seem to be the same age. But I have a special fondness for Pyrola, my youngest daughter, and it is only through her that you can bring about the final salvation. You must be able to recognize from her breath which one of the three has eaten the honey although two thousand years have passed."

After he had said this, the unfortunate king led the prince outside and opened the third door. All the rooms were decorated with precious gems of different colors. Sweet odors and soft stones drifted out of the background. Fresh air floated toward them. There in a bedstead that was surrounded by foliage of green and colored gems were Rubina, Briza, and Pyrola, who were laying like dead marble statues in the highest part of the middle hall. Each one of them was exceptionally beautiful, and they all looked alike. The splendor of the hall and the beauty of the princesses, the music and the nice odors stupefied him so that he no longer knew what he should be doing until the king of the castle reminded him and said, "It is already noon, and when the sun sets and you have not recognized who my youngest daughter is, you will suffer the same fate as your brothers, and I must sit here mute as I did before until another stranger loses his way and enters the castle. If you can recognize my daughter Pyrola without guessing, then she will be your wife, and you will inherit my kingdom."

But the youngest prince rushed outside where he wept and moaned, and the forest echoed with his laments. And as he was moaning and lamenting, he heard a voice call to him and say, "What are you grieving about, dear stranger?"

When he looked up, he recognized the queen of the bees, who was sitting on the branch of a tree.

"Alas!" he cried. "How can I know which of the three princesses ate honey two thousand years ago?"

"What?" asked the queen of the bees. "Is that all that's bothering you? How can you grieve so much about this? I'll give you a bee to take with you, and she will fly around all three daughters, and the one she lands on will be the princess that you are seeking."

Upon saying this, the queen flew into the beehive, and out came a bee that flew to his shoulder and perched on it. Then the prince carried the bee into the hall to the sleeping princesses, and the bee flew to all of them and fluttered above and around them until it finally landed on the lips of the one in the middle. Then the prince said to the hoary king, "The one in the middle is Pyrola, your youngest daughter!"

And no sooner did he say this than lightning and thunder erupted, and it was as if the earth was collapsing, and soon everything was changed. The small gray little man stood there as a worthy, majestic old king. The princesses stood in blooming beauty and embraced their father, and Pyrola, the youngest, approached the prince and thanked her savior. In response, the young prince embraced her and called her his bride. Servants went in and out, and there was a trampling in the castle courtyard. They went to the window, and the old wilderness was no longer there. Instead, they saw a splendid city, and beyond the city were fertile fields and many pretty meadows and villages. There was a bustling crowd in the streets, and everything was happening in such an orderly way that it appeared as if no miracle had occurred and everything was just as it used to be. Nobody seemed to recall what had happened.

Some servants came into the hall, and the king let them take the prince and his daughter Pyrola, who were ushered into a magnificent open coach which the king had harnessed with twelve white horses. Then he ordered twenty-four men dressed in purple and gold to ride out in advance with trumpets, and he had them announce that the prince and his daughter Pyrola were now the king and queen of the land. Thereafter a sumptuous banquet was held, and nothing was lacking to make it a glorious day.

And as they were sitting there in great jubilation, two unknown knights had themselves announced. They were allowed to enter, and lo and behold, the prince's brothers appeared. Immediately thereafter, another stranger was announced, and as he entered, the three princes sprang from their seats and greeted him with cries of joy: it was their father. He had set out in search of his lost sons and had just arrived in this city.

The father of the princes remained three months, and as long as he was there, the celebrations continued, and each feast was more splendid than the next. Then he departed for his home with his two oldest sons. They had supposedly changed for the better and divided and ruled the old king's realm. The oldest son is said to have married the oldest princess, Rubina, and the second son, the princess Briza, and both couples are said to have lived happily and ruled their kingdoms for a long time. However, the youngest prince and Pyrola lived to be more than a hundred years old and made their subjects happy. After the prince's death, however, a foreign king came to rule, and because of him the condition of the people became so bad again that a flood devastated the land. And since then this land, which is the land of fairy tales, has sunk and disappeared, and this legend is the only thing that remains of it.

JACOB AND WILHELM GRIMM

The Queen Bee†

Once two princes went forth in search of adventure, and after they fell into a wild decadent way of life, they never returned home again. Their youngest brother, who was called simpleton, went out to look for them, but when he finally found them, they ridiculed him for thinking that he, as naive as he was, could make his way in the world when they, who were much more clever, had not been able to succeed.

Eventually, the three of them traveled together and came to an anthill. The two oldest wanted to smash it and watch the small ants crawl around in fright and carry away their eggs, but Simpleton said, "Leave the little creatures in peace. I won't let you disturb them."

They continued on their way and came to a lake where a great many ducks were swimming. The two brothers wanted to catch a few and roast them, but Simpleton would not let them.

"Leave the creatures in peace," he said. "I won't let you kill them."

Next they came to a beehive, and there was so much honey in the hive that it had dripped down the tree trunk. The two brothers wanted to build a fire underneath it and suffocate the bees to get at the honey. However, Simpleton prevented them and again said, "Leave the creatures in peace. I won't let you burn them."

At last, the three brothers came to a castle, and they saw nothing but stone horses standing in the stables. Not a living soul could be seen. They went through all the halls until they reached the end, where there was a door with three locks hanging on it. In the middle of the door there was a peephole through which one could look into the room. In there they saw a gray dwarf sitting at a table. They called to him once, then twice, but he did not hear them. Finally, they called a third time, and he got up, opened the locks, and came out. However, he did not say a word. Instead, he just led them to a richly spread table, and after they had something to eat and drink, he brought each one to his own bedroom.

The next morning the gray dwarf went to the oldest brother, beckoned to him, and conducted him to a stone tablet on which were inscribed three tasks that had to be performed if the castle was to be disenchanted. The first task involved gathering one thousand pearls that were lying in

† Jacob and Wilhelm Grimm, "The Queen Bee"—"Die Bienenkönigin" (1857), No. 62 in *Kinder-und Hausmärchen. Gesammelt durch die Brüder Grimm* (Göttingen: Dieterich, 1857).

the moss of the forest. They belonged to the king's daughter and had to be collected from the moss before sundown. If one single pearl was missing, the seeker would be turned to stone.

The oldest brother went to the moss and searched the entire day, but when the day drew to a close, he had found only one hundred. Consequently, he was turned into stone as was ordained by the tablet. The next day the second brother undertook the adventure, but he did not fare much better than the oldest: he found only two hundred pearls and was turned into stone. Finally, it was Simpleton's turn to search for the pearls in the moss. However, because it was so difficult to find them and everything went so slowly, he sat down on a stone and began to weep. While he was sitting on the stone and weeping, the king of the ants whose life he had once saved came along with five thousand ants, and it did not take long before the little creatures had gathered the pearls together and stacked them in a pile.

Now, the second task was to fetch the key to the bedroom of the king's daughter from the lake. When Simpleton came to the lake, the ducks whose lives he had once saved came swimming toward him and then dived down to fetch the key from the depths.

Next came the third task, which was the hardest. The king had three daughters who lay asleep, and Simpleton had to pick out the youngest and the loveliest. However, they all looked exactly alike, and the only difference between them was that they each had eaten a different kind of sweet before falling asleep: the oldest had eaten a piece of sugar, the second a little syrup, the youngest a spoonful of honey. Just then the queen bee whom Simpleton had protected from the fire came along and tested the lips of all three princesses. At last she settled on the mouth of the princess who had eaten honey, and thus Simpleton was able to recognize the right daughter. Now the magic spell was broken, and everyone was set free from the deep sleep. All those who had been turned into stone regained their human forms. Simpleton married the youngest and loveliest daughter and became king after her father's death, while his two bothers were married to the other two sisters.

The Beast as Bridegroom

Most scholars generally agree that the *literary* development of the children's fairy tale "Beauty and the Beast," conceived by Madame Leprince de Beaumont in 1756 as part of *Le magasin des enfants,* translated into English in 1761 as *The Young Misses Magazine Containing Dialogues between a Governess and Several Young Ladies of Quality, Her Scholars,* owes its origins to the Roman writer Apuleius, who published the tale of *Cupid and Psyche* in *The Golden Ass* in the middle of the second century C.E. It is also clear that the oral folktale type 425A, the beast bridegroom, played a major role in the literary development. By the middle of the seventeenth century, the Cupid and Psyche tradition had been revived in France with a separate publication of Apuleius's tale in 1648; this revival inspired La Fontaine to write his long story "Amours de Psyche et de Cupidon" (1669) and Corneille and Molière to produce their tragédie-ballet *Psyché* (1671). The focus in La Fontaine's narrative and the play by Molière and Corneille is on the mistaken curiosity of Psyche. Her desire to know who her lover is almost destroys Cupid, and she must pay for her "crime" before she is reunited with Cupid. These two versions do not alter the main plot of Apuleius's tale, and they project an image of women who are either too curious (Psyche) or vengeful (Venus), and their lives must ultimately be ordered by Jove.

All this was changed by Madame d'Aulnoy, who was evidently familiar with different types of beast/bridegroom folktales and was literally obsessed by the theme of Psyche and Cupid and reworked it or mentioned it in several fairy tales: "Le mouton" ("The Ram," 1697), "La grenouille bienfaisante" ("The Beneficent Frog," 1698), "Serpentin vert" ("The Green Serpent," 1697), "Gracieuse et Percinet" ("Gracieuse and Percinet," 1697), and "Le prince Lutin" ("Prince Lutin," 1697). The two most important versions are "The Ram" and "The Green Serpent," and it is worthwhile examining some of the basic changes in the motifs and plot that break radically from the male literary tradition of Psyche and Cupid. In "The Ram," the heroine is actually punished by a relentless fairy. Based on the King Lear motif, this tale has Merveilleuse, the youngest daughter of a king, compelled to flee the court because her father believes mistakenly that she has insulted him. She eventually encounters a prince who has been transformed into a ram by a wicked fairy, and she is gradually charmed by his courteous manners and decides to wait five years until his enchantment will be over to marry him. However, she misses her father and two sisters, and through the ram's kind intervention she is able to visit them twice. The second time, however, she forgets about returning to the ram, who dies because of her neglect.

In "The Green Serpent," the heroine Laidronette acts differently. She runs away from home because she is ashamed of her ugliness. Upon encountering a prince who, as usual, has been transformed into a serpent by a wicked fairy, she is at first horrified. Gradually, after spending some time in his kingdom of the pagodes, who are exquisite little people that attend to her every wish, she becomes enamored of him and promises not to see him but to marry him in two years when his bewitchment will end. However, even though she reads the story of Psyche and Cupid, she breaks her promise and gazes upon him. This breech of promise enables the wicked fairy Magotine to punish her, and only after Laidronette performs three near-impossible tasks with the help of the fairy Protectrice is she able to transform herself into the beautiful Princess Discrète and the green serpent back into a handsome prince. Their love for each other eventually persuades the wicked fairy Magotine to mend her ways and reward them with the kingdom of Pagodaland.

The issue at hand in both fairy tales is fidelity and sincerity, or the qualities that make for tenderness, a topic of interest to women at that time. Interestingly, in Madame d'Aulnoy's two tales, the focus of the discourse is on the two princesses, who break their promises and learn that they will cause havoc and destruction if they do not keep their word. On the other hand, the men have been punished because they refused to marry old and ugly fairies and seek a more natural love. In other words, Madame d'Aulnoy sets conditions for both men and women that demand sincerity of feeling and constancy if they are to achieve true and happy love. Her tales may have had an influence on Jean-Paul Bignon's "Zeineb" (1714). They certainly were known by Madame Gabrielle de Villeneuve, who published her highly unique version of "Beauty and the Beast" in *La Jeune Amériquaine et les contes marins* in 1740, and it became the classic model for most of the Beauty and the Beast versions that followed in the eighteenth century. Indeed, in 1756 it served as the basis for Madame Leprince de Beaumont's most famous tale, which, in turn, provided the material for Countess de Genlis's dramatic adaptation, *The Beauty and the Monster,* in 1785 and for Jean-François Marmontel's libretto for the opera *Zemir et Azor* by André Modeste Grétry in 1788. Most significant by this time is the fact that Mme de Villeneuve wrote a tale of over two hundred pages (the length depends on which edition one reads) and was addressing a mixed audience of bourgeois and aristocratic adult readers. The social function of the fairy tale had changed: its basis was no longer the salon and the games that had been played there. Rather, the literary fairy tale's major reference point was another literary tale or an oral tale, and it was intended to amuse and instruct the isolated reader and listeners who may have heard the tale read aloud in a social situation.

Like Mme d'Aulnoy, Mme de Villeneuve was concerned with the self-realization of a young woman, and like the lesson preached by Madame d'Aulnoy, the message of Mme de Villeneuve for women is ambivalent. While all the rules and codes in her fairy tale are set by women—there are numerous parallel stories that involve a fairy kingdom and the laws of the fairies—Beauty is praised most for her submissiveness, docility, and earnestness. In Mme de Villeneuve's version, she does not break her vow to the Beast. Rather, she is steadfast and sees through the machinations of her five sisters in time for her to return to her beloved Beast. Then, after she saves him, and he is transformed into a charming prince, she is ready to sacrifice herself again by giving up her claim to him because she is merely bourgeois while he is a true nobleman. Her fairy protector, however, debates the prince's mother, who has arrived on the scene, and argues that Beauty's virtues are worth more than her class ranking. Eventually, though the fairy wins the debate, we learn that Beauty is really a princess who had been raised by her supposed merchant-father to escape death by enemies to her real father, a king.

With de Villeneuve's projection of Beauty, the person as an embodiment of the virtue of self-denial, the ground was prepared for a children's version of the Beauty and the Beast tale, and Mme Leprince de Beaumont did an excellent job of condensing and altering the tale in 1756 to address a group of young misses who were supposed to learn how to become ladies and that virtue meant denying themselves. In effect, the code of the tale was to delude them into believing that they would be realizing their goals in life by denying themselves.

By the time the Grimms wrote their version of "The Singing, Springing Lark," which they had heard from Henrietta Dorothea Wild in 1813, there were hundreds if not thousands of oral and literary versions that incorporated motifs from the oral beast-bridegroom cycle and the literary tradition of "Cupid and Psyche" and "Beauty and the Beast." For instance, even before the publication of the Grimms' tale, Charles Lamb wrote the long poem *Beauty and the Beast; or, A Rough Outside with a Gentle Heart* (1811), and there were important versions by Ludwig Bechstein, Walter Crane, and Andrew Lang in the nineteenth century. The proliferation of these tales up to the present has been strengthened by the classical film *La Belle et la Bête* (1946) by Jean Cocteau and later by the Walt Disney Corporation's production of *Beauty and the Beast* (1993). Betsy Hearne provides a comprehensive picture of the different versions of this tale-type in *Beauty and the Beast: Visions and Revisions of an Old Tale* (1989).

MARIE-CATHERINE D'AULNOY

The Ram†

In the happy times when fairies existed, there reigned a king who had three daughters. They were young and beautiful, and all three possessed considerable merit, but the youngest was the most charming and the favorite by far. They called her Merveilleuse. The king her father gave her more gowns and ribbons in a month than he gave the others in a year, and she was so good-natured that she shared everything with her sisters so that there were no misunderstandings among them.

The king had some very bad neighbors, who were weary of peace and formed such a powerful alliance against him that he was compelled to arm in self-defense. He raised a large army and took the field at its head. The three princesses remained with their tutors in a castle, where they received good news about the king every day. One time he took a city, another he won a battle. Finally, he succeeded completely in routing his enemies and driving them out of his dominions. He then returned to the castle as fast as he could to see his little Merveilleuse, whom he adored so much.

The three princesses had ordered three satin gowns to be made for themselves—one green, one blue, and the third white. Their jewels were selected to match their dresses. The green was enriched with emeralds; the blue with turquoises; and the white with diamonds. Thus attired, they went to meet the king, singing the following verses, which they had written to celebrate his victories:

† Marie-Catherine d'Aulnoy, "The Ram"—"Le mouton" (1697), in *Les contes de fées,* 4 vols. (Paris: Claude Barbin, 1697).

> "With conquest crown'd on many a glorious plain,
>   What joy to greet our king and sire again!
>   Welcome him back, victorious, to these halls,
> With new delights and countless festivals;
> Let shouts of joy and songs of triumph prove
> His people's loyalty, his daughters' love!"

When the king saw his lovely daughters in such splendid dresses, he embraced them all tenderly, but caressed Merveilleuse more than he did the others. A magnificent banquet was set up, and the king and his three daughters sat down to eat. Since it was his custom to draw inferences from everything, he said to the eldest, "Tell me, please, why have you put on a green gown?"

"Sire," she answered, "having heard of your achievements, I fancied that green would express the joy and hope with which your return inspired me."

"That is very prettily said!" the king exclaimed. "And you, my child," he continued, "why are you wearing a blue gown?"

"My liege," the princess said, "I want to indicate that we should constantly implore the gods to protect you. Moreover, your sight is to me like that of heaven and all the heavenly host!"

"You speak like an oracle!" the king said. "And you, Merveilleuse, why have you dressed yourself in white?"

"Because, sire," she answered, "it becomes me better than any color."

"What!" the king cried out, very much offended. "Was that your only motive, you little coquette?"

"My motive was to please you," said the princess. "It seems to me that I ought to have no other."

The king, who loved her dearly, was so perfectly satisfied with this explanation that he declared himself quite pleased by the little turn she had given to her meaning, and the art with which she had at first concealed the compliment.

"There! There!" he said. "I have had an excellent supper, and I shall not go to bed yet. Tell me what you all dreamed of the night before my return."

The eldest said she had dreamed that he had brought her a gown with the gold and jewels that glistened brighter than the sun. The second said she had dreamed that he had brought her a golden distaff to spin herself some shifts. The youngest said she had dreamed that he had married off her second sister, and that on the wedding day he had offered a golden vase and said, "Merveilleuse, come here. Come here so you can wash."

The king was indignant at this dream. He knit his brow and made an exceedingly wry face. Everybody saw he was very angry. He retired to his room and flung himself into bed. He could not forget his daughter's dream. "This insolent little creature," he said, "she wants to turn me into her servant. I wouldn't be surprised if she had put on white satin without thinking of me at all. She doesn't take me seriously. But I'll frustrate her wicked designs while there's still time." He rose in a fury, and though it was still dark outside, he sent for the captain of his guards and said to him,

"You heard Merveilleuse's dream. It forecasts strange things against me. I command you to seize her immediately, to take her into the forest, and to kill her, after which you will bring me her heart and her tongue so that I may be sure you have not deceived me, or I'll have you put to death in the most cruel manner possible."

The captain of the guards was astounded by this barbarous order. However, he did not dare argue with the king, for fear of increasing his anger and causing him to give the horrible order to another. He assured him he would take the princess and kill her and bring him her heart and her tongue.

The captain went directly to the princess's apartment, where he had some difficulty in obtaining permission to enter, for it was still very early. He informed Merveilleuse that the king desired to see her. She arose immediately, and a little Moorish girl, named Patypata, carried her train. A young ape and a little dog, who always accompanied her, ran after her. The ape was called Grabugeon, and the little dog, Tintin. The captain of the guards made Merveilleuse descend into the garden, where he told her the king was taking in the fresh morning air. She entered it, and the captain pretended to look for the king. When he did not find him, he said, "No doubt his majesty has walked further on into the wood." He opened a little door and led the princess into the forest. It was just getting light, and the princess looked at her escort, who had tears in his eyes and was so dejected that he could not speak.

"What's the matter?" she inquired in the kindest tone. "You seem very much distressed."

"Ah, madame!" he exclaimed. "How could I be otherwise, for I've been given the most dreadful order that has ever been given! The king has commanded me to kill you in this forest and to take your heart and your tongue to him. If I fail to do so, he will put me to death."

The poor princess turned pale with terror and began to weep silently. She looked like a little lamb about to be sacrificed. She fixed her beautiful eyes on the captain of the guards, and looking at him without anger, she said, "Do you really have the heart to kill me—me, who never did you any harm, and who always spoke well of you to the king? If I really deserved my father's hate, I would suffer the consequences without a murmur. But, alas, I have always shown him so much respect and affection that he cannot with justice complain of me."

"Fear not, beautiful princess," said the captain of the guards, "I am incapable of such a barbarous deed. I'd rather suffer the death he has threatened me with, but if I were to kill myself, you would not be much better off. We must find some way which will allow me to return to the king and convince him that you are dead."

"What way is there?" asked Merveilleuse. "He has ordered you to bring him my tongue and my heart, and if you don't do this, he won't believe you."

Patypata had witnessed everything that had happened, and neither the captain of the guards nor the princess was aware of her presence because they were so overcome by sadness. So she advanced with courage and threw herself at Merveilleuse's feet. "Madame," she said, "I want to offer you my life. You must kill me. I shall be most happy to die for such a good mistress."

"Oh! I can never permit it, my dear Patypata," the princess said, kissing her. "After such an affectionate proof of your friendship, your life is as dear to me as my own."

Then Grabugeon stepped forward and said, "You have good reason, princess, to love such a faithful slave as Patypata; she can be of much more use to you than I. Now it's my turn to offer you my tongue and heart with joy, for I wish to immortalize myself in the annals of the empire of monkeys."

"Ah, my darling Grabugeon," Merveilleuse replied, "I cannot bear the idea of taking your life!"

"I'd find it intolerable," exclaimed Tintin, "good little dog as I am, if anyone but myself were to sacrifice their life for my mistress. Either I will die, or nobody shall die."

Upon saying this, a great dispute arose between Patypata, Grabugeon, and Tintin, and they exchanged harsh words. At last, Grabugeon, who was quicker than the others, ran up to the very top of a tree and flung herself down headfirst, killing herself on the spot. Much as the princess grieved over her loss, she agreed to let the captain of the guards cut out her tongue since the poor thing was dead. But it was so small (for the creature was not much bigger than one's fist) that, to their dismay, they felt certain the king would not be deceived by it.

"Alas, my dear little ape," cried the princess, "there you are dead without my life saved by your sacrifice!"

"That honor has been reserved for me," interrupted the Moor, and as she spoke, she snatched the knife that had been used on Grabugeon and plunged it into her bosom. The captain of the guards would have taken her tongue, but it was so black that he knew he would not be able to deceive the king with it.

"Look at my misfortune!" the princess said in tears. "I lose all those I love, and yet my fate remains unchanged."

"Had you accepted my offer," Tintin said, "you would have only had to mourn my loss, and I would have had the satisfaction of being the only one mourned."

Merveilleuse kissed her little dog, weeping so bitterly over him that she was quite exhausted. She turned hastily away, and when she ventured to look around again, her escort was gone, and she found herself alone with the dead bodies of her Moor, her ape, and her little dog. She could not leave the spot until she had buried them in a hole which she found by chance at the foot of a tree. Afterward she scratched these words into the tree:

> Three faithful friends lie buried in this grave,
> Who gave themselves my life to save.

Then she began to think of her own safety. There was certainly none for her in that forest. It was so close to her father's castle that the first person who saw her would recognize her, or she might be eaten like a chicken by the lions and wolves that infested it. So she set off walking as fast as she could. However, the forest was so enormous and the sun so strong that she was soon ready to die from heat, fear, and weariness. She looked around her everywhere and was unable to see the end of the forest. Everything frightened her. She continually imagined that the king was in pursuit and sought to kill her, and she uttered so many sad lamentations that it is impossible to repeat them here.

She walked on without following any particular path. The thickets tore her beautiful dress and scratched her white skin. Finally she heard some sheep bleat. "There are probably some shepherds here with their flocks," she said. "Perhaps they'll be able to direct me to some village where I may disguise myself in the dress of a peasant. Alas!" she continued. "Sovereigns and princes are not always the happiest persons in the world. Who in all this kingdom would believe that I am a fugitive, that my father without cause or reason seeks my life, and that to save it I must disguise myself?"

As she made these observations, she approached the spot where she had heard the bleating. Upon reaching an open space surrounded by trees, she was most surprised to see a large ram who was whiter than snow and had gilded horns. He had a garland of flowers around his neck; his legs were entwined with ropes of pearls of enormous size; and chains of diamonds hung about him while he lay on a couch of orange blossoms. A pavilion of cloth of gold suspended in the air sheltered him from the rays of the sun. There were a hundred brightly decked sheep around him, and instead of browsing on the grass, some were having coffee, sherbet, ices, and lemonade; others, strawberries and cream, and sweetmeats. Some were playing at basset, others at lansquenet.[1] Several wore collars of gold, ornamented with numerous fine emblems, earrings, and ribbons, and flowers. Merveilleuse was so astonished that she remained almost motionless. Her eyes wandered in search of the shepherd in charge of this extraordinary flock, when the beautiful ram ran over to her in a sprightly manner. "Approach, divine princess," he said to her. "You have nothing to fear from such gentle and peaceful animals of our kind."

"What a miracle! A talking ram!" the princess exclaimed.

"Eh, madam," the ram replied, "your ape and your little dog spoke very prettily. Why weren't you surprised by that?"

"A fairy endowed them with the gift of speech, which made everything less miraculous," Merveilleuse stated. "Perhaps we had a similar experience," the ram answered, smiling in a sheepish manner. "But what has caused you to come our way, my princess?"

"A thousand misfortunes, my lord ram," she said to him. "I am the most unhappy person in the world. I'm looking for asylum from the fury of my father."

"Come, madame," the ram replied, "come with me. I can offer you one which will be known only by you, and you shall be completely in charge of everything there."

"I can't follow you," Merveilleuse said. "I'm about to die from exhaustion."

The ram with the golden horns called for his chariot, and immediately

---

1. A card game of German origin. "Basset": a card game similar to faro.

six goats were led forward. They were harnessed to a pumpkin of such a tremendous size that two persons could sit in it with the greatest ease. The pumpkin was dry, and the inside hollowed out and fitted with splendid down cushions and lined with velvet all over. The princess got into the pumpkin and admired such a novel equipage. The master-ram seated himself in the pumpkin beside her, and the goats took them at full gallop to a cave. The entrance was blocked by a large stone, and the golden-horned ram touched the stone with his foot, and it immediately fell. He told the princess to enter without fear; she thought the cave was a horrible place, and if her fear about being captured had been less, nothing could have induced her to go into it, but her anxiety was so great that she would even have thrown herself into a well to avoid capture. So she followed the ram without hesitation, and he walked in front of her to show her the way down, which ran so deep, so very deep, that she thought she was going at least to the other end of the earth, and at times she feared he was conducting her to the region of the dead.

Eventually, she discovered all at once a vast plain covered with a thousand different flowers, whose delicious perfume surpassed that of any she had ever smelled. A broad river of orange-flower water flowed around it; fountains of Spanish wine, rossolis, hippocras,[2] and a thousand other sorts of liqueurs formed charming cascades and little rivulets. The plain was covered with unusual trees. There were entire avenues of them, with partridges greased and dressed better than you could get at La Guerbois', hanging on the branches. In other avenues, the branches carried quails, young rabbits, turkeys, chickens, pheasants, and ortolans.[3] In certain parts, where the atmosphere appeared a little hazy, it rained bisques d'écrevisse, and other soups; foies gras, ragouts of sweetbreads, white puddings, sausages, tarts, patties, jam, and marmalade. There were also louis-d'ors, crowns, pearls, and diamonds. Showers so rare, as well as so useful, would no doubt have attracted some very excellent company if the great ram had been more inclined to mix with society in general, but all the chronicles in which he is mentioned concur in assuring us that he was as reserved as a Roman senator.

Since Merveilleuse had arrived in these beautiful regions during the finest time of the year, she only saw the palace that was formed by long lines of orange trees, jasmins, honeysuckles, and little musk roses, whose interlaced branches formed cabinets, halls, and chambers, all hung with gold and silver gauze, and furnished with large mirrors, lusters,[4] and remarkable paintings.

The master-ram told the princess to regard herself as the sovereign of these regions, that for some years he had had much cause for sorrow and tears, and it was now up to her to make him forget all his misfortunes.

"There is something very generous in your behavior, charming ram," she said to him, "and everything I see here appears to me so extraordinary that I don't know what to make of it."

2. A cordial drink made of wine flavored with spices. "Rossolis": a liqueur called "dew of the sun."
3. Small birds highly regarded for their delicate flavor.
4. Prismatic glass pendants attached to a chandelier; sometimes an entire chandelier is referred to as a luster.

She had barely uttered these words when a troop of the most remarkable and beautiful nymphs appeared before her. They gave her fruit in baskets of amber, but when she stepped toward them, they gradually withdrew. When she extended her hands to touch them, she felt nothing and discovered that they were only phantoms. "Oh! What does this mean?" she exclaimed. "Who are these things around me?" She began to weep, and King Ram (for so they called him), who had left her for a few minutes, returned and found her in tears, causing him such despair that he felt he would die at her feet.

"What is the matter, lovely princess?" he inquired. "Has anyone in these dominions been disrespectful to you?"

"No," she answered, "I cannot complain. It is only that I am not accustomed to living among the dead and with sheep that talk. Everything here frightens me, and though I am greatly obliged to you for bringing me here, I'll be more obliged if you will bring me back into the world."

"Don't be alarmed," the ram replied. "Please just deign to listen to me calmly, and you shall hear my sad story.

"I was born to inherit a throne. A long line of kings, my ancestors, had made sure that I would take possession of the finest kingdom in the universe. My subjects loved me. I was feared and envied by my neighbors and justly respected. It was said that no king had ever been more worthy of such homage. My personal appearance was not without its attractions for those who saw me. I was exceedingly fond of hunting, and once when I zealously pursued a stag, I became separated from my attendants. Suddenly I saw the stag plunge into a pond and spurred my horse in after him. This was just as imprudent as it was bold. But, instead of the coldness of the water, I felt an extraordinary heat. The pond dried up, and through an opening that gushed with terrible flames, I fell to the bottom of a precipice where nothing was to be seen but fire.

"I thought I was lost, when I heard a voice which said to me, 'No less fire could warm your heart, ungrateful one!' 'Hah! Who is it that complains of my coldness?' I said. 'An unfortunate who adores you without hope,' the voice replied. Just then the flames were extinguished, and I perceived a fairy whom I had known from early childhood and whose age and ugliness had always horrified me. She was leaning on a young slave of incomparable beauty; the golden chains she wore sufficiently betokened her condition. 'What miracle is this, Ragotte?' I said to her (as that was the fairy's name). 'Have you really ordered this?' 'Who else should have ordered it?' the fairy replied. 'Has it taken you this long to learn the way I feel? Must I undergo the shame of explaining myself? Have my eyes, once so certain of their power, lost all their influence? Consider how low I stoop! 'Tis I who make this confession of my weakness to you, who, great king as you may be, are less than an ant compared to a fairy like me.' 'I am whatever you please,' I said to her impatiently, 'but what is it you demand of me? Is it my crown, my cities, my treasures?' 'Ah, wretch!' she replied disdainfully. 'If I desired, my scullions would be more powerful than you. I demand your heart. My eyes have asked you for it thousands and thousands of times. You have not understood them, or rather, you don't want to understand them. If you had been desperately in love with someone else,' she continued, 'I wouldn't have interrupted the progress of your emotions, but I had too great an interest in you not to discover the indifference that reigned in your heart. Well, then, love me!' she added, pursing up her mouth to make it look more pleasant, and rolling her eyes about. 'I'll be your little Ragotte, and I'll add twenty kingdoms to what you have already, a hundred towers full of gold, five hundred full of silver—in a word, all you can wish for.' 'Madame Ragotte,' I said to her, 'I would never think of declaring myself to a person of your merit at the bottom of a pit in which I expect to be roasted. I implore you by all the charms that you possess to set me free and then we shall consider together what we can do to satisfy you.' 'Hah, traitor!' she exclaimed, 'if you loved me, you would not seek the road back to your kingdom. You'd be happy in a grotto, in a fox-house, in the woods, or in the deserts. Don't think that I'm such a novice. You hope to escape, but I warn you that you shall remain here, and your first task will be to keep my sheep. They are intelligent animals and speak just as well as you do.'

"Upon saying this, she took me to the plain where we now are and showed me her flock. I paid little attention to them, for I was struck by the marvelous beauty of the slave beside her, and my eyes betrayed me. The cruel Ragotte noticed my admiration and attacked her. She plunged a bodkin into one of her eyes with such violence that the adorable girl fell dead on the spot. At this horrible sight I threw myself on Ragotte, and with my sword in hand, I would have made her into a sacrificial victim for the spirits of the underworld if she had not used her power to make me motionless. All my efforts were in vain; I fell to the ground and sought some way to slay myself and to end my agony. But the fairy said to me with an ironical smile, 'I want you to get to know my power. You are a lion at present, but you will become a sheep.'

"As she said this, she touched me with her wand, and I found myself transformed as you now behold me. I have not lost the faculty of speech, nor the sense of torment due to my condition. 'You shall be a sheep for five years,' she said, 'and absolute master of these beautiful realms, while I shall move far from here and your handsome face and . . . only brood over the hate I owe you.'

"She disappeared, and if anything could have relieved my misfortune, it would have been her absence. The talking sheep you see here acknowledged me as their king; they informed me that they were unfortunate mortals who had in various ways offended the vindictive fairy. They had been changed into a flock and the penance of some was of less duration than that of others. In fact," he added, "every now and then they become what they were before and leave the flock. As for the shadows you have seen, they are Ragotte's rivals and enemies of Ragotte whom she has deprived of life for a century or so, and who will return to the world later on. The young slave I mentioned is among them. I have seen her several times with great pleasure, although she did not speak to me. When I approached her, I was disturbed to discover it was nothing but her shadow. However, I noticed that one of my sheep paid close attention to this little phantom, and learned that he was her lover. Ragotte had taken him from her out of jealousy, and this is the reason why I have since avoided the shadow of the slave and have sighed for nothing but my liberty during the past three years.

"In the hope of regaining it, I frequently wander into the forest. There I saw you, beautiful princess," he continued. "Sometimes you were in a chariot which you drove yourself with more skill than the sun does his own. Sometimes you followed the chase on a steed that seemed as if he would obey no other rider, or you were in a race with the ladies of your court, flying lightly over the plain, and you won the prize like another Atalanta.[5] Ah, princess, if, during all this time in which my heart paid you its secret homage, I had dared to address you, what wouldn't I have said? But how would you have received the declaration of an unhappy sheep like me?"

Merveilleuse was so stirred by all she had heard that she scarcely knew how to answer him. She said some civil thing to him, however, which gave him some hope, and told him that she was less alarmed at the ghosts now that she knew their owners would revive again. "Alas," she continued, "if my poor Patypata, my dear Grabugeon, and the pretty Tintin, who died to save me, could meet with a similar fate, I would not be so melancholy here."

Despite the disgrace of the royal ram, he still possessed some very remarkable prerogatives. "Go," he said to his grand equery (a very good-looking sheep), "go fetch the Moor, the ape, and the little dog. Their shadows will amuse our princess." One moment later they appeared, and although they did not approach Merveilleuse close enough for her to touch them, their presence was a great consolation to her.

The royal ram possessed all the sense and delicacy required for pleasant conversation. He adored Merveilleuse so much that she began to have some regard for him and soon came to love him. A pretty sheep, very gentle and very affectionate, is not unlikely to please one, particularly when one knows he is a king, and that his transformation will eventually end. Thus the princess spent her days in peace and awaited a happier future. The gallant ram devoted himself entirely to her. He gave fêtes, concerts, and hunts; his flock helped him, and even the shadows played their part in the entertainments.

One day, when his couriers arrived—for he regularly sent out couriers for news and always obtained the best—he learned that the eldest sister of Princess Merveilleuse was about to marry a great prince, and the most magnificent preparations were being made for the nuptials.

"Ah!" the young princess said. "How unfortunate I am to be deprived of the sight of so many fine things! Here I am underground, among ghosts and sheep, while my sister is about to be made a queen. Everybody will pay court to her, and I alone shall not be able to share in her joy."

"What reason do you have to complain, madame?" asked the king of the sheep. "Have I refused you permission to attend the wedding? Depart as soon as you please; only give me your word that you will return. If you

5. In Greek mythology, a virgin huntress who never wanted to marry. Suitors who desired to marry the beautiful princess had to run a footrace with her. If they lost, their heads were cut off. Many suitors did, indeed, lose their lives until Prince Melanion defeated her in a race.

do not agree to that, I shall perish at your feet, for my attachment to you is too passionate for me to lose you and live."

Merveilleuse was quite touched and promised the ram that nothing in the world would prevent her return. So he provided her with an equipage befitting her birth. She was superbly dressed, and nothing was omitted that would increase her beauty. She got into a chariot of mother-of-pearl drawn by six Isabella-colored hypogriffins[6] that had just arrived from the other end of the earth. She was accompanied by a great number of exceedingly handsome officers, who were richly attired. The royal ram had ordered them to come from a distant land to form the princess's train.

She arrived at her father's court at the moment the marriage was being celebrated. As soon as she appeared, she dazzled everybody by her glittering beauty and the jewels which adorned her. She heard nothing but acclamations and praises. The king gazed at her with such zeal and pleasure that she was afraid he would recognize her, but he was so convinced she was dead that he did not have the least inkling she was his daughter.

Nevertheless, she was so afraid that she might be detained that she did not stay to the end of the ceremony. She departed abruptly, leaving a little coral box garnished with emeralds, and it had these words on it in diamond sparks: "Jewels for the Bride." They opened it immediately, and it was extraordinary what they found! The king, who had hoped to see her again and was burning to know who she was, was in despair at her departure. He gave strict orders that, if she ever returned, they were to shut the gates and detain her.

Brief as had been the absence of Merveilleuse, it had seemed ages to the ram. He waited for her by the side of a fountain in the thickest part of the forest. He had immense treasures displayed there with the intention of presenting them to her in gratitude for her return. As soon as he saw her, he ran toward her, romping and frisking like a true sheep. He lay down at her feet, kissed her hands, and told her all about his anxiety and impatience. His passion inspired him so much that he spoke with an eloquence that charmed the princess a great deal.

Some short time afterward the king married off his second daughter. Merveilleuse heard about it and asked the ram once again for permission to attend a fête in which she took great interest.

At this request he felt a pang which he could not suppress. A secret presentiment warned him about a catastrophe. But since we cannot always avoid evil, and since his consideration for the princess overruled every other feeling, he did not have the heart to refuse her. "You desire to leave me, madame," he said, "and I must blame my sad fate for this unfortunate situation more than you. I consent to your wish, and I shall never be able to make you a sacrifice greater than this."

She assured him that she would return as quickly as she did the first time, that she would be deeply grieved if anything were to keep her from him, and implored him not to worry about her. She went in the same state as before and arrived just as they were beginning the marriage cere-

6. An enormous fabulous animal of Greek mythology, said to have the wings of an eagle and the body and hindquarters of a lion.

mony. Despite the attention the people were paying to it, her presence caused exclamations of joy and admiration, which drew the eyes of all the princes to her. They could not stop looking at her and felt her beauty to be so extraordinary that they could easily have been convinced that she was something more than mortal.

The king was charmed to see her once more. He never took his eyes off her, except to order all the doors to be closed to prevent her departure. When the ceremony was nearly concluded, the princess rose hastily, so that she might disappear in the crowd, but she was extremely surprised and distressed to find that all the gates were locked. The king approached her with great respect and a submissive air that reassured her. He begged her not to deprive them so soon of the pleasure of seeing her and requested that she remain and grace the banquet he was about to give the princes and princesses who had honored him with their presence on this occasion. He led her into a magnificent salon in which the entire court was assembled and offered her a golden basin and a vase filled with water so that she might wash her beautiful hands. But this time she could no longer suppress her emotions. She flung herself at his feet, embraced his knees, and exclaimed, "Behold, my dream has come true! You have offered me water to wash with on my sister's wedding day without anything evil happening to you."

The king had no difficulty recognizing her, for he had been struck by her great resemblance to Merveilleuse more than once. "Ah! my dear daughter," he said, embracing her with tears in his eyes, "can you forget my cruelty? I sought your life because I thought your dream predicted the loss of my crown. Indeed, it did just that," he continued, "for here your two sisters are married, and each has a crown of her own. Therefore, mine shall be yours." Upon saying this, he rose and placed his crown on the princess's head, crying, "Long live Queen Merveilleuse!"

The entire court repeated the shout. The two sisters came and threw their arms around her neck and kissed her a thousand times. Merveilleuse was so happy she could not express her feelings. She cried and laughed at the same moment. She embraced one, talked to another, thanked the king, and, in the midst of all this, she recalled the captain of the guard to whom she was much indebted, and asked eagerly to see him, but they informed her he was dead. She felt his loss deeply.

When they sat down to dinner, the king asked her to relate all that had happened to her since the day he had given such orders with regard to her fate. She immediately began telling the story with the most remarkable grace, and everybody listened to her attentively. But while she was engrossed in telling her story to the king and her sisters, the enamored ram watched the hour set for the return of the princess pass, and his anxiety became so extreme that he could not control it. "She'll never return!" he cried. "My miserable sheep's face disgusts her. Oh, unfortunate lover that I am, what will become of me if I have lost Merveilleuse? Ragotte! Barbarous fairy! How you have avenged yourself for my indifference to you!" He indulged in such lamentations for a long time, and then, as night was approaching without any signs of the princess, he ran to the city. When he reached the king's palace, he asked to see Merveilleuse, but since ev-

erybody was now aware of her adventures and did not want her to return
to the ram's realm, they harshly refused to admit him to her presence. He
uttered cries and lamentations capable of moving anyone except the Swiss
guard[7] who stood sentry at the palace gates. At length, broken-hearted, he
flung himself on the ground and breathed his last sigh.

The king and Merveilleuse knew nothing of the sad tragedy which had
taken place. The king suggested to his daughter that she ride in a trium-
phal coach and show herself to everyone in the city by the lights of
thousands and thousands of torches which illuminated the windows and
all the great squares. But what a horrible spectacle she encountered as she
left the palace gates—to see her dear ram stretched breathless on the pavement! She jumped out of the coach and ran to him. She wept and sobbed,
for she knew that her delay in returning had caused the royal ram's death.
In her despair, she felt she would die herself.

It was then acknowledged that persons of the highest rank are subject,
like others, to the blows of fortune, and that they frequently experience
the greatest misery at the very moment they believe themselves to have
attained the goal of their wishes.

> The choicest blessings sent by Heaven
> Oft to our ruin only tend;
> The charms, the talents, to us given,
> But bring to us a mournful end.
> The royal ram had happier been
> Without the graces which first led
> Ragotte to love, then hurl her mean
> But fatal vengeance on his head.
> Sure he deserved a better fate,
> Who spurn'd a sordid Hymen's[8] chains;
> Honest his love—unmask'd his hate—
> How different from our modern swains!
> Even his death may well surprise
> The lovers of the present day,—
> Only a silly sheep now dies,
> Because his ewe has gone astray.

JEAN-PAUL BIGNON

Princess Zeineb and King Leopard†

I am the daughter of King Batoche, who rules over the easternmost part
of the island of Gilolo. My name is Zeineb, and I have five older sisters.
One day, my father went hunting in the mountains, and after he had gone

7. Swiss guards were mercenary soldiers from Switzerland used as a special bodyguard by former
   sovereigns of France and other monarchs.
8. In Greek and Roman mythology, the god of marriage, represented by a young man carrying a
   torch and veil.
† Jean-Paul Bignon, "Zeineb"—"Princess Zeineb and King Leopard" (1714), in *Les aventures
   d'Abdalla* (Paris: P. Witte, 1710–14).

a long way, he eventually reached a desolate spot and was extremely surprised to find a superb palace that he had never seen before. Anxious to
find out more about this unknown building, he started to approach it, but
a terrifying voice called him by name, stopped him, and threatened him
with immediate death unless he sent one of his daughters within three
days to the creature speaking to him. King Batoche raised his eyes and
saw a leopard at a window, and this beast terrified him by the fire emanating from his eyes. In fact, my father's fright was so great that he quickly
left the spot with his men without daring to reply.

My sisters and I were all upset by the sadness that overcame our father,
especially since it was quite visible on his face. We hugged him and urged
him to tell us what was troubling his heart. We had to persist for a long
time, and finally he told us.

"It's a matter of my life or yours," he said. "Ah, I'd rather die than lose
my children, whom I love with such tender feelings!"

Tears were in his eyes as he began telling us what he had seen and how
he had been threatened in such a dangerous way.

"If that's the only dreadful thing that's been disturbing you, my dear
father," our oldest sister said, "you can console yourself. I'm going to depart
tomorrow. Perhaps this leopard won't be as merciless as you think."

The king vainly tried to oppose her plan. She let herself be guided to
the secluded palace. The doors opened, and the leopard let himself be
seen. But my sister found him so horrible that she forgot all her good
resolutions, turned around, and fled. When my three other sisters saw her
return, they scolded her harshly for having so little courage, and the next
day they all tried their luck together. But their courage failed them in the
same way that it had failed our oldest sister. As a result, the king's life
depended solely on me.

When I took my turn, I was more fearless than they were. Not only did
I withstand the dreadful gaze of the leopard, who was at the window when
I arrived, but I also had the courage to enter the marvelous palace with
my mind firmly made up not to leave until I had completely brought
everything to light. As soon as I was in the courtyard, the doors closed,
and a group of nymphs, who were quite comely but, due to some miracle,
could not talk, appeared before me and began serving me. I was led into
a magnificent apartment, and I spent the entire day regarding the beautiful
features of the palace and its gardens. In the evening, my dinner was
delicious, and I went to sleep in a bed that was better than any in King
Batoche's palace. But a thousand troubling things were soon to follow.

Shortly after I was in bed, I heard his steps, and it would not have taken
much to have frightened me to death. He rushed into my room and made
a terrible noise with his teeth, claws, and tail. Then he stretched his whole
body alongside me. I had left him plenty of space because I did not occupy
much myself. The beast behaved himself in an astonishingly discreet way:
he did not touch me at all and left before daybreak. I would have liked
to have taken advantage of this time to have slept, but my fear was much
too overwhelming. The same nymphs who had served me the day before
came to wake me and get me dressed. They did not neglect a thing to
make me comfortable. I had a royal lunch and heard a musical concert

during the afternoon. My pleasure was made complete when I observed that the leopard did not appear during the entire day. Indeed, this day set the tone for all the days that followed. But, to tell the truth, I spent many nights without daring to sleep. Finally, however, the discretion demonstrated by the leopard enabled me to regain my tranquility. In short, I can tell you that ten months went by like this, and at the end of this time, I succumbed to a curious desire that had taken hold of me from the beginning and that I had continually resisted: I wanted to know whether my leopard was also a leopard during the night as he was during the day.

So I got up from the bed while he was sleeping, and I avoided touching him. Then I tiptoed and searched all around the room for something to light it. I suspected that the beast's skin was lying on the ground. In fact, I found it and was then overcome by a mad whim—for, what else could I call my behavior? I boldly tore the skin to pieces without considering what might happen. After this rash act, I went and lay down again in my corner of the bed as if nothing had happened.

My companion got up at his usual time, and when he discovered that his skin was no longer there to serve him, he began to wail, and I responded by coughing to make him aware that I was awake.

"It's superfluous now to continue to take precautions," the man who had groaned said to me sadly. "I'm a powerful king, and I was placed under a magic spell by a magician who worked for my enemies. My enchantment is over now, and I had decided to share my throne and my bed with you. But alas, your curiosity has set me back, and it is now as if I had never suffered anything! Why did you act against your better judgment? Reason should always tell you that any kind of reckless action is prohibited in a place where you don't know the laws."

I confessed my mistake in a frank way and begged him to consider that girls are naturally very curious. I told him he should be grateful to me for not having looked sooner for the clarification that I found. This excuse spoiled everything and drew a new flood of reproaches that he heaped upon me. Finally, the enchanted king calmed down, and he momentarily revealed his splendid face, which radiated a sudden light. But as he felt the dark forces about to act on him again, he said farewell to me and taught me some words that were to be pronounced against anyone I wanted to restrain from doing something until I pronounced some other words that would free that person to continue his actions. No sooner did I learn them than the palace disappeared along with all its pleasant things, and I found myself alone and completely naked lying on a rock.

Tears poured out of my eyes as I cursed my curiosity and imprudence. Daylight came, and I was obliged out of shame to look around and see if I could find something to cover me. I noticed some clothes near the spot where I was lying and went over to pick them up. They were my own clothes, which had been exposed over ten months to all the abuses of time and were almost worn out. I put on those sad rags as best I could, and fearing that my mistake had caused my father's death, I thought it would be wiser to leave my country and to go begging rather than to appear before my sisters in the condition in which I was. So I smeared my face with dirt and summoned up my courage to begin my wandering.

After a long and fatiguing journey, I arrived at a seaport where an old Muslim, who was heading toward Borneo to do some trading, had pity on me and took me on board his ship. We had a safe voyage and let down the anchor in a bay of that large island, even though I was not sure why we did this. After descending with many other people who were tired of the sea, I left their company without anyone noticing since I had no desire to go with their leader, who was on his way to the coastal cities where business called him. I went into the interior of the island, which was very populous, and in three months I reached the pretty city of Soucad, which received its name from the large river that crosses it.

I noticed from the very first days that the embroidery that decorated the clothes of the women was extremely coarse, and I was convinced that I was more skillful in doing this simple work than the women of Borneo, and that I had found a source that would provide me with work. Once my skill became known, it was not long before I had success beyond my greatest expectations. I rented a small cottage, and in a short time I established an honest business for myself. I did not have any difficulty learning the language because people use approximately the same language in Soucad as they do in Gilolo. For six or seven months I was able to live in peace doing my work, and I gradually regained the beauty that people had flattered me with having—a beauty that had almost entirely disappeared due to the misery I had suffered and my exhaustion. As my looks changed, I drew the attention of many people, and among them were three of the most distinguished young men of the city, who conspired together to discover whether I was cruel. They agreed among themselves that one of them, who was considered a very artful seducer, would make the first attempt. He came to my house that very evening and began the conversation by asking me to make an embroidered belt for him. Then he talked about his feelings for me: no beauty intended to be an easy conquest has ever heard so many professions of friendship and favors all at once. When dinnertime arrived, he wanted to entertain me, and though he saw that I was repulsed by the idea, he insisted, and I consented. The meal tasted fine, and he did not forget little sweet songs to accompany it. In fact, my lover made it quite clear from several fresh looks that he expected me to be most obliging to him.

Since an open window in my room made him feel uncomfortable, he went over to shut it. However, while he was closing it, I pronounced those powerful words that the King Leopard had taught me, and I put him into a trance so that he had to keep doing what he was doing. As for me, I went to bed as I ordinarily did without any difficulties. The poor man, who was under a spell, spent the entire night doing what he was doing. The next morning I released him and let him go with a good warning to behave better in the future.

His comrades, who had been waiting impatiently for him in a street since daybreak, ran toward him as soon as they caught sight of him. He cleverly led them to believe that he had been perfectly well received and described his good fortune to them in glowing colors that set them afire. They drew lots to see which one would enjoy the expected happiness next, and the day seemed long to the one who had won. However, the night was much more tedious for him because he was obliged to wind a reel of silk for the exact same amount of time that the other had spent closing the window. The third young man was tricked just like his friends, and he had to comb my hair the entire night on account of my orders.

These young men did not have the strength to conceal their misadventures for a long time. All three were outraged, and their tenderness changed into obsessive hate. Therefore, they agreed to denounce me to the judges as the most despicable sorceress in the world. As a result, I was taken from my house and imprisoned. They worked feverishly at getting ready for my trial, and my adversaries were powerful and very motivated. Besides, I did not deny a single fact which they accused me of. Thus, the affair would not have lasted four days if I had not distributed some money among some of the judges through the help of a good friend, who was kind enough to do this. The decision was postponed for three whole months in part due to the money and in part due to the fact that two of the other judges were appreciative of the charms that they believed to see in me. They did everything they could to save me and were convinced that I would not be ungrateful after such a great service. Nevertheless, in the end my persecutors won, and I was condemned to be burned alive.

After this cruel sentence had been pronounced, I was led to the stake that had been set up in the middle of the most beautiful square in Soucad. When I arrived there, they made sure to tell me everything that one tells a person in that country when one is to be executed in a public ceremony, and they bound me to the stake with a large chain. The people hurled insults at me as if I were a sorceress and an enemy of the human race. They accused me of all the bad things that had happened naturally or accidentally to all those people who had bought my works. They were delighted to see the executioner advance toward the stake with a flaming torch in his hand. But this unsuspecting crowd was greatly surprised a moment later to see this same executioner become immobile and entranced. The only thing he could do was to hold his burning torch. This effect had been induced by the words that I had secretly pronounced against him. Everyone was in suspense due to this strange incident. Then their mood changed all at once, and they could not stop themselves from laughing as they watched this truly ridiculous figure that was supposed to be the executioner.

The three young men were present and had a large number of partisans in the crowd. They became extraordinarily furious at seeing an event that reminded them of what had happened to them. They cried out that this was public proof of my guilt and that they should quickly reduce a woman to ashes who, even at the point of death, had abominable ties with evil spirits. The mob was moved by these words and ran to the nearby houses to fetch firebrands. I prepared myself again to stop this rage when a noise that was mixed with acclamations caught their attention in the main street that emptied into the square.

It was the king of Soucad who had caused this pleasant commotion. After a long absence, he had wanted to surprise his people by making a sudden appearance. Since he was greatly beloved, everyone's attention was drawn to him and taken away from the stake, the executioner, the victim, and the judges.

The king had gotten out of his carriage and was riding slowly on horse-back in order to appear more popular. He advanced right into the middle of the square and saw a spectacle, which he found rather strange, since it did not fit the public joy that had been aroused by his happy return. When he turned toward the stake, he granted me the reprieve that only he could give, and he had me untied. Immediately, I ran to embrace the knees of my liberator, who looked at me very attentively. He dismounted and em-braced me with a joy that equaled the amazement of all the spectators. I did not dare to raise my eyes, but finally, once I glimpsed the person from whom I had received such a surprising reprieve, I recognized the King Leopard, whose image had remained deeply engraved in my mind.

It is impossible to express the feelings of my heart, my thoughts, and what I wanted to say. I could not form a single coherent sentence. My gratitude and joy took away all the words that came to my mind. The king had me get into his carriage without getting in himself and conducted me to his palace in triumph. Some days later, he married me in a solemn ceremony and empowered me to reign in his dominions. The first merciful act I asked him to perform was to pardon my accusers. Then I gave the judges who had let themselves be bribed by my money the punishment they deserved. On the other hand, those judges who had been moved by my beauty were punished in a more lenient way.

JEANNE-MARIE LEPRINCE DE BEAUMONT

Beauty and the Beast†

Once upon a time, there was an extremely rich merchant who had six children, three boys and three girls. Since he was a sensible man, the merchant spared no expense in educating his children, and he hired all kinds of tutors for their benefit.

His daughters were very pretty, but everyone admired the youngest one in particular. When she was a small child, they simply called her "Little Beauty." As a result, the name stuck and led to a great deal of jealousy on the part of her sisters. Not only was the youngest girl prettier than her sisters, but she was also better. The two elder girls were very arrogant because they were rich. They pretended to be ladies and refused to receive the visits of daughters who belonged to merchant families. They chose only people of quality for their companions. Every day they went to the balls, the theater, and the park, and they made fun of their younger sister, who spent most of her time reading books.

Since these girls were known to be very rich, many important merchants sought their hand in marriage. But the two elder sisters maintained that

† Jeanne-Marie Leprince de Beaumont, "Beauty and the Beast"—"La Belle et la Bête" (1756), in *Magasin des enfants* (Lyon: Reguilliat, 1756).

they would never marry unless they found a duke, or, at the very least, a count. But Beauty—as I have mentioned, this was the name of the youngest daughter—thanked all those who proposed marriage to her and said that she was too young and that she wanted to keep her father company for some years to come.

Suddenly the merchant lost his fortune, and the only property he had left was a small country house quite far from the city. With tears in his eyes, he told his children that they would have to go and live in this house and work like farmers to support themselves. His two elder daughters replied that they did not want to leave the city and that they had many admirers who would be only too happy to marry them, even though they no longer had a fortune. But these fine young ladies were mistaken. Their admirers no longer paid them any attention now that they were poor. Moreover, since they were so arrogant, everyone disliked them and said, "They don't deserve to be pitied. It's quite nice to see their pride take a fall. Now let's see them pretend to be ladies while minding the sheep in the country."

Yet, at the same time, people said, "As for Beauty, we're disturbed about her misfortune. She's such a good girl. She was always kind to poor people. She's such a good girl, so sweet and so forthright!"

There were even several gentlemen who wanted to marry her, despite the fact that she told them that she could not bring herself to abandon her poor father in his distress, and that she was going to follow him to the country to console him and help him in his work. Poor Beauty had been greatly upset by the loss of her fortune, but she said to herself, "My tears will not bring back my fortune. So I must try to be happy without it."

When they arrived at the country house, the merchant and his three daughters began farming the land. Beauty got up at four o'clock in the morning and occupied herself by cleaning the house and preparing breakfast for the family. At first she had a great deal of difficulty because she was not accustomed to working like a servant. But after two months she became stronger, and the hard work improved her health. After finishing her chores, she generally read, played the harpsichord, or sung while spinning. On the other hand, her two sisters were bored to death. They arose at ten o'clock in the morning, took walks the entire day, and entertained themselves bemoaning the loss of their beautiful clothes and the fine company they used to have.

"Look at our little sister," they would say to each other. "Her mind is so dense, and she's so stupid that she's quite content in this miserable situation."

The good merchant did not agree with his daughters. He knew that Beauty was more suited to stand out in company than they were. He admired the virtues of this young girl—especially her patience, for her sisters were not merely content to let her do all the work in the house, but they also insulted her at every chance they got.

After living one year in this secluded spot, the merchant received a letter informing him that one of his ships that contained some of his merchandise had just arrived safely. This news turned the heads of the two elder girls, for they thought that they would finally be able to leave the countryside where they had been leading a life of boredom. When they saw their father getting ready to depart for the city, they begged him to bring them back dresses, furs, caps, and all sorts of finery. Beauty asked for nothing because she thought that all the profit from the merchandise would not be sufficient to buy what her sisters had requested.

"Don't you want me to buy you something?" her father said to her.

"Since you are so kind to think of me," she replied, "please bring me a rose, for there are none here."

Beauty was not really anxious to have a rose, but she did not want to set an example that would disparage her sisters, who would have said that she had requested nothing to show how much better she was than they were.

The good man set out for the city, but when he arrived, he found there was a lawsuit concerning his merchandise, and after a great deal of trouble, he began his return journey much poorer than he had been before. He had only thirty miles to go before he would reach his house, and he was already looking forward to seeing his children again. But he had to pass through a large forest to get to his house, and he got lost. There was a brutal snowstorm, and the wind was so strong that he was knocked from his horse two times. When nightfall arrived, he was convinced that he would die of hunger and cold or be eaten by the wolves that were howling all around him. Suddenly he saw a big light at the end of a long avenue of trees. It appeared to be quite some distance away, and he began walking in that direction. Soon he realized that the light was coming from a huge palace that was totally illuminated. The merchant thanked God for sending this help, and he hurried to the castle, but he was very surprised to find nobody in the courtyards. His horse, which had followed him, saw a large open stable and entered. Upon finding hay and oats, the poor animal, who was dying of hunger, began eating with a rapacious appetite. The merchant tied the horse up in the stable and walked toward the palace without encountering a soul. However, when he entered a large hall, he discovered a good fire and a table covered with food that was set for just one person. Since the rain and snow had soaked him from head to foot, he approached the fire to dry himself. "The master of this house will forgive the liberty I'm taking," he said to himself, "and I'm sure that he'll be here soon."

He waited a considerable time, but when the clock struck eleven, and he still did not see anyone, he could not resist his hunger anymore and took a chicken that he devoured in two mouthfuls while trembling all over. As he became more hardy, he left the hall and went through several large and magnificently furnished apartments. Finally he found a room with a good bed, and since it was past midnight and he was tired, he decided to shut the door and go to bed. It was ten o'clock in the morning when he awoke the next day, and he was greatly surprised to find very clean clothes in place of his own, which had been completely tarnished.

"Surely," he said to himself, "this palace belongs to some good fairy who has taken pity on my predicament."

He looked out the window and no longer saw snow but arbors of flowers that gave rise to an enchanting view. He went back to the large hall where he had dined the night before and saw a small table with a cup of chocolate on it.

"I want to thank you, madame fairy," he said aloud, "for being so kind as to think of my own breakfast."

After drinking his chocolate, the good man went to look for his horse, and as he passed under an arbor of roses, he remembered that Beauty had asked for one, and he plucked a rose from a branch filled with roses. All of a sudden he heard a loud noise and saw a beast coming toward him. It was so horrible-looking that he almost fainted.

"You're very ungrateful," the beast said in a ferocious voice. "I saved your life by offering you hospitality in my castle, and then you steal my roses, which I love more than anything else in the world. You shall have to die for this mistake. I'll give you just a quarter of an hour to ask for God's forgiveness."

The merchant threw himself on his knees and pleaded with his hands clasped. "Pardon me, my lord. I didn't think that I'd offend you by plucking a rose for one of my daughters who had asked me to bring her one."

"I'm not called lord," replied the monster, "but Beast. I don't like compliments and prefer that people speak their minds. So don't think that you can move me by flattery. But you didn't tell me that you had daughters. Now I'll pardon you on the condition that one of your daughters will come here voluntarily to die in your place. Don't try to reason with me. Just go. And if your daughters refuse to die for you, swear to me that you'll return within three months."

The good man did not intend to sacrifice one of his daughters to this hideous monster, but he thought, "At least I'll have the pleasure of embracing them one more time."

So he swore he would return, and the beast told him he could leave whenever he liked. "But," he added, "I don't want you to leave empty-handed. Go back to the room where you slept. There you'll find a large empty chest. You may fill it with whatever you like, and I shall have it carried home for you."

Meanwhile, the Beast withdrew, and the good man said to himself, "If I must die, I shall still have the consolation of leaving my children with something to sustain themselves."

He returned to the room where he had slept, and upon finding a large quantity of gold pieces, he filled the big chest that the Beast had mentioned. After closing it, he went to his horse, which he found in the stable, and he left the palace with a sadness that matched the joy that he had experienced upon entering it. His horse took one of the forest roads on its own, and within a few hours the good man arrived at his small house, where his children gathered around him. But instead of responding to their caresses, the merchant burst into tears at the sight of them. His hand held the branch of roses that he had brought for Beauty, and he gave it to her saying, "Beauty, take these roses. They will cost your poor father dearly."

Immediately thereafter he told his family about the tempestuous adventure that he had experienced. On hearing the tale, the two elder daughters uttered loud cries and berated Beauty, who did not weep.

"See what this measly creature's arrogance has caused!" they said. "Why didn't she settle for the same gifts as ours. But no, our lady had to be different. Now she's going to be the cause of our father's death, and she doesn't even cry."

"That would be quite senseless," replied Beauty. "Why should I lament my father's death when he is not going to perish. Since the monster is willing to accept one of his daughters, I intend to offer myself to placate his fury, and I feel very happy to be in a position to save my father and prove my affection for him."

"No, sister," said her three brothers, "you won't die. We shall go and find this monster, and we'll die under his blows if we can't kill him."

"Don't harbor any such hopes, my children," said the merchant. "The Beast's power is so great that I don't have the slightest hope of having him killed. I'm delighted by the goodness of Beauty's heart, but I won't expose her to death. I'm old, and I don't have much longer to live. Therefore, I'll only lose a few years of my life, which I won't regret losing on account of you, my dear children."

"Rest assured, Father," said Beauty, "you won't go to this palace without me. You can't prevent me from following you. Even though I'm young, I'm not all that strongly tied to life, and I'd rather be devoured by this monster than to die of the grief that your loss would cause me."

Words were in vain. Beauty was completely determined to depart for this beautiful palace. And her sisters were delighted by this because the virtues of their younger sister had filled them with a good deal of jealousy. The merchant was so concerned by the torment of losing his daughter that he forgot all about the chest that he had filled with gold. But as soon as he returned to his room to sleep, he was quite astonished to find it by the side of his bed. He decided not to tell his children that he had become rich because his daughters would have wanted to return to the city, and he was resolved to die in the country. However, he confided his secret to Beauty, who informed him that several gentlemen had come during his absence and that there were two who loved her sisters. She pleaded with her father to let her sisters get married, for she was of such a kind nature that she loved them and forgave the evil they had done her with all her heart.

When Beauty departed with her father, the two nasty sisters rubbed their eyes with onions to weep. But her brothers wept in reality as did the merchant. Beauty was the only one who did not cry because she did not want to increase their distress.

The horse took the road to the palace, and by nightfall, they spotted it totally illuminated as before. The horse was installed in the stable all alone, and the good man entered the large hall with his daughter. There they found a table magnificently set for two people. However, the merchant did not have the heart to eat. On the other hand, Beauty forced herself to appear calm, and she sat down at the table and served him. Then she said to herself, "It's clear that the Beast is providing such a lovely feast to fatten me up before eating me."

After they had finished supper, they heard a loud noise, and the merchant said good-bye to his daughter with tears in his eyes, for he knew it was the Beast. Beauty could only tremble at the sight of this horrible figure, but she summoned her courage. The monster asked her if she had come of her own accord, and she responded yes and continued to shake.

"You are, indeed, quite good," said the Beast, "and I am very much obliged to you. As for you, my good man, you are to depart tomorrow, and never think of returning here. Good-bye, Beauty."

"Good-bye, Beast," she responded.

Suddenly the Beast disappeared.

"Oh, my daughter!" said the merchant embracing Beauty. "I'm half dead with fear. Believe me, it's best if I stay."

"No, my father," Beauty said firmly. "You're to depart tomorrow morning, and you'll leave me to the mercy of heaven. Perhaps heaven will take pity on me."

After they had gone to bed, they thought they would not be able to sleep the entire night. But they were hardly in their beds when their eyes closed shut. During her sleep, Beauty envisioned a lady who said to her, "Your kind heart pleases me, Beauty. The good deed you're performing to save your father's life shall not go unrewarded."

When Beauty awoke the next morning, she told her father about the dream, and though this consoled him somewhat, it did not prevent him from sobbing loudly when he had to separate himself from his dear child. After he departed, Beauty sat down in the great hall and also began to weep. Yet, since she had a great deal of courage, she asked God to protect her and resolved not to grieve any more during the short time she had to live. She firmly believed that the Beast was going to eat her that night, and in the meantime she decided to take a walk and explore this splendid castle. She could not help but admire its beauty, and she was quite surprised when she found a door on which were written the words "Beauty's Room." She opened the door quickly, and she was dazed by the magnificence that radiated throughout the room. But what struck her most of all was a large library, a harpsichord, and numerous books of music. "They don't want me to get bored," she whispered to herself. "If I'm only supposed to spend one day here, they wouldn't have made all these preparations."

This thought renewed her courage. She opened the library, saw a book, and read these letters on it: "Your wish is our command. You are queen and mistress here."

"Alas!" she said with a sigh. "My only wish is to see my poor father again and to know what he's doing at this very moment."

She had said this only to herself, so you can imagine her surprise when she glanced at a large mirror and saw her home, where her father was arriving with an extremely sad face. Her sisters went out to meet him, and despite the grimaces they made to pretend to be distressed, the joy on their faces at the loss of their sister was visible. One moment later, everything in the mirror disappeared, and Beauty could not but think that the Beast had been most compliant and that she had nothing to fear from him.

At noon she found the table set, and during her meal she heard an excellent concert, even though she did not see a soul. That evening, as she was about to sit down at the table, she heard the noise made by the Beast and could not keep herself from trembling.

"Beauty," the monster said to her, "would you mind if I watch you dine?"

"You're the master," replied Beauty trembling.

"No," responded the Beast. "You are the mistress here, and you only have to tell me to go if I bother you. Then I'll leave immediately. Tell me, do you find me very ugly?"

"Yes, I do," said Beauty. "I don't know how to lie. But I believe that you're very good."

"You're right," said the monster. "But aside from my ugliness, I'm not all that intelligent. I know quite well that I'm just a beast."

"A stupid person doesn't realize that he lacks intelligence," Beauty replied. "Fools never know what they're missing."

"Enjoy your meal, Beauty," the monster said to her, "and try to amuse yourself in your house, for everything here is yours. I'd feel upset if you were not happy."

"You're quite kind," Beauty said. "I assure you that I am most pleased with your kind heart. When I think of that, you no longer seem ugly to me."

"Oh, yes," the Beast answered, "I have a kind heart, but I'm still a monster."

"There are many men who are more monstrous than you," Beauty said, "and I prefer you with your looks rather than those who have a human face but conceal false, ungrateful, and corrupt hearts."

"If I had the intelligence," the Beast responded, "I'd make you a fine compliment to thank you. But I'm stupid so that I can only say that I'm greatly obliged to you."

Beauty ate with a good appetite. She was no longer afraid of the Beast, but she nearly died of fright when he said, "Beauty, will you be my wife?"

She did not answer right away, for she was fearful of enraging the monster by refusing him. At last, however, she said, trembling, "No, Beast."

At that moment, the poor monster wanted to sigh, but he made such a frightful whistle that it echoed through the entire palace. Beauty soon regained her courage, for the Beast said to her in a sad voice, "Farewell, then, Beauty."

He left the room, turning to look at her from time to time as he went. When Beauty was alone, she felt a great deal of compassion for the Beast. "It's quite a shame," she said, "that he's so ugly, for he's so good."

Beauty spent three months in the palace in great tranquillity. Every evening the Beast paid her a visit and entertained her at supper in conversation with plain good sense, but not what the world calls wit. Every day Beauty discovered new qualities in the monster. She had become so accustomed to seeing him that she adjusted to his ugliness, and far from dreading the moment of his visit, she often looked at her watch to see if it was already nine o'clock, for the Beast never failed to appear at that hour.

There was only one thing that troubled Beauty. Before she went to bed each night, the Beast would always ask her if she would be his wife, and he seemed deeply wounded when she refused.

"You're making me uncomfortable, Beast," she said one day. "I'd like to be able to marry you, but I'm too frank to allow you to believe that this could ever happen. I'll always be your friend. Try to be content with that."

"I'll have to," responded the Beast. "To be honest with myself, I know I'm quite horrible-looking. But I love you very much. However, I'm happy enough with the knowledge that you want to stay here. Promise me that you'll never leave me."

Beauty blushed at these words, for she had seen in her mirror that her father was sick with grief at having lost her, and she wished to see him again.

"I could very easily promise never to leave you," she said to the Beast. "But I have such a desire to see my father again that I would die of grief if you were to refuse me this request."

"I'd rather die myself than to cause you grief," the monster said. "I'll send you to your father's home. You shall stay with him, and your poor beast will die of grief."

"No," Beauty said to him with tears in her eyes. "I love you too much to want to cause your death. I promise to return in a week's time. You've shown me that my sisters are married and my brothers have left home to join the army. Just let me stay a week with my father since he's all alone."

"You shall be there tomorrow morning," the Beast said. "But remember your promise. You only have to place your ring on the table before going to bed if you want to return. Farewell, Beauty."

As was his custom, the Beast sighed when he said these words, and Beauty went to bed very sad at having disturbed him. When she awoke the next morning, she found herself in her father's house, and when she rang a bell that was at her bedside, it was answered by a servant who uttered a great cry upon seeing her. Her good father came running when he heard the noise and almost died of joy at seeing his dear daughter again. They kept hugging each other for more than a quarter of an hour. After their excitement subsided, Beauty recalled that she did not have any clothes to wear. But the servant told her that he had just found a chest in the next room, and it was full of dresses trimmed with gold and diamonds. Beauty thanked the good Beast for looking after her. She took the least rich of the dresses and told the servant to lock up the others, for she wanted to send them as gifts to her sisters. But no sooner had she spoken those words than the chest disappeared. Her father told Beauty that the Beast probably wanted her to keep them for herself, and within seconds the dresses and the chest came back again.

While Beauty proceeded to get dressed, a message was sent to inform her sisters of her arrival, and they came running with their husbands. Both sisters were exceedingly unhappy. The oldest had married a young gentleman who was remarkably handsome but was so enamored of his own looks that he occupied himself with nothing but his appearance from morning until night, and he despised his wife's beauty. The second sister had married a man who was very intelligent, but he used his wit only to enrage everyone, first and foremost his wife. The sisters almost died of grief when they saw Beauty dressed like a princess and more beautiful than daylight. It was in vain that she hugged them, for nothing could stifle their jealousy, which increased when she told them how happy she was.

The two envious sisters went down into the garden to vent their feelings in tears. "Why is this little snip happier than we are?" they asked each other. "Aren't we just as pleasing as she is?"

"Sister," said the oldest, "I've just had an idea. Let's try to keep her here more than a week. That stupid beast will become enraged when he finds out that she's broken her word, and perhaps he'll devour her."

"Right you are, sister," responded the other. "But we must show her a great deal of affection to succeed."

Having made this decision, they returned to the house and showed Beauty so much attention that Beauty wept with joy. After a week had passed, the two sisters tore their hair and were so distressed by her departure that she promised to remain another week. However, Beauty reproached herself for the grief she was causing her poor Beast, whom she loved with all her heart. In addition, she missed not being able to see him any longer. On the tenth night that she spent in her father's house, she dreamt that she was in the palace garden and saw the Beast lying on the grass nearly dead and reprimanding her for her ingratitude. Beauty awoke with a start and burst into tears.

"Aren't I very wicked for causing grief to a beast who's gone out of his way to please me?" she said. "Is it his fault that he's so ugly and has so little intelligence? He's so kind, and that's worth more than anything else. Why haven't I wanted to marry him? I'm more happy with him than my sisters are with their husbands. It is neither handsome looks nor intelligence that makes a woman happy. It is good character, virtue, and kindness, and the Beast has all these good qualities. It's clear that I don't love him, but I have respect, friendship, and gratitude for him. So there's no reason to make him miserable, and if I'm ungrateful, I'll reproach myself my entire life."

With these words Beauty arose, placed her ring on the table, and lay down again. No sooner was she in her bed than she fell asleep, and when she awoke the next morning, she saw with joy that she was in the Beast's palace. She put on her most magnificent dress to please him and spent a boring day waiting for nine o'clock in the evening to arrive. But the clock struck in vain, for the Beast did not appear.

Now Beauty feared that she had caused his death. She ran throughout the palace sobbing loudly and was terribly despondent. After searching everywhere, she recalled her dream and ran into the garden toward the canal where she had seen him in her sleep. There she found the poor Beast stretched out and unconscious, and she thought he was dead. She threw herself on his body without being horrified by his looks, and she felt his heart still beating. So she fetched some water from the canal and threw it on his face.

Beast opened his eyes and said to Beauty, "You forgot your promise. The grief I felt upon having lost you made me decide to die of hunger. But I shall die content since I have the pleasure of seeing you one more time."

Beauty and the Beast. Walter Crane, 1875.

"No, my dear Beast, you shall not die," said Beauty. "You shall live to become my husband. From this moment on, I give you my hand and swear that I belong only to you. Alas! I thought that I only felt friendship for you, but the torment I am feeling makes me realize that I cannot live without you."

Beauty had scarcely uttered these words when the castle radiated with light. Fireworks and music announced a feast. But these attractions could not hold her attention. She returned her gaze toward her dear Beast, whose dangerous condition made her tremble. But how great was her surprise! The Beast had disappeared, and at her feet was a prince more handsome than Eros himself, and he thanked her for having put an end to his enchantment. Although the prince merited her undivided attention, she could not refrain from asking what had happened to the Beast.

"You're looking at him right at your feet," the prince said. "A wicked fairy had condemned me to remain in this form until a beautiful girl would consent to marry me, and she had prohibited me from revealing my intelligence. You were the only person in the world kind enough to allow the goodness of my character to touch you, and in offering you my crown, I'm only discharging the obligations I owe you."

Beauty was most pleasantly surprised and assisted the handsome prince in rising by offering her hand. Together they went to the castle, and Beauty was overwhelmed by joy in finding her father and entire family in the hall, for the beautiful lady who had appeared to her in her dream had transported them to the castle.

"Beauty," said this lady, who was a grand fairy, "come and receive the reward for your good choice. You've preferred virtue over beauty and wit, and you deserve to find these qualities combined in one and the same person. You're going to become a great queen, and I hope that the throne will not destroy your virtues. As for you, my young ladies," the fairy said to Beauty's two sisters, "I know your hearts and all the malice they contain. You shall become statues, but you shall retain your ability to think beneath the stone that encompasses you. You shall stand at the portal of your sister's palace, and I can think of no better punishment to impose on you than to witness her happiness. I'll only allow you to return to your original shape when you recognize your faults. But I fear that you'll remain statues forever. Pride, anger, gluttony, and laziness can all be corrected, but some sort of miracle is needed to convert a wicked and envious heart."

All at once the fairy waved her wand and transported everyone in the hall to the prince's realm. His subjects rejoiced upon seeing him again, and he married Beauty, who lived with him a long time in perfect happiness because their relationship was founded on virtue.

JACOB AND WILHELM GRIMM

The Singing, Springing Lark†

Once upon a time there was a man who was about to go on a long journey, and right before his departure he asked his three daughters what he should bring back to them. The oldest wanted pearls, the second diamonds, but the third said, "Dear father, I'd like to have a singing, springing lark."

"All right," said the father. "If I can get one, you shall have it."

So he kissed all three daughters good-bye and went on his way. When the time came for his return journey, he had purchased pearls and diamonds for the two oldest, but even though he had looked all over, he had not been able to find the singing, springing lark for his youngest daughter. He was particularly sorry about that because she was his favorite. In the meantime, his way took him through a forest, in the middle of which he discovered a magnificent castle. Near the castle was a tree, and way on top of this tree he saw a lark singing and springing about.

"Well, you've come just at the right time," he said, quite pleased, and he ordered his servant to climb the tree and catch the little bird. But when the servant went over to the tree, a lion jumped out from under it, shook himself, and roared so ferociously that the leaves on the trees trembled.

"If anyone tries to steal my singing, springing lark," he cried, "I'll eat him up."

"I didn't know that the bird belonged to you," said the man. "I'll make up for my trespassing and give you a great deal of gold if only you'll spare my life."

"Nothing can save you," said the lion, "unless you promise to give me the first thing you meet when you get home. If you agree, then I'll not only grant you your life, but I'll also give you the bird for your daughter."

At first the man refused and said, "That could be my youngest daughter. She loves me most of all and always runs to meet me when I return home."

But the servant was very scared of the lion and said, "It doesn't always have to be your daughter. Maybe it'll be a cat or a dog."

The man let himself be persuaded and took the singing, springing lark. Then he promised the lion he would give him the first thing that met him when he got home.

Upon reaching his house, he walked inside, and the first thing that met him was none other than his youngest and dearest daughter. Indeed, she came running up to him, threw her arms around him, and kissed him. When she saw that he had brought her a singing, springing lark, she was overcome with joy. But her father could not rejoice and began to weep.

"My dearest child," he said, "I've had to pay a high price for this bird.

---

† Jacob and Wilhelm Grimm, "The Singing, Springing Lark"—"Das singende, springende Löweneckerchen" (1857), No. 88 in *Kinder- und Hausmärchen. Gesammelt durch die Brüder Grimm* (Göttingen: Dieterich, 1857).

In exchange I was compelled to promise you to a wild lion, and when he gets you, he'll tear you to pieces and eat you up." Then he went on to tell her exactly how everything had happened and begged her not to go there, no matter what the consequences might be. Yet she consoled him and said, "Dearest father, if you've made a promise, you must keep it. I'll go there, and once I've made the lion nice and tame, I'll be back here safe and sound."

The next morning she had her father show her the way. Then she took leave of him and walked calmly into the forest. Now it turned out that the lion was actually an enchanted prince. During the day he and his men were lions, and during the night they assumed their true human forms. When she arrived there, she was welcomed in a friendly way, and they conducted her to the castle. When night came, the lion became a handsome man, and the wedding was celebrated in splendor. They lived happily together by remaining awake at night and asleep during the day. One day he came to her and said, "Tomorrow there will be a celebration at your father's house since your oldest sister is to be married. If you wish to attend, my lions will escort you there."

She replied that, yes, she would very much like to see her father again, and she went there accompanied by the lions. There was great rejoicing when she arrived, for they all had believed that she had been torn to pieces by the lions and had long been dead. But she told them what a handsome husband she had and how well off she was. She stayed with them just as long as the wedding celebration lasted. Then she went back to the forest.

When the second daughter was about to be married, she was again invited to the wedding, but this time she said to the lion, "I don't want to go without you."

However, the lion said it would be too dangerous for him because he would be changed into a dove and have to fly about with the doves for seven years if the ray of a burning candle were to fall upon him.

"Please come with me," she said. "I'll be sure to take good care of you and protect you from the light."

So they went off together and took their small child with them. Once there she had a hall built for him so strong and thick that not a single ray of light could penetrate it. That was the place where he was to sit when the wedding candles were lit. However, its door was made out of green wood, and it split and developed a crack that nobody saw. The wedding was celebrated in splendor, but when the wedding procession with all the candles and torches came back from church and passed by the hall, a ray about the width of a hair fell upon the prince, and he was instantly transformed. When his wife entered the hall to look for him, she could find only a white dove sitting there, and he said to her, "For seven years I shall have to fly about the world, but for every seven steps you take I shall leave a drop of red blood and a little white feather to show you the way. And if you follow the traces, you'll be able to set me free."

Then the dove flew out the door, and she followed him. At every seventh step she took, a drop of blood and a little white feather would fall and show her the way. Thus she went farther and farther into the wide world and never looked about or stopped until the seven years were almost up. She was looking forward to that and thought they would soon be free. But they were still quite far from their goal.

Once, as she was moving along, she failed to find any more feathers or drops of blood, and when she raised her head, the dove had also vanished. "I won't be able to get help from a mortal," she thought, and so she climbed up to the sun and said to her, "You shine into every nook and cranny. Is there any chance that you've seen a white dove flying around?"

"No," said the sun, "I haven't, but I'll give you a little casket. Just open it when your need is greatest."

She thanked the sun and continued on her way until the moon came out to shine in the evening. "You shine the whole night through and on all fields and meadows. Is there any chance that you've seen a white dove flying around?"

"No," said the moon, "I haven't, but I'll give you an egg. Just crack it open when your need is greatest."

She thanked the moon and went farther until the night wind stirred and started to blow at her. "You blow over every tree and under every leaf. Is there any chance that you've seen a white dove flying around?"

"No," said the night wind, "I haven't, but I'll ask the three other winds. Perhaps they've seen one."

The east wind and the west wind came and reported they had not seen a thing, but the south wind said, "I've seen the white dove. It's flown to the Red Sea and has become a lion again, for the years are over. The lion's now in the midst of a fight with a dragon that's really an enchanted princess."

Then the night wind said to her, "Here's what I would advise you to do: Go to the Red Sea, where you'll find some tall reeds growing along the shore. Then count them until you come to the eleventh one, which you're to cut off and use to strike the dragon. That done, the lion will be able to conquer the dragon, and both will regain their human forms. After that, look around, and you'll see the griffin[1] sitting by the Red Sea. Get on his back with your beloved, and the griffin will carry you home across the sea. Now, here's a nut for you. When you cross over the middle of the sea, let it drop. A nut tree will instantly sprout out of the water, and the griffin will be able to rest on it. If he can't rest there, he won't be strong enough to carry you both across the sea. So if you forget to drop the nut into the sea, he'll let you fall into the water."

She went there and found everything as the night wind had said. She counted the reeds by the sea, cut off the eleventh, and struck the dragon with it, whereupon the lion conquered the dragon, and both immediately regained their human forms. But when the princess who had previously been a dragon was set free from the magic spell, she picked the prince up in her arms, got on the griffin, and carried him off with her. So the poor maiden, who had journeyed so far, stood alone and forsaken again, and

---

1. In Greek mythology, a fabulous creature with the wings of an eagle and the hindquarters of a lion.

sat down to cry. Eventually, she took heart and said, "I'll keep going as far as the wind blows and so long as the cock crows until I find him." And off she went and wandered a long, long way until she came to the castle where the two were living together. Then she heard that their wedding celebration was soon to take place. "God will come to my aid," she remarked as she opened the little casket that the sun had given her. There she found a dress as radiant as the sun itself. She took it out, put it on, and went up to the castle. Everyone at the court and the bride herself could not believe their eyes. The bride liked the dress so much she thought it would be nice to have it for her wedding and asked if she could buy it.

"Not for money or property," she answered, "but for flesh and blood."

The bride asked her what she meant by that, and she responded, "Let me sleep one night in the bridegroom's room."

The bride did not want to let her, but she also wanted the dress very much. Finally, she agreed, but the bridegroom's servant was ordered to give him a sleeping potion. That night when the prince was asleep, she was led into his room, sat down on his bed, and said, "I've followed you for seven years. I went to the sun, the moon, and the four winds to find out where you were. I helped you conquer the dragon. Are you going to forget me forever?"

But the prince slept so soundly that it merely seemed to him as if the wind were whispering in the firs. When morning came, she was led out again and had to give up her golden dress.

Since her ploy had not been of much use, she was quite sad and went out to a meadow, where she sat down and wept. But as she was sitting there, she remembered the egg that the moon had given her. She cracked it open, and a hen with twelve chicks came out, all in gold. The peeping chicks scampered about and then crawled under the mother hen's wings. There was not a lovelier sight to see in the world. Shortly after that she stood up and drove them ahead of her over the meadow until they came within sight of the bride, who saw them from her window. She liked the little chicks so much that she came right down and asked if she could buy them.

"Not with money or possessions, but for flesh and blood. Let me sleep another night in the bridegroom's room."

The bride agreed and wanted to trick her as she had done the night before. But when the prince went to bed, he asked the servant what had caused all the murmuring and rustling during the night, and the servant told him everything: that he had been compelled to give him a sleeping potion because a poor girl had secretly slept in his room, and that he was supposed to give him another one that night.

"Dump the drink by the side of my bed," said the prince.

At night the maiden was led in again, and when she began to talk about her sad plight, he immediately recognized his dear wife by her voice, jumped up, and exclaimed, "Now I'm really free from the spell! It was like a dream. The strange princess had cast a spell over me and made me forget you, but God has delivered me from the spell just in time."

That night they left the castle in secret, for they were afraid of the princess's father, who was a sorcerer. They got on the griffin, who carried them over the Red Sea, and when they were in the middle, she let the nut drop. Immediately a big nut tree sprouted, and the griffin was able to rest there. Then he carried them home, where they found their child, who had grown tall and handsome. From then on they lived happily until their death.

Author Biographies

Friedmund von Arnim

Friedmund von Arnim (1815–1883) was born into an illustrious family in Berlin and grew up in the city and on the family estate in Wiepersdorf in northern Germany. His father, Achim von Arnim, was one of the foremost Romantic writers; he published an important collection of folksongs with the poet Clemens Brentano, among other important stories and novels. His mother, Bettina, was a gifted writer of social tracts, letters, and fairy tales. Both Arnim's father and his mother were close friends of the Brothers Grimm, who actually dedicated one of their editions to Bettina. Arnim spent his youth in Berlin and was known for his eccentric ways and love of nature. When he completed school in 1834, he undertook the customary tour of the world that most nobles did at that time and eventually traveled to Munich and Schlesia. It was during this period that he collected the folktales of Schlesia, which he published in his book *Hundert neue Mährchen im Gebirge gesammelt (A Hundred New Fairy Tales Gathered in the Mountains*, 1844). He also became very involved in revolutionary movements and published *Die Rechte jedes Menschen (The Rights of Man*, 1843–44), which addressed the poor working conditions of peasants and laborers. By the late 1840s, Arnim had returned to the family estate in Wiepersdorf, which had been in ruins, and there he conducted various agrarian experiments and lived his life in a natural style that Rousseau had proposed. He wrote two other books, *Neue Heillehre (New Medicinal Teachings*, 1868) and *Eine deutsche Sprachlehhre für den Dorfschulunterricht (A German Language Textbook for Teaching in Village Schools*, 1877), the first was concerned with natural medicine and the second with improving language lessons in villages. His collection of Schlesian tales never became very popular, but the Brothers Grimm thought highly of the simple folk tone and style and used some of Arnim's versions as the basis for editing some of their own tales such as "Iron Hans."

Marie-Catherine d'Aulnoy

Marie-Catherine Le Jumel de Barneville, Comtesse d'Aulnoy (ca. 1650–1705), was born in Barneville, Normandy, into a wealthy aristocratic family. During her youth, she heard numerous folktales from her aunt and was encouraged by her mother to live as independently as possible. At the age of fifteen, she was married to François de la Motte, Baron d'Aulnoy, who was thirty years her senior and a notorious gambler and libertine. She had some children with him, but due to his poor character, she soon became disenchanted with her marriage and had several lovers. In 1669, with the help of her mother, Madame Guadagne, who had remarried after Baron de Barneville's death, and two men, Jacques-Antoine de Courboyer and Charles de la Moizière, who were their lovers, Mme d'Aulnoy tried to implicate her husband as a traitor in a crime against the king that would have meant his death. However, the Baron d'Aulnoy managed to extricate himself from the affair and turned the tables on his wife: de Courboyer and de la Moizière were executed; Madame Guadagne escaped and made her way to England; Mme d'Aulnoy was arrested briefly and then also managed to flee Paris. After taking refuge in a convent, Mme d'Aulnoy supposedly traveled extensively in Holland, England, and Spain and may have acted along with her adventurous mother as a secret agent for France in those foreign countries. She also had some more children and different lovers. In 1685, she received permission to return to Paris, and she set up house in the rue Saint-Benoit, which became one of the most interesting literary salons of the period.

By 1690 Mme d'Aulnoy, an exceedingly bright and beautiful woman, had begun her public literary career with the publication of the novel *L'histoire d'Hipolyte, comte de Douglas*, which contained the prose fairy tale "L'île de la Félicité" ("The Island of Happiness"), which was to anticipate the great fairy tale vogue that was to commence five years later. Her novel was extremely successful, and that same year, she published *Mémoires de la cour d'Espagne*, which appears to have been largely taken from an English book, since there is no evidence that Mme d'Aulnoy had ever been at the Spanish court; the same holds true for her next book, *Relation du voyage d'Espagne* (1791), which contained the tale "Histoire de Mira," based on the theme of Melusine. Her last book about journeys to foreign countries was *Mémoires de la cour d'Angleterre* (1795), which may also have been a fictive account based on Mme d'Aulnoy's own readings about the English court.

It became customary at Mme d'Aulnoy's salon to recite fairy tales and on festive occasions to dress up like characters from fairy tales. She herself became one of the most gifted storytellers at her salon, and eventually she published several volumes of fairy tales: *Les contes des fées*, vols. I–III (1697–98); *Les contes des fées* (1698), vol. IV; and *Contes nouveaux; ou Les fées à la mode*, vols. I–IV (1698). More than Charles Perrault, it was Mme d'Aulnoy who was responsible for the extraordinary vogue of French fairy tales that swept the Parisian literary circles during the next ten years and continued less intensely until the publication of the *Cabinet des fées* (1786–89).

On the basis of her so-called memoirs and fairy tales, Mme d'Aulnoy was elected a member of the Académie des Ricovrati in Padova, and she continued to be active in the literary field by publishing other works such as *Sentiments d'une ame pénitente* (*Feelings of a Repentant Soul*, 1698) and *Le Comte de Warwick* (1703). In addition, Mme d'Aulnoy managed to make time for intrigue. In 1799, she supposedly assisted her friend Mme Ticquet, who assassinated her husband M. Ticquet, a member of parliament, because he had allegedly abused her. Mme Ticquet was beheaded, and Mme d'Aulnoy was fortunately exculpated from any wrongdoing. In 1800, her husband died, and since she had been on terrible terms with him, his last act before death was to disinherit her. Nevertheless, she continued to maintain her salon and participate in the cultural life in Paris until her death in 1705.

Although Mme d'Aulnoy was a mediocre stylist and her poetry could be maudlin, she had such a powerful imagination and remarkable command of folktale motifs and characters that her fairy tales never ceased to astonish and captivate her readers. Moreover, Mme d'Aulnoy paid close attention to the details of dress, architecture, speech, and manners of her day, and she described these details in her fairy tales so accurately that they always had a ring of authenticity. Of course, her descriptions tended to be hyperbolic: her heroines were the most beautiful; her heroes were the most charming and handsome; the castles were the most splendid. One refrain continues throughout her tales: "never has anyone seen anything so magnificent as this." This "never" that becomes "forever" in her tales revealed her longing for a different kind of world than the one to which she had been exposed.

Mme d'Aulnoy did not like constraints. In particular, she did not like the manner in which women were treated and compelled to follow patriarchal codes, and, as we know, she did not stop short of aiding and abetting the execution or murder of men whom she considered unworthy or tyrannical. All her tales are filled with violence and violation of some kind or another that must be resolved, and in some cases, as in "The Ram" and "The Pigeon and the Dove," the resolution is not entirely satisfying. Mme d'Aulnoy's tales are nightmarish because the fairies themselves are not always in agreement with one another, and thus humans must try to live under laws that they do not always understand and under fairy powers that are arbitrary, not unlike Louis XIV and his ministers. The only saving grace in the tales is love, or *tendresse*—that is, true natural feelings between a man and woman—and these feelings are constantly tested in extreme if not macabre ways. Mme d'Aulnoy's repertoire of tortures and bestial transformations was immense. She stopped at nothing to make her lovers suffer, only to make their rescue all the sweeter.

Literary critics have often commented that Mme d'Aulnoy's tales emanated from the boredom that the aristocracy felt during the ancien régime and that the tales were a form of compensation for the frustration that she and others felt. However, Mme d'Aulnoy was anything but bored, and her tales that originated from her active social life in the salons of that time were a means of confronting the frustrating conditions under which she lived and of projecting possibilities for change. Like her heroine Belle-Belle or the Chevalier Fortune, Mme d'Aulnoy disguised her dreams in her symbolical tales and was not afraid to imagine or try anything if it meant the fulfillment of these very dreams.

Giambattista Basile

Born most likely in the village of Posillipo near Naples, Giambattista Basile (ca. 1576–1632) came from a large middle-class family and spent his youth in his native town, where he evidently received an excellent education. He sought to find a noble patron and establish himself as a writer in Naples and vicinity as a young man but had little success. Therefore, he left his hometown and became a soldier of fortune to earn his living. It is not certain where Basile went at first, but he eventually made his way to Venice, where he was sent to Candia, a Venetian outpost, to defend the city against the Turks. It was during this time that he began writing poetry and became a member of the Accademia degli Stravaganti in Venice. In 1608, he returned to Naples and, thanks to his sister Adriana, who had become a famous singer, he was able to make connections in literary circles and found employment as a professional courtier, which meant that he organized cultural events and performed administrative tasks for a particular court or nobleman. It was in 1608 that he published his first poem in Italian, followed by a book of odes and madrigals, *Madriali et ode*, in 1609. From this point on in his life, Basile held various positions as administrator or magistrate in districts around Naples, while trying to establish a name for himself as a poet, intellectual, and scholar who wrote both in Italian and in the Neapolitan dialect. From 1610 to 1620, he published numerous occasional poems as well as *Le avventurose disavventure* (*The Adventurous Misadventure*, 1611), a marine pastoral; *Egloghe amorose e lugubri* (*Amorous and Lugubrious Ecologues*, 1612), a musical drama; *Opere poetiche* (*Poetical Works*, 1613); and an edition of Pietro Bembo's *Rime* (1616), followed by studies on Bembo and other mannerist poets. It was probably around 1615/16 that Basile began work on his two major dialect works, *Le muse napoletane* (*Neapolitan Muses*) and *Lo cunto de li cunti* (*The Tale of Tales*). After the appearance of his pastoral idyll *Aretusa* in 1619, he returned to Naples and was appointed royal governor in nearby Lagolibero and, in 1626, governor of Anversa. He continued having success as a poet and became a member of various literary academies such as the Accademia degli Incauti. He wrote poems and odes in Latin, Spanish, and Italian, used in court spectacles and masquerades. Yet it was not his poetry that was to make him famous, but his fairy tales in Neapolitan prose dialect, which he most likely recited in various courts and which formed the basis of *Lo cunto de li cunti*. Unfortunately, he never saw the published version, for he died during a flu epidemic in 1632, which had been caused by the eruption of Mount Vesuvius in 1631. His sister Adriana arranged for the publication of *Lo cunto de li cunti*, which appeared in four separate books between 1634 and 1636, under the pseudonym "Gian Alessio Abbattutis," an anagram for his name. By the fourth edition in 1674, the title of the collection of tales was changed to *Il Pentamerone*.

Most of Basile's mature life was spent traveling from court to court and working as an administrator and governor for the nobility. Despite the many poems that he wrote in praise of his patrons, there are strong signs that he was discontent with his employment, which did not provide him enough time for his writing, and that he was very critical of the customs and behavior of the nobility. Though fond of the peasantry, he was also critical of their crude manners and superstitions and was disposed to depicting the humorous side of their lives in his tales. A pioneer in dialect literature, Basile had a brilliant knack of combining baroque forms of expression with familiar proverbs and was a master of the pun. Like Straparola, Basile set a frame for his tales, but unlike Straparola, he used a fairy tale as his "tale of tales" to set the stage for fifty marvelous stories. In this frame tale, Zoza, the daughter of the king of Vallepelosa, cannot laugh, and her father is so concerned about her happiness that he invites people from all over to try to make her laugh. She is eventually incited to laugh when she watches an old woman sop up oil in front of her window, but her laughter also brings about a curse. To get rid of the curse she must free a sleeping prince named Tadeo, and after numerous adventures that involve ten coarse women who tell a total of forty-nine fairy tales to please a false bride, Zoza is able to prove that she is the true bride of Prince Tadeo and causes the death of the imposter. Basile's tales are a combination of the baroque and the grotesque. A master of social commentary and insight into the machinations of all diverse types from the peasantry, mercantile class, and aristocracy, he created inimitable tales about the foibles of human beings who will stoop as low as they can for success, power, and money, and these tales still ring true today.

Catherine Bernard

Catherine Bernard (1662–1712) was born in Rouen and went to Paris during her youth. Since she was related to Corneille and Fontenelle, she was soon introduced to the literary circles of Paris and established herself in 1687 as a talented author with a series of novels under the general title *Les malheurs de l'amour (The Misfortunes of Love): Eléonor d'Yvrée* (1687), *Le Comte d'Amboise* (1688), and *Inès de Cordue* (1696). It was, however, as a writer of tragedies that she became famous during her lifetime. In 1689 her first play, *Léodamie*, was performed twenty times, and it was followed by *Brutus* (1690), which had even greater success than the play by Voltaire, who had influenced her work.

Like many women writers of her time who were not independently wealthy and remained single, Mlle Bernard led an austere and modest life. In addition to her novels and tragedies, she wrote a number of poems that were published in different anthologies of the seventeenth century. Since she could not support herself by her writing alone, she accepted the patronage of the Chancelière de Pontchartrain, one of the more influential ladies at Louis XIV's court.

Mlle Bernard's "Riquet with the Tuft" ("Riquet à la houppe") appeared in her novel Inès de Cordoue in 1696 along with one other tale, "Le Prince Rosier." There is some question as to whether she wrote her tale first and influenced Charles Perrault, or vice versa. It is more than likely, since they moved in the same literary circles, that there was a mutual influence, and that both may have been acquainted with an oral folktale that served as the basis of "Riquet." The differences between the two versions are very interesting. Perrault's tale is more imaginative and optimistic from a male viewpoint. To bring about the happy end, he has his princess comply with a male code of reasoning. Bernard's version is more realistic and corresponds to the general theme of her novel, "the misfortunes of love." Unlike Perrault, she took a more critical view of forced marriages and depicted the quandary that many women felt when they were obliged to enter into contractual marriages. To this extent, Bernard's tale, one of the first to inaugurate the fairy tale mode in France, is a significant social document that can be considered part of the debate about the role of women and women's education, which was prevalent during the ancien régime.

Jean-Paul Bignon

Jean-Paul Bignon (1662–1743) was the son of Jérome II and Suzanne Phélypeaux de Pontchartrain, and he chose to enter the ecclesiastical orders at an early age in order to be able to pursue his scholarly interests. In 1684 he was accepted into the Novitiate de l'Oratoire, and in 1685 he went to a retreat at St.-Paul-aux-Bois, the diocese of Soissons, for five years in order to devote himself to a systematic study of the classics. At the beginning of 1691, he was ordained as a priest and became director of all the academies in the kingdom, one of the most important positions with regard to education in the ancien régime. In 1693 he was made abbot of St.-Quentin-en-Isle but continued to function as the director of academies. Bignon endeavored to keep out of the quarrels between the Jansenites and Jesuits, and he gradually became one of the most influential figures in the domain of the arts and sciences during his lifetime. As a member of the Académie Française and president of the Academy of Sciences for forty years, he constantly supported the work of the most promising intellectuals in France.

In 1700 he was appointed director of the libraries and the bureau of censorship. At one point, in 1702, Bignon took over the directorship of the *Journal des scavans* (*Journal of Scholars*) and reorganized it so that more intellectuals could contribute to the publication and enhance the quality of the articles. Bignon constantly sought ways to improve the conditions of scholarship in France, and after he became royal librarian in 1718, he brought about major changes in the library system, increasing the holdings and providing great public access to the libraries. Toward the end of his life, he had an expensive chateau built for himself near Melun, and he gave his retreat the name *Isle-Belle*, or Beautiful Island.

Bignon was more than a great administrator. He was a noted public speaker, poet, and scholar. He published numerous essays and wrote an important biography entitled *Vie de François Lévesque, prêtre de l'Oratoire* (*The Life of François Lévesque, Priest of the Oratory*, 1684). Since he was most active in intellectual circles during the height of the fairy tale vogue, he evidently decided to make a contribution to it by writing a collection of tales entitled *Les aventures d'Abdalla, fils d'Anif* (*The Adventures of*

Abdalla, Son of Anif, 1712–14). Bignon combined oriental motifs with French folklore to depict the exotic adventures of Abdalla, who encounters Zeineb during his travels. Each episode of the book is a tale unto itself, and Zeineb's first-person narrative is extremely important because of the role it plays in the Beauty and the Beast tradition. It is more than likely that Mme de Villeneuve knew this version, and it may have served as the basis for her own tale, which later influenced Mme Leprince de Beaumont.

Ser Giovanni Fiorentino

Nothing whatsoever is known about Ser Giovanni Fiorentino (fourteenth century) who produced *Il Pecorone*, a collection of fifty novelle, in 1378. There have been many speculations about who the writer was, but his identity has not been determined. His work, however, had a clear impact on other Italian writers of the novelle. The fifty stories, which use material from legends, fairy tales, and fables, are told over twenty-five days in a convent by a nun and chaplain. As in many stories of this time, there is a strong didactic vein, and "Dionigia and the King of England" is a good example of the moral tone that characterizes his tales.

Antoine Galland

Antoine Galland (1646–1714) was born in Picardy, and since his family did not have enough money to support him at school, he received aid from religious patrons that enabled him to study Latin, Greek, and Hebrew in Noyon until the age of fourteen. In 1661, thanks again to generous patrons, he moved to Paris, where he studied at the Collège du Plessus. His major field was classical Greek and Latin, but he also began learning some Oriental languages. In 1670, due to his expertise with classical and Oriental languages, he was called upon to assist the French ambassador in Greece, Syria, and Palestine. After a brief return to Paris in 1674, he worked with the ambassador in Constantinople from 1677 to 1688, during which time he perfected his knowledge of Turkish, modern Greek, Arabic, and Persian. In addition, he collected valuable manuscripts and coins for the ambassador and the French East Indian Company. Back in Paris, he devoted the rest of his life to Oriental studies and published historical and philological works such as *Paroles remarkables, bons mots et maximes des Orientaux* (*Remarkable Words, Sayings and Maxims of the Orientals*, 1694). One of his great achievements was to assist Barthélemy d'Herbelot in compiling the *Bibliothèque orientale*, which was the first major encyclopedia of Islam, with over eight thousand entries about Middle Eastern people, places, and things. When d'Herbelot died in 1695, Galland continued his work and published the completed dictionary in 1697. But by far Galland's major contribution to European and Oriental literature was his translation, or, one could say, "creation," of *The Thousand and One Nights*, which began during the 1690s when he obtained a manuscript of

"The Voyages of Sinbad" and published the Sinbad stories in 1701. Due to the success of this work, he began translating and adapting a four-volume Arabic manuscript in French. By the time the last volume of his *Nights* was published, posthumously in 1717, he had fostered a vogue for Oriental literature and had altered the nature of the literary fairy tale in Europe and North America. Galland's accomplishment in making the Arabic fairy tales known in the West is great because there was never a so-called finished text by an identifiable author or editor. In fact, there were never 1001 nights or stories, and the title was originally *One Thousand Nights*. When and why the tales came to be called *The Thousand and One Nights* is unclear. The change in the title may stem from the fact that an odd number in Arabic culture is associated with luck and fortune, and it also indicates an exceedingly large number. The editions vary with regard to content and style, and though there is a common nucleus, the versions of the same tale are often different. Not only did Galland embellish his translations, which were more adaptations than literal translations, but he also added eight tales for which there were no manuscripts: "The Tale of Sayn-Asnam," "Aladdin, or The Wonderful Lamp," "Adventures of Khudadad and His Brothers," "History of the Caliph's Night Adventure," "Story of Ali Baba and the Forty Thieves," "Story of Ali Khwajah and the Merchant of Baghdad," "Adventures of Prince Ahmad and the Fairy Peribanu," and "The Two Sisters Who Envied their Cadette." Some of these narratives were oral tales that Galland recorded in Paris from a Maronite Christian Arab from Aleppo named Youhenna Diab or Hanna Diab, but it is quite clear from his French texts that Galland introduced many European fairy tale motifs and that he had his own distinct style in re-creating these Arabic tales.

Albert Ludwig Grimm

Albert Ludwig Grimm (1786–1872) was the son of a minister and was born in Helibronn. A contemporary of Jacob and Wilhelm Grimm, he was unrelated to them and felt that they had taken too much credit for publishing fairy tales for young readers, whereas he had actually begun publishing such tales several years before them. He studied theology and philology at the universities of Tübingen and Heidelberg, and after working a couple of years as a private tutor, he accepted a position to teach at the Pädagogium, a famous school, in Weinheim, and he eventually became its director. Given his pedagogical bent, it was not surprising that he did indeed begin working on revising fairy tales for the young before the Grimms and published his first collection of stories, *Kindermährchen* (*Children's Fairy Tales*), in 1809. This volume contained his fairy tale "Die drei Brüder" ("The Three Brothers"), which served as the basis for "Die Bienkönigin" ("The Queen Bee") by the Brothers Grimm, who denied ever being influenced by Albert Grimm. In addition, Grimm's *Children's Fairy Tales* also included a dramatic version of "Snow White," in which the queen does not die such a ghastly death. In fact, Grimm published numerous volumes of literary fairy tales that aimed at young readers' amusement and education and sought to cultivate good and appropriate taste according to social class and religious strictures. While he continued to teach at the Pädagogium, Grimm became active in politics and was twice elected the mayor of Weinheim. At the same time, he maintained an ambitious program of revising literary and oral fairy tales for the young, paying careful attention to their moral messages. Among his more important works are *Lina's Mährchenbuch* (*Lina's Fairy Tale Book*, 1816), *Mährchen der Tausend und Einen Nacht* (*Fairy Tales of the Thousand and One Nights*, 1820–24), *Märchen der alten Griechen* (*Tales of the Ancient Greeks*, 1824), a seven-volume *Mährchen-Bibliothek für Kinder* (*Fairy Tale Library for Children*, 1826), and *Mährchen aus dem Morgenlande* (*Fairy Tales from the Orient*, 1843). After his retirement from the Pädagogium in 1854 due to illness, he moved to Baden and continued to edit such works as *Deutsche Sagen und Mährchen* (*German Legends and Tales*, 1867) and republished the fairy tales of J. K. A. Musäus (1868) and of Wilhelm Hauff (1870) for young people.

Jacob and Wilhelm Grimm

Jacob (1785–1863) and Wilhelm (1786–1859) Grimm were born in the village of Hanau, where their father, Philip Grimm, served the count of Hanau as a lawyer. In 1791 the family moved to Steinau, near Kassel, where their father obtained an excellent position as district judge and soon became a leading figure of the town. However, Philip Grimm died suddenly in 1796 at the age of forty-four, and his death was traumatic for the entire family. Two years later, Jacob and Wilhelm were sent to an aunt in Kassel to study at a famous Lyzeum. Each one graduated at the head of his class, Jacob in 1802 and Wilhelm in 1803, and each went to the University of Marburg to study law. However, under the influence of Friedrich Karl von Savigny, they became interested in the philological aspects of law and ancient German literature. By 1805, they both decided that they would dedicate themselves to the study of old German literature and customs. Jacob went to work with Savigny in Paris for a year, and when he returned to Germany, he eventually obtained a position as private librarian to King Jerome Napoleon in 1808 when the French troops were occupying Kassel. Since the Grimms' mother died in 1807, this job enabled him to pursue his studies and help his brothers and sister. From 1809 to 1813 there was a period of relative stability and security for the Grimm family, and Jacob and Wilhelm collected oral and literary tales and other historical materials. Gradually, they began publishing the results of their research on old German literature; Jacob wrote *Über den altdeutschen Meistergesang* (*On the Old German Meistersang*), and Wilhelm, *Altdänische Heldenlieder* (*Danish Heroic Songs*), both in 1811. Together they published in 1812 a study of *Das Lied von Hildebrand* (*Song of Hildebrand*) and *Das Wessobrunner Gebet* (*Wessobrunner Prayer*). Of course, their major publication at this time was the first volume of the *Kinder- und Hausmärchen* (*Children's and Household Tales*) with scholarly annotations in 1812. When the French withdrew from Kassel in 1813 and the French armies were defeated throughout Central Europe, Jacob was appointed a member of the Hessian peace delegation and did diplomatic work in Paris and Vienna. During his absence, Wilhelm was able to procure the position of secretary to the royal librarian in Kassel and to concentrate on bringing out the second volume of the *Children's and Household Tales* in 1815. After Jacob secured the position of second librarian in the royal library of Kassel, he joined Wilhelm in editing the first volume of *Deutsche Sagen* (*German Legends*) in 1816. During the next thirteen years, the Grimms enjoyed a period of relative calm and prosperity. They could devote themselves to scholarly research and the publication of their findings. Together they published the second volume of *German Legends* (1818) and *Irische Land- und Seemärchen* (*Irish Elf Tales*, 1826), while Jacob wrote the first volume of *Deutsche Grammatik* (*German Grammar*, 1819) and *Deutsche Rechtsaltertümer* (*Ancient German Law*, 1828) by himself, and Wilhelm produced *Die deutsche Heldensage* (*The German Heroic Legend*, 1829). In 1829, however, when the first librarian died and his position in Kassel became vacated, the Grimms' domestic tranquillity was broken. Jacob, who had already become famous for his scholarly publications, had expected to be promoted to this position. But he did not have the right connections or the proper conservative politics and was overlooked. In response to this slight, he and Wilhelm resigned their posts, and one year later they traveled to Göttingen, where Jacob became professor of old German literature and head librarian, and Wilhelm librarian and, eventually, professor in 1835. Both were considered gifted teachers, and they broke new ground in the study of German literature, which had only recently become an accepted field of study at the German university. Aside from their teaching duties, they continued to write and publish important works: Jacob wrote the third volume of *German Grammar* (1831) and a major study entitled *Deutsche Mythologie* (*German Mythology*, 1835), while Wilhelm prepared the third edition of *Children's and Household Tales*. In 1837, when King Ernst August II succeeded to the throne of Hannover, he revoked the constitution of 1833, dissolved parliament, and declared that all civil servants had to pledge an oath to serve him personally. Since the Grimms refused, they were compelled to leave Göttingen, and after spending three years in Kassel, both brothers received offers to become professors at the University of Berlin and to do research at the Academy of Sciences. It was not until March 1841, however, that the Grimms took up residence in Berlin and were able to continue their work on the *Deutsches Wörterbuch* (*German Dictionary*), one of the most ambitious lexicographical undertakings of the nineteenth century, which they had begun in Kassel. When the Revolution of 1848 occurred in Germany, the Grimms were elected to the civil parliament, and Jacob was considered one of the most prominent men among the representatives at the National Assembly held in Frankfurt am Main. After the demise of the revolutionary movement, both brothers retired from active politics. In fact, Jacob resigned from his position as professor in 1848, the same year he published his significant study *Geschichte der deutschen Sprache* (*The History of the German Language*). Wilhelm retired from his post as professor in 1852. For the rest of their lives, the Grimms devoted most of their energy to completing the monumental *German Dictionary*, but they got only as far as the letter F. Though they did not finish the *Dictionary*, a task that had to be left to scholars in the twentieth century, they did produce an astonishing number of remarkable books during their lifetimes. The Grimms made scholarly contributions to the areas of folklore, history, ethnology, religion, jurisprudence, lexicography, and literary criticism. When Wilhelm died in 1859, the loss affected Jacob deeply. He became even more solitary but did not abandon the projects that he had held in common with his brother. Jacob died in 1863 after completing the fourth volume of his book *Deutsche Weistümer* (*German Precedents*).

There were seven major editions of the *Children's and Household Tales*, known in German as *Kinder- und Hausmärchen*. The first edition appeared in two volumes and was not intended for children or a general audience. Thereafter, the tales were always published in one volume:

1st edition 1812, vol. I	86 tales
1815, vol. II	70 tales
2nd edition 1819	170 tales
3rd edition 1837	177 tales
4th edition 1840	187 tales
5th edition 1843	203 tales
6th edition 1850	203 tales
7th edition 1857	210 tales

There was also a small edition that included fifty of the more popular tales, which went through ten editions from 1825 to 1858. Beginning with the second edition of the complete tales in 1819, Wilhelm Grimm was chiefly responsible for revising and expanding the collection of tales, and most of the additions after 1819 came from literary rather than oral sources. During the initial stages of their collecting, the Grimms relied mainly on people within the region of Kassel and on the so-called Bökendorfer Circle in Westphalia. Wilhelm Grimm visited the estate of Freiherr Adolf von Haxthausen in Bökendorf and became friendly with a group of young people there who provided him with numerous tales. Contrary to popular belief, the Grimms obtained most of their oral and literary tales from educated members of the middle and aristocratic classes. Indeed, the majority of their informants were women, and the Grimms did not travel widely to collect their tales. Instead, to their credit, they established a vast international network of scholars, friends, and acquaintances who did research for them and provided them with materials that were relevant to all fields of their work.

Charlotte-Rose de La Force

Charlotte-Rose de Caumont de La Force (ca. 1654–1724) was born into one of the oldest and most esteemed families of France in Bazadois. Due to the family lineage, she was accepted at King Louis XIV's court under the tutelage of Madame de Maintenon and was named the maiden of honor to the queen and the dauphine. During her adolescence, she developed into one of the most scheming young ladies at the court and became involved in various intrigues and had numerous love affairs despite the fact that she was notoriously ugly. She had a penchant for younger men, and at one point she fell in love with Charles Briou, the son of the president of parliament, who was indeed much younger than she was and very naive. Since his family did not sanction this relationship, they carried on a clandestine love affair. Eventually, through her connections, she managed to obtain the king's permission to marry Briou in 1687. However, his father and her family interfered and had the marriage annulled. Some years later, in 1697, there was another great scandal, caused this time by some impious verses she wrote, and this act led to Mlle de La Force's expulsion from the court: Louis XIV gave her the option of having her pension taken away, which would have left her penniless, or allowing her to keep it and live in a convent. She chose the convent.

Before her exile, Mlle de La Force had begun publishing historical romances, *Histoire secrète du duc de Bourgogne* (1694), *Histoire sècrete de Marie de Bourgogne* (1696), and *Histoire de Marguerite de Valois* (1696), which were extremely well-received because they depicted abductions, scandals, love affairs, disguises, and duels in a fascinating manner that had little to do with history and a great deal to do with the court society of that time. Mlle de la Force had a great flare for writing exciting romances and continued publishing works in this vein, such as *Gustave Vasa* (1698) and *Histoire secrète de Catherine Bourbon* (1703), after her banishment from the court.

With regard to her fairy tales, Mlle de La Force was considered an entertaining storyteller, and she had often attended salons and soirées in Paris, where she had recited her tales. Among her acquaintances were such well-known fairy tale writers as Antoine Hamilton, Mme d'Aulnoy, and Mme de Murat. She circulated her tales in manuscript form and revised them before she eventually published them anonymously under the title *Les contes des contes* (*The Tales of Tales*, 1697). They contained "Plus belle que fée" ("More Beautiful Than Fairy"), "Persinette," "L'enchanteur" ("The Sorcerer"), "Tourbillon," "Vert et bleu" ("Green and Blue"), "Le pays des délices" ("The Country of Delights"), "La puissance d'amour" ("The Power of Love"), and "La bonne femme" ("The Good Woman"). There is a great similarity between these tales and her romances. Mlle de la Force wrote long if not somewhat verbose fairy tales for an aristocratic audience that were filled with motifs taken largely from the courtly romance tradition. Her favorite plots involved crossed lovers, infidelity, and the power of love.

Eustache Le Noble

Eustache Le Noble, Baron de Saint-Georges et de Tenelière (1643–1711), was born in Troyes and had all the privileges of a wealthy aristocratic family. He began his career as an attorney general in the parliament of Metz. However, he led a dissolute life, and after accumulating many debts, he was accused of fraud and imprisoned. Yet he soon managed to escape and spent many years evading the authorities. Once he was recaptured, he began writing in prison and continued to write after his release. To pay off his debts, he produced an enormous quantity of books that catered to the tastes of the newly founded libraries in France. Many of his works were also politically motivated, as he sought the good graces of Louis XIV. Therefore, he published a series of books, *Relation de l'État de Gennes* (*The Relation of the State of Gennes*, 1685), *Le Cibisme* (1688), *Les travaux d'Hercule* (*The Labors of Hercules*, 1692–94), among others, that glorified France's history and celebrated the power of Louis XIV. In addition, Le Noble translated the Psalms of David and Horace's satires. He wrote fables and tales in imitation of La Fontaine and many prose works that captured life in the French provinces. Perhaps his most important work was the long didactic treatise *Uranie; ou, Les tableaux des philosophes* (*Uranie; or, The Tablets of Philosophers*, 1694–97), in which he explained classical and modern philosophy and developed his own philosophical principles based on astrology.

 Le Noble's fairy tale output was small. He included two tales, "L'oiseau de vérité" ("The Bird of Truth") and "L'apprenti magicien" ("The Apprentice Magician") in his collection of stories, *Le gage touché* (*The Wager Paid*, 1700). The frame of the tales is typical of its time: they are told by young girls who had heard the tales from their governesses. The emphasis on the oral tradition is significant because it harkens back to Straparola and Basile and looks forward to Mme Leprince de Beaumont, whose tales were told by a governess. "The Apprentice Magician" recalls many oral and literary tales in which a young magician or thief appropriates the power of his master and eventually kills him in a duel. "The Bird of Truth" was probably influenced by Mme d'Aulnoy's "The Princess Belle-Etoile and the Prince Cheri," and he may even have known Straparola's "Ancilotto, King of Provino," but Le Noble's style is immensely different from that of either Straparola or d'Aulnoy. He tends to be succinct and dry, and nothing is left to the imagination.

Marie-Jeanne Lhéritier

Marie-Jeanne de Villandon Lhéritier (1664–1734) was a niece of Charles Perrault and the daughter of Nicolas Lhéritier, seigneur de Nouvelon et de Villandon, a noted historian and writer. Her mother was reported to be quite erudite; her brother led a distinguished career as mathematician and man of letters; her sister, Mlle de Nouvelon, was a poet. Given such a literary and scholarly family, it was not by chance that Mlle Lhéritier decided to dedicate herself to writing. Unlike many other women writers of her time, however, she did not become involved in any scandals, nor was she banished to a convent. She never married, nor did she have any lovers. She was known for being studious, clever, and honorable and on close terms with the most influential women of her times. She was invited to attend gatherings at the more illustrious of the salons in Paris and eventually maintained her own literary salon, in which she often recited her tales, poetry, and other works before she would publish them.

Mlle Lhéritier's first major work was *Oeuvres méslées* (1695–98), which contained "L'innocente tromperie" ("The Innocent Fraud"), "L'avare puni" ("The Punished Miser"), "Les enchantements de l'eloquence; ou, Les effets de la douceur" ("The Enchantments of Eloquence; or, The Effects of Sweetness"), and "L'adroite princesse; ou, Les aventures de Finette" ("The Discreet Princess; or, The Adventures of Finette"), which was dedicated to Henriette Julie de Murat. It was followed immediately by *Bigarrures ingénieuses* (1696), which reprinted "The Enchantments of Eloquence" and "The Discreet Princess" and included a new fairy tale entitled "Ricdin-Ricdon." These early collections were influenced by Perrault, Mme d'Aulnoy, and Mme de Murat, who were all close friends of hers, and contained her major contributions to the fairy tale mode. In addition, though it has never been documented, it is apparent that Lhéritier was familiar with the tales of Basile.

As her reputation grew, she won various literary prizes and was elected a member of the Académie des Ricovrati de Padova in 1697. Mlle Lhéritier was supported in her work by her patron, the duchess of Nemours, Marie d'Orleans de Longueville, whose memoirs she edited in 1709. After her death, she received a modest pension from Chauvelin that enabled her to live in a comfortable way until her death. In addition, she inherited the salon of Mlle de Scudéry, for whom she wrote the eulogy "L'apothéose de Mlle Scudéry" (1702).

All Mlle Lhéritier's works tended to be moralistic and conformed to the general literary taste of the day. For example, two of her works, *La pompe dauphine* (1711) and *Le tombeau du dauphin* (1711), were dedicated to the king and the royal family and are filled with short, didactic pieces, which celebrated virtuous courtly manners. Mlle Lhéritier also liked to display her extensive knowledge in works such as *L'erudition enjouée* (1703) and *Les caprices du destin* (1718), which included short literary essays, histories, poems, and tales.

Even though Mlle Lhéritier published very few fairy tales after her three major works in 1795, she is historically important because her first three prose tales signaled the beginning of the mode of fairy tale writing that was to become so popular in France for the next hundred years and continued the experiments with the genre that the Italians had begun in the sixteenth and early part of the seventeenth century. "The Discreet Princess" is undoubtedly her most significant tale and reveals Mlle Lhéritier's attitudes toward the standards of proper comportment for young ladies as is also the case with "Ricdin-Ricdon" and "The Enchantments of Eloquence." The magical elements and the imagination are not celebrated so much in her tales as are reason and sobriety. In particular, "The Discreet Princess" was written in such a dry, succinct manner that it was considered to be one of Perrault's tales for over 150 years. However, Perrault would never have allowed a young woman to triumph over a man, no matter how villainous he was. To Mlle Lhéritier's credit, she demonstrated the qualities women needed to survive in courtly society, and her skillful transformation of folk motifs and themes rendered "The Discreet Princess" one of the more amusing narratives of that period. Her other tales are more serious and didactic and tend to be more programmatic statements about virtue and tender love. Consistent with her beliefs and drawing on her critical attitude toward Louis XIV's court, Mlle Lhéritier depicted clever and resilient women who are always rewarded for their virtuousness and purity despite the moral corruption of courtiers.

Jeanne-Marie Leprince de Beaumont

Jeanne-Marie Leprince de Beaumont (1711–1780) was born in Rouen and was given an excellent education. She married M. de Beaumont, a dissolute libertine, in 1745, and the marriage was annulled after two years. In 1745 she departed for England, where she earned her living as a governess, and she often returned to France for visits. She also married a certain M. Pichon and raised several children in England. At the same time, she began publishing novels and stories with a strong didactic bent. Her first work was a novel entitled *Le triomphe de la vérité* (*The Triumph of Truth*, 1748), which was published in France. However, it was in London that she made a name for herself by publishing short stories in magazines and producing collections of anecdotes, stories, fairy tales, commentaries, and essays directed at specific social and age groups. For instance, she published a series of pedagogical works with the following titles: *Le magasin des enfants* (1757), *Le magasin des adolescents* (1760), *Le magasin des pauvres* (1768), *Le mentor moderne* (1770), *Manuel de la jeunesse* (1773), and *Magasin des dévotes* (1779).

In 1762, she returned to France, where she continued her voluminous production and retired to a country estate in Haute-Savoie in 1768. Among her major works of this period were *Mémoires de La Baronne de Batteville* (1776), *Contes moraux* (1774), and *Oeuvres mêlées* (1775). By the time of her death, she had written over seventy different books.

Mme Leprince de Beaumont's major fairy tales were all published in *Le Magasin des enfants*, and they include "La Belle et la Bête" ("Beauty and the Beast"), "Le Prince Chéri," "Le Prince Désir," "Fatal et Fortuné," "Le Prince Charmante," "La veueve et les deux filles" ("The Widow and the Two Daughters"), "Aurore et Aimée," "Le Pêcheur et le voyageur" ("The Fisherman and the Voyager"), "Joliette," and "Bellotte et Laidronette." Her version of "Beauty and the Beast," which was based on Mme de Villeneuve's longer narrative, is perhaps the most famous in the world. Her emphasis was on the proper upbringing of young girls like Beauty, and in all her tales she continually stressed industriousness, self-sacrifice, modesty, and diligence as the qualities young ladies must possess to attain happiness. She was one of the first French writers to write fairy tales explicitly for children, and thus one can see from the two tales presented in this volume that she keeps her language and plot simple to convey her major moral messages. Though her style is limited by the lesson she wants to teach, the magic in her tales triumphs despite her preaching.

Jean de Mailly

Jean de Mailly (?–1724) was a godson of Louis XIV and the illegitimate son of one of the members of the de Mailly family. He spent his youth in the army, and at one time he caused a scandal by endeavoring to force his family in a trial to admit that he was illegitimate and that all the most honorable men were bastards and died in obscurity. Not much else is known about the chevalier's life except that he was a prolific writer and published over twenty books from the early 1690s until his death. These works dealt with such diverse subjects as history, nature, hunting, literature, and culture, and among the more important are *Rome galante* (1685), *Les disgrâces des amants* (*The Disgrace of the Lovers*, 1695), *Avantures et lettres galantes, avec la Promenade des Tuilleries* (*Adventures and Gallant Letters, with the Promenade of the Tuilleries*, 1697), *Les entretiens des cafés de Paris* (*Conversations of the Cafes of Paris*, 1702), *Diverses avantures de France et d'Espagne* (*Diverse Adventures of France and Spain*, 1707), *L'eloge de la chasse* (*In Praise of the Hunt*, 1723), and *Principales merveilles de la nature* (*Marvelous Principles of Nature*, 1723).

Since there were few literary genres that the Chevalier de Mailly did not attempt to cultivate and few topics that he did not treat, it is not surprising that he also tried his hand at writing and translating fairy tales. His major works were *Les illustres fées* (*The Illustrious Fairies*, 1698), *Recueil de contes galans* (*A Collection of Gallant Tales*, 1699), and the translation of Persian tales, *Le voyage et les avantures des trois princes de Sarendip* (*The Voyage and the Adventures of the Three Princes of Sarendip*, 1719). Mailly's fairy tales were often based on oral folktales and were filled with action and very little description. He was obviously fascinated by the marvels of nature and how things were transformed in mysterious ways. In particular, animals played an important role in his fairy tales and were often depicted as helpers. Mailly was not a great stylist, nor did he develop extraordinary plots as did most of the women writers of fairy tales. His best tale was clearly "The Queen of the Island of Flowers" ("La reine de l'isle des fleurs"), which appeared in *Les illustres fées*, in which he included three tales ("Fortunio," "Prince Guerini," and "Blanche Belle") adapted freely from Straparola's *Le piacevoli notti*. Since not much is known about Mailly's life, it is difficult to determine how well he knew Italian and how familiar he was with Italian fairy tales. What is fascinating about his adaptations is the manner in which he focuses on "illegitimate" protagonists, who always prove that they are from "royal" lineage. Also important in Mailly's tales are the autobiographical elements, which reveal a strong sense of his desire to belong to court society.

Girolamo Morlini

Not much is known about Girolamo Morlini (fifteenth/sixteenth centuries) except that he was a copyist and a lawyer who lived in Naples. He was influenced very much by Apuleius and the oral tradition, and he published

Novellae, fabulae, comoedia, a collection of eighty-one prose novelle with an appendix of twenty favole and a comedy, in 1520. These tales, written in Latin, are not novellas in the modern sense. They consist of anecdotes, fables, legends, and fairy tales that are satiric commentaries on the customs and attitudes of his day. Though there is a certain amount of didacticism in his tales, Morlini tended to stress the comical side of life and evidently had an influence on Straparola.

Henriette Julie de Murat

Henriette Julie de Castelnau, Countess de Murat (1670–1716), was born in Brest, Brittany, and was strongly influenced by the traditions and folklore of that region. Both her parents came from old noble families in Brittany, and at the time she was born, her father was governor of Brest. When Henriette Julie turned sixteen, she was sent to Louis XIV's court in Paris to marry Count de Murat. Soon after her arrival and marriage, she caused a sensation and impressed Queen Marie-Thérèse by wearing the traditional peasant costumes of Brittany.

Mme de Murat was known for her great beauty, wit, and independence. However, since she was courted by numerous famous people, she let this flattery go to her head. In addition, her nonconformism and flare for attention made important members of the court extremely jealous. Given the enemies she made and her zest for adventure, she was often in trouble with Louis XIV. Finally, in 1694, when she published a pamphlet entitled *Histoire de la courtisane Rhodope,* which was a political satire about Scarron, Louis XIV, and Madam de Maintenon, she was banished. It appears that her husband, who had played a minor role in her life, had died before this banishment. At any rate, Mme de Murat was sent alone to Loches, a small city in the provinces of France, where she remained until 1715.

It was in Loches from 1694 to 1715 that Mme de Murat wrote and published her most significant works: *Histoire galante des habitants de Loches (The Gallant History of the Inhabitants of Loches,* 1696), *Les mémoires de la Comtesse de Murat; ou, La defense des dames (The Memoirs of the Comtesse de Murat; or, The Defense of Women,* 1697), *Contes de fées* (1698), *Les nouveaux contes de féés* (1698), and *Histoires sublimes et allégoriques (Sublime and Allegorical Stories,* 1699). As in Paris, Mme de Murat, who missed the cultural life of the court, caused somewhat of a commotion in Loches. Given her vivacious temperament, she organized all kinds of gatherings at her house that were reported to be scandalous. In fact, however, Mme de Murat simply endeavored to re-create an atmosphere similar to Paris in Loches, and she loved to converse, dance, and stay up late telling fairy tales with some of her best friends like Charlotte-Rose de Caumont de La Force, who also published tales during this period. In addition to these soirées and numerous mysterious journeys, Mme de Murat astonished the people of this city by wearing a red cloak to church every Sunday.

Though Mme de Murat constantly sought to obtain a pardon from Louis XIV, she was never successful. She returned to Paris briefly in 1715, after Louis XIV's death. But even then, the duration of her residence there was very short because she was already suffering from chronic nephritis and kidney stones that caused her extreme pain. Therefore, she retired to her chateau, La Buzadière, where she died in 1716.

Madame de Murat composed her fairy tales during her exile in Loches to relieve herself of the boredom she experienced there. A born storyteller, she recalled the tales and legends that she had heard during her childhood in Brittany, and she amused herself by retelling them in her own versions to her friends. Then she would either record these oral versions in a journal or prepare them for publication. Most of her tales concern the issue of *tendresse*, marriage, and power struggles among the aristocracy. Mme de Murat's basic philosophy—live for the moment, and live according to your feelings—is the dominant theme in her tales. But she does not preach or predict a happy end when one subscribes to such a philosophy. In fact, nothing is predictable in her tales because even the power of fairies was never sufficient in her mind to guarantee a happy end.

Charles Perrault

Charles Perrault (1628–1703) was born in Paris into one of the more distinguished bourgeois families of that time. His father, Pierre Perrault, was a lawyer and member of parliament, and his four brothers—he was the youngest—all went on to fame in such fields as architecture and law. In 1637 Perrault began studying at the Collège de Beauvais (near the Sorbonne), and at the age of fifteen he stopped attending school and largely taught himself all he needed to know so he could later take his law examinations.

It was about this time that Perrault took an interest in the popular movement against Louis XIV, and his early poetry expressed a sympathy for bourgeois opposition to the crown. However, Perrault became somewhat fearful and gradually switched his position to support the king. In 1651 he passed the law examinations at the University of Orléans, and after working three years as a lawyer, he left the profession to become a secretary to his brother Pierre, who was the tax receiver of Paris.

After publishing some minor poems, Perrault began taking more and more of an interest in literature. In 1659 he produced two important poems, "Portrait d'Iris" and "Portrait de la voix d'Iris," and his public career as a poet was in full swing by 1660, when he published several poems in honor of Louis XIV. In 1663 Perrault was appointed secretary to Jean Baptiste Colbert, controller general of finances, perhaps the most influential minister in Louis XIV's government. For the next twenty years, until Colbert's death, Perrault was able to accomplish a great deal in the arts and sciences due to Colbert's power and influence.

In 1671 he was elected to the French Academy and was also placed in charge of the royal buildings. He continued writing poetry and took an active interest in cultural affairs of the court. In 1672 he married Marie Guichon, with whom he had three sons. She died in childbirth in 1678, and he never remarried, supervising the education of his children by himself.

When Colbert died in 1683, Perrault was dismissed from government service, but he had a pension and was able to support his family until his death. Released from governmental duties, Perrault could concentrate more on literary affairs, and in 1687, he helped inaugurate the "Quarrel of the Ancients and the Moderns" ("Querelle des Anciens et des Modernes") by reading a poem entitled "Le siècle de Louis le Grand." Perrault took the side of modernism and believed that France and Christianity—here he sided with the Jansenists—could only progress if they incorporated pagan beliefs and folklore and developed a culture of enlightenment. On the other hand, Nicolas Boileau, the literary critic, and Jean Racine, the dramatist, took the opposite viewpoint and argued that France had to imitate the great empires of Greece and Rome and maintain stringent classical rules in respect to the arts. This literary quarrel, which had great cultural implications, lasted until 1697, at which time Louis XIV decided to end it in favor of Boileau and Racine. However, this decision did not stop Perrault from trying to incorporate his ideas into his poetry and prose.

Perrault had always frequented the literary salons of his niece Mlle Lhéritier, Mme d'Aulnoy, and other women, and he had been annoyed by Boileau's satires against women. Thus, he wrote three verse tales, "Griseldis" (1691), "Les souhaits ridicules" ("The Foolish Wishes," 1693), and "Peau d'ane" ("Donkey-Skin," 1694), along with a long poem, "Apologie des femmes" (1694), in defense of women. Whether these works can be considered pro-woman today is a question. However, Perrault was definitely more enlightened in regard to this question than either Boileau or Racine, and his poems make use of a highly mannered style and folk motifs to stress the necessity of assuming an enlightened moral attitude toward women and exercising just authority.

In 1696, Perrault embarked on the more ambitious project of transforming several popular folktales with all their superstitious beliefs and magic into moralistic tales that would appeal largely to adults and demonstrate a modern approach to literature. He had a prose version of "Sleeping Beauty" ("La belle au bois dormant") printed in the journal *Mercure galant* in 1696, and in 1697 he published an entire collection of tales entitled *Histoires ou contes du temps passé*, which consisted of a new version of "Sleeping Beauty," "Le petit chaperon rouge" ("Little Red Riding Hood"), "Barbe bleue" ("Bluebeard"), "Cendrillon" ("Cinderella"), "Le petit poucet" ("Tom Thumb"), "Riquet à la houppe" ("Riquet with the Tuft"), "Le chat botté" ("Puss in Boots"), and "Les fées" ("The Fairies").

Although *Histoires ou contes du temps passé* was published under the name of Pierre Perrault Darmancour, Perrault's son, and although some critics have asserted that the book was indeed written or at least co-authored by his son, recent evidence has shown clearly that this could not have been the case, especially since his son had not published anything up to that point. Perrault was simply using his son's name to mask his own identity so that he would not be blamed for re-igniting the "Quarrel of the Ancients and the Moderns."

Numerous critics have regarded Perrault's tales as written directly for children, but they overlook the fact that there was no children's literature *per se* at that time and that most writers of fairy tales were composing and reciting their tales for their peers in the literary salons. Certainly, if Perrault intended them to make a final point in the "Quarrel of the Ancients and the Moderns," then he obviously had in mind an adult audience that would understand his humor and the subtle manner in which he transformed folklore superstition to convey his position about the "modern" development of French civility.

There is no doubt but that, among the writers of fairy tales during the 1690s, Perrault was the greatest stylist, which accounts for the fact that his tales have withstood the test of time. Furthermore, Perrault claimed that literature must become modern, and his transformations of folk motifs and literary themes into refined and provocative fairy tales still speak to the modern age, ironically in a way that may compel us to ponder whether the age of reason has led to the progress and happiness promised so charmingly in Perrault's tales.

Friedrich Schulz

(Joachim Christoph) Friedrich Schulz (1762–1798) was a German novelist who rose from rags to riches through his travel writings. Schulz was born in Magdeburg, and after an unhappy childhood, he managed to begin studying theology at the University of Halle in 1779. However, due to lack of funds, he was obliged to discontinue his studies after a year, and he briefly joined a traveling theater troupe which he abandoned to devote himself to writing. His first sentimental novel, *Karl Treumann und Wilhelmine Rosenfeld*, appeared in 1781, and it was quickly followed by another bestseller for those times, *Ferdinand von Löwenbain*. Aside from these novels, he wrote for almanacs and journals, and with his earnings he began traveling to other cities such as Berlin, Vienna, and Weimar, where he continued to succeed as a novelist and freelance writer. In 1789 he traveled to Paris and described the French Revolution in his popular *Geschichte der großen Revolution in Frankreich* (*History of the Great Revolution in France*, 1789) and in *Paris und die Pariser* (*Paris and the Parisians*, 1791). By 1791 he had been appointed professor of history at a gymnasium in the small city of Mitau, in eastern Germany. He became involved in politics and often wrote against the privileged aristocracy while continuing his career as historian and travel writer. Schulz had a strong interest in folklore, and he published numerous stories and novellas that were connected to legends, fairy tales, and customs in *Kleine Romane*, 5 volumes, 1788–90. Since he was very knowledgeable about French literature, it is clear that his version of "Rapunzel," which was published in *Kleine Romane*, owed a great debt to Mlle de La Force's "Persinette."

Caroline Stahl

Caroline Stahl, neé Dumpf (1776–1837), grew up in a German upper-class family on an estate near Dorpat in Livonia. As a young girl, she developed an early interest in literature and education and moved to Germany after she married. From 1808 to 1829, she lived in Weimar, Nuremberg, and Vienna and began writing moral and didactic tales for children that were published in the magazines *Deutsches Unterhaltungsblatt* and *Das Morgenblatt*. Her first book, *Fabeln, Märchen und Erzählungen (Fables, Fairy Tales, and Stories*, 1818), contained "Der undankbare Zwerg" ("The Ungrateful Dwarf"), which served as the model for the Grimms' "Rose Red and Snow White." Stahl went on to write another eleven books, among them *Allwinens Abendstunden: Ein Lesebuch für die Jugend (Alvin's Evening Hours: A Primer for the Young,* 1819), *Märchen für Kinder (Fairy Tales for Children,* 1823), and *Rosalinde; oder, Die Wege des Schicksals, den Töchtern gebildeter Stände gewidmet (Rosalind; or, The Ways of Fate, Dedicated to the Daughters of the Educated Classes,* 1834). Her works were similar to those of Mme Leprince de Beaumont in their didactic intention: she preached good conduct and celebrated virtues, particularly those that reflected the interests of the upper classes, in rewriting traditional oral and literary fairy tales. In 1820 she returned to Dorpat to work as an educator, and with the exception of a brief return to Nuremberg from 1828 to 1832, she spent the rest of her life in Livonia, dedicated to writing moral books for the young.

Giovan Francesco Straparola

Giovan Francesco Straparola (ca. 1480–1558), Italian writer and poet, is generally considered the "father" or progenitor of the literary fairy tale in Europe. He was born in Caravaggio, Italy, and left few documents, so little is known about his life. Even the name "Straparola" itself may be a pen name, for it indicates someone who is loquacious. Whoever this author was, Straparola was the first truly gifted author to write numerous fairy tales in the vernacular and cultivate for this kind of narrative a form and function that made it an acceptable genre among the educated classes in Italy and soon after in France, Germany, and England. Aside from a small volume of poems published in Venice in 1508, his major work is *Le piacevoli notti* (1550–53), translated as *The Facetious Nights* or *The Delectable Nights*. The collection has a framework similar to Boccaccio's *Decameron*. In this case, the tales are told over thirteen consecutive nights by a group of ladies and gentlemen gathered at the Venetian palace of Ottaviano Maria Sforza, former bishop of Lodi, who has fled Milan with his widowed daughter, Lucretia, to avoid persecution and capture by his political enemies. The framework and tales influenced other Italian and European writers, among them Giambattista Basile, Charles Perrault, and the Brothers Grimm. Of the seventy-five stories, there are fourteen fairy tales that can be traced to the Grimms' *Children's and Household Tales* and many other collections: "Cassandrino the Thief," "The Priest Scarpacifico," "Tebaldo," "Galeotto," "Pietro the Fool," "The Snake and the Maiden," "Fortunio, and the Siren" "Constanza/Constanzo," "Ancilotto, King of Provino," "Guerrino and the Wild Man," "The Three Brothers," "Maestro Lattantio," "Cesarino, the Dragon Slayer," and "Constantino Fortunato."

CRITICISM

JACK ZIPES

Cross-Cultural Connections and the Contamination of the Classical Fairy Tale†

For a long time it has commonly been assumed that our classical fairy tales were representative of particular cultures. Charles Perrault's tales are considered very French, the Grimms' collection is clearly German, and Hans Christian Andersen's stories are certainly Danish. While there is some truth to these assumptions, they conceal the cross-cultural and multi-layered origins and meanings of these pan-European tales that also have fascinating connections to the Orient, which includes the Middle and Far East. The present collection of literary fairy tales intends to shed more light on the fabulous sources and secrets of European literary fairy tales by presenting a panorama of the most significant narratives written before the Grimms' collection, those narratives that contributed to the making of the classical literary tradition of the fairy tale in Europe and North America.

Of course there can be no denying that the tales in this collection are culturally marked: they are informed by the writers, their respective cultures, and the socio-historical context in which the narratives were created. In this regard one can discuss the particular Italian, French, German, or English affiliation of a tale. Nevertheless, the tales have a great general paradoxical appeal that transcends their particularity: they contain "universal" motifs and components that the writers borrowed consciously and unconsciously from other cultures in an endeavor to imbue their symbolical stories with very specific commentaries on the mores and manners of their times. Fairy tales have always been truthful metaphorical reflections of the customs of their times—that is, of the private and public interrelations of people from different social classes seeking power to determine their lives. The truth value of a fairy tale is dependent on the degree to which a writer is capable of using a symbolical narrative strategy and stereotypical characterization to depict, expose, or celebrate the modes of behavior that were used and justified to attain power in the civilizing process of a given society. Whether oral or literary, the tales have sought to uncover truths about the delights of existence and the intricacies of our civilizing processes.

For the past three hundred years or more, scholars and critics have sought to define and classify the oral folktale and the literary fairy tale, as though they could be clearly distinguished from one another, and as though we could trace their origins to some primeval source. This is an impossible task because there are very few if any records, with the exception of paintings, drawings, etchings, inscriptions and other cultural arti-

† First published in this Norton Critical Edition.

facts, that reveal how tales were told and received thousands of years ago. In fact, even when written records came into existence, we have very little information about storytelling among the majority of people, except for bits and pieces that highly educated writers gathered and presented in their works. It is really not until the late eighteenth century and the early nineteenth century that scholars began studying and paying close attention to folktales and fairy tales, and it was also at this time that the Brothers Grimm, and many others to follow, sought to establish national cultural identities by uncovering the "pure" tales of their so-called people, the folk, and their imagined nations.

From a contemporary perspective, the efforts of the Brothers Grimm—and the numerous efforts that they helped to inspire by Peter Christen Asbjornsen and Jorgen Moe (*Norwegian Folktales*, 1841), George Stephens (*Swedish Folktales and Folk Stories*, 1844–49), Ludwig Bechstein (*German Fairy Tale Book*, 1845), Friedrich Wolf (*German Popular Tales and Legends*, 1845), Ignaz Vinzenz and Joseph Zingerle (*Children's and Household Tales from Tyrol*, 1852), Aleksandr Afanasyev (*Russian Fairy Tales*, 1855–63), Otto Sutermeister (*German and Household Tales*, Switzerland, 1869), Vittorio Imbriani (*Florentine Tales*, 1871), Giuseppe Pitré (*Popular Sicilian Tales, Novellas, and Stories*, 1875), Jerome Curtin (*Myths and Folk-Lore of Ireland*, 1890), and Joseph Jacobs (*English Fairy Tales*, 1890), to name but a few—have led to a misconception about the nature of folktales and fairy tales: there is no such thing as pure national folktale or literary fairy tale, and neither genre, the oral folktale or the literary fairy tale—if one can call them genres—is a "purebreed"; in fact, they are both very much mixed breeds, and it is the very way that they "contaminated" one another historically through cross-cultural exchange that has produced fruitful and multiple versions of similar social and personal experiences.

Naturally, the oral folktales that were told in many different ways thousands of years ago preceded the literary narratives, but we are not certain who told the tales, why, and how. We do know, however, that scribes began writing down different kinds of tales that reflected an occupation with rituals, historical anecdotes, customs, startling events, miraculous transformations, and religious beliefs. The recording of these various tales was extremely important because the writers preserved an oral tradition for future generations, and in the act of recording, they changed the tales to a greater or lesser degree, depending on what their purpose was in recording them. Albert Wesselski has clearly demonstrated in his *Versuch einer Theorie des Märchens* (*An Attempt to Conceive a Theory of the Fairy Tale*, 1931) that the literary fairy tale has deep roots in the oral tradition and that it was shaped in the Christian era through the repeated transmission of tales that were written down and retold and mutually influenced one another. There is no evidence that a separate oral wonder tale tradition or literary fairy tale tradition existed in Europe before the medieval period. But we do have evidence that people told all kinds of tales about gods, animals, catastrophes, wars, heroic deeds, rituals, customs, and simple daily incidents. What we call folktale or fairy tale motifs are indeed ancient and appear in many pre-Christian epics, poems, myths, fables, histories, and religious narratives.[1] However, the formation of the narrative structure that is common to the oral wonder tale and the literary fairy tale does not begin to take shape in Europe until some time during the early medieval period. How this occurred, where it occurred, and exactly when it occurred—these are questions that are practically impossible to answer because the tales developed as a process largely through talk, conversations, and performances that caught the imagination of many different people and were gradually written down first in Latin and then in different vernacular languages, when they became more acceptable in the late Middle Ages.[2] Clearly, the literary fairy tale developed as an appropriation of a particular oral storytelling tradition that gave birth to the wonder folktale, often called the *Zaubermärchen* (magic tale) or the *conte merveilleux* (marvelous tale). As more and more wonder tales were written down from the twelfth to the fifteenth centuries, they constituted the genre of the literary fairy tale, and writers began establishing the genre's own conventions, motifs, topoi, characters, and plots, based to a large extent on those developed in the oral tradition but altered to address a reading public formed largely by the aristocracy and the middle classes. Though the peasants were excluded in the formation of this literary tradition, their material, tone, style, and beliefs were also incorporated into the new genre, and their experiences were recorded, albeit from the perspective of the literate scribe or writer. The wonder tales were always considered somewhat suspect by the ruling and educated classes. The threatening aspect of wondrous change, turning the world upside-down, was something that ruling classes always tried to channel through codified celebrations like Carnival and religious holidays. Writers staked out political and property claims to wonder tales as they recorded and created them, and official cultural authorities sought to judge and control the new genre as it sought to legitimate itself.

It is extremely difficult to describe what the oral wonder tale was because our evidence is based on written documents. In Vladimir Propp's now famous study, *The Morphology of the Folk Tale* (Russian, 1928; English, 1968), he outlined thirty-one basic functions that constitute the formation of a paradigm, which was and still is common in Europe and North America. Though I have some reservations about Propp's categories because he does not discuss the social function of the wonder tale or its diverse aspects, his structuralist approach can be helpful in understanding plot formation and the reasons why certain tales have become so memorable. By functions, Propp meant the fundamental and constant components of a tale that are the acts of a character and necessary for driving the action forward. The plot generally involves a protagonist who is confronted with an interdiction or prohibition which he or she violates in some way. Therefore, there is generally a departure or banishment, and the protagonist either is

1. For two excellent studies regarding this point, see Alan Dundes, *Holy Writ: The Bible as Folklore* (Lanham, MD: Rowman & Littlefield, 1999), and Graham Anderson, *Fairy Tale in the Ancient World* (London: Routledge, 2000).
2. Some of the best work on the dissemination of folktales of many different types has been done by Rudolf Schenda, who has written numerous books on this topic. For instance, see his excellent study *Von Mund zu Ohr: Bausteine zu einer Kulturgeschichte volkstümlichen Erzählens in Europa* (Göttingen: Vandenhoeck and Ruprecht, 1993).

given a task or assumes a task related to the interdiction of prohibition. The protagonist is *as-signed* a task, and the task is a *sign*. That is, his or her character will be stereotyped and marked by the task that is his or her sign. Names are rarely used in a folktale. Characters function according to their social class or profession, and they often cross boundaries or transform themselves. Inevitably, there will be a significant or signifying encounter. Depending on the situation, the protagonist will meet either enemies or friends. The antagonist often takes the form of a witch, monster, or evil fairy; the friend is a mysterious individual or creature who gives the protagonist gifts. Sometimes there are three different animals or creatures who are helped by the protagonist and promise to repay him or her. Whatever the occasion, the protagonist somehow acquires gifts that are often magical agents, which bring about a miraculous or marvelous change or transformation. Soon after, the protagonist, endowed with gifts, is tested and overcomes inimical forces. However, this is not the end because there is generally a peripeteia or sudden fall in the protagonist's fortunes that is only a temporary setback. A miracle or marvelous intervention is needed to reverse the wheel of fortune. Frequently, the protagonist makes use of endowed gifts (and this includes magical agents and cunning) to achieve his or her goal. The success of the protagonist usually leads to marriage; the acquisition of money; survival and wisdom; or any combination of the first three. Whatever the case may be, the protagonist is transformed in the end. The functions form a transformation.

The significance of the paradigmatic functions of the wonder tale is that they facilitate recall for teller and listeners. Over hundreds of years they have enabled people to store, remember, and reproduce the plot of the tale and to change it to fit their experiences and desires due to the easily identifiable characters who are associated with particular social classes, professions, and assignments. The characters, settings, and motifs are combined and varied according to specific functions to induce *wonder* and *hope* for change in the audience of listeners/readers, who are to marvel or admire the magical changes that occur in the course of events. It is this earthy, sensual, and secular sense of wonder and hope that distinguished the wonder tales from other oral tales such as the legend, the fable, the anecdote, and the myth; it is clearly the sense of wonder that distinguishes the *literary* fairy tale from the moral story, novella, sentimental tale, and other modern short literary genres. Wonder causes astonishment, and as marvelous object or phenomenon, it is often regarded as a supernatural occurrence and can be an omen or portent. It gives rise to admiration, fear, awe, and reverence. In the oral wonder tale, we are to marvel about the workings of the universe where anything can happen at any time, and these *fortunate* and *unfortunate* events are never to be explained. Nor do the characters demand an explanation—they are opportunistic and hopeful. They are encouraged to be so, and if they do not take advantage of the opportunity that will benefit them in their relations with others, they are either dumb or mean-spirited. The tales seek to awaken our regard for the miraculous condition of life and to evoke profound feelings of awe and respect for life as a miraculous process, which can be altered and changed to compensate for the lack of power, wealth, and pleasure that most people experience. Lack, deprivation, prohibition, and interdiction motivate people to look for signs of fulfillment and emancipation. In the wonder tales, those who are naive and simple are able to succeed because they are untainted and can recognize the wondrous signs. They have retained their belief in the miraculous condition of nature, and revere nature in all its aspects. They have not been spoiled by conventionalism, power, or rationalism. In contrast to the humble characters, the villains are those who use words and power intentionally to exploit, control, transfix, incarcerate, and destroy for their benefit. They have no respect or consideration for nature and other human beings, and they actually seek to abuse magic by preventing change and causing everything to be transfixed according to their interests. The marvelous protagonist wants to keep the process of natural change flowing and indicates possibilities for overcoming the obstacles that prevent other characters or creatures from living in a peaceful and pleasurable way.

The focus on the marvelous and hope for change in the oral folktale does not mean that all wonder tales, and later the literary fairy tales, served and serve a radical transforming purpose. The nature and meaning of folktales have depended on the stage of development of a tribe, community, or society. Oral tales have served to stabilize, conserve, or challenge the common beliefs, laws, values, and norms of a group. The ideology expressed in wonder tales always stemmed from the position that the narrator assumed with regard to the relations and developments in his or her community, and the narrative plot and changes made in it depended on the sense of wonder, marvel, admiration, or awe that the narrator wanted to evoke. In other words, the sense of the miraculous in the tale and the intended emotion sought by the narrator are ideological.

Since these wonder tales have been with us for thousands of years and have undergone so many different changes in the oral tradition, it is difficult to determine the ideological intention of the narrator, and when we disregard the narrator's intention, it is often difficult to reconstruct (and/or deconstruct) the ideological meaning of a tale. In the last analysis, however, even if we cannot establish whether a wonder tale is ideologically conservative, radical, sexist, progressive, etc., it is the celebration of miraculous or fabulous transformation in the name of hope that accounts for its major appeal. People have always wanted to improve and/or change their personal status or have sought magical intervention on their behalf. The emergence of the literary fairy tale during the latter part of the medieval period bears witness to the persistent human quest for an existence without oppression and constraints. It is a utopian quest that we continue to mark down or record through the metaphors of the fairy tale.

Two more important points should be made about the oral tradition of transmission that concern the magical contents of the tales and the mode in which they were disseminated. It has often been assumed that the magic properties and gifts in the tales, along with the supernatural and incredible events, could have been believed only by the gullible and superstitious "folk," i.e., the peasantry and children. Over the years, the wonder tales and the fairy tales were gradually associated with untruths or silly women's tales. Allegedly, only an old goose would tell them, or gossips.[3] But this notion of what constituted the meaning of a wonder tale or fairy tale for people of the past is misleading, if not fallacious, and it is perhaps the case today as well. During the Middle Ages, most people in all social classes believed in magic, the supernatural, and the miraculous, and they were also smart enough to distinguish between probable and improbable events. The marvelous and the magical in all their forms were not considered abnormal, and thus all genres of literature that recorded marvelous and supernatural incidents were not judged to be absurd or preposterous. On the contrary, they were told and retold because they had some connection to the material conditions and relations in their societies. To a certain degree, they carried truths, and the people of all classes believed in these stories, either as real possibilities or as parables. Magic and marvelous rituals were common throughout Europe, and it is only with the gradual rise of the Christian Church, which began to exploit magic and miraculous stories and to codify what would be acceptable for its own interests, that wonder tales and fairy tales were declared sacrilegious, heretical, dangerous, and untruthful. However, the Church could not prevent these stories from being circulated; it could only stigmatize, censure, or criticize them. At the same time, the Church created its own "fairy tale" tradition of miraculous stories in which people were to believe and still believe. This is true of all organized religions and continues to be the case today. The magical tales of Bibles and religious texts have always been compelled to compete with the secular tradition of folk and fairy tales for truth value.

Aside from displacing oral wonder tales and fairy tales and/or replacing them with their own myths since the early Middle Ages, organized religions, their schools, and their believers began "feminizing" the tradition of wonder and fairy tales and thereby dismissing it as not relevant to the "real world" or the true world of belief. If women were regarded as the originators and disseminators of these tales, then the texts themselves had to be suspicious, for they might reflect the fickle, duplicitous, wild, and erotic character of women, who were not to be trusted. Thus their stories were not to be trusted. The association of women with the fairy tale, Mother Goose, the gander, the nursery, bedtime, and the unbelievable belies how tales were told and disseminated in Europe and North America from the Middle Ages to the present. We have absolutely no proof that women were the "originators" and/or prime tellers of tales, the primeval spinners. Tales were told in all walks of life in the Middle Ages and during the Enlightenment, as they are today, and both sexes contributed to and continue to contribute to the tale-telling tradition. Merchants, slaves, servants, sailors, soldiers, spinners, seamstresses, woodcutters, tailors, innkeepers, nuns, monks, preachers, charcoal burners, and knights carried tales as did chil-

3. See Marina Warner's admirable study on this topic, *From the Beast to the Blonde: On Fairy Tales and Their Tellers* (London: Chatto and Windus, 1994). In her introduction she states, "Prejudices against women, especially old women and their chatter, belong in the history of fairy tale's changing status, for the pejorative image of the gossip was sweetened by influences from the tradition of Sibyls and the cult of St. Anne, until the archetypal crone by the hearth could emerge as a mouthpiece of homespun wisdom" (xx).

dren. It would be an exaggeration to insist that everyone in society told
tales or that they were good and interesting tale tellers. But we must imagine that everyone was interested in news from afar and local events, and
we know that the original terms for fairy tales stemmed from terms like
Mär, cunto or *conte*, which simply meant tale, any kind of tale, and often
a tale that brought news to the listeners. These tales were often embellished, or they were ritual tales that brought the members of a community
closer together. Since we cannot prove one way or the other how frequently and by whom the tales were told, we must be cautious about
making generalizations about who the "caretakers" of the tales were. But
one factor is clear: the folk were not just made up of the peasantry or the
lower classes. The great majority of people in the Middle Ages up through
the beginning of the nineteenth century were nonliterate, and thus everyone participated in one way or the other (as teller or listener) in the oral
tradition. Everyone was exposed to some kind of storytelling, and nobody
can claim "true authorship," despite many claims made in the name of
the "folk."

When it comes to the literary tradition of the fairy tale, however, the
situation is different because men were privileged when it came to education, and the literary tradition, though it consisted of appropriated tales
from women and men alike, was firmly in the hands of men. The motifs,
characters, topoi, and magical properties of the literary tradition can be
traced back to tale collections from the Orient that predate Christianity.
They are apparent in Indian, Egyptian, Greek, and Roman myths and in
tales that constitute Oriental and Occidental religions. However, they were
never gathered or institutionalized in the short forms that we recognize in
the West until the late Middle Ages. Then male scribes began recording
them in collections of tales, epics, romances, and poetry from the tenth
century onward. In Italy fairy tale motifs can be found in the anonymous
thirteenth-century *Novellino* (*The Hundred Old Tales*), Giovanni Boccaccio's *Decameron* (1349–50), Ser Giovanni Fiorentino's *Il pecorone* (*The
Big Sheep*), Giovanni Sercambi's *Novelle* (*Novellas*, 1390–1402), Poggio
Bacciolino's *Facetiae* (ca. 1450), Luigi Pulci's *Morgante* (1483), Matteo
Maria Boiardo's *Orlando innamorato* (*Orlando in Love*, 1495), and Ludovico Ariosto's *Orlando furioso* (1516); in France, in Marie de France's
Lais (ca. 1189), Chrétien de Troyes's *Yvain, or the Knight of the Lion* (ca.
1190) and *Perceval* (ca. 1195), *Les cent nouvelles nouvelles* (*The Hundred
Tales*, 1456–61), and François Rabelais's *Gargantua and Pantagruel*
(1532–64); in Germany, in the anonymous *König Rother* (ca. 1150), the
thirteenth-century verse novella *Asinarius*, Wolfram von Eschenbach's *Par-
zifal* (ca. 1210), Hartmann von Aue's *Erek* (1180/85), *Armer Heinrich* (*Poor
Henry*, 1195), and *Iwein* (ca. 1205), Martin Montanus's *Wegkürtzer* (1560),
Andreas Strobl's *Ovum Paschale Novum* (1694), and Johann von Grim-
melshausen's *Simpliccismus* (1669); in England, in *Beowulf* (eighth century), *Sir Gawain and the Green Knight* (fourteenth-century poem),
Geoffrey of Monmouth's *Vita Merlini* (ca. 1150), Geoffrey Chaucer's *The
Canterbury Tales* (ca. 1387), Sir Thomas Malory's *The Death of Arthur*
(1469), Edmund Spenser's *The Faerie Queene* (1590–96), William Shakespeare's *Midsummer Night's Dream* (1595/96) and *The Tempest* (1611),

and Ben Jonson's *The Alchemist* (1610); in Spain, the Oriental influence was important in such translated works as *Disciplina clercalis* (ca. twelfth century), *Sendebar* (1253), and *Kalila e Dimna* (thirteenth century) and in the chivalric novels *Cavallero Zifar* (1300) and *Amades de Gaula* (1508). In general Oriental tales were spread around Europe both through oral retellings and through translations into various European languages. Some key works that influenced European writers of fairy tales are *The Fables of Bidpai* (the Persian/Arabic adaptation of the Indian *Pancatantra*), *Navigatio sancti brendani*, Christoforo Armeno's *Peregrinaggio di tre giovani figliuoli del re di Seren* (*Voyage of the Three Young Sons of the King of Ceylon*, 1557). In addition, such works as the thirteenth-century *Gesta Romanorum* (*Deeds of the Romans*) and *Legenda aurea* (*The Golden Legend*) written by Jacobus de Voraigne were used as primers for young children and contained folklore and fairy tale motifs as did many of the sermons and instructional books that were published from the fifteenth century onward.

The rise of the literary fairy tale as a short narrative form stemmed from the literary activity that flourished in Florence during the fourteenth century and led to the production of various collections of *novelle* in Italian and Latin under the influence of Boccaccio's *Decameron*. The *novella*, also called *conto*, was a short tale which adhered to principles of unity of time and action and clear narrative plot. The focus was on surprising events of *everyday* life, and the tales (influenced by oral wonder tales, fairy tales, *fabliaux*, chivalric romances, epic poetry, and fables) were intended for the amusement and instruction of the readers. Before Boccaccio turned his hand to writing his tales, the most famous collection was the *Novellino* written by an anonymous Tuscan author in the thirteenth century. But it was Boccaccio who set a model for all future writers of this genre with his frame narrative and subtle and sophisticated style. It was Boccaccio who expanded the range of topics of the novella and created unforgettable characters that led to numerous imitations by writers such as Ser Giovanni Fiorentino, Giovanni Sercambi, Franco Sachetti, Piovano Arlotto, and Matteo Bandello, to name but a few.

It was undoubtedly due to Boccaccio's example and the great interest in the novella that Giovan Francesco Straparola came to publish his collection, *Le piacevoli notti* (*The Pleasant Nights*,[4] 1550/53) in two volumes. Straparola is a fascinating figure because he was the first European writer to include fairy tales in his collection of novelle, and because we know next to nothing about him. Straparola was probably born about 1480 in Caravaggio, but there are no records that confirm this as a fact, especially since his surname Straparola, which means "the loquacious one," may have been a pseudonym. We have information only from the first volume of *Le piacevoli notti* that he was born in Caravaggio and that he was the author of another work, *Opera nova de Zoan Francesco Straparola da Caravazo* (1508), a collection of sonnets and poems, published in Venice.

---

4. The book was translated by W. G. Waters as *The Facetious Nights* (London: Society of Bibliophiles, 1898), and the title can also be translated as *The Entertaining Nights* or *The Delectable Nights*.

Nor are we certain of his death in 1557. Most likely he had moved to Venice as a young man, and it is clear from his collection of novelle, which he called *favole*, that he was very well educated. He knew Latin and various Italian dialects, and his references to other literary works and understanding of literary forms indicate that he was well versed in the humanities. Whoever Straparola may have been, his *Piacevoli notti* had great success: it was reprinted twenty-five times from 1553 to 1613 and translated into French in 1560 and 1580 and into German in 1791.

The allure of his work can be attributed to several factors: his use of erotic and obscene riddles,[5] his mastery of polite Italian used by the narrators in the frame narrative, his introduction of plain earthy language into the stories, the critical view of the power struggles in Italian society and lack of moralistic preaching, his inclusion of fourteen unusual fairy tales in the collection, and his interest in magic, unpredictable events, duplicity, and the supernatural. Similar to Boccaccio, Straparola exhibited an irreverence for authorities, and the frame narrative itself reveals a political tension and somewhat ironic if not pessimistic outlook on the possibilities of living a harmonious happy-ever-after life.

In the opening of the book, which sets the frame for all the *favole*, Straparola depicts how Ottoviano Maria Sforza, the bishop-elect of Lodi (most likely the real Sforza, who died in 1540), was forced to leave Milan because of political plots against him. He takes his daughter, Signora Lucretia, a widow, with him, and since her husband had died in 1523, it can be assumed that the setting for the *Nights* is approximately sometime between 1523 and 1540. The bishop and his daughter flee first to Lodi, then to Venice, and finally settle on the island of Murano. They gather a small group of congenial people around them: ten gracious ladies, two matronly women, and four educated and distinguished gentlemen. Since it is the time of Carnival, Lucretia proposes that the company take turns telling stories during the two weeks before Lent, and consequently, there are thirteen nights in which stories are told, amounting to seventy-four in all.

As was generally the case in upper-class circles, a formal social ritual is followed. Each night there is a dance by the young ladies. Then Lucretia draws the names of five ladies from a vase, and those five ladies are to tell the tales that evening. But before the storytelling, one of the men must sing a song, and after the song a lady tells a tale followed by a riddle in verse. Most of the riddles are examples of the double entendre and have strong sexual connotations, especially those told by the men. The object is to discuss erotic subjects in a highly refined manner. During the course of the thirteen nights, the men are invited every now and then to replace a woman and tell a tale. In addition, Lucretia herself tells two tales.

To a certain extent, the fictional company on the island of Murano can be regarded as an ideal representation of how people can relate to one another and comment in pleasing and instructive ways about all types of experience. The stories created by Straparola are literary fairy tales, revised oral tales, anecdotes, erotic tales, buffo tales of popular Italian life, didactic

5. The book was condemned by the ecclesiastical authorities in 1604 and placed on the *Index librorum prohibitorum*.

tales, fables, and tales based on writers who preceded him such as Boccaccio, Franco Sachetti, Ser Giovanni Fiorentino, Giovanni Sercambi,
and others. In the fairy tales, as well as in most of the other narratives,
Straparola focuses on power and fortune. Without luck (magic, fairies,
miracles), the hero cannot succeed in his mission, and without knowing
how to use the power of magic or taking advantage of a fortuitous event
or gift, the hero cannot succeed. Though wicked people are punished, it
is clear that moral standards are set only by the people in power. Thus
Galeotto can kill his brides at will, and fathers can seek to punish or sleep
with their daughters at will. The majority of the tales centers on active
male protagonists who are heroic mainly because they know how to exploit
opportunities that bring them wealth, power, and money. Straparola begins
most of his tales in small towns or cities in Italy and sends his protagonists
off to other countries, realms, and, of course, into woods or onto the sea.
His heroes are adventurers, and there is a sense that the fairy tales have
been gathered from far and wide.

    If Straparola did indeed spend most of his life in Venice, it would not
be by chance that the tales that he read and heard came to this port city
from far and wide. Venice was a thriving and wealthy city in the sixteenth
century, and Straparola would have had contact with foreigners from all
over Italy, Europe, and the Orient. Or he would have had news about
them. This real "news" formed the basis of the *fiabe* (fairy tales) in his
collection, and it is a collection that also traveled far and wide. But its
significance for the development of the literary fairy tale in Europe has
generally been neglected. Of course, he alone did not trigger the development, but there are clear signs that his tales circulated throughout Europe and had a considerable influence among educated writers: Basile was
apparently familiar with his book, and it is obvious that Mme d'Aulnoy,
Mme de Murat, Eustache Le Noble, and Jean de Mailly knew his tales,
and through them they spread to Germany and eventually influenced the
Brothers Grimm, who wrote about Straparola and Basile.[6] In short, Straparola initiated and influenced the genre of the literary fairy tale in Europe, and though it would be misleading to talk about a diachronic history
of the literary fairy tale with a chain reaction that begins with Straparola,
leads to Basile, then the French writers of the 1690s, and culminates in
the work of the Brothers Grimm, I would like to suggest that they form a
historical frame in which the parameters of the early literary fairy tale were
set, and within that frame there was an institutionalization of what we now
call fairy tale characters, topoi, motifs, metaphors, and plots. Their con-
ventionalization enabled numerous writers (and storytellers in the oral tradition) to experiment and produce highly original fairy tales at the same
time. These writers were also tellers, for the split between oral and literary
narrators was never as great as we imagine it to be, and their familiarity

---

6. In fact, Jacob Grimm wrote the preface to Giambattista Basile, *Der Pentamerone oder: Das
   Märchen aller Märchen*, trans. Felix Liebrecht (Breslau: Max und Komp, 1846). The Brothers
   Grimm probably knew about Basile's work as early as 1806 through their contact with Clemens
   Brentano, who was already adapting Basile. At the very latest, they were familiar with Straparola's
   work in 1817, when the first extensive translation appeared: *Die Märchen des Straparola*, trans.
   Friedrich Wilhelm Schmidt (Berlin: Duncker und Humlot, 1817).

with the folklore of their respective societies played a role in their literary representations in the fairy tale. Giambattista Basile's work is a case in point. And I want briefly to sketch the further development of the literary fairy tale beginning with Basile, then moving to the French writers of the 1690s, and concluding with the Brothers Grimm.

In contrast to Straparola, we know a great deal about Basile.[7] Born in a small village near Naples or perhaps in Naples itself about 1575, he came from a middle-class family, and in 1603 he left Naples and traveled north, eventually settling in Venice, where he earned his living as a soldier and began writing poetry. By 1608, he had returned to the region of Naples and held various positions as administrator and governor in different principalities and courts while pursuing a career as poet and writer until his death in 1632. Though he became well-known for his poems, odes, eclogues, and dramas, written in Italian, and helped organize court spectacles, his fame today is due to his astounding collection of fifty fairy tales written in Neapolitan dialect, *Lo cunto de li cunti* (*The Tale of Tales*, 1634–36), also known as the *Pentamerone* (*The Pentameron*), published posthumously thanks to the efforts of his sister Adriana, a famous opera singer.

There is no clear proof that Basile knew Straparola's tales, but it is more than likely that he was acquainted with them in some form, especially since he had spent about three years in Venice, where Straparola's tales were published. However important Straparola might have been for Basile's conception of his fairy tales, he was a pale light in comparison with the fiery imaginative Basile. To my mind, Basile is the most original and brilliant writer of fairy tales in Europe until the German romantic E. T. A. Hoffmann came on the scene in 1814. Not only did he draw on an abundance of literary and historical sources to create his hilarious ironical tales, but he was deeply acquainted with the folklore of a vast region around Naples and was familiar with Oriental tales. His command of the Neapolitan dialect is extraordinary, for he managed to combine an elevated form of the dialect with vulgar expressions, metaphors, idioms and brilliant proverbs,[8] many of which he created himself. The frame narrative (following Boccaccio, of course) is fascinating in and of itself. His "tale of tales" sets the stage for forty-nine marvelous stories. In this frame tale, Zoza, the daughter of the king of Vallepelosa, cannot laugh, and her father is so concerned about her happiness that he invites people from all over to try to make her laugh. Yet nobody can succeed until an old woman attempting to sop up oil in front of the palace has her jug broken by a mischievous court page. The ensuing argument between the old woman and the page, each hurling coarse and vulgar epithets at one another, is so delightful that Zoza bursts into laughter. However, this laughter does not make the old woman happy, and she curses Zoza by saying, "Be off with you, and

7. For more recent works on Basile, see the excellent studies by Barbara Broggini, "*Lo cunto de li cunti*" *von Giambattista Basile: Ein Ständepoet in Streit mit der Plebs, Fortuna, und der höfischen Korruption* (Frankfurt am Main: Lang, 1990), and Nancy Canepa, *From Court to Forest: Giambattista Basile's Lo cunto de li cunti and the Birth of the Literary Fairy Tale* (Detroit: Wayne State University Press, 1999).
8. See Charles Speroni, "Proverbs and Proverbial Phrases in Basile's *Pentameron*," *University of California Publications in Modern Philology* 24.2 (1941): 181–288.

may you never see the bud of a husband unless it is the prince of Cam-
porotondo!" To her dismay, Zoza learns that this prince, named Tadeo,
is under the spell of a wicked fairy and is in a tomb. He can only be
wakened and liberated by a woman who fills a pitcher with her tears that
is hanging on a nearby wall.

In need of help, Zoza visits three different fairies and receives a walnut,
a chestnut, and a hazelnut as gifts. Then she goes to Tadeo's tomb and
weeps into the pitcher for two days. When the pitcher is almost full, she
falls asleep because she is tired from all the crying. While she is sleeping,
however, a slave girl steals the pitcher, fills it, wakes Tadeo, and takes the
credit for bringing him back to life. Consequently, Tadeo marries her, and
she becomes pregnant.

But Zoza, whose happiness depends on Tadeo, is not about to concede
the prince to a slave girl. She rents a house across from Tadeo's palace
and manages to attract the attention of Tadeo. But the slave girl threatens
to beat the baby if Tadeo spends any time with Zoza, who now uses
another tactic to gain entrance to Tadeo's palace. On three different occasions she opens the nuts. One contains a little dwarf, who sings; the
next, twelve chickens made of gold; and the third, a doll that spins gold.
The slave girl demands these fascinating objects, and Tadeo sends for
them, offering Zoza whatever she wants. To his surprise, Zoza gives the
objects as gifts. Yet the final one, the doll, stirs an uncontrollable passion
in the slave girl to hear stories during her pregnancy, and she threatens
Tadeo again: unless women come to tell her tales, she will kill their unborn baby. So Tadeo invites ten women from the rabble known for their
storytelling: lame Zeza, twisted Cecca, goitered Meneca, big-nosed Tolla,
hunchback Popa, drooling Antonella, snout-faced Ciulla, rheummy Paola,
mangy Ciommetella, and diarrhetic Iacoba. The women spend the day
chattering and gossiping, and after the evening meal, one tale is told by
each one of the ten for five nights. Finally, on the last day, Zoza is invited
to tell the last tale, and she recounts what happened to her. The slave girl
tries to stop her, but Tadeo insists that Zoza be allowed to tell the tale to
the end. When he realizes that Zoza's tale is true, Tadeo has the slave girl
buried alive pregnant, and he marries Zoza to bring the tale of tales to a
"happy" conclusion.

Unlike the narratives by Boccaccio and Straparola, Basile's tales, which
are told during banquets with music, games, and dance, are entirely fairy
tales and are told by lower-class figures. There are constant local references
to Naples and the surrounding area and to social customs, political intrigues, and family conflicts. Basile was an astute social commentator, who
despaired of the corruption in the courts that he served and was obviously
taken with the country folk, their surprising antics, and their need and
drive for change. As Michele Rak has observed,

> In the case of the *Cunto* the plots are all filled with the same theme:
> the change of status. The situation of each tale evolves rapidly to bring
> wealth and beauty to some of the characters and poverty and ruin to
> others. This change is only realized amidst conflict, foremost in the

interior of the minimal social unit—the family about which there are many stories of fathers, mothers, stepmothers, sons, brothers—and then in the elementary reports of relations in the family—about which there are many stories about marriages and above all about unequal marriages between princes and shepherdesses. The change of status of these fairy-tale characters can be read as a metaphor of a much broader change: the acceleration of the time and mode of the cultural process characteristic of this phase of the modern era. In the *Cunto* the most evident signs of this transformation of the cultural regime are registered explicitly: the emergence of symbolical traditions, the opening of new dimensions of communication, the restructuring of the system and hierarchy of family relations, a broader literacy, the amplification and identification of the types of readers who also read the new novel, the client of the literature of celebration, the participant at the feasts and the theatricalization of public life.[9]

Similar to Straparola, Basile shared a concern with power and transformation and was fascinated by the wheel of fortune and how Lady Fortuna intervened in people's lives to provide them with the opportunity to advance in society or to gain some measure of happiness. Of course, he also depicted how Lady Fortuna could devastate people and cause destruction. Again, like Straparola he was not overly optimistic about establishing social equality and harmonious communities. Conflict reigns in his tales, in one of which a usually demure Cinderella chops off the head of her stepmother and in another a discreet princess virtually liquidates a seducer in a battle of the sexes. Nevertheless, his tales exude mirth because of the manner in which he turns language inside-out and creates a carnivalesque atmosphere. Just as the frame tale leads to the exposure of the stealthy slave girl with no holds barred, all the narratives seek to reveal the contradictory nature in which all members of society pretend to comport themselves according to lofty standards but will stoop as low as they must to achieve wealth and happiness. Basile takes great delight in minimizing the differences between coarse peasants and high aristocrats, and certainly if his tales had been written and published in Italian, they would have found their way to the Church's Index.

As it was, Basile's tales were—remarkable to say—reprinted several times in the seventeenth century despite the Neapolitan dialect and through translations into Italian and then French became fairly well known in Italy and France. It is apparent that Mlle Lhéritier was very familiar with his tales, and three of hers, "The Discreet Princess," "The Enchantments of Eloquence," and "Ricdin-Ricdon," depend heavily on three of his stories. In fact, the Italian influence in France during the 1790s was much more profound than scholars have suspected. At least six of Mme d'Aulnoy's fairy tales can be traced to Straparola's *fiabe*; two of Mme de Murat's tales owe a great debt to Straparola; and three of Mailly's tales and two of Le Noble's are very imitative of Straparola's works. Finally, almost all of Perrault's tales have models in the collections of Straparola and Basile. The

9. *Fiabe campane*, trans. Domenico Rea (Milan: Mondadori, 1984) 25.

Italian influence was certainly there, and it is not necessary or even important to undertake an assiduous philological comparison to prove theft,
imitation, or appropriation. What is significant and fascinating is the manner in which French writers began about 1790 to be attracted to folktales
and fairy tales and created a vogue[1] of writing that was to last approximately
a century and firmly institutionalized the fairy tale as a literary genre
throughout Europe and North America.

Perhaps I should say French women writers, or to be even more specific,
Mme d'Aulnoy, because she and they almost single-handedly transformed
the Italian and Oriental tales as well as oral tales into marvelous fairy tales
that were serious commentaries on court life and cultural struggles at the
end of the eighteenth century in Versailles and Paris. As Patricia Hannon
has remarked, "Whether denigrated by learned men such as Villiers or
praised by the modernist *Mercure*, tale writing was considered a group
phenomenon largely because the majority of narratives were published by
salon women who displayed their authorial identity through interior sign-
ings and intratextual references to each other's work. At the end of the
century when . . . French women were writing in heretofore unprece-
dented numbers, the *salonnières* Aulnoy, Bernard, Lhéritier, and their colleagues transformed what Erica Harth has described as the salon of space
of conversation into the space of writing."[2]

It was Mme d'Aulnoy who coined the term *conte de fée* (fairy tale), and
she began the vogue by incorporating a tale, "L'Isle de la félicité" ("The
Island of Happiness"), into her novel *L'histoire d'Hipolyte, comte de Duglas*
(1790), through the means of conversation. Talk and the oral tradition in
all its forms are key to understanding the rise and institution of the literary
genre. Interestingly, the tale does not end happily because the protagonist
Adolph does not follow the commands of Princess Felicity and is whisked
away by Father Death. As a consequence, the disappointed Princess Felicity does not show herself on earth, and perfect happiness is unattainable.
Mme d'Aulnoy went on to write another sixteen tales published in *Les
contes des fées* and *Contes nouveaux; ou, Les fées à la mode* between 1696
and 1698. These tales are intricate and long discourses about the importance of natural love and tenderness (*tendresse*), subjects dear to her heart.
In addition, they tend to embody a critique of conventional court manners
from an aristocratic woman's perspective that is further enhanced by the
dialogues in the narrative frames in which her tales are installed. The
conversations surrounding her tales are very important because the tales

1. There have been several excellent studies about this vogue: Mary Elizabeth Storer, *Un episode
littéraire de la fin du XVIIe siècle: la mode des contes de fées, 1685–1700* (Paris: Champion, 1928);
Jacques Barchilon, *Le conte merveilleux français de 1690 à 1790: Cent ans de féerie et de poésie
ignorées de l'histoire littéraire* (Paris: Champion, 1975); Teresa Di Scanno, *Les contes de fées à
l'époque classique, 1680–1715* (Naples: Liguori, 1975); and Raymonde Robert, *Le conte de fées
littéraire en France, de la fin du XVIIe à la fin du XVIIIe siècle* (Nancy: Presses Universitaires de
Nancy, 1982).
2. *Fabulous Identities: Women's Fairy Tales in Seventeenth-Century France* (Amsterdam: Rodopi,
1998) 172. Other pertinent books that deal with this topic and are also important for understanding
the vogue are Erica Harth, *Cartesian Women: Versions and Subversions of Rational Discourse in
the Old Regime* (Ithaca: Cornell University Press, 1992); Linda Timmermans, *L'accès des femmes
à la culture, 1598–1715. Un débat d'idées de Saint François à la Marquise de Lambert* (Paris:
Champion, 1993); and Lewis Seifert, *Fairy Tales, Sexuality and Gender in France, 1690–1715:
Nostalgic Utopias* (Cambridge: Cambridge University Press, 1996).

themselves grew out of literary entertainment and parlor games that had become common in many of the literary salons in France by the 1690s. It was in the salons and elsewhere that the French literary fairy tale was conventionalized and institutionalized. Marie-Jeanne Lhéritier, Catherine Bernard, Charlotte-Rose Caumont de La Force, Henriette Julie de Murat, Jean de Mailly, Eustache Le Noble, Charles Perrault, and other writers frequented many of the same salons or knew of one another. Interested in participating in a social discourse about the civilizing process in France, modern culture, and the role of women and aware of the unique potential that the fairy tale possessed as metaphorical commentary, these writers produced remarkable collections of tales within a short period of time: Mlle Lhéritier, *Oeuvres meslées* (1695); Mlle Bernard, *Inès de Cordoue* (1695), a novel, which includes "Riquet à la houppe"; Mlle de la Force, *Les contes des contes* (1797); Charles Perrault, *Histories ou contes du temps passé* (1697); Chevalier de Mailly, *Les illustres fées, contes galans* (1698); Mme de Murat, *Contes de fées* (1798); Paul-François Nodot, *Histoire de Mélusine* (1698); Sieur de Prechac', *Contes moins contes que les autres* (1698); Mme Durand, *La comtesse de Mortane* (1699); Mme de Murat, *Histoires sublimes et allégoriques* (1699); Eustache Le Noble, *Le gage touché* (1700); Mme d'Auneuil, *La tiranie des fées détruite* (1702); and Mme Durand, *Les petits soupers de l'année 1699* (1702).

Though the quality of the writing varied among these authors, they all participated in a notable modernist movement, for this was the period of French cultural wars when Nicolas Boileau and Perrault debated the merits of classical Greek and Roman models versus new French innovative art in the famous *Querelle des Anciens et des Modernes* (*Quarrel of the Ancients and Moderns*, 1687–96) and when the "infamous" *Querelle des femmes* (*Quarrel about Women*) pervaded various aspects of French culture. This was not an official debate, but it still raged in public during the latter part of the seventeenth century, as men continued to publish tomes about the proper role of women and how to control their bodies and demeanor, if not their identities.[3] The transformation of literary and oral tales into *contes de fées* was not superficial or decorative. The aesthetics that the aristocratic and bourgeois women and men developed in their conversational games and in their written tales had a serious aspect to it. As Patricia Hannon maintains, "Women at once embrace and manipulate modernist *mondain* ideology. Ostentatiously adopting the consecrated aristocratic aesthetic of negligence, the *conteuses* cultivate a positive class and gender identity in order equally to write beyond it. Claims of frivolity, amuseurism, amateurism, all found in women's metacommentaries on their chosen genre, at once denote their own ambivalence in crossing over into the 'masculine' territory of writing and publishing, and ensconce them safely in an ideological social frame which their fictional narratives will at times challenge. If the notion of the female author came of age during the last years of the century, it is perhaps because the salon appears to have conflated the notions of conversation and composition."[4]

3. See Timmermans, *L'accès des femmes à la culture*.
4. *Fabulous Identities*, 177.

Though they differed in style, perspective, and content, the writers of fairy tales, female and male,[5] were all anti-classical, and their narratives were implicitly written in opposition to the leading critic of the literary establishment, Boileau, and his followers. As Lewis Seifert has made clear, "The use of the marvelous in the *contes de fées* differs from that in both the mythological and the Christian epic. . . . By contrast, the *contes de fées* do not reduce the marvelous to allegorical systems of aesthetic, moral, or religious plausibility. Although they do have recourse to a moralizing pretext with the use of interspersed maxims and/or appended final morals, these serve to motivate the representation of individual characters or traits that are thereby plausible, and not the marvelous setting as a whole, which remains *invraisemblable*. Even further, the fairy tales make deliberate use of the marvelous and are thus deliberately implausible. This self-conscious and playful use of both the supernatural setting and the moralizing pretext distances any real belief in fairy magic, but also contributes to the readability of the text."[6]

In this regard, the French writers continued the remarkable experimentation with the marvelous that the Italians, namely Straparola and Basile, had begun many years before them, but they were able to ground them and institutionalize them as a genre more effectively than the Italians had done through the salon culture. Like Straparola and Basile, they exploited the marvelous in conscious narrative strategies to deal with real social issues of their time. Paradoxically, the more implausible they made their stories, the more plausible and appealing were their hidden meanings that struck readers as truthful and have not lost their truth content today. The accomplishments of the French writers were many: (1) They reacted to social and political events with great sensitivity, and since this was a period of Louis XIV's great wars that devastated the country and also a period of famine, there was great discontent with his reign and with the court that was mirrored in many of the tales. (2) They were ingenious in the manner in which they combined the salon conversations and games in their tales and at the same time "refined" the vulgar folk idiom to address their concerns that covered the role of precocious women, the relations and conditions of court society, tender and natural love, war, duplicity, class status, taste, morality, and power relations. (3) Almost all the marvelous realms they created, whether they were male or female writers, were governed by fairies and had little if any reference to Greek, Roman, and Christian allegorical systems. Fairies were omniscient and omnipotent and ruled their universes, and there was no explanation of why or how they had achieved such great power. Clearly, however, their "feminine" reign was in opposition to the mundane reign of Louis XIV and the Church. (4) The cross-cultural connections—the motifs they wove in their tales— are vast and stem from Italy, the Orient, the French countryside, and other

5. It is interesting to note that three of the important male writers of this vogue were marginalized types. Perrault was retired from his governmental position and had lost the support of the king. Mailly was an illegitimate son of an aristocrat and did not find favor at court. Le Noble was a libertine who had served some time in prison.
6. "Marvelous Realities: Reading the *Merveilleux* in the Seventeenth-Century French Fairy Tale," *Out of the Woods: The Origins of the Literary Fairy Tale in Italy and France*, ed. Nancy Canepa (Detroit: Wayne State University Press, 1997) 138–39.

European cultures. Although the French language and particular cultural references stamp these tales as French, they are also filled with and enriched by a pan-European tradition that helped form them.

The first French vogue was not a vogue in the sense of a fad, for shortly after the turn of the century it helped give rise to a second phase that consisted of Oriental tales and diverse experiments that themselves consisted of farces, parodies, innovative narratives, and moral tales for the young. Perhaps the most momentous event was the publication of Antoine Galland's *Les mille et une nuits* (*The Thousand and One Nights*, 1704–17) in twelve volumes. Galland had traveled and lived in the Middle East and had mastered Arabic, Hebrew, Persian, and Turkish, and, since he lived in Paris, he was also thoroughly familiar with the first vogue of fairy tales. After he published the first four volumes of *The Thousand and One Nights*, they became extremely popular, and he continued translating the tales until his death. The final two volumes were published posthumously and contained tales for which there are no manuscripts. Galland did more than translate. He actually adapted the tales to suit the tastes of his French readers, and he invented some of the plots and drew material together to form some of his own tales. His example was followed by Pétis de La Croix (1653–1713), who translated a Turkish work by Sheikh Zadah, the tutor of Amriath II, entitled *L'histoire de la sultane de Perse et des visirs. Contes turcs* (*The Story of the Sultan of the Persians and the Visirs. Turkish Tales*), in 1710. Moreover, he also translated a Persian imitation of *The Thousand and One Days*, which borrowed material from Indian comedies. Finally, there was the Abbé Jean-Paul Bignon's collection *Les aventures d'Abdalla, fils d'Anif* (1712–14), which purported to be an authentic Arabic work in translation but was actually Bignon's own creative adaptation of Oriental tales mixed with French folklore. All of the Oriental collections had a great exotic appeal to readers of fairy tales and not only in France. European readers had a strong interest in other "exotic" countries and cultures, and the tales, though highly implausible and marvelous, attracted readers because they appeared to represent these "other" diverse and strange people and fulfilled obvious wish-fulfillments and escape fantasies. In addition, the material, motifs, settings, and plots of the tales furnished European writers and storytellers with a greater repertoire and stimulated their imaginations for centuries to come, for the Arabian tales in particular were translated in hundreds of editions and many different European languages.

By 1720 the literary fairy tale was firmly entrenched in France, and its dissemination was to increase throughout the eighteenth century in different forms. Perhaps the most significant way was through the chapbooks of the Bibliothèque Bleue, which were series of popularized tales published in a cheap format in Troyes during the early part of the seventeenth century by Jean Oudot and his son, Nicolas, and Pierre Garnier. These collections (which were later translated and imitated in Germany as the Blaue Bibliothek and spread to England in chapbook form) were at first dedicated to the Arthurian romances, lives of saints, and legends. They were carried by peddlers to towns and cities in the country and made works originally written for an upper-class audience available for all classes. It was not until the latter part of the eighteenth century that Oudot, Garnier, and other publishers began including fairy tales and other stories in the Bibliothèque Bleue format. By this time, there were over 150 publishers in approximately seventy different places that were printing series of chapbooks.[7] Most of the fairy tales were abridged, and the language and style were changed so that they became comprehensible for all readers including the young. They were read aloud and appropriated by the lower classes, who, in turn, changed them in the oral tradition, and their "folk" versions would filter back into the literary tradition through writers who heard them. In addition to the popularization of the literary fairy tale through chapbooks and the oral tradition, there were numerous French writers who grew up with fairy tales of the first vogue whose attitude toward the tradition had become more satirical. As Mary Louise Ennis remarks, "The Comte de Caylus, himself the author of the *Contes orientaux*, commented that one hardly read anything else but fairy tales in his youth. In fact, so obsessed was the public by 1755 that Frédéric-Melchior Grimm opined that just about everyone had put his hand to one. Fairy tales and oriental intrigues became so popular that they influenced aristocrats and commoners alike. Accordingly, parodists could count upon the public's recognition of primary texts to decipher the encoded humor of their rewritten tales."[8]

Among the more important French writers of fairy tales during the first half of the eighteenth century were Philippe de Caylus (*Féerie novelles*, 1741, and *Contes orientaux tirés des manuscrits de la bibliothèque du roi de France*, 1743), Marie-Antoinette Fagnan (*Kanor, conte traduit du turc*, 1750; *Minet bleu et Louvette*, 1753; *Le miroir des princesses orientales*, 1755), Antoine Hamilton (*Le Bélier*, 1705, *L'histoire de Fleur d'Epine*, 1710, *Quatre facardins*, 1710–15), Louise Cavelier Levesque (*Le prince des Aigues*, 1722, and *Le prince invisible*, 1722), Catherine Caillot de Lintot (*Trois nouveaux contes de fées avec une préface qui n'est pasmoins serieuse*, 1735), Marguerite de Lubert (*Sec et noir, ou las princesse des fleurs et le prince des autruches*, 1737; *La princesse Camion*, 1743; *Le prince Glacé et la princesse Etincelante*, 1743), Henri Pajon ("Eritzine & Parelin," 1744, "L'enchanteur, ou la bague de puissance," 1745, and "Histoire des trois fils d'Hali Bassa," 1745), Gabrielle-Suzanne de Villeneuve (*La jeune Amériquaine et les contes marins*, 1740, and *Les belles solitaires*, 1745), and Claude-Henri de Voisenon (*Zulmis et Zelmaïde*, 1745, and *Le Sultan Mispouf et al Princesse Gismine*, 1746).

Although not all these writers wrote parodies, they were so well-versed in the conventions of fairy tale writers that they enjoyed playing with the motifs and audience expectations. Consequently, their tales often bordered on the burlesque and even on the macabre and grotesque. The fairies did outrageous things with their power. Humans were turned into talking fish and all kinds of bizarre animals. Sentimental love was parodied. Numerous

---

7. For two excellent accounts of this development, see Robert Mandrou, *De la culture populaire aux XVIIe et XVIIIe siècles. La Bibliothèque bleue* (Paris: Stock, 1965), and Geneviève Bollème, *La Bibliothèque bleue* (Paris: Juillard, 1971).
8. "Fractured Fairy Tales: Parodies for the Salon and Foire," *Out of the Woods: The Origins of the Literary Fairy Tale in Italy and France*, ed. Nancy Canepa (Detroit: Wayne State University Press, 1997) 223.

tales abandoned morality for pornography and eroticism. Thomas-Simon Gueullette endeavored to make his collection of *Mille et un quarts d'heure* (*Thousand and One Quarter Hours*, 1715) like Galland's *Thousand and One Nights*, just as he had sought to give a folklore aspect to *Soirées bretonnes* (*Breton Evenings*, 1712). Most of the tales in the second wave have clear textual references to a literary genre that had established itself, but it should not be regarded as separate from the oral tradition, for conversation, talk, discussions, and readings often formed the basis for literary production, no matter what the social class of the author was.

In 1741, Charles Duclos, Philippe de Caylus, and Claude-Henri de Voisenon were challenged by Mlle Quinault in her salon to write a tale based on designs by Boucher, and the result was not only Duclos's acerbic fairy tale "Acajou et Zirphile" (1744), which poked fun at fairy tale conventions and criticized a libertine society, but also probably Jean-Jacques Rousseau's "La Reine Fantasque" (1758), which ridicules monarchy and satirizes women. Rousseau attended Mlle Quinault's salon, and it has generally been assumed that he participated in the wager to see who could write the best tale based on Boucher's engravings. The tales by de Caylus and de Voisenon have not survived, but their other collections of comic fairy tales such as *Contes orienteaux* and *Zulmis et Zelmaïde* reveal to what extent they were familiar with written and oral versions of tales and discussions about them. French fairy tale writers of the eighteenth century were very conscious of how talk and conversation formed the basis of their tales and continually embedded their tales within frame narratives which highlighted the exchange of literary fairy tales and dialogue. Two of the most famous versions of "Beauty and the Beast" function as exemplary tales within a storytelling frame narrative. Mme de Villeneuve's *La jeune Amériquaine et les contes marins* (1740) recounts the voyage of a young girl returning to Saint Domingue, where her parents are plantation owners, after finishing her studies in France. During the trip, the girl's chambermaid is joined by everyone on board in telling stories. This volume contains two fairy tales, "Les Naïades" and "La Belle et al Bête," and it is notable that de Villeneuve's long and complicated version of "Beauty and the Beast"—it is close to two hundred pages in its original publication—indicates a familiarity with Mme d'Aulnoy's narratives and at the same time presents an elaborate discourse on blood lines, social class, and the merits of the bourgeoisie that reveals how she sought to interject her ideas of the civilizing process into the debates about appropriate marriages and the morals of her time. This is even more clearly the case in Mme Leprince de Beaumont's version of "Beauty and the Beast" (1757). It is to her credit that she was one of the first writers to compose eminently didactic fairy tales for young readers, particularly girls, to improve their social status. A governess in England for many years, she published *Le Magasin des enfants* (1757) in the form of a series of dialogues of a governess with her young pupils ranging in age from five to twelve. Interspersed with lessons in geography, history, and religion are about eighteen fairy tales that are metaphorical accounts of how proper moral and ethical behavior can bring about happiness for young ladies. While Mme Leprince de Beaumont advocated more equality and autonomy for women in society, her tales are contradictory insofar as they depict how girls should domesticate themselves, support men, and prove their worth through industriousness and good manners. It was through reading, dialogue, and lessons that girls could socialize themselves to advance their status in society, and Mme Leprince de Beaumont's "faith" in the power of reading the right reading material was to have a powerful effect on how fairy tales for children were to be composed and shaped in the latter part of the eighteenth century and up through the nineteenth century.

In fact, the French influence on the development of the literary fairy tale for young and old was prevalent throughout Europe and culminated in Charles-Joseph Mayer's remarkable forty-volume collection, *Cabinet des fées* (1785–89), which brought together a good deal of the most important fairy tales, including many of the Arabian tales by Galland, published during the past hundred years in France. Discreet if not prudish, Mayer excluded the erotic and satirical tales. Nevertheless, his collection, which was reprinted several times, had a profound influence because it was regarded as the culmination of an important trend and gathered tales that were representative and exemplary for the institution of a genre. Ironically, its most immediate impact was in Germany, where the literary fairy tale had not been flowering, and thanks to the French influence, it began to flourish in the last three decades of the eighteenth century. As Manfred Graetz has indicated in his significant study *Das Märchen in der deutschen Aufklärung. Vom Feenmärchen zum Volksmärchen*,[9] the German educated class was largely fluent in French and could read most of the French works in the original. However, German translations of numerous French fairy tales helped German writers to form their versions in their own language to establish the "German" literary genre in German-speaking principalities. It should be noted that most of these early translated tales were very free and could be considered adaptations. The first translations began as early as 1710, and they were based on Galland's *Thousand and One Nights*. Some of the other more important translations were Friedrich Eberhard Rambach's *Die Frau Maria le Prince de Beaumont Lehren der Tugend und Weisheit für die Jugend* (1758), based on Mme Leprince de Beaumont's *Le Magasin des enfants*; Wilhelm Christhelf Siegmund Mylius's *Drei hübsche kurzweilige Märlein* (1777), three fairy tales by Hamilton; Justin Bertuch's *Ammen-Mährchen* (1790), based on Perrault's *Histoires ou contes du temps passé*; and *Feen-Märchen der Frau Gräfin von Aulnoy*, four volumes (1790–96), fairy tales by Mme D'Aulnoy that appeared in Die Blaue Bibliothek. Most significant was the publication of the *Cabinet der Feen* (1761–66) in nine volumes translated by Friedrich Immanuel Bierling. This collection provided the German reading public with key French fairy tale texts and sparked imitations of different kinds. The work of Martin Christian Wieland was in part inspired by the French fairy tale, and he in turn was crucial as a cultural mediator. A famous German novelist and poet, closely associated with Weimar culture, Wie-

9. Stuttgart: Metzler, 1988. The one drawback in Graetz's work is that he discounts the influence of the oral tradition without adequately dealing with the diverse manner in which tales circulated in the medieval period up through the Enlightenment. Nor does he deal adequately with the concept of the "Volk," or people, as oral transmitters of tales.

land published an important collection of tales entitled *Dschinnistan* (1786–90), which included adaptations from the French *Cabinet des fées* as well as three original tales "Der Stein der Weisen" ("The Philosopher's Stone"), "Timander und Melissa," and "Der Druide oder die Salamanderin und die Bildsäule" ("The Druid or the Salamander and the Painted Pillar"). Typical of all these tales is the triumph of rationalism over mysticism. Among his other works that incorporated fairy tale motifs are *Der Sieg der Natur über die Schwärmerei oder die Abenteuer des Don Sylvio von Rosalva*,[1] (*The Victory of Nature over Fanaticism; or, The Adventures of Don Sylvio von Rosalva*, 1764), *Der goldene Spiegel* (*The Golden Mirror*, 1772), and *Oberon* (1780). In addition, he wrote "Pervonte" (1778/79), a remarkable verse rendition of Basile's "Peruonto," which concerns a poor simpleton whose heart is so good that he is blessed by the fairies and thus rises in society. Minor writers (Friedrich Maximilian Klinger, Christoph Wilhelm Guenther, Albert Ludwig Grimm, Friedrich Schulz) as well as major writers were influenced by the French vogue, German translations, and Wieland's works. Though Johann Karl August Musäus called his important collection of fairy tales *Volksmärchen der Deutschen* (*Folk tales of the Germans*, 1782–86) and Benedikte Naubert entitled her volume *Neue Volksmärchen der Deutschen* (*New Folktales of the Germans*, 1789–93), these works and others were pan-European and were also influenced by translations of Oriental tales into French and German. One of the first important collections for young readers, *Palmblätter* (*Palm Leaves*, 1786–90), four volumes edited by August Jakob Liebeskind with contributions by Johann Gottfried Herder and Friedrich Adolf Krummacher, had the subtitle "erlesene morgendländische Erzählungen" ("selected oriental stories"), and one of the key Romantic texts by Wilhelm Heinrich Wackenroder had the title "Ein wunderbares morgendländisches Märchen von einem nackten Heiligen" ("A Wondrous Oriental Tale of a Naked Saint," 1799).

In fact, by the time the German Romantics came on the literary scene, the fairy tale had been more or less well established in Germany, and they could abandon the conventional structure and themes and begin to experiment in a vast number of ways. All the major Romantic writers, Ludwig Tieck, Novalis, Clemens Brentano, Achim von Arnim, Joseph von Eichendorff, Friedrich de la Motte Fouqué, Adelbert Chamisso, and E. T. A. Hoffmann, wrote fairy tales that reveal a great familiarity with the French and oriental literary tradition as well as the oral tradition and folklore in Germany. Tieck composed a series of fairy tale plays, *Der gestiefelte Kater* (*Puss in Boots*, 1797), *Die verkehrte Welt* (*The Topsy-Turvy World*, 1799), *Der Blaubart* (*Bluebeard*, 1797), *Rotkäppchen* (*Little Red Riding Hood*, 1800), *Däumling* (*Thumbling*, 1812), and *Fortunat* (1816), that were based largely on Perrault's stories. However, his plays are more ex-

1. This fascinating fairy tale novel was translated into French and included in the *Cabinet des fées*. Wieland had an ambivalent attitude toward the fairy tale. In this novel, he depicts how a young man is too easily carried away by his imagination and warns against having too much fantasy. At the same time, Wieland incorporates a highly unusual fairy tale into the novel and employs fairy tale motifs in innovative ways. After writing this novel, he did not abandon the fairy tale, and it is interesting from the viewpoint of cultural interconnections that his novel, influenced by the French, should then be translated into French as part of the *Cabinet des fées*.

traordinary parodies that toyed with audience expectations and combined motifs from the literary and oral tradition in unconventional ways. His "Little Red Riding Hood," which the Grimms knew, was turned into a serious tragedy with an apparent commentary on the French Revolution. Almost all the Romantic tales reflected social conditions during the Napoleonic wars and French occupation of Germany. Clemens Brentano, a good friend of the Brothers Grimm and a staunch German patriot, began experimenting with Basile's *Pentamerone* about 1805 and planned to adapt twenty or more tales in German. He succeeded in rewriting only eleven. Some were published separately during his lifetime, and after his death they were published as *Italienische Märchen (Italian Fairy Tales)* in 1845.

Brentano, who was also a talented lyric poet, is a pivotal figure in the development of the Grimms' collection. In 1805 he published *Des Knaben Wunderhorn (The Boy's Wunderhorn)*, an important book of German folksongs, with Achim von Arnim, and he wanted to produce a similar book of folktales and sought help from various contributors. In 1806 he turned to the Brothers Grimm, who, by that time, had collected a great deal of material pertaining to German folklore. They agreed to save tales for Brentano, and between 1807 and 1812 they gathered approximately forty-nine tales from oral and written sources. Ironically, the tales did not come directly from the "simple folk," but from educated aristocratic and middle-class informants. For instance, in Kassel there was a group of young women from the Wild family (Dortchen, Gretchen, Lisette, and Marie Elisabeth) and their mother, Dorothea, and young women (Ludowine, Jeanette, and Marie) from the Hassenpflug family. They gathered together regularly to relate tales that they had read or heard from their nursemaids, governesses, and servants. In 1808 Jacob formed a friendship with Werner von Haxthausen in Westphalia, and he and Wilhelm visited the Haxthausen estate and recorded tales from a group of young men and women. Other important informants in Kassel were Dorothea Viehmann, a tailor's wife, and Johann Friedrich Krause, an old retired soldier. Many of the tales that the Grimms collected were French in origin because the Hassenpflugs were of Huguenot ancestry and spoke French at home. In addition, the French occupied the Rhineland during this time, and there was a strong French influence throughout this region. In short, from the beginning, the Grimms did not make great distinctions with regard to the "nationality" of their tales, nor did they rule out literary tales. Their "folk" included every social class of people. Just as the formation of the literary genre emanated from the mutual influence and interchange of the oral and literary tales that circulated in the medieval period, the Grimms' collection was drawn from the same sources.

In 1810, Brentano requested that the Grimms forward the tales that they had gathered to him, and they copied down forty-nine stories that were in rough form and kept a copy for themselves. By this time, they were skeptical of Brentano's project and feared that he might tamper with the tales and change them into poetic literary versions. Ironically, Brentano had lost interest in compiling a collection of folktales, whereas it was the Grimms who transformed the tales into exquisite literary narratives. Through some kind of oversight, Brentano left the forty-nine tales in the Ölenberg Monastery in Alsace, while the Grimms destroyed theirs after using it as the basis for the first edition of the *Kinder- und Hausmärchen* (*Children's and Household Tales*), published in two volumes in 1812 and 1815. Therefore, it is thanks to Brentano that we can understand how the Grimms altered the tales. His copy of the manuscript, now known as the Ölenberg manuscript, was first rediscovered in 1920 and published in different editions in 1924, 1927, and 1974.[2]

The first two volumes of *Children's and Household Tales* contained 156 tales and copious notes in the appendixes and were not at all intended for children. It was not until 1819, when the second edition appeared in one volume with 170 texts with the notes published separately, that the Grimms decided to cater to young readers as well as to a growing middle-class reading audience of adults. After the publication of the second edition, there were five more editions until 1857 as well as ten printings of a smaller edition of 50 tales. The final edition of 1857 contained 210 tales, which had been carefully stylized by Wilhelm so that they reflected what he and Jacob considered a popular "folk" tone and genuine customs and beliefs that the German people had cultivated. Like Basile, they made ample use of proverbs, for they felt that the truth of experience was to be found through the sayings and rituals of the folk and their metaphorical narratives.

The folk, as we know, is an imagined corpus just as the notion of a nation, and though the Grimms deceived themselves by believing there was something essentially German about their tales, there was something admirable in their endeavor to create a body of tales through which all Germans, young and old, could relate and develop a sense of community. This was their utopian and idealistic gesture in the name of democratic nationalism. But they certainly knew that their tales were very pan-European and contained strong Oriental influences. Just a look at the notes published separately in 1856 reveals how knowledgeable they were about the historical development of the fairy tale. There are important entries in the "Literatur" section on Straparola, Basile, Perrault, Mme d'Aulnoy, and the entire French school as well as short commentaries on the fairy tale in Spain, England, Scotland, Ireland, Greece, Sweden, Denmark, the Slavic countries, and the Orient. The Grimms saw in the tales from other countries numerous parallels and similarities that they could trace in their "German tales." Little did they know that these "foreign" ingredients were going to help their collection become the most famous anthology of fairy tales throughout the entire world. Indeed, the appeal of their tales may have something to do with the history of their cross-cultural connections.

In 1823 Edgar Taylor translated a selection of the Grimms' tales as *German Popular Stories* with illustrations by the famous George Cruikshank. The book was an immediate success, and there was a second printing in 1826. From that time on, there have been hundreds if not thousands of translations of the Grimms' tales in English and other languages

---

2. The most important edition is Heinz Rölleke, ed., *Die älteste Märchensammlung der Brüder Grimm* (Cologny-Geneva: Fondation Martin Bodmer, 1975). Rölleke's thorough scholarship enables us to trace the sources of the tales and to see the great changes in style and content that the Grimms made in preparing them for publication.

throughout the world. In 1868, John Ruskin, whose quaint fairy tale "The King of the Golden River" was greatly influenced by the Grimms, wrote an introduction to an enlarged edition of *German Popular Stories*, in which he stated: "For every fairy tale worth recording at all is the remnant of a tradition possessing true historical value;—historical, at least in so far as it has naturally arisen out of the mind of a people under special circumstances, and risen not without meaning, nor removed altogether from their sphere of religious faith. It sustains afterwards natural chances from the sincere action of the fear or fancy of successive generations; it takes new colour from their manner of life, and new form from their changing moral tempers. As long as these changes are natural and effortless, accidental and inevitable, the story remains essentially true, altering its form, indeed, like a flying cloud, but remaining a sign of the sky; a shadowy image, as truly part of the great firmament of the human mind as the light of reason which it seems to interrupt. But the fair deceit and innocent error of it cannot be interpreted nor restrained by a wilful purpose, and all additions to it by art do but defile, as the shepherd disturbs the flakes of morning mist with smoke from his fire of dead leaves."[3]

This is a curious statement from an author who used his art willfully to transform what he believed to be folklore from the Grimms into one of the most well-known and imaginative fairy tales of the Victorian period. But, despite its contradiction, Ruskin put his finger on what lies behind the constant transformation and transmission of fairy tales. Historically specific, they have indeed arisen out of the minds of human beings in search for the truth of their experiences, and they have been passed on through word of mouth and the written word. With each repetition through the oral and literary traditions that mutually influenced one another, diverse cultural experiences became intertwined and interlaced, and they formed the foundations of the Grimms' collection and other collections to follow.

The Grimms' *Children's and Household Tales* was not the culmination of the oral and literary tradition, but it did bring together representative tales in a style and ideology that suited middle-class taste throughout Europe and North America, and the subsequent value of the tales has been determined by the manner in which people throughout the world have regarded them as universal and classic. Although it is difficult to gather accurate figures, the Grimms' tales are probably the most reprinted and best known in the world and serve as reference points for all kinds of cultural productions for opera, theater, radio, cinema, mass media, and advertising. The metaphorical manner of our speech communication and modes in which we reflect upon ourselves incorporate fairy tale lore as we frequently seek to make our lives like fairy tales. Though we do not realize it, we bring ourselves closer to people from many different cultures through the cross-cultural connections of the tales, even though we endow them with our own specific individual and cultural meanings as we appropriate them. There was never such a thing as a "pure" folktale or a

3. Edgar Taylor, ed., *German Popular Stories*, intr. John Ruskin (London: John Camden Hotten, 1868) ix–x.

"pure" fairy tale. The genuine quality of all folk and fairy tales, as the present collection hopes to make clear, depends very much on their original contamination.

W. G. WATERS

[The Mysterious Giovan Francesco Straparola, Founding Father of the Fairy Tale]†

The name of Giovanni Francesco Straparola has been handed down to later ages as the author of the "Piacevoli Notti" (Facetious Nights), and on no other account, for the reason that he is one of those fortunate men of letters concerning whom next to nothing is known. He writes himself down as "da Caravaggio;" so it may be reasonably assumed that he first saw the light in that town, but no investigator has yet succeeded in indicating the year of his birth, or in bringing to light any circumstances of his life, other than certain facts connected with the authorship and publication of his works. The ground has been closely searched more than once, and in every case the seekers have come back compelled to admit that they have no story to tell or new fact to add to the scanty stock which has been already garnered. Straparola as a personage still remains the shadow he was when La Monnoie summed up the little that was known about him in the preface to the edition, published in 1725, of the French translation of the "Notti."

He was doubtless baptized by the Christian names given above, but it is scarcely probable that Straparola can ever have been the surname or style of any family in Caravaggio or elsewhere. More likely than not it is an instance of the Italian predilection for nicknaming,—a coined word designed to exhibit and perhaps to hold up to ridicule his undue loquacity; just as the familiar names of Masaccio, and Ghirlandaio, and Guercino, were tacked on to their illustrious wearers on account of some personal peculiarity or former calling. Caravaggio is a small town lying near to Crema, and about half way between Cremona and Bergamo. It enjoyed in the Middle Ages some fame as a place of pilgrimage on account of a spring of healing water which gushed forth on a certain occasion when the Virgin Mary manifested herself. Polidoro Caldara and Michael Angelo Caravaggio were amongst its famous men, and of these it keeps the memory, but Straparola is entirely forgotten. Fontanini, in the "Biblioteca dell' eloquenza Italiana,"[1] does not name him at all. Quadrio, "Storia e ragione d'ogni poesia,"[2] mentions him as the author of the "Piacevoli Notti," and remarks on his borrowings from Morlini. Tiraboschi, in the index to the

---

† Originally published as "Terminal Essay" in vol. IV of *The Facetious Nights of Straparola*, 4 vols. (London: The Society of Bibliophiles, 1891) 237–74.
1. *Library of Italian Eloquence* (Italian).
2. *The History and Discourse of Every Poetry* (Italian).

"Storia della letteratura Italiana,"[3] does not even give his name, and Crescimbeni concerns himself only with the enigmas which are to be found at the end of the fables. It is indeed a strange freak of chance that such complete oblivion should have fallen over the individuality of a writer so widely read and appreciated.

The first edition of the first part of the "Piacevoli Notti" was published at Venice in 1550, and of the second part in 1553. It would appear that the author must have been alive in 1557, because, at the end of the second part of the edition of that year, there is a paragraph setting forth the fact that the work was printed and issued "ad instanza dell' autore."[4] Some time before 1553 he seems to have been stung sharply on account of some charges of plagiarism which were brought against him by certain detractors, for in all the unmutilated editions of the "Notti" published after that date there is to be found a short introduction to the second part, in which he somewhat acrimoniously throws back these accusations, and calls upon all "gratiose et amorevole donne"[5] to accept his explanations thereof, admitting at the same time that these stories are not his own, but a faithful transcript of what he heard told by the ten damsels in their pleasant assembly. La Monnoie, in his preface to the French translation (ed. 1726), maintains that this juggling with words can only be held to be an excuse on his part for having borrowed the subject-matter for his fables and worked it into shape after his own taste. "Il declare qu'il ne se les est jamais attribuées, et se contente du mérite de les avoir fidèlement rapportées d'après les dix damoiselles. Cela, comme tout bon entendeur le comprend, ne signifie autre chose sinon qu'il avoit tiré d'ailleurs la matière de ces Fables, mais qu'il leur avoit donné la forme."[6]

This contention of La Monnoie seems reasonable enough, but Grimm, in the notes to "Kinder und Hausmärchen," has fallen into the strange error of treating Straparola's apology as something grave and seriously meant, and in the same sentence improves on his mistake by asserting that Straparola took all the fairy tales from the mouths of the ten ladies. "Von jenem Schmutz sind die Märchen ziemlich frei, wie sie ohnehin den besten Theil des ganzen Werkes ausmachen. Straparola hat sie, wie es in der Vorrede zum zweiten Bande (vor der sechsten Nacht) heisst, aus dem Munde zehn junger Fräulein aufgenommen und ausdrücklich erklärt, dass sie nicht sein Eigenthum seien."[7]

The most reasonable explanation of this mistake lies in the assumption that Grimm never saw the introduction to the second part at all. Indeed, the fact that he often uses French spelling of the proper names suggests that he may have worked from the French translation. Straparola makes

3. *History of Italian Literature* (Italian).
4. At the insistence of the author (Italian).
5. Gracious and lovely ladies (Italian).
6. He declares that he never attributed them to himself, and he is just content to have had the honor of having faithfully recorded the tales the way the ten damsels told them. As any good listener knows, this can only mean that he borrowed the subject matter for his tales and then gave them their form (French).
7. The tales are quite devoid of vulgarity, and they make for the best part of the entire work. As Straparola says in the preface to the second volume (right before the sixth night), he took the tales from the mouths of ten young ladies, and he explicitly explains that they were not his own (German).

no distinction between fairy tales and others. His words are, "che le piacevoli favole da me scritte, et in questo, et nell' altro volumetto raccolte
non siano mie, ma da questo, et quello ladronescamente rubbate. Io a dir
il vero, il confesso, che non sono mie, e se altrimente dicessi, me ne
mentirei, ma ben holle fedelmente scritte secondo il modo che furono da
dieci damigelle nel concistorio raccontate."[8]

Besides the "Notti" only one other work of Straparola's is known to
exist—a collection of sonnets and other poems published at Venice in
1508, and (according to a citation of Zanetti in the "Novelliero Italiano,"
t. iii., p. xv., Ven. 1754, Bindoni) in 1515 as well. A comparison of these
dates will serve to show that, as he had already brought out a volume in
the first decade of the century, the "Piacevoli Notti" must have been the
work of his maturity or even of his old age. With this fact the brief catalogue of the known circumstances of his life comes to an end.

Judging from the rapidity with which the successive editions of the
"Notti" were brought forth from the press after the first issue—sixteen
appeared in the twenty years between 1550 and 1570—we may with reason
assume that it soon took hold of the public favour. Its fame spread early
into France, where in 1560 an edition of the first part, translated into
French by Jean Louveau, appeared at Lyons, to be followed some thirteen
years later by a translation of the second part by Pierre de la Rivey, who
thus completed the book. He likewise revised and re-wrote certain portions
of Louveau's translation, and in 1725 an edition was produced at Amsterdam, enriched by a preface by La Monnoie, and notes by Lainez. There
are evidences that a German translation of the "Notti" was in existence at
the beginning of the seventeenth century, for in the introduction to Fischart's "Gargantua" (1608) there is an allusion to the tales of Straparola,
brought in by way of an apology for the appearance of the work, the writer
maintaining that, if the ears of the ladies are not offended by Boccaccio,
Straparola, and other writers of a similar character, there is no reason why
they should be offended by Rabelais. The author of the introduction to a
fresh edition of the same work (1775) remarks that he knows the tales of
Straparola from a later edition published in 1699. Of this translation no
copy is known to exist.

In the "Palace of Pleasure" Painter has given only one of the fables, the
second Fable of the second Night; and in Roscoe's "Italian Novelists"
another one appears, the fourth Fable of the tenth Night. At the end of
the last century the first Fable of the first Night was printed separately in
London under the title, "Novella cioe copia d'un Caso notabile interven-
uto a un gran gentiluomo Genovese."[9] A translation of twenty-four of the
fables, prefaced by a lengthy and verbose disquisition on the author, reputed to be from the pen of Mazzuchelli, appeared at Vienna in 1791;
but Brackelmann, in his "Inaugural Dissertation" (Gottingen, 1867), has

8. That the pleasant tales which I have written and collected in this volume and in the other small
   one are not mine but stories that I have feloniously stolen from various people. To tell the truth,
   I confess they are not mine, and if I were to say otherwise, I would be lying. However, I have
   faithfully written them down according to the manner in which they were told by the ten ladies
   during our gatherings (Italian).
9. Novella, or the transcription of a remarkable event involving a great gentleman of Genoa (Italian).

an examination of the introduction above named, which goes far to prove that Mazzuchelli had little or nothing to do with it. In 1817 Dr. F. W. V. Schmidt published at Berlin a translation into German of eighteen fables selected from the "Notti," to which he gave the title "Die Märchen des Straparola."[1] To his work Dr. Schmidt affixed copious notes, compiled with the greatest care and learning, thus opening to his successors a rich and valuable storehouse both of suggestion and of accumulated facts. It is almost certain that he must have worked from one of the many mutilated or expurgated editions of the book, for in the complete work there are several stories unnoticed by him which he would assuredly have included in his volume had he been aware of their existence.

Four of Straparola's fables are slightly altered versions of four of the stories in the "Thousand and One Nights," which, as it will scarcely be necessary to remark, were not translated into any European language till Galland brought out his work at the beginning of the eighteenth century. One of these, the third Fable of the fourth Night, is substantially the same as the story of the Princess Parizade and her envious sisters, given in Galland's translation. To account for this close resemblance we may either assume that Galland may have looked at Straparola's fable, or that Straparola may have listened to it from the mouth of some wandering oriental or of some Venetian traveller recently come back from the East—the tale, as he heard it, having been faithfully taken from the same written page which Galland afterwards translated. Another one, the story of the Three Hunchbacks—the third Fable of the fifth Night—has less likeness to the original, and has been imitated by Gueulette in his "Contes Tartares." The treatment of the story of the Princess Parizade by Straparola furnishes an illustration to prove that he was by no means deficient in literary skill and taste. He brings into due prominence the wicked midwife, who is *particeps criminis* with the queen-mother and the sisters in the attempted murder of the children, and who has on this account full and valid motive for acting as she did, seeing that interest and self-preservation as well would have prompted her to compass their destruction. On the other hand, in the Arabian tale it is hard to understand why the female fakir should have been led to persuade the princess to send her brothers off on their quest. Again, in the fable of Prince Guerrino Straparola has displayed great ingenuity in weaving together a good story out of some half-dozen of the widely-known fairy motives, any one of which might well have been fashioned into a story by itself.

After reading the "Facetious Nights" through one can hardly fail to be struck by the amazing variety of the themes therein handled. Besides the fairy tales—*many of them classic*—to which allusion has already been made, there is *the world-famous story* of "Puss in Boots," an original product of Straparola's brain. There are others which may rather be classed as romances of chivalry, in the elaboration of which a generous amount of magic and mystery is employed. The residue is made up of stories of intrigue and buffo tales of popular Italian life, some of which are fulsome in subject and broad in treatment, but with regard to the majority of these

---

1. *The Fairy Tales of Straparola.*

one is disposed to be lenient, inasmuch as the fun, though somewhat indelicate, is real fun. When the duped husband, a figure almost as inevitable in the Italian Novella as in the modern French novel, is brought forward, he is not always exhibited as the contemptible creature who seems to have sat for the part in the stories of the better known writers. Indeed, it sometimes happens that he turns the tables on his betrayers; and, although Straparola is laudably free from the vice of preaching, he now and then indulges in a brief homily by way of pointing out the fact that violators of the Decalogue generally come to a bad end, and that his own sympathies are all on the side of good manners. It is true that one misses in the "Notti" those delicious invocations of Boccaccio, commonly to be found at the end of the more piquant stories, in which he piously calls on Heaven to grant to himself and to all Christian men *bonnes fortunes* equal to those which he has just chronicled.

In the Proem to the work it is set forth how Ottaviano Maria Sforza, the bishop-elect of Lodi—the same probably who died in 1540, after a life full of vicissitude—together with his daughter Lucretia, is compelled by the stress of political events to quit Milan. The Signora Lucretia is described as the wife of Giovanni Francesco Gonzaga, cousin of Federico, Marquis of Mantua, but as no mention of this prince is made it may be assumed that she was already a widow. Seeing that her husband died in 1523, an approximate date may be fixed for the "Piacevoli Notti," but historical accuracy in cases of this sort is not to be expected or desired. After divers wanderings the bishop elect and his daughter find a pleasant refuge on the island of Murano, where they gather around them a company of *congenial spirits*, consisting of a group of *lovely and accomplished damsels, and divers cavaliers* of note. Chief amongst the latter is the learned Pietro Bembo, the renowned humanist and *the most distinguished man of letters* Venice ever produced. With him came his friend Gregorio Casali, who is described as "Casal Bolognese, a bishop, and likewise ambassador of the King of England." Both Gregorio Casali and his brother Battista were entrusted by Henry VIII, with the conduct of affairs of state pending between him and the Pope, and the former certainly visited England more than once. The king showed him many signs of favour during his stay, and when in 1527 Casali found himself shut up in Rome by the beleaguering army of the Constable of Bourbon, he was allowed free exit on the ground of his ambassadorial rank. Bernardo Cappello, another friend of Bembo, is also of the company, and a certain Antonio Molino, *a poet of repute*, who subsequently tells a fable in the dialect of Bergamo—a feat which leads to a similar display of local knowledge on the part of Signor Benedetto Trivigiano, who discourses in Trevisan. It may be remarked, however, that by far the greater number of the fables are told by the ladies.

But the joyous company assembled in the palace at Murano find divers other forms of recreation beside story-telling. They dance and they sing ballads, which are for the most part in praise of the gracious Signora Lucretia, but *the chief byplay of the entertainment* consists in the setting and solving of riddles. As soon as a fable is brought to an end the narrator is always called upon by the Signora to complete the task by propounding an enigma. This is then duly set forth in puzzling verses, put together as a rule in terms obscure enough to baffle solution, often entirely senseless, and now and again of a character fulsome enough to call down upon the propounder the Signora's rebuke on account of the seeming impropriety of the subject. A certain number of these enigmas are broad examples of the *double entendre*. The first reading of them makes one agree with the Signora, but when the graceful and modest damsel, who may have been the author, proceeds to give the true explanation of her riddle she never fails to demonstrate clearly to the gentle company that her enigma, from beginning to end, is entirely free from all that is unseemly. In "French and English" Mr. Philip Gilbert Hamerton tells a story illustrating the late survival of this sort of witticism in France. In the early days of Louis Philippe, on one occasion when the court was at Eu, the mayor of the town and certain other local notables were bidden to *déjeuner* at the chateau, and after banquet the mayor, in accordance with an old French fashion, asked leave to sing a song of his own making. This composition had two meanings, one lying on the surface and perfectly innocent, and the other, slightly veiled, which, though not immoral, was prodigiously indecent. When the true nature of the song was realized, there was for a second or two silence and confusion amongst the company; but at last, by good luck, someone laughed. The dangerous point was safely rounded, and the mayor brought his song to an end amidst loud applause.

When he published his translation into French of the second part of the "Notti," Pierre de la Rivey made alterations in almost all the enigmas therein contained, and re-wrote many of those which had already been translated by Louveau, but in neither case did his work tend to improve them.

Notwithstanding the foregoing, there will be found in the "Notti" a smaller proportion of stories objectionable to modern canons of taste than in any of the better known collections of Italian *novelle*. The judgments which have been dealt out to Straparola on the score of ribaldry by Landau, by the writer of the article in the "Biographie Universelle," and by Grimm in his notes to "Kinder und Hausmärchen," seem to be unduly severe. In certain places he is no doubt somewhat broad, but the number of these fables is not large. If one were to take the trouble to compare the rendering given by Basile in the "Pentamerone," of stories told also by Straparola, with the rendering of the same in the "Notti," the award for propriety of language would assuredly not always be given to the Neapolitan, who, it should be remembered, was writing a book for young children. In few of the collections of a similar character is there to be found so genuine a vein of comedy, and for the sake of this one may perhaps be permitted to beg indulgence for occasional lapses—lapses which are assuredly fewer in number and probably not more lax in character than those of novelists of greater fame. Straparola turns naturally towards *the cheerful side of things*, the lives of the men and women he deals with seem to be less oppressed with the *tædium vitæ* than are the creatures of the Florentine and Sienese and Neapolitan novel-writers, and the reason of this is not far to seek. Life in Venice, when once the political constitution was firmly and finally fixed on an oligarchic basis, was more stable, more secure, more luxurious than in any of the other ruling cities of Italy. Social and political convulsion of the sort which vexed the neighbouring states was almost unknown, and, though the forces of the Republic might occasionally suffer defeat and disaster in distant seas and in the Levant, life went on peacefully and pleasantly within the shelter of the Lagunes. The religious conscience of the people was easy-going, orthodox, and laudably inclined to listen to the voice of authority; neither disposed to nourish within the hidden canker of heresy, nor to let itself be worked up into ecstatic fever by any sudden conviction of ungodliness such as led to the lighting of the Bonfire of Vanities in Florence. In a society thus constituted it was inevitable that life should be easier, more gladsome, and more secure than in Milan, with the constant struggle of Pope against Emperor, and later on under the turbulent despotism of the Viscontis and Sforzas; or that in Florence, with its constant civil broils and licentious public life, which not even the craft and power of the leaders of the Medici could discipline into public order; or than in Naples, dominated by the Aragonese kings and harried by the greedy mercenaries in the royal employ; or than in Rome itself, vexed continually by intrigue, political and religious, and by the tumults generated by the violence and ambition of the ruling families.

A reflection of the gracious and placid life the Venetians led will be apparent to all who may observe and compare the art of Venice with the art of Milan, or Florence, or Naples. What a contrast is there between that charming idyll which Titian has made of the marriage of St. Catherine, a group full of joy, and beauty, and sunlight, and set in the midst of one of those delightful subalpine landscapes which he painted with such rare skill and insight, and the many other renderings of the same subject by Lombard or Tuscan masters, who, almost invariably, put on the canvas some foreshadowing of the coming tragedy in the shape of the boding horror of the toothed wheel! The Madonnas of Carpaccio and Bellini are stately ladies, well nourished, and having about them that unmistakable air of distinction which grows up with the daily use and neighbourhood of splendid and luxurious modes of life. There is no doubt a look of gravity and holiness upon their handsome faces, but there is no sign, either in the pose or in the glance of them, that they are conscious of any embarrassment, and it would take a very keen eye to discern a trace of quasi-divinity, or of any trouble aroused by the caress of the mysterious child, or of the burden of that "intolerable honour" which has been thrust upon them unsought—a mood which latter-day preachers have detected in renderings of the same theme conceived and executed in the more emotional atmosphere of the Val d'Arno. Take these Venetian Madonnas out of their pictured environment, and put on them a gala dress and sumptuous jewels, and one will find a bevy of comely dames who might well have kept company with the Signora Lucretia of the "Notti" in the fair garden at Murano, and listened to some sprightly story from Messer Pietro Bembo or from Messer Antonio Molino; or they might have gone out with the youths and damsels of whom Browning sings,

"Did young people take their pleasure when the sea was warm in May?
Balls and masks began at midnight, burning ever to mid-day,
When they made up fresh adventures for the morrow, do you say?"

In the pictures he draws Straparola illustrates a life like this, with now and then a touch of pathos, perhaps undesigned, as in the prologue to the second Night, *where he tells of the laughter of the blithe company*, ringing so loud and so hearty that it seemed to him as if the sound of their merriment yet lingered in his ears. There was, therefore, good reason why Straparola's imaginary exiles from the turbulent court of Milan should have sought at Murano, under the sheltering wings of St. Mark's lion, that ease and gaiety which they would have looked for in vain at home; there were also reasons equally valid why he should make the genius of the place inspire with its jocund spirit the stories with which the gentle company gathered around the Signora Lucretia wiled away the nights of carnival. In the whole of the seventy-four fables there are hardly half-a-dozen which can be classed as tragic in tone, but of these one, the story of Malgherita Spolatina, is the finest of the whole collection. It is rarely one meets with anything told with such force and sincerity; yet, in placing before his readers this vivid picture of volcanic passion and studied ruthless revenge, Straparola uses the simplest treatment and succeeds *à merveille*. The fact that this fable and certain others of more than average merit belong to the category of stories to which no source or origin in other writings has been assigned, raises a regret that Straparola did not trust more to his own inventive powers and draw less freely upon Ser Giovanni and Morlini. Of these creations of his own the story of Flamminio Veraldo is admirably told and strikingly original and dramatic in subject; so is that of Maestro Lattantio, and, for a display of savage cynicism and withering rage, it would be hard to find anything more powerfully portrayed than the death of Andrigetto.

In the fables of adventure, and in every other case where such treatment is possible, Straparola deals largely with the supernatural. All the western versions, except Straparola's, of the story best known to us as "Giletta of Narbonne" and as "All's Well that Ends Well," are worked out without calling in auxiliaries of an unearthly character. Boccaccio and Shakespeare bring together the husband and the forsaken wife by methods which, if somewhat strained, are quite natural; but Straparola at once calls for the witch and the magic horse, and whisks Isabella off to Flanders forthwith. The interest of the reader is kept alive by accounts of the trials and dangers—a trifle bizarre now and again—which heroes and heroines are called to undergo, the taste of the age preferring apparently this stimulant to *the intense dramatic power exhibited in the story of Malgherita*, and demanding that the ending should be a happy one, for the pair of lovers nearly always marry in the end, and live long and blissful years. In the tales of country life and character *the fun is boisterous and even broad, but it is always real fun*, and the laugh rings true. Straparola is often as broad as Bandello, but, unlike Bandello, he never smirches his pages merely for the sake of setting forth some story of simple brutality, or of leading up to a climax which is at the same time painfully shocking and purposeless. Il

Lasca in "Le Cene" makes as free use of the *beffe* and the *burle* as Straparola, but the last-named showed in the "Notti" that *he was incomparably the better hand* in dealing with his material. Il Lasca as a rule sets out his subject on the lines of the broadest farce, but he cannot keep to genuine farce, his natural bent of mind leading him always to elaborate his theme in some unseemly and offensive fashion. Very often he is obscene and savage at the same time, and the abominable practical jokes he makes his characters play the one on the other must surely have outraged even the coarse feeding taste of the age in which he wrote. He delights in working up long stories of lust, and of infidelity, and of vengeance worked on account of these, in a spirit of heartless cruelty which, more often than not, is horrible without being in the least impressive, for the reason that, fine stylist as he was, he lacked the touch of the artist. Masuccio, though his savage indignation against the vices of the priests and monks occasionally became mere brutality, sounded now and then the note of real tragedy, and, inferior as he was to Il Lasca in style, was by far the better story-teller of the two. Both of these would be commonly set down as, abler writers than Straparola, yet, by some means or other, *the latter could put a touch upon his work which was beyond the power of the others*—something *which enables one to read* the "Notti" without being conscious of that unpleasant aftertaste which one almost always feels on laying down either "Le Cene" or "Il Novellino."

Straparola's Italian is much more like the Italian of the present day than the English of Sidney or the German of Hans Sachs is like modern English or German, but this is not remarkable, considering how much earlier prose writing as an art came to perfection in Italy than in the rest of Europe. The impression gained by reading his prose is that he cared vastly more for the subject than for treatment. He laid hold of whatever themes promised to suit his purpose best as a story-teller, careless as to whether other craftsmen had used them before or not, and these he set forth in the simplest manner possible, taking little heed of his style or even of his grammar. He hardly ever indulges in a metaphor. One never feels that he has gone searching about fastidiously for some particular turn of phrase or neatly-fitting adjective; on the other hand, one is often obliged to pause in the middle of some long sentence and search for his meaning in the strange mixture of phrases strung together. Perhaps this spontaneity, this absence of studied design, may have helped to win for him the wide popularity he enjoyed. His aim was to lead his readers into some enchanted garden of fairyland; to thrill them with the woes and perils of his heroes and heroines; to shake their sides with laughter over the misadventures of some too amorous monk or lovesick cavalier, rather than to send them into ecstasy over the measured elegance of his phrases. In many of the later editions of the "Notti," the meaning has been further obscured, and the style rendered more rugged than ever, owing to the frequent and clumsy excisions made by the censors of morals. The early exclusion of the fourth Fable of the ninth Night shows that the eye of authority was soon attracted towards the popular novelist of the age. The motive for this activity was nominally the care of public morals, and one of the few extant references to Straparola is with regard to the expurgation of his works. In

"Cremona Illustrata," by Franciscus Arisius (Cremona, 1741), we read concerning Caravaggio: "In hoc enim oppido inclytæ stirpis Sfortiadum antiquo feudo ortum habuit Io. Franciscus Straparola cujus liber sæpe editus circumfertur italice hoc programmate: 'Le tredici piacevolissime notti overo favole ed enimmi.' Liber vetitus a sacra indicis congregatione et jure quidem merito cum obscenitates sordidas contineat moribus plerumque obnoxias et pluribi vulgatas. Optime quippe animadvertit Possevinus S. J. de cultura ingeniorum cap. 52, quod expediens esset homines potius nasci mutos et rationis expertes, quam in propriam et aliorum perniciam divinæ providentiæ dona convertere, imo ante eum ejusdem sententiæ fuisse M. F. Quintilianum licet gentilem, ipse Possevinus confirmat."

On reading even the most severely castrated edition of the "Notti," one may be at first a little surprised to find that some of the most fulsome stories have been left almost untouched, and it is not until one realizes the fact that expurgation has been held to mean the cutting out of every word *concerning religion and its professors*, that one fully understands the principle upon which "Possevinus S. J." and his colleagues worked. The presence of matter injurious to public morals had evidently less to do with the action of these reformers than certain anecdotes describing the presence of priests and nuns in certain places where, by every rule of good manners, they ought not to have been found. In plain words, the book was prohibited and castrated on account of the ugly picture of clerical morals which was exhibited in its pages. A glance at any of the editions issued "con licenza de' superiori" will show that the revisers went to their work with set purpose, caring nought as to the mangled mass of letterpress they might leave behind them. In some fables bits are cut out so clumsily that the point of the story is entirely lost; in others the feelings of orthodoxy are spared by changing the hero of amorous intrigue from a *Prete* to a *Giovene*. In one a pope is reduced to a mere initial (of course standing for a layman), and the famous story of Belphegor is left out altogether. It was surely little short of impertinent to ask for a condemnation of the "Notti" on the ground of offence to public decency from a generation which read such books as "Les facétieuses journées" of Chapuys and "Les contes aux heures perdues;" which witnessed the issue of Morlini's novels and of Cinthio degli Fabritii's book, "Dell' origine delli volgari proverbii,"[2] printed "cum privilegio summi pontificis et sacræ Cæsareæ majestatis;" a generation for which Poggio's obscene fables were favourite reading, and which remembered that Pietro Bembo had been a cardinal and Giovanni di Medici a pope.

It is impossible to indicate precisely the sources of the fables *seriatim*, seeing that in many cases there was available for Straparola a choice of origins. An approximate reckoning would give fifteen fables to the novelists who preceded him, twenty-two to Jerome Morlini, four to mediæval and seven to oriental legends, thus leaving twenty-eight to be classed as original. From beginning to end he certainly made free use of all the storehouses of materials which were available, selecting therefrom whatever subjects

2. On the Origins of Vulgar Proverbs (Italian).

pleased him, and working them up to the best of his skill. It was unrea-
sonable to censure him on this score, seeing that in what he did he merely
followed the fashion of the age. He borrowed from Ser Giovanni, and Ser
Giovanni borrowed also from the "Directorium" and the "Gesta Romanorum." Folk-lorists have discovered for us the fact that all the stories the
world ever listened to may, by proper classification, be shown to be derived
from some half-dozen sources. As the sorting and searching goes on, new
facts constantly come to light, the drift of which tends to prove that the
charge of plagiarism is now almost meaningless. It is hard to say what new
and strange fruits may not be gathered from the wide field now covered
by the folk-lorist. Formerly he hunted only in the East; now we find him
amongs the Lapps and the Zulus—in Labrador, and in the South Pacific
as well. A still more extended search will very likely find a fresh source
for those of the fables in the "Notti" which have heretofore been classed
as the original work of Straparola, and will discover for us a new and
genuine author of "Puss in Boots."

> Hide thou whatever here is found of fault;
> And laud the Faultless and His might exalt!

BENEDETTO CROCE

[The Fantastic Accomplishment of Giambattista Basile and His *Tale of Tales*]†

Lo Cunto de li Cunti as a Literary Work

ORIGIN AND FORM

Lo Cunto de li Cunti is a book of fairy-stories, *i.e.* of those traditional
tales in which superhuman and non-human beings from popular mythology play their parts—fairies, ogres, talking animals, vegetables and minerals
of prodigious virtue, and so on. The philologists of the nineteenth century
made accurate investigation of this variety of story, and put forward an
infinity of theories to account for its origin. But in previous centuries such
stories were merely a source of amusement and pleasure to children who
listened to them greedily, then, as now; learned folk disdained to consider
them, and they were rarely handled even by artists.

Among the first, and in a certain sense the very first, to pay attention to
them was Basile. Although fairy-stories were, indeed, scattered through the
works of the antecedent novelists and poets, in the *Pecorone*, in Sercambi's
work, in the *Mambriano* by Cieco da Ferrara, in the tales of Morlino,
while Gian Francesco Straparola da Caravaggio drew the argument of
many of the stories in his *Piacevoli notti* (1550) (in which respect he may

---

† Originally published as "*Lo Cunto de li Cunti* as a Literary Work" in the "Introduction" to
vol. I of *The Pentamerone of Giambattista Basile*, 2 vols., trans. N. M. Penzer (London: John
Lane and the Bodley Head, 1932). Unless otherwise indicated, all notes are by the editor of this
Norton Critical Edition.

be regarded as a precursor of our Basile) from popular fables and witticisms, yet in the pages of all these writers the tales were regularised and often metamorphosed into bourgeois stories shorn as far as possible of the marvellous, and nearly always related in the traditional style of the Italian *novellieri*. This was the case even with Straparola, of whom Grimm wrote that "he strove to tell his stories according to the prescribed and customary form and did not know how to strike a new cord," and only on two occasions, almost as if he foresaw the need of a new form, did he resort to dialect. It might be said that the fairy-story had, indeed, as it were, entered the field of literature with these *novellieri*, but was, so to speak, hidden, unnoticed, masked by the robe of the Boccaccio-like Epigoni. In *Lo Cunto de li Cunti*, on the contrary, they make an overt and clamorous entry, parading with all the pomp of popular imagination, and speaking its ingenuous and picturesque language.

What was the atmosphere with which Basile endowed and animated the traditional material? From the tales, as raw material, the most diverse works of art could be derived: from the allegorical and moral tale, the *conte philosophique*, in which fables are treated as symbols of ideas, to a simple heart-burning lyric sighing after youth. "Ah," says Heine as he wanders through the Tyrol and sees the green and white huts on the mountains, the flowery meadows, images of saints and children's faces, "here we should stay for ever and the aged grandmother should recite for us the most intimate stories." This feeling of tenderness is expressed in La Fontaine's famous apostrophe: "Si Peau d'âne m'était conté, j'y prendrais un plaisir extrême,"[1] nor is it lacking in Carlo Gozzi's gay mentality, when he writes *à propos* of the *Amore delle tre melarance* (love of the three oranges), "I confess that I laughed at myself and felt my soul's humiliation at enjoying those childish images which took me back to the time of my infancy."

But what attracted Basile, who was neither an intellectual nor a romantic, but merely a Secentist writer, in this popular literature was, above all, the unusual, the rustic, the absurd—all motives to him of "witty" comedy. For fancies and extravaganzas he could listen to the *cunti che soleno dire le vecchie pe trattenemiento de peccerille*, "tales solemnly told by the old women to amuse the young," and prompted by caprice or love of the bizarre he repeated them, now forgetting himself in these phantasies, so that the populace itself spoke with his mouth; now, by a rapid recovery of himself, caricaturing and parodying them—instincts that appear to be contradictory, and yet are harmonious, because they correspond to a peculiar psychological character. Basile does not take the whole thing seriously, nor does he treat it as a continuous jest, because this would become insipid; but he amuses himself by presenting the popular mind, and embroiders the presentation with humour.

In the *trattenemiente*, "diversions," of *Lo Cunto de li Cunti* the shrewd and smiling countenance of Cav. Basile flashes out at every turn, between the grinning faces of the old mischief-mongers.

Accordingly, while he is no modern transcriber, the tales in his hands

---

1. If "Donkey-Skin" had been told to me, I would have been extremely pleased (French).

preserve their ingenuous popular intonation, and also present us with a variety of elements proper to the time and to the character of the author. Among which we must reckon primarily the frame itself that encloses the *cunti* in a vaster *cunto*, and binds up the fifty stories into a *Pentamerone* in the same manner as the *Decamerone*.

STYLE AND CONTENT

Lo Cunto de li Cunti, then, is a living book, and no mere collection of Sicilian, Tuscan or Venetian tales, of which there are now so many; much rather is it spiritually related to the Italian "letteratura d'arte" of Pulci, of Lorenzo the Magnificent, of Folengo, akin in some respects to Boiardo and Ariosto. It gaily remodels the subject-matter of the chivalrous romances and of popular literature, and is, in a certain sense, the last unadulterated work on these lines, produced at a late date in Naples, no longer in the atmosphere of the Renaissance, but in that of the Seicento and of the Baroque. It is pervaded by the Baroque: Basile was not content to give dignity to his tales of ogres and fairies by presenting them in the setting that had become classical from the classic *Decamerone*, and giving the place held by Pampinea and Fiammetta, Neifile and Elisa, to his Zezas, Ciullas, Popas and Ciommetellas, but imparts to them all the strongest flavour of secentist literature.

The dawn cannot rise nor the sun set, in these tales, but he must find some new and bizarre metaphor to describe the daily phases, some circumlocution such as: "At dawn, the birds had but just shouted, 'Hail to the Sun!' "; "When the Sun issued into the open to disperse the humidity absorbed in the river of India"; "When the Sun with the golden broom of his rays sweeps away the impurities of Night from the fields sprinkled by the Dawn"; "When the Dawn emerges to seek fresh eggs to comfort her aged lover"; or "At the hour when the golden balls with which the Sun plays in the fields of Heaven take an inclined course towards the west"; "When the Sun, like a Genoese lady, draws the black taffeta round his face"; "When Night rises to light the candles of the catafalque of the heavens for the funeral obsequies of the Sun"; "When Earth spreads a vast black sheet to receive the wax that drops from the torches of Night"; and so on.

There is a mass of similar imagery, and still more in infinite variety, to describe the dark woods, the bubbling streams and rivers, the sparkling fountains. Kings and queens, princes and princesses, rustics, servingwenches and peasants, express their passions in introductions, progressions, reiterations and perorations, with wit and puns and clever quips in accordance with the rules and models of the treatises of flowery rhetoric. "Now be off and bake yourself, Cyprian Goddess!" exclaims the prince (I.2) admiring the beautiful fairy who is sleeping beside him, "go hang yourself, Helen! go home, Fiorella, your beauty pales before this beauty of double worth—beauty that is absolute, complete, solid, firm-planted; this marvellous grace, the grace of Siviglia, rare, enchanting, splendid. . . . Oh, sleep, sweet sleep, heap poppies on the eyes of this fair jewel! spoil not my delight in gazing my fill at this triumph of loveliness! Oh, fair tress that holds me captive! Oh, lovely eyes that inflame me! Oh, sweet lips that give me life afresh! Oh, soft breast that consoles me! Oh, lovely hand that wounds me! Where, where, in what workshop of nature's marvels, was this living statue fashioned? What India furnished the threads of gold for this hair? What Ethiopia the ivory for this brow? What shore the carbuncles for these eyes? What Tyre the crimson to tint these cheeks? . . ." And the other prince (I.6), who has in his hands the tiny slipper dropped by Cenerentola: "If the foundation is so fair, what must be the mansion? Oh, lovely candlestick which holds the candle that consumes me! Oh, tripod of the lovely cauldron in which my life is boiling! Oh, beauteous corks attached to the fishing-line of Love, with which he has caught this soul! Behold, I embrace and enfold you, and if I cannot reach the plant, I worship the roots; and if I cannot possess the capitals, I kiss the bases: you first imprisoned a white foot, now you have ensnared a stricken heart! Through you, she who sways my life was taller by a span and a half, through you, my life grows by that much in sweetness so long as I keep you in my possession."

At times even the characters take care to place themselves at a suitable spot, in a well-arranged scene, for the effusion of their sentiments, and, like Princess Renza (III.3), go under a mulberry tree to recite their stylistic lamentations beneath its shade. Hyperboles abound, pushed to such an extreme that they evaporate in the unspeakable and the ineffable, and the detailed descriptions of beauty or brutality, which read like inventories, are replete with everything attractive or repulsive that can be introduced. Metaphors, now extravagant and now subtle, follow without respite. The prince and the supposed monk meet, start a conversation, and walk on together, "cooling themselves in the heat of the way with the fan of conversation" (III.3).

The cat that has benefited Gagliuso (II.4) and now discovers his cold ingratitude reproaches him severely and turns his back on him; and the culprit tries to get round him by a peace-offering of the "lung of humility"—the lung being the tit-bit given in Neapolitan houses to the domestic cats and which is awaited with eager impatience. Penta (III.2), sent into exile with her babe, "takes her infant in her arms and waters it with milk and tears." And no less frequent are witticisms, as when the dying queen (*ibid.*) advises her husband to marry the good maimed girl, and the husband, upset as he is by his wife's proposal, has a humorous idea, and thinks without saying it aloud, "All right; if I have to marry again, I will gladly take the cripple, because with sorry creatures like women it is as well to take as little of them as possible."

Did Basile intend in these passages to satirise the Baroque literature of the day? This was the belief and conviction of Luigi Serio in the Settecento; but any such theory is put out of court by Basile's Italian works, which were certainly unknown to Serio, and which are in the most ornate Baroque style. Basile did not deprecate, and even gave high praise to, the literary mode of his period, and was himself a satellite of the great Marino; but in relating his tales he used it jocosely, just as, in caressing and playing with a child, in order to make it laugh, one puts a tall hat on its head, or eye-glasses on its nose. No satire is implied on the tall hat or the eye-glasses, and still less on the child. Nevertheless, by such means he unconsciously and artistically produces an ironical presentation of Baroque, which—whatever may be said by those who now extol it—is insupportable if taken seriously, and to-day seems ponderous and meaningless, while it is not only tolerable, but becomes animated and pleasing when illuminated by a flash of cunning and refreshed by a fountain of good-humour. In this respect, we may even say that Basile's *Pentamerone* is the finest Italian book of the Baroque period, which the verbose and inflated *Adone* certainly is not: the finest just because the Baroque here treads a lively measure, and only appears to vanish again: it was once turbid and obscure, it now becomes limpid gaiety.

This light Baroque succeeds in keeping the mind of the author and the readers above the material of the tales by a continuous distinction between culture and non-culture, the developed mind and raw mentality, the lettered and the vulgar—a method well understood and particularly appreciated by those who know and dislike the pedantries and affectations of would-be popular literature, in which adults vainly try to become children again, and only fall into pitiful parodies of the simple and ingenuous.

But this method does not prevent human participation in the action of the tales, which are staged by Basile with plastic imagination, concrete and detailed (as was the fashion with our Pulcis and Folenghis), combined with sentiments of fear, compassion, admiration or abhorrence. He shows us (I.3) a bundle of wood, which, when bestridden by the happy man whose every wish comes true, sets off like a horse, trots and prances, leaps and turns, followed by a crowd of urchins, while the women hang out of the windows in curiosity; or the assembly of beggars (*ibid.*), summoned by the King to a banquet in his palace, where they sit down, solemn and contented, to the table "like so many fine Counts"; or there is the roasting of the sea-dragon's heart (I.9), when the odour emitted from it induces the prodigious pregnancy of the cook and all the equipment of the kitchen, which brings forth its young in kind—the table a little table, the bed a little bed, the chairs small chairs, and finally the chamber-pot a beautiful little glazed pot, which was a joy to behold; or the ropes gnawed through, and the stratagems by which the mouse and the cockchafer (III.5) managed to reach the body of the fat German, whose nuptials they want to prevent; or Forteschiena (III.8), who heaps all the riches of the State and of private individuals on his unyielding back; or Parmetella (V.4), who runs, dazed and screaming, after the musical instruments she has let out of the box, which are now floating and resounding in the air. And sometimes we are soothed by a fresh, woodland scene, as when Nella (II.2), clinging to the tree in the silence of the night, overhears the conversation that goes on in the solitary hut of the ogre; or the little princess (II.5) who goes out of the city gate at night, by moonlight, accompanied by a fox, and sleeps with it under a canopy of leaves, on a mattress of tender herbage near a bubbling fountain, and listens, when she wakes at dawn, to the song of the innumerable birds that perch on the trees and delight her with their warbling.

In other places Basile makes us feel the modest virtue of his maidens, persecuted by vice and rewarded by good fortune, such as Viola (II.3), who is imperilled by the old procuress who is her aunt, but is saved by her resolution, and rushes at the old woman and slices off her ears as a punishment; Penta (III.2), who cuts off her beautiful hands, which have tempted her brother to an evil passion for her, and presents them to him in a basin; Sapia (III.4), who avoids all the pitfalls by which her sisters try to make her fall as they have fallen. He bids us admire the courage of the Baroness' intelligent daughter (V.6), who boxes the ears of the King's son, by which he is roused from his obstinate ignorance and redeemed; after which she fearlessly endures the vendetta, and finally marries him. The favourite comedy of the two lovers (II.3), who seek each other only to squabble as enemies, with insulting thrusts and tricks, like the Shakespearean Benedick and Beatrice, is here gracefully rendered. Again, we feel affection for the poor child (IV.7), who takes the cake from her mouth to give to the ragged crone who begs for it, and who remains modest and amiable when blessed by wealth and fortune. Among a group of dishonest and ferocious women Basile singles out the youngest (I.2), who shows her pity by refusing to murder the beautiful maiden who is their rival in the prince's affections. Anon, we shudder with terror at the old beggar-woman (II.7), whose pot of hardly begged beans is shattered by a cruel joker, and dies of hunger, to reappear suddenly as an evil shade to the heedless prince in the midst of his wedding festivities. In Corvetto (III.7), again, we have the fierce and implacable hatred of the courtiers for the King's favourite, and the endless plots contrived and carried out to encompass his destruction. There is Penta's joy (III.2) when she finds her husband again, and frisks around him like a little dog that wags its tail at seeing its master. There is the miracle of maternity in the tale of the sleeping beauty in the wood (V.5), who becomes a mother in her sleep, and whose two infants, Sun and Moon, hang on her breast while she is still asleep, and groping for the nipple suck her finger instead—drawing out the fatal thorn that had thrown her into the lethargy, and thus restoring her to life.

The mysterious charm of poetry is delineated in the prince (III.3) who loses the memory of his beloved, and hears from her lips, though unrecognised and disguised, the canzone of the "bianco viso," and all unknowing why, is suffused by its sweetness, and by a vague, expectant desire, so that he never wearies of listening to the song.

These are some of the many emotional tendencies reflected in these tales, whether Basile takes them from the people and resuscitates them, or whether he introduces them himself as new *motifs* giving fresh significance and human value to the bare and generalised legends.

He brings the fabulous into relation with actual daily life, with the life of his own time and his own Naples. The ogress figures as a countrywoman (II.1) watching over her garden, fierce in the protection of her property, vindictive against all who lay hands on what is hers; or again we hear her chattering at the evening meal to her husband on his return from his day's work, and asking what is being said and done in the world. Cenerentola (I.6), splendidly dressed in the fine coach provided by the fairy, with her train of servants and pages, is compared to a beautiful Neapolitan courtesan surprised and surrounded by the guards in the forbidden public walk at Chiaia and taken off to prison. Cienzo (I.7) is exiled from Naples because he has unwittingly broken the head of the King's son in one of the contests with stones, or "petriate," that are common in the Arenaccia. The Moorish slaves move and speak like the many slaves who were to be found at that time in Neapolitan houses, owing to the raids on the pirates. Rosella (III.9), the daughter of the Grand Turk, who is led by love into Christian lands, is courted as a fair adventuress by the Neapolitan barons, who, in order to provide the presents she asks for, fall into the hands of the usurers and are reduced to borrowing and spunging. The sisters of Sapia (III.4) refuse to submit to the confinement imposed by their father, and become two possessed "fenestrere," or ladies of easy virtue, behaving exactly like the unruly girls of southern countries; and when the windows are nailed up, they clamber on to the skylights, and thrust their heads out, chattering and flirting.

Basile's moral sentiments and emotions, which appear in his mode of handling the characters and actions, are expressed in the form of reflections in the introductions and conclusions to each tale, which are full of aphorisms on ingratitude, jealousy, envy, the invincible curiosity of women, their shrewdness, the fortune that favours the ignorant and cowardly, and in the maxims that underlie the tales, or are put into the mouths of the characters. Indeed, he has so much to say to this effect that these casual and scattered observations are inadequate, so he is impelled to pour out the superabundance of his feelings in four dialogues or "Egloghe" that follow the first four days respectively, and in which he satirises the difference between appearance and reality (*La coppella*), the juggling of words by which evil appears as good, and good as evil (*La tintura*), the tedium in which all human ambitions and pleasures terminate (*La stufa*), and the universal cupidity which leads everyone to seek their own prey and profit (*La volpara o l'uncino*). He gives us moral portraits and pictures of manners in a style between the hyperbolic and the grotesque, but so vigorously drawn that they remind us of the work of Jean Callot. We see the great lord, the soldier, the noble vaunting his rank, the braggart, the courtier, the bravo, the flatterer, the light woman, the poet, the lover, the astrologist, the alchemist, the miser who is praised for his economies, the coward who is extolled as prudent, and he who lives at his wife's expense, regarded as a man of breeding; while, on the other hand, the warm-hearted honourable man is discredited as a scamp and the man of taste is called a savage; the tyrannical lord and his agents who sell justice, and the merchant and the tailor and innkeepers with their imbroglios are here; and many other types and figures, along with the eventual disillusion suffered from love, military life, amusements, spectacles, and the arts—nothing escaping from the general depreciation but virtue and wealth or power, from which man obtains the only abiding satisfaction in the world.

RABELAIS AND BASILE

Whoever reads *Lo Cunto de li Cunti* for the first time with the great book of *Pantagruel* in mind cannot fail to be struck by the resemblance in the style of the two writers. Like Basile, Rabelais takes a popular tradition as the material for his own work; and, like Basile, he relates it in a semi-popular style, mixing up jokes, reflections, digressions and allusions of all sorts. He dedicates his book to the *beuveurs tres illustres*; and seems, in fact, to be in the condition of a man of great mental endowment, who after copious libations abandons the reins to all his most varied tendencies.

From this potent but disordered medley of intellect, fancy, memory and imagination, Rabelais pours out together in a torrent, profound ideas and play upon words, learned reminiscences and prodigious and monstrous tales to instruct and amuse the young, interspersed with the most delicate descriptions and meaningless extravaganzas. Basile is as much the poorer, in comparison with Rabelais, in intellectual content, as can be gauged by the distance between an Italian *littérateur* of the decadence and a Renaissance scholar. But there is an affinity in their literary procedure; the popular theme is embroidered by both, identically, in many places; both are prolific in long, emphatic or facetious enumerations, and there are many resemblances in style. Felix Liebrecht has gone even further, and declares outright that Basile had Rabelais in mind and followed him faithfully:

"After reading Rabelais repeatedly," he says, "we are persuaded that Basile imitated this writer's mode of expressing himself with the utmost exactitude: accordingly, the hypothesis put forward in our translation of *Lo Cunto de li Cunti* in regard to the imitation of a passage of Rabelais in the details of one tale (V.1) becomes more probable. Our decision is based on the astonishing conformity between the two authors in matters of style and expression, which cannot be entirely casual; and since a complete statement would take up too much space we shall confine ourselves to certain examples. Rabelais, *e.g.*, amuses himself by enumerating one after the other various objects of a given kind; *e.g.* birds (I.37), and so in Basile (II.5; IV.8); plants (I.13), and Basile (II.5); utensils (I.51), and Basile (II.5); words of abuse (I.25), and Basile (Intro. I.1, 3); games (I.22), and Basile (II and IV); clothes (I.56), and Basile (III.10). Further: synonyms— Rabelais (I.22), 'après avoir bien joué, sassé, passé et beluté temps,' etc., and Basile (II.10), 'che, comm' a sacco scosuto, se norcava, cannariava, ciancolava, ngorfeva, gliotteva, devacava, scervecchiava, piuziava, arravogliava, scrofoniava, schianava, petteneva, sbatteva, smorfeva ed arresidiava'; Rabelais (I, IV, new prologue), 'Sera beliné, corbiné, trompé et affiné,' and Basile (I.1), 'stimmano facile cosa de cecare, nzavorre, ngannare, mbrogliare e dare a vedere ceste pe lanterne a no maialone, marrone, maccarone, vervecone, nsempprecone,' etc. Again: incidental rhyming— Rabelais (*l.c.*), 'au soir, un chascun d'eux eut les mules au talon, le petit cancre au menton, la mal toux au poulmon, la catarrhe au gavion, le gros froncle au croupion,' etc. (also in I.52); and Basile (I.6), 'spampanate, sterliccate, impallaccate, tutte zagarelle, campanelle e scartabelle, tutte shiure, adure, cose e rose,' etc. As we have said, we can only cite a few of these examples, but they could be multiplied extensively, bearing in mind the abundance of proverbs common to both writers. Moreover, anyone who is willing to be convinced of Basile's imitation should compare *Pantagruel*, IV.9, and the Introduction to Basile, Day 5; the result stands out clearly."

This thesis of Liebrecht encounters an initial objection in the very slight acquaintance of Rabelais current in Italy in the Cinque and Seicento, Guerrini, who made researches on the subject, only succeeded in finding one passing allusion to him in Della Torre's *Facezie*; and Martinozzi, who unearthed a few more, entirely confirms Guerrini's negative conclusions. Nor has it ever been shown that Basile was acquainted with the French language or with its literature.

Nor are the only two specific and flagrant imitations cited by Liebrecht as convincing as he supposed. In the first Diversion of the Fifth Day there is the story of a magic goose (*papara*) and of a prince, who having retired into a narrow lane "a scarrecare lo ventre . . . , non trovannose carta a la saccoccia pe stoiarese, vista chella papara, accisa de frisco, se ne servette pe pezza."[2] The same tale had already been used by Straparola, but here, instead of a goose, the object used by the prince is a doll (*poavola*). And a Sicilian story, collected by Pitrè and entitled "La pupidda," which is similar in all respects to Basile's tale, also has the doll instead of the goose. What made Basile alter the doll into a goose? Liebrecht refers to the famous chapter of *Gargantua* about the "invention d'un torchecul"[3] in which we read: "en concluant ie dy et maintiens qu'il n'y a tel torchecul que d'un oison bien dumeté, pourveu qu'on luy tienne sa tête entre les jambes,"[4] etc.; and supposes that this suggested to Basile the idea of the substitution. But let alone the fact that the likeness between the use of a dead goose in Basile, and that upheld as the best in Rabelais, viz. a warm and living animal, is sufficiently vague, it appears to us that we should rather conclude from the analogy that Rabelais was unknown to Basile; because nothing in the matter cited corresponds to Rabelais' long dissertation, and the Neapolitan writer is unaware of the plethora of jokes the French author creates from this detail.

How the change from doll to goose occurred, whether (as Grimm supposes) from the similarity of the two dialect words *pipata* and *papara*, or for some other reason, we cannot tell.

The other comparison made by Liebrecht is between the beginning of the Fifth Day in which Basile describes a pastime which consisted in suggesting a game to each of the ladies: "la quale, senza pensarence, m'ha da dicere subeto ca no le piace, e la causa perché non le dace a l'omore"[5] and Book IV, Ch. IX of *Pantagruel*, which describes "les etranges alliances"[6] of the island of Ennaisin on which Pantagruel lands and repeats a long series of thrusts and parries exchanged between the inhabitants of the country; as: "en pareille alliance, l'un appelloit une sienne mon homelaicte, elle le nommoit mon oeuf; et estoient alliés comme une omelaicte d'oeufz. De mesmes un autre appelloit une sienne ma trippe, elle l'appelloit son fagot,"[7] and so on. Here, too, the supposed imitation is very doubtful. The purely artistic consideration remains; but, as a matter of

---

2. To relieve himself . . . he could not find any paper in his pocket and noticed the freshly killed goose. So he decided to use part of the bird instead (Italian).
3. The invention of an ass wiper (French).
4. In conclusion, I say that there is now no better ass wipe than a fluffy goose if you keep its head between your legs (French).
5. And she, without stopping to think, must say immediately that it does not please her and give the reason why (Italian).
6. The strange relationships (French).
7. So, too, one of them called a woman "my omelet," and she called him "my egg"; and they were indeed related to each other as eggs in an omelet. In the same way, one of them called a woman "my bundle," and she, in turn, called him "my stick," and so on (French).

fact, the literary imitators of the time follow situations, ideas and imagery without steeping themselves in the mentality of a foreign author and translating it into new form so that it is present throughout the work, and cannot be picked out in particular details. At any rate, Basile's style is not so unusual that it needs to be explained by any excursions into past times and foreign countries. It is a spontaneous product of the literary Seicento and of the southern temperament; spontaneous as was the spontaneity of Giordano Bruno, who, by the way, has also been labelled an imitator of Rabelais.

If we run through Basile's works in chronological order, taking first the *Lettere,* then the *Muse,* and finally *Lo Cunto de li Cunti,* we watch the development of an artistic temperament which seeks its proper outlet, experiments, progresses, and finally pursues its true path.

Liebrecht admits that Basile imitated Rabelais' artistic methods "in the happiest fashion" (*auf das glücklichste*); but—even granting that Basile had read Rabelais—it would seem that this very "happiness" of the imitation is the most obvious proof of non-imitation.

<h2 style="text-align:center">EARLY CRITICS</h2>

A two-sided work, which still forms a serio-burlesque, ingenuously malicious entity, such as *Lo Cunto de li Cunti,* was not easily understood or rightly estimated by the earlier critics. Ferdinando Galiani did not fathom it, when, after observing that Basile had unfortunately tried to compete with Boccaccio and to write a dialectical Decamerone to serve as a text for the Neapolitan vernacular, he says he was "totally lacking in the talent for such an enterprise" and "entirely devoid of all qualifications, whether inspiration, or philosophy, or knack of invention, or wealth of concepts, to enable him to invent and embellish graceful, interesting, tragic, witty or moral tales; the only thing he could think of was a jumble of stories about fairies and ogres which are so insipid, so monstrous and so revolting that the very Arabs who initiated this most depraved taste would have blushed to have invented them." Which is as much as to say (as observed by Imbriani) that Galiani, looking in *Lo Cunto de li Cunti* for the philosophy of Voltaire's *Contes philosophiques,* is disillusioned, and never discovers the true character of the book.

On the other hand, a spurious value is given to the facetious part by Galiani's witty adversary, Luigi Serio, who interprets the *Cunto de li Cunti* as a literary satire.

The criticism of Giuseppe Ferrari is more acute. He notes how Basile's characters "quelle que soit la bizarrerie des aventures où ils s'engagent, gardent constamment cette simplicité, entrainent avec cette force qui n'appartient qu'aux traditions populaires. C'est le peuple qui est le grand magicien et le premier créateur de cette fantasmagorie . . . ."[8] He further remarks that in Basile the fabulous episodes are "réduits toujours à des

---

8. No matter how bizarre the adventures are in which they become involved, they constantly maintain a certain simplicity, and they are captivating because of this force that belongs to the popular folk tradition. It is the people who are the great magician and the original creator of this phantasmagoria (French).

proportions triviales, et altérés par je ne sais quelle atmosphère de cuisine et de ménage: la fantaisie napolitaine au lieu d'embellir, d'idéaliser l'univers, l'a enlaidi à dessein; pour en développer la vitalité, elle l'a peuplé de monstres."[9]

Better still, Jacob Grimm writes that Basile "has told his stories altogether in the spirit of a lively, witty, and facetious people, with continued allusions to manners and customs, and even to ancient history and mythology, a knowledge of which is usually tolerably diffused among the Italians. This is the very reverse of the quiet and simple style of German stories. He abounds too much in picturesque and proverbial forms of speech, and witty turns present themselves to him every moment, and for the most part make their mark. Frequently too his expressions are of the rustic kind, bold, free, and outspoken, and therefore offend us; as, for instance, in the story of the doll, which could not well be told here in all its details, though we cannot exactly call it indecent, as that of Straparola is. A certain exuberance and glow of language are natural to Basile, for example, in Day Three, Tale 3, the complaint of Renza extends over two pages. This, however, is due only to the peculiar pleasure which southern nations take in ever-new impressions, and in lingering over the objects which give rise to them, and not to any attempt to conceal poverty in the subject itself. . . . As the superabundance of similes is for the most part prompted by fun and wit, the strangest and most laughable expressions may be used without being nonsensical. . . ."

A few years later, in 1846, in the Introduction to Liebrecht's translation after reasserting the superiority of Basile to Straparola, he adds: "When one has become familiar with it, the attractive form of the tales affords real delight. How inexhaustible, for instance, is the varied imagery with which dawn and sunset are depicted on every page! and if at times such phrases seem out of place or dragged in, yet in practically every case they will appear à propos and pertinent. The most charming and varied similes express the rushing and murmuring of the brooks, the sombre darkness of the silvern shades, the singing of the birds; and in the midst of Oriental flights of imagination, one comes unawares upon these gentle observations of nature. The language overflows with metaphors, puns, aphorisms and rhymes (for which our [the German] language in most cases is inadequate); and here, as in the unadulterated tales of all nations, we come across simple but inimitable rhymes at the important and decisive moments of the tale, which rivet the attention of the story-teller and similarly of the listener. So in Peruonto: 'Damme passa e fico Si vuoi che te lo dico'; in Schiavottella: 'Chiave ncinto E Martino drinto'; and in Cenerentola: 'Spoglia a me E vieste a te.' "[1]

Few, however, were by similarity of temperament and artistic nature so well qualified to understand Basile as Vittorio Imbriani, who not only collected strange tales, but also embellished and invented them. "In Ba-

---

9. Always reduced to trivial proportion and altered by some kind of kitchen and household atmosphere. Instead of embellishing or idealizing the world, the Neapolitan imagination makes it ugly by design. In order to develop the vitality in it, this imagination peoples it with monsters (French).
1. *Peruonto*: Give me raisins and figs if you want me to say what you wish. *Schiavottella*: Keys by my side, my opponent inside. *Cenerentola*: Now strip yourself and address me. (All Italian.)

sile," he writes, "everything is might: he has managed to give the correct form to these impersonal narratives, and at the same time to stamp this form with the seal of his own personality. Anyone who has the least acquaintance with popular literature will understand the difficulties of such an achievement. The peculiar charm of everything popular is the tinge of the epic that pervades it, and of the typical: the lack of individuality; and this charm is apt to vanish directly we attempt to handle it. . . . But Basile has succeeded in reconciling two things that had seemed to be irreconcilable, above all in style—distinct personality and popular impersonality. The voice of the people speaks from his books, and yet the Secentist *littérateur* is here, with all his merits and all his defects, which latter he seems to turn into jokes against himself. And in so doing he was greatly assisted both by having lived in the Seicento and by having employed the Neapolitan dialect. That dialect gives him an indescribable blend of ingenuousness and raillery at one and the same time; and withal we can detect the implicit irony."

BASILE'S USE OF DIALECT

Various observations have been made on the syntax and phraseology of Basile.

Galiani exaggerates in saying that he imitates Boccaccio; yet it is true that owing to the characteristic features of his stories, as described above, he neither could nor should have conformed to popular simplicity. He ran his sentences into long periods, deficient in cohesion and balance. As Liebrecht rightly notes, while his style exhibits a tiresome excess of participial constructions, his sentences are only hung together without being properly connected. They usually begin with the same word, generally with "ma" ("but"), and consequently lose in roundness and variety. The rhythm of the Basilian prose is often neglected: more relief and perspective are wanted, and the intervals seen by the imagination in the development of an event require a corresponding change in narrative. In these respcts a follower of Basile Pompeo Sarnelli, who composed a book of fables in the second half of the same century, was a much better writer. Imbriani declared that the defects in style would almost totally disappear with good punctuation to replace that which was absent or capricious in the old editions; but this would merely alleviate, without abolishing them, because they are integral to the construction of the period. It is well, moreover, to remember that Basile's work was posthumously published, and the author cannot have given it his final supervision.

With regard to the language, Galiani (preceded in this by Francesco Oliva in his unfinished but important *Grammatica della lingua napoletana*, which has remained unpublished) states that Basile had "the most incredible and minute acquaintance with all the terms, proverbs, modes of speech and curious and bizarre expressions used by the vulgar," but that in order to show off this opulence he abused it, "whence it follows that he frequently puts together in the wrong connection words and phrases that do not bear the sense in which he employs them." In fact, "there are great numbers of Tuscan words which he has forced and contorted into our language, although we have never made use of them. The amount of labour and trouble he has given himself to avoid such terms as are really Italian, and which we use commonly and have adopted, and to substitute for them the most obsolete and the most squalid expressions of the lowest of the people, simply because they are prohibited in the general language of Italy, is incredible."

Indeed we need only open the first pages of Lo Cunto de li Cunti to find examples of such modifications from the vernacular. Basile managed, by a kind of artistic coherence, to make the Neapolitan dialect even more Neapolitan than it really is; he excluded many forms in common with Italian, and gives strange inflections to purely Italian words. Morever, his strivings after comic effects led him to select all the popular phrases that were disparaging, burlesque or uncouth, and to use them as if equivalent to the serious and normal phraseology: as e.g. where Tadeo says to the crone in the Introduction): "Devo scusare moglierema se s'ha schiaffato ncuorpo st'omore malenconeco de sentire cunte; e, perzò, se ve piace de dare mbrocca a lo sfiolo della prencepessa mia e de cogliere miezo le voglie soie, sarrite contente, pe sti quatto o cinco iuorne che starrà a scarrecare la panza";[2] and so on. Again, for the requirements of his style and of his caricatures he was obliged to invent many terms, particularly in the abstract, that do not exist in popular parlance; and on the other hand he delighted in using certain classical forms (e.g. the articles lo, la, li, le, instead of o(u), a, i) which correspond with the tendency to elevate the dialect to the dignity of a language.

Leaving to others the grammatical and verbal analysis, it will here suffice to formulate the conclusion that the language of Lo Cunto de li Cunti (even taking into account the disparity which it, as being three centuries old, naturally presents to the dialect of to-day) would seem in its general physiognomy to be one of the languages, such as doggerel (maccheronico) and pedantry (fidenziano) which are created by artists and for artistic purposes, rather than one which was actually spoken. This must lead us to judge it by very different criteria from those adopted by the grammarians and legislators of the Neapolitan dialect. If in the syntax we must censure the lack of taste and smoothness we must equally, in considering the linguistic material, respect the mind of Basile, who—as has been said—was no straightforward realistic story-teller, but a satirist and a humorist.

IV. The Fortunes of Lo Cunto de li Cunti

IMITATORS OF BASILE

The first edition of Lo Cunto de li Cunti of which we have spoken was followed in 1644, by the second, dedicated to Signor Felice Basile, and in 1645 by the third, dedicated to Padre Daniele.

In 1674 the publisher, Antonio Bulifon, a Frenchman who had set up

2. Therefore, I must excuse my wife, who has become obsessed and in her melancholy state wants to hear fairy tales. So, if you would please, I ask you to fulfill the wish of my princess and fulfill my desires halfway, content yourselves during the four or five days that remain for her belly to deflate (Italian).

a shop in Naples, "seeing," as he says, "that this *Pentamerone* from the lively and bizarre mind of Cav. Giovan. Battista Basile, as witty as it is facetious, is in constant demand," so arranged matters that "having edited the text, he gave it new life by printing it afresh."

The reader for this edition was an Apulian priest, Pompeo Sarnelli, afterwards Bishop of Bisceglie, and at that time proof-reader in Bulifon's establishment. Sarnelli not unreasonably deplores the grave inaccuracies of the last edition, and proposes, as far as the text is concerned, to return to the first edition; but he frankly begins by correcting a number of forms that appear to him not to be pure Neapolitan, in which task he sometimes succeeds very well, at other times makes sad blunders, but is always dogmatic. For the rest, if he substitutes certain words or phrases for those of Basile, he neither subtracts nor adds anything substantial to the text, save one curious interpolation (which would appear unique) in the Fifth Diversion of the First Day [read "Third Day"], where Basile's words: "arrevato all' acqua de Sarno" are followed by Sarnelli's addition, "chillo bello shiummo c'ha dato nomme a la famiglia antica de li Sarnelli."

In Sarnelli's edition the work for the first time bears the title of Pentamerone on the title-page, under which name it was reprinted at Rome in 1679 and at Naples in 1697.

The *Muse napolitane* also had five reprints during the course of the seventeenth century.

These reprints, and probably others unknown to us, confirm what was written by Nicodemo in 1683 of *Lo Cunto de li Cunti*: "most gallant and most pleasant of books, which is in the hands of everyone."

And along with its readers and admirers Basile's work soon found its imitators, as befalls such books as have an individual and definite character.

Among the admiring readers was that strange Neapolitan intellect, Salvator Rosa, who not merely imitated Basile in his satires and copied part of the Eclogues of *Lo Cunto de li Cunti* at several places, but published his book in Florence; so that in the satires of Menzini we again find imitations of the Neapolitan eclogues. And it is said that when Lorenzo Lippi began to write the *Malmantile riacquistato*, "he derived an enormous stimulus from the work of Salvator Rosa . . ." and that the Napolitan painter provided him with "the book entitled *Lo Cunto de li Cunti* or *Tratteneminto de li peccerille*, composed in the Neapolitan mode of speech, from which he extracted some very fine tales, and putting these into rhyme set them here and there in his poem."

In the *Malmantile* (posthumously published in 1676, twelve years after the death of its author) we perceive an intention analogous to that which inspired Basile, namely, to attest the richness of his own dialect, the Florentine vernacular. But whereas in *Lo Cunto de li Cunti* this aim is subordinated to Basile's taste for grotesque representation, in the *Malmantile* it predominates: hence the coldness of this poem, which seems to be written solely for the purpose of being overloaded, as it was, by the pedantic annotations of Paolo Minucci.

It may seem strange that Lippi should resort to Basile for the tales which he introduces into his poem, seeing that these pertain to the heritage of everyone and were approximately as vigorous at that time in Florence as in Naples. But Basile, by drawing the attention of his readers to these tales and giving them a literary form, had regenerated them and indicated their artistic potentialities.

No one so far has pointed out which really are the imitations by Lippi from *Lo Cunto de li Cunti*, but, if we are not mistaken, they may be reduced to three. The second canto of the *Malmantile* is nothing but a rendering in verse of the *Cerva fatata* (I.9). In this tale the passage describing the marvellous efficiency of the dragon's heart is a good example of the way in which Lippi turned Basile's prose into verse: "Lo re . . . lo dette a cocinare a na bella dammecella. La quale, serratose a na cammara, non cossì priesto mese a lo fuoco lo core e scette lo fummo de lo vullo, che non sulo sta bella coca deventaie prena, che tutte li mobele de la casa ntorzaro. E, ncapo de poche iuorne, figliattero; tanto che la travacca fece no lettecciulo, lo forziero fece no scrignetiello, le seggie facettero seggiolelle, la tavola no tavolino, e lo cantaro fece no cantariello mpetenato, accossì bello ch'era no sapore!"[3] And in Lippi (II.16–17) we have:

> Ed egli, preso il prelibato cuore,
> lo diede al cuoco; al qual mentre lo cosse,
> si fece una trippaccia, la maggiore
> che ai dì dei nati mai veduta fosse.
> Le robe e masserizie, a quell'odore,
> anch'elle diventaron tutte grosse;
> e in poco tempo a un'otta tutte quante
> fecer d'accordo il pargoletto infante.
> Allor vedesti partorire il letto
> un tenero e vezzoso lettuccino;
> di qua l'armadio fece uno stipetto;
> la seggiola di là un seggiolino;
> la tavola figliò un bel buffetto;
> la cassa, un vago e picciol cassettino;
> e il destro un canterello mandò fuore,
> che una bocchina avea tutto sapore.[4]

There are evident echoes of *Lo Cunto de li Cunti* in the tale that is put into Psyche's mouth in the fourth canto (29–82) when she comes to seek her spouse in Malmantile: the beginning is taken from a part of the Fifth Diversion of the Second Day; passages in the middle are derived from the Introduction, from the Fifth Diversion of the Third Day, and also from

---

3. The king . . . gave it to a beautiful maiden to cook. She locked herself in a room and put the heart on the fire to boil, and as soon as the fumes arose from the stew, the beautiful cook became pregnant. Moreover, all the furniture in the house began to swell. And at the end of a few days, they all gave birth. The large bed had a little bed; the chest had a small casket; the big chairs had little chairs; the table had a little table; and the chamber pot produced a glazed chamber pot that was so beautiful it was a delight to behold (Italian).

4. And he took the exquisite heart and gave it to the cook. And while he cooked it, he made a tripe stew, the best that had ever been seen. However, when the odor spread, all the things began to swell and become big. In a short time, they all at once began producing baby infants. Then you saw the bed bring forth a dainty charming cot; the wardrobe a chest of drawers; the big chair a little chair; the table's son was a fine sideboard, and the big chest had a lovely little casket; the commode gave forth a little night stool, whose small opening was all sweet-scented. The cook, too, was no fool, for he felt in his side a gash, and out of it came, first, a turnspit, then a white-aproned cook's boy (Italian).

the Fourth of the First Day; and others from the Introduction are transported bodily to the close.

Finally, the tale of Nardino and Brunetto is a corruption of *Lo cuoruo* (IV. 9) and of the *Tre cetre* (V.9), with a certain admixture of new details.

How far Lippi imitated Basile's style may be seen from his description of the "uom selvatico Magorto" (VII.53–55), which echoes the many happy descriptions of ogres in Basile:

> Ma io ti vuò dar adesso un'abbozzata,
> qui presto presto, della sua figura.
> Ei nacque d'un folletto e d'una fata,
> a Fiesole, 'n una buca delle mura;
> ed è si brutto poi che la brigata,
> solo al suo nome, crepa di paura.
> Oh questo è il caso a por fra i nocentini,
> a far mangiar la pappa a quei bambini!
> Oltre ch'ei pute come una carogna,
> ed è piú nero della mezzanotte,
> ha il ceffo d'orso e il collo di cicogna,
> ed una pancia come una gran botte;
> va sui balestri ed ha bocca di fogna,
> da dar ripiego a un tin di mele cotte;
> zanne ha di porco e naso di civetta,
> che piscia in bocca e del continuo getta.
> Gli copron gli ossi i peli delle ciglia,
> ed ha cert'ugna lunghe mezzo braccio;
> gli uomini mangia e, quando alcun ne piglia,
> per lui si fa quel giorno un Berlingaccio,
> con ogni pappalecco e gozzoviglia;
> ch'ei fa, prima, col sangue il suo migliaccio,
> la carne assetta in varî e buon bocconi,
> e della pelle ne fa maccheroni.[5]

Basile had a greater influence on the Neapolitan writers; and since he was almost the Dante of that dialect, and became its lexicon and phrasebook for literary purposes, the writers who followed him for some century and a half all studied his works rather than the living language of the people.

One writer alone adhered to the general style of Basile, and related his *cunti* in prose: this was the 1674 editor, Pompeo Sarnelli, who ten years

5. But I want now to give you a brief sketch about his appearance. He was born from the union of a hobgoblin and a fairy at Fiesole in a hole in the wall. And he was so ugly that everyone around him trembled with fear just at the mention of his name. Such was the case that parents threatened their children that he would come unless they ate their food. Aside from that, he stank like a rotten corpse and was darker than midnight. He had the snout of a bear and the neck of a stork and a belly as large as a barrel. He walked bow-legged and had the mouth of a sewer. He looked like a makeshift vat of baked apples. He had the tusks of a wild boar and the nose of a screech owl, and he pissed in people's mouths without stopping. His body was covered with hair from head to toe, and his nails were as long as half an arm. He ate humans, and whenever he caught one, it was for him like a great day of Carnival so that he celebrated with gluttony and debauchery. First, he made a blood pudding with the blood and prepared the meat in various good pieces. Then he made macaroni out of the skin (Italian).

later published the *Posilecheata* under the anagrammatical name of Mesillo Reppone.

"Si be millanta valentuommene," he says in the Preface, "hanno scritto, dapò lo Cortese, vierze napoletane, nesciumo, dapò Gianalesio Abbattutis, ha scritto cunte."

The Frame to these tales is, as the title tells us, the account of an excursion to Posilipo, whither Masillo Reppone betakes himself to spend the day in a friend's villa. The day culminates in a grand feast, enlivened by the company and co-operation of Dr. Marchionno, a glutton and *bon viveur* of the first order. He devours three-quarters of the meal as his own share, chattering incessantly without a moment's pause; for every dish that is set on the table he has an appropriate proverb, or motto, or learned comment; and he asks, with the most amiable shamelessness, now for one thing, now for another, sure that he is pleasing his friend and conscientiously living up to his reputation as a glutton. After dinner five women of the people arrive, and each tells a story. The themes of the five tales do not resemble those of Basile, and present the further novelty of giving a kind of mythology of some of the most famous and popular monuments of Naples—the Giant of the Palazzo, the Neptune of the Fontana Medina, the so-called Testa di Napoli, the Quattro del Molo, and so on—because Sarnelli, even in writing fiction, never forgets that he is the author of a *Guida di Napoli*. In his narrative form, his introductions, the expression of his style, his quips or jests, he follows Basile, as an intelligent and elegant imitator, while he surpasses him in care and fluency. He promised to follow up this little book with a big volume of tales (*no libro gruosso*), but it never saw the light.

REPRINTS AND TRANSLATIONS—CARLO GOZZI

In the first half of the eighteenth century there were at least four reprints of *Lo Cunto de li Cunti*, based on the text of Sarnelli. Also in 1713 there appeared the first translation, which was from one dialect to another— from Neapolitan into Bolognese: the translators were Maddalena and Teresa Manfredi (sisters of the celebrated Eustachio) and their friends Teresa and Angiola Zanotti (sisters of the no less celebrated Giampietro and Francesco), and they called it: *La chiaqlira dla banzola o per dir mìi fol divers tradutt dal parlar Napulitan in lengua Bulgnesa*.

This translation ignores the divisions into five days, as well as the introductions to the days and to the several tales, and the four Interludes or Eclogues; the Introduction is abbreviated, and the fiftieth tale follows on the forty-ninth as a conclusion. Besides this, many of the embellishments with which Basile enriches the tales are omitted, such as the descriptions of dawn, of sunset, of night, as well as the longer speeches, and taking it as a whole, the style is generally accelerated. But even thus denuded and abbreviated, the tales retain their beauty, since they have gained on the one hand what they have lost on the other, and thus become more lively, simple and popular.

This work was reprinted several times and was the means (writes Guerini) "of fixing the rules of orthography of the dialect, and became the codex of the best spoken Bolognese, and is still being reprinted, and although now a century and a half old, it shows no signs of old age, even in the external and orthographical forms of the dialect." The anonymous translator of 1754 does not deserve the same praise, for he not only omits the Eclogues and the whole of certain tales, abridging others and changing the names of the characters, etc., besides making many blunders,[6] but he constantly adopts a most tasteless style, as can be seen in the following extract, which is the beginning of the first tale:

Eravi nella città di Biserta una donna dabbene chiamata Drusilla, la quale, oltre a sei figlie femmine, avea un figlio maschio tanto sciocco e scimunito, che la povera madre perciò ne stava scontentissima; né v'era giorno che non l'avvertiva, ora correggendolo dolcemente, ed ora al dolce delle correzioni vi mescolava l'asprezza delle invettive, od anche, se v'era di bisogno, delle bastonate; con tutto ciò non furone queste cose bastanti a far sí che Rodimonte si fosse riavuto della sua dappocaggine; per la qual cosa, vedendo Drusilla non esservi speranza che suo figlio ravveduto si fosse dalla sua sciocchezza (quasiché il difetto di natura fosse stato in lui cagionato per colpa sua), un giorno fra gli altri con un bastone lo batté di maniera che poco vi mancò a non romperle tutte le ossa. . . .[7]

Putting aside the translator's garbled style, however, it is certain that in view of the mentality of that century and of the quantity and quality of the language then available, any adequate translation of an author like Basile, which demanded a lively fancy and a rich vocabulary, must have been a hopeless task. The experiment might be tried again with a more confident outlook in our own day.

Nevertheless, Basile encountered another sympathetic soul in the Settecento, to whom he could narrate his *cunti*: Carlo Gozzi (1720–1808), who approximates to him in his dramatic fairy-tales. The third act of *Amore delle tre melarance*, played in 1761, and of which there now remains only a kind of scenario, is taken from the *Tre cetre* (V.9); and a further trace of *Lo Cunto de li Cunti* may be seen in the first act of the same play, in the expedient resorted to by Truffaldino to make the Prince Tartaglia laugh. The second of his tales, *Il corvo*, staged in the same year, 1761, is again derived from Basile and from his imitator Sarnelli in the *Augel belverde*.

Gozzi, even more than Basile, did not aim exclusively at reproducing the popular folk-lore, but used his dramatic compositions to express a mass of literary theories and polemics. But even so, while altering the creations of the people—and that in no slight degree—he did not change them fundamentally; hence popular sentiment survived in his stories, which

6. "Uorco" is always rendered "Orca," so that the King gives his daughter in marriage to an ogress! *La gatta cennerentola*, which is feminine, becomes "il gatto," and so on [*Croce's note*].

7. Once upon a time in the town of Biserta, there was a woman called Drusilla, who, aside from having six daughters, had a son who was so stupid and foolish that the poor mother was extremely unhappy. Not a day went by that she did not admonish him. Sometimes she would reprimand him sweetly, and other times, instead of sweet reprimands, she mixed them with harsh invectives, and also, if she had to, with beatings. But, despite all of that, it was not enough to bring about a change in Rodimonte. He remained unfit. Therefore, seeing that there was no hope for her son to overcome his stupidity (as if this were a natural defect of his and his own fault), Drusilla took a stick one day and began beating him in such a manner that it would not have taken much before all the bones in his body were broken (Italian).

therefore held a great fascination for the romantic Teutons. As De Sanctis puts it, the literary aims of Gozzi were transitory aims "which were to win his cause in polemics and in the theatre, and which to-day form the extinct part of his work"; but the live part is "the concept of the popular as against bourgeois comedy . . . its content is the poetic world, as it is conceived by the people, who are avid for marvels and mysteries, impressionable, ready to laugh or to cry."

THE BOOK OUTSIDE ITALY

Outside Italy, the first to be inspired by Basile was Wieland, who, in 1778, drew from certain extracts published in the *Bibliothèque des romans*, the material for a story in verse called *Peruonte oder die Wünsche*, which corresponds with *Peruonto* in *Lo Cunto de li Cunti* (I.3). In the first two parts the story follows that of the Neapolitan author, step by step, developing the situations more amply and with more detail. The tone is playful, but the touch of a moral concept is not lacking. A king of Salerno had a lovely daughter, named Vastolla, who, although she was most attractive and much coveted, entertained no thoughts of matrimony:

> Blieb mitten in den Flammen,
> Nach wahrer Salamanderart,
> Stets unversengt, eiskalt und felsenart.[8]

[The tale is given in Vol. I., and follows Wieland to the point where the unfortunate couple are saved from the barrel and Peruonto has acquired both brains and good-looks.]

From this point Wieland ceases to follow Basile, who concludes with the arrival of the father at the castle of the pair, where with mutual explanations the peace and happiness of all are established. The third part of Wieland's narrative, on the contrary, relates how after a few weeks Vastolla grew weary of this life of peaceful happiness. By persuading Peruonto to the further use of his gift she gets herself transported with him now to Salerno to assist at a banquet given by the King, now to Naples, where they lead an ostentatious life, now to Venice for the ceremony of the Bucintoro, and finally invites an elegant society to their castle; on which occasion Vastolla falls in love with one of her guests. She then asks Peruonto to let her journey to Sorrento, provided with an inexhaustible purse. Peruonto consents, but when he is left alone he invokes the fairies, imploring them to take back their gift:

> Hört mich, ihr gute Feen,
> An denen ich, trotz meinem bessern Sinn,
> So oft durch Wünschen mich vergangen,
> Hört meinen letzten Wunsch! Nehmt Alles wieder hin
> Was ich von euer Huld empfangen.
> Und setzt in diesem Augenblick

---

8. She remained in the middle of the flames, / According to the true way of the salamander, / Unscorched, ice-cold, and like a rock (German).

Mich in den Stand, worin ich war zurück,
Als ich zu wünschen angefangen![9]

The fairies grant his wish; the castle vanishes; Vastolla finds herself back at her father's Court, as though nothing had happened, and Peruonto is once more with his aged mother, chopping wood—his intellect alone being left him of all the benefits received.

Wieland, says one of his critics, seeks in this tale to foreshadow the concept set forth by Schiller in the verses: "was kein Verstand der Verständigen sieht, Das übet in Einfalt ein kindlich Germüht";[1] or rather he satirises and criticises mere desire, which loses itself in infinity.

A final and less happy edition of the Neapolitan text of *Lo Cunto de li Cunti* was published, together with the rest of Basile's works, at Naples, in 1788, in the *Collezione dei poemi in lingua napoletana* by Porcelli. A few years previously there had been a polemical discussion, as above indicated, between Galiani and Serio as to the significance and value of this work. But just as Galiani had failed to appreciate its artistic merit, so too he missed its philological and scientific importance. It was left to one of the fathers of modern philology and mythological science, Jacob Grimm, to throw light on this side of Basile's work, which for two centuries had been regarded merely as a source of mirth and entertainment.

V. *Lo Cunto de li Cunti* and Comparative Folk-Lore

GERMAN AND ENGLISH VERSIONS

It would be superfluous to repeat the history of the origins and formation of what is known as "comparative folk-lore."

Everyone knows how from the legends brought together at various times by Italian, French, Portuguese and German writers for artistic or educational purposes, we come in 1812 to the first scientific collection of them in the *Kinder- und Hausmärchen* of the Brothers Grimm.

The third volume of this fundamental work, published in 1822, assigns capital importance to Basile's *Lo Cunto de li Cunti* in a retrospective survey of these collections of stories.

"This collection," writes Grimm, "was for a long time the best and richest that had been found by any nation. Not only were the traditions at that time more complete in themselves, but the author had a special talent for collecting them, and besides that an intimate knowledge of the dialect. The stories are told with hardly any break, and the tone, at least in the Neapolitan tales, is perfectly caught. . . . We may therefore look on this collection of fifty tales as the basis of many others; for although it was not so in actual fact, and was indeed not known beyond the country in which it appeared, and was never translated into French, it still has all the importance of a basis, owing to the coherence of its traditions. Two-thirds

---

9. Listen to me, you good fairies, / Whom I have wronged often through wishing, / Despite my better sense, / Hear my last wish! Take everything back / That I have received from your good graces. / And return me immediately to that condition in which you found me / When I began to wish! (German).
1. What no mind of reasonable people sees, a naïve person can do in all simplicity (German).

of them are, so far as their principal incidents are concerned, to be found in Germany, and are current there at this very day. Basile has not allowed himself to make any alteration, scarcely even any addition of importance, and that gives his work a special value."

Thanks to this laudatory notice Basile's book emerged from the obscurity to which it had been relegated as a work in dialect, and that a dialect of Southern Italy, and became known to the world of students. After certain of his *cunti* had been translated at intervals by the said Brothers Grimm and others, Felix Liebrecht, in 1846, published a complete German translation of the book, to enable it to be used for research in comparative folklore. In his preface to this Jacob Grimm observes, in confirmation and illustration of his previous verdict on the importance of Basile: "It was by no means easy to translate the *Pentamerone* of Basile into German, since it presents all the idiosyncrasies by which the Neapolitan dialect differs in important respects from ordinary Italian. If it is hard enough to penetrate into the significance of the almost Eastern glow and sparkle of these metaphors, comparisons, jests, and expressions of love, abuse, or malediction, burning and vivid as Oriental poetry, the difficulty becomes ten times greater when we attempt to translate them into a language which is not subtle enough for the rendering of this bombast in its native grace and charm. Our modern German and our times are too formal for this; a Fischart with the language and manners of the sixteenth century might, if such a book had come into his hands, have taken the bit between his teeth and have succeeded in reaching or even surpassing the original, by means of the still unproscribed words and expressions which ingenuously render the modest and the immodest, the polished and the unpolished. I, for my part, had advised the translator, of whose profound insight into the original text no one can doubt, to omit everything that might give offence, and can understand that it would seem to him to be a delicate matter to interfere with the veracity and integrity of the text; but words and inflections that sound vulgar to us to-day, even when they correspond exactly with the original Italian, have become harsher and cruder to our ears because we have other standards of decency, and what then was an innocent *trattenemiento de li peccerille* would be impossible for our wives and children."

To all of which Liebrecht reasonably replies, that "Basile did not write his *Cunto de li Cunti* for children, despite its sub-title: 'Tales for the little ones,' nor yet merely for the ordinary man in the street."

We cannot but admire the manner in which Liebrecht carried out his task, facing, and almost always happily surmounting, the colossal difficulties which this text presents to a foreigner. The difficulty was even greater in 1846, owing to the lack of a complete Neapolitan dictionary (the only vocabulary being that which accompanied Porcelli's Collection); so that Liebrecht had to guide himself by his general philological knowledge, and by the direst study of the other Neapolitan writers. Notwithstanding this, his mistakes are infinitesimal, and are almost invariably due to the editions he had at hand. Of the older editions he only had access to Sarnelli, which appeared to him (as indeed it is) to be better than those which followed it, even the last and most widely known by Porcelli. The literary merit of his translation is no less striking, for he managed to find equivalents to

Basile's romantic expressions, so that Liebrecht's German prose is a true rendering of the exuberant and capricious author of the South.

He gives few notes to the text (mindful of Johnson's remark, "notes are often necessary, but they are necessary evils"), but they are very valuable, and the Appendix has a good account of the Neapolitan dialect and dialect literature.

The German translation was followed by an English version. As early as 1832 Sir Walter Scott, who was staying at Naples, and frequented the Biblioteca Bourbon, had come across Basile's book,[2] and was sufficiently interested to prepare an essay on the Neapolitan dialect.

Two years later some of the tales appeared in English in Keightley's *Tales and Popular Fictions*, and attracted the attention of J. E. Taylor, who got the original from Naples and begun to translate it with the sole help of the notes to Gabriele Fosano's *Tasso napoletano*; and later, with the aid of the poet Gabriele Rossetti; then in exile in England, and lastly with that of Liebrecht's translation; he confined his work to thirty tales, because he wished the book to be suitable for the general reader. This fine English edition was brought out in 1843 [read 1848] in a volume now very rare and sought after, illustrated with drawings by George Cruikshank; and Liebrecht praises it highly in the note to Dunlop, in which he makes various additions and corrections to his already published version. There is, on the other hand, no French version, save for a few tales, included in the *Journal pour tous* of 1865, and translated by one Della Corte di Somma. Later on there was another German version, or rather abridgment, of forty tales and one in Italian of only eighteen tales; in England, after several republications of the part-translation of Taylor, Sir Richard F. Burton made a complete and literal version.

The best works illustrative of *Lo Cunto de li Cunti* are in Italy; besides the studies by Imbriani (who examined it chiefly from the literary side) there is the collection of popular tales by the same Imbriani, those by Pitrè and others (in which we frequently find comparisons with Basile's tales), and the industrious research into comparative folk-lore with which we especially connect the name of Rua.

ORIGINS OF THE TALES AND SUBJECT-MATTER

Basile culled his tales directly from the people, as is attested by the virgin freshness of their form. And what otherwise could have been their literary history? Only certain of his stories are to be found in Straparola: *Peruonto* (I.3) corresponds to the first tale of the third night of Straparola; *Cagliuso* (II.4) to the first of the eleventh; *Lilla e Lolla* (V.I) to the second of the fifth; *Li cinco figlie* (V.7) to the fifth of the seventh. To these

---

2. It can be none other to which Sir Walter alludes when he writes: "One work in this dialect, for such it is, was described to me as a history of ancient Neapolitan legends—quite in my way; and it proves to be a dumpy fat 12mo. edition of Mother Goose's Tales with my old friend Puss in Boots, Bluebeard, and almost the whole stock of this very collection. If this be the original of this charming book, it is very curious, for it shows the right of Naples to the authorship, but there are French editions very early also; for there are two—whether French or Italian I am uncertain—of different dates, both having claims to the original edition, each omitting some tales which the other has." *Journal of Sir Walter Scott, 1825–32, from the original manuscript at Abbotsford*, Edinburgh, David Douglas, 1891, p. 873; on the Neapolitan dialect, cf. p. 875 [*Croce's note*].

coincidences, already noted by Grimm, we must add a few others, as between the story of *Cienzo* (I.7) and that of Cesarino of Berni (X.3) who frees a princess doomed to be devoured by a monster, slays the brute, and cuts out its tongue, making use of it subsequently to baffle a countryman who claims that he had killed the monster. Nevertheless, this critic is still of the opinion that, after due comparison, it is evident that Basile wrote independently of Straparola.

Other analogies can be detected with various authors. *Vardiello* (I.4) and the novel of Morlino (XLI): *De matre quæ filium custoditum reliquit*; but why should Basile have gone to Morlino for such a popular tale? and how did he manage to give it this very popular character? *Verdeprato* (II.2) is quite similar to a tale contained in the *Angitia Cortigiana de natura del cortigiano* (Roma, 1550) of M. A. Biondo, which is summarised by Passano as follows: "It tells of how a gentleman, named Pennaverde, passed through a crystal tube to reach his beloved, how the tube broken by the craft of the sister of his mistress lacerates his flesh so that he is on the point of death, and in what manner the lover is saved by his mistress": this too was a very well-known tale current under numerous versions. *Rosella* (III.9) corresponds in all points (save one of little importance) to the story of Filenia in Mambriano (c. XXI); and here the hypothesis of imitation acquires a certain probability "when we observe that the lack of all popular features, common to every version, in the novel of Cieco and in that of Basile, suggests a remodelling by the poet of the popular tale.

However this may be, we are forced to recognise that the literary element, if not altogether lacking in *Lo Cunto de li Cunti*, is very exiguous and negligible.

The variations introduced by Basile into the traditional legends consist almost entirely of formal embellishments; and it is but very seldom that we light on some non-popular detail, as, *e.g.*, in the Eighth Diversion of the Fourth Day, the spirited description of the *Casa del Tempo*.

Few of Basile's *trattenementi* fall outside the category of fairy-tales. Some are comical stories, as *Lo compare* (II.10), which relates how a good man resolved and succeeded in ousting an intruder from his home. *Li due fratelli* (IV.2), a tale of the varied fortunes of two brothers, one wealthy and vicious, the other poor and virtuous, is really, as Grimm remarks, a didactic tale. Among the citizen's wives-tales there are other narratives: *Vardiello* (I.4) is about a treasure found by a fool in consequence of his folly; *La serva d' aglie* (III.6) tells of a lady who disguised herself as a man, she is beloved, and after divers experiments is discovered to be a woman, and marries; *La soperbia castecata* (IV.10) is a king who is scorned by a princess. In revenge he gets her into his possession and makes her lead a miserable life, but eventually pardons and marries her. *La sapia* (V.6) tells of a young woman who by a judicious box on the ear converts the King's son into a man of intelligence. He marries her out of revenge, puts her to a thousand torments, and as in the preceding story there is a reconciliation. All the other tales belong to the world of fairies or ogres; these are strange, or even ordinary adventures, but always helped or hindered by the actions of these super-normal beings.

The fairies, as Grimm noted, are good or beneficent beings, and the

ogres and ogresses the bad or malevolent ones; in character, although they
have a Latin name, they greatly resemble the *gute* or *weise Frau*, and the
wilder Mann or *Riese* of German mythology. In the German legends we
often meet with Christian figures as well, angels, demons, the Madonna,
which are entirely wanting in the Italian stories; the devil and other malign
influences are named occasionally, but they are vague and are never presented as distinct personalities.

Besides ogres and fairies, certain personifications play a part in Basile's
tales, such as Time, the months (IV.8; V.2); men endowed with prodigious
faculties (I.5; III.8); enchanted animals such as the ass that voids gold (I.1);
a dragon (I.7); cats (II.4; III.10); a cockchafer, a mouse and a grasshopper
(III.5); birds (IV.5); fairies, ogres and princes transformed by caprice or
destiny into animals or plants, into a lizard (I.8); a hind (I.9); a serpent
(II.5); doves (IV.5); a myrtle (I.2); objects endowed with strange virtues,
as a herb that resuscitated the dead (I.7); the heart of an animal or the
petal of a rose that causes pregnancy (I.9; II.8); acorns, napkins, sticks,
rings, date-palms (II.1; I.1; III.4; IV.1; I.6); the fat of a wolf, as remedies
for mortal diseases (II.5; II.2); lastly, causes from the fatal effect of which
it is difficult to escape (Intro.; II.7; III.9).

The ethical element is that common to all fairy-tales: a rigorous distribution of rewards and punishments according to deserts, not without a
certain ferocity of procedure that seems to invoke the records of a distant
past or primitive civilisation.

LEWIS SEIFERT

The Marvelous in Context: The Place of the *Contes de Fées* in Late Seventeenth-Century France†

Praising the restraint with which Perrault uses the marvelous, Mary-
Elizabeth Storer asserts that in his tales "fairy magic (féerie) is made plausible, contemporary so to speak, and an atmosphere of reality is created
by details to which a La Fontaine or a La Bruyère could not have given
more attention" (*La Mode*, 103). Storer's statement relies on what continues to be a fundamental and largely unchallenged assumption in much
criticism on the *contes de fées*: the marvelous is acceptable to the extent
that it is used sparingly and plausibly. But in so far as fantasy literature,
by its very definition, defies an empirical or realistic explanation of narrative action, observations such as Storer's are bewildering. Why should
fairy tales be expected to minimize their use of the marvelous? Why should
a fundamentally *implausible* narrative effect be judged in terms of *plausibility*? At least part of the answer can be found in critical stereotypes that
take rationality to be the defining feature of French "classical" literature.
In this perspective, the *contes de fées* are an aberration to be ignored,

† From *Fairy Tales, Sexuality and Gender in France, 1690–1715: Nostalgic Utopias* (Cambridge:
Cambridge UP, 1996) 59–97. Reprinted with the permission of Cambridge University Press.

explained away, or at best subjected to this standard. To be sure, much
recent work militates against a simplistic view of "reason" and even "classicism" as the hallmarks of seventeenth-century French literature.[1] The
fact remains, however, that the first vogue of fairy tales, because of its
merveilleux, is strikingly original in the history of seventeenth-century
French literary forms. And it is perhaps this originality or specificity that
has caused critics to underscore the genre's implausibility.

Over and beyond its potential to subvert prevailing notions of verisimilitude and to define the text's readability, the marvelous leads to questions
about why the genre appeared when it did as well as its roles in the social
and cultural forces of the 1690s and early 1700s. To date, the explanations
offered by critics have failed by and large to account for the specific historical moment of the vogue. In her groundbreaking study, Mary-Elizabeth
Storer mentions without extensive analysis five conditions that in her view
contributed to the explosion of *contes de fées*: readers' boredom with the
long *romans* from the middle of the century; the tradition of fantasy literature extending back to the Middle Ages; the use of the *merveilleux* in
seventeenth-century court pastimes, opera, and salons; the sentiment of
decline at the end of Louis XIV's reign; and the personal misfortune of
many of the *conteurs* and *conteuses* (Storer, *La Mode*, 9–13, 252–253).
While any or even all of these factors doubtless contributed to the first
vogue of fairy tales, they do not necessarily explain why so many writers
were attracted to this specific genre at this particular time.[2] By contrast,
Raymonde Robert offers a considerably more complex picture. She concentrates at length on the ways that the *contes de fées* "mirror" (the term
is Robert's) late seventeenth-century society and culture—not only the elite
pastimes evoked by Storer, but also architecture, the decorative arts, attitudes of the privileged classes toward *le peuple* (the lower classes), and the
ideals of *mondain* culture (Robert, *Le Conte de fées*, 327–430). Central to
Robert's understanding of the genre is the assertion that it "is framed as
the ideal space for complete self-recognition and thus plays a sociological
role as a mirror intended to reinforce the image that the social group
claims for itself" (*La Mode*, 327). However, by insisting that the fairy tales
simply *reflect* a set of predetermined values, Robert tends to exclude from
consideration the complex ways that they *produce* and, especially, alter
ideological meanings.[3] What Robert leaves unstated, then, is that the fairy
tales' purported "realism" is both a reflection of and a response to a precise
social and cultural context. Moreover, she does not explain how the "mirroring" of the *contes de fées* differs from that of other art forms. The
seventeenth-century novel, as many critics have shown, also reinforced the

1. See Domna C. Stanton, "Classicism (Re)constructed: Notes on the Mythology of Literary History,"
   Continuum: Problems in French Literature from the Late Renaissance to the Early Enlightenment,
   vol. 1: "Rethinking Classicism: Overviews" (New York: AMS Press, 1990): 3–29.
2. Robert refutes Storer's simplistic understanding of escapism as a cause for the vogue (*Le Conte
   de fées*, 17). She also underscores Storer's imprecise literary chronology: by the 1690s, the *romans*
   had long been surpassed by the much shorter *nouvelles*, which continued to be published in great
   numbers throughout the first vogue (*Le Conte de fées*, 18).
3. On several occasions, Robert rejects interpretations of the *contes de fées* as "escape" from reality
   —such as Storer's (see especially *Le Conte de fées*, 16–20 and 327–330). However, her own analysis
   often suggests a more nuanced reading (see *Le Conte de fées*, 328).

ideological underpinnings of the aristocracy and in some instances the bourgeoisie.[4] As a result, Robert's otherwise magisterial analysis begs the question as to why a plethora of *contes de fées* appeared and why contemporaries found fairy tales so attractive during the final years of the seventeenth century.

In the current state of research on late seventeenth-century French culture, it is admittedly difficult to explain the rise of the genre in great detail. In particular, much remains to be explored concerning the transition from the seventeenth- to the eighteenth-century salon and, more generally, the changes within the reading public during the final decades of Louis XIV's reign. Far from resolving these questions or claiming exhaustive treatment of the appearance of the *contes de fées*, I will nonetheless argue that the fairy-tale vogue had strategic meanings in the context of the Quarrel of the Ancients and the Moderns as well as the *fin de siècle* attacks against *mondain* society. This chapter will also demonstrate that women writers found in the fairy-tale form a means of defining and defending their own stake in these conflicts. The meanings the genre assumed as an exemplar of "modernist" and *mondain* culture help us understand why it became so popular.

Ancient Tales/Modern Storytelling

Why would readers of the literate elite become interested in narratives they associated with the illiterate masses? Why would they desire to tell and write stories they treated with condescension not unlike that reserved for the popular tale-spinners themselves? What purposes did this recuperation or rewriting of such stories serve? Answers to these questions concern first of all the status of folklore in the seventeenth-century *contes de fées*. The link between folklore and this literary vogue is a matter of discernible traces of tale-types and motifs as well as the perception of folklore at the time.

Literary fairy tales are usually defined as written narratives based, in however minimal a way, on folktales, the oral narratives preserved and told by literate and non-literate groups alike. However, to conclude that the folkloric tradition was exclusively oral would be an over-generalization, for the historical study of folkloric tale-types and motifs has revealed that it is often impossible to separate written from oral versions.[5] As they were told and retold, tales were transformed, truncated, and combined with other motifs or tale-types in accordance with both printed and oral narratives. The reception of many of the seventeenth-century *contes de fées* proves this point quite clearly. Mainly through the *Bibliothèque bleue*, many of these versions of tale-types (re)entered the oral folkloric tradition, only to be collected later by folklorists.[6]

Unlike the Grimms and other nineteenth-century German fairy-tale writers in particular, none of the seventeenth-century *conteurs* and con-

---

4. See especially DiPiero, *Dangerous Truths*, and Harth, *Ideology and Culture*.
5. See Velay-Vallantin, *L'Histoire des contes*.
6. On the influence of publication on oral folklore, see especially, Velay-Vallantin, "Le Miroir des contes: Perrault dans les Bibliothèques bleues," *Les Usages de l'imprimé*, ed. Roger Chartier (Paris: Fayard, 1987) 129–185; and Velay-Vallantin, "Introduction," *L'Histoire des contes*.

teuses endeavored to transcribe folkloric narratives out of anything resembling ethnographic interest. This does not mean that folkloric tale-types (collected and indexed in the early twentieth century) are not to be found in many of the seventeenth-century *contes de fées*. Indeed, one of the most significant aspects of the seminal studies by both Marc Soriano and Raymonde Robert is their painstaking research into how and to what extent folkloric tale-types and motifs are used in the seventeenth-century *contes de fées*. Soriano shows that complex intertextual (literary and folkloric) networks inform the *Contes en vers* and the *Histoires ou contes du temps passé, avec des moralités* and that Perrault himself was an avid but unsentimental observer of popular folklore. Synthesizing the work of folklorists and literary historians, Robert concludes that fully one-half of the *contes de fées* published between 1690 and 1715 were based at least in part on tale-types (*Le Conte de fées*, 71).[7] As we will see in a moment, several *conteurs* and *conteuses* explicitly acknowledge their debt to folkloric sources. Of those who do not, several nonetheless display a thoroughgoing knowledge of traditional tale-types in their narratives.[8] These tales might be said to exploit a *direct* recuperation of folklore.[9]

In a general sense, the entire vogue represents what can be termed an *indirect* recuperation of folklore since the *contes de fées* were read as a derivation of folktales and, more importantly, as a genre that bore the imprint of the lower classes.[1] Indeed, the fairy tales were predicated on the presumption that they could be traced to folklore, that is, stories whose social indignity was sealed by their association in the minds of aristocratic and bourgeois readers with the superstition of the marvelous. Certain textual features, and especially marvelous characters such as fairies, ogres, dwarfs (among others) were associated, correctly or incorrectly, with folkloric tradition and served to remind readers of the popular "origins" of the vogue. It is the evocation of these purported origins more than the actual rewriting of folkloric narratives that is put to strategic uses in the social and cultural conflicts of the late seventeenth century.

The presumed folkloric origins of the *contes de fées* take on precise meanings within the *Querelle des Anciens el des Modernes* (Quarrel of the Ancients and the Moderns). Although various incarnations of this debate appeared from the sixteenth to the eighteenth centuries, its most famous battles in France took place during the second half of the seventeenth century, especially between 1687 (the year Perrault's poem "Le Siècle de Louis le Grand" was read in the Académie Française) and 1694 (when

7. This percentage compares with one-tenth for the eighteenth-century vogue (*Le Conte de fées*, 171).
8. Besides Perrault, d'Aulnoy demonstrates a wide and detailed knowledge of folkloric narratives. Robert finds traces of folkloric tale-types in eighteen of her twenty-five *contes de fées* (*Le Conte de fées*, 127–129).
9. See the "Recensement des contes types folkloriques utilisés par les contes de fées littéraires entre 1690 et 1778" in Robert, *Le Conte de fées*, 127–129.
1. What I discuss as the "indirect" recuperation of folklore has been studied in detail with respect to the German *Märchen* and their rewriting of the seventeenth- and eighteenth-century French literary fairy tales (see Manfred Grätz, *Das Märchen in der deutschen Aufklärung: Vom Feenmärchen zum Volksmärchen* [Stuttgart: J. B. Metzlersche Verlagsbuchhandlung, 1988]). I am grateful to Jack Zipes for this reference.

Boileau and Perrault were publicly reconciled). Complex in its aims and ramifications, this Quarrel centered around the status of modern cultural artifacts in relation to those inherited from Greek and Roman antiquity. Whereas the Ancients maintained that the latter were a universal bench-mark against which all artistic endeavors should be measured, the Moderns promoted the ideal of progress, which allowed the possibility that modern artistic creation could surpass that of antiquity. Where the Ancients saw a fundamental *stasis* and unchanging essence as the norm for cultural pro-duction, the Moderns perceived historical and cultural relativity.

Developed, at least ostensibly, from indigenous French and not ancient classical sources, fairy tales constituted a somewhat radical *exemplum* of the Moderns' theses. In their "theoretical" discussions, both Lhéritier and Perrault explicitly compared French folktales to the myths and fables of antiquity. In the context of the Quarrel, such comparisons required a good deal of audacity and polemic motivation. The ancient "tales" enjoyed the legitimacy of educational institutions not to mention a privileged place in the hierarchy of literary values. Folktales, by contrast, were accessible to anyone, but were above all the province of the uneducated and the illit-erate. To compare folkloric narratives to ancient myths and fables was to drive home the relativity of the latter prestigious forms. For both Lhéritier and Perrault, it was also to make a strategic attack on the Ancients. With only a few exceptions, Boileau and other partisans of the Ancients virtually ignored the fairy tales published by Perrault and the other *conteurs* and *conteuses*. In all likelihood they could not take the vogue seriously, given its association with folklore and children's literature, nor would they want to dignify it by openly denouncing it.[2]

Safe from counterattacks, then, Lhéritier and Perrault aggressively de-fended the value of folkloric tales and, thus, the capacity of a heretofore neglected generic form to serve the lofty goals of literature. "Contes pour contes" (Tales for tales), concludes the narrator in Lhéritier's "Les En-chantements de l'éloquence" (The Enchantments of Eloquence), "il me paraît que ceux de l'antiquité gauloise valent bien à peu près ceux de l'antiquité grecque; et les fées ne sont pas moins en droit de faire des prodiges que les dieux de la Fable" (it seems to me that those of Gallic antiquity are more or less comparable to those from Grecian antiquity; and fairies are no less capable of miracles than the gods of mythology).[3] To make this comparison, both Perrault and Lhéritier must show that their *contes* have every bit as much moral value as the classical *fable* (mythology, but also tales and fables). In the *Préface* to his *Contes en vers*, Perrault goes even further and argues for the moral superiority of the *conte de fées*: "Je prétends même que mes Fables méritent mieux d'être racontées que la plupart des Contes anciens, et particulièrement celui de la Matrone

---

2. The Abbé de Villiers, a virulent critic of novels and fairy tales, devotes an entire chapter of an anti-novel tract to denouncing the vogue, only to conclude by excusing himself: "mais c'est, ce me semble, assez parler de Contes, je craindrais que si quelque sérieux nous entendait, il ne trouvât notre conversation indigne de nous" (*Entretiens sur les contes de fées, et sur quelques autres ouvrages du temps. Pour servir de préservatif contre le mauvais goût* [Paris: J. Collombat, 1699] 110).

3. Marie-Jeanne Lhéritier de Villandon, "Les Enchantements de l'éloquence," *Contes de Perrault*, ed. Gilbert Rouger (Paris: Garnier, 1967) 256.

d'Ephèse et celui de Psyché, si l'on les regarde du côté de la Morale, chose principale dans toute sorte de Fables, et pour laquelle elles doivent avoir été faites" (I even claim that my Fables deserve more to be told than most of the ancient Tales, and particularly those of the Matron of Ephesus and Psyche, if one looks at them from the perspective of Morality, a principal aspect of every kind of Fable, and for which they ought to have been created [50; 121]). Calling his own tales *"fables"* and the "ancient" fables *"contes,"* the advocate for the *Modernes* makes his genre even more canonical than the canon itself. Perrault gives his tales a name of prestige and official sanction, the better to emphasize their moral quality. Later in the *Préface*, Perrault does not hesitate to attribute the moral value of folktales to their "originary" storytellers:

> Tout ce qu'on peut dire, c'est que cette Fable de même que la plupart de celles qui nous restent des Anciens n'ont été faites que pour plaire sans égard aux bonnes mœurs qu'ils négligeaient beaucoup. Il n'en est pas de même des contes que nos aïeux ont inventés pour leurs Enfants. Ils ne les ont pas contés avec l'élégance et les agréments dont les Grecs et les Romains ont orné leurs Fables; mais ils ont toujours eu un très grand soin que leurs contes renfermassent une moralité louable et instructive.

> All that one can say is that this Fable, like most of the Fables remaining to us from the Ancients, was created only to please, without regard for good morals, which they greatly neglected. It is not the same with the tales that our forefathers invented for their Children. They did not tell them with the same elegance and embellishment with which the Greeks and the Romans ornamented their Fables; but they always took great care that their tales should incorporate a praiseworthy and instructive moral. (51; 121)

What the folkloric narratives lack in elegance and ornament, they gain through their "moral" developed by the anonymous "forefathers" to edify their children. Significantly, then, Perrault substantiates the superiority of the French "fables" by evoking both the moralizing and infantilizing pretexts we saw in the previous chapter. So doing, he idealizes not only the folkloric tales but also the archetypal tale-spinners. Popular narratives and narrators lose their brute reality to become worthy models of modern culture. Moreover, the decidedly non-literary form of folklore—its lack of "elegance and embellishment with which the Greeks and the Romans ornamented their fables—becomes the guarantor of its exemplary content. By contrast, the form of the ancient *fables*, Perrault argues, pleases "without regard for good morals." The very literariness of these "tales" is tied, at least implicitly, to moral dissolution.

In her "Lettre à Madame D.G.**," Lhéritier presents a considerably more complex justification of folklore and its use in literature. Rather than deliver a frontal attack on the Ancients, as does Perrault, she concentrates on (what she perceives to be) the history and forms of folklore, which she traces to the Middle Ages. It was the troubadours, Lhéritier claims, who created what were to become folktales (*contes*), but also the epic novels (*romans*) of the mid-seventeenth century. Over the course of time, both of these offspring of the medieval poets became corrupted. Referring to the *nouvelles* of the second half of the century, Lhéritier declares that, with the notable exception of *La Princesse de Clèves*, "les Romans ont perdu beaucoup de leurs beautés: On les a réduits en petit, et dans cet état, il y en a peu qui conservent les grâces du style et les agréments de l'invention" (Novels have lost much of their beauty: they have been reduced in size, and in this state, there are few that preserve stylistic grace and the charms of innovation).[4] Similarly, many (but not all) folktales were filled with "aventures scandaleuses" (scandalous adventures), which Lhéritier attributes to the social standing of their popular storytellers. "Je crois . . . que ces Contes se sont remplis d'impuretés en passant dans la bouche du petit peuple, de même qu'une eau pure se charge toujours d'ordures en passant par un canal sale" (I think . . . that these Tales were filled with impurities by passing through the mouths of lowly people, just as pure water is laden with garbage when it passes through a dirty gutter [312–313]). Other popular storytellers are responsible for obscuring the moral function of folktales (313). By contrast, the fairy tales told/written for polite society attempt to recapture the inherent moral purity of the troubadours' storytelling and, thereby, simultaneously regenerate both the novel and folklore (306–307). More than a return to an indigenous intertext, the "Contes au style des troubadours" (Tales in the style of the troubadours), as Lhéritier calls them, are rewritten to exemplify the perfection of modern literary expectations, which only adds to the original stories: "la bienséance des mots n'ôte rien à la singularité des choses; et si le peuple ou les Troubadours s'étaient exprimés comme nous, leurs Contes n'en auraient que mieux valu" (the propriety of the words takes nothing from the singularity of things; and if the people or the Troubadours had expressed themselves as we do, their Tales would only have been better for it [314–315]).

Whether they rely on the storytelling of the popular masses or the troubadours, both Perrault and Lhéritier convey nostalgic and, thus, idealized visions of folklore. However, their nostalgia has less to do with a conviction for the pedagogical value of folklore than with strategic polemical interest. If the fundamental role of the literary text is to please and instruct (*plaire et instruire*), or more precisely, to please in order to instruct, then folklore is just as worthy of literary status as the ancient narratives. The point Lhéritier and Perrault seem to be making, then, is that the Ancients' insistence on both the imitation of classical models and the preeminence of the *plaire et instruire* ideal leads to a logical *aporia*. Classical literature does not have a privileged relationship to moral value. Rewritings of popular folklore are just as capable of fulfilling this function, and by extension, just as, if not more deserving of critical recognition as literature.

Lhéritier's and Perrault's manifestoes are strategic defenses of the "modernist" cause in another way as well. Both the "Lettre à Madame D.G**" and the *Préface* to the *Contes en vers* appeared in 1695, a year after Boileau and Perrault (the leaders of the Ancient and Modern camps respectively) had been publicly reconciled after many heated public disputes. Although

---

4. Marie-Jeanne Lhéritier de Villandon, "Lettre à Madame D.G.**," *Euvres meslées* (Paris: J. Guignard, 1696) 306.

this reconciliation was billed as the end of the Quarrel, Lhéritier's and Perrault's manifestoes, appearing when they did, continued the debate while bringing to it new material from which to make the "modernist" case. Subsequently, of course, both the *conteuse* and the *conteur* published still more tales as what might be considered practical applications of their theories. I would argue that the same might be said for the entire vogue of *contes de fées*. Apart from Lhéritier and Perrault, none of the fairy-tale writers make explicit allusions to the Quarrel. Yet, written and published in the polemical climate defined by Lhéritier and Perrault, the fairy tales published from 1696 on demonstrate, in a *de facto* manner, the recuperability of popular folklore and, thus, the "modernist" conception of literature. More decisive by far, the success of the vogue proved that there was wide-spread support for a resolutely modern literary form.

Popular Storytelling *and* Mondain *Culture*

Folklore plays a paradoxical role in the first vogue of *contes de fées*. On the one hand, of course, folklore is, either directly or indirectly, the *sine qua non* of these and all literary fairy tales. On the other hand, the fairy tales distance themselves from the popular origins of folktales by recycling them for the literary consumption of an elite readership. This paradox is crucial to the genre's defense of "modernist" literature: folklore provides a strategic source of cultural renewal, yet that renewal is predicated on an effacement of the reality of popular storytelling. At the same time, the paradoxical role of folklore enables the genre to (re)affirm precise sociocultural identities. As rewritings of folklore, the *contes de fées* posit, simultaneously, both a link and a distinction between the literate upper classes and the illiterate lower classes. Within the collective unconscious of the *mondain* public by and for whom the fairy tales were written, the popular (ie. lower class) tale-spinner becomes a model of sociable storytelling, which, in turn, (re)enunciates an elite socio-cultural ideal.[5] To understand why folklore and popular storytellers fulfilled this function, we must first consider the definition and status of *mondain* culture in the final years of the seventeenth century.

Not unlike current semantic usage, the adjective *mondain* in seventeenth-century France had ambiguous meanings. In religious parlance, of course, it took on negative connotations and designated persons who are excessively attached to worldly (as opposed to spiritual) values. In the positive sense that I use here, this term could also refer to an elite sociological group and the ideal of sociability that exemplified it. It is from this perspective that Furetière designates one of the meanings of *le monde* as "des manières de vivre et de converser avec les hommes. Les gens qui hantent

5. My analysis at this point parallels that of Robert, who concludes that "by playing with the material of popular stories, by mimicking their oral character, the *mondains* search for a form of self-affirmation in this confrontation with the alterity of popular discourse" (*Le Conte de fées*, 384). However, in the course of her analysis, Robert emphasizes not so much the appropriation of popular storytelling by the *conteurs* and *conteuses* (as I do here) as what she calls "the caesura between official culture and popular culture" (*Le Conte de fées*, 384). Moreover, while Robert interprets the *conte de fées* as a form of self-valorization, she does not connect the rise of the vogue with attacks on *mondain* culture.

la Cour sont appelés les gens du *monde,* le beau *monde,* le *monde* poli"
(ways of living and conversing with men. The people who live at court
are called people of the *world,* the beautiful *world,* the polite *world*).[6] Referring to a similar semantic network, Richelet defines *le monde poli, le
beau monde* as "les honnêtes gens et les gens de qualité, qui d'ordinaire
sont propres, polis et bien mis" (*honnête* people and people of quality who
are ordinarily clean, polite, and well dressed).[7] The adjective *mondain,*
then, referred to an exclusive public recognizable by the elevated socio-
economic station, outward appearance, and demeanor of its members, as
well as their coveted social contacts. The *mondains* belonged to what Alain
Viala has called the "intermediate stratum" of the three sociological groups
of readers of seventeenth-century France.[8] Neither erudites in the limited
sense nor "popular" consumers of pamphlets and chapbooks, this "intermediary" public, including both aristocrats and bourgeois, read and produced most of the literature of the period.

Throughout the seventeenth century, specific aspects of what might be
broadly called *mondain* culture were repeatedly attacked by various conservative religious interests, including among others the Compagnie du
Saint Sacrement and the Jansenists. Religious critics railed against everything from fashion to pastimes. These attacks were not always confined to
verbal admonitions. As the famous controversies surrounding Molière's *Le
Tartuffe* and *Dom Juan* attest, for instance, religious cabals could even
exert pressure to have plays banned. However, the final years of the century
witnessed an intensification of religious piety that translated into overt hostility toward *mondain* culture. What differentiated these attacks from the
preceding ones was that the court at Versailles, following what was probably Madame de Maintenon's lead, had become an important center of
this religious conservatism. The renowned bishop and orator Jacques-
Bénigne Bossuet, for instance, argued vigorously against "worldly" pleasures. In 1694, he wrote two polemical pieces, *Traité de la concupiscence*
and *Maximes et réflexions sur la comédie,* in which he staked out an un-
compromising position *vis-à-vis* artistic and, particularly, literary endeavors.[9] Not content to decry the secular *sciences,* Bossuet was one of a
number of ecclesiastical authorities to press for increased regulation if not
outright abolition of the theater in the 1690s. Even if public pressure
prevented any drastic measures, officials of both Church and State in-

6. Antoine Furetière, *Dictionnaire universal* (1690; Paris: S.N.L.-Le Robert, 1978).
7. Pierre Richelet, *Dictionnaire françois* (1680; Geneva: Slatkine Reprints, 1970). The *Dictionnaire
   de l'Académie françoise* (1694) does not give a corresponding definition for "monde."
8. Alain Viala, *Naissance de l'écrivain: sociologie de la littérature à l'âge classique* (Paris: Minuit,
   1985) 143–147.
9. In the following passage from the *Traité de la concupiscence,* for instance, Bossuet echoes Pascal
   in warning about the dangerous diversion from spiritual introspection caused by "sciences" ranging
   from history and philosophy to novels and poetry: "Pour ce qui est des véritables [sciences], on
   excède encore beaucoup à s'y livrer trop ou à contretemps, ou au préjudice de plus grandes
   obligations, comme il arrive à ceux qui dans le temps de prier ou de pratiquer la vertu, s'adonnent
   ou à l'histoire ou à la philosophie ou à toute sorte de lectures, surtout des livres nouveaux, des
   romans, des comédies, des poésies, et se laissent tellement posséder au désir de savoir qu'ils ne
   se possèdent plus euxmêmes. Car tout cela n'est autre chose qu'une intempérance, une maladie,
   un dérèglement de l'esprit, un dessèchement du cœur, une misérable captivité qui ne nous laisse
   pas le loisir de penser à nous, et une source d'erreurs" (Jacques-Bénigne Bossuet, *Traité de la
   concupiscence,* Les Textes français [Paris: Fernand Roches, 1930] 26).

creased their control over the theater. The atmosphere of suspicion and repression was endorsed, if only indirectly, by Louis XIV who, although an avid sponsor in his earlier years, appears to have totally abandoned the theater after 1692.[1] The most famous indication of this hostility came in 1697 with the expulsion from France of the Comédiens italiens, probably for staging a play with satirical allusions to Madame de Maintenon (Adam, *Histoire*, 5: 257, n. 12). Considering this climate, Antoine Adam is most likely justified to conclude that during the final years of Louis XIV's reign, "the theater was . . . subjected to a surveillance and regulations unknown in previous periods" (Adam, *Histoire*, 5: 258).

Opposition to the theater was only the more palpable of attacks against *mondain* culture in general. Compared to preceding decades, the 1690s and 1700s witnessed the publication of far more "moralist" tracts and treatises aimed at reforming sociable conduct and denouncing the dangers of *divertissements* such as opera, theater, novels, and gambling.[2] It is possible that the mushrooming of such publications is at least in part attributable to an expansion of the reading public in this period and a corresponding (but paradoxical) desire to make the demands of sociable conduct more stringent. Jacques Revel has noted that during the last third of the seventeenth century, when civility became a common point of reference for a socially heterogeneous public, an aristocratic reaction developed against a code of civility perceived to be too accessible.[3] The insistence on the difficulty of "transparent" and "simple" politeness corresponds to this socio-historical interpretation. Whatever the motivation, the regularity with which *mondain* entertainments and activities are scrutinized is striking. They are most often denounced as impeding the authenticity of "vrai mérite" (true merit) and "honnêteté sans artifice" (nobility without artifice) essential to acquiring moral and thus social distinction.[4] Consistently undergirding these critiques is a religious discourse not unrelated to the Church's attacks on theater. Thus, when the Duchesse de Liancourt advises her granddaughter to shun novels, the reasons she gives involve piety: "le démon vous présentera aussi des romans qui auront de la vogue . . . mais il y a un venin dans ces sortes de livres . . . on se sent si froid pour la prière et pour la lecture spirituelle, et si fort en goût pour les folies du monde qu['] . . . on demeure avec un cœur tout changé" (the devil will show you novels in vogue . . . but there is a venom in that sort of books . . . one feels so cold for prayer and spiritual readings, and so inclined for the follies of the world that . . . one comes away with a

1. Antoine Adam, *Histoire de la littérature française au XVIIe siècle*, 5 vols. (Paris: del Duca, 1968) 5: 253, n. 4. On hostility to the theater in late seventeenth-century France, see Adam, *Histoire*, 5: 251–266.
2. I base this observation on Raymond Toinet's extremely useful "Les Ecrivains moralistes au XVIIe siècle," *Revue d'Histoire littéraire de la France*, 23 (1916): 570–610; 24 (1917): 296–306, 656–675; 25 (1918): 310–320, 655–671; 33 (1926): 395–407. Roughly half of all the titles inventoried were published in the period 1690–1715.
3. Jacques Revel, "The Uses of Civility," *A History of Private Life: Passions of the Renaissance*, ed. Philippe Ariès and Georges Duby, trans. Arthur Goldhammer (Cambridge, MA: Harvard University Press, 1989) 201–203.
4. I borrow these terms from the Abbé Morvan de Bellegarde, *Réflexions sur ce qui peut plaire ou déplaire ans le commerce du monde* (Lyon: Horace Molin, 1696). See also his *Réflexions sur la politesse des mœrs, avec des maximes pour la société civile* (Paris: J.-F. Broncart, 1699).

completely changed heart.)[5] Just as significant as the reality of these attacks were the perceptions on the part of *mondains* themselves. In what amounted to the counterpart of religious denunciations of public immorality, many writers observed the oppressive piety of official circles. In 1696, for example, the Abbé du Bos wrote: "si Dieu ne nous assiste, on mettra bientôt la moitié de la ville en couvents, et la moitié des bibliothèques en livres de dévotion" (if God does not help us, half of the city will soon turn into convents and half of the libraries into devotional books [quoted in Adam, *Histoire*, 5: 8]). Perceptions such as these lead to more concrete reactions: after a highly public campaign by the Church against the theater in 1694, the numbers of play-goers increased dramatically.

If we consider that the vogue of *contes de fées* appeared against this backdrop of hostility to and reaction of the *mondain* sphere, then the cultural function of the genre comes into sharper focus. Although the vogue did not represent anything like a direct reply to the pietistic condemnations of polite society and its pastimes, it did appear as a revalorization and reenunciation of the sociable ideals of the *mondains* (including their literary tastes) at a time when they were drawing considerable criticism. In other words, the *contes de fées* were more of the order of a compensation for this criticism than a counterattack. Traces of this *mondain* response are perhaps visible when, at the end of "La Princesse Carpillon," d'Aulnoy decries the "*censeurs* odieux / Qui voulez qu'un héros résiste à la tendresse" (odious *critics* / Who want a hero to resist the tenderness of love [NCF, 4: 307–308; emphasis added]) and again at the end of "La Princesse Belle-Etoile et le Prince Chéri" when she declares: "L'Amour, n'en déplaise aux *censeurs*, / Est l'origine de la gloire" (Love, in spite of its *critics*, / Is the origin of glory [NCF, 5: 266; emphasis added]). But the clearest indication that the *conteurs* and *conteuses* were conscious of the prevailing religious rigorism while writing their tales is to be found in Lhéritier's "Lettre à Madame D.G**," which announces the new vogue but also preempts pietistic critics:

> Je sais, Madame, que le grand nombre de vos pieuses occupations ne vous empêche pas de vous divertir quelquefois par la lecture des ouvrages d'esprit, et que vous souhaitez d'être informée du caractère des nouveautés qu'il produit. Cette humeur chagrine qui paraît dans certaines personnes qu'on nomme pieuses, et qui les rend farouches, ne se trouve point en vous, quoique vous remplissiez tous les devoirs d'une piété profonde et solide. Ainsi je me fais un plaisir de vous annoncer aujourd'hui, qu'on est devenu depuis quelque temps du goût dont vous êtes. On voit de petites Histoires répandues dans le monde, dont tout le dessein est de prouver agréablement la solidité des Proverbes.
>
> I know, Madam, that your numerous pious activities do not prevent you from sometimes entertaining yourself by reading works of the

5. See Jeanne de Schomberg, Duchesse de Liancourt, *Règlement donné par une dame de haute qualité à sa petite-fille. Pour sa Conduite, et pour celle de sa Maison. Avec un autre Règlement que celle Dame avoit dressé pour ellemême* (1694; Paris: Florentin, 1718), 34.

mind and that you wish to be informed of the nature of the new works that it produces. That disgruntled mood which appears in certain persons who are called pious and which makes them inflexible is not to be found in you, even though you fulfill all the duties of a profound and solid piety. Thus it is a pleasure for me to announce to you today that people have come to be of your taste as of late. One sees little Stories told throughout polite society, the entire purpose of which is to prove agreeably the solidity of Proverbs. ("Lettre," 299–300)

If only implicitly, Lhéritier distinguishes between the authentic piety of both her addressee as well as the "little stories told throughout polite society" and the more questionable piety of "certain persons." More than a counterattack on euphemistically designated individuals, Lhéritier's description defends the moral integrity not only of the fairy-tale vogue but also of *mondain* culture itself. Against the arguments of Bossuet and others, the *conteuse* argues that piety and secular diversions are not inherently incompatible. To the contrary, the "petites Histoires," based on "the solidity of proverbs," serve as proof of their compatibility.

    * * * [T]he moral defense of the fairy-tale genre is most often an ironic pretext for saying something else. In the case of the above passage from the "Lettre à Madame D.G**," it is clear that Lhéritier is not only defending the moral function of the "petites Histoires" but also using it to legitimize the reading of secular "works of the mind" as well as the social context that receives them and makes them possible. Far from being unusual, the reaffirmation of *mondain* culture is central to the seventeenth-century *contes de fées*. Whether in the prefaces, frame-narratives, or the tales themselves, the ideals of polite society are the essential ideological framework. Paradoxically, however, these ideals are conveyed through gentrified folktales. But how can narratives associated with the lowest classes become a means of self-affirmation for a social and cultural elite?

Few of the *conteurs* and the *conteuses* make explicit reference to their tales' folkloric intertexts. Those who do, most notably Lhéritier and Perrault, trace these narratives to the storytelling of lower class women, namely nurses and governesses who spin tales for children. From all appearances, allusions to this type of storytelling reflect a widely held assumption on the part of the upper classes at the time.[6] If the *contes de fées* were predicated on an infantilizing pretext, it is because folktales were thought to be, above all, what women domestics told to the children of their masters and mistresses. More important, however, is the importance this storytelling scene assumes as the vogue's phantasmatic origin.

    Historians of folklore have established that most folktales were recounted

6. Soriano hypothesizes that Lhéritier and Perrault subconsciously occulted the fact that folklore was addressed almost exclusively to adults in popular settings (*Les Contes*, 96). Whatever the case, the existence of expressions such as "conte de vieille," "conte de ma Mère l'Oye," etc. in seventeenth-century France, attest not only to an undeniable social reality (storytelling by nurses and governesses to upper class children) but also, and more decisively, to a cultural stereotype.

among adults, and by women *and* men.[7] Thus, the storytelling scene prevalent in the seventeenth-century elite imagination is a reductive recuperation of a more varied popular tradition. Nonetheless, this scene figures
prominently in the theoretical discussions of both Perrault and Lhéritier.
In what is doubtless a strategic jibe at the Ancients, Perrault cites the
similar origins of the classical myth of "Psyche and Cupid" and the folkloric "Peau d'Ane":

> La Fable de Psyché écrite par Lucien et par Apulée est une fiction
> toute pure et un conte de Vieille comme celui de Peau d'Ane. Aussi
> voyons-nous qu'Apulée le fait raconter par une vieille femme à une
> jeune fille que des voleurs avaient enlevée, de même que celui de
> Peau d'Ane est conté tous les jours à des Enfants par leurs Gouver-
> nantes, et par les Grands-mères.

> The Fable of Psyche written by Lucian and by Apuleius is a pure
> fiction, and an Old Woman's tale like that of Donkey-skin. Therefore
> we see that Apuleius has it told by an old woman to a young woman
> whom thieves had abducted, just as Donkey-skin is told every day to
> Children by their Governesses, and by their Grandmothers. (50; 121)

In spite of her otherwise harsh judgment of popular storytelling, Lhéritier
affirms the pedagogical motivation of the women who appropriated the
contes of the troubadours: "la tradition nous a conservé les Contes des
Troubadours, et comme ils sont ordinairement remplis de faits surpren-
ants, et qu'ils enferment une bonne morale, les Grands-mères et les Gou-
vernantes les ont toujours racontés aux Enfants pour leur mettre dans
l'esprit la haine du vice et l'amour de la vertu" (tradition has preserved for
us the Tales of the Troubadours, and since they are ordinarily filled with
surprising details and include a good moral, Grandmothers and Governesses have always told them to Children in order to instill in their minds
hatred of vice and love of virtue ["Lettre," 305–306]).

But what is the purpose of evoking the transmission of folklore by
women of the popular classes? One answer can be found in the inherent
class configuration of this storytelling scene. Be she *grand-mère*, *nourrice*,
or *gouvernante*, the storyteller is a lower-class woman given the responsibility of entertaining children with traditional stories. Identifying with these
children, readers and writers of the *contes de fées* rely on the imaginary
storytelling of the surrogate mothers to reassert the values of their own
class. The mediation of this radical other (who is both lower class and a
woman) does not threaten the hegemonic system since she is constructed
as complicitous with it and since, as Michèle Farrell has argued, she "functions symbolically as a symptom of the asymmetry of the class relationship
obtaining between the aristocracy and the people . . ."[8] Given this ambiv-

---

7. Robert, *Le Conte de fées*, 8. Tale-telling was wide-spread in peasant *veillées* until the Revolution.
   See Edward Shorter, "The 'Veillée' and the Great Transformation," *The Wolf and the Lamb:
   Popular Culture in France from the Old Régime to the Twentieth Century*, ed. Jacques Beauroy,
   Marc Bertrand, and Edward T. Gargan (Saratoga, CA: Anma Libri, 1976) 127–140. See also
   Michèle Simonsen, *Perrault: "Contest"*, Etudes littéraires, 35 (Paris: Presses Universitaires de
   France, 1992) 20–24.
8. Michèle L. Farrell, "Celebration and Repression of Feminine Desire in Mme d'Aulnoy's Fairy
   Tale: *La Chatte Blanche*," *L'Esprit créateur* vol. 29, no. 3 (1989): 53.

alence, she is at the very center of an outlook perhaps best described as "aristocratic romanticism,"[9] the elitist, idealized vision of peasant life enabling members of the upper classes to capitalize on the advantages of what Norbert Elias calls the "civilizing process" (such as a decrease in the amount of interpersonal violence) while simultaneously retreating from its constraints. In this sense, the figure of the "originary" *conteuse* is profoundly nostalgic. As an imagined point of origin in the earthly immanence of base materiality, she guarantees the authenticity of experience and identity for a group in need of such reassurance. Specifically, the popular female storyteller reaffirms the exclusive socio-economic boundaries of *mondain* culture at a time when censors were calling into question its moral legitimacy. She represents a nostalgic fixation on social hierarchy as a means of displacing and compensating for the ethical attacks on the elite group.[1] She is also significant as a maternal figure: she comes to resemble the primal mother of psychoanalytic theory since she is an object of longing that both resolves and bespeaks deep-seated anxieties.

Ultimately, of course, the storytelling of the real *conteuses* is effaced by the seventeenth-century fairy tales and is transformed into narratives that reflect the elevated social stature of their audience. As a result, the *contes de fées* endorse an ethic of sociability central to *mondain* culture. That is, the entire vogue (with the exception of Fénelon's tales) is an extension or recreation of salon storytelling and the ideal of social interaction it implied. The inscription of this particular ideal of sociability had itself been waning since the middle of the seventeenth century and is, thus, one of the central nostalgic characteristics of the genre.

In Durand's novel, *La Comtesse de Mortane*, which contains two *contes de fées*, the countess expresses her pleasure when her suitor offers to spin a tale for her assembled salon: "Ah! . . . ne différez pas un moment, j'aime les contes comme si j'étais encore enfant . . ." (Ah! . . . don't wait a moment longer, I love fairy tales as if I were still a child),[2] thus inscribing this infantilizing genre within the activities of the privileged space of seventeenth-century sociability. The little evidence that remains suggests that storytelling based on folktales was an activity of the salons and the court from at least the mid-century.[3] However, without more substantial information, it is impossible to know how wide-spread this practice was, what the nature was of the tales told, and even (as has been suggested) if the published tales replaced the oral practice.[4] It is somewhat helpful, then,

9. See Elias, especially chapter 8, "On the Sociogenesis of Aristocratic Romanticism in the Process of Courtization," *The Court Society*, trans. Edmund Jephcott (Oxford: Basil Blackwell, 1983) 214–267.

1. Again, the obvious exception is Fénelon who figures among the most vocal critics of *mondain* culture.

2. Catherine Durand Bédacier, *La Comtesse de Mortane par Madame**** (Paris: Veuve de C. Barbin, 1699) 244.

3. See Introduction, 8–9. Tale-telling also existed at court. See Sévigné's letter of 6 August 1677 and Storer, *La Mode*, 12–14.

4. Robert hypothesizes that fairy tales stopped being told in the salons after 1698, the highpoint of the vogue (*Le Conte de fées*, 92–93). However, her own discussion of the second vogue shows that *contes de fées* were both told and discussed in eighteenth-century salons (see especially 342–349). Furthermore, in manuscript letters dating from 1708–1709, Murat makes reference to salon tale-telling (*Ouvrages de Mme la Comtesse de Murat*, ms. 3471, Bibliothèque de l'Arsenal, Paris, f° 278).

that many of the seventeenth-century *contes de fées* appear in frame-narratives that feature salon settings.[5] Although these fictional accounts obviously cannot be taken as historical records, they do suggest something of the ideology of sociability that the oral and the written vogues exemplified. Robert concludes that the frame-narratives and the tales told therein uphold "the image of an exclusive social group arrogantly turned in on itself" (*Le Conte de fées*, 341). In this analysis, the effect of storytelling in the frame-narratives is no different from that of other representations of the salon in seventeenth-century literature.[6] To be sure, it is crucial to recognize the elitist prejudice that is conveyed by these representations of storytelling. But it is also crucial to examine the precise nature of the sociable ideals on which the genre is predicated, whether in the frame-narratives, the meta-commentaries on the genre, or the tales themselves.

It is not insignificant that the seventeenth-century fairy tales are often embedded in frame-narratives as a *jeu d'esprit*,[7] a salon game in which one player improvises according to certain rules while the others guess the meaning of the riddle-like piece (Baader, *Dames de lettres*, 49–52). For, like the other *jeux d'esprit*, *contes de fées* involve a recognition of (what is perceived to be) polite society's fundamental need for variety. Consequently, they are coded as a short-lived vogue, as the title of one of d'Aulnoy's *recueils*, *Contes nouveaux ou les Fées à la mode* (New Tales or Fairies in Fashion), makes explicit. The fairy-tale genre thus provides the spontaneous "give and take" of salon conversation, which is intended to stave off the boredom *les honnêtes gens* must never display (Stanton, *The Aristocrat as Art*, 100–101). In opposition to the trivialization of *divertissements* by a long line of moralists,[8] the *conteurs* and *conteuses* follow the lead of writers such as Madeleine de Scudéry in justifying the need for multiple diversions: "depuis qu'on commence à parler jusqu'à ce qu'on cesse de vivre, les plaisirs changent, et doivent changer" (from the time one begins to speak until one stops living, diversions change and must change), says the narrator in Madeleine de Scudéry's *Les Ieux*;[9] "c'est proprement dans les plaisirs qu'il faut de la variété et des intervalles, et que le cœur et l'esprit ont besoin de se délasser" (it is especially in diversions that there must be variety and change and that the heart and the mind need to be able to relax ["Les Ieux," 16]).

Spinning, reading, or listening to tales is part of the seventeenth-century *art de la conversation*—an esthetic enabling interlocutors to interact poet-

5. This is true for tales by d'Aulnoy (*Le Gentilhomme bourgeois* and *Dom Gabriel Ponce de Léon*), Bernard (*Inès de Cardoue*), Durand (*La Comtesse de Mortane* and *Les Petits Soupers de l'été de l'année 1699*), and Murat (*Le Voyage de campagne*).
6. See Elizabeth Goldsmith, *Exclusive Conversations: The Art of Interaction in Seventeenth-Century France* (Philadelphia: University of Pennsylvania Press, 1988).
7. For a general discussion of the salons' *jeux d'esprit*, see Baader, *Dames de Lettres*, especially 44–61.
8. Pascal is undoubtedly the best known of these critics. In the *Pensées*, *divertissements* refer either to the activities people falsely believe will give them serenity or to those they use to escape a *repos* that has become an intolerable *ennui*. On this Pascalian notion and its relation to the seventeenth-century ideal of *repos*, see Stanton, "The Ideal of *Repos* in Seventeenth-Century French Literature," *L'Esprit créateur* vol. 15, nos. 1–2 (Spring-Summer 1975): 92–93.
9. "Les Ieux servant de préface à Mathilde," *Mathilde d'Aguilar* (1667; Geneva: Slatkine Reprints, 1979) 15.

ically and to display the "natural" superiority of the elite group.[1] Like
sociable conversation, contes de fées are to reflect an ease or naturalness
of expression—a stylistic trait that is consistently emphasized in discussions
of the genre.[2] The terms used to describe this quality, such as naiveté,
simplicité, and engouement (literally, playfulness), all reflect the contemporary esthetic ideal of négligence—a refinement designed to give the appearance of being innate, effortless, and aristocratic. Not surprisingly, this
quality is dependent on an intuitive perception that is difficult to achieve.
As Lhéritier observes, "Il faut être très-éclairé pour connaître les différences
des styles et l'usage qu'on en doit faire. La naïveté bien entendue, n'est
pas connue de tout le monde" (One must be very enlightened to know
the differences among styles and the use one must make of them. Well-
understood naïveté is not known to everyone ["Lettre," 317]). Lhéritier
further connects this stylistic simplicity with the ethical purity she perceives
in the purportedly original medieval fairy tales: "il me paraît qu'on fait
mieux de retourner au style des Troubadours . . . Ce qui serait à souhaiter,
est qu'en nous ramenant le goût de l'antiquité Gauloise, on nous ramenât
aussi cette belle simplicité de mœurs, qu'on prétend avoir été si commune
dans ces temps heureux" (it seems to me that we are better off returning
to the style of the Troubadours . . . What we could hope for is that by
bringing back the taste for Gallic antiquity, that beautiful simplicity of
morals which is supposed to have been so common in those happy times
would be brought back to us as well ["Lettre," 309–310]). Through her
own eccentric genealogy of fairy-tale storytelling, Lhéritier gives unique
expression to the moralizing pretext of the entire genre: its elusive negligence calls forth the ethical purity of a golden age. The deceptively natural
quality of l'art de la conversation communicates a profoundly nostalgic
vision of society.

More important, however, is the fact that the sociable ideals in the
telling of contes de fées are imbued with nostalgia. Just how nostalgic they
are becomes apparent when they are contrasted with the growing emphasis
on "sincerity" in epistolary writing at the end of the century. Whereas
early letter manuals concentrate on models as the best way to learn the
rhetoric of a "balanced verbal dialogue," after about 1670, writers such as
Grimarest and La Fevrerie begin to valorize the frankness, personal attitudes and sentiment best exemplified in the lettre d'amour (love letter).[3]
This particular change leads Elizabeth Goldsmith to conclude that by the
end of the century the ideology of sociability was being replaced by an
emphasis on "sincerity" (35). By contrast, the fairy-tale storytelling rejects

1. On l'art de la conversation in seventeenth-century France, see Goldsmith, Exclusive Conversations;
   Stanton, The Aristocrat as Art: A Study of the "Honnête Homme" and the "Dandy" in Seventeenth-
   and Nineteenth-Century French Literature (New York: Columbia University Press, 1980), 140–
   145.
2. For instance, in d'Aulnoy's Dom Gabriel Ponce de Léon, a frame-narrative containing several of
   her contes de fées, a discussion about the genre's stylistic qualities prompts one character to pre-
   scribe the following: "Il me semble . . . qu'il ne faut les rendre ni empoulés ni rampants, qu'ils
   doivent tenir un milieu qui soit plus enjoué que sérieux, qu'il y faut un peu de morale, et surtout
   les proposer comme une bagatelle où l'auditeur a seul droit de mettre le prix" (Dom Gabriel
   Ponce de Léon, Les Contes des fées, 1697, NCF, 3: 471).
3. Goldsmith, Exclusive Conversations, 29–36.

this tendency toward individualism in favor of an earlier ideal of *honnêteté* in which the exclusivity of the group predominates. Like other forms of "aristocratic romanticism" and like nostalgia generally, the prescribed enunciation and reception of the *contes de fées* portray the present as a decline from an idealized past. This nostalgia for a disappearing form of sociability might also be a longing for a vanishing dynamic within the salons. It is possible, for instance, that the seventeenth-century fairy tales are an early form of the nostalgic allusions to the mid-seventeenth-century salons that are prevalent in certain eighteenth-century circles.[4] In any event, the entire vogue of fairy tales can be read as an inscription of *mondain* culture within a backward-looking vision of social interaction, the evocation of an idealized past.

Fairy Tales and Novels

In the *contes de fées*, folklore is subjected to a radical transformation. It is no longer conveyed in the dialect of the peasants or lower classes, nor can it be said to reflect their worldview. Rather, it is poured into the mold of the period's elite literary forms. Among these, the most important is the novel. Characters, motifs, plot situations, and other devices common in seventeenth-century novels (especially those of the mid-century *romans*) are prominent in most of the *contes de fées*.[5] These are far from being the only literary fairy tales in which folklore is melded with the topoi of novels.[6] In the case of the vogue, such features package unadulterated folktales for an elite audience. They allow *mondain* readers to recognize their own literary tastes in the folklore of the masses by effacing the disconcerting traces of popular storytelling.

The link between the *contes de fées* and the novel was perceived by seventeenth-century readers and, more importantly, by those hostile to such productions of polite society. For the acerbic Abbé de Villiers, the vogue of fairy tales is decisive proof of the indefensibility of *all* prose fiction: "Rien ne marque mieux qu'on a aimé les Romans par esprit de bagatelle que de voir qu'on leur compare des contes à dormir debout et que les femmes autrefois charmées de *la Princesse de Clèves* sont aujourd'hui entêtées de *Griselidis* et de *la Belle aux cheveux d'or*" (Nothing better proves the trivial nature of people who like novels than to see that they are compared to old wives' tales and that the women who used to be enchanted by the *Princesse de Clèves* are today stubbornly attached to *Griselidis* and *la Belle aux cheveux d'or*).[7] Implicit in this critic's statement is a widely articulated attack on the (supposed) implausibility of novels,

---

4. See Harth's discussion of Genlis in *Cartesian Women: Versions and Subversions of Rational Discourse in the Old Regime* (Ithaca, NY: Cornell University Press, 1992) 117–118.
5. Even in Perrault's tales, in which the use of such devices is minimal, there is often a play on novelistic expectations (see, for instance, the conclusion to "Le Petit Poucet").
6. Folklorists have often perceived admixtures of oral and patently literary intertexts as an unreliable "contamination" of the "pure" folkloric tradition. Recently, historical studies of folklore have questioned this assumption and suggested the difficulty of speaking about an oral folklore that does not reflect in some way literary or written sources. See Velay-Vallantin, "Introduction," *L'Histoire des contes*.
7. Quoted in Storer, *La Mode*, 212. "Griselidis" is by Perrault and "La Belle aux cheveux d'or" by d'Aulnoy.

and particularly the mid-century *romans*. An explicit example of this kind of critique can be found in Boileau's *Dialogue des héros de roman*. In the *Discours* that precedes this dialogue, Boileau insists on the puerility of the novels that appeared after d'Urfé's *L'Astrée*: "On vantait surtout ceux de Gomberville, de La Calprenède, de Desmarets, et de Scudéry. Mais ces Imitateurs, s'efforçant mal-à-propos d'enchérir sur leur Original, et prétendant anoblir ses caractères, tombèrent, à mon avis, dans une très grande puerilité" (Those of Gomberville, La Calprenède, Desmarets, and Scudéry were especially praised. But these Imitators, inappropriately trying to exceed their Original and claiming to make its characteristics noble, slipped into a very great puerility in my opinion).[8] When we remember the infantilizing pretext on which the first vogue is predicated, Boileau's reference to implausibility as puerility reveals an important link between seventeenth-century novels and *contes de fées*: fairy tales are but a radical infantilization of the *romans*. For *mondain* writers and readers of fairy tales, though, this link shows the genre to be a strategic redeployment of the attacks on the novel's purported *invraisemblance* and puerility. The genre is a defiant illustration of such criticisms and exposes itself to an irony which * * * critics seem unable or at least unwilling to perceive.

The use of novelistic devices by the *contes de fées* is also noteworthy as a sign of nostalgia. Not only does the vogue display features that go against the grain of narrative fiction of the second half of the seventeenth century, in many respects it also harks back to the earlier *romans*. So doing, the great majority of fairy tales betray a longing for an idealized aristocratic identity.

During the second half of the century, the novel developed a different relation to history than had previous forms. Whereas the epic-length *romans*, published mostly before 1660, were set in a remote past and presented idealized characters in complex adventures, the *nouvelles* (novellas), which flourished during the 1660s and 1670s (Lafayette's masterpiece *La Princesse de Clèves* among them), had more recent time-settings and presented fewer characters in simpler plots. Both of these forms were predicated on an ambiguity between historiography and fiction.[9] In the *romans*, writers "appropriated history for those [nobles] who were beginning to be excluded from it" (Harth, *Ideology and Culture*, 141), resulting in "mock histories" and *romans à clef*. In the *nouvelles*, novelists purported to present truth in the form of "secret history" unrecorded by historians (Harth, *Ideology and Culture*, 147). * * * [T]hese developments in narrative fiction reflect a change in the status of the categories of the *vrai* and the *vraisemblable* in seventeenth-century esthetics. While the romances claim to be plausible and thus give a moral corrective to truth, the novellas favor truth (understood as an objective view) over verisimilitude. Hence, the

8. Boileau, *Œuvres complètes*, 444. See Georges May (*Le Dilemme du roman*, 16–23) for a discussion of similar criticisms of the novel in seventeenth- and eighteenth-century France.
9. On this ambiguity, see Faith E. Beasley, *Revising Memory: Women's Fiction and Memoirs in Seventeenth-Century France* (New Brunswick: Rutgers University Press, 1990), especially 19–41. See also Harth, *Ideology and Culture*, 129–221; and Marie-Thérèse Hipp, *Mythes et réalités: enquête sur le roman et les mémoires (1660–1700)* (Paris: Klincksieck, 1976).

romans and the *nouvelles* have diverging ideological foundations. The romances "offered a class of people whose political integrity was being threatened the image of historical and ideological continuity with the golden age of French aristocracy" (DiPiero, *Dangerous Truths*, 90–91). The *nouvelles*, on the contrary, "articulated the historical construction of images of grandeur by reveling in the seamier sides of monarchic splendor" (DiPiero, *Dangerous Truths*, 231).

Now, in the last years of the seventeenth century, the *nouvelles* tended to portray ambivalent social and political stances so as to appeal to both aristocratic and bourgeois readers.[1] From all appearances, the fairy tales too enjoyed a wide readership composed of both nobles and non-nobles, and yet the ideological position they endorse is unequivocally aristocratic. Perhaps nowhere is this more apparent than in the similarities the *contes de fées* share with the pastoral and heroic romances that flourished in the early and mid-part of the century. Beyond their complicated, extraordinary plots and non-linear exposition, many of the tales feature pastoral settings that bespeak a nostalgic return to the romances and the ideological universe they construct.[2] The pastoral topoi found in several of the fairy tales recreate an elusive and exclusive location that resembles d'Urfé's *L'Astrée*. In that novel, shepherds and shepherdesses, acting more like "nobles dressed up as if for an amateur theatrical in a local château" (Harth, *Ideology and Culture*, 39) than sheep-herders, are engaged in amorous intrigues against the backdrop of the beautiful rolling hills and forests of fifth-century Forez (in southeastern France). As Erica Harth has shown, this retreat to nature and peasant life had a precise function in the context of early seventeenth-century France. "The ambition of the noble in the real world is replaced by love in the world of Forez . . . Loss of social and economic privilege is transmuted into a world-weary flight from the world" (*Ideology and Culture*, 47). The *contes de fées* offered a similar imaginary compensation. But I would argue that the pastoral topoi in particular reveal a nostalgia for the discursive realization of a (seemingly) lost or endangered aristocratic essence.

In d'Aulnoy's "La Princesse Belle-Etoile et le Prince Chéri," the pastoral topoi are used to highlight the characters' quest for identity. Involving the misfortunes of two generations, this tale depicts the refuge and, ultimately, the benefits afforded by a retreat to a simpler life. The story begins with an impoverished queen, along with her three daughters, leaving court to set up shop as a cook in the country. When they serve a crotchety old fairy with undeserved graciousness, the daughters are rewarded with marriages befitting their true social rank. Another round of misfortune befalls

1. As DiPiero explains, "since it was no longer possible to court an exclusively aristocratic clientele with fictions designed to reaffirm what they already knew or believed, authors needed to invoke multiple and often conflicting political stances in their works . . . Noble readers might heed the warning this fiction issued about middle-class upstarts who attempted to usurp their traditional positions of ascendancy and authority, and bourgeois readers could learn . . . the contrived nature of the elaborate sign systems they would have to penetrate in order to accede to the ranks of power and privilege" (*Dangerous Truths*, 231).
2. Besides the fairy tales, a group of novels that appeared in the 1690s also recycled the exoticism and extraordinary adventures characteristic of the earlier romances (see Henri Coulet, *Le Roman jusqu'à la Révolution*, 2 vols. [Paris: Colin, 1967] 2: 288–289). Literary fairy tales are doubtless a continuation of and a deviation from this strain of the novel.

their offspring, who are banished by an evil queen-mother. But they are miraculously saved by a pirate couple who retire to a forest upon discovering that the children's hair produces jewels whenever it is combed. The pirates, inspired by innate goodness and an intuitive understanding of the children's high birth, give them a proper education. After unknowingly arriving at their birthplace, the children must endure a series of tests imposed by the queen-mother before their true identities are revealed to them. Finally, Chéri and Belle-Etoile are married, and the impoverished queen, their grandmother, returns to court.

This ending is evidence enough that the pastoral motifs in this tale reinstate a lost or obscured identity. During the pastoral "retreats" of both generations—when the queen and her daughters become cooks and when the children of these latter are raised as the pirates' offspring—their inborn nobility is always clearly in evidence. The queen's daughters grow out of childhood, "leur beauté n'aurait pas fait moins de bruit que les sauces de la Princesse [ie, the queen] si elle ne les aurait cachées dans une chambre . . ." (their beauty would not have been any less appreciated than the Princess's sauces if she had not hidden them in a room.)[3] And later, the banished children of this queen's daughters "passaient pour être les leurs [les enfants des corsaires], quoiqu'ils marquassent, par toutes leurs actions, qu'ils sortaient d'un sang plus illustre" (passed as their own [the pirates' children], even though they displayed, by all their actions, that they descended from a more illustrious family [197–198]). Finally, the characters' pastoral retreat is a time for solidifying and proving the merit of their aristocratic existence.

The fact that the characters in this tale and the vast majority of the *contes de fées* are of noble birth and abide by heroic ideals demonstrates how similar they are to the heroes and heroines of the *romans*.[4] By contrast, the existence of protagonists in the *nouvelles* is anything but idealized; in fact, their world is often marked by the conflict between the real nature of the world and an ideal set of norms or expectations. The characters of the fairy tales inhabit a universe in which their aristocratic nature—their physical, emotional, and intellectual superiority—is destined to prevail. Rather than problematize this existence, these characters serve as a superlative model for noble conduct (Bannister, *Privileged Mortals*, 20–26). The adventures of the characters in "La Princesse Belle-Etoile et le Prince Chéri," for instance, are designed to show the validity of the maxim "un bienfait n'est jamais perdu" (a good deed is never lost), recalling the magnanimity of the queen and her daughters toward the old fairy, who then promised to grant their wishes. At the end of the tale, the fairy tells the queen how, out of gratitude for her initial act of kindness, she protected her children and grandchildren. The inborn goodness of the queen and her daughter perpetuates itself and, ultimately, receives the recognition and power it deserves—regained social status. In the end, so the tale seems to say, aristocratic essence always wins out.

3. "La Princesse Belle-Etoile et le Prince Chéri," *Contes nouveaux ou les Fées à la mode*, 1698, NCF, 5: 180.
4. The heroes and/or heroines in Perrault's "Grisélidis," "Les Souhaits ridicules," "Le Petit Chaperon Rouge," "Le Maître chat," and "Le Petit Poucet" and in Le Noble's "L'Apprenti magicien" are the notable exceptions to this rule. Thus, my remarks here apply only partially to these two *conteurs*.

It is not implausible that the requirement of noble birth for the vast majority of fairy-tale heroes and heroines represents a reaction against the diminishing significance of the distinction between noble and non-noble in late seventeenth-century France.[5] The fairy tales' valorization of aristocratic class identity parallels the entrenchment at the end of Louis XIV's reign of *marques de noblesse* (chief among which was the requirement of noble birth) as a means of compensating for the loss of socio-political recognition.[6] No less compensatory is the sumptuous wealth lavished upon protagonists throughout this corpus. As Raymonde Robert has shown, the *contes de fées* equate spectacular displays of wealth with authentic aristocratic superiority (*Le Conte de fées*, 362–363). And ultimately, noble birth is always recognized by the material trappings of a socio-economic elite.

Nostalgia, then, governs not only the fairy tales' rewriting of folklore but also their rewriting of early seventeenth-century romances; and between these two intertexts there is a mutual interdependence. The structures of an identifiable literary form legitimize the recourse to folkloric narratives. At the same time, since the *contes de fées* rely on folklore and the *merveilleux* associated with it, they give new life to an aristocratic ethos promulgated by the *romans* and make it a means of wish-fulfillment. In "La Princesse Belle-Etoile et le Prince Chéri," for example, the quest for aristocratic identity is woven into the folkloric tale-type AT707 (The Three Golden Sons), whose protagonists are non-nobles in most recorded oral versions.[7] A purportedly popular narrative is made to purvey a distinctively aristocratic worldview in a form that reflects elite literary tastes. Melding folkloric and novelistic features, the *contes de fées* reify the contingencies of *mondain* culture into the certainty of aristocratic essence. Culture, in this case, is tied to being. The nostalgic return to both the romances and popular storytelling provides an escape from the constraints on *mondain* culture as well as a reaffirmation of its validity.

Gendered Storytelling and the Empire de Féerie

As a product of polite society that embodies the ideals of "modernist" culture and e(xc)lusive sociability, the vogue of fairy tales had strategic value for writers and readers of both sexes. It is nevertheless striking, especially in the context of seventeenth-century literary production, that so many women published so many of the *contes de fées* that appeared between 1690 and 1715. Accounting for nearly half of the writers of the vogue, the *conteuses* published two-thirds of all the fairy tales in this period. Significantly, the proportion of female-authored tales within the corpus is even higher than the comparatively large number of novels written by women in roughly the same period. The question we are led to ask, then, is why women were drawn to this genre in such numbers. What attraction did the fairy-tale form hold for the *conteuses*, distinct from the *conteurs*? To be sure, there are considerable differences among the female writers

---

5. See Ellery Schalk, *From Valor to Pedigree: Ideas of Nobility in France in the Sixteenth and Seventeenth Centuries* (Princeton University Press, 1986).
6. Ibid., 213–214.
7. In most folkloric versions of AT707, the princesses in d'Aulnoy's text are commoners who have the good fortune to marry a king. See Delarue and Tenèze, *Le Conte populaire français*, 2: 637.

of the vogue, as indeed there are among the male writers. In spite of these, the fairy-tale form does have a strategic value for the *conteuses* as a group. It allows them to assert their role as women writers in the production of literary and, more specifically, *mondain* culture. In other words, the *conteuses* highlight their own *gendered* relation to the genre and the creation of cultural artifacts in general.

The vogue takes on clear tactical significance for the *conteuses* when we consider that the attacks on *mondain* culture during the last decade of the seventeenth century gave particular attention to women. Among the fiercest were those formulated by Madame de Maintenon, who founded and oversaw an orphanage for girls at Saint-Cyr, and Fénelon, who wrote a treatise on the education of women (*De l'éducation des filles*, 1687) and served for a time as secret advisor to Madame de Maintenon. Both saw in women the instrument by which the French aristocracy, having (in their view) fallen into moral and genealogical decline, could be renewed. If women of noble extraction were to assume the responsibilities of pious virtue, they argued, then the purity of French nobility would be restored and the social order reinstated. For women to perform this essential role, they would have to turn away from the pleasures of *mondain* life, including all forms of "worldly" *divertissements* and sociability, to take on instead the duties of domesticity. As Carolyn Lougee has argued, "the perception of the antithesis between domesticity and polite society was implicit in Maintenon's thought as in Fénelon's. The family, the source of both individual and social salvation, was, Maintenon felt, vulnerable to the temptations of *mondain* life. All was lost if girls were allowed to aim at the pleasures of *sociabilité*, acquiring 'the taste for wit and for conversations that they will not find within their families' " (*Le Paradis des femmes*, 190–191). Assailed by both of these reformers was what they called *bel esprit*, the mastery of verbal and intellectual skills that were an integral part of *l'art de la conversation* and, thus, prized by polite society. In its place, they promoted an ideal of femininity that privileged domesticity over sociability, submission over assertiveness, and silence over conversation. The result was women who, by respecting the proper limits of their own so-called capacities, eschewed the pitfalls of "worldly" women.

Although Maintenon and Fénelon are primarily concerned with education, they rely on many of the same arguments expounded by "moralist" critics concerning the moral dangers that novels, plays, operas, and gambling pose for women. Above all, they deemed the representation of love in these works to be pernicious to women, who are said to possess more vulnerable imaginations than men and who are, thus, more easily led into debauchery.[8] In the eyes of such censors, female sociability represented the most visible of the dangers produced by *mondain* culture. To restrict

8. In *De l'éducation des filles*, Fénelon warns: "Celles qui ont de l'esprit s'érigent souvent en précieuses, et lisent tous les livres qui peuvent nourrir leur vanité; elles se passionnent pour des romans, pour des comédies, pour des récits d'aventures chimériques où l'amour profane est mêlé; elles se rendent l'esprit visionnaire en s'accoutumant au langage magnifique des héros de romans; elles se gâtent même par là pour le monde: car tous ces beaux sentiments en l'air, toutes ces passions généreuses, toutes ces aventures que l'auteur du roman a inventées pour le plaisir, n'ont aucun rapport avec les vrais motifs qui font agir dans le monde, et qui décident des affaires, ni avec les mécomptes qu'on trouve dans tout ce qu'on entreprend" (95).

women's access to the cultural sphere, in their view, was to fight against a pervasive corruption of society. In the domain of literature, it was also to fight against the corruption of taste in the marketplace, for which women above all were responsible. "Les femmes n'ont-elles pas quand elles veulent le talent de donner du débit aux plus mauvaises choses?" (When women desire to do so, don't they have the talent to sell the worst things?), asks one of the speakers in the Abbé de Villiers's *Entretiens sur les contes de fées*. "Pour moi je croirais que de tous les moyens de faire valoir les Livres qui ne valent rien, le meilleur c'est d'engager les femmes à les prôner" (As for me, I would tend to think that of all the ways to promote Books that are worth nothing, the best is to get women to praise them.)[9] The other speaker affirms this opinion by explaining: "Tout ce qui demande un peu d'application les fatigue et les ennuie [les femmes]; elles s'amusent d'un Livre avec le même esprit dont elles s'occupent d'une mouche ou d'un ruban, êtes-vous étonné après cela que les Contes et les Historiettes aient du débit?" (Anything that requires a little effort tires and bores them [women]. They have the same mindset when amusing themselves with a Book as when attending to a mouche or a ribbon. Are you surprised then that *Contes* and *Historiettes* are a commercial success? [286]). Over and beyond a condemnation of women's frivolity if not to say bad taste, these statements testify to the fear that women's power as readers evoked in opponents of *mondain* culture. Arguably, the attacks on women promulgated by critics such as the Abbé de Villiers were in part a reaction against women's increased control of literary taste, if not the book trade itself, during the seventeenth century.[1] Whatever its causes, Villiers's attacks are similar to those of the moral reformers in their ultimate effects on women. For, all of these critics share a desire to make women the scapegoat for the perceived evils of polite society. All of them argue either explicitly or implicitly that the only way to reform the cultural public sphere is to exclude women from it.

Now it is particularly significant that the vogue of seventeenth-century *contes de fées*, dominated numerically by the *conteuses*, appeared at a time of such hostility to women's activity in *mondain* culture. By developing a genre that in many ways seems to confirm the attacks on women's frivolity, the *conteuses* openly defy such critiques. Even further, they develop a strategic affirmation of their own *mondain* literary activity as a group of women writers. So doing, they might be said to capitalize on the period's prevalent lexical association of folk- and fairy tales with women in such expressions as "*contes de quenoville*" (tales of the distaff), "*contes de vieille*" (old wives' tales), "*contes de ma Mère l'Oye*" (Mother Goose tales). Of course, before the advent of the vogue, this association had considerable

9. Abbé de Villiers, *Entretiens sur les contes de fées, et sur quelques autres ouvrages du temps. Pour servir de préservatif contre le mauvais goût* (Paris: J. Collombat, 1699) 284–285.
1. See DeJean, *Tender Geographies*, 127–158. See also Lewis C. Seifert, "*Les Fées Modernes*: Women, Fairy Tales, and the Literary Field in Late Seventeenth-Century France," *Going Public: Women and Publishing in Early Modern France*, ed. Elizabeth Goldsmith and Dena Goodman (Ithaca, NY: Cornell University Press, 1995) 129–145, and Linda Timmermans, *L'Accès des femmes à la culture, 1598–1715: un débat d'idées de Saint François de Sales à la Marquise de Lambert* (Paris: Champion, 1993) 152–176, 224–236.

negative connotations. Even in its midst, a hostile reader like the Abbé de Villiers uses the link between fairy tales and popular women storytellers to denounce the fairy-tale vogue as "ce ramas de contes qui nous assassinent depuis un an ou deux" (this heap of tales that has plagued us for a year or two [*Entretiens sur les contes de fées*, 69]). Finding in the *contes de fées* a lack of erudition that he attributes to the gender of their authors (regardless of their class), Villiers's Provincial speaker makes the perception of female attribution the reality of female authorship: "l'invention en est due à des Nourrices ignorantes; et on a tellement regardé cela comme le partage des femmes, que ce ne sont que des femmes qui ont composé ceux qui ont paru depuis quelque temps en si grand nombre" (they were originally created by ignorant Nurses, and they are considered to be the domain of women, so much so that only women have composed those [tales] that have recently appeared in such great numbers [76–77]). The *Parisien*, Villiers's alter ego, concurs with this assessment in further condemning the tales of the *conteuses*:

> Ce n'est pas à dire que ces Contes ne pussent être bons. Il y a des femmes capables de quelque chose de meilleur encore; et si celles qui ont entrepris d'en composer, s'étaient souvenues que ces Contes n'ont été inventés que pour développer et rendre sensible quelque moralité importante, on ne les aurait point regardés comme le partage des ignorants et des femmes.

> This is not to say that these Tales could not be good. Some women are capable of something even better; and if those who endeavored to compose some had remembered that these Tales were only invented to develop an important moral and make it understandable, people would not have looked on them [the tales] as the domain of the ignorant and women. (77)

To the mind of the *Parisien*, the association of the *contes de fées* with women is something that the *conteuses* should have attempted to overcome by infusing their tales with moral significance. In other words, they should have written so that readers like Villiers would not be able to recall the tradition of female authorship that produces folkloric narratives. The *Parisien* is clearly appalled that this tradition continues uninterrupted.

By conjoining fairy tales, women, and ignorance, Villiers attacks the legitimacy of the *conteuses* as women writers. Yet, these same writers engage in a sexual/textual politics that contradicts Villiers's phallocentrism by constructing a positive collective identity, an emphasis on the interconnections between themselves and their tales that is non-existent in the texts of the *conteurs*. In her "Lettre à Madame D.G**," Lhéritier evokes this identity when she reminds her addressee of a conversation they had on fairy tales:

> Je me souviens parfaitement combien vous vous étonniez qu'on ne s'avisât point de faire des Nouvelles, ou des Contes, qui roulassent sur [des] maximes antiques. On y est enfin venu, et je me suis hasardée à me mettre sur les rangs, pour marquer mon attachement à

de charmantes Dames, dont vous connaissez les belles qualités. Les personnes de leur mérite et de leurs caractères, semblent nous ramener le temps des Fées, où l'on vovait tant de gens parfaits.

I remember perfectly well how astonished you were that no one had thought to write Novellas or Tales based on ancient maxims. People have finally gotten around to doing it, and I have attempted to place myself among their ranks in order to show my connection with some charming Ladies, whose beautiful qualities you are aware of. Persons of their merit and character seem to bring back the time of the Fairies, when so many perfect people could be seen. (302)[2]

Lhéritier's linkage of the "charmantes Dames" and fairies is repeated in several texts of the *conteuses*. In Murat's "Anguillette," for instance, the narrator makes an explicit intertextual reference to d'Aulnoy and her tale, "La Princesse Carpillon," when describing prince Atimir: "Le Prince qui alors régnait descendait en droite ligne de la célèbre Princesse Carpillon, et de son charmant époux, dont une Fée moderne, plus savante et plus polie que celles de l'antiquité, nous a si galamment conté les merveilles" (The Prince who reigned at that time descended directly from the famous Princess Carpillon and her charming husband, about whom a modern Fairy, more learned and polite than those of antiquity, has so gallantly told us the marvels [277–278]).[3] In fact, Murat develops this comparison at length in the dedication letter to the "Fées modernes" preceding her *Histoires sublimes et allégoriques,* in which the household chores and popular magic of peasant women storytellers are contrasted with the courtly refinement of the *conteuses* and their fairies. Dramatizing as it does the tensions between the recuperation of a gendered storytelling tradition and the investment of the vogue of *contes de fées* in "aristocratic romanticism," this passage is worth quoting at length:

Les anciennes Fées vos devancières ne passent plus que pour des badines auprès de vous. Leurs occupations étaient basses et puériles, ne s'amusant qu'aux Servantes et aux Nourrices. Tout leur soin consistait à bien balayer la maison, mettre le pot au feu, faire la lessive, remuer et endormir les enfants, traire les vaches, battre le beurre, et mille autres pauvretés de cette nature; et les effets les plus considérables de leur Art se terminaient à faire pleurer des perles et des diamants, moucher des émeraudes, et cracher des rubis.

Your predecessors the ancient Fairies pass for little more than jesters next to you. Their activities were lowly and puerile, interesting only

2. This collective identity is also evident in Lhéritier's dedication of "L'Adroite Princesse" to Murat and in the *avertissement* preceding Murat's *Histoires sublimes et allégoriques:* "Je suis bien aise d'avertir le Lecteur de deux choses. La première que j'ai pris les idées de quelques-uns de ces Contes dans un Auteur ancien intitulé, *les Facétieuses nuits du Seigneur Straparolle,* imprimé pour la seizième fois en 1615. Les Contes apparemment étaient bien en vogue dans le siècle passé, puisque l'on a fait tant d'impressions de ce livre. Les Dames qui ont écrit jusqu'ici en ce genre ont puisé dans la même source au moins pour la plus grande partie. La seconde chose que j'ai à dire, c'est que mes Contes sont composés dès le mois d'Avril dernier, que si je me suis rencontrée avec une de ces Dames en traitant quelquesuns des mêmes sujets, je n'ai point pris d'autre modèle que l'original, ce qui serait aisé à justifier par les routes différentes que nous avons prises" (*Histoires sublimes et allégoriques par Mme la comtesse D***, dédiées aux fées modernes* [Paris: J. et P. Delaulme, 1699] n.p.)
3. Murat, "La Princesse Carpillon," *Histoires sublimes et allégoriques,* 277–278.

to Servants and Nurses. Their only cares were to sweep the house well, put the pot on the fire, do the laundry, rock the children and put them to sleep, milk cows, churn butter, and a thousand other miserable things of that sort. And the most important effects of their Art consisted of making people cry pearls and diamonds, sneeze emeralds, and spit rubies. (unpaginated preface)

She then contrasts these "ancient" fairies with her *dédicataires*, the "Fées modernes":

> Mais pour vous, MESDAMES, vous avez bien pris une autre route: Vous ne vous occupez que de grandes choses, dont les moindres sont de donner de l'esprit à ceux et celles qui n'en ont point, de la beauté aux laides, de l'éloquence aux ignorants, des richesses aux pauvres, et de l'éclat aux choses les plus obscures . . . Pour prévenir toutes les marques de reconnaissance que chacun s'efforcera de vous donner, je vous offre quelques Contes de ma façon, qui tous faibles et peu corrects qu'ils sont, ne laisseront pas de vous persuader qu'il n'y a personne dans l'Empire de Féerie qui soit plus véritablement à vous que LA COMTESSE D***.

> But as for you, MESDAMES, you have taken a very different path: You are only concerned with great things, the least of which are giving wit to those men and women who have none, beauty to ugly women, eloquence to the ignorant, riches to the poor, and clarity to obscure things . . . To anticipate all the marks of gratitude that everyone will attempt to give you, I offer you a few Tales in my own style which, however feeble and incorrect they are, will nonetheless convince you that there is no one in the Empire of Fairy Magic who is more truly devoted to you than THE COUNTESS OF *** (unpaginated preface)

Ostensibly a comparison of "ancient" and "modern" fairies as they appear in folktales and *contes de fées*, this letter is also (and not without a little ambiguity) a comparison of the "ancient" and "modern" *conteuses*. Beyond the fact that Murat's authorial voice identifies herself as belonging to the *Empire de féerie*, the title *"Fée,"* as we have already seen, was a conceit given to many salon women in the seventeenth century.[4] Consequently, the *fées* referred to in this letter can be read as both fairies who performed the deeds mentioned themselves, and storytellers who perform them in their tales. The description of the *fées modernes* given here is both a flattering portrait *of* the *conteuses* and an attribution of the powers of fairies *to* the *conteuses*—a wish-fulfillment for discursive powers. Yet, these are opposed to, if not derived from, the more lowly ones of the "ancient" fairies/*conteuses*. On one level, of course, these "popular" fairies/women storytellers are mentioned *in order to* be rejected. But the *fées modernes* and the *conteuses* can only ever be a refinement of the traditions they seemingly negate. While distancing themselves from the "originary" story-

---

4. From all appearances, when the *conteuses* refer to themselves as fairies, they are imitating a practice in the salons whereby certain women were given the title, *Fée*. For instance, Madame de Rambouillet was called "la grande Fée" by Voiture, and the duchesse du Maine insisted on being called "Fée Ludovise" (see Storer, *La Mode*, 12). Moreover, allusions to fairy magic were frequently used in panegyrical works about Louis XIV's reign (see Delaporte, *Du Merveilleux*, 44–46).

tellers, the *conteuses* nonetheless appropriate to their own ends the over-determined genderedness of these women's folkloric talespinning. And so doing, they idealize the figure of the learned *conteuse* who demonstrates the refinements of the salon setting and the importance of women within it.[5]

Besides asserting and illustrating women's activity in *mondain* culture, the fairy tales of the *conteuses* also reveal their affinities, as women writers, with the "modernist" side of the Quarrel of the Ancients and the Moderns. For the most part, the connections between the *conteuses* and the Moderns are implicit rather than explicit, and therefore somewhat difficult to assess. If the seventeenth-century *contes de fées* are a demonstration of the Moderns' arguments, though, at the very least the *conteuses* are indirectly linked to their side of the Quarrel. Nonetheless, it is a widely held assumption that women, and especially women writers, generally supported and had a vested interest in the "modernist" arguments of the quarrel.[6] The vast majority of literate women were denied direct access to formal education —especially to the classical learning vaunted by the Ancients—and women writers excelled in genres, such as the novel and the letter, that lacked recognized classical models. To date, however, scarely any work has been devoted to just which women might be classified as Moderns, and the complex interests they might have had in adopting this viewpoint are unclear. It is not my aim here to resolve this problem, but rather to examine the evidence for a link between the *conteuses* and the "modernist" cause in order to further understand the large numbers and strategic functions of the tales written by women.

This link is all the more convincing when we consider that the majority of the *contes de fées* appeared in the wake of one of the most heated confrontations of the Quarrel, namely the controversy surrounding the publication in 1694 of Boileau's *Satire X* (often called "Contre les femmes" [Against Women]). In this vicious text reminiscent of an earlier tradition of *gauloiserie*, a thoroughly misogynistic narrator dialogues with a nephew who has just announced his imminent marriage. Attempting to curtail the nephew's optimism, the uncle argues that wives are almost always unvirtuous and husbands miserable as a result. Infidelity is rampant among wives, declares the narrator, and women are prone to a multitude of vices. Among other things, this text proclaims that they are likely to become coquettes, spendthrifts, gamblers, misers, hypochondriacs, pedants, and religious hypocrites. As much as it was an assault on women, this satire was a direct attack on Perrault (who was mentioned by name in the original version) and the Moderns in general. Perrault immediately fired back with his *Apologie des femmes*, and numerous other responses were published by partisans of the Moderns.[7] For them, Boileau's deni-

5. On this point, see Gabrielle Verdier's "Figures de la conteuse dans les contes de fées féminins," *XVIIe siècle* 180 (July–September 1993): 481–499. Verdier shows how the storytelling figure promoted by the *conteuses*, with all the qualities of a refined salon woman, differs from Perrault's archetypal "popular" female storyteller. However, Lhéritier's position is more complex since she endorses both figures simultaneously.
6. Harth, *Cartesian Women*, 81.
7. See Adam, *Histoire*, 5: 61–66.

gration of women was tantamount to an offensive against polite society, the most receptive public for "modernist" literature and culture.[8] The father in Perrault's *L'Apologie des femmes* makes this clear when arguing against his son's misogyny: "Peux-tu ne savoir pas que la Civilité / Chez les Femmes naquit avec l'Honnêteté? / Que chez elles se prend la fine politesse, / Le bon air, le bon goût, et la délicatesse? (Can you not know that Civility / In the company of Women is born with *Honnêteté*? / That in their company is acquired refined politeness, / Good demeanor, good taste, and refinement?)[9] To understand how Boileau's satire could be interpreted as an assault on the Moderns and, further, how the *conteuses* are connected with their cause, we must briefly consider the role of women in "modernist" esthetics.

Among the Moderns and, more generally, the polite society of seventeenth-century France, women's language was considered to display a naturalness and ease of expression that served as a model for men, who were otherwise confined to the strictures of rhetorical exercise. Moreover, women's judgment of artistic taste was taken to be more immediate and thus more reliable than men's, which depended on erudite standards of taste. Underlying all of these qualities, according to the Moderns and polite society, was the fact that women were deemed to incarnate the "negligent" (seemingly effortless and refined) esthetic ideal of *naïveté*. Speaking of women, the "modernist" abbé in Perrault's *Parallèle des anciens et des modernes* declares: "on sait la justesse de leur discernement pour les choses fines et délicates, la sensibilité qu'elles ont pour ce qui est clair, vif, naturel et de bon sens, et le dégoût subit qu'elles témoignent à l'abord de tout ce qui est obscur, languissant, contraint et embarrassé" (we know the precision of their discernment for fine and delicate things, the sensitivity they have for that which is clear, lively, natural and of good sense, and the sudden disgust they show when approaching all that is obscure, languorous, forced and awkward).[1] The models that women furnished regarding polite discourse and artistic judgment provided a middle ground between erudite and polite, but non-erudite publics. This indigenous cultural domain, which Marc Fumaroli has termed the *mémoire parallèle* (parallel memory), was a common point of reference for these two groups, enabling the "*sçavans*" and the "*ignorans*" to counterbalance each other. As Fumaroli has put it:

> Between the culture of the small elite of *sçavans* and the "mémoire parallèle" that the vast and heterogeneous community of *ignorans* conveys in the vernacular tongue, one must introduce a mediation—*mondain* culture—which should not be confused with "learned culture." For, this mediation . . . sketches out an unstable compromise between two extremes—the Latin and erudite memory and the collective French memory.[2]

8. Ibid., 5: 63.
9. Charles Perrault, *L'Apologie des femmes, par Monsieur P** * (Paris: Veuve Coignard, 1694) 7.
1. Perrault, *Parallèle des anciens et des modernes* 1: 31; 108.
2. Marc Fumaroli, "Les Enchantements de l'éloquence: *Les Fées* de Charles Perrault ou De la littérature," *Le Statut de la littérature: mélanges offertes à Paul Bénichou,* ed. Marc Fumaroli (Geneva: Droz, 1982) 158.

The compromise of the *mémoire parallèle* was accessible to polite society, but even more significantly, offered an esthetic model of simplicity and grace grounded on indigenous or "natural" sources. As Fumaroli goes on to show, it was women who best incarnated the common ground shared by both the learned and the polite ("Les Enchantements de l'éloquence," 158). It was women who held together an otherwise disparate cultural community.

Ultimately, however, women's "innate" qualities were appropriated by men to enhance their own position in the Quarrel of the Ancients and the Moderns as well as the polite society of the salons.[3] Indeed, concerned above all to answer Boileau's vendetta, Perrault, in *L'Apologie des femmes*, lauds above all the ideals of feminine domesticity and subservience.[4] Therefore, by exploiting and developing the fairy tale, the *conteuses* might be said to reappropriate their mediating agency and their relation to language. Implicitly, at least, their rewriting of a genre associated with the *naïveté* of peasant women italicizes the role of women in "modernist" and *mondain* circles. However, many of the tales by the *conteuses* inscribe this reappropriation in more overt ways, not least of which is a foregrounding of women's speech as innate and stylistically perfect.

Such a link between women and "modernist" culture is dramatically illustrated in Lhéritier's "Les Enchantements de l'éloquence." From the very beginning of this tale, the heroine, Blanche, is a model of natural and captivating eloquence; indeed, her adventures repeatedly demonstrate the tale's moral: "Doux et courtois langage / Vaut mieux que riche héritage" (Sweet and courtly speech / Is more valuable than a wealthy inheritance). Blanche's speech enchants a prince and causes two fairies with names evoking the prized qualities of the heroine—Dulcicula and Eloquentia nativa—to bestow her with the gifts of being "toujours plus que jamais douce, aimable, bienfaisante, et d'avoir la plus belle voix du monde" (always more than ever sweet, nice, doing good and having the most beautiful voice in the world [258]) and having spew from her mouth "des perles, des diamants, des rubis et des émeraudes chaque fois qu'elle ferait un sens fini en parlant" (pearls, diamonds, rubies, and emeralds every time she spoke concisely [260]). As Fumaroli has demonstrated,[5] the descriptions of Blanche's speech are reminiscent of seventeenth-century rhetorical ideals, as are the names of the fairies: "Dulcicula" evoking *douceur*, and thus the ideals of *suavitas* and *effeminatio*, and "Eloquentia nativa" reminiscent of *neglegentia diligens*. Yet, Blanche's eloquence is not the

---

3. See the illuminating discussion of this question in Elizabeth L. Berg, "Recognizing Differences: Perrault's Modernist Esthetic in *Parallèle des Anciens et des Modernes*," *Papers on French Seventeenth-Century Literature* vol. 10, no. 18 (1983): 135–148.

4. In the *Préface* to his *Apologie*, Perrault attempts to preempt the criticism this stance is likely to draw from women inclined toward the Moderns: "Je suis encore persuadé que quelques femmes de la haute volée n'aimeront pas ces mères et ces filles, qui, travaillant chez elles,

> *Ne songent qu'à leur tâche, et qu'à bien recevoir*
> *Leur père ou leur époux quand il revient le soir.*

Elles trouveront ces manières bien bourgeoises, et le sentiment que j'ai là-dessus, bien antique pour un Défenseur des Modernes. Mais quoi qu'elles puissent dire, et quelque autorisées qu'elles soient par l'usage et par la mode, il sera toujours plus honnête pour elles de s'occuper à des ouvrages convenables à leur sexe et à leur qualité, que de passer leur vie dans une oisiveté continuelle" (unpaginated preface).

5. See "Les Enchantements de l'éloquence."

result of learning, but a gift of the fairies, who are anxious to embellish her pleasing way with words. Blanche, then, is the innate demonstration of rhetorical eloquence, the natural and effortless incarnation of what could (usually) only be learned with great effort. The importance of Blanche's speech does not stop here, however, for, at the end of the tale, it is used by the narrator to assert the superiority of modern over ancient, but also female over male eloquence. Before leaving home to join her husband-to-be, Blanche attracts a crowd with her oratorical gifts:

> Les choses brillantes qui sortaient de sa bouche attiraient encore plus de monde que celles qui sortent de la bouche de Mr. de******, toutes belles qu'elles sont. Ce peuple avait raison: n'était-il pas bien plus agréable de voir sortir des pierres préciecuses d'une belle petite bouche comme celle de Blanche qu'il ne l'était de voir sortir des éclairs de la grande bouche de cet orateur tonnant qui était cependant si couru des Athéniens.

> The brilliant things that came from her mouth attracted still more people than those that come from the mouth of Mr. de ******, as beautiful as they are. These people were right: wasn't it much more agreeable to see precious stones come from a beautiful little mouth like Blanche's than it was to see lightening bolts come from the big mouth of that thundering orator who was, however, so appreciated by the Athenians. (264)

While it is unclear exactly to whom Lhéritier is referring in this passage, the male figures represent erudite and ancient models of rhetoric to which Blanche's speech is compared. In the final paragraph of the tale, the narrator connects Blanche's example to "modernist" ideals even more explicitly:

> [Ce conte] ne me paraît pas plus incroyable que beaucoup d'histoires que nous a faites l'ancienne Grèce; et j'aime autant dire qu'il sortait des perles et des rubis de la bouche de Blanche, pour désigner les effets de l'éloquence, que de dire qu'il sortait des éclairs de celle de Périclès. Contes pour contes, il me paraît que ceux de l'antiquité gauloise valent bien à peu près ceux de l'antiquité grecque; et les fées ne sont pas moins en droit de faire des prodiges que les dieux de la Fable.

> To me, [this tale] does not seem to be any more unbelievable than many of the stories that ancient Greece handed down to us; and I am just as disposed to say that pearls and rubies came out of the mouth of Blanche, in order to indicate the effects of eloquence, as to say that lightning came out of Pericles'. Tales for tales, it seems to me that those of Gallic antiquity are more or less comparable to those of Grecian antiquity; and fairies are no less able to perform miracles than the gods of mythology. (265)

Blanche is the representative of this "modern" genre, but she is also an example of the link the literary fairy tale allows the *conteuses* to forge between themselves and the "modernist" cause. She is the expression and realization of Lhéritier's utopian desire for discursive powers that resist the recuperation and subordination of women by the Moderns.

Both nostalgic and utopian impulses are at work in the appropriation of folklore by the *conteuses*. On the one hand, these writers posit an idealized narrative tradition of an unspecified past as the origin for their own writing. On the other, they affirm through their intertextual and interpersonal allusions a group consciousness that contrasts with or even defies the attacks on women's activities in polite society. They might even be contributing to the "invention" of a female literary and cultural tradition occurring at this time through eulogies of French women writers published by Lhéritier and Vertron, among others.[6] However fleetingly, the *conte de fées* also afforded women writers the opportunity to recapture the mediating agency of women in "modernist" esthetics. All in all, the *conteuses* use the fairy-tale form to create a counterideology in which women assert their own abilities and desires to participate in cultural and, especially, literary production. Not unlike the tensions in the Moderns' recuperation of folklore, so too are there profound ambiguities in the storytelling of the *conteuses*. The nostalgic return to folklore makes possible the creation of a utopian counter-ideology. By the same token, the utopian function of this story-telling is inseparable from the nostalgic reification of the real popular women storytellers. The *Empire de Féerie* is indeed a liberatory space, but not for everyone.[7]

The marvelous offered the *conteuses* the possibility of presenting a strategic (re)inscription of women's literary activity. But it mediated many other desires as well. In a genre recognized but also dismissed as collective daydreaming, the *merveilleux* made it possible for writers and readers to reiterate and/or reimagine what is taken to be plausible and real. Moreover, the ironic distance provided by the infantilizing and moralizing pretexts was a cover through which a sophisticated public could find wish-fulfillment in an otherwise lowly literary form. The vogue of fairy tales conveyed longings that varied according to the particular notions of plausibility or reality perceived as most crucial by three distinct but potentially interdependent groups—the Moderns, polite society, and women writers and readers. For all of these, the marvelous allowed a retreat from the strictures of an oppressive present, a refuge in an idealized past and/or a partially imagined future. It mediated the conflicting nostalgic and utopian desires inherent in a period of cultural crisis and transition.

6. See Lhéritier, *Le Triomphe de Madame Deshoulières, Reçue dixième muse au Pantasse* (np: 1694) and *L'Apothéose de Mademoiselle de Scudéry* (Paris: J. Moreau, 1702); Claude Charles Guionet, seigneur de Vertron, *La Nouvelle Pandore ou les femmes illustres du siècle de Louis le Grand*, 2 vols. (Paris: Veuve Mezuel, 1698).
7. Even in elite circles, not all women shared the enthusiasm for fairy tales. In a letter to Huet, an early theorist and apologist of the novel, the Marquise de Lambert writes (probably around 1711): "Je voudrais bien que vous le puissiez guérir [notre sexe] du mauvais goût qui règne à présent. Ce sont les contes qui ont pris la place des romans: puisqu'on nous bannit, Monseigneur, du pays de la raison et du savoir, et qu'on ne nous laisse que l'empire de l'imagination, au moins faudrait-il rêver noblement, et que l'esprit et les sentiments eussent quelque part à nos illusions" (quoted in Roger Marchal, *Madame de Lambert et son milieu*, Studies on Voltaire and the Eighteenth Century, 289 [Oxford: The Voltaire Foundation, 1991] 227). Marchal explains Lambert's disdain for the *contes de fées* as part of a broader rejection of the novel, which was to last until the beginning of Louis XV's reign (*Madame de Lambert*, 228).

BIBLIOGRAPHY

DiPiero, Thomas. *Dangerous Truths and Criminal Passions: The Evolution of the French Novel, 1569–1791.* Stanford: Stanford University Press, 1992.
Harth, Erica. *Ideology and Culture in Seventeenth-Century France.* Ithaca, NY: Cornell University Press, 1983.
Robert, Raymonde. *Le conte des fées littéraire en France de la fin du XVIIe à la fin du XVIIIe siècle.* Nancy: Presses Universitaires de Nancy, 1982.
Stanton, Domna C. *The Aristocrat as Art: A Study of the 'Honnete Homme' and the 'Dandy' in Seventeenth- and Nineteenth-Century French Literature.* New York: Columbia University Press, 1980.
Storer, Mary Elizabeth. *La Mode des contes des fées (1685–1700).* Paris: Champion, 1928.

PATRICIA HANNON

Corps cadavres: Heroes and Heroines in the Tales of Perrault†

"Griselidis"

Before he published the 1697 collection *Contes du temps passé avec des moralités*, Charles Perrault depicted the ideal wife in the verse tale "Griselidis" which he recited to his colleagues at the Académie française in 1691.[1] Since, as Gilbert Rouger has pointed out, "Griselidis" participates in the debate on women's virtue or lack thereof,[2] it can be considered an avatar of those texts centered around the *Querelle des femmes****. "Griselidis" was conceived and presented to illustrate the moral art associated with the cause of the moderns championed by Perrault.[3] Yet, as Perrault's dedication to "Mademoiselle" avows, modern Parisians like herself will find it difficult if not impossible to identify with the sublime patience of the persecuted heroine: "Je ne me suis jamais flatté," admits Perrault, "Que par vous de tout point il [Griselidis' example] serait imité" (57).[4] Instead, the subjugated female sensuality embodied by the heroine will evolve into a subdued and perhaps more "modern" version as the serene housewife of Perrault's later *Apologie des femmes*. After all, admits the academician, Parisian society would merely ridicule the "trop antiques leçons" of this modern fairy tale. Indeed, this tension between ancient and modern, tradition and innovation, subjugated and dominant, hierarchy and its reversal, runs like a subversive thread through Perrault's tales, both in verse and in prose.

Griselidis' docility, and especially her modesty—"un air chaste et modeste/Charmait uniquement et plus que tout le reste" (68)[5]—compel the smitten prince to risk a misalliance, defined and decried by the century as a marriage between social unequals. As we shall see, this initial mis-

---

† From *Fabulous Identities: Women's Fairy Tales in Seventeenth-Century France* (Amsterdam: Rodopi, 1998) 46–77. Reprinted by permission of the publisher. All translations in footnotes are by the editor of this Norton Critical Edition.
1. Unless otherwise noted, all quotations refer to Jean-Pierre Collinet's edition of the *Contes*.
2. *Contes*, ed. Gilbert Rouger, 13.
3. See Mark Soriano, *Les Contes de Perrault*, 314.
4. I have never expected . . . that Griselidis's example at all be imitated by you.
5. A chaste and modest air that had a unique charm, more than any other woman.

marriage appears to proliferate into a recurrent and problematic figure in five of Perrault's seven subsequently published prose tales. After straying from his hunting companions, the hero serendipitously discovers the humble shepherdess, who spins as she tends her sheep. Huntsman-like aggressivity and dominance prefigure the prince's authoritative role in the couple's eventual marriage, at which time the warrior enters the house and is transformed into a tyrannical mate. However, for the moment, the hunter-prince's perspective focuses on a lovely peasant girl who, "D'une main sage et ménagère / Tournait son agile fuseau" (64).[6] This spindle, which makes an ominous reappearance in the "Belle au bois dormant," defines the parameters of Griselidis' submission and ensures her confinement to a traditionally "feminine" role. More important, the prince's initial gaze provokes the requisite modesty of this beauty who "S'était toujours sauvée à l'ombre des bocages" (64).[7] Clearly, the invasive hero's vision foreshadows the heroine's loss of innocence: "Dès qu'elle se vit aperçue / D'un brillant incarnat la prompte et vive ardeur / De son beau teint redoubla la splendeur, / Et sur son visage épandue, / Y fit triompher la pudeur" (65).[8] Griselidis' "brillant incarnat," synonymous with the "*vermillon de la vertu*" defining *pudeur* in the *Dictionnaire universel*,[9] is a guarantee that female sensuality, once encoded by a male perspective grounded in theories on women's nature, will be relegated to the conjugal house.

Perrault's tale appears to subscribe to that view of human sexuality offered by the literature on women: identified with and confined to the female body, sexuality is circumvented through the codes of propriety entrusted to women. Griselidis, who recalls the veiled Roman goddess Pudicité described in Furetière's dictionary,[1] at once dissimulates her own and the prince's desire "Sous le voile innocent de cette aimable honte,"[2] which reiterates her refuge "à l'ombre des bocages." The heroine's blushing together with the amorous hero's gaze, contrasts with the somber "shadows" and "veil" in an eloquent rendering of repression. Chastity, the unique province of women, subdues the expression of passion, "l'autre en moi," in order that it be channeled into a conjugal society presided over by a male mind. The body and by extension sexuality, women's symbolic double, is subdued and mastered through the prism of a rational consciousness. Such optical appropriation of the female body is pervasive in Perrault's tales, including "Peau d'Ane," which features another hero-prince who first spies his beloved through a keyhole, then loses his heart to her "sage et modeste pudeur" (108).[3] According to Philip Lewis, Cartesian rationalism, which provides the conceptual foundation for the cen-

6. Was turning her agile spindle with a clever and well-trained hand.
7. Had always been preserved by the shadow of the grove.
8. The moment she realized she had been seen, she blushed deeply, and the lively color added splendor to her beauty and spread throughout her face, bringing about a triumph for modesty.
9. Furetière, *Dictionnaire universel*, 1727.
1. *Pudicité* is in part defined as: "Divinité adorée par les Romains sous la forme d'une femme voilée & dans une contenance trés modeste."
2. Under the innocent veil of that lovable shame.
3. Good and unpretentious modesty.

tury's privileging of the visual, legitimates the value system articulated in Perrault's writings.[4]

Griselidis agrees with her future husband's assertion that "On ne peut jamais vivre heureux / Quand on y commande tous deux" (62).[5] Nonetheless, Griselidis' "bonne honte," as Richelet calls *pudeur*, merely serves to encourage her husband's erratic behavior. One might even say that her virtue incites the prince's Sadean impulses. Although the narrator ascribes the hero's deviant character traits to melancholy, defined as an illness according to seventeenth-century medicine, his unconventional flouting of the marriage contract together with his sadistic persecution of the unbearably saintly heroine, suggest a rebellious nature impatient with tradition. From the outset, Perrault's characters, first the heroes, then the heroines, display a willingness to tempt the strictures of conventional hierarchies. The royal hero's "maligne humeur" is a severe character flaw which provokes his unflinching mistreatment of Griselidis, and at the same time anticipates the ineffectual husbands and fathers who dominate the later prose tales. Perrault is generally unforgiving in his depiction of father figures, who, excepting the present case, seem far removed from the "little kings in the home" that abound in didactic writings.[6]

Ideologically speaking, the Perraldian disdain for the patriarch informs his modernist stance in the Quarrel of the Ancients and Moderns: he challenges the "fathers" of culture, the ancients with whom he identified his intellectual rival Boileau. Indeed, the misogynist frame that defines the melancholic hero's perception of *le sexe* is nearly identical to the scathing antifeminism expressed in Boileau's 1694 *Satire* X. By attributing the hero's mistrust of women to his unstable temperament, Perrault implies that the ancient perspective on women initiated by Aristotle is flawed in quite the same way that the body is weakened by illness. The "capricious" prince of "Griselidis" profits from his new-found husbandly authority to put his wife's patience and fidelity to the test. Clearly, he uses marriage as a subterfuge in order to engage in a variety of abuses of spousal power. Experimenting with the hierarchical conjugal figure traced by the era's tracts on women, the adventuresome prince endangers without dismissing the ordained familial relations of subordination and dominance. When the deceitful hero repudiates the long-suffering Griselidis and perversely introduces their own daughter as his future bride, his obstinate cruelty is nothing short of subversive. It at once suggests the theme of incest underlying the 1694 verse tale "Peau d'Ane," and foreshadows the simultaneously threatened and reinforced family hierarchies in the *Contes du temps passé*.

Since, at this time, the patriarchal family was being strengthened and the metaphors of family and marriage were widely used to describe the

---

4. See Lewis' *Seeing Through the Mother Goose Tales: Visual Turns in the Writings of Charles Perrault*, ch. 1, 10–41. This chapter studies Perrault's *Parallèle* and reveals its reliance on the Cartesian tradition of rationalism.
5. One can only live happily [in a marriage] if one is in charge of the couple.
6. In "Louis Marin Lecteur de Charles Perrault," Catherine Velay-Vallantin interprets the donkey skin worn by the heroine of "Peau d'Ane" as "un meurtre symbolique du père-roi, désargenté et dépossédé sans son animal surnaturel" (274).

state,[7] there is a seditious ring to the tampering with conjugal bliss found in "Griselidis." Addressing the tale's intimate relation to the symbolics of power, Michèle Longino has shown how both the paratext—Preface, dedication and closing epistle—and the tale itself can be read as "an incitement to question authority," whether that of abusive hero or absolutist king. According to Longino, "Griselidis," a study in relations of power and authority, is a potentially subversive political statement that does not, for all that, abandon its ambivalent tone.[8]

The unstable notion of marital power relations suggested by the prince's restless experimenting with the traditional ideals of male dominance and female subservience, is transposed to the prose tales. In many of the latter, the family can be likened to a battleground where power struggles are delineated along the fault lines of gender: opportunistic stepmothers defy cowardly noblemen, ogresses endanger the royal lineage, disobedient wives challenge the master's word. The modernist world of the *Contes* is plagued by mismatched couples and shifting conjugal hierarchies. Gender-specific in the tracts on women, but paradoxically exceeded in "Griselidis," the foundations of household authority are now undermined and the state is consequently unsteady. When one examines the successors of the idealized Griselidis—"D'une obéissance achevée . . . . Et qui n'ait point de volonté"—[9] it becomes clear that their protean nature, reinforced by the narrator's pervasive irony, merely serves to accentuate the question of women's—and by extension the body's—place in what is not always the master's house.

"La Belle au bois dormant"

A case in point is "La Belle au Bois dormant," the first tale included in the *Contes du temps passé*. The tale's characteristic undecidability results from a comic opposition between a complacently impassive princess heroine and her aggressively voracious mother-in-law. On the one hand, female sensuality is ordered through the perspective of a rational consciousness, whereas on the other, it defies all constraint in order to indulge its unavowable appetites. The spindle that first appeared in *Griselidis* resurfaces as the spinning wheel which, once again, circumscribes women's sphere of action. Forcibly symbolizing women's work, the spinning wheel puts an end to the heroine's wanderings as she circulates about the palace, too far from her assigned place: "c'est principalement aux

---

7. According to Sarah Hanley's "Engendering the State: Family Formation and State Building in Early Modern France," the metaphors of family and marriage used to describe the state outlasted those of divine right (27).
8. See Michèle Farrell, "*Griselidis*: Issues of Gender, Genre and Authority." Farrell's reading of the paratext reveals the bi-dimensional aspect of the tale, which participates in both the *conte* and the *nouvelle*. As a *conte* (the dedication to "Mademoiselle"), it furnishes didactic lessons for a female readership, whereas its *nouvelle* (the letter to "Monsieur") dimension invites the reader to reflect on questions of authority. This generic intersection along with the two implied audiences, characterizes the entire collection and accounts for the undecidable tone of the tales. As Farrell points out, Perrault's version of this folktale differs from that of others such as Boccacio's rendition, in that Perrault's prince severs the marriage contract.
   Louis Marin's analyses of Perrault's tales were perhaps the first to focus on the important theme of power that traverses the *Contes*. See Marin's *Food for Thought*.
9. Complete obedience . . . and without any will.

hommes qu'il appartient de se promener,"[1] warns Grenaille. The princess, "fort vive, un peu étourdie,"[2] resembles Fénelon's hypothetical young girl, whose unseemly curiosity and "vivacité d'imagination" must be restrained at all costs. For Perrault as for Fénelon, domesticity, here symbolized by the prick of the spinning-wheel, serves to suppress female unruliness. At the same time, this first hint of bloodshed foretells the carnage that will afflict the noble heroines of "La Barbe bleue" and "Le Petit Poucet."

The needle draws blood, causing the princess to evanesce into a hundred-years' sleep, an eloquent metaphor for the feminine passivity and contained sensuality so vaunted by theorists who extolled women's chastity. Frozen in time but not lifeless, the heroine's subdued body represents those disruptive impulses to be distanced from the newly assertive rational consciousness. The unconscious body overtaken by endless sleep is ceremonially sealed within a palace by "une si grande quantité de grands arbres et de petits, de ronces d'épines entrelacées les unes dans les autres que bête ni homme n'y aurait pu passer" (134).[3] Sexual repression is poeticized by such ritualized enclosure that is yet another rendition of "the laws of God and those of the world," which according to the theorist Le Moyne, encircle and imprison women.[4] The societal dicta evoked by Le Moyne seem to be outlined in the interlaced trees and bushes surrounding the princess, since the palace they protect will soon shelter yet another familial "little state," consisting of the royal couple along with their children Aurore and Jour. Albeit with disarming irony that counters the mysteries of reproduction so prevalent in theories of women's nature, Perrault's closing *moralités* do allude to women's prescribed role by using the terms *"le sexe"* and *"femelle"* to designate them. When the beautiful princess at last awakens to behold the prince's gaze, she is transformed into "le plus bel spectacle qu'il eût jamais vu" (135).[5] After all, as the feminist Grenaille concedes, "elle est . . . toujours morte, tant qu'elle n'a point au dedans de soy de principe, qui se mouvant luy communique sa vie, & les facultez d'agir."[6]

Symbol of sensuality, the heroine comes into existence only insofar as she is fashioned through the prism of the hero's rational perspective. The relation between the viewing subject and the perceived object has affinities with Cartesianism, and reminds one of Heidegger's description of Descartes' metaphysics as involving a scrutinizing subject who transforms the world into a picture.[7] While the Cartesian frame involves a scientific mind in search of truth and knowledge, Perrault's fictional transposition features a hunter in quest of ideal feminine beauty. In this fairy tale as in "Griselidis," royal hunters "discover" their unsuspecting prey while exploring the confines of their domains in search of adventure. Again, both heroes focus

1. It is principally men who should do the promenading.
2. Very vivacious, a little heedless.
3. Such a great quantity of trees, large and small, interlaced by brambles and thorns, that neither man nor beast could penetrate them.
4. *La Gallerie des femmes fortes*, 149. See also ch. I.
5. The most beautiful spectacle he had ever seen.
6. *L'Honneste Mariage*, 322.
7. See Lewis, 16–17. Lewis cites Heidegger's "The Age of the World Picture," in which the philosopher relates Descartes' metaphysics to modern science. In Heidegger's view, Cartesian truth is situated in the subject, for whom the world is an object to be examined.

their perspectives on docile beauties who are consequently transformed into "spectacle," enchanting pictures for pleasurable viewing. Living portraits of the passivity enshrined by writings on women's nature, these submissive heroines exemplify the ideal of female chastity. In fact, the heroine of "La Belle au bois dormant" surpasses that ideal in the second part of the tale often expurgated from versions for children.

Since "Sleeping Beauty" as originally written by Perrault includes two versions of *le sexe*, one inspired by and concordant with his century's theories on the nature of women, the other shaped by the Gallic tradition of folkloric misogyny, this tale and others like it represent female sensuality as simultaneously mastered and asserted. The breach in the sanctified hierarchy illustrated by the prince's act of envisioning, then animating the paralyzed heroine, coincides with the tale's inscription of the contemporary practice of *mésalliance*. Decried by all manner of elites, from the ancient nobility of the sword to the newly ennobled, intermarriages between persons of unequal social status was not, for all that, unique to the seventeenth century. On the contrary, misalliance was prevalent since the Middle Ages. However, the perception of this accepted practice underwent significant changes in the course of time, changes that relate in part to the identity crisis suffered by the nobility as a result of the social and economic changes that characterized the nascent state.[8] Historians stress the complexity of the issue of misalliance, yet all concur that, for many of Perrault's contemporaries, intermarriages symbolized disorder and instability at its worst. Nonetheless, even if alliances involving parvenus and ancient nobility were met with official contempt, intermarriage was frequent, especially between the ancient nobility and the legally noble.[9]

Clearly, certain forms of intermarriage elicited more public outcry than others. Such were the marriages involving financiers, arguably "the most controversial social grouping in seventeenth-century France."[1] There is every reason to believe that the mother of "Sleeping Beauty" 's hero-prince might very well have been the daughter of a financier. The first in a succession of domineering matriarchs, Sleeping Beauty's stepmother was sought out by the prince's deceased father because of her fabulous wealth, "à cause de ses grands biens" (137).[2] A misalliance is indicated, the catalyst that disrupts conventional household protocol in so many tales of the Perraldian corpus. Perrault's mismatches, signifying as they most often do that women have usurped what the century considered to be the province of men's authority, exemplify what Davis first identified as "woman on top," the engravings and other images of sexual inversion that were pervasive in preindustrial Europe. According to Davis, these imagined reversals express the conflicts that ensued when emerging redistributions of power challenged traditional forms of order.[3]

8. See Gayle K. Brunelle, "Dangerous Liaisons: *Mésalliance* and Early Modern French Noblewomen," 81–83; 100.
9. See Collins, *The State in Early Modern France*, 132, and Brunelle, 99.
1. Lougee, *Le Paradis des femmes*, 134.
2. Because of her great wealth.
3. Davis, *Society and Culture in Early Modern France*, 150.

Certain of Perrault's contemporaries including the Sieur de Mainville, would have exonerated the deceased father of the prince for having married below his station in order to secure his financial interests: "Il n'a proprement que les femmes qui se mesallient," asserted Mainville.[4] For while Boileau would likely have protested that the departed king had "By a cowardly contract sold all his ancestors,"[5] rare were those who shunned a financially promising match with the daughter of a wealthy financier.[6] Considering that the husband's rank determined the status of the children, *mésalliance* had less overt consequences for male as opposed to female nobility.[7] However, money was widely seen as a threat to social cohesion, a disruptive force that signaled a breach in social stratification.[8] Given that early modern Europe unanimously considered the female sex to be the disorderly one,[9] what better figure than the daughter of a financier, doubly unruly by sex and by heritage, to infringe upon household decorum? Surely, "Sleeping Beauty"'s ogress-queen mother embodies the destructive appetites that accompanied rapid social change and threatened the established order.

Upon the death of his father, the prince officially marries Sleeping Beauty, who takes up residence with him at the royal court. There is no hint of trouble until the newly-anointed king departs for war. During her son's absence, the ogress will reign over the kingdom while simultaneously unleashing her monstrous appetite. To satisfy her cravings, she promptly orders that the heroine and her children be slaughtered and served for dinner. Violent death is avoided thanks to a wily and compassionate servant, yet not before the heroine, possessed of the same morbid passivity that afflicted Griselidis, offers herself to her would-be assassin: "Faites votre devoir, lui dit-elle en lui tendant le col" (139).[1] Although Sleeping Beauty's disabling complacency is diametrically opposed to her mother-in-law's aggressive bestiality, both characters are associated with the body, whether created by contemporary theorists or philosophers of antiquity. Nevertheless, solely the ogress-queen assumes the functions of the male sovereign. That the queen is so grotesquely equated with the body and its unspeakable desires serves to underscore the dangers incurred when sensuality assumes control and asserts itself as dominant rather than dominated.

Perhaps the ogress inherited certain of her voracious female instincts from her father, who may have resembled the infamous seventeenth-century financier Claude Cornuel. Castigated by his peers as the "king of the harpies," Cornuel was publicly scorned because he was thought to

---

4. *Du bonheur et du malheur du mariage et des considérations qu'il faut faire avant que de s'y engager*, 132–33. [It is only proper for women to enter into a misalliance.]
5. Boileau, "Satire V," "De l'Abus," quoted by Lougee, 104.
6. See Collins, 132.
7. See Brunelle, 99.
8. See Lougee, 72–77. Lougee explains that the salon was associated with money, which was in turn viewed as unsettling the social order. Contemporaries represented the salon as a crossroads of social mobility, in which money, venality, and luxury were rampant. Because the salons were directed by women, women too were associated with the disorder thought to result from the convergent influences of wealth and venality.
9. Davis, 124.
1. Do your duty, she said to him and extended her neck.

have enriched himself and his relatives by bankrupting others. The financier was described as a veritable ogre in "La Voix du Peuple au Roy," which protested Richelieu's policies while condemning Cornuel as "more criminal than all the men who have *devoured* the people (emphasis added)." Like the women invented by the misogynist Boileau, Cornuel was identified with disruptive appetites and unbridled passions: he lavished riches on his mistress, ruined or saved men according to the dictates of his passion.[2]

As Louis Marin has pointed out, ogres are a metaphor for bestiality that expresses itself in culture as deviance.[3] While it is true that the ogress-regent eventually meets her doom by plunging headlong into a cauldron of toads and snakes, the chaos and violence endemic to the sensual female haunt Perrault's fairy tales. As a result, the generally conservative values extolled by the *Contes* are contradicted by suggestive alternatives to existing family structures. Davis has in fact argued that, although most anthropologists interpret comic inversion as ultimately reinforcing stable hierarchy, gender role reversal may also prompt innovation.[4]

"La Barbe bleue"

The blood shed by the prick of the spinning-wheel needle and suggested in the image of the young Sleeping Beauty, offering her outstretched neck to her executioner, reappears, virulent and degraded, in the third tale of the collection, "La Barbe bleue." Misalliance, contamination of the bloodlines, is here the agent of terrifying carnage. "On s'indigne beaucoup plus contre une femme, que contre un homme qui se mesallie,"[5] warns Furetière. The century's professed loathing of marriages of mixed rank fell disproportionately upon women, perhaps because noblewomen who married commoners forfeited the right to noble status for their offspring.[6] Moreover, marrying beneath one's status implies an act of passion, which, according to theorists on women's nature, was best repressed. Decidedly, passion is not the impetus behind this heroine's attraction to her betrothed. Rather, the prosperous Bluebeard, whose possessions include "de belles maisons à la Ville et à la Campagne, de la vaisselle d'or et d'argent, des

---

2. Quoted by Lougee, 160. From "Sur la Mort de Cornuel," Bibliothèque de l'Arsenal, Conrart MS 5131, p. 198. The entire reference reads as follows: "[Cornuel] ruins and saves whom he pleases according to the movements of his hatred, his love, his interests; who buys houses and builds palaces for his trollop, on whom he spends more than fifty thousand livres annually . . . this pox should be punished with a double torment for having led a rollicking life. . . ."

3. "Robert Sauce ('Sleeping Beauty in the Forest')," in *Food for Thought*, 144. Marin defines the ogre in fiction as "a kind of living metaphor for a wild and ferocious bestiality that has been deviated into culture and society."

4. See Davis, 129–31; 143–44. Davis argues that "the image of the disorderly woman did not always function to keep women in their place" (131). Literary examples of inversion "kept open alternate ways of conceiving family structure" (143). To illustrate how "the unruly option" can embolden one to action, Davis cites the example of Antoinette de Bourguignon, who took the first step toward her future career by disguising herself as a hermit and fleeing an arranged marriage (144).

5. It is much more shocking when a woman enters a misalliance than when a man does.

6. Brunelle states that "From the male point of view, focused as it was on preserving the nobility of the parental lineage, derogation in the female line mattered little" (83). This was perhaps true in practice, however, one cannot deny the indignation expressed by theorists and other male writers against the noblewomen who contracted marriages with social unequals. According to these theorists, women's misalliances were more blameworthy than those of men.

meubles en broderie, et des carrosses tout dorés" (150),[7] offers luxury in abundance to this daughter of a "femme de qualité."[8]

Mainville explains how this financier was able to attract noble wives[9]: "Le Brocart ouvre les oreilles de l'une; la petite Calle qui suit ou qui porte la queue persuade l'autre; les Perles adoucissent la plus fière; & le Carrosse enlève la plus difficile."[1] It was not uncommon for fathers and brothers to seek intermarriage of their daughters and sisters to commoners, in order to secure the financial interests of the family. In some cases, sacrificing a noble daughter, particularly a younger one such as the heroine, was the only alternative to maintaining the lineage.[2] Perhaps encouraged by her family, "Bluebeard" 's heroine, seduced by the hero's splendid possessions and gallant sociability, finally concedes that he is a "fort honnête homme," despite his horrid beard. Reiterated inventories of the evil hero's magnificent riches assert his power while entrapping the noble heroine, who appears oblivious to her villainous husband's dubious history and family lineage. Dazzled, she pays ever less attention to the unnatural color of the villain's beard, the blue chosen to designate both the kings of France and the royal system of justice.[3] Instead, Bluebeard's sumptuous dwelling entrances her into "forgetting" that her mate's several previous wives have mysteriously disappeared, one by one. Like the nobility described by Boileau, the heroine and her family seem to ally themselves with the infamous while substituting money for virtue. "For, if the glitter of gold does not enhance the blood, In vain does one make the splendor of his rank shine," warns Boileau.[4] Yet, Bluebeard's ostentatious urban and country estates blur the distinctions of rank, while convincing the heroine to expose herself to the uncertainties of a misalliance.

When her new husband departs on a business trip, the young wife receives her women friends, who tour this magnificent abode worthy of Louis' finance minister Fouquet. A variation on the salon gathering, the art of conversation practiced by the admiring ladies in Bluebeard's mansion is inspired by a glittering display of riches. If one assumes that Bluebeard is a financier, this scene, which situates a salon reunion in his palatial residence, bespeaks the intimate relation between *salonnières* and

---

7. Fine town and country houses, gold and silver plates, embroidered furniture, and gilded coaches . . . lady of quality.

8. According to Furetière's dictionary, "Quand on dit absolument, un homme de *qualité*, c'est un homme qui tient un des premiers rangs dans l'Etat, soit par sa noblesse, soit par ses emplois, ou ses dignités."

9. Jean-Pierre Collinet points out in his *Notices* to the *Contes du temps passé* that Gilles de Rais was perhaps not the model for "Barbe bleue." Collinet too believes that Bluebeard's sumptuous dwelling signals his profession as a financier. "Le mariage du début ressemble à ces alliances monstrueuses qu'une aristocratie désargentée conclut avec des roturiers enrichis (284)." Others who have speculated on Bluebeard's identity as a financier include Jacques Barchilon, Catherine Velay-Vallantin, and Jean-Marie Apostolidès.

1. Mainville, 132–33. [Flattery opens the ears of one lady; the little page who follows one's steps or brings up the rear persuades the others while pearls soften the proudest ones; and the carriage carries off the most difficult.]

2. See Brunelle, 98–99.

3. In "Des Choses cachées dans le château de Barbe Bleue" (187), Apostolidès notes that the color blue, normally associated with the noble virtues of loyalty and obedience, connotes infamy when associated with the villainous commoner. His strange beard sets the villain apart from the rest of the community, yet Bluebeard refuses to rid himself of it, perhaps because it conceals a diabolical mark. It is known that inquisitors of the century's witch hunts ordered their suspects to be shaven in order to reveal any diabolical marks concealed beneath the hair.

4. "Satire V," quoted in Lougee, 104.

financiers as set forth by Carolyn Lougee. For many of Perrault's contemporaries, the salon was a crossroads where the forces transforming seventeenth-century France converged. Salons were associated with social
mobility and the accompanying effects wrought by luxury, venality or the
selling of offices, and money. Financiers often patronized salons whose
members included significant numbers of their wives and daughters.[5] Bluebeard's wife invites her friends to tour the house, including the *garde
meubles*, encumbered with such collected treasures as "des tapisseries, des
lits, des sofas, des cabinets, des guéridons, des tables et des miroirs, où l'on
se voyait depuis les pieds jusqu'à la tête . . ." (150).[6] These same mirrors,
one of the era's luxury items, reappear in "Cendrillon," where they are
associated with opportunistic arrivistes who lack the most basic rudiments
of acceptable behavior. Bluebeard's valued possessions can reflect the art
market newly organized under Louis XIV; merchants opened boutiques
and tempted wealthy consumers with priceless objects. Bluebeard merely
emulates the king, the first collector of the kingdom.[7]

While the ladies feast their eyes on Bluebeard's prized collection, their
noble hostess scurries precipitously to the room below, the only one whose
entry was strictly forbidden by her husband. She dashes to the forbidden
chamber with such abandon that she nearly breaks her neck: "elle pensa
se rompre le cou deux ou trois fois" (151).[8] Recalling the image of Sleeping Beauty's extended neck awaiting the executioner's knife, the heroine's
endangered body presages the scene of the corpses whose throats have
been slashed as well as her own subsequent brush with the same gruesome
death. The newlywed, conscious of her husband's interdiction, pauses on
the threshold of the forbidden chamber: "songeant à la défense que son
Mari lui avait faite, et considérant qu'il pourrait lui arriver malheur d'avoir
été désobéissante . . ." (151).[9] Deliberately transgressing Poullain's notion
of "reasonable" family hierarchy, the heroine unlocks the door and becomes simultaneously the point of perspective and the usurper of forbidden knowledge:

> après quelques moments elle commença à voir que le plancher était
> couvert de sang caillé, et que dans ce sang se miraient les corps de
> plusieurs femmes mortes attachées le long des murs (c'était toutes les
> femmes que la Barbe bleue avait epousées, et qu'il avait egorgées
> l'une après l'autre). (151)[1]

In juxtaposition with the preceding description of the *garde-meubles*, the
heroine's vision suggests that these dead women, so many collectors' trophies, are barely distinguishable from the precious objects located directly

---

5. See Lougee, 134; 161. According to Somaize's list in the *Dictionnaire des précieuses*, numerous
   salon women were wedded to financiers.
6. Tapestries, beds, sofas, cabinets, stands, tables and mirrors in which they see themselves from head
   to foot.
7. See Apostolidès, *Le Roi machine*, 123.
8. She thought she broke her neck on two or three occasions.
9. Recalling her husband's prohibition and considering what misfortune might befall her if she
   disobeyed.
1. After a short time she began to perceive that the floor was covered with clotted blood of the dead
   bodies of several women suspended from the walls. These were all the former wives of Blue Beard,
   who had cut their throats one after the other.

above them. Richelet indeed defines the *cabinet* which conceals this horrible secret as a room containing valuable art works, "les tableaux de prix." The interchangeability of the victims, murdered in orderly succession—"l'une après l'autre"—suggests their fate as the prey of a serial killer.[2] Perhaps these unfortunate women consulted a marriage list such as the one published in Furetière's *Roman bourgeois*, which ranked eligible marriage partners according to their wealth.[3] If such were the case, they entered unwisely into an economic transaction in which their noble blood was exchanged for Bluebeard's enhanced social status. Clearly, putting financial solvency before the interests of the bloodline unleashes lethal instincts.

Upon entering the prohibited room, the heroine is confronted with a sinister vision which eerily evokes Grenaille's "Il faut qu'elles s'attachent à une maison," as well as Le Moyne's "les liens de la bien-séance l'attachent au logis."[4] This grotesque scene visually renders the ultimate sacrifice required by the "little state." It also serves to underscore that, excepting the three animals devoured by the ogress of "La Belle au bois dormant," the sheep consumed by the ogre of "Le Petit Poucet," and Bluebeard himself, the victims of Perrault's fairy tales are women, most of noble blood. If one assumes the noble origin of Bluebeard's slain wives, this bloodshed bespeaks the loss of certain legal and economic powers suffered by the era's women of rank.[5] Gone, in one powerful image, the immense cultural influence, to say nothing of the sexual liberty, enjoyed by women of the seventeenth-century urban elite. Nowhere, perhaps, has the violence inherent in domesticity been more forcefully rendered than in this depiction of slain wives literally hanging from the walls of the conjugal house. This macabre vision corrects inappropriate female curiosity and disobedience by hyperbolizing in a morbid register, women's confinement to domesticity promoted by theorists and moralists alike.

Clearly, Bluebeard's spouse cannot infringe on sanctified marital hierarchy without impunity; rather, her challenge to the villain's power, the latter synonymous with the secret knowledge locked in the chamber, threatens to exact the price of blood. Lewis has argued that Bluebeard's authority rests on this dreadful secret, equivalent to the knowledge that his wife strives to possess and that he endeavors to keep from her. The bloody crypt celebrates "an abject relation of subjugation" in which power is based on sexual difference, a difference essential to Bluebeard's brute dominance. At all costs, the hideous financier must maintain his identity by asserting his exclusive right to knowledge, a secret he himself has created, a fantasy sustained by female blood.[6] One can follow the trail of blood

2. In *From the Beast to the Blonde*, Marina Warner relates that one of the main causes of women's deaths before the nineteenth century was childbirth. According to Warner, the scene of the bloody crypt represents the situation in which widowers remarried in quick succession upon the not uncommon death of their wives in labor. Warner interprets Bluebeard's several marriages as a form of "serial murder" (263).

3. See Erica Harth, *Ideology and Culture in Seventeenth-Century France*, 122.

4. Francois de Grenaille, *L'Honneste Veuve*, 22; Pierre Le Moyne, *La Gallerie des femmes fortes*, 268. [They must attach themselves to a house . . . the bonds of propriety are attached to the dwelling.]

5. See Joan Kelly, *Women, History and Theory*, 67.

6. Lewis, 208–37. Lewis' valuable analysis of the power relation between Bluebeard and his wife should be read in its entirety. Drawing upon Luce Irigary, he interprets the blood on the key as the "darkly figurative and positive blood-value of womanhood, of matriarchy or maternal power" (235).

from Griselidis' blushing modesty, to the curious Sleeping Beauty's wounded finger, and, after bypassing the present heroine's failed beheading, to the disobedient wives' caked blood.

The ghastly vision of mutilated corpses also signals the demise of the symbolism of blood which was linked with the nobility: the loss of noble blood accompanied by its transformation into "sang caillé," reflects the weakening currency of the aristocratic ideology of lineage, in conflict with the emerging power of the monetary. The identity of the nobility had traditionally been defined through a "symbolics of blood." Noble selfhood was confirmed through ancestry and its corresponding system of alliances.[7] In the stable society of orders, blue blood and power were indissociable. However, since the very meaning of the term "nobility" was in flux during the seventeenth century,[8] images of corrupted blood abound: "si tous les grands Seigneurs préféroient les amourettes aux véritables amours, l'illustre Sang seroit bien-tost *tary*, les grandes Familles seroient bien-tost éteintes, & les Estats seroient bien-tost affaiblis" (emphasis added).[9] Caked blood is synonymous with tainted blood, whether it stems from sexual peccadilloes or intermarriages between persons of unequal status. The suspended cadavers surrounded by a mirror of dried blood signify that the nobility, suffering from the moral bankruptcy decried by Boileau, is "in the red." The ancestral houses of the old aristocracy are symbolically demolished as the feudal ethos competes with that of the market place.

Purged of noble blood, the body that sustained the system of alliances through its progeny is reduced to a lifeless object, a monument to past glory. Female sensuality is reified, frozen motionless in the reflection of dried blood, poised to enter into an economic transaction. Perrault relies on the identification of women with the body already posited in the tracts on women's nature. However, he goes one step further when he imposes a mathematical perspective on female nature. Strung along the chamber walls one after another, "l'une après l'autre," the slaughtered wives have been subjected to a quantifying operation not foreign to the calculating Bluebeard, who counts on his wives' disobedience: he relies on their perception of the bloody chamber in order to confirm his power. Once confronted by the necrophilic husband, their terrified eyes reflect Bluebeard's brutal superiority over all members of their sex, "one after another." Bluebeard's career is devoted to self-affirmation; he fatally reiterates his identity as "le maistre & comme le propriétaire de la personne de sa femme . . . il en devient le possesseur, le maître et le seigneur.[1]

When Bluebeard's wife contemplates her slain predecessors, a macabre configuration of the traditional subordination of women, the body she represents accedes to the knowledge that Cartesian rationalism reserves for

7. Michel Foucault, "La Volonté de savoir," in *Histoire de la sexualité*, Vol. I, 164–66; 194–95.
8. Brunelle, 94.
9. Rene Bary, *L'Esprit de cour ou les conversations galantes*, 219. [If all the great lords preferred love affairs rather than true love, the illustrious blood would soon be tarnished, the great families would soon be extinguished, and the estates would soon be weakened.]
1. Antoine de Courtin, *Traité de la jalousie*, 179; 151–52. Lewis' analysis stresses the role played by the headless corpses in Bluebeard's identity. If one conceives of the villain's castle as a construction of the self, the cadavers, erotically connoting absorption and consumption, are centrally situated in the *cabinet*, at the very core of Bluebeard's identity. Lewis, 211. [The master and as the owner of the person of his wife . . . he becomes the possessor of her, her lord and master.]

the mind, the latter being masculinized in the writings on female nature. In a reversal of the century's theorized marital protocol, the heroine occupies the center of vision usually reserved for a male character. Timmermans has shown how the *femme savante*, the learned woman, was nearly unanimously discredited by the latter seventeenth century. Perceived as a threat to order, women's intellectual aspirations would presumably enable them to assume public functions traditionally exercised by men: "La femme savante dans la littérature sert de repoussoir à la femme idéale, que celle-ci soit connue comme une ménagère ignorante, une ménagère instruite, ou comme une mondaine cultivée."[2] Bluebeard challenges this disruption of order by attempting to reinstate his dominance in the customary fashion: "il allait lui abattre la tête."[3] Clearly, this symbolic yet potentially deadly gesture literally seeks to cut off the heroine from the knowledge she dared claim as her own. According to her mate's grisly calculations, only the fall of the cutlass will force his imprudent wife to take her prescribed place in the bloody tomb.

Bluebeard's fantasy of power is sustained at the high price of female blood. Therefore, the tale's first moral appropriately condemns *le sexe*, as Perrault refers to women, whose unfortunate intellectual curiosity "*Coûte* souvent bien des regrets," and "*coûte* trop cher" (emphasis added).[4] Fitting terms, one might add, for fairy-tale characters who almost without exception view the marriage contract as an economic transaction. From the very beginning, this shrewd daughter of a noblewoman proves herself a fitting match for her conniving husband. Both Bluebeard and his wife wed out of financial interest, both break contracts, both are mutually deceptive.[5] The heroine enters into the marriage contract with a great deal of self-interest and very few if any romantic illusions. Every bit as artful as her mate, this young aristocrat shows a remarkable flexibility, a willingness to compromise with the ideals of her class in order to flourish in the newly emerging order of things. When condemned to die by the knife and join her predecessors, the heroine buys time until the arrival of her avenging brothers. Then, in a stunning theatrical reversal, the wife inherits Bluebeard's enormous fortune and enriches her family with the spoils of the murdered financier: "Il se trouva que la Barbe bleue n'avait point d'héritiers, et qu'ainsi sa femme demeura maîtresse de tous ses biens" (153).[6]

Combining equal parts of noble generosity and "bourgeois" commercial sense,[7] the heroine parcels out her wealth a bit like a careful business woman: "Elle employa *une partie* à marier sa soeur. Anne avec un jeune gentilhomme . . . *une autre partie* à acheter des Charges de Capitaine à

---

2. See Timmermans, *L'Acces des femmes a la culture*, 330; 352; 359. [The educated woman in literature serves as a foil of the ideal woman, whether she is known as an ignorant housewife, a trained housewife, or a cultivated, worldly woman.]
3. He went to cut off her head.
4. Often costs regrets . . . costs too much.
5. Lewis rightfully stresses the parallelism between Bluebeard and his wife in regard to knowledge, transgression and self-interest (205–08).
6. Since Blue Beard had no heirs, his widow inherited all his wealth.
7. Lewis has arrived at a similar conclusion. He interprets the ending as a "definitive sign of the aristocracy's drift into complicity and accommodation with the power and values of an ascendant bourgeoisie" (285).

ses deux frères; et *le reste* à se marier à un fort honnête homme . . ." (153–54, emphasis added).[8] Clearly, this enterprising heroine seems to have greater affinities with Sleeping Beauty's famished mother-in-law than with the self-effaced wives of "Griselidis" and "Sleeping Beauty." She enriches her family without sacrificing her own happiness. Indeed, since the epithet "fort honnête homme" designates both her former and present mate, it would not be surprising if Bluebeard's replacement is yet another financier or other parvenu meant to further embellish the coffers of the heroine and her family. Perhaps, in time, this noble daughter will even join the ranks of Perrault's obstreperous matriarchs.

The second moral surely reinforces this interpretation. Referring to the concluding role reversal, the narrator tauntingly asserts that "On a peine à juger qui des deux est le maître." While certain critics have viewed this "modern" moral as indicative of women's potentially equal position in the marital hierarchy,[9] its parentage with Perrault's earlier conservative *Apologie* would appear to argue otherwise. Describing the wife who violates the traditional conjugal chain of command, Perrault's sympathies seem unambivalent: "Si l'on la [the wife] voit souvent résoudre et décider, / C'est que le foible époux ne sçait pas commander."[1] However, ambiguity marks this tale in which the portrait of a newly assertive heroine is haunted by the tableau of her slain sisters at the center of the sinister castle. Like the indelible mark of blood on the key to the forbidden chamber, this morbid image taints the unstable mirror of memory.

"Cendrillon"

The weak husband mocked in the *Apologie* reappears in "Cendrillon," the sixth tale of the collection. By all appearances a member of the lesser nobility or an impoverished noble, this widower gentleman takes as his second wife a haughty woman who "le gouvernait entièrement" (171).[2] Cinderella's father, who welcomes this wealthy woman and her daughters into the heart of his family, becomes in so doing the agent of his own daughter's disgrace; the young noblewoman, who "n'osait s'en plaindre à son père qui l'aurait grondée,"[3] demurs to the newcomers because she fears her father's displeasure. The evil stepmother, perhaps the daughter of a financier or other successful parvenu, shares important traits with her

---

8. She employed part of it to arrange a marriage between her sister Anne and a young gentleman . . . another part paid for commissions for her two brothers so they could become captains. The rest she used for her marriage to a worthy man.

9. See, for example, Lewis, 203. Lewis interprets the tale's conclusion as a reinstatement of the masculine order. The heroine will no longer challenge authority, rather, she chooses a second marriage to another "fort honnête homme." According to Lewis, patriarchal order is reestablished because the true *honnête homme* dissimulates the differences between men and women that Bluebeard insists on underscoring (245). Yet, it should be remembered that the notion of sexual difference played an important role in promoting women's prominent position in polite *honnête* society: those who explained women's prominent place in a society based on the art of sociability, cited women's essential difference from men as the basis for their superiority in well-defined cultural matters.

Jeanne Morgan was one of the first Perraudian scholars to analyze the dual morals in the *Contes*. See *Perrault's Morals for Moderns*.

1. *Apologie des femmes*, 9. [If one sees the wife often determining and deciding, / It is because the weak husband does not know how to command.]

2. Completely governed him.

3. Did not dare complain to her father, who would have only scolded her.

predecessor Bluebeard. Most especially, she too is associated with luxury, since she has provided the magnificent apparel and fine appointments that distinguish her own daughter's circumstances from those of the shoddily clothed and ill-housed heroine. "La Barbe bleue" and "Cendrillon," which refer to the exact same "miroirs où elles se voyaient depuis les pieds jusqu'à la tête,"[4] engage in an uneasy celebration of materialism. Both at once denigrate and promote an ideology fashioned on conspicuous wealth, both focus on misalliances in order to incorporate gender role reversals that mock traditional notions of marital hierarchy. Whether her reign be provisional as in "La Belle au bois dormant," or lasting, as implied by the conclusion of "Barbe bleue," the female head of household gives fair warning that, although the body synonymous with women is still in the moralists' house, that house is in disarray.

"Cendrillon"'s disordered household is built upon the authority of the domineering stepmother: "qui dit une belle-mère, dit une marastre; qui dit une marastre dit une tigresse . . . on donne indifféremment le nom de marastre à tout ce qui est cruel."[5] The despised stepmother or mother-in-law reflects the conflicting interests that could pit younger and older generations of women from different families against one another. New wives of widowers were particularly sensitive to the needs of their own children, whose interests could be compromised by the offspring of their husband's first marriage.[6] In Perrault's tales, this negative figure impinges on the sanctity of the noble household sustained by respect for the purity of the bloodline. Cinderella's stepmother embodies the forces of luxury which were blamed for undermining the society of orders by obscuring the distinctions of rank. Ostentation and expense mark the new wife, who insinuates herself into the aristocratic milieu by rectifying the gentlemanly widower's financial distress.

From the standpoint of the aristocratic ideology of lineage, misalliances "ne sont pas moins communes que fatales à la décadence des Maisons."[7] It would appear that the father is not reluctant to endanger his own daughter's welfare in exchange for securing his precarious economic situation. Perhaps he resembled others of the century's indigent nobles, who, faced with financial ruin, felt that they had little choice but to bargain with the interests of their daughters or younger sons. It is well known that, during the second half of the century, marriages between men of the high nobility and daughters of the newly ennobled or the wealthy were not uncommon. Nobles sought to provide for their increasingly expensive life style, while the commoners they wed sought the prestige conferred by a title.

The stepmother's two daughters, who, we are told, resemble their mother in every way, are but an extension of the latter's nefarious presence. Cinderella's noble demeanor, ridiculed by the menial tasks imposed on her, is particularly challenged by a new set of power relations based on conspicuous consumption. Resembling many of the socially mobile *salon-*

4. Mirrors in which they could regard themselves from head to foot.
5. Courtin, 238–39. [Whoever says stepmother says harsh mother; whoever says harsh mother says tigress . . . the name harsh mother is used for any woman who is cruel.]
6. See Warner on the rivalry between the mother-in-law and the daughter-in-law, 226–28.
7. Mainville, 67.

nières,[8] the stepsisters subscribe to a sartorial code that equates status with luxury.[9] These "Demoiselles," a term usually referring to young noble-women, assert their claim to high birth by flaunting their red velvet gowns and diamond jewelry. However, the system of alliances that sustained aristocratic ideology is undermined by these false damsels. Cinderella's fashion-conscious stepsisters, like the *salonnières* described by Michel de Pure and Madeleine de Scudéry,[1] negate the family and the ideology of lineage implied by the previous, presumably idyllic relations between Cinderella and her father. "On donne par abus ce nom ["Demoiselle"] aux filles et aux femmes qui sont un peu bien-mises, qui ont quelque air, quelque bien considérable,"[2] explains Richelet.

To be sure, our pretentious arrivistes are invited to the prince's ball because they have established a name for themselves—"elles faisaient grande figure dans le Pays" (172)[3]—and not on account of their noble status. "Always in front of their mirror," the stepsisters are continuously obliged to recreate their identity according to the dictates of court society, which demanded increasingly elaborate attire as a measure of social distinction. Fénelon for one, recognized that sartorial elegance facilitated social ascent and assimilation of the newly ennobled into the old nobility. With this in mind, the stepsisters' seemingly innocuous conversation involving floral-patterned gold coats and intricate hairstyles indicates an obsession with power. This was precisely the view of Fénelon, who interpreted women's preoccupation with fashion as a desire for authority: "les chemins qui conduisent les hommes à l'autorité et à la gloire leur étant fermés, elles tâchent de dédommager . . . de la vient qu'elles aspirent tant à la beauté et à toutes les graces extérieures . . . ."[4] According to Fénelon, women's attachment to finery and novelty threatened the established order: "Dès qu'il n'y a plus de règle pour les habits et les meubles, il n'y en a plus d'effectives pour les conditions. . . ."[5] When Cinderella's nouveau riche stepsisters are invited to the prince's ball, their ascendancy as well as her debasement is recognized by the monarchy. In the aftermath, a new configuration of power emerges, one that bespeaks the conflicting values embraced by the ideology of race and the life styles of the court. The former called for the surveillance of the sexes, whereas the latter promoted a degree of sexual freedom.[6]

When the stepmother assumes direction of the household, female sensuality does indeed transgress the ideal of "mute eloquence" promoted by

---

8. A good half of the salon women listed in Antoine de Somaize's *Dictionnaire des précieuses* come from newly ennobled families rather than from the ancient nobility. See Lougee, 113–37.
9. See Lougee, 72–73. According to the era's antifeminists, exquisite apparel served to blur class distinctions and endanger established social strictures.
1. De Pure, *La Prétieuse ou le mystère des ruelles*, published in 1656–57; Scudéry. "Histoire de Sapho," in *Artamène ou le Grand Cyrus*, published in 1649–53. See also Lougee, 90.
2. The name damsel is used pejoratively for girls and women who are a little well-dressed, who have an air about them, a considerable air.
3. They cut a grand figure in the country.
4. Since the ways that conduct men to authority and glory were closed to them [women], they tried to compensate . . . this is why they aspire so much to beauty and to all those outward charms . . .
5. For both citations, see *De L'education des femmes*, 149. [Ever since there were no longer rules for clothes and furniture, there were no longer any effective forces to set conditions . . .]
6. See Dewald, *Aristocratic Experience and the Origins of Modern Culture*, 126.

Lescale,[7] nonetheless its expression is fettered by the very wealth through which it speaks. Once enlightened by her fairy-godmother's "lessons" on how to transform lowly objects into high culture, pumpkins into carriages and rats into coachmen, Cinderella, too, will adopt the new materialism that has overtaken her father's house. The fairy compensates for the ill-intentioned stepmother by providing her noble charge with the accounterments required to make her debut in high society. For although the heroine is naturally gracious and eloquent, she must be initiated into the realities of social life in a seventeenth-century world in which the old aristocracy is obliged to compete with newcomers in order to survive.

In a litany of metamorphoses that underscore beneficial exchanges, the fairy godmother, "la dressant," "l'instruisant,"[8] initiates Cinderella into the art of compromise.[9] The dynamic fairy dispels the tearful heroine's inertia, while introducing her to the rudimentary principles of economic exchange. The instant wealth occasioned by the fairy's magic wand can symbolize the new power of the monetary, visible to all Perrault's contemporaries, whether they be found at court, salon, or in the streets of Paris depicted in Sorel's *Francion*. Yet, the treasures meted out by the fairy, from fabulous equipage to priceless ball gown, include neither the freedom of movement nor the autonomy that limitless wealth can imply. On the contrary, the profusion of gifts signaling the fairy's beneficence take on a quite different meaning in light of the very last item to embellish her body: the glass slippers, "the prettiest in the world."

Antithesis of the seven-league boots seized by the hero of the last tale of the collection, "Le Petit Poucet," Cinderella's shimmering footwear at once assures her immobility and ensures that she will never accomplish Poucet's marvelous feats. Rather, the heroine's fragile slippers suggest fettered mobility, while recalling the unfortunate destiny of another heroine, Little Red Riding Hood, who ventures outside the house and into the jaws of a ravenous ogre-like wolf. Cinderella's glass slippers should keep the heroine well within the bounds prescribed for her by the century's theorists on the nature of women. As we have seen, Fénelon warned that "les fréquentes sorties de la maison et les conversations qui peuvent donner l'envie de sortir souvent, doivent être évitées."[1] Grenaille too, conceded that, while "les Dames doivent estre un peu remuantes . . . J'ayme bien mieux qu'elles soient invisibles dans les maisons."[2]

When Cinderella arrives at the prince's ball, her precarious liberty symbolized by the shoes of glass is further imperiled. Recalling the mirrors that reflect the stepsisters' image through the prism of an elite sartorial

7. See ch. 1.
8. Forming her; instructing her.
9. My reading of "Cendrillon" presumes the heroine's original noble status, which is temporarily obscured by the measures taken by her father to relieve his impoverishment. This fairy tale thus conforms to the structure of the genre, which presents an initial fall from grace that is consequently rectified. Lewis, citing Norbert Elias, interprets the tale as inscribing the heroine's trajectory from low to high status. The latter is accomplished by the civilizing process as represented by the magnificent gown, an emblem of the court society's ideology of controlled, magnificent appearance (158–59).
1. The frequent outings and conversations that could bring about the desire to leave the house even more often have to be avoided.
2. Fenelon, 112; Grenaille, *Le Plaisirs des dames*, 210. [The ladies should bustle about a little . . . I prefer that they are invisible in the homes.]

code, the mirror of the court, that collective point of perspective through which the heroine achieves social recognition, transforms her into spectacle: "on était attentif à contempler les grandes beautés de cette inconnue;" "Toutes les Dames étaient attentives à considérer sa coiffure et ses habits" (174). The king himself authorizes this celebration of beauty enhanced by wealth: "Le Roi même, tout vieux qu'il était, ne laissait pas de la regarder" (174).[3] Exchanging its admiration for her autonomy, the rapt adulation of the court integrates Cinderella into its midst. Like his fellow heroes in "Griselidis" and "La Belle au bois dormant", "Cendrillon" 's prince, "occupé à la considérer" (174), perceives the heroine as a spectacle not because of his gender, but as an inevitable consequence of his participation in the courtly sphere. While it may be true that Cinderella's freedom is circumscribed by the hero's romanticized vision, his own independence has long since been compromised. To a certain degree, his very love for the heroine is conditional upon the court society, whose enraptured gaze dictates in part the desire of its sovereign.

In a communal expression of satisfaction and pleasure, wealth is sanctioned by the court, for whom Cinderella serves as the emblem of luxury. The insistent gaze of the court society radiates out like a centrifugal force from the king and prince to engulf the heroine in a sea of praise—"On n'entendait qu'un bruit confus" (174). Focusing entirely on the heroine, whose individual identity is appropriated by the collective perspective, the ball scene presents in tableau form what has long been recognized as women's central role in court culture. "Natural" authorities on taste, language, and manners, women were at the epicenter of the new values of civility that flourished in worldly circles. Once passed through the sieve of the civilizing gaze, the heroine's natural superiority is transformed into a product of culture. Nonetheless, Cinderella's perfection is emphatically associated with her physical nature; her body is indeed highlighted by the jewel-studded finery with which it is assimilated. Having been metamorphosed into a precious gem, the ornamented female body is poised to become an object of pleasurable consumption. To illustrate the point, one need only mention the case of André du Chesne, whose version of Neo-Platonism expanded the notion of the equivalence between beauty and goodness by including luxurious ornamentation in his definition of beauty. Inviting women to deck themselves in precious jewels and vestments, Du Chesne argued the cause of luxury, while implicitly offering the portrait of women as objects of conspicuous consumption.[4]

Cinderella's pedestal at the heart of the court economy appears to be yet another version, albeit palatial, of the confinement of le sexe advocated by theoreticians on the nature of women. And yet, the reifying of female sensuality typical of the Contes du temps passé, appears to dispel the mys-

---

3. The king himself, old as he was, could not take his eyes off her.
4. See Lougee, 39–40. It is interesting to note that Du Chesne's apology of luxury is included in a book dedicated to a financier. "While other feminists were content to argue that luxury was ethically neutral, intrinsically neither good nor bad, Du Chesne urged women to ornament themselves, drawing explicitly the portrait of women as objects of conspicuous consumption which was implicit in the abstractions of Neo-Platonism from the beginning."

teries of femininity so evident in the tracts defining women. Instead, the *Contes* often subject the female body to a quantifying process with economic overtones. For example, Jeanne Morgan has shown that in "Les Fées," the royal hero gives short shrift to his bride's high birth and noble qualities in order to focus on the diamonds and pearls that accompany her every utterance: "Le fils du Roi en devint amoureux, et considérant qu'un tel don valait mieux que tout ce qu'on pourrait donner en mariage à une autre, l'amena au Palais du Roi son père où il l'épousa" (167).[5] This son of royalty adopts a mercantile perspective usually considered anathema to his class. In the same vein, the king of "Le Chat botté" exercises his parental prerogative of choosing a mate for his daughter after a perusal of the "marquis" 's treasures, to which his daughter is suggestively assimilated by metonymy.

The reification implied by the lavishly ornamented body is eloquently summarized by the glass slippers, the sole item of Cinderella's marvelous garb to withstand the demystifying power of the stroke of midnight. Ever attentive that her noble protégé assimilate her mentor's lessons on the art of compromise, the fairy punishes Cinderella for reneging on their contract by transforming her exquisite apparel into rags. The shimmering footwear alone remains intact, a promise of final integration into the space reserved for the newly savvy heroine in the emerging order of things. Unfit for travel, the dainty slippers serve to restrain adventurous impulses while at the same time acting as a kind of symbolic double for the heroine. Once the prince retrieves Cinderella's lost shoe, its status as a precious synecdoche of the female body is clear: we learn that "le fils du Roi l'avait ramassée" and that "il n'avait fait que la regarder pendant tout le reste du bal" (176).[6] The prince's gaze passes from the heroine to the slipper with which she is equated by metonymy. Indeed, the captured slipper is the accomplished hunter's prize, since the heroine flees the ball as light-footedly as a "doe" that the prince fails to "trap." The hero's envisioning of the slipper is at once a metaphor for arrested movement and a pledge that the heroine, representing the nobility, will be co-opted into the dominant order of the court; the future sovereign's masterful perspective assures that the stepmother's provisional rule will cede to the king's, the matriarchy to Salic law. Suggesting a compromise between the throne and the nobility that Cinderella embodies, the transfixed slipper implies that the aristocracy will forego a certain degree of freedom while exchanging traditional privileges for new ones.

The perfect fit of the heroine's foot to the slipper, which "était juste comme de cire,"[7] clarifies its synecdochic status as an integral part of her body, a representation or possible substitute for that body. The term "synecdoche," whose Greek origin signifies "act of taking together," "understand-

---

5. See Morgan, 91. [The king's son fell in love with her, and when he considered that such a gift was worth more than a dowry anyone else could bring, he took her to the palace of the king, his father, where he married her.]
6. The king's son had picked it up; he had done nothing but gaze at it during the remainder of the evening.
7. Was exactly like wax.

ing one thing with another,"[8] implies, as Kenneth Burke has noted, "a relation of convertibility between the two terms."[9] The prince thus envisions his lady love through the intermediary of a fantastic object, which, according to Freud, represents female sexuality. The foot itself was often conceived of as a sexual symbol in ancient mythology.[1] More specifically in this case, the frail slipper of glass renders visual a central tenet of the treatises on women, that is, the frequent assimilation of women's nature with the valorized engendering body. As Berriot-Salvadore's study of the depiction of women in Renaissance medicine makes clear, the notion of woman as a precious but fragile container, "précieux instrument de la génération,"[2] has its roots in the sixteenth century.[3] Cinderella's magic slipper metaphorically encloses her within what the century considered women's most valued and mysterious function.

However, Perrault departs from the ideologies expressed by theoreticians on women's nature by focusing more intently on the object as opposed to the generative process itself. Such an object-mediated expression of sexual desire can be related to the economic dimension which permeates the *Contes du temps passé* as a whole.[4] "Cendrillon" 's fetishism was announced by the preceding "Peau d'Ane," whose hero-prince tenderly guards the heroine's ring, while publicizing his intention to marry the damsel whose finger fits the jewel. In both tales, the focus on the limbs' extremities suggests a concern with movement. Fitting the body to the object restricts its mobility by confining it to the courtly sphere of established order. Neither Peau d'Ane's adventure on the margins of society nor Cinderella's brush with magic in her stepmother's household can challenge the finality of the perfect fit, whether through ring or slipper. Taking possession of the errant body, the glass shoe, that is the body riveted and sublimated by the prince's rational gaze, suggests Descartes' dream of the diamond-like body—"d'une matière aussi peu corruptible que les diamants."[5] Both the chimerical ideal of the dazzling "corps diamant" and the scintillating slipper can represent not only arrested mobility, but arrested development as well. Fetishism, not unlike the Cartesian dismissal of sexual differences, is in part defined as the denial of difference and the desire for sexual sameness.[6]

8. *Princeton Encyclopedia of Poetry and Poetics*, 840.
9. Burke, *A Grammar of Motives*, 508.
1. Freud, *Trois Essais sur la théorie de la sexualité*, 40 and note 20, 172.
2. Precious instrument of the generation.
3. *Un Corps, un destin: la femme dans la médecine de la Renaissance*, 202. Berriot-Salvadore thus describes the depiction of women in Renaissance medicine: "Mais délivrée de son imperfection originelle, la femme semble alors un monde clos dont le centre est ce mystérieux organe appelé utérus. La théorie de "l'utérocentrisme" devient origine et confluent de toute une symbolique féminine. L'incertitude même de la terminologie scientifique enrichit le pouvoir fantasmatique de ce qui n'est d'abord qu'une description anatomique. Ulérus, matrice, mère: des mots qui désignent tantôt l'organe, tantôt l'être tout entier" (199).
4. In note 14 to the First Essay on sexuality, Freud wrote: "La différence la plus caractéristique entre notre vie érotique et celle de l'antiquité consiste en ce que, dans l'antiquité, l'accent était mis sur la pulsion, alors que nous le mettons sur l'objet. Pendant l'antiquité, on glorifiait la pulsion, et cette pulsion ennoblissait l'objet . . . tandis que, dans les temps modernes, nous méprisons l'activité sexuelle en elle-même et ne l'excusons en quelque sorte que par suite des qualités que nous retrouvons dans son objet" (171).
5. René Descartes, *Discours de la Méthode* in *Oeuvres et lettres*, 143. [Made of a material that, like diamonds, cannot be tarnished.]
6. See Charles Bernheimer, "Fetishism and Allegory in *Bouvard et Pécuchet*" in *Flaubert and Postmodernism*, 160–61. Descartes elides the question of sexual difference; the Cartesian *corps machine* is asexual.

Sacrificial Bodies

From another perspective, Cinderella's shoes of glass suggest the threat of spilled blood that plagues Perrault's aristocratic female characters. Throughout the *Contes*, the woman of nobility, guarantor of the blood line, is menaced by a panoply of potentially lethal instruments including spinning-wheel needles, knives, and cutting glass. To a certain degree, Perrault's tales enact a death wish for the aristocracy, which is symbolically menaced through the constantly endangered female progenitor. In effect, the degradation of noble birth is no stranger to the Perraldian corpus. A case in point is "Riquet à la houppe," which depicts royal maternity in a state of unmitigated affliction. "Riquet" 's bereaved queens give birth to monsters whose defects are distributed according to a sexual polarity originating in the *Querelle des femmes*. However, the most emphatic dismissal of female nobility, the matriarchal house, and the body's disorderly reign, is found in "Le Petit Poucet," the concluding tale of the *Contes du temps passé*.

"Le Petit Poucet" rejoins "La Barbe bleue" through the sanguine image of the ogre's seven crown-bearing daughters "egorgées et nageant dans leur sang" (198).[7] Although their deceived father slaughters them unwittingly, this immolation of female "royalty"—"il coupa sans balancer la gorge à ses sept filles" (197)[8]—is a complicitous wink at Salic law. These talented princesses, who "promettaient beaucoup, car elles mordaient déjà les petits enfants pour en sucer le sang" (196)[9]—are excluded from succession to their father's reign of terror with the fall of a knife. Their destiny recalls that of the "Belle au bois dormant" 's ogress-queen, who dives into a cauldron of vipers and thereby signals an end to her matriarchal power. At a time when women's increasing prominence elicits repressive legislation and diatribes against society ladies, Perrault responds by a symbolic eradication of female sovereignty. His fairy tales mockingly yet decisively put severe limits on the reign of women. Perrault at times appears to agree with Fénelon, who asserted that women's functions should correspond to their "natural" gifts for housewifery: "Voici donc les occupations des femmes . . . une maison à régler, un mari à rendre heureux, des enfants à bien élever."[1]

The aristocratic blood that flows so abundantly in Perrault's tales rivals the spilling of royal blood that haunts Racine's *Thebaïde*. Clearly, if the newly emerging state relied on a family model, it was not inspired by the aristocratic example. Both Racine and Perrault represent either the destruction or transformation of the royal family, whether through incest or misalliance. As we have seen, misalliance resembles incest in that it can signal perverted or corrupted blood together with endangered family hierarchies. The bloodletting in Racine's play and in the tales can be conceived of as a rite signaling the imminent passage from one world order to another. The shedding of noble blood suggests an unstable world in

7. Murdered and swimming in their blood.
8. He cut the throats of his seven daughters without hesitating.
9. Showed great promise, for they had already begun to bite little children to suck their blood.
1. Fenelon, 92–93. [Here are then women's occupations . . . to keep a house in order, to make a husband happy, and to raise children in a proper way.]

transition toward a newly emerging order in which aristocrats share power with bourgeois.[2] In Perrault's prose tales, female sovereigns in particular are purged of the noble blood that symbolized the power of ancestral alliances. The noble female, symbolically divorced from the ideology of lineage that underlay the aristocracy, is then poised to take part in the enterprise of state-building through the intermediary of *mésalliance*.

Perrault's metaphorical sacrifice of the noble female takes on new meaning in the light of René Girard's analysis of violence in primitive societies.[3] According to Girard, those societies lacking a judicial system act to contain violence through a system of sacrifice. Foregoing direct retaliation against the guilty party, the sacrificial ceremony seeks to arrest the interminable cycle of violence involved in murder and ensuing acts of retaliation. Sacrifice is meant to prevent the escalation of violence by victimizing an outsider, whether an animal, a foreigner, or a society member considered inessential or inferior. According to sacrificial logic, outsider status ensures that the victim will not be avenged by powerful kin or allies. By dint of the same line of reasoning, grounded in the avoidance of the vengeance that sacrifice is meant to defuse, the victim can resemble yet not be identical to the real object of violence. In some primitive societies, the victim substitutes for and is offered to all members of society in order to protect the community from its own violence (18).

Although "primitive" scarcely describes the time frame of the very contemporary *Contes du temps passé*, the fairy-tale genre by definition involves an indeterminate or abstract temporal framework. The Perraldian tales do indeed seem to offer a textual transposition of those sacrifices, which according to Girard, effect a collective transfer at the victim's expense. One might surmise that the violence inherent in the changing society of seventeenth-century France is figuratively deflected from the social body to the body of women; the blood of women is symbolically offered to appease the violence and conflict arising from social change. Female characters are merely the sacrificial substitute for the real object of violence, social change itself, perhaps as embodied in the king. And while the century's code of propriety would scarcely admit of attacking even a fictive king, the royal or noble heroine is fair game. She is, unequivocally, the progenitor of the ruling class. Girard does recognize women's status as inconsequential members of society, yet he asserts that they are never sacrificed since such an act would encourage either the husband's or the father's retaliation (25). Our *conteur*, however, can claim the immunity of fiction in electing women, especially noble ones, as his victims. Moreover, as Girard himself admits, "Plus la crise est aiguë, plus la victime doit être précieuse" (33).[4]

The sacrificial role assigned to many of Perrault's heroines can also be linked to the century's equation of women with (repressed or domesti-

2. See Terrance Cave, "Between Corneille and Racine: *La Thébaïde*," and Roland Barthes, *Sur Racine*. For Cave, Racine's play represents the social instability of the modern world in which absolute truth is absent. Barthes equates Créon with what he defines as the emerging bourgeois order and the voice of the individual.
3. Girard, *La Violence et le sacré*.
4. The more acute the crisis, the more the victim must be precious.

cated) sexuality. While it is true that Perrault's women have for the most part a more conflicted relation to their sexual natures, echoes of Le Moyne and Poullain, from the "principe qui engendre," to the periphrastic "c'est en elles qui se passe ce qu'il y a de plus curieux à connoistre, sçavoir, comment se produit l'homme,"[5] resound throughout the *Contes du temps passé*.[6] For Perrault as for the theoreticians on women's nature, sensuality and sexuality are the province of the female. And, as Girard has shown, sexuality in many societies is considered to be a site of disorder, associated as it is with the violence of rape, the pain of childbirth and the transgressions of incest and adultery. Sexuality is thought impure because associated with violence and bloodshed, a violence often symbolized by the female body.[7] Just as the seventeenth-century woman invented by theorists and moralists is associated with the blood of childbirth, Perrault's women, from Sleeping Beauty to the seven ogresses, are tainted with the trace of spilled blood.

The female body, overdetermined in the contemporary consciousness through its association with sexuality and specifically childbirth, serves as a kind of magnet for violence. Attracting or absorbing violence unto itself, the sensual female symbolically eradicates this social plague from the surrounding community. The mystery enshrouding the female body evoked by feminist and antifeminist theorists alike, is perhaps related to this phantasmic yet no less real, violence inseparable from the era's notions of female sexuality. One might even surmise that theoreticians' recourse to the inexplicable plays a protective role in deflecting aggression, both real and imagined, from *le sexe*. Small wonder then, that both hypothetical women and fairy-tale heroines can scarcely forego the ubiquitous chastity necessary to contain the violence that symbolically marks them. In an age of change and disorder, the body's unbridled sexuality, identified almost exclusively with women, is one disorder too many.

"Le Sexe" Revisited

While Perrault's fairy tales enact in part the theories of gendered hierarchy expressed in the writings on the nature of women, they often belie the ideal of chaste, silenced femininity as articulated in those tracts. Taking as our point of departure Foucault's definition of sexuality, we can detect an evolution in the era's notions of female sensuality, and by extension, sexuality itself. Foucault conceived of sexuality as a point of juncture between biology and history, a convergence between the body and a given configuration of power. The "notion of sex" is a historical construct, a

5. From the "engendering principle" to the periphrastic. "The most curious thing that one could ever know or understand takes place in women: the reproduction of man himself," resound throughout . . .
6. The first citation is from Le Moyne's *La Gallerie des femmes fortes*, the second from Poullain's *De l'égalité des deux sexes*, 94. See also ch. 1 of this study.
7. Girard, 55–58. Girard thus explains the link between women, sexuality, and violence: "Il y a lieu de se demander en outre si le processus de symbolisation ne répond pas á une 'volonté' obscure de rejeter toute la violence sur la femme exclusivement. Par le biais du sang menstruel, un transfert de violence s'effectue, un monopole de fait s'établit au détriment du sexe féminin" (58–59). As Berriot Salvadore points out, the menstruating woman has been considered impure since Antiquity. For Aristotle, the glance of a menstruating woman can tarnish a mirror. The Renaissance *conteurs* subscribe to this tradition that considers menstrual blood to be a kind of venom (24–25).

discursive creation by which power invests and consequently defines the human body. Foucault's analysis then, emphasizes the speculative dimension of sexuality, an ideal point, a "dense transfer point for relations of power."[8]

Clearly, seventeenth-century speculation on women's nature *** sought first to confine sexuality to the parameters of the female body, second to domesticate the latter, all the while alluding to its irrepressible mystery. In the era's musings on women's essential nature, the pervasive discourse on female chastity attempts to integrate the "unruly" body into the existing power system. The body effaced by *pudeur*, is nonetheless compensated by the promise of a special form of intuitive knowledge that owes little to rationality and everything to women's imagined essence. One might even surmise that the mythologies inspired by women's procreative role served as a kind of restitution for the loss of political and legal power.

According to Lougee, the preoccupation with female chastity in the era's writings on women expresses the desire for a stable society respective of hereditary status.[9] If this be true, one must acknowledge that the *pudeur* distinguishing Griselidis and Peau d'Ane is challenged by a bevy of haughty stepmothers, regal mothers-in-law, and financially savvy heroines who populate the *Contes du temps passé*. This need not be surprising, since Perrault's ironic and even duplicitous tales incorporate paradox and contradiction at every turn. For each submissive Griselidis and docile Sleeping Beauty, there is a dominating stepmother and a calculating wife. In large part dismissive of the reputed mysteries of femininity cited by many theoreticians, Perrault elects instead to lower the veil of chastity while liberating the body to speak. Indeed, this master storyteller tests the values grounded in sexual repression, all the while appearing to valorize them.

Perhaps more than any of the contemporary mores incorporated into the Perraldian corpus, it is the controversial practice of *mésalliance* which promotes a heretofore unimaginable dialogue between the newly voluble body (of female sensuality) and the increasingly unsteady (rational) perspective through which it viewed. While the nostalgia for a more stable society of orders resurfaces in the gentle demeanor of Cinderella and the obsequious inclinations of Sleeping Beauty, a future encompassing women who compete with men for power creates a palpable tension that undermines vague longings for the past. Misalliance and the economic exchanges that define it usher in a line of articulate heroines whose prominence has much to do with the increasing importance of wealth in regulating social and political life. Unequal matches destabilize traditional forms of social stratification, and in so doing, encourage enterprising females to calculate their self-interests and those of their kin, according to the new universal measure of monetary exchange.

8. Foucault, 136. The "notion of sex" involves a mystification that obscures the "real" body. In this sense, sexuality is a "point of support" for relations of power.
9. Lougee associates the demand for chastity solely with those writers whom she defines as antifeminist, that is, those who confined women's role to the private as opposed to the public sphere (92). However, both women's advocates and detractors were nearly unanimous in citing chastity as the preeminent feminine virtue.

When money vies with the noble system of power built on blood alliances, a certain democratizing exchange takes place between male and female characters. Bluebeard's wife survives her husband's morbid instincts to inherit his wealth and enrich herself, as well as her family. Cinderella, having interiorized the fairy's lessons on the beneficial effects of exchange, emulates her predecessor by enhancing her status and establishing her sisters at court. Like the roturier Petit Poucet, these two heroines engage in venality to advance their own aristocratic interests; the morals condoning *arrivisme* in both "Cendrillon" and "Le Chat botté" attest that both aristocrats and commoners, men and women, used their wits to benefit from the buying and selling of offices. Stepmothers and mothers-in-law enter the noble household via their fortunes, while buying the right to disdain hierarchy and practice self-affirmation, however provisional. Denigrated as it may be, the matriarchal example suggests an alternate way of envisioning the distribution of familial authority. Clearly, misalliance is a paradoxical figure in the *Contes*. Although it is derided when it results in tyrannical female misrule, it is exonerated or simply ignored when it enables a clever noblewoman to outwit her diabolical mate.

Might one then assume that, on some counts, Perrault can be counted among women's advocates? Yes, in part. For although his *Apologie* confines women to the private sphere, his *Parallèle* highlights women's role as arbiters of culture and thus situates them, albeit ambiguously, in public life. The fairy tales present the same conflicting view of women's place in society. Female characters' aspirations to power are alternately derided and enabled. And while the sensual dimension that the century associated with women is often restrained, even reified, the Perraldian heroine can be assertively calculating. Enterprising female characters such as Bluebeard's wife, owe their superiority not to intuition or sentiment, but rather to their deliberate and careful reasoning.

Once again, the tales' inscription of *mésalliance* appears to be pivotal in ferreting out the feminist tendencies of these texts. Lougee has stressed that women's advocates, substituting behavior for birth, praised personal wealth, venality, and other controversial means of social advancement.[1] Perrault was probably intimately acquainted with these practices, since his own father was a lawyer and administrator involved in the creation and selling of offices. In certain of the *Contes*, women who engage in marriages with social unequals simultaneously enter into economic transactions that seem to disregard, or at the very least, underplay gender differences. It would appear that *mésalliance* and the unsettling of traditional hierarchies that it entails, is a passport to a degree of equality between the sexes largely unknown to tracts on women's nature. Yet, the underlying current of violence that is from time to time directed at female characters throughout the academician's fairy tales renders his ambivalent "feminism" disturbingly problematical.[2]

1. See Lougee, 45; 47; 49.
2. Davis has stressed that women in early modern Europe had a conflicted relation to power. However, one need not assume that they were powerless. Women's problematical relation to power is eloquently inscribed in Perrault's fairy tales.

HARRY VELTEN

The Influence of Charles Perrault's
Contes de ma Mère L'oie on German Folklore†

Perrault's *Contes de ma mère l'oie* had a vast and instantaneous success. Within a year after their first publication a new edition was printed in Holland, a copy of which can be found in the former Hofbibliothek in Karlsruhe.[1] How well known the book became, not only in France but also at an early date in Germany, can be surmised from Gottsched's account of the reception of the French fairy tales in Germany in his *Versuch einer kritischen Dichtkunst*, which appeared in 1730, as well as from Herder's rather disparaging remarks on Perrault in *Andrastea*, II, 6.

The comparatively late occurrence of translations need not astonish us, if we take into consideration that French was the language of educated people in Central Europe at the time, and that Perrault's tales were read primarily in the French original. There even appeared French reprints in Germany. Sander in Berlin published the book in French in 1770. In the same year another Berlin edition was printed by Wever, containing the original together with a German translation. It was not until ten years later that Perrault's tales were translated again, when Mylius in Berlin edited a selection of them under the title *Einige Feenmärchen für Kinder*. Again ten years later, in 1790, two complete translations appeared.[2]

The early dissemination of the *contes* in German-speaking territory was also most probably due to oral transmission. For throughout the eighteenth century the upper classes in Germany were accustomed to have their children educated by French governesses or tutors, who doubtless told the stories to their pupils. The children, in turn, may have told them to the German servants in their household, so that the tales may have spread even among the common people early in the century.

At all events, the stories were popular in Germany for approximately a hundred years before the first genuine German fairy tales appeared in literature. A close investigation of the traces which the *contes* left in German folklore will show to how considerable an extent Perrault influenced German popular tradition.

I. Les fées

Perrault's *Les fées* is a wide-spread type of tale, related to the Cinderella theme, in which the heroine is rewarded for her diligence, kindness and modesty, while her sister is punished for her laziness, rudeness and greed. In the *Anmerkungen zu den Kinder- und Hausmärchen der Brüder*

† From *The Germanic Review* 5 (1930): 14–18. Reprinted with the permission of the Helen Dwight Reid Educational Foundation. Published by Heldref Publications, 1319 Eighteenth Street NW, Washington DC 20036-1802. Copyright © 1930.

1. *Contes de ma mère l'oye, Histoires ou Contes du Temps passé. Avec des Moralitéz. Par le Fils de Monsieur Perrault de l'Académie Françoise. MDCXCVIII,* a Dutch reprint of the original Paris edition of 1697.
2. In Bertuch's *Blaue Bibliothek aller Nationen,* published in Gotha, and in a Weimar edition entitled, *Sämtliche Feenmärchen von Ch. Perrault, Frau v. Lintot und J. J. Rousseau.*

Grimm[3] Perrault's story is listed among the parallels to *Frau Holle*, the best known German tale of this type. The tasks by which the character of the sisters is tested in *Frau Holle* are, however, much more elaborate than in *Les fées*, and the nature of the reward and punishment differs considerably. The French story is much more closely related to No. 13 of the Grimm collection, *Die drei Männlein im Walde*.

Both stories agree completely as to their main contents. The younger of two sisters is ill treated by the mother. She renders a small service to a supernatural being, represented in *Les fées* by a fairy, in Grimm No. 13 by three dwarfs. For her kind deed she is rewarded by having precious stones or gold coins drop from her lips whenever she speaks. The older sister, trying to obtain the same gift, inadvertently shows her natural rudeness and is duly punished by having toads leap from her mouth. She meets a miserable death, while her sister marries a prince.

The only essential difference of the two tales consists in the ending of Grimm No. 13, which contains the very common folklore motif of the ugly sister's substitution for the beautiful bride. This is due to a contamination with a different type of fairy tale, represented by Grimm Nos. 11, 89 and 135.[4]

An influence of *Les fées* on *Die drei Männlein im Walde* is virtually certain, if we take into consideration that the exact manner of the reward and punishment as related in Perrault occurs in no other German variant.[5] Our assumption can, therefore, not be refuted by contending that the motif itself is not infrequent in folklore, and that it is already contained, in part and in a somewhat different form, in Basile's *Pentamerone*, IV, 7, where the heroine breathes roses and jasmin and has pearls fall out of her hair.

All other German versions of our fairy tale[6] are closely related to *Frau Holle*, without showing any traceable connection with *Les fées*. The German parallels to Grimm No. 13[7] agree with Grimm as to the main motifs, while diverging from both Grimm and Perrault in their account of the method of reward and punishment. *Die drei Männlein im Walde*, therefore, appears to be the only German version which was influenced by the French tale.

II. *La belle au bois dormant*

The task of tracing the influence of *La belle au bois dormant* on German folklore is made comparatively easy by the fact that there exists only one German parallel to this Perrault tale, i.e., the well-known *Dornröschen* (Grimm No. 50). For Bechstein's and Dähnhardt's versions are doubtless derived directly from Grimm.[8] The same is the case with two German folksongs, to be found in Kretschmer-Zuccalmaglio's and in Böhme's col-

---

3. By J. Bolte and G. Polivka. Leipzig, 1913–18, I, 215 (Grimm No. 24).
4. This contamination may have taken place at a comparatively early time. For the same motif appears already in a sixteenth century story, i.e., in the ending of the tenth story of the third day in Basile's *Pentamerone*.
5. R. Köhler, in *Kleinere Schriften*, Weimar, 1898, I, 126–7, investigates this motif. His list of parallels does not mention any Germanic version of *Les fées* which contains the motif.
6. Cf. Bolte-Polivka, I, 207ff.
7. Cf. Bolte-Polivka, I, 99ff.
8. Cf. Bolte-Polivka, I, 434.

lections.[9] The only remaining German variant, No. 41 of Jahn's Pomeranian stories,[1] is obviously a combination of Grimm's *Dornröschen* with Grimm No. 55.

Owing to lack of space, we can quote below merely a selection of the many striking verbal agreements of the two tales, which, in certain passages, make Grimm No. 50 appear almost like a translation of Perrault.

During a festival, arranged by a king and queen to celebrate the birth of a princess, a fairy who had not been invited pronounces a curse upon the child. Another fairy tries to mitigate the curse. The stories read:

Perrault	Grimm No. 50[2]
"It's true that I don't have sufficient power to undo entirely what my elder has done. The princess will pierce her hand with a spindle. But instead of dying, she'll only fall into a deep slumber that will last one hundred years. At the end of that time, a king's son will come to wake her."	She still had her wish to make, and although she could not undo the evil spell, she could nevertheless soften it.
	"The princess will not die," she said. "Instead, she shall fall into a deep sleep for one hundred years."
In hope of avoiding the misfortune predicted by the old fairy, the king immediately issued a public edict forbidding all the people to spin with a spindle or to have spindles in their house under pain of death.	Since the king wanted to guard his dear child against such a catastrophe, he issued an order that all spindles in his kingdom were to be burned. . . .
After fifteen or sixteen years had passed, the king and queen went away to one of their country residences, and one day the princess happened to be running about the castle. She went from one chamber up to another, and after arriving at the top of a tower, she entered a little garret, where an honest old woman was sitting by herself, spinning with her distaff and spindle. This good woman had never heard of the king's prohibition with respect to spinning with a spindle.	Now, on the day she turned fifteen, it happened that the king and queen were not at home. . . . So she wandered all over the place and explored as many rooms and chambers . . . and she saw an old woman in a little room sitting with a spindle and busily spinning flax.
	"Good day, old granny," said the princess. "What are you doing there?"
	"I'm spinning," said the old woman, and she nodded her head.
"What are you doing there, my good woman?" asked the princess.	"What's the thing that's bobbing about in such a funny way?" asked the maiden, who took the spindle and wanted to spin too, but just as she touched the spindle, the magic spell began working, and she pricked her finger with it.
"I'm spinning, my lovely child," answered the old woman, who did not know her.	

9. Cf. Bolte-Polivka, I, 434.
1. Cf. Bolte-Polivka, I, 434.
2. Not having been able to obtain the 1812 edition, I quote the text of the edition of 1857.

"Oh, how pretty it is!" the princess responded. "How do you do it?
Let me try and see if I can do it as
well."

No sooner had she grasped the
spindle than she pricked her hand
with the point and fainted, for she
had been hasty, a little thoughtless,
and moreover, the sentence of the
fairies had ordained it to be that
way.

Both stories continue in an almost identical manner, telling of the profound sleep that overcame all inhabitants of the castle; of the hedge that
grew around it; and of the arrival of the rescuer after a hundred years.
While, however, *Dornröschen* ends with the marriage of princess and rescuer, Perrault's tale goes on, relating that later the princess and her two
children *Aurore* and *Jour* were cruelly persecuted by the prince's mother,
who was an ogress.

The only essential point of divergence in Grimm's tale is the omission
of this continuation. On the strength of this fact, it has been contended
that Grimm No. 50 embodies an independent Germanic tradition of our
fairy tale. Petsch,[3] e.g., argues that *Dornröschen* is not the only variant that
gives the shorter version. It is true that Bolte-Polivka[4] list six parallels, a
French, a Croatian, a Greek and three Russian tales, which close with the
wedding of the rescued maiden and her deliverer. However, in all other
respects, these stories are very remote from both Grimm and Perrault.
Moreover, they were recorded such a long time after Grimm's *Märchen*
that they may quite well represent degenerate derivatives of *Dornröschen*
itself.

It is significant that all remaining versions, including the earliest ones,
tell a longer story than Grimm and are, at the same time, much more
closely related to Perrault than are the six variants quoted above.[5]

Thimme[6] and Rutgers[7] are hardly justified in maintaining that the last
part of *La belle* is an unmotivated continuation. For the mother of the
prince simply takes the part which in an older version[8] was played by his
wife, who certainly did *not* lack a motive for the persecution. The motif
of jealousy is, however, by no means the original one. There can be no
doubt that in the original version of our folk-tale the children were to be
killed because they were twins. As J. Rendel Harris[9] has pointed out, the

3. In *Paul und Braunes Beiträge*, XLII, 80 ff.
4. *Op. cit.*, I, 437.
5. The tale first appears in the *Perceforest*, a French prose novel of the fourteenth century. The hero
   has to go through an enchanted sleep himself and has to conquer a rival before he is united with
   the princess. Concerning other early variants, see Bolte-Polivka.
6. Cf. *Das Märchen*, p. 97.
7. Cf. *Märchen und Sage*, Dissertation, Groningen, 1923, p. 69.
8. Such a version is found in the story "Sole, Luna e Talia" In Basile's *Pentamerone*, V, 5, the ending
   of which agrees completely with that of *La belle*, except for the fact that the fiendish woman
   appears as the rescuer's wife.
9. *The Cult of the Heavenly Twins*, Cambridge University Press, 1906.

fear of twins was found among all Aryan and Semitic peoples, as well as among the natives of Africa. To this day, many African tribes regard the birth of twins as an evil omen.

The frequent occurrence in folklore of the motif of the fiendish mother-in-law does, therefore, not permit us to infer that the end of Perrault's tale is an inorganic addition. Moreover, this ending must originally have been taken over by German folklore with the rest of the Perrault story; for we find it in the Bruchstück No. 5 in the Grimm collection.[1] This fragment shows such a striking conformity with the end of *La belle* that there cannot be any doubt about its derivation.[2]

Apart from the ending and the minor difference between Perrault's more artful and slightly ironical style and Grimm's more simple and childlike manner of rendering the story, the French and the German tales are so utterly alike that Grimm's story must be considered a mutilated transmission of *La belle*. The two tales are the only versions (excepting one of the Russian variants quoted above) that contain the motifs of the magic sleep which overtakes all inmates of the castle, and of the hedge that grows around the palace. A Breton tale[3] in which a thorn bush plays a prominent part is apparently more closely connected with Grimm No. 31 than with *Dornröschen*.

Grimm and Perrault furthermore agree in relating the immediate awakening of the sleeping princess at the arrival of her rescuer, while in the *Perceforest* and the *Pentamerone* she does not wake up until she has borne a child to her rescuer. Lastly, the Grimm version has preserved, in conformity with Perrault, the story of the fairy who is angered because of a missing favor. This motif occurs already in the *Perceforest*, where one of the three goddesses, invited to the festival, does not find any knife at her place.[4]

We may safely conclude that *Dornröschen* was embodied in German folklore for the first time in consequence of the wide dissemination of Perrault's *contes* in Western and Central Europe.

III. Cendrillon

The Cinderella type belongs to the most widely cultivated fairy tales in existence.[5] It is closely related to *Peau d'âne*, treated under IV. Both types count among a group of stories that can be divided, according to the method of Bolte-Polivka,[6] into the following main motifs:

A1, She is maltreated by her step-mother and step-sisters, or

1. Cf. Bolte-Polivka, III, 488.
2. There is no trace of the tale in Germany before the time of the Grimms. The mere mention of the name in the title of Gryphius' play *Die geliebte Dornrose* of 1660 does not warrant any conclusions. Few will still share the view of the Grimms, who regarded *Dornröschen* as a degenerative derivative of the Valkyrie story in the Sigrdrifumol; and the assumption that this Germanic legend was influenced by a fairy tale of the *Dornröschen* type is at least highly doubtful, as Panzer has shown in *Studien sur germanischen Sagengeschichte*, Munich, 1912, II, 136. In Europe the tale obviously was first known in Romance territory, whatever its ultimate source may be.
3. Cf. Spiller, *Zur Geschichte des Märchens vom Dornröschen*, Frauenfeld, 1893, p. 18.
4. It is true, however, that this motif is not infrequently found in folk-tales; it appears even in Icelandic stories. Cf. Dr. Konrad Maurer, *Isländische Volkssagen der Gegenwart*, Leipzig, 1860, p. 283, 287.
5. Cf. Miss M. R. Cox, *Cinderella, Three Hundred and Forty-five Variants*, London, 1893.
6. 168; the above tabulation differs from that of Bolte-Polivka chiefly in the subdivision of B.

A2, she flees in a disfiguring disguise from her father, who wants to marry her.

B1, While doing menial work, she receives aid from her dead mother, from a tree on her mother's grave,

B2, from a supernatural being, or

B3, from birds.

C1, Magnificently dressed, she dances several times with a prince, who vainly tries to retain her.

C2, She alludes to the abuse she endured while a servant.

C3, The prince beholds her in her chamber, donning beautiful raiment, or he sees her in church.

D1, She is discovered by a shoe-test, or

D2, by a ring which she puts in the food of the prince.

E, She marries the prince.

Perrault's *Cendrillon* is composed of the motifs A1, B2, C1, D1, E, while the best known German parallel, the *Aschenputtel*, Grimm No. 21, consists of A1, B1, B3, C1, D1, E. Grimm is altogether different from Perrault in all details, and contains numerous incidents and digressions not found in *Cendrillon*. The only two Germanic variants[7] which, like Perrault, show the sequence A1, B2, C1, D1, E are Meier's *Aschengrittel*[8] and Zingerle's *Die drei Schwestern*.[9]

Meier No. 4 differs from Grimm, and is brought somewhat closer to Perrault by the omission of the motifs B1 and B3. The heroine is aided by a dwarf, whose part resembles that of the fairy in *Cendrillon*. The story, furthermore, omits several incidents of the Grimm tale, such as the stories of the pigeon house, the pear trees, and the stepsisters' punishment. Aschengrittel is denied permission to go to the ball without first having to perform a futile task. In all other respects, however, Meier No. 4 follows Grimm, embodying even the story of the father's journey.[1]

The German version which most closely resembles Perrault is Zingerle's tale. Both stories proceed in the same simple, straightforward manner, telling that the heroine was left at home to do menial work while her sisters went to the ball. A fairy—according to Zingerle, an angel—provides her with splendid finery and sends her to the ball, where the prince is greatly impressed by her. She manages to disappear unnoticed. The stories continue as follows:

Perrault	Zingerle
On the third day she *loses*, during her hasty retreat, *one of her glass-slippers*. The prince picks it up, proclaiming that he will wed its owner.	On the last evening she is pursued by the king's servants. She scatters gold to detain them and *drops her slipper*, which is brought to the

7. The tale No. 23 in Bondeson's *Svenska Folk-Sagor*, Stockholm, 1880, which consists of the same sequence, is a direct derivative of *Cendrillon*. This is not surprising; for a translation of the French story was published in Stockholm as early as 1787 under the title *Sagan om Ask-fis, eller den lilla Glas-Toffelen*.

8. No. 4 in E. Meier's *Deutsche Volksmärchen aus Schwaben*, Stuttgart, 1852.

9. *Kinder- und Hausmärchen aus Tirol*, Innsbruck, 1852 and 1911, p. 130 ff.

1. This incident, by the way, does not appear in the first Grimm edition of 1812. It was added later from a different version.

In vain the *shoe is tried on all the ladies of the court* and on the step-sisters. They mock at Cendrillon, *dissuading her from putting on the slipper; but the emissary of the prince insists.* The shoe fits, and Cendrillon *is taken to the prince as his bride.*

king. He orders it *to be tried on every girl in town.* The older sisters attempt a fraud, but the deception is revealed by birds. *The king's messenger makes the heroine put on the slipper in spite of the sisters' protests.* Seeing she is the right bride, he *conducts her to the king, whom she weds.*

The deception attempted by the heroine's sisters and the warning by birds, contained in Zingerle's tale, are obviously incidents which are drawn from the Grimm version. The scattering of gold by the heroine is an extraneous feature. All the rest of the story agrees more closely with Perrault than with Grimm. This conformity is made the more significant by the fact that Zingerle's collection also contains a parallel to Perrault's *Peau d'âne*—a parallel which shows the same affinity to Perrault regarding the motif of supernatural help. The prominence of the fairies is peculiar to French folklore. We also find there quite frequently the substitution of angels or the Virgin Mary for the fairies. This makes it most probable that *Cendrillon* influenced Zingerle's *Die drei Schwestern*, notwithstanding the fact that the Tyrolese tale is somewhat deformed in that the heroine does not bear the name of "Cinderella" or a German equivalent, but is called merely "Else."

IV. Peau d'âne

Peau d'âne is composed of the motifs A2, B2, C3, D2, E, according to the tabulation under III. The tale differs from the Cinderella type in the beginning, which relates the flight of the heroine from her father, who wants to marry her, and in the recognition scene, which is effected, not by a shoe but by a ring. Most of the German parallels to *Peau d'âne* lack the important motif A2. Moreover, other essential divergences from Perrault are found in all these variants except one—Zingerle No. 2, which contains the motifs B2, C3, D2, E.

Only four German versions show the motif A2. Two of these, Bartsch's *Aschenpüster*[2] and Vernaleken No. 33,[3] contain the motif C2 and deviate from Perrault also in other respects. The two remaining variants are Grimm's *Allerleirauh* and a story in Lemke's collection.[4] *Allerleirauh*, Grimm No. 65, consists of A2, C1, D2, E.

In the beginning Grimm's tale is virtually identical with *Peau d'âne*. Both stories tell that a king promised his dying wife he would never marry again unless he found a woman whose beauty equalled hers. Perceiving the resemblance of his daughter to her dead mother, he decided to make her his wife. In order to prevent it, the maiden first demanded several

2. K. Bartsch, *Sagen, Märchen und Gebräuche aus Meckiensburg*, Vienna, 1879.
3. Th. Vernaleken, *Österreichische Kinder- und Hausmärchen*, Vienna, 1892.
4. *Volkstümliches aus Ostpreußen*, Allenstein, 1899, II, p. 214. The tale is apparently a derivative of Grimm No. 65.

robes colored like the stars of heaven. When she had received these, she asked, according to Perrault, for the skin of a gold-producing ass—according to Grimm, for a cloak made out of a thousand different kinds of fur. All her wishes having been granted, she resolved to flee. She blackened her face and hands, donned her ass's skin or cloak, and left her father's castle.

In Perrault's version the heroine is assisted by her fairy godmother, whereas in Grimm supernatural aid is merely hinted at in a passage where we are told that the heroine packed all her beautiful dresses into a nutshell. But despite this minor divergence there can be no doubt that the beginning of *Allerleirauh* goes back to Perrault. For Grimm No. 65 is the only German variant which contains the motif of the promise exacted by the dying queen.

The latter part of the Grimm tale deviates considerably from *Peau d'âne*. The meeting of heroine and king which takes place at three consecutive festivals clearly shows a contamination with the Cinderella type of story. The account of the recognition, likewise, is repeated three times. Allerleirauh puts, in the food of the king, first her ring, then her spinning-wheel, and, on the last day, her gold reel.

The beginning of Zingerle No. 2, *Cistl im Körbl*, has very little in common with either Perrault or Grimm, except for the fact that the part of a mysterious hunter who provides the heroine with beautiful robes resembles the rôle of the fairy in *Peau d'âne*. But in its latter part the Tyrolese story follows Perrault much more closely than Grimm No. 65 does.

The two tales relate that the heroine became a lowly and despised servant in a castle. On the first Sunday the master happened to see her in her sun-colored dress and fell in love with her. After returning to the castle, he fell ill and no doctor could cure him. The heroine baked a cake for him, dropping a ring into it, by means of which she was recognised. The master became well again and made her his wife.

If we consider the striking agreement of details, we can hardly doubt that *Peau d'âne* has influenced Zingerle No. 2. *Cistl im Körbl* is, moreover, the only German version containing, in conformity with Perrault, the motif C_3—that is to say, the only variant in which the meeting of heroine and prince is not told according to the version of the Cinderella tale. Both Zingerle and Grimm agree to a great extent with Perrault regarding the nature and color of the heroine's dresses.

Peau d'âne has belonged among the most popular French folk-tales[5] since very early times, whereas it is not traceable in German tradition before the time of Musaeus' collection, which was published in 1787.[6]

V. *Le Petit Chaperon Rouge*

There exist five German parallels to *Le Petit Chaperon Rouge*, which are all extremely similar to Perrault's tale. *Rotkäppchen*, Grimm No. 26,

5. *Peaus d'âne* is said to be derived from the tale I, 4 in Straparola's *Le piacevoli notti*; but the first trace of it appears in the *nouvelle* 129 of Des Perier's *Nouvelles récréations* of 1558.
6. Musaeus drew on *Peau d'âne* in one of his highly artificial fairy tales, *Die Nymphe des Brunnens*, in *Volksmärchen der Deutschen* (reprint, Berlin, 1908).

is by far the earliest on record and shows an almost literal conformity with Perrault, except for the ending. Since the four later German variants[7] agree with Grimm and diverge from Perrault regarding the end of the story, it is very probable that they are derived from Grimm. At any rate, a connection between the Perrault and the Grimm versions is irrefutable, as a synopsis of the original texts will prove, which unfortunately can be given here only in part.

Perrault	Grimm No. 26
Once upon a time there was a little village girl, the prettiest that had ever been seen. Her mother doted on her, and her grandmother even more. This good woman made her a little red hood which suited her so well that she was called Little Red Riding Hood wherever she went.	Once upon a time there was a sweet little maiden. Whoever laid eyes upon her could not help but love her. But it was her grandmother who loved her most. She could never give the child enough. One time she made her a present, a small, red velvet cap, and since it was so becoming and the maiden insisted on always wearing it, she was called Little Red Cap.
One day, after her mother had baked some biscuits, she said to Little Red Riding Hood, "Go see how your grandmother's feeling. I've heard that she's sick. You can take her some biscuits and this small pot of butter."	One day her mother said to her, "Come, Little Red Cap, take this piece of cake and bottle of wine and bring them to your grandmother. She's sick and weak—"

The two tales continue in well nigh literal conformity, the most striking agreement of all occurring in the conversation of the little girl with the wolf who impersonates the grandmother. The passage, which represents an almost exact translation, reads as follows:

"What big ears you have, grandmother!"	"Oh, grandmother, what big ears you have!"
"The better to hear you with, my child."	"The better to hear you with."
"What big eyes you have, grandmother!"	"Oh, grandmother, what big hands you have!"
"The better to see you with, my child."	"The better to grab you with."
"What big teeth you have, grandmother!"	"Oh, grandmother, what a terribly big mouth you have!"
"The better to eat you with."	"The better to eat you with!"
And upon saying these words, the wicked wolf pounced on Little Red Riding Hood and ate her up.	No sooner did the wolf say that than he jumped out of bed and gobbled up poor Little Red Cap.

7. *Rotkäppchen* in L. Bechstein's *Deutsches Märchenbuch*, Leipzig, 1874, and in J. Kehrein's *Volkssprache und Volkssitte im Herzogium Nassau*, Weilburg, 1862, Wirth's *Rautkappl* in *Archiv für die Geschichte von Oberfranken*, XX, 229, and a Tyrolese tale in *Zeitschrift für Volkskunde*, X, 415.

At this point Perrault's tale ends, while Grimm No. 26 continues, relating that a hunter who happened to pass looked in, saw the wolf, cut his body open, and found the grandmother and the girl still alive. They then filled the wolf with stones, so that he broke down and died when he tried to escape. Grimm also tells a second version of the ending, according to which the wolf does not eat the old woman or the girl but is outwitted by the grandmother and drowned.

The end of the *Rotkäppchen* may be merely an anorganic addition to the tale, caused by a contamination with the Grimm story No. 5, which ends in an almost identical manner. The fact that Grimm found a second version seems to justify the conclusion that the continuation was not yet firmly connected with the tale. On the other hand, Perrault may have reported a mutilated variant. This assumption is also quite plausible; for, as A. Lang pointed out in *Custom and Myth*, folk-tales of this type are probably related to the Greek myth of Cronos, who ate his own children and disgorged them again after a stone had been given him in place of Zeus.

However that may be, there are so many passages in Grimm's version that agree verbally with the French tale that we are forced to assume that *Le Petit Chaperon Rouge* became by oral transmission the direct source of Grimm's *Rotkäppchen*.

VI. *Les souhaits ridicules*

Les souhaits ridicules belongs to a well-known type of tale, in which a supernatural being promises to one or more persons the fulfilment of a certain number of wishes. The wishes are all granted, but owing to the thoughtlessness of those who express them they bring no profit at all. The only German version that agrees with Perrault's rhymed story regarding the number and exact nature of the wishes is the tale "Drei Wünsche" in J. P. Hebel's *Schatzkästlein*, which was first published in 1811.

The two stories run as follows:

Perrault	
To a poor woodcutter Jupiter granted three wishes. While his wife was preparing supper the man, in his thoughtlessness, remarked he would like a sausage of a yard's length. Immediately the sausage appeared from out the chimney. The woman angered the man so much with her reproaches that he shouted:	A poor man and his wife were permitted by a fairy to express three wishes. Without thinking of the fairy's gift, the woman wished for a sausage to go with their supper. No sooner had she spoken than the sausage came down the chimney. Seeing one of the precious wishes wasted, the irate husband exclaimed:
"I wish to God that the sausage was hanging from your nose, you vile creature!"	"I only wish that the sausage would grow on your nose!"

Both tales end alike, relating that after due deliberation the man employed the remaining wish to remove the sausage from his wife's nose.

In *Les souhaits ridicules* the man utters all three wishes,[8] while in Hebel's version it is the woman who wastes the first wish. This is the only essential point of divergence. It is easy to account for the substitution of the fairy for Jupiter, a figure altogether unfamiliar to German popular tradition.

In the numerous variants to our folk-tale the nature of the wishes varies greatly. This is a matter of course. For if a person is at liberty to procure himself anything on earth, there is certainly not the slightest necessity that he should wish for a yard's length of sausage. If, therefore, two versions agree in this point, it can be considered as irrefutable evidence that the tales are related. Hebel's *Drei Wünsche* is doubtless derived from *Les souhaits ridicules*. This seems all the more plausible, if we take into consideration that Hebel was well read in French literature and that he was an ardent admirer of France.

Conclusion

Only two of Perrault's eleven stories have left no ascertainable traces in German folklore: namely, *Grisélidis*, which Perrault avowedly drew from Boccaccio's *Decamerone*, and *Riquet à la houppe*, for which there exist only two parallels in all.[9] The following table will summarize the result of our investigation. It includes also those stories whose influence on German popular tradition is already more or less known; that is to say, *Le petit poucet*, *La barbe bleue*, and *Le chat bollé*, which, owing to limited space, could not be treated here in detail.

Perrault's tale	is the only source of	influenced
Les fées		Grimm No. 13
Les belle au bois	Grimm No. 50	
Cendrillon		Zingerle's *Drei Schwestern*
Peau d'âne		Grimm No. 65; Zingerle No. 2
Le petit chaperon	Grimm No. 26	
Les souhaits	Hebel's *Drei Wünsche*	
Le petit poucet	Bechstein's *Der Kleine Däumling*[1]	Grimm No. 15[2]
La barbe bleue	Grimm, 1812, No. 62;[3] Bechstein's *Vom Ritter Blaubart*[4]	Bechstein's *Drei Bräute*; Meier's *König Blaubart*; Weddigen-Hartmann, p. 199[5]
Le chat botté	Grimm, 1812, No. 33[6]	

8. Bédier's rendition of Perrault's story in his tabulation in *Les Fabliaux*, Paris, 1925, p. 217, is incorrect regarding this point.
9. One French and one Hungarian variant; cf. Otto Meier, *Zeitschrift für vergleichende Literaturgeschichte*, V, 122, and A. F. Doerfler, *ibidem*, VI, 393.
1. Pointed out by Gaston Paris, *Mémoires de la Société de Linguistique*, I, 394.
2. This was known already to the Grimms. Cf. Bolte-Polivka, I, 115.
3. Purposely omitted from the later editions because of the obvious identity with Perrault's tale.
4. Cf. Bolte-Polivka, I, 407.
5. The story in Weddigen-Hartmann's *Sagenschatz Westfalens*, 1884, p. 199, and Bechstein's and Meier's tales are all contaminated with Grimm No. 46; Meier's story is, moreover, influenced by Grimm No. 40. Cf. Bolte-Polivka, I, p. 407, and J. A. MacCulloch, *The Childhood of Fiction*, London, 1905, p. 308.
6. Purposely omitted from the later editions because of the obvious identity with Perrault's tale.

SIEGFRIED NEUMANN

The Brothers Grimm as Collectors and Editors of German Folktales†

The names of Jacob and Wilhelm Grimm inevitably evoke thoughts of Grimms' *Fairy Tales*. In the form given them by Wilhelm in the last edition he produced in 1857, the *Kinder- und Hausmärchen* have been printed so often and become so widely known that this book constitutes in public consciousness the ultimate achievement linked with the name Grimm. In fact, none of their works occupied the brothers—at least Wilhelm—over so long a period as the collecting, editing, and annotating of the fairy tales. Spanning almost fifty years, this work represents in terms of duration alone the "work of a lifetime." And, indeed, fairy tale research seems to be the one area of their work in which the Grimms not only achieved the strongest resonance, but also in which they determined with particular clarity the course of future research.[1] So in essence the *Kinder- und Hausmärchen* are still the standard source work on which our knowledge of the German folktale is based;[2] and even in the folkloric research of other countries one can still find today traces of the Grimms' influence.[3]

Assessments of the Brothers Grimm as collectors and students of the fairy tale, however, run the risk of focusing on the final form of the *Kinder- und Hausmärchen* and its success. In doing so, one all too easily overlooks the fact that the collection represents basically an early work. When Jacob and Wilhelm began to devote themselves intensively to German folk literature in 1805, they were not yet scholars but only twenty-year-old university students who were reacting to newly experienced stimuli. Their teacher in Marburg, the legal historian Friedrich Karl von Savigny, had awakened their inclination for historical studies and steered their interest towards "Old Germanic" literature. And Clemens Brentano, one of the leaders of the Heidelberg Romantic circle, had won the brothers over and enlisted them in his search for surviving forms of traditional folk poetry, which he planned to publish.[4]

There were certainly models for these efforts, such as Johann Karl Au-

† From *The Reception of Grimms' Fairy Tales: Responses, Reactions, Revisions*, ed. Donald Haase (Detroit: Wayne State UP, 1993) 24–40. Reprinted by permission of the publisher. This essay is based on the author's articles "Zur Entstehung und zum Charakter der Grimmschen 'Kinder- und Hausmärchen': Bemerkungen aus volkskundlicher Sicht," *Jacob und Wilhelm Grimm: Vorträge anläßlich der 200. Wiederkehr ihrer Geburtstage*, Sitzungsberichte der Akademie der Wissenschaften der DDR: Gesellschaftswissenschaften, 1985, 6/G (Berlin: Akademie-Verlag, 1986) 55–64; and "Die Brüder Grimm als Sammler und Herausgeber deutscher Volksmärchen," *Die Brüder Grimm: Beiträge zu ihrem Schaffen*, ed. Kreisheimatmuseum Haldensleben and Die Stadt- und Bezirksbibliothek "Wilhelm Weitling" (Magdeburg: Druckhaus Haldensleben, 1988) 36–45. Translated by Donald Haase.

1. Denecke 63–87; Woeller, "Die Bedeutung der Brüder Grimm"; and Bolte and Polívka. See also the bibliographical references that follow.
2. This is the case even though the folkloric content of the collection has been critically examined for years. See, for example, Schoof; Karl Schmidt; Woeller, "Der soziale Gehalt"; and Grimm, *Kinder- und Hausmärchen: Ausgabe letzter Hand*.
3. See Briggs; Gašparíková; Horák; Leitinger; Michaelis-Jena; Nişcov; Ortutay; Peeters; Pomeranceva; Pulmer; Leopold Schmidt; Ziel, "A.N. Afanas'evs Märchensammlung"; Ziel, "Wirkungen."
4. On the intellectual and ideological development of the Brothers Grimm, see Stern 4–14.

gust Musäus—however problematic his *Volksmährchen der Deutschen* (1782–86) appeared even to his contemporaries. And above all there was the example of Johann Gottfried Herder, whose high assessment of the song (*Lied*) and fairy tale as the poetry of the folk was echoed by the Romantic movement.[5] This echo is especially evident in Clemens Brentano and Achim von Arnim's folk song collection *Des Knaben Wunderhorn* (1806–08), to which the Brothers Grimm themselves had already contributed.

A corresponding fairy-tale collection was supposed to follow *Des Knaben Wunderhorn*, and the fairy-tale narratives that the Grimms excerpted from old books or transcribed from friends in the Wild and Hassenpflug families in Kassel during and after 1807 were intended solely for Brentano's projected publication. But already in a letter to Arnim on 19 October 1807, Brentano writes that he had found the brothers "after two years of long, diligent and very rigorous study, so erudite and so rich in notes, experiences, and the most varied perspectives regarding all romantic poetry" that he was "shocked" "at their modesty concerning the treasures" they possessed. They were working, he writes, "in order one day to write a proper history of German poetry" (Steig, *Achim von Arnim und Clemens Brentano* 224). Nonetheless in 1810 the Grimms sent Brentano their fairy-tale notes upon his request—but not, of course, without first having their own copies made. And in 1811, when Brentano still had made no arrangements for his projected fairy-tale book, they conceived the plan of preparing their own, for which the copies would serve as a starting point.

At this time, under the influence of Napoleon's foreign rule, the Brothers Grimm not only sought "in the history of German literature and language consolation and refreshment . . . from the enemy's high spirits," as Jacob formulated it retrospectively in 1841 (*Kleinere Schriften* 546); they also felt that by collecting and publishing surviving forms of "Old Germanic" literature and folk poetry they were fostering national self-reflection. Like Herder, from whom the Romantic movement borrowed the concept of natural poetry (*Naturpoesie*), the Grimms also saw in folk poetry—in the songs, fairy tales, and legends of the common people—the original source of poetry and the echo of ancient literature. And in this context they understood "folk poetry" largely in an ethnic sense—as the poetry of Germans, Poles, and so on (*Geschichte der deutschen Volksdichtung* 91). At the same time the Grimms viewed fairy tales as belonging "to those poetic works whose content had most purely and powerfully preserved the essence of early epic poetry" (Ginschel 250). As Wilhelm emphasized already in 1811: "These fairy tales deserve better attention than they have so far received, not only because of their poetry, which has its own loveliness and gives to everyone who heard them as a child a golden moral and a happy memory for life; but also because they belong to our national poetry, since it can be shown that they have lived throughout several centuries among the folk" (*Altdänische Heidenlieder* xxvi–xxvii). And writing of the fairy-tale book he had prepared in collaboration with Wilhelm, Jacob observed: "I would not have found any pleasure in work-

5. See Jahn; Arnold; and Benz.

ing on it if I were not of the belief that it could become to the most serious and oldest people, as well as to me, important for poetry, mythology, and history."[6] And in 1860 he emphasized explicitly that he had "immediately recognized the value of these traditional forms for mythology" and had therefore "insisted vigorously on the faithfulness of the collection and rejected embellishments."[7]

But what about this "faithfulness"? The fairy-tale manuscripts originally intended for Brentano, which were preserved among his unpublished papers, range from mere notes to relatively complete texts. And these exhibit certain individual differences. Fairy tales in the original manuscript taken down by Jacob are in most cases texts characterized by concise language and which in part only outline a tale's subject. Wilhelm's transcriptions, on the other hand, constitute tales with a more polished content and smoother narration. But for publication even these had to be shaped and polished as narratives. To what extent this was or was not also true of the subsequent sketches specifically intended for their own book of fairy tales we do not know, because these manuscripts were not preserved. However, the revision of the original manuscript for the first edition reveals that the Grimms, who were novices at such literary activity, largely followed their models, so that hardly any stylistic differences are discernable between texts edited by Jacob and Wilhelm (Rölleke; Ginschel 222–24). When the preface to the first volume of the *Kinder- und Hausmärchen* in 1812 states that "no details have been added or embellished or changed" (XVIII; trans. in Tatar 210), that applies only to the content, but not to the linguistic appearance of the printed fairy-tale texts.

Nevertheless, the brothers were in fact intent upon tales issuing genuinely from the oral folk tradition and considered it important that such tales be recorded in their own right. Consequently, they often provided the same tale type in two or three versions, sometimes even under the same heading, as with Nos. 20, 32, and 36. This alleged faithfulness to the sources (even if they were only limitedly accessible) constitutes for the brothers a primary scientific concern, as suggested in the quoted statements from Jacob. This is corroborated as well by the following facts: (1) the Grimms preferred stories from oral sources to texts with a literary character (so that part of their literary excerpts in the original manuscript were not printed along with the other pieces); (2) besides the most diverse kinds of fairy tales and comical tales (*Schwänke*), the brothers also included in their edition legends, tall tales, and horror stories, among which were thematically uninteresting or poorly told pieces;[8] (3) the Grimms gave their book a programmatic preface and scholarly notes. At the same time, the *Kinder- und Hausmärchen* were naturally supposed to make these stories available to wider circles, as indicated already by the title. And here pedagogical factors played a role, for the book was supposed to become a "manual of education"—"ein eigentliches Erziehungsbuch" (*Kinder- und Haus-*

6. Jacob's letter of 28 Jan. 1813 to Arnim (Steig, *Achim von Arnim und Jacob und Wilhelm Grimm* 271).
7. Jacob's letter of 18 Feb. 1860 to Franz Pfeiffer ("Zur Geschichte der deutschen Philologie" 249).
8. An itemized and somewhat original overview of the generic diversity is given by Berendsohn 33–127.

märchen: 1812 und 1815 2: VIII). But because of the problematic content and awkward narrative style of certain texts, as critics noted, such an effect was apparently not possible. As a consequence the nine hundred copies of the first volume seemed for some years to be almost unmarketable.[9]

On the basis of the criticism their book received, against which the Grimms defended themselves and which they privately had to acknowledge, they apparently imposed a different standard for the selection and revision of tales for the projected second volume. This standard was defined by two widely praised tales from the first volume that had come from Philipp Otto Runge: "The Fisherman and His Wife" (No. 19) and "The Juniper Tree" (No. 47). With these texts as their models, the Grimms themselves developed an ideal fairy-tale form that in the end could be produced only by talented storytellers or retellers and could find its counterpart only in artistically shaped texts. They found both in the intellectually active bourgeois and aristocratic circles in which they moved. Particularly in enlisting the aristocratic Haxthausen family of Westphalia as tale collectors and informants, and in discovering the *Märchenfrau* Dorothea Viehmann from Niederzwehren near Kassel, the Grimms became the beneficiaries of a string of aesthetically pleasing fairy tales. Moreover, the tales in Westphalian dialect and those of Viehmann appear to be directly transcribed from the oral narration. That the tales in the second volume of 1815 (with thirty-three of seventy texts from the Haxthausen family and fifteen from Viehmann) were as a rule better told than those in the first volume was very substantially related to the greater storytelling talent of the new sources. But Wilhelm, who for the most part attended to the editing of the newly collected material, seems to have also exercised a stronger editorial hand wherever his experience with the first volume suggested it might be necessary. "You have," wrote Arnim to Wilhelm after receiving the second volume on 10 February 1815, "genially collected, and have sometimes right genially helped, which of course you don't mention to Jacob; but you should have done it even more often" (Steig, *Achim von Arnim und Jacob und Wilhelm Grimm* 319). The preface and notes demonstrate that the Grimms adhered to the scientific intentions they had applied to the first volume, but this time the emphasis lay visibly on the presentation of a more appealing text, which was aimed at larger groups of readers. Nonetheless, the second volume sold as poorly as the first (Schoof 27; Grimm, *Kinder- und Hausmärchen: 1819* 2: 541–43).

Therefore, in the course of being prepared for the second edition of 1819, Grimms' collection underwent an extensive revision. Twenty-seven of the texts contained in the first volume and seven of those in the second were deleted, either because they no longer met the aesthetic demands of the Grimms or because they were otherwise questionable (e.g., due to their cruelty). Eighteen texts of the first edition were merged with newly collected variants of specific tales or so substantially changed by other thematic or formal revisions that virtually new texts resulted. And forty-five texts, revised in varying degrees, were incorporated as new texts in the

---

9. Lemmer 107–16; Grimm, *Kinder- und Hausmärchen: 1819* 2: 536; and Ginschel 230–31.

collection, which now grew to 170 tales.[1] Thus resulted almost by half a new book of fairy tales; and in it Wilhelm Grimm's poetically atuned stylizing—his unique fairy-tale voice—became distinct for the first time. Consistent with this development, the heavily expanded annotations were relegated in 1822 to their own separate volume, which addressed itself especially to readers with a specialized scholarly interest (Grimm, *Kinder- und Hausmärchen: 1819* 2: 548, 556–64).

But popular success came first in 1825 with the Small Edition of the *Kinder- und Hausmärchen*, which was conceived primarily for children and included fifty selected texts and seven engravings. This edition smoothed the way for the reception of the large edition, which Wilhelm sought continuously with every new edition to enrich through the addition of new or better fairy-tale texts. Up until the seventh and final edition of 1857, Wilhelm not only adopted new stories from other contemporary collections (e.g., Nos. 171–72 from Mecklenburg, Nos. 181 and 186 from Oberlausitz, Nos. 184–85 and 188–89 from Bavaria); he also replaced weak texts with better narrated variants of the same tales, which accordingly appeared under new titles (e.g., No. 101 "Der Bärenhäuter" instead of "Der Teufel Grünrock," No. 107 "Die beiden Wanderer" instead of "Die Krähen," No. 136 "Der Eisenhans" instead of "De wilde Mann," etc.).

Simultaneously Wilhelm further honed the texts stylistically from edition to edition. The opening lines of "The Frog King" (No. 1) serve as a good example. The first edition of 1812 reads:

> Es war einmal eine Königstochter, die ging hinaus in den Wald und setzte sich an einen kühlen Brunnen. Sie hatte eine goldene Kugel, die war ihr liebstes Spielwerk, die warf sie in die Höhe und fing sie wieder in der Luft und hatte ihre Lust daran. (*Kinder- und Haus- märchen: 1812 und 1815* 1: 1)

> Once upon a time there was a king's daughter who went into the forest and sat down at a cool well. She had a golden ball that was her favorite toy. She would throw it up and catch it in the air and was amused by this.

The second edition of 1819 already shows distinct changes, which aim at greater concreteness:

> Es war einmal eine Königstochter, die wußte nicht was sie anfangen sollte vor langer Weile. Da nahm sie eine goldene Kugel, womit sie schon oft gespielt hatte und ging hinaus in den Wald. Mitten in dem Wald aber war ein reiner, kühler Brunnen, dabei seizte sie sich nieder, warf die Kugel in die Höhe, fing sie wieder, und das war ihr so ein Spielwerk. (*Kinder- und Hausmärchen: 1819* 1: 9)

> Once upon a time there was a king's daughter who was so bored she didn't know what to do. So she took a golden ball that she often played with and went into the forest. Now in the middle of the forest

---

1. Here again twenty-nine contributions came from the Haxthausens and eighteen from Dorothea Viehmann.

there was a clear, cool well and she sat down next to it, threw the ball into the air, and she would play this way.

In the last edition edited by Wilhelm from 1857, the scene has been so thoroughly painted that it can nearly stand alone:

> In den alten Zeiten, wo das Wünschen noch geholfen hat, lebte ein König, dessen Töchter waren alle schön, aber die jüngste war so schön, daß die Sonne selber, die doch so vieles gesehen hat, sich verwunderte, sooft sie ihr ins Gesicht schien. Nahe bei dem Schlosse des Königs lag ein großer dunkler Wald, und in dem Walde unter einer alten Linde war ein Brunnen; wenn nun der Tag recht heiß war, so ging das Königskind hinaus in den Wald und setzte sich an den Rand des kühlen Brunnens; und wenn sie Langeweile hatte, so nahm sie eine goldene Kugel, warf sie in die Höhe und fing sie wieder; und das war ihr liebstes Spielwerk. (*Kinder- und Hausmärchen: Ausgabe letzter Hand* 1: 29)

> In olden times, when wishing still helped, there lived a king whose daughters were all beautiful, but the youngest was so beautiful that the sun itself, which had seen so many things, was always filled with amazement each time it cast its rays upon her face. Now, there was a great dark forest near the king's castle, and in this forest, beneath an old linden tree, was a well. Whenever the days were very hot, the king's daughter would go into the forest and sit down by the edge of the cool well. If she became bored, she would take her golden ball, throw it into the air, and catch it. More than anything else she loved playing with this ball. (Trans. in Zipes 2)

The Grimm fairy-tale style is fully developed here. But what also clearly emerges is Wilhelm's manner and art of narration, which seek—in this case to the extreme—to plumb the fairy-tale events down to their very details. One can respond to the result in two ways—by lamenting the loss of the folktale's simplicity, or by welcoming the poetic enrichment.[2] In any case, these examples clearly demonstrate the growth of an aesthetically oriented attitude.

The orientation towards fairy tales as linguistic-artistic survivals is certainly also one of the reasons that the Grimms did not turn their attention more closely to those who told these fairy tales. Moreover, in viewing folk literature as natural poetry (*Naturpoesie*), the Grimms were inclined to view their informants less as individual storytellers than as oral sources. If they nonetheless described their best storyteller in the preface to the second volume, that was done largely from this very perspective. Dorothea Viehmann, a "peasant woman" who told "genuine Hessian tales," as the preface claims (in reality she was a tailor's wife from a Huguenot family), corresponded to the Grimms' image of an ideal tale teller from the simple folk, among whom they expected to find the guardians of the oral story-telling tradition: "Devotion to tradition is far stronger among people who always adhere to the same way of life than we (who tend to want to change) can understand" (*Kinder- und Hausmärchen: 1812 und 1815* 2: V–VI;

---

2. See, respectively, Panzer 1: xlii–xlvii; and Grimm, *Kinder- und Hausmärchen: 1819* 2: 570.

trans. in Tatar 212). Also in the letters of the Haxthausen family there is talk of trips into the surrounding villages "to gather from the mouths of the old rural population the tales, folk songs, and children's songs that still live" (Schoof 38, 74, 81, 95). However, we know little about storytellers who came from the working classes of the population. On the other hand, the fact that Grimms' informants belonged above all to the educated classes and to the aristocracy does not at all mean that their tales reflect principally the tradition as it existed in these social circles. Yet vast areas of oral folktale tradition remained inevitably unknown to the Grimms; and vulgar stories, which even then made up a large part of the popular tradition, were very likely consciously overlooked in the course of collecting. Consequently, on the basis of sources alone, the popular tradition is only partially represented in Grimms' collection—even if one takes into account that the repertoire of oral tales established in the middle-class homes of Kassel or among the Haxthausens depended largely on the folk tradition or found its motifs reflected in it.[3]

The Brothers Grimm themselves apparently did not consider this manner of transmission to be a shortcoming. Already in the preface to the first volume we find the idea that although fairy tales are "never fixed and always changing from one region to another, from one teller to another, they still preserve a stable core" (*Kinder- und Hausmärchen: 1812 und 1815* 1: XIII; trans. in Tatar 208). In this respect the Grimms saw all their informants as well as themselves as links in a chain of storytellers, each having a certain right to retell the tales in his or her own way. At the same time, whenever faced with several versions of the same tale, Wilhelm endeavored in each case to give the best one in terms of content and narrative. And when he thought it possible to expand or to "improve" this version with another transmission, he would do it—convinced that in this way the "genuine" folktale could be reconstructed. In doing so—as the 1856 volume of annotations attests—he had no inhibitions about blending texts from Hesse, Westphalia, and Mecklenburg, or from an older written tradition and recent oral tradition. He was concerned above all with a text's inner coherence and the completeness of individual motifs. Further revision focused on conforming the tale's content to childlike understanding, portraying the tale's characters (they were supposed to be as vivid as possible), and attempting to animate the depictions through direct speech, linguistic expressions, verses, and so forth (Ginschel 215–17). All this spoke to a concern already expressed in the second volume of the first edition: "The aim of our collection was not just to serve the cause of the history of poetry: it was also our intention that the poetry living in it be effective" (*Kinder- und Hausmärchen: 1812 und 1815* 2: XIII; trans. in Tatar 214). Through his textual revisions, however, Wilhelm—despite all his efforts to reconstruct the "genuine" voice of the folk—increasingly endowed the fairy tales with a poetic art form of his own making. In other words, the Grimms' original striving to record the oral tradition was gradually replaced (at least from our contemporary perspective) by literary principles: "Despite loving

---

3. See the overview of Grimm's contributors and informants compiled by Heinz Rölleke in Grimm, *Kinder- und Hausmärchen: Ausgabe letzter Hand* 3: 559–74.

fidelity towards the folk tradition, the Brothers Grimm created from it a work of literature" (Berendsohn 26).

Consequently, the final edition of 1857 can be used only in a limited way if one seeks to discover clues in the tales' content that point to their origin in the contemporary folk tradition. This edition contains in large measure very beautiful fairy tales, which are by the same token Grimms' own versions and in which some elements of social criticism have been deleted in order not to offend the groups of readers the Grimms were addressing. For example, in the first published version of the tale "God-father Death" (1812, No. 44), the poor man answers the "good Lord" with these words: " 'I don't want you to be godfather! You give to the rich and let the poor go hungry.' With that he left him standing there and went on" (Kinder- und Hausmärchen: 1812 und 1815 1: 193). In later editions, however, this commentary follows: "The man said that because he did not know how wisely God distributes wealth and poverty" (Kinder- und Haus-märchen: 1819 1: 153; trans. in Zipes 161). With that interpolation, the original message of this passage is fundamentally changed and turned into its opposite (Steinitz). On the other hand, a tale such as "The Tablecloth, the Knapsack, the Cannon Hat, and the Horn" (1812, No. 37), which was told to the Grimms by the retired dragoon Johann Friedrich Krause and in which the king and his royal household are ultimately massacred, was replaced in the second edition by a variant in which the same events are even more drastically depicted (No. 54).

To be sure, the tales printed in the first edition, which were repeatedly recorded at the beginning of the nineteenth century, clearly reveal that it was primarily young women of the bourgeoisie and aristocracy who sup-plied the Grimms with these stories. Their tales, especially those like "Cinderella" (No. 21), "Brier Rose" (No. 50), and "Snow White" (No. 53), which are favorites among later generations of children, depict the fate of young girls, whose lives are miraculously fulfilled through love for a prince. But in the case of the tailor's wife Dorothea Viehmann, it is not only an outstanding storyteller who speaks, but also a representative of the simple folk. One needs only to read her tale "The Clever Farmer's Daughter" (1815, No. 8),[4] whose plot is embedded in critical depictions of the social milieu that show the feudal lords' oppression of peasants. Here, as in Vieh-mann's tale of the battle of the animals (1815, No. 16),[5] the victory of the weak over the strong is painted with obvious engagement. And it is hardly coincidental that the impoverished old dragoon Krause should tell the tale of the faithful dog Old Sultan, whose master threatens to destroy him in his old age now that his useful days are over (1812, No. 48). So the Grimms' collection does contain features in which one can recognize directly the views of the oppressed, the "voice of the folk." And in some cases these traces survive even into the last edition of 1857.

In sum: With a remarkable feel for the nature of folk literature, the Brothers Grimm collected as much of the oral narrative tradition and

4. In the second and subsequent editions this tale appeared, with few changes, as No. 94.
5. In the second and subsequent editions this tale appeared, with few changes, as No. 102.

documented it as "faithfully" and as comprehensively as was possible for them under the existing conditions. The *Kinder- und Hausmärchen* became a world-wide success "because here for the first time significant national and international traditions of the intellectual culture from the broadest spectrum of the folk appeared elevated to the level and clothed in the language of 'belles lettres,' without their content or message having been decisively altered" (*Geschichte der deutschen Volksdichtung* 90).

What distinguished the Grimm collection most clearly of all from its precursors was the wealth and diversity of the tales it presented.[6] Even the first edition of the *Kinder- und Hausmärchen* of 1812–15 included nearly the complete stock of tale types that have been found subsequent to the Grimms in the folk traditions of the various German regions. That makes the Grimms' collection even to this day *the* book of German fairy tales. And the brothers were not content just to reproduce the texts; in the volumes of commentary published both in 1822 and 1856,[7] they also attempted to place each fairy tale, comical tale (*Schwank*), and legend in the context of German and non-German oral narrative traditions. From these volumes of commentary and the important work of Bolte and Polívka that they generated, there runs a straight line to the tale type and motif indices as well as to the comparative oral narrative research of recent decades.[8] In this respect the Brothers Grimm can be regarded without question as the fathers of international folktale research. Even much of what they documented, as it were, in passing has had a stimulating effect. For example, the brief characterization of Dorothea Viehmann in the second volume of the *Kinder- und Hausmärchen* in 1815 became the starting point for world-wide narrator research (Dégh, *Märchen* 47–65; Lüthi 83–105).

But above all, ever since the Grimms folktales have been collected in nearly all regions of the earth. And for this purpose collectors have increasingly made use of tape recordings, which capture the exact wording of a spoken narration. Modern folk narrative research demands unconditional authenticity in recording from informants, whereas this was still not possible for the Grimms. Yet in their work one observes at least the demand for authenticity—for instance, in Jacob's *Circular* of 1815, where he writes: "It is above all important that these objects be recorded faithfully and accurately, without make-up or accessories, from the mouths of the tellers, when feasible in and with their very own words, with the greatest exactitude and detail; and whatever might be gotten in the living regional dialect would therefore be doubly valuable, although even sketchy fragments are not to be rejected." Whoever follows these principles in collecting oral materials circulating today is still well advised. Of course, narrative research is no longer just interested in the narrated material itself, but also in the narrator and audience, in the context and motivation of

6. See Wesselski; and Neumann, *Es war einmal.*
7. The 1856 volume is vol. 3 of Grimm, *Kinder- und Hausmärchen: Ausgabe letzter Hand.*
8. See the monographs published in the series *Folklore Fellows Communications*; and the progressively appearing volumes of the *Enzyklopädie des Märchens.* English-speaking readers can find more information about this important latter work in Uther.

the narrative event, and in the role of storytelling in the intellectual and cultural life of people today.[9] In this respect we have achieved so far only limited results that—in the distant wake of the Grimms—urgently need further study and elaboration.[1]

Whoever conducts oral narrative research today—especially in German-speaking regions—will repeatedly hear tales, particularly fairy tales, that directly or indirectly go back to the Grimms' collection. In those instances, good storytellers—even when they use dialect to retell what they have read—strive to stay as close as possible to the published model. For it is generally expected of contemporary storytellers to retell fairy tales "properly"—that is, in the "Grimm version." But one can readily observe that storytellers of an impulsive or imaginative nature, despite their acknowledged debt to this source, break away from the original and endow the Grimms' tales with innovations in content and a different linguistic guise.[2] In both cases we are faced with the distinct reverse influence of the Grimms' collection on the oral folktale itself—in other words, the reception of Grimms' tales by the oral tradition. This is a phenomenon that deserves the special attention of scholars of oral narrative.[3]

WORKS CITED

Altdänische Heldenlieder, Balladen und Märchen. Trans. Wilhelm Grimm. Heidelberg: Mohr und Zimmer, 1811.

Arnold, Günter. "Herders Projekt einer Märchensammlung." *Jahrbuch für Volkskunde und Kulturgeschichte* 27 (1984): 99–106.

Benz, Richard. *Märchen-Dichtung der Romantiker: Mil einer Vorgeschichte.* Gotha: Perthes, 1908.

Berendsohn, Walter A. *Grundformen volkstümlicher Erzählerkunst in den Kinder- und Hausmärchen der Brüder Grimm.* Hamburg: Gente, 1921.

Bolte, Johannes, and Georg Polívka. *Anmerkungen zu den Kinder- und Hausmärchen der Brüder Grimm.* 5 vols. Leipzig: Dieterich, 1913–32.

Briggs, Katharine M. "The Influence of the Brothers Grimm in England." *Brüder Grimm Gedenken* 1 (1963): 511–24.

Dégh, Linda. *Märchen, Erzähler und Erzählgemeinschaft.* Trans. Johanna Till. Berlin: Akademie-Verlag, 1962.

——. "What Did the Grimm Brothers Give to and Take from the Folk?" *The Brothers Grimm and Folktale.* Ed. James M. McGlathery. Urbana: U of Illinois P, 1988. 66–90.

Denecke, Ludwig. *Jacob Grimm und sein Bruder Wilhelm.* Stuttgart: Metzler, 1971.

Eichler, Ingrid. *Sächsische Märchen und Geschichten—erzählt von Otto Vogel.* Berlin: Akademie-Verlag, 1971.

Enzyklopädie des Märchens. Ed. Kurt Ranke. Vols. 1 ff. Berlin: De Gruyter, 1975–.

Folklore Fellows Communications. Vols. 1 ff. Helsinki: Soumalainen Tiedeakatemia, 1910–.

Fraenger, Wilhelm, and Wolfgang Steinitz, eds. *Jacob Grimm zur 100. Wiederkehr seines Todestages: Festschrift des Instituts für deutsche Volkskunde.* Berlin: Akademie-Verlag, 1963.

Gašparíková, Viera. "Die Folkloreprosa in der Slowakei im zweiten Drittel des 19. Jahrhunderts unter dem Blickwinkel des Werkes der Brüder Grimm." *Brüder Grimm Gedenken* 8 (1988): 240–50.

Geschichte der deutschen Volksdichtung. Ed. Hermann Strobach. Berlin: Akademie-Verlag, 1981.

Ginschel, Gunhild. *Der junge Jacob Grimm: 1805–1819.* Berlin: Akademie-Verlag, 1967.

Grimm, Brothers. *Kinder- und Hausmärchen: Ausgabe letzter Hand mit den Originalanmerkungen der Brüder Grimm.* Ed. Heinz Rölleke. 3 vols. Stuttgart: Reclam, 1980.

——. *Kinder- und Hausmärchen gesammelt durch die Brüder Grimm: Vergrößerter Nachdruck der zweibändigen Erstausgabe von 1812 und 1815.* Ed. Heinz Rölleke and Ulrike Marquardt. 2 vols. and suppl. Göttingen: Vandenhoeck & Ruprecht, 1986.

——. *Kinder- und Hausmärchen: Nach der 2. vermehrten und verbesserten Auflage von 1819.* Ed. Heinz Rölleke. 2 vols. Cologne: Diederichs, 1982.

9. See Strobach et al. 5–26; and Neumann, "Volkserzählung heute."
1. For the former German Democratic Republic see Neumann, "Volkserzähler unserer Tage in Mecklenburg"; *Ein mecklenburgischer Volkserzähler; Eine mecklenburgische Märchenfrau;* "Mecklenburgische Erzähler"; as well as Eichler.
2. See Neumann, *Eine mecklenburgische Märchenfrau* 31–40.
3. See Ranke; Dégh, "Grimm Brothers"; and Neumann, *Mecklenburgische Volksmärchen* 35.

Grimm, Jacob. *Circular wegen Aufsammlung der Volkspoesie.* Wien, 1815. Ed. Ludwig Denecke. Afterword by Kurt Ranke. Kassel: Brüder Grimm-Museum, 1968.

——. *Kleinere Schriften.* Vol. 8. Ed. Eduard Ippel. Gütersloh: Bertelsmann, 1890.

Horák, Jiří. "Jacob Grimm und die slawische Volkskunde." Fraenger and Steinitz 11–70.

Jahn, Erwin. "Die *Volksmärchen der Deutschen* von Johann Karl August Musäus." Diss. U of Leipzig, 1914.

Leitinger, Doris. "Die Wirkung von Jacob Grimm auf die Slaven, insbesondere auf die Russen." *Brüder Grimm Gedenken* 2 (1975): 66–130.

Lemmer, Manfred, ed. *Grimms Märchen in ursprünglicher Gestalt.* Leipzig: Insel, 1963.

Lüthi, Max. *Märchen.* 7th ed. Stuttgart: Metzler, 1979.

Michaelis-Jena, Ruth. "Die schottischen Beziehungen der Brüder Grimm." *Brüder Grimm Gedenken* 2 (1975): 334–42.

Neumann, Siegfried Armin. *Es war einmal . . . Volksmärchen aus fünf Jahrhunderten.* 2 vols. Rostock: Hinstorf, 1982.

——. "Mecklenburgische Erzähler der Gegenwart und ihre Märchen." *Märchen in unserer Zeit: Zu Erscheinungsformen eines populären Erzählgenres.* Ed. Hans-Jörg Uther. Munich: Diederichs, 1990. 102–14.

——. *Eine mecklenburgische Märchenfrau: Bertha Peters erzählt Märchen, Schwänke und Geschichten.* Berlin: Akademie-Verlag, 1974.

——. *Mecklenburgische Volksmärchen.* Berlin: Akademie-Verlag, 1971.

——. *Ein mecklenburgischer Volkserzähler: Die Geschichten des August Rust.* 2nd ed. Berlin: Akademie-Verlag, 1970.

——. "Volkserzähler unserer Tage in Mecklenburg: Bemerkungen zur Erzähler-Forschung in der Gegenwart." *Deutsches Jahrbuch für Volkskunde* 15 (1969): 31–49.

——. "Volkserzählung heute: Bemerkungen zu Existenzbedingungen und Daseinsformen der Volksdichtung in der Gegenwart." *Jahrbuch für Volkskunde und Kulturgeschichte* 23 (1980): 92–102.

Nişcov, Viorica. "Über den Widerhall der volkskundlichen Beschäftigung der Brüder Grimm in Rumänien." *Brüder Grimm Gedenken* 2 (1975): 146–67.

Ortutay, Gyula. "Jacob Grimm und die ungarische Folkloristik." Fraenger and Steinitz 169–89.

Panzer, Friedrich, ed. *Die Kinder- und Hausmärchen der Brüder Grimm in ihrer Urgestalt.* 2 vols. Munich: Beck, 1913.

Peeters, Karel C. "Der Einfluß der Brüder Grimm und ihrer Nachfolger auf die Volkskunde in Flandern." *Brüder Grimm Gedenken* 1 (1963): 405–20.

Pomeranceva, Erna. "A.N. Afanas'ev und die Brüder Grimm." Fraenger and Steinitz 94–103.

Pulmer, Karin. "Zur Rezeption der Grimmschen Märchen in Dänemark." *Brüder Grimm Gedenken* 8 (1988): 181–203.

Ranke, Kurt. "Der Einfluß der Grimmschen Kinder- und Hausmärchen auf das volkstümliche deutsche Erzählgut." *Papers of the International Congress of European and Western Ethnology, Stockholm 1951.* Ed. Sigurd Erixon. Stockholm: International Commission of Folk Arts and Folklore, 1956. 126–35.

Rölleke, Heinz, ed. *Die älteste Märchensammlung der Brüder Grimm: Synopse der handschriftlichen Urfassung von 1810 und der Erstdrucke von 1812.* Cologny/Geneva: Fondation Martin Bodmer, 1975.

Schmidt, Karl. *Die Entwicklung der Grimmschen Kinder- und Hausmärchen seit der Urhandschrift.* Halle: Niemeyer, 1932.

Schmidt, Leopold. "Die Brüder Grimm und der Entwicklungsgang der östereichischen Volkskunde." *Brüder Grimm Gedenken* 1 (1963): 309–31.

Schoof, Wilhelm. "Zur Entstehungsgeschichte der Grimmschen Märchen." *Hessische Blätter für Volkskunde* 29 (1930): 1–118.

Steig, Reinhold. *Achim von Arnim und Clemens Brentano.* Stuttgart: Cotta, 1894.

——. *Achim von Arnim und Jacob und Wilhelm Grimm.* Stuttgart: Cotta, 1904.

Steinitz, Wolfgang. "Lied und Märchen als Stimme des Volkes." *Deutsches Jahrbuch für Volkskunde* 2 (1956): 11–32.

Stern, Leo. *Der geistige und politische Standort von Jacob Grimm in der deutschen Geschichte.* Berlin: Akademie-Verlag, 1963.

Strobach, Hermann, et al. *Deutsche Volksdichtung: Eine Einführung.* Leipzig: Reclam, 1979.

Tatar, Maria. *The Hard Facts of the Grimms' Fairy Tales.* Princeton: Princeton UP, 1987.

Uther, Hans-Jörg. "The Encyclopedia of the Folktale." *Fairy Tales and Society: Illusion, Allusion, and Paradigm.* Ed. Ruth B. Bottigheimer. Philadelphia: U of Pennsylvania P, 1986. 187–93.

Wesselski, Albert. *Deutsche Märchen vor Grimm.* 2 vols. 2nd ed. Brünn: Rohrer, 1942.

Woeller, Waltraud. "Die Bedeutung der Brüder Grimm für die Märchen- und Sagenforschung." *Wissenschaftliche Zeitschrift der Humboldt-Universität zu Berlin.* Gesellschafts- und sprachwissenschaftliche Reihe 14 (1965): 507–14.

——. "Der soziale Gehalt und die soziale Funktion der deutschen Volksmärchen." *Wissenschaftliche Zeitschrift der Humboldt-Universität zu Berlin.* Gesellschafts- und sprachwissenschaftliche Reihe 10 (1961): 395–459; 11 (1962): 281–307.

Ziel, Wulfhild. "A.N. Afanas'evs Märchensammlung 'Narodnye russkie skazki' (1855–1863)—geplant nach dem Vorbild der 'Kinder- und Hausmärchen' der Brüder Grimm: Beispiele ausführlicher Anmerkungen, in denen auf Jacob und Wilhelm Grimm verwiesen wird." *Brüder Grimm Gedenken* 8 (1988): 204–21.

———. "Wirkungen von Jacob und Wilhelm Grimm auf die Sammlung russischer Volksbilderbogen 'Russkie narodnye kartinki' von Dmitrij Aleksandrovič Rovinskij (St. Petersburg 1881)." *Brüder Grimm Gedenken* 9 (1990): 171–83.

Zipes, Jack, trans. *The Complete Fairy Tales of the Brothers Grimm.* New York: Bantam, 1987.

"Zur Geschichte der deutschen Philologie. I: Briefe von Jacob Grimm." *Germania: Vierteljahrsschrift für deutsche Alterthumskunde* 11 (1866): 239–56.

Selected Bibliography

FAIRY TALE COLLECTIONS AND RELATED LITERATURE

Al-Mas'udi. *El-Mas'udi's Historical Encyclopedia, entitled Meadows of Gold and Mines of Gems.* London: Oriental Translation Fund of Great Britain and Ireland, 1841.

Almanni, Luigi. "Bianca, Figliuola del Conte di Tolosa" (1531). *Novelle del Cinquecento.* Ed. Giambattista Salinari. 2 vols. Turin: Unione Tipografico-Editrice Tornese, 1955.

Andersen, Hans Christian. *Wonderful Stories for Children.* Trans. Mary Botham Howitt. 1st English ed. London: Chapman and Hall, 1846.

——. *Danish Fairy Legends and Tales.* Trans. Caroline Peachey. 2nd ed., with a memoir of the author. London: Addey, 1852.

——. *The Complete Fairy Tales and Stories.* Trans. Erik Christian Haugaard. New York: Doubleday, 1974.

Arnim, Friedmund von. *Hundert neue Mährchen im Gebirge gesammelt.* Charlottenburg: Egbert Bauer, 1844.

——. *Hundert neue Mährchen im Gebirge gesammelt.* Ed. Heinz Röllecke. Cologne: Eugen Diederichs, 1986.

Asbjornsen, Peter Christen. *Norske huldreeventyr of folkesagn.* Christiania: C. A. Oybwad, 1848.

——. *Round the Yule, Norwegian Folk and Fairy Tales.* Trans. H. L. Braekstad. London: Sampson Low, Marston, Seaarle, & Rivington, 1881.

Asbjornsen, Peter Christen, and Jorgen Moe. *Norske folke-eventyr.* Christiania: J. Dahl, 1852.

——. *Popular Tales from the Norse.* Intro. George Dasent. Edinburgh: Edmonstron & Douglas, 1859.

Aubailly, Jean-Claude, ed. *Fabliaux et contes moraux du Moyen Age.* Pref. Jean Joubert. Paris: Livre de Poche, 1987.

Aulnoy, Marie-Catherine Le Jumel de Barneville, Baronne de. *Les contes de fées.* 4 vols. 1st ed. Paris: Claude Barbin, 1697.

——. *Contes nouveaux ou les fées à la mode.* 2 vols. Paris: Veuve de Théodore Girard, 1698.

——. *Suite des contes nouveaux ou les fées à la mode.* 2 vols. Paris: Veuve de Théodore Girard, 1698.

——. *The Fairy Tales of Madame d'Aulnoy.* Trans. Annie Macdonell. Intro. Anne Thackeray Ritchie. London: Lawrence & Bullen, 1895.

——. *Contes.* Ed. Philippe Houcade. Intro. Jacques Barchilon. 2 vols. Paris: Société des Textes Français Modernes, 1997–98.

Barchilon, Jacques, ed. *Nouveau cabinet des fées.* 18 vols. Geneva: Slatkine Reprints, 1978. Partial reprint of *Le cabinet des fées.* Ed. Charles-Joseph Mayer.

Basile, Giambattista. *Lo cunto de le cunti overo lo trattenemiento de peccerille.* De Gian Alessio Abbattutis. 5 vols. Naples: Ottavio Beltrano, 1634–36.

——. *The Pentamerone of Giambattista Basile.* Trans. and ed. N. M. Penzer. 2 vols. London: John Lane and the Bodley Head, 1932.

——. *Lo cunto de li cunti.* Ed. Michele Rak. 1634. Milan: Garazanti, 1986.

——. *Il racconto dei racconti.* Ed. Alessandra Burani and Ruggero Guarini. Trans. Ruggero Guarini. Milan: Adelphi Edizioni, 1994.

——. *The Pentamerone.* Trans. Richard Burton. London: Spring, n.d.

Bebel, Heinrich. *Facetiarum . . . libri tres, a mendis repurgati, & in lucem rursus redditi.* Tübingen: Morhard, 1542.

Bechstein, Ludwig. *Deutsches Märchenbuch.* Leipzig: Wigand, 1845.

——. *Ludwig Bechsteins Märchenbuch.* Leipzig: Wigand, 1853.

——. *Neues Deutsches Märchenbuch.* Vienna: Hartleben, 1856.

——. *Sämtliche Märchen.* Ed. Walter Scherf. Munich: Winkler, 1968.

Bernard, Catherine. *Inès de Cardoue, nouvelle espagnole.* Paris: Jouvenol, 1696; Geneva: Slatkine Reprints, 1979.

Bierling, Friedrich Immanuel, ed. *Cabinet der Feen.* 9 vols. Nürnberg: Raspe, 1761–66.

Bignon, Abbé Jean-Paul. *Les Aventures d'Abdalla, fils d'Hani, envoyé par le sultan des Indes à la découverte de l'île de Borico.* Paris: P. Witte, 1710–14.

Blackwell, Jeannine, and Susanne Zantop, eds. *Bitter Healing: German Women Writers, 1700–1830. An Anthology.* Lincoln: University of Nebraska Press, 1990.

Calvi, Francois de. *Histoire Générale des Larrons.* Paris: Martin Collet, 1623.

Calvino, Italo, ed. *Fiabe.* Torino: Einaudi, 1970.

————, ed. *Italian Folktales*. Trans. George Martin. New York: Harcourt Brace Jovanovich, 1980.
Cambell of Islay, John Francis, ed. *Popular Tales of the West Highlands*. 4 vols. Orally collected. Translated. 3ʳᵈ ed. Hounslow, Middlesex: Wildwood House, 1983–84.
Ciccuto, Marcello, ed. *Novelle italiene; Il Cinquecento*. Milan: Garzanti, 1982.
Crane, Thomas Frederick. *Italian Popular Tales*. Boston: Houghton, Mifflin, 1889.
Deulin, Charles. *Les contes de ma Mère l'Oye avant Perrault*. Paris: Dentu, 1878.
Delarue, Paul, and Marie-Louise Tenèze. *Le conte populaire français. Un catalogue raisonné des versions de France et des pays de langue française et d'Outre-mer*. 4 vols. Paris: Maisonneuve et Larose, 1957–76.
Delarue, Paul, ed. *French Fairy Tales*. Illus. Warren Chappell. New York: Knopf, 1968.
Ehrismann, Otfrid, ed. *Der Stricker: Erzählungen, Fabeln, Reden*. Stuttgart: Philipp Reclam, 1992.
Ey, Karl August Eduard, ed. *Harzmärchenbuch. Oder Sagen und Märchen aus der Oberharze*. 4ᵗʰ ed. 1862.
Fatini, Guiseppe, ed. *Novelle del Cinquecento*. Turin: Unione Tipografico-Editrice Tornese, 1930.
Fiorentino, Ser Giovanni. *Il Pecorone*. Milan: Giovanni Antonio, 1554; rep. and ed. by Enzo Esposito, Ravena: Longo, 1974.
Galland, Antoine. *Les milles et une nuit*. 12 vols. Vols. 1–4. Paris: Florentin Delaulne, 1704; vols. 5–7, ibid., 1706; vol. 8, ibid., 1709; vols. 9–10, Florentin Delaulne, 1712; vols. 11–12, Lyon: Briasson, 1717.
Gonzenbach, Laura. *Sicilianische Märchen*. 2 vols. Leipzig: W. Engelmann, 1870.
Grimm, Albert Ludwig. *Kindermährchen*. Heidelberg: Morhr und Zimmer, 1808.
————. *Lina's Mährchenbuch*. Frankfurt am Main: Wilmans, 1816.
Grimm, Jacob, and Wilhelm. *Kinder- und Hausmarchen. Gesammelt durch die Bruder Grimm*. Berlin: Realschulbuchhandlung, 1812.
————. *Kinder- und Hausmarchen. Gesammelt durch die Bruder Grimm*. Vol. 2. Berlin: Realschul-buchhandlung, 1815.
————. *Kinder- und Hausmarchen. Gesammelt durch die Bruder Grimm*. 7th rev. and exp. edition. 2 vols. Göttingen: Dieterich, 1857.
————. *German Popular Stories, Translated from the Kinder und Haus Märchen*. Trans. Edgar Taylor. London: C. Baldwin, 1823.
————. *Household Stories from the Collection of the Brothers Grimm*. Trans. Lucy Crane. London: Macmillan, 1882.
Grimm, Jacob, and Wilhelm. *The Complete Fairy Tales of the Brothers Grimm*. Ed. and trans. Jack Zipes. New York: Bantam, 1987.
Gueullette, Thomas Simon. *Les mille et un quarts d'heure, contes tartares*. Paris: 1715.
Guglielminetti, Marziano. *Novelliei del Cinquecento*. Milan: Ricciardi, 1972.
Haltrich, Josef, ed. *Deutsche Volksmärchen aus dem Sachsenlande in Siebenbürgen*. Hermannstadt: Krafft, 1885.
Histoire de la belle Héleine de Constantinople. Troyes: Garnier, 1700.
Husain, Shahrukh. *Handsome Heroines: Women as Men in Folklore*. New York: Doubleday, 1995.
Imbriani, Vittorio. *La novellaja fiorentina*. Livorno: F. Vigo, 1877.
Jacobs, Joseph, ed. *English Fairy Tales*. London: Nutt, 1890.
Jamieson, Robert. *Popular Ballads and Songs from Tradition, Manuscripts and Scarce Editions*. Edinburgh: A. Constable, 1806.
Joisten, Charles. *Contes populaires du Dauphiné*. Vol. 1. Grenoble: Publications du Musée Dauphinois, 1971.
Karlinger, Felix, ed. *Der abenteuerliche Glückstopf: Märchen des Barock*. Munich: Bruckmann, 1965.
La Force, Charlotte-Rose Caumont de. *Les contes des contes par Mlle de ****. Paris: S. Bernard, 1698.
————. *Les Jeux d'esprit ou la promenade de la Princesse de Conti à Eu par Mademoiselle de La Force*. Ed. M. le marquis de la Grange. Paris: Auguste Aubry, 1862.
Lang, Andrew, ed. and trans. *Perrault's Popular Tales*. Oxford: Clarendon Press, 1888.
Lhéritier de Villandon, Marie-Jeanne. *Oeuvres meslées, contenant l'Innocente tromperie, l'Avare puni, les Enchantements de l'éloquence, les Aventures de Finette, nouvelles, et autres ouvrages, en vers et en prose, de Mlle de L'H**** — avec le Triomphe de Mme Des-Houlières tel qu'il a été composé par Mlle ****. Paris: J. Guignard, 1696.
————. *La Tour ténébreuse et les jours lumineux, contes anglois, accompagnés d'historiettes et tirés d'une ancienne chronique composée par Richard, surnommé Coeur de Lion, roi d'Angleterre, avec le récit des diverse aventures de ce roi*. Paris: Veuve de Claude Barbin, 1705.
Le Noble, Eustache. *Le gage touché, hisoires galantes*. Amsterdam: Jaques Desbordes, 1700.
Leprince de Beaumont, Marie. *Magasin des enfans, ou Dialogue d'une sage gouvernante avec ses élèves de la première distinction*. Lyon: Reguilliat, 1756.
Maier, Bruno, ed. *Novelle italiane del Cinquecento*. Milan: Il Club del Libro, 1962.
Mailly, Jean de. *Les illustres fées, contes galans. Dédié aux dames*. Paris: M-M. Brunet, 1698.
Martines, Lauro, ed. *An Italian Renaissance Sextet: Six Tales in Historical Context*. Trans. Murtha Baca. New York: Marsilo, 1994.
Massignon, Geneviève, ed. *Folktales of France*. Trans. Jacqueline Hyland. Chicago: U of Chicago P, 1968.
Mas'udi. *The Meadows of Gold. The Abbasids*. London: Kegan Paul, 1989.
Mayer, Charles-Joseph, ed. *Le cabinet des fées; ou, Collection choisie des contes des fées, et autres contes merveilleux*. 41 vols. Amsterdam: s.n., 1785.

Mieder, Wolfgang, ed. *Grimms Märchen—modern*. Stuttgart: Reclam, 1979.

Millien, A., and P. Delarue. *Contes du Nivernais et du Morvan*. Paris: Érasme, 1953.

Morlini, Girolamo. *Novellae, fabulae, comoedia*. Naples: Joan. Pasquet de Sallo, 1520.

——. *Hieronimi Morlini Parthenopei Novellae, Fabulae, Comoedia*. Paris: P. Jannet, 1855.

——. *Novelle e favole*. Ed. Giovanni Villani. Rome: Salerno, 1983.

Murat, Henriette Julie de Castelnau, Comtesse de. *Contes de fées dédiez à S. A. S. Madame la princesse douairière de Conty, par Mad, la comtesse de M****. Paris: Claude Barbin, 1698.

——. *Les nouveaux contes de fées par Mme de M****. Paris: Claude Barbin, 1698.

——. *Histoires sublimes et allégoriques*. Paris: Florentin Delaulne, 1699.

Musäus, Johann Karl August. *Volksmährchen der Deutschen*. 5 vols. Gotha: Ettinger, 1782–87.

Painter, William, trans. *The Palace of Pleasure: Elizabethan Versions of Italian and French Novels from Boccaccio, Bandello, Cinthio, Straparola, Queen Margaret of Navarre, and Others*. 3 vols. 1890. New York: Dover Publications, 1966.

Perrault, Charles. *Histoires ou contes du temps passé*. Paris: Claude Barbin, 1697.

——. *Contes*. Ed. Jean Pierre Collinet. Folio, 1281. Paris: Gallimard, 1981.

——. *Contes de Perrault*. Ed. Gilbert Rouger. Paris: Garnier, 1967.

——. *Contes*. Ed. Marc Soriano. Paris: Flammarion, 1989.

——. *Contes*. Ed. Catherine Magnien. Paris: Le Livre de Poche, 1990.

——. *Perrault's Complete Fairy Tales*. Trans. A. E. Johnson et al. Illus. W. Heath Robinson. New York: Dodd, Mead, 1961.

Pitré, Giuseppe. *Fiabe e leggende populari Siciliani*. Palermo: L. Pedone Lauriel, 1870.

——. *Fiabe, novelle e racconti populari Siciliani*. 4 vols. Palermo: L. Pedone Laùriel, 1875.

Rak, Michele, ed. *Fiabe campane*. Milan: Mondadori, 1984.

Ricci, Lucia Battaglia, ed. *Novelle italiene: Il Duecento, Il Trecento*. Milan: Garzanti, 1982.

Robbins, Rossell Hope, ed. and trans. *The Hundred Tales (Les Cent Nouvelles Nouvelles)*. New York: Crown, 1960.

Robert, Raymonde, ed. *Il était une fois les fées: contes du XVIIe et XVIIIe siècles*. Nancy: PU de Nancy, 1984.

——, ed. *Contes parodiques et licencieux du 18e siècle*. Nancy: PU de Nancy, 1987.

Röllecke, Heinz, ed. *Die älteste Märchensammlung der Brüder Grimm*. Cologny-Geneva: Fondation Martin Bodmer, 1975.

——, ed. *Märchen aus dem Nachlaß der Brüder Grimm*. 3rd rev. ed. Bonn: Bouvier, 1983.

——, ed. *Die wahren Märchen der Brüder Grimm*. Frankfurt am Main: Fischer, 1995.

——, ed. *Grimms Märchen und ihre Quellen: Die literarischen Vorlagen der Grimmschen Märchen synoptisch vorgestellt und kommentiert*. Trier: Wissenschaftlicher Verlag Trier, 1998.

Ryder, Arthur W., trans. *The Panchatantra*. Chicago: U of Chicago P, 1956.

Saal, Justus Heinrich. *Abendstunden in lehrreichen und anmuthungen Erzählungen*. Breslau: Johann Friedrich Korn, 1767.

Sacchetti, Franco. *Il Trecentonovelle*. Ed. Antonio Lanza. Florence: Sansoni, 1984.

Salinari, Giambattista, ed. *Novelle del Cinquecento*. 2 vols. Turin: Unione Tipografico-Editice Tornese, 1955.

Sarnelli, Pompeo. *Posilecheata*. Naples: Morano, 1684.

Schulz, Friedrich. *Kleine Romane*. 5 vols. Leipzig: Georg Joachim Göschen, 1788–90.

Scrivano, Riccardo, ed. *Cinquecento minore*. Bologne: Zanichelli, 1966.

Somadeva. *The Ocean of Story*. Ed. N. M. Penzer. Trans. Charles H. Tawney. 10 vols. Indian Edition. Delhi: Motilal Banarsidass, 1968.

Stahl, Caroline. *Fabeln und Erzählungen für Kinder*. Nuremberg, 1818.

Straparola, Giovan Francesco. *Le piacevoli notti*. 2 vols. Venice: Comin da Trino, 1550/1553.

——. *Le piacevoli notti*. Ed. Pastore Stocchi. Rome-Bari: Laterza, 1979.

——. *The Facetious Nights of Straparola*. Trans. William G. Waters. Illus. Jules Garnier and E. R. Hughes. 4 vols. London: Lawrence and Bullen, 1894.

Tatar, Maria, ed. *The Classic Fairy Tales*. New York: W. W. Norton, 1999.

Tomkowiak, Ingrid, and Ulrich Marzolph, eds. *Grimms Märchen International*. 2 vols. Paderborn: Schöningh, 1996.

Uther, Hans-Jörg, ed. *Märchen vor Grimm*. Munich: Eugen Diederichs Verlag, 1990.

Villeneuve, Gabrielle-Suzanne Barbot de. *La jeune Amériquaine et les contes marins*. La Haye aux dépes de la Compagnie, 1740.

Wesseleski, Albert, ed. *Deutsche Märchen vor Grimm*. Brünn: Rudolf M. Rohrer, 1938.

Windling, Terri, ed. *The Armless Maiden and Other Tales for Childhood's Survivors*. New York: Tor, 1995.

Wolf, Johann Wilhelm, ed. *Deutsche Märchen und Sagen*. Leipzig: F. A. Brockhaus, 1845.

——. *Deutsche Hausmärchen*. Göttingen: Dieterich, 1851.

Zingerele, Ignanz Vinzenz, and Joseph. *Tirols Volksdichtungen und Volksbräuche*. Innsbruck: Wagner, 1852.

Zipes, Jack, ed. *Beauties, Beasts, and Enchantment: French Classical Fairy Tales*. New York: New American Library, 1989.

——, ed. *Spells of Enchantment: The Wondrous Fairy Tales of Western Culture*. New York: Viking, 1991.

REFERENCE WORKS

Aarne, Antti. *The Types of the Folktales. A Classification and Bibliography.* Rev. and enl. by Stith Thompson. 2nd rev. ed. FF Communications No. 3. Helsinki: Suomalainen Tiedeakatemia, 1961.

Adams, D. J. "The 'Contes de fées' of Madame d'Aulnoy: Reputation and Re-Evaluation." *Bulletin of the John Rylands University Library of Manchester* 76.3 (Autumn 1994): 5–22.

Anderson, Graham. *Fairy Tale in the Ancient World.* London: Routledge, 2000.

Apel, Friedmar. *Die Zaubergärten der Phantasie. Zur Theorie und Geschichte des Kunstmärchens.* Heidelberg: Winter 1978.

———. "Die bezauberte Vernunft." *Das Kabinett der Feen des 17. und 18. Jahrhunderts.* Eds. Friedmar Apel and Norbert Miller. Munich: Winkler, 1984. 5–40.

Baader, Renate. *Dames de Lettres: Autorinnen des preziosen, hocharistokratischen und 'modernen' Salons (1646–1698): Mlle de Scudéry-Mlle de Montpensier-Mme d'Aulnoy.* Stuttgart: J. B. Metzlersche Verlagsbuchh., 1986.

Bang, Ilse. *Die Entwicklung der deutschen Marchenillustration.* Munich: F. Bruckmann, 1944.

Barchilon, Jacques. "Uses of the Fairy Tale in the Eighteenth Century." *Studies on Voltaire and the Eighteenth Century* 24 (1963): 111–38.

———. *Le conte merveilleux français de 1690 à 1790.* Paris: Champion, 1975.

———. "Vers l'inconscient de *La Belle au Bois Dormant*." *Cermeil* 2 (Feb. 1986): 88–92.

———. "L'Ironie et l'humour dans les 'Contes' de Perrault." *Studi francese* 32 (1967): 258–70.

Barchilon, Jacques, and Peter Flinders. *Charles Perrault.* Boston: Twayne, 1981.

Bausinger, Hermann. " 'Historisierende' Tendenzen im deutschen Märchen seit der Romantik. Requisitenverschiebung und Requisitenerstarrung." *Wirkendes Wort* 10 (1960): 279–86.

———. *Märchen, Phantasie und Wirklichkeit.* Frankfurt am Main: dipa-Verlag, 1987.

Berendsohn, Walter A. *Grundformen volkstümlicher Erzählkunst in den Kinder- und Hausmärchen der Brüder Grimm.* 2nd rev. ed. Wiesbaden: Sändig, 1968.

Berlioz, Jacques, Claude Bremond, and Catherine Velay-Vallentin, eds. *Formes médievales du conte merveilleux.* Paris: Stock, 1989.

Böhm-Korff, Regina. *Deutung und Bedeutung von "Hänsel und Gretel."* Frankfurt am Main: Peter Lang, 1991.

Bolte, Johannes, and George Polivka. *Anmerkungen zu den "Kinder- und Hausmärchen."* 5 vols. Leipzig: 1913–32. Rep.: Hildesheim: Georg Olms, 1963.

Bolte, Johannes, and Lutz Mackensen. *Handworterbuch des deutschen Marchens.* Berlin: W. de Gruyter & Co., 1931.

Bottigheimer, Ruth B. "Tale Spinners: Submerged Voices in Grimms' Fairy Tales." *New German Critique* 27 (1982): 141–50.

———, ed. *Fairy Tales and Society: Illusion, Allusion, and Paradigm.* Philadelphia: U of Pennsylvania P, 1986.

———. *Grimms' Bad Girls and Bold Boys: The Moral and Social Vision of the Tales.* New Haven: Yale UP, 1987.

———. "Fairy Tales, Folk Narrative Research and History." *Social History* 14.3 (1989): 343–57.

———. "Cupid and Psyche vs. Beauty and the Beast: The Milesian and the Modern." *Merveilles et Contes* 3.1 (May 1989): 4–14.

———. "Luckless, Witless, and Filthy-footed. A Sociocultural Study and Publishing History Analysis of 'The Lazy Boy.' " *Journal of American Folklore* 106 (1993): 259–84.

Brackert, Helmut, ed. *Und wenn sie nicht gestorben sind: Perspektiven auf das Märchen.* Frankfurt am Main: Suhrkamp, 1980.

Brednich, Rolf Wilhelm, ed. *Enzyklopädie des Märchens.* 11 vols. Berlin: Walter de Gruyter, 1977–2000.

Broggini, Barbara. *"Lo cunto de li cunti" von Giambattista Basile: Ein Ständepoet in Streit mit der Plebs, Fortuna und der höfischen Korruption.* Frankfurt am Main: Peter Lang, 1990.

Bürger, Christa. "Die soziale Funktion volkstümlicher Erzählformen—Sage und Märchen." *Projekt Deutschunterricht 1.* Ed. Heinz Ide. Stuttgart: Metzler, 1971. 26–56.

Burke, Peter. *The Art of Conversation.* Ithaca: Cornell UP, 1993.

Butor, Michel. "On Fairy Tales." *European Literary Theory and Practice.* Ed. Vernon W. Gras. New York: Delta, 1973. 351–56.

Calabrese, Stefano. *Gli arabeschi della fiaba dal Basile ai romantici.* Pisa: Pacini, 1984.

———. *Fiaba.* Florence: La Nuova Italia, 1997.

Canepa, Nancy L. "From Court to Forest: The Literary Itineraries of Giambattista Basile." *Italica* 71.3 (Fall 1994): 291–310.

———, ed. *Out of the Woods: The Origins of the Literary Fairy Tale in Italy and France.* Detroit: Wayne State UP, 1997.

———. *From Court to Forest: Giambattista Basile's Lo cunto de li cunti and the Birth of the Literary Fairy Tale.* Detroit: Wayne State UP, 1999.

Canton, Katia. *The Fairy Tale Revisited: A Survey of the Evolution of the Tales, from Classical Literary Interpretations to Innovative Contemporary Dance-Theater Productions.* New York: Peter Lang, 1994.

Caracciolo, Peter L., ed. *The 'Arabian Nights' in English Literature: Studies in the Reception of 'The Thousand and One Nights' into British Culture.* New York: St. Martin's Press, 1988.

Charrière, G. "Du social au sacré dans les contes de Perrault." *Revue des histoires des religions* 197.2 (1980): 159–89.

Chartier, Roger, ed. *Les usages de l'imprimé*. Paris: Fayard, 1987.

Clancy, Patricia. "A French Writer and Educator in England: Mme Le Prince de Beaumont." *Studies on Voltaire and the Eighteenth Century* 201 (1982): 195–208.

Clodd, Edward. *Tim Tit Tot: An Essay of Savage Philosophy*. London: Duckworth, 1898.

Cocchiara, Giuseppe. *Storia del folklore in Europa*. Collezione di studi religiosi, etnologici e psicologici 20. Turin: Einaudi, 1954.

Collins, James B. *The State in Early Modern France*. Cambridge: Cambridge UP, 1995.

Cox, Marian Emily Roalfe. *Cinderella: Three Hundred and Forty-Five Variants of Cinderella, Catskin, and Cap o'Rushes, Abstracted and Tabulated with a Discussion of Medieval Analogues, and Notes*. Intro. Andrew Lang. Nendeln, Liechtenstein: Kraus Reprint, 1967.

Crane, Thomas Frederick. *Italian Popular Tales*. Boston: Houghton Mifflin, 1885.

Craveri, Benedetta. "Talk!" *New York Review of Books* 47 (Jan. 20, 2000): 60–64.

Croce, Benedetto. "Giambattista Basile el'elaborazione artistica delle fiabe popolari." *Il Pentamerone*. Ed. and trans. Benedetto Croce. Naples: 1891. xiii–xxxv.

Cromer, Sylvie. " 'Le Sauvage' Histoire Sublime et allégorique de Madame de Murat." *Merveilles et contes* 1.1 (May 1987): 2–19.

Dégh, Linda. *Folktales and Society. Storytelling in a Hungarian Peasant Community*. Trans. Emily M. Schlossberg. Bloomington: Indiana UP, 1969.

——. "Grimms' Household Tales and Its Place in the Household: The Social Relevance of a Controversial Classic." *Western Folklore* 38 (1979): 83–103.

——. "What Did the Grimm Brothers Give To and Take From the Folk?" *The Brothers Grimm and Folktale*. Ed. James McGlathery et al. Urbana: U of Illinois P, 1988. 66–90.

DeGraff, Amy Vanderlyn. *The Tower and the Well: A Psychological Interpretation of the Fairy Tales of Madame d'Aulnoy*. Birmingham: Summa Publications, 1984.

Deguise, Alix. "Mme Le prince de Beaumont: conteuse ou moraliste?" *Femmes savantes et femmes d'esprit: Women Intellectuals of the French Eighteenth Century*. Ed. Roland Bonnel and Catherine Rubinger. New York: Peter Lang, 1994. 155–82.

DeJean, Joan. *Tender Geographies: Women and the Origins of the Novel in France*. New York: Columbia UP, 1991.

——. *Ancients Against Moderns: Culture Wars and the Making of a Fin de Siècle*. Chicago: U of Chicago P, 1997.

Delaporte, P. Victor. *Du merveilleux dans la littérature française sous le règne de Louis XIV*. 1891. Genève: Slatkine Reprints, 1968.

Delarue, Paul. "Les contes merveilleux de Perrault et la tradition populaire." *Bulletin Folklorique d'Ile-de-France* 12 (1951): 221–28, 251–61, 283–91.

Demnati, Faouzia. *Le merveilleux et le realisme et leurs implications sociales et culturelles dans les "Piacevoli notti" de Giovan Francesco Straparola*. Tunis: Université Tunis I, Faculté des lettres de Manouba, 1989.

Démoris, René. "Du littéraire au littéral dans 'Peau d'âne' de Perrault." *Revue des Sciences Humaines* 166 (1977): 261–79.

Denecke, Ludwig. *Jacob Grimm und sein Bruder Wilhelm*. Stuttgart: Metzler, 1971.

——, ed. *Brüder Grimm Gedenken*. Vol. 1. Marburg: Elwert, 1963.

——, ed. *Brüder Grimm Gedenken*. Vol. 2. Marburg: Elwert, 1975.

——, ed. *Brüder Grimm Gedenken*. Vol. 3. Marburg: Elwert, 1981.

——, ed. *Brüder Grimm Gedenken*. Vol. 4. Marburg: Elwert, 1984.

——, ed. *Brüder Grimm Gedenken*. Vol. 5. Marburg: Elwert, 1985.

——, ed. *Brüder Grimm Gedenken*. Vol. 6. Marburg: Elwert, 1986.

——, ed. *Brüder Grimm Gedenken*. Vol. 7. Marburg: Elwert, 1987.

Dewald, Jonathan. *Aristocratic Experience and the Origins of Modern Culture: France, 1570–1715*. Berkeley: U of California P, 1993.

Di Scanno, Teresa. *Les contes de fées à l'époque classique (1680–1715)*. Naples: Liguori, 1975.

Diederichs, Ulf. *Who's Who im Märchen*. Munich: Deutscher Taschenbuch Verlag, 1997.

DiPiero, Thomas. *Dangerous Truths and Criminal Passions: The Evolution of the French Novel, 1569–1791*. Stanford: Stanford UP, 1992.

Dundes, Alan, ed. *Cinderella: A Folklore Casebook*. New York: Garland, 1982.

——. "The Psychoanalytic Study of the Grimms' Tales with Special Reference to 'The Maiden without Hands' (AT 706)." *The Germanic Review* 42 (Spring 1987): 50–65.

——, ed. *The Study of Folklore*. Englewood Cliffs, N.J.: Prentice-Hall, 1962.

——, ed. *Little Red Riding Hood: A Casebook*. Madison: U of Wisconsin P, 1989.

——. *Holy Writ: The Bible as Folklore*. Lanham, MD: Rowman & Littlefield, 1999.

Escarpit, Denise. *Histoire d'un conte: Le Chat Botté en France et en Angleterre*. 2 vols. Paris: Didier, 1985.

Falassi, Alessandro. *Folklore by the Fireside: Text and Context of the Tuscan Veglia*. Austin: U of Texas P, 1980.

Farrell, Michele L. "Celebration and Repression of Feminine Desire in Mme d'Aulnoy's Fairy Tale: *La Chatte Blanche*." *Esprit Créateur* 29.3 (1989): 52–75.

Fehling, Detlev. *Amor und Psyche: Die Schöpfung des Apuleius und ihre Einwirkung auf das Märchen*. Wiesbaden: Steiner, 1977.

Fink, Gonthier-Louis. *Naissance et apogée du conte merveilleux en Allemagne 1740–1800*. Paris: Les Belles Lettres, 1966.

——. "Les avatars de Rumpelstilzchen. La vie d'un conte populaire." *Deutsche-Französisches Gespräch im Lichte der Märchen*. Ed. Ernst Kracht. Münster: Aschendorff, 1964. 46–72.

Franci, Giovanna, and Ester Zago. *La bella addormentata. Genesi e metamorfosi di una fiaba.* Bari: Dedalo, 1984.

Freudmann, Felix R. "Realism and Magic in Perrault's Fairy Tales." *'Esprit Créateur* 3 (1963): 116–22.

Fumaroli, Marc. "Les Enchantements de l'éloquence: *Les Fées* de Charles Perrault ou De la littérature." *Le Statut de la littérature: mélanges offertes á Paul Bénichou.* Ed. Marc Fumaroli. Genève: Droz, 1982. 152–86.

Ginschel, Gunhild. *Der junge Jacob Grimm.* Berlin: Akademie Verlag, 1967.

Girou-Swiderski, Marie-Laure. "La Belle ou la bête? Mme de Villeneuve, la méconnue." *Femmes savantes et femmes d'esprit: Women Intellectuals of the French Eighteenth Century.* Ed. Roland Bonnel and Catherine Rubinger. New York: Peter Lang, 1994. 199–228.

Göttner-Abendroth, Heide. *Die Göttin und ihr Heros: Die matriarchalen Religionen in Mythose, Märchen und Dichtung.* Munich: Frauenoffensive, 1980.

Goldberg, Christine. *The Tale of the Three Oranges.* Helsinki: Academia Scientiarum Fennica, 1997.

———. "The Donkey Skin Folktale Cycle (AT 501B)." *Journal of American Folklore* 110 (Winter 1997): 28–46.

Goldsmith, Elizabeth C. *Exclusive Conversations: The Art of Interaction in Seventeenth-Century France.* Philadelphia: U of Pennsylvania P, 1988.

Goodman, Dena. *The Republic of Letters: A Cultural History of the French Enlightenment.* Ithaca: Cornell UP, 1994.

Grätz, Manfred. *Das Märchen in der deutschen Aufklärung. Vom Feenmärchen zum Volksmärchen.* Stuttgart: Metzler, 1988.

Guaragnella, Pasquale. "Sventura e maschere di eros nella societa di corte: La fiaba della 'belia dormiente' fra Basile e Perrault." *Eros in Francia nel Seicento.* Intro. Paolo Bari Carile. Paris: Adriatica, Nizet, 1987. 323–65.

Gunkel, Hermann. *The Folktale in the Old Testament.* Sheffield: Almond Press, 1987.

Hagen, Rolf. "Perraults Märchen und die Brüder Grimm." *Zeitschrift für deutsche Philologie* 74 (1955): 392–410.

Hamann, Hermann. *Die literarischen Vorlagen der "Kinder- und Hausmärchen" und ihre Berarbeitung durch die Brüder Grimm.* Berlin: Mayer und Müller, 1906.

Hamman, A.-G. *L'Epopée du Livre: La transmission des textes anciens, du scribe à l'imprimerie.* Paris: Perrin, 1985.

Hannon, Patricia. *Fabulous Identities: Women's Fairy Tales in Seventeenth-Century France.* Amsterdam: Rodopi, 1998.

Harf-Lancner, Laurence. *Les Fées au Moyen Age: Morgane et Mélusine. La naissance des fées.* Paris: Honoré Champion, 1984.

Harries, Elizabeth W. "Simulating Oralities: French Fairy Tales of the 1690s." *College Literature* 23 (June 1996): 100–115.

Harth, Erica. *Ideology and Culture in Seventeenth-Century France.* Ithaca: Cornell UP, 1983.

———. *Cartesian Women: Versions and Subversions of Rational Discourse in the Old Regime.* Ithaca: Cornell UP, 1992.

Hearne, Betsy Gould. *Beauty and the Beast: Visions and Revisions of an Old Tale.* Chicago: U of Chicago P, 1989.

Heindrichs, Ursula and Heinz-Albert. *Zauber Märchen: Forschungsberichte aus der Welt der Märchen.* Munich: Diederichs, 1998.

Hellegouarc'h, Jacqueline, ed. *L'art de la conversation.* Paris: Classiques Garnier, 1999.

Hennig, Dieter, and Bernhard Lauer, eds. *Die Brüder Grimm. Dokumente ihres Lebens und Wirkens.* Kassel: Weber & Weidemeyer, 1985.

Herranen, Gun. " 'The Maiden without Hands' (AT 706)." *D'un Conte à l'autre: La variabilité dans la littérature orale.* Ed. Veronika Gorog-Karady. Paris: 1987. 105–15.

Hetmann, Frederik. "Die mündlichen Quellen der Grimms oder die Rolle der Geschichtenerzähler in den *Kinder- und Hausmärchen.*" *The Germanic Review* 42 (Spring 1987): 83–89.

Heyden, Franz. *Volksmärchen und Volksmärchen-Erzähler. Zur literarischen Gestaltung des deutschen Volksmärchens.* Hamburg: Hanseatische Verlagsanstalt, 1922.

Hildebrandt, Irma. *Es waren ihrer Fünf. Die Brüder Grimm und ihre Familie.* Cologne: Diederichs, 1984.

Hoffmann, Kathryn. "Of Innocents and Hags: The Status of the Female in the Seventeenth-Century Fairy Tale." *Cahiers du Dix-Septième* 2 (1997): 205–14.

Holbek, Bengt. *Interpretation of Fairy Tales: Danish Folklore in a European Perspective.* Helsinki: Academia Scientarium Fennica, 1987.

Horn, Katalin. *Der aktive und der passive Märchenheld.* Basel: Schweizerische Gesellschaft für Volkskunde, 1983.

Jolles, André. *Einfache Formen.* Tübingen: Niemeyer, 1958.

Jones, Steven Swann. *The Fairy Tale: The Magic Mirror of Imagination.* New York: Twayne, 1995.

Kamenetsky, Christa. *The Brothers Grimm and Their Critics: Folktales and the Quest for Meaning.* Athens: Ohio UP, 1992.

Karlinger, Felix, ed. *Wege der Märchenforschung.* Darmstadt: Wissenschaftliche Buchgesellschaft, 1973.

———. *Grundzüge einer Geschichte des Märchens im deutschen Sprachraum.* Darmstadt: Wissenschaftliche Buchgesellschaft, 1983.

Kiefer, Emma Emily. *Albert Wesselski and Recent Folktale Theories*. Indiana University Publications: Folklore Series 3. Bloomington: Indiana UP, 1947.

Klone, Ursula. *Die Aufnahme des Marchens in der italienischen Kunstprosa von Straparola bis Basile*. Marburg/Lahn: Philipps-Universitat zu Marburg, 1961.

Klotz, Volker. *Das europäische Kunstmärchen*. Stuttgart: Metzler, 1985.

Laiblin, Wilhelm, ed. *Märchenforschung und Tiefenpsychologie*. Darmstadt: Wissenschaftliche Buchgesellschaft, 1969.

Lauer, Bernhard, ed. *Rapunzel: Traditionen eines euopäischen Märchenstoffes in Dichtung und Kunst*. Kassel: BrüderGrimm-Museum, 1993.

Lewis, Philip. *Seeing Through the Mother Goose Tales: Visual Turns in the Writings of Charles Perrault*. Stanford: Stanford UP, 1996.

Leyen, Friedrich von der. *Das Märchen*. Leipzig: Quelle & Meyer, 1917.

——. *Das deutsche Märchen und die Brüder Grimm*. Düsseldorf: Diederichs, 1964.

Liebs, Elke. *Kindheit und Tod: Der Rattenfänger-Mythos als Beitrag zu einer Kulturgeschichte der Kindheit*. Munich: Wilhelm Fink, 1986.

Lods, Jeanne. *Le Roman de Perceforest*. Geneva: Droz, 1951

Loskoutoff, Yvan. *La Sainte et la fée; dévotion à l'Enfant Jésus et mode des contes merveilleux à la fin du régne de Louis XIV*. Geneva: Droz, 1987.

Lougee, Carolyn C. *Le Paradis des femmes: Women, Salons and Social Stratification in Seventeenth-Century France*. Princeton: Princeton UP, 1976.

Lüthi, Max. *Die Gabe im Märchen und in der Sage*. Bern: Francke, 1943.

——. *Das europäische Volksmärchen*. 2nd rev. ed. Bern: Francke, 1960.

——. *Volksmärchen und Volkssage*. 2nd rev. ed. Bern: Francke, 1966.

——. *Once Upon a Time. On the Nature of Fairy Tales*. Trans. Lee Chadeayne & Paul Gottwald. New York: Ungar, 1970.

——. *Das Volksmärchen als Dichtung*. Cologne: Diederichs, 1975.

——. *The European Folktale: Form and Nature*. Trans. John D. Niles. Philadelphia: Institute for the Study of Human Issues, 1982.

——. *The Fairy Tale as Art Form and Portrait of Man*. Trans. Jon Erickson. Bloomington: U of Indiana P, 1985.

Malarte, Claire-Lise. "Les *Contes* de Perrault, Oeuvre 'Moderne.' " *D'un Siècle à L'Autre: Anciens et Modernes*. Ed. Louise Godard de Donville. Marseilles: C.M.R., 1987. 91–100.

——. *Perrault à travers la critique depuis 1960*. Tübingen: Biblio 17, 1989.

Marin, Louis. *Food for Thought*. Trans. Mette Hjort. Baltimore: Johns Hopkins UP, 1989.

——. "Puss-in-Boots: Power of Signs—Signs of Power." *Diacritics* 7 (Summer 1977): 54–63.

——. *La parole mangée et autres essais théologico-politiques*. Paris: Meridiens Klincksieck, 1986.

Mazenauer, Beat, and Severin Perrig. *Wie Dornröschen seine Unschuld gewann: Archäologie der Märchen*. Leipzig: Kiepenheuer, 1995.

Mazon, Jeanne Roche. *En marge de l'Oiseau bleu*. Paris: Artisan du livre, 1930.

Mazzacurati, Giancarlo. "Sui materiali in opera nelle *Piacevoli Notti* di Giovan Francesco Straparola" and "La Narrativa di Giovan Francesco Straparola: sociologia e structura del personaggio fiabesco." *Società e strutture narrative dal Trecento al Cinquecento*. Naples: Liguori, 1971.

McGlathery, James M., ed. *The Brothers Grimm and Folktale*. Champaign: U of Illinois P, 1988.

——. *Fairy Tale Romance: The Grimms, Basile, and Perrault*. Urbana: U of Illinois P, 1991.

——. *Grimms' Fairy Tales: A History of Criticism on a Popular Classic*. Columbia, SC: Camden House, 1993.

Metzger, Michael M., and Katharina Mommsen, eds. *Fairy Tales as Ways of Knowing: Essays on Marchen in Psychology, Society, and Literature*. Bern, Las Vegas: P. Lang, 1981.

Mieder, Wolfgang, ed. *Grimms Märchen—modern*. Stuttgart: Reclam, 1979.

——. "Survival Forms of 'Little Red Riding Hood' in Modern Society." *International Folklore Review: Folklore Studies from Overseas* 2 (1982): 23–40.

——. "Wilhelm Grimm's Proverbial Additions in the Fairy Tales." *Proverbium* 3 (1986): 59–83.

——. "Sprichwörtliche Schwundstufen des Märchens. Zum 200. Geburtstag der Brüder Grimm." *Proverbium* 3 (1986): 257–71.

——. "*Findet, so werdet ih suchen!*" *Die Brüder Grimm und das Sprichwort*. Bern: Peter Lang, 1986.

——. *Tradition and Innovation in Folk Literature*. Hanover: UP of New England, 1987.

——. "Grimm Variations: From Fairy Tales to Modern Anti-Fairy Tales." *The Germanic Review* 42 (Spring 1987): 90–102.

Mitchell, Jane Tucker. *A Thematic Analysis of Mme d'Aulnoy's Contes de fées*. University, MS: Romance Monographs, 1978.

Morgan, Jeanne. *Perrault's Morals for Moderns*. Frankfurt am Main: Peter Lang, 1985.

Motley, Mark. *Becoming a French Aristocrat: The Education of the Court Nobility, 1580–1715*. Princeton: Princeton UP, 1990.

Motte-Gillet, Anne. "Giovan Francesco Straparola: "Les Facétieuses Nuits."" *Conteurs italiens de la Renaissance*. Ed. A. Motte-Gillet. Intro. Giancarlo Mazzacurati. Trans. Georges Kempf. Paris: Gallimard, 1993. 1386–1440.

Mourey, Lilyane. *Introduction aux contes de Grimm et de Perrault*. Paris: Minard, 1978.

Nissen, Walter. *Die Brüder Grimm und ihre Märchen*. Göttingen: Vandenhoeck & Ruprecht, 1984.

Nitschke, August. *Soziale Ordnungen im Spiegel der Märchen*. 2 vols. Stuttgart: Frommann-Holzboog, 1976–77.

——. "Aschenputtel aus der Sicht der historischen Verhaltensforschung." *Und wenn sie nicht gestorben sind . . . Perspektiven auf das Märchen.* Ed. Helmut Brackert. Frankfurt am Main: Suhrkamp, 1980. 71–88.

Nobis, Helmut. *Phantasie und Moralität: Das Wunderbare in Wielands "Dschinnistan" und der "Geschichte des Prinzen Biribinker."* Kronberg: Scriptor, 1976.

Ong, Walter. *Orality and Literacy.* London: Methuen, 1982.

Opie, Iona, and Peter Opie, eds. *The Classic Fairy Tales.* Oxford: Oxford UP, 1974.

Palacio, Jean de. *Les perversions du merveilleux: Ma mère l'Oye au tournant du siècle.* Paris: Séguier, 1993.

Palmer, Melvin D. "Madame d'Aulnoy in England." *Comparative Literature* 27 (1975): 237–53.

Pellowski, Anne. *The World of Storytelling.* Rev. ed. Bronx, NY: Wilson, 1990.

Petrini, Mario. *La fiaba di magia nella letteratura italiana.* Verona: Del Bianco, 1983.

Philippson, Ernst. *Der Märchen Typus von König Drosselbart.* F. F. Communications No. 50. Greifswald: Suomalainen Tiedeakatemia, 1923.

Pozzi, Victoria Smith. "Straparola's *Le Piacevoli notti*: Narrative Technique and Ideology." Diss. University of California, Los Angeles, 1981.

Prisco, Michele, ed. *Giambattista Basile: Protagonisti della Storia di Napoli.* Naples: Elio de Rosa, 1995.

Propp, Vladimir. *Morphology of the Folktale.* Eds. Louis Wagner and Alan Dundes. Trans. Laurence Scott. 2nd rev. ed. Austin: U of Texas P, 1958.

——. "Les Transformations des Contes Fantastiques." *Théorie de la littérature.* Ed. Tzvetan Todorov. Paris: Seuil, 1965. 234–62.

——. *Theory and History of Folklore.* Trans. Ariadna Y. Martin and Richard P. Martin. Ed. Anatoly Liberman. Minneapolis: U of Minnesota P, 1984.

Rak, Michele. *La maschera della fortuna: Letture del Basile toscano.* Naples: Liguori, 1975.

——. *Napoli gentile: La letturatura in "lingua napoletana" nella cultura barocca (1596–1632).* Bologna: Il Mulino, 1994.

Ranke, Kurt. "Betrachtungen zum Wesen und Funktion des Märchens." *Studium Generale* 11 (1958): 647–64.

——. "Der Einfluß der Grimmischen 'Kinder- und Hausmärchen' auf das volkstümliche deutsche Erzählgut." *Papers of the International Congress of Western Ethnology.* Ed. Sigurd Erixon. Stockholm: International Commission on Folk Arts and Folklore, 1951.

Richardson, Brian. *Printing, Writers and Readers in Renaissance Italy.* Cambridge: Cambridge UP, 1999.

Richter, Dieter, and Johannes Merkel. *Märchen, Phantasie und soziales Lernen.* Berlin: Basis, 1974.

——. *Schlaraffenland. Geschichte einer populären Phantasie.* Cologne: Eugen Diederichs, 1984.

——. "Brentano als Leser Basiles und die italienische Übersetzung des *Cunto del li cunti.*" *Jahrbuch des Freien Deutschen Hochstifts* (1986): 234–41.

——. *Das fremde Kind: Zur Entstehung des bürgerlichen Zeitalters.* Frankfurt am Main: Fischer, 1987.

Robert, Raymonde. *Le conte des fées littéraire en France de la fin du XVIIe à la fin du XVIIIe siècle.* Nancy: PU de Nancy, 1982.

——. "L'Infantalisation du conte merveilleux au XVIIe siècle." *Littératures classiques* 14 (January 1991): 33–46.

Roberts, Warren E. *The Tale of the Kind and the Unkind girls: AA-TH 480 and Related Titles.* Detroit: Wayne State UP, 1994.

Roche-Mazon, Jeanne. *Autour des Contes des Fées.* Paris: Didier, 1968.

Röhrich, Lutz. *Gebärden—Metapher—Parodie.* Düsseldorf: Schwann, 1967.

——. *Märchen und Wirklichkeit.* Wiesbaden: Steiner, 1974.

——. *Sagen und Märchen. Erzählforschung heute.* Freiburg: Herder, 1976.

——. "Der Froschkönig." *Das selbstverständliche Wunder: Beiträge germanistischer Märchenforschung.* Ed. Wilhelm Solms. Marburg: Hitzeroth, 1986. 7–41.

Rölleke, Heinz, ed. "Texte, die beinahe 'Grimms Märchen' geworden wären." *Zeitschrift für deutsche Philologie* 102 (1983): 481–500.

——. *Die Märchen der Brüder Grimm.* Munich: Artemis, 1985.

——. "Wo das Wünschen noch geholfen hat." *Gesammelte Aufsätze zu den "Kinder- und Hausmärchen" der Brüder Grimm.* Bonn: Bouvier, 1985.

——. "Die 'Kinder- und Hausmärchen' der Brüder Grimm in neuer Sicht." *Diskussion Deutsch* 91 (Oct. 1986): 458–64.

Rooth, Anna Birgitta. *The Cinderella Cycle.* Lund: Gleerup, 1951.

Rumpf, Marianne. *Ursprung und Entstehung von Warn- und Schreckmärchen.* Folklore Fellows' Communications 160. Helsinki: Suomalainen Tiedeakatemia/Academia scientificarum fennica, 1955.

Santucci, Luigi. *Das Kind, sein Mythos und sein Märchen.* Hannover: Schrödel, 1964.

Saupé, Yvette. *Les Contes de Perrault et la mythologie: Rapproachements et influences.* Paris: Biblio 17, Papers on French Seventeenth-Century Literature, 1997.

Schauf, Susanne. *Die verlorene Allmacht der Feen: Untersuchungen zum französischen Kunstmärchen des 19. Jahrhunderts.* Frankfurt am Main: Peter Lang, 1986.

Schenda, Rudolf. *Volk ohne Buch.* Frankfurt am Main: Klostermann, 1970.

——. *Die Leserstoffe der Kleinen Leute.* Munich: Beck, 1976.

———. "Folkloristik und Sozialgeschichte." *Erzählung und Erzählforschung im 20. Jahrhundert*. Eds. Rolf Kloepfer and Gisela Janetke-Dillner. Stuttgart: Kohlhammer, 1981. 441–48.

———. "Alphabetisierung und Literasierung in Westeuropa im 18. und 19. Jahrhundert." *Sozialer und kultureller Wandel der ländlichen Welt des 18. Jahrhunderts*. Eds. Ernst Hinrichs and Günter Wiegelmann. Wolfenbüttel: Herzog August Bibliothek, 1982. 1–20.

———. "Mären von deutschen Sagen. Bemerkungen zur Produktion 'Volkserzählungen' zwischen 1850 und 1870." *Geschichte und Gesellschaft* 9 (1983): 26–48.

———. "Volkserzählung und nationale Identität: Deutsche Sagen im Vormärz." *Fabula* 25 (1984): 296–303.

———. "Volkserzählung und Sozialgeschichte." *Il Confronto Lettario* 1.2 (1984): 265–79.

———. "Orale und literarische Kommunikationsformen im Bereich von Analphabeten und Gebildeten im 17. Jahrhundert." *Literatur und Volk im 17. Jahrhundert. Probleme populärer Kultur in Deutschland*. Eds. Wolfgang Brückner, Peter Blickle, and Dieter Breuer. Wiesbaden: Harrasowitz, 1985. 447–64.

———. "Vorlesen: Zwischen Analphabetentum und Bücherwissen." *Bertelsmann Briefe* 119 (1986): 5–14.

———. "Telling Tales—Spreading Tales: Change in the Communicative Forms of a Popular Genre." *Fairy Tales and Society. Illusion, Allusion, and Paradigm*. Ed. Ruth B. Bottigheimer. Philadelphia: U of Pennsylvania P, 1986.

———. *Folklore e Letteratura Popolare: Italia—Germania—Francia*. Rome: Istituto della Enciclopedia Italiana, 1986.

———. *Von Mund zu Ohr: Baustein zu einer Kulturgeschichte volkstümlichen Erzählens in Europa*. Göttingen: Vandenhoeck & Ruprecht, 1993.

———. "Basiles *Pentamerone* (1634) neu übersetzen?" *Fabula* 39 (1998): 219–42.

Scherf, Walter. "Family Conflicts and Emancipation in Fairy Tales." *Children's Literature* 3 (1974): 77–93.

———. *Lexikon der Zaubermärchen*. Stuttgart: Kröner, 1982.

———. "Das Märchenpublikum. Die Erwartung der Zuhörer und Leser und die Antwort des Erzählers." *Diskussion Deutsch* 91 (Oct. 1986): 479–96.

———. *Das Märchen Lexikon*. 2 vols. Munich: Beck, 1995.

Schödel, Siegfried, ed. *Märchenanalysen*. Stuttgart: Reclam, 1977.

Schoof, Wilhelm. *Zur Entstehungsgeschichte der Grimmschen Märchen*. Hamburg: Hauswedell, 1959.

Scott, Carole. "Magical Dress: Clothing and Transformation in Folk Tales." *Children's Literature Quarterly* 21 (Winter 1996–97): 151–57.

Seifert, Lewis C. "Disguising the Storyteller's 'Voice': Perrault's Recuperation of the Fairy Tale." *Cincinnati Romance Review* 8 (1989): 13–23.

———. "Female Empowerment and Its Limits: The conteuses' Active Heroines." *Cahiers du Dix-septième* 4.2 (Fall 1990): 17–34.

———. "Tales of Difference: Infantilization and the Recuperation of Class and Gender in 17th-Century contes de fées." *Actes de Las Vegas: Théorie dramatique, Théophile de Viau, Les Contes de fées*. Ed. Marie-France Hilgar. Paris: PFSCL, 1991. 179–94.

———. "Marie-Catherine le Jumel de Barneville, Comtesse d'Aulnoy." *French Women Writers: A Bio-Bibliographical Source Book*. Eds. Eva Martin Sartori and Dorothy Wynne Zimmerman. New York: Greenwood, 1991. 11–20.

———. "*Les Fées Modernes*: Women, Fairy Tales, and the Literary Field in Late Seventeenth-Century France." Ed. Elizabeth C. Goldsmith and Dena Goodman. *Going Public: Women and Publishing in Early Modern France*. Ithaca: Cornell UP, 1995. 129–45.

———. *Fairy Tales, Sexuality, and Gender in France, 1690–1715: Nostalgic Utopias*. Cambridge: Cambridge UP, 1996.

Seitz, Gabriele. *Die Brüder Grimm. Leben—Werk—Zeit*. Munich: Winkler, 1984.

Siegmund, Wolfdietrich, ed. *Antiker Mythos in unseren Märchen*. Kassel: Röth-Verlag, 1984.

Sielaff, Erich. "Zum deutschen Volksmärchen." *Der Bibliothekar* 12 (1952): 816–29.

———. "Bemerkungen zur kritischen Aneignung der deutschen Volksmärchen." *Wissenschaftliche Zeitschrift der Universität Rostock* 2 (1952/53): 241–301.

Solms, Wilhelm, and Annegret Hofius. "Der wunderbare Weg zum Glück. Vorschlag für die Behandlung der 'Kinder- und Hausmärchen' der Brüder Grimm im Deutschunterricht." *Diskussion Deutsch* 91 (Oct. 1986): 511–34.

Soriano, Marc. *Les Contes de Perrault. Culture savante et traditions populaires*. Paris: Gallimard, 1968.

———. "Le petit chaperon rouge." *Nouvelle Revue Française* 16 (1968): 429–43.

———. "From Tales of Warning to Formulettes. The Oral Tradition in French Children's Literature." *Yale French Studies* 43 (1969): 24–43.

———. *Le Dossier Charles Perrault*. Paris: Hachette, 1972.

———. *Guide de littérature pour la jeunesse*. Paris: Flammarion, 1975.

Speroni, Charles. *Proverbs and Proverbial Phrases in Basile's "Pentamerone."* Berkeley: U of California P, 1943.

Squarotti, Giorgio Barberi. "Problemi di technica narrativa cinquecentesca." *Sigma* II (1965): 84–108. Translation in German as "Probleme der Erzähltechnik im 16. Jahrhundert: Lo Straparola." *Die romanische Novelle*. Ed. W. Eitel. Darmstadt: Wissenschaftliche Buchgesellschaft, 1977. 143–74.

Stanton, Domna C. *The Aristocrat as Art: A Study of the 'Honnete Homme' and the 'Dandy' in Seventeenth- and Nineteenth-Century French Literature*. New York: Columbia UP, 1980.

Steinlein, Rüdiger. *Die domestizierte Phantasie. Studien zur Kinderliteratur, Kinderlektüre und Literaturpädogik des 18. und 19. Jahrhunderts*. Heidelberg: Carl Winter, 1987.

———. "Marchen als poetische Erziehungsform: Zum kinderliterarischen Status der Grimmschen 'Kinder- und Hausmarchen.' " *Zeitschrift fur Germanistik* 5.2 (1995): 301–16.

Stewart, Susan. *Nonsense: Aspects of Intertextuality in Folklore and Literature*. Baltimore: Johns Hopkins UP, 1978.

———. *On Longing: Narratives of the Miniature, the Gigantic, the Souvenir, the Collection*. Baltimore: Johns Hopkins UP, 1984.

Storer, Mary Elizabeth. *La Mode des contes des fées (1685–1700)*. Paris: Champion, 1928.

———. *Contes de Féés du Grand Siècle*. New York: Publications of the Institute of French Studies, Columbia University, 1934.

Strosetzki, Christoph. *Rhétorique de la conversation: Sa dimension littéraire et linguistique dans la societé française du XVIIe siècle*. Paris-Tübingen: Biblio 17–20, 1984.

Tatar, Maria M. "From Nags to Witches: Stepmothers in the Grimms' Fairy Tales." *Opening Texts: Psychoanalysis and the Culture of the Child*. Ed. Joseph H. Smith and William Kerrigan. Baltimore: Johns Hopkins UP, 1985. 28–41.

———. "Tests, Tasks, and Trials in the Grimms' Fairy Tales." *Children's Literature*. Vol. 13. New Haven: Yale UP, 1985. 31–48.

———. "Born Yesterday: Heroes in the Grimms' Fairy Tales." *Fairy Tales and Society: Illusion Allusion, and Paradigm*. Ed. Ruth B. Bottigheimer. Philadelphia: U of Pennsylvania P, 1986.

———. *The Hard Facts of the Grimms' Fairy Tales*. Princeton: Princeton UP, 1987.

———. *Off with Their Heads: Fairy Tales and the Culture of Childhood*. Princeton: Princeton UP, 1992.

Tenèze, Marie Louise, ed. *Approaches de nos traditions orales*. Paris: Maisonneuve et Larose, 1970.

Thompson, Stith. *Motif Index of Folk Literature*. 6 vols. 1932–36. Bloomington: U of Indiana P, 1955.

———. *The Folktale*. New York: Holt Rinehart & Winston, 1946.

Timmermans, Linda. *L'Accès des femmes à la culture, 1598–1715. Un débat d'idées de Saint François de Sales à la Marquise de Lambert*. Paris: Champion, 1993.

Tismar, Jens. *Kunstmärchen*. Stuttgart: Metzler, 1977.

———. *Das deutsche Kunstmärchen des zwanzigsten Jahrhunderts*. Stuttgart: Metzler, 1981.

Tonnelat, Ernest. *Les contes des frères Grimm: Etudes sur la composition et le style du recueil des 'Kinder- und Hausmärchen.'* Paris: Armand Colin, 1912.

Trost, Caroline. "Belle Belle ou le chevalier Fortuné: A Liberated Woman in a Tale by Mme d'Aulnoy." *Merveilles & Contes* 5 (1991): 57–66.

Velay-Vallantin, Catherine. "Le miroir des contes. Perrault dans les Bibliothèques bleues." *Les usages de l'imprimé*. Ed. Roger Chartier. Paris: Fayard, 1987. 129–85.

———. *L'histoire des contes*. Paris: Fayard, 1992.

Velten, Harry. "The Influence of Charles Perrault's Contes de ma Mère L'Oie on German Folklore." *The Germanic Review* 5 (1930): 14–18.

Verdi, Laura. *Il regno incantato: il contesto sociale e culturale della fiaba in Europa*. Padua: Centro studi sociologia religiosa di Padova, 1980.

Verdier, Gabrielle. "Les Contes de fées." *Actes de Las Vegas: Théorie dramatique, Théophile de Viau. Les Contes de fées*. Ed. Marie-France Hilgar. Paris: Papers on French Seventeenth-Century Literature, 1991.

———. "Figures de la conteuse dans les contes de fées feminins." *XVIIe Siècle* 180 (1993): 481–99.

———. "Gracieuse vs. Grognon, or How To Tell The Good Guys From the Bad in the Literary Fairy Tale." *Cashiers du Dix-Septième* 4.2 (1997): 13–20.

Verdier, Yvonne. "Grand-méres, si vous saviez: le Petit Chaperon Rouge dans la tradition orale." *Cahiers de Littérature Orale* 4 (1978): 17–55.

Viala, Alain. *La Naissance de l'écrivain*. Paris: Minuit, 1985.

Von der Leyen, Friedrich. *Das deutsche Märchen*. 1917. Leipzig: Quelle & Meyer, 1930.

Vries, Jan de. "Dornröschen." *Fabula* (1959): 110–21.

Warner, Marina. *From the Beast to the Blonde: On Fairy Tales and Their Tellers*. London: Chatto & Windus, 1995.

———. *No Go the Bogeyman: Scaring, Lulling, and Making Mock*. London: Chatto & Windus, 1998.

Welch, Marcelle Maistre. "Les Jeux de l'écriture dans les Contes de fées de Mme d'Aulnoy." *Romanische Forschungen* CI.1 (1989): 75–80.

———. "Rébellion et résignation dans les contes de fées de Mme d'Aulnoy et Mme de Murat." *Cahiers du dix-septième* 2 (1989): 131–42.

———. "La Satire du rococo dans les contes de fées de Madame d'Aulnoy." *Revue Romane* 28 (1993): 75–85.

Wesselski, Albert. *Versuch einer Theorie des Märchens*. Reichenberg: Prager Deutsche Studien 45, 1931.

———. *Märchen des Mittelalters*. Berlin: Stubenrauch, 1942.

Wetzel, Hermann Hubert. *Märchen in den französischen Novellensammlungen der Renaissance*. Berlin: Erich Schmidt, 1974.

Wittmann, Reinhard, ed. *Buchmarkt und Lektüre im 18, und 19. Jahrhundert. Beiträge zum literarischen Leben 1750–1880*. Tübingen: Max Niemeyer, 1982.

Woeller, Waltraut. *Der soziale Gehalt und die soziale Funktion der deutschen Volksmärchen.* Habilitations-Schrift der Humboldt-Universität zu Berlin, 1955.

Wolfzettel, Friedrich. "La lutte contre les mères: quelques exemples d'une valorisation émancipatrice du conte de fées au dix-huitième siècle." *Réception et identification du conte depuis le moyen âge.* Ed. Michel Zink and Xavier Ravier. Toulouse: Université de Toulouse-Le Mirail, 1987. 123–31.

Wührl, Paul-Wolfgang. *Das deutsche Kunstmärchen.* Heidelberg: Quelle & Meyer, 1984.

Zago, Esther. "Some Medieval Versions of Sleeping Beauty: Variations on a Theme." *Studi Francesci* 69 (1979): 417–31.

——. "La Belle au Bois Dormant: Sens et Structure." *Cermeil* 2 (Feb. 1986): 92–96.

——. "Carlo Collodi as Translator: From Fairy Tale to Folk Tale." *Lion and Unicorn* 12 (1988): 61–73.

——. "Giambattista Basile: Il suo pubblico e il suo metodo." *Selecta: Journal of the Pacific Northwest Council on Foreign Languages* 2 (1981): 78–80.

Zarucchi, Jeanne Morgan. *Perrault's Morals for Moderns.* New York: Peter Lang, 1985.

Zipes, Jack. *Breaking the Magic Spell: Radical Theories of Folk and Fairy Tales.* London: Heinemann, 1979.

——. *The Trials and Tribulations of Little Red Riding Hood: Versions of the Tale in Socio-Cultural Context.* South Hadley: Bergin & Garvey, 1983; 2nd rev. ed. New York: Routledge, 1993.

——. *Fairy Tales and the Art of Subversion. The Classical Genre for Children and the Process of Civilization.* London: Heinemann, 1983.

——. *The Brothers Grimm: From Enchanted Forests to the Modern World.* New York: Routledge, 1988.

——. *Fairy Tale as Myth/Myth as Fairy Tale.* Lexington: UP of Kentucky, 1994.

——. *Happily Ever After: Fairy Tales, Children, and the Culture Industry.* New York: Routledge, 1997.

——. *When Dreams Came True: Classical Fairy Tales and Their Tradition.* New York: Routledge, 1999.

——. *The Oxford Companion to Fairy Tales: The Western Fairy Tale Tradition from Medieval to Modern.* Oxford: Oxford UP, 2000.